Rage of Angels
Bloodline
Master of the Game

Sidney Sheldon

Diamond Books,
An Imprint of HarperCollins*Publishers*,
77–85 Fulham Palace Road
Hammersmith, London W6 8JB

This Diamond Books Omnibus edition first published 1993
9 8 7 6 5 4 3 2 1

ISBN 1 85813 248 7 (UK)
ISBN Diamond Books 0261 66152 3 (international edition)

Phototypeset in Ehrhardt by Intype, London

Printed in Great Britain by Mackays of Chatham Ltd

Contents

By the same author

If Tomorrow Comes
A Stranger in the Mirror
The Other Side of Midnight
The Naked Face
Windmills of the Gods
The Sands of Time
Memories of Midnight
The Doomsday Conspiracy
The Stars Shine Down

Rage of Angels

This book is dedicated with love to Mary
The Eighth Wonder of the World

The characters and events in this novel are fictional. The background, however, is real, and I am indebted to those who generously helped to fill it in for me. In a few instances I have taken what I believe to be necessary dramatic license. Any legal or factual errors are mine alone.

My deep gratitude for sharing with me their courtroom lives and experiences goes to F. Lee Bailey, Melvin Belli, Paul Caruso, William Hundley, Luke McKissack, Louis Nizer, Jerome Shestack and Peter Taft.

In California, the Honorable Wm. Matthew Byrne, of the United States District Court, was most helpful.

In New York, I owe special thanks to Mary de Bourbon of the New York District Attorney's office for showing me the inner workings of the court system; to Phil Leshin, former Assistant Commissioner for Public Affairs of the New York City Department of Correction, for escorting me through Riker's Island; and to Pat Perry, the Assistant Deputy Warden at Riker's Island.

Barry Dastin's legal supervision and counsel have proved invaluable.

My appreciation to Alice Fisher for her assistance in researching this book.

And finally, a thank you to Catherine Munro, who patiently and cheerfully transcribed and typed what began as a thousand-page manuscript, more than a dozen times over a period of almost three years.

SIDNEY SHELDON

"... Tell us of the secret hosts of evil, O Cimon ..."
"Their names may not be spake aloud
lest they profane mortal lips,
for they came out of unholy darknesses
and attacked the heavens,
but they were driven away by the rage of angels ..."

from *Dialogues of Chios*

Book One

1

New York: September 4, 1969

The hunters were closing in for the kill.

Two thousand years ago in Rome, the contest would have been staged at the Circus Neronis or the Colosseum, where voracious lions would have been stalking the victim in an arena of blood and sand, eager to tear him to pieces. But this was the civilized twentieth century, and the circus was being staged in the Criminal Courts Building of downtown Manhattan, Courtroom Number 16.

In place of Suetonius was a court stenographer, to record the event for posterity, and there were dozens of members of the press and visitors attracted by the daily headlines about the murder trial, who queued up outside the courtroom at seven o clock in the morning to be assured of a seat.

The quarry, Michael Moretti, sat at the defendant's table, a silent, handsome man in his early thirties. He was tall and lean, with a face formed of converging planes that gave him a rugged, feral look. He had fashionably styled black hair, a prominent chin with an unexpected dimple in it and deeply set olive-black eyes. He wore a tailored gray suit, a light blue shirt with a darker blue silk tie, and polished, custom-made shoes. Except for his eyes, which constantly swept over the courtroom, Michael Moretti was still.

The lion attacking him was Robert Di Silva, the fiery District Attorney for the County of New York, representative of The People. If Michael Moretti radiated stillness, Robert Di Silva radiated dynamic movement; he went through life as though he were five minutes late for an appointment. He was in constant motion, shadowboxing with invisible opponents. He was short and powerfully built, with an unfashionable graying crew cut. Di Silva had been a boxer in his youth and his nose and face bore the scars of it. He had once killed a man m the ring and he had never regretted it. In the years since then, he had yet to learn compassion.

Robert Di Silva was a fiercely ambitious man who had fought his way up to his present position with neither money nor connections to help him. During his climb, he had assumed the veneer of a civilized servant of the people; but underneath, he was a gutter fighter, a man who neither forgot nor forgave.

Under ordinary circumstances, District Attorney Di Silva would not have been in this courtroom on this day. He had a large staff, and any one of his senior assistants was capable of prosecuting this case. But Di Silva had known from the beginning that he was going to handle the Moretti case himself.

Michael Moretti was front-page news, the son-in-law of Antonio Granelli, *capo di capi*, head of the largest of the five eastern Mafia Families. Antonio Granelli was getting old and the street word was that Michael Moretti was being groomed to take his father-in-law's place. Moretti had been involved in dozens of crimes ranging from mayhem to murder, but no district attorney had ever been able to prove anything. There were too many careful layers between Moretti and those who carried out his orders. Di Silva himself had spent three frustrating years trying to get evidence against Moretti. Then, suddenly, Di Silva had gotten lucky.

Camillo Stela, one of Moretti's *soldati*, had been caught in a murder committed during a robbery. In exchange for his life, Stela agreed to sing. It was the most beautiful music Di Silva had ever heard, a song that was going to bring the most powerful Mafia Family in the east to its knees, send Michael Moretti to the electric chair, and elevate Robert Di Silva to the governor's office in Albany. Other New York governors had made it to the White House: Martin Van Buren, Grover Cleveland, Teddy Roosevelt and Franklin Roosevelt. Di Silva intended to be the next.

The timing was perfect. The gubernatorial elections were coming up next year.

Di Silva had been approached by the state's most powerful political boss. "With all the publicity you're getting on this case, you'll be a shoo-in to be nominated and then elected governor, Bobby. Nail Moretti and you're our candidate."

Robert Di Silva had taken no chances. He prepared the case against Michael Moretti with meticulous care. He put his assistants to work assembling evidence, cleaning up every loose end, cutting off each legal avenue of escape that Moretti's attorney might attempt to explore. One by one, every loophole had been closed.

It had taken almost two weeks to select the jury, and the District Attorney had insisted upon selecting six "spare tires" – alternate jurors – as a precaution against a possible mistrial. In cases where important Mafia figures were involved, jurors had been known to disappear or to have unexplained fatal accidents. Di Silva had seen to it that this jury was sequestered from the beginning, locked away every night where no one could get to it.

The key to the case against Michael Moretti was Camillo Stela, and Di Silva's star witness was heavily protected. The District Attorney remembered only too vividly the example of Abe "Kid Twist" Reles, the government witness who had "fallen" out of a sixth-floor window of the Half Moon Hotel in Coney Island while being guarded by half a dozen policemen. Robert Di Silva had selected Camillo Stela's guards personally, and before the trial Stela had been secretly moved to a different location every night. Now, with the trial under way, Stela was kept in an isolated holding cell, guarded by four armed deputies. No one was allowed to get near him, for Stela's willingness to testify rested on his belief that District Attorney Di Silva was capable of protecting him from the vengeance of Michael Moretti.

It was the morning of the fifth day of the trial.

*

It was Jennifer Parker's first day at the trial. She was seated at the prosecutor's table with five other young assistant district attorneys who had been sworn in with her that morning.

Jennifer Parker was a slender, dark-haired girl of twenty-four with a pale skin, an intelligent, mobile face, and green, thoughtful eyes. It was a face that was attractive rather than beautiful, a face that reflected pride and courage and sensitivity, a face that would be hard to forget. She sat ramrod straight, as though bracing herself against unseen ghosts of the past.

Jennifer Parker's day had started disastrously. The swearing-in ceremony at the District Attorney's office had been scheduled for eight A.M. Jennifer had carefully laid out her clothes the night before and had set the alarm for six so that she would have time to wash her hair.

The alarm had failed to go off. Jennifer had awakened at seven-thirty and panicked. She had gotten a run in her stocking when she broke the heel of her shoe, and had had to change clothes. She had slammed the door of her tiny apartment at the same instant she remembered she had left her keys inside. She had planned to take a bus to the Criminal Courts Building, but now that was out of the question, and she had raced to get a taxi she could not afford and had been trapped with a cab driver who explained during the entire trip why the world was about to come to an end.

When Jennifer had finally arrived, breathless, at the Criminal Courts Building at 155 Leonard Street, she was fifteen minutes late.

There were twenty-five lawyers gathered in the District Attorney's office, most of them newly out of law school, young and eager and excited about going to work for the District Attorney of the County of New York.

The office was impressive, paneled and decorated in quiet good taste. There was a large desk with three chairs in front of it and a comfortable leather chair behind it, a conference table with a dozen chairs around it, and wall cabinets filled with law books.

On the walls were framed autographed pictures of J. Edgar Hoover, John Lindsay, Richard Nixon and Jack Dempsey.

When Jennifer hurried into the office, full of apologies, Di Silva was in the middle of a speech. He stopped, turned his attention on Jennifer and said, "What the hell do you think this is – a tea party?"

"I'm terribly sorry, I – "

"I don't give a damn whether you're sorry. Don't you ever be late again!"

The others looked at Jennifer, carefully hiding their sympathy.

Di Silva turned to the group and snapped, "I know why you're all here. You'll stick around long enough to pick my brains and learn a few courtroom tricks, and then when you think you're ready, you'll leave to become hotshot criminal lawyers. But there may be one of you – maybe – who will be good enough to take my place one day." Di Silva nodded to his assistant. "Swear them in."

They took the oath, their voices subdued.

When it was over, Di Silva said, "All right. You're sworn officers of the court, God help us. This office is where the action is, but don't get your hopes up. You're going to bury your noses in legal research, and draft documents – subpoenas, warrants – all those wonderful things they taught you in law school. You won't get to handle a trial for the next year or two."

Di Silva stopped to light a short, stubby cigar. "I'm prosecuting a case now. Some of you may have read about it." His voice was edged with sarcasm. "I can use half a dozen of you to run errands for me." Jennifer's hand was the first one up. Di Silva hesitated a moment, then selected her and five others.

"Get down to Courtroom Sixteen."

As they left the room, they were issued identification cards. Jennifer had not been discouraged by the District Attorney's attitude. *He has to be tough*, she thought. *He's in a tough job.* And she was working for him now. She was a member of the staff of the District Attorney of the County of New York! The interminable years of law school drudgery were over. Somehow her professors had managed to make the law seem abstract and ancient, but Jennifer had always managed to glimpse the Promised Land beyond: the real law that dealt with human beings and their follies. Jennifer had been graduated second in her class and had been on Law Review. She had passed the bar examination on the first try, while a third of those who had taken it with her had failed. She felt that she understood Robert Di Silva, and she was sure she would be able to handle any job he gave her.

Jennifer had done her homework. She knew there were four different bureaus under the District Attorney – Trials, Appeals, Rackets and Frauds – and she wondered to which one she would be assigned. There were over two hundred assistant district attorneys in New York City and five district attorneys, one for each borough. But the most important borough, of course, was Manhattan: Robert Di Silva.

Jennifer sat in the courtroom now, at the prosecutor's table, watching Robert Di Silva at work, a powerful, relentless inquisitor.

Jennifer glanced over at the defendant, Michael Moretti. Even with everything Jennifer had read about him, she could not convince herself that Michael Moretti was a murderer. *He looks like a young movie star in a courtroom set*, Jennifer thought. He sat there motionless, only his deep, black eyes giving away whatever inner turmoil he might have felt. They moved ceaselessly, examining every corner of the room as though trying to calculate a means of escape. There was no escape. Di Silva had seen to that.

Camillo Stela was on the witness stand. If Stela had been an animal, he would have been a weasel. He had a narrow, pinched face, with thin lips and yellow buckteeth. His eyes were darting and furtive and you disbelieved him before he even opened his mouth. Robert Di Silva was aware of his witness's shortcomings, but they did not matter. What mattered was what Stela had to say. He had horror stories to tell that had never been told before, and they had the unmistakable ring of truth.

The District Attorney walked over to the witness box where Camillo Stela had been sworn in.

"Mr. Stela, I want this jury to be aware that you are a reluctant witness and that in order to persuade you to testify, the State has agreed to allow you to plead to the lesser charge of involuntary manslaughter in the murder you are charged with. Is that true?"

"Yes, sir." His right arm was twitching.

"Mr. Stela, are you acquainted with the defendant, Michael Moretti?"

"Yes, sir." He kept his eyes away from the defendant's table where Michael Moretti was sitting.

"What was the nature of your relationship?"

"I worked for Mike."

"How long have you known Michael Moretti?"

"About ten years." His voice was almost inaudible.

"Would you speak up, please?"

"About ten years." His neck was twitching now.

"Would you say you were close to the defendant?"

"Objection!" Thomas Colfax rose to his feet. Michael Moretti's attorney was a tall, silver-haired man in his fifties, the *consigliere* for the Syndicate, and one of the shrewdest criminal lawyers in the country. "The District Attorney is attempting to lead the witness."

Judge Lawrence Waldman said, "Sustained."

"I'll rephrase the question. In what capacity did you work for Mr. Moretti?"

"I was kind of what you might call a troubleshooter."

"Would you be a little more explicit?"

"Yeah. If a problem comes up – someone gets out of line, like – Mike would tell me to go straighten this party out."

"How would you do that?"

"You know – muscle."

"Could you give the jury an example?"

Thomas Colfax was on his feet. "Objection, Your Honor. This line of questioning is immaterial."

"Overruled. The witness may answer."

"Well, Mike's into loan-sharkin', right? A coupla years ago Jimmy Serrano gets behind in his payments, so Mike sends me over to teach Jimmy a lesson."

"What did that lesson consist of?"

"I broke his legs. You see," Stela explained earnestly, "if you let one guy get away with it, they're all gonna try it."

From the corner of his eye, Robert Di Silva could see the shocked reactions on the faces of the jurors.

"What other business was Michael Moretti involved in besides loan-sharking?"

"Jesus! You name it."

"I would like *you* to name it, Mr. Stela."

"Yeah. Well, like on the waterfront, Mike got a pretty good fix in with the union. Likewise the garment industry. Mike's into gamblin', juke boxes, garbage collectin', linen supplies. Like that."

"Mr. Stela, Michael Moretti is on trial for the murders of Eddie and Albert Ramos. Did you know them?"

"Oh, sure."

"Were you present when they were killed?"

"Yeah." His whole body seemed to twitch.

"Who did the actual killing?"

"Mike." For a second, his eyes caught Michael Moretti's eyes and Stela quickly looked away.

"Michael Moretti?"

"That's right."

"Why did the defendant tell you he wanted the Ramos brothers killed?"

"Well, Eddie and Al handled a book for – "

"That's a bookmaking operation? Illegal betting?"

"Yeah. Mike found out they was skimmin'. He had to teach em a lesson 'cause they was his boys, you know? He thought – "

"Objection!"

"Sustained. The witness will stick to the facts."

"The facts was that Mike tells me to invite the boys – "

"Eddie and Albert Ramos?"

"Yeah. To a little party down at The Pelican. That's a private beach club." His arm started to twitch again and Stela, suddenly aware of it, pressed against it with his other hand.

Jennifer Parker turned to look at Michael Moretti. He was watching impassively, his face and body immobile.

"What happened then, Mr. Stela?"

"I picked Eddie and Al up and drove 'em to the parkin' lot. Mike was there, waitin'. When the boys got outta the car, I moved outta the way and Mike started blastin'."

"Did you see the Ramos brothers fall to the ground?"

"Yes, sir."

"And they were dead?"

"They sure buried 'em like they was dead."

There was a ripple of sound through the courtroom. Di Silva waited until there was silence.

"Mr. Stela, you are aware that the testimony you have given in this courtroom is self-incriminating?"

"Yes, sir."

"And that you are under oath and that a man's life is at stake?"

"Yes, sir."

"You witnessed the defendant, Michael Moretti, cold-bloodedly shoot to death two men because they had withheld money from him?"

"Objection! He's leading the witness."

"Sustained."

District Attorney Di Silva looked at the faces of the jurors and what he saw there told him he had won the case. He turned to Camillo Stela.

"Mr. Stela, I know that it took a great deal of courage for you to come into this courtroom and testify. On behalf of the people of this state, I want to thank you." Di Silva turned to Thomas Colfax. "Your witness for cross."

Thomas Colfax rose gracefully to his feet. "Thank you, Mr. Di Silva." He glanced at the clock on the wall, then turned to the bench. "If it please Your Honor, it is now almost noon. I would prefer not to have my cross-examination interrupted. Might I request that the court recess for lunch now and I'll cross-examine this afternoon?"

"Very well." Judge Lawrence Waldman rapped his gavel on the bench. "This court stands adjourned until two o'clock."

Everyone in the courtroom rose as the judge stood up and walked through the side door to his chambers. The jurors began to file out of the room. Four armed deputies surrounded Camillo Stela and escorted him through a door near the front of the courtroom that led to the witness room.

At once, Di Silva was engulfed by reporters.

"Will you give us a statement?"

"How do you think the case is going so far, Mr. District Attorney?"

"How are you going to protect Stela when this is over?"

Ordinarily Robert Di Silva would not have tolerated such an intrusion in the courtroom, but he needed now, with his political ambitions, to keep the press on his side, and so he went out of his way to be polite to them.

Jennifer Parker sat there, watching the District Attorney parrying the reporters' questions.

"Are you going to get a conviction?"

"I'm not a fortune teller," Jennifer heard Di Silva say modestly. "That's what we have juries for, ladies and gentlemen. The jurors will have to decide whether Mr. Moretti is innocent or guilty."

Jennifer watched as Michael Moretti rose to his feet. He looked calm and relaxed. *Boyish* was the word that came to Jennifer's mind. It was difficult for her to believe that he was guilty of all the terrible things of which he was accused. *If I had to choose the guilty one*, Jennifer thought, *I'd choose Stela, the Twitcher.*

The reporters had moved off and Di Silva was in conference with members of his staff. Jennifer would have given anything to hear what they were discussing.

Jennifer watched as a man said something to Di Silva, detached himself from the group around the District Attorney, and hurried over toward Jennifer. He was carrying a large manila envelope. "Miss Parker?"

Jennifer looked up in surprise. "Yes."

"The Chief wants you to give this to Stela. Tell him to refresh his memory about these dates. Colfax is going to try to tear his testimony apart this afternoon and the Chief wants to make sure Stela doesn't foul up."

He handed the envelope to Jennifer and she looked over at Di Silva. *He remembered my name*, she thought. *It's a good omen.*

"Better get moving. The D.A. doesn't think Stela's that fast a study."

"Yes, sir." Jennifer hurried to her feet.

She walked over to the door she had seen Stela go through. An armed deputy blocked her way.

"Can I help you, miss?"

"District Attorney's office," Jennifer said crisply. She took out her identification card and showed it. "I have an envelope to deliver to Mr. Stela from Mr. Di Silva."

The guard examined the card carefully, then opened the door, and Jennifer found herself inside the witness room. It was a small, uncomfortable-looking room containing a battered desk, an old sofa and wooden chairs. Stela was seated in one of them, his arm twitching wildly. There were four armed deputies in the room.

As Jennifer entered, one of the guards said, "Hey! Nobody's allowed in here."

The outside guard called, "It's okay, Al. D.A.'s office."

Jennifer handed Stela the envelope. "Mr. Di Silva wants you to refresh your recollection about these dates."

Stela blinked at her and kept twitching.

2

As Jennifer was making her way out of the Criminal Courts Building on her way to lunch, she passed the open door of a deserted courtroom. She could not resist stepping inside the room for a moment.

There were fifteen rows of spectators' benches on each side of the rear area. Facing the judge's bench were two long tables, the one on the left marked *Plaintiff* and the one on the right marked *Defendant*. The jury box contained two rows of eight chairs each. *It's an ordinary courtroom*, Jennifer thought, *plain – even ugly – but it's the heart of freedom*. This room and all the courtrooms like it represented the difference between civilization and savagery. The right to a trial by a jury of one's peers was what lay at the heart of every free nation. Jennifer thought of all the countries in the world that did not have this little room, countries where citizens were taken from their beds in the middle of the night and tortured and murdered by anonymous enemies for undisclosed reasons: Iran, Uganda, Argentina, Peru, Brazil, Romania, Russia, Czechoslovakia . . . the list was depressingly long.

If the American courts were ever stripped of their power, Jennifer thought, *if citizens were ever denied the right to a trial by jury, then America would cease to exist as a free nation*. She was a part of the system now and, standing there, Jennifer was filled with an overwhelming feeling of pride. She would do everything she could to honor it, to help preserve it. She stood there for a long moment, then turned to leave.

From the far end of the hall there was a distant hum that got louder and louder, and became pandemonium. Alarm bells began to ring. Jennifer heard the sound of running feet in the corridor and saw policemen with drawn guns racing toward the front entrance of the courthouse. Jennifer's instant thought was that Michael Moretti had escaped, had somehow gotten past the barrier of guards. She hurried out into the corridor. It was bedlam. People were racing around frantically, shouting orders over the din of the clanging bells. Guards armed with riot guns had taken up positions at the exit doors. Reporters who had been telephoning in their stories were hurrying into the corridor to find out what was happening. Far down the hall, Jennifer saw District Attorney Robert Di Silva wildly issuing instructions to half a dozen policemen, his face drained of color.

My God! He's going to have a heart attack, Jennifer thought.

She pushed her way through the crowd and moved toward him, thinking that perhaps she could be of some use. As she approached, one of the deputies who had been guarding Camillo Stela looked up and saw Jennifer. He raised an arm and pointed to her, and five seconds later Jennifer Parker found herself being grabbed, handcuffed and placed under arrest.

There were four people in Judge Lawrence Waldman's chambers: Judge Waldman, District Attorney Robert Di Silva, Thomas Colfax, and Jennifer.

"You have the right to have an attorney present before you make any statement," Judge Waldman informed Jennifer, "and you have the right to remain silent. If you – "

"I don't need an attorney, Your Honor! I can explain what happened."

Robert Di Silva was leaning so close to her that Jennifer could see the throbbing of a vein in his temple. "Who paid you to give that package to Camillo Stela?"

"Paid me? Nobody paid me!" Jennifer's voice was quavering with indignation.

Di Silva picked up a familiar looking manila envelope from Judge Waldman's desk. "No one paid you? You just walked up to my witness and delivered *this?*" He shook the envelope and the body of a yellow canary fluttered onto the desk. Its neck had been broken.

Jennifer stared at it, horrified. "I – one of your men – gave me – "

"Which one of my men?"

"I – I don't know."

"But you know he was one of my men." His voice rang with disbelief.

"Yes. I saw him talking to you and then he walked over to me and handed me the envelope and said you wanted me to give it to Mr. Stela. He – he even knew my name."

"I'll bet he did. How much did they pay you?"

It's all a nightmare, Jennifer thought. *I'm going to wake up any minute and it's going to be six o'clock in the morning, and I'm going to get dressed and go to be sworn in on the District Attorney's staff.*

"*How much?*" The anger in him was so violent that it forced Jennifer to her feet.

"Are you accusing me of – ?"

"Accusing you!" Robert Di Silva clenched his fists. "Lady, I haven't even started on you. By the time you get out of prison you'll be too old to spend that money."

"There is no money." Jennifer stared at him defiantly.

Thomas Colfax had been sitting back, quietly listening to the conversation. He interrupted now to say, "'excuse me, Your Honor, but I'm afraid this isn't getting us anywhere."

"I agree," Judge Waldman replied. He turned to the District Attorney. "Where do you stand, Bobby? Is Stela still willing to be cross-examined?"

"Cross-examined? He's a basket case! Scared out of his wits. He won't take the stand again."

Thomas Colfax said smoothly, "If I can't cross-examine the prosecution's chief witness, Your Honor, I'm going to have to move for a mistrial."

Everyone in the room knew what that would mean: Michael Moretti would walk out of the courtroom a free man.

Judge Waldman looked over at the District Attorney. "Did you tell your witness he can be held in contempt?"

"Yes. Stela's more scared of them than he is of us." He turned to direct a venomous look at Jennifer. "He doesn't think we can protect him anymore."

Judge Waldman said slowly, "Then I'm afraid this court has no alternative but to grant the defense's request and declare a mistrial."

Robert Di Silva stood there, listening to his case being wiped out. Without Stela, he had no case. Michael Moretti was beyond his reach now, but Jennifer Parker was not. He was going to make her pay for what she had done to him.

Judge Waldman was saying, "I'll give instructions for the defendant to be freed and the jury dismissed."

Thomas Colfax said, "Thank you, Your Honor." There was no sign of triumph in his face.

"If there's nothing else . . . ," Judge Waldman began.

"There is something else!" Robert Di Silva turned to Jennifer Parker. "I want her held for obstructing justice, for tampering with a witness in a capital case, for conspiracy, for . . ." He was incoherent with rage.

In her anger, Jennifer found her voice. "You can't prove a single one of those charges because they're not true. I – I may be guilty of being stupid, but that's *all* I'm guilty of. No one bribed me to do anything. I thought I was delivering a package for you."

Judge Waldman looked at Jennifer and said, "Whatever the motivation, the consequences have been extremely unfortunate. I am going to request that the Appellate Division undertake an investigation and, if it feels the circumstances warrant it, to begin disbarment proceedings against you."

Jennifer felt suddenly faint. "Your Honor, I – "

"That is all for now, Miss Parker."

Jennifer stood there a moment, staring at their hostile faces. There was nothing more she could say.

The yellow canary on the desk had said it all.

3

Jennifer Parker was not only on the evening news – she *was* the evening news. The story of her delivering a dead canary to the District Attorney's star witness was irresistible. Every television channel had pictures of Jennifer leaving Judge Waldman's chambers, fighting her way out of the courthouse, besieged by the press and the public.

Jennifer could not believe the sudden horrifying publicity that was being showered on her. They were hammering at her from all sides: television reporters, radio reporters and newspaper people. She wanted desperately to flee from them, but her pride would not let her.

"Who gave you the yellow canary, Miss Parker?"

"Have you ever met Michael Moretti?"

"Did you know that Di Silva was planning to use this case to get into the governor's office?"

"The District Attorney says he's going to have you disbarred. Are you going to fight it?"

To each question Jennifer had a tight-lipped "No comment."

On the CBS evening news they called her "Wrong-Way Parker," the girl who had gone off in the wrong direction. An ABC newsman referred to her as the "Yellow Canary." On NBC, a sports commentator compared her to Roy Riegels, the football player who had carried the ball to his own team's one-yard line.

In Tony's Place, a restaurant that Michael Moretti owned, a celebration was taking place. There were a dozen men in the room, drinking and boisterous.

Michael Moretti sat alone at the bar, in an oasis of silence, watching Jennifer Parker on television. He raised his glass in a salute to her and drank.

Lawyers everywhere discussed the Jennifer Parker episode. Half of them believed she had been bribed by the Mafia, and the other half that she had been an innocent dupe. But no matter which side they were on, they all concurred on one point: Jennifer Parker's short career as an attorney was finished.

She had lasted exactly four hours.

She had been born in Kelso, Washington, a small timber town founded in 1847 by a homesick Scottish surveyor who named it for his home town in Scotland.

Jennifer's father was an attorney, first for the lumber companies that dominated the town, then later for the workers in the sawmills. Jennifer's earliest memories of growing up were filled with joy. The state of Washington was a storybook place for a child, full of spectacular mountains and glaciers and national parks. There were skiing and canoeing and, when she was older, ice climbing on glaciers and pack trips to places with wonderful names: Ohanapecosh and Nisqually and Lake Cle Elum and Chenuis Falls and Horse Heaven and the Yakima Valley. Jennifer learned to climb on Mount Rainier and to ski at Timberline with her father.

Her father always had time for her, while her mother, beautiful and restless, was mysteriously busy and seldom at home. Jennifer adored her father. Abner Parker was a mixture of English and Irish and Scottish blood. He was of medium height, with black hair and green-blue eyes. He was a compassionate man with a deep-rooted sense of justice. He was not interested in money, he was interested in people. He would sit and talk to Jennifer by the hour, telling her about the cases he was handling and the problems of the people who came into his unpretentious little office, and it did not occur to Jennifer until years later that he talked to her because he had no one else with whom to share things.

After school Jennifer would hurry over to the courthouse to watch her father at work. If court was not in session she would hang around his office, listening to him discuss his cases and his clients. They never talked about her going to law school; it was simply taken for granted.

When Jennifer was fifteen she began spending her summers working for her father. At an age when other girls were dating boys and going steady, Jennifer was absorbed in lawsuits and wills.

Boys were interested in her, but she seldom went out. When her father would ask her why, she would reply, "They're all so *young*, Papa." She knew that one day she would marry a lawyer like her father.

On Jennifer's sixteenth birthday, her mother left town with the eighteen-year-old son of their next-door neighbor, and Jennifer's father quietly died. It took seven years for his heart to stop beating, but he was dead from the moment he heard the news about his wife. The whole town knew and was sympathetic, and that, of course, made it worse, for Abner Parker was a proud man. That was when he began to drink. Jennifer did everything she could to comfort him but it was no use, and nothing was ever the same again.

The next year, when it came time to go to college, Jennifer wanted to stay home with her father, but he would not bear of it.

"We're going into partnership, Jennie," he told her. "You hurry up and get that law degree."

When she was graduated she enrolled at the University of Washington in Seattle to study law. During the first year of school, while Jennifer's classmates were flailing about in an impenetrable swamp of contracts, torts, property, civil procedure and criminal law, Jennifer felt as though she had come home. She moved into the university dormitory and got a job at the Law Library.

Jennifer loved Seattle. On Sundays, she and an Indian student named Ammini Williams and a big, rawboned Irish girl named Josephine Collins would go rowing on Green Lake in the heart of the city, or attend the Gold Cup races on Lake Washington and watch the brightly colored hydroplanes flashing by.

There were great jazz clubs in Seattle, and Jennifer's favorite was Peter's Poop Deck, where they had crates with slabs of wood on top instead of tables.

Afternoons, Jennifer, Ammini and Josephine would meet at The Hasty Tasty, a hangout where they had the best cottage-fried potatoes in the world.

There were two boys who pursued Jennifer: a young, attractive medical student named Noah Larkin and a law student named Ben Munro; and from time to time Jennifer would go out on dates with them, but she was far too busy to think about a serious romance.

The seasons were crisp and wet and windy and it seemed to rain all the time. Jennifer wore a green-and-blue-plaid lumber jacket that caught the raindrops in its shaggy wool and made her eyes flash like emeralds. She walked through the rain, lost in her own secret thoughts, never knowing that all those she passed would file away the memory.

In spring the girls blossomed out in their bright cotton dresses. There were six fraternities in a row at the university, and the fraternity brothers would gather on the lawn and watch the girls go by, but there was something about Jennifer that made them feel unexpectedly shy. There was a special quality about her that was difficult for them to define, a feeling that she had already attained something for which they were still searching.

Every summer Jennifer went home to visit her father. He had changed so much. He was never drunk, but neither was he ever sober. He had retreated into an emotional fortress where nothing could touch him again.

He died when Jennifer was in her last term at law school. The town remembered, and there were almost a hundred people at Abner Parker's funeral, people he had helped and advised and befriended over the years. Jennifer did her grieving in private. She had lost more than a father. She had lost a teacher and a mentor.

After the funeral Jennifer returned to Seattle to finish school. Her father had left her less than a thousand dollars and she had to make a decision about what to do with her life. She knew that she could not return to Kelso to practice law, for there she would always be the little girl whose mother had run off with a teenager.

Because of her high scholastic average, Jennifer had interviews with a dozen top law firms around the country, and received several offers.

Warren Oakes, her criminal law professor, told her: "That's a real tribute, young lady. It's very difficult for a woman !o get into a good law firm."

Jennifer's dilemma was that she no longer had a home or roots. She was not certain where she wanted to live.

Shortly before graduation Jennifer's problem was solved for her. Professor Oakes asked her to see him after class.

"I have a letter from the District Attorney's office in Manhattan, asking me to recommend my brightest graduate for his staff. Interested?"

New York. "Yes, sir." Jennifer was so stunned that the answer just popped out.

She flew to New York to take the bar examination, and returned to Kelso to close her father's law office. It was a bittersweet experience, filled with memories of the past and it seemed to Jennifer that she had grown up in that office.

She got a job as an assistant in the law library of the university to tide her over until she heard whether she had passed the New York bar examination.

"It's one of the toughest in the country," Professor Oakes warned her.

But Jennifer *knew*.

She received her notice that she had passed and an offer from the New York District Attorney's office on the same day.

One week later, Jennifer was on her way east.

She found a tiny apartment (*Spc W/U fpl gd loc nds sm wk*, the ad said) on lower Third Avenue, with a fake fireplace in a steep fourth-floor walk-up. *The exercise will do me good*, Jennifer told herself. There were no mountains to climb in Manhattan, no rapids to ride. The apartment consisted of a small living room with a couch that turned into a lumpy bed, and a tiny bathroom with a window that someone long ago had painted over with black paint, sealing it shut. The furniture looked like something that could have been donated by the Salvation Army. *Oh, well, I won't be living in this place long*. Jennifer thought. *This is just temporary until I prove myself as a lawyer.*

That had been the dream. The reality was that she had been in New York less than seventy-two hours, had been thrown off the District Attorney's staff and was facing disbarment.

Jennifer quit reading newspapers and magazines and stopped watching television, because wherever she turned she saw herself. She felt that people were staring at her on the street, on the bus, and at the market. She began to hide out in her tiny apartment, refusing to answer the telephone or the doorbell. She thought about packing her suitcases and returning to Washington. She thought about getting a job in some other field. She thought about suicide. She spent long hours composing letters to District Attorney Robert Di Silva. Half the letters were scathing indictments of his insensitivity and lack of understanding. The other half were abject apologies, with a plea for him to give her another chance. None of the letters was ever sent.

For the first time in her life Jennifer was overwhelmed with a sense of desperation. She had no friends in New York, no one to talk to. She stayed locked in her apartment all day, and late at night she would slip out to walk the deserted streets of the city. The derelicts who peopled the night never accosted her. Perhaps they saw their own loneliness and despair mirrored in her eyes.

Over and over, as she walked, Jennifer would envision the courtroom scene in her mind, always changing the ending.

A man detached himself from the group around Di Silva and hurried toward her. He was carrying a manila envelope.

Miss Parker?

Yes.

The Chief wants you to give this to Stela.

Jennifer looked at him coolly. Let me see your identification, please.

The man panicked and ran.

A man detached himself from the group around Di Silva and hurried toward her. He was carrying a manila envelope.

Miss Parker?

Yes.

The Chief wants you to give this to Stela. He thrust the envelope into her hands.

Jennifer opened the envelope and saw the dead canary inside. I'm placing you under arrest.

A man detached himself from the group around Di Silva and hurried toward her. He was carrying a manila envelope. He walked past her to another young assistant district attorney and handed him the envelope. The Chief wants you to give this to Stela.

She could rewrite the scene as many times as she liked, but nothing was changed. One foolish mistake had destroyed her. And yet – who said she was destroyed? The press? Di Silva? She had not heard another word about her disbarment, and until she did she was still an attorney. *There are law firms that made me offers*, Jennifer told herself.

Filled with a new sense of resolve, Jennifer pulled out the list of the firms she had talked to and began to make a series of telephone calls. None of the men she asked to speak to was in, and not one of her calls was returned. It took her four days to realize that she was the pariah of the legal profession. The furor over the case had died down, but everyone still remembered.

Jennifer kept telephoning prospective employers, going from despair to indignation to frustration and back to despair again. She wondered what she was going to do with the rest of her life, and each time it came back to the same thing: All she wanted to do, the one thing she really cared about, was to practice law. She was a lawyer and, by God, until they stopped her she was going to find a way to practice her profession.

She began to make the rounds of Manhattan law offices. She would walk in unannounced, give her name to the receptionist and ask to see the head of personnel. Occasionally she was granted an interview, but when she was, Jennifer had the feeling it was out of curiosity. She was a freak and they wanted to see what she looked like in person. Most of the time she was simply informed there were no openings.

At the end of six weeks, Jennifer's money was running out. She would have moved to a cheaper apartment, but there *were* no cheaper apartments. She began to skip breakfast and lunch, and to have dinner at one of the little corner dinettes where the food was bad but the prices were good. She discovered the Steak & Brew and Roast-and-Brew, where for a modest sum she was able to get a main course, all the salad she could eat, and all the beer she could drink. Jennifer hated beer, but it was filling.

When Jennifer had gone through her list of large law firms, she armed herself with a list of smaller firms and began to call on them, but her reputation had preceded her even there. She received a lot of propositions from interested males, but no job offers. She was beginning to get desperate. *All right*, she thought defiantly, *if no one wants to hire me, I'll open my own law office.* The catch was that that took money. Ten thousand dollars, at least. She would need enough for rent, telephone, a secretary, law books, a desk and chairs, stationery . . . she could not even afford the stamps.

Jennifer had counted on her salary from the District Attorney's office but that, of course, was gone forever. She could forget about severance pay. She had not been severed; she had been beheaded. No, there was no way she could afford to open her own office, no matter how small. The answer was to find someone with whom to share offices.

Jennifer bought a copy of *The New York Times* and began to search through the want ads. It was not until she was near the bottom of the page that she came across a small advertisement that read: *Wanted/Prof man sh sm off w/2 oth/prof men. Rs rent.*

The last two words appealed to Jennifer enormously. She was not a professional man, but her sex should not matter. She tore out the ad and took the subway down to the address listed.

It was a dilapidated old building on lower Broadway. The office was on the tenth floor and the flaking sign on the door read:

KENNETH BAILEY

ACE INVEST GA IONS

Beneath it:

ROCKEFELLER C LLECTION AG NCY

Jennifer took a deep breath, opened the door and walked in. She was standing in the middle of a small, windowless office. There were three scarred desks and chairs crowded into the room, two of them occupied.

Seated at one of the desks was a bald, shabbily dressed, middle-aged man working on some papers. Against the opposite wall at another desk was a man in his early thirties. He had brick-red hair and bright blue eyes. His skin was pale and freckled. He was dressed in tight-fitting jeans, a tee shirt, and white canvas shoes without socks. He was talking into the telephone.

"Don't worry, Mrs. Desser, I have two of my best operatives working on your case. We should have news of your husband any day now. I'm afraid I'll have to ask you for a little more expense money . . . No, don't bother mailing it. The mails are terrible. I'll be in your neighborhood this afternoon. I'll stop by and pick it up."

He replaced the receiver and looked up and saw Jennifer.

He rose to his feet, smiled and held out a strong, firm hand. "I'm Kenneth Bailey. And what can I do for you this morning?"

Jennifer looked around the small, airless room and said uncertainly, "I – I came about your ad."

"Oh." There was surprise in his blue eyes.

The bald-headed man was staring at Jennifer.

Kenneth Bailey said, "This is Otto Wenzel. He's the Rockefeller Collection Agency."

Jennifer nodded. "Hello." She turned back to Kenneth Bailey. "And you're Ace Investigations?"

"That's right. What's your scam?"

"My – ?" Then, realizing, "I'm an attorney."

Kenneth Bailey studied her skeptically. "And you want to set up an office *here?*"

Jennifer looked around the dreary office again and visualized herself at the empty desk, between these two men.

"Perhaps I'll look a little further," she said. "I'm not sure – "

"Your rent would only be ninety dollars a month."

"I could *buy* this building for ninety dollars a month," Jennifer replied. She turned to leave.

"Hey, wait a minute."

Jennifer paused.

Kenneth Bailey ran a hand over his pale chin. "I'll make a deal with you. Sixty. When your business gets rolling we'll talk about an increase."

It was a bargain. Jennifer knew that she could never find any space elsewhere for that amount. On the other had, there was no way she could ever attract clients to this hellhole. There was one other thing she had to consider. She did not have the sixty dollars.

"I'll take it," Jennifer said.

"You won't be sorry," Kenneth Bailey promised. "When do you want to move your things in?"

"They're in."

Kenneth Bailey painted the sign on the door himself. It read:

JENNIFER PARKER

ATTORNEY AT LAW

Jennifer studied the sign with mixed feelings. In her deepest depressions it had never occurred to her that she would have her name under that of a private investigator and a bill collector. Yet, as she looked at the faintly crooked sign, she could not help feeling a sense of pride. She was an attorney. The sign on the door proved it.

Now that Jennifer had office space, the only thing she lacked was clients.

Jennifer could no longer afford even the Steak & Brew. She made herself a breakfast of toast and coffee on the hot plate she had set up over the radiator in her tiny bathroom. She ate no lunch and had dinner at Chock Full O'Nuts or Zum Zum, where they served large pieces of wurst, slabs of bread and hot potato salad.

She arrived at her desk promptly at nine o'clock every morning, but there was nothing for her to do except listen to Ken Bailey and Otto Wenzel talking on the telephone.

Ken Bailey's cases seemed to consist mostly of finding runaway spouses and children, and at first Jennifer was convinced that he was a con man, making extravagant promises and collecting large advances. But Jennifer quickly learned that Ken Bailey worked hard and delivered often. He was bright and he was clever.

Otto Wenzel was an enigma. his telephone rang constantly. He would pick it up, mutter a few words into it, write something on a piece of paper and disappear for a few hours.

"Oscar does repo's," Ken Bailey explained to Jennifer one day.

"Repo's?"

"Yeah. Collection companies use him to get back auto mobiles, television sets, washing machines – you name it." He looked at Jennifer curiously. "You got *any* clients?"

"I have some things coming up," Jennifer said evasively.

He nodded. "Don't let it get you down. Anyone can make a mistake."

Jennifer felt herself flushing. So he knew about her.

Ken Bailey was unwrapping a large, thick roast-beef sandwich. "Like some?"

It looked delicious. "No, thanks," Jennifer said firmly. "I never eat lunch."

"Okay."

She watched him bite into the juicy sandwich. He saw her expression and said, "You sure you – ?"

"No, thank you. I – I have a appointment."

Ken Bailey watched Jennifer walk out of the office and his face was thoughtful. He prided himself on his ability to read character, but Jennifer Parker puzzled him. From the television and newspaper accounts he had been sure someone had paid this girl to destroy the case against Michael Moretti. After meeting Jennifer, Ken was less certain. He had been married once and had gone through hell, and he held women in low esteem. But something told him that this one was special. She was beautiful, bright and very proud. *Jesus! he* said to himself. *Don't be a fool! One murder on your conscience is enough.*

Emma Lazarus was a sentimental idiot, Jennifer thought. "Give me your tired, your poor, your huddled masses yearning to breathe free . . . Send these, the homeless, tempest-tossed, to me." Indeed! Anyone manufacturing welcome mats in New York would have gone out of business in an hour. In New York no one cared whether you lived or died. Stop feeling sorry for yourself! Jennifer told herself. But it was difficult. Her resources had dwindled to eighteen dollars, the rent on her apartment was overdue, and her share of the office rent was due in two days. She did not have enough money to stay in New York any longer, and she did not have enough money to leave.

Jennifer had gone through the Yellow Pages, calling law offices alphabetically, trying to get a job. She made the calls from telephone booths because she was too embarrassed to let Ken Bailey and Otto Wenzel hear her conversations. The results were always the same. No one was interested in hiring her. She would have to return to Kelso and get a job as a legal aide or as a secretary to one of her father's friends. How he would have hated that! It was a bitter defeat, but there were no choices left. She would be returning home a failure. The immediate problem facing her was transportation. She looked through the afternoon *New York Post* and found an ad for someone to share driving expenses to Seattle. There was a telephone number and Jennifer called it. There was no answer. She decided she would try again in the morning.

The following day, Jennifer went to her office for the last time. Otto Wenzel was out, but Ken Bailey was there, on the telephone, as usual. He was wearing blue jeans and a vee-neck cashmere sweater.

"I found your wife," he was saying. "The only problem, pal, is that she doesn't want to go home. . . . I know. Who can figure women out? . . . Okay. I'll tell you where she's staying and you can try to sweet-talk her into coming back." He gave the address of a midtown hotel. "My pleasure." He hung up and swung around to face Jennifer. "You're late this morning."

"Mr. Bailey, I – I'm afraid I'm going to have to be leaving. I'll send you the rent money I owe you as soon as I'm able to."

Ken Bailey leaned back in his chair and studied her. His look made Jennifer uncomfortable.

"Will that be all right?" she asked.

"Going back to Washington?"

Jennifer nodded.

Ken Bailey said, "Before you leave, would you do me a little favor? A lawyer friend's been bugging me to serve some subpoenas for him, and I haven't got time. He pays twelve-fifty for each subpoena plus mileage. Would you help me out?"

One hour later Jennifer Parker found herself in the plush law offices of Peabody & Peabody. This was the kind of firm she had visualized working in one day, a full partner with a beautiful corner suite. She was escorted to a small back room where a harassed secretary handed her a stack of subpoenas.

"Here. Be sure to keep a record of your mileage. You do have a car, don't you?"

"No, I'm afraid I – "

"Well, if you use the subway, keep track of the fares."

"Right."

Jennifer spent the rest of the day delivering subpoenas in the Bronx, Brooklyn and Queens in a downpour. By eight o'clock that evening, she had made fifty dollars. She arrived back at her tiny apartment chilled and exhausted. But at least she had earned some money, her first since coming to New York. And the secretary had told her there were plenty more subpoenas to serve. It was hard work, running all over town, and it was humiliating. She had had doors slammed in her face, had been cursed at, threatened, and propositioned twice. The prospect of facing another day like that was dismaying; and yet, as long as she could remain in New York there was hope, no matter how faint.

Jennifer ran a hot bath and stepped into it, slowly sinking down into the tub, feeling the luxury of the water lapping over her body. She had not realized how exhausted she was. Every muscle seemed to ache. She decided that what she needed was a good dinner to cheer her up. She would splurge. *I'll treat myself to a real restaurant with tablecloths and napkins*, Jennifer thought. *Perhaps they'll have soft music and I'll have a glass of white wine and –*

Jennifer's thoughts were interrupted by the ringing of the doorbell. It was an alien sound. She had not had a single visitor since she had moved in two months earlier. It could only be the surly landlady about the overdue rent. Jennifer lay still, hoping she would go away, too weary to move.

The doorbell rang again. Reluctantly, Jennifer dragged herself from the warm tub. She slipped on a terry-cloth robe and went to the door.

"Who is it?"
A masculine voice on the other side of the door said, "Miss Jennifer Parker?"
"Yes."
"My name is Adam Warner. I'm an attorney."
Puzzled, Jennifer put the chain on the door and opened it a crack. The man standing in the hall was in his middle thirties, tall and blond and broad-shouldered, with gray-blue inquisitive eyes behind horn-rimmed glasses. He was dressed in a tailored suit that must have cost a fortune.
"May I come in?" he asked.
Muggers did not wear tailored suits, Gucci shoes and silk ties. Nor did they have long, sensitive hands with carefully manicured nails.
"Just a moment"
Jennifer unfastened the chain and opened the door. As Adam Warner walked in, Jennifer glanced around the one-room apartment, seeing it through his eyes, and winced. He looked like a man who was used to better things.
"What can I do for you, Mr. Warner?"
Even as she spoke, Jennifer suddenly knew why he was there, and she was filled with a quick sense of excitement. It was about one of the jobs she had applied for! She wished that she had on a nice, dark blue tailored robe, that her hair was combed, that –
Adam Warner said, "I'm a member of the Disciplinary Committee of the New York Bar Association, Miss Parker. District Attorney Robert Di Silva and Judge Lawrence Waldman have requested the Appellate Division to begin disbarment proceedings against you."

4

The law offices of Needham, Finch, Pierce and Warner were located at 30 Wall Street, occupying the entire top floor of the building. There were a hundred and twenty-five lawyers in the firm. The offices smelled of old money and were done in the quiet elegance befitting an organization that represented some of the biggest names in industry.
Adam Warner and Stewart Needham were having their ritual morning tea. Stewart Needham was a dapper, trim man in his late sixties. He had a neat Vandyke beard and wore a tweed suit and vest. He looked as though he belonged to an older era, but as hundreds of opponents had learned to their sorrow through the years, Stewart Needham's mind belonged very much to the twentieth century. He was a titan, but his name was known only in the circles where it mattered. He preferred to remain in the background and use his considerable influence to affect the outcome of legislation, high government appointments

and national politics. He was a New Englander, born and reared taciturn.

Adam Warner was married to Needham's niece Mary Beth, and was Needham's protégé. Adam's father had been a respected senator. Adam himself was a brilliant lawyer. When he had been graduated *magna cum laude* from Harvard Law School, he had had offers from prestigious law firms all over the country. He chose Needham, Finch and Pierce, and seven years later became a partner. Adam was physically attractive and charming, and his intelligence seemed to add an extra dimension to him. He had an easy sureness about himself that women found challenging. Adam had long since developed a system for dissuading over-amorous female clients. He had been married to Mary Beth for fourteen years and did not approve of extramarital affairs.

"More tea, Adam?" Stewart Needham asked.

"No, thanks." Adam Warner hated tea, and he had been drinking it every morning for the last eight years only because he did not want to hurt his partner's feelings. It was a brew that Needham concocted himself and it was dreadful.

Stewart Needham had two things on his mind and, typically, he began with the pleasant news. "I had a meeting with a few friends last night," Needham said. *A few friends* would be a group of the top power brokers in the country. "They're considering asking you to run for United States senator, Adam."

Adam felt a sense of elation. Knowing Stewart Needham's cautious nature, Adam was certain that the conversation had been more than casual or Needham would not have brought it up now.

"The big question, of course, is whether you're interested. It would mean a lot of changes in your life."

Adam Warner was aware of that. If he won the election, it would mean moving to Washington, D.C., giving up his law practice, starting a whole new life. He was sure that Mary Beth would enjoy it; Adam was not so sure about himself. And yet, he had been reared to assume responsibility. Also, he had to admit to himself that there was a pleasure in power.

"I'd be very interested, Stewart."

Stewart Needham nodded with satisfaction. "Good. They'll be pleased." He poured himself another cup of the dreadful brew and casually broached the other subject that was on his mind. "There's a little job the Disciplinary Committee of the Bar Association would like you to handle, Adam. Shouldn't take you more than an hour or two."

"What is it?"

"It's the Michael Moretti trial. Apparently, someone got to one of Bobby Di Silva's young assistants and paid her off."

"I read about it. The canary."

"Right. Judge Waldman and Bobby would like her name removed from the roster of our honorable profession. So would I. It reeks."

"What do they want me to do?"

"Just make a quick check, verify that this Parker girl behaved illegally or unethically, and then recommend disbarment proceedings. She'll be served with a notice to show cause and they'll handle the rest of it. It's just routine."

Adam was puzzled by something. "Why me, Stewart? We have a couple of dozen young lawyers around here who could handle this."

"Our revered District Attorney specifically asked for you. He wants to make sure nothing goes wrong. As we're both aware," he added dryly, "Bobby's not the most forgiving man in the world. He wants the Parker woman's hide nailed up on his wall."

Adam Warner sat there, thinking about his busy schedule.

"You never know when we might need a favor from the D.A.'s office, Adam. Quid pro quo. It's all cut and dried."

"All right, Stewart." Adam rose to his feet.

"Sure you won't have some more tea?"

"No, thanks. It was as good as always."

When Adam Warner returned to his office he rang for one of his paralegal assistants, Lucinda, a bright, young Black woman.

"Cindy, get me all the information you can on an attorney named Jennifer Parker."

She grinned and said, "The yellow canary."

Everybody knew about her.

Late that afternoon Adam Warner was studying the transcript of the court proceedings in the case of *The People of New York v. Michael Moretti.* Robert Di Silva had had it delivered by special messenger. It was long past midnight when Adam finished. He had asked Mary Beth to attend a dinner party without him, and had sent out for sandwiches. When Adam was through reading the transcript, there was no doubt in his mind that Michael Moretti would have been found guilty by the jury if fate had not intervened in the form of Jennifer Parker. Di Silva had prosecuted the case flawlessly.

Adam turned to the transcript of the deposition that had been taken in Judge Waldman's chambers afterward.

DI SILVA: *You are a college graduate?*

PARKER: *Yes, sir.*

DI SILVA: *And a law school graduate?*

PARKER: *Yes, sir.*

DI SILVA: *And a stranger hands you a package, tells you to deliver it to a key witness in a murder trial and you just do it? Wouldn't you say that went beyond the bounds of stupidity?*

PARKER: *It didn't happen that way.*

DI SILVA: *You said it did.*

PARKER: *What I mean is, I didn't think he was a stranger. I thought he was on your staff.*

DI SILVA: *What made you think that?*

PARKER: *I've told you. I saw him talking to you and then he came over to me with this envelope and he called me by name, and he said you wanted me to deliver it to the witness. It all happened so fast that –*

DI SILVA: *I don't think it happened that fast. I think it took time to set it up. It took time to arrange for someone to pay you off to deliver it.*

PARKER: *That's not true. I –*

DI SILVA: *What's not true? That you didn't know you were delivering the envelope?*

PARKER: *I didn't know what was in it.*

DI SILVA: *So it's true that someone paid you.*

PARKER: *I'm not going to let you twist my words around. No one paid me anything.*

DI SILVA: *You did it as a favor?*

PARKER: *No. I thought I was acting on your instructions.*

DI SILVA: *You said the man called you by name.*

PARKER: *Yes.*

DI SILVA: *How did he know your name?*

PARKER: *I don't know.*

DI SILVA: *Oh, come on. You must have some idea. Maybe it was a lucky guess. Maybe he just looked around that courtroom and said, There's someone who looks like her name could be Jennifer Parker. Do you think that was it?*

PARKER: *I've told you. I don't know.*

DI SILVA: *How long have you and Michael Moretti been sweethearts?*

PARKER: *Mr. Di Silva, we've gone all over this. You've been questioning me now for five hours. I'm tired. I have nothing more to add. May I be excused?*

DI SILVA: *If you move out of that chair I'll have you placed under arrest. You're in big trouble, Miss Parker. There's only one way you're going to get out of it. Stop lying and start telling the truth.*

PARKER: *I've told you the truth. I've told you everything I know.*

DI SILVA: *Except the name of the man who handed you the envelope. I want his name and I want to know how much he paid you.*

There were thirty more pages of transcript. Robert Di Silva had done everything but beat Jennifer Parker with a rubber hose. She had stuck to her story.

Adam closed the transcript and wearily rubbed his eyes. It was two A.M. Tomorrow he would dispose of the Jennifer Parker matter.

To Adam Warner's surprise, the Jennifer Parker case would not be disposed of so easily. Because Adam was a methodical man he ran a check on Jennifer Parker's background. As far as he could determine, she had no crime connections, nor was there anything to link her with Michael Moretti.

There was something about the case that disturbed Adam. Jennifer Parker's defense was too flimsy. If she were working for Moretti, he would have protected her with a reasonably plausible story. As it was, her story was so transparently naïve that it had a ring of truth about it.

At noon Adam received a call from the District Attorney. "How goes it Adam?"

"Fine, Robert."

"I understand you're handling the hatchet-man job on the Jennifer Parker matter."

Adam Warner winced at the phrase. "I've agreed to make a recommendation, yes."

"I'm going to put her away for a long time." Adam was taken aback by the hatred in the District Attorney's voice.

"Easy, Robert. She's not disbarred yet."

Di Silva chuckled. "I'll leave that to you, my friend." His tone changed. "I hear on the grapevine that you may be moving to Washington soon. I want you to know that you can count on my full support."

Which was considerable, Adam Warner knew. The District Attorney had been around a long time. He knew where the bodies were buried and he knew how to squeeze the most out of that information.

"Thanks, Robert. I appreciate that."

"My pleasure, Adam. I'll wait to hear from you."

Meaning Jennifer Parker. The quid pro quo Stewart Needham had mentioned, with the girl used as a pawn. Adam Warner thought about Robert Di Silva's words: *I'm going to put her away for a long time.* From reading the transcript, Adam judged that there was no real evidence against Jennifer Parker. Unless she confessed, or unless someone came forward with information that proved criminal complicity, Di Silva would not be able to touch the girl. He was counting on Adam to give him his vengeance.

The cold, harsh words of the transcript were clear-cut, and yet Adam wished he could have heard the tone of Jennifer Parker's voice when she denied her guilt.

There were pressing matters claiming Adam's attention, important cases involving major clients. It would have been easy to go ahead and carry out the wishes of Stewart Needham, Judge Lawrence Waldman and Robert Di Silva, but some instinct made Adam Warner hesitate. He picked up Jennifer Parker's file again, scribbled some notes and began to make some long-distance telephone calls.

Adam had been given a responsibility and he intended to carry it through to the best of his ability. He was all too familiar with the long, back-breaking hours of study and hard work it took to become an attorney and to pass the bar. It was a prize that took years to attain, and he was not about to deprive someone of it unless he was certain there was justification.

The following morning Adam Warner was on a plane to Seattle, Washington. He had meetings with Jennifer Parker's law professors, with the head of a law firm where she had clerked for two summers, and with some of Jennifer's former classmates.

Stewart Needham telephoned Adam in Seattle. "What are you doing up there, Adam? You've got a big case load waiting for you back here. That Parker thing should have been a snap."

"A few questions have arisen," Adam said carefully. "I'll be back in a day or so, Stewart."

There was a pause. "I see. Let's not waste any more time on her than we have to."

By the time Adam Warner left Seattle, he felt he knew Jennifer Parker almost as well as she knew herself. He had built up a portrait of her in his mind, a mental identikit, with pieces filled in by her law professors, her landlady, members of the law firm where she had served as a clerk, and classmates. The picture that Adam had acquired bore no resemblance to the picture Robert Di Silva had given him. Unless Jennifer Parker was the most consummate actress who ever lived, there was no way she could have been involved in a plot to free a man like Michael Moretti.

Now, almost two weeks after he had had that morning conversation with Stewart Needham, Adam Warner found himself facing the girl whose past he had been exploring. Adam had seen newspaper pictures of Jennifer, but they had not prepared him for the impact she made in person. Even in an old robe, without makeup, and her dark brown hair bath-damp, she was breathtaking.

Adam said, "I've been assigned to investigate your part in the Michael Moretti trial, Miss Parker."

"Have you now!" Jennifer could feel an anger rising in her. It started as a spark and became a flame that exploded inside her. They still were not through with her. They were going to make her pay for the rest of her life. Well, she had had enough.

When Jennifer spoke, her voice was trembling. "I have nothing to say to you! You go back and tell them whatever you please. I did something stupid, but as far as I know, there's no law against stupidity. The District Attorney thinks someone paid me off." She waved a scornful hand in the air. "If I had any money, do you think I'd be living in a place like this?" Her voice was beginning to choke up. "I – I don't care what you do. All I want is to be left alone. Now please go away!"

Jennifer turned and fled into the bathroom, slamming the door behind her.

She stood against the sink, taking deep breaths, wiping the tears from her eyes. She knew she had behaved stupidly. *That's twice*, she thought wryly. She should have handled Adam Warner differently. She should have tried to explain, instead of attacking him. Maybe then she would not be disbarred. But she knew that was wishful thinking. Sending someone to question her was a charade. The next step would be to serve her with an order to show cause, and the formal machinery would be set in motion. There would be a trial panel of three attorneys who would make their recommendation to the Disciplinary Board which would make its report to the Board of Governors. The recommendation was a foregone conclusion: disbarment. She would be forbidden to practice law in the state of New York. Jennifer thought bitterly, *There's one bright side to this. I can get into the* Guinness Book of Records *for the shortest law career in history.*

She stepped into the bath again and lay back, letting the still-warm water lap at her, soothing away her tension. At this moment she was too tired to care what happened to her. She closed her eyes and let her mind drift. She was half asleep when the chill of the water awakened her. She had no idea how long she had lain in the tub. Reluctantly she stepped out and began toweling herself dry. She was no longer hungry. The scene with Adam Warner had taken her appetite away.

Jennifer combed her hair and creamed her face and decided she would go to bed without dinner. In the morning she would telephone about the ride to Seattle. She opened the bathroom door and walked into the living room.

Adam Warner was seated in a chair, leafing through a magazine. He looked up as Jennifer came into the room, naked.

"I'm sorry," Adam said. "I

Jennifer gave a small cry of alarm and fled to the bathroom, where she put on her robe. When she stepped out to confront Adam again, Jennifer was furious.

"The inquisition is over. I asked you to leave."

Adam put the magazine down and said quietly, "Miss Parker, do you think we could discuss this calmly for a moment?"

"No!" All the old rage boiled up in Jennifer again. "I have nothing more to say to you or your damned disciplinary committee. I'm tired of being treated like – like I'm some kind of criminal!"

"Have I said you were a criminal?" Adam asked quietly.

"You – isn't that why you're here?"

"I told you why I'm here. I'm empowered to investigate and recommend for or against disbarment proceedings. I want to get your side of the story."

"I see. And how do I buy you off?"

Adam's face tightened. "I'm sorry, Miss Parker." He rose to his feet and started for the door.

"Just a minute!" Adam turned. "Forgive me," she said. "I – everybody seems to be the enemy. I apologize."

"Your apology is accepted."

Jennifer was suddenly aware of the flimsy robe she was wearing. "If you still want to ask me questions, I'll put some clothes on and we can talk."

"Fair enough. Have you had dinner?"

She hesitated. "I – "

"I know a little French restaurant that's just perfect for inquisitions."

It was a quiet, charming bistro on 56th Street on the East Side.

"Not too many people know about this place," Adam Warner said when they had been seated. "It's owned by a young French couple who used to work at Les Pyrénées. The food is excellent."

Jennifer had to take Adam's word for it. She was incapable of tasting anything. She had not eaten all day, but she was so nervous that she was unable to force any food down her throat. She tried to relax, but it was impossible. No matter how much he pretended, the charming man seated opposite her was the enemy. And he *was* charming, Jennifer had to admit. He was amusing and attractive, and under other circumstances Jennifer would have enjoyed the evening enormously; but these were not other circumstances. Her whole future was in the hands of this stranger. The next hour or two would determine in which direction the rest of her life would move.

Adam was going out of his way to try to relax her. He had recently returned from a trip to Japan where he had met with top government officials. A special banquet had been prepared in his honor.

"Have you ever eaten chocolate-covered ants?" Adam asked.

"No."

He grinned. "They're better than the chocolate-covered grasshoppers."

He talked about a hunting trip he had taken the year before in Alaska, where he had been attacked by a bear. He talked about everything but why they were there.

Jennifer had been steeling herself for the moment when Adam would begin to interrogate her, yet when he finally brought up the subject, her whole body went rigid.

He had finished dessert and he said quietly, "I'm going to ask you some questions, and I don't want you to get upset. Okay?"

There was a sudden lump in Jennifer's throat. She was not sure she would be able to speak. She nodded.

"I want you to tell me exactly what happened in the courtroom that day. Everything you remember, everything you felt. Take your time."

Jennifer had been prepared to defy him, to tell him to do whatever he pleased about her. But somehow, sitting across from Adam Warner, listening to his quiet voice, Jennifer's resistance was gone. The whole experience was still so vivid in her mind that it hurt just to think about it. She had spent more than a month trying to forget it. Now he was asking her to go through it again.

She took a deep, shaky breath and said, "All right."

Haltingly, Jennifer began to recount the events in the courtroom, gradually speaking more rapidly as it all came to life again. Adam sat there quietly listening, studying her, saying nothing.

When Jennifer had finished, Adam said, "The man who gave you the envelope – was he in the District Attorney's office earlier that morning when you were sworn in?"

"I've thought about that. I honestly don't remember. There were so many people in the office that day and they were all strangers."

"Had you ever seen the man before, anywhere?"

Jennifer shook her head helplessly. "I can't recall. I don't think so."

"You said you saw him talking to the District Attorney just before he walked over to give you the envelope. Did you see the District Attorney hand him the envelope?"

"I – no."

"Did you actually see this man talking to the District Attorney, or was he just in the group around him?"

Jennifer closed her eyes for a second, trying to bring back that moment. "I'm sorry. Everything was so confused. I – I just don't know."

"Do you have any idea how he could have known your name?"

"No."

"Or why he selected you?"

"That one's easy. He probably knew an idiot when he saw one." She shook her head. "No. I'm sorry, Mr. Warner, I have no idea."

Adam said, "A lot of pressure is being brought to bear on this. District Attorney Di Silva has been after Michael Moretti for a long time. Until you came along, he had an airtight case. The D.A.'s not very happy with you."

"I'm not very happy with me, either." Jennifer could not blame Adam Warner for what he was about to do. He was just carrying out his job. They were out to get her and they had succeeded. Adam Warner was not responsible; he was merely the instrument they were using.

Jennifer felt a sudden, overwhelming urge to be alone. She did not want anyone else to see her misery.

"I'm sorry," she apologized. "I – I'm not feeling very well. I'd like to go home, please."

Adam studied her a moment. "Would it make you feel any better if I told you I'm going to recommend that disbarment proceedings against you be dropped?"

It took several seconds for Adam's words to sink in. Jennifer stared at him, speechless, searching his face, looking into those gray-blue eyes behind the horn-rimmed glasses. "Do – do you really mean that?"

"Being a lawyer is very important to you, isn't it?" Adam asked.

Jennifer thought of her father and his comfortable little law office, and of the conversations they used to have, and the long years of law school, and their hopes and dreams. *We're going into partnership. You hurry up and get that law degree.*

"Yes," Jennifer whispered.

"If you can get over a rough beginning, I have a feeling you'll be a very good one."

Jennifer gave him a grateful smile. "Thank you. I'm going to try."

She said the words over again in her mind. *I'm going to try!* It did not matter that she shared a small and dingy office with a seedy private detective and a man who repossessed cars. It was a *law* office. She was a member of the legal profession, and they were going to allow her to practice law. She was filled with a feeling of exultation. She looked across at Adam and knew she would be forever grateful to this man.

The waiter had begun to clear the dishes from the table. Jennifer tried to speak, but it came out a cross between a laugh and a sob. "Mr. Warner – "

He said gravely, "After all we've been through together, I think it should be Adam."

"Adam – "

"Yes?"

"I hope it won't ruin our relationship, but – " Jennifer moaned, "I'm starved!"

5

The next few weeks raced by. Jennifer found herself busy from early morning until late at night, serving summonses – court orders to appear to answer a legal action – and subpoenas – court orders to appear as a witness. She knew that her chances of getting into a large law firm were nonexistent, for after the fiasco she had been involved in, no one would dream of hiring her. She would just have to find some way to make a reputation for herself, to begin all over.

In the meantime, there was the pile of summonses and subpoenas on her desk from Peabody & Peabody. While it was not exactly practicing law, it was twelve-fifty and expenses.

Occasionally, when Jennifer worked late, Ken Bailey would take her out to dinner. On the surface he was a cynical man, but Jennifer felt that it was a facade. She sensed that he was lonely. He had been graduated from Brown University and was bright and well-read. She could not imagine why he was satisfied to spend his life working out of a dreary office, trying to locate stray husbands and wives. It was as though he had resigned himself to being a failure and was afraid to try for success.

Once, when Jennifer brought up the subject of his marriage, he growled at her, "It's none of your business," and Jennifer had never mentioned it again.

Otto Wenzel was completely different. The short, potbellied little man was happily married. He regarded Jennifer as a daughter and he constantly brought her soups and cakes that his wife made. Unfortunately, his wife was a terrible cook, but Jennifer forced herself to eat whatever Otto Wenzel brought in, because she did not want to hurt his feelings. One Friday evening Jennifer was invited to the Wenzel home for dinner. Mrs. Wenzel had prepared stuffed cabbage, her specialty. The cabbage was soggy, the meat inside was hard, and the rice half-cooked. The whole dish swam in a lake of chicken fat. Jennifer attacked it bravely, taking small bites and pushing the food around on her plate to make it seem as though she were eating.

"How do you like it?" Mrs. Wenzel beamed.

"It – it's one of my favorites."

From that time on, Jennifer had dinner at the Wenzel's every Friday night, and Mrs. Wenzel always prepared Jennifer's favorite dish.

Early one morning, Jennifer received a telephone call from the personal secretary of Mr. Peabody, Jr.

"Mr. Peabody would like to see you this morning at eleven o'clock. Be prompt, please."

"Yes, ma'am."

In the past, Jennifer had only dealt with secretaries and law clerks in the Peabody office. It was a large, prestigious firm, one that young lawyers dreamed of being invited to join. On the way to keep her appointment, Jennifer began to fantasize. If Mr. Peabody himself wanted to see her, it had to be about something important. He probably had seen the light and was going to offer her a job as a lawyer with his firm, to give her a chance to show what she could do. She was going to surprise all of them. Some day it might even be Peabody, Peabody & Parker.

Jennifer killed thirty minutes in the corridor outside the office, and at exactly eleven o'clock, she entered the reception room. She did not want to seem too eager. She was kept waiting for two hours, and was finally ushered into the office of Mr. Peabody, Jr. He was a tall, thin man wearing a vested suit and shoes that had been made for him in London.

He did not invite her to sit down. "Miss Potter – " He had an unpleasant, high-pitched voice.

"Parker."

He picked up a piece of paper from his desk. "This is a summons. I would like you to serve it."

At that instant, Jennifer sensed that she was not going to become a member of the firm.

Mr. Peabody, Jr., handed Jennifer the summons and said, "Your fee will be five hundred dollars."

Jennifer was sure she had misunderstood him. "Did you say five hundred dollars?"

"That is correct. If you are successful, of course."

"There's a problem," Jennifer guessed.

"Well, yes," Mr. Peabody, Jr., admitted. "We've been trying to serve this man for more than a year. His name is William Carlisle. He lives on an estate in Long Island and he never leaves his house. To be quite truthful, a dozen people have tried to serve him. He has a bodyguard-butler who keeps everyone away."

Jennifer said, "I don't see how I – "

Mr. Peabody, Jr. leaned forward. "There's a great deal of money at stake here.

But I can't get William Carlisle into court unless I can serve him, Miss Potter." Jennifer did not bother to correct him. "Do you think you can handle it?"

Jennifer thought about what she could do with five hundred dollars "I'll find a way."

At two o'clock that afternoon, Jennifer was standing outside the imposing estate of William Carlisle. The house itself was Georgian, set in the middle of ten acres of beautiful, carefully tended grounds. A curving driveway led to the front of the house, which was framed by graceful fir trees. Jennifer had given a lot of thought to her problem. Since it was impossible to get into the house, the only solution was to find a way to get Mr. William Carlisle to come out.

Half a block down the street was a gardener's truck. Jennifer studied the truck a moment, then walked over to it, looking for the gardeners. There were three of them at work, and they were Japanese.

Jennifer walked up to the men. "Who's in charge here?"

One of them straightened up. "I am."

"I have a little job for you . . ." Jennifer began

"Sorry, miss. Too busy."

"This will only take five minutes."

"No. Impossible to – "

"I'll pay you one hundred dollars."

The three men stopped to look at her. The chief gardener said, "You pay us one hundred dollars for five minutes' work?"

"That's right."

"What we have to do . . . ?"

Five minutes later, the gardener's truck pulled into the driveway of William Carlisle's estate and Jennifer and the three gardeners got out. Jennifer looked around, selected a beautiful tree next to the front door and said to the gardeners, "Dig it up."

They took their spades from the truck and began to dig. Before a minute had gone by, the front door burst open and an enormous man in a butler's uniform came storming out.

"What the hell do you think you're doing?"

"Long Island Nursery," Jennifer said crisply. "We're takin' out all these trees."

The butler stared at her. "You're *what?*"

Jennifer held up a piece of paper. "I have an order here to dig up these trees."

"That's impossible! Mr. Carlisle would have a fit!" He turned to the gardeners. "You stop that!"

"Look, mister," Jennifer said, "I'm just doin' my job." She looked at the gardeners. "Keep diggin', fellas."

"No!" the butler shouted. "I'm telling you there's been a mistake! Mr. Carlisle didn't order any trees dug up."

Jennifer shrugged and said, "My boss says he did."

"Where can I get in touch with your boss?"

Jennifer looked at her watch. "He's out on a job in Brooklyn. He should be back in the office around six."

The butler glared at her, furious. "Just a minute! Don't do anything until I return."

"Keep diggin'," Jennifer told the gardeners.

The butler turned and hurried into the house, slamming the door behind him. A few moments later the door opened and the butler returned, accompanied by a tiny middle-aged man.

"Would you mind telling me what the devil is going on here?"

"What business is it of yours?" Jennifer demanded.

"I'll tell you what business it is of mine," he snapped. "I'm William Carlisle and this happens to be my property."

"In that case, Mr. Carlisle," Jennifer said, "I have something for you." She reached in her pocket and put the summons in his hand. She turned to the gardeners. "You can stop digging now."

Early the next morning Adam Warner telephoned. Jennifer recognized his voice instantly.

"I thought you would like to know," Adam said, "that the disbarment proceedings have been officially dropped. You have nothing more to worry about."

Jennifer closed her eyes and said a silent prayer of thanks. "I – I can't tell you how much I appreciate what you've done."

"Justice isn't always blind."

Adam did not mention the scene he had had with Stewart Needham and Robert Di Silva. Needham had been disappointed, but philosophical.

The District Attorney had carried on like a raging bull. "You let that bitch get away with this? Jesus Christ, she's Mafia, Adam! Couldn't you see that? She's conning you!"

And on and on, until Adam had tired of it.

"All the evidence against her was circumstantial, Robert. She was in the wrong place at the wrong time and she got mouse-trapped. That doesn't spell Mafia to me."

Finally Robert Di Silva had said, "Okay, so she's still a lawyer. I just hope to God she practices in New York, because the minute she sets foot in any of my courtrooms, I'm going to wipe her out."

Now, talking to Jennifer, Adam said nothing of this. Jennifer had made a deadly enemy, but there was nothing that could be done about it. Robert Di Silva was a vindictive man, and Jennifer was a vulnerable target. She was bright and idealistic and achingly young and lovely.

Adam knew he must never see her again.

There were days and weeks and months when Jennifer was ready to quit. The sign on the door still read *Jennifer Parker, Attorney at Law*, but it did not deceive anyone, least of all Jennifer. She was not practicing law. Her days were spent running around in rain and sleet and snow, delivering subpoenas and summons to people who hated her for it. Now and then she accepted a *pro bono* case, helping the elderly get food stamps, solving various legal problems of ghetto Blacks and Puerto Ricans and other underprivileged people. But she felt trapped.

The nights were worse than the days. They were endless, for Jennifer had insomnia and when she did sleep, her dreams were filled with demons. It had begun the night her mother had deserted Jennifer and her father, and she had not been able to exorcise whatever it was that was causing her nightmares.

She was consumed by loneliness. She went out on occasional dates with young lawyers, but inevitably she found herself comparing them to Adam Warner, and they all fell short. There would be dinner and a movie or a play, followed by a struggle at her front door. Jennifer was never sure whether they expected her to go to bed with them because they had bought her dinner, or because they had had to climb up and down four steep flights of stairs. There were times when she was strongly tempted to say *Yes*, just to have someone with her for the night, someone to hold, someone to share herself with. But she needed more in her bed than a warm body that talked; she needed someone who cared, someone for whom she could care.

The most interesting men who propositioned Jennifer were all married, and she flatly refused to go out with any of them, She remembered a line from Billy Wilder's wonderful film *The Apartment*: "When you're in love with a married man you shouldn't wear mascara." Jennifer's mother had destroyed a marriage, had killed Jennifer's father. She could never forget that.

Christmas came and New Year's Eve, and Jennifer spent them alone. There had been a heavy snowfall and the city looked like a gigantic Christmas card. Jennifer walked the streets, watching pedestrians hurrying to the warmth of their homes and families, and she ached with a feeling of emptiness: She missed her father terribly. She was glad when the holidays were over. *Nineteen seventy is going to be a better year*, Jennifer told herself.

On Jennifer's worst days, Ken Bailey would cheer her up. He took her out to Madison Square Garden to watch the Rangers play, to a disco club and to an occasional play or movie. Jennifer knew he was attracted to her, and yet he kept a barrier between them.

In March, Otto Wenzel decided to move to Florida with his wife.

"My bones are getting too old for these New York winters," he told Jennifer.

"I'll miss you." Jennifer meant it. She had grown genuinely fond of him.

"Take care of Ken."

Jennifer looked at him quizzically.

"He never told you, did he?"

"Told me what?"

He hesitated, then said, "His wife committed suicide. He blames himself"

Jennifer was shocked. "How terrible! Why – why did she do it?"

"She caught Ken in bed with a young blond man."

"Oh, my God!"

"She shot Ken and then turned the gun on herself. He lived. She didn't."

"How awful! I had no idea that . . . that – "

"I know. He smiles a lot, but he carries his own hell with him."

"Thanks for telling me."

When Jennifer returned to the office, Ken said, "So old Otto's leaving us."

"Yes."

Ken Bailey grinned. "I guess it's you and me against the world."

"I guess so."

And in a way, Jennifer thought, *it is true.*

Jennifer looked at Ken with different eyes now. They had lunches and dinners together, and Jennifer could detect no signs of homosexuality about him but she knew that Otto Wenzel had told her the truth: Ken Bailey carried his own private hell with him.

A few clients walked in off the street. They were usually poorly dressed, bewildered and, in some instances, out-and-out nut cases.

Prostitutes came in to ask Jennifer to handle their bail, and Jennifer was amazed at how young and lovely some of them were. They became a small but steady source of income. She could not find out who sent them to her. When she mentioned it to Ken Bailey, he shrugged in a gesture of ignorance and walked away.

Whenever a client came to see Jennifer, Ken Bailey would discreetly leave. He was like a proud father, encouraging Jennifer to succeed.

Jennifer was offered several divorce cases and turned them down. She could not forget what one of her law professors had once said: *Divorce is to the practice of law what proctology is to the practice of medicine.* Most divorce lawyers had bad reputations. The maxim was that when a married couple saw red, lawyers saw green. A high-priced divorce lawyer was known as a *bomber,* for he would use legal high explosives to win a case for a client and, in the process, often destroyed the husband, the wife and the children.

A few of the clients who came into Jennifer's office were different in a way that puzzled her.

They were well dressed, with an air of affluence about them, and the cases they brought to her were not the nickel-and-dime cases Jennifer had been accustomed to handling. There were estates to be settled that amounted to substantial sums of money, and lawsuits that any large firm would have been delighted to represent.

"Where did you hear about me?" Jennifer would ask.

The replies she got were always evasive. From a friend . . . I read about you . . . your name was mentioned at a party . . . It was not until one of her clients, in the course of explaining his problems, mentioned Adam Warner that Jennifer suddenly understood.

"Mr. Warner sent you to me, didn't he?"

The client was embarrassed. "Well, as a matter of fact, he suggested it might be better if I didn't mention his name."

Jennifer decided to telephone Adam. After all, she did owe him a debt of thanks. She would be polite, but formal. Naturally, she would not let him get the impression that she was calling him for any reason other than to express her appreciation. She rehearsed the conversation over and over in her mind. When Jennifer finally got up enough nerve to telephone, a secretary informed her that Mr. Warner was in Europe and was not expected back for several weeks. It was an anticlimax that left Jennifer depressed.

She found herself thinking of Adam Warner more and more often. She kept remembering the evening he had come to her apartment and how badly she had behaved. He had been wonderful to put up with her childish behavior when she had taken out her anger on him. Now, in addition to everything else he had done for her, he was sending her clients.

Jennifer waited three weeks and then telephoned Adam again. This time he was in South America.

"Is there any message?" his secretary asked.

Jennifer hesitated. "No message."

Jennifer tried to put Adam out of her mind, but it was impossible. She wondered whether he was married or engaged. She wondered what it would he like to be Mrs. Adam Warner. She wondered if she were insane.

From time to time Jennifer came across the name of Michael Moretti in the newspapers or weekly magazines. There was an in-depth story in the *New Yorker* magazine on Antonio Granelli and the eastern Mafia Families. Antonio Granelli was reported to be in falling health and Michael Moretti, his son-in-law, was preparing to take over his empire. *Life* magazine ran a story about Michael Moretti's lifestyle, and at the end of the story it spoke of Moretti's trial. Camillo Stela was serving time in Leavenworth, while Michael Moretti was free. It reminded its readers how Jennifer Parker had destroyed the case that would have sent him to prison or the electric chair. As Jennifer read the article, her stomach churned. The electric chair? She could cheerfully have pulled the switch on Michael Moretti herself.

Most of Jennifer's clients were unimportant, but the education was priceless. Over the months, Jennifer came to know every room in the Criminal Courts Building at 100 Centre Street and the people who inhabited them.

When one of her clients was arrested for shoplifting, mugging, prostitution or drugs, Jennifer would head downtown to arrange bail, and bargaining was a way of life.

"Bail is set at five hundred dollars."

"Your Honor, the defendant doesn't have that much money. If the court will reduce bail to two hundred dollars, he can go back to work and keep supporting his family."

"Very well. Two hundred."

"Thank you, Your Honor."

Jennifer got to know the supervisor of the complaint room, where copies of the arrest reports were sent.

"You again, Parker! For God's sake, don't you ever sleep?"

"Hi, Lieutenant. A client of mine was picked up on a vagrancy charge. May I see the arrest sheet? The name is Connery. Clarence Connery."

"Tell me something, honey. Why would you come down here at three A.M. to defend a vagrant?"

Jennifer grinned. "It keeps me off the streets."

She became familiar with night court, held in Room 218 of the Centre Street courthouse. It was a smelly, overcrowded world, with its own arcane jargon. Jennifer was baffled by it at first.

"Parker, your client is booked on bedpain."

"My client is booked on *what?*"

"Bedpain. Burglary, with a Break, Enter, Dwelling, Person, Armed, Intent to kill, at Night. Get it?"

"Got it."

"I'm here to represent Miss Luna Tarner."

"Jesus H. Christ!"

"Would you tell me what the charges are?"

"Hold on. I'll find her ticket. Luna Tarner. That's a hot one . . . here we are. Pross. Picked up by CWAC, down below."

"*Quack?*"

"You're new around here, huh? *CWAC* is the City-Wide Anti-Crime unit. A *pross* is a hooker, and *down below* is south of Forty-Second Street. Capish?"

"Capish."

*

Night court depressed Jennifer. It was filled with a human tide that ceaselessly surged in and out, washed up on the shores of justice.

There were more than a hundred and fifty cases heard each night. There were whores and transvestites, stinking, battered drunks and drug addicts. There were Puerto Ricans and Mexicans and Jews and Irish and Greeks and Italians, and they were accused of rape and theft and possession of guns or dope or assault or prostitution. And they all had one thing in common: they were poor. They were poor and defeated and lost. They were the dregs, the misfits whom the affluent society had passed by. A large proportion of them came from Central Harlem, and because there was no more room in the prison system, all but the most serious offenders were dismissed or fined. They returned home to St. Nicholas Avenue and Morningside and Manhattan Avenues, where in three and one-half square miles there lived two hundred and thirty-three thousand Blacks, eight thousand Puerto Ricans, and an estimated one million rats.

The majority of clients who came to Jennifer's office were people who had been ground down by poverty, the system, themselves. They were people who had long since surrendered. Jennifer found that their fears fed her self-confidence. She did not feel superior to them. She certainly could not hold herself up as a shining example of success, and yet she knew there was one big difference between her and her clients: she would never give up.

Ken Bailey introduced Jennifer to Father Francis Joseph Ryan. Father Ryan was in his late fifties, a radiant, vital man with crisp gray-and-black hair that curled about his ears. He was always in serious need of a haircut. Jennifer liked him at once.

From time to time, when one of his parishioners would disappear, Father Ryan would come to Ken and enlist his services. Invariably, Ken would find the errant husband, wife, daughter or son. There would never be a charge.

"It's a down payment on heaven," Ken would explain.

One afternoon when Jennifer was alone Father Ryan dropped by the office.

"Ken's out, Father Ryan. He won't be back today."

"It's really you I wanted to see, Jennifer," Father Ryan said. He sat down in the uncomfortable old wooden chair in front of Jennifer's desk. "I have a friend who has a bit of a problem."

That was the way he always started out with Ken.

"Yes, Father?"

"She's an elderly parishioner, and the poor dear's having trouble getting her Social Security payments. She moved into my neighborhood a few months ago and some damned computer lost all her records, may it rust in hell."

"I see."

"I knew you would," Father Ryan said, getting to his feet. "I'm afraid there won't be any money in it for you."

Jennifer smiled. "Don't worry about that. I'll try to straighten things out."

She had thought it would be a simple matter, but it had taken her almost three days to get the computer reprogrammed.

One morning a month later, Father Ryan walked into Jennifer's office and said, "I hate to bother you, my dear, but I have a friend who has a bit of a problem. I'm afraid he has no – " He hesitated.

" – Money," Jennifer guessed.

"Ah! That's it. Exactly. But the poor fellow needs help badly."

"All right. Tell me about him."

"His name is Abraham. Abraham Wilson. He's the son of one of my parishioners. Abraham is serving a life sentence in Sing Sing for killing a liquor store owner during a holdup."

"If he was convicted and is serving his sentence, I don't see how I can help, Father."

Father Ryan looked at Jennifer and sighed. "That's not his problem."

"It isn't?"

"No. A few weeks ago Abraham killed another man – a fellow prisoner named Raymond Thorpe. They're going to try him for murder, and go for the death penalty."

Jennifer had read something about the case. "If I remember correctly, he beat the man to death."

"So they say."

Jennifer picked up a pad and a pen. "Do you know if there were any witnesses?"

"I'm afraid so."

"How many?"

"Oh, a hundred or so. It happened in the prison yard, you see."

"Terrific. What is it you want me to do?"

Father Ryan said simply, "Help Abraham."

Jennifer put down her pen. "Father, it's going to take your Boss to help him." She sat back in her chair. "He's going in with three strikes against him. He's Black, he's a convicted murderer, and he killed another man in front of a hundred witnesses. Assuming he did it, there just aren't any grounds for defense. If another prisoner was threatening him, there were guards he could have asked to help him. Instead, he took the law into his own hands. There isn't a jury in the world that wouldn't convict him."

"He's still a fellow human being. Would you just talk to him?"

Jennifer sighed. "I'll talk to him if you want me to, but I won't make any commitment."

Father Ryan nodded, "I understand. It would probably mean a great deal of publicity."

They were both thinking the same thing. Abraham Wilson was not the only one who had strikes against him.

Sing Sing Prison is situated at the town of Ossining, thirty miles upstate of Manhattan on the east bank of the Hudson River, overlooking the Tappan Zee and Haverstraw Bay.

Jennifer went up by bus. She had telephoned the assistant warden and he had made arrangements for her to see Abraham Wilson, who was being held in solitary confinement.

During the bus ride, Jennifer was filled with a sense of purpose she had not felt in a long time. She was on her way to Sing Sing to meet a possible client charged with murder. This was the kind of case she had studied for, prepared herself for. She felt like a lawyer for the first time in a year, and yet she knew she was being unrealistic. She was not on her way to see a client. She was on her way to tell a man she could not represent him. She could not afford to become involved in a highly publicized case that she had no chance of winning.

Abraham Wilson would have to find someone else to defend him.

A dilapidated taxi took Jennifer from the bus station to the penitentiary, situated on seventy acres of land near the river. Jennifer rang the bell at the side entrance and a guard opened the door, checked off her name against his list, and directed her to the assistant warden's office.

The assistant warden was a large, square man with an old-fashioned military haircut and an acne-pitted face. His name was Howard Patterson.

"I would appreciate anything you can tell me about Abraham Wilson," Jennifer began.

"If you're looking for comfort, you're not going to get it here." Patterson glanced at the dossier on the desk in front of him. "Wilson's been in and out of prisons all his life. He was caught stealing cars when he was eleven, arrested on a mugging charge when he was thirteen, picked up for rape when he was fifteen, became a pimp at eighteen, served a sentence for putting one of his girls in the hospital . . ." He leafed through the dossier. "You name it – stabbings, armed robbery and finally the big time – murder."

It was a depressing recital.

Jennifer asked, "Is there any chance that Abraham Wilson *didn't* kill Raymond Thorpe?"

"Forget it. Wilson's the first to admit it, but it wouldn't make any difference even if he denied it. We've got a hundred and twenty witnesses."

"May I see Mr. Wilson?"

Howard Patterson rose to his feet "Sure, but you're wasting your time."

Abraham Wilson was the ugliest human being Jennifer Parker had ever seen. He was coal-black, with a nose that had been broken in several places, missing front teeth and tiny, shifty eyes set in a knife-scarred face. He was about six feet four inches and powerfully built. He had huge flat feet which made him lumber. If Jennifer had searched for one word to describe Abraham Wilson, it would have been *menacing*. She could imagine the effect this man would have on a jury.

Abraham Wilson and Jennifer were seated in a high-security visiting room, a thick wire mesh between them, a guard standing at the door. Wilson had just been taken out of solitary confinement and his beady eyes kept blinking against the light. If Jennifer had come to this meeting feeling she would probably not want to handle this case, after seeing Abraham Wilson she was positive. Merely sitting opposite him she could feel the hatred spewing out of the man.

Jennifer opened the conversation by saying, "My name is Jennifer Parker. I'm an attorney. Father Ryan asked me to see you."

Abraham Wilson spat through the screen, spraying Jennifer with saliva. "That mothafuckin' do-gooder."

It's a wonderful beginning, Jennifer thought. She carefully refrained from wiping the saliva from her face. "Is there anything you need here, Mr. Wilson?"

He gave her a toothless smile. "A piece of ass, baby. You innersted?"

She ignored that. "Do you want to tell me what happened?"

"Hey, you lookin' for my life story, you gotta pay me for it. I gonna sell it for da movin' pitchurs. Maybe I'll star in it mysef."

The anger coming out of him was frightening. All Jennifer wanted was to get out of there. The assistant warden had been right. She was wasting her time.

"I'm afraid there's really nothing I can do to help you unless you help me, Mr. Wilson. I promised Father Ryan I would at least come and talk to you."

Abraham Wilson gave her a toothless grin again. "That's mighty white of ya, sweetheart. Ya sure ya don't wanna change your mind 'bout that piece of ass?"

Jennifer rose to her feet. She had had enough. "Do you hate everybody?"

"Tell ya what, doll, you crawl inta my skin and I'll crawl inta yours, and then you'n me'll rap 'bout hate."

Jennifer stood there, looking into that ugly black face, digesting what he had said, and then she slowly sat down. "Do you want to tell me your side of the story, Abraham?"

He stared into her eyes, saying nothing. Jennifer waited, watching him, wondering what it must be like to wear that scarred black skin. She wondered how many scars were hidden inside the man.

The two of them sat there in a long silence. Finally, Abraham Wilson said, "I killed the somabitch."

"Why did you kill him?"

He shrugged. "The motha' was comin' at me with this great big butcher knife, and – "

"Don't con me. Prisoners don't walk around carrying butcher knives."

Wilson's face tightened and he said, "Get the fuck outa here, lady. I din't sen' for ya." He rose to his feet. "An' don't come round heah botherin' me no more, you heah? I'm a busy man."

He turned and walked over to the guard. A moment later they were both gone. That was that. Jennifer could at least tell Father Ryan that she had talked to the man. There was nothing further she could do.

A guard let Jennifer out of the building. She started across the courtyard toward the main gate, thinking about Abraham Wilson and her reaction to him. She disliked the man and, because of that, she was doing something she had no right to do: she was judging him. She had already pronounced him guilty and he had not yet had a trial. Perhaps someone *had* attacked him, not with a knife, of course, but with a rock or a brick. Jennifer stopped and stood there indecisively. Every instinct told her to go back to Manhattan and forget about Abraham Wilson.

Jennifer turned and walked back to the assistant warden's office.

"He's a hard case," Howard Patterson said. "When we can, we try rehabilitation instead of punishment, but Abraham Wilson's too far gone. The only thing that will calm him down is the electric chair."

What a weird piece of logic, Jennifer thought. "He told me the man he killed attacked him with a butcher knife."

"I guess that's possible."

The answer startled her. "What do you mean, 'that's possible'? Are you saying a convict in here could get possession of a knife? A butcher knife?"

Howard Patterson shrugged. "Miss Parker, we have twelve hundred and forty convicts in this place, and some of them are men of great ingenuity. Come on. I'll show you something."

Patterson led Jennifer down a long corridor to a locked door. He selected a key from a large key ring, opened the door and turned on the light. Jennifer followed him into a small, bare room with built-in shelves.

"This is where we keep the prisoners' box of goodies." He walked over to a large box and lifted the lid.

Jennifer stared down into the box unbelievingly.

She looked up at Howard Patterson and said, "I want to see my client again."

6

Jennifer prepared for Abraham Wilson's trial as she had never prepared for anything before in her life. She spent endless hours in the law library checking for procedures and defenses, and with her client, drawing from him every scrap of information she could. It was no easy task. From the beginning, Wilson was truculent and sarcastic.

"You wanna know about me, honey? I got my first fuck when I was ten. How ole was you?"

Jennifer forced herself to ignore his hatred and his contempt, for she was aware that they covered up a deep fear. And so Jennifer persisted, demanding to know what Wilson's early life was like, what his parents were like, what had shaped the boy into the man. Over a period of weeks, Abraham Wilson's reluctance gave way to interest, and his interest finally gave way to fascination. He had never before had reason to think of himself in terms of what kind of person he was, or why.

Jennifer's prodding questions began to arouse memories, some merely unpleasant, others unbearably painful. Several times during the sessions when Jennifer was questioning Abraham Wilson about his father, who had regularly given him savage beatings, Wilson would order Jennifer to leave him alone. She left, but she always returned.

If Jennifer had had little personal life before, she now had none. When she was not with Abraham Wilson, she was at her office, seven days a week, from early morning until long after midnight, reading everything she could find about the crimes of murder and manslaughter, voluntary and involuntary. She studied hundreds of appellate court decisions, briefs, affidavits, exhibits, motions, transcripts. She pored over files on intent and premeditation, self-defense, double jeopardy, and temporary insanity.

She studied ways to get the charge reduced to manslaughter.

Abraham had not planned to kill the man. But would a jury believe that? Particularly a local jury. The townspeople hated the prisoners in their midst. Jennifer moved for a change of venue, and it was granted. The trial would be held in Manhattan.

Jennifer had an important decision to make: should she allow Abraham Wilson to testify? He presented a forbidding figure, but if the jurors were able to hear his side of the story from his own lips, they might have some sympathy for him. The problem was that putting Abraham Wilson on the stand would allow the prosecution to reveal Wilson's background and past record, including the previous murder he had committed.

Jennifer wondered which one of the assistant district attorneys Di Silva would assign to be her adversary. There were half a dozen very good ones who prosecuted murder trials, and Jennifer familiarized herself with their techniques.

She spent as much time as possible at Sing Sing, looking over the scene of the killing in the recreation yard, talking to guards and Abraham, and she interviewed dozens of convicts who had witnessed the killing.

"Raymond Thorpe attacked Abraham Wilson with a knife," Jennifer said. "A large butcher knife. You must have seen it."

"Me? I didn't see no knife."

"You must have. You were right there."

"Lady, I didn't see nothin'."

Not one of them was willing to get involved.

Occasionally Jennifer would take time out to have a regular meal, but usually she grabbed a quick sandwich at the coffee shop on the main floor of the courthouse. She was beginning to lose weight and she had dizzy spells.

Ken Bailey was becoming concerned about her. He took her to Forlini's across from the courthouse, and ordered a large lunch for her.

"Are you trying to kill yourself?" he demanded.

"Of course not."

"Have you looked in a mirror lately?"

"No."

He studied her and said, "If you have any sense, you'll drop this case."

"Why?"

"Because you're setting yourself up as a clay pigeon. Jennifer, I hear things on the street. The press is peeing in its collective pants, they're so eager to start taking potshots at you again."

"I'm an attorney," Jennifer said stubbornly. "Abraham Wilson is entitled to a fair trial. I'm going to try to see that he gets one." She saw the look of concern on Ken Bailey's face. "Don't worry about it. The case isn't going to get *that* much publicity."

"It isn't, huh? Do you know who's prosecuting?"

"No."

"Robert Di Silva"

Jennifer arrived at the Leonard Street entrance of the Criminal Courts Building and pushed her way past the people churning through the lobby, past the uniformed policemen, the detectives dressed like hippies, the lawyers identified by the briefcases they carried. Jennifer walked toward the large circular information desk, where no attendant had ever been posted, and took the elevator to the sixth floor. She was on her way to see the District Attorney. It had been almost a year since her last encounter with Robert Di Silva, and Jennifer was not looking forward to this one. She was going to inform him that she was resigning from Abraham Wilson's defense.

It had taken Jennifer three sleepless nights to make her decision. What it came down to finally was that the primary consideration had to be the best interests of her client. The Wilson case was not important enough for Di Silva to handle himself. The only reason, therefore, for the District Attorney's giving it his personal attention was because of Jennifer's involvement. Di Silva wanted vengeance. He was planning to teach Jennifer a lesson. And so she had finally decided she had no choice but to withdraw from Wilson's defense. She could not let him be executed because of a mistake she had once made. With her off the case, Robert Di Silva would probably deal with Wilson more leniently. Jennifer was on her way to save Abraham Wilson's life.

There was an odd feeling of reliving the past as she got off at the sixth floor and walked toward the familiar door marked District *Attorney, County of New*

York. Inside, the same secretary was seated at the same desk.

"I'm Jennifer Parker. I have an appointment with – "

"Go right in," the secretary said. "The District Attorney is expecting you."

Robert Di Silva was standing behind his desk, chewing on a wet cigar, giving orders to two assistants. He stopped as Jennifer entered.

"I was betting you wouldn't show up."

"I'm here."

"I thought you would have turned tail and run out of town by now. What do you want?"

There were two chairs opposite Robert Di Silva's desk, but he did not invite Jennifer to sit.

"I came here to talk about my client, Abraham Wilson."

Robert Di Silva at down, leaned back in his chair and pretended to think. "Abraham Wilson . . . oh, yes. That's the nigger murderer who beat a man to death in prison. You shouldn't have any trouble defending him." He glanced at his two assistants and they left the room.

"Well, counselor?"

"I'd like to talk about a plea."

Robert Di Silva looked at her with exaggerated surprise. "You mean you came in to make a deal? You amaze me. I would have thought that someone with your great legal talent would be able to get him off scot-free."

"Mr. Di Silva, I know this looks like an open-and-shut case," Jennifer began, "but there are extenuating circumstances. Abraham Wilson was – "

District Attorney Di Silva interrupted. "Let me put it in legal language you can understand, counselor. You can take your extenuating circumstances and shove them up your ass!" He got to his feet and when he spoke his voice was trembling with rage. "Make a deal with you, lady? You fucked up my life! There's a dead body and your boy's going to burn for it. Do you hear me? I'm making it my personal business to see that he's sent to the chair."

"I came up here to withdraw from the case. You could reduce this to a manslaughter charge. Wilson's already in for life. You could – "

"No way! He's guilty of murder plain and simple!"

Jennifer tried to control her anger. "I thought the jury was supposed to decide that."

Robert Di Silva smiled at her without mirth. "You don't know how heart-warming it is to have an expert like you walk into my office and explain the law to me."

"Can't we forget our personal problems? I – "

"Not as long as I live. Say hello to your pal Michael Moretti for me."

Half an hour later, Jennifer was having coffee with Ken Bailey.

"I don't know what to do," Jennifer confessed. "I thought if I got off the case Abraham Wilson would stand a better chance. But Di Silva won't make a deal. He's not after Wilson – he's after me."

Ken Bailey looked at her thoughtfully. "Maybe he's trying to psych you out. He wants you running scared."

"I *am* running scared." She took a sip of her coffee. It tasted bitter. "It's a bad case. You should see Abraham Wilson. All the jury will have to do is *look* at him and they'll vote to convict."

"When does the trial come up?"

"In four weeks."

"Anything I can do to help?"

"Uh-huh. Put out a contract on Di Silva."

"Do you think there's any chance you can get Wilson an acquittal?"

"Looking at it from the pessimist's point of view, I'm trying my first case against the smartest District Attorney in the country, who has a vendetta against me, and my client is a convicted Black killer who killed again in front of a hundred and twenty witnesses."

"Terrific. What's the optimist's point of view?"

"I could get hit by a truck this afternoon."

The trial date was only three weeks now. Jennifer arranged for Abraham Wilson to be transferred to the prison at Riker's Island. He was put in the House of Detention for Men, the largest and oldest jail on the island. Ninety-five percent of his prison mates were there awaiting trial for felonies: murder, arson, rape, armed robbery and sodomy.

No private cars were allowed on the island, and Jennifer was transported in a small green bus to the gray brick control building where she showed her identification. There were two armed guards in a green booth to the left of the building, and beyond that a gate where all unauthorized visitors were stopped. From the control building, Jennifer was driven down Hazen Street, the little road that went through the prison grounds, to the Anna M. Kross Center Building, where Abraham Wilson was bought to see her in the counsel room, with its eight cubicles reserved for attorney-client meetings.

Walking down the long corridor on her way to meet with Abraham Wilson, Jennifer thought: *This must be like the waiting room to hell.* There was an incredible cacophony. The prison was made of brick and steel and stone and tile. steel gates were constantly opening and clanging shut. There were more than one hundred men in each cellblock, talking and yelling at same time, with two television sets tuned to different channels and a music system playing country rock. Three hundred guards were assigned to the building, and their bellowing could be heard over the prison symphony.

A guard had told Jennifer, "Prison society is the politest society in the world. If a prisoner ever brushes up against another one, he immediately says, 'Excuse me.' Prisoners have a lot on their minds and the least little thing . . ."

Jennifer sat across form Abraham Wilson and she thought: *this man's life is in my hands. If he dies, it will be because I failed him.* She looked into his eyes and saw the despair there.

Three days before the Abraham Wilson trial was to begin, Jennifer learned that the presiding judge was to be the Honorable Lawrence Waldman, who had presided over the Michael Moretti trial and had tried to get Jennifer disbarred.

7

At four o'clock on a Monday morning in late September of 1970, the day the trial of Abraham Wilson was to begin, Jennifer awakened feeling tired and heavy-eyed. She had slept badly, her mind filled with dreams of the trial. In one of the dreams, Robert Di Silva had put her in the witness box and asked her about Michael Moretti. Each time Jennifer tried to answer the questions, the jurors interrupted her with a chant: *Liar! Liar! Liar!*

Each dream was different, but they were all similar. In the last one, Abraham Wilson was strapped in the electric chair. As Jennifer leaned over to console him, he spit in her face. Jennifer awoke trembling, and it was impossible for her to go back to sleep. She sat up in a chair until dawn and watched the sun come up. She was too nervous to eat. She wished she could have slept the night before. She wished that she were not so tense. She wished that this day was over.

As she bathed and dressed she had a premonition of doom. She felt like wearing black, but she chose a green Chanel copy she had bought on sale at Loehmann's.

At eight-thirty, Jennifer Parker arrived at the Criminal Courts Building to begin the defense in the case of The People of the State of New York against Abraham Wilson. There was a crowd outside the entrance and Jennifer's first thought was that there had been an accident. She saw a battery of television cameras and microphones, and before Jennifer realized what was happening, she was surrounded by reporters.

A reporter said, "Miss Parker, this is your first time in court, isn't it, since you fouled up the Michael Moretti case for the District Attorney?"

Ken Bailey had warned her. *She* was the central attraction, not her client. The reporters were not there as objective observers; they were there as birds of prey and she was to be their carrion.

A young woman in jeans pushed a microphone up to Jennifer's face. "Is it true that District Attorney Di Silva is out to get you?"

"No comment." Jennifer began to fight her way toward the entrance of the building.

"The District Attorney issued a statement last night that he thinks you shouldn't be allowed to practice law in the New York courts. Would you like to say anything about that?"

"No comment." Jennifer had almost reached the entrance.

"Last year Judge Waldman tried to get you disbarred. Are you going to ask him to disqualify himself from – ?"

Jennifer was inside the courthouse.

The trial was scheduled to take place in Room 37. The corridor outside was crowded with people trying to get in, but the courtroom was already full. It was buzzing with noise and there was a carnival atmosphere in the air. There were extra rows reserved for members of the press. *Di Silva saw to that*, Jennifer thought.

Abraham Wilson was seated at the defense table, towering over everyone around him like an evil mountain. He was dressed in a dark blue suit that was too small for him, and a white shirt and blue tie that Jennifer had bought him. They did not help. Abraham Wilson looked like a ugly killer in a dark blue suit. *He might just as well have worn his prison clothes*, Jennifer thought, discouraged.

Wilson was staring defiantly around the courtroom, glowering at everyone who met his look. Jennifer knew her client well enough now to understand that his belligerence was a cover-up for his fright; but what would come over to everyone – including the judge and the jury – was an impression of hostility and hatred. The huge man was a threat. They would regard him as someone to be feared, to be destroyed.

There was not a trace in Abraham Wilson's personality that was loveable. There was nothing about his appearance that could evoke sympathy. There was only that ugly, scarred face with its broken nose and missing teeth, that enormous body that would inspire fear.

Jennifer walked over to the defense table where Abraham Wilson was sitting and took the seat next to him. "Good morning, Abraham."

He glanced over at her and said, "I didn't think you was comin'."

Jennifer remembered her dream. She looked into his small, slitted eyes. "You knew I'd be here."

He shrugged indifferently. "It don't matter one way or another. They's gonna get me, baby. They's gonna convict me of murder and then they's gonna pass a law makin' it legal to boil me in oil, then they's gonna boil me in oil. This ain't gonna be no trial. This is gonna be a show. I hope you brung your pop-corn."

There was a stir around the prosecutor's table and Jennifer looked up to see District Attorney Di Silva taking his place at the table next to a battery of assistants. He looked at Jennifer and smiled. Jennifer felt a growing sense of panic.

A court officer said, "All rise," and Judge Lawrence Waldman entered from the judge's robing room.

"Hear ye, Hear ye. All people having business with Part Thirty-seven of this Court, draw near, give your attention and you shall be heard. The Honorable Justice Lawrence Waldman presiding."

The only one who refused to stand was Abraham Wilson. Jennifer whispered out of the corner of her mouth, "Stand up!"

"Fuck 'em, baby. They gonna have to come and drag me up."

Jennifer took his giant hand in hers. "On your feet, Abraham. We're going to beat them."

He looked at her for a long moment, then slowly got to his feet, towering over her.

Judge Waldman took his place on the bench. The spectators resumed their seats. The court clerk handed a court calendar to the judge.

"The People of the State of New York versus Abraham Wilson, charged with the murder of Raymond Thorpe."

Jennifer's instinct normally would have been to fill the jury box with Blacks, but because of Abraham Wilson she was not so sure. Wilson was not one of them. He was a renegade, a killer, "a disgrace to their race." They might convict him more readily than would whites. All Jennifer could do was try to keep the more obvious bigots off the jury. But bigots did not go around advertising. They would keep quiet about their prejudices, waiting to get their vengeance.

By late afternoon of the second day, Jennifer had used up her ten peremptory challenges. She felt that her *voir dire* – the questioning of the jurors – was clumsy and awkward, while Di Silva's was smooth and skillful. He had the knack of putting the jurors at ease, drawing them into his confidence, making friends of them.

How could I have forgotten what a good actor Di Silva is? Jennifer wondered.

Di Silva did not exercise his peremptory challenges until Jennifer had exhausted hers, and she could not understand why. When she discovered the reason, it was too late. Di Silva had outsmarted her. Among the final prospective jurors questioned were a private detective, a bank manager and the mother of a doctor – all of them *Establishment* – and there was nothing now that Jennifer could do to keep them off the jury. The District Attorney had sandbagged her.

Robert Di Silva rose to his feet and began his opening statement.

"If it please the court" – he turned to the jury – "and you ladies and gentlemen of the jury, first of all I would like to thank you for giving up your valuable time to sit in this case." He smiled sympathetically. "I know what a disruption jury service can be. You all have jobs to get back to, families needing your attention."

It's as though he's one of them, Jennifer thought, *the thirteenth juror.*

"I promise to take up as little of your time as possible. This is really a very simple case. That's the defendant sitting over there – Abraham Wilson. The defendant is accused by the State of New York of murdering a fellow inmate at Sing Sing Prison, Raymond Thorpe. There's no doubt that he did. He's admitted it. Mr. Wilson's attorney is going to plead self-defense."

The District Attorney turned to look at the huge figure of Abraham Wilson, and the eyes of the jurors automatically followed him. Jennifer could see the reactions on their faces. She forced herself to concentrate on what District Attorney Di Silva was saying.

"A number of years ago twelve citizens, very much like yourselves, I am sure, voted to put Abraham Wilson away in a penitentiary. Because of certain legal technicalities, I am not permitted to discuss with you the crime that Abraham Wilson committed. I *can* tell you that that jury sincerely believed that locking Abraham Wilson up would prevent him from committing any further crimes. Tragically, they were wrong. For even locked away, Abraham Wilson was able to strike, to kill, to satisfy the blood lust in him. We know now, finally, that there is only one way to prevent Abraham Wilson from killing again. And that is to execute him. It won't bring back the life of Raymond Thorpe, but it can save the lives of other men who might otherwise become the defendant's next victims."

Di Silva walked along the jury box, looking each juror in the eye. "I told you that this case won't take up much of your time. I'll tell you why I said that. The defendant sitting over there – Abraham Wilson – murdered a man in cold blood. He has confessed to the killing. But even if he had not confessed, we have witnesses who saw Abraham Wilson commit that murder in cold blood. More than a hundred witnesses, in fact.

"Let us examine the phrase, 'in cold blood.' Murder for *any* reason is as distasteful to me as I know it is to you. But sometimes murders are committed for reasons we can at least understand. Let's say that someone with a weapon is threatening your loved one – a child, or a husband or a wife. Well, if you had a gun you might pull that trigger in order to save your loved one's life. You and I might not *condone* that kind of thing, but I'm sure we can at least understand it. Or, let's take another example. If you were suddenly awakened in the middle of the night by an intruder threatening your life and you had a chance to kill him to save yourself, and you killed him – well, I think we can all understand how *that* might happen. And that wouldn't make us desperate criminals or evil people, would it? It was something we did in the heat of the moment." Di Silva's voice hardened. "But *cold-blooded murder* is something else again. To take the life of another human being, without the excuse of any feelings or passions, to do it for money or drugs or the sheer pleasure of killing – "

He was deliberately prejudicing the jury, yet not overstepping the bounds, so that there could be no error calling for mistrial or reversal.

Jennifer watched the faces of the jurors, and there was no question but that

Robert Di Silva had them. They were agreeing with every word he said. They shook their heads and nodded and frowned. They did everything but applaud him. He was an orchestra leader and the jury was his orchestra. Jennifer had never seen anything like it. Every time the District Attorney mentioned Abraham Wilson's name – and he mentioned it with almost every sentence – the jury automatically looked over at the defendant. Jennifer had cautioned Wilson not to look at the jury. She had drilled it into him over and over again that he was to look anywhere in the courtroom except at the jury box, because the air of defiance he exuded was enraging. To her horror now, Jennifer found that Abraham Wilson's eyes were fastened on the jury box, locking eyes with the jurors. Aggression seemed to be pouring out of him.

Jennifer said in a low voice, "Abraham . . ."

He did not turn.

The District Attorney was finishing his opening address. "The Bible says, 'An eye for an eye, a tooth for a tooth.' That is vengeance. The State is not asking for vengeance. It is asking for justice. Justice for the poor man whom Abraham Wilson cold-bloodedly – *cold-bloodedly* – murdered Thank you."

The District Attorney took his seat.

As Jennifer rose to address the jury, she could feel their hostility and impatience. She had read books about how lawyers were able to read juries' minds, and she had been skeptical. But no longer. The message from the jury was coming at her loudly and clearly. They had already decided her client was guilty, and they were impatient because Jennifer was wasting their time, keeping them in court when they could be out doing more important things, as their friend the District Attorney had pointed out. Jennifer and Abraham Wilson were the enemy.

Jennifer took a deep breath and said, "If Your Honor please," and then she turned back to the jurors. "Ladies and gentlemen, the reason we have courtrooms, the reason we are all here today, is because the law, in its wisdom, knows that there are always two sides to every case. Listening to the District Attorney's attack on my client, listening to him pronounce my client guilty without benefit of a jury's verdict – *your* verdict – one would not think so."

She looked into their faces for a sign of sympathy or support. There was none. She forced herself to go on. "District Attorney Di Silva used the phrase over and over, '*Abraham Wilson is guilty.*' That is a lie. Judge Waldman will tell you that no defendant is guilty until a judge or jury declares that he is guilty. That is what we are all here to find out, isn't it? Abraham Wilson has been charged with murdering a fellow inmate at Sing Sing. But Abraham Wilson did not kill for money or for dope. He killed to save his own life. You remember those clever examples that the District Attorney gave you when he explained the difference between killing in cold blood and in hot blood. Killing in hot blood is when you're protecting someone you love, or when you're defending yourself. Abraham Wilson killed in self-defense, and I tell you now that any of us in this courtroom, under identical circumstances, would have done exactly the same thing.

"The District Attorney and I agree on one point: Every man has the right to protect his own life. If Abraham Wilson had not acted exactly as he did, he would be dead." Jennifer's voice was ringing with sincerity. She had forgotten her nervousness in the passion of her conviction. "I ask each of you to remember one thing: under the law of this state, the prosecution must prove beyond any reasonable doubt that the act of killing was not committed in self-defense. And before this trial is over we will present solid evidence to show you that Raymond Thorpe was killed in order to prevent his murdering my client. Thank you."

The parade of witnesses for the State began. Robert Di Silva had not missed a single opportunity. His character witnesses for the deceased, Raymond Thorpe, included a minister, prison guards and fellow convicts. One by one they took the stand and testified to the sterling character and pacific disposition of the deceased.

Each time the District Attorney was finished with a witness, he turned to Jennifer and said, "Your witness."

And each time Jennifer replied, "No cross-examination."

She knew that there was no point in trying to discredit the character witnesses. By the time they were finished, one would have thought that Raymond Thorpe had been wrongfully deprived of sainthood. The guards, who had been carefully coached by Robert Di Silva, testified that Thorpe had been a model prisoner who went around Sing Sing doing good works, intent only on helping his fellow man. The fact that Raymond Thorpe was a convicted bank robber and rapist was a tiny flaw in an otherwise perfect character.

What badly damaged Jennifer's already weak defense was the physical description of Raymond Thorpe. He had been a slightly built man, only five feet nine inches tall. Robert Di Silva dwelt on that, and he never let the jurors forget it. He painted a graphic picture of how Abraham Wilson had viciously attacked the smaller man and had smashed Thorpe's head against a concrete building in the exercise yard, instantly killing him. As Di Silva spoke, the jurors' eyes were fastened on the giant figure of the defendant sitting at the table, dwarfing everyone near him.

The District Attorney was saying, "We'll probably never know what caused Abraham Wilson to attack this harmless, defenseless little man – "

And Jennifer's heart suddenly leaped. One word that Di Silva had said had given her the chance she needed.

" – We may never know the reason for the defendant's vicious attack, but one thing we *do* know, ladies and gentlemen – it wasn't because the murdered man was a threat to Abraham Wilson."

"Self-defense?" He turned to Judge Waldman. "Your Honor, would you please direct the defendant to rise?"

Judge Waldman looked at Jennifer. "Does counsel for the defense have any objection?"

Jennifer had an idea what was coming, but she knew that any objection on her part could only be damaging. "No, Your Honor."

Judge Waldman said, "Will the defendant rise, please?"

Abraham Wilson sat there a moment, his face defiant; then he slowly rose to his full height of six feet four inches.

Di Silva said, "There is a court clerk here, Mr. Galin, who is five feet nine inches tall, the exact height of the murdered man, Raymond Thorpe. Mr. Galin, would you please go over and stand next to the defendant?"

The court clerk walked over to Abraham Wilson and stood next to him. The contrast between the two men was ludicrous. Jennifer knew she had been outmaneuvered again, but there was nothing she could do about it. The visual impression could never be erased. The District Attorney stood there looking at the two men for a moment, and then said to the jury, his voice almost a whisper, "*Self-defense?*"

The trial was going worse than Jennifer had dreamed in her wildest nightmares. She could feel the jury's eagerness to get the trial over with so they could deliver a verdict of guilty.

Ken Bailey was seated among the spectators and, during a recess, Jennifer had a chance to exchange a few words with him.

"It's not an easy case," Ken said sympathetically. "I wish you didn't have King Kong for a client. Christ, just looking at him is enough to scare the hell out of anybody."

"He can't help that."

"As the old joke goes, he could have stayed home. How are you and our esteemed District Attorney getting along?"

Jennifer gave him a mirthless smile. "Mr. Di Silva sent me a message this morning. He intends to remove me from the law business."

When the parade of prosecution witnesses was over and Di Silva had rested his case, Jennifer rose and said, "I would like to call Howard Patterson to the stand."

The assistant warden of Sing Sing Prison reluctantly rose and moved toward the witness box, all eyes fixed on him. Robert Di Silva watched intently as Patterson took the oath. Di Silva's mind was racing, computing all the probabilities. He knew he had won the case. He had his victory speech all prepared.

Jennifer was addressing the witness. "Would you fill the jury in on your background, please, Mr. Patterson?"

District Attorney Di Silva was on his feet. "The State will waive the witness's background in order to save time, and we will stipulate that Mr. Patterson is the assistant warden at Sing Sing Prison."

"Thank you," Jennifer said. "I think the jury should be informed that Mr. Patterson had to be subpoenaed to come here today. He is here as a hostile witness." Jennifer turned to Patterson. "When I asked you to come here voluntarily and testify on behalf of my client, you refused. Is that true?"

"Yes."

"Would you tell the jury *why* you had to be subpoenaed to get you here?"

"I'll be glad to. I've been dealing with men like Abraham Wilson all my life. They're born troublemakers."

Robert Di Silva was leaning forward in his chair, grinning, his eyes locked on the faces of the jurors. He whispered to an assistant, "Watch her hang herself."

Jennifer said, "Mr. Patterson, Abraham Wilson is not on trial here for being a troublemaker. He's on trial for his life. Wouldn't you be willing to help a fellow human being who was unjustly accused of a capital crime?"

"If he were unjustly accused, yes." The emphasis on *unjustly* brought a knowing look to the faces of the jurors.

"There have been killings in prison before this case, have there not?"

"When you lock up hundreds of violent men together in an artificial environment, they're bound to generate an enormous amount of hostility, and there's – "

"Just yes or no, please, Mr. Patterson."

"Yes."

"Of those killings that have occurred in your experience, would you say that there have been a variety of motives?"

"Well, I suppose so. Sometimes – "

"Yes or no, please."

"Yes."

"Has self-defense ever been a motive in any of those prison killings?"

"Well, sometimes – " He saw the expression on Jennifer's face. "Yes."

"So, based on your vast experience, it is entirely possible, is it not, that Abraham Wilson was actually defending his own life when he killed Raymond Thorpe?"

"I don't think it – "

"I asked if it is possible. Yes or no."

"It is highly unlikely," Patterson said stubbornly.

Jennifer turned to Judge Waldman. "Your Honor, would you please direct the witness to answer the question?"

Judge Waldman looked down at Howard Patterson. "The witness will answer the question."

"Yes."

But the fact that his whole attitude said *no* had registered on the jury.

Jennifer said, "If the court please, I have subpoenaed from the witness some material I would like to submit now in evidence."

District Attorney Di Silva rose. "What kind of material?"

"Evidence that will prove our contention of self-defense."

"Objection, Your Honor."

"What are you objecting to?" Jennifer asked. "You haven't seen it yet."

Judge Waldman said, "The court will withhold a ruling until it sees the evidence. A man's life is at stake here. The defendant is entitled to every possible consideration."

"Thank you, Your Honor." Jennifer turned to Howard Patterson. "Did you bring it with you?" she asked.

He nodded, tight-lipped. "Yes. But I'm doing this under protest."

"I think you've already made that very clear, Mr. Patterson. May we have it, please?"

Howard Patterson looked over to the spectator area where a man in a prison guard uniform was seated. Patterson nodded to him. The guard rose and came forward, carrying a covered wooden box.

Jennifer took it from him. "The defense would like to place this in evidence as Exhibit A, Your Honor."

"What is it?" District Attorney Di Silva demanded.

"It's called a *goodie box*."

There was a titter from the spectators.

Judge Waldman looked down at Jennifer and said slowly, "Did you say a *goodie* box? What is in the box, Miss Parker?"

"Weapons. Weapons that were made in Sing Sing by the prisoners for the purpose of – "

"Objection!" The District Attorney was on his feet, his voice a roar. He hurried toward the bench. "I'm willing to make allowances for my colleague's inexperience, Your Honor, but if she intends to practice criminal law, then I would suggest she study the basic rules of evidence. There is no evidence linking anything in this so-called *goodie box* with the case that is being tried in this court."

"This box proves – "

"This box proves nothing." The District Attorney's voice was withering. He turned to Judge Waldman. "The State objects to the introduction of this exhibit as being immaterial and irrelevant."

"Objection sustained."

And Jennifer stood there, watching her case collapse. Everything was against her: the judge, the jury, Di Silva, the evidence. Her client was going to the electric chair unless . . .

Jennifer took a deep breath. "Your Honor, this exhibit is absolutely vital to our defense. I feel – "

Judge Waldman interrupted. "Miss Parker, this court does not have the time or the inclination to give you instructions in the law, but the District Attorney is quite right. Before coming into this courtroom you should have acquainted yourself with the basic rules of evidence. The first rule is that you cannot introduce evidence that has not been properly prepared for. Nothing has been put into the record about the deceased being armed or not armed. Therefore, the question of these weapons becomes extraneous. You are overruled."

Jennifer stood there, the blood rushing to her cheeks. "I'm sorry," she said stubbornly, "but it is *not* extraneous."

"That is enough! You may file an exception."

"I don't want to file an exception, Your Honor. You're denying my client his rights."

"Miss Parker, if you go any further I will hold you in contempt of court."

"I don't care what you do to me," Jennifer said. "The ground *has* been prepared for introducing this evidence. The District Attorney prepared it himself."

Di Silva said, "What? I never – "

Jennifer turned to the court stenographer. "Would you please read Mr. Di Silva's statement, beginning with the line, 'We'll probably never know what caused Abraham Wilson to attack . . .'?"

The District Attorney looked up at Judge Waldman. "Your Honor, are you going to allow – ?"

Judge Waldman held up a hand. He turned to Jennifer. "This court does not need you to explain the law to it, Miss Parker. When this trial is ended, you will be held in contempt of court. Because this is a capital case, I am going to hear you out." He turned to the court stenographer. "You may proceed."

The court stenographer turned some pages and began reading. "We'll probably never know what caused Abraham Wilson to attack this harmless, defenseless little man – "

"That's enough," Jennifer interrupted. "Thank you." She looked at Robert Di Silva and said slowly, "Those are your words, Mr. Di Silva. *We'll probably never know what caused Abraham Wilson to attack this harmless, defenseless little man . . .*" She turned to Judge Waldman. "The key word, Your Honor, is *defenseless.* Since the District Attorney himself told this jury that the victim was defenseless, he left an open door for us to pursue the fact that the victim might *not* have been defenseless, that he might, in fact, have had a weapon. Whatever is brought up in the direct is admissible in the cross."

There was a long silence.

Judge Waldman turned to Robert Di Silva. "Miss Parker has a valid point. You did leave the door open"

Robert Di Silva was looking at him unbelievingly. "But I only – "

"The court will allow the evidence to be entered as Exhibit A."

Jennifer took a deep, grateful breath. "Thank you, Your Honor." She picked up the covered box, held it up in her hands and turned to face the jury. "Ladies and gentlemen, in his final summation the District Attorney is going to tell you that what you are about to see in this box is not direct evidence. He will be correct. He is going to tell you that there is nothing to link any of these weapons to the deceased. He will be correct. I am introducing this exhibit for another reason. For days now, you have been hearing how the ruthless, trouble-making defendant, who stands six feet four inches tall, wantonly attacked Raymond Thorpe, who stood only five feet nine inches tall. The picture that has been so carefully, and falsely, painted for you by the prosecution is that of a sadistic, murdering bully who killed another inmate for no reason. But ask yourselves this: isn't there always *some* motive? Greed, hate, lust, *something?* I believe – and

I'm staking my client's life on that belief – that there *was* a motive for that killing. The *only* motive, as the District Attorney himself told you, that justifies killing someone: self-defense. A man fighting to protect his own life. You have heard Howard Patterson testify that in his experience murders *have* occurred in prison, that convicts *do* fashion deadly weapons. What that means is that it was possible that Raymond Thorpe was armed with such a weapon, that indeed it was *he* who was attacking the defendant, and the defendant, trying to protect himself, was forced to kill him – *in self-defense.* If you decide that Abraham Wilson ruthlessly – and without any motivation at all – killed Raymond Thorpe, then you must bring in a verdict of guilty as charged. If, however, after seeing this evidence, you have a reasonable doubt in your minds, then it is your duty to return a verdict of not guilty." The covered box was becoming heavy in her hands. "When I first looked into this box I could not believe what I saw. You, too, may find it hard to believe – but I ask you to remember that it was brought here under protest by the assistant warden of Sing Sing Prison. This, ladies and gentlemen, is a collection of confiscated weapons secretly made by the convicts at Sing Sing."

As Jennifer moved toward the jury box, she seemed to stumble and lose her balance. The box fell out of her grasp, the top flew off, and the contents spilled out over the courtroom floor. There was a gasp. The jurors began to get to their feet so they could have a better look. They were staring at the hideous collection of weapons that had tumbled from the box. There were almost one hundred of them, of every size, shape and description. Homemade hatchets and butcher knives, stilettos and deadly looking scissors with the ends honed, pellet guns, and a large, vicious-looking cleaver. There were thin wires with wooden handles, used for strangling, a leather sap, a sharpened ice pick, a machete.

Spectators and reporters were on their feet now, craning to get a better look at the arsenal that lay scattered on the floor. Judge Waldman was angrily pounding his gavel for order.

Judge Waldman looked at Jennifer with an expression she could not fathom. A bailiff hurried forward to pick up the spilled contents of the box. Jennifer waved him away.

"Thank you," she said, "I'll do it."

As the jurors and spectators watched, Jennifer got down on her knees and began picking up the weapons and putting them back in the box. She worked slowly, handling the weapons gingerly, looking at each one without expression before she replaced it. The jurors had taken their seats again, but they were watching every move she made. It took Jennifer a full five minutes to return the weapons to the box, while District Attorney Di Silva sat there, fuming.

When Jennifer had put the last weapon in the deadly arsenal back in the box, she rose, looked at Patterson, then turned and said to Di Silva, "Your witness."

It was too late to repair the damage that had been done. "No cross," the District Attorney said.

"Then I would like to call Abraham Wilson to the stand."

8

"Your name?"

"Abraham Wilson."

"Would you speak up, please?"

"Abraham Wilson."

"Mr. Wilson, did you kill Raymond Thorpe?"

"Yes, ma'am."

"Would you tell the court why?"

"He was gonna kill me."

"Raymond Thorpe was a much smaller man than you. Did you really believe that he would be able to kill you?"

"He was comin' at me with a knife that made him purty tall."

Jennifer had kept out two objects from the goodie box. One was a finely honed butcher knife; the other was a large pair of metal tongs. She held up the knife. "Was this the knife that Raymond Thorpe threatened you with?"

"Objection! The defendant has no way of knowing – "

"I'll rephrase the question. Was this similar to the knife that Raymond Thorpe threatened you with?"

"Yes, ma'am."

"And these tongs?"

"Yes, ma'am."

"Had you had trouble with Thorpe before?"

"Yes, ma'am."

"And when he came at you armed with these two weapons, you were forced to kill him in order to save your own life?"

"Yes, ma'am."

"Thank you."

Jennifer turned to Di Silva. "Your witness."

Robert Di Silva rose to his feet and moved slowly toward the witness box.

"Mr. Wilson, you've killed before, haven't you? I mean, this wasn't your first murder?"

"I made a mistake and I'm payin' for it. I – "

"Spare us your sermon. Just answer yes or no."

"Yes."

"So a human life doesn't have much value to you."

"That ain't true. I – "

"Do you call committing two murders valuing human life? How many people would you have killed if you *didn't* value human life? Five? Ten? Twenty?"

He was baiting Abrabam Wilson and Wilson was falling for it. His jaw was clenched and his face was filling with anger. *Be careful!*

"I only kilt two people."

"Only! You *only* killed two people!" The District Attorney shook his head in mock dismay. He stepped close to the witness box and looked up at the defendant. "I'll bet it gives you a feeling of power to be so big. It must make you feel a little bit like God. Any time you want to, you can take a life here, take a life there . . ."

Abraham Wilson was on his feet, rising to his full height. "You somabitch!"

No! Jennifer prayed. *Don't!*

"Sit down!" Di Silva thundered. "Is that the way you lost your temper when you killed Raymond Thorpe?"

"Thorpe was tryin' ta kill me."

"With these?" Di Silva held up the butcher knife and the pair of tongs. "I'm sure you could have taken that knife away from him." He waved the tongs around. "And you were afraid of this?" He turned back to the jury and held up the tongs deprecatingly. "This doesn't look so terribly lethal. If the deceased had been able to hit you over the head with it, it might have caused a small bump. What exactly is this pair of tongs, Mr. Wilson?"

Abraham Wilson said softly, "They're testicle crushers."

The jury was out for eight hours.

Robert Di Silva and his assistants left the courtroom to take a break, but Jennifer stayed in her seat, unable to tear herself away.

When the jury filed out of the room, Ken Bailey came up to Jennifer. "How about a cup of coffee?"

"I couldn't swallow anything."

She sat in the courtroom, afraid to move, only dimly aware of the people around her. It was over. She had done her best. She closed her eyes and tried to pray, but the fear in her was too strong. She felt as though she, along with Abraham Wilson, was about to be sentenced to death.

The jury was filing back into the room, their faces grim and foreboding, and Jennifer's heart began to beat faster. She could see by their faces that they were going to convict. She thought she would faint. Because of her, a man was going to be executed. She should never have taken the case in the first place. What right had she to put a man's life in her hands? She must have been insane to think she could win over someone as experienced as Robert Di Silva. She wanted to run up to the jurors before they could give their verdict and say, *Wait! Abraham Wilson hasn't had a fair trial. Please let another attorney defend him. Someone better than I am.*

But it was too late. Jennifer stole a look at Abrabam Wilson's face. He sat there as immobile as a statue. She could feel no hatred coming from him now, only a deep despair. She wanted to say something to comfort him, but there were no words.

Judge Waldman was speaking. "Has the jury reached a verdict?"

"It has, Your Honor."

The judge nodded and his clerk walked over to the foreman of the jury, took a slip of paper from him and handed it to the judge. Jennifer felt as though her heart were going to come out of her chest. She could not breathe. She wanted to hold back this moment, to freeze it forever before the verdict was read.

Judge Waldman studied the slip of paper in his hands; then he slowly looked around the courtroom. His eyes rested on the members of the jury, on Robert Di Silva, on Jennifer and finally on Abraham Wilson.

"The defendant will please rise."

Abraham Wilson got to his feet, his movements slow and tired, as though all the energy had been drained out of him.

Judge Waldman read from the slip of paper. "This jury finds the defendant, Abraham Wilson, not guilty as charged."

There was a momentary hush and the judge's further words were drowned out in a roar from the spectators. Jennifer stood there, stunned, unable to believe what she was hearing. She turned toward Abraham Wilson, speechless. He stared at her for an instant with those small, mean eyes. And then that ugly face broke into the broadest grin that Jennifer had ever seen. He reached down and hugged her and Jennifer tried to fight back her tears.

The press was crowding around Jennifer, asking for a statement, barraging her with questions.

"How does it feel to beat the District Attorney?"

"Did you think you were going to win this case?"

"What would you have done if they had sent Wilson to the electric chair?"

Jennifer shook her head to all questions. She could not bring herself to talk to them. They had come here to watch a spectacle, to see a man being hounded to his death. If the verdict had gone the other way . . . she could not bear to think about it. Jennifer began to collect her papers and stuff them into a briefcase.

A bailiff approached her. "Judge Waldman wants to see you in his chambers, Miss Parker."

She had forgotten that there was a contempt of court citation waiting for her but it no longer seemed important. The only thing that mattered was that she had saved Abraham Wilson's life.

Jennifer glanced over at the prosecutor's table. District Attorney Silva was savagely stuffing papers into a briefcase, berating one of his assistants. He caught Jennifer's look. His eyes met hers and he needed no words.

Judge Lawrence Waldman was seated at his desk when Jennifer walked in. He said curtly, "Sit down, Miss Parker." Jennifer took a seat. "I will not allow you or anyone else to turn my courtroom into a sideshow."

Jennifer flushed. "I tripped. I couldn't help what – "

Judge Waldman raised a hand. "Please. Spare me." Jennifer clamped her lips tightly together.

Judge Waldman leaned forward in his chair. "Another thing I will not tolerate in my court is insolence." Jennifer watched him warily, saying nothing. "You overstepped the bounds this afternoon. I realize that your excessive zeal was in defense of a man's life. Because of that, I have decided not to cite you for contempt."

"Thank you, Your Honor." Jennifer had to force the words out.

The judge's face was unreadable as be continued: "Almost invariably, when a case is finished 1 have a sense of whether justice has been served or not. In this instance, quite frankly, I'm not sure." Jennifer waited for him to go on.

"That's all, Miss Parker."

In the evening editions of the newspapers and on the television news that night, Jennifer Parker was back in the headlines, but this time she was the heroine. She was the legal David who had slain Goliath. Pictures of her and Abraham Wilson and District Attorney Di Silva were plastered all over the front pages. Jennifer hungrily devoured every word of the stories, savoring them. It was such a sweet victory after all the disgrace she had suffered earlier.

Ken Bailey took her to dinner at Luchow's to celebrate, and Jennifer was recognized by the captain and several of the customers. Strangers called Jennifer by name and congratulated her. It was a heady experience.

"How does it feel to be a celebrity?" Ken grinned.

"I'm numb."

Someone sent a bottle of wine to the table.

"I don't need anything to drink," Jennifer said. "I feel as though I'm already drunk."

But she was thirsty and she drank three glasses of wine while she rehashed the trial with Ken.

"I was scared. Do you know what it's like to hold someone else's life in your hands? It's like playing God. Can you think of anything scarier than that? I mean, I come from *Kelso* . . . could we have another bottle of wine, Ken?"

"Anything you want."

Ken ordered a feast for them both, but Jennifer was too excited to eat.

"Do you know what Abraham Wilson said to me the first time I met him? He said, 'You crawl into my skin and I'll crawl into yours and then you and me will rap about hate.' Ken, I was *in* his skin today, and do you know something? I thought the jury was going to convict *me*. I felt as though I was going to be executed. I love Abraham Wilson. Could we have some more wine?"

"You haven't eaten a bite."

"I'm thirsty."

Ken watched, concerned, as Jennifer kept filling and emptying her glass. "Take it easy."

She waved a hand in airy dismissal. "It's California wine. It's like drinking water." She took another swallow. "You're my best friend. Do you know who's not my best friend? The great Robert Di Sliva. Di Sivla."

"Di Silva."

"Him, too. He hates me. D'ja see his face today? O-o-oh, he was mad! He said he was gonna run me out of court. But he didn't, did he?"

"No, he – "

"You know what I think? You know what I *really* think?"

"I – "

"Di Sliva thinks I'm Ahab and he's the white whale."

"I think you have that backwards."

"Thank you, Ken. I can always count on you. Let's have 'nother bottle of wine."

"Don't you think you've had enough?"

"Whales get thirsty." Jennifer giggled. "Tha's me. The big old white whale. Did I tell you I love Abraham Wilson? He's the most beautiful man I ever met. I looked in his eyes, Ken, my frien', 'n' he's beautiful! Y'ever look in Di Sivla's eyes? O-o-oh! They're cold! I mean, he's 'n iceberg. But he's not a bad man. Did I tell you 'bout Ahab 'n' the big white whale?"

"Yes."

"I love old Ahab. I love everybody. 'N' you know why, Ken? 'Cause Abraham Wilson is alive tonight. He's alive. Le's have 'nother bottle a wine to celebrate . . ."

It was two A.M. when Ken Bailey took Jennifer home. He helped her up the four flights of stairs and into her little apartment. He was breathing hard from the climb.

"You know," Ken said, "I can feel the effects of all that wine."

Jennifer looked at him pityingly. "People who can't handle it shoudn' drink."

And she passed out cold.

She was awakened by the shrill screaming of the telephone. She carefully reached for the instrument, and the slight movement sent rockets of pain through every nerve ending in her body.

"'Lo . . ."

"Jennifer? This is Ken."

"'Lo, Ken."

"You sound terrible. Are you all right?"

She thought about it. "I don't think so. What time is it?"

"It's almost noon. You'd better get down here. All hell is breaking loose."

"Ken – I think I'm dying."

"Listen to me. Get out of bed – slowly – take two aspirin and a cold shower, drink a cup of hot black coffee, and you'll probably live."

When Jennifer arrived at the office one hour later, she was feeling better. *Not good*, Jennifer thought, but *better*.

Both telephones were ringing when she walked into the office.

"They're for you." Ken grinned. "They haven't stopped! You need a switchboard."

There were calls from newspapers and national magazines and television and radio stations wanting to do in-depth stories on Jennifer. Overnight, she had become big news. There were other calls, the kind of which she had dreamed. Law firms that had snubbed her before were telephoning to ask when it would be convenient for her to meet with them.

In his office downtown, Robert Di Silva was screaming at his first assistant. "I want you to start a confidential file on Jennifer Parker. I want to be informed of every client she takes on. Got it?"

"Yes, sir."

"Move!"

9

"He ain't no button guy anymore'n I'm a fuckin' virgin. He's been workin' on the arm all his life."

"The asshole came suckin' up to me askin' me to put in the word with Mike. I said, 'Hey, paesano, I'm only a soldier, ya know?" If Mike needs another shooter he don't have to go lookin' in shit alley."

"He was tryin' to run a game on you, Sal."

"Well, I clocked him pretty good. He ain't connected and in this business, if you ain't connected, you're nothin'."

They were taking in the kitchen of a three-hundred-year-old Dutch farmhouse in upstate New Jersey.

There were three of them in the room: Nick Vito, Joseph Colella and Salvatore "Little Flower" Fiore.

Nick Vito was a cadaverous-looking man with thin lips that were almost invisible, and deep green eyes that were dead. He wore two hundred dollar shoes and white socks.

Joseph "Big Joe" Colella was a huge slab of a man, a granite monolith, and when he walked he looked like a building moving. Someone had once called him a vegetable garden. "Colella's got a potato nose, cauliflower ears and a pea brain."

Colella had a soft, high-pitched voice and a deceptively gentle manner. He owned a race horse and had an uncanny knack for picking winners. He was a family man with a wife and six children. His specialties were guns, acid and chains. Joe's wife, Carmelina, was a strict Catholic, and on Sundays when Colella was not working, he always took his family to church.

The third man, Salvatore Fiore, was almost a midget. He stood five feet three inches and weighed a hundred and fifteen pounds. He had the innocent face of a choirboy and was equally adept with a gun or a knife. Women were greatly attracted to the little man, and he boasted a wife, half a dozen girl friends, and a beautiful mistress. Fiore had once been a jockey, working the tracks from Pimlico to Tijuana. When the racing commissioner at Hollywood Park banned Fiore for doping a horse, the commissioner's body was found floating in Lake Tahoe a week later.

The three men were *soldati* in Antonio Granelli's Family, but it was Michael Moretti who had brought them in, and they belonged to him, body and soul.

In the dining room, a Family meeting was taking place. Seated at the head of the table was Antonio Granelli, *capo* of the most powerful Mafia Family on the east coast. Seventy-two years old, he was such a powerful-looking man with the shoulders and broad chest of a laborer, and a shock of white hair. Born in Palermo, Sicily, Antonio Granelli came to America when he was fifteen and went to work on the waterfront on the west side of lower Manhattan. By the time he was twenty-one, he was lieutenant to the dock boss. The two men had a argument, and when the boss mysteriously disappeared, Antonio Granelli had taken over. Anyone who wanted to work on the docks had to pay him. He had used the money to begin his climb to power, and had expanded rapidly, branching out into loan-sharking and the numbers racket, prostitution and gambling and drugs and murder. Over the years he had been indicted thirty-two times and had only been convicted once, on a minor assault charge. Granelli was a ruthless man with the down-to-earth cunning of a peasant, and a total amorality.

To Granelli's left sat Thomas Colfax, the Family *consigliere*. Twenty-five years earlier, Colfax had had a brilliant future as a corporation lawyer, but he had defended a small olive-oil company which turned out to be Mafia-controlled and, step by step, had been lured into handling other cases for the Mafia until finally, through the years, the Granelli Family had become his sole client. It was a very lucrative client and Thomas Colfax became a wealthy man, with extensive real estate holdings and bank accounts all over the world.

To the right of Antonio Granelli sat Michael Moretti, his son-in-law. Michael was ambitious, a trait that made Granelli nervous. Michael did not fit into the pattern of the Family. His father, Giovanni, a distant cousin of Antonio Granelli, had been born not in Sicily but in Florence. That alone made the Moretti family suspect – everybody knew that Florentines were not to be trusted.

Giovanni Moretti had come to America and opened a shop as a shoemaker, running it honestly, without even a back room for gambling or loan-sharking or girls. Which made him stupid.

Giovanni's son, Michael, was entirely different He had put himself through

Yale and the Wharton School of Business. When Michael had finished school, he had gone to his father with one request: he wanted to meet his distant relative, Antonio Granelli. The old shoemaker had gone to see his cousin and the meeting had been arranged. Granelli was sure that Michael was going to ask for a loan so that he could go into some kind of business, maybe open a shoe shop like his dumb father. But the meeting had been a surprise.

"I know how to make you rich," Michael Moretti had begun.

Antonio Granelli had looked at the impudent young man and had smiled tolerantly. "I am rich."

"No. You just *think* you're rich."

The smile had died away. "What the hell you talkin' about, kid?"

And Michael Moretti had told him.

Antonio Granelli had moved cautiously at first, testing each piece of Michael's advice. Everything had succeeded brilliantly. Where before, the Granelli Family had been involved in profitable illegal activities, under Michael Moretti's supervision it branched out. Within five years the Family was into dozens of legitimate businesses, including meat-packing, linen supplies, restaurants, trucking companies and pharmaceuticals. Michael found ailing companies that needed financing and the Family went in as a minor partner and gradually took over, stripping away whatever assets there were. Old companies with impeccable reputations suddenly found themselves bankrupt. The businesses that showed a satisfactory profit, Michael hung on to and he increased the profits tremendously, for the workers in those businesses were controlled by his unions, and the company took their insurance through one of the Family-owned insurance companies, and they bought their automobiles from one of the Family's automobile dealers. Michael created a symbiotic giant, a series of businesses through which the consumer was constantly being milked – and the milk flowed to the Family.

In spite of his successes, Michael Moretti was aware that he had a problem. Once he had shown Antonio Granelli the rich, ripe horizons of legitimate enterprise, Granelli no longer needed him. He was expensive, because in the beginning he had persuaded Antonio Granelli to give him a percentage of what everyone was sure would be a small pot. But as Michael's ideas began to bear fruit and the profits poured in, Granelli had second thoughts. By chance, Michael learned that Granelli had held a meeting to discuss what the Family should do with him.

"I don't like to see all this money goin' to the kid," Granelli had said. "We get rid of him."

Michael had circumvented that scheme by marrying into the Family. Rosa, Antonio Granelli's only daughter, was nineteen years old. Her mother had died giving birth to her, and Rosa had been brought up in a convent and was allowed to come home only during the holidays. Her father adored her, and he saw to it that she was protected and sheltered. It was on a school holiday, an Easter, that

Rosa met Michael Moretti. By the time she returned to the convent, she was madly in love with him. The memory of his dark good looks drove her to do things when she was alone that the nuns told her were sins against God.

Antonio Granelli was under the delusion that his daughter thought he was merely a successful businessman, but over the years, Rosa's classmates had shown her newspaper and magazine articles about her father and his real business, and whenever the government made an attempt to indict and convict one of the Granelli Family, Rosa was always aware of it. She never discussed it with her father, and so he remained happy in his belief that his daughter was an innocent and that she was spared the shock of knowing the truth.

The truth, if he had know it, would have surprised Granelli for Rosa found her father's business terribly exciting. She hated the discipline of the nuns at the convent and that, in turn, led her to hate all authority. She daydreamed about her father as a kind of Robin Hood, challenging authority, defying the government. The fact that Michael Moretti was an important man in her father's organization made him that much more exciting to her.

From the beginning, Michael was very careful how he handled Rosa. When he managed to be alone with her they exchanged ardent kisses and embraces, but Michael never let it go too far. Rosa was a virgin and she was willing – eager – to give herself to the man she loved. It was Michael who held back.

"I respect you too much, Rosa, to go to bed with you before we're married."

In reality, it was Antonio Granelli he respected too much. *He'd chop my balls off*, Michael thought.

And so it happened that at the time Antonio Granelli was discussing the best way to get rid of Michael Moretti, Michael and Rosa came to him and announced that they were in love and intended to get married. The old man screamed and raged and gave a hundred reasons why it would happen only over someone's dead body. But in the end, true love prevailed and Michael and Rosa were married in an elaborate ceremony.

After the wedding the old man had called Michael aside. "Rosa's all I got, Michael. You take good care of her, huh?"

"I will, Tony."

"I'm gonna be watchin' you. You better make her happy. You know what I mean, Mike?"

"I know what you mean."

"No whores or chippies. Understand? Rosa likes to cook. You see that you're home for dinner every night. You're gonna be a son-in-law to be proud of."

"I'm going to try very hard, Tony."

Antonio Granelli had said casually, "Oh, by the way, Mike, now that you're a member of the Family, that royalty deal I gave you – maybe we oughta change it."

Michael had clapped him on the arm. "Thanks, Papa, but it's enough for us. I'll be able to buy Rosa everything she wants."

And he had walked away, leaving the old man staring after him.

That had been seven years earlier, and the years that followed had been wonderful for Michael. Rosa was pleasant and easy to live with and she adored him, but Michael knew that if she died or went away, he would get along without her. He would simply find someone else to do the things she did for him. He was not in love with Rosa. Michael did not think he was capable of loving another human being; it was as though something was missing in him.

He had no feelings for people, only for animals. Michael had been given a collie puppy for his tenth birthday. The two of them were inseparable. Six weeks later the dog had been killed in a hit-and-run accident, and when Michael's father offered to buy him another dog, Michael had refused. He had never owned another dog after that.

Michael had grown up watching his father slaving his life away for pennies, and Michael had resolved that would never happen to him. He had known what he wanted from the time he had first heard talk about his famous distant cousin Antonio Granelli. There were twenty-six Mafia Families in the United States, five of them in New York City, and his cousin Antonio's was the strongest. From his earliest childhood, Michael thrived on tales of the Mafia. His father told him about the night of the Sicilian Vespers, September 10, 1931, when the balance of power had changed hands. In that single night, the *Young Turks* in the Mafia staged a bloody coup that wiped out more than forty *Mustache Petes*, the old guard who had come over from Italy and Sicily.

Michael was of the new generation. He had gotten rid of the old thinking and had brought in fresh ideas. A nine-man national commission controlled all the Families now, and Michael knew that one day he would run that commission.

Michael turned now to study the two men seated at the dining room table of the New Jersey farmhouse. Antonio Granelli still had a few years left but, with luck, not too many.

Thomas Colfax was the enemy. The lawyer had been against Michael from the beginning. As Michael's influence with the old man had increased, Colfax's had decreased.

Michael had brought more and more of his own men into the Organization, men like Nick Vito and Salvatore Fiore and Joseph Colella, who were fiercely loyal to him. Thomas Colfax had not liked that.

When Michael had been indicted for the murders of the Ramos brothers, and Camillo Stela had agreed to testify against him in court, the old lawyer had believed that he was finally going to be rid of Michael, for the District Attorney had an airtight case.

Michael had thought of a way out in the middle of the night. At four in the morning, he had gone out to a telephone booth and called Joseph Colella.

"Next week some new lawyers are going to be sworn in on the District Attorney's staff. Can you get me their names?"

"Sure, Mike. Easy."

"One more thing. Call Detroit and have them fly in a cherry – one of their boys who's never been tagged." And Michael had hung up.

Two weeks later, Michael Moretti had sat in the courtroom studying the new assistant district attorneys. He had looked them over carefully, his eyes traveling from face to face, searching and judging. What he planned to do was dangerous, but its very daring could make it work. He was dealing with young beginners who would be too nervous to ask a lot of questions, and anxious to be helpful and make their mark. Well, someone was certainly going to make his mark.

Michael had finally selected Jennifer Parker. He liked the fact that she was inexperienced and that she was tense and trying to hide it. He liked the fact that she was female and would feel under more pressure than the men. When Michael was satisfied with his decision, he turned to a man in a gray suit sitting among the spectators and nodded toward Jennifer. That was all.

Michael had watched as the District Attorney had finished his examination of that son-of-a-bitch, Camillo Stela. He had turned to Thomas Colfax and said, *Your witness for cross.* Thomas Colfax had risen to his feet. *If it please Your Honor, it is now almost noon. I would prefer not to have my cross-examination interrupted. Might I request that the court recess for lunch now and I'll cross-examine this afternoon?*

And a recess had been declared. Now was the moment!

Michael saw his man casually drift up to join the men who were crowded around the District Attorney. The man made himself a part of the group. A few moments later, he walked over to Jennifer and handed her a large envelope. Michael sat there, holding his breath, willing Jennifer to take the envelope and move toward the witness room. She did. It was not until he saw her return without it that Michael Moretti relaxed.

That had been a year ago. The newspapers had crucified the girl, but that was *her* problem. Michael had not given any further thought to Jennifer Parker until the newspapers had begun recently to feature the Abraham Wilson trial. They had dragged up the old Michael Moretti case and Jennifer Parker's part in it. They had run her picture. She was a stunning-looking girl, but there was something more – there was a sense of independence about her that stirred something in him. He stared at the picture for a long time.

Michael began to follow the Abraham Wilson trial with increasing interest. When the boys had celebrated with a victory dinner after Michael's mistrial was declared, Salvatore Fiore had proposed a toast. "The world got rid of one more fuckin' lawyer."

But the world had not gotten rid of her, Michael thought. Jennifer Parker had bounced back and was still in there, fighting. Michael liked that.

He had seen her on television the night before, discussing her victory over Robert Di Silva, and Michael had been oddly pleased.

Antonio Granelli had asked, "Ain't she the mouthpiece you set up, Mike?"

"Uh-huh. She's got a brain, Tony. Maybe we can use her one of these days."

10

The day after the Abraham Wilson verdict, Adam Warner telephoned. "I just called to congratulate you."

Jennifer recognized his voice instantly and it affected her more than she would have believed possible.

"This is – "

"I know." Oh, *God*, Jennifer thought. *Why did I say that?* There was no reason to let Adam know how often she had thought about him in the past few months.

"I wanted to tell you I thought you handled the Abraham Wilson case brilliantly. You deserved to win it."

"Thank you." *He's going to hang up*, Jennifer thought. *I'll never see him again. He's probably too busy with his harem.*

And Adam Warner was saying, "I was wondering if you'd care to have dinner with me one evening?"

Men hate overeager girls. "What about tonight?"

Jennifer heard the smile in his voice. "I'm afraid my first free night is Friday. Are you busy?"

"No." She had almost said, *Of course not*.

"Shall I pick you up at your place?"

Jennifer thought about her dreary little apartment with its lumpy. sofa, the ironing board set up in a corner. "It might be easier if we met somewhere."

"Do you like the food at Lutèce?"

"May I tell you after I've eaten there?"

He laughed. "How's eight o'clock?"

"Eight o'clock is lovely."

Lovely. Jennifer replaced the receiver and sat there in a glow of euphoria. *This is ridiculous*, she thought. *He's probably married and has two dozen children*. Almost the first thing Jennifer had noticed about Adam when they had had dinner was that he was not wearing a wedding ring. *Inconclusive evidence*, she thought wryly. There definitely should be a law forcing all husbands to wear wedding rings.

Ken Bailey walked into the office. "How's the master attorney?" He looked at her more closely. "You look like you just swallowed a client."

Jennifer hesitated, then said, "Ken, would you run a check on someone for me?"

He walked over to her desk, picked up a pad and pencil. "Shoot. Who is it?"

She started to say Adam's name, then stopped, feeling like a fool. What business had she prying into Adam Warner's private life? *For God's sake*, she told herself, *all he did is ask you to have dinner with him, not marry him.* "Never mind."

Ken put the pencil down. "Whatever you say."

"Ken – "

"Yes?"

"Adam Warner. His name is Adam Warner."

Ken looked at her in surprise. "Hell, you don't need me to run a check on him. Just read the newspapers."

"What do you know about him?"

Ken Bailey flopped into a chair across from Jennifer and steepled his fingers together. "Let me see. He's a partner in Needham, Finch, Pierce and Warner; Harvard Law School; comes from a rich socialite family; in his middle thirties – "

Jennifer looked at him curiously. "How do you know so much about him?"

He winked. "I have friends in high places. There's a rumor they're going to run Mr. Warner for the United States Senate. There's even a little presidential ground swell going on. He's got what they call charisma."

He certainly has, Jennifer thought. She tried to make her next question sound casual. "What about his personal life?"

Ken Bailey looked at her oddly. "He's married to the daughter of an ex-Secretary of the Navy. She's the niece of Stewart Needham, Warner's law partner."

Jennifer's heart sank. So that was that.

Ken was watching her, puzzled. "Why this sudden interest in Adam Warner?"

"Just curious."

Long after Ken Bailey had left, Jennifer sat there thinking about Adam. *He asked me to dinner as a professional courtesy. He wants to congratulate me. But he's already done that over the telephone. Who cares why? I'm going to see him again. I wonder whether he'll remember to mention he has a wife. Of course not. Well, I'll have dinner with Adam on Friday night and that will be the end of that.*

Late that afternoon, Jennifer received a telephone call from Peabody & Peabody. It was from the senior partner himself.

"I've been meaning to get around to this for some time," he said. "I wondered if you and I might have lunch soon."

His casual tone did not deceive Jennifer. She was sure the idea of having lunch with her had not occurred to him until after he had read about the Abraham Wilson decision. He certainly did not want to meet with her to discuss serving subpoenas.

"What about tomorrow?" he suggested. "My club."

They met for lunch the following day. The senior Peabody was a pale, prissy man, an older version of his son. His vest failed to conceal a slight paunch. Jennifer liked the father just as little as she had liked the son.

"We have an opening for a bright young trial attorney in our firm, Miss Parker. We can offer you fifteen thousand dollars a year to start with."

Jennifer sat there listening to him, thinking how much that offer would have meant to her a year earlier when she had desperately needed a job, needed someone who believed in her.

He was saying, "I'm sure that within a few years there would be room for a partnership for you in our firm."

Fifteen thousand dollars a year and a partnership. Jennifer thought about the little office she shared with Ken, and her tiny, shabby four-flight walk-up apartment with its fake fireplace.

Mr. Peabody was taking her silence for acquiescence. "Good. We'd like you to begin as soon as possible. Perhaps you could start Monday. I – "

"No."

"Oh. Well, if Monday's not convenient for you – "

"I mean, no, I can't take your offer, Mr. Peabody," Jennifer said, and amazed herself.

"I see." There was a pause. "Perhaps we could start you at twenty thousand dollars a year." He saw the expression on her face. "Or twenty-five thousand. Why don't you think it over?"

"I've thought it over. I'm going to stay in business for myself."

The clients were beginning to come. Not a great many and not very affluent, but they were clients. The office was becoming too small for her.

One morning after Jennifer had kept two clients waiting outside in the hallway while she was dealing with a third, Ken said, "This isn't going to work. You're going to have to move out of here and get yourself a decent office uptown."

Jennifer nodded. "I know. I've been thinking about it."

Ken busied himself with some papers so that he did not have to meet her eyes. "I'll miss you."

"What are you talking about? You have to go with me."

It took a moment for the words to sink in. He looked up and a broad grin creased his freckled face.

"Go with you?" He glanced around the cramped, windowless room. "And give up all this?"

The following week, Jennifer and Ken Bailey moved into larger offices in the five hundred block on Fifth Avenue. The new quarters were simply furnished and consisted of three small rooms: one for Jennifer, one for Ken and one for a secretary.

The secretary they hired was a young girl named Cynthia Ellman fresh out of New York University.

"There won't be a lot for you to do for a while," Jennifer apologized, "but things will pick up."

"Oh, I know they will, Miss Parker." There was heroine worship in the girl's voice.

She wants to be like me, Jennifer thought. *God forbid!*

Ken Bailey walked in and said, "Hey, I get lonely in that big office all by myself. How about dinner and the theater tonight?"

"I'm afraid I – " She was tired and had some briefs to read, but Ken was her best friend and she could not refuse him.

"I'd love to go."

They went to see *Applause*, and Jennifer enjoyed it tremendously. Lauren Bacall was totally captivating. Jennifer and Ken had supper afterward at Sardi's.

When they had ordered, Ken said, "I have two tickets for the ballet Friday night. I thought we might – "

Jennifer said, "I'm sorry, Ken. I'm busy Friday night."

"Oh." His voice was curiously flat.

From time to time, Jennifer would find Ken staring at her when he thought he was unobserved, and there was an expression on his face that Jennifer found hard to define. She knew Ken was lonely, although he never talked about any of his friends and never discussed his personal life. She could not forget what Otto had told her, and she wondered whether Ken himself knew what he wanted out of life. She wished that there were some way she could help him.

It seemed to Jennifer that Friday was never going to arrive. As her dinner date with Adam Warner drew closer, Jennifer found it more and more difficult to concentrate on business. She found herself thinking about Adam constantly. She knew she was being ridiculous. She had seen the man only once in her life, and yet she was unable to get him out of her mind. She tried to rationalize by telling herself that it was because he had saved her when she was facing disbarment proceedings, and then had sent her clients. That was true, but Jennifer knew it was more than that. It was something she could not explain, even to herself. It was a feeling she had never had before, an attraction she had never felt for any other man. She wondered what Adam Warner's wife was like. She was undoubtedly one of the chosen women who, every Wednesday, walked through the red door at Elizabeth Arden's for a day of head-to-toe pampering. She would be sleek and sophisticated, with the polished aura of the wealthy socialite.

*

On the magic Friday morning at ten o'clock, Jennifer made an appointment with a new Italian hairdresser Cynthia had told her all the models were going to. At ten-thirty, Jennifer called to cancel it. At eleven, she rescheduled the appointment.

Ken Bailey invited Jennifer to lunch, but she was too nervous to eat anything. Instead, she went shopping at Bendel's, where she bought a short, dark green chiffon dress that matched her eyes, a pair of slender brown pumps and a matching purse. She knew she was far over her budget, but she could not seem to stop herself.

She passed the perfume department on the way out, and on an insane impulse bought a bottle of Joy perfume. It was insane because the man was married.

Jennifer left the office at five o'clock and went home to change. She spent two hours bathing and dressing for Adam, and when she was finished she studied herself critically in the minor. Then she defiantly combed out her carefully coiffured hair and tied it back with a green ribbon. *That's better*, she thought. *I'm a lawyer going to have dinner with another lawyer.* But when she closed the door she left behind a faint fragrance of rose and jasmine.

Lutèce was nothing like what Jennifer had expected. A French tricolor flew above the entrance of the small town house. Inside, a narrow hall led to a small bar and beyond was a sunroom, bright and gay, with porch wicker and plaid tablecloths. Jennifer was met at the door by the owner, André Soltner.

"May I help you?"

"I'm meeting Mr. Adam Warner. I think I'm a little early."

He waved Jennifer toward the small bar. "Would you care for a drink while you are waiting, Miss Parker?"

"That would be nice," Jennifer said. "Thank you."

"I'll send a waiter over."

Jennifer took a seat and amused herself watching the bejeweled and mink-draped women arriving with their escorts. Jennifer had read and heard about Lutèce. It was reputed to be Jacqueline Kennedy's favorite restaurant and to have excellent food.

A distinguished-looking gray-haired man walked up to Jennifer and said, "Mind if I join you for a moment?"

Jennifer stiffened. "I'm waiting for someone," she began. "He should be here – "

He smiled and sat down. "This isn't a pickup, Miss Parker." Jennifer looked at him in surprise, unable to place him. "I'm Lee Browning, of Holland and Browning." It was one of the most prestigious law firms in New York. "I just wanted to congratulate you on the way you handled the Wilson trial."

"Thank you, Mr. Browning."

"You took a big chance. It was a no-win case." He studied her a moment. "The rule is, when you're on the wrong side of a no-win case, make sure it's one where there's no publicity involved. The trick is to spotlight the winners and kick the losers under the rug. You fooled a lot of us. Have you ordered a drink yet?"

"No – "

"May I – ?" He beckoned to a waiter. "Victor, bring us a bottle of champagne, would you? Dom Perignon."

"Right away, Mr. Browning."

Jennifer smiled. "Are you trying to impress me?"

He laughed aloud. "I'm trying to hire you. I imagine you've been getting a lot of offers."

"A few."

"Our firm deals mostly in corporate work, Miss Parker, but some of our more affluent clients frequently get carried away and have need of a criminal defense attorney. I think we could make you a very attractive proposal. Would you care to stop by my office and discuss it?"

"Thank you, Mr. Browning. I'm really flattered, but I just moved into my own offices. I'm hoping it will work out."

He gave her a long look. "It will work out." He raised his eyes as someone approached and got to his feet and held out his hand. "Adam, how are you?"

Jennifer looked up and Adam Warner was standing there shaking hands with Lee Browning. Jennifer's heart began to beat faster and she could feel her face flush. *Idiot schoolgirl!*

Adam Warner looked at Jennifer and Browning and said, "You two know each other?"

"We were just beginning to get acquainted," Lee Browning said easily. "You arrived a little too soon."

"Or just in time." He took Jennifer's arm. "Better luck next time, Lee."

The captain came up to Adam. "Would you like your table now, Mr. Warner, or would you like to have a drink at the bar first?"

"We'll take a table, Henri."

When they had been seated, Jennifer looked around the room and recognized half a dozen celebrities.

"This place is like a *Who's Who*," she said.

Adam looked at her. "It is now."

Jennifer felt herself blush again. *Stop it, you fool.* She wondered how many other girls Adam Warner had brought here while his wife was sitting at home, waiting for him. She wondered if any of them ever learned that he was married, or whether he always managed to keep that a secret from them. Well, she had an advantage. *You're going to be in for a surprise, Mr. Warner,* Jennifer thought.

They ordered drinks and dinner and busied themselves making small talk. Jennifer let Adam do most of the talking. He was witty and charming, but she was armored against his charm. It was not easy. She found herself smiling at his anecdotes, laughing at his stories.

It won't do him any good, Jennifer told herself. She was not looking for a fling.

The specter of her mother haunted her. There was a deep passion within Jennifer that she was afraid to explore, afraid to release.

They were having dessert and Adam still had not said one word that could be misconstrued. Jennifer had been building up her defenses for nothing, fending off an attack that had never materialized, and she felt like a fool. She wondered what Adam would have said if he had known what she had been thinking all evening. Jennifer smiled at her own vanity.

"I never got a chance to thank you for the clients you sent me," Jennifer said. "I did telephone you a few times, but – "

"I know." Adam hesitated, then added awkwardly, "I didn't want to return your phone calls." Jennifer looked at him in surprise. "I was afraid to," he said simply.

And there it was. He had taken her by surprise, caught her off guard, but his meaning was unmistakable. Jennifer knew what was coming next. And she did not want him to say it. She did not want him to be like all the others, the married men who pretended they were single. She despised them and she did not want to despise this man.

Adam said quietly, "Jennifer, I want you to know I'm married." She sat there staring at him, her mouth open.

"I'm sorry. I should have told you sooner." He smiled wryly. "Well, there really was no sooner, was there?"

Jennifer was filled with a strange confusion. "Why – why did you ask me to dinner, Adam?"

"Because I had to see you again."

Everything began to seem unreal to Jennifer. It was as though she were being pulled under by some giant tidal wave. She sat there listening to Adam saying all the things he felt, and she knew that every word was true. She knew be cause she felt the same way. She wanted him to stop before he said too much. She wanted him to go on and say more.

"I hope I'm not offending you," Adam said.

There was a sudden shyness about him that shook Jennifer. "Adam, I – I – "

He looked at her and even though they had not touched, it was as if she were in his arms.

Jennifer said shakily, "Tell me about your wife."

"Mary Beth and I have been married fifteen years. We have no children."

"I see."

"She – we decided not to have any. We were both very young when we got married. I had known her a long time. Our families were neighbors at a summer place we had in Maine. When she was eighteen, her parents were killed in a plane crash. Mary Beth was almost insane with grief. She was all alone. I – we got married."

He married her out of pity and he's too much of a gentleman to say so, Jennifer thought.

"She's a wonderful woman. We've always had a very good relationship."

He was telling Jennifer more than she wanted to know, more than she could handle. Every instinct in her warned her to get away, to flee. In the past she had easily been able to cope with the married men who had tried to become involved with her, but Jennifer knew instinctively that this was different. If she ever let herself fall in love with this man, there would be no way out. She would have to be insane ever to begin anything with him.

Jennifer spoke carefully. "Adam, I like you very much. I don't get involved with married men"

He smiled, and his eyes behind the glasses held honesty and warmth. "I'm not looking for a backstreet affair. I enjoy being with you. I'm very proud of you. I'd like us to see each other once in a while."

Jennifer started to say, *What good would that* do? but the words came out, "That would be good."

So we'll have lunch once a month, Jennifer thought. *It can't hurt anything.*

11

One of Jennifer's first visitors to her new office was Father Ryan. He wandered around the three small rooms and said, "Very nice, indeed. We're getting up in the world, Jennifer."

Jennifer laughed. "This isn't exactly getting up in the world, Father. I have a long way to go."

He eyed her keenly. "You'll make it. By the way, I went to visit Abraham Wilson last week."

"How is he getting along?"

"Fine. They have him working in the prison machine shop. He asked me to give you his regards."

"I'll have to visit him myself one day soon."

Father Ryan sat in his chair, staring at her, until Jennifer said, "Is there something I can do for you, Father?"

He brightened. "Ah, well, I know you must be busy, but now that you've brought it up, a friend of mine has a bit of a problem. She was in an accident. I think you're just the one to help her."

Automatically Jennifer replied, "Have her come in and see me, Father."

"I think you'll have to go to her. She's a quadruple amputee."

Connie Garrett lived in a small, neat apartment on Houston Street. The door was opened for Jennifer by an elderly white-haired woman wearing an apron.

"I'm Martha Steele, Connie's aunt. I live with Connie. Please come in. She's expecting you."

Jennifer walked into a meagerly furnished living room. Connie Garrett was propped up with pillows in a large armchair. Jennifer was shocked by her youth. For some reason, she had expected an older woman. Connie Garrett was about twenty-four, Jennifer's age. There was a wonderful radiance in her face, and Jennifer found it obscene that there was only a torso with no arms or legs attached to it. She repressed a shudder.

Connie Garrett gave her a warm smile and said, "Please sit down, Jennifer. May I call you Jennifer? Father Ryan has told me so much about you. And, of course, I've seen you on television. I'm so glad you could come."

Jennifer started to reply, "My pleasure," and realized how inane it would have sounded. She sat down in a soft comfortable chair opposite the young woman.

"Father Ryan said you were in an accident a few years ago. Do you want to tell me what happened?"

"It was my fault, I'm afraid. I was crossing an intersection and I stepped off the sidewalk and slipped and fell in front of a truck."

"How long ago was this?"

"Three years ago last December. I was on my way to Bloomingdale's to do some Christmas shopping."

"What happened after the truck hit you?"

"I don't remember anything. I woke up in the hospital. They told me that an ambulance brought me there. There was an injury to my spine. Then they found bone damage and it kept spreading until – " She stopped and tried to shrug. It was a pitiful gesture. "They tried to fit me with artificial limbs, but they don't work on me."

"Did you bring suit?"

She looked at Jennifer, puzzled. "Father Ryan didn't tell you?"

"Tell me what?"

"My lawyer sued the utility company whose truck hit me, and we lost the case. We appealed and lost the appeal."

Jennifer said, "He should have mentioned that. If the appellate court turned you down, I'm afraid there's nothing that can be done."

Connie Garrett nodded. "I didn't really believe there was. I just thought – well, Father Ryan said you could work miracles."

"That's *his* territory. I'm only a lawyer."

She was angry with Father Ryan for having given Connie Garrett false hope. Grimly, Jennifer decided she would have a talk with him.

The older woman was hovering in the background. "Can I offer you something, Miss Parker? Some tea and cake, perhaps?"

Jennifer suddenly realized she was hungry, for she had had no time for lunch. But she visualized sitting opposite Connie Garrett while she was being fed by hand, and she could not bear the thought.

"No, thanks," Jennifer lied. "I just had lunch."

All Jennifer wanted to do was get out of there as quickly as possible. She tried to think of some cheering note she could leave on, but there was nothing. *Damn Father Ryan!*

"I – I'm really sorry. I wish I – "

Connie Garrett smiled and said, "Please don't worry about it."

It was the smile that did it. Jennifer was sure if she had been in Connie Garrett's place she would never have been able to smile.

"Who was your lawyer?" Jennifer heard herself asking.

"Melvin Hutcherson. Do you know him?"

"No, but I'll look him up." She went on, without meaning to, "I'll have a talk with him."

"That would be so nice of you." There was warm appreciation in Connie Garrett's voice.

Jennifer thought of what the girl's life must be like, sitting there totally helpless, day after day, month after month, year after year, unable to do anything for herself.

"I can't promise anything, I'm afraid."

"Of course not. But do you know something, Jennifer? I feel better just because you came."

Jennifer rose to her feet. It was a moment to shake hands, but there was no hand to shake.

She said awkwardly, "It was nice meeting you, Connie. You'll hear from me."

On the way back to her office, Jennifer thought about Father Ryan and resolved that she would never succumb to his blandishments again. There was nothing anyone could do for that poor crippled girl, and to offer her any kind of hope was indecent. But she would keep her promise. She would talk to Melvin Hutcherson.

When Jennifer returned to her office there was a long list of messages for her. She looked through them quickly, looking for a message from Adam Warner. There was none.

12

Melvin Hutcherson was a short, balding man with a tiny button nose and washed-out pale blue eyes. He had a shabby suite of offices on the West Side that reeked of poverty. The receptionist's desk was empty.

"Gone to lunch," Melvin Hutcherson explained.

Jennifer wondered if he had a secretary. He ushered her into his private office, which was no larger than the reception office.

"You told me over the phone you wanted to talk about Connie Garrett."

"That's right."

He shrugged. "There's not that much to talk about. We sued and we lost. Believe me, I did a bang-up job for her."

"Did you handle the appeal?"

"Yep. We lost that, too. I'm afraid you're spinning your wheels." He regarded her a moment. "Why do you want to waste your time on something like this? You're hot. You could be working on big money cases."

"I'm doing a friend a favor. Would you mind if I looked at the transcripts?"

"Help yourself," Hutcherson shrugged. "They're public property."

Jennifer spent the evening going over the transcripts of Connie Garrett's lawsuit. To Jennifer's surprise, Melvin Hutcherson had told the truth: he had done a good job. He had named both the city and the Nationwide Motors Corporation as co-defendants, and had demanded a trial by jury. The jury had exonerated both defendants.

The Department of Sanitation had done its best to cope with the snowstorm that had swept the city that December; all its equipment had been in use. The city had argued that the storm was an act of God, and that if there was any negligence, it was on the part of Connie Garrett.

Jennifer turned to the charges against the truck company. Three eyewitnesses had testified that the driver had tried to stop the truck to avoid hitting the victim, but that he had been unable to brake in time, and the truck had gone into an unavoidable spin and had hit her. The verdict in favor of the defendant had been upheld by the Appellate Division and the case had been closed.

Jennifer finished reading the transcripts at three o'clock in the morning. She turned off the lights, unable to sleep. On paper, justice had been done. But the image of Connie Garrett kept coming into her mind. A girl in her twenties, without arms or legs. Jennifer visualized the truck hitting the young girl, the awful agony she must have suffered, the series of terrible operations that had been performed, each one cutting away parts of her limbs. Jennifer turned on the light and sat up in bed. She dialed Melvin Hutcherson's home number.

"There's nothing in the transcripts about the doctors," Jennifer said into the telephone. "Did you look into the possibility of malpractice?"

A groggy voice said, "Who the fuck is this?"

"Jennifer Parker. Did you – "

"For Christ's sake! It's – it's four o'clock in the morning! Don't you have a watch?"

"This is important. The hospital wasn't named in the suit. What about those operations that were performed on Connie Garrett? Did you check into them?"

There was a pause while Melvin Hutcherson tried to gather his thoughts. "I talked to the heads of neurology and orthopedics at the hospital that took care of her. The operations were necessary to save her life. They were performed by the top men there and were done properly. That's why the hospital wasn't named in the suit."

Jennifer felt a sharp sense of frustration. "I see."

"Look, I told you before, you're wasting your time on this one. Now why don't we both get some sleep?"

And the receiver clicked in Jennifer's ear. She turned out the light and lay back again. But sleep was farther away than ever. After a while, Jennifer gave up the struggle, arose and made herself a pot of coffee. She sat on her sofa drinking it, watching the rising sun paint the Manhattan skyline, the faint pink gradually turning into a bright, explosive red.

Jennifer was disturbed. For every injustice there was supposed to be a remedy at law. Had justice been done in Connie Garrett's case? She glanced at the clock on the wall. It was six-thirty. Jennifer picked up the telephone again and dialed Melvin Hutcherson's number.

"Did you check out the record of the truck driver?" Jennifer asked.

A sleepy voice said, "Jesus Christ! Are you some kind of crazy? When do you sleep?"

"The driver of the utility truck. Did you check out his record?"

"Lady, you're beginning to insult me."

"I'm sorry," Jennifer insisted, "but I have to know."

"The answer is yes. He had a perfect record. This was his first accident."

So that avenue was closed. "I see." Jennifer was thinking hard.

"Miss Parker," Melvin Hutcherson said, "do me a big favor, will you? If you have any more questions, call me during office hours."

"Sorry," Jennifer said absently. "Go back to sleep."

"Thanks a lot!"

Jennifer replaced the receiver. It was time to get dressed and go to work.

13

It had been three weeks since Jennifer had had dinner with Adam at Lutèce. She tried to put him out of her mind, but everything reminded her of Adam: a chance phrase, the back of a stranger's head, a tie similar to the one he had worn. There were many men who tried to date her. She was propositioned by clients, by attorneys she had opposed in court and by a night-court judge, but Jennifer wanted none of them. Lawyers invited her out for what was cynically referred to as "funch," but she was not interested. There was an independence about her that was a challenge to men.

Ken Bailey was always there, but that fact did nothing to assuage Jennifer's loneliness. There was only one person who could do that, damn him!

He telephoned on a Monday morning. "I thought I'd take a chance and see if you happened to be free for lunch today."

She was not. She said, "Of course I am."

Jennifer had sworn to herself that if Adam ever called her again she would be friendly yet distant, and courteous but definitely not available.

The moment she heard Adam's voice she forgot all those things and said, *Of course I am.*

The last thing in the world she should have said.

They had lunch at a small restaurant in Chinatown, and they talked steadily for two hours that seemed like two minutes. They talked about law and politics and the theater, and solved all the complex problems of the world. Adam was brilliant and incisive and fascinating. He was genuinely interested in what Jennifer was doing, and took a joyous pride in her successes. *He has a right to*, Jennifer thought. If not for him, *I'd be back in Kelso, Washington.*

When Jennifer returned to the office, Ken Bailey was waiting for her.

"Have a good lunch?"

"Yes, thank you."

"Is Adam Warner going to become a client?" His tone was too casual.

"No, Ken. We're just friends."

And it was true.

The following week, Adam invited Jennifer to have lunch in the private dining room of his law firm. Jennifer was impressed with the huge, modern complex of offices. Adam introduced her to various members of the firm, and Jennifer felt like a minor celebrity, for they seemed to know all about her. She met Stewart Needham, the senior partner. He was distantly polite to Jennifer, and she remembered that Adam was married to his niece.

Adam and Jennifer had lunch in the walnut-paneled dining room run by a chef and two waiters.

"This is where the partners bring their problems."

Jennifer wondered whether he was referring to her.

It was hard for her to concentrate on the meal.

Jennifer thought about Adam all that afternoon. She knew she had to forget about him, had to stop seeing him. He belonged to another woman.

That night, Jennifer went with Ken Bailey to see *Two by Two*, the new Richard Rodgers show.

As they stepped into the lobby there was an excited buzz from the crowd, and Jennifer turned to see what was happening. A long, black limousine had pulled up to the curb and a man and woman were stepping out of the car.

"It's him!" a woman exclaimed, and people began to gather around the car. The burly chauffeur stepped aside and Jennifer saw Michael Moretti and his wife. It was Michael that the crowd focused on. He was a folk hero, handsome enough to be a movie star, daring enough to have captured everyone's imagination. Jennifer stood in the lobby watching as Michael Moretti and his wife made their way through the crowd. Michael passed within three feet of Jennifer, and for an instant their eyes met. Jennifer noticed that his eyes were so black that she could not see his pupils. A moment later he disappeared into the theater.

Jennifer was unable to enjoy the show. The sight of Michael Moretti had brought back a flood of fiercely humiliating memories. Jennifer asked Ken to take her home after the first act.

Adam telephoned Jennifer the next day and Jennifer steeled herself to refuse his invitation. *Thank you, Adam, but I'm really very busy.*

But all Adam said was, "I have to go out of the country for a while."

It was like a blow to the stomach. "How – how long will you be gone?"

"Just a few weeks. I'll give you a call when I get back."

"Fine," Jennifer said brightly. "Have a nice trip."

She felt as though someone had died. She visualized Adam on a beach in Rio, surrounded by half-naked girls, or in a penthouse in Mexico City, drinking margaritas with a nubile, dark-eyed beauty, or in a Swiss chalet making love to – *Stop it!* Jennifer told herself. She should have asked him where he was going. It was probably a business trip to some dreary place where he would have no time for women, perhaps the middle of some desert where be would be working twenty-four hours a day.

She should have broached the subject, very casually, of course. *Will you be taking a long plane trip? Do you speak any foreign languages? If you get to Paris, bring me back some Vervaine tea. I suppose the shots must be painful. Are you taking your wife with you? Am I losing my mind?*

Ken had come into her office and was staring at her. "You're talking to yourself. Are you okay?"

No! Jennifer wanted to shout. *I need a doctor. I need a cold shower. I need Adam Warner.*

She said, "I'm fine. Just a little tired."

"Why don't you get to bed early tonight?"

She wondered whether Adam would be going to bed early.

Father Ryan called. "I went to see Connie Garrett. She told me you've dropped by a few times."

"Yes." The visits were to assuage her feeling of guilt because she was unable to be of any help. It was frustrating.

*

Jennifer plunged herself into work, and still the weeks seemed to drag by. She was in court nearly every day and worked on briefs almost every night.

"Slow down. You're going to kill yourself," Ken advised her.

But Jennifer needed to exhaust herself physically and mentally. She did not want to have time to think. *I'm a fool*, she thought. *An unadulterated fool.*

It was four weeks before Adam called.

"I just got back," he said. The sound of his voice thrilled her. "Can we meet for lunch somewhere?"

"Yes. I'd enjoy that, Adam." She thought she had carried that off well. A simple *Yes, I'd enjoy that, Adam.*

"The Oak Room in the Plaza?"

"Fine."

It was the most businesslike, unromantic dining room in the world, filled with affluent middle-aged wheelers and dealers, stockbrokers and bankers. It had long been one of the few remaining bastions of privacy for men, and its doors had only recently been opened to women.

Jennifer arrived early and was seated. A few minutes later, Adam appeared. Jennifer watched the tall, lean figure moving toward her and her mouth suddenly went dry. He looked tanned, and Jennifer wondered if her fantasies about Adam on some girl-ridden beach had been true. He smiled at her and took her hand, and Jennifer knew in that moment that it did not matter what logic she used about Adam Warner or married men. She had no control over herself. It was as though someone else were guiding her, telling her what she should do, telling her what she must do. She could not explain what was happening to her, for she had never experienced anything like it. *Call it chemistry*, she thought. *Call it karma, call it heaven.* All Jennifer knew was that she wanted to be in Adam Warner's arms more than she had ever wanted anything in her life. Looking at him, she visualized his making love to her, holding her, his hard body on top of her, inside her, and she felt her face becoming red.

Adam said apologetically, "Sorry about the short notice. A client canceled a luncheon date."

Jennifer silently blessed the client.

"I brought you something," Adam said. It was a lovely green and gold silk scarf. "It's from Milan."

So *that's* where he had been. *Italian girls.* "It's beautiful, Adam. Thank you."

"Have you ever been to Milan?"

"No. I've seen pictures of the cathedral there. It's lovely."

"I'm not much of a sightseer. My theory is that if you've seen one church, you've seen them all."

Later, when Jennifer thought about that luncheon, she tried to remember what they had talked about, what they had eaten, who had stopped by the table to say hello to Adam, but all she could remember was the nearness of Adam, his touch, his looks. It was as though he had her in some kind of spell and she was mesmerized, helpless to break it.

At one point Jennifer thought, *I know what to do. I'll make love with him. Once. It can't be as wonderful as my fantasies. Then I'll be able to get over him.*

When their hands touched accidentally, it was like an electric charge between them. They sat there talking of everything and nothing, and their words had no meaning. They sat at the table, locked in an invisible embrace, caressing each other, making fierce love, naked and wanton. Neither of them had any idea what they were eating or what they were saying. There was a different, more demanding hunger in them and it kept mounting and mounting, until neither of them could stand it any longer.

In the middle of their luncheon, Adam put his hand over Jennifer's and said huskily, "Jennifer – "

She whispered, "Yes. Let's get out of here."

Jennifer waited in the busy, crowded lobby while Adam registered at the desk. They were given a room in the old section of the Plaza Hotel, overlooking 58th Street. They used the back bank of elevators, and it seemed to Jennifer that it took forever to reach their floor.

If Jennifer was unable to remember anything about the luncheon, she remembered everything about their room. Years later, she could recall the view, the color of the drapes and carpets, and each picture and piece of furniture. She could remember the sounds of the city, far below, that drifted into the room. The images of that afternoon were to stay with her the rest of her life. It was a magic, multicolored explosion in slow motion. It was having Adam undress her, it was Adam's strong, lean body in bed, his roughness and his gentleness. It was laughter and passion. Their hunger had built to a greed that had to be satisfied. The moment Adam began to make love to her, the words that flashed into Jennifer's mind were, *I'm lost.*

They made love again and again, and each time was an ecstasy that was almost unbearable.

Hours later, as they lay there quietly, Adam said, "I feel as though I'm alive for the first time in my life."

Jennifer gently stroked his chest and laughed aloud.

Adam looked at her quizzically. "What's so funny?"

"Do you know what I told myself? That if I went to bed with you once, I could get you out of my system."

He twisted around and looked down at her. "And – ?"

"I was wrong. I feel as though you're a part of me. At least" – she hesitated – "*part* of you is a part of me."

He knew what she was thinking.

"We'll work something out," Adam said. "Mary Beth is leaving Monday for Europe with her aunt for a month."

14

Jennifer and Adam Warner were together almost every night.

He spent the first night at her uncomfortable little apartment and in the morning he declared, "We're taking the day off to find you a decent place to live."

They went apartment hunting together, and late that afternoon Jennifer signed a lease in a new high-rise building off Sutton Place, called The Belmont Towers. The sign in front of the building had read *Sold Out*.

"Why are we going in?" Jennifer asked.

"You'll see."

The apartment they looked at was a lovely five-room duplex, beautifully furnished. It was the most luxurious apartment Jennifer had ever seen. There was a master bedroom and bath upstairs, and downstairs a guest bedroom with its own bath and a living room that had a spectacular view of the East River and the city. There was a large terrace, a kitchen and a dining room.

"How do you like it?" Adam asked.

"Like it? I love it," Jennifer exclaimed, "but there are two problems, darling. First of all, I couldn't possibly afford it. And secondly, even if I could, it belongs to someone else."

"It belongs to our law firm. We leased it for visiting VIP's. I'll have them find another place."

"What about the rent?"

"I'll take care of that. I – "

"No."

"That's crazy, darling. I can easily afford it and – "

She shook her head. "You don't understand, Adam. I have nothing to give you except me. I want that to be a gift."

He took her in his arms and Jennifer snuggled against him and said, "I know what – I'll work nights."

Saturday they went on a shopping spree. Adam bought Jennifer a beautiful silk nightgown and robe at Bonwit Teller, and Jennifer bought Adam a Turnbull & Asser shirt. They purchased a chess game at Gimbel's and cheesecake in Junior's near Abraham & Straus. They bought a Fortnum & Mason plum pudding at Altman's, and books at Doubleday. They visited the Gammon Shop and Caswell-Massey, where Adam bought Jennifer enough potpourri to last for ten years. They had dinner around the corner from the apartment.

They would meet at the apartment in the evening after work and discuss the day's events, and Jennifer would cook dinner while Adam set the table. Afterward, they read or watched television or played gin rummy or chess. Jennifer prepared Adam's favorite dishes.

"I'm shameless," she told him. "I won't stop at anything."

He held her close. "Please don't."

It was strange, Jennifer thought. Before they began their affair they saw each other openly. But now that they were lovers, they dared not appear in public together, so they went to places where they were not apt to run into friends: small family restaurants downtown, a chamber music concert at the Third Street Music School Settlement. They went to see a new play at the Omni Theatre Club on 18th Street and had dinner at the Grotta Azzurra on Broome Street, and ate so much that they swore off Italian food for a month. *Only we don't have a month*, Jennifer thought. Mary Beth was returning in fourteen days.

They went to The Half Note to hear avant-garde jazz in the Village, and peeked into the windows of the small art galleries.

Adam loved sports. He took Jennifer to watch the Knicks play, and Jennifer got so caught up in the game she cheered until she was hoarse.

On Sunday they lazed around, having breakfast in their robes, trading sections of the *Times*, listening to the church bells ring across Manhattan, each offering up its own prayer.

Jennifer looked over at Adam absorbed in the crossword puzzle and thought: *Say a prayer for* me. She knew that what she was doing was wrong. She knew that it could not last. And yet, she had never known such happiness, such euphoria. Lovers lived in a special world, where every sense was heightened, and the joy Jennifer felt now with Adam was worth any price she would have to pay later. And she knew she was going to have to pay.

Time took on a different dimension. Before, Jennifer's life had been measured out in hours and meetings with clients. Now her time was counted by the minutes she could spend with Adam. She thought about him when she was with him, and she thought about him when she was away from him.

Jennifer had read of men having heart attacks in the arms of their mistresses, and so she put the number of Adam's personal physician in her private telephone book by her bedside so that if anything ever happened it could be handled discreetly and Adam would not be embarrassed.

Jennifer was filled with emotions that she had not known existed in her. She had never thought of herself as being domestic, but she wanted to do everything for Adam. She wanted to cook for him, to clean for him, to lay out his clothes in the morning. To take care of him.

Adam kept a set of clothes at the apartment, and he would spend most nights with Jennifer. She would lie next to him, watching him fall asleep, and she would try to stay awake as long as possible, terrified of losing a moment of their precious time together. Finally, when Jennifer could keep her eyes open no longer, she would snuggle in Adam's arms and fall asleep, contented and safe. The insomnia that had plagued Jennifer for so long had vanished. Whatever night devils had tormented her had disappeared. When she curled up in Adam's arms, she was instantly at peace.

She enjoyed walking around the apartment in Adam's shirts, and at night she would wear his pajama top. If she was still in bed in the morning when he left, Jennifer would roll over to his side of the bed. She loved the warm smell of him.

It seemed that all the popular love songs she heard had been written for Adam and her, and Jennifer thought, *Noel Coward was right. It's amazing how potent cheap music can be.*

In the beginning, Jennifer had thought that the overwhelming physical feeling they had for each other would diminish in time, but instead it grew stronger.

She told Adam things about herself that she had never told another human being. With Adam, there were no masks. She was Jennifer Parker, stripped naked, and still he loved her. It was a miracle. And they shared another miracle together: laughter.

Impossibly, she loved Adam more each day. She wished that what they had would never end. But she knew it would. For the first time in her life, she became superstitious. There was a special blend of Kenya coffee that Adam liked. Jennifer bought some every few days.

But she bought only one small can at a time.

One of Jennifer's terrors was that something would happen to Adam when he was away from her and that she would not know it until she read about it, or heard about it on a news program. She never told Adam of her fears.

Whenever Adam was going to be late he would leave notes for Jennifer around the apartment where she would come upon them unexpectedly. She would find them in the bread-box or in the refrigerator, or in her shoe; they delighted her, and she saved each one.

Their last remaining days together raced by in a blur of joyous activity. Finally, it was the night before Mary Beth was to return. Jennifer and Adam had dinner in the apartment, listened to music and made love. Jennifer lay awake all night, Adam in her arms. Her thoughts were of the happiness they had shared.

The pain would come later.

At breakfast, Adam said, "Whatever happens, I want you to know this – you're the only woman I've ever truly loved."

The pain came then.

15

The anodyne was work, and Jennifer immersed herself in it totally so that she had no time to think.

She had become the darling of the press, and her courtroom successes were highly publicized. More clients came to her than she could handle, and while Jennifer's chief interest was in criminal law, at Ken's urging she began to accept a variety of other cases.

Ken Bailey had become more important than ever to Jennifer. He handled the investigations on her cases, and he was brilliant. She was able to discuss other problems with him and she valued his advice.

Jennifer and Ken moved again, this time into a large suite of offices on Park Avenue. Jennifer hired two bright young attorneys, Dan Martin and Ted Harris, both from Robert Di Silva's staff, and two more secretaries.

Dan Martin was a former football player from Northwestern University and he had the appearance of an athlete and the mind of a scholar.

Ted Harris was a slight, diffident young man who wore thick milk-bottle spectacles and was a genius.

Martin and Harris took care of the legwork and Jennifer handled the appearances at trials.

The sign on the door read: *JENNIFER PARKER & ASSOCIATES.*

The cases that came into the office ranged from defending a large industrial corporation on a pollution charge to representing a drunk who had suffered whiplash when he was bounced from a tavern. The drunk, of course, was a gift from Father Ryan.

"He has a bit of a problem," Father Ryan told Jennifer. : "He's really a decent family man, but the poor fellow has such pressures that he sometimes takes a drop too much."

Jennifer could not help but smile. As far as Father Ryan was concerned, none of his parishioners was guilty and his only desire was to help them get out of the difficulty they had carelessly gotten themselves into. One reason Jennifer understood the priest so well was that basically she felt the same as he did. They were dealing with people in trouble who had no one to help them, with neither the money nor the power to fight the Establishment, and in the end they were crushed by it.

The word *justice* was honored mostly in the breach. In the courtroom, neither the prosecuting attorney nor the defense attorney sought justice: The name of the game was to win.

*

From time to time, Jennifer and Father Ryan talked about Connie Garrett, but the subject always left Jennifer depressed. There was an injustice there and it rankled her.

In his office in the back room of Tony's Place, Michael Moretti watched as Nick Vito carefully swept the office with an electronic device, looking for gypsy taps. Through his police connections, Michael knew that no electronic surveillance had been authorized by the authorities, but once in a while a overzealous tin hotdog, a young detective, would set up a gypsy – or illegal – tap, hoping to pick up information. Michael was a careful man. His office and home were swept every morning and every evening. He was aware that he was the number one target for half a dozen different law agencies, but he was not concerned. He knew what they were doing, but they did not know what he was doing; and if they did, they could not prove it.

Sometimes late at night Michael would look through the peephole of the restaurant's back door and watch the FBI agents pick up his garbage for analysis, and substitute other garbage for it.

One night Nick Vito said, "Jesus, boss, what if the jokers dig up something?"

Michael laughed. "I hope they do. Before they get here we switch our garbage with the restaurant next door."

No, the federal agents were not going to touch him. The Family's activities were expanding, and Michael had plans that he had not even revealed yet. The only stumbling block was Thomas Colfax. Michael knew he had to get rid of the old lawyer. He needed a fresh young mind. And again and again, his thoughts turned to Jennifer Parker.

Adam and Jennifer met for lunch once a week, and it was torture for both of them, for they had no time to be alone together, no privacy. They talked on the telephone every day, using code names. He was Mr. Adams and she was Mrs. Jay.

"I hate sneaking around like this," Adam said.

"I do too." But the thought of losing him terrified her.

The courtroom was where Jennifer escaped from her own private pain. The courtroom was a stage, an area where she matched wits against the best that the opposition could offer. Her school was the courtroom and she learned well. A trial was a game played within certain rigid rules, where the better player won, and Jennifer was determined to be the better player.

Jennifer's cross-examinations became theatrical events, with a skilled speed and rhythm and timing. She learned to recognize the leader of a jury and to concentrate on him, knowing he could swing the others into line.

A man's shoes said something about his character. Jennifer looked for jurors who wore comfortable shoes, because they were inclined to be easygoing.

She learned about strategy, the overall plan of a trial, and about tactics, the day-by-day maneuvers. She became an expert at shopping for friendly judges.

Jennifer spent endless hours preparing each case, heeding the adage, *Most cases are won or lost before the trial begins.* She became adept at mnemonics so that she could remember jurors' names: Smith – a muscular man who could handle an anvil; Helm – a man steering a boat; Newman – a new-born baby.

The court usually recessed at four o'clock, and when Jennifer was cross-examining a witness in the late afternoon, she would stall until a few minutes before four and then hit the witness with a verbal blow that would leave a strong overnight impression on the jury.

She learned to read body language. When a witness on the stand was lying, there would be telltale gestures: stroking the chin, pressing the lips together, covering the mouth, pulling the earlobes or grooming the hair. Jennifer became an expert at reading those signs, and she would zero in for the kill.

Jennifer discovered that being a woman was a disadvantage when it came to practicing criminal law. She was in macho territory. There were still very few women criminal attorneys and some of the male lawyers resented Jennifer. On her briefcase one day Jennifer found a sticker that read: *Women Lawyers Make the Best Motions.* In retaliation, Cynthia put a sign on her desk that read: *A Woman's Place is in the House . . . and in the Senate.*

Most juries started out by being prejudiced against Jennifer, for many of the cases she handled were sordid, and there was a tendency to make an association between her and her client. She was expected to dress like Jane Eyre and she refused, but she was careful to dress in such a fashion that she would not arouse the envy of the women jurors, and at the same time appear feminine enough so as not to antagonize the men who might feel she was a lesbian. At one time, Jennifer would have laughed at any of these considerations. But in the courtroom she found them to be stern realities. Because she had entered a man's world she had to work twice as hard and be twice as good as the competition. Jennifer learned to prepare thoroughly not only her own cases, but the cases of her opposition as well. She would lie in bed at night or sit at the desk in her office and plot her opponent's strategy. What would she do if she were on the other side? What surprises would she try to pull? She was a general, planning both sides of a lethal battle.

Cynthia buzzed on the intercom. "There's a man on line three who wants to talk to you, but he won't give his name or tell me what its about."

Six months earlier, Cynthia would simply have hung up on the man. Jennifer had taught her never to turn anyone away.

"Put him through," Jennifer said.

A moment later she heard a man's voice ask cautiously, "Is this Jennifer Parker?"

"Yes."

He hesitated. "Is this a safe line?"

"Yes. What can I do for you?"

"It's not for me. It's for – for a friend of mine."

"I see. What's your friend's problem?"

"This has to be in confidence, you understand."

"I understand."

Cynthia walked in and handed Jennifer the mail. "Wait," Jennifer mouthed.

"My friend's family locked her up in an insane asylum. She's sane. It's a conspiracy. The authorities are in on it."

Jennifer was only half-listening now. She braced the telephone against her shoulder while she went through the morning's mail.

The man was saying, "She's rich and her family's after her money."

Jennifer said, "Go on," and continued examining the mail.

"They'd probably have me put away, too, if they found I was trying to help her. It could be dangerous for me, Miss Parker."

A nut case, Jennifer decided. She said, "I'm afraid I can't do anything, but I'd suggest you get hold of a good psychiatrist to help your friend."

"You don't understand. They're all in on it."

"I do understand," Jennifer said soothingly. "I – "

"Will you help her?"

"There's nothing I can – I'll tell you what. Why don't you give me your friend's name and address and if I get a chance, I'll look into it."

There was a long silence. Finally the man spoke. "This is confidential, remember."

Jennifer wished he would get off the telephone. Her first appointment was waiting in the reception room. "I'll remember."

"Cooper. Helen Cooper. She had a big estate on Long Island, but they took it away from her."

Obediently, Jennifer made a note on a pad in front of her. "Fine. What sanatorium did you say she was in?" There was a click and the line went dead. Jennifer threw the note into the waste basket.

Jennifer and Cynthia exchanged a look. "It's a weird world out there," Cynthia said. "Miss Marshall is waiting to see you."

Jennifer had talked to Loretta Marshall on the telephone a week earlier. Miss Marshall had asked Jennifer to represent her in a paternity suit against Curtis Randall III, a wealthy socialite.

Jennifer had spoken to Ken Bailey. "We need information on Curtis Randall III. He lives in New York, but I understand he spends a lot of time in Palm Beach. I want to know what his background is, and if he's been sleeping with a girl named Loretta Marshall."

She had told Ken the names of the Palm Beach hotels that the woman had given her. Two days later, Ken Bailey had reported back.

"It checks out. They spent two weeks together at hotels in Palm Beach, Miami and Atlantic City. Loretta Marshall gave birth to a daughter eight months ago."

Jennifer sat back in her chair and looked at him thoughtfully. "It sounds as though we might have a case."

"I don't think so."

"What's the problem?"

"The problem is our client. She's slept with everybody including the Yankees."

"You're saying that the father of the baby could be any number of men."

"I'm saying it could be half the world."

"Are any of the others wealthy enough to give child support?"

"Well, the Yankees are pretty rich, but the big league moneyman is Curtis Randall III."

He handed her a long list of names.

Loretta Marshall walked into the office. Jennifer had not been sure what to expect. A pretty, empty-headed prostitute, in all probability. But Loretta Marshall was a complete surprise. Not only was she not pretty, she was almost homely. Her figure was ordinary. From the number of Miss Marshall's romantic conquests, Jennifer had expected nothing less than a sexy raving beauty. Loretta Marshall was the stereotype of an elementary grade schoolteacher. She was clad in a plaid wool skirt, a button-down-collar shirt, a dark blue cardigan and sensible shoes. At first, Jennifer had been sure that Loretta Marshall was planning to use her to force Curtis Randall to pay for the privilege of raising a baby that was not his. After an hour's conversation with the girl, Jennifer found that her opinion had changed. Loretta Marshall was transparently honest.

"Of course, I have no proof that Curtis is Melanie's father," she smiled shyly. "Curtis isn't the only man I've slept with."

"Then what makes you think he's the father of your child, Miss Marshall?"

"I don't *think*. I'm sure of it. It's hard to explain, but I even know the night Melanie was conceived. Sometimes a woman can feel those things."

Jennifer studied her, trying to find any sign of guile or deceit. There was none. The girl was totally without pretense. Perhaps, Jennifer thought, men found that part of her charm.

"Are you in love with Curtis Randall?"

"Oh, yes. And Curtis said he loved me, Of course, I'm not sure he still does, after what's happened."

If you loved him, Jennifer wondered, *how could you have slept with all those other men?* The answer might have lain in that sad, homely face and plain figure.

"Can you help me, Miss Parker?"

Jennifer said cautiously, "Paternity cases are always difficult. I have a list of more than a dozen men you've slept with in the past year. There are probably others. If I have such a list, you can be sure that Curtis Randall's attorney will have one."

Loretta Marshall frowned. "What about blood samples, that kind of thing . . .?"

"Blood tests are admissible in evidence only if they prove that the defendant could not be the father. They're legally inconclusive."

"I don't really care about me. It's Melanie I want protected. It's only right that Curtis should take care of his daughter."

Jennifer hesitated, weighing her decision. She had told Loretta Marshall the truth. Paternity cases were difficult. To say nothing about being messy and unpleasant. The attorneys for the defense would have a field day when they got this woman on the stand. They would bring up a parade of her lovers and, before they were through, they would make her look like a whore. It was not the type of case that Jennifer wanted to become involved in. On the other hand, she believed Loretta Marshall. This was no ordinary gold digger out to gouge an ex-lover. The girl was convinced that Curtis Randall was the father of her child. Jennifer made her decision.

"All right," she said, "we'll take a crack at it."

Jennifer set up a meeting with Roger Davis, the lawyer representing Curtis Randall. Davis was a partner in a large Wall Street firm and the importance of his position was indicated by the spacious corner suite he occupied. He was pompous and arrogant, and Jennifer disliked him on sight.

"What can I do for you?" Roger Davis asked.

"As I explained on the telephone, I'm here on behalf of Loretta Marshall."

He looked at her and said impatiently, "So?"

"She's asked me to institute a paternity suit against Mr. Curtis Randall III. I would prefer not to do that."

"You'd be a damned fool if you did."

Jennifer held her temper in check. "We don't wish to drag your client's name through the courts. As I'm sure you know, this kind of case always gets nasty. Therefore, we're prepared to accept a reasonable out-of-court settlement."

Roger Davis gave Jennifer a wintry smile. "I'm sure you are. Because you have no case. None at all."

"I think we have."

"Miss Parker, I haven't time to mince words. Your client is a whore. She'll have intercourse with anything that moves. I have a list of men she's slept with. It's as long as my arm. You think my client is going to get hurt? Your client will be *destroyed*. She's a schoolteacher, I believe. Well, when I get through with her she'll never teach anywhere again as long as she lives. And I'll tell you something else. Randall believes he's the father of that baby. But you'll never prove it in a million years."

Jennifer sat back, listening, her face expressionless.

"Our position is that your client could have become impregnated by anyone in the Third Army. You want to make a deal? Fine. I'll tell you what we'll do. We'll buy your client birth-control pills so that it doesn't happen again."

Jennifer stood up her cheeks burning. "Mr. Davis," she said, "that little speech of yours is going to cost your client half a million dollars."

And Jennifer was out the door.

Ken Bailey and three assistants could turn up nothing against Curtis Randall III. He was a widower, a pillar of society, and he had had very few sexual flings.

"The son of a bitch is a born-again puritan," Ken Bailey complained.

They were seated in the conference room at midnight, the night before the paternity trial was to begin. "I've talked to one of the attorneys in Davis's office, Jennifer. They're going to destroy our client. They're not bluffing."

"Why are you sticking your neck out for this girl?" Dan Martin asked.

"I'm not here to judge her sex life, Dan. She believes that Curtis Randall is the father of her baby. I mean, she really *believes* it. All she wants is money for her daughter – nothing for herself. I think she deserves her day in court."

"We're not thinking about her," Ken replied. "We're thinking about you. You're on a hot roll. Everybody's watching you. I think this is a no-win case. It's going to be a black mark against you."

"Let's all get some sleep," Jennifer said. "I'll see you in court."

The trial went even worse than Ken Bailey had predicted. Jennifer had had Loretta Marshall bring her baby into the courtroom, but now Jennifer wondered if she had not made a tactical error. She sat there, helpless, as Roger Davis brought witness after witness to the stand and forced each of them to admit they had slept with Loretta Marshall. Jennifer did not dare cross-examine them. They were victims, and they were testifying in public only because they had been forced to. All Jennifer could do was sit by while her client's name was besmirched. She watched the faces of the jurors, and she could read the growing hostility there. Roger Davis was too clever to characterize Loretta Marshall as a whore. He did not have to. The people on the stand did it for him.

Jennifer had brought in her own character witnesses to testify to the good work that Loretta Marshall had done as a teacher, to the fact that she attended church regularly and was a good mother; but all this made no impression in the face of the horrifying array of Loretta Marshall's lovers. Jennifer had hoped to play on the sympathy of the jury by dramatizing the plight of a young woman who had been betrayed by a wealthy playboy and then abandoned when she had become pregnant. The trial was not working out that way.

Curtis Randall III was seated at the defendant's table. He could have been chosen by a casting director. He was an elegant-looking man in his late fifties, with striking gray hair and tanned, regular features. He came from a social background, belonged to all the right clubs and was wealthy and successful. Jennifer could feel the women on the jury mentally undressing him.

Sure, Jennifer thought. *They're thinking that they're worthy to go to* bed *with Mr. Charming, but not that what-does-he-see-in-her slut sitting in the courtroom with a ten-month old baby in* her *arms.*

Unfortunately for Loretta Marshall, the child looked nothing like its father. Or its mother, for that matter. It could have belonged to anybody.

As though reading Jennifer's thoughts, Roger Davis said to the jury, "There they sit, ladies and gentlemen, mother and child. Ah! But *whose* child? You've seen the defendant. I defy anyone in this courtroom to point out *one single point of resemblance* between the defendant and this infant. Surely, if my client were the father of this child, there would be *some* sign of it. Something in the eyes, the nose, the chin. Where is that resemblance? It doesn't exist, and for a very simple reason. The defendant is not the father of this child. No, I'm very much afraid that what we have here is the classic example of a loose woman who was careless, got pregnant, and then looked around to see which lover could best afford to pay the bills."

His voice softened. "Now, none of us is here to judge her. What Loretta Marshall chooses to do with her personal life is her own business. The fact that she is a teacher and can influence the minds of small children, well, that is not in my purview, either. I am not here to moralize; I'm simply here to protect the interests of an innocent man."

Jennifer studied the jury and she had the sinking feeling that every one of them was on the side of Curtis Randall. Jennifer still believed Loretta Marshall. If only the baby looked like its father! Roger Davis was right. There was no resemblance at all. And he had made sure the jury was aware of that.

Jennifer called Curtis Randall to the stand. She knew that this was her only chance to try to repair the damage that had been done, her final opportunity to turn the case around. She studied the man in the witness chair for a moment.

"Have you ever been married, Mr. Randall?"

"Yes. My wife died in a fire." There was an instinctive reaction of sympathy from the jury.

Damn! Jennifer moved on quickly. "You never remarried?"

"No. I loved my wife very much, and I – "

"Did you and your wife have any children?"

"No. Unfortunately, she was not able to."

Jennifer gestured toward the baby. "Then Melanie is your only – "

"Objection!"

"Sustained. Counsel for the plaintiff knows better than that."

"I'm sorry, Your Honor. It slipped out." Jennifer turned back to Curtis Randall. "Do you like children?"

"Yes, very much."

"You're the chairman of the board of your own corporation, are you not, Mr. Randall?"

"Yes."

"Haven't you ever wished for a son to carry on your name?"

"I suppose every man wants that."

"So if Melanie had been born a boy instead of – "

"Objection!"

"Sustained." The judge turned to Jennifer. "Miss Parker, I will ask you again to stop doing that."

"Sorry, Your Honor." Jennifer turned back to Curtis Randall. "Mr. Randall, are you in the habit of picking up strange women and taking them to hotels?"

Curtis Randall ran his tongue nervously over his lower lip. "No, I am not."

"Isn't it true that you first met Loretta Marshall in a bar and took her to a hotel room?"

His tongue was working at his lips again. "Yes, ma'am, but that was just – that was just sex."

Jennifer stared at him. "You say 'that was just sex' as though you feel sex is something dirty."

"No, ma'am." His tongue flicked out again.

Jennifer was watching it, fascinated, as it moved across his lips. She was filled with a sudden, wild sense of hope. She knew now what she had to do. She had to keep pushing him. And yet she could not push him so hard that the jury would become antagonistic toward her.

"How many women have you picked up in bars?"

Roger Davis was on his feet. "Irrelevant, Your Honor. And I object to this line of questioning. The only woman involved in this case is Loretta Marshall. We have already stipulated that the defendant had sexual intercourse with her. Aside from that, his personal life has no relevance in this courtroom."

"I disagree, Your Honor. If the defendant is the kind of man who – "

"Sustained. Please discontinue that line of questioning, Miss Parker."

Jennifer shrugged. "Yes, Your Honor." She turned back to Curtis Randall. "Let's get back to the night you picked up Loretta Marshall in a bar. What kind of bar was it?"

"I – I really don't know. I'd never been there before."

"It was a singles bar, wasn't it?"

"I have no idea."

"Well, for your information, the *Play Pen* was and is a singles bar. It has the reputation of being a pickup place, a rendezvous where men and women go to meet partners they can take to bed. Isn't that why you went there, Mr. Randall?"

Curtis Randall began to lick his lips again. "It – it may have been. I don't remember."

"You don't remember?" Jennifer's voice was weighted with sarcasm. "Do you happen to remember the date on which you first met Loretta Marshall in that bar?"

"No, I don't. Not exactly."

"Then let me refresh your memory."

Jennifer walked over to the plaintiff's table and began looking through some papers. She scribbled a note as though she were copying a date and handed it to Ken Bailey. He studied it, a puzzled expression on his face.

Jennifer moved back toward the witness box. "It was on January eighteenth, Mr. Randall."

Out of the corner of her eye, Jennifer saw Ken Bailey leaving the courtroom.

"It could have been, I suppose. As I said, I don't remember."

For the next fifteen minutes, Jennifer went on questioning Curtis Randall. It was a rambling, gentle cross-examination, and Roger Davis did not interrupt, because he saw that Jennifer was making no points with the jurors, who were beginning to look bored.

Jennifer kept talking, keeping an eye out for Ken Bailey. In the middle of a question, Jennifer saw him hurry into the courtroom, carrying a small package.

Jennifer turned to the judge. "Your Honor, may I ask for a fifteen-minute recess?"

The judge looked at the clock on the wall. "Since it's almost time for lunch, the court will adjourn until one-thirty."

At one-thirty the court was in session again. Jennifer had moved Loretta Marshall to a seat closer to the jury box, with the baby on her lap.

The judge said, "Mr. Randall, you are still under oath. You will not have to be sworn in again. Take the stand, please."

Jennifer watched as Curtis Randall sat down in the witness box. She walked up to him and said, "Mr. Randall, how many illegitimate children have you sired?"

Roger Davis was on his feet. "Objection! This is outrageous, Your Honor. I will not have my client subjected to this kind of humiliation."

The judge said, "Objection sustained." He turned to Jennifer. "Miss Parker, I have warned you – "

Jennifer said contritely, "I'm sorry, Your Honor."

She looked at Curtis Randall and saw that she had accomplished what she had wanted. He was nervously licking his lips. Jennifer turned toward Loretta Marshall and her baby. The baby was busily licking its lips. Jennifer slowly walked over to the baby and stood in front of her a long moment, focusing the attention of the jury.

"Look at that child," Jennifer said softly.

They were all staring at little Melanie, her pink tongue licking her underlip.

Jennifer turned and walked back to the witness box. "And look at this man."

Twelve pairs of eyes turned to focus on Curtis Randall. He sat there nervously licking his underlip, and suddenly the resemblance was unmistakable. Forgotten was the fact that Loretta Marshall had slept with dozens of other men. Forgotten was the fact that Curtis Randall was a pillar of the community.

"This is a man," Jennifer said mournfully, "of position and means. A man everyone looks up to. I want to ask you only one question: What kind of man is it who would deny his own child?"

The jury was out less than one hour, returning with a judgment for the plaintiff. Loretta Marshall would receive two hundred thousand dollars in cash and two thousand dollars a month for child support.

When the verdict came in, Roger Davis strode up to Jennifer, his face flushed with anger. "Did you do something with that baby?"

"What do you mean?"

Roger Davis hesitated, unsure of himself. "That lip thing. That's what won the jury over, the baby licking her lips like that. Can you explain it?"

"As a matter of fact," Jennifer said loftily, "I can. It's called heredity." And she walked away.

Jennifer and Ken Bailey disposed of the bottle of corn syrup on the way back to the office.

16

Adam Warner had known from almost the beginning that his marriage to Mary Beth had been a mistake. He had been impulsive and idealistic, trying to protect a young girl who seemed lost and vulnerable to the world.

He would give anything not to hurt Mary Beth, but Adam was deeply in love with Jennifer. He needed someone to talk to, and he decided on Stewart Needham. Stewart had always been sympathetic. He would understand Adam's position.

The meeting turned out to be quite different from what Adam had planned. As Adam walked into Stewart Needham's office, Needham said, "Perfect timing. I've just been on the phone with the election committee. They're formally asking you to run for the United States Senate. You'll have the full backing of the party."

"I – that's wonderful," Adam said.

"We have a lot to do, my boy. We have to start organizing things. I'll set up a fund-raising committee. Here's where I think we should begin . . ."

For the next two hours, they discussed plans for the campaign.

When they had finished, Adam said, "Stewart, there's something personal I'd like to talk to you about."

"I'm afraid I'm late for a client now, Adam."

And Adam had the sudden feeling that Stewart Needham had known what was on Adam's mind all the while.

Adam had a date to meet Jennifer for lunch at a dairy restaurant on the West Side. She was waiting for him in a rear booth.

Adam walked in, charged with energy, and from his expression Jennifer knew that something had happened.

"I have some news for you," Adam told her. "I've been asked to run for the United States Senate."

"Oh, Adam!" Jennifer was filled with a sudden excitement. "That's wonderful! You'll make such a great senator!"

"The competition's going to be fierce. New York's a tough state."

"It doesn't matter. No one can stop you." And Jennifer knew it was true. Adam was intelligent and courageous, willing to fight the battles he believed in. As he had once fought her battle.

Jennifer took his hand and said warmly, "I'm so proud of you, darling."

"Easy, I haven't been elected yet. You've heard about cups, lips and slips."

"That has nothing to do with my being proud of you. I love you so much, Adam."

"I love you, too."

Adam thought about telling Jennifer of the discussion he had almost had with Stewart Needham, but he decided not to. It could wait until he had straightened things out.

"When will you start campaigning?"

"They want me to announce that I'm running right away. I'll have unanimous party backing."

"That's wonderful!"

There was something that was *not* wonderful tugging at the back of Jennifer's mind. It was something she did not want to put into words, but she knew that sooner or later she was going to have to face it. She wanted Adam to win, but the Senate race would be a sword of Damocles hanging over her head. If Adam won, Jennifer would lose him. He would be running on a reform ticket and there would be no margin in his life for any scandal. He was a married man and if it was learned he had a mistress, it would be political suicide.

That night, for the first time since she had fallen in love with Adam, Jennifer had insomnia. She was awake until dawn battling the demons of the night.

Cynthia said, "There's a call waiting for you. It's the Martian again."

Jennifer looked at her blankly.

"You know, the one with the story about the insane asylum."

Jennifer had put the man completely out of her mind. He obviously was someone in need of psychiatric help.

"Tell him to – " She sighed. "Never mind. I'll tell him myself."

She picked up the telephone. "Jennifer Parker."

The familiar voice said, "Did you check the information I gave you?"

"I haven't had a chance." She remembered she had thrown away the notes she had made. "I'd like to help you. Will you give me your name?"

"I can't," he whispered. "They'll come after me, too. You just check it out. Helen Cooper. Long Island."

"I can recommend a doctor who – " The line went dead.

Jennifer sat there a moment, thinking, and then asked Ken Bailey to come into the office.

"What's up, Chief?"

"Nothing – I think. I've had a couple of crank calls from someone who won't leave his name. Would you please see if you can find out anything about a woman named Helen Cooper. She's supposed to have had a large estate on Long Island."

"Where is she now?"

"Either in some insane asylum or on Mars."

Two hours later, Ken Bailey walked in and surprised Jennifer by saying, "Your Martian has landed. There's a Helen Cooper committed at The Heathers Asylum in Westchester."

"Are you sure?" Ken Bailey looked hurt. "I didn't mean that," Jennifer said. Ken was the best investigator she had ever known. He never said anything unless he was positive of it, and he never got his facts wrong.

"What's our interest in the lady?" Ken asked.

"Someone thinks she's been framed into the asylum. I'd like you to check out her background. I want to know about her family."

The information was on Jennifer's desk the following morning. Helen Cooper was a dowager who had been left a fortune of four million dollars by her late husband. Her daughter had married the superintendent of the building where they lived and, six months after the marriage, the bride and groom had gone to court to ask that the mother be declared incompetent, and that the estate be put under their control. They had found three psychiatrists who had testified to Helen Cooper's incompetency and the court had committed her to the asylum.

Jennifer finished reading the report and looked up at Ken Bailey. "The whole thing sounds a little fishy, doesn't it?"

"Fishy? You could wrap it up in a newspaper and serve it with chips. What are you going to do about it?"

It was a difficult question. Jennifer had no client. If Mrs. Cooper's family had had her locked away, they certainly would not welcome Jennifer's interference, and since the woman herself had been declared insane, she was not competent to hire Jennifer. It was an interesting problem. One thing Jennifer knew: client or not, she was not going to stand by and see someone railroaded into an insane asylum.

"I'm going to pay a visit to Mrs. Cooper," Jennifer decided.

The Heathers Asylum was located in Westchester in a large, wooded area. The grounds were fenced in and the only access was through a guarded gate. Jennifer was not yet ready to let the family know what she was doing, so she had telephoned around until she had found an acquaintance with a connection to the sanatorium. He had made arrangements for her to pay a visit to Mrs. Cooper.

The head of the asylum, Mrs. Franklin, was a dour, hard-faced woman who reminded Jennifer of Mrs. Danvers in *Rebecca*.

"Strictly speaking," Mrs. Franklin sniffed, "I should not be letting you talk to Mrs. Cooper. However, we'll call this an unofficial visit. It won't go in the records."

"Thank you."

"I'll have her brought in."

Helen Cooper was a slim, attractive-looking woman in her late sixties. She had vivid blue eyes that blazed with intelligence, and she was as gracious as though she were receiving Jennifer in her own home.

"It was good of you to come and visit me," Mrs. Cooper said, "but I'm afraid I'm not quite sure why you're here."

"I'm an attorney, Mrs. Cooper. I received two anonymous telephone calls telling me you were in here and that you didn't belong here."

Mrs. Cooper smiled gently. "That must have been Albert."

"Albert?"

"He was my butler for twenty-five years. When my daughter, Dorothy, married, she fired him." She sighed. "Poor Albert. He really belongs to the past, to another world. I suppose, in a sense, I do too. You're very young, my dear, so perhaps you're not aware of how much things have changed. Do you know what's missing today? Graciousness. It's been replaced, I'm afraid, by greed."

Jennifer asked quietly, "Your daughter?"

Mrs. Cooper's eyes saddened. "I don't blame Dorothy. It's her husband. He's not a very attractive man, not morally, at least. I'm afraid my daughter is not very attractive physically. Herbert married Dorothy for her money and found out that the estate was entirely in my hands. He didn't like that."

"Did he say that to you?"

"Oh, yes indeed. My son-in-law was quite open about it. He thought I should give my daughter the estate then, instead of making her wait until I died. I would have, except that I didn't trust him. I knew what would happen if he ever got his hands on all that money."

"Have you ever had any history of mental illness, Mrs. Cooper?"

Helen Cooper looked at Jennifer and said wryly, "According to the doctors, I'm suffering from schizophrenia and paranoia."

Jennifer had the feeling that she had never spoken to a more sane person in her life.

"You are aware that three doctors testified that you were incompetent?"

"The Cooper estate is valued at four million dollars, Miss Parker. You can influence a lot of doctors for that kind of money. I'm afraid you're wasting your time. My son-in-law controls the estate now. He'll never let me leave here."

"I'd like to meet your son-in-law."

The Plaza Towers was on East 72nd Street, in one of the most beautiful residential areas of New York. Helen Cooper had her own penthouse there. Now the name plate on the door read *Mr. and Mrs. Herbert Hawthorne.*

Jennifer had telephoned ahead to the daughter, Dorothy, and when Jennifer arrived at the apartment, both Dorothy and her husband were waiting for her. Helen Cooper had been right about her daughter. She was not attractive. She was thin and mousy-looking, with no chin, and her right eye had a cast in it. Her husband, Herbert, looked like a clone of Archie Bunker. He was at least twenty years older than Dorothy.

"Come on in," he grunted.

He escorted Jennifer from the reception hall into an enormous living room, the walls of which were covered with paintings by French and Dutch masters.

Hawthorne said to Jennifer bluntly, "Now, suppose you tell me what the hell this is all about."

Jennifer turned to the girl. "It's about your mother."

"What about her?"

"When did she first start showing signs of insanity?"

"She – "

Herbert Hawthorne interrupted. "Right after Dorothy and me got married. The old lady couldn't stand me."

That's certainly one proof of sanity, Jennifer thought.

"I read the doctors' reports," Jennifer said. "They seemed biased."

"What do you mean, biased?" His tone was truculent.

"What I mean is that the reports indicated that they were dealing in gray areas where there were no clear-cut criteria for establishing what society calls sanity. Their decision was shaped, in part, by what you and your wife told them about Mrs. Cooper's behavior."

"What are you tryin' to say?"

"I'm saying that the evidence is not clear-cut. Three other doctors could have come up with an entirely different conclusion."

"Hey, look," Herbert Hawthorne said, "I dunno what you think you're tryin' to pull, but the old lady's a looney. The doctors said so and the court said so."

"I read the court transcript," Jennifer replied. "The court also suggested that her case be periodically reviewed."

There was consternation on Herbert Hawthorne's face. "You mean they might let her out?"

"They're *going* to let her out," Jennifer promised. "I'm going to see to it."

"Wait a minute! What the hell is goin' on here?"

"That's what I intend to find out." Jennifer turned to the girl. "I checked out your mother's previous medical history. There has never been anything wrong with her, mentally or emotionally. She – "

Herbert Hawthorne interrupted. "That don't mean a damn thing! These things can come on fast. She – "

"In addition," Jennifer continued to Dorothy, "I checked on your mother's social activities before you had her put away. She lived a completely normal life."

"I don't care what you or anybody else says. She's crazy!" Herbert Hawthorne shouted.

Jennifer turned to him and studied him a moment. "Did you ask Mrs. Cooper to give the estate to you?"

"That's none of your goddamned business!"

"I'm making it my business. I think that's all for now." Jennifer moved toward the door.

Herbert Hawthorne stepped in front of her, blocking her way. "Wait a minute. You're buttin' in where you're not wanted. You're lookin' to make a little cash for yourself, right? Okay, I understand that, honey. Tell you what I'll do. Why don't I give you a check right now for a thousand dollars for services rendered and you just drop this whole thing. Huh?"

"Sorry," Jennifer replied. "No deal."

"You think you're gonna get more from the old lady?"

"No," Jennifer said. She looked him in the eye. "Only one of us is in this for the money."

It took six weeks of hearings and psychiatric consultations and conferences with four different state agencies. Jennifer brought in her own psychiatrists and when they were finished with their examinations and Jennifer had laid out all the facts at her disposal, the judge reversed his earlier decision and Helen Cooper was released and her estate restored to her control.

The morning of Mrs. Cooper's release she telephoned Jennifer.

"I want to take you to lunch at Twenty-One."

Jennifer looked at her calendar. She had a crowded morning, a luncheon date and a busy afternoon in court, but she knew how much this meant to the elderly woman. "I'll be there," Jennifer said.

Helen Cooper's voice was pleased. "We'll have a little celebration."

*

The luncheon went beautifully. Mrs. Cooper was a thoughtful hostess, and obviously they knew her well at 21.

Jerry Berns escorted them to a table upstairs, where they were surrounded by beautiful antiques and Georgian silver. The food and service were superb.

Helen Cooper waited until they were having their coffee. Then she said to Jennifer, "I'm very grateful to you, my dear. I don't know how large a fee you were planning to charge, but I want to give you something more."

"My fees are high enough."

Mrs. Cooper shook her head. "It doesn't matter." She leaned forward, took Jennifer's hands in hers and dropped her voice to a whisper.

"I'm going to give you Wyoming."

17

The front page of *The New York Times* carried two stories of interest, side by side. One was an announcement that Jennifer Parker had obtained an acquittal for a woman accused of slaying her husband. The other was an article about Adam Warner running for the United States Senate.

Jennifer read the story about Adam again and again. It gave his background, told about his service as a pilot in the Viet Nam War, and gave an account of his receiving the Distinguished Flying Cross for bravery. It was highly laudatory, and a number of prominent people were quoted as saying that Adam Warner would be a credit to the United States Senate and to the nation. At the end of the article, there was a strong hint that if Adam were successful in his campaign, it could easily be a stepping-stone to his running for the presidency of the United States.

In New Jersey, at Antonio Granelli's farmhouse, Michael Moretti and Antonio Granelli were finishing breakfast. Michael was reading the article about Jennifer Parker.

He looked up at his father-in-law and said, "She's done it again, Tony."

Antonio Granelli spooned up a piece of poached egg. "Who done what again?"

"That lawyer. Jennifer Parker. She's a natural."

Antonio Granelli grunted. "I don' like the idea of no woman lawyer workin' for us. Women are weak. You never know what the hell they gonna do."

Michael said cautiously, "You're right, a lot of them are, Tony."

It would not pay for him to antagonize his father-in-law. As long as Antonio Granelli was alive, he was dangerous; but watching him now, Michael knew he would not have to wait much longer. The old man had had a series of small strokes and his hands trembled. It was difficult for him to talk, and he walked with a cane. His skin was like dry, yellowed parchment. All the juices had been sucked out of him. This man, who was at the head of the federal crime list, was a toothless tiger. His name had struck terror into the hearts of countless *mafiosi* and hatred in the hearts of their widows. Now, very few people got to see Antonio Granelli. He hid behind Michael, Thomas Colfax, and a few others he trusted.

Michael had not been *raised* – made the head of the Family – yet, but it was just a question of time. "Three-Finger Brown" Lucchese had been the strongest of the five eastern Mafia chieftains, then Antonio Granelli, and soon . . . Michael could afford to be patient. He had come a long, long way from the time when, as a cocky, fresh-faced kid, he had stood in front of the major dons in New York and held a flaming scrap of paper in his hand and sworn: "This is the way I will burn if I betray the secrets of Cosa Nostra."

Now, sitting at breakfast with the old man, Michael said, "Maybe we could use the Parker woman for small stuff. Just to see how she does."

Granelli shrugged. "Just be careful, Mike. I don' wan' no strangers in on Family secrets."

"Let me handle her."

Michael made the telephone call that afternoon.

When Cynthia announced that Michael Moretti was calling, it brought an instant spate of memories, all of them unpleasant. Jennifer could not imagine why Michael Moretti would be calling her.

Out of curiosity, she picked up the telephone. "What is it you want?"

The sharpness of her tone took Michael Moretti aback. "I want to see you. I think you and I should have a little talk."

"What about, Mr. Moretti?"

"It's nothing I'd care to discuss on the telephone. I can tell you this, Miss Parker – it's something that would be very much in your interest."

Jennifer said evenly, "I can tell you this, Mr. Moretti. Nothing you could ever do or say could be of the slightest interest to me," and she slammed down the receiver.

Michael Moretti sat at his desk staring at the dead phone in his hand. He felt a stirring within him, but it was not anger. He was not sure what it was, and he was not sure he liked it. He had used women all his life and his dark good looks and innate ruthlessness had gotten him more eager bed partners than he could remember.

Basically, Michael Moretti despised women. They were too soft. They had no spirit. *Rosa, for example. She's like a little pet dog who does everything she's told*, Michael thought. *She keeps my house, cooks for me, fucks me when I want to be fucked, shuts up when I tell her to shut up.*

Michael had never known a woman of spirit, a woman who had the courage to defy him. Jennifer Parker had had the nerve to hang up on him. What was it she had said? *Nothing you could ever do or say could be of the slightest interest to me.* Michael Moretti thought about that and smiled to himself. She was wrong. He was going to show her how wrong she was.

He sat back, remembering what she had looked like in court, remembering her face and her body. He suddenly wondered what she would be like in bed. A wildcat, probably. He started thinking about her nude body under his, fighting him. He picked up the telephone and dialed a number.

When a girl's voice answered he said, "Get naked. I'm on my way over."

On her way back to the office after lunch, as Jennifer was crossing Third Avenue she was almost run down by a truck. The driver slammed on his brakes and the rear end of the truck skidded sideways, barely missing her.

"Jesus Christ, lady!" the driver yelled. "Why don't you watch where the hell you're goin'!"

Jennifer was not listening to him. She was staring at the name on the back of the truck. It read *Nationwide Motors Corporation.* She stood there watching, long after the truck had disappeared from sight. Then she turned and hurried back to the office.

"Is Ken here?" she asked Cynthia.

"Yes. He's in his office."

She went in to see him. "Ken, can you check out Nationwide Motors Corporation? We need a list of all the accident cases their trucks have been involved in for the past five years."

"That's going to take a while."

"Use LEXIS." That was the national legal computer.

"You want to tell me what's going on?"

"I'm not sure yet, Ken. It's just a hunch. I'll let you know if anything comes of it."

She had overlooked something in the case of Connie Garrett, that lovely quadruple amputee who was destined to spend the rest of her life as a freak. The driver may have had a good record, but what about the *trucks?* Maybe somebody was liable, after all.

The next morning Ken Bailey laid a report in front of Jennifer. "Whatever the hell you're after, looks like you've hit the jackpot. Nationwide Motors Corporation has had fifteen accidents in the last five years. and some of their trucks have been recalled."

Jennifer felt an excitement begin to build in her. "What was the problem?"

"A deficiency in the braking system that causes the rear end of the truck to swing around when the brakes are hit hard."

It was the rear end of the truck that had hit Connie Garrett.

Jennifer called a staff meeting with Dan Martin, Ted Harris and Ken Bailey.

"We're going into court on the Connie Garrett case," Jennifer announced.

Ted Harris stared at her through his milk-bottle glasses. "Wait a minute, Jennifer, I checked that out. She lost on appeal. We're going to get hit with *res judicata*."

"What's *res judicata?*" Ken Bailey asked.

Jennifer explained, "It means for civil cases what double jeopardy means for criminal cases. 'There must be an end to litigation.' "

Ted Harris added, "Once a final judgment has been made on the merits of a case, it can only be opened again under very special circumstances. We have no grounds to reopen."

"Yes, we have. We're going after them on *discovery*."

The principle of discovery read: *Mutual knowledge of all relevant facts gathered by both parties is essential to proper litigation.*

"The deep-pocket defendant is Nationwide Motors. They held back information from Connie Garrett's attorney. There's a deficiency in the braking system of their trucks and they kept it out of the record."

She looked at the two lawyers. "Here's what I think we should do . . ."

Two hours later, Jennifer was seated in Connie Garrett's living room.

"I want to move for a new trial. I believe we have a case."

"No. I couldn't go through another trial."

"Connie – "

"Look at me, Jennifer. I'm a freak. Every time I look in the mirror I want to kill myself. Do you know why I don't?" Her voice sank to a whisper. "Because I can't. I *can't!*"

Jennifer sat there, shaken. How could she have been so insensitive?

"Suppose I try for an out-of-court settlement? I think that when they hear the evidence they'll be wilting to settle without going to trial."

The offices of Maguire and Guthrie, the attorneys who represented the Nationwide Motors Corporation, were located on upper Fifth Avenue in a modern glass and chrome building with a splashing fountain in front. Jennifer announced herself at the reception desk. The receptionist asked her to be seated, and fifteen minutes later Jennifer was escorted into the offices of Patrick Maguire. He was the senior partner in the firm, a tough, hard-bitten Irishman with sharp eyes that missed nothing.

He motioned Jennifer to a chair. "It's nice to meet you, Miss Parker. You've gotten yourself quite a reputation around town."

"Not all bad, I hope."

"They say you're tough. You don't look it."

"I hope not."

"Coffee? Or some good Irish whiskey?"

"Coffee, please."

Patrick Maguire rang and a secretary brought in two cups of coffee on a sterling silver tray.

Maguire said, "Now what is it I can do for you?"

"It's about the Connie Garrett case."

"Ah, yes. As I recall, she lost the case and the appeal."

As I recall. Jennifer would have bet her life that Patrick Maguire could have recited every statistic in the case.

"I'm going to file for a new trial."

"Really? On what grounds?" Maguire asked politely.

Jennifer opened her attaché case and took out the brief she had prepared. She handed it to him.

"I'm requesting a reopening on failure to disclose."

Maguire leafed through the papers, unperturbed. "Oh, yes," he said. "That brake business."

"You knew about it?"

"Of course." He tapped the file with a stubby finger. "Miss Parker, this won't get you anywhere. You would have to prove that the same truck involved in the accident had a faulty brake system. It's probably been overhauled a dozen times since the accident, so there would be no way of proving what its condition was then." He pushed the file back toward her. "You have no case."

Jennifer took a sip of her coffee. "All I have to do is prove what a bad safety record those trucks have. Ordinary diligence should have made your client know that they were defective."

Maguire said casually, "What is it you're proposing?"

"I have a client in her early twenties who's sitting in a room she'll never leave for the rest of her life because she has no arms or legs. I'd like to get a settlement that would make up a little bit for the anguish she's going through."

Patrick Maguire took a sip of his coffee. "What kind of settlement did you have in mind?"

"Two million dollars."

He smiled. "That's a great deal of money for someone with no case."

"If I go to court, Mr. Maguire, I promise you I'll have a case. And I'll win a lot more than that. If you force us to sue, we're going to sue for five million dollars."

He smiled again. "You're scaring the bejeezus out of me. More coffee?"

"No, thanks." Jennifer arose.

"Wait a minute! Sit down, please. I haven't said no."

"You haven't said yes."

"Have some more coffee. We brew it ourselves."

Jennifer thought of Adam and the Kenya coffee.

"Two million dollars is a lot of money, Miss Parker."

Jennifer said nothing.

"Now, if we were talking about a lesser amount, I might be able to – " He waved his hands expressively.

Jennifer remained silent.

Finally Patrick Maguire said, "You really want two million, don't you?"

"I really want five million, Mr. Maguire."

"All right. I suppose we might be able to arrange something."

It had been easy!

"I have to leave for London in the morning, but I'll be back next week."

"I want to wrap this up. I'd appreciate it if you would talk to your client as soon as possible. I'd like to give my client a check next week."

Patrick Maguire nodded. "That can probably be worked out."

All the way back to the office, Jennifer was filled with a sense of unease. It had been too simple.

That night on her way home, Jennifer stopped at a drugstore. When she came out and started across the street, she saw Ken Bailey walking with a handsome young blond man. Jennifer hesitated, then turned into a side street so that she would not be seen. Ken's private life was his own business.

On the day that Jennifer was scheduled to meet with Patrick Maguire, she received a call from his secretary.

"Mr. Maguire asked me to give you his apologies, Miss Parker. He's going to be tied up in meetings all day. He'll be happy to meet with you at your convenience tomorrow."

"Fine," Jennifer said. "Thank you."

The call sounded an alarm in Jennifer's mind. Her instincts had been right. Patrick Maguire was up to something.

"Hold all my calls," she told Cynthia.

She locked herself in her office, pacing back and forth, trying to think of every possible angle. Patrick Maguire had first told Jennifer she had no case. With almost no persuasion, he had then agreed to pay Connie Garrett two million dollars. Jennifer remembered how uneasy she had been at the time. Since then, Patrick Maguire had been unavailable. First London – if he had really gone to London – and then the conferences that had kept him from returning Jennifer's telephone calls all week. And now another delay.

But why? The only reason would be if – Jennifer stopped pacing and picked up the interoffice telephone and called Dan Martin.

"Check on the date of Connie Garrett's accident, would you, Dan? I want to know when the statute of limitations is up."

Twenty minutes later, Dan Martin walked into Jennifer's office, his face white.

"We blew it," he said. "Your hunch was right. The statute of limitations ran out today."

She felt suddenly sick. "There's no chance of a mistake?"

"None. I'm sorry, Jennifer. One of us should have checked it out before. It – it just never occurred to me."

"Or me." Jennifer picked up the telephone and dialed a number. "Patrick Maguire, please. Jennifer Parker."

She waited for what seemed an eternity, and then she said brightly into the telephone, "Hello there, Mr. Maguire. How was London?" She listened. "No, I've never been there . . . Ah, well, one of these days . . . The reason I'm calling," she said casually, "is that I just talked to Connie Garrett. As I told you before, she really doesn't want to go to court unless she has to. So if we could settle this today – "

Patrick Maguire's laugh boomed through the receiver. "Nice try, Miss Parker. The statute of limitations is up today. No one is going to sue anybody. If you'd like to settle for a lunch sometime we can talk about the fickle finger of fate."

Jennifer tried to keep the anger out of her voice. "That's a pretty rotten trick, friend."

"It's a pretty rotten world, friend," Patrick Maguire chuckled.

"It's not how you play the game, it's whether you win or not, right?"

"You're pretty good, honey, but I've been at it a lot longer than you. Tell your client I said better luck next time."

And he rang off.

Jennifer sat there holding the telephone in her hand. She thought of Connie Garrett sitting at home, waiting for the news. Jennifer's head began to pound and a film of perspiration popped out on her forehead. She reached in her desk drawer for an aspirin and looked at the clock on the wall. It was four o'clock. They had until five o'clock to file with the Clerk of the Superior Court.

"How long would it take you to prepare the filing?" Jennifer asked Dan Martin, who stood there suffering with her.

He followed her glance. "At least three hours. Maybe four. There's no way."

There has to be a way, Jennifer thought.

Jennifer said, "Doesn't Nationwide have branches all over the United States?"

"Yes."

"It's only one o'clock in San Francisco. We'll file against them there and ask for a change of venue later."

Dan Martin shook his head. "Jennifer, all the papers are here. If we got a firm in San Francisco and briefed them on what we need and they drew up new papers, there's no way they could make the five o'clock deadline."

Something in her refused to give up. "What time is it in Hawaii?"

"Eleven in the morning."

Jennifer's headache disappeared as if by magic, and she leapt from her chair in excitement. "That's it, then! Find out if Nationwide does business there. They must have a factory, sales office, garage – anything. If they do, we file there."

Dan Martin stared at her for a moment and then his face lit up. "Gotcha!" He was already hurrying toward the door.

Jennifer could still hear Patrick Maguire's smug tone on the telephone. *Tell your client, better luck next time*. There would never be a next time for Connie Garrett. It had to be *now*.

Thirty minutes later Jennifer's intercom buzzed and Dan Martin said excitedly, "Nationwide Motors manufactures their drive shafts on the island of Oahu."

"We've got them! Get hold of a law firm there and have them file the papers immediately."

"Did you have any special firm in mind?"

"No. Pick someone out of Martindale-Hubbell. Just make sure they serve the papers on the local attorney for National. Have them call us back the minute those papers are filed. I'll be waiting here in the office."

"Anything else I can do?"

"Pray."

The call from Hawaii came at ten o'clock that evening. Jennifer grabbed the phone and a soft voice said, "Miss Jennifer Parker, please."

"Speaking."

"This is Miss Sung of the law firm of Gregg and Hoy in Oahu. We wanted to let you know that fifteen minutes ago we served the papers you requested on the attorney for Nationwide Motors Corporation."

Jennifer exhaled slowly. "Thank you. Thank you very much."

Cynthia sent in Joey La Guardia. Jennifer had never seen the man before. He had telephoned, asking her to represent him in an assault case. He was short, compactly built and wore an expensive suit that looked as though it had been carefully tailored for someone else. He had an enormous diamond ring on his little finger.

La Guardia smiled with yellowed teeth and said, "I come to you 'cause I need some help. Anybody can make a mistake, right, Miss Parker? The cops picked me up 'cause I did a little number on a coupla guys, but I thought they was out to get me, you know? The alley was dark and when I seen them comin' at me – well, it's a rough neighborhood down there. I jumped them before they could jump me."

There was something about his manner that Jennifer found distasteful and false. He was trying too hard to be ingratiating.

He pulled out a large wad of money.

"Here. A grand down an' another grand when we go to court. Okay?"

"My calendar is full for the next few months. I'll be glad to recommend some other attorneys to you."

His manner became insistent. "No. I don't want nobody else. You're the best."

"For a simple assault charge you don't need the best."

"Hey, listen," he said, "I'll give you more money." There was a desperation in his voice. "*Two* grand down and – "

Jennifer pressed the buzzer under her desk and Cynthia walked in. "Mr. La Guardia's leaving, Cynthia."

Joey La Guardia glared at Jennifer for a long moment, scooped up his money and thrust it back in his pocket. He walked out of the office without a word. Jennifer pressed the intercom button.

"Ken, could you please come in here a minute?"

It took Ken Bailey less than thirty minutes to get a complete report on Joey La Guardia.

"He's got a rap sheet a mile long," he told Jennifer. "He's been in and out of the pen since he was sixteen." He glanced at the piece of paper in his hand. "He's out on bail. He was picked up last week for assault and battery. He beat up two old men who owed the Organization money."

Everything suddenly clicked into place. "Joey La Guardia works for the Organization?"

"He's one of Michael Moretti's enforcers."

Jennifer was filled with a cold fury. "Can you get me the telephone number of Michael Moretti?"

Five minutes later, Jennifer was speaking to Moretti.

"Well, this is an unexpected pleasure, Miss Parker. I – "

"Mr. Moretti, I don't like being set up."

"What are you talking about?"

"Listen to me. And listen well. I'm not for sale. Not now, not ever. I won't represent you or anyone who works for you. All I want is for you to leave me alone. Is that clear?"

"Can I ask you a question?"

"Go ahead."

"Will you have lunch with me?"

Jennifer hung up on him.

Cynthia's voice came over the intercom. "A Mr. Patrick Maguire is here to see you, Miss Parker. He has no appointment, but he said – "

Jennifer smiled to herself. "Have Mr. Maguire wait."

She remembered their conversation on the telephone. *It's not how you play the game, it's whether you win or not, right? You're pretty good, honey, but I've been at it a lot longer than you. Tell your client I said better luck next time.*

Jennifer kept Patrick Maguire waiting for forty-five minutes, and then buzzed Cynthia.

"Send Mr. Maguire in, please."

Patrick Maguire's genial manner was gone. He had been outwitted, and he was angry and did not bother to conceal it.

He walked over to Jennifer's desk and snapped, "You're causing me a lot of problems, friend."

"Am I, friend?"

He sat down, uninvited. "Let's stop playing games. I had a call from the general counsel of Nationwide Motors. I underestimated you. My client is willing to make a settlement." He reached into his pocket, pulled out an envelope and handed it to Jennifer. She opened it. Inside was a certified check made out to Connie Garrett. It was for one hundred thousand dollars.

Jennifer slipped the check back in the envelope and returned it to Patrick Maguire.

"It's not enough. We're suing for five million dollars."

Maguire grinned. "No, you're not. Because your client's not going into court. I just paid her a visit. There's no way you can ever get that girl into a courtroom. She's terrified and, without her, you haven't got a chance."

Jennifer said angrily, "You had no right to talk to Connie Garrett without my being present"

"I was only trying to do everybody a favor. Take the money and run, friend."

Jennifer got to her feet. "Get out of here. You turn my stomach."

Patrick Maguire rose. "I didn't know your stomach *could* be turned."

And he walked out, taking the check with him.

Watching him go, Jennifer wondered whether she had made a terrible mistake. She thought of what a hundred thousand dollars could do for Connie Garrett. But it was not enough. Not for what that girl would have to endure every day for the rest of her life.

Jennifer knew that Patrick Maguire was right about one thing. Without Connie Garrett in the courtroom, there was no chance that a jury would return a verdict for five million dollars. Words could never persuade them of the horror of her life. Jennifer needed the impact of Connie Garret's presence in the courtroom, with the jury looking at her day after day; but there was no way Jennifer could persuade the young woman to go into court. She had to find another solution.

Adam telephoned.

"I'm sorry I couldn't call you before," he apologized. "I've been having meetings on the Senate race and – "

"It's all right, darling. I understand." *I've got to understand*, she thought.

"I miss you so much."

"I miss you, too, Adam." *You'll never know how much.*

"I want to see you."

Jennifer wanted to say, *When?* but she waited.

Adam went on. "I have to go to Albany this afternoon. I'll call you when I get back."

"All right." There was nothing else she could say. There was nothing she could do.

At four o'clock in the morning, Jennifer awakened from a terrible dream and knew how she was going to win five million dollars for Connie Garrett.

18

"We've set up a series of fund-raising dinners across the state. We'll hit the larger towns only. We'll get to the whistle-stops through a few national television shows like *Face The Nation*, the *Today* show and *Meet the Press.* We figure that we can pick up – Adam, are you listening?"

Adam turned to Stewart Needham and the other three men in the conference room – top media experts. Needham had assured him – and said, "Yes, of course, Stewart."

He had been thinking of something else entirely. Jennifer. He wanted her here at his side, sharing the excitement of the campaign, sharing this moment, sharing his life.

Adam had tried several times to discuss his situation with Stewart Needham, but each time his partner had managed to change the subject.

Adam sat there thinking about Jennifer and Mary Beth. He knew that it was unfair to compare them, but it was impossible not to.

Jennifer is stimulating to be with. She's interested in everything and makes me feel alive. Mary Beth lives in her own private little world . . .

Jennifer and I have a thousand things in common. Mary Beth and I have nothing in common but our marriage . . .

I love Jennifer's sense of humor. She knows how to laugh at herself. Mary Beth takes everything seriously . . .

Jennifer makes me feel young. Mary Beth seems older than her years . . .

Jennifer is self-reliant. Mary Beth depends on me to tell her what to do . . .

Five important differences between the woman I'm in love with and my wife.

Five reasons why I can never leave Mary Beth.

19

On a Wednesday morning in early August the trial of *Connie Garrett v. Nationwide Motors Corporation* began. Ordinarily, the trial would only have been worth a paragraph or two in the newspapers, but because Jennifer Parker was representing the plaintiff, the media were out in full force.

Patrick Maguire sat at the defense table, surrounded by a battery of assistants dressed in conservative gray suits.

The process of selecting a jury began. Maguire was casual, almost to the point of indifference, for he knew that Connie Garrett was not going to appear in court. The sight of a beautiful young quadruple amputee would have been a powerful emotional lever with which to pry a large sum of money out of a jury – but there would be no girl and no lever.

This time, Maguire thought, *Jennifer Parker has outsmarted herself.*

The jury was impaneled and the trial got underway. Patrick Maguire made his opening statement and Jennifer had to admit to herself that he was very good indeed. He dwelt at length on the plight of poor young Connie Garrett, saying all the things that Jennifer had planned to say, stealing her emotional thunder. He spoke of the accident, stressing the fact that Connie Garrett had slipped on ice and that the truck driver had not been at fault.

"The plaintiff is asking you ladies and gentlemen to award her five million dollars." Maguire shook his head incredulously. "*Five million dollars!* Have you ever seen that much money? I haven't. My firm handles some affluent clients, but I want to tell you that in all my years of practicing law, I have never even seen *one* million dollars – or *half* a million dollars."

He could see by the looks on the faces of the jurors that neither had they.

"The defense is going to bring witnesses in here who will tell you how the accident happened. And it *was* an accident. Before we're through, we'll show you that Nationwide Motors had no culpability in this matter. You will have noticed that the person bringing the suit, Connie Garrett, is not in court today. Her attorney has informed Judge Silverman that she will not make an appearance at all. Connie Garrett is not in this courtroom today where she belongs, but I can tell you where she is. Right now, as I'm standing here talking to you, Connie Garrett is sitting at home counting the money she thinks you're going to give her. She's waiting for her telephone to ring and for her attorney to tell her how many millions of dollars she suckered out of you.

"You and I know that any time there's an accident where a big corporation is involved – no matter how indirectly – there are people who are immediately going to say, 'Why, that company is rich. It can afford it. Let's take it for all we can.' "

Patrick Maguire paused.

"Connie Garrett's not in this courtroom today because she couldn't face you. She knows that what she's trying to do is immoral. Well, we're going to send her away empty-handed as a lesson to other people who might be tempted to try the same thing in the future. A person has to take responsibility for his or her own actions. If you slip on a piece of ice on the street, you can't blame big brother for it. And you shouldn't try to swindle five million dollars out of him. Thank you."

He turned to bow to Jennifer, and then walked over to the defense table and sat down.

Jennifer rose to her feet and approached the jury. She studied their faces, trying to evaluate the impression that Patrick Maguire had made.

"My esteemed colleague has told you that Connie Garrett will not be in this courtroom during the trial. That is correct." Jennifer pointed to an empty space at the plaintiff's table. "That is where Connie Garrett would be sitting if she were here. Not in that chair. In a special wheelchair. The chair she lives in.

Connie Garrett won't be in this courtroom, but before this trial is over you will all have an opportunity to meet her and get to know her as I have gotten to know her."

There was a puzzled frown on Patrick Maguire's face. He leaned over and whispered to one of his assistants.

Jennifer was going on. "I listened as Mr. Maguire spoke so eloquently, and I want to tell you I was touched. I found my heart bleeding for this multi-billion-dollar corporation that's being mercilessly attacked by this twenty-four-year-old woman who has no arms or legs. This woman who, at this very moment is sitting at home, greedily awaiting that telephone call that will tell her she's rich." Jennifer's voice dropped.

"Rich to do what? Go out and buy diamonds for the hands she doesn't have? Buy dancing shoes for the feet she doesn't have? Buy beautiful dresses that she can *never* wear? A Rolls Royce to take her to parties she's not invited to? Just think of all the fun she's going to have with that money."

Jennifer spoke very quietly and sincerely as her eyes moved slowly across the faces of the jurors. "Mr. Maguire has never seen five million dollars at one time. Neither have I. But I'll tell you this. If I were to offer any one of you five million dollars in cash right now, and all I wanted in exchange was to cut off both your arms and both your legs, I don't think five million dollars would seem like very much money . . . "

"The law in this case is very clear," Jennifer explained. "In an earlier trial, which the plaintiff lost, the defendants were aware of a defect in the braking system in their trucks, and they withheld that knowledge from the defendant and from the court. In doing so, they acted illegally. That is the basis for this new trial. According to a recent government survey, the biggest contributors to truck accidents involve wheels and tires, brakes and steering systems. If you will just examine these figures for a moment . . ."

Patrick Maguire was appraising the jury and he was an expert at it. As Jennifer droned on about the statistics, Maguire could tell that the jurors were getting bored with this trial. It was becoming too technical. The trial was no longer about a crippled girl. It was about trucks and braking distances and faulty brake drums. The jurors were losing interest.

Maguire glanced over at Jennifer and thought, *She's not as clever as she's reputed to be.* Maguire knew that if he had been on the other side defending Connie Garrett, he would have ignored the statistics and mechanical problems and played on the jury's emotions. Jennifer Parker had done exactly the opposite.

Patrick Maguire leaned back in his chair now and relaxed.

Jennifer was approaching the bench. "Your Honor, with the court's permission, I have an exhibit I would like to introduce."

"What kind of exhibit?" Judge Silverman asked.

"When this trial began I promised the jury that they would get to know Connie Garrett. Since she is unable to be here in person, I would like permission to show some pictures of her."

Judge Silverman said, "I see no objection to that." He turned to Patrick Maguire. "Does the attorney for the defense have any objection?"

Patrick Maguire got to his feet, moving slowly, thinking fast. "What kind of pictures?"

Jennifer said, "A few pictures taken of Connie Garrett at home."

Patrick Maguire would have preferred not to have the pictures, but on the other hand, photographs of a crippled girl sitting in a wheelchair were certainly a lot less dramatic than the actual appearance of the girl herself would have been. And there was another factor to consider: if he objected, it would make him look unsympathetic in the eyes of the jury.

He said generously, "By all means, show the pictures."

"Thank you."

Jennifer turned to Dan Martin and nodded. Two men in the back row moved forward with a portable screen and a motion picture projector and began to set them up.

Patrick Maguire stood up, surprised. "Wait a minute! What is this?"

Jennifer replied innocently, "The pictures you just agreed to let me show."

Patrick Maguire stood there, silently fuming. Jennifer had said nothing about motion pictures. But it was too late to object. He nodded curtly and sat down again.

Jennifer had the screen positioned so the jury and Judge Silverman could see it clearly.

"May we have the room darkened, Your Honor?"

The judge signaled the bailiff and the shades were lowered. Jennifer walked over to the 16 mm projector and turned it on, and the screen came to life.

For the next thirty minutes there was not a sound to be heard in the courtroom. Jennifer had hired a professional cameraman and a young director of commercials to make the film. They had photographed a day in the life of Connie Garrett, and it was a stark, realistic horror story. Nothing had been left to the imagination. The film showed the beautiful young amputee being taken out of bed in the morning, being carried to the toilet, being cleaned like a small, helpless baby . . . being bathed . . . being fed and dressed . . . Jennifer had seen the film over and over and now, as she watched it again, she felt the same lump in her throat and her eyes filled with tears, and she knew that it must be having the same effect on the judge and the jury and the spectators in the courtroom.

When the film was ended, Jennifer turned to Judge Silverman. The plaintiff rests."

The jury had been out for more than ten hours, and with each passing hour Jennifer's spirits sank lower. She had been sure of an immediate verdict. If they had been as affected by the film as she had been, a verdict should not have taken more than an hour or two.

*

When the jury had filed out, Patrick Maguire had been frantic, certain that he had lost his case, that he had underestimated Jennifer Parker once again. But as the hours passed and the jury still did not return, Maguire's hopes began to rise. It would not have taken the jury this long to make an emotional decision. "We're going to be all right. The longer they're in there arguing, the more their emotions are going to cool off."

A few minutes before midnight, the foreman sent a note to Judge Silverman for a legal ruling. The judge studied the request, then looked up. "Will both attorneys approach the bench, please?"

When Jennifer and Patrick Maguire were standing in front of him, Judge Silverman said, "I want to apprise you of a note I have just received from the foreman. The jury is asking whether they are legally permitted to award Connie Garrett more than the five million dollars her attorney is suing for."

Jennifer felt suddenly giddy. Her heart began to soar. She turned to look at Patrick Maguire. His face was drained of color.

"I'm informing them," Judge Silverman said, "that it is within their province to set any amount they feel is justified."

Thirty minutes later the jury filed back into the courtroom. The foreman announced they had found in favor of the plaintiff. The amount of damages she was entitled to was six million dollars.

It was the largest personal injury award in the history of the State of New York.

20

When Jennifer walked into her office the following morning she found an array of newspapers spread across her desk. She was on the front page of every one of them. There were four dozen beautiful red roses in a vase. Jennifer smiled. Adam had found time to send her flowers.

She opened the card. It read: *Congratulations. Michael Moretti.*

The intercom buzzed and Cynthia said, "Mr. Adams is on the line."

Jennifer grabbed the telephone. She tried to keep her voice calm. "Hello, darling."

"You've done it again."

"I got lucky."

"Your client got lucky. Lucky to have you as an attorney. You must be feeling wonderful."

Winning cases made her feel good. Being with Adam made her feel wonderful. "Yes."

"I have something important to tell you," Adam said. "Can you meet me for a drink this afternoon?"

Jennifer's heart sank. There was only one thing Adam could have to tell her: he was never going to see her again.

"Yes. Yes, of course . . ."

"Mario's? Six o'clock?"

"Fine."

She gave the roses to Cynthia.

Adam was waiting in the restaurant, seated at a back table. *So he won't be embarrassed if I get hysterical*, Jennifer thought. Well, she was determined not to cry. Not in front of Adam.

She could tell from his gaunt, haggard face what he had been going through, and she intended to make this as easy as possible for him. Jennifer sat down and Adam took her hand in his.

"Mary Beth is giving me a divorce," Adam said, and Jennifer stared at him, speechless.

It was Mary Beth who had begun the conversation. They had returned from a fund-raising dinner where Adam had been the main speaker. The evening had been an enormous success. Mary Beth had been quiet during the ride home, a curious tension about her.

Adam said, "I thought the evening went well, didn't you?"

"Yes, Adam."

Nothing more was said until they reached the house. "Would you like a nightcap?" Adam asked.

"No, thank you. I think we should have a talk."

"Oh? About what?"

She looked at him and said, "About you and Jennifer Parker."

It was like a physical blow. Adam hesitated for a moment, wondering whether to deny it or–

"I've known it for some time. I haven't said anything because I wanted to make up my mind about what to do."

"Mary Beth, I – "

"Please let me finish. I know that our relationship hasn't been – well – all we hoped it would be. In some ways, perhaps I haven't been as good a wife as I should have been."

"Nothing that's happened is your fault. I – "

"Please, Adam. This is very difficult for me. I've made a decision. I'm not going to stand in your way."

He looked at her unbelievingly. "I don't – "

"I love you too much to hurt you. You have a brilliant political future ahead of you. I don't want anything to spoil that. Obviously, I'm not making you completely happy. If Jennifer Parker can make you happy, I want you to have her."

He had a feeling of unreality, as though the whole conversation were taking place underwater. "What will happen to you?"

Mary Beth smiled. "I'll be fine, Adam. Don't worry about me. I have my own plans."

"I – I don't know what to say."

"There's no need to say anything. I've said it all for both of us. If I held on to you and made you miserable, it wouldn't do either of us any good, would it? I'm sure Jennifer's lovely or you wouldn't feel about her the way you do." Mary Beth walked over to him and took him in her arms. "Don't look so stricken, Adam. What I'm doing is the best thing for everyone."

"You're remarkable."

"Thank you." She gently traced his face with her fingertips and smiled. "My dearest Adam. I'll always be your best friend. Always." Then she came closer and put her head on his shoulder. He could hardly hear her soft voice. "It's been such a long time since you held me in your arms, Adam. You wouldn't have to tell me you love me, but would you – would you like to – hold me in your arms once more and make love to me? Our last time together?"

Adam was thinking of this now as he said to Jennifer, "The divorce was Mary Beth's idea."

Adam went on talking, but Jennifer was no longer listening to the words; she was only hearing the music. She felt as though she were floating, soaring. She had steeled herself for Adam to tell her he could never see her again – and now this! It was too much to absorb. She knew how painful the scene with Mary Beth must have been for Adam, and Jennifer had never loved Adam more than she did at this moment. She felt as though a crushing load had been lifted from her chest, as though she could breathe again.

Adam was saying, "Mary Beth was wonderful about it. She's an incredible woman. She's genuinely happy for both of us."

"That's hard to believe."

"You don't understand. For some time now we've lived more like . . . brother and sister. I've never discussed it with you, but – " he hesitated and said carefully, "Mary Beth doesn't have strong . . . drives."

"I see."

"She'd like to meet you."

The thought of it disturbed Jennifer. "I don't think I could, Adam. I'd feel – uncomfortable."

"Trust me."

"If – if you want me to, Adam, of course"

"Good, darling. We'll go for tea. I'll drive you out."

Jennifer thought for a moment. "Wouldn't it be better if I went alone?"

The following morning, Jennifer drove out the Saw Mill River Parkway, headed upstate. It was a crisp, clear morning, a lovely day for a drive. Jennifer turned on the car radio and tried to forget her nervousness about the meeting facing her.

The Warner house was a magnificently preserved house of Dutch origin, overlooking the river at Croton-on-Hudson, set on a large estate of rolling green acres. Jennifer drove up the driveway to the imposing front entrance. She rang the bell and a moment later the door was opened by an attractive woman in her middle thirties. The last thing Jennifer had expected was this shy southern woman who took her hand, gave her a warm smile and said, "I'm Mary Beth. Adam didn't do you justice. Please come in."

Adam's wife was wearing a beige wool skirt that was softly full, and a silk blouse opened just enough to reveal a mature but still lovely breast. Her beige-blond hair was worn long and slightly curling about her face, and was flattering to her blue eyes. The pearls around her neck could never be mistaken as cultured. There was an air of old-world dignity about Mary Beth Warner.

The interior of the house was lovely, with wide, spacious rooms filled with antiques and beautiful paintings.

A butler served tea in the drawing room from a Georgian silver tea service.

When he had left the room, Mary Beth said, "I'm sure you must love Adam very much."

Jennifer said awkwardly, "I want you to know, Mrs. Warner, that neither of us planned – "

Mary Beth Warner put a hand on Jennifer's arm. "You don't have to tell me that. I don't know whether Adam told you, but our marriage has turned into a marriage of politeness. Adam and I have known each other since we were children. I think I fell in love with Adam the first time I saw him. We went to the same parties and had the same friends, and I suppose it was inevitable that one day we would get married. Don't misunderstand. I still adore Adam and I'm sure he adores me. But people do change, don't they?"

"Yes."

Jennifer looked at Mary Beth and she was filled with a deep feeling of gratitude. What could have been an ugly and sordid scene had turned into something friendly and wonderful. Adam had been right. Mary Beth was a lovely lady.

"I'm very grateful to you," Jennifer said.

"And I'm grateful to you," Mary Beth confided. She smiled shyly and said, "You see, I'm very much in love, too. I was going to get the divorce immediately but I thought, for Adam's sake, we'd best wait until after the election."

Jennifer had been so busy with her own emotions that she had forgotten about the election.

Mary Beth went on: "Everyone seems sure that Adam is going to be our next senator, and a divorce now would gravely hurt his chances. It's only six months away, so I decided it would be better for him if I delayed it." She looked at Jennifer. "But forgive me – is that agreeable with you?"

"Of course it is," Jennifer said.

She would have to completely readjust her thinking. Her future would now be tied to Adam. If he became senator, she would live with him in Washington, D.C. It would mean giving up her law practice here, but that did not matter. Nothing mattered except that they could be together.

Jennifer said, "Adam will make a wonderful senator."

Mary Beth raised her head and smiled. "My dear, one day Adam Warner is going to make a wonderful *President*."

The telephone was ringing when Jennifer arrived back at the apartment. It was Adam. "How did you get along with Mary Beth?"

"Adam, she was wonderful!"

"She said the same thing about you."

"You read about old southern charm, but you don't come across it very often. Mary Beth has it. She's quite a lady."

"So are you, darling. Where would you like to be married?"

Jennifer said, "Times Square, for all I care. But I think we should wait, Adam."

"Wait for what?"

"Until after the election. Your career is important. A divorce could hurt you right now."

"My private life is – "

" – going to become your public life. We mustn't do anything that might spoil your chances. We can wait six months."

"I don't want to wait."

"I don't either, darling." Jennifer smiled. "We won't really be waiting, will we?"

21

Jennifer and Adam had lunch together almost every day, and once or twice a week Adam spent the night at their apartment. They had to be more discreet than ever, for Adam's campaign had actively begun, and he was becoming a nationally prominent figure. He gave speeches at political rallies and fund-raising dinners, and his opinions on national issues were quoted more and more frequently in the press.

Adam and Stewart Needham were having their ritual morning tea.

"Saw you on the *Today* show this morning," Needham said. "Fine job, Adam. You got every single point across. I understand they've invited you back again."

"Stewart, I hate doing those shows. I feel like some goddamned actor up there, performing."

Stewart nodded, unperturbed. "That's what politicians are, Adam – actors. Playing a part, being what the public wants them to be. Hell, if politicians acted like themselves in public – what expression do the kids use? – letting it all hang out? – this country'd be a damned monarchy."

"I don't like the fact that running for public office has become a personality contest."

Stewart Needham smiled. "Be grateful you've got the personality, my boy. Your ratings in the polls keep going up every week." He stopped to pour more tea. "Believe me, this is only the beginning. First the Senate, then the number one target. Nothing can stop you." He paused to take a sip of his tea. "Unless you do something foolish, that is."

Adam looked up at him. "What do you mean?"

Stewart Needham delicately wiped his lips with a damask napkin.

"Your opponent is a gutter fighter. I'll bet you that right now he's examining your life under a microscope. He won't find any ammunition, will he?"

"No." The word came to Adam's lips automatically.

"Good," Stewart Needham said. "How's Mary Beth?"

Jennifer and Adam were spending a lazy weekend at a country house in Vermont that a friend of Adam's had loaned him. The air was crisp and fresh, hinting at the winter to come. It was a perfect weekend, comfortable and relaxed, with long hikes during the day and games and easy conversation before a blazing fire at night

They had carefully gone through all the Sunday papers. Adam was moving up in every poll. With a few exceptions, the media were for Adam. They liked his style, his honesty, his intelligence and his frankness. They kept comparing him to John Kennedy.

Adam sprawled in front of the fireplace, watching flame shadows dancing across Jennifer's face. "How would you like to be the wife of the President?"

"Sorry. I'm already in love with a senator."

"Will you be disappointed if I don't win, Jennifer?"

"No. The only reason I want it is because you want it, darling."

"If I do win, it will mean living in Washington."

"If we're together, nothing else matters."

"What about your law practice?"

Jennifer smiled. "The last time I heard, they had lawyers in Washington."

"What if I asked you to give it up?"

"I'd give it up."

"I don't want you to. You're too damned good at it."

"All I care about is being with you. I love you so much, Adam."

He stroked her soft dark brown hair and said, "I love you, too. So much."

They went to bed, and later, they slept.

On Sunday night they drove back to New York. They picked up Jennifer's car at the garage where she had parked it, and Adam returned to his home. Jennifer went back to their apartment in New York.

Jennifer's days were unbelievably full. If she had thought she was busy before, now she was besieged. She was representing international corporations that had bent a few laws and been caught, senators with their fingers in the till, movie stars who had gotten into trouble. She represented bank presidents and bank robbers, politicians and heads of unions.

Money was pouring in, but that was not important to Jennifer. She gave large bonuses to the office staff, and lavish gifts.

Corporations that came up against Jennifer no longer sent in their second string of lawyers, so Jennifer found herself pitted against some of the top legal talent of the world.

She was admitted into the American College of Trial Lawyers, and even Ken Bailey was impressed.

"Jesus," he said, "you know, only one percent of the lawyers in this country can get in?"

"I'm their token woman," Jennifer laughed.

When Jennifer represented a defendant in Manhattan, she could be certain that Robert Di Silva would either prosecute the case personally or mastermind it. His hatred of Jennifer had grown with every victory she had.

During one trial in which Jennifer was pitted against the District Attorney, Di Silva put a dozen top experts on the stand as witnesses for the prosecution.

Jennifer called no experts. She said to the jury: "If we want a spaceship built or the distance of a star measured, we call in the experts. But when we want something really important done, we collect twelve ordinary folks to do it. As I recall, the founder of Christianity did the same thing."

Jennifer won the case.

One of the techniques Jennifer found effective with a jury was to say, "I know that the words 'law' and 'courtroom' sound a little frightening and remote from your lives, but when you stop to think about it, all we're doing here is dealing with the rights and wrongs done to human beings like ourselves. Let's forget we're in a courtroom, my friends Let's just imagine we're sitting around in my living room, talking about what's happened to this poor defendant, this fellow human being."

And, in their minds, the jurors *were* sitting in Jennifer's living room, carried away by her spell.

This ploy worked beautifully for Jennifer until one day when she was defending a client against Robert Di Silva. The District Attorney rose to his feet and made the opening address to the jury.

"Ladies and gentlemen," Di Silva said, "I'd like for you to forget you're in a court of law. I want you to imagine that you're sitting at home in my living room and *we're* just sitting around informally chatting about the terrible things the defendant has done."

Ken Bailey leaned over and whispered to Jennifer, "Do you hear what that bastard's doing? He's stealing your stuff!"

"Don't worry about it," Jennifer replied coolly.

When Jennifer got up to address the jury, she said:

"Ladies and gentlemen, I've never heard anything as outrageous as the remarks of the District Attorney." Her voice rang with righteous indignation. "For a minute, I couldn't believe I had heard him correctly. How dare he tell you to *forget* you're sitting in a court of law! This courtroom is one of the most precious possessions our nation has! It is the foundation of our freedom. Yours and mine and the defendant's. And for the District Attorney to suggest that you forget where you are, that you forget your sworn duty, I find both shocking and contemptible. I'm asking you, ladies and gentlemen, to *remember* where you are, to remember that all of us are here to see that justice is done and that the defendant is vindicated."

The jurors were nodding approvingly.

Jennifer glanced toward the table where Robert Di Silva was sitting. He was staring straight ahead, a glazed look in his eyes.

Jennifer's client was acquitted.

After each court victory, there would be four dozen red roses on Jennifer's desk, with a card from Michael Moretti. Each time, Jennifer would tear up the cards and have Cynthia take away the flowers. Somehow they seemed obscene coming from him. Finally Jennifer sent Michael Moretti a note, asking him to stop sending her flowers.

When Jennifer returned from the courtroom after winning her next case, there were five dozen red roses waiting for her.

22

The Rainy Day Robber case brought Jennifer new headlines. The accused man had been called to her attention by Father Ryan.

"A friend of mine has a bit of a problem – " he began, and they both burst out laughing.

The friend turned out to be Paul Richards, a transient, accused of robbing a bank of a hundred and fifty thousand dollars. A robber had walked into the bank wearing a long black raincoat, under which was hidden a sawed-off shotgun. The collar of the raincoat was raised so that his face was partially hidden. Once inside the bank, the man had brandished the shotgun and forced a teller to hand over all his available cash. The robber had then fled in a waiting automobile. Several witnesses had seen the getaway car, a green sedan, but the license number had been covered with mud.

Since bank robberies were a federal offense, the FBI had entered the case. They had put the *modus operandi* into a central computer and it had come up with the name of Paul Richards.

Jennifer went to visit him at Riker's Island.

"I swear to God I didn't do it," Paul Richards said. He was in his fifties, a red-faced man with cherubic blue eyes, too old to be running around pulling bank robberies.

"I don't care whether you're innocent or guilty," Jennifer explained, "but I have one rule. I won't represent a client who lies to me."

"I swear on my mother's life I didn't do it."

Oaths had ceased to impress Jennifer long ago. Clients had sworn their innocence to her on the lives of their mothers, wives, sweethearts and children. If God had taken those oaths seriously, there would have been a serious decline in the population.

Jennifer asked, "Why do you think the FBI arrested you?"

Paul Richards answered without hesitation. "Because about ten years ago I pulled a bank job and was dumb enough to get caught."

"You used a sawed-off shotgun under a raincoat?"

"That's right. I waited until it was raining, and then hit a bank."

"But you didn't do this last job?"

"No. Some smart bastard copied my act."

The preliminary hearing was before Judge Fred Stevens, a strict disciplinarian. It was rumored that he was in favor of shipping all criminals off to some inaccessible island where they would stay for the rest of their lives. Judge Stevens believed that anyone caught stealing for the first time should have his right hand chopped off, and if caught again, should have his left hand chopped off, in ancient Islamic tradition. He was the worst judge Jennifer could have asked for. She sent for Ken Bailey.

"Ken, I want you to dig up everything you can on Judge Stevens."

"Judge Stevens? He's as straight as an arrow. He – "

"I know he is. Do it, please."

The federal prosecutor who was handling the case was an old pro named Carter Gifford.

"How are you going to plead him?" Gifford asked.

Jennifer gave him a look of innocent surprise. "Not guilty, of course."

He laughed sardonically. "Judge Stevens will get a kick out of that. I suppose you're going to move for a jury trial."

"No."

Gifford studied Jennifer suspiciously. "You mean you're going to put your client in the hands of the hanging judge?"

"That's right."

Gifford grinned. "I knew you'd go around the bend one day, Jennifer. I can't wait to see this."

"The United States of America versus Paul Richards. Is the defendant present?"

The court clerk said, "Yes, Your Honor."

"Would the attorneys please approach the bench and identify themselves?"

Jennifer and Carter Gifford moved toward Judge Stevens.

"Jennifer Parker representing the defendant."

"Carter Gifford representing the United States Government."

Judge Stevens turned to Jennifer and said brusquely, "I'm aware of your reputation, Miss Parker. So I'm going to tell you right now that I do not intend to waste this court's time. I will brook no delays in this case. I want to get on with this preliminary hearing and get the arraignment over with. I intend to set a trial date as speedily as possible. I presume you will want a jury trial and – "

"No, Your Honor."

Judge Stevens looked at her in surprise. "You're not asking for a jury trial?"

"I am not. Because I don't think there's going to be an arraignment."

Carter Gifford was staring at her. "What?"

"In my opinion, you don't have enough evidence to bring my client to trial."

Carter Gifford snapped, "You need another opinion!" He turned to Judge Stevens. "Your Honor, the government has a very strong case. The defendant has already been convicted of committing exactly the same crime in exactly the same manner. Our computer picked him out of over two thousand possible suspects. We have the guilty man right here in this courtroom, and the prosecution has no intention of dropping the case against him."

Judge Stevens turned to Jennifer. "It seems to the court that there is enough *prima facie* evidence here to have an arraignment and a trial. Do you have anything more to say?"

"I do, Your Honor. There is not one single witness who can positively identify Paul Richards. The FBI has been unable to find any of the stolen money. In fact, the only thing that links the defendant to this crime is the imagination of the prosecutor."

The judge stared down at Jennifer and said with ominous softness, "What about the computer that picked him out?"

Jennifer sighed. "That brings us to a problem, Your Honor."

Judge Stevens said grimly, "I imagine it does. It is easy to confuse a live witness, but it is difficult to confuse a computer."

Carter Gifford nodded smugly, "Exactly, Your Honor."

Jennifer turned to face Gifford. "The FBI used the IBM 370/168, didn't it?"

"That's right. It's the most sophisticated equipment in the world."

Judge Stevens asked Jennifer, "Does the defense intend to challenge the efficiency of that computer?"

"On the contrary, Your Honor. I have a computer expert here in court today who works for the company that manufactures the 370/168. He programmed the information that turned up the name of my client."

"Where is he?"

Jennifer turned and motioned to a tall, thin man seated on a bench. He nervously came forward.

Jennifer said, "This is Mr. Edward Monroe."

"If you've been tampering with my witness," the prosecuting attorney exploded, "I'll – "

"All I did was to request Mr. Monroe to ask the computer if there were other possible suspects. I selected ten people who had certain general characteristics similar to my client. For purposes of identification, Mr. Monroe programmed in statistics on age, height, weight, color of eyes, birthplace – the same kind of data that produced the name of my client."

Judge Stevens asked impatiently, "What is the point of all this, Miss Parker?"

"The point is that the computer identified one of the ten people as a prime suspect in the bank robbery."

Judge Stevens turned to Edward Monroe. "Is this true?"

"Yes, Your Honor." Edward Monroe opened his briefcase and pulled out a computer readout.

The bailiff took it from Monroe and handed it to the judge. Judge Stevens glanced at it and his face became red.

He looked at Edward Monroe. "Is this some kind of joke?"

"No, sir."

"The computer picked *me* as a possible suspect?" Judge Stevens asked.

"Yes, sir, it did."

Jennifer explained, "The computer has no reasoning power, Your Honor. It can only respond to the information it is given. You and my client happen to be the same weight, height and age. You both drive green sedans, and you both come from the same state. That's really as much evidence as the prosecuting attorney has. The only other factor is the way in which the crime was done. When Paul Richards committed that bank robbery ten years ago, millions of people read about it. Any one of them could have imitated his *modus operandi*. Someone did." Jennifer indicated the piece of paper in Judge Stevens' hand. "That shows you how flimsy the State's case really is."

Carter Gifford sputtered, "Your Honor – " and stopped. He did not know what to say.

Judge Stevens looked again at the computer readout in his hand and then at Jennifer.

"What would you have done," he asked, "if the court had been a younger man, thinner than I, who drove a *blue* car?"

"The computer gave me ten other possible suspects," Jennifer said. "My next choice would have been New York District Attorney Robert Di Silva."

Jennifer was sitting in her office, reading the headlines, when Cynthia announced, "Mr. Paul Richards is here."

"Send him in, Cynthia."

He came into the office wearing a black raincoat and carrying a candy box tied with a red ribbon.

"I just wanted to tell you thanks."

"You see? Sometimes justice *does* triumph."

"I'm leaving town. I decided I need a little vacation." He handed Jennifer the candy box. "A little token of my appreciation."

"Thank you, Paul."

He looked at her admiringly. "I think you're terrific."

And he was gone.

Jennifer looked at the box of candy on her desk and smiled. She had received less for handling most of Father Ryan's friends. If she got fat, it would be Father Ryan's fault.

Jennifer untied the ribbon and opened the box. Inside was ten thousand dollars in used currency.

One afternoon as Jennifer was leaving the courthouse, she noticed a large, black, chauffeured Cadillac limousine at the curb. As she started to walk past it, Michael Moretti stepped out. "I've been waiting for you."

Close up, there was an electric vitality to the man that was almost overpowering.

"Get out of my way," Jennifer said. Her face was flushed and angry, and she was even more beautiful than Michael Moretti had remembered.

"Hey," he laughed, "cool down. All I want to do is talk to you. All you have to do is listen. I'll pay you for your time."

"You'll never have enough money."

She started to move past him. Michael Moretti put a conciliatory hand on her arm. Just touching her increased his excitement.

He turned on all of his charm. "Be reasonable. You won't know what you're turning down until you hear what I have to say. Ten minutes. That's all I want. I'll drop you off at your office. We can talk on the way."

Jennifer studied him a moment and said, "I'll go with you on one condition. I want the answer to a question."

Michael nodded. "Sure. Go ahead."

"Whose idea was it to frame me with the dead canary?"

He answered without hesitation. "Mine."

So now she knew. And she could have killed him. Grimly she stepped into the limousine and Michael Moretti moved in beside her. Jennifer noted that he gave the driver the address of her office building without asking.

As the limousine drove off, Michael Moretti said, "I'm glad about all the great things that are happening to you."

Jennifer did not bother to reply.

"I really mean that."

"You haven't told me what it is you want."

"I want to make you rich."

"Thanks. I'm rich enough." Her voice was filled with the contempt she felt toward him.

Michael Moretti's face flushed. "I'm trying to do you a favor and you keep fighting me."

Jennifer turned to look at him. "I don't want any favors from you."

He made his voice conciliatory. "Okay. Maybe I'm trying to make up a little for what I did to you. Look, I can send you a lot of clients. Important clients. Big money. You have no idea – "

Jennifer interrupted. "Mr. Moretti, do us both a favor. Don't say another word."

"But I can – "

"I don't want to represent you or any of your friends."

"Why not?"

"Because if I represented one of you, from then on you'd own me."

"You've got it all wrong," Michael protested. "My friends are in legitimate businesses. I mean banks, insurance companies – "

"Save your breath. My services aren't available to the Mafia."

"Who said anything about the Mafia?"

"Call it whatever you like. No one owns me but me. I intend to keep it that way."

The limousine stopped for a red light.

Jennifer said, "This is close enough. Thank you for the lift." She opened the door and stepped out.

Michael said, "When can I see you again?"
"Not ever, Mr. Moretti."
Michael watched her walk away.
My God, he thought, *that's a woman!* He suddenly became aware that he had an erection and smiled, because he knew that one way or another, he was going to have her.

23

It was the end of October, two weeks before the election, and the senatorial race was in full swing. Adam was running against the incumbent Senator John Trowbridge, a veteran politician, and the experts agreed it was going to be a close battle.

Jennifer sat at home one night, watching Adam and his opponent in a television debate. Mary Beth had been right. A divorce now could easily have wrecked Adam's growing chances for victory.

When Jennifer walked into the office after a long business lunch, there was a urgent message for her to call Rick Arlen.

"He's called three times in the last half-hour," Cynthia said.

Rick Arlen was a rock star who had, almost overnight, become the hottest singer in the world. Jennifer had heard about the enormous incomes of rock stars, but until she got involved with Rick Arlen's affairs, she had had no idea what that really meant. From records, personal appearances, merchandising and now motion pictures, Rick Arlen's income was more than fifteen million dollars a year. Rick was twenty-five years old, an Alabama farm boy who had been born with a gold mine in his throat.

"Get him for me," Jennifer said.

Five minutes later he was on the line. "Hey, man, I've been tryin' to reach you for hours."

"Sorry, Rick. I was in a meeting."

"Problem. Gotta see you."

"Can you come in to the office this afternoon?"

"I don't think so. I'm in Monte Carlo, doin' a benefit for Grace and the Prince. How soon can you get here?"

"I couldn't possibly get away now," Jennifer protested. "I have a desk piled up – "

"Baby, I *need* you. You've got to get on a bird this afternoon."

And he hung up.

Jennifer thought about the phone call. Rick Arlen had not wanted to discuss his problem over the telephone. It could be anything from drugs to girls to boys. She thought about sending Ted Harris or Dan Martin to solve whatever the problem was, but she liked Rick Arlen. In the end, Jennifer decided to go herself.

She tried to reach Adam before she left, but he was out of the office.

She said to Cynthia, "Get me reservations on an Air France flight to Nice. I'll want a car to meet me and drive me to Monte Carlo."

Twenty minutes later she had a reservation on a seven o'clock flight that evening.

"There's a helicopter service from Nice directly to Monte Carlo," Cynthia said. "I've booked you on that."

"Wonderful. Thank you."

When Ken Bailey heard why Jennifer was leaving, he said, "Who does that punk think he is?"

"He *knows* who he is, Ken. He's one of our biggest clients."

"When will you be back?"

"I shouldn't be gone more than three or four days."

"Things aren't the same when you're not here. I'll miss you."

Jennifer wondered whether he was still seeing the young blond man.

"Hold down the fort until I get back."

As a rule, Jennifer enjoyed flying. She regarded her time in the air as freedom from pressures, a temporary escape from all the problems that beset her on the ground, a quiet oasis in space away from her endlessly demanding clients. This flight across the Atlantic, however, was unpleasant. It seemed unusually bumpy, and Jennifer's stomach became queasy and upset.

She was feeling a bit better by the time the plane landed in Nice the next morning. There was a helicopter waiting to fly her to Monte Carlo. Jennifer had never ridden in a helicopter before and she had looked forward to it. But the sudden lift and the swooping motions made her ill again, and she was unable to enjoy the majestic sights of the Alps below and the Grande Corniche, with miniature automobiles winding up the steep mountainside.

The buildings of Monte Carlo appeared, and a few minutes later the helicopter was landing in front of the modern white summer casino on the beach.

Cynthia had telephoned ahead and Rick Arlen was there to meet Jennifer.

He gave her a big hug. "How was the trip?"

"A little rough."

He took a closer look at her and said, "You don't look so hot. I'll take you up to my pad and you can rest up for the big do tonight."

"What big do?"

"The gala. That's why you're here."

"*What*?"

"Yeah. Grace asked me to invite anyone I liked. I like you."

"Oh, Rick!"

Jennifer could cheerfully have strangled him. He had no idea how much he had disrupted her life. She was three thousand miles away from Adam, she had clients who needed her, court cases to try – and she had been lured to Monte Carlo to attend a party!

Jennifer said, "Rick, how could – ?"

She looked at his beaming face and started to laugh.

Oh, well, she was here. Besides, the gala might turn out to be fun.

The gala was spectacular. It was a milk fund concert for orphans, sponsored by Their Serene Highnesses, Grace and Rainier Grimaldi, and it was held outdoors at the summer casino. It was a lovely evening. The night was balmy and the slight breeze coming off the Mediterranean stirred the tall palm trees. Jennifer wished Adam could have been here to share it with her. There were fifteen hundred seats occupied by a cheering audience.

Half a dozen international stars performed, but Rick Arlen was the headliner. He was backed up by a raucous three-piece band and flashing psychedelic lights that stained the velvet sky. When he finished, he received a standing ovation.

There was a private party afterward at the *piscine*, below the Hotel de Paris. Cocktails and a buffet supper were served around the enormous pool, in which dozens of lighted candles floated on lily pads.

Jennifer estimated that there were more than three hundred people there. Jennifer had not brought an evening gown, and just looking at the splendidly dressed women made her feel like the poor little match girl. Rick introduced her to dukes and duchesses and princesses. It seemed to Jennifer that half the royalty of Europe was there. She met heads of cartels and famous opera singers. There were fashion designers and heiresses and the great soccer player, Pele. Jennifer was in the midst of a conversation with two Swiss bankers when a wave of dizziness engulfed her.

"Excuse me," Jennifer said.

She went to find Rick Arlen. "Rick, I – "

He took one look at her and said, "You're white as a sheet, baby. Let's split."

Thirty minutes later, Jennifer was in bed in the villa that Rick Arlen had rented.

"A doctor's on his way," Rick told her.

"I don't need a doctor. It's just a virus or something."

"Right. It's the 'or something' he's gonna check out."

Dr. André Monteux was an elderly wisp of a man somewhere in his eighties. He wore a neatly trimmed full beard and carried a black medical case.

The doctor turned to Rick Arlen. "If you would leave us alone, please."

"Sure. I'll wait outside."

The doctor moved closer to the bed. "Alors. What have we here?"

"If I knew that," Jennifer said weakly, "I'd be making this house call and you'd be lying here."

He sat down on the edge of the bed. "How are you feeling?"

"Like I've come down with the bubonic plague."

"Put out your tongue, please."

Jennifer put out her tongue and began to gag. Dr. Monteux checked her pulse and took her temperature.

When he had finished, Jennifer asked, "What do you think it is, Doctor?"

"It could be any one of a number of things, beautiful lady. If you are feeling well enough tomorrow, I would like you to come to my office where I can do a thorough examination."

Jennifer felt too ill to argue. "All right," she said. "I'll be there."

In the morning Rick Arlen drove Jennifer into Monte Carlo where Dr. Monteux gave her a complete examination.

"It's a bug of some kind, isn't it?" Jennifer asked.

"If you wish a prediction," the elderly doctor replied, "I will send out for fortune cookies. If you wish to know what is wrong with you, we will have to be patient until the laboratory reports come back."

"When will that be?"

"It usually takes two or three days."

Jennifer knew there was no way she was going to stay there for two or three days. Adam might need her. She knew she needed him.

"In the meantime, I would like you to stay in bed and rest." He handed her a bottle of pills. "These will relax you."

"Thank you." Jennifer scribbled something on a piece of paper. You can call me here."

It was not until Jennifer had gone that Dr. Monteux looked at the piece of paper. On it was written a New York telephone number.

At the Charles de Gaulle Airport in Paris, where she changed planes, Jennifer took two of the pills Dr. Monteaux had given her and a sleeping pill. She slept fitfully during most of the trip back to New York, but when she disembarked from the plane she was feeling no better. She had not arranged for anyone to meet her and she took a taxi to her apartment.

In the late afternoon, the telephone rang. It was Adam.

"Jennifer! Where have you – "

She tried to put energy into her voice. "I'm sorry, darling. I had to go to Monte Carlo to see a client and I couldn't reach you."

"I've been worried sick. Are you all right?"

"I'm fine. I – I've just been running around a lot."

"My God! I was imagining all kinds of terrible things."

"There's nothing to worry about," Jennifer assured him. "How's everything going with the campaign?"

"Fine. When am I going to see you? I was supposed to leave for Washington but I can postpone – "

"No, you go ahead," Jennifer said. She did not want Adam to see her like this. "I'll be busy. We'll spend the weekend together."

"All right." His tone was reluctant. "If you're not doing anything at eleven, I'm on the CBS news."

"I'll watch, darling."

Jennifer was asleep five minutes after she had replaced the receiver.

In the morning Jennifer telephoned Cynthia to tell her she was not coming into the office. Jennifer had slept restlessly, and when she awakened she felt no better. She tried to eat breakfast but could not keep anything down. She felt weak and realized she had had nothing to eat for almost three days.

Her mind unwillingly went over the frightening litany of things that could be wrong with her. Cancer first, naturally. She felt for lumps in her breast, but she could not feel anything amiss. Of course, cancer could strike anywhere. It could be a virus of some kind, but the doctor surely would have known that immediately. The trouble was that it could be almost anything. Jennifer felt lost and helpless. She was not a hypochondriac, she had always been in wonderful health, and now she felt as though her body had somehow betrayed her. She could not bear it if anything happened to her. Not when everything was so wonderful.

She was going to be fine. Of course she was.

Another wave of nausea swept through her.

At eleven o'clock that morning, Dr. André Monteux called from Monte Carlo. A voice said, "Just a moment. I'll put the doctor on."

The moment stretched into a hundred years, and Jennifer clutched the telephone tightly, unable to bear the waiting.

Finally, Dr. Monteux's voice came on and he said, "How are you feeling?"

"About the same," Jennifer replied nervously. "Are the results of the tests in?"

"Good news," Dr. Monteux said. "It is not the bubonic plague."

Jennifer could stand no more. "What is it? What's the matter with me?"

"You are going to have a baby, Mrs. Parker."

Jennifer sat there numbly staring at the telephone. When she found her voice again she asked, "Are – are you sure?"

"Rabbits never lie. I take it this is your first baby."

"Yes."

"I would suggest you see an obstetrician as soon as possible. From the severity of the early symptoms, there may be some difficulties ahead for you."

"I will," Jennifer replied. "Thank you for calling, Dr. Monteux."

She replaced the receiver and sat there, her mind in a turmoil. She was not sure when it could have happened, or what her feelings were. She could not think straight.

She was going to have Adam's baby. And suddenly Jennifer knew how she felt. She felt *wonderful*; she felt as though she had been given some indescribably precious gift.

The timing was perfect, as though the gods were on their side. The election would soon be over and she and Adam would be married as quickly as possible. It would be a boy. Jennifer knew it. She could not wait to tell Adam.

She telephoned him at his office.

"Mr. Warner is not in," his secretary informed her. "You might try his home."

Jennifer was reluctant to call Adam at home, but she was bursting with her news. She dialed his number. Mary Beth answered.

"I'm sorry to bother you," Jennifer apologized. "There's something I have to talk to Adam about. This is Jennifer Parker."

"I'm pleased that you called," Mary Beth said. The warmth in her voice was reassuring. "Adam had some speaking engagements, but he's returning tonight. Why don't you come up to the house? We can all have dinner together. Say, seven o'clock?"

Jennifer hesitated for a moment. "That will be lovely."

It was a miracle that Jennifer did not have an accident driving to Croton-on-Hudson. Her mind was far away, dreaming of the future. She and Adam had often discussed having children. She could remember his words. *I want a couple that look exactly like you.*

As Jennifer drove along the highway, she thought she could feel a slight stirring in her womb, but she told herself that that was nonsense. It was much too early. But it would not be long now. Adam's baby was in her. It was alive and would soon be kicking. It was awesome, overwhelming. She –

Jennifer heard someone honking at her, and she looked up and saw that she had almost forced a truck driver off the road. She gave him an apologetic smile and drove on. Nothing could spoil this day.

It was dusk when Jennifer pulled up in front of the Warner house. A fine snow was beginning to fall, lightly powdering the trees. Mary Beth, wearing a long blue brocade gown, opened the front door to greet Jennifer, taking her arm and warmly welcoming her into the house, reminding Jennifer of the first time they had met.

Mary Beth looked radiantly happy. She was full of small talk, putting her visitor at ease. They went into the library where there was a cheerful fire crackling in the hearth.

"I haven't heard from Adam yet," Mary Beth said. "He's probably been detained. In the meantime, you and I can have a nice long chat. You sounded excited on the telephone." Mary Beth leaned forward conspiratorially. "What's your big news?"

Jennifer looked at the friendly woman across from her and blurted out, "I'm going to have Adam's baby."

Mary Beth leaned back in her chair and smiled. "Well! Now isn't that something! So am I!"

Jennifer stared at her. "I – I don't understand."

Mary Beth laughed. "It's really quite simple, my dear. Adam and I *are* married, you know."

Jennifer said slowly, "But – but you and Adam are getting a divorce."

"My dear girl, why on earth would I divorce Adam? I adore him."

Jennifer felt her head beginning to spin. The conversation was making no sense. "You're – you're in love with someone else. You said you – "

"I said that I'm in love. And I am. I'm in love with Adam. I told you, I've been in love with Adam since the first time I saw him."

She could not mean what she was saying. She was teasing Jennifer, playing some kind of silly game.

"Stop it!" Jennifer said. "You're like a brother and sister to each other. Adam doesn't make love to – "

Mary Beth's voice tinkled with laughter. "My poor dear! I'm surprised that someone as clever as you are could – " She leaned forward with concern. "You believed him! I'm so sorry. I am. I really am."

Jennifer was fighting to keep control of herself. "Adam is in love with me. We're getting married."

Mary Beth shook her head. Her blue eyes met Jennifer's and the naked hatred in them made Jennifer's heart stop for an instant.

"That would make Adam a bigamist. I'll never give him a divorce. If I had let Adam divorce me and marry you, he would lose the election. As it is, he's going to win it. Then we'll go on to the White House, Adam and I. There's no room in his life for anyone like you. There never was. He only thinks he's in love with you. But he'll get over that when he finds out I'm carrying his baby. Adam's always wanted a child."

Jennifer squeezed her eyes shut, trying to stop the terrible pain in her head.

"Can I get you something?" Mary Beth was asking solicitously.

Jennifer opened her eyes. "Have you told him you're having a baby?"

"Not yet." Mary Beth smiled. "I thought I'd tell him to night when he gets home and we're in bed."

Jennifer was filled with loathing. "You're a monster . . ."

"It's all in the point of view, isn't it, honey? I'm Adam's wife. You're his whore."

Jennifer rose to her feet, feeling dizzy. Her headache had become an unbearable pounding. There was a roaring in her ears and she was afraid she was going to faint. She was moving toward the entrance, her legs unsteady.

Jennifer stopped at the door, pressing herself against it, trying to think. Adam had said he loved her, but he had slept with this woman, had made her pregnant.

Jennifer turned and walked out into the cold night air.

24

Adam was on a final campaign swing around the state. He telephoned Jennifer several times, but he was always surrounded by his entourage and it was impossible to talk, impossible for Jennifer to tell him her news.

Jennifer knew the explanation for Mary Beth's pregnancy: she had tricked Adam into sleeping with her. But Jennifer wanted to hear it from Adam.

"I'll be back in a few days and we'll talk then," Adam said.

The election was only five days away now. Adam deserved to win it; he was the better man. Jennifer felt that Mary Beth was right when she said it could be the stepping-stone to the presidency of the United States. She would force herself to wait and see what happened.

If Adam was elected senator, Jennifer would lose him. Adam would go to Washington with Mary Beth. There would be no way he could get a divorce. The scandal of a freshman senator divorcing a pregnant wife to marry his pregnant mistress would be too juicy a story for him ever to live down. But if Adam should lose the race, he would be free. Free to go back to his law practice, free to marry Jennifer and not worry or care about what anyone else thought. They would be able to live the rest of their lives together. Have their child.

Election Day dawned cold and rainy. Because of the interest in the senate race, a large voter turnout was expected at the polls despite the weather.

In the morning, Ken Bailey asked, "Are you going to vote today?"

"Yes."

"Looks like a close race, doesn't it?"

"Very close."

She went to the polls late that morning, and as she stepped into the voting booth she thought dully, *A vote for Adam Warner is a vote against Jennifer Parker.* She voted for Adam and left the booth. She could not bear to go back to her office. She walked the streets all afternoon, trying not to think, trying not to feel; thinking and feeling, knowing that the next few hours were going to determine the rest of her life.

25

"This is one of the closest elections we have had in years," the television announcer was saying.

Jennifer was at home alone watching the returns on NBC. She had made herself a light dinner of scrambled eggs and toast, and then was too nervous to eat anything. She sat in a robe huddled up on the couch, listening to her fate being broadcast to millions of people. Each viewer had his own reason for watching, for wanting one of the candidates to win or to lose, but Jennifer was sure that none of them was as deeply involved in the outcome of this election as she was. If Adam won, it would mean the end of their relationship . . . and the end of the baby in her womb.

There was a quick shot of Adam on the screen, and by his side, Mary Beth. Jennifer prided herself on being able to read people, to understand their motives, but she had been completely taken in by the moonlight-and-magnolias routine of the honey-voiced bitch. She kept pushing back the picture of Adam going to bed with that woman, making her pregnant.

Edwin Newman was saying, "Here are the latest returns in the senate race between the incumbent, John Trowbridge, and challenger Adam Warner. In Manhattan, John Trowbridge has a total of 221,375 votes. Adam Warner has a total of 214,895."

"In the Forty-fifth Election District of the Twenty-ninth Assembly District in Queens, John Trowbridge is two percentage points ahead."

Jennifer's life was being measured in percentage points.

"The totals from The Bronx, Brooklyn, Queens, Richmond and the counties of Nassau, Rockland, Suffolk and Westchester add up to 2,300,000 for John Trowbridge, and 2,120,000 for Adam Warner, with the votes from upstate New York just beginning to come in. Adam Warner has made a surprisingly strong showing against Senator Trowbridge, who is serving his third term. From the beginning, the polls have been almost evenly divided in this race. According to the latest returns, with sixty-two percent of the votes counted, Senator Trowbridge is beginning to pull ahead. When we read the last returns one hour ago, Senator Trowbridge was two percentage points ahead. The returns now indicate that he has increased his lead to two and a half percentage points. If this trend continues, the NBC computer will predict Senator Trowbridge to be the victor in the senatorial race for the United States Senate. Moving on to the contest between . . ."

Jennifer sat there, looking at the set, her heart pounding. It was as though millions of people were casting a vote to decide whether it would be Adam and Jennifer, or Adam and Mary Beth. Jennifer felt light-headed and giddy. She must remember to eat sometime. But not now. Nothing mattered now except what was happening on the screen in front of her. The suspense kept building, minute by minute, hour by hour.

At midnight, Senator John Trowbridge's lead was three percentage points. At two in the morning, with seventy-one percent of the votes counted, Senator Trowbridge was leading by a margin of three and a half percentage points. The computer declared that Senator John Trowbridge had won the election.

Jennifer sat there staring at the television set, drained of all emotion, of all feeling. Adam had lost. Jennifer had won. She had won Adam and their son. She was free to tell Adam now, to tell him about their baby, to plan for their future together.

Jennifer's heart ached for Adam, for she knew how much the election had meant to him. And yet in time, Adam would get over his defeat. One day he would try again, and she would help him. He was still young. The world lay before both of them. Before the three of them.

Jennifer fell asleep on the couch, dreaming about Adam and the election and the White House. She and Adam and their son were in the Oval Office. Adam was making his acceptance speech. Mary Beth walked in and began to interrupt. Adam started to yell at her and his voice got louder and louder. Jennifer woke up. The voice was the voice of Edwin Newman. The television set was still on. It was dawn.

Edwin Newman, looking exhausted, was reading the final election returns. Jennifer listened to him, her mind still half asleep.

As she started to rise from the couch she heard him say, "And here are the final results on the New York State senatorial election. In one of the most stunning upsets in years, Adam Warner has defeated the incumbent, Senator John Trowbridge, by a margin of less than one percent."

It was over. Jennifer had lost.

26

When Jennifer walked into the office late that morning, Cynthia said, "Mr. Adams is on the line, Miss Parker. He's been calling all morning."

Jennifer hesitated, then said, "All right, Cynthia, I'll take it." She went into her office and picked up the telephone. "Hello, Adam. Congratulations."

"Thanks. We have to talk. Are you free for lunch?" Jennifer hesitated. "Yes."

It had to be faced sometime.

*

It was the first time Jennifer had seen Adam in three weeks. She studied his face. Adam looked haggard and drawn. He should have been flushed with victory, but instead he seemed oddly nervous and uncomfortable. They ordered a lunch which neither of them ate, and they talked about the election, their words a camouflage to hide their thoughts.

The charade had become almost unbearable when, finally, Adam said, "Jennifer . . ." He took a deep breath and plunged ahead. "Mary Beth is going to have a baby."

Hearing the words from him somehow made it an unbearable reality. "I'm sorry, darling. It – it just happened. It's difficult to explain."

"You don't have to explain." Jennifer could see the scene clearly. Mary Beth in a provocative negligee – or naked – and Adam –

"I feel like such a fool," Adam was saying. There was an uncomfortable silence and he went on. "I got a call this morning from the chairman of the National Committee. There's talk about grooming me as their next presidential candidate." He hesitated. "The problem is that with Mary Beth pregnant, this would be an awkward time for me to get a divorce. I don't know what the hell to do. I haven't slept in three nights." He looked at Jennifer and said, "I hate to ask this of you, but – do you think we could wait a little while until things sort themselves out?"

Jennifer looked across the table at Adam and felt such a deep ache, such an intolerable loss, that she did not think she could stand it.

"We'll see each other as often as possible in the meantime," Adam told her. "We – "

Jennifer forced herself to speak. "No, Adam. It's over."

He stared at her. "You don't mean that. I love you, darling. We'll find a way to – "

"There is no way. Your wife and baby aren't going to disappear. You and I are finished. I've loved it. Every moment of it."

She rose to her feet, knowing that if she did not get out of the restaurant she would start screaming. "We must never see each other again."

She could not bear to look at his pain-filled eyes.

"Oh, God, Jennifer! Don't do this. Please don't do this! We – "

She did not hear the rest. She was hurrying toward the door, running out of Adam's life.

27

Adam's telephone calls were neither accepted nor returned. His letters were sent back unopened. On the last letter Jennifer received, she wrote the word "deceased" on the envelope and dropped it in the mail slot. *It's true*, Jennifer thought. *I am dead.*

She had never known that such pain could exist She had to be alone, and yet she was not alone. There was another human being inside her, a part of her and a part of Adam. And she was going to destroy it.

She forced herself to think about where she was going to have the abortion. A few years earlier an abortion would have meant some quack doctor in a dirty, sleazy back-alley room, but now that was no longer necessary. She could go to a hospital and have the operation performed by a reputable surgeon. Somewhere outside of New York City. Jennifer's photograph had been in the newspapers too many times, she had been on television too often. She needed anonymity, someplace where no one would ask questions. There must never, never be a link between her and Adam Warner. *United States Senator* Adam Warner. Their baby must die anonymously.

Jennifer allowed herself to think of what the baby would have been like, and she began to weep so hard that it was difficult to breathe.

It had started to rain. Jennifer looked up at the sky and wondered whether God was crying for her.

Ken Bailey was the only person Jennifer could trust to help her.

"I need an abortion," Jennifer said without preamble. "Do you know of a good doctor?"

He tried to mask his surprise, but Jennifer could see the variety of emotions that flickered across his face.

"Somewhere out of town, Ken. Someplace where they won't know me."

"What about the Fiji Islands?" There was an anger in his voice.

"I'm serious."

"Sorry. I – you caught me off guard." The news had taken him completely by surprise. He worshipped Jennifer. He knew that he loved her, and there were times when he thought he was in love with her; but he could not be sure, and it was torture. He could never do to Jennifer what he had done to his wife. *God*, Ken thought, *why the hell couldn't You make up Your mind about me?*

He ran his hands through his red hair and said, "If you don't want to have it in New York, I'd suggest North Carolina. It's not too far away."

"Can you check it out for me?"

"Yeah. Fine. I – "

"Yes?"

He looked away from her. "Nothing."

Ken Bailey disappeared for the next three days. When he walked into Jennifer's office on the third day, he was unshaven and his eyes were hollow and red-rimmed.

Jennifer took one look at him and asked, "Are you all right?"

"I guess so."

"Is there anything I can do to help?"

"No." *If God can't help me, love, there's nothing you can do.*

He handed Jennifer a slip of paper. On it was written, *Dr. Eric Linden, Memorial Hospital, Charlotte, North Carolina.*

"Thank you, Ken."

"*De nada.* When are you going to do it?"

"I'll go down there this weekend."

He said awkwardly, "Would you like me to go with you?"

"No, thanks. I'll be fine."

"What about the return trip?"

"I'll be all right."

He stood there a moment, hesitating. "It's none of my business, but are you sure this is what you want to do?"

"I'm sure."

She had no choice. She wanted nothing more in the world than to keep Adam's baby, but she knew it would be insane to try to bring the baby up by herself.

She looked at Ken and said again, "I'm sure."

The hospital was a pleasant old two-story brick building on the outskirts of Charlotte.

The woman behind the registration desk was gray-haired, in her late sixties. "May I help you?"

"Yes," Jennifer said. "I'm Mrs. Parker. I have an appointment with Dr. Linden to – to – " She could not bring herself to say the words.

The receptionist nodded understandingly. "The doctor's expecting you, Mrs. Parker. I'll have someone show you the way."

An efficient young nurse led Jennifer to an examining room down the hall and said, "I'll tell Dr. Linden you're here. Would you like to get undressed? There's a hospital gown on the hanger."

Slowly, possessed by a feeling of unreality, Jennifer undressed and put on the white hospital gown. She felt as though she were putting on a butcher's apron. She was about to kill the life inside her. In her mind, the apron became spattered with blood, the blood of her baby. Jennifer found herself trembling.

A voice said, "Here, now. Relax."

Jennifer looked up to see a burly bald-headed man wearing horn-rimmed glasses that gave his face an owlish appearance.

"I'm Dr. Linden." He looked at the chart in his hand. "You're Mrs. Parker."

Jennifer nodded.

The doctor touched her arm and said soothingly, "Sit down." He went to the sink and filled a paper cup with water. "Drink this."

Jennifer obeyed. Dr. Linden sat in a chair, watching her until the trembling had subsided.

"So. You want to have an abortion."

"Yes."

"Have you discussed this with your husband, Mrs. Parker?"

"Yes. We – we both want it."

He studied her. "You appear to be in good health."

"I feel – I feel fine."

"Is it an economic problem?"

"No," Jennifer said sharply. Why was he bothering her with questions? "We – we just can't have the baby."

Dr. Linden took out a pipe. "This bother you?"

"No."

Dr. Linden lit the pipe and said, "Nasty habit." He leaned back and blew out a puff of smoke.

"Could we get this over with?" Jennifer asked.

Her nerves were stretched to the breaking point. She felt that at any moment she was going to scream.

Dr. Linden took another long, slow puff from his pipe. "I think we should talk for a few minutes."

By an enormous effort of will, Jennifer controlled her agitation. "All right."

"The thing about abortions," Dr. Linden said, "is that they're so final. You can change your mind now, but you can't change it after the baby's gone."

"I'm not going to change my mind."

He nodded and took another slow puff of the pipe. "That's good."

The sweet smell of the tobacco was making Jennifer nauseous. She wished he would put away his pipe. "Doctor Linden – "

He rose to his feet reluctantly and said, "All right, young lady, let's have a look at you."

Jennifer lay back on the examining table, her feet in the cold metal stirrups. She felt his fingers probing inside her body. They were gentle, and skilled, and she felt no embarrassment, only an ineffable sense of loss, a deep sorrow. Unbidden visions came into her mind of her young son, because she knew with certainty it would have been a boy, running and playing and laughing. Growing up in the image of his father.

Dr. Linden had finished his examination. "You can get dressed now, Mrs. Parker. You may stay here overnight, if you like, and we'll perform the operation in the morning."

"No!" Jennifer's voice was sharper than she had intended. "I'd like it done now, please."

Dr. Linden was studying her again, a quizzical expression on his face.

"I have two patients ahead of you. I'll have the nurse come in and get a lab work-up and then put you in your room. We'll go ahead with surgery in about four hours. All right?"

Jennifer whispered, "All right"

She lay on the narrow hospital bed, her eyes closed, waiting for Dr. Linden to return. There was an old-fashioned clock on the wall and its ticking seemed to fill the room. The ticktock became words: *Young Adam, Young Adam, Young Adam, our son, our son, our son.*

Jennifer could not shut the vision of the baby out of her mind. At this moment it was inside her body, comfortable and warm and alive, protected against the world in its amniotic womb. She wondered whether it had any primeval fear of what was about to happen to it. She wondered whether it would feel pain when the knife killed it. She put her hands over her ears to shut out the ticking of the clock. She found she was beginning to breathe hard, and her body was covered with perspiration. She heard a sound and opened her eyes.

Dr. Linden was standing over her, a look of concern on his face. "Are you all right, Mrs. Parker?"

"Yes," Jennifer whispered. "I just want it finished."

Dr. Linden nodded. "That's what we're going to do." He took a syringe from the table next to her bed and moved toward her.

"What's in that?"

"Demerol and Phenergan to relax you. We'll be going into the operating room in a few minutes." He gave Jennifer the injection. "I take it that this is your first abortion?"

"Yes."

"Then let me explain the procedure to you. It's painless and relatively simple. In the operating room you'll be given nitrous oxide, a general anesthesia, and oxygen by mask. When you're unconscious, a speculum will be inserted into the vagina, so that we can see what we're doing. We will then begin dilating the cervix with a series of metal dilators, in increasing sizes, and scraping out the uterus with a curette. Any questions so far?"

"No."

A warm, sleepy feeling was stealing over her. She could feel her tension vanishing as though by magic, and the walls of the room began to blur. She wanted to ask the doctor something, but she could not remember what it was . . . something about the baby . . . it no longer seemed important. The important thing was that she was doing what she had to do. It would all be over in a few minutes, and she could start her life again.

She found herself drifting off into a wonderful, dreamy state . . . she was aware of people coming into the room, lifting her onto a metal table with wheels . . . she could feel the coldness of the metal on her back through her thin hospital gown. She was being rolled down the hallway and she started to count the lights overhead. It seemed important to get the number right, but she was not sure why. She was being wheeled into a white, antiseptic operating room and Jennifer thought, *This is where my baby is going to die. Don't worry, little Adam. I won't let them hurt you.* And without meaning to, she began to cry.

Dr. Linden patted her arm. "It's all right. This won't hurt."

Death without pain, Jennifer thought. *That was nice.* She loved her baby. She did not want him to be hurt.

Someone put a mask over her face and a voice said, "Breathe deeply."

Jennifer felt hands raise the hospital gown and spread her legs apart.

It was going to happen. It was going to happen now. Young Adam, Young Adam, Young Adam.

"I want you to relax," Dr. Linden said.

Jennifer nodded. *Good-bye, my baby.* She felt a cold, steel object begin to move between her thighs and slowly slide up inside her. It was the alien instrument of death that was going to murder Adam's baby.

She heard a strange voice scream out, "Stop it! Stop it! Stop it!"

And Jennifer looked up at the surprised faces staring down at her and realized that the screams were coming from her. The mask pressed down harder against her face. She tried to sit up, but there were straps holding her down. She was being sucked into a vortex that was moving faster and faster, drowning her.

The last thing she remembered was the huge white light in the ceiling whirling above her, spinning down and going deep inside her skull.

When Jennifer awakened, she was lying in the hospital bed in her room. Through the window she could see that it was dark outside. Her body felt sore and battered, and she wondered how long she had been unconscious. She was alive, but her baby – ?

She reached for the bell pinned to her bed and pressed it. She kept pressing it, frantic, unable to stop herself.

A nurse appeared in the doorway, then quickly left. A few moments later Dr. Linden hurried in. He moved to the side of the bed and gently pried Jennifer's fingers away from the bell.

Jennifer grabbed his arm fiercely and said in a hoarse voice, "My baby – he's dead!" – !"

Dr. Linden said, "No, Mrs. Parker. He's alive. I hope it's a boy. You kept calling him Adam."

28

Christmas came and went, and it was a new year, 1973. The snows of February gave way to the brisk winds of March, and Jennifer knew that it was time to stop working.

She called a meeting of the office staff.

"I'm taking a leave of absence," Jennifer announced. "I'll be gone for the next five months."

There were murmurs of surprise.

Dan Martin asked, "We'll be able to reach you, won't we?"

"No, Dan. I'll be out of touch."

Ted Harris peered at her through his thick spectacles. "Jennifer, you can't just – "

"I'll be leaving at the end of this week."

There was a finality in her tone that brooked no further questions. The rest of the meeting was taken up with a discussion of pending cases.

When everyone else had left, Ken Bailey asked, "Have you really thought this thing through?"

"I have no choice, Ken."

He looked at her. "I don't know who the son of a bitch is, but I hate him."

Jennifer put her hand on his arm. "Thank you. I'll be all right."

"It's going to get rough, you know. Kids grow up. They ask questions. He'll want to know who his father is."

"I'll handle it."

"Okay." His tone softened. "If there's anything I can do – anything – I'll always be around."

She put her arms around him. "Thank you, Ken. I – thank you."

Jennifer stayed in her office long after everyone else had left, sitting alone in the dark, thinking. She would always love Adam. Nothing could ever change that, and she was sure that he still loved her. *Somehow*, Jennifer thought, *it would be easier if he did not*. It was an unbearable irony that they loved each other and could not be together, that their lives were going to move farther and farther apart. Adam's life would be in Washington now with Mary Beth and their child. Perhaps one day Adam would be in the White House. Jennifer thought of her own son growing up, wanting to know who his father was. She could never tell him, nor must Adam ever know that she had borne him a child, for it would destroy him.

And if anyone else ever learned about it, it would destroy Adam in a different way.

Jennifer had decided to buy a house in the country, somewhere outside of Manhattan, where she and her son could live together in their own little world.

She found the house by sheer accident. She had been on her way to see a client on Long Island and had turned off the Long Island Expressway at Exit 36, then had taken a wrong turn and found herself in Sands Point. The streets were quiet and shaded with tall, graceful trees, and the houses were set back from the road, each in its private little domain. There was a *For Sale* sign in front of a white colonial house on Sands Point Road. The grounds were fenced in and there was a lovely wrought-iron gate in front of a sweeping driveway, with lamp posts lighting the way, and a large front lawn with a row of yews sheltering the house. From the outside it looked enchanting. Jennifer wrote down the name of the realtor and made an appointment to see the house the following afternoon.

The real estate agent was a hearty, high-pressure type, the kind of salesman Jennifer hated. But she was not buying his personality, she was buying a house.

He was saying, "It's a real beauty. Yessir, a *real* beauty. About a hundred years old. It's in tip-top condition. Absolutely tip-top."

Tip-top was certainly an exaggeration. The rooms were airy and spacious, but in need of repair. *It would be fun*, Jennifer thought, *to fix up this house and decorate it.*

Upstairs, across from the master suite, was a room that could be converted into a nursery. She would do it in blue and –

"Like to walk around the grounds?"

It was the tree house that decided Jennifer. It was built on a platform high up in a sturdy oak tree. Her son's tree house. There were three acres, with the back lawn gently sloping down to the sound, where there was a dock. It would be a wonderful place for her son to grow up in, with plenty of room for him to run around. Later, he would have a small boat. There would be all the privacy here that they would need, for Jennifer was determined that this was going to be a world that belonged only to her and her child.

She bought the house the following day.

Jennifer had had no idea how painful it would be to leave the Manhattan apartment she and Adam had shared. His bathrobe and pajamas were still there, and his slippers and shaving kit. Every room held hundreds of memories of Adam, memories of a lovely, dead past. Jennifer packed her things as quickly as possible and got out of there.

At the new house, Jennifer kept herself busy from early morning until late at night, so that there would be no time to think about Adam. She went into the shops in Sands Point and Port Washington to order furniture and drapes. She bought Porthault linens, and silver and china. She hired local workmen to come in and repair the faulty plumbing and leaky roof and worn-out electrical equipment. From early morning until dusk, the house was filled with painters, carpenters, electricians and wallpaper hangers. Jennifer was everywhere, supervising everything. She wore herself out during the day, hoping she would be able to sleep at night, but the demons had returned, torturing her with unspeakable nightmares.

She haunted antique shops, buying lamps and tables and objets d'art. She bought a fountain and statues for the garden, a Lipschitz, a Noguchi and a Miró.

Inside the house, everything was beginning to look beautiful.

Bob Clement was a California client of Jennifer's and the area rugs he had designed for the living room and the nursery made the rooms glow with subdued color.

Jennifer's abdomen was getting bigger, and she went into the village to buy maternity clothes. She had an unlisted telephone installed. It was there only for emergencies, and she gave no one the telephone number and expected no calls. The only person in the office who knew where she lived was Ken Bailey, and he was sworn to secrecy.

He drove out to see Jennifer one afternoon, and she showed him around the house and grounds and took enormous pleasure in his delight.

"It's beautiful, Jennifer. Really beautiful. You've done a hell of a job." He looked at her swollen abdomen. "How long is it going to be?"

"Another two months." She put his hand against her belly and said, "Feel this."

He felt a kick.

"He's getting stronger every day," Jennifer said proudly.

She cooked dinner for Ken. He waited until they were having dessert before he brought up the subject.

"I don't want to pry," he said, "but shouldn't whoever the proud papa is be doing something – ?"

"Subject closed."

"Okay. Sorry. The office misses you like hell. We have a new client who – "

Jennifer held up a hand "I don't want to hear about it."

They talked until it was time for Ken to leave, and Jennifer hated to see him go. He was a dear man and a good friend.

Jennifer shut herself off from the world in every possible way. She stopped reading the newspapers and would not watch television or listen to the radio. Her universe was here within these four walls. This was her nest, her womb, the place where she was going to bring her son into the world.

She read every book she could get her hands on about raising children, from Dr. Spock to Ames and Gesell and back again.

When Jennifer finished decorating the nursery, she filled it with toys. She visited a sporting goods shop and looked at footballs and baseball bats and a catcher's mitt. And she laughed at herself. *This is ridiculous. He hasn't even been born yet.* And she bought the baseball bat and the catcher's mitt. The football tempted her, but she thought, *That can wait.*

It was May, and then June.

The workmen finished and the house became quiet and serene. Twice a week Jennifer would drive into the village and shop at the supermarket, and every two weeks she would visit Dr. Harvey, her obstetrician. Jennifer obediently drank more milk than she wanted, took vitamins and ate all the proper, healthy foods. She was getting large now and clumsy, and it was becoming difficult for her to move about.

She had always been active, and she had thought she would loathe getting heavy and awkward, having to move slowly; but somehow, she did not mind it. There was no reason to hurry anymore. The days became long and dreamy and peaceful. Some diurnal clock within her had slowed its tempo. It was as though she were reserving her energy, pouring it into the other body living inside her.

One morning, Dr. Harvey examined her and said, "Another two weeks, Mrs. Parker."

It was so close now. Jennifer had thought she might be afraid. She had heard all the old wives' tales of the pain, the accidents, the malformed babies, but she felt no fear, only a longing to see her child, an impatience to get his birth over with so she could hold him in her arms.

Ken Bailey drove out to the house almost every day now, bringing with him *The Little Engine That Could, Little Red Hen, Pat the Bunny*, and a dozen Dr. Seuss books.

"He'll love these," Ken said.

And Jennifer smiled, because he had said "he." *An omen.*

They strolled through the grounds and had a picnic lunch at the water's edge and sat in the sun. Jennifer was self-conscious about her looks. She thought, *Why would he want to waste his time with the ugly fat lady from the circus?*

And Ken was looking at Jennifer and thinking: *She's the most beautiful woman I've ever seen.*

The first pains came at three o'clock in the morning. They were so sharp that Jennifer was left breathless. A few moments later they were repeated and Jennifer thought exultantly, *It's happening!*

She began to count the time between the pains, and when they were ten minutes apart she telephoned her obstetrician. Jennifer drove to the hospital, pulling over to the side of the road every time a contraction came. An attendant was standing outside waiting for her when she arrived, and a few minutes later Dr. Harvey was examining her.

When he finished, he said reassuringly, "Well, this is going to be an easy delivery, Mrs. Parker. Just relax and we'll let nature take its course."

It was not easy, but neither was it unbearable. Jennifer could stand the pain because out of it something wonderful was happening. She was in labor for almost eight hours, and at the end of that time, when her body was wracked and contorted with spasms and she thought that it was never going to stop, she felt a quick easing and then a rushing emptiness, and a sudden blessed peace.

She heard a thin squeal and Dr. Harvey was holding up her baby, saying, "Would you like to take a look at your son, Mrs. Parker?"

Jennifer's smile lit the room.

29

His name was Joshua Adam Parker and he weighed in at eight pounds, six ounces, a perfectly formed baby. Jennifer knew that babies were supposed to be ugly at birth, wrinkled and red and resembling little apes. Not Joshua Adam. He was beautiful. The nurses at the hospital kept telling Jennifer what a handsome boy Joshua was, and Jennifer could not hear it often enough. The resemblance to Adam was striking. Joshua Adam had his father's gray-blue eyes and beautifully shaped head. When Jennifer looked at him, she was looking at Adam. It was a strange feeling, a poignant mixture of joy and sadness. How Adam would have loved to see his handsome son!

When Joshua was two days old he smiled up at Jennifer and she excitedly rang for the nurse.

"Look! He's smiling!"

"It's gas, Mrs. Parker."

"With other babies it might be gas," Jennifer said stubbornly. "My son is smiling."

Jennifer had wondered how she would feel about her baby, had worried whether she would be a good mother. Babies were surely boring to be around. They messed their diapers, demanded to be fed constantly, cried and slept. There was no communication with them.

I won't really feel anything about him until he's four or five years old, Jennifer had thought. How wrong, how wrong. From the moment of Joshua's birth, Jennifer loved her son with a love she had never known existed in her. It was a fiercely protective love. Joshua was so small, and the world so large.

When Jennifer brought Joshua home from the hospital, she was given a long list of instructions, but they only served to panic her. For the first two weeks a practical nurse stayed at the house. After that, Jennifer was on her own, and she was terrified she might do something wrong that would kill the baby. She was afraid he might stop breathing at any moment.

The first time Jennifer made Joshua's formula, she realized she had forgotten to sterilize the nipple. She threw the formula in the sink and started all over again. When she had finished she remembered she had forgotten to sterilize the bottle. She began again. By the time Joshua's meal was ready, he was screaming with rage.

There were times when Jennifer did not think she would be able to cope. At unexpected moments she was overwhelmed with feelings of unexplained depression. She told herself that it was the normal postpartum blues, but the explanation did not make her feel any better. She was constantly exhausted. It seemed to her that she was up all night giving Joshua his feedings and when she did finally manage to drop off to sleep, Joshua's cries would awaken her and Jennifer would stumble back into the nursery.

She called the doctor constantly, at all hours of the day and night.

"Joshua's breathing too fast" . . . "He's breathing too slowly" . . . "Joshua's coughing" . . . "He didn't eat his dinner" . . . "Joshua vomited."

In self-defense, the doctor finally drove to the house and gave Jennifer a lecture.

"Mrs. Parker, I've never seen a healthier baby than your son. He may *look* fragile, but he's as strong as an ox. Stop worrying about him and enjoy him. Just remember one thing – he's going to outlive both of us!"

And so Jennifer began to relax. She had decorated Joshua's bedroom with print curtains and a bedspread with a blue background sprigged with white flowers and yellow butterflies. There was a crib, a play pen, a miniature matching chest and desk and chair, a rocking horse, and the chest full of toys.

Jennifer loved holding Joshua, bathing and diapering him, taking him for airings in his shiny new perambulator. She talked to him constantly, and when Joshua was four weeks old he rewarded her with a smile. *Not gas*, Jennifer thought happily. *A smile!*

The first time Ken Bailey saw the baby, he stared at it for a long time. With a feeling of sudden panic, Jennifer thought, *He's going to recognize it. He's going to know it's Adam's baby.*

But all Ken said was, "He's a real beauty. He takes after his mother."

She let Ken hold Joshua in his arms and she laughed at Ken's awkwardness. But she could not help thinking, *Joshua will never have a father to hold him.*

Six weeks had passed and it was time to go back to work. Jennifer hated the idea of being away from her son, even for a few hours a day, but the thought of returning to the office filled her with excitement. She had completely cut herself off from everything for so long. It was time to re-enter her other world.

She looked in the mirror and decided the first thing she had to do was get her body back in shape. She had been dieting and exercising since shortly after Joshua's birth, but now she went at it even more strenuously, and soon she began to look like her old self.

Jennifer started to interview housekeepers. She examined them as though each one was a juror: she probed, looking for weaknesses, lies, incompetence. She interviewed more than twenty potential candidates before she found one she liked and trusted, a middle-aged Scotswoman named Mrs. Mackey, who had worked for one family for fifteen years and had left when the children had grown up and gone away to school.

Jennifer had Ken check her out, and when Ken assured her that Mrs. Mackey was legitimate, Jennifer hired her.

A week later Jennifer returned to the office.

30

Jennifer Parker's sudden disappearance had created a spate of rumors around Manhattan law offices.

When word got out on the grapevine that Jennifer was back, the interest was enormous. The reception that Jennifer received on the morning she returned kept swelling, as attorneys from other offices dropped by to visit her.

Cynthia, Dan and Ted had hung streamers across the room and a huge *Welcome Back* sign. There was champagne and cake.

"At nine o'clock in the morning?" Jennifer protested.

But they insisted.

"It's been a madhouse here without you," Dan Martin told her. "You're not planning to do this again, are you?"

Jennifer looked at him and said, "No. I'm not planning to do this again."

Unexpected visitors kept dropping in to make sure Jennifer was all right and to wish her well.

She parried questions about where she had been with a smile and "We're not allowed to tell."

She held conferences all day with the members of her staff. Hundreds of telephone messages had accumulated.

When Ken Bailey was in Jennifer's office alone with her, he said, "You know who's been driving us nuts trying to reach you?"

Jennifer's heart leaped. "Who?"

"Michael Moretti."

"Oh."

"He's weird. When we wouldn't tell him where you were, he made us swear you were all right."

"Forget about Michael Moretti."

Jennifer went over all the cases that were being handled by the office. Business was excellent. They had acquired a lot of important new clients. Some of the older clients refused to deal with anyone but Jennifer, and were waiting for her return.

"I'll call them as soon as I can," Jennifer promised.

She went through the rest of the telephone messages. There were a dozen calls from Mr. Adams. Perhaps she should have let Adam know that she was all right, that nothing had happened to her. But she knew she could not bear hearing his voice, knowing he was close and that she would not be able to see him, touch him, hold him. Tell him about Joshua.

Cynthia had clipped news stories she thought would be of interest to Jennifer. There was a syndicated series on Michael Moretti, calling him the most important Mafia leader in the country. There was a photograph of him and under it the caption, *I'm just an insurance salesman.*

It took Jennifer three months to catch up on her backlog of cases She could have handled it more rapidly, but she insisted on leaving the office at four o'clock every day, no matter what she was involved in. Joshua was waiting.

Mornings, before Jennifer went to the office, she made Joshua's breakfast herself and spent as much time as possible playing with him before she left.

When Jennifer came home in the afternoon, she devoted all of her time to Joshua. She forced herself to leave her business problems at the office, and turned down any cases that would take her away from her son. She stopped working weekends. She would let nothing intrude on her private world.

She loved reading aloud to Joshua.

Mrs. Mackey protested, "He's an infant, Mrs. Parker. He doesn't understand a word you're saying."

Jennifer would reply confidently, "Joshua understands."

And she would go on reading.

Joshua was a series of unending miracles. When he was three months old he began cooing and trying to talk to Jennifer. He amused himself in his crib with a large, tinkling ball and a toy bunny that Ken had brought him. When he was six months old, he was already trying to climb out of his crib, restless to explore the world. Jennifer held him in her arms and he grabbed her fingers with his tiny hands and they carried on long and serious conversations.

Jennifer's days at the office were full. One morning she received a call from Philip Redding, president of a large oil corporation.

"I wonder if we could meet," he said. "I have a problem."

Jennifer did not have to ask him what it was. His company had been accused of paying bribes in order to do business in the Middle East. There would be a large fee for handling the case, but Jennifer simply did not have the time.

"I'm sorry," she said. "I'm not available, but I can recommend someone who's very good."

"I was told not to take no for an answer," Philip Redding replied.

"By whom?"

"A friend of mine. Judge Lawrence Waldman."

Jennifer heard the name with disbelief. "Judge Waldman asked you to call me?"

"He said you're the best there is, but I already knew that."

Jennifer held the receiver in her hand, thinking of her previous experiences with Judge Waldman, how sure she had been that he hated her and was out to destroy her.

"All right. Let's have breakfast tomorrow morning," Jennifer said.

When she had hung up, she placed a call to Judge Waldman.

The familiar voice came on the telephone. "Well. I haven't talked to you in some time, young lady."

"I wanted to thank you for having Philip Redding call me."

"I wanted to make certain he was in good hands."

"I appreciate that, Your Honor."

"How would you like to have dinner with an old man one evening?"

Jennifer was taken by surprise. "I'd love having dinner with you."

"Fine. I'll take you to my club. They're a bunch of old fogies and they're not used to beautiful young women. It'll shake them up a bit."

Judge Lawrence Waldman belonged to the Century Association on West 43rd Street, and when he and Jennifer met there for dinner she saw that he had been teasing about old fogies. The dining room was filled with authors, artists, lawyers and actors.

"It is the custom not to make introductions here," Judge Waldman explained to Jennifer. "It's assumed that every person is immediately recognizable."

Seated at various tables, Jennifer recognized Louis Auchincloss, George Plimpton and John Lindsay, among others.

Socially, Lawrence Waldman was totally different from what Jennifer had expected. Over cocktails he said to Jennifer, "I once wanted to see you disbarred because I thought you had disgraced our profession. I'm convinced that I was wrong. I've been watching you closely. I think you're a credit to the profession."

Jennifer was pleased. She had encountered judges who were venal, stupid or incompetent. She respected Lawrence Waldman. He was both a brilliant jurist and a man of integrity.

"Thank you, Your Honor."

"Off the bench, why don't we make it Lawrence and Jennie?"

Her father was the only one who had ever called her Jennie.

"I'd like that, Lawrence."

The food was excellent and that dinner was the beginning of a monthly ritual they both enjoyed tremendously.

31

It was the summer of 1974. Incredibly, a year had flown by since Joshua Adam Parker had been born. He had taken his first tottering steps and he understood the words for nose and mouth and head.

"He's a genius," Jennifer flatly informed Mrs. Mackey.

Jennifer planned Joshua's first birthday party as though it were being given at the White House. On Saturday she shopped for gifts. She bought Joshua clothes and books and toys, and a tricycle he would not be able to use for another year or two. She bought favors for the neighbors' children she had invited to the party, and she spent the afternoon putting up streamers and balloons. She baked the birthday cake herself and left it on the kitchen table. Somehow, Joshua got hold of the cake and grabbed handfuls of it and crammed it into his mouth, ruining it before the other guests arrived.

Jennifer had invited a dozen children from the neighborhood, and their mothers. The only adult male guest was Ken Bailey. He brought Joshua a tricycle, a duplicate of the one Jennifer had bought.

Jennifer laughed and said, "That's ridiculous, Ken. Joshua's not old enough for that."

The party only lasted two hours, but it was splendid. The children ate too much and were sick on the rug, and fought over the toys and cried when their balloons burst, but all in all, Jennifer decided, it was a triumph. Joshua had been a perfect host, handling himself, with the exception of a few minor incidents, with dignity and aplomb.

That night, after all the guests had left and Joshua had been put to bed, Jennifer sat at his bedside watching her sleeping son, marveling at this wonderful creature that had come from her body and the loins of Adam Warner. Adam would have been so proud to have seen how Joshua had behaved. Somehow, the joy was diminished because it was hers alone.

Jennifer thought of all the birthdays to come. Joshua would be two years old, then five, then ten and twenty. And he would be a man and he would leave her. He would make his own life for himself.

Stop it! Jennifer scolded herself. *You're feeling sorry for yourself.* She lay in bed that night, wide awake, reliving every detail of the party, remembering it all.

One day, perhaps, she could tell Adam about it.

32

In the months that followed, Senator Adam Warner was becoming a household word. His background, ability and charisma had made him a presence in the Senate from the beginning. He won a place on several important committees and he sponsored a piece of major labor legislation that passed quickly and easily. Adam Warner had powerful friends in Congress. Many had known and respected his father. The consensus was that Adam was going to be a presidential contender one day. Jennifer felt a bittersweet pride.

Jennifer received constant invitations from clients, associates and friends to dinner and the theater and various charity affairs, but she refused almost all of them. From time to time she would spend an evening with Ken. She enjoyed his company immensely. He was funny and self-deprecating, but beneath the facade of lightness, Jennifer knew, there was a sensitive, tormented man. He would sometimes come to the house for lunch or dinner on weekends, and he would play with Joshua for hours. They loved each other.

Once, when Joshua had been put to bed and Jennifer and Ken were having dinner in the kitchen, Ken kept staring at Jennifer until she asked, "Is anything wrong?"

"Christ, yes," Ken groaned. "I'm sorry. What a bitch of a world this is."

And he would say nothing further.

Adam had not tried to get in touch with Jennifer in almost nine months now, but she avidly read every newspaper and magazine article about him, and watched him whenever he appeared on television. She thought about him constantly. How could she not? Her son was a living reminder of Adam's presence. Joshua was two years old now and incredibly like his father. He had the same serious blue eyes and the identical mannerisms. Joshua was a tiny, dear replica, warm and loving and full of eager questions.

To Jennifer's surprise, Joshua's first words had been *car-car*, when she took him for a drive one day.

He was speaking in sentences now and he said *please* and *thank you*. Once, when Jennifer was trying to feed him in his high chair, he said impatiently, "Mama, go play with your toys."

Ken had bought Joshua a paint set, and Joshua industriously set about painting the walls of the living room.

When Mrs. Mackey wanted to spank him, Jennifer said, "Don't. It will wash off. Joshua's just expressing himself."

"That's all *I* wanted to do," Mrs. Mackey sniffed. "Express myself. You'll spoil that boy rotten."

But Joshua was not spoiled. He was mischievous and demanding, but that was normal for a two-year-old. He was afraid of the vacuum cleaner, wild animals, trains and the dark.

Joshua was a natural athlete. Once, watching him at play with some of his friends, Jennifer turned to Mrs. Mackey and said, "Even though I'm Joshua's mother, I'm able to look at him objectively, Mrs. Mackey. I think he may be the Second Coming."

Jennifer had made it a policy to avoid any cases that would take her out of town and away from Joshua, but one morning she received an urgent call from Peter Fenton, a client who owned a large manufacturing firm.

"I'm buying a factory in Las Vegas and I'd like you to fly down there and meet with their lawyers."

"Let me send Dan Martin," Jennifer suggested. "You know I don't like to go out of town, Peter."

"Jennifer, you can wrap the whole thing up in twenty-four hours. I'll fly you down in the company plane and you'll be back the next day."

Jennifer hesitated. "All right."

She had been to Las Vegas and was indifferent to it. It was impossible to hate Las Vegas or to like it. One had to look upon it as a phenomenon, an alien civilization with its own language, laws and morals. It was like no other city in the world. Huge neon lights blazed all night long, proclaiming the glories of the magnificent palaces that had been built to deplete the purses of tourists who flocked in like lemmings and lined up to have their carefully hoarded savings taken away from them.

Jennifer gave Mrs. Mackey a long and detailed list of instructions about taking care of Joshua.

"How long are you going to be away, Mrs. Parker?"

"I'll be back tomorrow."

"Mothers!"

Peter Fenton's Lear jet picked Jennifer up early the next morning and flew her to Las Vegas. Jennifer spent the after noon and evening working out the details of the contract. When they finished, Peter Fenton asked Jennifer to have dinner with him.

"Thank you, Peter, but I think I'll stay in my room and get to bed early. I'm returning to New York in the morning."

Jennifer had talked to Mrs. Mackey three times during the day and had been reassured each time that little Joshua was fine. He had eaten his meals, he had no fever and he seemed happy.

"Does he miss me?" Jennifer asked.

"He didn't say," Mrs. Mackey sighed.

Jennifer knew that Mrs. Mackey thought she was a fool, but Jennifer did not care.

"Tell him I'll be home tomorrow."

"I'll give him the message, Mrs. Parker."

Jennifer had intended to have a quiet dinner in her suite, but for some reason, the rooms suddenly became oppressive, the walls seemed to be closing in on her. She could not stop thinking about Adam.

How could he have made love to Mary Beth and made her pregnant when . . .

The game Jennifer always played, that her Adam was just away on a business trip and would soon return to her, did not work this time. Jennifer's mind kept returning to a picture of Mary Beth in her lace negligee and Adam.

She had to get out, to be somewhere where there were noisy crowds of people. *Perhaps,* Jennifer thought, *I might even see a show.* She quickly showered, dressed and went downstairs.

Marty Allen was starring in the main show room. There was a long line at the entrance to the room for the late show, and Jennifer regretted that she had not asked Peter Fenton to make a reservation for her.

She went up to the captain at the head of the line and said, "How long a wait will there be for a table?"

"How many in your party?"

"I'm alone."

"I'm sorry, miss, but I'm afraid – "

A voice beside her said, "My booth, Abe."

The captain beamed and said, "Certainly, Mr. Moretti. This way, please."

Jennifer turned and found herself looking into the deep black eyes of Michael Moretti.

"No, thank you," Jennifer said. "I'm afraid I – "

"You have to eat." Michael Moretti took Jennifer's arm and she found herself walking beside him, following the captain to a choice banquette in the center of the large room. Jennifer loathed the idea of dining with Michael Moretti, but she did not know how to get out of it now without creating a scene. She wished fervently that she had agreed to have dinner with Peter Fenton.

They were seated at a banquette facing the stage and the captain said, "Enjoy your dinner, Mr. Moretti, miss."

Jennifer could feel Michael Moretti's eyes on her and it made her uncomfortable. He sat there, saying nothing. Michael Moretti was a man of deep silences, a man who distrusted words, as though they were a trap rather than a form of communication. There was something riveting about his silence. Michael Moretti used silence the way other men used speech.

When he finally spoke, Jennifer was caught off guard.

"I hate dogs," Michael Moretti said. "They die."

And it was as though he was revealing a private part of himself that came from some deep wellspring. Jennifer did not know what to reply.

Their drinks arrived and they sat there drinking quietly, and Jennifer listened to the conversation they were not having.

She thought about what he had said: *I hate dogs. They die.* She wondered what Michael Moretti's early life had been like. She found herself studying him. He was attractive in a dangerous, exciting way. There was a feeling of violence about him, ready to explode.

Jennifer could not say why, but being with this man made her feel like a woman. Perhaps it was the way his ebony black eyes looked at her, then looked away from her, as though fearful of revealing too much. Jennifer realized it had been a long time since she had thought of herself as a woman. From the day she had lost Adam. *It takes a man to make a woman feel female*, Jennifer thought, *to make her feel beautiful, to make her feel wanted.*

Jennifer was grateful he could not read her mind.

Various people approached their booth to pay their respects to Michael Moretti: business executives, actors, a judge, a United States senator. It was power paying tribute to power, and Jennifer began to feel a sense of how much influence he wielded.

"I'll order for us," Michael Moretti said. "They prepare this menu for eight hundred people. It's like eating on an airline."

He raised his hand and the captain was at his side instantly. "Yes, Mr. Moretti. What would you like tonight, sir?"

"We'll have a *Chateaubriand*, pink and charred."

"Of course, Mr. Moretti."

"*Pommes soufflées* and an endive salad."

"Certainly, Mr. Moretti."

"We'll order dessert later."

A bottle of champagne was sent to the table, compliments of the management.

Jennifer found herself beginning to relax, enjoying herself almost against her will. It had been a long while since she had spent an evening with an attractive man. And even as the phrase came into Jennifer's mind, she thought, *How can I think of Michael Moretti as attractive? He's a killer, an amoral animal with no feelings.*

Jennifer had known and defended dozens of men who had committed terrible crimes, but she had the feeling that none of them was as dangerous as this man. He had risen to the top of the Syndicate and it had taken more than a marriage to Antonio Granelli's daughter to accomplish that.

"I telephoned you once or twice while you were away," Michael said. According to Ken Bailey, he had called almost every day. "Where were you?" He made the question sound casual.

"Away."

A long silence. "Remember that offer I made you?"

Jennifer took a sip of her champagne. "Don't start that again, please."

"You can have any – "

"I told you, I'm not interested. There's no such thing as an offer you can't refuse. That's only in books, Mr. Moretti. I'm refusing."

Michael Moretti thought of the scene that had taken place in his father-in-law's home a few weeks earlier. There had been a meeting of the Family and it had not gone well. Thomas Colfax had argued against everything that Michael had proposed.

When Colfax had left, Michael had said to his father-in-law, "Colfax is turning into an old woman. I think it's time to put him out to pasture, Papa."

"Tommy's a good man. He's saved us a lot of trouble over the years."

"That's history. He doesn't have it anymore."

"Who would we get to take his place?"

"Jennifer Parker."

Antonio Granelli had shaken his head. "I told you, Michael. It ain't good to have a woman know our business."

"This isn't just a woman. She's the best lawyer around."

"We'll see," Antonio Granelli had said. "We'll see."

Michael Moretti was a man who was used to getting what he wanted, and the more Jennifer stood up to him, the more he was determined to have her. Now, sitting next to her, Michael looked at Jennifer and thought, *One day you're going to belong to me, baby – all the way.*

"What are you thinking about?"

Michael Moretti gave Jennifer a slow, easy smile, and she instantly regretted the question. It was time to leave.

"Thank you for a wonderful dinner, Mr. Moretti. I have to get up early, so – "

The lights began to dim and the orchestra started an overture.

"You can't leave now. The show is starting. You'll love Marty Allen."

It was the kind of entertainment that only Las Vegas could afford to put on, and Jennifer thoroughly enjoyed it. She told herself she would leave immediately after the show, but when it was over and Michael Moretti asked Jennifer to dance, she decided it would be ungracious to refuse. Besides, she had to admit to herself that she was having a good time. Michael Moretti was a skillful dancer, and Jennifer found herself relaxing in his arms. Once, when another couple collided with them, Michael was pushed against Jennifer and for an instant she felt his male hardness, and then he immediately pulled away, careful to hold her at a discreet distance.

Afterward, they walked into the casino, a vast terrain of bright lights and noise, packed with gamblers engrossed in various games of chance, playing as though their lives depended on their winning. Michael took Jennifer to one of the dice tables and handed her a dozen chips.

"For luck," he said.

The pit boss and dealers treated Michael with deference, calling him *Mr. M.* and giving him large piles of hundred-dollar chips, taking his markers instead of cash. Michael played for large stakes and lost heavily, but he seemed unperturbed. Using Michael's chips, Jennifer won three hundred dollars, which she insisted on giving to Michael. She had no intention of being under any obligation to him.

From time to time during the course of the evening, various women came up to greet Michael. All of them were young and attractive, Jennifer noticed. Michael was polite to them, but it was obvious that he was only interested in Jennifer. In spite of herself, she could not help feeling flattered.

Jennifer had been tired and depressed at the beginning of the evening, but there was such a vitality about Michael Moretti that it seemed to spill over, charging the air, enveloping Jennifer.

Michael took her to a small bar where a jazz group was playing, and afterward they went on to the lounge of another hotel to hear a new singing group. Everywhere they went Michael was treated like royalty. Everyone tried to get his attention, to say hello to him, to touch him, to let him know they were there.

During the time they were together, Michael did not say one word at which Jennifer could take offense. And yet, Jennifer felt such a strong sexuality coming from him that it was like a series of waves beating at her. Her body felt bruised, violated. She had never experienced anything like it. It was a disquieting feeling and, at the same time, exhilarating. There was a wild, animal vitality about him that Jennifer had never encountered before.

It was four o'clock in the morning when Michael finally walked Jennifer back to her suite. When they reached Jennifer's door, Michael took her hand and said, "Good night. I just want you to know this has been the greatest night of my life."

His words frightened Jennifer.

33

In Washington, Adam Warner's popularity was growing. He was written up in the newspapers and magazines with increasing frequency. Adam started an investigation of ghetto schools, and headed a Senate committee that went to Moscow to meet with dissidents. There were newspaper photographs of his arrival at Sheremetyevo Airport, being greeted by unsmiling Russian officials. When Adam returned ten days later, the newspapers gave warm praise to the results of his trip.

The coverage kept expanding. The public wanted to read about Adam Warner and the media fed their appetite. Adam became the spearhead for reform in the Senate. He headed a committee to investigate conditions in federal penitentiaries, and he visited prisons around the country. He talked to the inmates and guards and wardens, and when his conmittee's report was turned in, extensive reforms were begun.

In addition to the news magazines, women's magazines ran articles about him. In *Cosmopolitan*, Jennifer saw a picture of Adam, Mary Beth and their little daughter, Samantha. Jennifer sat by the fireplace in her bedroom and looked at the picture for a long, long time. Mary Beth was smiling into the camera, exuding sweet, warm southern charm. The daughter was a miniature of her mother. Jennifer turned to the picture of Adam. He looked tired. There were small lines around his eyes that had not been there before, and his sideburns were beginning to be tinged with gray. For a moment, Jennifer had the illusion that she was seeing the face of Joshua, grown up. The resemblance was uncanny. The photographer had had Adam turn directly into the camera, and it seemed to Jennifer that he was looking at her. She tried to read the expression in his eyes, and she wondered whether he ever thought about her.

Jennifer turned to look again at the photograph of Mary Beth and her daughter. Then she threw the magazine into the fireplace and watched it burn.

Adam Warner sat at the head of his dinner table, entertaining Stewart Needham and half a dozen other guests. Mary Beth sat at the other end of the table, making small talk with a senator from Oklahoma and his bejeweled wife. Washington had been like a stimulant to Mary Beth. She was in her element here. Because of Adam's increasing importance, Mary Beth had become one of Washington's top hostesses and she reveled in that position. The social side of Washington bored Adam, and he was glad to leave it to Mary Beth. She handled it well and he was grateful to her.

"In Washington," Stewart Needham was saying, "more deals get made over dinner tables than in the hallowed halls of Congress."

Adam looked around the table and wished that this evening were over. On the surface, everything was wonderful. Inside, everything was wrong. He was married to one woman and in love with another. He was locked into a marriage from which there was no escape. If Mary Beth had not become pregnant, Adam knew he would have gone ahead with the divorce. It was too late now; he was committed. Mary Beth had given him a beautiful little daughter and he loved her, but it was impossible to get Jennifer out of his mind.

The wife of the governor was speaking to him.

"You're so lucky, Adam. You have everything in the world a man could want, don't you?"

Adam could not bring himself to answer.

34

The seasons came and went and they revolved around Joshua. He was the center of Jennifer's world. She watched him grow and develop, day by day, and it was a never-ending wonder as he began to walk and talk and reason. His moods changed constantly and he was, in turn, wild and aggressive and shy and loving. He became upset when Jennifer had to leave him at night, and he was still afraid of the dark, so Jennifer always left a night light on for him.

When Joshua was two years old he was impossible, a typical "Terrible Two." He was destructive and stubborn and violent. He loved to "fix" things. He broke Mrs. Mackey's sewing machine, ruined the two television sets in the house and took Jennifer's wristwatch apart. He mixed the salt with the sugar and fondled himself when he thought he was alone. Ken Bailey brought Jennifer a German shepherd puppy, Max, and Joshua bit it.

When Ken came to the house to visit, Joshua greeted him with, "Hi! Do you have a ding-dong? Can I see it?"

That year, Jennifer would gladly have given Joshua away to the first passing stranger.

At three, Joshua suddenly became an angel, gentle, affectionate and loving. He had the physical coordination of his father, and he loved doing things with his hands. He no longer broke things. He enjoyed playing outdoors, climbing and running and riding his tricycle.

Jennifer took him to the Bronx Zoo and to marionette plays. They walked along the beach and saw a festival of Marx Brothers movies in Manhattan, and had ice cream sodas afterward at Old Fashioned Mr. Jennings on the ninth floor of Bonwit Teller.

Joshua had become a companion. As a Mother's Day gift, Joshua learned a favorite song of Jennifer's father – *Shine On, Harvest Moon* – and sang it to Jennifer. It was the most touching moment of her life.

It's true, Jennifer thought, *that we do not inherit the world from our parents; we borrow it from our children.*

Joshua had started nursery school and was enjoying it. At night when Jennifer came home, they would sit in front of the fireplace and read together. Jennifer would read *Trial Magazine* and *The Barrister* and Joshua would read his picture books. Jennifer would watch Joshua as he sprawled out on the floor, his brow knit in concentration, and she would suddenly be reminded of Adam. It was still like an open wound. She wondered where Adam was and what he was doing.

What he and Mary Beth and Samantha were doing.

Jennifer managed to keep her private and professional life separate, and the only link between the two was Ken Bailey.

He brought Joshua toys and books and played games with him and was, in a sense, a surrogate father.

One Sunday afternoon Jennifer and Ken stood near the tree house, watching Joshua climb up to it.

"Do you know what he needs?" Ken asked.

"No."

"A father." He turned to Jennifer. "His real father must be one prize shit."

"Please don't, Ken."

"Sorry. It's none of my business. That's the past. It's the future I'm concerned about. It isn't natural for you to be living alone like – "

"I'm not alone. I have Joshua."

"That's not what I'm talking about." He took Jennifer in his arms and kissed her gently. "Oh, God damn it, Jennifer. I'm sorry . . ."

Michael Moretti had telephoned Jennifer a dozen times. She returned none of his calls. Once she thought she caught a glimpse of him sitting in the back of a courtroom where she was defending a case, but when she looked again he was gone.

35

Late one afternoon as Jennifer was getting ready to leave the office, Cynthia said, "There's a Mr. Clark Holman on the phone."

Jennifer hesitated, then said, "I'll take it."

Clark Holman was an attorney with the Legal Aid Society.

"Sorry to bother you, Jennifer," he said, "but we have a case downtown that no one wants to touch, and I'd really appreciate it if you could help us out. I know how busy you are, but – "

"Who's the defendant?"

"Jack Scanlon."

The name registered instantly. It had been on the front pages of the newspapers for the past two days. Jack Scanlon had been arrested for kidnapping a four-year-old girl and holding her for ransom. He had been identified from a composite drawing the police had obtained from witnesses to the abduction.

"Why me, Clark?"

"Scanlon asked for you."

Jennifer looked at the clock on the wall. She was going to be late for Joshua. "Where is he now?"

"At the Metropolitan Correctional Center."

Jennifer made a quick decision. "I'll go down and talk to him. Make the arrangements, will you?"

"Right. Thanks a million. I owe you one."

Jennifer telephoned Mrs. Mackey. "I'm going to be a little late. Give Joshua his dinner and tell him to wait up for me."

Ten minutes later, Jennifer was on her way downtown.

To Jennifer, kidnapping was the most vicious of all crimes, particularly the kidnapping of a helpless young child; but every accused person was entitled to a hearing no matter how terrible the crime. That was the foundation of the law: justice for the lowliest as well as the highest.

Jennifer identified herself to the guard at the reception desk and was taken to the Lawyers' Visiting Room.

The guard said, "I'll get Scanlon for you."

A few minutes later a thin, aesthetic-looking man in his late thirties, with a blond beard and light blond hair was brought into the room. He looked almost Christlike.

He said, "Thank you for coming, Miss Parker." His voice was soft and gentle. "Thank you for caring."

"Sit down."

He took a chair opposite Jennifer.

"You asked to see me?"

"Yes. Even though I think only God can help me. I've done a very foolish thing."

She regarded him distastefully. "You call kidnapping a helpless little girl for ransom a 'foolish thing'?"

"I didn't kidnap Tammy for ransom."

"Oh? Why *did* you kidnap her?"

There was a long silence before Jack Scanlon spoke. "My wife, Evelyn, died in childbirth. I loved her more than anything in the world. If ever there was a saint on earth, it was that woman. Evelyn wasn't a strong person. Our doctor advised her not to have a baby, but she didn't listen." He looked down at the floor in embarrassment. "It – it may be hard for you to understand, but she said she wanted it anyway, because it would be like having another part of me."

How well Jennifer understood that.

Jack Scanlon had stopped speaking, his thoughts far away.

"So she had the baby?"

Jack Scanlon nodded. "They both died." It was difficult for him to go on. "For a while, I – I thought I would . . . I didn't want to go on living without her. I kept wondering what our child would have been like. I kept dreaming about how it would have been if they had lived. I kept trying to turn the clock back to the moment before Evelyn – " He stopped, his voice choked with pain. "I turned to the Bible and it saved my sanity. *Behold, I have set before you an open door which no one is able to shut*. Then, a few days ago, I saw a little girl playing on the street, and it was as though Evelyn had been reincarnated. She had her eyes, her hair. She looked up at me and smiled and I – I know it sounds crazy, but it was Evelyn smiling at me. I must have been out of my head. I thought to myself, *This is the daughter Evelyn would have had. This is our child.*"

Jennifer could see his fingernails digging into his flesh.

"I know it was wrong, but I took her." He looked up into Jennifer's eyes. "I wouldn't have harmed that child for anything in the world."

Jennifer was studying him closely, listening for a false note. There was none. He was a man in agony.

"What about the ransom note?" Jennifer asked.

"I didn't send a ransom note. The last thing in the world I cared about was money. I just wanted little Tammy."

"*Someone* sent the family a ransom note."

"The police keep saying I sent it, but I didn't."

Jennifer sat there, trying to fit the pieces together. "Did the story of the kidnapping appear in the newspapers before or after you were picked up by the police?"

"Before. I remember wishing they'd stop writing about it. I wanted to go away with Tammy and I was afraid someone would stop us."

"So anyone could have read about the kidnapping and tried to collect a ransom?"

Jack Scanlon twisted his hands helplessly. "I don't know. All I know is I want to die."

His pain was so obvious that Jennifer found herself moved by it. If he was telling the truth – and it was naked in his face – then he did not deserve to die for what he had done. He should be punished, yes, but not executed.

Jennifer made her decision. "I'm going to try to help you."

He said quietly, "Thank you. I really don't care anymore what happens to me."

"I do."

Jack Scanlon said, "I'm afraid I – I have no money to give you."

"Don't worry about it. I want you to tell me about yourself."

"What do you want to know?"

"Start from the beginning. Where were you born?"

"In North Dakota, thirty-five years ago. I was born on a farm. I guess you could call it a farm. It was a poor piece of land that nothing much wanted to grow on. We were poor. I left home when I was fifteen. I loved my mother, but I hated my father. I know the Bible says it's wrong to speak evil of your parents, but he was a wicked man. He enjoyed whipping me."

Jennifer could see his body tighten as he went on.

"I mean, he really enjoyed it. If I did the smallest thing he thought was wrong, he would whip me with a leather belt that had a big brass buckle on it. Then he'd make me get down on my knees and pray to God for forgiveness. For a long time I hated God as much as I hated my father." He stopped, too filled with memories to speak.

"So you ran away from home?"

"Yes. I hitchhiked to Chicago. I didn't have much schooling, but at home I used to read a lot. Whenever my father caught me, that was an excuse for another whipping. In Chicago, I got a job working in a factory. That's where I met Evelyn. I cut my hand on a milling machine and they took me to the dispensary, and there she was. She was a practical nurse. He smiled at Jennifer. "She was the most beautiful woman I'd ever seen. It took about two weeks before my hand was healed, and I went to her for a treatment every day. After that, we just kind of started going together. We talked about getting married, but the company lost a big order and I was laid off with the rest of the people in my department. That didn't matter to Evelyn. We got married and she took care of me. That was the only thing we ever argued about. I was brought up to believe that a man should take care of a woman. I got a job driving a truck and the money was good. The only part I hated was that we were separated, sometimes for a week at a time. Outside of that, I was awfully happy. We were both happy. And then Evelyn got pregnant."

A shudder ran through him. His hands began to tremble.

"Evelyn and our baby girl died." Tears were running down his cheeks. "I don't know why God did that. He must have had a reason, but I don't know why." He was rocking back and forth in his chair, unaware of what he was doing, his arms clasped in front of his chest, holding in his grief. "*I will instruct you and teach you the way you should go; I will counsel you.*"

Jennifer thought, *This one the electric chair is not going to get!*

"I'll be back to see you tomorrow," Jennifer promised him.

Bail had been set at two hundred thousand dollars. Jack Scanlon did not have the bond money and Jennifer had it put up for him. Scanlon was released from the Correctional Center and Jennifer found a small motel on the West Side for him to move into. She gave him a hundred dollars to tide him over.

"I don't know how," Jack Scanlon said, "but I'll pay you back every cent. I'll start looking for a job. I don't care what it is. I'll do anything."

When Jennifer left him, he was searching through the want ads.

The federal prosecutor, Earl Osborne, was a large, heavy-set man with a smooth round face and a deceptively bland manner. To Jennifer's surprise, Robert Di Silva was in Osborne's office.

"I heard you were taking on this case," Di Silva said. "Nothing's too dirty for you to handle, is it?"

Jennifer turned to Earl Osborne. "What's he doing here? This is a federal case."

Osborne replied, "Jack Scanlon took the girl away in her family's car."

"Auto theft, grand larceny," Di Silva said.

Jennifer wondered if Di Silva would have been there if she were not involved. She turned back to Earl Osborne.

"I'd like to make a deal," Jennifer said. "My client – "

Earl Osborne held up a hand. "Not a chance. We're going all the way on this one."

"There are circumstances – "

"You can tell us all about it at the preliminary."

Di Silva was grinning at her.

"All right," Jennifer said. "I'll see you in court."

Jack Scanlon found a job working at a service station on the West Side near his motel, and Jennifer stopped by to see him.

"The preliminary hearing is the day after tomorrow," Jennifer informed him. "I'm going to try to get the government to agree to a plea bargain and plead you guilty to a lesser charge. You'll have to serve some time, Jack, but I'll try to see that it's as short as possible."

The gratitude in his face was reward enough.

At Jennifer's suggestion, Jack Scanlon had bought a respectable suit to wear at the preliminary hearing. He had had his hair cut and his beard trimmed, and Jennifer was pleased with his appearance.

They went through the court formalities. District Attorney Di Silva was present. When Earl Osborne had presented his evidence and asked for an indictment, Judge Barnard turned to Jennifer.

"Is there anything you would like to say, Miss Parker?"

"There is, Your Honor. I'd like to save the government the cost of a trial. There are mitigating circumstances here that have not been brought out. I would like to plead my client guilty to a lesser charge."

"No way," Earl Osborne said. "The government will not agree to it."

Jennifer turned to Judge Barnard. "Could we discuss this in Your Honor's chambers?"

"Very well. I'll set a date for the trial after I've heard what counsel has to say."

Jennifer turned to Jack Scanlon, who was standing there, bewildered.

"You can go back to work," Jennifer told him. "I'll drop by and let you know what happened."

He nodded and said quietly, "Thank you, Miss Parker."

Jennifer watched him turn and leave the courtroom.

Jennifer, Earl Osborne, Robert Di Silva and Judge Barnard were seated in the judge's chambers.

Osborne was saying to Jennifer, "I don't know how you could even ask me to plea-bargain. Kidnapping for ransom is a capital offense. Your client is guilty and he's going to pay for what he did."

"Don't believe everything you read in the newspapers, Earl. Jack Scanlon had nothing to do with that ransom note."

"Who you trying to kid? If it wasn't for ransom, what the hell *was* it for?"

"I'll tell you" Jennifer said.

And she told them. She told them about the farm and the beatings and about Jack Scanlon falling in love with Evelyn and marrying her, and losing his wife and daughter in child-birth.

They listened in silence, and when Jennifer was finished, Robert Di Silva said, "So Jack Scanlon kidnapped the girl because it reminded him of the kid he would have had? And Jack Scanlon's wife died in childbirth?"

"That's right." Jennifer turned to Judge Barnard. "Your Honor, I don't think that's the kind of man you execute."

Di Silva said unexpectedly, "I agree with you."

Jennifer looked at him in surprise.

Di Silva was pulling some papers out of a briefcase. "Let me ask you something," he said. "How would you feel about executing *this* kind of man?" He began to read from a dossier. "Frank Jackson, age thirty-eight. Born in Nob Hill, San Francisco. Father was a doctor, mother a prominent socialite. At fourteen, Jackson got into drugs, ran away from home, picked up in Haight-Ashbury and returned to his parents. Three months later Jackson broke into his father's dispensary, stole all the drugs he could get his hands on and ran away. Picked up in Seattle for possession and selling, sent to a reformatory, released when he was eighteen, picked up one month later on a charge of armed robbery with intent to kill . . ."

Jennifer could feel her stomach tightening. "What does this have to do with Jack Scanlon?"

Earl Osborne gave her a frosty smile. "Jack Scanlon is. Frank Jackson."

"I don't believe it!"

Di Silva said, "This yellow sheet came in from the FBI an hour ago. Jackson's a con artist and a psychopathic liar. Over the last ten years he's been arrested on charges raging from pimping to arson to armed robbery. He did a stretch in Joliet. He's never held a steady job and he's never been married. Five years ago he was picked up by the FBI on a kidnapping charge. He kidnapped a three-year-old girl and sent a ransom note. The body of the little girl was found in a wooded area two months later. According to the coroner's report, the body was partially decomposed, but there were visible signs of small knife cuts all over her body. She had been raped and sodomized."

Jennifer felt suddenly ill.

"Jackson was acquitted on a technicality that some hotshot lawyer cooked up." When Di Silva spoke again his voice was filled with contempt. "That the man you want walking around the streets?"

"May I see that dossier, please?"

Silently, Di Silva handed it to Jennifer and she began reading it. It was Jack Scanlon. There was no question about it. There was a police mug shot of him stapled to the yellow sheet. He had looked younger then and he had no beard, but there was no mistaking him. Jack Scanlon – Frank Jackson – had lied to her about everything. He had made up his life story and Jennifer had believed every word. He had been so convincing that she had not even taken the trouble to have Ken Bailey check him out.

Judge Barnard said, "May I see that?"

Jennifer handed the dossier to him. The judge glanced through it and then looked at Jennifer. "Well?"

"I won't represent him."

Di Silva raised his eyebrows in mock surprise. "You shock me, Miss Parker. You're always saying that everyone is entitled to a lawyer."

"Everyone is," Jennifer replied evenly, "but I have a hard and fast rule: I won't represent anyone who lies to me. Mr. Jackson will have to get himself another lawyer."

Judge Barnard nodded. "The court will arrange that."

Osborne said, "I'd like his bail revoked immediately, Your Honor. I think he's too dangerous to be walking the streets."

Judge Barnard turned to Jennifer. "As of this moment you're still the attorney of record, Miss Parker. Do you have any objection to that?"

"No," Jennifer said tightly. "None."

Judge Barnard said, "I'll order his bail revoked."

Judge Lawrence Waldman had invited Jennifer to a charity dinner that evening. She had felt drained after the events of the afternoon and would have preferred to go home and have a quiet evening with Joshua, but she did not want to disappoint the judge. She changed clothes at the office and met Judge Waldman at the Waldorf-Astoria, where the party was taking place.

It was a gala event, with half a dozen Hollywood stars entertaining, but Jennifer was unable to enjoy it. Her mind was elsewhere. Judge Waldman had been watching her.

"Is anything wrong, Jennie?"

She managed a smile. "No, just a business problem, Lawrence."

And what kind of business am I really in, Jennifer wondered, *dealing with the dregs of humanity, the rapists and killers and kidnappers?* She decided it would be a wonderful night to get drunk.

The captain came over to the table and whispered in Jennifer's ear. "Excuse me, Miss Parker, there's a telephone call for you."

Jennifer felt an instant sense of alarm. The only one who knew where to reach her was Mrs. Mackey. She could only be calling because something was wrong.

"Excuse me," Jennifer said.

She followed the captain to a small office off the lobby.

Jennifer picked up the receiver and a man's voice whispered, "You bitch! You double-crossed me."

Jennifer felt her body begin to tremble. "Who is this?" she asked.

But she knew.

"You told the cops to come and get me."

"That's not true! I – "

"You promised to help me."

"I will help you. Where are – ?"

"You lying cunt!" His voice dropped so low she could hardly make out his words. "You're going to pay for this. Oh, you're going to pay for this!"

"Wait a min – "

The telephone was dead. Jennifer stood there, chilled. Something had gone terribly wrong. Frank Jackson, alias Jack Scanlon, had somehow escaped and he was blaming Jennifer for what had happened. How had he known where she was? He must have followed her here. He could be waiting outside for her now.

Jennifer was trying to control the trembling of her body, trying to think, to reason out what had happened. He had seen the police coming to arrest him, or perhaps they had picked him up and he had gotten away from them. *How* did not matter. The important thing was that he was blaming her for what had happened.

Frank Jackson had killed before and he could kill again. Jennifer went into the ladies' room and stayed there until she was calm again. When she had regained control of herself, she returned to the table.

Judge Waldman took one look at her face. "What on earth's happened?"

Jennifer told him briefly. He was aghast.

"Good God! Would you like me to drive you home?"

"I'll be all right, Lawrence. If you could just make sure I get to my car safely, I'll be fine."

They quietly slipped out of the large ballroom and Judge Waldman stayed with Jennifer until the attendant brought her car.

"You're certain you don't want me to come with you?"

"Thanks. I'm sure the police will pick him up before morning. There aren't many people walking around who look like him. Good night."

Jennifer drove off, making sure no one was following her. When she was certain she was alone, she turned onto the Long Island Expressway and headed for home.

She kept looking in her rearview mirror, checking the cars behind her. Once she pulled off the road to let all the traffic pass her, and when the road behind her was clear, she drove on. She felt safer now. It could not be many hours before the police picked up Frank Jackson. There would be a general alert out for him by this time.

Jennifer turned into her driveway. The grounds and the house, which should have been brightly lighted, were dark. She sat in the car staring at the house unbelievingly, her mind beginning to shriek with alarm. Frantically, she tore the car door open and raced to the front door. It was ajar. Jennifer stood there for an instant, filled with terror, then stepped into the reception hall. Her foot kicked something warm and soft and she let out an involuntary gasp. She turned on the lights. Max lay on the blood-soaked rug. The dog's throat had been cut from ear to ear.

"Joshua!" It was a scream. "Mrs. Mackey!"

Jennifer ran from room to room, switching on all the lights and calling out their names, her heart pounding so hard that it was difficult for her to breathe. She raced up the stairs to Joshua's bedroom. His bed had been slept in, but it was empty.

Jennifer searched every room in the house, then raced downstairs, her mind numb. Frank Jackson must have known all along where she lived. He had followed her home one night from her office or after she left the service station. He had taken Joshua and he was going to kill him to punish her.

She was passing the laundry room when she heard a faint scrabbling sound coming from the closet. Jennifer moved toward the closed door slowly and pulled it open. It was black inside.

A voice whimpered, "Please don't hurt me any more."

Jennifer turned on the light. Mrs. Mackey was lying on the floor, her hands and feet tightly bound with wire. She was only half-conscious.

Jennifer quickly knelt beside her. "Mrs. Mackey!"

The older woman looked up at Jennifer and her eyes began to focus.

"He took Joshua." She began to sob.

As gently as she could, Jennifer untwisted the wire that was cutting into Mrs.

Mackey's arms and legs. They were raw and bleeding. Jennifer helped the housekeeper to her feet.

Mrs. Mackey cried hysterically. "I c-couldn't stop him. I t-tried. I – "

The sound of the telephone cut into the room. The two women were instantly silenced. The telephone rang again and again, and somehow it had an evil sound. Jennifer walked over to it and picked it up.

The voice said, "I just wanted to make sure you got home all right."

"*Where is my son?*"

"He is a beautiful boy, isn't he?" the voice asked.

"Please! I'll do anything. Anything you like!"

"You've already done everything, Mrs. Parker."

"No, please!" She was sobbing helplessly.

"I like to hear you cry," the voice whispered. "You'll get your son back, Mrs. Parker. Read tomorrow's papers."

And the line went dead.

Jennifer stood there, fighting against the faintness, trying to think. Frank Jackson had said, "He *is* a beautiful boy, isn't he?" That could mean Joshua was still alive. Otherwise, wouldn't he have said *was* beautiful? She knew she was simply playing games with words, trying to keep her sanity. She had to do something quickly.

Her first impulse was to telephone Adam, ask him to help. It was his son who had been kidnapped, his son who was going to be killed. But she knew there was nothing Adam could do. He was two hundred and thirty-five miles away. She had only two choices: one was to call Robert Di Silva, tell him what had happened and ask him to throw out a dragnet to try to catch Frank Jackson. *Oh, God, that will take too long!*

The second choice was the FBI. They were trained to handle kidnappings. The problem was that this was not like other kidnapping. There would be no ransom note for them to trace, no chance to try to trap Frank Jackson and save Joshua's life. The FBI moved according to its own strict ritual. It would not be of any help in this instance. She had to decide quickly . . . while Joshua was still alive. Robert Di Silva or the FBI. It was difficult to think.

She took a deep breath and made her decision. She looked up a telephone number. Her fingers were trembling so badly she had to dial the number three times before she got it right.

When a man answered, Jennifer said, "I want to speak to Michael Moretti."

36

"Sorry, lady. This is Tony's Place. I don't know no Mike Moretti."

"Wait!" Jennifer screamed. "Don't hang up!" She forced a calmness into her voice. "This is urgent. I'm a – a friend of his. My name is Jennifer Parker. I need to talk to him right away."

"Look, lady, I said – "

"Give him my name and this telephone number."

She gave him the number. Jennifer was beginning to stutter so badly she could hardly speak. "T-t-tell him – "

The line went dead.

Numbly, Jennifer replaced the receiver. She was back to one of her first two choices. Or both of them. There was no reason why Robert Di Silva and the FBI could not join forces to try to find Joshua. The thing that was driving her mad was that she knew how little chance they would have of finding Frank Jackson. There was no time. *Read tomorrow's papers.* There was a finality about his last words that made Jennifer certain he would not telephone her again, would not give anyone a chance to trace him. But she had to do *something.* She would try Di Silva. She reached for the telephone again. It rang as she touched it, startling her.

"This is Michael Moretti."

"Michael! Oh, Michael, help me, please! I – " She began to sob uncontrollably. She dropped the telephone, then picked it up again quickly, terrified he had hung up. "*Michael?*"

"I'm here." His voice was calm. "Get hold of yourself and tell me what's wrong."

"I – I'll – " She took in quick, deep breaths, trying to stop the trembling. "It's my son, Joshua. He's – he's been kidnapped. They're going to – kill him."

"Do you know who took him?"

"Y-yes. His name is F-Frank Jackson." Her heart was pounding.

"Tell me what happened." His voice was quiet and confident.

Jennifer forced herself to talk slowly, recounting the sequence of events.

"Can you describe what Jackson looks like?"

Jennifer conjured up a picture of him in her mind. She put the picture into words, and Michael said, "You're doing fine. Do you know where he served time?"

"At Joliet. He told me he's going to kill – "

"Where was the gas station he worked at?"

She gave Michael the address.

"Do you know the name of the motel he was staying at?"

"Yes. No." She could not remember. She dug her fingernails into her forehead until it began to bleed, forcing herself to think. He waited patiently.

It came to her suddenly. "It's the Travel Well Motel. It's on Tenth Avenue. But I'm sure he isn't there now."

"Well see."

"I want my son back alive."

Michael Moretti did not reply and Jennifer understood why.

"If we find Jackson – ?"

Jennifer took a deep, shuddering breath. "*Kill him!*"

"Stay by your telephone."

The connection was broken. Jennifer replaced the receiver. She felt strangely calmer, as though something had been accomplished. There was no reason to feel the confidence she did in Michael Moretti. From a logical point of view, it was a wild, insane thing to have done; but logic had nothing to do with this. Her son's life was at stake. She had deliberately sent a killer to catch a killer. If it did not work . . . She thought of the little girl whose body had been raped and sodomized.

Jennifer went to tend to Mrs. Mackey. She took care of her cuts and bruises and put her to bed. Jennifer offered her a sedative, but Mrs. Mackey pushed it away

"I couldn't sleep," she cried. "Oh, Mrs. Parker! He gave that baby sleeping pills."

Jennifer stared at her in horror.

Michael Moretti sat at his desk, facing the seven men he had summoned. He had already given instructions to the first three.

He turned to Thomas Colfax. "Tom, I want you to use your connections. Go down and see Captain Notaras and have him pull the package on Frank Jackson. I want everything they've got on him."

"We're wasting a good connection, Mike. I don't think – "

"Don't argue! Just do it."

Colfax said stiffly, "Very well."

Michael turned to Nick Vito. "Check out the gas station where Jackson worked. Find out if he hung around any of the bars there, if he had any friends."

To Salvatore Fiore and Joseph Colella: "Get over to Jackson's motel. He's probably gone by now, but find out if he palled around with anyone. I want to know who his buddies were. He looked at his watch. "It's midnight. I'm giving you eight hours to find Jackson."

The men started out the door.

Michael called after them, "I don't want anything to happen to the kid. Keep calling in. I'll be waiting."

Michael Moretti watched them leave, then picked up one of the telephones on his desk and began to dial.

1:00 A.M.

The motel room was not large, but it was very neat. Frank Jackson liked things neat. He felt it was part of being brought up properly. The venetian blinds were rolled down and slanted so that no one could see into the room. The door was locked and chained, and he had pressed a chair against it. He walked over to the bed where Joshua lay. Frank Jackson had forced three sleeping pills down the boy's throat, and he was still sleeping soundly. Still, Jackson prided himself on being a man who took no chances, so Joshua's hands and feet were tightly bound together with the same kind of wire that had been used to tie up the old lady in the house. Jackson looked down at the sleeping boy and he was filled with a sense of sadness.

Why in God's name did people keep forcing him to do these terrible things? He was a gentle, peaceful man, but when everyone was against you, when everyone attacked you, you had to defend yourself. The trouble with everybody was that they always underestimated him. They failed to realize until too late that he was smarter than all of them.

He had known the police were coming for him half an hour before they arrived. He had been filling the tank of a Chevrolet Camaro and had seen his boss go inside the office to answer the telephone. Jackson had not been able to hear the conversation, but it was not necessary. He saw the covert looks his boss. gave him as he whispered into the telephone. Frank Jackson knew immediately what was happening. The police were coming for him. The Parker bitch had double-crossed him, had told the police to lock him up. She was like all the rest of them. His boss was still talking on the telephone when Frank Jackson grabbed his jacket and disappeared. It had taken him less than three minutes to find an unlocked car on the street and hot-wire it, and moments later he was headed for Jennifer Parker's house.

Jackson really had to admire his own intelligence. Who else would have thought of following her to find out where she lived? He had done that the day she had gotten him out on bail. He had parked across the street from her house and had been surprised when Jennifer had been met at the gate by a little boy. He had watched them together and sensed even then that the kid might come in handy. He was an unexpected bonus, what the poets called a hostage to fate.

Jackson smiled to himself at how terrified the old bitch of a housekeeper had been. He had enjoyed twisting the wire into her wrists and ankles. No, not enjoyed, really. He was being too hard on himself. It had been *necessary.* The housekeeper had thought he was going to rape her. She disgusted him. All women did, except for his sainted mother. Women were dirty, unclean, even his whore of a sister. It was only the children who were pure. He thought of the last little girl he had taken. She had been beautiful, with long blond curls, but she had had to pay for her mother's sins. Her mother had had Jackson fired from his job. People tried to keep you from earning an honest living and then punished you when you broke their stupid laws. The men were bad enough, but the women were worse. Pigs who wanted to soil the temple of your body. Like the waitress, Clara, he was going to take to Canada. She was in love with him. She thought he was such a gentleman because he had never touched her. If she only knew! The idea of making love to her sickened him. But he was going to take her out of the country with him because the police would be looking for a man alone. He would shave off his beard and trim his hair, and when he crossed the border he would get rid of Clara. That would give him great pleasure.

Frank Jackson walked over to a battered cardboard suitcase on a luggage rack, opened it and took out a tool kit. From it he removed nails and a hammer. He laid them on the bed side table next to the sleeping boy. Then he went into the bathroom and lifted a two-gallon gasoline can from the bath tub. He carried it into the bedroom and set the can on the floor. Joshua was going to go up in flames. But that would be *after* the crucifixion.

2:00 A.M.

Throughout New York and around the country, the word was spreading. It started in bars and flophouses. A cautious word here and there, dropped into a willing ear. It began as a trickle and spread to cheap restaurants and noisy discotheques and all-night newsstands. It was picked up by taxi drivers and truckers and girls working the midnight streets. It was like a pebble dropped into a deep, dark lake, with the ripples beginning to widen and spread. Within a couple of hours everyone on the street knew that Michael Moretti wanted some information and wanted it fast. Not many people were given a chance to do a favor for Michael Moretti. This was a golden opportunity for somebody, because Moretti was a man who knew how to show his appreciation. The word was that he was looking for a thin blond guy who looked like Jesus. People began searching their memories.

2:15 A.M.

Joshua Adam Parker stirred in his sleep and Frank Jackson moved to his side. He had not yet removed the boy's pajamas. Jackson checked to make sure that the hammer and nails were in place and ready. It was important to be meticulous about these things. He was going to nail the boy's hands and feet to the floor before he set the room on fire. He could have done it while the boy was asleep, but that would have been wrong. It was important that the boy be awake to see what was happening, to know he was being punished for the sins of his mother. Frank Jackson looked at his watch. Clara was coming to the motel to pick him up at seven-thirty. Five hours and fifteen minutes left. Plenty of time.

Frank Jackson sat down and studied Joshua, and once he tenderly fondled an errant lock of the small boy's hair.

3:00 A.M.

The first of the telephone calls began coming in.

There were two telephones on Michael Moretti's desk and it seemed that the moment he picked up one, the other started ringing.

"I got a line on the guy, Mike. A couple years ago he was workin' a scam in Kansas City with Big Joe Ziegler and Mel Cohen."

"Fuck what he was doing a couple of years ago. Where is he *now?*"

"Big Joe says he ain't heard from him in about six months. I'm tryin' to get hold of Mel Cohen."

"Do it!"

The next phone call was no more productive.

"I went over to Jackson's motel room. He checked out. He was carryin' a brown suitcase and a two-gallon can that coulda had gasoline in it. The clerk has no idea where he went."

"What about the neighborhood bars?"

"One of the bartenders recognized his description, but he says he wasn't a regular. He went in two or three times after work."

"Alone?"

"Accordin' to the bartender, yeah. He didn't seem interested in the girls there."

"Check out the gay bars."

The telephone rang again almost as soon as Michael had hung up. It was Salvatore Fiore.

"Colfax talked to Captain Notaras. The police property clerk got a record of a pawn ticket in Frank Jackson's personal effects. I got the number of the ticket and the name of the pawn shop. It's owned by a Greek, Gus Stavros, who fences hot rocks."

"Did you check it out?"

"We can't check it out until mornin', Mike. The place is closed. I – "

Michael Moretti exploded. "We can't *wait* until morning! Get your ass down there!"

There was a telephone call from Joliet. It was hard for Michael to follow the conversation because his caller had had a laryngectomy and his voice sounded as if it was coming from the bottom of a box.

"Jackson's cellmate was a man named Mickey Nicola. They were pretty tight."

"Any idea where Nicola is now?"

"Last I heard he was back east somewhere. He's a friend of Jackson's sister. We have no address on her."

"What was Nicola sent up for?"
"They nailed him on a jewelry heist."

3:30 A.M.

The pawnshop was located in Spanish Harlem at Second Avenue and 124th Street. It was in an unloved two-story building, with the shop downstairs and living quarters upstairs.

Gus Stavros was awakened by a flashlight shining in his face. He instinctively started to reach for the alarm button at the side of his bed.

"I wouldn't," a voice said.

The flashlight moved away and Gus Stavros sat up in bed. He looked at the two men standing on either side of him and knew he had been given good advice. A giant and a midget. Stavros could feel an asthma attack coming on.

"Go downstairs and take whatever you want," he wheezed. "I won't make a move."

The giant, Joseph Colella said, "Get up. Slow."

Gus Stavros rose from his bed, cautious not to make any sudden movements.

The small man, Salvatore Fiore, shoved a piece of paper under his nose. "This is the number of a pawn ticket. We want to see the merchandise."

"Yes, sir."

Gus Stavros walked downstairs, followed by the two men. Stavros had installed an elaborate alarm system only six months earlier. There were bells he could have pushed and secret places on the floor he could have stepped on and help would be on its way. He did none of those things because his instincts told him he would be dead before anyone could reach him. He knew that his only chance lay in giving the two men what they wanted. He only prayed he would not die from a goddamned asthma attack before he got rid of them.

He turned on the downstairs lights and they all moved toward the front of the shop. Gus Stavros had no idea what was going on, but he knew it could have been a great deal worse. If these men had come merely to rob him, they could have cleaned out the pawn shop and been gone by now. It seemed they were only interested in one piece of merchandise. He wondered how they had circumvented the elaborate new alarms on the doors and windows, but he decided not to ask.

"Move your ass," Joseph Colella said.

Gus looked at the pawn ticket number again and began to sort through his files. He found what he was looking for, nodded in satisfaction, and went to the large walk-in strong room and opened it, the two men close behind him. Stavros searched along a shelf until he found a small envelope. Turning to the two men, he opened the envelope and took out a large diamond ring that sparkled in the overhead lights.

"This is it," Gus Stavros said. "I gave him five hundred for it." The ring was worth at least twenty thousand dollars.

"You gave five hundred to who?" little Salvatore Fiore asked.

Gus Stavros shrugged. "A hundred customers a day come in here. The name on the envelope is John Doe."

Fiore pulled a piece of lead pipe out of nowhere and smashed it savagely against Gus Stavros' nose. He fell to the floor screaming with pain, drowning in his own blood.

Fiore asked quietly, "Who did you say brought it in?"

Fighting for breath, Gus Stavros gasped, "I don't know his name. He didn't tell me. I swear to God!"

"What did he look like?"

The blood was flowing into Gus Stavros' throat so fast he could hardly speak. He was beginning to faint, but he knew if he passed out before he talked he would never wake up.

"Let me think," he pleaded.

Stavros tried to focus, but he was so dizzy from the pain that it was difficult. He forced himself to remember the customer walking in, taking the ring out of a box and showing it to him. It was coming back to him.

"He – he was kind of blond and skinny – " He choked on some blood. "Help me up."

Salvatore Fiore kicked him in the ribs. "Keep talkin'."

"He had a beard, a blond beard . . ."

"Tell us about the rock. Where did it come from?"

Even in his extreme pain, Gus Stavros hesitated. If he talked, he would be a dead man later. If he did not, he would die now. He decided to postpone his death as long as possible.

"It came from the Tiffany job."

"Who was in on the job with the blond guy?"

Gus Stavros was finding it harder to breathe. "Mickey Nicola."

"Where can we find Nicola?"

"I don't know. He – he shacks up with some girl in Brooklyn."

Fiore lifted a foot and nudged Stavros' nose. Gus Stavros screamed with pain.

Joseph Colella asked, "What's the broad's name?"

"Jackson. Blanche Jackson."

4:30 A.M.

The house was set back from the street, surrounded by a small white picket fence with a carefully tended garden in front. Salvatore Fiore and Joseph Colella tramped through the flowers and made their way to the back door. It took them less than five seconds to open it. They stepped inside and moved toward the stairs. From a bedroom above they could hear the sounds of a bed creaking and the voices of a man and a woman. The two men pulled out their guns and started to move quietly up the stairs.

The woman's voice was saying, "Oh, Christ! You're wonderful, Mickey! Give it to me harder, baby."

"It's all for you, honey, every bit of it. Don't come yet."

"Oh, I won't," the woman moaned. "Let's come to – "

She looked up and screamed. The man whirled around. He started to reach under the pillow but decided against it.

"Okay," he said. "My wallet's in my pants on the chair. Take it and get the hell out of here. I'm busy."

Salvatore Fiore said, "We don't want your wallet, Mickey."

The anger on Mickey Nicola's face turned to something else. He sat up in bed, moving cautiously, trying to figure out the situation. The woman had pulled the sheets up over her breasts, her face a combination of anger and fright.

Nicola carefully swung his feet over the side of the bed, sitting on the edge, ready to spring. His penis had gone limp. He was watching both men, waiting for an opportunity.

"What do you want?"

"Do you work with Frank Jackson?"

"Go fuck yourselves."

Joseph Colella turned to his companion. "Shoot his balls off."

Salvatore Fiore raised his gun and aimed.

Mickey Nicola screamed, "Wait a minute! You guys must be crazy!" He looked into the little man's eyes and said quickly, "Yeah. I've worked with Jackson."

The woman cried out angrily, "Mickey!"

He turned on her savagely. "Shut up! You think I want to be a fuckin' eunuch?"

Salvatore Fiore turned to the woman and said, "You're Jackson's sister, ain't you?"

Her face was filled with fury. "I never heard of him."

Fiore raised his gun and moved closer to the bed. "You got two seconds to talk to me or you two are gonna be splashed all over the wall."

There was something in his voice that chilled her. He raised his gun and the blood began to drain from the woman's face.

"Tell them what they want to know," Mickey Nicola cried.

The gun moved up to press against the woman's breast.

"Don't! Yes! Frank Jackson's my brother."

"Where can we find him?"

"I don't know. I don't see him. I swear to God I don't know! I – "

His hand tightened on the trigger.

She screamed, "*Clara*! Clara would know! Ask Clara!"

Joseph Colella said, "Who's Clara?"

"She's – she's a waitress Frank knows."

"Where can we find her?"

This time there was no hesitation. The words spilled out. "She works at a bar called The Shakers in Queens." Her body began to tremble.

Salvatore Fiore looked at the two of them and said politely, "You can go back to your fuckin' now. Have a nice day."

And the two men departed.

5:30 A.M.

Clara Thomas (nee Thomachevsky) was about to fulfill her lifelong dream. She hummed happily to herself as she packed her cardboard suitcase with the clothes she would need in Canada. She had taken trips with gentlemen friends before, but this was different. This was going to be her honeymoon trip. Frank Jackson was like no other man she had known. The men who came into the bar, pawing her and pinching her buttocks, were nothing but animals. Frank Jackson was different. He was a real gentleman. Clara paused in her packing to think about that word: *gentle man*. She had never thought of it that way before, but that was Frank Jackson. She had seen him only four times in her life, but she knew she was in love with him. She could tell he had been attracted to her from the very beginning, because he always sat at her booth. And after the second time he had walked her home when the bar had closed.

I must still have it, Clara thought smugly, *if I can get a handsome young guy like that*. She stopped her packing to walk over to the closet mirror to study herself. Maybe she was a little too heavy and her hair was a couple of shades too red, but dieting would take care of the extra pounds and she would be more careful the next time she dyed her hair. All in all, she wasn't too dissatisfied with what she saw. *The old broad's still pretty good-lookin'*, she told herself. She knew that Frank Jackson wanted to take her to bed, even though he had never touched her. He was really special. There was an almost – Clara furrowed her forehead, trying to think of the word – *spiritual* quality about him. Clara had been brought up a good Catholic and she knew it was sacrilegious to even think such a thought, but Frank Jackson reminded her a little bit of Jesus. She wondered what Frank would be like in bed. Well, if he was shy, she would show him a trick or two. He had talked about their getting married as soon as they got to Canada. Her dream come true. Clara looked at her watch and decided she had better hurry. She had promised to pick Frank up at his motel at seven-thirty.

She saw them in the mirror as they walked into her bedroom. They had come out of nowhere. A giant and a little fellow. Clara watched as the two of them moved toward her.

The small man looked at the suitcase. "Where you goin', Clara?"

"None of your business. Just take what you want and get out of here. If there's anything in this joint worth more than ten bucks, I'll eat it."

"I got something you can eat," the big man Colella said.

"Up yours, buster," Clara snapped. "If this is gonna be a rape job, I want you to know the doctor's treatin' me for gonorrhea."

Salvatore Fiore said, "We ain't gonna hurt you. We just wanna know where Frank Jackson is."

They could see the change that came over her. Her body suddenly stiffened and her face became a mask.

"Frank Jackson?" There was a note of deep puzzlement in her voice. "I don't know any Frank Jackson."

Salvatore Fiore pulled a lead pipe out of his pocket and took a step toward her.

"You don't scare me," Clara said, "I – "

His arm lashed out across her face, and in the midst of the blinding pain she could feel her teeth crumbling inside her mouth like tiny pieces of grit. She opened her mouth to speak and blood began pouring out. The big man raised his pipe again.

"No, please don't!" She gagged.

Joseph Colella said politely, "Where can we find this Frank Jackson?"

"Frank is – is – "

Clara thought of her sweet, gentle man in the hands of these two monsters. They were going to hurt him and, instinctively, she knew that Frank would not be able to stand the pain. He was too sensitive. If she could only find a way to save him, he would be grateful to her forever.

"I don't know."

Salvatore Fiore moved forward and Clara heard the sound of her leg breaking at the same instant she felt the excruciating pain. She fell to the floor, unable to scream because of all the blood in her mouth.

Joseph Colella stood over her and said pleasantly, "Maybe you don't unnerstand. We ain't gonna kill you. We're just gonna keep breakin' things. When we're through with you, you'll look like a piece of garbage the cat threw away. Do you believe me?"

Clara believed him. Frank Jackson would never want to look at her again. She had lost him to these two bastards. No dream come true, no marriage. The little man was moving forward with the lead pipe again.

Clara moaned, "Don't. Please don't. Frank's at the – the Brookside Motel on Prospect Avenue. He – "

She fainted.

Joseph Colella walked over to the telephone and dialed a number.

Michael Moretti answered. "Yes?"

"Brookside Motel on Prospect Avenue. Want us to take him?"

"No. I'll meet you there. Make sure he doesn't leave."

"He won't go anywhere."

6:30 A.M.

The boy was beginning to stir again. The man watched as Joshua opened his eyes. The boy looked down at the wire on his wrists and legs, and then looked up and saw Frank Jackson, and the memories came flooding back.

This was the man who had pushed those pills down his throat and kidnapped him. Joshua knew all about kidnappings from television. The police would come and save him and put the man in jail. Joshua was determined not to show his fear, because he wanted to be able to tell his mother how brave he had been.

"My mother will be here with the money," Joshua assured the man, "so you don't have to hurt me."

Frank Jackson walked over to the bed and smiled down at the boy. He really was a beautiful child. He wished he could take the boy to Canada instead of Clara. Reluctantly, Frank Jackson looked at his watch. It was time to get things ready.

The boy held up his bound wrists. The blood had caked dry.

"Would you mind taking this off, please?" he asked politely. "I won't run away."

Frank Jackson liked it that the boy had said "please." It showed good manners. These days, most kids had no manners at all. They ran around the streets like wild animals.

Frank Jackson went into the bathroom where he had put the can of gasoline back in the tub so that it would not stain the rug in the living room. He prided himself on details like that. He carried the can into the bedroom and set it down. He moved to the boy's side, lifted up the bound figure and placed him on the floor. Then he picked up the hammer and two large nails and knelt next to the boy.

Joshua Parker was watching him, wide-eyed. "What are you going to do with that?"

"Something that will make you very happy. Have you ever heard of Jesus Christ?" Joshua nodded. "Do you know how he died?"

"On the cross."

"That's very good. You're a bright boy. We don't have a cross here, so we'll have to do the best we can."

The boy's eyes were beginning to fill with fear.

Frank Jackson said, "There's nothing to be afraid of. Jesus wasn't afraid. You mustn't be afraid."

"I don't want to be Jesus," Joshua whispered. "I want to go home."

"I'm going to send you home," Frank Jackson promised. "I'm going to send you home to Jesus."

Frank Jackson took a handkerchief out of his back pocket and moved it toward the boy's mouth. Joshua gritted his teeth together.

"Don't make me angry."

Frank Jackson pressed his thumb and forefinger against Joshua's cheeks and forced his mouth open. He shoved the handkerchief into Joshua's mouth and slapped a piece of tape across it to hold the handkerchief in place. Joshua was straining against the wires that bound his wrists and hands, and they began to bleed again. Frank Jackson ran his hands over the fresh cuts.

"The blood of Christ." he said softly.

He picked up one of the boy's hands, turned it over and held it down against the floor. Then he picked up a nail. Holding it against Joshua's palm with one hand, Frank Jackson picked up the hammer with his other. He drove the nail through the boy's hand into the floor.

*

7:15 A.M.

Michael Moretti's black limousine was stalled on the Brooklyn-Queens Expressway in early morning traffic, held up by a vegetable truck that had overturned and spilled its cargo across the road. Traffic had come to a standstill.

"Pull over to the other side of the road and get past him," Michael Moretti ordered Nick Vito.

"There's a police car up ahead, Mike."

"Go up and tell whoever's in charge that I want to talk to him."

"Right, boss."

Nick Vito got out of the car and hurried toward the squad car. A few moments later he returned with a police sergeant. Michael Moretti opened the window of the car and held out his hand. There were five one hundred dollar bills in it.

"I'm in a hurry, officer."

Two minutes later the police car, red light flashing, was guiding the limousine past the wreckage on the road. When they were clear of the traffic, the sergeant got out of the police car and walked back to the limousine.

"Can I give you an escort somewhere, Mr. Moretti?"

"No, thank you," Michael said. "Come and see me Monday." To Nick Vito: "Move it!"

7:30 A.M.

The neon sign in front read:

BROOKSIDE MOTEL
SINGLES – DOUBLES
DAILY AND WEEKLY RATES
INDIVIDUALES – DOBLES
PRECIOS ESPECIALES

Joseph Colella and Salvatore Fiore sat in their car across from Bungalow 7. A few minutes earlier they had heard a thump from inside, so they knew that Frank Jackson was still there.

We oughta jump in and cool him, Fiore thought. But Michael Moretti had given instructions.

They settled back to wait.

7:45 A.M.

Inside Bungalow 7, Frank Jackson was making his final preparations. The boy was a disappointment. He had fainted. Jackson had wanted to wait until Joshua regained consciousness before the other nails were driven in, but it was getting late. He picked up the can of gasoline and sprinkled it across the boy's body, careful not to let it touch that beautiful face. He visualized the body under the pajamas and wished that he had time to – but, no, that would be foolish. Clara would be here any moment. He must be ready to leave when she arrived. He reached in his pockets, pulled out a box of matches, and set them neatly beside the can of gasoline, the hammer and the nails. People simply did not appreciate how important neatness was.

Frank Jackson looked at his watch again and wondered what was keeping Clara.

7:50 A.M.

Outside Bungalow 7, the limousine skidded to a stop and Michael Moretti jumped out of the car. The two men in the sedan hurried over to join him.

Joseph Colella pointed to Bungalow 7. "He's in there."

"What about the kid?"

The big man shrugged. "Dunno. Jackson's got the curtains drawn."

"Should we go in now and take him?" Salvatore Fiore asked.

"Stay here."

The two men looked at him in surprise. He was a *caporegime*. He had soldiers to make hits for him while he sat back in safety. And yet he was going in himself. It was not right.

Joseph Colella said, "Boss, Sal and I can – "

But Michael Moretti was already moving to the door of Bungalow 7, a gun fitted with a silencer in his hand. He paused for a second to listen, then stepped back and smashed the door open with one powerful kick.

Moretti took in the scene in a single frozen moment: the bearded man kneeling on the floor beside the small boy; the boy's hand nailed to the floor, the room reeking of gasoline.

The bearded man had turned toward the door and was staring at Michael. The last sounds he ever uttered were, "You're not Cl – "

Michael's first bullet took him in the center of his forehead. The second bullet shattered his pharynx, and the third bullet took him in the heart. But by that time he no longer felt anything.

Michael Moretti stepped to the door and waved to the two men outside. They hurried into the cabin. Michael Moretti knelt beside the boy and felt his pulse. It was thin and thready, but he was still alive. He turned to Joseph Colella.

"Call Doc Petrone. Tell him we're on our way over."

9:30 A.M.

The instant the telephone rang, Jennifer snatched it up, squeezing it tightly. "Hello!"

Michael Moretti's voice said, "I'm bringing your son home."

Joshua was whimpering in his sleep. Jennifer leaned over and put her arms around him, holding him gently. He had been asleep when Michael had carried him into the house. When Jennifer had seen Joshua's unconscious body, his wrists and ankles heavily bandaged, his body swathed in gauze, she had nearly gone out of her mind. Michael had brought the doctor with him and it had taken him half an hour to reassure Jennifer that Joshua was going to be all right.

"His hand will heal," the doctor assured her. "There will be a small scar there, but fortunately no nerves or tendons were damaged. The gasoline burns are superficial. I bathed his body in mineral oil. I'll look in on him for the next few days. Believe me, he's going to be fine."

Before the doctor left, Jennifer had him attend to Mrs. Mackey.

Joshua had been put to bed and Jennifer stayed at his side, waiting to reassure him when he awakened. He stirred now and his eyes opened.

When he saw his mother, he said tiredly, "I knew you'd come, Mom. Did you give the man the ransom money?"

Jennifer nodded, not trusting her voice.

Joshua smiled. "I hope he buys too much candy with the money and gets a stomachache. Wouldn't that be funny?"

She whispered, "Very funny, darling. Do you know what you and I are going to do next week? I'm going to take you to – "

Joshua was asleep again.

It was hours later when Jennifer walked back into the living room. She was surprised to see that Michael Moretti was still there. Somehow it reminded her of the first time she had met Adam Warner, when he had waited for her in her little apartment.

"Michael – " It was impossible to find the words. "I – I can't tell you how – how grateful I am."

He looked at her and nodded.

She forced herself to ask the question. "And – and Frank Jackson?"

"He won't bother anyone again."

So it was over. Joshua was safe. Nothing else mattered.

Jennifer looked at Michael Moretti and thought, *I owe him so much. How can I ever repay him?*

Michael was watching her, wrapped in silence.

Book Two

37

Jennifer Parker stood naked, staring out of the large picture window that overlooked the Bay of Tangier. It was a beautiful, crisp autumn day and the bay was filled with skimming white sails and deep-throated power boats. Half a dozen large yachts bobbed at anchor in the harbor. Jennifer felt his presence and turned.

"Like the view?"

"Love it."

He looked at her naked body. "So do I." His hands were on her breasts, caressing them. "Let's go back to bed."

His touch made Jennifer shiver. He demanded things that no man had ever dared ask of her, and he did things to her that had never been done to her before.

"Yes, Michael."

They walked back into the bedroom and there, for one fleeting moment, Jennifer thought of Adam Warner, and then she forgot everything except what was happening to her.

Jennifer had never known anyone like Michael Moretti. He was insatiable. His body was athletic, lean and hard, and it became a part of Jennifer's body, catching her up in its own frenzy, carrying her along on a rising wave of pounding excitement that went on and on until she wanted to scream with a wild joy. When they had finished making love and Jennifer lay there, spent, Michael began once more, and Jennifer was caught up with him again and again in an ecstasy that became almost too much to bear.

Now he lay on top of her, staring into her flushed, happy face. "You love it, don't you, baby?"

"Yes."

There was a shame in it, a shame at how much she needed him, needed his lovemaking.

Jennifer remembered the first time.

It was the morning Michael Moretti had brought Joshua safely back home. Jennifer had known that Frank Jackson was dead and that Michael Moretti had killed him. The man standing in front of her had saved her son for her, had killed for her. It filled Jennifer with some deep, primordial feeling.

"How can I thank you?" Jennifer had asked.

And Michael Moretti had walked over to her, taken her in his arms and kissed her. Out of some old loyalty to Adam, Jennifer had pretended to herself that it would end with that kiss; but instead, it became a beginning. She knew what Michael Moretti was, and yet all that counted as nothing against what he had done. She stopped thinking and let her emotions take over.

They went upstairs to her bedroom, and Jennifer told herself that she was repaying Michael for what he had done for her, and then they were in bed and it was an experience beyond anything that Jennifer had ever dreamed.

Adam Warner had made love to her, but Michael Moretti possessed her. He filled every inch of her body with exquisite sensations. It was as though he were making love in bright, flashing colors, and the colors kept changing from one moment to the next, like some wonderful kaleidoscope. One moment he made love gently and sensitively, and the next moment he was cruel and pounding and demanding, and the changes made Jennifer frantic. He withdrew from her, teasing her, making her want more, and when she was on the verge of fulfillment he pulled away.

When she could stand it no longer, she begged, "Please take me! Take me!"

And his hard organ began to pound into her again until she screamed with pleasure. She was no longer a woman paying back a debt. She was a slave to something she had never known before. Michael stayed with her for four hours, and when he left, Jennifer knew that her life had changed.

She lay in her bed thinking about what had happened, trying to understand it. How could she be so much in love with Adam and still have been so overwhelmed by Michael Moretti? Thomas Aquinas had said that when you got to the heart of evil, there was nothing there. Jennifer wondered if it was also true of love. She was aware that part of what she had done was out of a deep loneliness. She had lived too long with a phantom, a man she could neither see nor have, yet she knew she would always love Adam. Or was it just a memory of that love?

Jennifer was not sure what she felt about Michael. Gratitude, yes. But that was a small part of it. It was more. Much more. She knew who and what Michael Moretti was. He had killed for her, but he had killed for others, too. He had murdered men for money, for power, for vengeance. How could she feel as she did about a man like that? How could she have let him make love to her and have been so excited by him? She was filled with a sense of shame and she thought, *What kind of person am I?*

She had no answer.

The afternoon newspapers reported the story of a fire in a Queens motel. The remains of an unidentified man were found in the ruins. Arson was suspected.

After Joshua's return, Jennifer had tried to make everything as normal for him as possible, fearful of the trauma the preceding night might have inflicted upon him. When Joshua woke up, Jennifer prepared a meal and brought it to him in bed. It was a ridiculous meal, consisting of all the junk foods he loved: a hot dog and a peanut butter sandwich and Fritos and Hostess Twinkies and root beer.

"You should have seen him, Mom," Joshua said between bites. "He was crazy!" He held up his bandaged hand. "Do you think he really thought I was Jesus Christ?"

Jennifer repressed a shudder. "I – I don't know, darling."

"Why do people want to kill other people?"

"Well – " and Jennifer's thoughts suddenly went back to Michael Moretti. Did she have the right to judge him? She did not know the terrible forces that had shaped his life, that had turned him into what he had become. She had to learn more about him, to get to know and understand him.

Joshua was saying, "Do I have to go to school tomorrow?"

Jennifer put her arms around him. "No, darling. We're both going to stay home and play hooky all week. We – "

The telephone rang.

It was Michael. "How's Joshua?"

"He's wonderful – thank you."

"And how are you feeling?"

Jennifer felt her throat thickening with embarrassment. "I'm – I – I feel fine."

He chuckled. "Good. I'll see you for lunch tomorrow. Donato's on Mulberry Street. Twelve-thirty."

"All right, Michael. Twelve-thirty."

Jennifer spoke those words and there was no turning back.

The captain at Donato's knew Michael, and the best table in the restaurant had been reserved for him. People kept stopping by to say hello, and Jennifer was again amazed at the way everyone kowtowed to him. It was strange how much Michael Moretti reminded her of Adam Warner, for each, in his own way, was a man of power.

Jennifer started to question Michael about his background, wanting to learn how and why he had gotten trapped into the life he led.

He interrupted her. "You think I'm in this because of my family or because someone put pressure on me?"

"Well – yes, Michael. Of course."

He laughed. "I worked my butt off to get where I am. I love it. I love the money. I love the power. I'm a king, baby, and I love being king."

Jennifer looked at him, trying to understand. "But you can't enjoy – "

"Listen!" His silence had suddenly turned into words and sentences and confidences, pouring out as though they had been stored inside him for years, waiting for someone to come along to share them with. "My old man was a Coca-Cola bottle."

"A Coca-Cola bottle?"

"Right. There are billions of them in the world and you can't tell one from another. He was a shoemaker. He worked his fingers to the bone, trying to put food on the table. We had nothing. Being poor is only romantic in books. In real life, it's smelly rooms with rats and cockroaches and bad food that you can never get enough of. When I was a young punk, I did anything I could to make a buck.

I ran errands for the big shots, I brought them coffee and cigars, I found them girls – anything to stay alive. Well, one summer I went down to Mexico City. I had no money, nothing. My ass was hanging out. One night a girl I met invited me to a large dinner party at a fancy restaurant. For dessert they served a special Mexican cake with a little clay doll baked inside it. Someone at the table explained that the custom was that whoever got the clay doll had to pay for the dinner. I got the clay doll." He paused. "I swallowed it."

Jennifer put her hand over his. "Michael, other people have grown up poor and – "

"Don't confuse me with other people." His tone was hard and uncompromising. "I'm me. I know who I am, baby. I wonder if you know who you are."

"I think I do."

"Why did you go to bed with me?"

Jennifer hesitated. "Well, I – I was grateful and – "

"Bullshit! You wanted me"

"Michael, I – "

"I don't have to buy my women. Not with money and not with gratitude."

Jennifer admitted to herself that he was right. She *had* wanted him, just as he had wanted her. *And yet*, Jennifer thought, *this man deliberately tried to destroy me once. How can I forget that?*

Michael leaned forward and took Jennifer's hand, palm up. Slowly, he caressed each finger, each mound, never taking his eyes from her.

"Don't play games with me. Not ever, Jennifer."

She felt powerless. Whatever there was between them transcended the past.

It was when they were having dessert that Michael said, "By the way, I have a case for you."

It was as though he had slapped her in the face.

Jennifer stared at him. "What kind of case?"

"One of my boys, Vasco Gambutti, has been arrested for killing a cop. I want you to defend him."

Jennifer sat there filled with hurt and anger that he was still trying to use her.

She said evenly, "I'm sorry, Michael. I told you before. I can't get involved with – with your . . . friends."

He gave her a lazy grin. "Did you ever hear the story about the little lion cub in Africa? He leaves his mother for the first time to go down to the river to get a drink, and a gorilla knocks him down. While he's picking himself up, a big leopard shoves him out of the way. A herd of elephants comes along and almost tramples him to death. The little cub returns home all shaken up and he says, 'You know something, Ma – it's a jungle out there!' "

There was a long silence between them. It *was* a jungle out there, Jennifer thought, but she had always stood at the edge of it, outside it, free to flee whenever she wanted to. She had made the rules and her clients had had to live by them. But now, Michael Moretti had changed all that. This was *his* jungle.

Jennifer was afraid of it, afraid to get caught up in it. Yet, when she thought about what Michael had done for her, she decided it was a small thing he was asking.

She would do Michael this one favor.

38

"We're going to handle the Vasco Gambutti case," Jennifer informed Ken Bailey.

Ken looked at Jennifer in disbelief. "He's Mafia! One of Michael Moretti's hit men. That's not the kind of client we take."

"We're taking this one."

"Jennifer, we can't afford to get mixed up with the mob."

"Gambutti's entitled to a fair trial, just like anyone else." The words sounded hollow, even to her.

"I can't let you – "

"As long as this is my office, I'll make the decisions." She could see the surprise and hurt that came into his eyes.

Ken nodded, turned and walked out of the office. Jennifer was tempted to call him back and try to explain. But how could she? She was not sure she could even explain it to herself.

When Jennifer had her first meeting with Vasco Gambutti, she tried to regard him as just another client. She had handled clients before who were accused of murder, but somehow, this was different. This man was a member of a vast network of organized crime, a group that bled the country of untold billions of dollars, an arcane cabal that would kill when necessary to protect itself.

The evidence against Gambutti was overwhelming. He had been caught during the holdup of a fur shop and had killed an off-duty policeman who had tried to stop him. The morning newspapers announced that Jennifer Parker was going to be the defense attorney.

Judge Lawrence Waldman telephoned. "Is it true, Jennie?"

Jennifer knew instantly what he meant. "Yes, Lawrence."

A pause. "I'm surprised. You know who he is, of course."

"Yes, I know."

"You're getting into dangerous territory."

"Not really. I'm just doing a friend a favor."

"I see. Be careful."

"I will," Jennifer promised.

It was only afterward that Jennifer realized he had said nothing about their having dinner together.

After looking over the material her staff had assembled, Jennifer decided that she had no case at all.

Vasco Gambutti had been caught red-handed in a robbery-murder, and there were no extenuating circumstances. Furthermore, there was always a strong emotional pull in the minds of the jurors when the victim was a policeman.

She called Ken Bailey in and gave him his instructions.

He said nothing, but Jennifer could feel his disapproval and was saddened. She promised herself that this was the last time she would work for Michael.

Her private phone rang and she picked it up. Michael said, "Hello, baby. I'm hungry for you. Meet me in half an hour."

She sat there, listening, already feeling his arms around her, his body pressing against hers.

"I'll be there," Jennifer said.

The promise to herself was forgotten.

The Gambutti trial lasted ten days. The press was there in full force, eager to watch District Attorney Di Silva and Jennifer Parker in open combat again. Di Silva had done his homework thoroughly, and he deliberately understated his case, letting the jurors take the suggestions he dropped and build on them, creating horrors in their minds even greater than the ones he depicted.

Jennifer sat quietly through the testimony, seldom bothering to raise objections.

On the last day of the trial, she made her move.

There is an adage in law that when you have a weak defense, you put your opponent on trial. Because Jennifer had no defense for Vasco Gambutti, she had made a decision to put Scott Norman, the slain policeman, on trial. Ken Bailey had dug up everything there was to know about Scott Norman. His record was not good, but before Jennifer was through she made it seem ten times worse than it was. Norman had been on the police force for twenty years, and in that period had been suspended three times on charges of unnecessary violence. He had shot and almost killed an unarmed suspect, he had beaten up a drunk in a bar and he had sent to the hospital a man involved in a domestic quarrel. Although these incidents had taken place over a period of twenty years, Jennifer made it seem as though the deceased had committed an unbroken series of despicable acts. Jennifer had a parade of witnesses on the stand giving testimony against the dead police officer, and there was not one thing Robert Di Silva could do about it.

In his summation, Di Silva said, "Remember, ladies and gentlemen of the jury, that Officer Scott Norman is not the one on trial here. Officer Scott Norman was the victim. He was killed by" – pointing – "the defendant, Vasco Gambutti."

But even as the District Attorney spoke, he knew it was no use. Jennifer had made Officer Scott Norman appear to be as worthless a human being as Vasco Gambutti. He was no longer the noble policeman who had given his life to apprehend a criminal. Jennifer Parker had distorted the picture so that the victim was no better than the accused slayer.

The jury returned a verdict of not guilty on the charge of murder in the first degree and convicted Vasco Gambutti of manslaughter. It was a stunning defeat for District Attorney Di Silva, and the media were quick to announce another victory for Jennifer Parker.

"Wear your chiffon. It's a celebration," Michael told her.

They had dinner at a seafood restaurant in the Village. The restaurant owner sent over a bottle of rare champagne and Michael and Jennifer drank a toast.

"I'm very pleased."

Coming from Michael, it was an accolade.

He placed a small red-and-white-wrapped box in her hands. "Open it."

He watched as she untied the gold thread and removed the lid. In the box lay a large, square-cut emerald, surrounded by diamonds.

Jennifer stared at it. She started to protest. "Oh, Michael!" And she saw the look of pride and pleasure on his face.

"Michael – what am I going to do with you?"

And she thought: *Oh. Jennifer, what am I going to do with you?*

"You need it for that dress." He placed the ring on the third finger of her left hand.

"I – I don't know what to say. I – thank you. It's really a celebration, isn't it!"

Michael grinned. "The celebration hasn't started yet. This is only the foreplay."

They were riding in the limousine on their way to an apartment that Michael kept uptown. Michael pressed a button and raised the glass that separated the rear of the car from the driver.

We're locked away in our own little world, Jennifer thought. Michael's nearness excited her.

She turned to look into his black eyes and he moved toward her and slid his hand along her thighs, and Jennifer's body was instantly on fire.

Michael's lips found hers and their bodies were pressed together. Jennifer felt the hard maleness of him and she slid down to the floor of the car. She began to make love to him, caressing him and kissing him until Michael began to moan, and Jennifer moaned with him, moving faster and faster until she felt the spasms of his body.

The celebration had begun.

*

Jennifer was thinking of the past now as she lay in bed in the hotel room in Tangier, listening to the sounds of Michael in the shower. She felt satisfied and happy. The only thing missing was her young son. She had thought of taking Joshua with her on some of her trips, but instinctively she wanted to keep him and Michael Moretti far away from each other. Joshua must never be touched by that part of her life. It seemed to Jennifer that her life was a series of compartments: there was Adam, there was her son and there was Michael Moretti. And each had to be kept separate from the others.

Michael walked out of the bathroom wearing only a towel. The hair on his body glistened from the dampness of the shower. He was a beautiful, exciting animal.

"Get dressed. We have work to do."

39

It happened so gradually that it did not seem to be happening at all. It had begun with Vasco Gambutti, and shortly afterward Michael asked Jennifer to handle another case, then another, until soon it became a steady flow of cases.

Michael would call Jennifer and say, "I need your help, baby. One of my boys is having a problem."

And Jennifer was reminded of Father Ryan's words, *A friend of mine has a bit of a problem.* Was there really any difference? America had come to accept the Godfather syndrome. Jennifer told herself that what she was doing now was the same as what she had been doing all along. The truth was that there was a difference – a big difference.

She was at the center of one of the most powerful organizations in the world.

Michael invited Jennifer to the farmhouse in New Jersey, where she met Antonio Granelli for the first time, and some of the other men in the Organization.

At a large table in the old-fashioned kitchen were Nick Vito, Arthur "Fat Artie" Scotto, Salvatore Fiore and Joseph Colella.

As Jennifer and Michael came in and stood in the doorway, listening, Nick Vito was saying, " . . . like the time I did a Pound in Atlanta. I had a heavy H book goin". This popcorn pimp comes up and tries to fuck me over 'cause he wants a piece of the action."

"Did you know the guy?" Fat Artie Scotto asked.

"What's to know? He wants to get his lights turned on. He tried to put the arm on me."

"On *you?*"

"Yeah. His head wasn't wrapped too tight."

"What'd you do?"

"Eddie Fratelli and me got him over in the ghinny corner of the yard and burned him. What the hell, he was doin' bad time, anyway."

"Hey, whatever happened to Little Eddie?"

"He's doin' a dime at Lewisburg."

"What about his bandit? She was some class act."

"Oh, yeah. I'd love to make her drawers."

"She's still got the hots for Eddie. Only the Pope knows why."

"I liked Eddie. He used to be an up-front guy."

"He went ape-shit. Speakin' of that, do you know who turned into a candy man . . . ?"

Shop talk.

Michael grinned at Jennifer's puzzled reaction to the conversation and said, "Come on – I'll introduce you to Papa."

Antonio Granelli was a shock to Jennifer. He was in a wheelchair, a feeble skeleton of a man, and it was hard to imagine him as he once must have been.

An attractive brunette with a full figure walked into the room, and Michael said to Jennifer, "This is Rosa, my wife."

Jennifer had dreaded this moment. Some nights after Michael had left her – fulfilled in every way a woman could be – she had fought with a guilt that almost overpowered her. *I don't want to hurt another woman. I'm stealing. I've got to stop this! I must!* And, always, she lost the battle.

Rosa looked at Jennifer with eyes that were wise. *She knows*, Jennifer thought.

There was a small awkwardness, and then Rosa said softly, "I'm pleased to meet you, Mrs. Parker. Michael tells me you're very intelligent."

Antonio Granelli grunted. "It's not good for a woman to be too smart. It's better to leave the brains to the men."

Michael said with a straight face, "I think of Mrs. Parker as a man, Papa."

They had dinner in the large, old-fashioned dining room.

"You sit next to me," Antonio Granelli commanded Jennifer.

Michael sat next to Rosa. Thomas Colfax, the *consigliere*, sat opposite Jennifer and she could feel his animosity.

The dinner was superb. An enormous antipasto was served, and then *pasta fagioli*. There was a salad with garbanzo beans, stuffed mushrooms, veal *piccata*, linguini and baked chicken. It seemed that the dishes never stopped coming.

There were no visible servants in the house, and Rosa was constantly jumping up and clearing the table to bring in new dishes from the kitchen.

"My Rosa's a great cook," Antonio Granelli told Jennifer. "She's almost as good as her mother was. Hey, Mike?"

"Yes," Michael said politely.

"His Rosa's a wonderful wife," Antonio Granelli went on, and Jennifer wondered whether it was a casual remark or a warning.

Michael said, "You're not finishing your veal."

"I've never eaten so much in my life," Jennifer protested.

And it was not over yet.

There was a bowl of fresh fruit and a platter of cheese, and ice cream with a hot fudge sauce, and candy and mints.

Jennifer marveled at how Michael managed to keep his figure.

The conversation was easy and pleasant and could have been taking place in any one of a thousand Italian homes, and it was hard for Jennifer to believe that this family was different from any other family.

Until Antonio Granelli said, "You know anythin' about the *Unione Siciliana?*"

"No," Jennifer said.

"Let me tell you about it, lady."

"Pop – her name is Jennifer."

"That's not no Italian name, Mike. It's too hard for me to remember. I'll call you lady, lady. Okay?"

"Okay," Jennifer replied.

"The *Unione Siciliana* started in Sicily to protect the poor against injustices. See, the people in power, they robbed the poor. The poor had nothin' – no money, no jobs, no justice. So the *Unione* was formed. When there was injustice, people came to the members of the secret brotherhood and they got vengeance. Pretty soon the *Unione* became stronger than the law, because it was the *people's* law. We believe in what the Bible says, lady." He looked Jennifer in the eye. "If anyone betrays us, we get vengeance."

The message was unmistakable.

Jennifer had always known instinctively that if she ever worked for the Organization she would be taking a giant step, but like most outsiders, she had a misconception of what the Organization was like. The Mafia was generally depicted as a bunch of mobsters sitting around ordering people murdered and counting the money from loan-sharking and whorehouses. That was only a part of the picture. The meetings Jennifer attended taught her the rest of it: These were businessmen operating on a scale that was staggering. They owned hotels and banks, restaurants and casinos, insurance companies and factories, building companies and chains of hospitals. They controlled unions and shipping. They were in the record business and sold vending machines. They owned funeral parlors, bakeries and construction companies. Their yearly income was in the billions. How they had acquired those interests was none of Jennifer's concern. It was her job to defend those of them who got into trouble with the law.

Robert Di Silva had three of Michael Moretti's men indicted for shaking down a group of lunch wagons. They were charged with conspiracy to interfere with commerce by extortion and seven counts of interference with commerce. The only witness willing to testify against the men was a woman who owned one of the stands.

"She's going to blow us away," Michael told Jennifer. "She's got to be handled."

"You own a piece of a magazine publishing company, don't you?" Jennifer asked.

"Yes. What does that have to do with lunch wagons?"

"You'll see."

Jennifer quietly arranged for the magazine to offer a large sum of money for the witness's story. The woman accepted. In court, Jennifer used that to discredit the woman's motives, and the charges were dismissed.

Jennifer's relationship with her associates had changed. When the office had begun to take a succession of Mafia cases, Ken Bailey had come into Jennifer's office and said, "What's going on? You can't keep representing these hoodlums. They'll ruin us."

"Don't worry about it, Ken. They'll pay."

"You can't be that naïve, Jennifer. You're the one who's going to pay. They'll have you hooked."

Because she had known he was right, Jennifer said angrily, "Drop it, Ken."

He had looked at her for a long moment, then said, "Right. You're the boss."

The Criminal Courts was a small world, and news traveled swiftly. When word got out that Jennifer Parker was defending members of the Organization, well-meaning friends went to her and reiterated the same things that Judge Lawrence Waldman and Ken Bailey had told her.

"If you get involved with these hoodlums, you'll be tarred with the same brush."

Jennifer told them all: "Everyone is entitled to be defended."

She appreciated their warnings, but she felt that they did not apply to her. She was not a part of the Organization; she merely represented some of its members. She was a lawyer, like her father, and she would never do anything that would have made him ashamed of her. The jungle was there, but she was still outside it.

Father Ryan had come to see her. This time it was not to ask her to help out a friend.

"I'm concerned about you, Jennifer. I hear reports that you're handling – well – the wrong people."

"Who are the wrong people? Do you judge the people who come to you for help? Do you turn people away from God because they've sinned?"

Father Ryan shook his head. "Of course not. But it's one thing when an individual makes a mistake. It's something else when corruption is organized. If you help those people, you're condoning what they do. You become a part of it."

"No. I'm a lawyer, Father. I help people in trouble."

Jennifer came to know Michael Moretti better than anyone had ever known him. He exposed feelings to her that he had never revealed to anyone else. He was basically a lonely, solitary man, and Jennifer was the first person who had ever been able to penetrate his shell.

Jennifer felt that Michael *needed her*. She had never felt that with Adam. And Michael had forced her to admit how much she needed him. He had brought out feelings in her that she had kept suppressed – wild, atavistic passions that she had been afraid to let loose. There were no inhibitions with Michael. When they were in bed together, there were no limits, no barriers. Only pleasure, a pleasure Jennifer had never dreamed possible.

Michael confided to Jennifer that he did not love Rosa, but it was obvious that Rosa worshiped Michael. She was always at his service, waiting to take care of his needs.

Jennifer met other Mafia wives, and she found their lives fascinating. Their husbands went out to restaurants and bars and racetracks with their mistresses while their wives stayed home and waited for them.

A Mafia wife always had a generous allowance, but she had to be careful how she spent it, lest she attract the attention of the Internal Revenue Service.

There was a pecking order ranging from the lowly *soldato* to the *capo di tutti capi*, and the wife never owned a more expensive coat or car than the wife of her husband's immediate superior.

The wives gave dinner parties for their husbands' associates, but they were careful not to be more lavish than their position permitted in relation to the others.

At ceremonies such as weddings or baptism, where gifts were called for, a wife was never allowed to spend more than the wife above her station in the hierarchy.

The protocol was as stringent as that at U.S. Steel, or any other large business corporation.

The Mafia was an incredible moneymaking machine, but Jennifer became aware that there was another element in it that was equally important: power.

"The Organization is bigger than the government of most of the countries of the world," Michael told Jennifer. "We gross more than a half a dozen of the largest companies in America, put together."

"There's a difference," Jennifer pointed out. "They're legitimate and – "

Michael laughed. "You mean the ones that haven't been caught. Dozens of the country's biggest companies have been indicted for violating one law or another. Don't kid yourself about heroes, Jennifer. The average American today can't name two astronauts who have been up in space, but they know the names of Al Capone and Lucky Luciano."

Jennifer realized that in his own way, Michael was equally as dedicated as Adam was. The difference was that their lives had gone in opposite directions.

When it came to business, Michael had a total lack of empathy. It was his strong point. He made decisions based solely on what was expedient for the Organization.

In the past, Michael had been completely dedicated to fulfilling his ambitions. There had been no emotional room for a woman in his life. Neither Rosa nor Michael's girl friends had ever been a part of his real needs.

Jennifer was different. He needed her as he had needed no other woman. He had never known anyone like her. She excited him physically, but so had dozens of others. What made Jennifer special was her intelligence, her independence. Rosa obeyed him; other women feared him; Jennifer challenged him. She was his equal. He could talk to her, discuss things with her. She was more than intelligent. She was smart.

He knew that he was never going to let her go.

Occasionally Jennifer took business trips with Michael, but she tried to avoid traveling whenever she could because she wanted to spend as much time as possible with Joshua. He was six years old now and growing unbelievably fast. Jennifer had enrolled him in a private school nearby, and Joshua loved it.

He rode a two-wheel bicycle and had a fleet of toy racing cars and carried on long and earnest conversations with Jennifer and Mrs. Mackey.

Because Jennifer wanted Joshua to grow up to be strong and independent, she tried to walk a carefully balanced line, letting Joshua know how much she loved him, making him aware that she was always there when he needed her and yet giving him a sense of his own independence.

She taught him to love good books and to enjoy music. She took him to the theater, avoiding opening nights because there would be too many people there who might know her and ask questions. On weekends she and Joshua would have a movie binge. On Saturday they would see a movie in the afternoon, have dinner at a restaurant and then see a second movie. On Sunday they would go sailing or bicycling together. Jennifer gave her son all the love that was stored in her, but she was careful to try not to spoil him. She planned her strategy with Joshua more carefully than she had planned any court case, determined not to fall into the traps of a one-parent home.

Jennifer felt no sacrifice in spending so much time with Joshua; he was great fun. They played word games and Impressions and Twenty Questions, and Jennifer was delighted by the quickness of her son's mind. He was at the head of his class and an outstanding athlete, but he did not take himself seriously. He had a marvelous sense of humor.

When it did not interfere with his schoolwork, Jennifer would take Joshua on trips. During Joshua's winter vacation, Jennifer took time off to go skiing with him in the Poconos. In the summer she took him to London on a business trip with her, and they spent two weeks exploring the countryside. Joshua adored England.

"Could I go to school here?" he asked.

Jennifer felt a pang. It would not be long before he left her to go away to school, to seek his fortune, to get married and have his own home and family. Was that not what she wanted for him? Of course it was. When Joshua was ready, she would let him go with open arms, and yet she knew how difficult it was going to be.

Joshua was looking at her, waiting for an answer. "Can I, Mom?" he asked. "Maybe Oxford?"

Jennifer held him close. "Of course. They'll be lucky to get you."

On a Sunday morning when Mrs. Mackey was off, Jennifer had to go into Manhattan to pick up a transcript of a deposition. Joshua was visiting some friends. When Jennifer returned home, she started to prepare dinner for the two of them. She opened the refrigerator – and stopped dead in her tracks. There was a note inside, propped up between two bottles of milk. Adam had left her notes like that. Jennifer stared at it, mesmerized, afraid to touch it. Slowly, she reached for the note and unfolded it. It said, *Surprise! Is it okay if Alan has dinner with us?*

It took half an hour for Jennifer's pulse to return to normal.

From time to time, Joshua asked Jennifer about his father.

"He was killed in Viet Nam, Joshua. He was a very brave man."

"Don't we have a picture of him anywhere?"

"No, I'm sorry, darling. We – we weren't married very long before he died."

She hated the lie, but she had no choice.

Michael Moretti had only asked once about Joshua's father.

"I don't care what happened before you belonged to me – I'm just curious."

Jennifer thought about the power that Michael would have over Senator Adam Warner if Michael ever learned the truth.

"He was killed in Viet Nam. His name's not important."

40

In Washington, D.C., a Senate investigating committee headed by Adam Warner was in its final day of an intensive inquiry into the new XK-1 bomber that the Air Force was trying to get the Senate to approve. For weeks, expert witnesses had paraded up to Capitol Hill, half of them testifying that the new bomber would be an expensive albatross that would destroy the defense budget and ruin the country, and the other half testifying that unless the Air Force could get the bomber approved, America's defenses would be so weakened that the Russians would invade the United States the following Sunday.

Adam had volunteered to test-fly a prototype of the new bomber, and his colleagues had eagerly seized on his offer. Adam was one of them, a member of the club, and he would give them the truth.

Adam had taken the bomber up early on a Sunday morning with a skeleton crew and had put the plane through a series of rigorous tests. The flight had been an unqualified success, and he had reported back to the Senate committee that the new XK-1 bomber was an important advance in aviation. He recommended that the airplane go into production immediately. The Senate approved the funds.

The press enthusiastically played up the story. They described Adam as one of the new breed of investigative senators, a lawmaker who went out into the field to study the facts for himself instead of taking the word of lobbyists and others who were concerned with protecting their own interests.

Newsweek and *Time* both did cover stories on Adam, and the *Newsweek* story ended with:

> The Senate has found an honest and capable new guardian to investigate some of the vital problems that plague this country, and to bring to them light instead of heat. There is a growing feeling among the kingmakers that Adam Warner has the qualities that would grace the presidency.

Jennifer devoured the stories about Adam and she was filled with pride. And pain. She still loved Adam and she loved Michael Moretti, and she did not understand how it was possible, or what kind of woman she had become. Adam had created the loneliness in her life. Michael had erased it.

The smuggling of drugs from Mexico had increased enormously, and it was obvious that organized crime was behind it. Adam was asked to head an investigating committee. He coordinated the efforts of half a dozen United States law enforcement agencies, and flew to Mexico and obtained the cooperation of the Mexican government. Within three months, the drug traffic had slowed to a trickle.

In the farmhouse in New Jersey, Michael Moretti was saying, "We've got a problem."

They were seated in the large, comfortable study. In the room were Jennifer, Antonio Granelli and Thomas Colfax. Antonio Granelli had suffered a stroke and it had aged him twenty years overnight. He looked like a shrunken caricature of a man. The paralysis had affected the right side of his face so that when he spoke, saliva drooled from the corners of his mouth. He was old and almost senile, and he leaned more and more on Michael's judgment. He had even reluctantly come to accept Jennifer.

Not so Thomas Colfax. The conflict between Michael and Colfax had grown stronger. Colfax knew it was Michael's intention to replace him with this woman. Colfax admitted to himself that Jennifer Parker was a clever lawyer, but what could she possibly know of the traditions of the *borgata?* Of what had made the brotherhood work so smoothly all these years? How could Michael bring in a stranger – worse, a woman! – and trust her with their life-and-death secrets? It was an untenable situation. Colfax had talked to the *caporegimi* – the squad lieutenants – and the *soldati* – the soldiers – one by one, voicing his fears, trying to win them over to his side, but they were afraid to go against Michael. If he trusted this woman, then they felt they must trust her also.

Thomas Colfax decided he would have to bide his time. But he would find a way to get rid of her.

Jennifer was well aware of his feelings. She had replaced him, and his pride would never let him forgive her for that. His loyalty to the Syndicate would keep him in line and protect her, but if his hatred for her should become stronger than that loyalty . . .

Michael turned to Jennifer. "Have you ever heard of Adam Warner?"

Jennifer's heart stopped for an instant. It was suddenly hard for her to breathe. Michael was watching her, waiting for an answer.

"You – you mean the senator?" Jennifer managed to say.

"Uh – huh. We're going to have to cool the son of a bitch."

Jennifer could feel the blood drain from her face. "Why, Michael?"

"He's hurting our operation. Because of him, the Mexican government is closing down factories belonging to friends of ours. Everything's starting to come apart. I want the bastard out of our hair. He's got to go."

Jennifer's mind was racing. "If you touch Senator Warner," she said, choosing her words carefully, "you'll destroy yourself."

"I'm not going to let – "

"Listen to me, Michael. Get rid of him, and they'll send ten men to take his place. A hundred. Every newspaper in the country will be after you. The investigation that's going on now will be nothing compared to what will happen if Senator Warner is harmed."

Michael said angrily, "I'm telling you we're *hurting!*"

Jennifer changed her tone. "Michael, use your head. You've seen these investigations before. How long do they last? Five minutes after the senator is finished, he'll be investigating something else and all this will be over. The factories that are closed down will open up again and you'll be back in business. That way there won't be any repercussions. You try to do it your way and you'll never hear the end of it."

"I disagree," Thomas Colfax said. "In my opinion – "

Michael Moretti growled, "No one asked for your opinion."

Thomas Colfax jerked as though he had been slapped. Michael paid no attention. Colfax turned to Antonio Granelli for support. The old man was asleep.

Michael said to Jennifer, "Okay, counselor, we'll leave Warner alone for now."

Jennifer realized she had been holding her breath. She exhaled slowly. "Is there anything else?"

"Yeah." Michael picked up a heavy gold lighter and lit a cigarette. "A friend of ours, Marco Lorenzo, has been convicted of extortion and robbery."

Jennifer had read about the case. According to the newspapers, Lorenzo was a congenital criminal with a long string of arrests for crimes of violence.

"Do you want me to file an appeal?"

"No, I want you to see that he goes to jail."

Jennifer looked at him in surprise.

Michael put the cigarette lighter back on his desk. "I got word that Di Silva wants to ship him back to Sicily. Marco's got enemies there. If they send him back he won't live twenty-four hours. The safest place for him is Sing Sing. When the heat's off in a year or two we'll get him out. Can you swing it?"

Jennifer hesitated. "If we were in another jurisdiction I could probably do it. But Di Silva won't plea-bargain with me."

Thomas Colfax said quickly, "Perhaps we should let someone else take care of this."

"If I had wanted someone else to take care of it," Michael snapped, "I would have said so." He turned back to Jennifer. "I want you to handle it."

Michael Moretti and Nick Vito watched from the window as Thomas Colfax climbed into his sedan and drove off.

Michael said, "Nick, I want you to get rid of him."

"*Colfax?*"

"I can't trust him anymore. He's living in the past with the old man."

"Whatever you say, Mike. When do you want me to do it?"

"Soon. I'll let you know."

Jennifer was seated in Judge Lawrence Waldman's chambers. It was the first time she had seen him in more than a year. The friendly telephone calls and dinner invitations had stopped. Well, that could not be helped, Jennifer thought. She liked Lawrence Waldman and she regretted losing his friendship, but she had made her choice.

They were waiting for Robert Di Silva and they sat there in an uncomfortable silence, neither bothering to make small talk. When the District Attorney walked in and took a seat, the meeting began.

Judge Waldman said to Jennifer, "Bobby says that you want to discuss a plea bargain before I pass sentence on Lorenzo."

"That's right." Jennifer turned to District Attorney Di Silva. "I think it would be a mistake to send Marco Lorenzo to Sing Sing. He doesn't belong here. He's an illegal alien. I feel he should be shipped back to Sicily where he came from."

Di Silva looked at her in surprise. He had been going to recommend deportation, but if that was what Jennifer Parker wanted, then he would have to re-evaluate his decision.

"Why do you recommend that?" Di Silva asked.

"For several reasons. First of all, it will keep him from committing any more crimes here, and – "

"So will being in a cell in Sing Sing."

"Lorenzo is an old man. He can't stand being confined. He'll go crazy if you put him in jail. All his friends are in Sicily. He can live there in the sun and die in peace with his family."

Di Silva's mouth tightened with anger. "We're talking about a hoodlum who's spent his life robbing and raping and killing, and you're worried about whether he's with his friends in the sun?" He turned to Judge Waldman. "She's unreal!"

"Marco Lorenzo has a right to – "

Di Silva pounded his fist on the desk. "He has no rights at all! He's been convicted of extortion and armed robbery."

"In Sicily, when a man – "

"He's not in Sicily, goddamn it!" Di Silva yelled. "He's here! He committed the crimes here and he's going to pay for them here." He stood up. "Your Honor, we're wasting your time. The state refuses any plea bargaining in this case. We're asking that Marco Lorenzo be sentenced to Sing Sing."

Judge Waldman turned to Jennifer. "Do you have any thing more to say?"

She looked at Robert Di Silva angrily. "No, Your Honor."

Judge Waldman said, "Sentencing will be tomorrow morning. You are both excused."

Di Silva and Jennifer rose and left the office.

In the corridor outside, the District Attorney turned to Jennifer and smiled. "You've lost your touch, counselor."

Jennifer shrugged. "You can't win them all."

Five minutes later, Jennifer was in a telephone booth talking to Michael Moretti.

"You can stop worrying. Marco Lorenzo will be going to Sing Sing."

41

Time was a swiftly flowing river that had no shores, no boundaries. Its seasons were not winter, spring, fall or summer, but birthdays and joys and troubles and pain. They were court battles won, and cases lost; the reality of Michael, the memories of Adam. But mainly, it was Joshua who was time's calendar, a reminder of how quickly the years were passing.

He was, incredibly, seven years old. Overnight, it seemed, he had gone from crayons and picture books to airplane models and sports. Joshua had grown tall and he resembled his father more every day, and not merely in his physical appearance. He was sensitive and polite, and he had a strong sense of fair play. When Jennifer punished him for something he had done, Joshua said stubbornly, "I'm only four feet tall, but I've got my rights."

He was a miniature Adam. Joshua was athletic, as Adam was. His heroes were the Bebble brothers and Carl Stotz.

"I never heard of them," Jennifer said.

"Where have you *been*, Mom? They invented Little League."

"Oh. *That* Bebble brothers and Carl Stotz."

On weekends, Joshua watched every sports event on television – football, baseball, basketball – it did not matter. In the beginning, Jennifer had let Joshua watch the games alone, but when he tried to discuss the plays with her afterward and Jennifer was completely at sea, she decided she had better watch with him. And so the two of them would sit in front of the television set, munching popcorn and cheering the players.

One day Joshua came in from playing ball, a worried expression on his face, and said, "Mom, can we have a man-to-man talk?"

"Certainly, Joshua."

They sat down at the kitchen table and Jennifer made him a peanut butter sandwich and poured a glass of milk.

"What's the problem?"

His voice was sober and filled with concern. "Well, I heard the guys talkin' and I was just wonderin' – do you think there'll still be sex when I grow up?"

Jennifer had bought a small Newport sailboat, and on weekends she and Joshua would go out on the sound for a sail. Jennifer liked to watch his face when he was at the helm. He wore an excited little smile, which she called his "Eric the Red" smile. Joshua was a natural sailor, like his father. The thought brought Jennifer up sharply. She wondered whether she was trying to live her life with Adam vicariously through Joshua. All the things she was doing with her son –

the sailing, the sporting events – were things she had done with his father. Jennifer told herself she was doing them because Joshua liked doing them, but she was not sure she was being completely honest. She watched Joshua sheet in the jib, his cheeks tanned from the wind and the sun, his face beaming, and Jennifer realized that the reasons did not matter. The important thing was that her son loved his life with her. He was not a surrogate for his father. He was his own person and Jennifer loved him more than anyone on earth.

42

Antonio Granelli died and Michael took over full control of his empire. The funeral was lavish, as befitted a man of the Godfather's stature. The heads and members of Families from all over the country came to pay their respects to their departed friend, and to assure the new *capo* of their loyalty and support. The FBI was there, taking photographs, as well as half a dozen other government agencies.

Rosa was heartbroken, because she had loved her father very much, but she took consolation and pride in the fact that her husband was taking her father's place as head of the Family.

Jennifer was proving more valuable to Michael every day. When there was a problem, it was Jennifer whom Michael consulted. Thomas Colfax was becoming an increasingly bothersome appendage.

"Don't worry about him," Michael told Jennifer. "He's going to retire soon."

The soft chimes of the telephone awakened Jennifer. She lay in bed, listening a moment, then sat up and looked at the digital clock on the nightstand. It was three o'clock in the morning.

She lifted the receiver. "Hello."

It Was Michael. "Can you get dressed right away?"

Jennifer sat up straighter and tried to blink the sleep from her eyes. "What's happened?"

"Eddie Santini was just picked up on an armed robbery charge. He's a two-time loser. If they convict him, they'll throw the key away."

"Were there any witnesses?"

"Three, and they all got a good look at him."

"Where is he now?"

"The Seventeenth Precinct"

"I'm on my way, Michael."

Jennifer put on a robe and went down to the kitchen and made herself a steaming pot of coffee. She sat drinking it in the breakfast room, staring out at the night, thinking. *Three witnesses. And they all got a good look at him.*

She picked up the telephone and dialed. "Give me the City Desk."

Jennifer spoke rapidly. "I got some information for you. A guy named Eddie Santini's just been picked up on an armed robbery charge. His attorney's Jennifer Parker. She's gonna try to spring him."

She hung up and repeated the call to two other newspapers and a television station. When Jennifer was through telephoning, she looked at her watch and had another leisurely cup of coffee. She wanted to make certain the photographers had time to get to the precinct on 51st Street. She went upstairs and got dressed.

Before Jennifer left, she went into Joshua's bedroom. His night-light was on. He was sound asleep, the blankets twisted around his restless body. Jennifer gently straightened the blankets, kissed him on the forehead and started to tiptoe out of the room.

"Where you goin'?"

She turned and said, "I'm going to work. Go back to sleep."

"What time is it?"

"It's four o'clock in the morning."

Joshua giggled. "You sure work funny hours for a lady."

She came back to his bedside. "And you sure sleep funny hours for a man."

"Are we going to watch the Mets game tonight?"

"You bet we are. Back to Dreamland."

"Okay, Mom. Have a good case."

"Thanks, pal."

A few minutes later, Jennifer was in her car, on her way into Manhattan.

When Jennifer arrived, a lone photographer from the *Daily News* was waiting. He stared at Jennifer and said, "It's true! You really handling the Santini case?"

"How did you know that?" Jennifer demanded.

"A little birdie, counselor."

"You're wasting your time. No pictures."

She went inside and arranged for Eddie Santini's bail, stalling the proceedings until she was sure the television cameraman and a reporter and photographer had arrived from *The New York Times*. She decided she could not wait for the *Post*.

The police captain on duty said, "There're some reporters and television people out front, Miss Parker. You can go out the back way if you want."

"It's all right," Jennifer said. "I'll handle them."

She led Eddie Santini to the front corridor where the photographers and reporters were waiting.

She said, "Look, gentlemen, no pictures, please."

And Jennifer stepped aside while the photographer and television cameraman took pictures.

A reporter asked, "What makes this case big enough for you to handle?"

"You'll find out tomorrow. Meanwhile, I would advise you not to use those pictures."

One of the reporters called out, "Come on, Jennifer! Haven't you heard of freedom of the press?"

At noon Jennifer got a call from Michael Moretti. His voice was angry. "Have you seen the newspapers?"

"No."

"Well, Eddie Santini's picture is all over the front pages and on the television news. I didn't tell you to turn this goddamned thing into a circus!"

"I know you didn't. It was my own idea."

"Jesus! What's the point?"

"The point, Michael, is those three witnesses."

"What about them?"

"You said they got a good look at Eddie Santini. Well, when they get up in court to identify him, they're going to have to prove they didn't identify him because they saw his picture all over the newspapers and television."

There was a long silence, and then Michael's voice said admiringly, "I'm a son of a bitch!"

Jennifer had to laugh.

Ken Bailey was waiting in her office that afternoon when Jennifer walked in, and she knew instantly from the look on his face that something was wrong.

"Why didn't you tell me?" Ken demanded.

"Tell you what?"

"About you and Mike Moretti."

Jennifer checked the retort that rose to her lips. Saying *It's none of your business* was too easy. Ken was her friend; he cared. In a way, it was his business. Jennifer remembered it all, the tiny office they had shared, how he had helped her. *I've got a lawyer friend who's been bugging me to serve some subpoenas for him. I haven't got time. He pays twelve-fifty for each subpoena plus mileage. Would you help me out?*

"Ken, let's not discuss this."

His tone was filled with cold fury. "Why not? Everybody else is discussing it. The word is that you're Moretti's girl." His face was pale. "Jesus!"

"My personal life – "

"He lives in a sewer and you brought that sewer into the office! You've got us all working for Moretti and his hoodlums."

"Stop it!"

"I am. That's what I came to tell you. I'm leaving."

His words were a shock. "You can't leave. You're wrong about what you think of Michael. If you'll just meet him, you'll see – "

The moment the words were out, Jennifer knew she had made a mistake.

He looked at her sadly and said, "He's really wrapped you up, hasn't he? I remember you when you knew who you were. That's the girl I want to remember. Say good-bye to Joshua for me."

And Ken Bailey was gone.

Jennifer felt the tears begin to come, and her throat constricted so tightly that she could hardly breathe. She put her head down on the desk and closed her eyes, trying to shut out the hurt.

When she opened her eyes, night had fallen. The office was in darkness except for the eerie red glow cast by the city lights. She walked over to the window and stared out at the city below. It looked like a jungle at night, with only a dying campfire to keep away the encroaching terrors.

It was Michael's jungle. There was no way out of it.

43

The Cow Palace in San Francisco was a madhouse, filled with noisy, chanting delegates from all over the country. There were three candidates vying for the presidential nomination, and each had done well in the primaries. But the star, the one who outshone them all, was Adam Warner. The nomination was his on the fifth ballot, and it was made unanimous. His party finally had a candidate they could put forward with pride. The incumbent President, the leader of the opposition party, had a low credibility rating and was considered by the majority of people to be inept.

"Unless you take your cock out and pee in front of a camera on the six o'clock news," Stewart Needham told Adam, "you're going to be the next President of the United States."

After his nomination, Adam flew to New York for a meeting at the Regency Hotel with Needham and several influential members of the party. Present in the room was Blair Roman, head of the second largest advertising agency in the country.

Stewart Needham said, "Blair will be in charge of running the publicity end of your campaign, Adam."

"Can't tell you how glad I am to be aboard." Blair Roman grinned. "You're going to be my third President."

"Really?" Adam was not impressed with the man.

"Let me fill you in on some of the game plan." Blair Roman started pacing the room, swinging an imaginary golf club as he walked. "We're going to saturate the country with television commercials, build an image of you as the man who can solve America's problems. Big Daddy – only a young, good-looking Big Daddy. You get it, Mr. President?"

"Mr. Roman."

"Yes?"

"Would you mind not calling me "Mr. President?"

Blair Roman laughed. "Sorry. Slip of the tongue, A.W. In my mind you're already in the White House. Believe me, I know you're the man for the job or I wouldn't be undertaking this campaign. I'm too rich to have to work for money."

Beware of people who say they're too rich to have to work for money, Adam thought.

"*We* know you're the man for the job – now we have to let the *people* know it. If you'll just take a look at these charts I've prepared, I've broken down different sections of the country into various ethnic groups. We're going to send you to key places where you can press the flesh."

He leaned forward into Adam's face and said earnestly, "Your wife is going to be a big asset. Women's magazines will go crazy for stuff on your family life. We're going to *merchandise* you, A.W."

Adam found himself beginning to get irritated. "Just how do you plan to do that?"

"It's simple. You're a product, A.W. We're going to sell you just like we'd sell any other product. We – "

Adam turned to Stewart Needham. "Stewart, could I see you alone?"

"Certainly." Needham turned to the others and said, "Let's break for dinner and meet back here at nine o'clock. We'll continue the discussion then."

When the two men were alone, Adam said, "Jesus, Stewart? He's planning to turn this thing into a circus! 'You're a product, A.W. We're going to sell you just like we'd sell any other product.' He's disgusting!"

"I know how you feel, Adam," Stewart Needham said soothingly, "but Blair gets results. When he said you're his third President, he wasn't kidding. Every President since Eisenhower has had an advertising agency masterminding his campaign. Whether you like it or not, a campaign needs salesmanship. Blair Roman knows the psychology of the public. As distasteful as it may be, the reality is that if you want to be elected to any public office, you have to be sold – you have to be merchandised."

"I hate it."

"That's part of the price you're going to have to pay." He walked over to Adam and put an arm across his shoulder. "All you have to do is keep the objective in mind. You want the White House? All right. We're going to do everything we can to get you there. But you have to do your part. If being the ringmaster in a three-ring circus is part of it, bear with it."

"Do we really need Blair Roman?"

"We need *a* Blair Roman. Blair's as good as there is. Let me handle him. I'll keep him away from you as much as possible."

"I'd appreciate that."

The campaign began. It started with a few television spots and personal appearances and gradually grew bigger and bigger until it spanned the nation. Wherever one went, there was Senator Adam Warner in living color. In every part of the country he could be watched on television, heard on radio, seen on billboards. Law and order was one of the key issues of the campaign, and Adam's crime investigation committee was heavily stressed.

Adam taped one-minute television spots, three-minute television spots and five-minute spots, geared for different sections of the country. The television spots that went to West Virginia dealt with unemployment and the vast supply of underground coal that could make the area prosperous; the television segments for Detroit talked about urban blight; in New York City, the subject was the rising crime rate.

Blair Roman confided to Adam, "All you have to do is hit the highlights, A.W. You don't have to discuss key issues in depth. We're selling the product, and that's *you*."

Adam said, "Mr. Roman, I don't care what your goddamned statistics say. I'm not a breakfast food and I don't intend to be sold like one. I *will* talk about issues in depth because I think the American people are intelligent enough to want to know about them."

"I only – "

"I want you to try to set up a debate between me and the President, to discuss the basic issues."

Blair Roman said, "Right. I'll take a meeting with the President's boys right away, A.W."

"One more thing," Adam said.

"Yes? What's that?"

"Stop calling me A.W."

44

In the mail was a notice from the American Bar Association announcing its annual convention in Acapulco. Jennifer was in the midst of handling half a dozen cases, and ordinarily she would have ignored the invitation, but the convention was going to take place during Joshua's school vacation and Jennifer thought about how much Joshua would enjoy Acapulco.

She said to Cynthia, "Accept. I'll want three reservations."

She would take Mrs. Mackey along.

At dinner that evening, Jennifer broke the news to Joshua. "How would you like to go to Acapulco?"

"That's in Mexico," he announced. "On the west coast."

"That's right."

"Can we go to a topless beach?"

"Joshua!"

"Well, they have them there. Being naked is only natural."

"I'll think about it."

"And can we go deep-sea fishing?"

Jennifer visualized Joshua trying to pull in a large marlin and she contained her smile. "We'll see. Some of those fish get pretty big."

"That's what makes it exciting," Joshua explained seriously. "If it's easy, it's no fun. There's no sport to it."

It could have been Adam talking.

"I agree."

"What else can we do there?"

"Well, there's horseback riding, hiking, sightseeing – "

"Let's not go to a bunch of old churches, okay? They all look alike."

Adam saying, *If you've seen one church, you've seen them all.*

The convention began on a Monday. Jennifer, Joshua and Mrs. Mackey flew to Acapulco on Friday morning on a Braniff jet. Joshua had flown many times before, but he was still excited by the idea of airplanes. Mrs. Mackey was petrified with fear.

Joshua consoled her. "Look at it this way. Even if we crash, it'll only hurt for a second."

Mrs. Mackey turned pale.

The plane landed at Benito Juarez Airport at four o'clock in the afternoon, and an hour later the three of them arrived at Las Brisas. The hotel was eight miles outside of Acapulco, and consisted of a series of beautiful pink bungalows built on a hill, each with its private patio. Jennifer's bungalow, like several of the others, had its own swimming pool. Reservations had been difficult to get, for there were half a dozen other conventions and Acapulco was overcrowded, but Jennifer had made a telephone call to one of her corporate clients, and an hour later she had been informed that Las Brisas was eagerly expecting her.

When they had unpacked, Joshua said, "Can we go into town and hear them talk? I've never been to a country where nobody speaks English." He thought a moment and added, "Unless you count England."

They went into the city and wandered along the Zocalo, the frenetic center of downtown, but to Joshua's disappointment the only language to be heard was English. Acapulco was crowded with American tourists.

They strolled along the colorful market on the main pier opposite Sanborn's in the old part of town, where there were hundreds of stalls selling a bewildering variety of merchandise.

In the late afternoon, they took a *calandria*, a horse-drawn carriage, to Pie de la Cuesta, the sunset beach, and then returned to town.

They had dinner at Armando's Le Club, and it was excellent.

"I *love* Mexican food," Joshua declared.

"I'm glad," Jennifer said. "Only this is French."

"Well, it has a Mexican flavor."

Saturday was a full day. They went shopping in the morning at the Quebrada, where the nicer stores were, and then stopped for a Mexican lunch at Coyuca 22. Joshua said "I suppose you're going to tell me this is French, too."

"No, this is the real thing, gringo."

"What's a gringo?"

"You are, amigo."

They walked by the *fronton* building near the Plaza Caleta, and Joshua saw the billboards advertising jai alai inside.

He stood there, wide-eyed, and Jennifer asked, "Would you like to see the jai alai games?"

Joshua nodded. "If it's not too expensive. If we run out of money we won't be able to get home."

"I think we can manage."

They went inside and watched the furious play of the teams. Jennifer placed a bet for Joshua and his team won.

When Jennifer suggested returning to the hotel, Joshua said, "Gosh, Mom, can't we see the divers first?"

The hotel manager had mentioned them that morning.

"Are you sure you wouldn't like to rest, Joshua?"

"Oh, if you're too tired, sure. I keep forgettin' about your age."

That did it. "Never mind my age." Jennifer turned to Mrs. Mackey. "Are you up to it?"

"Certainly," Mrs. Mackey groaned.

The diving act was at La Quebrada cliffs. Jennifer, Joshua and Mrs. Mackey stood on a public viewing platform while divers carrying lighted torches plunged one hundred and fifty feet into a narrow, rock-lined cove, timing their descent to coincide with the arrival of incoming breakers. The slightest miscalculation would have meant instant death.

When the exhibition was over, a boy came around to collect a donation for the divers.

"*Uno peso, por favor.*"

Jennifer gave him five pesos.

She dreamed about the divers that night.

Las Brisas had its own beach, La Concha, and early Sunday morning Jennifer, Joshua and Mrs. Mackey drove down in one of the pink canopied jeeps that the hotel supplied to its guests. The weather was perfect. The harbor was a sparkling blue canvas dotted with speedboats and sailboats.

Joshua stood at the edge of the terrace, watching the water skiers race by.

"Did you know water skiing was invented in Acapulco, Mom?"

"No. Where did you hear that?"

"I either read it in a book or I made it up."

"I vote for 'made it up.' "

"Does that mean I can't go water skiing?"

"Those speedboats are pretty fast. Aren't you afraid?"

Joshua looked out at the skiers skimming over the water. "That man said, 'I'm going to send you home to Jesus.' And then he put a nail in my hand."

It was the first reference he had made to the terrible ordeal he had gone through.

Jennifer knelt and put her arms around her son. "What made you think of that, Joshua?"

He shrugged. "I don't know. I guess because Jesus walked on water and everyone out there is walking on water." He saw the stricken look on his mother's face. "I'm sorry, Mom. I don't think about it much, honest."

She hugged him tightly and said, "It's all right, darling. Of course you can go water skiing. Let's have lunch first."

The outdoor restaurant at La Concha had wrought-iron tables set with pink linen, shaded by pink-and-white-striped umbrellas. Lunch was a buffet and the long serving table was crowded with an incredible assortment of dishes. There were fresh lobster and crab and salmon, selections of cold and hot meats, salads, a variety of raw and cooked vegetables, cheeses and fruits. There was a separate table for an array of freshly baked desserts. The two women watched Joshua fill and empty his plate three times before he sat back, satisfied.

"It's a very good restaurant," he pronounced. "I don't care *what* kind of food it is." He stood up. "I'll go check on the water skiing."

Mrs. Mackey had barely picked at her food.

"Are you feeling all right?" Jennifer asked. "You haven't eaten anything since we arrived."

Mrs. Mackey leaned forward and whispered darkly, "I don't want Montezuma's Revenge!"

"I don't think you have to worry about that in a place like this."

"I don't hold with foreign food," Mrs. Mackey sniffed.

Joshua ran back to the table and said, "I got a boat. Is it okay if I go now, Mom?"

"Don't you want to wait a while?"

"What for?"

"Joshua, you'll sink with all you've eaten."

"Test me!" he begged.

While Mrs. Mackey watched on shore, Jennifer and Joshua got into the speedboat and Joshua had his first water-skiing lesson. He spent the first five minutes falling down, and after that, performed as though born to water skiing. Before the afternoon was over, Joshua was doing tricks on one ski, and finally skiing on his heels with no skis.

They spent the rest of the afternoon lazing on the sand and swimming.

On the way back to Las Brisas in the jeep, Joshua snuggled up against Jennifer and said, "You know something, Mom? I think this was probably the best day of my whole life."

Michael's words flashed through her mind: *I just want you to know this has been the greatest night of my life.*

Early Monday morning Jennifer arose and got dressed to attend the convention. She put on a full-flowing dark green skirt and an off-the-shoulder blouse embroidered in giant red roses, that revealed her patina of suntan. She studied herself in the mirror and was pleased. Despite the fact that her son thought she was over the hill, Jennifer was aware that she looked like Joshua's beautiful thirty-four-year-old sister. She laughed to herself and thought that this vacation was one of her better ideas.

Jennifer said to Mrs. Mackey, "I have to go to work now. Take good care of Joshua. Don't let him get too much sun."

The huge convention center was a cluster of five buildings joined by roofed circulation terraces, sprawled over thirty-five acres of lush greenery. The carefully tended lawns were studded with pre-Columbian statues.

The Bar Association Convention was being held in *Teotihuacan*, the main hall, holding an audience of seventy-five hundred people.

Jennifer went to the registration desk, signed in and entered the large hall. It was packed. In the crowd she spotted dozens of friends and acquaintances. Nearly all of them had changed from conservative business suits and dresses to brightly colored sport shirts and pants. It was as though everyone was on vacation. *There is a good reason*, Jennifer thought, *for holding the convention in a place like Acapulco instead of in Chicago or Detroit*. They could take off their stiff collars and somber ties and let themselves go under a tropical sun.

Jennifer had been given a program at the door but, deep in conversation with some friends, had paid no attention to it.

A deep voice boomed over the loudspeaker, "Attention, please! Would you all please take your seats? Attention, please! We would like to get the meeting started. Would you sit down, please!"

Reluctantly the small groups began to break up as people started to find seats. Jennifer looked up to see that half a dozen men had mounted the dais.

In the center was Adam Warner.

Jennifer stood there, frozen, as Adam walked to the chair next to the microphone and took a seat. She felt her heart begin to pound. The last time she had seen Adam had been when they had had lunch at the little Italian restaurant, the day he had told her that Mary Beth was pregnant.

Jennifer's immediate impulse was to flee. She had had no idea Adam would be there and she could not bear the thought of facing him. Adam and his son being in the same city filled her with panic. Jennifer knew she had to get out of there quickly.

She turned to leave as the chairman announced over the loudspeaker, "If the rest of you ladies and gentlemen will take your seats, we will begin."

As people around her began sitting down, Jennifer found herself conspicuous by standing. Jennifer slid into a seat, determined to slip away at the first opportunity.

The chairman said, "We are honored this morning to have as our guest speaker a nominee for the presidency of the United States. He is a member of the New York Bar Association and one of the most distinguished members of the United States Senate. It is with great pride that I introduce *Senator Adam Warner.*"

Jennifer watched as Adam rose, accepting the warm applause. He stepped to the microphone and looked out across the room. "Thank you, Mr. Chairman, ladies and gentlemen."

Adam's voice was rich and resonant, and he had an air of authority that was mesmerizing. The silence in the room was total.

"There are many reasons why we are gathered here today." He paused. "Some of us like to swim and some of us like to snorkel . . ." There was a swell of appreciative laughter. "But the main reason we are here is to exchange ideas and knowledge and discuss new concepts. Today, lawyers are under greater attack than at any time in my memory. Even the Chief Justice of the Supreme Court has been sharply critical of our profession."

Jennifer loved the way he used *our*, making him one with the rest of them. She let his words wash over her, content just to look at him, to watch the way he moved, to hear his voice. At one point he stopped to run his fingers through his hair, and it gave Jennifer a sharp pang. It was a gesture of Joshua's. Adam's son was only a few miles away and Adam would never know.

Adam's voice grew stronger, more forceful. "Some of you in this room are criminal lawyers. I must admit I have always considered that to be the most exciting branch of our profession. Criminal lawyers often deal in life and death. It is a very honorable profession and one of which we can all be proud. However" – his voice grew hard – "there are some of them" – and now Jennifer noticed that Adam was disassociating himself by his choice of the pronoun – "who are a disgrace to the oath they have taken. The American system of jurisprudence is based on the inalienable right of every citizen to have a fair trial. But when the law is made a mockery of, when lawyers spend their time and energy, imagination and skill, finding ways to defy that law, finding ways to subvert justice, then I think it is time something must be done." Every eye in the room was fastened on Adam as he stood there, eyes blazing. "I am speaking, ladies and gentlemen, out of personal experience and a deep anger for some of the things I see happening. I am currently heading a Senate committee conducting an investigation of organized crime in the United States. My committee has found itself thwarted and frustrated time after time by men who hold themselves to be more powerful than the highest enforcement agencies of our nation. I have seen judges suborned, the families of witnesses threatened, key witnesses disappear. Organized crime in our country is like a deadly python that is squeezing our economy, swallowing up our courts, threatening our very lives. The great majority of lawyers are honorable men and women doing honorable jobs, but I want to give warning to that small minority who think their law is above our law: you're making a grave mistake and you're going to pay for that mistake. Thank you."

Adam sat down to a tumultuous burst of applause that became a standing ovation. Jennifer found herself on her feet applauding with the others, but her thoughts were on Adam's last words. It was as though he had been speaking directly to her. Jennifer turned and headed toward the exit, pushing her way through the crowd.

As Jennifer approached the door she was hailed by a Mexican lawyer with whom she had worked a year earlier.

He kissed her hand gallantly and said, "What an honor to have you in our country again, Jennifer. I insist you have dinner with me this evening."

Jennifer and Joshua had planned to go to The Maria Elena that night to watch the native dancers. "I'm sorry, Luis. I have an engagement."

His large, liquid eyes showed his disappointment. "Tomorrow then?"

Before Jennifer could answer, an assistant district attorney from New York was at her side.

"Hello, there," he said. "What are you doing slumming with the common folk? How about having dinner with me tonight? There's a Mexican disco called Nepentha, where they have a glass floor lit from underneath and a mirror overhead."

"It sounds fascinating, thanks, but I'm busy tonight."

A few moments later Jennifer found herself surrounded by lawyers she had worked for and against all over the country. She was a celebrity and they all wanted to talk to her. It was half an hour before Jennifer could break free. She hurried toward the lobby, and as she moved to the exit, Adam was walking toward her, surrounded by the press and secret service men. Jennifer tried to retreat, but it was too late. Adam had seen her.

"Jennifer!"

For an instant she thought of pretending she had not heard him, but she could not embarrass him in front of the others. She would say hello quickly and be on her way.

She watched as Adam moved toward her, saying to the press, "I have no more statements to make now, ladies and gentlemen."

A moment later Adam was touching her hand, looking into her eyes, and it was as though they had never been apart. They stood there in the lobby, surrounded by people, and yet they might have been completely alone. Jennifer had no idea bow long they stood there looking at each other.

Finally, Adam said, "I – I think we'd better have a drink."

"It would be wiser if we didn't" She had to get out of this place.

Adam shook his head. "Overruled."

He took her arm and led her into the crowded bar. They found a table at the rear of the room.

"I've called you and I've written to you," Adam said. "You never called me back and my letters were returned."

He was watching her, his eyes filled with questions. "There isn't a day that's gone by that I haven't thought about you. Why did you disappear?"

"It's part of my magic act," Jennifer said lightly.

A waiter came to take their order. Adam turned to Jennifer. "What would you like?"

"Nothing. I really have to leave, Adam."

"You can't go now. This is a celebration. The anniversary of the revolution."

"Theirs or ours?"

"What's the difference?" He turned to the waiter. "Two margaritas."

"No. I – " *All right*, she thought, *one drink*. "Make mine a double," Jennifer said recklessly.

The waiter nodded and left.

"I read about you all the time," Jennifer said. "I'm very proud of you, Adam."

"Thank you." Adam hesitated. "I've been reading about you, too."

She responded to the tone in his voice. "But you're not proud of me."

"You seem to have a lot of Syndicate clients."

Jennifer found her defenses going up. "I thought your lecture was over."

"This isn't a lecture, Jennifer. I'm concerned about you. My committee is after Mike Moretti, and we're going to get him."

Jennifer looked around the bar filled with lawyers. "For God's sake, Adam, we shouldn't be having this discussion, especially in here."

"Where, then?"

"Nowhere. Michael Moretti is my client I can't discuss him with you."

"I want to talk to you. Where?"

She shook her head. "I told you I – "

"I have to talk about us."

"There is no us." Jennifer started to rise.

Adam put his hand on her arm. "Please, don't go. I can't let you go. Not yet."

Reluctantly, Jennifer sat down.

Adam's eyes were fastened on her face. "Do you ever think of me?"

Jennifer looked up at him and did not know whether to laugh or cry. Did she ever think of him! He lived in her house. She kissed him good morning every day, made his breakfast, went sailing with him, loved him. "Yes," Jennifer said finally, "I think of you."

"I'm glad. Are you happy?"

"Of course." She knew she had said it too quickly. She made her voice more casual. "I have a successful practice, I'm well off financially, I travel a great deal, I see a lot of attractive men. How is your wife?"

"She's fine." His voice was low.

"And your daughter?"

He nodded, and there was pride in his face. "Samantha's wonderful. She's just growing up too fast."

She would be Joshua's age.

"You've never married?"

"No."

There was a long moment, and then Jennifer tried to continue, but she had hesitated too long. It was too late. Adam had looked into her eyes and he had known instantly.

He clasped her hand in his. "Oh, Jennifer. Oh, my darling!"

Jennifer could feel the blood rushing to her face. She had known all along that this would be a terrible mistake.

"I have to go, Adam. I have an appointment."

"Break it," he urged.

"I'm sorry. I can't." All she wanted to do was get out of there, to get her son away from there, to flee back home.

Adam was saying, "I'm supposed to fly back to Washington on an afternoon plane. I can arrange to stay over if you'll see me tonight."

"No. No!"

"Jennifer, I can't let you go again. Not like this. We have to talk. Just have dinner with me."

He was pressing her hand tighter. She looked at him and fought with all her strength and found herself weakening.

"Please, Adam," she begged. "We shouldn't be seen together. If you're after Michael Moretti – "

"This has nothing to do with Moretti. A friend of mine has offered me the use of his boat It's called the *Paloma Blanca*. It's docked at the Yacht Club. Eight o'clock."

"I won't be there."

"I will. I'll be waiting for you."

Across the room, at the crowded bar, Nick Vito was sitting with two Mexican *puttanas* a friend had delivered to him. Both were pretty and coarse and underage, the way Nick Vito liked them. His friend had promised they would be special, and he had been right. They were rubbing up against him, whispering exciting promises in his ear, but Nick Vito was not listening. He was staring across the room at the booth where Jennifer Parker and Adam Warner were seated.

"Why don't we go up to your room now, *querido?*" one of the girls suggested to Nick.

Nick Vito was tempted to walk over to Jennifer and the stranger she was with and say hello, but both girls had their hands between his legs and were stroking him. He was going to make one hell of a sandwich.

"Yeah, let's go upstairs," Nick Vito said.

45

The *Paloma Blanca* was a motor sailer and it shone proud and white and gleaming in the moonlight. Jennifer approached it slowly, looking around to make sure that no one had observed her. Adam had told her he would elude the secret service men and apparently he had succeeded. After Jennifer had seated Joshua and Mrs. Mackey at Maria Elena, she had taken a taxi and had had the driver drop her off two blocks before the pier.

Jennifer had picked up the phone half a dozen times to call Adam to say she would not meet him. She had started to write a note, then had torn it up. From the moment she had left Adam at the bar, Jennifer had been in an agony of indecision. She thought of all the reasons why she should not see Adam. Nothing good could possibly come of it, and it could lead to a tremendous amount of harm. Adam's career could be at stake. He was riding on a crest of public popularity, an idealist in a time of cynicism, the country's hope for the future. He was the darling of the media, but the same press that had helped to create him would be out there waiting to push him into the abyss if he betrayed their image of him.

And so Jennifer had made up her mind not to see him. She was another woman, living a different life, and she belonged to Michael now.

Adam was waiting for her at the top of the gangplank.

"I was so afraid you weren't coming," he said.

And she was in his arms and they were kissing.

"What about the crew, Adam?" Jennifer finally asked.

"I sent them away. Do you still remember how to sail?"

"I still remember."

They hoisted the sail and sheeted in for a starboard tack, and ten minutes later the *Paloma Blanca* was heading through the harbor toward the open sea. For the first half hour they were busy navigating, but there was not a moment when they were not acutely aware of each other. The tension kept mounting, and they both knew that what was going to happen was inevitable.

When they finally cleared the harbor and were sailing into the moonlit Pacific, Adam moved to Jennifer's side and put has arms around her.

They made love on the deck under the stars, with the soft, fragrant breeze cooling their naked bodies.

The past and the future were swept away and there was only the present holding the two of them together in its swiftly fleeting moments. For Jennifer knew that this night in Adam's arms was not a beginning; it was an ending. There was no way to bridge the worlds that separated them. They had traveled too far from each other and there was no road back. Not now, not ever. She would always have a part of Adam in Joshua, and that would be enough for her, would have to be enough for her.

This night would have to last her the rest of her life.

They lay there together, listening to the gentle susurration of the sea against the boat.

Adam said, "Tomorrow – "

"Don't talk," Jennifer whispered. "Just love me, Adam."

She covered his lips with small kisses and fluttered her fingers delicately along the strong, lean lines of his body. She moved her hands down in slow circles until she found him, and her fingers began to stroke him.

"Oh God, Jennifer," Adam whispered, and his mouth began to move slowly down her naked body.

46

"The cocksucker kept givin' me the *malocchio,*" little Salvator Fiore was complaining, "so I finally hadda burn 'im."

Nick Vito laughed, for anyone who was stupid enough to fool around with the Little Flower had to be out to lunch. Nick Vito was enjoying himself in the farmhouse kitchen with Salvatore Fiore and Joseph Colella, talking over old times, waiting for the conference in the living room to end. The midget and the giant were his best friends. They had gone through the fire together. Nick Vito looked at the two men and thought happily, *They're like my brothers.*

"How's your cousin Pete?" Nick asked the giant Colella.

"He did cancer and he's under the hammer, but be's gonna be okay."

"He's beautiful."

"Yeah. Pete's good people; he's just had a little bad luck. He was back-up man on a bank job, but it wasn't his stick, and the fuckin' cops tagged him and put him away. He did hard time. The hacks tried to turn him around but they was spinnin' their wheels."

"Hell, yes. Pete's got class."

"Yeah. He always went for big bucks, big broads and big cars."

From the living room there came the sound of raised, angry voices. They listened a moment.

"Sounds like Colfax has a bug up his ass."

Thomas Colfax and Michael Moretti were alone in the room, discussing a large gambling operation that the Family was about to start in the Bahamas. Michael had put Jennifer in charge of making the business arrangements.

"You can't do it, Mike," Colfax protested. "I know all the boys down there. She doesn't. You must let me handle it." He knew he was talking too loudly, but he was unable to control himself.

"Too late," Michael said.

"I don't trust the girl. Neither did Tony."

"Tony's not with us anymore." Michael's voice was dangerously quiet.

Thomas Colfax knew that this was the moment to back down. "Sure, Mike. All I'm saying is that I think the girl's a mistake. I grant you she's smart, but I'm warning you, before she's through she could send us all away."

It was Thomas Colfax whom Michael was concerned about. The Warner Crime Commission investigation was in full swing. When they reached Colfax, how long would the old man stand up to them before he cracked? He knew more about the Family than Jennifer Parker could ever know. Colfax was the one who could destroy them all, and Michael did not trust him.

Thomas Colfax was saying, "Send her away for awhile. Just until this investigation cools down. She's a woman: If they start putting pressure on her, she'll talk."

Michael studied him and made his decision. "All right, Tom. Maybe you've got a point there. Jennifer may not be dangerous, but on the other hand, if she's not with us a hundred percent, why take unnecessary chances?"

"That's all I'm suggesting, Mike." Thomas Colfax rose from his chair, relieved. "You're doing the wise thing."

"I know." Michael turned toward the kitchen and yelled out, "Nick!"

A moment later Nick Vito appeared.

"Drive the *consigliere* back to New York, will you, Nick?"

"Sure thing, boss."

"Oh. On the way I want you to stop and deliver a package for me." He turned to Thomas Colfax. "You don't mind?"

"Of course not, Mike." He was flushed with his victory.

Michael Moretti said to Nick Vito, "Come on. It's upstairs."

Nick followed Michael up to his bedroom. When they were inside, Michael closed the door.

"I'd like you to make a stop before you get out of New Jersey."

"Sure, boss."

"I want you to drop off some garbage." Nick Vito looked puzzled. "The *consigliere*," Michael explained.

"Oh. Okay. Whatever you say."

"Take him out to the dump. There won't be anyone around at this time of night"

Fifteen minutes later the limousine was headed for New York. Nick Vito was at the wheel, with Thomas Colfax in the passenger seat beside him.

"I'm glad Mike decided to sideline that bitch," Thomas Colfax said.

Nick glanced sideways at the unsuspecting lawyer seated beside him. "Uh-huh."

Thomas Colfax looked at the gold Baume & Mercier watch on his wrist. It was three o'clock in the morning, long past his bedtime. It had been a long day and he was tired. *I'm getting too old for these battles*, he thought.

"How far out are we driving?"

"Not far," Nick mumbled.

Nick Vito's mind was in a turmoil. Killing was a part of his job and it was a part he enjoyed, because of the sense of power it gave him. Nick felt like a god when he killed; he was omnipotent. But tonight, he was bothered. He could not understand why he had been ordered to blow away Thomas Colfax. Colfax was the *consigliere*, the man everyone turned to when they were in trouble. Next to the Godfather, the *consigliere* was the most important man in the Organization. He had kept Nick out of the slammer a dozen times.

Shit! Nick thought. *Colfax was right. Mike should never have let a woman come into the business. Men thought with their brains. Women thought with their pussies.*

Oh, how he'd love to get his hands on Jennifer Parker! He'd fuck her until she cried 'Uncle' and then –

"Watch it! You're going off the road!"

"Sorry." Nick quickly steered the car back into his lane.

The dump was a short distance ahead. Nick could feel the perspiration popping out under his arms. He glanced over again at Thomas Colfax.

Snuffing him out would be a cinch. It would be like putting a baby to sleep but, goddamn it! it was the wrong baby! Someone was giving Mike a hand job. This was a sin. It was like murdering his old man.

He wished he could have talked it over with Salvatore and Joe. They could have told him what to do.

Nick could see the dump ahead to the right of the highway. His nerves began to tighten, just as they always did before a hit. He pressed his left arm against his side and felt the reassuring bulk of the short-barreled .38 Smith & Wesson nestling there.

"I could use a good night's sleep," Thomas Colfax yawned.

"Yeah." He was going to get a long, long sleep.

The car was nearing the dump now. Nick checked the rear-view mirror and scanned the road ahead. There were no cars in sight

He put his foot on the brake suddenly and said, "Goddamn it, it feels like I'm getting a flat"

He brought the car to a stop, opened the door and stepped out onto the road. He slipped the gun out of its holster and held it at his side. Then he moved around to the passenger side of the car and said, "Could you give me a hand?"

Thomas Colfax opened the door and stepped out. "I'm not very good at – " He saw the raised gun in Nick's hand and stopped. He tried to swallow. "W-What's the matter, Nick?" His voice cracked. "What have I done?"

That was the question that had been burning inside Nick Vito's mind all evening. Someone was running a game on Mike. Colfax was on *their* side, he was one of them. When Nick's younger brother had gotten in trouble with the Feds, it had been Colfax who had stepped in and saved the boy. He had even gotten him a job. *I owe him, goddamn it*, Nick thought.

He let his gun hand drop. "Honest to God, I don't know, Mr. Colfax. It ain't right."

Thomas Colfax looked at him a moment and sighed. "Do what you have to do, Nick."

"Jesus, I can't do this. You're my *consigliere.*"

"Mike will kill you if you let me go."

Nick knew that Colfax was telling the truth. Michael Moretti was not a man to tolerate disobedience. Nick thought of Tommy Angelo. Angelo had been the wheel man on a fur heist. Michael had ordered him to take the car they had used and have it crushed in a compactor in a New Jersey junkyard the Family owned. Tommy Angelo had been in a hurry to keep a date, so he had dumped the car on an East Side street, where investigators had found it. Angelo had disappeared the next day, and the story was that his body had been put in the trunk of an old

Chevy and compacted. No one crossed Michael Moretti and lived. *But there is a way,* Nick thought.

"Mike don't have to know it," Nick said. His usually slow brain was working rapidly, with an unnatural clarity. "Look," he said, "all you gotta do is blow the country. I'll tell Mike I buried you under the garbage so they'll never find you. You can hide out in South America or somewhere. You must have a little dough stashed away."

Thomas Colfax tried to keep the sudden hope out of his voice. "I have plenty, Nick. I'll give you whatever – "

Nick shook his head fiercely. "I ain't doin' this for money. I'm doin' it because" – *How could he put it into words?* – "I got *respect* for you. The only thing is, you gotta protect me. Can you catch a mornin' plane to South America?"

Thomas Colfax said, "No problem, Nick. Just drop me off at my house. My passport's there."

Two hours later, Thomas Colfax was on an Eastern Airlines jet. It was bound for Washington, D.C.

47

It was their last day in Acapulco, a perfect morning with warm, soft breezes playing melodies through the palm trees. The beach at La Concha was crowded with tourists greedily soaking up the sun before returning to the routine of their everyday lives.

Joshua came running up to the breakfast table wearing a bathing suit, his athletic little body fit and tan. Mrs. Mackey lumbered along behind him.

Joshua said, "I've had plenty of sufficient time to digest my food, Mom. Can I go water skiing now?"

"Joshua, you just finished eating."

"I have a very high metabolism rate," he explained earnestly. "I digest food fast."

Jennifer laughed. "All right. Have a good time."

"I will. Watch me, huh?"

Jennifer watched as Joshua raced along the pier to a waiting speedboat. She saw him engage the driver in earnest conversation, and then they both turned to look at Jennifer. She signaled an okay, and the driver nodded and Joshua began to put on water skis.

The motor boat roared into life and Jennifer looked up to see Joshua beginning to rise on his water skis.

Mrs. Mackey said proudly, "He's a natural athlete, isn't he?"

At that moment, Joshua turned to wave at Jennifer and lost his balance, falling against the pilings. Jennifer leaped to her feet and began racing toward the pier. An instant later, she saw Joshua's head appear above the surface of the water and he looked at her, grinning.

Jennifer stood there, her heart beating fast, and watched as Joshua put the water skis back on. As the boat circled and began to move forward again, it gained enough momentum to pull Joshua to his feet. He turned once to wave at Jennifer and then was racing away on top of the waves. She stood there watching, her heart still pounding from fright. If anything happened to him . . . She wondered whether other mothers loved their children as much as she loved her son, but it did not seem possible. She would have died for Joshua, killed for him. *I have killed for him*, she thought, *with the hand of Michael Moretti*.

Mrs. Mackey was saying, "That could have been a nasty fall."

"Thank God it wasn't."

Joshua was out on the water for an hour. When the boat pulled back into the slip, he let go of the tow rope and gracefully skied up onto the sand.

He ran over to Jennifer, filled with excitement. "You should have seen the accident, Mom. It was incredible! A big sailboat tipped over and we stopped and saved their lives."

"That's wonderful, son. How many lives did you save?"

"There were six of them."

"And you pulled them out of the water?"

Joshua hesitated. "Well, we didn't exactly pull them out of the water. They were kinda sittin' on the side of their boat. But they probably would have starved to death if we hadn't come along."

Jennifer bit her lip to keep from smiling. "I see. They were very lucky you came along, weren't they?"

"I'll say."

"Did you hurt yourself when you fell, darling?"

"Course not." He felt the back of his head. "I got a little bump."

"Let me feel it."

"What for? You know what a bump feels like."

Jennifer reached down and gently ran her hand along the back of Joshua's head.

Her fingers found a large lump. "It's as big as an egg, Joshua."

"It's nothing."

Jennifer rose to her feet. "I think we'd better get started back to the hotel."

"Can't we stay a little while longer?"

"I'm afraid not. We have to pack. You don't want to miss your ball game Saturday, do you?"

He sighed. "No. Old Terry Waters is just waitin' to take my place."

"No chance. He pitches like a girl."

Joshua nodded smugly. "He does, doesn't he?"

When they returned to Las Brisas, Jennifer telephoned the manager and asked him to send a doctor to the room. The doctor arrived thirty minutes later, a portly, middle-aged Mexican dressed in an old-fashioned white suit. Jennifer admitted him into the bungalow.

"How may I serve you?" Dr. Raul Mendoza asked.

"My son had a fall this morning. He has a nasty bump on his head. I want to make sure he's all right."

Jennifer led him into Joshua's bedroom, where he was packing a suitcase.

"Joshua, this is Doctor Mendoza."

Joshua looked up and asked, "Is somebody sick?"

"No. No one's sick, my lad. I just wanted the doctor to take a look at your head."

"Oh, for Pete's sake, Mom! What's the matter with my head?"

"Nothing. I would just feel better if Doctor Mendoza checked it over. Humor me, will you?"

"Women!" Joshua said. He looked at the doctor suspiciously. "You're not going to stick any needles in me or anything, are you?"

"No, señor, I am a very painless doctor."

"That's the kind I like."

"Please sit down."

Joshua sat on the edge of the bed and Dr. Mendoza ran his fingers over the back of Joshua's head. Joshua winced with pain but he did not cry out. The doctor opened his medical bag and took out an ophthalmoscope. "Open your eyes wide, please."

Joshua obeyed. Dr. Mendoza stared through the instrument.

"You see any naked dancin' girls in there?"

"Joshua!"

"I was just askin'."

Dr. Mendoza examined Joshua's other eye. "You are fit as a fiddle. That is the American slang expression, no?" He rose to his feet and closed his medical bag. "I would put some ice on that," he told Jennifer. "Tomorrow the boy will be fine."

It was as though a heavy load had been lifted from Jennifer's heart. "Thank you," she said.

"I will arrange the bill with the hotel cashier, señora. Good bye, young man."

"Good-bye, Doctor Mendoza."

When the doctor had gone, Joshua turned to his mother. "You sure like to throw your money away, Mom."

"I know. I like to waste it on things like food, your health – "

"I'm the healthiest man on the whole team."

"Stay that way."

He grinned. "I promise."

They boarded the six o'clock plane to New York and were back in Sands Point late that night. Joshua slept all the way home.

48

The room was crowded with ghosts. Adam Warner was in his study, preparing a major television campaign speech, but it was impossible to concentrate. His mind was filled with Jennifer. He had been able to think of nothing else since he had returned from Acapulco. Seeing her had only confirmed what Adam had known from the beginning. He had made the wrong choice. He should never have given up Jennifer. Being with her again was a reminder of all that he had had, and thrown away, and he could not bear the thought of it.

He was in an impossible situation. A *no-win* situation, Blair Roman would have called it.

There was a knock on the door and Chuck Morrison, Adam's chief assistant, came in carrying a cassette. "Can I talk to you a minute, Adam?"

"Can it wait, Chuck? I'm in the middle of – "

"I don't think so." There was excitement in Chuck Morrison's voice.

"All right. What's so urgent?"

Chuck Morrison moved closer to the desk. "I just got a telephone call. It could be some crazy, but if it's not, then Christmas came early this year. Listen to this."

He placed a cassette in the machine on Adam's desk, pressed a switch and the tape began to play.

What did you say your name was?

It doesn't matter. I won't talk to anyone except Senator Warner.

The Senator is busy just now. Why don't you drop him a note and I'll see to –

No! Listen to me. This is very important. Tell Senator Warner I can deliver Michael Moretti to him. I'm taking my life in my hands making this phone call. Just give Senator Warner the message.

All right. Where are you?

I'm at the Capitol Motel on Thirty-second Street. Room Fourteen. Tell him not to come until after dark and to make sure he's not followed. I know you're taping this. If you play the tape for anyone but him, I'm a dead man.

There was a click and the tape ended.

Chuck Morrison said, "What do you think?"

Adam frowned. "The town is full of cranks. On the other hand, our boy sure knows what bait to use, doesn't he? Michael – by God-Moretti!"

At ten o'clock that night, Adam Warner, accompanied by four secret service men, cautiously knocked at the door of Room 14 of the Capitol Motel. The door was opened a crack.

The moment Adam saw the face of the man inside, he turned to the men with him and said, "Stay outside. Don't let anyone near this place."

The door opened wider and Adam stepped into the room.
"Good evening, Senator Warner."
"Good evening, Mr. Colfax."
The two men stood there appraising each other.
Thomas Colfax looked older than when Adam had last seen him, but there was another difference, almost indefinable. And then Adam realized what it was. Fear. Thomas Colfax was frightened. He had always been a self-assured, almost arrogant man, and now that self-assurance had disappeared.
"Thank you for coining, Senator." Colfax's voice sounded strained and nervous.
"I understand you want to talk to me about Michael Moretti."
"I can lay him in your lap."
"You're Moretti's attorney. Why would you want to do that?"
"I have my reasons."
"Let's say I decided to go along with you. What would you expect in return?"
"First, complete immunity. Second, I want to get out of the country. I'll need a passport and papers – a new identity."
So Michael Moretti had put out a contract on Thomas Colfax. It was the only explanation for what was happening. Adam could hardly believe his good fortune. It was the best possible break he could have had.
"If I get immunity for you," Adam said, " – and I'm not promising you anything yet – you understand that I would expect you to go into court and testify fully. I would want everything you've got"
"You'll have it."
"Does Moretti know where you are now?"
"He thinks I'm dead." Thomas Colfax smiled nervously. "If he finds me, I will be."
"He won't find you. Not if we make a deal."
"I'm putting my life in your hands, Senator."
"Frankly," Adam informed him, "I don't give a damn about you. I want Moretti. Let's lay down the ground rules. If we come to an agreement, you'll get all the protection the government can give you. If I'm satisfied with your testimony, we'll provide you with enough money to live in any country you choose under an assumed identity. In return for that, you'll have to agree to the following: I'll want full testimony from you regarding Moretti's activities. You'll have to testify before a grand jury, and when we bring Moretti to trial, I'll expect you to be a witness for the government. Agreed?"
Thomas Colfax looked away. Finally he said, "Tony Graelli must be turning over in his grave. What happens to people? Whatever happened to honor?"
Adam had no answer. This was a man who had cheated the law a hundred times, who had gotten paid killers off scot-free, who had helped mastermind the activities of the most vicious crime organization the civilized world had ever known. And he was asking what had happened to honor.
Thomas Colfax turned to Adam. "We have a deal. I want it in writing, and I want it signed by the Attorney General."

"You'll have it." Adam looked around the shabby motel room. "Let's get out of this place."

"I won't go to a hotel. Moretti's got ears everywhere."

"Not where you're going."

At ten minutes past midnight a military truck and two jeeps, manned by armed marines, rolled up in front of Room 14. Four military police went into the room id came out a few moments later, closely escorting Thomas Colfax into the back of the truck. The procession pulled away from the motel with one jeep in front of the truck and the second jeep following in the rear, headed for Quantico, Virginia, thirty-five miles south of Washington. The three-car caravan proceeded at high speed, and forty minutes later arrived at the United States Marine Corps base at Quantico.

The commandant of the base, Major General Roy Wallace, and a detail of armed marines were waiting at the gate. As the caravan came to a stop, General Wallace said to the captain in charge of the detail, "The prisoner is to be taken directly to the stockade. There is to be no conversation with him."

Major General Wallace watched as the procession entered the compound. He would have given a month's pay to know the identity of the man in the truck. The general's command consisted of a 310–acre Marine Corps air station and part of the FBIs Academy, and was the principal center for training officers of the United States Marine Corps. He had never before been asked to house a civilian prisoner. It was totally outside regulations.

Two hours earlier, he had received a telephone call from the commandant of the Marine Corps himself. "There's a man on his way to your base, Roy. I want you to clear out the stockade and keep him in there until further orders."

General Wallace thought he had heard wrong. "Did you say *clear out the stockade*, sir?"

"That's right. I want this man in there by himself. No one is to be allowed near him. I want you to double the stockade guard. Understood?"

"Yes, General."

"One more thing, Roy. If anything happens to that man while he's in your custody, I'm going to have roasted ass for breakfast"

And the commandant had hung up.

General Wallace watched the truck lumber toward the stockade, then returned to his office and rang for his aide, Captain Alvin Giles.

"About the man we're putting in the stockade – " General Wallace said.

"Yes, General?"

"Our primary objective is his safety. I want you to hand pick the guards yourself. No one else is to go near him. No visitors, no mail, no packages. Understood?"

"Yes, sir."

"I want you personally to be in the kitchen when his food is being prepared."

"Yes, General."

"If anyone shows any undue curiosity about him, I want that reported to me immediately. Any questions?"

"No, sir."

"Very good, Al. Stay on top of it. If anything goes wrong, I'll have roasted ass for breakfast."

49

Jennifer was awakened by the soft drumming of the early morning rain, and she lay in bed listening to it gently hammering against the house.

She glanced at the alarm clock. It was time to begin her day.

Half an hour later, Jennifer walked downstairs into the dining room to join Joshua for breakfast. He was not there.

Mrs. Mackey came in from the kitchen. "Good morning, Mrs. Parker."

"Good morning. Where's Joshua?"

"He seemed so tired that I thought I'd let him sleep a little longer. He doesn't have to start back to school until tomorrow."

Jennifer nodded. "Good idea."

She ate her breakfast and went upstairs to say good-bye to Joshua. He was lying in his bed, sound asleep.

Jennifer sat on the edge of the bed and said softly, "Hey, sleepyhead, do you want to say good-bye?"

He slowly opened one eye. "Sure, friend. 'Bye." His voice was heavy with sleep. "Do I have to get up?"

"No. Tell you what. Why don't you laze around today. You can stay inside and have fun. It's raining too hard to go outdoors."

He nodded drowsily. "Okay, Mom."

His eyes closed again and he was asleep.

Jennifer spent the afternoon in court, and by the time she finished and arrived home it was after seven o'clock. The rain, which had been a drizzle all day, was coming down in torrents, and as Jennifer drove up the driveway, the house looked like a besieged castle surrounded by a gray, churning moat.

Mrs. Mackey opened the front door and helped Jennifer out of her dripping raincoat.

Jennifer shook the damp out of her hair and said, "Where's Joshua?"

"He's asleep."

Jennifer looked at Mrs. Mackey with concern. "Has he been sleeping all day?"

"Heavens, no. He's been up and around. I fixed his dinner, but when I went upstairs to get him be had dozed off again, so I just thought I'd let him be."

"I see."

Jennifer went upstairs into Joshua's room and quietly entered. Joshua was asleep. Jennifer leaned over and touched his forehead. He had no fever; his color was normal. She felt his pulse. There was nothing wrong except her imagination. She was letting it run away with her. Joshua had probably been playing too hard all day and it was natural that he was tired. Jennifer slipped out of the room and returned downstairs.

"Why don't you make some sandwiches for him, Mrs. Mackey? Leave them at the side of the bed. He can have them when he wakes up."

Jennifer had dinner at her desk, working on briefs, preparing a trial deposition for the next day. She thought about calling Michael to tell him she was back, but she was hesitant about speaking to him so soon after the night with Adam . . . He was too perceptive. It was after midnight when she finished reading. She stood up and stretched, trying to relieve the tension in her back and neck. She put her papers in her attaché case, turned out the lights and went upstairs. She passed by Joshua's room and looked in. He was still asleep.

The sandwiches on the stand beside the bed were untouched.

The following morning when Jennifer went down to breakfast, Joshua was there, dressed and ready for school.

"Morning, Mom."

"Good morning, darling. How are you feeling?"

"Great. I was really tired. Must have been that Mexican sun."

"Must have been."

"Acapulco's really neat. Can we go back there on my next vacation?"

"I don't know why not. You glad to be getting back to school?"

"I refuse to answer on the grounds that it might incriminate me."

In the middle of the afternoon, Jennifer was taking a deposition when Cynthia buzzed.

"I'm sorry to disturb you, but there's a Mrs. Stout on the line and – "

Joshua's homeroom teacher. "I'll take it."

Jennifer picked up the telephone. "Hello, Mrs. Stout. Is anything wrong?"

"Oh no, everything's fine, Mrs. Parker. I didn't mean to alarm you. I just thought I might suggest to you that it would be a good idea if Joshua got more sleep."

"What do you mean?"

"He slept through most of his classes today. Miss Williams and Mrs. Toboco both mentioned it. Perhaps you could see to it that he gets to bed a bit earlier."

Jennifer stared at the telephone. "I – yes, I'll do that"

Slowly, she replaced the receiver and turned to the people in the room watching her.

"I – I'm sorry," she said. "Excuse me."

She hurried out to the reception room. "Cynthia, find Dan. Ask him to finish the deposition for me. Something has come up."

"All – " Jennifer was already out the door.

She drove home like a madwoman, exceeding the speed limit, going through red lights, her mind filled with visions of something terrible having happened to Joshua. The drive seemed interminable and when her house appeared in the distance, Jennifer half expected to see the driveway filled with ambulances and police cars. The driveway was deserted. Jennifer pulled up beside the front door and hurried into the house.

"Joshua!"

He was in the den watching a baseball game on television.

"Hi, Mom. You're home early. Did you get fired?"

Jennifer stood in the doorway staring at him, her body flooding with relief. She felt like an idiot.

"You should have seen the last inning. Craig Swan was fantastic!"

"How do you feel, son?"

"Great."

Jennifer put her hand on his forehead. He had no fever.

"You sure you're all right?"

"Of course I am. Why do you look so funny? You worried about something? You want to have a man-to-man talk?"

She smiled. "No, darling, I just – does anything hurt you?"

He groaned. "I'll say. The Mets are losing six to five. You know what happened in the first inning?"

He began an excited replay of his favorite team's exploits. Jennifer stood there looking at him, adoring him, thinking, *Damn my imagination! Of course he's all right.*

"You go on and watch the rest of the game. I'll see about dinner."

Jennifer went into the kitchen, lighthearted. She decided to make a banana cake, one of Joshua's favorite desserts.

Thirty minutes later, when Jennifer returned to the study, Joshua was lying on the floor, unconscious.

The ride to Blinderman Memorial Hospital seemed to take forever. Jennifer sat in the back of the ambulance clutching Joshua's hand. An attendant was holding an oxygen mask over Joshua's face. He had not regained consciousness. The ambulance's siren was keening, but the traffic was heavy and the ambulance went slowly while curious people gaped through the windows, staring at the white-faced woman and the unconscious boy. It seemed to Jennifer a sickening violation of privacy.

"Why can't they use one-way glass in ambulances?" Jennifer demanded.

The attendant looked up, startled. "Ma'am?"

"Nothing . . . nothing."

After what seemed an eternity, the ambulance pulled up at the emergency entrance at the back of the hospital. Two interns were waiting at the door. Jennifer stood there held less, watching as Joshua was removed from the ambulance and transferred to a gurney.

An attendant asked, "Are you the boy's mother?"

"Yes."

"This way, please."

What followed was a blurred kaleidoscope of sound and light and movement Jennifer watched Joshua being wheeled down a long, white corridor to an X-ray room.

She started to follow, but the attendant said, "You'll have to check him in first."

A thin woman at the front desk was saying to Jennifer, "How do you plan to pay for this? Do you have Blue Cross or some other form of insurance?"

Jennifer wanted to scream at the woman, wanted to get back to Joshua's side, but she forced herself to answer the questions, and when they were over and Jennifer had filled out several forms, the woman allowed Jennifer to leave.

She hurried down to the X-ray room and went inside. The room was empty. Joshua was gone. Jennifer ran back to the hallway, looking around frantically. A nurse passed by.

Jennifer clutched her arm. "Where's my son?"

The nurse said, "I don't know. What's his name?"

"Joshua. Joshua Parker."

"Where did you leave him?"

"He – he was having X-rays – he – " Jennifer was beginning to be incoherent. "What have they done with him! Tell me!"

The nurse took a closer look at Jennifer and said, "Wait here, Mrs. Parker. I'll see if I can find out."

She came back a few minutes later. "Dr. Morris would like to see you. Come this way, please."

Jennifer found that her legs were trembling. It was difficult to walk.

"Are you all right?" The nurse was staring at her.

Her mouth was dry with fear. "I want my son."

They came to a room filled with strange-looking equipment. "Wait here, please."

Dr. Morris came in a few moments later. He was a very fat man with a red face and nicotine stains on his fingers. "Mrs. Parker?"

"Where's Joshua?"

"Step in here a moment, please." He led Jennifer into a small office across from the room with the strange-looking equipment. "Please sit down."

Jennifer took a seat. "Joshua is – it's – it's nothing serious, is it, Doctor?"

"We don't know yet." His voice was surprisingly soft for a man of his size. "I need some information. How old is your son?"

"He's only seven."

The *only* had slipped out, a reprimand to God.

"Was he in an accident recently?"

A vision flashed through Jennifer's mind of Joshua turning to wave and losing his balance and hitting the pilings. "He – he had a water skiing accident. He bumped his head."

The doctor was making notes. "How long ago was that?"

"I – a few – a few days ago. In Acapulco." It was difficult to think straight.

"Did he seem all right after the accident?"

"Yes. He had a lump on the back of his head, but otherwise he – he seemed fine."

"Did you notice any lapse of memory?"

"No."

"Any personality changes?"

"No."

"No convulsions or stiff neck or headache?"

"No."

The doctor stopped writing and looked up at Jennifer. "I've had an X-ray done, but it's not enough. I want to do a CAT scan."

"A – ?"

"It's a new computerized machine from England that takes pictures of the inside of the brain. I may want to make some additional tests afterward. Is that all right with you?"

"If – if – if" – she was stammering – "it's necessary. It – it won't hurt him, will it?"

"No. I may also need to do a spinal puncture."

He was frightening her.

She forced the question out of her mouth. "What do you think it is? What's the matter with my son?" She did not recognize the sound of her own voice.

"I'd prefer not to make any guesses, Mrs. Parker. We'll know in an hour or two. He's awake now, if you'd like to see him."

"Oh, please!"

A nurse led her to Joshua's room. He was lying in bed, a pale small figure. He looked up as Jennifer entered.

"Hi, Mom."

"Hi there." She sat at the edge of his bed. "How do you feel?"

"Kind of funny. It's like I'm not here."

Jennifer reached out and took his hand. "You're here, darling. And I'm with you."

"I can see two of everything."

"Did – did you tell the doctor that?"

"Uh – huh. I saw two of him. I hope he doesn't send you two bills."

Jennifer gently put her arms around Joshua and hugged him. His body seemed frail and shrunken.

"Mom?"

"Yes, darling?"

"You won't let me die, will you?"

Her eyes were suddenly stinging. "No, Joshua, I won't let you die. The doctors are going to make you well and then I'm going to take you home."

"Okay. And you promised we can go back to Acapulco sometime."

"Yes. As soon as – "

He was asleep.

Dr. Morris came into the room with two men wearing white jackets.

"We'd like to begin the tests now, Mrs. Parker. They won't take long. Why don't you wait in here and make yourself comfortable?"

Jennifer watched them take Joshua out of the room. She sat on the edge of the bed, feeling as though she had been physically beaten. All the energy had drained out of her. She sat there, staring at the white wall, in a trance.

A moment later a voice said, "Mrs. Parker – "

Jennifer looked up and Dr. Morris was there.

"Please go ahead and do the tests," Jennifer said.

He looked at her oddly. "We've finished."

Jennifer looked at the clock on the wall. She had been sitting there for two hours. Where had the time gone? She looked into the doctor's face, reading it, searching for the small, tell-tale signs that would reveal whether he had good news or bad news for her. How many times had she done this before, reading the faces of jurors, knowing in advance from their expressions what the verdict would be? A hundred times? Five hundred? Now, because of the panic raging within her, Jennifer could tell nothing. Her body began to shake uncontrollably.

Dr. Morris said, "Your son is suffering from a subdural hematoma. In layman's terms, there has been a massive trauma to his brain."

Her throat was suddenly so dry that no words could come out.

"Wh – " She swallowed and tried again. "What does that – ?" She could not finish the sentence.

"I want to operate immediately. I'll need your permission."

He was playing some kind of cruel prank on her. In a moment he was going to smile and tell her that Joshua was fine. I was just punishing you, Mrs. Parker, for wasting my time. There's nothing wrong with your son except that he needs sleep. He's a growing boy. You mustn't take up our time when we have patients to look after who are really ill. He was going to smile at her and say, "You can take your son home now."

Dr. Morris was going on. "He's young and his body seems strong. There's every reason to hope the operation will be a success."

He was going to cut open her baby's brain, tear into it with his sharp instruments, perhaps destroy whatever it was that made Joshua, Joshua. Perhaps – kill him.

"No!" It was an angry cry.

"You won't give us permission to operate?"

"I – " Her mind was so confused she could not think. "Wh – what will happen if you don't operate?"

Dr. Morris said simply, "Your son will die. Is the boy's father here?"

Adam! Oh, how she wanted Adam, how she wanted to feel his arms around her, comforting her. She wanted him to tell her that everything was going to be all right, that Joshua was going to be fine.

"No," Jennifer replied finally, "he's not. I – I give you my permission. Go ahead with the operation."

Dr. Morris filled out a form and handed it to her. "Would you sign this, please?"

Jennifer signed the paper without looking at it. "How long will it take?"

"I won't know until I open – " He saw the look on her face. "Until I begin the operation. Would you like to wait here?"

"No!" The walls were closing in on her, choking her. She could not breathe. "Is there a place where I can pray?"

It was a small chapel with a painting of Jesus over the altar. The room was deserted except for Jennifer. She knelt, but she was unable to pray. She was not a religious person; why would God listen to her now? She tried to quiet her mind so that she could talk to God, but her fear was too strong; it had taken complete possession of her. She kept berating herself mercilessly. *If I only hadn't taken Joshua to Acapulco*, she thought . . . *If I hadn't let him go water skiing . . . If I hadn't trusted that Mexican doctor . . . If. If. If.* She made bargains with God. *Make him well again and I'll do anything you ask of me.*

She denied God. *If there was a God, would he do this to a child who had never harmed anyone? What kind of God lets innocent children die?*

Finally, out of sheer exhaustion, Jennifer's thoughts slowed and she remembered what Dr. Morris had said. *He's young and his body seems strong. There's every reason to hope the operation will be a success.*

Everything was going to be all right. Of course it was. When this was over, she would take Joshua away someplace where he could rest. Acapulco, if he liked. They would read and play games and talk . . .

When finally Jennifer was too exhausted to think any longer, she slumped into a seat, her mind a dazed blank, empty. Someone was touching her arm and she looked up and Dr. Morris was standing over her. Jennifer looked into his face and had no need to ask any questions.

She lost consciousness.

50

Joshua lay on a narrow metal table, his body eternally still. He looked I though be were peacefully asleep, his handsome young face filled with secret, far-off dreams. Jennifer had seen that expression a thousand times as Joshua had snuggled into his warm bed while Jennifer had at sat his side, studying the face of her young son, filled with a love that was so strong it choked her. And how many times had she gently tucked his blanket around him to protect him from the cold of the night?

Now the cold was deep inside Joshua's body. He would never be warm again. Those bright eyes would never open again and look at her, and she would never see the smile on his lips, or hear his voice, or feel his small, strong arms around her. He was naked beneath the sheet.

Jennifer said to the doctor, "I want you to cover him with a blanket. He'll be cold."

"He can't – " and Dr. Morris looked into Jennifer's eyes and what he saw there made him say, "Yes, of course, Mrs. Parker," and he turned to the nurse and said, "Get a blanket."

There were half a dozen people in the room, most of them in white uniforms and they all seemed to be talking to Jennifer, but she could not hear what they were saying. It was as though she were in a bell jar, shut off from the rest of them. She could see their lips moving, but there was no sound. She wanted to yell at them to go away, but she was afraid of frightening Joshua. Someone was shaking her arm and the spell was broken and the room was suddenly filled with a roar of sound, and everyone seemed to be talking at once.

Dr. Morris was saying, " . . . necessary to perform an autopsy."

Jennifer said quietly, "If you touch my son again, I'll kill you."

And she smiled at everyone around her because she did not want them to become angry with Joshua.

A nurse was trying to persuade Jennifer to leave the room, but she shook her head. "I can't leave him alone. Someone might turn out the lights. Joshua is afraid of the dark."

Someone squeezed her arm and Jennifer felt the prick of a needle, and a moment later a feeling of great warmth and peace engulfed her, and she slept.

When Jennifer awakened, it was late afternoon. She was in a small room in the hospital and someone had undressed her and clothed her in a hospital gown. She rose to her feet and dressed and went looking for Dr. Morris. She was supernaturally calm.

Dr. Morris said, "We'll make all the funeral arrangements for you, Mrs. Parker. You won't have to – "

"I'll take care of it."

"Very well." He hesitated, embarrassed. "About the autopsy, I know you didn't mean what you said this morning. I – "

"You're wrong."

During the next two days, Jennifer went through all the rituals of death. She went to a local undertaker and made the funeral arrangements. She selected a white casket with a satin lining. She was self-possessed and dry-eyed and, later, when she tried to think about it, she had no recollection of any of it. It was as though someone else had taken over her body and mind and was acting for her. She was in a state of deep shock, hiding behind its protective shell to keep from going insane.

As Jennifer was leaving the undertaker's office, he said, "If there are any special clothes you would like your son buried in, Mrs. Parker, you can have them brought in and we'll dress him."

"I'll dress Joshua myself."

He looked at her in surprise. "If you wish, of course, but – " He watched her leave, wondering if she knew what it was like to dress a corpse.

Jennifer drove home, pulled the car into the driveway and entered the house.

Mrs. Mackey was in the kitchen, her eyes red, her face twisted with grief. "Oh, Mrs. Parker! I can't believe – "

Jennifer neither saw nor heard her. She moved past Mrs. Mackey and walked upstairs into Joshua's room. It was exactly the same. Nothing had changed, except that the room was empty. Joshua's books and games and baseball and skiing equipment were all there, waiting for him. Jennifer stood in the doorway, staring at the room, trying to remember why she had come there. *Oh, yes. Clothes for Joshua.* She walked over to the closet. There was a dark blue suit she had bought for him on his last birthday. Joshua had worn it the evening she had taken him to dinner at Lutéce. She remembered that evening vividly. Joshua had looked so grown up and Jennifer had thought with a pang, *One day he'll be sitting here with the girl he's going to marry.* That day would never come now. There would be no growing up. No girl. No life.

Next to the blue suit were several pairs of blue jeans and slacks and tee shirts, one with the name of Joshua's baseball team on it. Jennifer stood there running her hands aimlessly over the clothes, losing all track of time.

Mrs. Mackey appeared at her aide. "Are you all right Mrs. Parker?"

Jennifer said politely, "I'm fine, thank you, Mrs. Mackey."

"Can I help you with something?"

"No, thank you. I'm going to dress Joshua. What do you think he would like to wear?" Her voice was bright and cheerful, but her eyes were dead.

Mrs. Mackey looked into them and was frightened. "Why don't you lie down a bit, dear? I'm going to call the doctor."

Jennifer's hands moved across the clothes hanging in the closet. She pulled the baseball uniform from the hanger. "I think Joshua would like this. Now, what else will he need?"

Mrs. Mackey watched helplessly as Jennifer went over to the dresser and took out underwear, socks and a shirt. *Joshua needed these things because he was going away on a holiday. A long holiday.*

"Do you think he'll be warm enough in this?"

Mrs. Mackey burst into tears. "Please, don't," she begged. "Leave those things. I'll take care of it"

But Jennifer was already on her way downstairs with them.

The body was in the mortuary's slumber room. They had placed Joshua on a long table that dwarfed the small figure.

When Jennifer returned with Joshua's clothes, the mortician tried once again. "I spoke to Doctor Morris. We both agree that it would be much better, Mrs. Parker, if you would let us handle this. We're quite used to it and – "

Jennifer smiled at him. "Get out."

He swallowed and said, "Yes, Mrs. Parker."

Jennifer waited until he had left the room and then she turned to her son.

She looked into his sleeping face and said, "Your mother is going to take care of you, my darling. You're going to wear your baseball uniform. You'll like that, won't you?"

She pulled the sheet away and looked at his naked, shrunken body, and then she began to dress him. She started to slip his shorts on him and she recoiled from the icy cold of his flesh. It was as hard and stiff as marble. Jennifer tried to tell herself that this piece of chill, lifeless flesh was not her son, that Joshua was away somewhere, warm and happy, but she was unable to make herself believe it. It was Joshua on this table. Jennifer's body began to shake. It was as though the cold inside Joshua had gotten inside her, chilling her to the marrow. She said fiercely to herself, *Stop it! Stop it! Stop it! Stop it! Stop it!*

She took deep, shuddering breaths, and when she was finally calmer she resumed dressing her son, talking to him all the while. She pulled his shorts on, then his trousers, and when she lifted him up to put his shirt on, his head slipped and fell against the table and Jennifer cried out, "I'm sorry, Joshua, forgive me!" and she began to weep.

It took Jennifer almost three hours to dress Joshua. He was wearing his baseball uniform and favorite tee shirt, white socks and sneakers. The baseball cap shadowed his face, so Jennifer finally laid it on his chest. "You can carry it with you, my darling."

When the undertaker came and looked into the room, Jennifer was standing over the dressed body, holding Joshua's hand and talking to him.

The man walked over and said gently, "We'll take care of him now."

Jennifer took one last look at her son. "Please be careful with him. He hurt his head, you know."

The funeral was simple. Jennifer and Mrs. Mackey were the only ones there to watch the small white coffin being lowered into the freshly dug grave. Jennifer had thought of telling Ken Bailey, for Ken and Joshua had loved each other, but Ken was no longer in their lives.

When the first shovelful of dirt had been thrown on the coffin, Mrs. Mackey said, "Come along, dear. I'll take you home."

Jennifer said politely, "I'm fine. Joshua and I won't be needing you any more, Mrs. Mackey. I'll see that you get a years wages and I'll give you a reference. Joshua and I thank you for everything."

Mrs. Mackey stood there staring as Jennifer turned and walked away. She walked carefully, standing very straight, as though she were going down an eternal corridor wide enough for only one person.

The house was still and peaceful. She went up to Joshua's room and closed the door behind her and lay on his bed, looking at all the things that belonged to him, all the things he had loved. Her whole world was in this room. There was nothing for her to do now, nowhere for her to go. There was only Joshua. Jennifer started with the day he was born and relived all her memories of him.

Joshua taking his first steps . . . Joshua saying *car-car* and *Mama*, go *play with your toys*. . . Joshua going off to school alone for the first time, a tiny, brave figure . . . Joshua lying in bed with the measles, his body racked with misery . . . Joshua hitting a home run and winning the game for his team . . . Joshua sailing . . . Joshua feeding an elephant at the zoo . . . Joshua singing *Shine On, Harvest Moon* on Mother's Day . . . The memories flowed on, home movies in her mind. They stopped on the day Jennifer and Joshua were to leave for Acapulco.

Acapulco . . . where she had seen Adam and made love with him. She was being punished because she had thought only of herself. *Of course*, Jennifer thought, *This is my punishment. This is my hell.*

And she started all over again, beginning with the day Joshua was born . . . Joshua taking his first steps . . . Joshua saying *car-car*, and *Mama, go play with your toys* . . .

Time slipped away. Sometimes Jennifer would hear a telephone ring in some distant recess of the house, and once she heard someone knocking at the front door, but those sounds had no meaning for her. She would not allow anything to interrupt her being with her son. She stayed in the room, eating nothing and drinking nothing, lost in her own private world with Joshua. She had no sense of time, no idea how long she lay there.

It was five days later that Jennifer heard the front door bell again and the sound of someone pounding on the door, but she paid no attention Whoever it was would go away and leave her alone. Dimly she heard the sound of glass breaking, and a few moments later the door to Joshua's room burst open and Michael Moretti loomed in the doorway.

He took one look at the gaunt, hollow-eyed figure staring up at him from the bed and he said, "Jesus Christ!"

It took all of Michael Moretti's strength to get Jennifer out of the room. She fought him hysterically, punching him and clawing at his eyes. Nick Vito was waiting downstairs and it took the two of them to force Jennifer into the car. Jennifer had no idea who they were or why they were there. She only knew that they were taking her away from her son. She tried to tell them that she would die if they did this to her, but she was finally too exhausted to fight any longer. She fell asleep.

When Jennifer awakened, she was in a bright, clean room with a picture window with a view of a mountain and a blue lake in the distance. A uniformed nurse was seated in a chair next to the bed, reading a magazine. She looked up as Jennifer opened her eyes.

"Where am I?" It hurt her throat to speak.

"You're with friends, Miss Parker. Mr. Moretti brought you here. He's been very concerned about you. He'll be so pleased to know you're awake."

The nurse hurried out of the room. Jennifer lay there, her mind blank, willing herself not to think. But the memories began to return, unbidden, and there was nowhere to hide from them, nowhere to escape to. Jennifer realized that she had been trying to commit suicide without actually having the courage to do it. She simply had wanted to die and was willing it to happen. Michael had saved her. It was ironic. Not Adam, but Michael. She supposed it was unfair to blame Adam. She had kept the truth from him, had kept him ignorant of the son who had been born and who was now dead. Joshua was dead. Jennifer could face that now. The pain was deep and agonizing, and she knew it was a pain that would be with her for as long as she lived. But she could bear it. She would have to. It was justice, demanding its payment.

Jennifer heard footsteps and looked up. Michael had come into the room. He stood there, looking at her with wonder. He had been like a wild man when Jennifer had disappeared. He had nearly been out of his mind for fear that something had happened to her.

He walked over to her bed and looked down at her. "Why didn't you tell me?" Michael sat down on the side of the bed. "I'm sorry."

She took his had. "Thank you for bringing me here. I – think I was a little crazy."

"A little."

"How long have I been here?"

"Four days. The doctor's been feeding you intravenously."

Jennifer nodded, and even that small movement caused great effort. She felt inordinately weary.

"Breakfast is on the way. He gave me orders to fatten you up."

"I'm not hungry. I don't think I ever want to eat again."

"You'll eat."

And to Jennifer's surprise, Michael was right. When the nurse brought her soft-boiled eggs and toast and tea on a tray, Jennifer found she was famished.

Michael stayed there and watched her, and when Jennifer was finished Michael said, "I've got to go back to New York to take care of a few things. I'll return in a couple of days."

He leaned over and kissed her gently. "See you Friday." He slowly traced his fingers across her face. "I want you well, quick. You hear?"

Jennifer looked at him and said, "I hear."

51

The large conference room at the United States Marine Corps base was filled to overflowing. Outside the room, a squad of armed guards was on the alert. Inside was an extraordinary gathering. A special grand jury was seated in chairs against the wall. On one side of a long table sat Adam Warner, Robert Di Silva and the assistant director of the FBI. Across from them sat Thomas Colfax.

Bringing the grand jury to the base had been Adam's idea.

"It's the only way we can be sure of protecting Colfax."

The grand jury had agreed to Adam's suggestions, and the secret session was about to begin.

Adam said to Thomas Colfax, "Would you identify yourself, please?"

"My name is Thomas Colfax."

"What is your occupation, Mr. Colfax?"

"I'm an attorney, licensed to practice in the State of New York, as well as in many other states in this country."

"How long have you been practicing law?"

"For more than thirty-five years."

"Do you have a general practice?"

"No, sir. I have one client."

"Who is your client?"

"For most of those thirty-five years it was Antonio Graelli, now deceased. His place was taken by Michael Moretti. I represent Michael Moretti and his Organization."

"Are you referring to organized crime?"

"I am, sir."

"Because of the position you held for so many years, is it a fair assumption to say that you are in a unique position to know the inner workings of what we shall call the Organization?"

"Very little went on there that I did not know about."

"And criminal activities were involved?"

"Yes, Senator."

"Would you describe the nature of some of the activities?"

For the next two hours, Thomas Colfax spoke. His voice was steady and sure. He named names, places and dates, and at times his recital was so fascinating that the people in the room forgot where they were, caught up in the horror stories Colfax was telling.

He talked of murder contracts given out, of witnesses killed so they could not testify; of arson, mayhem, white slavery – it was a catalogue out of Hieronymus Bosch. For the first time, the innermost operation of the largest crime syndicate in the world was being exposed, laid bare for everyone to see.

Occasionally, Adam or Robert Di Silva would ask a question, prompting Thomas Colfax, having him fill in gaps wherever necessary.

The session was going far better than Adam could have wished when suddenly, near the end, with only a few minutes' left, the catastrophe occurred.

One of the men on the grand jury had asked a question about a money-laundering operation.

"That happened about two years ago. Michael kept me away from some of the later stuff. Jennifer Parker handled that."

Adam froze.

Robert Di Silva said, "Jennifer Parker?" There was a bursting eagerness in his question.

"Yes, sir." A vindictive note crept into Thomas Colfax's voice. "She's the Organization's house counsel now."

Adam wanted desperately to quiet him, to keep what he was saying off the record, but it was too late. Di Silva was going for the jugular vein and nothing would stop him.

"Tell us about her," Di Silva said tightly.

Thomas Colfax went on. "Jennifer Parker's involved in setting up dummy corporations, laundering money . . ."

Adam tried to break in. "I don't – "

" . . . murder."

The word hung in the room.

Adam broke the silence. "We – we have to stick to the facts, Mr. Colfax. You're not trying to tell us that Jennifer Parker was involved in a killing?"

"That's exactly what I'm telling you. She ordered a hit on a man who kidnapped her son. The man's name was Frank Jackson. She told Moretti to kill him and he did."

There was an excited murmur of voices.

Her son! Adam was thinking: *There has to be some mistake.*

He stammered, "I think – I think we have enough evidence without hearsay. We – "

"It's not hearsay," Thomas Colfax assured him. "I was in the room with Moretti when she called."

Adam's hands under the table were pressing together so hard that they were drained of blood. "The witness looks tired. I think that's enough for this session."

Robert Di Silva said to the special grand jury, "I'd like to make a suggestion about procedure . . ."

Adam was not listening. He was wondering where Jennifer was. She had disappeared again. Adam had repeatedly tried to find her. But now he was desperate. He had to reach her, and quickly.

52

The largest undercover operation in law enforcement in the United States began to move ahead.

The Federal Strike Force Against Organized Crime and Racketeering worked side by side with the FBI, the Postal and Customs Services, the Internal Revenue Service, the Federal Bureau of Narcotics, and half a dozen other agencies.

The scope of the investigation included murder, conspiracy to commit murder, racketeering, extortion, income tax evasion, union frauds, arson, loan-sharking and drugs.

Thomas Colfax had given them the key to a Pandora's box of crime and corruption that was going to help wipe out a major part of organized crime.

Michael Moretti's Family would be hardest hit, but the evidence touched dozens of other Families around the country.

Across the United States and abroad, government agents were quietly questioning friends and business associates of the men on their lists. Agents in Turkey, Mexico, San Salvador, Marseilles and Honduras were liaising with their counterparts, giving them information on illegal activities taking place in those countries. Small-time crooks were pulled into the net, and when they talked they were given their freedom in exchange for evidence against the top crime figures. It was all being handled discreetly, so that the main quarry would have no warning of the storm that was about to break over their heads.

As chairman of the Senate Investigating Committee, Adam Warner received a steady stream of visitors at his home in Georgetown, and the sessions in his study often lasted until the small hours of the morning. There was little doubt that when this was over and Michael Moretti's Organization was broken, the presidential race would be an easy victory for Adam.

He should have been a happy man. He was miserable, facing the greatest moral crisis of his life. Jennifer Parker was deeply involved, and Adam had to warn her, to tell her to escape while she still had a chance. And yet, he had another obligation: an obligation to the committee that bore his name, an obligation to the United States Senate itself. He was Jennifer's prosecutor. How could he be her protector? If he warned her and it was discovered, it would destroy the credibility of his investigating committee and everything it had accomplished. It would destroy his future, his family.

Adam had been stunned by Colfax's mention of Jennifer having a child.

He knew he had to speak to Jennifer.

Adam dialed her office number and a secretary said, "I'm sorry, Mr. Adams, Miss Parker is not in."

"It's – it's very important. Do you know where I can reach her?"

"No, sir. Can someone else help you?"

No one could help him.

During the next week, Adam tried to reach Jennifer several times each day. Her secretary would only say, "I'm sorry, Mr. Adams, but Miss Parker is away from the office."

Adam was sitting in the study starting to call Jennifer for the third time that day when Mary Beth walked into the room. Adam casually replaced the receiver.

Mary Beth walked up to him and ran her fingers through his hair. "You look tired, darling."

"I'm fine."

She moved over to a suede armchair across from Adam's desk and sat down. "It's all coming together, isn't it, Adam?"

"It looks that way."

"I hope it's over soon, for your sake. The strain must be terrible."

"I'm bearing up under it, Mary Beth. Don't worry about me."

"But I do worry. Jennifer Parker's name is on that list, isn't it?"

Adam looked at her sharply. "How did you know that?"

She laughed. "Angel, you've turned this house into a public meeting place. I can't help but hear a little of what goes on. Everybody seems so terribly excited about catching Michael Moretti and his woman friend." She watched Adam's face, but there was no reaction.

Mary Beth looked at her husband fondly and thought, *How naïve men are*. She knew more about Jennifer Parker than Adam did. It had always amazed Mary Beth how brilliant a man could be in business or politics, and yet be so silly when it came to women. Look how many truly great men had been married to cheap little floozies. Mary Beth understood about her husband having an affair with Jennifer Parker. After all, Adam was a very attractive and desirable man. And like all men, he was susceptible. Her philosophy was to forgive and never forget.

Mary Beth knew what was best for her husband. Everything she did was for Adam's own good. Well, when all this was over, she would take Adam away somewhere. He *did* look tired. They would leave Samantha with the housekeeper and go someplace romantic. Perhaps Tahiti.

Mary Beth glanced out the window and saw two of the secret service men talking. She had mixed feelings about their presence. Mary Beth disliked the intrusion on her privacy, but at the same time, their being there was a reminder that her husband was a candidate for the presidency of the United States. No, how foolish of her. Her husband was going to *be* the next President of the United States. Everyone said so. The idea of living in the White House was so tangible that just thinking about it warmed her. Her favorite occupation, while Adam was busy with all his meetings, was to redecorate the White House. She would sit alone in her room for hours, changing furniture around in her mind, planning all the exciting things she was going to do when she became First Lady.

She had seen the rooms that most visitors were not allowed in: the White House Library with its almost thee thousand books, the China Room and the Diplomatic Reception Room, and the family quarters and the seven guest bedrooms on the second floor.

She and Adam would live in that house, become a part of its history. Mary Beth shuddered at the thought of how close Adam had come to throwing away their chances because of that Parker woman. Well, that was all over, thank God.

She watched Adam now as he sat at his desk, looking drawn and haggard.

"Can I fix you a cup of coffee, darling?"

Adam started to say no, then changed his mind. "That would be nice."

"It will just take a jiffy."

The moment Mary Beth left the room, Adam picked up the telephone again and began to dial. It was evening and he knew Jennifer's office was closed, but there should be someone at the answering service. Alter what seemed an interminable period of time, the operator answered.

"This is urgent," Adam said. "I've been trying to reach Jennifer Parker for several days. This is Mr. Adams."

"One moment, please." The voice came back on the line. "I'm sorry, Mr. Adams. I have no word on where Miss Parker is. Do you want to leave a message?"

"No." Adam slammed down the receiver, filled with frustration, knowing that even if he did leave a message for Jennifer to call him, there was no way she could return that call.

He sat in his den, looking out at the night, thinking about the dozens of arrest warrants that would soon be drawn up. One of them would be for murder.

It would have Jennifer's name on it.

It was five days before Michael Moretti returned to the mountain cabin where Jennifer was staying. She had spent those days resting, eating, taking long walks around the paths. When she heard Michael's car drive up, Jennifer went out to greet him.

Michael looked her over and said, "You look a lot better."

"I feel better. Thank you."

They walked along the path leading to the lake.

Michael said, "I have something for you to do."

"What is it?"

"I want you to leave for Singapore tomorrow."

"Singapore?"

"An airline steward was picked up at the airport there, carrying a load of coke. His name is Stefan Bjork. He's in jail. I want you to bail him out before he starts talking."

"All right."

"Get back as fast as you can. I'll miss you"

He drew her close and kissed her very softly on her lips, then whispered, "I love you, Jennifer."

And she knew that he had never uttered those words to any one before.

But it was too late. It was finished. Something had died in her forever, and she was left with only the guilt and the loneliness. She had made up her mind to tell Michael that she was leaving. There would be no Adam and no Michael. She had to go away somewhere, alone, and start over. She had a debt to pay. She would do this last thing for Michael and tell him her plans when she returned.

She left for Singapore the next morning.

53

Nick Vito, Tony Santo, Salvatore Fiore and Joseph Colella were having lunch at Tony's Place. They sat at a front booth, and every time the door opened they automatically glanced up to check out the newcomers. Michael Moretti was in the back room, and while there was no current conflict among the Families, it was always better to play it safe.

"What happened to Jimmy?" the giant Joseph Colella was asking.

"*Astutatu-morte,*" Nick Vito told him. "The dumb son of a bitch fell for the sister of a detective. The broad was stacked, I'll give her that. She and her dick brother talked Jimmy into a flip. Jimmy arranged for a sit-down with Mike and he wore a wire hidden in his pants leg."

"So what happened?" Fiore asked.

"What happened was Jimmy got so nervous he had to pee. When he opened up his fly, the fuckin' wire came out"

"Oh, shit!"

"That's what Jimmy did. Mike turned him over to Gino. He used Jimmy's wire to strangle him. He went out *suppilu suppilu* – very slowly."

The door opened and the four men looked up. It was the newspaper boy with the afternoon *New York Post*.

Joseph Colella called out, "Over here, sonny." He turned to the others. "I wanna check the lineup at Hialeah. I got a hot horse runnin' today."

The newspaper boy, a weather-beaten man in his seventies, handed Joseph Colella a paper and Colella gave him a dollar. "Keep the change."

That was what Michael Moretti would have said. Joe Colella started to open the paper and Nick Vito's eye was caught by a photograph on the front page.

"Hey!" he said. "I seen that guy before!"

Tony Santo took a look over Vito's shoulder. "Of course you have, shmuck. That's Adam Warner. He's runnin' for President."

"No," Vito insisted. "I mean I *seen* him." He furrowed his brow, trying to remember. Suddenly it came to him.

"Got it! He was the guy in the bar down in Acapulco with Jennifer Parker."

"What're you talkin' about?"

"Remember when I was down there last month deliverin' a package? I saw this guy with Jennifer. They was havin' a drink together."

Salvatore Fiore was staring at him. "Are you sure?"

"Yeah. Why?"

Fiore said slowly, "I think maybe you better tell Mike."

Michael Moretti looked at Nick Vito and said, "You're out of your fucking mind. What would Jennifer Parker be doing with Senator Warner?"

"Beats me, boss. All I know is they was sittin' in this bar, havin' a drink."

"Just the two of them?"

"Yeah."

Salvatore Fiore said, "I thought you oughtta hear about it, Mike. This Warner asshole is investigatin' the shit outta us. Why would Jennifer be havin' a drink with him?"

That was exactly what Michael wanted to know. Jennifer had talked about Acapulco and the convention, and she had mentioned half a dozen people she had run into. But she had not said a word about Adam Warner.

He turned to Tony Santo. "Who's the business manager of the janitor's union now?"

"Charlie Corelli."

Five minutes later, Michael was speaking to Charles Corelli on the telephone.

". . . The Belmont Towers," Michael said. "A friend of mine lived there nine years ago. I'd like to talk to the guy who was the janitor there then." Michael listened for a moment. "I appreciate it, pal. I owe you one." He hung up.

Nick Vito, Santo, Fiore and Colella were watching him.

"Haven't you bastards got anything to do? Get the fuck out of here." The four men hurriedly left.

Michael sat there, thinking, picturing Jennifer and Adam Warner together. *Why had she never mentioned him? And Joshua's father, who had died in the Viet Nam war. Why hadn't Jennifer ever talked about him?*

Michael Moretti began to pace the office.

Three hours later Tony Santo ushered in a timid, badly dressed man in his sixties who was obviously terrified.

"This is Wally Kawolski," Tony said.

Michael rose and shook Kawolski's hand. "Thanks for coming over, Wally. I appreciate it. Sit down. Can I get you anything?"

"No, no thank you, Mr. Moretti. I'm fine, sir. Thank you very much." He was doing everything but bowing.

"Don't be nervous. I just want to ask you a couple of questions, Wally."

"Sure, Mr. Moretti. Anything you want to know. Anything at all."

"Are you still working at the Belmont Towers?"

"Me? No, sir. I left there, oh, about five years ago. My mother-in-law has bad arthritis and – "

"Do you remember the tenants?"

"Yes, sir. Most of 'em, I guess. They was kind of – "

"Do you remember a Jennifer Parker?"

Walter Kawolski's face lit up. "Oh, sure, She was a fine lady. I even remember her apartment number. Nineteen twenty-nine. Like the year the market crashed, you know? I liked her."

"Did Miss Parker have a lot of visitors, Wally?"

Wally slowly scratched his head. "Well, that's hard to say, Mr. Moretti. I only saw her when she was comin' in or goin' out, like."

"Did any men ever spend the night in her apartment?"

Walter Kawolski shook his head. "Oh, no, sir."

So all this had been about nothing. He felt a sharp wave of relief. He had known all along that Jennifer would never –

"Her boyfriend might have come home and caught her."

Michael thought he must have misunderstood. "Her boyfriend?"

"Yeah. The guy Miss Parker was livin' with there."

The words hit Michael in the stomach like a sledgehammer. He lost control of himself. He grabbed Walter Kawolski by the lapels and jerked him to his feet. "You stupid cocksucker! I *asked* you if – what was his name?"

The little man was terrified. "I don't know, Mr. Moretti. I swear to God, I don't know!"

Michael shoved him away. He picked up the newspaper and pushed it under Walter Kawolski's nose.

Kawolski looked at Adam Warner's photograph and said excitedly, "That's him! That's her boyfriend."

And Michael felt the world crashing down around him. Jennifer had lied to him all this time; she had betrayed him with Adam Warner! The two of them had been sneaking behind his back, conspiring against him, making a fool of him. She had put horns on him.

The ancient juices of vengeance stirred strongly within Michael Moretti, and he knew he was going to kill them both.

54

Jennifer flew from New York to London to Singapore, with a two-hour stopover in Bahrain. The almost-new airport at the oil emirate was already a slum, filled with men, women and children in native garb, sleeping on the floors and on benches. In front of the airport liquor store was a printed warning that anyone drinking in a public place was subject to imprisonment. The atmosphere was hostile, and Jennifer was glad when her flight was called.

The 747 jet landed at Changi Airport in Singapore at four-forty in the afternoon. It was a brand new airport, fourteen miles from the center of the city, replacing the old International Airport, and as the plane taxied down the runway Jennifer could see signs of construction still going on.

The Customs building was large and airy and modern, with rows of luggage carts for the convenience of passengers. The Customs officers were efficient and polite, and in fifteen minutes Jennifer was finished and headed for the taxi stand.

Outside the entrance, a heavy middle-aged Chinese man approached her. "Miss Jennifer Parker?"

"Yes."

"I am Chou Ling." Moretti's contact in Singapore. "I have a limousine waiting."

Chou Ling supervised the storing of Jennifer's luggage in the trunk of the limousine, and a few minutes later they were headed toward the city.

"Did you have a pleasant flight?" Chou Ling asked.

"Yes, thank you." But Jennifer's mind was on Stefan Bjork.

As though reading her thoughts, Chou Ling nodded to a building ahead of them. "That is Changi Prison. Bjork is in there."

Jennifer turned to look. Changi Prison was a large building off the highway, surrounded by a green fence and electrified barbed wire. There were watch-towers at each corner, manned by armed guards, and the entrance was blocked by a second barbed wire fence and, beyond that, more guards at the gate.

"During the war," Chou Ling informed Jennifer, "all British personnel on the island were interned there."

"When will I be able to get to see Bjork?"

Chou Ling replied delicately, "It is a very sensitive situation, Miss Parker. The government is most adamant about drug use. Even first offenders are dealt with ruthlessly. People who *deal* in drugs . . ." Chou Ling shrugged expressively. "Singapore is controlled by a few powerful families. The Shaw family, C. K. Tang, Tan Chin Tuan and Lee Kuan Yew, the Prime Minister. These families control the finance and commerce of Singapore. They do not wish drugs here."

"We must have some friends here with influence."

"There is a police inspector, David Touh – a most reasonable man."

Jennifer wondered how much "reasonable" cost, but she did not ask. There would be time enough for that later. She sat back and studied the scenery. They were passing through the suburbs of Singapore now, and the overwhelming impression was of greenery and flowers blooming everywhere. On both sides of MacPherson Road were modern shopping complexes alongside ancient shrines and pagodas. Some of the people walking along the streets wore ancient costumes and turbans, while others were smartly dressed in the latest western styles. The city seemed a colorful mixture of an ancient culture and a modern metropolis. The shopping centers looked new and everything was spotlessly clean. Jennifer commented on that.

Chou Ling smiled. "There is a simple explanation. There is a five-hundred-dollar fine for littering, and it is strictly enforced."

The car turned on to Stevens Road, and on a hill above them Jennifer saw a lovely white building completely surrounded by trees and flowers.

"That is the Shangri-La, your hotel."

The lobby was enormous, white and immaculately clean, with marble pillars and glass everywhere.

While Jennifer was checking in, Chou Ling said, "Inspector Touh will be in touch with you." He handed Jennifer a card. "You can always reach me at this number."

A smiling bellman took Jennifer's luggage and led her through an atrium to the elevator. There was an enormous garden under a waterfall, and a swimming pool. The Shangri-La was the most breathtaking hotel Jennifer had ever seen. Her suite on the second floor consisted of a large living room and bedroom, and a terrace overlooking a colorful sea of white and red anthuriums, purple bougainvillea and coconut palms. *It's like being in the middle of a Gauguin*, Jennifer thought.

A breeze was blowing. It was the kind of day Joshua loved. *Can we go sailing this afternoon, Mom? Stop doing that,* Jennifer told herself.

She walked over to the telephone. "I would like to place a call to the United States. New York City. Person-to-person to Mr. Michael Moretti." She gave the telephone number.

The operator said, "I'm so sorry. All the circuits are busy. Please try again later."

"Thank you."

Downstairs, the operator looked for approval to the man standing next to the switchboard.

He nodded. "Good," he said. "Very good."

The call from Inspector Touh came an hour after Jennifer checked into the hotel.

"Miss Jennifer Parker?"

"Speaking."

"This is Inspector David Touh." He had a soft, indefinable accent.

"Yes, Inspector. I've been expecting your call. I'm anxious to arrange – "

The inspector interrupted. "I wonder if I might have the pleasure of your company at dinner this evening."

A warning. He was probably afraid of the phone being bugged.

"I would be delighted."

The Great Shanghai was an enormous, noisy restaurant filled, for the most part, with natives who were loudly eating and talking. There was a three-piece band on a platform, and an attractive girl in a *cheongsam* was singing popular American songs.

The maître d' said to Jennifer, "A table for one?"

"I'm meeting someone. Inspector Touh."

The maître d's face broke into a smile. "The inspector is waiting for you. This way, please." He led Jennifer to a table at the front of the room, next to the bandstand.

Inspector David Touh was a tall, thin, attractive man in his early forties, with delicate features and dark, liquid eyes. He was beautifully and almost formally dressed in a dark suit.

He held Jennifer's chair for her, then sat down. The band was playing a deafening rock song.

Inspector Touh leaned across to Jennifer and said, "May I order a drink for you?"

"Yes, thank you."

"You must try a *chendol*."

"A – what?"

"It is made with coconut milk, coconut sugar and little pieces of gelatin. You will like it."

The inspector glanced up and a waitress was at his side instantly. The inspector ordered the two drinks and *dim sum*, Chinese appetizers. "I hope you do not mind if I order your dinner for you?"

"Not at all. I would be pleased."

"I understand that in your country women are used to taking command. Here it is still the man who is in charge."

A sexist, Jennifer thought, but she was in no mood to get into an argument.

She needed this man. Because of the incredible din and the music, it was almost impossible to carry on a conversation. Jennifer sat back and looked around the room. Jennifer had been to other Oriental countries, but the people in Singapore seemed extraordinarily beautiful, men and women both.

The waitress put Jennifer's drink in front of her. It resembled a chocolate soda with slippery lumps in it.

Inspector Touh read her expression. "You must stir it."

"I can't hear you."

He shouted, "You must stir it!"

Jennifer dutifully stirred her drink. She tasted it.

It was awful, much too sweet, but Jennifer nodded and said, "It's – it's different."

Half a dozen platters of dim sum appeared on the table. Some of them were odd shaped delicacies that Jennifer had never seen before, and she decided not to ask what they were. The food was delicious.

Inspector Touh explained, yelling over the roar of the room, "This restaurant is renowned for the *Nonya* style of food. That is a mixture of Chinese ingredients and Malay spices. No recipes have ever been written down."

"I'd like to talk to you about Stefan Bjork," Jennifer said.

"I can't hear you." The noise of the band was deafening.

Jennifer leaned closer. "I want to know when I can see Stefan Bjork."

Inspector Touh shrugged and pantomimed that he could not hear. Jennifer suddenly wondered whether he had chosen this table so they could talk safely, or whether he had selected it so they could not talk at all.

An endless succession of dishes followed the *dim sum* and it was a superb meal. The only thing that disturbed Jennifer was that she had not once been able to bring up the subject of Stefan Bjork.

When they had finished eating and were out on the street, Inspector Touh said, "I have my car here." He snapped his fingers and a black Mercedes that had been double-parked pulled up to them. The inspector opened the back door for Jennifer. A large uniformed policeman was behind the wheel. Something was not right. *If Inspector Touh wanted to discuss confidential matters with me*, Jennifer thought, *he would have arranged for us to be alone.*

She got into the back seat of the car and the inspector slid in beside her. "This is your first time in Singapore, is it not?"

"Yes."

"Ah, then, there is much for you to see."

"I didn't come here to sight-see, Inspector. I must return home as quickly as possible."

Inspector Touh sighed. "You Caucasians are always in such a rush. Have you heard of Bugis Street?"

"No."

Jennifer shifted in her seat so that she could study Inspector Touh. He had a face that was highly mobile and his gestures were expressive. He seemed outgoing and communicative, and yet he had spent the entire evening saying exactly nothing.

The car stopped for a *trishaw*, one of the three-wheeled carriages pedaled by natives. Inspector Touh watched with contempt as the *trishaw* carried two tourists down the street.

"We shall outlaw those one day."

Jennifer and Inspector Touh got out of the car a block away from Bugis Street.

"No automobiles are allowed in there," Inspector Touh explained.

He took Jennifer's arm and they started walking along the busy sidewalk. In a few minutes, the crowds were so thick it was almost impossible to move. Bugis Street was narrow, with stalls on both sides, fruit stalls and vegetable stands and stalls that sold fish and meat. There were outdoor restaurants with chairs set around small tables. Jennifer stood there, drinking in the sights and the sounds and the smells and the riot of colors. Inspector Touh took her arm and shouldered his way through the crowd, clearing a path. They reached a restaurant with three tables in front of it, all occupied. The inspector gripped the arm of a passing waiter, and a moment later the proprietor was at their side. The inspector said something to him in Chinese. The proprietor walked over to one of the tables, spoke to the guests, and they looked at the inspector and quickly rose and left. The inspector and Jennifer were seated at the table.

"Can I order something for you?"

"No, thank you." Jennifer looked at the teeming sea of people thronging the sidewalks and streets. Under other circumstances she might have enjoyed this. Singapore was a fascinating city, a city to share with someone you cared about.

Inspector Touh was saying, "Watch. It is almost midnight."

Jennifer looked up. At first she noticed nothing. Then she saw that all the shopkeepers were simultaneously beginning to close up their stands. In ten minutes, every stall was closed and locked and their owners had disappeared.

"What's happening?" Jennifer asked.

"You will see."

There was a murmur from the crowd at the far end of the street, and the people began to move toward the sidewalk, leaving a cleared place in the street. A Chinese girl in a long, tight-fitting evening gown was walking down the center of the street. She was the most beautiful woman Jennifer had ever seen. She walked proudly and slowly, pausing to greet people at various tables, then moving on.

As the girl neared the table where Jennifer and the inspector were sitting, Jennifer got a better look at her, and up close, she was even lovelier. Her features were soft and delicate, and her figure was breathtaking. Her white silk gown was slit at the sides so that one could see the delicately curved thigh and small, perfectly formed breasts.

As Jennifer turned to speak to the inspector, another girl appeared. She was, if possible, even lovelier than the first. Two more were walking behind her, and in a moment Bugis Street was filled with beautiful young girls. They were a mixture of Malaysian, Indian and Chinese.

"They're prostitutes," Jennifer guessed.

"Yes. Transsexuals."

Jennifer stared at him. It was not possible. She turned and looked at the girls again. She could see absolutely nothing masculine about any of them.

"You're joking."

"They are known as *Billy Boys.*"

Jennifer was bewildered. "But they – "

"They have all had an operation. They think of themselves as women." He shrugged. "So, why not? They do no harm. You understand," he added, "that prostitution is illegal here. But the *Billy Boys* are good for tourism and as long as they do not disturb the guests, the police close an eye to it."

Jennifer looked again at the exquisite young people moving down the street, stopping at tables to make deals with customers.

"They do well. They charge up to two hundred dollars. When they get too old to work, they become Mamasans."

Most of the girls were seated at tables now with men, dickering for their services. One by one, they began to rise and leave with their clients.

"They handle up to two or three transactions a night," the inspector explained. "They take over Bugis Street at midnight and they must be out by six in the morning so that the stands can open for business again. We can leave whenever you're ready."

"I'm ready."

As they moved along the street, an unbidden image of Ken Bailey flashed through Jennifer's mind and she thought, *I hope you are happy.*

On the drive back to the hotel, Jennifer made up her mind that, chauffeur or no chauffeur, she was going to bring up Bjork's name.

As the car turned on to Orchard Road, Jennifer said determinedly, "About Stefan Bjork – "

"Ah, yes. I have arranged for you to visit him at ten o'clock tomorrow morning."

55

In Washington, D.C., Adam Warner was summoned from a meeting to take an urgent telephone call from New York.

District Attorney Robert Di Silva was on the phone. He was jubilant. "The special grand jury just returned the indictments we asked for. Every one of them! We're all set to move." There was no response. "Are you there, Senator?"

"I'm here." Adam forced enthusiasm into his voice. "That's great news."

"We should be able to start closing in within twenty-four hours. If you can fly up to New York, I think we should have a final meeting tomorrow morning with all the agencies so we can coordinate our moves. Can you do that, Senator?"

"Yes," Adam said.

"I'll make the arrangements. Ten o'clock tomorrow morning."

"I'll be there." Adam replaced the receiver.

The special grand jury just returned the indictments we asked for. Every one of them!

Adam picked up the telephone again and began to dial.

56

The visitors' room at Changi Prison was a small, bare room with whitewashed stucco walls, containing one long table with hard wooden chairs set on either side. Jennifer was seated in one of the chairs, waiting. She looked up as the door opened and Stefan Bjork walked in, accompanied by a uniformed guard.

Bjork was in his thirties, a tall, sullen-faced man with protuberant eyes. *A thyroid condition*, Jennifer thought. There were vivid bruises on his cheeks and forehead. He sat down opposite Jennifer.

"I'm Jennifer Parker, your attorney. I'm going to try to get you out of here."

He looked at her and said, "You better make it soon."

It could have been a threat or a plea. Jennifer remembered Michael's words: *I want you to bail him out before he starts talking.*

"Are they treating you all right?"

He cast a covert look at the guard standing near the door. "Yeah. Okay."

"I've applied for bail for you."

"What are the chances?" Bjork was unable to conceal the hope in his voice.

"I think they're pretty good. It will be two or three days at the most."

"I have to get out of this place."

Jennifer rose to her feet. "I'll see you soon."
"Thanks," Stefan said. He held out his hand.
The guard said sharply, "No!"
They both turned.
"No touching."
Stefan Bjork gave Jennifer a look and then said hoarsely, "Hurry!"

When Jennifer returned to her hotel, there was a telephone message that Inspector Touh had called. As she was reading it, the phone rang. It was the inspector.

"While you are waiting, Miss Parker, I thought you might enjoy a little tour of our city."

Jennifer's first reaction was to say no, but she realized there was nothing she could do until she had Bjork safely on a plane out of here. Until then, it was important to keep Inspector Touh's goodwill.

Jennifer said, "Thank you. I would enjoy that."

They stopped to have lunch at Kampachi, and then headed for the countryside, driving north on Bukit Timah Road to Malaysia, going through a series of colorful little villages with a variety of food stands and shops. The people seemed well-dressed and prosperous looking. Jennifer and Inspector Touh stopped at the Kranji Cemetery and War Memorial, walking up the steps and through the open blue gates. In front of them was a large marble cross, and in the background an enormous column. The cemetery was a sea of white crosses.

"The war was very bad for us," Inspector Touh said. "We all lost many friends and family members."

Jennifer said nothing. Her mind could see a grave in Sands Point. But she could not let herself think about what lay beneath the small mound.

In Manhattan, a meeting of law enforcement agencies was in progress at the Police Intelligence Unit on Hudson Street. There was an air of jubilation in the crowded room. Many of the men had gone into the investigation with cynicism, for they had been through this kind of exercise before. Over the past years they had managed to accumulate overwhelming evidence against mobsters and murderers and blackmailers, and in case after case, high-priced legal talent had won acquittals for the criminals they represented. This time it was going to be different. They had the testimony of the *Consigliere* Thomas Colfax, and no one would be able to shake him. For more than twenty-five years he had been the linchpin of the mob. He would go into court, give names, dates, facts and figures. And now they were being given the go-ahead to move.

Adam had worked harder than anyone in the room to make this moment happen. It was to have been the triumphal carriage that would take him to the

White House. Now that the moment was here, it had turned to ashes. In front of Adam was a list of people who had been indicted by the special grand jury. The fourth name on the list was Jennifer Parker, and the charges opposite her name were murder and conspiracy to commit half a dozen different federal crimes.

Adam Warner looked around the room and forced himself to speak. "You're – you're all to be congratulated."

He tried to say more, but the words would not come out. He was filled with such self-loathing that it was a physical pain.

The Spanish are right, Michael Moretti thought. *Vengeance is a dish best eaten cold*. The only reason Jennifer Parker was still alive was because she was out of his reach. But she would be returning soon. And in the meantime, Michael could savor what was going to happen to her. She had betrayed him in every way a woman could betray a man. For that he was going to see that she received special attention.

In Singapore, Jennifer tried again to put a call through to Michael.

"I'm sorry," the switchboard operator told her, "the circuits to the United States are busy."

"Will you keep trying, please?"

"Of course, Miss Parker."

The operator looked up at the man standing guard beside the switchboard, and he gave her a conspiratorial smile.

At his downtown headquarters, Robert Di Silva was looking at a warrant that had just been delivered. It had Jennifer Parker's name on it.

I've finally got her, he thought. And he felt a savage satisfaction.

The telephone operator announced, "Inspector Touh is in the lobby to see you."

Jennifer was surprised, for she had not been expecting him. He must have some news about Stefan Bjork.

Jennifer took the elevator down to the lobby.

"Forgive me for not telephoning," Inspector Touh apologized. "I thought it best to speak to you personally."

"You have some news?"

"We can talk in the car. I want to show you something."

They drove along Yio Chu Kang Road.

"Is there a problem?" Jennifer asked.

"None at all. Bail will be set for the day after tomorrow."

Then where was he taking her?

They were passing a group of buildings on Jalan Goatopah Road, and the driver brought the car to a stop.

Inspector Touh turned to Jennifer. "I'm sure this will interest you."

"What is it?"

"Come along. You will see."

The interior of the building was old and dilapidated-looking, but the overpowering impression was of the smell, wild and primitive and musky. It was like nothing Jennifer had ever smelled before.

A young girl hurried forward and said, "Would you like an escort? I – "

Inspector Touh waved her aside. "We won't need you."

He took Jennifer's arm and they walked outside into the grounds. There were half a dozen large sunken tanks and from them came a series of strange slithering sounds. Jennifer and Inspector Touh reached the first pen. There was a sign: *Keep Your Hands Off the Pool. Danger.* Jennifer looked down. The tank was filled with alligators and crocodiles, dozens of them, all in continuous movement, sliding over and under one another.

Jennifer shuddered. "What is this?"

"It is a crocodile farm." He looked down at the reptiles. "When they are between three and six years old they are skinned and turned into wallets and belts and shoes. You see that most of them have their mouths open. That is the way they relax. It is when they close their mouths that you must be careful."

They moved on to a tank with two enormous alligators in it.

"These are fifteen years old. They are used only for breeding purposes."

Jennifer shivered. "They're so ugly. I don't know how they can stand each other."

Inspector Touh said, "They can't. As a matter of fact, they do not often mate."

"They're prehistoric."

"Precisely. They go back millions of years, with the same primitive mechanisms they had at the beginning of time."

Jennifer wondered why he had brought her here. If the inspector thought that these horrible-looking beasts would interest her, he was mistaken. "May we go now?" Jennifer asked.

"In a moment." The inspector looked up toward the young girl who had met them inside. She was carrying a tray toward the first tank.

"Today is feeding day," the inspector said. "Watch."

He moved with Jennifer toward the first tank. "They feed them fish and pigs' lungs once every three days."

The girl began throwing food into the pen, and instantly it erupted into a churning, swirling mass of activity. The alligators and crocodiles lunged for the raw, bloody food, tearing into it with their saurian fangs. As Jennifer watched, two of them went for the same piece of meat, and instantly they turned on each other, savagely attacking, biting and slashing until the pen started to fill with blood. The eyeball of one was torn loose, but its teeth were sunk into the jaws of its attacker and it would not let go. As the blood began pouring out more heavily, staining the water, the other crocodiles joined in, savaging their two wounded mates, ripping at their heads until the raw skin was exposed. They began to devour them alive.

Jennifer felt faint. "Please, let's get out of here."

Inspector Touh put his hand on her arm. "One moment."

He stood there watching, and after a while he led Jennifer away.

That night, Jennifer dreamt of the crocodiles clawing and tearing each other to pieces. Two of them suddenly turned into Michael and Adam, and in the middle of her nightmare Jennifer woke up, trembling. She was unable to go back to sleep.

The raids began. Federal and local law-enforcement agents struck in a dozen different states and in half a dozen foreign countries, and the raids were orchestrated to take place simultaneously.

In Ohio, a senator was arrested while making a speech to a women's club on honesty in government.

In New Orleans, an illegal national bookmaking operation was shut down.

In Amsterdam, a diamond smuggling operation was halted.

A bank manager in Gary, Indiana, was arrested on charges of laundering Organization money.

In Kansas City, a large discount house filled with stolen goods was raided.

In Phoenix, Arizona, half a dozen detectives on the vice squad were placed under arrest.

In Naples, a cocaine factory was seized.

In Detroit, a nationwide automobile theft ring was broken up.

Unable to reach Jennifer by telephone, Adam Warner went to her office.

Cynthia recognized him instantly.

"I'm sorry, Senator Warner, Miss Parker is out of the country."

"Where is she?"

"The Shangri-La Hotel in Singapore."

Adam's spirits rose. He could telephone her and warn her not to return.

The hotel housekeeper walked in as Jennifer was getting out of the shower.

"Excuse me. What time will you be checking out today?"

"I'm not checking out today. I'm leaving tomorrow."

The housekeeper looked puzzled. "I was told to get this suite ready for a party coming in late tonight."

"Who told you to do that?"

"The manager."

Downstairs, an overseas call was coming in at the switchboard. There was a different operator on duty and a different man was standing over her.

The operator spoke into her mouthpiece. "New York City calling Miss Jennifer Parker?"

She looked at the man standing next to her. He shook his head.

"I'm sorry. Miss Parker has checked out."

The sweeping raids continued. Arrests were made in Honduras, San Salvador, Turkey and Mexico. The net swept up dealers and killers and bank robbers and arsonists. There were crackdowns in Fort Lauderdale and Atlantic City and Palm Springs.

And they continued.

In New York, Robert Di Silva was keeping close track of the progress being made. His heart beat faster as he thought about the net that was closing in on Jennifer Parker and Michael Moretti.

Michael Moretti escaped the police dragnet by sheer chance. It was the anniversary of his father-in-law's death, and Michael and Rosa had gone to the cemetery to pay homage to her father.

Five minutes after they left, a carload of FBI agents arrived at Michael Moretti's house and another carload at his office. When they learned he was not in either place, the agents settled down to wait.

Jennifer realized that she had neglected to make a plane reservation for Stefan Bjork back to the States. She called Singapore Airlines.

"This is Jennifer Parker. I'm booked on your Flight One-Twelve leaving tomorrow afternoon for London. I'd like to make an additional reservation."

"Thank you. Would you hold the line, please?"

Jennifer waited and after a few minutes the voice came back on the line. Was that Parker? P-A-R-K-E-R?"

"Yes."

"Your reservation has been canceled, Miss Parker."

Jennifer felt a small shock. "Canceled? By whom?"

"I do not know. You have been taken off our passenger list."

"There's been some mistake. I'd like you to put me back on that list."

"I'm sorry, Miss Parker. Flight One-Twelve is full."

Inspector Touh was the one to straighten everything out, Jennifer decided. She had agreed to have dinner with him. She would find out what was happening then.

He picked her up early.

Jennifer told the inspector about the mix-up in her hotel and plane reservations.

He shrugged "Our famous inefficiency, I am afraid. I will look into it."

"What about Stefan Bjork?"

"Everything is arranged. He will be released tomorrow morning."

Inspector Touh said something to the driver in Chinese and the car made a U-turn.

"You have not seen Kallang Road. You will find it most interesting."

The car made a left turn on to Lavender Street, then one block later a right turn to Kallang Bahru. There were large signs advertising florists and casket companies. A few blocks later the car made another turn.

"Where are we?"

Inspector Touh turned to Jennifer and said quietly, "We are on the Street With No Name."

The car began to move very slowly. There were only undertakers on both sides of the street, row after row of them: Tan Kee Seng, Clin Noh, Ang Yung Long, Goh Soon. Ahead, a funeral was in progress. All the mourners were dressed in white and a three-piece band was playing: a tuba, a sax and drums. A body was laid out on a table with wreaths of flowers around it and a large photograph of the deceased sat on an easel facing the front. Mourners were sitting around, eating.

Jennifer turned to the inspector. "What is this?"

"These are the houses of death. The natives call them the *die houses.* The word death is difficult for them to pronounce." He looked at Jennifer and said, "But death is only a part of life, is it not?"

Jennifer looked into his cold eyes and was suddenly frightened.

They went to the Golden Phoenix, and it was not until they were seated that Jennifer had a chance to question him.

"Inspector Touh, did you have a reason for taking me to the crocodile farm and the die houses?"

He looked at her and said evenly, "Of course. I thought they would interest you. Especially since you came here to free your client, Mr. Bjork. Many of our young people are dying because of the drugs that are brought into our country, Miss Parker. I could have taken you to the hospital where we try to treat them, but I felt it might be more informative for you to see where they end up."

"All that has nothing to do with me."

"That is a matter of opinion." All the friendliness had gone out of his voice.

Jennifer said, "Look, Inspector Touh, I'm sure you're being well paid to – "

"There is not enough money in the world for anyone to pay me."

He stood up and nodded to someone, and Jennifer turned. Two men in gray suits were approaching the table.

"Miss Jennifer Parker?"

"Yes."

There was no need for them to pull out their FBI credentials. She knew before they spoke. "FBI. We have extradition papers and a warrant for your arrest. We're taking you back to New York on the midnight plane."

57

When Michael Moretti left his father-in-law's grave, he was already late for an appointment. He decided to call the office and reschedule it. He stopped at a telephone booth along the highway and dialed the number. The phone rang once and a voice answered, "Acme Builders."

Michael said, "This is Mike. Tell – "

"Mr. Moretti isn't here. Call back later."

Michael felt his body tightening. All he said was "Tony's Place."

He hung up and hurried back to the car. Rosa looked at his face and asked, "Is everything all right, Michael?"

"I don't know. I'm going to drop you off at your cousin's. Stay there until you hear from me."

Tony followed Michael into the office in the rear of the restaurant.

"I got word that the Feds are crawlin' all over your house and the downtown office, Mike."

"Thanks," Michael said. "I don't want to be disturbed."

"You won't be."

Michael waited until Tony walked out of the room and closed the door behind him. Then Michael picked up the telephone and furiously began to dial.

It took Michael Moretti less than twenty minutes to learn that a major disaster was taking place. As the reports of the raids and arrests began to filter in, Michael received them with mounting disbelief. All his soldiers and lieutenants were being picked up. Drops were being raided; gambling operations were being seized; confidential ledgers and records were being impounded. What was happening was a nightmare. The police had to be obtaining information from someone in his Organization.

Michael placed telephone calls to other Families around the country, and all of them demanded to know what was going on. They were being badly hurt and no one knew where the leak was coming from. They all suspected it was coming from the Moretti Family.

Jimmy Guardino, in Las Vegas, gave him an ultimatum. "I'm calling on behalf of the Commission, Michael." The National Commission was the supreme power that superseded the power of any individual Family when there was trouble. "The police are rounding up all the Families. Someone big is singing. The word we get is that it's one of your boys. We're giving you twenty-fours to find him and take care of him."

In the past, police raids had always netted the small fry, the expendables. Now, for the first time, the men at the top were being pulled in. *Someone big is singing. The word we get is that it's one of your boys.* They had to be right. Michael's Family had been the hardest hit, and the police were looking for him. Someone had given them solid evidence, or they never would have mounted a campaign this big. But who could it be? Michael sat back, thinking.

Whoever was tipping off the authorities had inside information that was known only to Michael and his two top lieutenants, Salvatore Fiore and Joseph Colella. Only the three of them knew where the ledgers were hidden, and the FBI had found them. The only other person who would have had the information was Thomas Colfax, but Colfax was buried under a garbage dump in New Jersey.

Michael sat there and thought about Salvatore Fiore and Joseph Colella. It was difficult to believe that either one of them could have broken *omertà* and talked. They had been with him from the beginning; he had hand picked them. He had allowed them to have their own loan-sharking operation on the side and to run a small prostitution ring. Why would they betray him? The answer, of course, was simple: the chair he was sitting in. They wanted his chair. Once he was out, they could move in and take over. They were a team; they had to be in it together.

Michael was filled with a murderous rage. The stupid bastards were trying to pull him down, but they would not live long enough to enjoy it. The first thing he had to do was arrange bail for his men who had been arrested. He needed a lawyer he could trust – Colfax was dead, and Jennifer – Jennifer! Michael could feel the coldness creeping around his heart again. In his head he could hear himself saying, *Get back as fast as you can. I'll miss you. I love you, Jennifer.* He had said that and she had betrayed him. She would pay for that.

Michael made a telephone call and sat back to wait, and fifteen minutes later Nick Vito hurried into the office.

"What's happening?" Michael asked.

"The place is still buzzin' with Feds, Mike. I drove around the block a couple of times, but I did like you said. I stayed away."

"I've got a job for you, Nick."

"Sure, boss. What can I do for you?"

"Take care of Salvatore and Joe."

Nick Vito stared at him. "I – I don't understand. When you say, *take care of them*, you don't mean – "

Michael shouted, "I mean blow their fucking brains out! Do you need a blueprint?"

"N-no," Nick Vito stammered. "It's just that I-I-I mean – Sal and Joe are your top men!"

Michael Moretti moved to his feet, his eyes dangerous. "You want to tell me how to run my business, Nick?"

"No, Mike. I – sure. I'll take care of them for you. When – ?"

"Now. Right away. I don't want them to live to see the moon tonight. Do you understand?"

"Yeah. I understand."

Michael's hands tightened into fists. "If I had time, I'd take care of them myself. I want them to hurt, Nick. Make it slow, you hear? *Suppilu suppilu.*"

"Sure. Okay."

The door opened and Tony hurried in, his face gray. "There's two FBI agents out there with a warrant for your arrest. I swear to God I don't know how they knew you was here. They – "

Michael Moretti turned to Nick Vito and snapped, "Out the back way. Move!" He turned to Tony. "Tell them I'm in the can. I'll be right with them."

Michael picked up the telephone and dialed a number. One minute later he was talking to a judge of the Superior Court of New York.

"There are two Feds out here with a warrant for my arrest."

"What are the charges, Mike?"

"I don't know and I don't give a shit. I'm calling you to set things up so that I'm bailed out. I can't sit around in the slammer. I've got things to do."

There was a silence and the judge's voice said carefully, "I'm afraid I won't be able to help you this time, Michael. The heat's on all over and if I try to interfere – "

When Michael Moretti spoke, there was an ominous note in his voice. "Listen to me, you asshole, and listen good. If I spend one hour in jail, I'll see to it that you're behind bars for the rest of your life. I've been taking good care of you for a long time. You want me to tell the D.A. how many cases you fixed for me? Would you like me to give the IRS the number of your Swiss bank account? Would you – "

"For God's sake, Michael!"

"Then move!"

"I'll see what I can do," Judge Lawrence Waldman said. I'll try to – "

"Try to, shit! Do it! Do you hear me, Larry? Do it!" Michael slammed down the receiver.

His mind was working swiftly and coolly. He was not concerned about being taken to jail. He knew that Judge Waldman would do as he was told, and he could trust Nick Vito to attend to Fiore and Colella. Without their testimony, the government could not prove a thing against him.

Michael looked in the small mirror on the wall, combed back his hair, straightened his tie, and went out to meet the two FBI agents.

Judge Lawrence Waldman came through, as Michael had known he would. At the preliminary hearing, an attorney selected by Judge Waldman requested bail, and it was set at five hundred thousand dollars.

Di Silva stood there, angry and frustrated, as Michael Moretti walked out of the courtroom.

58

Nick Vito was a man of limited intelligence. His value to the Organization lay in the fact that he followed orders without question and that he carried them out efficiently. Nick Vito had been up against guns and knives dozens of times, but he had never known fear. He knew it now. Something was happening that was beyond his understanding, and he had a feeling that somehow he was responsible for it.

All day he had been hearing about the raids that were taking place, the sweeping arrests that were being made. The street talk was that there was a traitor loose, someone high up in the Organization. Even with his limited intellect, Nick Vito was able to connect the fact that he had let Thomas Colfax live and that, shortly afterward, someone had started betraying the Family to the authorities. Nick Vito knew that it could not be Salvatore Fiore or Joseph Colella. The two men were like brothers to him and they were both as fanatically loyal to Michael Moretti as he was. But there was no way he could ever explain that to Michael, not without getting himself chopped into small pieces; because the only other one who could be responsible was Thomas Colfax, and Colfax was supposed to be dead.

Nick Vito was in a dilemma. He loved the Little Flower and the giant. Fiore and Colella had done him dozens of favors in the past, just as Thomas Colfax had; but he had helped Colfax out of a jam, and look what it had gotten him. So Nick Vito decided he was not going to be softhearted again. It was his own life he had to protect now. Once he killed Fiore and Colella, he would be in the clear. But because they were like brothers to him, he would see that they died quickly.

It was simple for Nick Vito to determine their whereabouts, for they always had to be available in case Michael needed them. Little Salvatore Fiore was visiting his mistress's apartment on 83rd Street near the Museum of Natural History.

Nick knew that Salvatore always left there at five o'clock to go home to his wife. It was now three. Nick debated with himself. He could either hang around the front of the apartment building or go upstairs and take Salvatore inside the apartment. He decided he was too nervous to wait. The fact that he was nervous made Nick Vito more nervous. The whole thing was beginning to get to him. *When this is over*, he thought, *I'm gonna ask Mike for a vacation. Maybe I'll take a couple of young girls and go down to the Bahamas.* Just thinking about that made him feel better.

Nick Vito parked his car around the corner from the apartment house and walked up to the building. He let himself in the front door with a piece of celluloid, ignored the elevator and walked up the stairs to the third floor. He moved toward the door at the end of the corridor, and when he reached it he pounded on it

"Open up! Police!"

He heard quick sounds from behind the door and a few moments later it opened on a heavy chain and he could see the face and part of the naked figure of Marina, Salvatore Fiore's mistress.

"Nick!" she said. "You crazy idiot. You scared the hell out of me."

She took the chain off the door and opened it. "Sal, it's Nick!"

Little Salvatore Fiore walked in from the bedroom, naked. "Hey, Nicky boy! What the fuck you doin' here?"

"Sal, I got a message for you from Mike."

Nick Vito raised a .22 automatic with a silencer and squeezed the trigger. The firing pin slammed into the .22 caliber cartridge, sending the bullet out of the muzzle at a thousand feet a second. The first bullet shattered the bridge of Salvatore Fiore's nose. The second bullet put out his left eye. As Marina opened her mouth to scream, Nick Vito turned and put a bullet in her head. As she fell to the floor, he put one more bullet in her chest, to make certain. *It's a waste of a beautiful piece of ass*, Nick thought, *but Mike wouldn't like it if I left any witnesses around.*

Big Joseph Colella owned a horse that was running in the eighth race at Belmont Park in Long Island. Belmont was a one-and-one-half-mile track, the perfect length for the filly that the giant was running. He had advised Nick to bet on it. In the past, Nick had won a lot on Colella's tips. Colella always put a little money on for Nick when his horses ran. As Nick Vito walked toward Colella's box, he thought regretfully about the fact that there would be no more tips. The eighth race had just started. Colella was standing up in his box, cheering his horse on. It was a large-purse race and the crowd was screaming and yelling as the horses rounded the first turn.

Nick Vito stepped into the box behind Colella and said, "How you doin', pal?"

"Hey, Nick! You got here just in time. Beauty Queen's gonna win this one. I put a little bet on it for you."

"That's great, Joe."

Nick Vito pressed the .22 caliber gun against Joseph Colella's spine and fired three times through his coat. The muffled noise went unnoticed in the cheering crowd. Nick watched Joseph Colella slump to the ground. He debated for an instant whether to take the pari-mutuel tickets out of Colella's pocket, then decided against it. After all, the horse could lose.

Nick Vito turned and unhurriedly walked toward the exit, one anonymous figure among thousands.

Michael Moretti's private line rag.

"Mr. Moretti?"

"Who wants him?"

"This is Captain Tanner."

It took Michael a second to place the name. A police captain. Queens precinct. On the payroll.

"This is Moretti."

"I just received some information I think might interest you."

"Where are you calling from?"

"A public telephone booth."

"Go ahead."

"I found out where all the heat's coming from."

"You're too late. They've been taken care of already."

"*They?* Oh. I only heard about Thomas Colfax."

"You don't know what the hell you're talking about. Colfax is dead."

It was Captain Tanner's turn to be confused. "What are *you* talking about? Thomas Colfax is sitting at the Marine Base in Quantico right now, spilling his guts to everybody who'll listen."

"You're out of your mind," Michael snapped. "I happen to know – " He stopped. What *did* he know? He had told Nick Vito to kill Thomas Colfax, and Vito had said that he had. Michael sat there thinking. "How sure are you about this, Tanner?"

"Mr. Moretti, would I be calling you if I wasn't sure?"

"I'll check it out. If you're right, I owe you one."

"Thank you, Mr. Moretti."

Captain Tanner replaced the receiver, pleased with himself. In the past he had found Michael Moretti to be a very appreciative man. This could be the *big* one, the one that could enable him to retire. He stepped out of the telephone booth into the cold October air.

There were two men standing outside the booth, and as the captain started to step around them, one of them blocked his way. He held up an identification card.

"Captain Tanner? I'm Lieutenant West, Internal Security Division. The Police Commissioner would like to have a word with you."

Michael Moretti hung up the receiver slowly. He knew with a sure animal instinct that Nick Vito had lied to him. Thomas Colfax was still alive. That would explain everything that was happening. *He* was the one who had turned traitor. And Michael had sent Nick Vito out to kill Fiore and Colella. Jesus, he had been stupid! Outsmarted by a dumb hired gunman into wasting his two top men! He was filled with an icy rage.

He dialed a number and spoke briefly into the telephone. After he made a second telephone call, he sat back and waited.

When he heard Nick Vito on the phone, Michael forced himself to keep the fury he felt out of his voice. "How did it go, Nick?"

"Okay, boss. Just like you said. They both suffered a lot."

"I can always count on you, Nick, can't I?"

"You know you can, boss."

"Nick, I want you to do me one last favor. One of the boys left a car at the corner of York and Ninety-fifth Street. It's a tan Camaro. The keys are behind the sun visor. We're going to use it for a job tonight. Drive it over here, will you?"

"Sure, boss. How soon do you need it? I was going to – "

"I need it now. Right away, Nick."

"I'm on my way."

"Good-bye, Nick."

Michael replaced the receiver. He wished he could be there to watch Nick Vito blow himself to hell, but he had one more urgent thing to do.

Jennifer Parker would be on her way back soon, and he wanted to get everything ready for her.

59

It's like some kind of goddamned Hollywood movie production, Major General Roy Wallace thought, *with my prisoner as the star.*

The large conference room at the United States Marine Corps base was filled with technicians from the Signal Corps, scurrying around setting up cameras and sound and lighting equipment, using an arcane jargon.

"Kill the brute and hit the inkies. Bring a baby over here . . ."

They were getting ready to put Thomas Colfax's testimony on film.

"It's extra insurance," District Attorney Di Silva had argued. "We know that no one can get to him, but it will be good to have it on the record, anyway." And the others had gone along with him.

The only person absent was Thomas Colfax. He would be brought in at the last minute, when everything was in readiness for him.

Just like a goddamn movie star.

Thomas Colfax was having a meeting in his cell with David Terry of the Justice Department, the man in charge of creating new identities for witnesses who wished to disappear.

"Let me explain a bit about the Federal Witness Security Program," Terry said. "When the trial is over, we'll send you to whichever country you choose. Your furniture and other belongings will be shipped to a warehouse in Washington, with a coded number. We'll forward it to you later. There won't be any way for anyone to trace you. We'll supply you with a new identity and background and, if you wish, a new appearance."

"I'll take care of that." He trusted no one to know what he was going to do with his appearance.

"Ordinarily when we set people up with a new identity, we find jobs for them in whatever field they're suited for, and we supply them with some money. In your case, Mr. Colfax, I understand that money is no problem."

Thomas Colfax wondered what David Terry would say if he knew how much money was salted away in his bank accounts in Germany, Switzerland and Hong Kong. Even Thomas Colfax had not been able to keep track of it all, but a modest estimate, he would guess, would be nine or ten million dollars.

"No," Colfax said, "I don't think money will be a problem."

"All right, then. The first thing to decide is where you would like to go. Do you have any particular area in mind?"

It was such a simple question, yet so much lay behind it. What the man was really saying was, *Where do you want to spend the rest of your life?* For Colfax knew that when he got to wherever he was going, he would never be able to leave. It would become his new habitat, his protective cover, and he would not be safe anywhere else in the world.

"Brazil."

It was the logical choice. He already owned a two-hundred-thousand-acre plantation there in the name of a Panamanian corporation that could not be traced back to him. The plantation itself was like a fortress. He could afford to buy himself enough protection so that even if Michael Moretti did finally learn where he was, no one would be able to touch him. He could buy anything, including all the women he wanted. Thomas Colfax liked Latin women. People thought that when a man reached the age of sixty-five he was finished sexually, that he no longer had any interest, but Colfax had found that his appetite had grown as he had gotten older. His favorite sport was to have two or three beautiful young women in bed with him at the same time, working him over. The younger the better.

"Brazil will be easy to arrange," David Terry was saying. "Our government will buy you a small house there, and – "

"That won't be necessary." Colfax almost laughed aloud at the thought of his having to live in a small house. "All I will require of you is that you provide me with the new identification and safe transportation. I'll take care of everything else."

"As you wish, Mr. Colfax." David Terry rose to his feet. "I think we've covered just about everything." He smiled reassuringly. "This is going to be one of the easy ones. I'll begin setting things in motion. As soon as you're finished testifying, you'll be on an airplane to South America."

"Thank you." Thomas Colfax watched his visitor leave and he was filled with a sense of elation. He had done it! Michael Moretti had made the mistake of underestimating him, and it was going to be Moretti's final mistake. Colfax was going to bury him so deep that he would never rise again.

And his testimony was going to be filmed. That would be interesting. He wondered whether they would use makeup on him. He studied himself in the small mirror on the wall. *Not bad*, he thought, *for a man my age. I still have my looks. Those young South American girls love older men with gray hair.*

He heard the sound of the cell door opening, and he turned. A marine sergeant was bringing in Colfax's lunch. There would be plenty of time to eat before the filming began.

The first day, Thomas Colfax had complained about the food that was served to him, and from then on General Wallace had arranged for all of Colfax's meals to be catered. In the weeks that Colfax had been confined at the fort, his slightest suggestion had become their command. They wanted to do everything they could to please him, and Colfax took full advantage of it. He had had comfortable furniture moved in, and a television set, and he received a daily supply of newspapers and current magazines.

The sergeant placed the tray of food on a table set for two, and he made the same comment he made every day.

"Looks good enough to eat, sir."

Colfax smiled politely and sat down at the table. Roast beef rare, the way he liked it, mashed potatoes and Yorkshire pudding. He waited as the marine pulled up a chair and sat down across from him. The sergeant picked up a knife and fork, cut off a piece of the meat and began to eat. Another of General Wallace's ideas. Thomas Colfax had his own taster. *Like the kings of ancient times*, he thought. He watched as the marine sampled the roast beef, the potatoes and the Yorkshire pudding.

"How is it?"

"To tell you the truth, sir, I prefer my beef on the well-done side."

Colfax picked up his own knife and fork and began to eat. The sergeant was mistaken. The meat was cooked perfectly, the potatoes were creamy and hot and the Yorkshire pudding was done to a turn.

Colfax reached for the horseradish and spread it lightly over the beef. It was with the second bite that Colfax knew something was terribly wrong. There was a sudden burning sensation in his mouth that seemed to shoot through his whole body. He felt as though he were on fire. His throat was closing, paralyzed, and he began gasping for air. The marine sergeant sitting across from him was staring at him. Thomas Colfax clutched his throat and tried to tell the sergeant what was happening, but no words would come out. The fire in him was spreading more swiftly now, filling him with an unbearable agony. His body stiffened in a terrible spasm and he toppled over backwards to the floor.

The sergeant watched him for a moment, then bent over the body and lifted Thomas Colfax's eyelid to make sure he was dead.

Then he called for help.

60

Singapore Airlines Flight 246 landed at Heathrow Airport in London at seven-thirty A.M. The other passengers were detained in their seats until Jennifer and the two FBI agents were out of the plane and in the airport's security office.

Jennifer was desperately anxious to see a newspaper to find out what was, happening at home, but her two silent escorts denied her request and refused to be drawn into conversation.

Two hours later, the three of them boarded a TWA plane bound for New York.

In the United States Court House at Foley Square an emergency meeting was taking place. Present were Adam Warner, Robert Di Silva, Major General Roy Wallace, and half a dozen representatives from the FBI, the Justice Department and the Treasury Department.

"How the hell could this have happened?" Robert Di Silva's voice was trembling with rage. He turned to the general. "You were told how important Thomas Colfax was to us."

The general spread his hands helplessly. "We took every precaution we could, sir. We're checking now to see how they could have smuggled prussic acid into – "

"I don't give a shit how they did it! Colfax is dead!"

The man from the Treasury Department spoke up. "How much does Colfax's death hurt us?"

"A hell of a lot," Di Silva replied. "Putting a man on a witness stand is one thing. Showing a lot of ledgers and accounts is something else. You can bet your ass that some smart attorney's going to start talking about how those books could have been faked."

"Where do we go from here?" a man from the Treasury Department asked.

The District Attorney replied, "We keep doing what we're doing. Jennifer

Parker's on her way back from Singapore. We have enough to put her away forever. While she's going down, we're going to get her to pull Michael Moretti down with her." He turned to Adam. "Don't you agree, Senator?"

Adam felt ill. "Excuse me."

He quickly left the room.

61

The signalman on the ground, wearing oversized earmuffs, waved his two semaphores, guiding the jumbo 747 toward the waiting ramp. The plane pulled up to a fixed circle and, at a signal, the pilot cut the four Pratt & Whitney turbofan engines.

Inside the giant plane a steward's voice came over the loudspeaker, "Ladies and gentlemen, we have just landed at New York's Kennedy Airport. We thank you for flying TWA. Will all passengers please remain in their seats until a further announcement. Thank you."

There were general murmurs of protest. A moment later the doors were opened by the ramp crew. The two FBI agents seated with Jennifer in the front of the plane rose to their feet.

One of them turned to Jennifer and said, "Let's go."

The passengers watched with curiosity as the three people left the plane. A few minutes later the steward's voice came over the loudspeaker again. "Thank you for your patience, ladies and gentlemen. You may now disembark."

A government limousine was waiting at a side entrance to the airport. The first stop was the Metropolitan Correctional Center at 150 Park Row, that connected into the United States Court House at Foley Square.

After Jennifer had been booked, one of the FBI men said, "Sorry, we can't keep you here. We have orders to take you out to Riker's Island."

The ride to Riker's Island was made in silence. Jennifer sat in the back seat between the two FBI men, saying nothing, but her mind was busy. The two men had been uncommunicative during the entire trip across the ocean, so Jennifer had no way of knowing how much trouble she was in. She knew that it was serious, for it was not easy to obtain a warrant of extradition.

She could do nothing to help herself while she was in jail. Her first priority was to get out on bail.

They were crossing the bridge to Riker's Island now, and Jennifer looked out at the familiar view, a view she had seen a hundred times on the way to talk to clients. And now *she* was a prisoner.

But not for long, Jennifer thought *Michael will get me out*.

The two FBI men escorted Jennifer into the reception building and one of the men handed the guard the extradition warrant.

"Jennifer Parker."

The guard glanced at it. "We've been expecting you, Miss Parker. You have a reservation in Detention Cell Three."

"I have the right to one phone call."

The guard nodded toward the telephone on his desk. "Sure."

Jennifer picked it up, silently praying that Michael Moretti was in. She began to dial.

Michael Moretti had been waiting for Jennifer's call. For the last twenty-four hours he had been able to think of nothing else. He had been informed when Jennifer had landed in London, when her plane had left Heathrow, and when she had arrived back in New York. He had sat at his desk, mentally tracking Jennifer on her way to Riker's Island. He had visualized her entering the prison. She would demand to make a phone call before they put her in a cell. She would call him. That was all he asked. He would have her out of there in an hour, and then she would be on her way to him. Michael Moretti was living for the moment when Jennifer Parker walked through the door.

Jennifer had done the unforgivable. She had given her body to the man who was trying to destroy him. And what else had she given him? What secrets had she told him?

Adam Warner was the father of Jennifer's son. Michael was certain of that now. Jennifer had lied to him from the beginning, had told him that Joshua's father was dead. *Well, that was a prophecy that will soon be fulfilled*, Michael told himself. He was caught in an ironic conflict. On the one hand, he had a powerful weapon he could use to discredit and destroy Adam Warner. He could blackmail Warner with the threat of exposing his relationship with Jennifer; but if he did that, he would be exposing himself. When the Families learned – and they would learn – that Michael's woman was the mistress of the head of the Senate Investigating Committee, Michael would become a laughing-stock. He would no longer be able to hold up his head or command his men. A cuckold was not fit to be a *don*. So the blackmail threat was a double-edged sword and, as tempting as it was, Michael knew that he dare not use it. He would have to destroy his enemies in another way.

Michael looked at the small, crudely drawn map on the desk in front of him. It was Adam Warner's route to where he was going to attend a private fund-raising dinner party that evening. The map had cost Michael Moretti five thousand dollars. It was going to cost Adam Warner his life.

The telephone rang on Michael's desk and he involuntarily started. He picked it up and heard Jennifer's voice on the other end. That voice that had whispered endearments into his ear, that had begged him to make love to her, that –

"Michael – are you there?"

"I'm here. Where are you?"

"They've got me at Riker's Island. They're holding me on a murder charge. Bail hasn't been set yet. When can you – ?"

"I'll have you out of there in no time. Just sit tight. Okay?"

"Yes, Michael." He could hear the relief in her voice.

"I'll have Gino pick you up."

A few moments later Michael reached for the telephone and dialed a number. He spoke into the phone for several minutes.

"I don't care how high the bail is. I want her out *now*."

He replaced the receiver and pressed a button on his desk. Gino Gallo came in.

"Jennifer Parker's at Riker's Island. She should be sprung in an hour or two. Pick her up and bring her here."

"Right, boss."

Michael leaned back in his chair. "Tell her we won't have to worry about Adam Warner after today."

Gino Gallo's face brightened. "No?"

"No. He's on his way to deliver a speech, but he'll never get there. He's going to have an accident at the bridge at New Canaan."

Gino Gallo smiled. "That's great, boss."

Michael gestured toward the door. "Move."

District Attorney Di Silva fought Jennifer's bail with every stratagem at his command. They were appearing before William Bennett, a judge of the Supreme Court of New York.

"Your Honor," Robert Di Silva said, "the defendant is charged with a dozen counts of felony. We had to extradite her from Singapore. If she's granted bail, she'll flee to someplace where there is no extradition. I ask that Your Honor deny bail."

John Lester, a former judge who was representing Jennifer, said, "The District Attorney is guilty of gross distortion, Your Honor. My client did not flee anywhere. She was in Singapore on business. If the government had asked her to return she would have done so voluntarily. She's a reputable attorney with a large practice here. It would be inconceivable that she would run away."

The arguments went on for more than thirty minutes.

At the end of that time, Judge Bennett said, "Bail is grated in the sum of five hundred thousand dollars."

"Thank you, Your Honor," Jennifer's attorney said. "We'll pay the bail."

Fifteen minutes later, Gino Gallo was helping Jennifer into the back of a Mercedes limousine.

"That didn't take long," he said.

Jennifer did not reply. Her mind was on what was happening. She had been completely isolated in Singapore. She had no idea of what had been going on in the United States, but she was certain that her arrest was not an unrelated incident. They would not be after her alone. She badly needed to talk to Michael and find out what had been happening. Di Silva had to be very sure of himself to have had her brought back on a murder charge. He –

Gino Gallo said two words that caught Jennifer's attention.

" . . . Adam Warner . . ."

Jennifer had not been listening.

"What did you say?"

"I said we won't have to worry about Adam Warner no more. Mike is havin' him took care of."

Jennifer could feel her heart begin to pound. "He is? When?"

Gino Gallo raised his hand from the wheel to glance at his watch. "In about fifteen minutes. It's set up to look like an accident."

Jennifer's mouth was suddenly dry. "Where – " She could not get the words out. "Where – where is it going to happen?"

"New Canaan. The bridge."

They were passing through Queens. Ahead was a shopping center with a pharmacy.

"Gino, will you pull up in front of that drugstore? I have to get something."

"Sure." He skillfully turned the wheel and swung into the entrance to the shopping center. "Can I help you?"

"No, no. I'll – I'll only be a minute."

Jennifer got out of the car and hurried inside, nerves screaming. There was a telephone booth at the back of the store. Jennifer reached into her purse. She had no change except for some Singapore coins. She hurried over to the cashier and pulled out a dollar.

"Could I have change, please?"

The bored cashier took Jennifer's money and gave her a handful of silver. Jennifer dashed back to the telephone. A stout woman was picking up the receiver and dialing.

Jennifer said, "I have an emergency. I wonder if I could – "

The woman glared at her and kept dialing.

"Hello, Hazel," the woman whooped. "My horoscope was right. I've had the worst day! You know the shoes I was going to pick up at Delman's? Would you believe they sold the only pair they had in my size?"

Jennifer touched the woman's arm and begged, "Please!"

"Get your own phone," the woman hissed. She turned back to the receiver. "Remember the suede ones we saw? Gone! So you know what I did? I said to that clerk . . ."

Jennifer closed her eyes and stood there, oblivious to everything but the torment inside her. Michael must not kill Adam. She had to do whatever she could to save him.

The woman hung up and turned to Jennifer. "I should make another call, just to teach you a lesson," she said.

As she walked away, smiling at her little victory, Jennifer made a grab for the phone. She called Adam's office.

"I'm sorry," his secretary said, "but Senator Warner is not in. Do you wish to leave a message?"

"It's urgent," Jennifer said. "Do you know where he can be reached?"

"No, I'm sorry. If you would like to – "

Jennifer hung up. She stood there a moment, thinking, then quickly dialed another number. "Robert Di Silva."

There was an interminable wait and then: "The District Attorney's office."

"I have to speak to Mr. Di Silva. This is Jennifer Parker."

"I'm sorry. Mr. Di Silva is in a conference. He can't be dis – "

"You get him on this telephone. This is an emergency. Hurry!" Jennifer's voice was trembling.

Di Silva's secretary hesitated. "Just a moment."

A minute later, Robert Di Silva was on the telephone. "Yes?" His voice was unfriendly.

"Listen, and listen carefully," Jennifer said. "Adam Warner's going to be killed. It's going to happen in the next ten or fifteen minutes. They're planning to do it at the New Canaan bridge."

She hung up. There was nothing more she could do. A brief vision of Adam's torn body came into her mind and she shuddered. She looked at her watch and silently prayed that Di Silva would be able to get help there in time.

Robert Di Silva replaced the receiver and looked at the half-dozen men in his office. "That was a weird call."

"Who was it?"

"Jennifer Parker. She said they're going to assassinate Senator Warner."

"Why did she call you?"

"Who knows?"

"Do you think it's on the level?"

District Attorney Di Silva said, "Hell, no."

Jennifer walked through the office door and, in spite of himself, Michael could not help reacting to her beauty. It was the same way he felt every time he saw her. Outside, she was the loveliest woman he had ever seen. But inside she was treacherous, deadly. He looked at the lips that had kissed Adam Warner and at the body that had lain in Adam Warner's arms.

She was walking in saying, "Michael, I'm so glad to see you. Thank you for arranging everything so quickly."

"No problem. I've been waiting for you, Jennifer." She would never know how much he meant that.

She sank into an armchair. "Michael, what in God's name is going on? What's happening?"

He studied her, half admiring her. She was responsible for helping to bring his empire crashing down, and she was sitting there innocently asking what was going on!

"Do you know why they brought me back?"

Sure, he thought. *So you can sing some more for them.* He remembered the little yellow canary with its broken neck. That would be Jennifer soon.

Jennifer looked into his black eyes. "Are you all right?"

"I've never been better." He leaned back in his chair. "In a few minutes, all our problems are going to be over."

"What do you mean?"

"Senator Warner is going to have an accident. That'll cool off the committee pretty good." He looked at the clock on the wall. "I should be getting a phone call any minute."

There was something odd in Michael's manner, something forbidding. Jennifer was filled with a sudden premonition of danger. She knew she had to get out of there.

She stood up. "I haven't had a chance to unpack. I'll go – "

"Sit down." The undertone in Michael's voice sent a chill down her back.

"Michael – "

"Sit down."

She glanced toward the door. Gino Gallo was standing there, his back against it, watching Jennifer with no expression on his face.

"You're not going anywhere," Michael told her.

"I don't under – "

"Don't talk. Don't say another word."

They sat there waiting, staring at each other, and the only sound in the room was the loud ticking of the clock on the wall. Jennifer tried to read Michael's eyes, but they were blank, filled with nothing, giving away nothing.

The sudden ringing of the telephone jarred the stillness of the room. Michael picked up the receiver. "Hello? . . . Are you sure? . . . All right. Get out of there." He replaced the receiver and looked up at Jennifer. "The bridge at New Canaan is swarming with cops."

Jennifer could feel the relief flooding through her body. It became a sense of exhilaration. Michael was watching her and she made an effort not to let her emotions show.

Jennifer asked, "What does that mean?"

Michael said slowly, "Nothing. Because that's not where Adam Warner is going to die."

62

The twin bridges of the Garden State Parkway were not named on the map. The Garden State Parkway crossed the Raritan River between the Amboys, splitting into the two bridges, one northbound and the other southbound.

The limousine was just west of Perth Amboy, heading toward the southbound bridge. Adam Warner was seated in the back, with a secret service man beside him, and two secret service men in front.

Agent Clay Reddin had been assigned to the senator's guard detail six months earlier, and he had come to know Adam Warner well. He had always thought of him as an open, accessible man, but all day the senator had been strangely silent and withdrawn. *Deeply troubled* were the words that came to Agent Reddin. There was no question in his mind but that Senator Warner was going to be the next President of the United States, and it was Reddin's responsibility to see that nothing happened to him. He reviewed again the precautions that had been taken to safeguard the senator, and he was satisfied that nothing could go wrong.

Agent Reddin glanced again at the probable President-to-be, and wondered what he was thinking.

Adam Warner's mind was on the ordeal that was confronting him. He had been informed by Di Silva that Jennifer Parker had been arrested. The thought of her being locked away like an animal was anathema to him. His mind kept returning to the wonderful moments they had shared together. He had loved Jennifer as he had never loved another woman.

One of the secret service men in the front seat was saying, "We should be arriving in Atlantic City right on schedule, Mr. President."

Mr. President. That phrase again. According to all the latest polls, he was far ahead. He was the country's new folk hero, and Adam knew it was due in no small measure to the crime investigation he had headed, the investigation that would destroy Jennifer Parker.

Adam glanced up and saw that they were approaching the twin bridges. There was a side road just before the bridge and a huge semitrailer truck was stopped at the entrance on the opposite side of the road. As the limousine neared the bridge, the truck started to pull out, so that the two vehicles arrived at the bridge at the same time.

The secret service driver applied his brakes and slowed down. "Look at that idiot."

The shortwave radio crackled into life. "Beacon One! Come in, Beacon One!"

The agent in the front seat next to the driver picked up the transmitter. "This is Beacon One."

The large truck was abreast of the limousine now as it started across the span. It was a behemoth, completely blocking out the view on the driver's side of the car. The limousine driver started to speed up to get ahead of it, but the truck simultaneously increased its speed.

"What the hell does he think he's doing?" the driver muttered.

"We've had an urgent call from the District Attorney's office. Fox One is in danger! Do you read me?"

Without warning, the truck veered to the right, hitting the side of the limousine, forcing it against the bridge railing. In seconds, the three secret service men in the car had their guns out.

"Get down!"

Adam found himself pushed down onto the floor, while Agent Reddin shielded Adam's body. The secret service agents rolled down the windows on the left side of the limousine, guns pointed. There was nothing at which to shoot. The side of the huge semitrailer blotted out everything. The driver was up ahead, out of sight. There was another jolt and a grinding crash as the limousine was knocked into the railing again. The driver swung the wheel to the left, fighting to keep the car on the bridge, but the truck kept forcing him back. The cold Raritan River swirled two hundred feet below them.

The secret service agent next to the driver had grabbed his radio microphone and was calling wildly into it, "This is Beacon One! Mayday! Mayday! Come in all units!"

But everyone in the limousine knew that it was too late for anyone to save them. The driver tried to stop the car, but the truck's huge fenders were locked into it, sweeping the limousine along. It was only a matter of seconds before the huge truck would edge them over the side of the bridge. The agent driving the car tried evasive tactics, alternately using the brake and the accelerator to slow down and speed up, but the truck had the car cruelly pinned against the bridge railing. There was no room for the car to maneuver. The truck blocked off any escape on the left side, and on the right side the limousine was being pushed against the iron railing of the bridge. The agent fought the wheel desperately as the truck pressed hard into the limousine once again, and everyone in the car could feel the bridge railing start to give way.

The truck was jamming harder now, forcing the limousine over the side. Those in the car could feel the sudden list as the front wheels broke through the railing and went over the edge of the bridge. The car was teetering on the brink and each man, in his own way, prepared to die.

Adam felt no fear, only an ineffable sadness at the loss, the waste. It was Jennifer he should have shared his life with, had children with – and suddenly Adam knew, from somewhere deep within himself, that they had had a child.

The limousine gave another lurch and Adam cried out once aloud at the injustice of what had happened, what was happening.

From overhead came the roar of two police helicopters as they swooped down out of the sky, and a moment later there was the sound of machine guns. The semitrailer lurched and all motion suddenly stopped. Adam and the others could hear the helicopters circling overhead. The men remained motionless, knowing that the slightest movement could send the car over the bridge, into the waters below.

There was the distant scream of police sirens drawing nearer, and a few minutes later the sound of voices barking out commands. The engine of the truck roared into life again. Slowly, carefully, the truck moved, inching away from the trapped car, removing the pressure against it. The limousine tilted for one terrible instant, and then was still. A moment later, the truck had been backed out of the way and Adam and the others could see out of the left-hand windows.

There were half a dozen squad cars and uniformed policemen with drawn guns swarming over the bridge.

A police captain was at the side of the battered car.

"We'll never get the doors open," he said. "We're going to bring you out through the windows – real easy."

Adam was lifted out of the window first, slowly and carefully, so as not to upset the balance of the car and send it over the side. The three secret service men were next.

When all the men had been removed from the car, the police captain turned to Adam and asked, "Are you all right, sir?"

Adam turned to look at the car hanging over the edge of the bridge, and then at the dark water of the river far below.

"Yes," he said. "I'm all right."

Michael Moretti glanced up at the clock on the wall. "It's all over." He turned to face Jennifer. "Your boyfriend's in the river by now."

She was watching him, her face pale. "You can't – "

"Don't worry. You're going to have a fair trial." He turned to Gino Gallo. "Did you tell her that Adam Warner was going to be blown away in New Canaan?"

"Just like you told me, boss."

Michael looked at Jennifer. "The trial's over."

He rose to his feet and walked over to where Jennifer was sitting. He grabbed her blouse and pulled her to her feet.

"I loved you," he whispered. He hit her hard across the face. Jennifer did not flinch. He hit her again, harder, then a third time, and she fell to the floor.

"Get up. We're taking a trip."

Jennifer lay there, dizzy from the blows, trying to clear her head. Michael hauled her roughly to her feet.

"You want me to take care of her?" Gino Gallo asked.

"No. Bring the car around the back."

"Right, boss." He hurried out of the room.

Jennifer and Michael were alone.

"Why?" he asked. "We owned the world, and you threw it away. *Why?*"

She did not answer.

"You want me to fuck you once more for old times' sake?" Michael moved toward her and grabbed her arm. "Would you, like that?" Jennifer did not respond. "You're never going to fuck anyone again, you hear? I'm going to put you in the river with your lover! You can keep each other company."

Gino Gallo came back into the room, his face white. "Boss! There's a – "

There was a crashing sound from outside the room. Michael dived for the gun in his desk drawer. He had it in his hand when the door burst open. Two federal agents came through the door, guns drawn.

"Freeze!"

In that split second, Michael made his decision. He raised the gun and turned and fired at Jennifer. He saw the bullets go into her a second before the agents started shooting. He watched the blood spurt out of her chest, then he felt a bullet tear into him, and then another. He saw Jennifer lying on the floor, and Michael did not know which was the greater agony, her death or his. He felt the hammer blow of another bullet, and then he felt nothing.

63

Two interns were wheeling Jennifer out of the operating room and into Intensive Care. A uniformed policeman followed at Jennifer's side. The hospital corridor was a bedlam of policemen, detectives and reporters.

A man walked up to the reception desk and said, "I want to see Jennifer Parker."

"Are you a member of her family?"

"No. I'm a friend."

"I'm sorry. No visitors. She's in Intensive Care."

"I'll wait."

"It could be a long time."

"That doesn't matter," Ken Bailey said.

A side door opened and Adam Warner, gaunt and haggard, entered, flanked by a team of secret service men.

A doctor was waiting to greet him. "This way, Senator Warner." He led Adam into a small office.

"How is she?" Adam asked.

"I'm not optimistic. We removed three bullets from her."

The door opened and District Attorney Robert Di Silva hurried in. He looked at Adam Warner and said, "I'm sure glad you're okay."

Adam said, "I understand I owe my thanks to you. How did you know?"

"Jennifer Parker called me. She told me they were setting you up in New Canaan. I figured it was probably some kind of diversionary ploy, but I couldn't take a chance, so I covered it. Meanwhile, I got hold of the route you were taking and we sent some choppers after you to protect you. My hunch is that Parker tried to set you up."

"No," Adam said. "No."

Robert Di Silva shrugged. "Have it your way, Senator. The important thing is that you're alive." As an afterthought he turned to the doctor. "Is she going to live?"

"Her chances are not very good."

The District Attorney saw the look on Adam Warner's face and misinterpreted it. "Don't worry. If she makes it, we've got her nailed down tight."

He looked at Adam more closely. "You look like hell. Why don't you go home and get some rest?"

"I want to see Jennifer Parker first."

The doctor said, "She's in a coma. She may not come out of it."

"I would like to see her, please."

"Of course, Senator. This way."

The doctor led the way out of the room, with Adam following and Di Silva behind him. They walked a few feet down the corridor to a sign that said INTENSIVE CARE UNIT – KEEP OUT.

The doctor opened the door and held it for the two men. "She's in the first room."

There was a policeman in front of the door, guarding it. He came to attention as he saw the District Attorney.

"No one gets near that room without written authorization from me. You understand?" Di Silva asked.

"Yes, sir."

Adam and Di Silva walked into the room. There were three beds, two of them empty. Jennifer lay in the third, tubes running into her nostrils and wrists. Adam moved close to the bed and stared down at her. Jennifer's face was very pale against the white pillows, and her eyes were closed. In repose, her face seemed younger and softer. Adam was looking at the innocent girl he had met years ago, the girl who had said angrily to him, *If anyone had paid me off, do you think I'd be living in a place like this? I don't care what you do. All I want is to be left alone.* He remembered her courage and idealism and her vulnerability. She had been on the side of the angels, believing in justice and willing to fight for it. What had gone wrong? He had loved her and he loved her still, and he had made one wrong choice that had poisoned all their lives, and he knew he would never feel free of guilt for as long as he lived.

He turned to the doctor. "Let me know when she – " He could not say the words. " – what happens."

"Of course," the doctor said.

Adam Warner took one long last look at Jennifer and said a silent good-bye.

Then he turned and walked out to face the waiting reporters.

Through a dim, misty haze of semiconsciousness, Jennifer heard the men leave. She had not understood what they were saying, for their words were blurred by the pain that gripped her. She thought she had heard Adam's voice, but she knew that could not be. He was dead. She tried to open her eyes, but the effort was too great.

Jennifer's thoughts began to. . . . Abraham Wilson came running into the room carrying a box. He stumbled and the box opened and a yellow canary flew out of it . . . Robert Di Silva was screaming, *Catch it! Don't let it get away!* . . . and Michael Moretti was holding it and laughing, and Father Ryan said, *Look, everybody! It's a miracle!* and Connie Garrett was dancing around the room and everyone applauded . . . Mrs. Cooper said, *I'm going to give you Wyoming . . . Wyoming . . . Wyoming* . . . and Adam came in with dozens of red roses and Michael said, *They're from me*, and Jennifer said, *I'll put them in a vase in water*, and they shriveled and died and the water spilled onto the floor and became a lake, and she and Adam were sailing, and Michael was chasing them on water skis and he became Joshua and he smiled at Jennifer and waved and started to lose his balance, and she screamed, *Don't fall . . . Don't fall . . . Don't fall* . . . and an enormous wave swept Joshua into the air and he held out his arms like Jesus and disappeared.

For an instant, Jennifer's mind cleared.

Joshua was gone.

Adam was gone.

Michael was gone.

She was alone. In the end, everyone was alone. Each person had to die his own death. It would be easy to die now.

A feeling of blessed peace began to steal over her. Soon there was no more pain.

64

It was a cold January day in the Capitol when Adam Warner was sworn in as the fortieth President of the United States. His wife wore a sable hat and a dark sable coat that did wonderful things for her pale complexion and almost concealed her pregnancy. She stood next to her daughter and they both watched proudly as Adam took the oath of office, and the country rejoiced for the three of them. They were the best of America: decent and honest and good, and they belonged in the White House.

In a small law office in Kelso, Washington, Jennifer Parker sat alone looking at the inauguration on television. She watched until the last of the ceremony was over and Adam and Mary Beth and Samantha had left the podium, surrounded by secret service men. Then Jennifer turned off the television set and watched the images fade into nothingness. And it was like turning off the past: shutting out all that had happened to her, the love and the death and the joy and the pain. Nothing had been able to destroy her. She was a survivor.

She put on her hat and coat and walked outside, pausing for a moment to look at the sign that said: *Jennifer Parker, Attorney at Law.* She thought for an instant of the jury that had acquitted her. She was still a lawyer, as her father had been a lawyer. And she would go on, searching for the elusive thing called justice. She turned and headed in the direction of the courthouse.

Jennifer walked slowly down the deserted, windswept street. A light snow had begun to fall, casting a chiffon veil over the world. From an apartment building nearby there came a sudden burst of merriment, and it was such an alien sound that she stopped for a moment to listen. She pulled her coat tighter about her and moved on down the street, peering into the curtain of snow ahead, as though she were trying to see into the future.

But she was looking into the past, trying to understand when it was that all the laughter died.

Bloodline

For Natalie with love

The physician will carefully prepare a mixture of crocodile dung, lizard flesh, bats' blood and camels' spit...

From a papyrus listing 811 prescriptions used by the Egyptians in 1550 BC

Acknowledgements While this is a work of fiction, the backgrounds are authentic, and I wish to express my gratitude to those who so generously contributed to my research. If, in adapting their information to the requirements of a novel, I have found it necessary to expand or contract certain time elements, I take full responsibility. My deepest appreciation goes to:

Dr Margaret M. McCarron
Associate Medical Director
Los Angeles County, University of Southern California

Dean Brady, USC Pharmacy School

Dr Gregory A. Thompson
Director, Drug Information Centre
Los Angeles County, University of Southern California

Dr Bernd W. Schulze
Drug Information Centre
Los Angeles County, University of Southern California

Dr Judy Flesh
Urs Jäggi, Hoffman-La Roche & Co. A.G., Basel

Dr Gunter Siebel, Schering A.G., Berlin

The Criminal Investigation Divisions of Scotland Yard, Zurich and Berlin

Charles Walford, Sotheby Parke Bernet, London

And to Jorja, who makes all things possible.

1

Istanbul
Saturday, September 5
10 p.m.

He was seated in the dark, alone, behind the desk of Hajib Kafir, staring unseeingly out of the dusty office window at the timeless minarets of Istanbul. He was a man who was at home in a dozen capitals of the world, but Istanbul was one of his favourites. Not the tourist Istanbul of Beyoglu Street, or the gaudy Lalezab Bar of the Hilton, but the out-of-the-way places that only the Moslems knew: the *yalis*, and the small markets beyond the *souks*, and the Telli Baba, the cemetery where only one person was buried, and the people came to pray to him.

His waiting had the patience of a hunter, the quiet stillness of a man in control of his body and his emotions. He was Welsh, with the dark, stormy good looks of his ancestors. He had black hair and a strong face, and quick intelligent eyes that were a deep blue. He was over six feet tall, with the lean, muscular body of a man who kept himself in good physical condition. The office was filled with the odours of Hajib Kafir, his sickly sweet tobacco, his acrid Turkish coffee, his fat, oily body. Rhys Williams was unaware of them. He was thinking about the telephone call he had received from Chamonix an hour earlier.

" . . . A terrible accident! Believe me, Mr Williams, we are all devastated. It happened so quickly that there was no chance to save him. Mr Roffe was killed instantly . . ."

Sam Roffe, president of Roffe and Sons, the second largest pharmaceutical company in the world, a multi-billion-dollar dynasty that girdled the globe. It was impossible to think of Sam Roffe as being dead. He had always been so vital, so full of life and energy, a man on the move, living in aeroplanes that raced him to company factories and offices all over the world, where he solved problems others could not deal with, created new concepts, pushed everyone to do more, to do better. Even though he had married, and fathered a child, his only real interest had been the business. Sam Roffe had been a brilliant and extraordinary man. Who could replace him? Who was capable of running the enormous empire he had left? Sam Roffe had not chosen an heir apparent. But then he had not planned to die at fifty-two. He had thought there would be plenty of time.

And now his time had run out.

The lights in the office suddenly flashed on and Rhys Williams looked towards the doorway, momentarily blinded.

"Mr Williams! I did not know anyone was here."

It was Sophie, one of the company secretaries, who was assigned to Rhys Williams whenever he was in Istanbul. She was Turkish, in her middle twenties, with an attractive face and a lithe, sensuous body, rich with promise. She had let Rhys know in subtle, ancient ways that she was available to bring him whatever pleasures he wished, whenever he desired them, but Rhys was not interested.

Now she said, "I returned to finish some letters for Mr Kafir." She added softly, "Perhaps there is something I can do for you?"

As she moved closer to the desk, Rhys could sense the musky smell of a wild animal in season.

"Where is Mr Kafir?"

Sophie shook her head regretfully. "He has left for the day." She smoothed the front of her dress with the palms of soft, clever hands. "Can I help you in some way?" Her eyes were dark and moist.

"Yes," Rhys said. "Find him."

She frowned. "I have no idea where he could – "

"Try the Kervansaray, or the Mermara." It would probably be the former, where one of Hajib Kafir's mistresses worked as a belly dancer. Although you never knew with Kafir, Rhys thought. He might even be with his wife.

Sophie was apologetic. "I will try, but I am afraid I – "

"Explain to him that if he's not here in one hour, he no longer has a job."

The expression on her face changed. "I will see what I can do, Mr Williams." She started towards the door.

"Turn out the lights."

Somehow, it was easier to sit in the dark with his thoughts. The image of Sam Roffe kept intruding. Mont Blanc should have been an easy climb at this time of the year, early September. Sam had tried the climb before, but storms had kept him from reaching the peak.

"I'll plant the company flag up there this time," he had promised Rhys, jokingly.

And then the telephone call a short while ago as Rhys was checking out of the Pera Palace. He could hear the agitated voice on the telephone." . . . They were doing a traverse over a glacier . . . Mr Roffe lost his footing and his rope broke . . . He fell into a bottomless crevasse."

Rhys could visualize Sam's body smashing against the unforgiving ice, hurtling downward into the crevasse. He forced his mind away from the scene. That was the past. There was the present to worry about now. The members of Sam Roffe's family had to be notified of his death, and they were scattered in various parts of the world. A press announcement had to be prepared. The news was going to travel through international financial circles like a shock wave. With the company in the midst of a financial crisis, it was vital that the impact of Sam Roffe's death be minimized as much as possible. That would be Rhys's job.

Rhys Williams had first met Sam Roffe nine years earlier. Rhys, then twenty-five, had been sales manager for a small drug firm. He was brilliant and innovative, and as the company had expanded, Rhys's reputation had quickly spread. He was offered a job at Roffe and Sons and when he turned it down,

Sam Roffe bought the company Rhys worked for and sent for him. Even now he could recall the overwhelming power of Sam Roffe's presence at their first meeting.

"You belong here at Roffe and Sons," Sam Roffe had informed him. "That's why I bought that horse-and-buggy outfit you were with."

Rhys had found himself flattered and irritated at the same time. "Suppose I don't want to stay?"

Sam Roffe had smiled and said confidently, "You'll want to stay. You and I have something in common, Rhys. We're both ambitious. We want to own the world. I'm going to show you how."

The words were magic, a promised feast for the fierce hunger that burned in the young man, for he knew something that Sam Roffe did not. There was no Rhys Williams. He was a myth that had been created out of desperation and poverty and despair.

He had been born near the coalfields of Gwent and Carmarthen, the red, scarred valleys of Wales where layers of sandstone and saucer-shaped beds of limestone and coal puckered the green earth. He grew up in a fabled land where the very names were poetry: Brecon and Pen-y-fan and Penderyn and Glyncorrwg and Maesteg. It was a land of legend, where the coal buried deep in the ground had been created 280 million years before, where the landscape was once covered with so many trees that a squirrel could travel from the Brecon Beacons to the sea without ever touching the ground. But the Industrial Revolution had come along and the beautiful green trees were chopped down by the charcoal-burners to feed the insatiable fires of the iron industry.

The young boy grew up with the heroes of another time and another world. Robert Farrer, burned at the stake by the Roman Catholic Church because he would not take a vow of celibacy and abandon his wife; King Hywel the Good, who brought the law to Wales in the tenth century; the fierce warrior Brychen who sired twelve sons and twenty-four daughters and savagely put down all attacks on his kingdom. It was a land of glorious histories in which the lad had been raised. But it was not all glory. Rhys's ancestors were miners, every one of them, and the young boy used to listen to the tales of hell that his father and his uncles recounted. They talked of the terrible times when there was no work, when the rich coalfields of Gwent and Carmarthen had been closed in a bitter fight between the companies and the miners, and the miners were debased by a poverty that eroded ambition and pride, that sapped a man's spirit and strength and finally made him surrender.

When the mines were open, it was another kind of hell. Most of Rhys's family had died in the mines. Some had perished in the bowels of the earth, others had coughed their blackened lungs away. Few had lived past the age of thirty.

Rhys used to listen to his father and his ageing young uncles discussing the past, the cave-ins and the cripplings and the strikes; talking of the good times and the bad, and to the young boy they seemed the same. All bad. The thought of spending his years in the darkness of the earth appalled Rhys. He knew he had to escape.

He ran away from home when he was twelve. He left the valleys of coal and went to the coast, to Sully Ranny Bay and Lavernock, where the rich tourists flocked, and the young boy fetched and carried and made himself useful, helping ladies down the steep cliffs to the beach, lugging heavy picnic baskets, driving a pony-cart at Penarth, and working at the amusement park at Whitmore Bay.

He was only a few hours away from home, but the distance could not be measured. The people here were from another world. Rhys Williams had never imagined such beautiful people or such glorious finery. Each woman looked like a queen to him and the men were all elegant and splendid. This was the world where he belonged, and there was nothing he would not do to make it his.

By the time Rhys Williams was fourteen, he had saved enough money to pay for his passage to London. He spent the first three days simply walking round the huge city, staring at everything, hungrily drinking in the incredible sights and the sounds and the smells.

His first job was as a delivery boy at a draper's shop. There were two male clerks, superior beings both, and a female clerk, who made the young Welsh boy's heart sing every time he looked at her. The men treated Rhys as he was meant to be treated, like dirt. He was a curiosity. He dressed peculiarly, had abominable manners and spoke with an incomprehensible accent. They could not even pronounce his name. They called him Rice, and Rye, and Rise. "It's pronounced Reese," Rhys kept telling them.

The girl took pity on him. Her name was Gladys Simpkins and she shared a tiny flat in Tooting with three other girls. One day she allowed the young boy to walk her home after work and invited him in for a cup of tea. Young Rhys was overcome with nervousness. He had thought this was going to be his first sexual experience, but when he began to put his arm around Gladys, she stared at him a moment, then laughed. "I'm not giving none of that to you," she said. "But I'll give you some advice. If you want to make somethin' of yourself, get yourself some proper clothes and a bit of education and learn yourself some manners." She studied the thin, passionate young face and looked into Rhys's deep blue eyes, and said softly, "You're gonna be a bit of all right when you grow up."

If you want to make somethin' of yourself . . . That was the moment when the fictitious Rhys Williams was born. The real Rhys Williams was an uneducated, ignorant boy with no background, no breeding, no past, no future. But he had imagination, intelligence and a fiery ambition. It was enough. He started with the image of what he wanted to be, who he intended to be. When he looked in his mirror, he did not see the clumsy, grubby little boy with a funny accent; his mirror image was polished and suave and successful. Little by little, Rhys began to match himself to the image in his mind. He attended night school, and he spent his weekends in art galleries. He haunted public libraries and went to the theatre, sitting in the gallery studying the fine clothes of the men seated in the stalls. He scrimped on food, so that once a month he could go to a good restaurant, where he carefully copied the table manners of others. He observed and learned and remembered. He was like a sponge, erasing the past, soaking up the future.

In one short year Rhys had learned enough to realize that Gladys Simpkins, his princess, was a cheap Cockney girl who was already beneath his tastes. He quit the draper's shop and went to work as a clerk at a chemist's shop that was part of a large chain. He was almost sixteen now, but he looked older. He had filled out and was taller. Women were beginning to pay attention to his dark Welsh good looks and his quick, flattering tongue. He was an instant success in the shop. Female customers would wait until Rhys was available to take care of them. He dressed well and spoke correctly, and he knew he had come a long way from Gwent and Carmarthen, but when he looked in the mirror, he was still not satisfied. The journey he intended to make was still ahead of him.

Within two years Rhys Williams was made manager of the shop where he worked. The district manager of the chain said to Rhys, "This is just the beginning, Williams. Work hard and one day you'll be the superintendent of half a dozen stores."

Rhys almost laughed aloud. To think that that could be the height of anyone's ambition! Rhys had never stopped going to school. He was studying business administration and marketing and commercial law. He wanted more. His image in the mirror was at the top of the ladder; Rhys felt he was still at the bottom. His opportunity to move up came when a drug salesman walked in one day, watched Rhys charm several ladies into buying products they had no use for, and said, "You're wasting your time here, lad. You should be working in a bigger pond."

"What did you have in mind?" Rhys asked.

"Let me talk to my boss about you."

Two weeks later Rhys was working as a salesman at the small drug firm. He was one of fifty salesmen, but when Rhys looked in his special mirror, he knew that that was not true. His only competition was himself. He was getting closer to his image now, closer to the fictitious character he was creating. A man who was intelligent, cultured, sophisticated and charming. What he was trying to do was impossible. Everyone knew that one had to be born with those qualities; they could not be created. But Rhys did it. He became the image he had envisaged.

He travelled around the country, selling the firm's products, talking and listening. He would return to London full of practical suggestions, and he quickly began to move up the ladder.

Three years after he had joined the company, Rhys was made general sales manager. Under his skilful guidance the company began to expand.

And four years later, Sam Roffe had come into his life. He had recognized the hunger in Rhys.

"You're like me," Sam Roffe had said. "We want to own the world. I'm going to show you how." And he had.

Sam Roffe had been a brilliant mentor. Over the next nine years under Sam Roffe's tutelage Rhys Williams had become invaluable to the company. As time went on, he was given more and more responsibility, reorganizing various divisions, troubleshooting in whatever part of the world he was needed, coordinating the different branches of Roffe and Sons, creating new concepts. In the end Rhys knew more about running the company than anyone except Sam Roffe himself. Rhys Williams was the logical successor to the presidency. One morning, when Rhys and Sam Roffe were returning from Caracas in a company jet, a luxurious converted Boeing 707–320, one of a fleet of eight planes, Sam Roffe had complimented Rhys on a lucrative deal that he had concluded with the Venezuelan government.

"There'll be a fat bonus in this for you, Rhys."

Rhys had replied quietly, "I don't want a bonus, Sam. I'd prefer some stock and a place on your board of directors."

He had earned it, and both men were aware of it. But Sam had said, "I'm sorry. I can't change the rules, even for you. Roffe and Sons is a privately held company. No one outside the family can sit on the board or hold stock."

Rhys had known that, of course. He attended all board meetings, but not as a member. He was an outsider. Sam Roffe was the last male in the Roffe bloodline. The other Roffes, Sam's cousins, were females. The men they had married sat on the board of the company. Walther Gassner, who had married Anna Roffe; Ivo Palazzi, married to Simonetta Roffe; Charles Martel, married to Hélène Roffe. And Sir Alec Nichols, whose mother had been a Roffe.

So Rhys had been forced to make a decision. He knew that he deserved to be on the board, that one day he should be running the company. Present circumstances prevented it, but circumstances had a way of changing. Rhys had decided to stay, to wait and see what happened. Sam had taught him patience. And now Sam was dead.

The office lights blazed on again, and Hajib Kafir stood in the doorway. Kafir was the Turkish sales manager for Roffe and Sons. He was a short, swarthy man who wore diamonds and his fat belly like proud ornaments. He had the dishevelled air of a man who had dressed hastily. So Sophie had not found him in a nightclub. Ah, well, Rhys thought. A side-effect of Sam Roffe's death. Coitus interruptus.

"Rhys!" Kafir was exclaiming. "My dear fellow, forgive me! I had no idea you were still in Istanbul! You were on your way to catch a plane, and I had some urgent business to – "

"Sit down, Hajib. Listen carefully. I want you to send four cables in company code. They're going to different countries. I want them hand-delivered by our own messengers. Do you understand?"

"Of course," Kafir said, bewildered. "Perfectly."

Rhys glanced at the thin, gold Baume & Mercier watch on his wrist. "The New City Post Office will be closed. Send the cables from Yeni Posthane Cad. I want them on their way within thirty minutes." He handed Kafir a copy of the cable he had written out. "Anyone who discusses this will be instantly discharged."

Kafir glanced at the cable and his eyes widened. "My God!" he said. "Oh, my God!" He looked up at Rhys's dark face. "How – how did this terrible thing happen?"

"Sam Roffe died in an accident," Rhys said.

Now, for the first time, Rhys allowed his thoughts to go to what he had been pushing away from his consciousness, what he had been trying to avoid thinking about: Elizabeth Roffe, Sam's daughter. She was twenty-four now. When Rhys had first met her she had been a fifteen-year-old girl with braces on her teeth, fiercely shy and overweight, a lonely rebel. Over the years Rhys had watched Elizabeth develop into a very special young woman, with her mother's beauty and her father's intelligence and spirit. She had become close to Sam. Rhys knew how deeply the news would affect her. He would have to tell her himself.

Two hours later, Rhys Williams was over the Mediterranean on a company jet, headed for New York.

2

Berlin
Monday, September 7
10 a.m.

Anna Roffe Gassner knew that she must not let herself scream again or Walther would return and kill her. She crouched in a corner of her bedroom, her body trembling uncontrollably, waiting for death. What had started out as a beautiful fairy-tale had ended in terror, unspeakable horror. It had taken her too long to face the truth: the man she had married was a homicidal maniac.

Anna Roffe had never loved anyone before she met Walther Gassner, including her mother, her father and herself. Anna had been a frail, sickly child who suffered from fainting spells. She could not remember a time when she had been free of hospitals, nurses, or specialists flown in from far-off places. Because her father was Anton Roffe, of Roffe and Sons, the top medical experts flew to Anna's bedside in Berlin. But when they had examined her and tested her and finally departed, they knew no more than they had known before. They could not diagnose her condition.

Anna was unable to go to school like other children, and in time she had become withdrawn, creating a world of her own, full of dreams and fantasies, where no one else was allowed to enter. She painted her own pictures of life, because the colours of reality were too harsh for her to accept. When Anna was eighteen, her dizziness and fainting spells disappeared as mysteriously as they had started. But they had marred her life. At an age when most girls were getting engaged or married, Anna had never even been kissed by a boy. She insisted to herself that she did not mind. She was content to live her own dream life, apart from everything and everyone. In her middle twenties suitors came calling, for Anna Roffe was an heiress who bore one of the most prestigious names in the world, and many men were eager to share her fortune. She received proposals from a Swedish count, an Italian poet and half a dozen princes from indigent countries. Anna refused them all. On his daughter's thirtieth birthday, Anton Roffe moaned, "I'm going to die without leaving any grandchildren."

On her thirty-fifth birthday Anna had gone to Kitzhübel, in Austria, and there she had met Walther Gassner, a ski instructor thirteen years younger than herself.

The first time Anna had seen Walther the sight of him had literally taken her breath away. He was skiing down the *Hahnenkamm*, the steep racing slope, and it was the most beautiful sight Anna had ever seen. She had moved closer to the bottom of the ski run to get a better look at him. He was like a young god, and Anna had been satisfied to do nothing but watch him. He had caught her staring at him.

"Aren't you skiing, *gnädiges Fräulein?*"

She had shaken her head, not trusting her voice, and he had smiled and said, "Then let me buy you lunch."

Anna had fled in a panic, like a schoolgirl. From then on, Walther Gassner had pursued her. Anna Roffe was not a fool. She was aware that she was neither pretty nor brilliant, that she was a plain woman, and that, aside from her name, she had seemingly very little to offer a man. But Anna knew that trapped within that ordinary façade was a beautiful, sensitive girl filled with love and poetry and music.

Perhaps because Anna was not beautiful, she had a deep reverence for beauty. She would go to the great museums and spend hours staring at the paintings and the statues. When she had seen Walther Gassner it was as though all the gods had come alive for her.

Anna was having breakfast on the terrace of the Tennerhof Hotel on the second day when Walther Gassner joined her. He did look like a young god. He had a regular, clean-cut profile, and his features were delicate, sensitive, strong. His face was deeply tanned and his teeth were white and even. He had blond hair and his eyes were a slate grey. Beneath his ski clothes Anna could see the movement of his biceps and thigh muscles, and she felt tremors going through her loins. She hid her hands in her lap so that he could not see the keratosis.

"I looked for you on the slope yesterday afternoon," Walther said. Anna could not speak. "If you don't ski, I'd like to teach you." He smiled, and added, "No charge."

He had taken her to the *Hausberg*, the beginners' slope, for her first lesson. It was immediately apparent to them both that Anna had no talent for skiing. She kept losing her balance and falling down, but she insisted on trying again and again because she was afraid that Walther would despise her if she failed. Instead, he had picked her up after her tenth fall and had said gently, "You were meant to do better things than this."

"What things?" Anna had asked miserably.

"I'll tell you at dinner tonight."

They had dined that evening and breakfasted the next morning, and then had lunch and dinner again. Walther neglected his clients. He skipped skiing lessons in order to go into the village with Anna. He took her to the casino in Der Goldene Greif, and they went sleigh-riding and shopping and hiking, and sat on the terrace of the hotel hour after hour, talking. For Anna, it was a time of magic.

Five days after they had met, Walther took her hands in his and said, "Anna, *liebchen*, I want to marry you."

He had spoiled it. He had taken her out of her wonderful fairyland and brought her back to the cruel reality of who and what she was. An unattractive, thirty-five-year-old virginal prize for fortune-hunters.

She had tried to leave but Walther had stopped her. "We love each other, Anna. You can't run away from that."

She listened to him lying, listened to him saying, "I've never loved anyone before," and she made it easy for him because she wanted so desperately to believe him. She took him back to her room, and they sat there, talking, and as Walther told Anna the story of his life, she suddenly began to believe, thinking with wonder, It is really the story of my own life.

Like her, Walther had never had anyone to love. He had been alienated from the world by his birth as a bastard, as Anna had been alienated by her illness. Like her, Walther had been filled with the need to give love. He had been brought up in an orphanage, and when he was thirteen and his extraordinary good looks were already apparent, the women in the orphanage had begun to use him, bringing him to their rooms at night, taking him to bed with them, teaching him how to please them. As a reward the young boy was given extra food and pieces of meat, and desserts made with real sugar. He received everything but love.

When Walther was old enough to run away from the orphanage, he found that the world outside was no different. Women wanted to use his good looks, to wear him as a badge; but it never went any deeper than that. They gave him gifts of money and clothes and jewellery, but never of themselves.

Walther was her soul-mate, Anna realized, her *doppelgänger.* They were married in a quiet ceremony at the town hall.

Anna had expected her father to be overjoyed. Instead, he had flown into a rage. "You're a silly, vain fool," Anton Roffe screamed at her. "You've married a no-good fortune-hunter. I've had him checked out. All his life he's lived off women, but he's never before found anyone stupid enough to marry him."

"Stop it!" Anna cried. "You don't understand him."

But Anton Roffe knew that he understood Walther Gassner only too well. He asked his new son-in-law to come to his office.

Walther looked around approvingly at the dark panelling and the old paintings hanging on the walls. "I like this place," Walther said.

"Yes, I'm sure it's better than the orphanage."

Walther looked up at him sharply, his eyes suddenly wary. "I beg your pardon?"

Anton said, "Let's cut out the *Scheiss*. You've made a mistake. My daughter has no money."

Walther's grey eyes seemed to turn to stone. "What are you trying to tell me?"

"I'm not trying to tell you anything. I'm telling you. You won't get anything from Anna because she hasn't got anything. If you had done your homework more thoroughly, you would have learned that Roffe and Sons is a close-held corporation. That means that none of its stock can be sold. We live comfortably, but that's it. There is no big fortune to be milked here. He fumbled in his pocket, drew out an envelope and threw it on the desk in front of Walther. "This will reimburse you for your trouble. I will expect you to be out of Berlin by six o'clock. I don't want Anna ever to hear from you again."

Walther said quietly, "Did it ever cross your mind that I might have married Anna because I fell in love with her?"

"No," Anton said acidly. "Did it ever cross yours?"

Walther looked at him a moment. "Let's see what my market price is." He tore open the envelope and counted the money. He looked up at Anton Roffe again. "I value myself at much higher than twenty thousand marks."

"It's all you're getting. Count yourself lucky."

"I do," Walther said. "If you want to know the truth, I think I am very lucky. Thank you." He put the money in his pocket with a careless gesture and a moment later was walking out of the door.

Anton Roffe was relieved. He experienced a slight sense of guilt and distaste for what he had done and yet he knew it had been the only solution. Anna would be unhappy at being deserted by her groom, but it was better to have it happen now than later. He would try to see to it that she met some eligible men of her own age, who would at least respect her if not love her. Someone who would be interested in her and not her money or her name. Someone who would not be bought for twenty thousand marks.

When Anton Roffe arrived home, Anna ran up to greet him, tears in her eyes. He took her in his arms and hugged her, and said, "Anna, *liebchen*, it's going to be all right. You'll get over him – "

And Anton looked over her shoulder, and standing in the doorway was Walther Gassner. Anna was holding up her finger, saying, "Look what Walther bought me! Isn't it the most beautiful ring you've ever seen? It cost twenty thousand marks."

In the end, Anna's parents were forced to accept Walther Gassner. As a wedding gift they bought them a lovely Schinkel manor-house in Wannsee, with French furniture mixed with antiques, comfortable couches and easy chairs, a Roentgen desk in the library, and bookcases lining the walls. The upstairs was furnished with elegant eighteenth-century pieces from Denmark and Sweden.

"It's too much," Walther told Anna. "I don't want anything from them or from you. I want to be able to buy you beautiful things, *liebchen.*" He gave her that boyish grin and said, "But I have no money."

"Of course you do," Anna replied. "Everything I have belongs to you."

Walther smiled at her sweetly and said, "Does it?"

At Anna's insistence – for Walther seemed reluctant to discuss money – she explained her financial situation to him. She had a trust fund that was enough for her to live on comfortably, but the bulk of her fortune was in shares of Roffe and Sons. The shares could not be sold without the unanimous approval of the board of directors.

Anna told him. Walther could not believe it. He made her repeat the sum.

"And you can't sell the stock?"

"No. My cousin Sam won't let it be sold. He holds the controlling shares. One day . . ."

Walther expressed an interest in working in the family business. Anton was against it.

"What can a ski bum contribute to Roffe and Sons?" he asked.

But in the end he gave in to his daughter, and Walther was given a job in administration with the company. He proved to be excellent at it and advanced rapidly. When Anna's father died two years later, Walther Gassner was made a member of the board. Anna was so proud of him. He was the perfect husband and lover. He was always bringing her flowers and little gifts, and he seemed content to stay at home with her in the evening, just the two of them. Anna's happiness was almost too much for her to bear. *Ach, danke, lieber Gott*, she would say silently.

Anna learned to cook, so that she could make Walther's favourite dishes. She made *choucroute*, a bed of crunchy sauerkraut and creamy mashed potatoes heaped with a smoked pork chop, a frankfurter and a Nuremberg sausage. She prepared fillet of pork cooked in beer and flavoured with cumin, and served it with a fat baked apple, cored and peeled, the centre filled with *airelles*, the little red berries.

"You're the best cook in the world, *liebchen*," Walther would say, and Anna would blush with pride.

In the third year of their marriage, Anna became pregnant.

There was a great deal of pain during the first eight months of her pregnancy, but Anna bore that happily. It was something else that worried her.

It started one day after lunch. She had been knitting a sweater for Walther, day-dreaming, and suddenly she heard Walther's voice, saying, "My God, Anna, what are you doing, sitting here in the dark?"

The afternoon had turned to dusk, and she looked down at the sweater in her lap and she had not touched it. Where had the day gone? Where had her mind been? After that, Anna had other similar experiences, and she began to wonder whether this sliding away into nothingness was a portent, an omen that she was going to die. She did not think she was afraid of death, but she could not bear the thought of leaving Walther.

Four weeks before the baby was due, Anna lapsed into one of her day-dreams, missed a step and fell down an entire flight of stairs.

She awakened in the hospital.

Walther was seated on the edge of the bed, holding her hand. "You gave me a terrible scare."

In a sudden panic she thought, The baby! I can't feel the baby. She reached down. Her stomach was flat. "Where is my baby?"

And Walther held her close and hugged her.

The doctor said, "You had twins, Mrs Gassner."

Anna turned to Walther, and his eyes were filled with tears. "A boy and a girl, *liebchen*."

And she could have died right then of happiness. She felt a sudden, irresistible longing to have them in her arms. She had to see them, feel them, hold them.

"We'll talk about that when you're stronger," the doctor said. "Not until you're stronger."

They assured Anna that she was getting better every day, but she was becoming frightened. Something was happening to her that she did not understand. Walther would arrive and take her hand and say goodbye, and she would look at him in surprise and start to say, "But you just got here . . ." And then she would see the clock, and three or four hours would have passed.

She had no idea where they had gone.

She had a vague recollection that they had brought the children to her in the night and that she had fallen asleep. She could not remember too clearly, and she was afraid to ask. It did not matter. She would have them to herself when Walther took her home.

The wonderful day finally arrived. Anna left the hospital room in a wheelchair, even though she insisted she was strong enough to walk. She actually felt very weak, but she was so excited that nothing mattered except the fact that she was going to see her babies. Walther carried her into the house, and he started to take her upstairs to their bedroom.

"No, no!" she said. "Take me to the nursery."

"You must rest now, darling. You're not strong enough to – "

She did not listen to the rest of what he was saying. She slipped out of his arms and ran into the nursery.

The blinds were drawn and the room was dark and it took Anna's eyes a moment to adjust. She was filled with such excitement that it made her dizzy. She was afraid she was going to faint.

Walther had come in behind her. He was talking to her, trying to explain something, but whatever it was was unimportant.

For there they were. They were both asleep in their cribs, and Anna moved towards them softly, so as not to disturb them, and stood there, staring down at them. They were the most beautiful children she had ever seen. Even now, she could see that the boy would have Walther's handsome features and his thick blond hair. The girl was like an exquisite doll, with soft, golden hair and a small, triangular face.

Anna turned to Walther and said, her voice choked, "They're beautiful. I – I'm so happy."

"Come, Anna," Walther whispered. He put his arms around Anna, and held her close, and there was a fierce hunger in him, and she began to feel a stirring within her. They had not made love for such a long time. Walther was right. There would be plenty of time for the children later.

The boy she named Peter and the girl Birgitta. They were two beautiful miracles that she and Walther had made, and Anna would spend hour after hour in the nursery, playing with them, talking to them. Even though they could not understand her yet she knew they could feel her love. Sometimes, in the middle of play, she would turn and Walther would be standing in the doorway, home from the office, and Anna would realize that somehow the whole day had slipped by.

"Come and join us," she would say. "We're playing a game."

"Have you fixed dinner yet?" Walther would ask, and she would suddenly feel guilty. She would resolve to pay more attention to Walther, and less to the children, but the next day the same thing would happen. The twins were like an irresistible magnet that drew her to them. Anna still loved Walther very much, and she tried to assuage her guilt by telling herself that the children were a part of him. Every night, as soon as Walther was asleep, Anna would slip out of bed and creep into the nursery, and sit and stare at the children until dawn started filtering into the room. Then she would turn and hurry back to bed before Walther awoke.

Once, in the middle of the night, Walther walked into the nursery and caught her. "What in God's name do you think you're doing?" he said.

"Nothing, darling. I was just – "

"Go back to bed!"

He had never spoken to her like that before.

At breakfast Walther said, "I think we should take a holiday. It will be good for us to get away."

"But Walther, the children are too young to travel."
"I'm talking about the two of us."
She shook her head. "I couldn't leave them."
He took her hand and said, "I want you to forget about the children."
"Forget about the children?" There was shock in her voice.
He looked into her eyes and said, "Anna, remember how wonderful it was between us before you were pregnant? What good times we had? How much joy it was to be together, just the two of us, with no one else around to interfere?"
It was then that she understood. Walther was jealous of the children.

The weeks and months passed swiftly. Walther never went near the children now. On their birthdays Anna bought them lovely presents. Walther always managed to be out of town on business. Anna could not go on deceiving herself for ever. The truth was that Walther had no interest in the children at all. Anna felt that perhaps it was her fault, because she was *too* interested in them. *Obsessed* was the word Walther had used. He had asked her to consult a doctor about it, and she had gone only to please Walther. But the doctor was a fool. The moment he had started talking to her, Anna had shut him out, letting her mind drift, until she heard him say, "Our time is up, Mrs Gassner. Will I see you next week?"
"Of course."
She never returned.
Anna felt that the problem was as much Walther's as hers. If her fault lay in loving the children too much, then his fault lay in not loving them enough.
Anna learned not to mention the children in Walther's presence, but she could hardly wait for him to leave for the office, so that she could hurry into the nursery to be with her babies. Except that they were no longer babies. They had had their third birthday, and already Anna could see what they would look like as adults. Peter was tall for his age and his body was strong and athletic like his father's. Anna would hold him on her lap and croon, "Ah, Peter, what are you going to do to the poor fräuleins? Be gentle with them, my darling son. They won't have a chance."
And Peter would smile shyly and hug her.
Then Anna would turn to Birgitta. Birgitta grew prettier each day. She looked like neither Anna or Walther. She had spun-gold hair and skin as delicate as porcelain. Peter had his father's fiery temper and sometimes it would be necessary for Anna to spank him gently, but Birgitta had the disposition of an angel. When Walther was not around, Anna played records or read to them. Their favourite book was *101 Märchen*. They would insist that Anna read them the tales of ogres and goblins and witches over and over again, and at night Anna would put them to bed, singing them a lullaby:

Schlaf, Kindlein, schlaf,
Der Vater hüt't die Schaf . . .

Anna had prayed that time would soften Walther's attitude, that he would change. He did change, but for the worse. He hated the children. In the beginning Anna had told herself that it was because Walther wanted all of her love for himself, that he was unwilling to share it with anyone else. But slowly she became aware that it had nothing to do with loving her. It had to do with hating her. Her father had been right. Walther had married her for her money. The children were a threat to him. He wanted to get rid of them. More and more he talked to Anna about selling the stock. "Sam has no right to stop us! We could take all that money and go away somewhere. Just the two of us."

She stared at him. "What about the children?"

His eyes were feverish. "No. Listen to me. For both our sakes we've got to get rid of them. We must."

It was then that Anna began to realize that he was insane. She was terrified. Walther had fired all the domestic help, and except for a cleaning woman who came in once a week, Anna and the children were alone with him, at his mercy. He needed help. Perhaps it was not too late to cure him. In the fifteenth century they gathered the insane and imprisoned them for ever on houseboats, *Narrenschiffe*, the ships of fools, but today, with modern medicine, she felt there must be something they could do to help Walther.

Now, on this day in September, Anna sat huddled on the floor in her bedroom, where Walther had locked her, waiting for him to return. She knew what she had to do. For his sake, as well as hers and the children's. Anna rose unsteadily and walked over to the telephone. She hesitated for only an instant, then picked it up and began to dial 110, the police emergency number.

An alien voice in her ear said, "*Hallo. Hier ist der Notruf der Polizei. Kann ich Ihnen helfen?*"

"*Ja, bitte!*" Her voice was choked. "*Ich* – "

A hand came out of nowhere and tore the receiver from her, and slammed it down into the cradle.

Anna backed away. "Oh, please," she whimpered, "don't hurt me."

Walther was moving towards her, his eyes bright, his voice so soft that she could hardly make out the words. "*Liebchen*, I'm not going to hurt you. I love you, don't you know that?" He touched her, and she could feel her flesh crawl. "It's just that we don't want the police coming here, do we?" She shook her head from side to side, too filled with terror to speak. "It's the children that are causing the trouble, Anna. We're going to get rid of them. I – "

Downstairs the front doorbell rang. Walther stood there, hesitating. It rang again.

"Stay here," he ordered. "I'll be back."

Anna watched, petrified, as he walked out of the bedroom door. He slammed it behind him and she could hear the click of the key as he locked it.

I'll be back, he had said.

Walther Gassner hurried down the stairs, walked to the front door and opened it. A man in a grey messenger's uniform stood there, holding a sealed manila envelope.

"I have a special delivery for Mr and Mrs Walther Gassner."

"Yes," Walther said. "I will take it."

He closed the door, looked at the envelope in his hand, then ripped it open. Slowly, he read the message inside.

DEEPLY REGRET TO INFORM YOU THAT SAM ROFFE WAS KILLED IN A CLIMBING ACCIDENT. PLEASE BE IN ZURICH FRIDAY NOON FOR AN EMERGENCY MEETING OF THE BOARD OF DIRECTORS.

It was signed "Rhys Williams".

3

Rome
Monday, September 7
6 p.m.

Ivo Palazzi stood in the middle of his bedroom, the blood streaming down his face. "*Mamma mia! Mi hai rovinato!*"

"I haven't begun to ruin you, you miserable *figlio di putana!*" Donatella screamed at him.

They were both naked in the large bedroom of their apartment in Via Montemignaio. Donatella had the most sensuous, exciting body Ivo Palazzi had ever seen, and even now, as his life's blood poured from his face, from the terrible scratches she had inflicted on him, he felt a familiar stirring in his loins. *Dio*, she was beautiful. There was an innocent decadence about her that drove him wild. She had the face of a leopard, high cheekbones and slant eyes, full ripe lips, that nibbled him and sucked him and – But he must not think of that now. He picked up a white cloth from a chair to staunch the flow of blood, and too late he realized that it was his shirt. Donatella was standing in the middle of their huge double bed, yelling at him. "I hope you bleed to death! When I've finished with you, you filthy whoremonger, there won't be enough left for a *gattino* to shit on!"

For the hundredth time Ivo Palazzi wondered how he had got himself into this impossible situation. He had always prided himself on being the happiest of men, and all his friends had agreed with him. His *friends? Everybody!* Because Ivo had no enemies. In his bachelor days he had been a happy-go-lucky Roman without a care in the world, a Don Giovanni who was the envy of half the males in Italy. His philosophy was summed up in the phrase *Farst onore con una donna*

– "Honour oneself with a woman." It kept Ivo very busy. He was a true romantic. He kept falling in love, and each time he used his new love to help him forget his old love. Ivo adored women, and to him they were all beautiful, from the *putane* who plied their ancient trade along the Via Appia, to the high-fashion models strutting along the Via Condotti. The only girls Ivo did not care for were the Americans. They were too independent for his tastes. Besides, what could one expect of a nation whose language was so unromantic that they would translate the name of Giuseppe Verdi to Joe Green?

Ivo always managed to have a dozen girls in various states of preparation. There were five stages. In stage one were the girls he had just met. They received daily phone calls, flowers, slim volumes of erotic poetry. In stage two were those to whom he sent little gifts of Gucci scarves and porcelain boxes filled with Perugina chocolates. Those in stage three received jewellery and clothes and were taken to dinner at El Toula, or Taverna Flavia. Those in stage four shared Ivo's bed and enjoyed his formidable skills as a lover. An assignation with Ivo was a production. His beautifully decorated little apartment on the Via Margutta would be filled with flowers, *garofani* or *papaveri*, the music would be opera, classical or rock, according to the chosen girl's taste. Ivo was a superb cook, and one of his specialities, appropriately enough, was *pollo alla cacciatora*, the hunter's chicken. After dinner, a bottle of chilled champagne to drink in bed . . . Ah, yes, Ivo loved stage four.

But stage five was probably the most delicate of them all. It consisted of a heartbreaking farewell speech, a generous parting gift and a tearful *arrivederci*.

But all that was in the past. Now Ivo Palazzi took a quick glance at his bleeding, scratched face in the mirror over his bed and was horrified. He looked as though he had been attacked by a mad threshing machine.

"Look at what you've done to me!" he cried. "*Cara*, I know you didn't mean it."

He moved over to the bed to take Donatella in his arms. Her soft arms flew around him and as he started to hug her, she buried her long fingernails in his naked back and clawed him like a wild animal. Ivo yelled with pain.

"Scream!" Donatella shouted. "If I had a knife, I'd cut off your *cazzo* and ram it down your miserable throat."

"Please!" Ivo begged. "The children will hear you."

"Let them!" she shrieked. "It's time they found out what kind of monster their father is."

He took a step towards her. "*Carissima* – "

"Don't you touch me! I'd give my body to the first drunken syphilitic sailor I met on the streets before I'd ever let you come near me again."

Ivo drew himself up, his pride offended. "That is not the way I expect the mother of my children to talk to me."

"You want me to talk nice to you? You want me to stop treating you like the vermin you are?" Donatella's voice rose to a scream. "*Then give me what I want!*"

Ivo looked nervously towards the door. "*Carissima* – I can't. I don't have it."

"Then get it for me!" she cried. "You promised!"

She was beginning to get hysterical again, and Ivo decided the best thing for him to do was to get out of there quickly before the neighbours called the *carabinieri* again.

"It will take time to get a million dollars," he said soothingly. "But I'll – I'll find a way."

He hastily donned his underpants and trousers, and socks and shoes, while Donatella stormed around the room, her magnificent, firm breasts waving in the air, and Ivo thought to himself, My God, what a woman! How I adore her! He reached for his bloodstained shirt. There was no help for it. He put it on, feeling the cold stickiness against his back and chest. He took a last look in the mirror. Small pools of blood were still oozing from the deep gashes where Donatella had raked her fingernails across his face.

"*Carissima*," Ivo moaned, "how am I ever going to explain this to my wife?"

Ivo Palazzi's wife was Simonetta Roffe, an heiress of the Italian branch of the Roffe family. Ivo had been a young architect when he had met Simonetta. His firm had sent him to supervise some changes in the Roffe villa at Porto Ercole. The instant Simonetta had set eyes on Ivo, his bachelor days were numbered. Ivo had got to the fourth stage with her on the first night, and found himself married to her a short time later. Simonetta was as determined as she was lovely, and she knew what she wanted: she wanted Ivo Palazzi. Thus it was that Ivo found himself transformed from a carefree bachelor to the husband of a beautiful young heiress. He gave up his architectural aspirations with no regrets and joined Roffe and Sons, with a magnificent office in EUR, the section of Rome started with such high hopes by the late, ill-fated Duce.

Ivo was a success with the firm from the beginning. He was intelligent, learned quickly and everyone adored him. It was impossible not to adore Ivo. He was always smiling, always charming. His friends envied him his wonderful disposition and wondered how he did it. The answer was simple. Ivo kept the dark side of his nature buried. In fact, he was a deeply emotional man, capable of great volatile hatreds, capable of killing.

Ivo's marriage with Simonetta thrived. At first, he had feared that marriage would prove to be a bondage that would strangle his manhood to death, but his fears proved to be unfounded. He simply put himself on an austerity programme, reducing the number of his girl friends, and everything went on as before.

Simonetta's father bought them a beautiful home in Olgiata, a large private estate twenty-five kilometres north of Rome, guarded by closed gates and manned by uniformed guards.

Simonetta was a wonderful wife. She loved Ivo and treated him like a king, which was no more than he felt he deserved. There was just one tiny flaw in

Simonetta. When she became jealous, she turned into a savage. She had once suspected Ivo of taking a female buyer on a trip to Brazil. He was righteously indignant at the accusation. Before the argument was over, their entire house was a shambles. Not one dish or piece of furniture was left intact, and much of it had been broken over Ivo's head. Simonetta had gone after him with a butcher's knife, threatening to kill him and then herself, and it had taken all of Ivo's strength to wrest the knife from her. They had wound up fighting on the floor, and Ivo had finally torn off her clothes and made her forget her anger. But after that incident Ivo became very discreet. He had told the buyer he could not take any more trips with her, and he was careful never to let the faintest breath of suspicion touch him. He knew that he was the luckiest man in the world. Simonetta was young and beautiful and intelligent and rich. They enjoyed the same things and the same people. It was a perfect marriage, and Ivo sometimes found himself wondering, as he transferred a girl from stage two to stage three, and another from stage four to stage five, why he kept on being unfaithful. Then he would shrug philosophically and say to himself, Someone has to make these women happy.

Ivo and Simonetta had been married for three years when Ivo met Donatella Spolini on a business trip to Sicily. It was more of an explosion than a meeting, two planets coming together and colliding. Where Simonetta had the slender, sweet body of a young woman sculpted by Manzu, Donatella had the sensuous, ripe body of a Rubens. Her face was exquisite and her green, smouldering eyes set Ivo aflame. They were in bed one hour after they had met, and Ivo, who had always prided himself on his prowess as a lover, found that he was the pupil and Donatella the teacher. She made him rise to heights he had never achieved before, and her body did things to his that he had never dreamed possible. She was an endless cornucopia of pleasure, and as Ivo lay in bed, his eyes closed, savouring incredible sensations, he knew he would be a fool to let Donatella go.

And so Donatella had become Ivo's mistress. The only condition she imposed was that he had to get rid of all the other women in his life, except his wife. Ivo had happily agreed. That had been eight years ago, and in all that time Ivo had never been unfaithful to either his wife or his mistress. Satisfying two hungry women would have been enough to exhaust an ordinary man, but in Ivo's case it was exactly the opposite. When he made love to Simonetta he thought about Donatella and her ripe, full body, and he was filled with lust. And when he made love to Donatella, he thought of Simonetta's sweet young breasts and tiny *culo* and he performed like a wild man. No matter which woman he was with, he felt that he was cheating the other. It added enormously to his pleasure.

Ivo bought Donatella a beautiful apartment in Via Montemignaio, and he was with her every moment that he could manage. He would arrange to be away on a sudden business trip and, instead of leaving, he would spend the time in bed with Donatella. He would stop by to see her on his way to the office, and he would spend his afternoon siestas with her. Once, when Ivo sailed to New York on the *QE 2* with Simonetta, he installed Donatella in a cabin one deck below. They were the five most stimulating days of Ivo's life.

On the evening that Simonetta announced to Ivo that she was pregnant, Ivo was filled with an indescribable joy. A week later Donatella informed Ivo that *she* was pregnant, and Ivo's cup ran over. Why, he asked himself, are the gods so good to me? In all humility, Ivo sometimes felt that he did not deserve all the great pleasures that were being bestowed upon him.

In due course Simonetta gave birth to a girl and a week later Donatella gave birth to a boy. What more could any man ask? But the gods were not finished with Ivo. A short time later, Donatella informed Ivo that she was pregnant again, and the following week Simonetta also became pregnant. Nine months later, Donatella gave Ivo another son and Simonetta presented her husband with another daughter. Four months later, both women were pregnant again and this time they gave birth on the same day. Ivo frantically raced from the Salvator Mundi, where Simonetta was ensconced, to the Santa Chiera Clinic where Ivo had taken Donatella. He sped from hospital to hospital, driving on the Raccordo Anulare, waving to the girls sitting in front of their little tents along the sides of the road, under pink umbrellas, waiting for customers. Ivo was driving too fast to see their faces, but he loved them all and wished them well.

Donatella gave birth to another boy and Simonetta to another girl.

Sometimes Ivo wished it had been the other way round. It was ironical that his wife had borne him daughters and his mistress had borne him sons, for he would have liked male heirs to carry on his name. Still, he was a contented man. He had three children with outdoor plumbing, and three children with indoor plumbing. He adored them and he was wonderful to them, remembering their birthdays, their saints' days, and their names. The girls were called Isabella and Benedetta and Camilla. The boys were Francesco and Carlo and Luca.

As the children grew older, life began to get more complicated for Ivo. Including his wife, his mistress and his six children, Ivo had to cope with eight birthdays, eight saints' days, and two of every holiday. He made sure that the children's schools were well separated. The girls were sent to Saint Dominique, the French convent on the Via Cassia, and the boys to Massimo, the Jesuit school in EUR. Ivo met and charmed all their teachers, helped the children with their homework, played with them, fixed their broken toys. It taxed all of Ivo's ingenuity to handle two families and keep them apart, but he managed. He was truly an exemplary father, husband and lover. On Christmas Day he stayed home with Simonetta, Isabella, Benedetta and Camilla. On *Befana*, the sixth of January, Ivo dressed up as the *Befana*, the witch, and handed out presents and *carbone*, the black rock candy prized by children, to Francesco, Carlo and Luca.

Ivo's wife and his mistress were lovely, and his children were bright and beautiful, and he was proud of them all. Life was wonderful.

And then the gods spat in Ivo Palazzi's face.

As in the case of most major disasters, this one struck without any warning.

Ivo had made love to Simonetta that morning before breakfast, and then had gone directly to his office where he did a profitable morning's work. At one o'clock he told his secretary – male, at Simonetta's insistence – that he would be at a meeting the rest of the afternoon.

Smiling at the thought of the pleasures that lay ahead of him, Ivo circled the construction that blocked the street along the Lungo Tevere, where they had been building a subway for the past seventeen years, crossed the bridge to the Corso Francia, and thirty minutes later was driving into his garage at Via Montemignaio. The instant Ivo opened the door of the apartment, he knew something was terribly wrong. Francesco, Carlo and Luca were clustered around Donatella, sobbing, and as Ivo walked towards Donatella, she looked at him with an expression of such hatred on her face that for a moment Ivo thought he must have entered the wrong apartment.

"*Stronzo!*" she screamed at him.

Ivo looked around him, bewildered. "*Carissima* – children – what's wrong? What have I done?"

Donatella rose to her feet. "Here's what you've done!" She threw a copy of the magazine *Oggi* in his face. "Look at it!"

Bewildered, Ivo reached down and picked up the magazine. Staring out from the cover was a photograph of himself, Simonetta and their three daughters. The caption read: *Padre di Famiglia.*

Dio! He had forgotten all about it. Months before, the magazine had asked permission to do a story about him and he had foolishly agreed. But Ivo had never dreamed that it would be given this prominence. He looked over at his sobbing mistress and children, and said, "I can explain this . . ."

"Their schoolmates have already explained it," Donatella shrieked. "My children came home crying because everybody at school is calling them bastards!"

"*Cara*, I – "

"My landlord and the neighbours have treated us like lepers. We can't hold up our heads any more. I have to get them out of here."

Ivo stared at her, shocked. "What are you talking about?"

"I'm leaving Rome, and I'm taking my sons with me."

"They're mine too," he shouted. "You can't do it."

"Try to stop me and I'll kill you!"

It was a nightmare. Ivo stood there, watching his three sons and his beloved mistress in hysterics, and he thought, This can't be happening to me.

But Donatella was not finished with him. "Before we go," she announced, "I want one million dollars. In cash."

It was so ridiculous that Ivo started to laugh. "A million – "

"Either that, or I telephone your wife."

That had happened six months earlier. Donatella had not carried out her threat

– not yet – but Ivo knew she would. Each week she had increased the pressure. She would telephone him at the office and say, "I don't care how you get the money. Do it!"

There was only one way that Ivo could possibly obtain such a huge sum. He had to be able to sell the stock in Roffe and Sons. It was Sam Roffe who was blocking the sale, Sam who was jeopardizing Ivo's marriage, his future. He had to be stopped. If one knew the right people, anything could be done.

What hurt Ivo more than anything was that Donatella – his darling, passionate mistress – would not let him touch her. Ivo was permitted to visit the children every day, but the bedroom was off limits.

"After you give me the money," Donatella promised, "then I will let you make love to me."

It was out of desperation that Ivo telephoned Donatella one afternoon and said, "I'm coming right over. The money is arranged."

He would make love to her first and placate her later. It had to work out that way. He had managed to undress her, and when they were both naked, he had told her the truth. "I don't have the money yet, *cara*, but one day soon–"

It was then that she had attacked him like a wild animal.

Ivo was thinking of these things now, as he drove away from Donatella's apartment (as he now thought of it) and turned north on to the crowded Via Cassia, towards his home at Olgiata. He glanced at his face in the rear-view mirror. The bleeding had lessened, but the scratches were raw-looking and discoloured. He looked down at his shirt, stained with blood. How was he going to explain to Simonetta the scratches on his face and his back? For one reckless moment Ivo actually considered telling her the truth, but he dismissed the thought as quickly as it came into his head. He might – just might – have been able to confess to Simonetta that in a moment of mental aberration he had gone to bed with a girl and got her pregnant, and he might – he just *might* – have got away with a whole skin. But *three children?* Over a period of *three years?* His life would not be worth a five-lire piece. There was no way he could avoid going home now, for they were expecting guests for dinner, and Simonetta would be waiting for him. Ivo was trapped. His marriage was finished. Only San Genaro, the patron saint of miracles, could help him. Ivo's eye was caught by a sign at the side of the Via Cassia. He suddenly slammed on the brakes, turned off the highway and brought the car to a stop.

Thirty minutes later, Ivo drove through the gates of Olgiata. Ignoring the stares of the guards as they saw his torn face and bloodstained shirt, Ivo drove along the winding roads, came to the turn that led to his driveway, and pulled up in front of his house. He parked the car, opened the front door of the house and walked into the living-room. Simonetta and Isabella, their eldest daughter, were in the room. A look of shock came over Simonetta's face as she saw her husband.

"Ivo! What happened?"

Ivo smiled awkwardly, trying to ignore the pain it cost, and admitted sheepishly, "I'm afraid I did something stupid, *cara* – "

Simonetta was moving closer, studying the scratches on his face, and Ivo could see her eyes begin to narrow. When she spoke, her voice was frosty. "Who scratched your face?"

"Tiberio," Ivo announced. From behind his back he produced a large, spitting, ugly grey cat that leaped out of his arms and raced off. "I bought it for Isabella, but the damned thing attacked me while I was trying to put it in its basket."

"*Povero amore mio!*" Instantly, Simonetta was at his side. "*Angelo mio!* Come upstairs and lie down. I'll get the doctor. I'll get some iodine. I'll – "

"No, no! I'm fine," Ivo said bravely. He winced as she put her arms around him. "Careful! I'm afraid he's clawed my back, too."

"*Amore!* How you must be suffering!"

"No, really," Ivo said. "I feel good." And he meant it.

The front doorbell rang.

"I'll go," Simonetta said.

"No, I'll go," Ivo said quickly. "I – I'm expecting some important papers from the office."

He hurried to the front door and opened it.

"Signor Palazzi?"

"*Sì.*"

A messenger, dressed in a grey uniform, handed him an envelope. Inside was a teletype from Rhys Williams. Ivo read the message rapidly. He stood there for a long, long time.

Then he took a deep breath and went upstairs to get ready for his guests.

4

Buenos Aires
Monday, September 7
3 p.m.

The Buenos Aires autodrome on the dusty outskirts of Argentina's capital city was crammed with fifty thousand spectators who had come to watch the championship classic. It was a 115–lap race over the almost four-mile circuit. The race had been running for nearly five hours, under a hot, punishing sun, and out of a starting field of thirty cars only a handful remained. The crowd was seeing history being made. There had never been such a race before, and perhaps never would be again. All the names that had become legend were on the track this day: Chris Amon from New Zealand, and Brian Redman from Lancashire.

There was the Italian Andrea di Adamici, in an Alfa-Romeo Tipo 33, and Carlos Maco of Brazil, in a March Formula 1. The prize-winning Belgian Jacky Ickx was there, and Sweden's Reine Wisell in a BRM.

The track looked like a rainbow gone mad, filled with the swirling reds and greens and black and white and golds of the Ferraris and Brabhams and McLaren M19–As and Lotus Formula 3s.

As lap after gruelling lap went by, the giants began to fall. Chris Amon was in fourth place when his throttle jammed open. He sideswiped Brian Redman's Cooper before he brought his own car under control by cutting the ignition, but both cars were finished. Reine Wisell was in first position, with Jacky Ickx close behind the BRM. On the far turn, the BRM gearbox disintegrated and the battery and electrical equipment caught fire. The car started spinning, and Jacky Ickx's Ferrari was caught in the vortex.

The crowd was in a frenzy.

Three cars were outpacing the rest of the field, Jorje Amandaris from Argentina, driving a Surtees; Nils Nilsson from Sweden in a Matra; and a Ferrari 312 B-2, driven by Martel of France. They were driving brilliantly, daring the straight track, challenging the curves, moving up.

Jorje Amandaris was in the lead, and because he was one of them, the Argentinians cheered him madly. Close behind Amandaris was Nils Nilsson, at the wheel of a red and white Matra, and behind him the black and gold Ferrari, driven by Martel of France.

The French car had gone almost unnoticed until the last five minutes, when it had started gaining on the field. It had reached tenth position, then seventh, then fifth. And it was coming on strongly. The crowd was watching now as the French driver started moving up on number two, driven by Nilsson. The three cars were travelling at speeds in excess of 180 miles an hour. That was dangerous enough at carefully contoured race tracks like Brands Hatch or Watkins Glen, but on the cruder Argentine track it was suicide. A red-coated referee stood at the side of the track, holding up a sign: FIVE LAPS.

The French black and gold Ferrari attempted to pass Nilsson's Matra on the outside, and Nilsson inched over, blocking the French car's way. They were lapping a German car on the inside track, moving up on it fast. Now it was opposite Nilsson's car. The French car dropped back and edged over so that it was positioned in the tight space behind the German car and Nilsson's Matra. With a quick burst of acceleration the French driver made for the narrow slot, forcing the two cars out of its way and shooting ahead into the number two spot. The crowd, which had been holding its breath, roared its approval. It had been a brilliant, dangerous manoeuvre.

It was Amandaris in the lead now, Martel second and Nilsson in third position, with three laps remaining. Amandaris had seen the move. The French driver is good, Amandaris told himself, but not good enough to beat me. Amandaris intended to win this race. Ahead of him he saw the sign being flashed – TWO LAPS. The race was almost over, and it was his. Out of the corner of his eye he could see the black and gold Ferrari trying to pull up alongside him. He got a glimpse of the driver's goggled, dirt-streaked face, tight and determined. Amandaris gave an inward sigh. He regretted what he was about to do, but he had no choice. Racing was not a game for sportsmen, it was a game for winners.

The two cars were approaching the north end of the oval, where there was a high banking turn, the most dangerous in the track, the scene of a dozen crashes. Amandaris shot another quick look at the French driver of the Ferrari and then tightened his grip on the wheel. As the two cars started to approach the curve, Amandaris imperceptibly lifted his foot from the accelerator, so that the Ferrari began to pull ahead. He saw the driver give him a quick, speculative look. Then the driver was abreast of him, falling into his trap. The crowd was screaming. Jorje Amandaris waited until the black and gold Ferrari was fully committed to passing him on the outside. At that moment Amandaris opened his throttles wide and started to move towards the right, cutting the French driver's path to the straight, so that the only choice was to head up the embankment.

Amandaris saw the sudden, dismayed expression on the French driver's face and silently said, *Salaud!* At that instant the driver of the French car turned the wheel directly into Amandaris's Surtees. Amandaris could not believe it. The Ferrari was on a crash course with him. They were only three feet apart and at that speed Amandaris had to make a split-second decision. *How could anyone have known that the French driver was completely loco?* In a swift, reflex action, Amandaris swung the wheel sharply to the left, trying to avoid the thousand pounds of metal hurtling at him, and braked hard, so that the French car missed him by a fraction of an inch, and shot past him towards the finish line. For a moment Jorje Amandaris's car fishtailed, then went out of control into a spin, flinging itself wildly across the track, rolling over and over until it burst into a tower of red and black flames.

But the crowd's attention was riveted on the French Ferrari, roaring across the finishing line to victory. There were wild screams from the spectators as they ran towards the car, surrounding it, cheering. The driver slowly stood up and took off the racing goggles and helmet.

She had wheat-coloured hair, cut short, and her face was sculptured with strong, firm features. There was a classic cold beauty about her. Her body was trembling, not with exhaustion, but with excitement, the memory of the moment when she had looked into Jorje Amandaris's eyes as she sent him to his death. Over the loudspeaker the announcer was excitedly yelling, "The winner is Hélène Roffe-Martel, from France, driving a Ferrari."

Two hours later, Hélène and her husband, Charles, were in their suite in the Ritz Hotel in downtown Buenos Aires, lying on the rug in front of the fireplace, and Hélène was naked on top of him in the classic position of *la diligence de Lyon*, and Charles was saying, "Oh, Christ! Please don't do that to me! Please!"

And his begging increased her excitement and she began to put on more pressure, hurting him, watching the tears come to his eyes. I'm being punished for no reason, Charles thought. He dreaded to think what Hélène would do to him if she ever found out about the crime he had committed.

Charles Martel had married Hélène Roffe for her name and for her money. After the ceremony she had kept her name, along with his, and she had kept her money. By the time Charles found out he had made a bad bargain, it was too late.

Charles Martel was a junior attorney in a large Paris law firm when he first met Hélène Roffe. He had been asked to bring some documents into the conference room, where a meeting was taking place. In the room were the four senior partners in the firm, and Hélène. Charles had heard of her. Everyone in Europe had. She was an heiress to the Roffe pharmaceutical fortune. She was wild and unconventional, and the newspapers and magazines adored her. She was a champion skier; flew her own Learjet, had led a mountain-climbing expedition in Nepal, raced cars and horses, and changed men as casually as she changed her wardrobe. Her photograph was constantly appearing in *Paris-Match* and *Jours de France*. She was in the law office now because the firm was handling her divorce. Her fourth or fifth, Charles Martel was not sure which, nor was he interested. The Roffes of the world were out of his reach.

Charles handed the papers to his superior, nervous, not because Hélène Roffe was in the room – he hardly glanced at her – but because of the presence of the four senior partners. They represented Authority, and Charles Martel respected Authority. He was basically a retiring man, content to make a modest living, reside in a little apartment in Passy and tend to his small stamp collection.

Charles Martel was not a brilliant attorney, but he was a competent one, thorough and reliable. He had a stiff *petsec* dignity about him. He was in his early forties and his physical appearance, while not unattractive, was certainly far from prepossessing. Someone had once said that he had the personality of wet sand, and the description was not an unjust one. It was with a good deal of surprise, therefore, that the day after he had met Hélène Roffe, Charles Martel received a summons to go to the office of M. Michel Sachard, the senior partner, where he was told, "Hélène Roffe wishes you to assume personal charge of her divorce case. You will take over at once."

Charles Martel was stunned. He asked, "Why me, Monsieur Sachard?"

Sachard looked him in the eye and replied, "I can't imagine. See that you service her well."

Being in charge of Hélène's divorce action made it necessary for Charles to see her frequently. Too frequently, he felt. She would telephone him and invite him to dinner at her villa in Le Vésinet to discuss the case, and to the opera and to her house in Deauville. Charles kept trying to explain to her that it was a simple case, that there would be no problem in obtaining the divorce, but Hélène – she insisted that he call her Hélène, to his acute embarrassment – told him she needed his constant reassurance. Later he was to think back on that with bitter amusement.

During the weeks that followed their first meeting, Charles began to suspect that Hélène Roffe was interested in him romantically. He could not believe it. He was a nobody, and she was a member of one of the great families, but Hélène left him in no doubt as to her intentions. "I'm going to marry you, Charles."

He had never thought of getting married. He was not comfortable with women. Besides, he did not love Hélène. He was not even certain he liked her. The fuss and attention that attended her wherever they went discomfited him. He was caught in the limelight of her celebrity and it was a role he was not accustomed to. He was also painfully aware of the contrast between them. Her flamboyance was an irritant to his conservative nature. She set fashion styles and was the epitome of glamour, while he – well, he was a simple, ordinary, middle-aged lawyer. He could not understand what Hélène Roffe saw in him. Nor could anyone else. Because of her well-publicized participation in dangerous sports that were normally the exclusive province of men, there were rumours that Hélène Roffe was an advocate of the women's liberation movement. In fact, she despised the movement, and had only contempt for its concept of equality. She saw no reason why men should be allowed to become the equal of women. Men were handy to have around, when required. They were not particularly intelligent, but they could be taught to fetch and light cigarettes, run errands, open doors and give satisfaction in bed. They made excellent pets, dressed and bathed themselves and were toilet-trained. An amusing species.

Hélène Roffe had had the playboys, the daredevils, the tycoons, the glamour boys. She had never had a Charles Martel. She knew exactly what he was: *Nothing*. A piece of blank clay. And that was precisely the challenge. She intended to take him over, mould him, see what she could make of him. Once Hélène Roffe made up her mind, Charles Martel never had a chance.

They were married in Neuilly and they honeymooned in Monte Carlo, where Charles lost his virginity and his illusions. He had planned to return to the law firm.

"Don't be a fool," his bride said. "Do you think I want to be married to a law clerk? You'll go into the family business. One day you'll be running it. *We'll* be running it."

Hélène arranged for Charles to work in the Paris branch of Roffe and Sons. He reported to her on everything that went on and she guided him, helped him, gave him suggestions to make. Charles's advancement was rapid. He was soon in charge of the French operation, and a member of the board of directors. Hélène Roffe had changed him from an obscure lawyer to an executive of one of the largest corporations in the world. He should have been ecstatic. He was miserable. From the first moment of their marriage Charles found himself totally dominated by his wife. She chose his tailor, his shoemaker and his shirtmaker. She got him into the exclusive Jockey Club. Hélène treated Charles like a gigolo. His salary went directly to her, and she gave him an embarrassingly small allowance. If Charles needed any extra money, he had to ask Hélène for it. She made him account for every moment of his time, and he was at her constant beck and call. She seemed to enjoy humiliating him. She would telephone him at the office and order him to come home immediately with a jar of massage cream, or something equally stupid. When he arrived, she would be in the bedroom, naked, waiting for him. She was insatiable, an animal. Charles had lived with his mother until he was thirty-two, when she had died of cancer. She had been an invalid for as long as Charles could remember, and he had taken care of her. There had been no time to think about going out with girls or getting married. His mother had been a burden and when she died, Charles thought he would feel a sense of freedom. Instead, he felt a sense of loss. He had no interest in women or sex. He had, in a naïve burst of candour, explained his feelings to Hélène when she had first mentioned marriage. "My – my libido is not very strong," he had said.

Hélène had smiled. "Poor Charles. Don't worry about sex. I promise you, you'll like it."

He hated it. That only seemed to add to Hélène's pleasure. She would laugh at him for his weakness, and force him to do disgusting things that made Charles feel degraded and sick. The sex act was debasing enough. But Hélène was interested in experimenting. Charles never knew what to expect. Once, at the moment he was having an orgasm, she had put crushed ice on his testicles, and another time she had shoved an electric prod up his anus. Charles was terrified of Hélène. She made him feel that she was the male and he was the female. He tried to salvage his pride but, alas, he could find no area in which Hélène was not superior to him. She had a brilliant mind. She knew as much about the law as he did, and much more about business. She spent hour after hour discussing the company with him. She never tired of it. "Think of all that power, Charles! Roffe and Sons can make or break more than half the countries in the world. I should be running the company. My great-grandfather founded it. It's part of me."

After one of these outbursts Hélène would be sexually insatiable, and Charles was forced to satisfy her in ways that did not bear thinking about. He came to despise her. His one dream was to get away from her, to escape. But for that he needed money.

One day, over lunch, a friend of his, René Duchamps, told Charles about an opportunity to make a fortune.

"An uncle of mine who owned a large vineyard in Burgundy has just died. The vineyard is going to be put up for sale – ten thousand acres of first-class *Appelation d'origine contrôlée*. I have the inside track," René Duchamps continued, "because it's my family. I don't have enough to swing the deal by myself, but if you came in with me, we could double our money in one year. At least, come and look at it."

Because Charles could not bear to admit to his friend that he was penniless, he went to the rolling red slopes of Burgundy to view the land. He was deeply impressed.

René Duchamps said, "We'll each put in two million francs. In a year we'll each have four million."

Four million francs! It would mean freedom, escape. He could go away to some place where Hélène could never find him.

"I'll think about it," Charles promised his friend.

And he did. Day and night. It was the chance of a life-time. But *how?* Charles knew that it would be impossible for him to try to borrow money without Hélène immediately learning about it. Everything was in her name, the houses, the paintings, the cars, the jewellery. The jewellery . . . those beautiful, useless ornaments she kept locked up in the safe in the bedroom. Gradually, the idea was born. If he could get hold of her jewellery, a little at a time, he could replace the pieces with copies and borrow money on the real jewellery. After he had made his killing in the vineyard, he would simply return the jewels. And have enough money to disappear for ever.

Charles telephoned René Duchamps and said, his heart pounding with excitement, "I've decided to go in with you."

The first part of the plan filled Charles with terror. He had to get into the safe and steal Hélène's jewellery.

The anticipation of the terrible thing he was about to do made Charles so nervous that he was barely able to function. He went through each day like an automaton, neither seeing nor hearing what was happening around him. Every time Charles saw Hélène he began to sweat. His hands would tremble at odd times. Hélène was concerned about him, as she would have been concerned about any pet. She had the doctor examine Charles, but the doctor could find nothing wrong. "He seems a bit tense. A day or two in bed, perhaps."

Hélène looked long at Charles, lying in bed, naked, and smiled. "Thank you, doctor."

The moment the doctor left, Hélène began getting undressed. "I – I'm not feeling very strong," Charles protested.

"I am," Hélène replied.

He had never hated her more.

Charles's opportunity came the following week. Hélène was going to Garmisch-Partenkirchen to ski with some friends. She decided to leave Charles in Paris.

"I want you home every night," Hélène told him. "I'll telephone you."

Charles watched her speed away, at the wheel of her red Jensen, and the moment she was out of sight he hurried to the wall safe. He had watched her open it often, and he knew most of the combination. It took him an hour to figure out the rest of it. With trembling fingers he pulled the safe open. There, in velvet-lined boxes, sparkling like miniature stars, lay his freedom. He had already located a jeweller, one Pierre Richaud, who was a master at duplicating jewellery. Charles had begun a long, nervous explanation about why he wanted the jewels copied, but Richaud said, matter-of-factly, "Monsieur, I am making copies for everyone. No-one with any sense wears real jewellery on the streets these days."

Charles gave him one piece at a time to work on, and when the copy was ready, he substituted it for the real piece. He borrowed money on the real jewellery from the Crédit Municipal, the state-owned pawnshop.

The operation took longer than Charles had anticipated. He could only get into the safe when Hélène was out of the house, and there were unforeseen delays in copying the pieces. But finally the day came when Charles was able to say to René Duchamps, "I'll have all the money for you tomorrow."

He had accomplished it. He was half-owner of a great vineyard. And Hélène had not the slightest suspicion of what he had done.

Charles had secretly begun to read up on the growing of vines. And why not? Was he not a vintner now? He learned about the different vines: *cabernet sauvignon* was the principal vine used, but others were planted alongside it: *gros cabernet, merlot, malbec, petit verdot*. The desk drawers of Charles's office were filled with pamphlets on soil and wine pressing. He learned about fermentation and pruning and grafting. And that the worldwide demand for wine kept growing.

He met regularly with his partner. "It's going to be even better than I thought," René told Charles. "Prices for wine are sky-rocketing. We should get three hundred thousand francs a *tonneau* for the first pressings."

More than Charles had dreamed! The grapes were red gold. Charles began to buy travel pamphlets on the South Sea Islands and Venezuela and Brazil. The very names had a magic about them. The only problem was that there were few places in the world where Roffe and Sons did not have offices, where Hélène could not find him. And if she found him, she would kill him. He knew that, with an absolute certainty. Unless he killed her first. It was one of his favourite fantasies. He murdered Hélène over and over again, in a thousand delicious ways.

Perversely, Charles now began to enjoy Hélène's abuse. All the time she was forcing him to do unspeakable things to her, he was thinking, I'll be gone soon, you *convasse*. I'll be rich on your money and there's nothing you can do about it.

And she would command, "Faster now," or "Harder," or "Don't stop!" and he would meekly obey her.

And smile inside.

In vine-growing, Charles knew the crucial months were in the spring and summer, for the grapes were picked in September and they had to have a carefully balanced season of sun and rain. Too much sun would burn the flavour, just as too much rain would drown it. The month of June began splendidly. Charles checked the weather in Burgundy once, then twice a day. He was in a fever of impatience, only weeks away from the fulfilment of his dream. He had decided on Montego Bay. Roffe and Sons had no office in Jamaica. It would be easy to lose himself there. He would not go near Round Hill or Ocho Rios, where any of Hélène's friends might see him. He would buy a small house in the hills. Life was cheap on the island. He could afford servants, and fine food, and in his own small way live in luxury.

And so in those first days of June, Charles Martel was a very happy man. His present life was an ignominy, but he was not living in the present: he was living in the future, on a tropical, sun-bathed, wind-caressed island in the Caribbean.

The June weather seemed to get better each day. There was sun, and there was rain. Perfect for the tender little grapes. And as the grapes grew, so did Charles's fortune.

On the fifteenth day of June it began to drizzle in the Burgundy region. Then it began to rain harder. It rained day after day, and week after week, until Charles could no longer bring himself to check the weather reports.

René Duchamps telephoned. "If it stops by the middle of July, the crop can still be saved."

July turned out to be the rainiest month in the history of the French weather bureau. By the first of August, Charles Martel had lost every centime of the money he had stolen. He was filled with a fear such as he had never known.

"We're flying to Argentina next month," Hélène had informed Charles. "I've entered a car race there."

He had watched her speeding round the track in the Ferrari, and he could not help thinking: *If she crashes, I'm free.*

But she was Hélène Roffe-Martel. Life had cast her in the role of a winner, just as it had cast him in the role of a loser.

Winning the race had excited Hélène even more than usual. They had returned to their hotel suite in Buenos Aires, and she had made Charles get undressed and lie on the rug, on his stomach. When he saw what she had in her hand as she straddled him, he said, "Please, no!"

There was a knock on the door.

"*Merde!*" Hélène said. She waited, silent, but the knocking was repeated.

A voice called, "Señor Martel?"

"Stay here!" Hélène commanded. She got up, whipped a heavy silk robe about her slim, firm body, walked over to the door and pulled it open. A man in a grey messenger's uniform stood there, holding a sealed manila envelope.

"I have a special delivery for Señor and Señora Martel."

She took the envelope and closed the door.

She tore the envelope open and read the message inside, then slowly read it again.

"What is it?" Charles asked.

"Sam Roffe is dead," she said. She was smiling.

5

London
Monday, September 7
2 p.m.

White's Club was situated at the top of St James's Street, near Piccadilly. Built as a gambling club in the eighteenth century, White's was one of the oldest clubs in England, and the most exclusive. Members put their sons' names down for membership at birth, for there was a thirty-year waiting list.

The façade of White's was the epitome of discretion. The wide bow-windows looking out on St James's Street were meant to accommodate those within rather than to satisfy the curiosity of the outsiders passing by. A short flight of steps led to the entrance but, aside from members and their guests, few people ever got past the door. The rooms in the club were large and impressive, burnished with the dark, rich patina of time. The furniture was old and comfortable – leather couches, newspaper racks, priceless antique tables and deep, stuffed armchairs that had held the posteriors of half a dozen Prime Ministers. There was a backgammon room with a large, open fireplace behind a bronze-covered rail, and a formal curved staircase led to the dining-room upstairs. The dining-room ran across the entire breadth of the house, and contained one huge mahogany table which seated thirty persons, and five side tables. At any luncheon or dinner the room contained some of the most influential men in the world.

Sir Alec Nichols, Member of Parliament, was seated at one of the small corner tables, having lunch with a guest, Jon Swinton. Sir Alec's father had been a baronet, and his father and grandfather before him. They had all belonged to White's. Sir Alec was a thin, pale man in his late forties, with a sensitive aristocratic face and an engaging smile. He had just motored in from his country estate in Gloucestershire, and was dressed in a tweed sports jacket and slacks, with loafers. His guest wore a pin-stripe suit with a loud, checked shirt and a red tie, and seemed out of place in this quiet, rich atmosphere.

"They really do you proud here," Jon Swinton said, his mouth full, as he chewed the remains of a large veal chop on his plate.

Sir Alec nodded. "Yes. Things have changed since Voltaire said, 'The British have a hundred religions and only one sauce.' "

Jon Swinton looked up. "Who's Voltaire?"

Sir Alec said, embarrassed, "A – a French chap."

"Oh." John Swinton washed his food down with a swallow of wine. He laid down his knife and fork and wiped a napkin across his mouth. "Well, now, Sir Alec. Time for you and I to talk a little business."

Alec Nichols said softly, "I told you two weeks ago I'm working everything out, Mr Swinton. I need a bit more time."

A waiter walked over to the table, balancing a high stack of wooden cigar boxes. He skilfully set them down on the table.

"Don't mind if I do," Jon Swinton said. He examined the labels on the boxes, whistled in admiration, pulled out several cigars which he put in his breast-pocket, then lit one. Neither the waiter nor Sir Alec showed any reaction to this breach of manners. The waiter nodded to Sir Alec, and carried the cigars to another table.

"My employers have been very lenient with you, Sir Alec. Now, I'm afraid, they've got impatient." He picked up the burned match, leaned forward and dropped it into Sir Alec's glass of wine. "Between you and I, they're not nice people when they're upset. You don't want to get them down on you, you know what I mean?"

"I simply don't have the money right now."

Jon Swinton laughed loudly. "Come off it, chum. Your mum was a Roffe, right? You've got a thousand-acre farm, a posh town house in Knightsbridge, a Rolls-Royce and a bloody Bentley. You're not exactly on the dole then, are you?"

Sir Alec looked around, pained, and said quietly, "None of them is a liquid asset. I can't – "

Swinton winked and said, "I'll bet that sweet little wife of yours, Vivian, is a liquid asset, eh? She's got a great pair of Bristols."

Sir Alec flushed. Vivian's name on this man's lips was a sacrilege. Alec thought of Vivian as he had left her that morning, still sweetly asleep. They had separate bedrooms, and one of Alec Nichols's great joys was to go into Vivian's room for one of his "visits". Sometimes, when Alec awakened early, he would walk into Vivian's bedroom while she was asleep and simply stare at her. Awake or asleep, she was the most beautiful girl he had ever seen. She slept in the nude, and her soft, curved body would be half exposed as she curled into the sheets. She was blonde, with wide, pale blue eyes and skin like cream.

Vivian had been a minor actress when Sir Alec had first met her at a charity ball. He had been enchanted by her looks, but what had drawn him to her was her easy, outgoing personality. She was twenty years younger than Alec, and filled with a zest for living. Where Alec was shy and introverted, Vivian was gregarious and vivacious. Alec had been unable to get her out of his mind, but it had taken him two weeks to summon up nerve enough to telephone her. To his surprise and delight Vivian had accepted his invitation. Alec had taken her to a play at the Old Vic, and then to dinner at the Mirabelle. Vivian lived in a dreary little basement flat in Notting Hill, and when Alec had brought her home, she had said, "Would you like to come in then?" He had stayed the night, and it had changed his whole life. It was the first time that any woman had been able to bring him to a climax. He had never experienced anything like Vivian. She was velvet tongue and trailing golden hair and moist, pulsing, demanding depths that Alec explored until he was drained. He could become aroused simply thinking about her.

There was something else. She made him laugh, she made him come alive.

She poked fun at Alec because he was shy and a bit stodgy, and he adored it. He was with her as often as Vivian would permit it. When Alec took Vivian to a party, she was always the centre of attention. Alec was proud of that, but jealous of the young men gathered around her, and he could not help wondering how many of them she had been to bed with.

On the nights when Vivian could not see him because she had another engagement, Alec was frantic with jealousy. He would drive to her flat and park down the block, to see what time she came home, and whom she was with. Alec knew that he was behaving like a fool, and yet he could not help himself. He was in the grip of something too strong to break.

He realized that Vivian was wrong for him, that it was out of the question for him to marry her. He was a respected Member of Parliament, with a brilliant future. He was part of the Roffe dynasty, on the board of directors of the company. Vivian had no background to help her cope with Alec's world. Her mother and father had been second-rate music-hall artists, playing the provincial circuit. Vivian had had no education except for what she had picked up in the streets, or backstage. Alec knew that she was promiscuous and superficial. She was shrewd but not particularly intelligent. And yet Alec was obsessed with her. He fought it. He tried to stop seeing her, but it was no use. He was happy when he was with her, and he was miserable when he was without her. In the end he proposed to her because he had to, and when Vivian accepted, Sir Alec Nichols was ecstatic.

His new bride moved into the family home, a beautiful old Robert Adam house in Gloucestershire, a Georgian mansion with Doric columns and a long sweeping driveway. It was set amid the green of a thousand acres of lush farmland, with its own private shooting, and running streams to fish. At the back of the house was a park that had been laid out by Capability Brown.

The interior of the house was stunning. The large front hall had a stone floor and walls of painted wood. There were pairs of old lanterns and marble-topped Adam gilt-wood tables and mahogany chairs. The library had original eighteenth-century built-in bookcases, and a pair of pedestal tables by Henry Holland, and chairs designed by Thomas Hope. The drawing-room was a mixture of Hepplewhite and Chippendale, with a Wilton carpet, and a pair of Waterford glass chandeliers. There was a huge dining-room that could seat forty guests, and a smoking-room. On the second floor were six bedrooms, each with an Adam fireplace, and on the third floor were the servants' quarters.

Six weeks after she had moved into the house, Vivian said, "Let's get out of this place, Alec."

He looked at her, puzzled. "You mean you'd like to go up to London for a few days?"

"I mean I want to *move* back to London."

Alec looked out of the window at the emerald-green meadows, where he had played as a child, and at the giant sycamore and oak trees, and he said hesitantly, "Vivian, it's so peaceful here. I – "

And she said, "I know, luv. That's what I can't stand – the fucking peace!"

They moved to London the following week.

Alec had an elegant four-storey town house in Wilton Crescent, off Knightsbridge, with a lovely drawing-room, a study, a large dining-room, and at the back of the house, a picture window that overlooked a grotto, with a waterfall and statues and white benches set amid a beautiful formal garden. Upstairs were a magnificent master suite and four smaller bedrooms.

Vivian and Alec shared the master suite for two weeks, until one morning Vivian said, "I love you, Alec, but you do snore, you know." Alec had not known. "I really must sleep alone, luv. You don't mind, do you?"

Alec minded deeply. He loved the feel of her soft body in bed, warm against him. But deep inside, Alec knew that he did not excite Vivian sexually the way other men excited her. That was why she did not want him in her bed. So now he said, "Of course I understand, darling."

At Alec's insistence, Vivian kept the master suite, and he moved into one of the small guest bedrooms.

In the beginning, Vivian had gone to the House of Commons and had sat in the Visitors' Gallery on days when Alec was to speak. He would look up at her and be filled with a deep, ineffable pride. She was undoubtedly the most beautiful woman there. And then came the day when Alec finished his speech and looking up for Vivian's approval, saw only an empty seat.

Alec blamed himself for the fact that Vivian was restless. His friends were older than Vivian, too conservative for her. He encouraged her to invite her young companions to the house, and brought them together with his friends. The results were disastrous.

Alec kept telling himself that when Vivian had a child, she would settle down and change. But one day, somehow – and Alec could not bear to know how – she picked up a vaginal infection and had to have a hysterectomy. Alec had longed for a son. The news had shattered him, but Vivian was unperturbed.

"Don't worry, luv," she said, smiling. "They took out the nursery, but they left in the playpen."

He looked at her for a long moment, then turned and walked away.

Vivian loved to go on buying sprees. She spent money indiscriminately, recklessly, on clothes and jewellery and cars, and Alec did not have the heart to stop her. He told himself that she had grown up in poverty, hungry for beautiful things. He wanted to buy them for her. Unfortunately, he could not afford it. His salary was consumed by taxes. His fortune lay in his shares of stock in Roffe and Sons but those shares were restricted. He tried to explain that to Vivian but she was not interested. Business discussions bored her. And so Alec let her carry on.

He had first learned of her gambling when Tod Michaels, the owner of Tod's Club, a disreputable gambling place in Soho, had dropped in to see him.

"I have your wife's IOUs here for a thousand pounds, Sir Alec. She had a rotten run at roulette."

Alec had been shocked. He had paid off the IOUs and had had a confrontation with Vivian that evening. "We simply can't afford it," he had told her. "You're spending more than I'm making."

She had been very contrite. "I'm sorry, angel. Baby's been bad."

And she had walked over to him and put her arms around him and pressed her body against his, and he had forgotten his anger.

Alec had spent a memorable night in her bed. He was sure now that there would be no more problems.

Two weeks later Tod Michaels had come to visit Alec again. This time Vivian's IOUs were five thousand pounds. Alec was furious. "Why did you let her have credit?" he demanded.

"She's your wife, Sir Alec," Michaels had replied blandly. "How would it look if we refused her?"

"I'll – I'll have to get the money," Alec had said. "I don't have that much cash at the moment."

"Please! Consider it a loan. Pay it back when you can."

Alec had been greatly relieved. "That's very generous of you, Mr Michaels."

It was not until a month later that Alec learned that Vivian had gambled away another twenty-five thousand pounds, and that he was being charged interest at the rate of ten per cent a week. He was horrified. There was no way he could raise that much cash. There was nothing that he could even sell. The houses, the beautiful antiques, the cars, all belonged to Roffe and Sons. His anger frightened Vivian enough so that she promised not to gamble any more. But it was too late. Alec found himself in the hands of loan sharks. No matter how much Alec gave them, he could not manage to pay off the debt. It kept mounting each month, instead of getting smaller, and it had been going on for almost a year.

When Tod Michael's hoodlums first began to press him for the money, Alec had threatened to go to the police commissioner. "I have connections in the highest quarters," Alec had said.

The man had grinned. "I got connections in the lowest." Now Sir Alec found himself sitting here at White's with this dreadful man, having to contain his pride, and beg for a little more time.

"I've already paid them back more than the money I borrowed. They can't – "

Swinton replied, "That was just on the interest, Sir Alec. You still haven't paid the principal."

"It's extortion," Alec said.

Swinton's eyes darkened. "I'll give the boss your message." He started to rise.

Alec said quickly, "No! Sit down. Please."

Slowly Swinton sat down again. "Don't use words like that," he warned. "The last chap who talked like that had both his knees nailed to the floor."

Alec had read about it. The Kray brothers had invented the punishment for their victims. And the people Alec was dealing with were just as bad, just as ruthless. He could feel the bile rising in his throat. "I didn't mean that," Alec said. "It's just that I – I don't have any more cash."

Swinton flicked the ash from his cigar into Alec's glass of wine, and said, "You have a big bundle of stock in Roffe and Sons, don't you, Alec baby?"

"Yes," Alec replied, "but it's non-saleable and non-transferable. It's no good to anyone unless Roffe and Sons goes public."

Swinton took a puff on his cigar. "And is it going public?"

"That's up to Sam Roffe. I've – I've been trying to persuade him."

"Try harder."

"Tell Mr Michaels he'll get his money," Alec said. "But please stop hounding me."

Swinton stared. "Hounding you? Why, Sir Alec, you little cocksucker, you'll know when we start hounding you. Your fucking stables will burn down, and you'll be eating roast horsemeat. Then your house will burn. And maybe your wife." He smiled, and Alec wished he had not. "Have you ever eaten cooked pussy?"

Alec had turned pale. "For God's sake – "

Swinton said soothingly, "I'm kidding. Tod Michaels is your friend. And friends help each other, right? We were talking about you at our meeting this morning. And do you know what the boss said? He said, 'Sir Alec's a good sort. If he hasn't got the money, I'm sure he'll think of some other way to take care of us.' "

Alec frowned. "What other way?"

"Well, it's not hard for a bright chap like you to work something out, is it? You're running a big drug company, right? You make things like cocaine, for example. Just between you and I, who'd ever know if you happened to accidentally misplace a few shipments here and there?"

Alec stared at him. "You're insane," he said. "I – I couldn't do that."

"It's amazing what people can do when they have to," Swinton said genially. He rose to his feet. "You either have our money for us, or we'll tell you where to deliver the merchandise."

He ground his cigar out on Alec's butter plate. "Give my regards to Vivian, Sir Alec. Ta."

And Jon Swinton was gone.

Sir Alec sat there alone, unseeing, surrounded by all the familiar, comfortable things that were so much a part of his past life, that were now threatened. The only alien thing was the obscene, wet, cigar butt on the plate. How had he ever allowed them to come into his life? He had permitted himself to be manoeuvred into a position where he was in the hands of the underworld. And now he knew that they wanted more than money from him. The money was merely the bait with which they had trapped him. They were after his connections with the drug company. They were going to try to force him to work with them. If it became known he was in their power, the Opposition would not hesitate to make capital of it. His own party would probably ask him to resign. It would be done tactfully and quietly. They would probably exert pressure on him to apply for the Chiltern Hundreds, a post that paid a nominal salary of a hundred pounds a year from the Crown. The one barrier to being an MP was that you could not be in receipt of pay from the Crown or the Government. So Alec would no longer be allowed to serve in Parliament. The reason could not be kept secret, of course. He would be in disgrace. Unless he could come up with a large sum of money. He had talked to Sam Roffe again and again, asking him to let the company go public, to let the shares of stock be marketed.

"Forget it," Sam had told him. "The minute we let outsiders in, we have a lot of strangers telling us how to run our business. Before you know it, they'll take over the board, and then the company. What's the difference to you, Alec? You have a big salary, an unlimited expense account. You don't *need* the money."

For a moment Alec had been tempted to tell Sam how desperately he needed it. But he knew it would do no good. Sam Roffe was a company man, a man without compassion. If he knew that Alec had in any way compromised Roffe and Sons, he would have dismissed him without a moment's hesitation. No, Sam Roffe was the last person to whom he could turn.

Alec was facing ruin.

The reception porter at White's walked towards Sir Alec's table with a man dressed in a messenger's uniform, carrying a sealed manila envelope.

"Excuse me, Sir Alec," the porter apologized, "but this man insists that he has instructions to deliver something to you personally."

"Thank you," Sir Alec said. The messenger handed him the envelope, and the porter led him back to the door.

Alec sat there a long time before he reached for the envelope and opened it. He read the message through three times, then he slowly crumpled the paper in his fist, and his eyes began to fill with tears.

6

New York
Monday, September 7
11 a.m.

The private Boeing 707–320 was making its final approach to Kennedy Airport, gliding out of the stacked-up traffic pattern. It had been a long, tedious flight and Rhys Williams was exhausted, but he had been unable to sleep during the night. He had ridden in this plane too often with Sam Roffe. His presence still filled it.

Elizabeth Roffe was expecting him. Rhys had sent her a cable from Istanbul, merely announcing that he would arrive the following day. He could have broken the news of her father's death over the telephone but she deserved more than that.

The plane was on the ground now, taxiing towards the terminal. Rhys carried very little luggage, and he was quickly ushered through Customs. Outside, the sky was grey and bleak, a foretaste of the winter to come. A limousine was waiting at the side entrance to drive him to Sam Roffe's Long Island estate, where Elizabeth would be waiting.

During the drive Rhys tried to rehearse the words that he would say to her to try to soften the blow, but the moment Elizabeth opened the front door to greet him the words flew out of his head. Each time Rhys saw Elizabeth her beauty caught him by surprise. She had inherited her mother's looks, the same patrician features, midnight black eyes framed by long, heavy lashes. Her skin was white and soft, her hair a shiny black. Her figure was rich and firm. She was wearing an open-necked, creamy silk blouse and a pleated grey-flannel skirt and fawn-coloured pumps. There was no sign of the awkward little girl Rhys had first met nine years earlier. She had become a woman, intelligent and warm and completely unselfconscious about her beauty. She was smiling at him now, pleased to see him. She took his hand and said, "Come in, Rhys," and led him into the large oak-panelled library. "Did Sam fly in with you?"

There was no way to break it gently. Rhys took a deep breath and said, "Sam had a bad accident, Liz." He watched the colour drain from her face. She waited for him to go on. "He was killed."

She stood there frozen. When she finally spoke, Rhys could barely hear her. "What-what happened?"

"We don't have any of the details yet. He was climbing Mont Blanc. A rope broke. He fell into a crevasse."

"Did they find – "

She closed her eyes for a moment, then opened them.

"A bottomless crevasse."

Her face had turned white. Rhys felt a quick sense of alarm. "Are you all right?"

She smiled brightly, and said, "Of course. I'm fine, thank you. Would you like some tea or something to eat?"

He looked at her in surprise and started to speak, and then he understood. She was in shock. She was rattling on, making no sense, her eyes unnaturally bright, her smile fixed.

"Sam was such a great athlete," Elizabeth was saying. "You've seen his trophies. He always won, didn't he? Did you know he climbed Mont Blanc before?"

"Liz – "

"Of course you did. You went with him once, didn't you, Rhys?"

Rhys let her talk, anaesthetizing herself against the pain, trying to build an armour of words to ward off the moment when she would have to face her own anguish. For an instant, as he listened to her, he was reminded of the vulnerable little girl he had first known, too sensitive and shy to have any protection against brutal reality. She was dangerously wound up now, tense and brittle, and there was a fragility about her that worried Rhys.

"Let me call a doctor," he said. "He can give you something to – "

"Oh, no. I'm really quite all right. If you don't mind, I think I'll lie down for a while. I'm feeling a bit tired."

"Would you like me to stay?"

"Thank you. That won't be necessary."

She walked him to the door, and as he started to get into the car Elizabeth called, "Rhys!"

He turned.

"Thank you for coming."

Jesus Christ.

Long hours after Rhys Williams had gone, Elizabeth Roffe lay in her bed, staring at the ceiling, watching the shifting patterns painted by the pale September sun.

And the pain came. She had not taken a sedative, because she wanted the pain. She owed that to Sam. She would be able to bear it, because she was his daughter. And so she lay there, all day and all night, thinking of nothing, thinking of everything, remembering, feeling. She laughed, and she cried, and she supposed that she was in a state of hysteria. It did not matter. There was no one to hear her. In the middle of the night, she suddenly became ravenously hungry and went down into the kitchen and devoured a large sandwich and then threw it up. She felt no better. Nothing could ease the pain that filled her. Her mind kept going back, back over the years with her father. Through her bedroom window she watched the sun rise. Some time later, one of the servants knocked at the door, and Elizabeth sent her away. Once the phone rang, and her heart leaped and she reached for it, thinking, It's Sam! Then she remembered, and snatched her hand away.

He would never call her again. She would never hear his voice again. She would never see him again.

A bottomless crevasse.

Bottomless.

Elizabeth lay there, letting the past wash over her, remembering, remembering it all.

7

The birth of Elizabeth Rowane Roffe was a double tragedy. The minor tragedy was that Elizabeth's mother died on the delivery table. The major tragedy was that Elizabeth was born a girl.

For nine months, until she emerged from the darkness of her mother's womb, she was the most eagerly awaited child in the world, heir to a colossal empire, the multi-billion-dollar giant, Roffe and Sons.

Sam Roffe's wife, Patricia, was a dark-haired woman of surpassing beauty. Many women had tried to marry Sam Roffe, for his position, his prestige, his wealth. Patricia had married him because she had fallen in love with him. It had proved to be the worst of reasons. Sam Roffe had been looking for a business arrangement, and Patricia had suited his requirements ideally. Sam had neither the time nor the temperament to be a family man. There was no room in his life for anything but Roffe and Sons. He was fanatically dedicated to the company, and he expected no less from those around him. Patricia's importance to him lay solely in the contribution she could make to the image of the company. By the time Patricia came to a realization of what kind of marriage she had made, it was too late. Sam gave her a role to play, and she played it beautifully. She was the perfect hostess, the perfect Mrs Sam Roffe. She received no love from her husband and in time Patricia learned to give none. She served Sam, and was as much an employee of Roffe and Sons as the lowliest secretary. She was on call twenty-four hours a day, ready to fly wherever Sam needed her, capable of entertaining a small company of world leaders or serving a gourmet dinner to a hundred guests at a day's notice, with crisp, heavily embroidered table cloths, gleaming Baccarat crystal, heavy Georgian silverware. Patricia was one of Roffe and Sons' unlisted assets. She worked at keeping herself beautiful, and exercised and dieted like a Spartan. Her figure was perfect, and her clothes were designed for her by Norell in New York, Chanel in Paris, Hartnell in London, and young Sybil Connolly in Dublin. The jewellery Patricia wore was created for her by Jean Schlumberger and Bulgari. Her life was busy and full and joyless and empty. Becoming pregnant had changed all that.

Sam Roffe was the last male heir of the Roffe dynasty, and Patricia knew how desperately he wanted a son. He was depending on her. And now she was the queen mother, busy with the baby within her, the young prince, who would one day inherit the kingdom. When they wheeled Patricia into the delivery room, Sam clasped her hand and said "Thank you".

She was dead of an embolism thirty minutes later, and the only blessing about Patricia's death was that she died without knowing that she had failed her husband.

Sam Roffe took time off from his gruelling schedule to bury his wife, and then turned his attention to the problem of what he should do with his infant daughter.

One week after Elizabeth was born, she was taken home and turned over to a nanny, the beginning of a long series of nannies. During the first five years of her life, Elizabeth saw very little of her father. He was barely more than a blur, a stranger who was always arriving or leaving. He travelled constantly and Elizabeth was a nuisance who had to be carted along, like a piece of extra luggage. One month Elizabeth would find herself living at their Long Island estate, with its bowling alley, tennis court, swimming pool and squash court. A few weeks later, her nanny would pack Elizabeth's clothes and she would be flown to their villa in Biarritz. It had fifty rooms and thirty acres of grounds and Elizabeth kept getting lost.

In addition, Sam Roffe owned a large duplex penthouse apartment on Beekman Place, and a villa on the Costa Smeralda in Sardinia. Elizabeth travelled to all these places, shunted from house to apartment to villa, and grew up amid all the lavish elegance. But always she felt like an outsider who had wandered by mistake into a beautiful birthday party given by unloving strangers.

As Elizabeth grew older, she came to know what it meant to be the daughter of Sam Roffe. Just as her mother had been an emotional victim of the company, so was Elizabeth. If she had no family life, it was because there was no family, only the paid surrogates and the distant figure of the man who had fathered her, who seemed to have no interest in her, only in the company. Patricia had been able to accept her situation, but for the child it was torment. Elizabeth felt unwanted and unloved, and did not know how to cope with her despair, and in the end she blamed herself for being unlovable. She tried desperately to win the affection of her father. When Elizabeth was old enough to go to school, she made things for him in class, childish drawings and watercolour paintings and lopsided ashtrays, and she would guard them fiercely, waiting for him to return from one of his trips, so that she could surprise him, please him, hear him say, *It's beautiful, Elizabeth. You're very talented.*

When he returned, Elizabeth would present her love offering, and her father would glance at it absently and nod, or shake his head. "You'll never be an artist, will you?"

Sometimes Elizabeth would awaken in the middle of the night, and walk down the long winding staircase of the Beekman Place apartment and through the large cavernous hall that led to her father's study. She would step into the empty room as if she were entering a shrine. This was *his* room, where he worked and signed important pieces of paper and ran the world. Elizabeth would walk over to his enormous leather-topped desk and slowly rub her hands across it. Then she would move behind the desk and sit in his leather chair. She felt closer to her father there. It was as though by being where he was, sitting where he sat, she could become a part of him. She would hold imaginary conversations with him, and he would listen, interested and caring as she poured out her problems. One night, as Elizabeth sat at his desk in the dark, the lights in the room suddenly came on. Her father was standing in the doorway. He looked at Elizabeth seated behind his desk, clad in a thin nightgown, and said, "What are you doing here alone in the dark?" And he scooped her up in his arms and carried her upstairs, to her bed, and Elizabeth had lain awake all night, thinking about how her father had held her.

After that, she went downstairs every night and sat in his office waiting for him to come and get her, but it never happened again.

No one discussed Elizabeth's mother with her, but there was a beautiful full-length portrait of Patricia Roffe hanging in the reception hall, and Elizabeth would stare at it by the hour. Then she would turn to her mirror. Ugly. They had put braces on her teeth, and she looked like a gargoyle. No wonder my father isn't interested in me, Elizabeth thought.

Overnight she developed an insatiable appetite, and began to gain weight. For she had arrived at a wonderful truth: if she were fat and ugly, no one would expect her to look like her mother.

When Elizabeth was twelve years old, she attended an exclusive private school on the East Side of Manhattan, in the upper seventies. She would arrive in a chauffeur-driven Rolls-Royce, walk into her class and sit there, withdrawn and silent, ignoring everyone around her. She never volunteered to answer a question. And when she was called upon, she never seemed to know the answer. Her teachers soon got into the habit of ignoring her. They discussed Elizabeth among themselves and unanimously agreed that she was the most spoiled child they had ever seen. In a confidential year-end report to the headmistress, Elizabeth's teacher wrote:

We have been able to make no progress with Elizabeth Roffe. She is aloof from her classmates and refuses to participate in any of the group activities, but it is difficult to tell if this is because she makes no effort, or because she is unable to handle the assignments. She is arrogant and egotistical. Were it not for the fact that her father is a major benefactor of this school, I would strongly recommend expelling her.

The report was light-years from the reality. The simple truth was that Elizabeth Roffe had no protective shield, no armour against the terrible loneliness that engulfed her. She was filled with such a deep sense of her own unworthiness that she was afraid to make friends, for fear they would discover that she was worthless, unlovable. She was not arrogant, she was almost pathologically shy. She felt that she did not belong in the same world that her father inhabited. She did not belong anywhere. She loathed being driven to school in the Rolls-Royce, because she knew she did not deserve it. In her classes she knew the answers to the questions the teachers asked, but she did not dare to speak out, to call attention to herself. She loved to read, and she would lie awake late at night in her bed, devouring books.

She day-dreamed, and oh! what lovely fantasies. She was in Paris with her father, and they were driving through the Bois in a horse-drawn carriage, and he took her to his office, an enormous room something like Saint Patrick's cathedral, and people kept walking in with papers for him to sign, and he would wave them away and say, "Can't you see I'm busy now? I'm talking to my daughter, Elizabeth."

She and her father were skiing in Switzerland, moving down a steep slope side by side, with an icy wind whipping past them, and he suddenly fell and cried out with pain, because his leg was broken, and she said, "Don't worry, Papa! I'll take care of you." And she skied down to the hospital and said, "Quickly, my father's hurt," and a dozen men in white jackets brought him there in a shiny ambulance and she was at his bedside, feeding him (it was probably his arm that was broken, then, not his leg), and her mother walked into the room, alive somehow, and her father said, "I can't see you now, Patricia. Elizabeth and I are talking."

Or they would be in their beautiful villa in Sardinia, and the servants would be away, and Elizabeth would cook dinner for her father. He would eat two helpings of everything and say, "You're a much better cook than your mother was, Elizabeth."

The scenes with her father always ended in the same way. The doorbell would ring and a tall man, who towered over her father, would come in and beg Elizabeth to marry him, and her father would plead with her, "Please, Elizabeth, don't leave me. I need you."

And she would agree to stay.

Of all the homes in which Elizabeth grew up, the villa in Sardinia was her favourite. It was by no means the largest, but it was the most colourful, the friendliest. Sardinia itself delighted Elizabeth. It was a dramatic, rock-bound island, some 160 miles south-west of the Italian coast, a stunning panorama of mountains, sea and green farmland. Its enormous volcanic cliffs had been thrown up thousands of years ago from the primal sea, and the shoreline swept in a vast crescent as far as the eye could follow, the Tyrrhenian Sea framing the island in a blue border.

For Elizabeth the island had its own special odours, the smell of sea breezes and forests, the white and yellow *macchia*, the fabled flower that Napoleon had loved. There were the *corbeccola* bushes that grew six feet high and had a red fruit that tasted like strawberries, and the *guarcias*, the giant stone oaks whose bark was exported to the mainland to be used for making corks for wine bottles.

She loved to listen to the singing rocks, the mysterious giant boulders with holes through them. When the winds blew through the holes, the rocks emitted an eerie keening sound, like a dirge of lost souls.

And the winds blew. Elizabeth grew to know them all. The mistral and the *ponente*, the tramontana and the *grecate* and the levanter. Soft winds and fierce winds. And then there was the dreaded sirocco, the warm wind that blew in from the Sahara.

The Roffe villa was on the Costa Smeralda, above Porto Cervo, set high atop a cliff overlooking the sea, secluded by juniper trees and the wild-growing Sardinian olive trees with their bitter fruit. There was a breathtaking view of the harbour far below, and around it, sprinkled over the green hills, a jumble of stucco and stone houses thrown together in a crazy hodge-podge of colours resembling a child's crayon drawing.

The villa was stone, with huge juniper beams inside. It was built on several levels, with large, comfortable rooms, each with its own fireplace and balcony. The living-room and dining-room had picture windows that gave a panoramic view of the island. A free-form staircase led to four bedrooms upstairs. The furniture blended perfectly with the surroundings. There were rustic refectory tables and benches, and soft easy chairs. Across the windows were fringed white wool curtains that had been hand-woven on the island, and the floors were laid with colourful *cerasarda* tiles from Sardinia and other tiles from Tuscany. In the bathrooms and bedrooms were native wool carpets, coloured with vegetable dyes in the traditional way. The house was ablaze with paintings, a mixture of French Impressionists, Italian masters and Sardo primitives. In the hallway hung portraits of Samuel Roffe and Terenia Roffe, Elizabeth's great-great-grandfather and grandmother.

The feature of the house that Elizabeth loved most was the tower room, under the sloping tile roof. It was reached by a narrow staircase from the second floor, and Sam Roffe used it as his study. It contained a large work desk and a comfortable, padded swivel chair. The walls were lined with bookcases and maps, most of them pertaining to the Roffe empire. French windows led to a small balcony built over a sheer cliff, and the view from there was heart-stopping.

It was in this house, when she was thirteen years old, that Elizabeth discovered the origins of her family, and for the first time in her life felt that she belonged, that she was part of something.

It began the day she found the Book. Elizabeth's father had driven to Olbia, and Elizabeth had wandered upstairs to the tower room. She was not interested in the books on the shelves, for she had long since learned that they were technical volumes on pharmacology and pharmacognosy, and on multinational corporations and international law. Dull and boring. Some of the manuscripts were rare, and these were kept in glass cases. There was a medical volume in Latin called *Circa Instans*, written in the Middle Ages, and another called *De Materia Medica*. It was because Elizabeth was studying Latin and was curious to see one of the old volumes that she opened the glass case to take it out. Behind it, tucked away out of sight, she saw another volume. Elizabeth picked it up. It was thick, bound in leather, and had no title.

Intrigued, Elizabeth opened it. It was like opening the door to another world. It was a biography of her great-great-grandfather, Samuel Roffe, in English, privately printed on vellum. There was no author given, and no date, but Elizabeth was sure that it was more than one hundred years old, for most of the pages were faded, and others were yellowed and flaking with age. But none of this was important. It was the story that mattered, a story that brought life to the portraits hanging on the wall downstairs. Elizabeth had seen the pictures of her great-great-grandparents a hundred times: paintings of an old-fashioned man and woman, dressed in unfamiliar clothes. The man was not handsome, but there was great strength and intelligence in his face. He had fair hair, high Slavic cheekbones and keen, bright blue eyes. The woman was a beauty. Dark hair, a flawless complexion and eyes as black as coal. She wore a white silk dress with a tabard over the top, and a bodice made of brocade. Two strangers who meant nothing to Elizabeth.

But now, alone in the tower room, as Elizabeth opened the Book and began to read, Samuel and Terenia Roffe became alive. Elizabeth felt as though she had been transported back in time, that she was living in the ghetto of Krakow in the year 1853, with Samuel and Terenia. As she read deeper and deeper into the Book, she learned that her great-great-grandfather Samuel, the founder of Roffe and Sons, was a romantic and an adventurer.

And a murderer.

8

Samuel Roffe's earliest memory, Elizabeth read, was of his mother being killed in a pogrom in 1855 when Samuel was five years old. He had been hidden in the cellar of the small wooden house the Roffes shared with other families in the ghetto of Krakow. When the rioting was finally over, endless hours later, and the only sound left was the weeping of the survivors, Samuel cautiously left his hiding place and went out into the streets of the ghetto to look for his mother. It seemed to the young boy that the whole world was on fire. The entire sky was red from the blazing wooden buildings that burned on every side, and clouds of thick black smoke hung everywhere. Men and women were frantically searching for their families, or trying to save their businesses and homes and meagre possessions. Krakow, in the mid-nineteenth century, had a fire department, but it was forbidden to the Jews. Here in the ghetto, at the edge of the city, they were forced to fight the holocaust by hand, with water drawn from their wells, and scores of people formed bucket brigades to drown the flames. Samuel saw death wherever he looked, mutilated bodies of men and women tossed aside like broken dolls; naked, raped women and children, bleeding and moaning for help.

Samuel found his mother lying in the street, half conscious, her face covered with blood. The young boy knelt down at her side, his heart pounding wildly. "Mama!"

She opened her eyes and saw him, and tried to speak, and Samuel knew that she was dying. He desperately wanted to save her, but he did not know how, and even as he gently wiped the blood away, it was already too late.

Later, Samuel stood there watching as the burial party carefully dug up the ground under his mother's body: for it was soaked in her blood, and according to the Scriptures, it had to be buried with her so that she could be returned to God whole.

It was at that moment that Samuel made up his mind that he wanted to become a doctor.

The Roffe family shared a three-storey, narrow, wooden house with eight other families. Young Samuel lived in one small room with his father and his Aunt Rachel, and in all his life he had never been in a room by himself or slept or eaten alone. He could not remember a single moment when he could not hear the sound of voices, but Samuel did not crave privacy, for he had no idea that it existed. He had always lived in a crowded maze.

Each evening Samuel and his relatives and friends were locked into the ghetto by the gentiles, as the Jews penned up their goats and cows and chickens.

At sundown the massive double wooden gates of the ghetto were closed and locked with a large iron key. At sunrise the gates were opened again, and the Jewish merchants were permitted to go into the city of Krakow to conduct business with the gentiles, but they were required to be back inside the ghetto walls before sunset.

Samuel's father had come from Russia, where he had fled from a pogrom in Kiev, and he had made his way to Krakow, where he had met his bride. Samuel's father was a stooped, grey-haired man, his face worn and wrinkled, a pushcart pedlar who hawked his wares of notions and trinkets and utensils through the narrow, winding streets of the ghetto. Young Samuel loved to roam the crowded, bustling, cobble-stoned streets. He enjoyed the smell of fresh-baked bread mingled with the odours of drying fish and cheeses and ripening fruit and sawdust and leather. He liked to listen to the pedlars singing out their wares, and the housewives bargaining with them in outraged, grieved tones. The variety of goods that the pedlars sold was staggering: linens and laces, ticking and yarn, leather and meats and vegetables and needles and soft soap and plucked whole chickens and candies and buttons and syrups and shoes.

On Samuel's twelfth birthday his father took him into the city of Krakow for the first time. The idea of going through the forbidden gates and seeing Krakow itself, the home of the gentiles, filled the boy with an almost unbearable excitement.

At six o'clock in the morning Samuel, wearing his one good suit, stood in the dark next to his father in front of the huge closed gates of the city, surrounded by a noisy crowd of men with crude, homemade pushcarts, wagons or barrows. The air was cold and raw, and Samuel huddled into his threadbare sheep's wool coat.

After what seemed hours, a bright orange sun peeped over the eastern horizon and there was an expectant stir from the crowd. Moments later, the huge wooden gates began to swing open and the merchants started to pour through them like a stream of industrious ants, heading towards the city.

As they approached the wonderful, terrible city, Samuel's heart begin to beat faster. Ahead he could see the fortifications towering over the Vistula. Samuel clung to his father more tightly. He was actually in Krakow, surrounded by the feared goyim, the people who locked them up every night. He stole quick, frightened glances at the faces of the passers-by and he marvelled at how different they looked. They did not wear *payves*, earlocks, and *bekeches*, the long black coats, and many of them were clean-shaven. Samuel and his father walked along the Plante towards the Rynek, the crowded market-place, where they passed the enormous cloth hall, and the twin-towered Church of Saint Mary. Samuel had never seen such magnificence. The new world was filled with wonders. First of all, there was an exciting feeling of freedom and space that left Samuel breathless. The houses on the streets were all set apart, not jumbled together, and most of them had a small garden in front. Surely, Samuel thought, everyone in Krakow must be a millionaire.

Samuel accompanied his father to half a dozen different suppliers, where his father bought goods which he tossed into the cart. When the cart was filled, he and the boy headed back towards the ghetto.

"Can't we stay longer?" Samuel begged.

"No, son. We have to go home."

Samuel did not want to go home. He had been outside the gates for the first time in his life, and he was filled with an elation that was so strong it almost choked him. That people could live like *this*, free to walk wherever they pleased, free to do whatever they wanted . . . Why could he not have been born outside the gate? Instantly, he was ashamed of himself for having such disloyal thoughts.

That night when Samuel went to bed, he lay awake for a long time, thinking about Krakow and the beautiful houses with their flowers and green gardens. He had to find a way to get free. He wanted to talk to someone about the things he felt, but there was no one who would understand him.

Elizabeth put the Book down and sat back, closing her eyes, visualizing Samuel's loneliness, his excitement, his frustration.

It was at that moment that Elizabeth began to identify with him, to feel that she was part of him, as he was a part of her. His blood ran in her veins. She had a wonderful, heady sense of belonging.

Elizabeth heard the sound of her father's car coming up the driveway, and she quickly put the Book away. She had no further chance to read it during her stay there, but when she returned to New York the Book was hidden at the bottom of her suitcase.

9

After the warm winter sunshine of Sardinia, New York seemed like Siberia. The streets were filled with snow and slush, and the wind blowing off the East River was frigid; but Elizabeth did not mind. She was living in Poland, in another century, sharing the adventures of her great-great-grandfather. Every afternoon after school, Elizabeth would rush up to her room, lock the door and take out the Book. She had thought of discussing it with her father, but she was afraid to, for fear he would take it away from her.

In a wonderful, unexpected way, it was old Samuel who gave Elizabeth encouragement. It seemed to Elizabeth that they were so much alike. Samuel was a loner. He had no one to talk to. Like me, thought Elizabeth. And because they were almost the same age – even though a century apart – she could identify with him.

Samuel wanted to be a doctor.

Only three physicians were allowed to take care of the thousands of people crowded into the insanitary, epidemic-ridden confines of the ghetto; and of the three, the most prosperous was Dr Zeno Wal. His house stood among its poorer neighbours like a castle in the midst of a slum. It was three storeys high, and through its windows could be seen freshly washed and starched white-lace curtains and glimpses of shining, polished furniture. Samuel could visualize the doctor inside, treating his patients, helping them, curing them: doing what Samuel longed to do. Surely, if someone like Dr Wal took an interest in him, Samuel thought, he could help him to become a doctor. But as far as Samuel was concerned, Dr Wal was as inaccessible as any of the gentiles living in the city of Krakow, outside the forbidden wall.

From time to time Samuel would catch glimpses of the great Dr Zeno Wal walking along the street, engaged in earnest conversation with a colleague. One day, as Samuel was passing the Wal house, the front door opened and the doctor came out with his daughter. She was about Samuel's age, and she was the most beautiful creature Samuel had ever seen. The moment Samuel looked at her, he knew she was going to be his wife. He did not know how he was going to manage that miracle, he only knew that he had to.

Every day after that, Samuel found an excuse to be near the house, hoping to get another glimpse of her.

One afternoon, as Samuel was walking by the Wal house on an errand, he heard piano music coming from inside, and he knew that *she* was playing. He had to see her. Looking around to make sure no one was observing him, Samuel walked to the side of the house. The music was coming from upstairs, directly above his head. Samuel stepped back and studied the wall. There were enough handholds for him to climb it, and without a moment's hesitation he started up. The second floor was higher than he had realized, and before he reached the window he was ten feet above the ground. He looked down and felt a momentary sense of dizziness. The music was louder now, and he felt as if she were playing for him. He grabbed another handhold so that he could peer over the sill. He found himself looking into an exquisitely furnished parlour. The girl was seated before a gold and white piano, playing, and behind her in an armchair, reading a book, was Dr Wal. Samuel had no eyes for him. He could only stare at the beautiful vision just a few feet away from him. He loved her! He would do something spectacular and daring so that she would fall in love with him. He would – So engrossed was Samuel in his daydream that he loosened his grip and began to fall into space. He let out a cry and saw two startled faces staring at him just before he plunged to the ground.

He woke up on an operating table in Dr Wal's office, a spacious room fitted with medical cabinets and an array of surgical equipment. Dr Wal was holding an awful-smelling piece of cotton under Samuel's nose. Samuel choked and sat up.

"That's better," Dr Wal said. "I should remove your brain but I doubt if you have one. What were you planning to steal, boy?"

"Nothing," Samuel replied indignantly.

"What's your name?"

"Samuel Roffe."

The doctor's fingers began to probe Samuel's right wrist, and the boy cried out with pain.

"Hm. You have a broken wrist, Samuel Roffe. Maybe we should let the police fix it."

Samuel groaned aloud. He was thinking about what would happen when the police brought him home in disgrace. His Aunt Rachel's heart would be broken; his father would kill him. But, even more important, how could he ever hope to win Dr Wal's daughter now? He was a criminal, a marked man. Samuel felt a sudden, agonizing jerk on his wrist, and looked up at the doctor in shocked surprise.

"It's all right," Dr Wal said. "I've set it." He went to work putting a splint on it. "Do you live around here, Samuel Roffe?"

"No, sir."

"Haven't I seen you hanging about?"

"Yes, sir."

"Why?"

Why? If Samuel told the truth, Dr Wal would laugh at him.

"I want to become a doctor," Samuel blurted out, unable to contain himself.

Dr Wal was staring at him in disbelief. "*That's* why you climbed the wall of my house like a burglar'?"

Samuel found himself telling his entire story. He told about his mother dying in the streets, and about his father, about his first visit to Krakow and his frustration at being locked inside the ghetto walls at night like an animal. He told how he felt about Dr Wal's daughter. He told everything, and the doctor listened in silence. Even to Samuel's ears his story sounded ridiculous; and when he was finished, he whispered. "I – I'm sorry."

Dr Wal looked at him for a long time, and then said, "I'm sorry, too. For you, for me, and for all of us. Every man is a prisoner, and the greatest irony of all is to be the prisoner of another man."

Samuel looked up at him, puzzled. "I don't understand, sir."

The doctor sighed. "One day you will." He rose to his feet, walked over to his desk, selected a pipe and slowly and methodically filled it. "I'm afraid this is a very bad day for you, Samuel Roffe."

He put a match to the tobacco, blew it out and then turned to the boy. "Not because of your broken wrist. That will heal. But I'm going to have to do something to you that may not heal so quickly." Samuel was watching him, his eyes wide. Dr Wal walked over to his side, and when he spoke his voice was gentle. "Very few people ever have a dream. You have two dreams. And I'm afraid I am going to have to break both of them."

"I don't – "

"Listen to me carefully, Samuel. You can never be a doctor – not in our world. Only three of us are allowed to practise medicine in the ghetto. There are dozens of skilled doctors here, waiting for one of us to retire or to die so that they can take our place. There's no chance for you. None. You were born at the wrong time, in the wrong place. Do you understand me, boy?"

Samuel swallowed. "Yes, sir."

The doctor hesitated, then went on. "About your second dream – I'm afraid that one is just as impossible. There is no chance of your ever marrying Terenia."

"Why?" Samuel asked.

Dr Wal stared at him. "*Why?* For the same reason you can't become a doctor. We live by the rules, by our traditions. My daughter will marry someone of her own class, someone who can afford to keep her in the same style in which she has been raised. She will marry a professional man, a lawyer, a doctor or a rabbi. You-well, you must put her out of your mind."

"But – "

The doctor was ushering him towards the door. "Have someone look at that splint in a few days. See that the bandage is kept clean."

"Yes, sir," Samuel said. "Thank you, Dr Wal."

Dr Wal studied the blond, intelligent-looking boy before him. "Goodbye, Samuel Roffe."

Early the next afternoon, Samuel rang the front doorbell of the Wal house. Dr Wal watched him through the window. He knew that he should send him away.

"Send him in," Dr Wal said to the maid.

After that, Samuel came to Dr Wal's house two or three times a week. He ran errands for the doctor, and in exchange Dr Wal let him watch as he treated patients or worked in his laboratory, concocting medicines. The boy observed and learned and remembered everything. He had a natural talent. Dr Wal felt a growing sense of guilt, for he knew that in a way he was encouraging Samuel, encouraging him to be something he could never be; and yet he could not bring himself to turn the boy away.

Whether it was by accident or design, Terenia was almost always around when Samuel was there. Occasionally he would get a glimpse of her walking past the laboratory, or leaving the house, and once he bumped into her in the kitchen, and his heart began to pound so hard that he thought he would faint. She studied him for a long moment, a look of speculation in her eyes, then she nodded coolly and was gone. At least she had noticed him! That was the first step. The rest was only a matter of time. There was not the slightest doubt in Samuel's mind. It was fated. Terenia had become a major part of Samuel's dreams about the future. Where once he had dreamed for himself, he now dreamed for the two of them. Somehow he would get them both out of this terrible ghetto, this stinking, overcrowded prison. And he would become a great success. But now his success would not be for him alone, but for both of them.

Even though it was impossible.

Elizabeth fell asleep, reading about old Samuel. In the morning when she awakened, she carefully hid the Book and began to get dressed for school. She could not get Samuel off her mind. How did he marry Terenia? How did he get out of the ghetto? How did he become famous? Elizabeth was consumed by the Book, and she resented the intrusions that tore her away from it and forced her to return to the twentieth century.

One of the classes that Elizabeth had to attend was ballet, and she loathed it. She would stuff herself into her pink tutu, and stare at her image in the mirror and try to tell herself that her figure was voluptuous. But the truth was there for her to see. She was fat. She would never be a ballet dancer.

Shortly after Elizabeth's fourteenth birthday, Mme Netturova, her dance teacher, announced that in two weeks the class would give its yearly dance recital in the auditorium, and that the students were to invite their parents. Elizabeth was in a state of panic. The mere thought of getting upon a stage in front of an audience filled her with dread. She could not go through with it.

A child was running across a street in front of a car. Elizabeth saw her, raced out and snatched the child from the jaws of death. Unfortunately, ladies and gentlemen, Elizabeth Roffe's toes were crushed by the wheels of the automobile, and she will not be able to dance at the recital this evening.

A careless maid left a bar of soap at the top of the stairs. Elizabeth slipped and fell down the long flight, breaking her hip. Nothing to worry about, the doctor said. It will heal in three weeks.

No such luck. On the day of the performance, Elizabeth was in perfect health, and in a state of hysteria. Again, it was old Samuel who helped her. She remembered how frightened he had been, but he had gone back to face Dr Wal. She would not do anything to disgrace Samuel. She would face up to her ordeal.

Elizabeth had not even mentioned the recital to her father. In the past she had often asked him to school meetings and parties which parents were requested to attend, but he had always been too busy.

On this evening, as Elizabeth was getting ready to leave for the dance recital, her father returned home. He had been out of town for ten days.

He passed her bedroom, saw her and said, "Good evening,' Elizabeth." Then, "You've put on some weight."

She flushed and tried to pull in her stomach. "Yes, Father."

He started to say something, then changed his mind. "How's school coming along?"

"Fine, thank you."

"Any problems?"

"No, Father."

"Good."

It was a dialogue they had had a hundred times over the years, a meaningless litany that seemed to be their only form of communication. How's-school-coming-along-fine-thank-you-any-problems-no-Father-good.
Two strangers discussing the weather, neither listening nor caring about the other's opinion. Well, one of us cares, Elizabeth thought.

But this time Sam Roffe stood there, watching his daughter, a thoughtful expression on his face. He was used to dealing with concrete problems and although he sensed that there was a problem here, he had no idea what it was, and if anyone had told him, Sam Roffe's answer would have been, "Don't be a fool. I've given Elizabeth everything."

As her father started to leave, Elizabeth heard herself say, "My – my – ballet class is giving a recital. I'm in it. You don't want to come, do you?"

And even as she said the words, she was filled with a sense of horror. She did not want him there to see her clumsiness. Why had she asked him? But she knew why. Because she was the only girl in the class whose parents would not be in that auditorium. It doesn't matter, anyway, she told herself, because he's going to say no. She shook her head, furious with herself, and turned away. And behind her, incredibly, she heard her father's voice saying, "I'd like that."

The auditorium was crowded with parents, relatives and friends, watching the students dance to the accompaniment of two grand pianos on either side of the stage. Mme Netturova stood off to one side, counting the beat aloud as the children danced, calling the attention of the parents to herself.

A few of the children were remarkably graceful, and showed signs of real talent. The others went through their performances determined to substitute enthusiasm for ability. The mimeographed programme announced three musical excerpts from *Coppélia, Cinderella* and, inevitably, *Swan Lake.* The *pièce de résistance* was to be the solos, when each child would have her moment of glory, alone.

Backstage, Elizabeth was in an agony of apprehension. She kept peering through the side curtain, and each time she saw her father sitting in the second row centre, she thought what a fool she had been to ask him. So far during the show, Elizabeth had been able to lose herself in the background, hidden behind the other dancers. But now her solo was coming up. She felt gross in her tutu, like something in a circus. She was certain they would all laugh at her when she came out on the stage – and she had *invited* her father to watch her humiliation! Elizabeth's only consolation was that her solo lasted for only sixty seconds. Mme Netturova was no fool. It would all be over so quickly that no one would even notice her. All Elizabeth's father had to do was to glance away for a minute, and her number would be finished.

Elizabeth watched the other girls as they danced, one by one, and they seemed to her like Markova, Maximova, Fonteyn. She was startled by a cold hand on her bare arm, and Mme Netturova hissed, "On your toes, Elizabeth, you're next."

Elizabeth tried to say, "Yes, madame," but her throat was so dry that no words came out. The two pianists struck up the familiar theme of Elizabeth's solo. She stood there, frozen, incapable of moving, and Mme Netturova was whispering, "Get out there!" and Elizabeth felt a shove against her back, and she was out on the stage, half naked, in front of a hundred hostile strangers. She did not dare look at her father. All she wanted was to get this ordeal over with as quickly as possible and flee. What she had to do was simple, a few pliés and jetés and leaps. She began to execute the steps, keeping time to the music, trying to think herself thin and tall and lithe. As she finished, there was a smattering of polite applause from the audience. Elizabeth looked down at the second row, and there was her father, smiling proudly and applauding – applauding her, and something inside Elizabeth snapped. The music had stopped. But Elizabeth kept on dancing, doing pliés and jetés and battements and turns, carried away, transported beyond herself. The confused musicians began to pick up her beat, first one pianist, then the other, trying to keep up with her. Backstage, Mme Netturova was signalling to Elizabeth wildly, her face filled with fury. But Elizabeth was blissfully unaware of her, transported beyond herself. The only thing that mattered to her was that she was onstage, dancing for her father.

"I am sure you understand, Mr Roffe, that this school simply cannot tolerate that type of behaviour." Mme Netturova's voice was trembling with anger. "Your daughter ignored everyone else and took over, as though – as though she were some kind of *star.*"

Elizabeth could feel her father turn to look at her, and she was afraid to meet his eyes. She knew that what she had done was unforgivable, but she had been unable to stop herself. For one moment on that stage she had tried to create something beautiful for her father, had tried to impress him, make him notice her, be proud of her. Love her.

Now she heard him say, "You're absolutely right Madame Netturova. I will see to it that Elizabeth is suitably punished."

Mme Netturova gave Elizabeth a look of triumph, and said, "Thank you, Mr Roffe. I will leave it in your hands."

Elizabeth and her father were standing outside the school. He had not said a word to her since leaving Mme Netturova's office. Elizabeth was trying to compose a speech of apology – but what could she say? How could she ever make her father understand why she had done what she had done? He was a stranger, and she was afraid of him. She had heard him vent his terrible anger on others for making mistakes, or for having disobeyed him. Now she stood there waiting for his wrath to fall upon her.

He turned to her and said, "Elizabeth, why don't we drop in at Rumpelmayer's and get a chocolate soda?"

And Elizabeth burst into tears.

She lay in her bed that night, wide awake, too stimulated to go to sleep. She kept replaying the evening over and over in her mind. The excitement of it had been almost more than she could bear. Because this was no made-up daydream. It had happened, it was real. She could see herself and her father, seated at the table at Rumpelmayer's surrounded by the large, colourful stuffed bears and elephants and lions and zebras. Elizabeth had ordered a banana split, which had turned out to be absolutely enormous, and her father had not criticized her. He was talking to her. No how's-school-coming-along-fine-thank-you-any-problems-no-Father-good. But really *talking*. He told her about his recent trip to Tokyo, and how his host had served chocolate-covered grasshoppers and ants as a special treat for him, and how he had had to eat them in order not to lose face.

When Elizabeth had scooped up the last drop of the ice cream, her father suddenly said, "What made you do it, Liz?"

She knew that everything was going to be spoiled now, that he was going to reprimand her, tell her how disappointed he was in her.

She said, "I wanted to be better than everyone else." She could not bring herself to add, *For you*.

He looked at her for what seemed a long time, and then he laughed. "You certainly surprised the hell out of everybody." There was a note of pride in his voice.

Elizabeth felt the blood rushing to her cheeks, and she said, "You're not angry with me?"

There was a look in his eyes that she had never seen before. "For wanting to be the best? That's what the Roffes are all about." And he reached over and squeezed her hand.

Elizabeth's last thoughts as she drifted off to sleep were: My father likes me, he really likes me. From now on, we'll be together all the time. He'll take me on trips with him. We'll talk about things and we'll become good friends."

The following afternoon her father's secretary informed her that arrangements had been made to send Elizabeth away to a boarding-school in Switzerland.

10

Elizabeth was enrolled in the International Château Lemand, a girls' school situated in the village of Sainte-Blaise, overlooking the Lake of Neuchâtel. The ages of the girls ranged from fourteen to eighteen. It was one of the finest schools in the excellent Swiss educational system.

Elizabeth hated every minute of it.

She felt exiled. She had been sent away from home, and it was like some dire punishment for a crime she had not committed. On that one magic evening she had felt that she was on the verge of something wonderful, discovering her father, and her father discovering her, and their becoming friends. But now he was farther away than ever.

Elizabeth was able to keep track of her father in the newspapers and magazines. There were frequent stories and photographs of him meeting with a Prime Minister or a President, opening a new pharmaceutical plant in Bombay, mountain climbing, dining with the Shah of Iran. Elizabeth pasted all the stories in a scrapbook which she constantly pored over. She hid it next to the book of Samuel.

Elizabeth remained aloof from the other students. Some of the girls shared rooms with two or three others, but Elizabeth had asked for a room by herself. She wrote long letters to her father, then tore up the ones that revealed her feelings. From time to time she received a note from him, and there were gaily wrapped packages from expensive stores on her birthday, sent by his secretary. Elizabeth missed her father terribly.

She was going to join him at the villa in Sardinia for Christmas, and as the time drew nearer, the waiting became almost unbearable. She was sick with excitement. She made a list of resolutions for herself and carefully wrote them down:

Do not be a pest.

Be interesting.

Do not complain about anything, especially school.

Do not let him know you are lonely.

Do not interrupt while he is speaking.

Be well groomed at all times, even at breakfast.

Laugh a lot so that he can see how happy you are.

The notes were a prayer, a litany, her offering to the gods. If she did all these things, maybe – maybe – Elizabeth's resolutions merged into fantasies. She would make profound observations about the Third World and the nineteen developing nations, and her father would say, "I didn't know you were so interesting" (rule number two). "You're a very bright girl, Elizabeth." Then he would turn to his secretary and say, "I don't think Elizabeth needs to go back to school. Why don't I keep her here with me?"

A prayer, a litany.

A company Learjet picked Elizabeth up at Zurich and flew her to the airport at Olbia, where she was met by a limousine. Elizabeth sat in the back of the car, silent, forcing her knees together to keep them from trembling. No matter what happens, she thought fiercely, I won't let him see me cry. He mustn't know how much I've missed him.

The car drove up the long, winding mountain highway that led to the Costa Smeralda, then turned off on to the small road that wound to the top. This road had always frightened Elizabeth. It was very narrow and steep, with the mountain on one side and a terrifying abyss on the other.

The car pulled up in front of the house, and Elizabeth stepped out and began walking towards the house and then running, her legs carrying her as fast as they could. The front door opened and Margherita, the Sardinian housekeeper, stood there smiling. "Hello, Miss Elizabeth."

"Where's my father?" Elizabeth asked.

"He had to go to Australia on some emergency. But he left a lot of pretty presents for you. It's going to be a lovely Christmas."

11

Elizabeth had brought the Book with her. She stood in the hallway of the villa, studying the painting of Samuel Roffe, and next to him, Terenia, feeling their presence as though they had come to life. After a long time Elizabeth turned and climbed up the ladder to the tower room, taking the Book. She spent hours every day in the tower room, reading and rereading, and each time she felt closer to Samuel and Terenia, the century that separated them disappearing.

Over the next few years, Elizabeth read, Samuel spent long hours in Dr Wal's laboratory, helping him mix ointments and medicines, learning how they worked. And always in the background was Terenia, haunting, beautiful. The very sight of her was enough to keep alive Samuel's dream that one day she would belong to him. Samuel got along well with Dr Wal, but Terenia's mother was another story. She was a sharp-tongued virago, a snob, and she hated Samuel. He tried to keep out of her way.

Samuel was fascinated by the many drugs that could heal people. A papyrus had been found that listed 811 prescriptions used by the Egyptians in 1550 BC. Life expectancy at birth then was fifteen years and Samuel could understand why when he read some of the prescriptions: crocodile dung, lizard flesh, bats' blood, camels' spit, lions' liver, toe of a frog, unicorn powder. The *Rx* sign on every prescription was the ancient prayer to Horae, the Egyptian god of healing. Even the word "chemistry" derived from the ancient name of Egypt, the land of Kahmi, or Chemi. The priest-physicians were called magi, Samuel learned.

The apothecaries' shops in the ghetto and in Krakow itself were primitive. Most of the bottles and jars were filled with untested and untried medicinal items, some useless, some harmful. Samuel became familiar with them all. There was castor oil, calomel and rhubarb, iodine compounds and codeine and ipecac. You could purchase panaceas for whooping cough, colic and typhoid fever. Because no sanitary precautions were taken, it was common to find ointments and gargles filled with dead insects, roaches, rat droppings and bits of feather and fur. The majority of patients who took the remedies died either of their diseases or from the remedies.

Several magazines were printed that were devoted to apothecary news, and Samuel read them all avidly. He discussed his theories with Dr Wal.

"It stands to reason," Samuel said, his voice ringing with conviction, "that there must be a cure for every disease. Health is natural, disease is unnatural."

"Perhaps," Dr Wal said, "but most of my patients won't even let me try the new medications on them." He added dryly, "And I think they're wise."

Samuel devoured Dr Wal's sparse library on pharmacy. And when he had read and reread those books, he felt frustrated by the unanswered questions that lay between the covers.

Samuel was fired by the revolution that was taking place. Some scientists believed that it was possible to counteract the cause of diseases by building up a resistance that would destroy the illness. Dr Wal tried it once. He took the blood of a patient with diphtheria, and injected it into a horse. When the horse died, Dr Wal gave up his experiments. But young Samuel was sure that Dr Wal had been on the right track.

"You can't stop now," Samuel said. "I know it will work."

Dr Wal shook his head. "That's because you're seventeen, Samuel. When you're my age, you won't be as sure of anything. Forget about it."

But Samuel was not convinced. He wanted to continue his experiments, but for that Samuel needed animals, and there were few available except for the stray cats and rats that he was able to catch. No matter how minute the doses that Samuel gave them, they died. They're too small, Samuel thought. I need a larger animal. A horse or a cow or a sheep. But where was he going to find one?

One late afternoon when Samuel arrived home, an ancient horse and cart stood in front of the house. On the side of the cart a crudely lettered sign read: "ROFFE & SON." Samuel stared at it unbelievingly, then raced into the house to find his father. "That – that horse out there," he said. "Where did you get it?"

His father smiled at him proudly. "I made a deal. We can cover more territory with a horse. Maybe in four or five years we can buy another horse. Think of it. We'll have *two* horses."

That was the extent of his father's ambition, owning two broken-down horses pulling carts through the dirty, crowded streets of the Krakow ghetto. It made Samuel want to weep.

That night when everyone was asleep, Samuel went out to the stable and examined the horse, which they had named Ferd. As horses went, this one was without question one of the lowest of the species. She was a very old horse, swaybacked and spavined. It was doubtful whether she could move much faster than Samuel's father. But none of that mattered. What was important was that Samuel now had his laboratory animal. He could do his experiments without having to worry about catching rats and stray cats. Of course, he would have to be careful. His father must never find out what he was doing. Samuel stroked the horse's head. "You're going into the drug business," he informed Ferd.

Samuel improvised his own laboratory, using a corner of the stable in which Ferd was kept.

He grew a culture of diphtheria germs in a dish of rich broth. When the broth turned cloudy, he removed some of it to another container and then weakened it, first by diluting the broth, then by heating it slightly. He filled a hypodermic needle with it and approached Ferd. "Remember what I told you?" Samuel whispered. "Well, this is your big day."

Samuel plunged the contents of the hypodermic into the loose skin of the horse's shoulder, as he had seen Dr Wal do. Ferd turned to look at him reproachfully, and sprayed him with urine.

Samuel estimated that it would take about seventy-two hours for the culture to develop in Ferd. At the end of that time Samuel would give her a larger dose. Then another. If the antibody theory was right, each dose would build up a stronger blood resistance to the disease. Samuel would have his vaccine. Later, he would have to find a human being to test it on, of course, but that should not be difficult. A victim of the dread disease should be only too happy to try something that might save his life.

For the next two days Samuel spent almost every waking moment with Ferd.

"I've never seen anyone love an animal so much," his father said. "You can't keep away from her, can you?"

Samuel mumbled an inaudible reply. He felt a sense of guilt about what he was doing, but he knew what would happen if he even mentioned it to his father. However, there was no need for his father to know. All Samuel had to do was extract enough blood from Ferd to make up a vial or two of serum, and no one would ever be the wiser.

On the morning of the third and crucial day, Samuel was awakened by the sound of his father's voice from in front of the house. Samuel got out of bed, hurried to the window and looked out. His father was standing in the street with his cart, bellowing at the top of his lungs. There was no sign of Ferd. Samuel threw on some clothes and raced outside.

"*Momser!*" his father was yelling. "Cheat! Liar! Thief! Thief!"

Samuel pushed past the crowd that was beginning to gather round his father.

"Where's Ferd?" Samuel demanded.

"I'm glad you asked me," his father moaned. "She's dead. She died in the streets like a dog."

Samuel's heart sank.

"We're going along as nice as you please. I'm tending to business, not rushing her, you understand, not whipping her, or pushing her like some of the other pedlars I could name. And how does she show her appreciation? She drops dead. When I catch that *gonif* who sold her to me, I'll kill him!"

Samuel turned away, sick at heart. More than Ferd had passed away. Samuel's dreams had died. With Ferd went the escape from the ghetto, the freedom, the beautiful house for Terenia and their children.

But a greater disaster was to befall.

The day after Ferd died, Samuel learned that Dr Wal and his wife had arranged for Terenia to marry a rabbi. Samuel could not believe it. Terenia belonged to *him!* Samuel raced over to the Wal house. He found Dr and Mrs Wal in the parlour. He walked up to them, took a deep breath and announced, "There's been a mistake, Terenia's mistake, Terenia's going to marry me."

They stared at him in astonishment.

"I know I'm not good enough for her," Samuel hurried on, "but she won't be happy married to anyone but me. The rabbi's too old for–"

"*Nebbich!* Out! Out!" Terenia's mother was apoplectic.

Sixty seconds later Samuel found himself standing out in the street, forbidden ever to enter the Wal house again.

In the middle of the night Samuel had a long talk with God.

"What do you want from me? If I can't have Terenia, why did you make me love her? Haven't you any feelings?" He raised his voice in frustration and yelled, "Can you hear me?"

And the others in the crowded little house yelled back, "We can all hear you, Samuel. For God's sake, shut up and let us get some sleep!"

The following afternoon, Dr Wal sent for Samuel. He was ushered into the parlour, where Dr and Mrs Wal and Terenia were gathered.

"It seems we have a problem," Dr Wal began. "Our daughter can be quite a stubborn young lady. For some reason she's taken a fancy to you. I cannot call it love, Samuel, because I don't believe that young girls know what love is. However, she has refused to marry Rabbi Rabinowitz. She thinks she wants to marry you."

Samuel sneaked a glance at Terenia, and she smiled at him and he almost burst with joy. It was short-lived.

Dr Wal was going on. "You said that you love my daughter."

"Y – y – yes, sir," Samuel stammered. He tried it again, his voice stronger. "Yes, sir."

"Then let me ask you something, Samuel. Would you like Terenia to spend the rest of her life married to a pedlar?"

Samuel instantly saw the trap, but there was no way out of it. He looked at Terenia again and said slowly, "No, sir."

"Ah. Then you see the problem. None of us wants Terenia to marry a pedlar. And you're a pedlar, Samuel."

"I won't always be, Dr Wal." Samuel's voice was strong and sure.

"And what *will* you be?" Mrs Wal snapped. "You come from a family of pedlars, you'll remain a family of pedlars. I will not allow my daughter to marry one."

Samuel looked at the three of them, his mind filled with confusion. He had come here with trepidation and despair, had been lifted to the heights of joy, and now he had been plunged into a black abyss again. What did they want from him?

"We've agreed on a compromise," Dr Wal said. "We're going to give you six months to prove that you're more than just a pedlar. If, by the end of that time, you cannot offer Terenia the kind of life she is accustomed to, then she is going to marry Rabbi Rabinowitz."

Samuel stared at him, aghast. "Six months!"

No one could become a success in six months! No one, certainly, who lived in the ghetto of Krakow.

"Do you understand?" Dr Wal asked.

"Yes, sir." Samuel understood only too well. He felt as if his stomach were filled with lead. He did not need a solution, he needed a miracle. The Wals would only be content with a son-in-law who was a doctor or a rabbi, or who was wealthy. Samuel quickly examined each possibility.

The law forbade him to become a doctor.

A rabbi? One had to start studying for the rabbinate by thirteen, and Samuel was almost eighteen now.

Wealthy? That was out of the question. If he worked twenty-four hours a day peddling his wares in the streets of the ghetto until he was ninety, he would still be a poor man. The Wals had set an impossible task for him. They had seemingly given in to Terenia by allowing her to postpone her marriage to the rabbi, while at the same time setting conditions that they knew would be impossible for Samuel to meet. Terenia was the only one who believed in him. She had confidence that he could find some kind of fame or fortune in six months. She's crazier than I am, Samuel thought in despair.

The six months began, and time flew. Samuel's days were spent as a pedlar, helping his father. But the moment the shadows of the setting sun began to fall on the walls of the ghetto, Samuel would hurry home, gulp down a bite to eat, and then go to work in his laboratory. He made hundreds of batches of serums, and injected rabbits and cats and dogs and birds, and all the animals died. They're too small, Samuel thought desperately. I need a larger animal.

But he had none, and time was racing by.

Twice a week Samuel would go into Krakow to replenish the merchandise that he and his father sold from the cart. He would stand inside the locked gates at dawn, surrounded by the other pedlars, but he neither saw nor heard them. His mind was in another world.

As Samuel stood there one morning, daydreaming, a voice yelled, "You! Jew! Move on!"

Samuel looked up. The gates had been opened and his cart was blocking the way. One of the guards was angrily motioning for Samuel to move. There were always two guards on duty in front of the gate. They wore green uniforms and special insignia and were armed with pistols and heavy clubs. On a chain around his waist one of the guards carried a large key that opened and locked the gates. Alongside the ghetto ran a small river spanned by an old wooden bridge. Across the bridge was the police garrison where the ghetto guards were stationed. More than once, Samuel had witnessed a hapless Jew being dragged across the bridge. It was always a one-way trip. Jews were required to be back inside the ghetto by sundown, and any Jew caught outside the gates after dark was arrested and deported to a labour camp. It was the nightmare of every Jew that he might be caught outside the ghetto after sunset.

Both guards were supposed to remain on duty, patrolling in front of the gates, all night; but it was common knowledge inside the ghetto that after the Jews were locked in, one of the guards would slip away for a night of pleasure in the city. Just before dawn he would return to help his partner open the gates for the new day.

The two guards that were usually stationed there were named Paul and Aram. Paul was a pleasant man with a genial disposition. Aram was an entirely different matter. He was an animal, swarthy and stockily built, with powerful arms and a body like a beer keg. He was a Jew-baiter, and whenever he was on duty, all the Jews outside the gates made sure that they returned early, because nothing delighted Aram more than to lock a Jew out, club him senseless and drag him across the bridge to the dreaded police barracks.

It was Aram now who stood yelling at Samuel to move his cart. He hurriedly went through the gates and headed for the city, and he could feel Aram's eyes boring into his back.

Samuel's six-months grace period quickly dwindled to five months and then to four months, then three. There was not a day, not an hour, when Samuel was not thinking about a solution to his problem, or feverishly working in his tiny laboratory. He tried to speak to some of the wealthy merchants of the ghetto, but few had time for him, and those who had time offered him useless advice.

"You want to make money? Save your pennies, boy, and one day you'll have enough to buy a fine business like mine."

That was easy enough for them to say – most of them had been born into wealthy homes.

Samuel thought of taking Terenia and running away. But where to? At the end of the journey would lie another ghetto, and he would still be a penniless *nebbich*. No, he loved Terenia too much to do that to her. That was the real trap in which he was caught.

Inexorably the clock ran on, and the three months became two, and then one. Samuel's only consolation during that time was that he was allowed to see his beloved Terenia three times a week, chaperoned, of course, and each time Samuel saw her, he loved her more deeply. It was a bitter-sweet feeling, for the more often he saw her, the closer he was coming to losing her. "You'll find a way," Terenia kept assuring him.

But now there were only three weeks left, and Samuel was no closer to a solution than when he had started.

Late one night Terenia came to see Samuel at the stable. She put her arms around him and said, "Let's run away, Samuel."

He had never loved her so much as he loved her at that moment. She was willing to disgrace herself, give up her mother and father, the wonderful life she lived, for him.

He held her close and said, "We can't. Wherever we went, I'd still be a pedlar."

"I don't mind."

Samuel thought of her beautiful home with the spacious rooms and the servants, and he thought of the tiny squalid room he shared with his father and his aunt, and he said, "*I* would mind, Terenia."

And she turned and left.

The following morning Samuel met Isaac, a former schoolmate, walking down the street, leading a horse. It had one eye, suffered from acute colic, was spavined and deaf.

"Morning, Samuel."

"Morning, Isaac. I don't know where you're going with that poor horse, but you'd better hurry. It doesn't look like it's going to last much longer."

"It doesn't have to. I'm taking Lottie to a glue factory."

Samuel eyed the animal with a sudden, quickened interest. "I shouldn't think they'd give you much for her."

"I know. I just want a couple of florins to buy a cart."

Samuel's heart began to beat faster. "I think I can save you a trip. I'll trade you my cart for your horse."

It took less than five minutes to conclude the bargain.

Now all Samuel had to do was build another cart and explain to his father how he had lost the old one, and how he had come into possession of a horse that was on its last legs.

Samuel led Lottie to the barn where he had kept Ferd. On closer examination the horse was an even more discouraging sight. Samuel patted the animal and said, "Don't worry, Lottie, you're going to make medical history."

A few minutes later Samuel was at work on a new serum.

Because of the crowded and insanitary conditions of the ghetto, epidemics were frequent. The latest plague was a fever that produced a choking cough, swollen glands and a painful death. The doctors did not know what caused it, or how to treat it. Isaac's father went down with the disease. When Samuel heard the news, he hurried over to see Isaac.

"The doctor has been here," the weeping boy told Samuel. "He said there's nothing to be done."

From upstairs they could hear the terrible sounds of a racking cough that seemed to go on for ever.

"I want you to do something for me," Samuel said. "Get me a handkerchief of your father's."

Isaac stared at him. "*What?*"

"One that he's used. And be careful how you handle it. It will be full of germs."

An hour later Samuel was back at the stable, carefully scraping the contents of the handkerchief into a dish filled with broth.

He worked all that night and all the next day and the following day, injecting small doses of the substance into the patient Lottie, then larger doses, fighting against time, trying to save the life of Isaac's father.

Trying to save his own life.

In later years Samuel was never sure whether God was looking out for him or for the old horse, but Lottie survived the gradually increased doses, and Samuel had his first batch of antitoxin. His next task was to persuade Isaac's father to let him use it on him.

As it turned out, it needed no persuasion. When Samuel reached Isaac's house, it was filled with relatives, mourning the dying man upstairs.

"He only has a little time left," Isaac told Samuel.

"Can I see him?"

The two boys went upstairs. Isaac's father was in bed, his face flushed with fever. Each racking cough sent his wasted frame into a spasm that left him weaker. It was obvious that he was dying.

Samuel took a deep breath and said, "I want to talk to you and your mother."

Neither of them had any confidence in the little glass vial that Samuel had brought, but the alternative was death. They took a chance simply because there was nothing to lose.

Samuel injected Isaac's father with the serum. He waited at the bedside for three hours, and there was no change. The serum had no effect. If anything, the coughing spells seemed more frequent. Finally Samuel left, avoiding Isaac's eyes.

At dawn the next day Samuel had to go into Krakow to buy goods. He was in a fever of impatience to get back to see whether Isaac's father was still alive.

There were large crowds at all the markets, and it seemed to Samuel that it took for ever to make his purchases. It was late afternoon by the time his cart was finally filled and he headed back towards the ghetto.

When Samuel was still two miles away from the gates, disaster struck. One of the wheels of the cart broke in half and the merchandise began to spill on to the pavement. Samuel was in a terrible dilemma. He had to find another wheel somewhere, and yet he did not dare leave the cart unguarded. A crowd had begun to gather, eyeing the spilled merchandise with avid eyes. Samuel saw a uniformed policeman approaching – a gentile – and he knew that he was lost. They would take everything away from him. The policeman pushed his way through the crowd and turned to the frightened boy. "Your cart needs a new wheel."

"Y – yes, sir."

"Do you know where to find one?"

"No, sir."

The policeman wrote something on a piece of paper. "Go there. Tell him what you need."

Samuel said, "I can't leave the cart."

"Yes, you can," the policeman said. He cast a stern eye over the crowd. "I'll be right here. Hurry!"

Samuel ran all the way. Following the directions on the piece of paper, he found himself in a blacksmith's shop, and when Samuel explained the situation, the blacksmith found a wheel that was the right size for the wagon. Samuel paid for the wheel out of the small bag of money he carried. He had half a dozen guldens left.

He raced back to his cart, rolling the wheel before him. The policeman was still there, and the crowd had dispersed. The merchandise was safe. With the policeman helping him, it took another half-hour to get the wheel on and secure it. Once more he started for home. His thoughts were on Isaac's father. Would Samuel find him dead or alive? He did not think he could stand the suspense of not knowing a moment longer.

He was only a mile from the ghetto now. Samuel could see the high walls rising against the sky. And even as he watched, the sun set on the western horizon, and the unfamiliar streets were bathed in darkness. In the excitement of what had happened, Samuel had forgotten about the time. It was past sundown and he was outside the gates! He began to run, pushing the heavy cart ahead of him, his heart pounding until it felt ready to burst. The ghetto gates would be closed. Samuel recalled all the terrible stories he had heard about Jews who were locked out of the ghetto at night. He began running faster. There would probably be only one guard on duty now. If it were Paul, the friendly one, then Samuel might have a chance. If it were Aram – Samuel could not bear to think about it.

The darkness was thickening now, closing in on him like a black fog, and a light rain began to fall. Samuel was nearing the ghetto walls, only two blocks away, and suddenly the huge gates loomed into view. They were locked.

Samuel had never seen them closed from the outside before. It was as though life had suddenly been turned inside out, and he shivered with terror. He was shut away from his family, from his world, from everything that was familiar. He slowed down, approaching the gates warily, looking for the guards. They were not in sight. Samuel was filled with a sudden wild hope. The guards had probably been called away on some emergency. Samuel would find a way to open the gates, or to scale the walls without being seen. As he reached the gates, the figure of a guard stepped out of the shadows.

"Keep coming," the guard commanded.

In the darkness Samuel could not see his face. But he recognized the voice. It was Aram.

"Closer. Come here."

Aram was watching Samuel approach, a thin grin on his face. The boy faltered.

"That's it," Aram called encouragingly. "Keep walking."

Slowly, Samuel moved towards the giant, his stomach churning, his head pounding. "Sir," Samuel said. "Please let me explain. I had an accident. My cart – "

Aram reached out with his hamlike fist, grabbed Samuel by the collar and lifted him into the air. "You dumb son-of-a-bitch of a Jew," he crooned softly. "Do you think I care why you're out? You're on the wrong side of the gates! Do you know what's going to happen to you now?"

The boy shook his head in terror.

"Let me tell you," Aram said. "We got a new edict last week. All Jews caught outside the gates after sundown are to be shipped to Silesia. Ten years of hard labour. How do you like that?"

Samuel could not believe it. "But I – I haven't done anything. I – "

With his right hand Aram hit Samuel hard across the mouth, then let him drop heavily to the ground. "Let's go," Aram said.

"Wh – where?" Samuel asked. His voice was choked with terror.

"To the police barracks. In the morning you'll be shipped out with the rest of the scum. Get up."

Samuel lay there, unable to bring his mind into focus. "I – I have to go inside to say goodbye to my family."

Aram grinned. "They won't miss you."

"Please!" Samuel pleaded. "Let me – let me at least send them a message."

The smile died on Aram's face. He stood over Samuel menacingly. When he spoke his voice was soft. "I said get up, Jew shit. If I have to say it once more, I'll kick your balls in for you."

Slowly, Samuel rose to his feet. Aram took his arm with an iron grip and started walking him towards the police barracks. *Ten years of hard labour in Silesia!* No one ever returned from there. He looked up at the man holding his arm, pulling him towards the bridge that led to the barracks.

"Please don't do this," Samuel pleaded. "Let me go."

Aram squeezed his arm tighter, so that the blood seemed to stop flowing. "Keep begging," Aram said. "I love to hear a Jew beg. Have you heard about Silesia? You'll be just in time for the winter. But don't worry, it's nice and warm underground in the mines. And when your lungs get black with coal and you start coughing them up, they'll leave you out in the snow to die."

Ahead of them across the bridge, barely visible in the rain, was the stark building that served as the police barracks.

"Faster!" Aram said.

And suddenly Samuel knew that he could not let anyone do this to him. He thought of Terenia and his family and Isaac's father. No one would take his life from him. Somehow he had to escape, to save himself. They were crossing the narrow bridge now, the river running noisily below, swollen by the winter rains. There were only thirty yards left to go. Whatever was going to be done had to be done now. But how could he escape? Aram had a gun and even without it the enormous guard could have killed him easily. He was almost twice as big as Samuel and much more powerful. They had reached the other side of the bridge now, and the barracks lay just ahead of them.

"Hurry up," Aram growled, pulling Samuel along. "I've got other things to do."

They were so close to the building now that Samuel could hear the laughter of the guards coming from inside. Aram tightened his grip and started to drag the boy across the cobblestoned yard that led to the police station. There were only seconds left. Samuel reached into his pocket with his right hand and felt the bag with the half-dozen guldens in it. His fingers closed around it, and his blood began to course with excitement. Carefully, he pulled the bag out of his pocket with his free hand, loosened the drawstring and dropped the bag. It landed on the stones with a loud tinkle of coins.

Aram stopped suddenly. "What was that?"

"Nothing," Samuel replied quickly.

Aram looked into the boy's eyes and grinned. Holding Samuel tightly, he took a step back, looked down at the ground and saw the open bag of money.

"You won't need money where you're going," Aram said.

He reached down to pick up the sack, and Samuel reached down at the same time. Aram snatched the sack of money away from him. But it was not the sack that Samuel was after. His hand closed on one of the large cobblestones lying on the ground, and as Samuel straightened up, he smashed it into Aram's right eye with all his strength, turning it into a red jelly, and he kept pounding at him, again and again. He watched the guard's nose cave in, and then his mouth, until the face was nothing but a gout of red blood. And still Aram stood there on his feet, like some blind monster. Samuel looked at him, sick with fear, unable to hit him again. Then, slowly, the giant body began to collapse. Samuel stared down at the dead guard, unable to believe what he had done. He heard the voices from the barracks and he became suddenly aware of the terrible danger he was in. If they caught him now, they would not send him to Silesia. They would flay him alive and hang him in the town square. The penalty for even *striking* a policeman was death. And Samuel had killed one of them. He must get away quickly. He could try to flee across the border, but then he would be a hunted fugitive for the rest of his life. There had to be another solution. He stared down at the faceless corpse and suddenly he knew what he had to do. He reached down and searched the guard's body until he found the large key that opened the gates. Then, overcoming his revulsion, Samuel grabbed Aram's boots and began pulling the guard towards the river bank. The dead man seemed to weigh a ton. Samuel kept pulling, spurred by the sounds coming from the barracks. He reached the river bank. He stopped a moment to regain his breath, then shoved the body over the edge of the steep embankment and watched it roll into the coursing waters below. One hand stuck to the side of the bank for what seemed an eternity, and then the body was slowly washed downstream, out of sight. Samuel stood there, hypnotized, filled with horror at what he had done. He picked up the rock he had used and threw it into the water. He was still in great danger. He turned and ran back across the bridge towards the huge, locked gates of the ghetto. There was no one around. With trembling fingers Samuel placed the giant key in the lock and turned it. He pulled against the great wooden gates. Nothing happened. They were too heavy for him to move. But on that night nothing was impossible for Samuel. He was filled with a strength that came from outside and he pulled the huge gates open. He shoved the cart inside, then closed the gates behind him, and ran towards his house, pushing the cart ahead of him. The tenants of the house were gathered in the living-room, and when Samuel walked in, they stared at him as if he were a living ghost.

"They let you come back!"

"I – I don't understand," his father stammered. "We thought you – "

Quickly, Samuel explained what had happened, and their looks of concern turned to expressions of terror.

Oh, my God!" groaned Samuel's father. "They'll murder us all!"

"Not if you listen to me," Samuel said. He explained his plan.

Fifteen minutes later Samuel and his father and two of their neighbours stood at the gates of the ghetto.

"Suppose the other guard comes back?" Samuel's father whispered.

Samuel said, "We have to take that chance. If he's there, I'll take all the blame."

Samuel pushed open the huge gates and slipped outside, alone, expecting to be pounced upon at any moment. He put the huge key in the lock and turned it. The gates of the ghetto were now locked from the outside. Samuel tied the key around his waist, and walked a few yards to the left of the gates. A moment later a rope slithered down the wall like a thick snake. Samuel clung to it while on the other side his father and the others began to haul him up. When Samuel reached the top of the wall, he made a noose of one end of the rope, fastened it to a projecting spike and lowered himself to the ground. When he was safely down, he shook the rope loose.

"Oh, my God!" his father was mumbling. "What's going to happen at sunrise?"

Samuel looked at him and replied. "We're going to be pounding on the gates, telling them to let us out."

At dawn the ghetto was swarming with uniformed police and soldiers. They had had to locate a special key to open the gates at sunrise for the merchants who were yelling to be let out. Paul, the second guard, had confessed to leaving his post and spending the night in Krakow, and he had been placed under arrest. But that still did not solve the mystery of Aram. Ordinarily the incident of a guard disappearing so close to the ghetto would have been a perfect excuse to start a pogrom. But the police were baffled by the locked gate. Since the Jews were safely locked up on the *inside*, they obviously could not have harmed him. In the end they decided that Aram must have run off with one of his many girl friends. They thought he might have thrown away the heavy, cumbersome key, and they searched for it everywhere, but they could not find it. Nor would they because it was buried deep in the ground, under Samuel's house.

Exhausted physically and emotionally, Samuel had fallen into his bed and was asleep almost instantly. He was awakened by someone yelling and shaking him. Samuel's first thought was: *They've found Aram's body. They've come to get me.*

He opened his eyes. Isaac was standing there in a state of hysteria. "It's stopped," Isaac was screaming. "The coughing's stopped. It's a *bracha!* Come back to the house."

Isaac's father was sitting up in bed. The fever had miraculously disappeared, and the coughing had stopped.

As Samuel walked up to his bedside, the old man said, "I think I could eat some chicken soup," and Samuel began to cry.

In one day he had taken a life and saved a life. The news about Isaac's father swept through the ghetto. The families of dying men and women besieged the Roffe house, pleading with Samuel for some of his magic serum. It was impossible for him to keep up with the demand. He went to see Dr Wal. The doctor had heard about what Samuel had done, but he was sceptical.

"I'll have to see it with my own eyes, he said. "Make up a batch and I'll try it out on one of my patients."

There were dozens to choose from, and Dr Wal selected the one he felt was closest to death. Within twenty-four hours the patient was on his way to recovery.

Dr Wal went to the stable where Samuel had been working day and night, preparing serum, and said, "It works, Samuel. You've done it. What do you want for your dowry?"

And Samuel looked up at him and replied wearily, "Another horse."

That year, 1868, was the beginning of Roffe and Sons.

Samuel and Terenia were married and Samuel's dowry was six horses and a small, well-equipped laboratory of his own. Samuel explained his experiments. He began to distil drugs from herbs, and soon his neighbours began coming to the little laboratory to buy remedies for whatever ills bothered them. They were helped, and Samuel's reputation spread. To those who could not afford to pay, Samuel would say, "Don't worry about it. Take it away." And to Terenia, "Medicine is for healing, not for profit."

His business kept increasing, and soon he was able to say to Terenia, "I think it's time to open a small apothecary's shop where we can sell ointments and powders and other things besides prescriptions."

The shop was a success from the beginning. The rich men who had refused to help Samuel before came to him now with offers of money.

"We'll be partners," they said. "We'll open a chain of shops."

Samuel discussed it with Terenia. "I'm afraid of partners. It's our business. I don't like the idea of strangers owning part of our lives."

Terenia agreed with him.

As the business grew and expanded into additional shops, the offers of money increased. Samuel continued to turn them all down.

When his father-in-law asked him why, Samuel replied, "Never let a friendly fox into your henhouse. One day he's going to get hungry."

As the business flourished, so did the marriage of Samuel and Terenia. She bore him five sons – Abraham, Joseph, Anton, Jan and Pitor – and with the birth of each son Samuel opened a new apothecary's shop, each one larger than the one before. In the beginning Samuel hired one man to work for him, then two, and soon he had more than two dozen employees.

One day Samuel received a visit from a government official. "We're lifting some of the restrictions on Jews," he told Samuel. "We would like you to open an apothecary's shop in Krakow."

And Samuel did. Three years later he had prospered enough to erect his own building in downtown Krakow and to buy Terenia a beautiful house in the city. Samuel had finally achieved his dream of escaping from the ghetto.

But he had dreams far beyond Krakow.

As the boys grew older, Samuel hired tutors for them, and each of the boys learned a different language.

"He's gone crazy," Samuel's mother-in-law said. "He's the laughing-stock of the neighbourhood, teaching Abraham and Jan English, Joseph German, Anton French and Pitor Italian. Who are they going to speak to? No one here speaks any of those barbaric languages. The boys won't even be able to talk to one another!"

Samuel merely smiled and said patiently, "It's part of their education." He knew to whom his sons would be talking.

By the time the boys reached their middle teens, they had all travelled to different countries with their father. On each of his trips Samuel laid the groundwork for his future plans. When Abraham was twenty-one years old,

Samuel called the family together and announced, "Abraham is going to America to live."

"America!" Terenia's mother shouted. "It's filled with savages! I will not let you do this to my grandson. The boy is staying here where he will be safe."

Safe. Samuel thought of the pogroms and Aram, and of his mother's murder.

"He's going abroad," Samuel declared. He turned to Abraham. "You'll open a factory in New York and be in charge of the business there."

Abraham said proudly, "Yes, Father."

Samuel turned to Joseph. "On your twenty-first birthday you will go to Berlin." Joseph nodded.

Anton said, "And I will go to France. Paris, I hope."

"Just watch yourself," Samuel growled. "Some of those gentiles are very beautiful."

He turned to Jan. "You will go to England."

Pitor, the youngest son, said eagerly, "And I'm going to Italy, Papa. How soon can I leave?"

Samuel laughed and replied. "Not tonight, Pitor. You'll have to wait until you're twenty-one."

And thus it worked out. Samuel accompanied his sons abroad and helped them establish offices and factories. Within the next seven years, there were branches of the Roffe family in five foreign countries. It was becoming a dynasty, and Samuel had his lawyer set it up so that while each company was independent, it was at the same time responsible to the parent company.

"No strangers," Samuel kept warning the lawyer. "The stock must never leave the family."

"It won't," the lawyer assured him. "But if your sons can't sell their stock, Samuel, how are they going to get along? I'm sure you'll want them to live in comfort."

Samuel nodded. "We'll arrange for them to live in beautiful homes. They'll have generous salaries and expense accounts, but everything else must go back into the business. If they ever want to sell the stock, it must be unanimous. The majority of the stock will belong to my eldest son and his heirs. We're going to be bigger than the Rothschilds."

Over the years Samuel's prophecy became a reality. The business grew and prospered. Though the family was widely scattered, Samuel and Terenia saw to it that they remained as closely-knit as possible. Their sons returned home for birthdays and high holidays. Their visits were more than festive occasions, however. The boys would closet themselves with their father and discuss business. They had their own private espionage system. Whenever one son in one country heard about a new drug development, he would dispatch couriers to report it to the others, and they would begin manufacturing it themselves, so that in this way they kept constantly ahead of their competitors.

As the wheel of the century turned, the boys married and had children and gave

Samuel grandchildren. Abraham had gone to America on his twenty-first birthday, in the year 1891. He had married an American girl seven years later and in 1905 she gave birth to Samuel's first grandchild, Woodrow, who sired a son named Sam. Joseph had married a German girl, who bore him a son and a daughter. The son in his turn married a girl, who bore a daughter, Anna. Anna married a German, Walther Gassner. In France, Anton had married a French girl, by whom he had two sons. One son committed suicide. The other married and had one daughter, Hélène. She married several times but had no children. Jan, in London, had married an English girl. Their only daughter had married a baronet named Nichols and had a son whom they christened Alec. In Rome, Pitor had married an Italian girl. They had a son and daughter. When the son, in his turn, married, his wife gave him a daughter, Simonetta, who fell in love with and married a young architect, Ivo Palazzi.

These then were the descendants of Samuel and Terenia Roffe.

Samuel lived long enough to see the winds of change that swept across the world. Marconi created wireless telegraphy and the Wright brothers launched the first aeroplane at Kitty Hawk. The Dreyfus affair captured the headlines and Admiral Peary reached the North Pole. Ford's Model Ts were in mass production; there were electric lights and telephones. In medicine, the germs that caused tuberculosis and typhoid and malaria were isolated and tamed.

Roffe and Sons, a little less than half a century after it had been founded, was a multi-national behemoth that circled the globe.

Samuel and his broken-down horse, Lottie, had created a dynasty.

When Elizabeth had finished reading the Book for perhaps the fifth time, she quietly returned it to its place in the glass case. She no longer needed it. She was a part of it, just as it was a part of her.

For the first time in her life, Elizabeth knew who she was, and where she had come from.

12

It was on her fifteenth birthday in the second term of her first year at school that Elizabeth first met Rhys Williams. He had dropped in at the school to bring Elizabeth a birthday present from her father.

"He wanted to come himself," Rhys explained, "but he couldn't get away." Elizabeth tried to conceal her disappointment but Rhys was quick to see it. There was something forlorn about the young girl, a naked vulnerability, that touched him. On an impulse he said, "Why don't you and I have dinner together?"

It was a terrible idea, Elizabeth thought. She could visualize the two of them walking into a restaurant together: him, incredibly good-looking and suave, and her, all braces and pudge. "Thank you, no," Elizabeth said stiffly. "I – I have some studying to do."

But Rhys Williams refused to accept no for an answer. He thought of the lonely birthdays he had spent by himself. He got permission from the headmistress to take Elizabeth out for dinner. They got into Rhys's car and started heading towards the airport.

"Neuchâtel is the other way," Elizabeth said.

Rhys looked at her and asked innocently, "Who said we were going to Neuchâtel?"

"Where are we going?"

"Maxim's. It's the only place to celebrate a fifteenth birthday."

They flew to Paris in a private jet, and had a superb dinner. It began with paté de foie gras with truffles, lobster bisque, crisp duck à l'orange and Maxim's special salad, and ended with champagne and a birthday cake. Rhys drove Elizabeth down the Champs-Elysées afterwards, and they returned to Switzerland late that night.

It was the loveliest evening of Elizabeth's life. Somehow Rhys had managed to make her feel interesting, and beautiful, and it was a heady experience. When Rhys dropped Elizabeth off at school, she said, "I don't know how to thank you. I – it's the nicest time I've ever had."

"Thank your father." Rhys grinned. "It was all his idea."

But Elizabeth knew that that was not true.

She decided that Rhys Williams was the most wonderful man she had ever met. And without doubt the most attractive. She got into her bed that night thinking about him. Then she rose and went to the small desk under the window. She took out a piece of paper and a pen, and wrote, "Mrs Rhys Williams".

She stared at the words for a long time.

Rhys was twenty-four hours late for his date with a glamorous French actress, but he was not concerned. They wound up at Maxim's, and somehow Rhys could not help thinking that his evening there with Elizabeth had been more interesting.

She would be someone to reckon with, one day.

Elizabeth was never certain who was more responsible for the change that began in her – Samuel or Rhys Williams – but she began to take a new pride in herself. She lost the compulsion to eat constantly, and her body began to slim down. She began to enjoy sport and started to take an interest in school. She made an effort to socialize with the other girls. They could not believe it. They had often invited

Elizabeth to their pyjama parties, and she had always declined. Unexpectedly, she appeared at a pyjama party one night.

The party was being held in a room shared by four girls, and when Elizabeth arrived the room was crammed with at least two dozen students, all in pyjamas or robes. One of the girls looked up in surprise and said, "Look who's here! We were betting you couldn't come."

"I – I'm here."

The air was filled with the pungent, sweet aroma of cigarette smoke. Elizabeth knew that many of the girls smoked marijuana, but she had never tried any. Her hostess, a French girl named Renée Tocar, walked up to Elizabeth, smoking a stubby brown cigarette. She took a deep puff, then held it out to Elizabeth. "You smoke?"

It was more of a statement than a question.

"Of course," Elizabeth lied. She took the cigarette, hesitated a moment, then put it between her lips and inhaled. She could feel her face going green, and her lungs rebelling, but she managed a smile and gasped, "Neat."

The moment Renée turned away, Elizabeth sank down on to a couch. She experienced a dizziness, but in a moment it passed. Experimentally she took another puff. She began to feel curiously light headed. Elizabeth had heard and read about the effects of marijuana. It was supposed to release inhibitions, take you out of yourself. She took another puff, deeper this time, and she began to feel a pleasant floating sensation, as if she were on another planet. She could see the girls in the room and hear them talking, but somehow they were all blurred, and the sounds were muted and far away. The lights seemed very bright, and she closed her eyes. The moment she did she was floating off into space. It was a lovely feeling. She could watch herself drifting over the roof of the school, up and up, over the snowy Alps into a sea of fluffy white clouds. Someone was calling her name, calling her back to earth. Reluctantly, Elizabeth opened her eyes. Renée was leaning over her, a look of concern on her face.

"Are you all right, Roffe?"

Elizabeth gave her a slow, contented smile, and said fuzzily, "I'm just wonderful." And in her infinite, euphoric state, she confessed, "I've never smoked marijuana before."

Renée was staring at her. "Marijuana? That's a Gauloise."

On the other side of the village of Neuchâtel was a boys' school, and Elizabeth's classmates sneaked away for trysts at every opportunity. The girls talked about the boys constantly. They talked about their bodies and the size of their penises and what they allowed the boys to do to them, and what they did to the boys in turn. At times it seemed to Elizabeth that she was trapped in a school full of raving nymphomaniacs. Sex was an obsession with them. One of the private games at school was *frôlage*. A girl would completely strip, and lie in bed on her back while another girl stroked her from her breasts to her thighs. The payment was a pastry bought in the village. Ten minutes of *frôlage* earned one pastry. By the end of ten minutes the girl usually reached orgasm, but if she had not, the one administering the *frôlage* would continue and earn an additional pastry.

Another favourite sexual *divertissement* was to be found in the bathroom. The school had large, old-fashioned bathtubs, with flexible hand showers that could be removed from the hook on the side of the wall. The girls would sit in a tub, turn on the shower, and then with the warm water gushing out, they would push the head of the shower between their legs and rub it gently back and forth.

Elizabeth indulged in neither *frôlage* nor the shower head, but her sexual urges were beginning to get stronger and stronger. It was at about this time that she made a shattering discovery.

One of Elizabeth's teachers was a small, slim woman named Chantal Harriot. She was in her late twenties, almost a schoolgirl herself. She was attractive-looking, and when she smiled she became beautiful. She was the most sympathetic teacher Elizabeth had, and Elizabeth felt a strong bond with her. Whenever Elizabeth was unhappy, she would go to Mlle Harriot and tell her her problems. Mlle Harriot was an understanding listener. She would take Elizabeth's hand and stroke it, and give her soothing advice and a cup of hot chocolate and cakes, and Elizabeth always felt better immediately.

Mlle Harriot taught French and also taught a class in fashion, in which she emphasized style and harmony of colours, and the proper accessories.

"Remember, girls," she would say, "the smartest clothes in the world will look terrible if you wear the wrong accessories." "Accessories" was Mlle Harriot's watchword.

Whenever Elizabeth lay in the warm tub, she found that she was thinking of Mlle Harriot, of the look on her face when they talked together, and of the way Mlle Harriot caressed her hand, softly and tenderly.

When Elizabeth was in other classes, she would find her mind drifting towards Mlle Harriot, and she would remember the times that the teacher had put her arms around her, consoling her, and had touched her breasts. At first Elizabeth had believed that the touches were accidental, but they had happened more and more often, and each time Mlle Harriot would give Elizabeth a soft, questioning look as though waiting for some response. In her mind Elizabeth could see Mlle Harriot, with her gently swelling breasts, and her long legs, and she would wonder what she looked like naked, in bed. It was then that the full realization stunned Elizabeth.

She was a Lesbian.

She was not interested in boys, because she was interested in girls. Not the kind of silly little girls who were her classmates, but someone sensitive and understanding, like Mlle Harriot. Elizabeth could visualize the two of them in bed together, holding and comforting each other.

Elizabeth had read and heard enough about Lesbians to know how difficult life was for them. Society did not approve. Lesbianism was considered a crime against nature. But what was wrong, Elizabeth wondered, in loving someone tenderly and deeply? Did it matter whether it was a man or a woman? Was it not the love itself that was the important thing? Was it better to have a loveless heterosexual marriage than a loving homosexual one?

Elizabeth thought about how horrified her father was going to be when he learned the truth about her. Well, she would just have to face up to it. She would have to readjust her thinking about the future. She could never have a so-called normal life like other girls, with a husband and children. Wherever she went, she would always be an outcast, a rebel, living outside the mainstream of society. She and Mlle Harriot – Chantal – would find a little apartment somewhere, or perhaps a small house. Elizabeth would decorate it beautifully in soft pastels, with all the proper accessories. There would be graceful French furniture and lovely paintings on the walls. Her father could help – no, she must not expect any help from her father. In all probability he would never even speak to her again.

Elizabeth thought about her wardrobe. She might be a Lesbian, but she was determined not to dress like one. No tweeds or slacks, tailored suits or vulgar mannish hats. They were the lepers' bells of emotionally crippled women. She would try to look as feminine as possible.

Elizabeth decided that she would learn to be a great cook so that she could prepare Mlle Harriot's – Chantal's – favourite dishes. She visualized the two of them sitting in their apartment, or small house, enjoying a candle-lit dinner that Elizabeth had prepared. First, there would be vichyssoise, followed by a lovely salad, then perhaps shrimps or lobster, or a Chateaubriand, with delicate ices for dessert. After dinner they would sit on the floor before a blazing fire in the hearth, watching the soft snowflakes fall outside. *Snowflakes.* So it would be winter. Elizabeth hastily revised the menu. Instead of a cold vichyssoise she would prepare a nice, hearty onion soup, and perhaps make a fondue. The dessert could be a soufflé. She would have to learn to time it so that it would not fall. *Then* the two of them would sit on the floor before a warming fire, and read poetry to each other. T. S. Eliot, perhaps. Or V. J. Rajadhon.

Time is the enemy of love,
The thief that shortens
All our golden hours.
I have never understood then
Why lovers count their happiness
In days and nights and years,
While our love can only be measured
In our joys and sighs and tears.

Ah, yes, Elizabeth could see the long years stretching out before the two of them, and the passage of time would begin to melt into a golden, warm glow.

She would fall asleep.

Elizabeth had been expecting it, and yet when it happened it caught her by surprise. She was awakened one night by the sound of someone entering her room and softly closing the door. Elizabeth's eyes flew open. She could see a shadow moving across the moon-dappled room towards her bed, and a ray of moonlight fell across Mlle Harriot's – Chantal's – face. Elizabeth's heart began to beat wildly.

Chantal whispered, "Elizabeth," and, standing there, slipped off her robe. She was wearing nothing underneath. Elizabeth's mouth went dry. She had thought of this moment so often, and now that it was actually happening, she was in a panic. In truth she was not sure exactly what she was supposed to do, or how. She did not want to make a fool of herself in front of the woman she loved.

"Look at me," Chantal commanded hoarsely. Elizabeth did. She let her eyes roam over the naked body. In the flesh Chantal Harriot was not quite what Elizabeth had envisioned. Her breasts looked a little like puckered apples, and they sagged a bit. She had a tiny potbelly, and her derrière seemed – this was the only word Elizabeth could think of – underslung.

But none of that was important. What mattered was what lay underneath, the soul of the woman, the courage and the daring to be different from everyone else, to defy the whole world and to want to share the rest of her life with Elizabeth.

"Move over, *mon petit ange*," she was whispering.

Elizabeth did as she was told, and the teacher slipped into bed beside her. There was a strong, feral smell about her. She turned towards Elizabeth and put her arms around her, and said, "Oh, *chérie*, I have dreamed of this moment." And she kissed Elizabeth on the lips, forcing her tongue into Elizabeth's mouth, and making quick, groaning noises.

It was, without doubt, the most unpleasant sensation Elizabeth had ever experienced. She lay there in shock. Chantal's – Mlle Harriot's – fingers were moving across Elizabeth's body, squeezing her breasts, slowly sliding down her stomach towards her thighs. And all the time her lips were on Elizabeth's, slobbering, like an animal.

This was it. This was the beautiful magic moment. *If we were one, you and I, together we would make a universe to shake the stars and move the heavens.*

Mlle Harriot's hands were moving downward, caressing Elizabeth's thighs, starting to reach between her legs. Quickly, Elizabeth tried to conjure up the candle-lit dinners and the soufflé and the evenings before the fireplace, and all the wonderful years the two of them would share together; but it was no use. Elizabeth's mind and flesh were repelled; she felt as though her body was being violated.

Mlle Harriot moaned, "Oh, *chérie*, I want to fuck you."

And all Elizabeth could think of to say was, "There's a problem. One of us has the wrong accessories."

And she began to laugh and cry hysterically, weeping for the beautiful candle-lit vision that had died, and laughing because she was a healthy, normal girl who had just learned that she was free.

The next day Elizabeth tried the shower nozzle.

13

In the Easter holiday, in her final year at school, when she was eighteen, Elizabeth went to the villa in Sardinia to spend ten days. She had learned to drive, and for the first time she was free to explore the island on her own. She took long drives along the beaches and visited tiny fishing villages. She swam at the villa, under the warm Mediterranean sun, and at night lay in her bed listening to the mournful sound of the singing rocks, as the wind gently blew through them. She went to a carnival in Tempio, where the entire village dressed up in national costume. Hidden behind the anonymity of domino masks, the girls invited the boys to dance, and everyone felt free to do things they would not dare do at any other time. A boy might *think* he knew which girl he made love to that night, but the next morning he could not be certain. It was, Elizabeth thought, like an entire village playing *The Guardsman*.

She drove to Punta Murra and watched the Sardos cook small lambs on open fires. The native islanders gave her *seada*, a goats' cheese covered in a dough, with hot honey over it. She drank the delicious *selememont*, the local white wine that could be had nowhere else in the world because it was too delicate to travel.

One of Elizabeth's favourite haunts was the Red Lion Inn at Porto Cervo. It was a little pub in a basement, with ten tables for dining, and an old-fashioned bar.

Elizabeth dubbed that holiday the Time of the Boys. They were the sons of the rich, and they came in swarms, inviting Elizabeth to a constant round of swimming and riding parties. It was the first move in the mating rite.

"They're all highly eligible," Elizabeth's father assured her.

To Elizabeth they were all clods. They drank too much, talked too much and pawed her. She was sure they wanted her not for herself, because she might be an intelligent or worthwhile human being, but because she was a Roffe, heiress to the Roffe dynasty. Elizabeth had no idea that she had grown into a beauty, for it was easier to believe the truth of the past than the reflection in her mirror.

The boys wined and dined her and tried to get her into bed. They sensed that Elizabeth was a virgin, and some aberration in the male ego deluded each boy into the conviction that if he could take away Elizabeth's virginity, she would fall madly in love with him and be his slave for ever. They refused to give up. No matter where they took Elizabeth, the evenings always ended up the same. "Let's go to bed." And always she politely refused them.

They did not know what to make of her. They knew she was beautiful, so it followed that she must be stupid. It never occurred to them that she was more intelligent than they. Who ever heard of a girl being both beautiful *and* intelligent?

And so Elizabeth went out with the boys to please her father, but they all bored her.

Rhys Williams came to the villa, and Elizabeth was surprised at how excited and pleased she was to see him again. He was even more attractive than she had remembered.

Rhys seemed glad to see her. "What's happened to you?" he asked.

"What do you mean?"

"Have you looked in your mirror lately?"

She blushed. "No."

He turned to Sam. "Unless the boys are all deaf, dumb and blind, I have a feeling Liz isn't going to be with us much longer."

Us! Elizabeth enjoyed hearing him say that. She hung around the two men as much as she dared, serving them drinks, running errands for them, enjoying just looking at Rhys. Sometimes Elizabeth would sit in the background, listening as they discussed business affairs, and she was fascinated. They spoke of mergers and of new factories, and products that had succeeded and others that had failed, and why. They talked about their competitors, and planned strategies and counter-strategies. To Elizabeth it was all heady stuff.

One day when Sam was up in the tower room, working, Rhys invited Elizabeth to lunch. She took him to the Red Lion and watched him play darts with the men at the bar. Elizabeth marvelled at how much at home Rhys was. He seemed to fit in anywhere. She had heard a Spanish expression that she had never understood, but she did now as she watched Rhys. *He's a man easy in his skin.*

They sat at a small corner table with a red and white tablecloth, and had shepherd's pie and ale, and they talked. Rhys asked her about school.

"It's really not too bad," Elizabeth confessed. "I'm learning how little I know."

Rhys smiled. "Very few people get that far. You finish in June, don't you?"

Elizabeth wondered how he had known. "Yes."

"Do you know what you want to do after that?"

It was the question she had been asking herself. "No. Not really."

"Interested in getting married?"

For one quick instant her heart missed a beat. Then she realized that it was a general question. "I haven't found anyone yet." She thought of Mlle Harriot and the cosy dinners in front of the fireplace and the snow falling, and she laughed aloud.

"Secret?"

"Secret." She wished she could share it with him, but she did not know him well enough. The truth was, Elizabeth realized, that she did not know Rhys at all. He was a charming, handsome stranger who had once taken pity on her and flown her to Paris for a birthday dinner. She knew that he was brilliant in business and that her father depended on him. But she knew nothing about his personal life, or what he was really like. Watching him, Elizabeth had the feeling that he was a many-layered man, that the emotions he showed were to conceal the emotions he felt, and Elizabeth wondered if anyone really knew him.

It was Rhys Williams who was responsible for Elizabeth losing her virginity.

The idea of going to bed with a man had become more and more appealing to Elizabeth. Part of it was the strong physical urge that sometimes caught her unawares and gripped her in waves of frustration, an urgent physical ache that would not leave. But there was also a strong curiosity, the need to know what *it* was like. She could not go to bed with just anyone, of course. He had to be someone special, someone she could cherish, someone who would cherish her.

On a Saturday night Elizabeth's father gave a gala at the villa.

"Put on your most beautiful dress," Rhys told Elizabeth. "I want to show you off to everyone."

Thrilled, Elizabeth had taken it for granted that she would be Rhys's date. When Rhys arrived, he had with him a beautiful blonde Italian princess. Elizabeth felt so outraged and betrayed that at midnight she left the party and went to bed with a bearded, drunken Russian painter named Vassilov.

The entire, brief affair was a disaster. Elizabeth was so nervous and Vassilov was so drunk that it seemed to Elizabeth that there was no beginning, middle or end. The foreplay consisted of Vassilov pulling down his pants and flopping on to the bed. At that point Elizabeth was tempted to flee, but she was determined to punish Rhys for his perfidy. She got undressed and crawled into bed. A moment later, with no warning, Vassilov was entering her. It was a strange sensation. It was not unpleasant, but neither did the earth shake. She felt Vassilov's body give a quick shudder, and a moment later he was snoring. Elizabeth lay there filled with self-disgust. It was hard to believe that all the songs and books and poems were about *this.* She thought of Rhys, and she wanted to weep. Quietly, Elizabeth put on her clothes and went home. When the painter telephoned her the next morning, Elizabeth had the housekeeper tell him that she was not in. The following day Elizabeth returned to school.

She flew back in the company jet with her father and Rhys. The plane, which had been built to carry a hundred passengers, had been converted into a luxury ship. It had two large, beautifully decorated bedrooms in the rear, with full bathrooms, a comfortable office, a sitting-room amidship, with paintings, and an elaborately equipped galley up front. Elizabeth thought of it as her father's magic carpet.

The two men talked business most of the time. When Rhys was free, he and Elizabeth played a game of chess. She played him to a draw, and when Rhys said, "I'm impressed," Elizabeth blushed with pleasure.

The last few months of school went by swiftly. It was time to begin thinking about her future. Elizabeth thought of Rhys's question, *Do you know what you want to do with your life?* She was not sure yet. But because of old Samuel, Elizabeth had become fascinated by the family business, and knew that she would like to become a part of it. She was not sure what she could do. Perhaps she could start by helping her father. She remembered all the tales of the wonderful hostess her mother had become, how invaluable she had been to Sam. She would try to take her mother's place.

It would be a start.

14

The Swedish Ambassador's free hand was squeezing Elizabeth's bottom, and she tried to ignore it as they danced round the room, her lips smiling, her eyes expertly scanning the elegantly dressed guests, the orchestra, the liveried servants, the buffet heaped with a variety of exotic dishes and fine wines, and she thought to herself with satisfaction, It's a good party.

They were in the ballroom of the Long Island estate. There were two hundred guests, all of them important to Roffe and Sons. Elizabeth became aware that the Ambassador was pressing his body closer to hers, trying to arouse her. He flicked his tongue in her ear and whispered, "You're a beautiful dancer."

"So are you," Elizabeth said with a smile, and she made a sudden mis-step and came down hard on his toe with the sharp heel of her shoe. He gave a cry of pain and Elizabeth exclaimed contritely, "I'm so sorry, Ambassador. Let me get you a drink."

She left him and threaded her way towards the bar, making her way easily through the guests, her eyes moving carefully around the room, checking to see that everything was perfect.

Perfection – that was what her father demanded. Elizabeth had been the hostess for a hundred of Sam's parties now, but she had never learned to relax. Each party was an event, an opening night, with dozens of things that could go wrong. Yet she had never known such happiness. Her girlhood dream of being close to her father, of his wanting her, needing her, had come true. She had learned to adjust to the fact that his needs were impersonal, that her value to him was based on how much she could contribute to the company. That was Sam Roffe's only criterion for judging people. Elizabeth had been able to fill the gap that had existed since her mother's death. She had become her father's hostess. But because Elizabeth was a highly intelligent girl, she had become much more than that. She attended business conferences with Sam, in aeroplanes and in foreign hotel suites and factories and at embassies and palaces. She watched her father wield his power, deploying the billions of dollars at his command to buy and sell, tear down and build. Roffe and Sons was a vast cornucopia, and Elizabeth watched her father bestow its largesse on its friends, and withhold its bounty from its enemies. It was a fascinating world, filled with interesting people, and Sam Roffe was the master of it all.

As Elizabeth looked around the ballroom now, she saw Sam standing at the bar, chatting with Rhys, a Prime Minister and a Senator from California. Her father saw Elizabeth and waved her over. As Elizabeth moved towards him, she thought of the time, three years earlier, when it had all begun.

Elizabeth had flown home the day of her graduation. She was eighteen. Home, at the moment, had been the apartment at Beekman Place in Manhattan. Rhys had been there with her father. She had somehow known that he would be. She carried pictures of him in the secret places of her thoughts, and whenever she was lonely or depressed or discouraged, she would take them out and warm herself with her memories. In the beginning it had seemed hopeless. A fifteen-year-old schoolgirl and a man of twenty-five. Those ten years might as well have been a hundred. But through some wonderful mathematical alchemy, at eighteen the difference in years was less important. It was as though she was growing older faster than Rhys, trying to catch up with him.

Both men rose as she walked into the library where they were talking business. Her father said casually, "Elizabeth. Just get in?"

"Yes."

"Ah. So school's finished."

"Yes."

"That's fine."

And that was the extent of her welcome home. Rhys was walking towards her, smiling. He seemed genuinely pleased to see her. "You look wonderful, Liz. How was the graduation? Sam wanted to be there but he couldn't get away."

He was saying all the things her father should have been saying.

Elizabeth was angry with herself for being hurt. It was not that her father did not love her, she told herself, it was just that he was dedicated to a world in which she had no part. He would have taken a son into his world; a daughter was alien to him. She did not fit into the Corporate Plan.

"I'm interrupting." She moved towards the door.

"Wait a minute," Rhys said. He turned to Sam. "Liz has come home just in time. She can help with the party on Saturday night."

Sam turned to Elizabeth, studying her objectively, as though newly assessing her. She resembled her mother. She had the same beauty, the same natural elegance. A flicker of interest came into Sam's eyes. It had not occurred to him before that his daughter might be a potential asset to Roffe and Sons. "Do you have a formal dress?"

Elizabeth looked at him in surprise. "I – "

"It doesn't matter. Go and buy one. Do you know how to give a party?"

Elizabeth swallowed and said, "Certainly." Wasn't that one of the advantages of going to a Swiss finishing-school? They taught you all the social graces. "Of course I know how to give a party."

"Good. I've invited a group from Saudi Arabia. There'll be about – " He turned to Rhys.

Rhys smiled at Elizabeth and said, "Forty. Give or take a few."

"Leave everything to me," Elizabeth said confidently.

The dinner was a complete fiasco.

Elizabeth had told the chef to prepare crab cocktails for the first course, followed by individual cassoulets, served with vintage wines. Unfortunately the cassoulet had pork in it, and the Arabs touched neither shellfish nor pork. Nor did they drink alcoholic beverages. The guests stared at the food, eating nothing. Elizabeth sat at the head of the long table, across the room from her father, frozen with embarrassment, dying inside.

It was Rhys Williams who saved the evening. He disappeared into the study for a few moments and spoke into the telephone. Then he came back into the dining-room and entertained the guests with amusing stories, while the staff began to clear the table.

In what seemed no time at all, a fleet of catering trucks drove up, and as if by magic a variety of dishes began appearing. Couscous and lamb en brochette and rice and platters of roast chicken and fish, followed by sweetmeats and cheese and fresh fruit. Everyone enjoyed the food except Elizabeth. She was so upset that she could not swallow a bite. Each time she looked up at Rhys, he was watching her, a conspiratorial look in his eyes. Elizabeth could not have said why, but she was mortified that Rhys should not only witness her shame but save her from it. When the evening finally ended, and the last of the guests had reluctantly departed in the early hours of the morning, Elizabeth and Sam and Rhys were in the drawing-room. Rhys was pouring a brandy.

Elizabeth took a deep breath and turned to her father, "I'm sorry about the dinner. If it hadn't been for Rhys – "

"I'm sure you'll do better next time," Sam said flatly.

Sam was right. From that time on, when Elizabeth gave a party, whether it was for four people or for four hundred, she researched the guests, found out their likes and dislikes, what they ate and drank, and what type of entertainment they enjoyed. She kept a catalogue with file cards on each person. The guests were flattered to find that their favourite brand of wine or whisky or cigars had been stocked for them, and that Elizabeth was able to discuss their work knowledgeably.

Rhys attended most of the parties, and he was always with the most beautiful girls there. Elizabeth hated them all. She tried to copy them. If Rhys brought a girl who wore her hair pinned up at the back, Elizabeth did her hair the same way. She tried to dress the way Rhys's girls dressed, to act the way they acted. But none of it seemed to make any impression on Rhys. He did not even seem to notice. Frustrated, Elizabeth decided that she might as well be herself.

On the morning of her twenty-first birthday, when Elizabeth came down to breakfast, Sam said, "Order some theatre tickets for tonight. Supper afterwards at 'Twenty-one'."

Elizabeth thought, He remembered, and she was inordinately pleased.

Then her father added, "There'll be twelve of us. We'll be going over the new Bolivian contracts."

She said nothing about her birthday. She received telegrams from a few former schoolmates, but that was it. Until six o'clock that evening, when an enormous bouquet of flowers arrived for her. Elizabeth was sure it was from her father. But the card read: "What a lovely day for a lovely lady." It was signed "Rhys".

Her father left the house at seven o'clock that evening on his way to the theatre. He noticed the flowers and said absently, "Got a beau, huh?"

Elizabeth was tempted to say, "They're a birthday present," but what would have been the point? If you had to remind someone you loved that it was your birthday, then it was futile.

She watched her father leave, and wondered what she would do with her evening. Twenty-one had always seemed such an important milestone. It signified growing up, having freedom, becoming a woman. Well, here was the magic day, and she felt no different from the way she had felt last year, or the year before. Why couldn't he have remembered? Would he have remembered if she were his son?

The butler appeared to ask her about dinner. Elizabeth was not hungry. She felt lonely and deserted. She knew she was feeling sorry for herself, but it was more than this uncelebrated birthday she was regretting. It was all the lonely birthdays of the past, the pain of growing up alone, without a mother or a father or anyone to give a damn.

At ten o'clock that night she was dressed in a robe, sitting in the living-room in the dark, in front of the fireplace, when a voice said, "Happy birthday".

The lights came on and Rhys Williams stood there. He walked over to her and said reprovingly, "This is no way to celebrate. How many times does a girl have a twenty-first birthday?"

"I – I thought you were supposed to be with my father tonight," Elizabeth said, flustered.

"I was. He mentioned that you were staying home alone tonight. Get dressed. We're going to dinner."

Elizabeth shook her head. She refused to accept his pity. "Thank you, Rhys. I – I'm really not hungry."

"I am, and I hate eating alone. I'm giving you five minutes to get into some clothes, or I'm taking you out like that."

They ate at a diner on Long Island, and they had hamburgers and chili and French-fried onions and root beer, and they talked, and Elizabeth thought it was better than the dinner she had had at Maxim's. All Rhys's attention was focused on her, and she could understand why he was so damned attractive to women. It was not just his looks. It was the fact that he truly liked women, that he enjoyed being with them. He made Elizabeth feel like someone special, that he wanted to be with her more than with anyone else in the world. No wonder, Elizabeth thought, everyone fell in love with him.

Rhys told her a little about his boyhood in Wales, and he made it sound wonderful and adventurous and gay. "I ran away from home," he said, "because there was a hunger in me to see everything and do everything. I wanted to be everyone I saw. *I* wasn't enough for me. Can you understand that?"

Oh, how well she understood it!

"I worked at the parks and the beaches and one summer I had a job taking tourists down the Rhosili in coracles, and – "

"Wait a minute," Elizabeth interrupted. "What's a Rhosili and what's a – a coracle?"

"The Rhosili is a turbulent, swift-flowing river, full of dangerous rapids and currents. Coracles are ancient canoes, made of wooden lathes and waterproof animal skins, that go back to pre-Roman days. You've never seen Wales, have you?" She shook her head. "Ah, you would love it." She knew she would. "There's a waterfall at the Vale of Neath that's one of the beautiful sights of this world. And the lovely places to see: Abereiddi and Caerbwdi, Porthclais, Kilgetty and Llangwm Uchaf," and the words rolled off his tongue like the lilt of music. "It's a wild, untamed country, full of magical surprises."

"And yet you left Wales."

Rhys smiled at her and said, "It was the hunger in me. I wanted to own the world."

What he did not tell her was that the hunger was still there.

Over the next three years Elizabeth became indispensable to her father. Her job was to make his life comfortable, so that he could concentrate on the thing that was all-important to him: the Business. The details of running his life were left entirely to Elizabeth. She hired and fired servants, opened and closed the various houses as her father's needs required, and entertained for him.

More than that, she became his eyes and ears. After a business meeting Sam would ask Elizabeth her impression of a man, or explain to her why he had acted in a particular fashion. She watched him make decisions that affected the lives of thousands of people and involved hundreds of millions of dollars. She heard heads of state plead with Sam Roffe to open a factory, or beg him not to close one down.

After one of those meetings Elizabeth said, "It's unbelievable. It's – it's as though you're running a country."

Her father laughed and replied, "Roffe and Sons has a larger income than three-quarters of the countries in the world."

In her travels with her father Elizabeth became reacquainted with the other members of the Roffe family, her cousins and their husbands or wives.

As a young girl Elizabeth had seen them during holidays when they had come to one of her father's houses, or when she had gone to visit them during brief school holidays.

Simonetta and Ivo Palazzi, in Rome, had always been the most fun to be with. They were open and friendly, and Ivo had always made Elizabeth feel like a woman. He was in charge of the Italian division of Roffe and Sons, and he had done very well. People enjoyed dealing with Ivo. Elizabeth remembered what a classmate had said when she had met him. "You know what I like about your cousin? He has warmth and charmth."

That was Ivo, warmth and charmth.

Then there was Hélène Roffe-Martel, and her husband, Charles, in Paris. Elizabeth had never really understood Hélène, or felt at ease with her. She had always been nice to Elizabeth, but there was a cool reserve that Elizabeth had never been able to break through. Charles was head of the French branch of Roffe and Sons. He was competent, though from what Elizabeth had overheard her father say, he lacked drive. He could follow orders, but he had no initiative. Sam had never replaced him, because the French branch ran very profitably. Elizabeth suspected that Hélène Roffe-Martel had a great deal to do with its success.

Elizabeth liked her German cousin, Anna Roffe Gassner, and her husband, Walther. Elizabeth remembered hearing family gossip that Anna Roffe had married beneath her. Walther Gassner was reputed to be a black sheep, a fortune-hunter, who had married an unattractive woman years older than himself, for her money. Elizabeth did not think her cousin was unattractive. She had always found Anna to be a shy, sensitive person, withdrawn, and a little frightened by life. Elizabeth had liked Walther on sight. He had the classic good looks of a movie star, but he seemed to be neither arrogant nor phony. He appeared to be genuinely in love with Anna, and Elizabeth did not believe any of the terrible stories she had heard about him.

Of all her cousins, Alec Nichols was Elizabeth's favourite. His mother had been a Roffe, and she had married Sir George Nichols, the third baronet. It was Alec to whom Elizabeth had always turned when she had a problem. Somehow, perhaps because of Alec's sensitivity and gentleness, he had seemed to the young child to be her peer, and she realized now what a great compliment that was to Alec. He had always treated her as an equal, ready to offer whatever aid and advice he could. Elizabeth remembered that once, in a moment of black despair, she had decided to run away from home. She had packed a suitcase and then, on a sudden impulse, had telephoned Alec in London to say goodbye. He had been in the middle of a conference, but he had come to the phone and talked to Elizabeth for more than an hour. When he had finished, Elizabeth had decided to forgive her father and give him another chance. That was Sir Alec Nichols. His wife, Vivian, was something else. Where Alec was generous and thoughtful, Vivian was selfish and thoughtless. She was the most self-centred woman Elizabeth had ever known.

Years ago, when Elizabeth was spending a weekend in their country home in Gloucestershire, she went on a picnic by herself. It had begun to rain, and she had returned to the house early. She had gone in by the back door, and as she had started down the hallway, she had heard voices from the study raised in a quarrel.

"I'm damned tired of playing nursemaid," Vivian was saying. "You can take your precious little cousin and amuse her yourself tonight. I'm going up to London. I have an engagement."

"Surely you can cancel it, Viv. The child is only going to be with us another day, and she – "

"Sorry, Alec. I feel like a good fuck, and I'm getting one tonight."

"For God's sake, Vivian!"

"Oh, shove it up your ass! Don't try to live my life for me."

At that moment, before Elizabeth could move, Vivian had stormed out of the study. She had taken one quick look at Elizabeth's stricken face, and said cheerily, "Back so soon, pet?" And strode upstairs.

Alec had come to the doorway. He had said gently, "Come in, Elizabeth."

Reluctantly she had walked into the study. Alec's face was aflame with embarrassment. Elizabeth had wanted desperately to comfort him, but she did not know how. Alec had walked over to a large refectory table, picked up a pipe, filled it with tobacco and lit it. It had seemed to Elizabeth that he took for ever.

"You must understand Vivian."

Elizabeth had replied, "Alec, it's none of my business. I – "

"But in a sense it is. We're all family. I don't want you to think harshly of her."

Elizabeth could not believe it. After the incredible scene she had just heard, Alec was defending his wife.

"Sometimes in a marriage," Alec had continued, "a husband and a wife have different needs." He had paused awkwardly, searching for the right phrase. "I don't want you to blame Vivian because I – I can't fulfil some of those needs. That's not her fault, you see."

Elizabeth had not been able to stop herself. "Does – does she go out with other men often?"

"I'm rather afraid she does."

Elizabeth had been horrified. "Why don't you leave her?"

He had given her his gentle smile. "I can't leave her, dear child. You see, I love her."

The next day Elizabeth had returned to school. From that time on, she had felt closer to Alec than to any of the others.

Of late, Elizabeth had become concerned about her father. He seemed preoccupied and worried about something, but Elizabeth had no idea what it was. When she asked him about it,' he replied, "Just a little problem I have to clear up. I'll tell you about it later."

He had become secretive, and Elizabeth no longer had access to his private papers. When he had said to her, "I'm leaving tomorrow for Chamonix to do a little mountain climbing," Elizabeth had been pleased. She knew he needed a rest. He had lost weight and had become pale and drawn-looking.

"I'll make the reservations for you," Elizabeth had said.

"Don't bother. They're already made."

That, too, was unlike him. He had left for Chamonix the next morning. That was the last time she had seen him. The last time she would ever see him.

Elizabeth lay there in her darkened bedroom, remembering the past. There was an unreality about her father's death, perhaps because he had been so alive.

He was the last to bear the name of Roffe. Except for her. What would happen to the company now? Her father had held the controlling interest. She wondered to whom he had left the stock.

Elizabeth learned the answer late the next afternoon. Sam's lawyer had appeared at the house. "I brought a copy of your father's will with me. I hate to intrude on your grief at a time like this, but I thought it best that you know at once. You are your father's sole beneficiary. That means that the controlling shares of Roffe and Sons are in your hands."

Elizabeth could not believe it. Surely he did not expect *her* to run the company. "Why?" she asked. "Why me?"

The attorney hesitated, then said, "May I be frank, Miss Roffe? Your father was a comparatively young man. I'm sure he didn't expect to die for many years. In time, I'm confident he would have made another will, designating someone to take over the company. He probably had not made up his mind yet." He shrugged. "All that is academic, however. The point is that the control now rests in your hands. You will have to decide what you want to do with it, who you want to give it to." He studied her for a moment, then continued, "There has never before been a woman on the board of directors of Roffe and Sons, but – well, for the moment you're taking your father's place. There's a board meeting in Zurich this Friday. Can you be there?"

Sam would have expected it of her.

And so would old Samuel.

"I'll be there," Elizabeth said.

Book Two

15

Portugal
Wednesday, September 9
Midnight

In the bedroom of a small rented apartment in Rua dos Bombeiros, one of the winding, dangerous back alleys of Alto Estoril, a motion-picture scene was being filmed. There were four people in the room. A cameraman, and on a bed the two actors in the scene, the man in his thirties and a young blonde girl with a stunning figure. She wore nothing except a vivid red ribbon tied round her neck. The man was large, with a wrestler's shoulders and a barrel-shaped, incongruously hairless chest. His phallus, even in detumescence, was huge. The fourth person in the room was a spectator, seated in the background, wearing a black broad-brimmed hat and dark glasses.

The cameraman turned to the spectator, questioningly, and the spectator nodded. The cameraman pressed a switch and the camera began to whir. He said to the actors, "All right. Action."

The man knelt over the girl and she took his penis in her mouth until it began to grow hard. The girl took it out and said, "Jesus, that's big!"

"Shove it in her," the cameraman ordered.

The man slid down over the girl and put his penis between her legs.

"Take it easy, honey." She had a high, querulous voice.

"Look as though you're enjoying it."

"How can I? It's the size of a fucking watermelon." The spectator was leaning forward, watching every move as the man entered her. The girl said, "Oh, my God, that feels wonderful. Just take it slow, baby."

The spectator was breathing harder now, staring at the scene on the bed. This girl was the third, and she was even prettier than the others.

She was writhing from side to side now, making little moaning noises. "Oh, yes," she gasped. "Don't stop!" She grasped the man's hips and began pulling them towards her. The man began to pump harder and faster, in a frantic, pounding motion. Her movements began to quicken, and her nails dug into the man's naked back. "Oh, yes," she moaned. "Yes, yes, yes! I'm coming!"

The cameraman looked towards the spectator, and the spectator nodded, eyes glistening behind the dark glasses.

"Now!" the cameraman called to the man on the bed.

The girl, caught in her own furious frenzy, did not even hear him. As her face filled with a wild ecstasy, and her body began to shudder, the man's huge hands closed round her throat and began to squeeze, closing off the air so that she could not breathe. She stared up at him, bewildered, and then her eyes filled with a sudden, terrified comprehension.

The spectator thought: *This is the moment. Now! Jesus God! Look at her eyes!* They were dilated with terror. She fought to tear away the iron bands around her throat, but it was useless. She was still coming, and the deliciousness of her orgasm and the frantic shudder of her death throes were blending into one.

The spectator's body was soaked with perspiration. The excitement was unbearable. In the middle of life's most exquisite pleasure the girl was dying, her eyes staring into the eyes of death. It was so beautiful.

Suddenly it was over. The spectator sat there, exhausted, shaken with spasms of pleasure, lungs filled with long, deep breaths. The girl had been punished.

The spectator felt like God.

16

Zurich
Friday, September 11
Noon

The world headquarters of Roffe and Sons occupied sixty acres along the Sprettenbach on the western outskirts of Zurich. The administration building was a twelve-storey modern, glass structure, towering over a nest of research buildings, manufacturing plants, experimental laboratories, planning divisions, and railway spurs. It was the brain centre of the far-flung Roffe and Sons empire.

The reception lobby was starkly modern, decorated in green and white, with Danish furniture. A receptionist sat behind a glass desk, and those who were admitted by her into the recesses of the building had to be accompanied by a guide. To the right rear of the lobby was a row of lifts, with one private express lift for the use of the company president.

On this morning the private lift had been used by the members of the board of directors. They had arrived within the past few hours from various parts of the world by plane, train, helicopter and limousine. They were gathered now in the enormous, high-ceilinged, oak-panelled boardroom: Sir Alec Nichols, Walther Gassner, Ivo Palazzi and Charles Martel. The only non-member of the board in the room was Rhys Williams.

Refreshments and drinks had been laid out on a sideboard, but no-one in the room was interested. They were tense, nervous, each preoccupied with his own thoughts.

Kate Erling, an efficient Swiss woman in her late forties, came into the room. "Miss Roffe's car has arrived."

Her eyes swept round the room to make sure that everything was in order:

pens, note pads, a silver carafe of water at each place, cigars and cigarettes, ashtrays, matches. Kate Erling had been Sam Roffe's personal secretary for fifteen years. The fact that he was dead was no reason for her to lower his standards, or hers. She nodded, satisfied, and withdrew.

Downstairs, in front of the administration building, Elizabeth Roffe was stepping out of a limousine. She wore a black, tailored suit with a white blouse. She had on no make-up. She looked much younger than her twenty-four years, pale and vulnerable.

The press was waiting for her. As she started into the building, she found herself surrounded by television and radio and newspaper reporters, with cameras and microphones.

"I'm from *L'Europeo*, Miss Roffe. Could we have a statement? Who's going to take over the company now that your father-?"

"Look this way, please, Miss Roffe. Can you give our readers a big smile?"

"Associated Press, Miss Roffe. What about your father's will?"

"New York *Daily News*. Wasn't your father an expert mountain climber? Did they find out how – ?"

"*Wall Street Journal*. Can you tell us something about the company's financial – ?"

"I'm from the London *Times*. We're planning to do an article on the Roffe – "

Elizabeth was fighting her way into the lobby, escorted by three security guards, pushing through the sea of reporters.

"One more picture, Miss Roffe – "

And Elizabeth was in the lift, the door closing. She took a deep breath and shuddered. Sam was dead. Why couldn't they leave her alone?

A few moments later, Elizabeth walked into the boardroom. Alec Nichols was the first to greet her. He put his arms around her shyly and said, "I'm so sorry, Elizabeth. It was such a shock to all of us. Vivian and I tried to telephone you but – "

"I know. Thank you, Alec. Thank you for your note."

Ivo Palazzi came up and gave her a kiss on each cheek. "*Cara*, what is there to say? Are you all right?"

"Yes, fine. Thank you, Ivo." She turned. "Hello, Charles."

"Elizabeth, Hélène and I were devastated. If there is anything at all – "

"Thank you."

Walther Gassner walked over to Elizabeth and said awkwardly, "Anna and I wish to express our great sorrow at what has happened to your father."

Elizabeth nodded, her head high. "Thank you, Walther."

She did not want to be here, surrounded by all the reminders of her father. She wanted to flee, to be alone.

Rhys Williams was standing off to one side, watching Elizabeth's face, and he was thinking, If they don't stop, she's going to break down. He deliberately moved through the group, held out his hand and said, "Hello, Liz."

"Hello, Rhys." She had last seen him when he had come to the house to bring her the news of Sam's death. It seemed like years ago. Seconds ago. It had been one week.

Rhys was aware of the effect it was costing Elizabeth to keep her composure. He said, "Now that everyone's here, why don't we begin." He smiled reassuringly. "This won't take long."

She gave him a grateful smile. The men took their accustomed places at the large, rectangular oak table. Rhys led Elizabeth to the head of the table and pulled out a chair for her. My father's chair, Elizabeth thought. Sam sat here, chairing these meetings.

Charles was saying, "Since we do not have a – " He caught himself and turned to Alec. "Why don't you take over?"

Alec glanced round, and the others murmured approval. "Very well."

Alec pressed a button on the table in front of him, and Kate Erling returned, carrying a notebook. She closed the door behind her and pulled up a straight chair, her notebook and pen poised.

Alec said, "I think that under the circumstances we can dispense with the formalities. All of us have suffered a terrible loss. But' – he looked apologetically at Elizabeth – "the essential thing right now is that Roffe and Sons show a strong public face."

"*D'accord.* We have been taking enough of a hammering in the press lately," Charles growled.

Elizabeth looked over at him and asked, "Why?"

Rhys explained, "The company is facing a lot of unusual problems just now, Liz. We're involved in heavy lawsuits, we're under government investigation, and some of the banks are pressing us. The point is that none of it is good for our image. The public buys pharmaceutical products because they trust the company that makes them. If we lose that trust, we lose our customers."

Ivo said reassuringly, "We have no problems that can't be solved. The important thing is to reorganize the company immediately."

"How?" Elizabeth asked.

Walther replied, "By selling our stock to the public."

Charles added, "In that way we can take care of all our bank loans, and have enough money left – " He let the sentence trail off.

Elizabeth looked at Alec. "Do you agree with that?"

"I think we're all in agreement, Elizabeth."

She leaned back in her chair, thoughtful. Rhys picked up some papers, rose and carried them to Elizabeth. "I've had all the necessary documents prepared. All you have to do is sign."

Elizabeth glanced at the papers lying before her. "If I sign these, what happens?"

Charles spoke up. "We have a dozen international brokerage firms ready to form a consortium to underwrite the stock issue. They will guarantee the sale at a price we mutually agree upon. In an offering as large as this one, there will be several institutional purchasers, as well as private ones."

"You mean like banks and insurance companies?" Elizabeth asked.

Charles nodded. "Exactly."

"And they'll put their people on the board of directors?"

"That's usual . . ."

Elizabeth said, "So, in effect, they would control Roffe and Sons."

"We would still remain on the board of directors," Ivo interposed quickly.

Elizabeth turned to Charles. "You said a consortium of stockbrokers is ready to move ahead."

Charles nodded. "Yes."

"Then why haven't they?"

He looked at her, puzzled. "I don't understand."

"If everyone is in agreement that the best thing for the company is to let it get out of the family and into the hands of outsiders, why hasn't it been done before?"

There was an awkward silence. Ivo said, "It has to be by mutual consent, *cara*. *Everyone* on the board must agree."

"Who didn't agree?" Elizabeth asked.

The silence was longer this time.

Finally Rhys spoke up. "Sam."

And Elizabeth suddenly realized what had disturbed her from the moment she had walked into this room. They had all expressed their condolences and their shock and grief over her father's death, and yet at the same time there had been an atmosphere of charged excitement in the room, a feeling of – strangely, the word that came into her mind was *victory*. They had had the papers all drawn up for her, everything ready. *All you have to do is sign*. But if what they wanted was right, then why had her father objected to it? She asked the question aloud.

"Sam had his own ideas," Walther explained. "Your father could be very stubborn."

Like old Samuel, Elizabeth thought. Never let a friendly fox into your hen-house. One day he's going to get hungry. And Sam had not wanted to sell. He must have had good reason.

Ivo was saying, "Believe me, *cara*, it is much better to leave all this to us. You don't understand these things."

Elizabeth said quietly, "I would like to."

"Why bother yourself with this?" Walther objected. "When your stock is sold, you will have an enormous amount of money – more than you'll ever be able to spend. You can go off anywhere you like and enjoy it."

What Walther said made sense. Why *should* she get involved? All she had to do was sign the papers in front of her, and leave.

Charles said impatiently, "Elizabeth, we're simply wasting time. You have no choice."

It was at that instant that Elizabeth knew she did have a choice. Just as her father had had a choice. She could walk away and let them do as they pleased with the company, or she could stay and find out why they were all so eager to sell the stock, why they were pressuring her. For she could feel the pressure. It was so strong it was almost physical. Everyone in that room was *willing* her to sign the papers.

She glanced over at Rhys, wondering what he was thinking. His expression was non-committal. Elizabeth looked at Kate Erling. She had been Sam's secretary for a long time. Elizabeth wished she could have had a chance to speak to her alone. They were all looking at Elizabeth, waiting for her to agree.

"I'm not going to sign," she said. "Not now."

There was a moment of stunned silence. Then Walther said, "I don't understand, Elizabeth." His face was ashen. "Of course you must! Everything is arranged."

Charles said angrily, "Walther's right. You must sign."

They were all speaking at once, in a confused and angry storm of words that beat at Elizabeth.

"*Why* won't you sign?" Ivo demanded.

She could not say: *Because my father would not sign. Because you're rushing me.* She had a feeling, an instinct that something was wrong, and she was determined to find out what it was. So now she merely said, "I'd like a little more time to think about it."

The men looked at one another.

"How much time, *cara?*" Ivo asked.

"I don't know yet. I'd like to get a better understanding of what's involved here."

Walther exploded. "Damn it, we can't – "

Rhys cut in firmly, "I think Elizabeth is right."

The others turned to look at him. Rhys went on, "She should have a chance to get a clear picture of the problems the company is facing, and then make up her own mind."

They were all digesting what Rhys had said.

"I agree with that," Alec said.

Charles said bitterly, "Gentlemen, it doesn't make any difference whether we agree with it or not. Elizabeth is in control."

Ivo looked at Elizabeth. "*Cara* – we need a decision quickly."

"You'll have it," Elizabeth promised.

They were all watching her, each busy with his own thoughts.

One of them was thinking, Oh, God. *She's going to have to die too.*

17

Elizabeth was awed.

She had been in her father's Zurich headquarters often, but always as a visitor. The power belonged to him. And now it belonged to her. She looked round the huge office and felt like an impostor. The room had been magnificently decorated by Ernst Hohl. At one end stood a Roentgen cabinet with a Millet landscape over it. There was a fireplace, and in front of it a chamois leather couch, a large coffee-table and four easy chairs. Around the walls were Renoirs, Chagalls, Klees and two early Courbets. The desk was a solid block of black mahogany. Next to it, on a large console table, was a communications complex – a battery of telephones with direct lines to company headquarters around the world. There were two red phones with scramblers, an intricate intercom system, a ticker-tape machine and other equipment. Hanging behind the desk was a portrait of old Samuel Roffe.

A private door led to a large dressing-room, with cedar closets and lined drawers. Someone had removed Sam's clothing, and Elizabeth was grateful. She walked through a tiled bathroom that included a marble bath and a stall shower. There were fresh Turkish towels hanging on warming racks. The medicine chest was empty. All the daily paraphernalia of her father's life had been taken away. Kate Erling, probably. Elizabeth idly wondered whether Kate had been in love with Sam.

The executive suite included a large sauna, a fully equipped gymnasium, a barber's shop, and a dining-room that could seat a hundred people. When foreign guests were being entertained, a little flag representing their country was placed in the floral centrepiece on the table.

In addition, there was Sam's private dining-room, tastefully decorated with murals.

Kate Erling had explained to Elizabeth, "There are two chefs on duty during the day, and one at night. If you are having more than twelve guests for luncheon or dinner, they need two hours' notice."

Now Elizabeth sat at the desk, piled high with papers, memoranda, and statistics and reports, and she did not know where to begin. She thought of her father sitting here, in this chair, behind this desk, and she was suddenly filled with a sense of unbearable loss. Sam had been so able, so brilliant. How she needed him now!

Elizabeth had managed to see Alec for a few moments before he returned to London.

"Take your time," he had advised her. "Don't let anyone pressure you."

So he had sensed her feelings.

"Alec, do you think I should vote to let the company go public?"

He had smiled at her and said awkwardly, "I'm afraid I do, old girl, but then

I've got my own axe to grind, haven't I? Our shares are no good to any of us until we can sell them. That's up to you now."

Elizabeth was remembering that conversation as she sat alone in the huge office. The temptation to telephone Alec was overpowering. All she had to say was, "I've changed my mind." And get out. She did not belong here. She felt so inadequate.

She looked at the set of intercom buttons on the console. Opposite one of them was the name RHYS WILLIAMS. Elizabeth debated a moment, then flicked down the switch.

Rhys was seated across from her, watching her. Elizabeth knew exactly what he must be thinking, what they were all thinking. That she had no business to be there.

"That was quite a bomb you dropped at the meeting this morning," Rhys said.

"I'm sorry if I upset everyone."

He grinned. " 'Upset' " is hardly the word. You put everyone in a state of shock. It was all supposed to have been cut and dried. The publicity releases were ready to send out." He studied her a moment. "What made you decide not to sign, Liz?"

How could she explain that it was nothing more than a feeling, an intuition? He would laugh at her. And yet Sam had refused to let Roffe and Sons go public. She had to find out why.

As though reading her thoughts, Rhys said, "Your great-great-grandfather set this up as a family business, to keep away outsiders. But it was a small company then. Things have changed. We're running one of the biggest drugstores in the world. Whoever sits in your father's chair has to make all the final decisions. It's one hell of a responsibility."

She looked at him and wondered whether this was Rhys's way of telling her to get out. "Will you help me?"

"You know I will."

She felt a rush of relief and she realized how much she had been counting on him.

"The first thing we'd better do," Rhys said, "is take you on a tour of the plant here. Do you know about the physical structure of this company?"

"Not much."

That was not true. Elizabeth had been at enough meetings with Sam over the past few years to have picked up a good deal of knowledge about the workings of Roffe and Sons. But she wanted to hear it from Rhys's point of view.

"We manufacture much more than drugs, Liz. We make chemicals and perfumes and vitamins and hair sprays and pesticides. We produce cosmetics and bio-electronic instruments. We have a food division, and a division of animal nitrates." Elizabeth was aware of all that, but she let Rhys go on. "We publish magazines for distribution to doctors. We make adhesives, and building protection agents and plastic explosives."

Elizabeth could sense that he was becoming caught up by what he was saying; she could hear the undertone of pride in his voice, and she was oddly reminded of her father.

"Roffe and Sons owns factories and holding companies in over a hundred countries. Every one of them reports to this office." He paused, as though to make sure that she understood the point. "Old Samuel went into business with a horse and a test tube. It's grown to sixty factories around the world, ten research centres and a network of thousands of salesmen and detail men and woman." They were the ones, Elizabeth knew, who called on the doctors and hospitals. "Last year, in the United States alone, they spent over fourteen billion dollars on drugs – and we have a healthy share of that market."

And yet Roffe and Sons was in trouble with the banks. Something was wrong.

Rhys took Elizabeth on a tour of the company's headquarters factory. In actuality, the Zurich division was a dozen factories, with seventy-five buildings on the sixty acres of ground. It was a world in microcosm, completely self-supporting. They visited the manufacturing plants, the research departments, the toxicology laboratories, the storage plants. Rhys brought Elizabeth to a sound stage, where they made motion pictures for research and for their world-wide advertising and product divisions. "We use more film here," Rhys told Elizabeth, "than the major Hollywood studios."

They went through the molecular biology department, and the liquid centre, where fifty giant, stainless steel, glass-lined tanks hung suspended from the ceiling, filled with liquids ready to be bottled. They saw the tablet-compression rooms, where powders were formed into tablets, sized, stamped with ROFFE AND SONS, packaged and labelled, without anyone ever touching them. Some of the drugs were ethical products, available only on prescription, others were proprietary items, sold over the counter.

Set apart from the other buildings were several small buildings. These were for the scientists: the analytical chemists, biochemists, organic chemists, parasitologists, pathologists.

"More than three hundred scientists work here, Rhys told Elizabeth. "Most of them are PhDs. Would you like to see our hundred-million-dollar room?"

Elizabeth nodded, intrigued.

It was in an isolated brick building, guarded by a uniformed policeman with a gun. Rhys showed his security pass, and he and Elizabeth were permitted to enter a long corridor with a steel door at the end of it. The guard used two keys to open the door, and Elizabeth and Rhys entered. The room contained no windows. It was lined from floor to ceiling with shelves filled with every variety of bottles, jars and tubes.

"Why do they call this the hundred-million-dollar room?" Elizabeth asked.

"Because that's what it cost to furnish it. See all those compounds on the shelves? None of them have names, only numbers. They're the ones that didn't make it. They're the failures."

"But a hundred million – "

"For every new drug that works, there are about a thousand that end up in this room. Some drugs are worked on for as long as ten years, and then abandoned. A single drug can cost five or ten million dollars in research before we find out that it's no good, or that someone else has beaten us to it. We don't throw any of these things away because now and then one of our bright young men will back into a discovery that can make something in this room valuable."

The amounts of money involved were awesome.

"Come on, Rhys said. "I'll show you the Loss Room."

It was in another building, this one unguarded, containing, like the other room, only shelves filled with bottles and jars.

"We lose a fortune here too," Rhys said. "But we plan it that way."

"I don't understand."

Rhys walked over to a shelf and picked up a bottle. It was labelled "Botulism". "Do you know how many cases of botulism there were in the United States last year? Twenty-five. But it costs us millions of dollars to keep this drug in stock." He picked up another bottle at random. "This is an antidote for rabies. This room is full of drugs that are cures for rare diseases – snakebites, poisonous plants. We furnish them free to the armed forces and to hospitals, as a public service."

"I like that," Elizabeth said. Old Samuel would have liked it too, she thought.

Rhys took Elizabeth to the capsule rooms, where empty bottles were carried in on a giant conveyor belt. By the time they had crossed the room, the bottles had been sterilized, filled with capsules, labelled, topped with cotton, and sealed. All done by automation.

There was a glass-blowing factory, an architectural centre to plan new buildings, a real estate division to acquire the land for them. In one building there were scores of writers turning out pamphlets in fifty languages, and printing presses to print them.

Some of the departments reminded Elizabeth of George Orwell's *1984*. The Sterile Rooms were bathed in eerie ultraviolet light. Adjoining rooms were painted in different colours – white, green or blue – and the workers wore uniforms to match. Each time they entered or left the room, they had to go through a special sterilizing chamber. Blue workers were locked in for the entire day. Before they could eat or rest or go to the toilet, they had to undress, enter a neutral green zone, put on other clothes, and reverse the process when they returned.

"I think you'll find this interesting," Rhys said.

They were walking down the grey corridor of a research building. They reached a door marked "RESTRICTED – DO NOT ENTER". Rhys pushed the door open, and he and Elizabeth walked through. They went through a second door and Elizabeth found herself in a dimly lit room filled with hundreds of cages containing animals. The room was hot and humid, and she felt as if she had suddenly been transported to a jungle. As her eyes grew accustomed to the half-light, she saw that the cages were filled with monkeys and hamsters and cats and white mice. Many of the animals had obscene-looking growths protruding from various parts of their bodies. Some had their heads shaven, and were crowned with electrodes that had been implanted in their brains. Some of the animals were screaming and gibbering, racing around in their cages, while others were comatose and lethargic. The noise and the stench were unbearable. It was like some kind of hell. Elizabeth walked up to a cage that contained a single white kitten. Its brain was exposed, enclosed in a clear plastic covering through which protruded half a dozen wires.

"What – what's going on here?" Elizabeth asked. A tall, bearded young man making notes in front of a cage explained. "We're testing a new tranquillizer."

"I hope it works," Elizabeth said weakly. "I think I could use it." And she walked out of the room before she could be sick.

Rhys was at her side in the corridor. "Are you all right?"

She took a deep breath. "I – I'm fine. Is all that really necessary?"

Rhys looked at her and replied. "Those experiments save a lot of lives. More than one third of the people born since nineteen fifty are alive only because of modern drugs. Think about that."

Elizabeth thought about it.

It took six full days to tour the key buildings, and when Elizabeth had finished, she was exhausted, her head spinning with the vastness of it. And she realized she was seeing just one Roffe plant. There were dozens of others scattered around the world.

The facts and figures were stunning. "It takes between five and ten years to market a new drug, and out of every two thousand compounds tested, we'll average only three products."

And " . . . Roffe and Sons has three hundred people working here in quality control alone."

And " . . . Worldwide, Roffe and Sons is responsible for over half a million employees . . ."

And " . . . our gross income last year was . . ."

Elizabeth listened, trying to digest the incredible figures that Rhys was throwing at her. She had known that the company was large, but "large" was such an anonymous word. Having it actually translated into terms of people and money was staggering.

That night as Elizabeth lay in bed, recalling all the things she had seen and heard, she was filled with an overpowering feeling of inadequacy.

Ivo *Believe me*, cara, *it is much better to leave all this to us. You don't understand these things.*

Alec *I think you should sell but I have an axe to grind.*

Walther *Why bother yourself with this? You can go off any where you like and enjoy your money.*

They were right, all of them, Elizabeth thought. I'm going to get out and let them do what they like with the company. I do not belong in this position.

The moment she made the decision, she felt a deep sense of relief. She fell asleep almost immediately.

The following day, Friday, was the beginning of a holiday weekend. When Elizabeth arrived at the office, she sent for Rhys to announce her decision.

"Mr Williams had to fly to Nairobi last night," Kate Erling informed her. "He said to tell you he would be back on Tuesday. Can anyone else help you?"

Elizabeth hesitated. "Put in a call to Sir Alec, please."

"Yes, Miss Roffe." Kate added, a note of hesitation in her voice, "A package for you was delivered this morning by the police department. It contains the personal belongings your father had with him at Chamonix."

The mention of Sam brought back that sharp sense of loss, of grief.

"The police apologized because they could not give it to your messenger. It was already on its way to you."

Elizabeth frowned. "My messenger?"

"The man you sent to Chamonix to pick it up."

"I didn't send anyone to Chamonix." It was obviously some bureaucratic mix-up. "Where is it?"

"I put it in your closet."

There was a Vuitton suitcase, containing Sam's clothes, and a locked attaché case with a key taped to it. Probably company reports. She would let Rhys handle them. Then she remembered that he was away. Well, she decided, she would go away for the weekend too. She looked at the attaché case and thought, Perhaps there's something personal belonging to Sam. I'd better look at it first.

Kate Erling buzzed. "I'm sorry, Miss Roffe. Sir Alec's out of the office."

"Leave a message for him to call me, please. I'll be at the villa in Sardinia. Leave the same message for Mr Palazzi, Mr Gassner and Mr Martel."

She would tell them all that she was leaving, that they could sell the stock, do as they pleased with the company.

She was looking forward to the long weekend. The villa was a retreat, a soothing cocoon, where she could be alone to think about herself and her future. Events had been flung at her so rapidly that she had had no chance to put things into any kind of perspective. Sam's accident – Elizabeth's mind tripped over the word "death"; inheriting the controlling stock of Roffe and Sons; the urgent pressure from the family to let the company go public. And the company itself. The awesome heartbeat of a behemoth whose power spanned the world. It was too much to cope with all at once.

When she flew to Sardinia late that afternoon, Elizabeth had the attaché case with her.

18

She took a taxi from the airport. There was no one at the villa because it had been closed, and Elizabeth had not told anyone she was coming. She let herself in and walked slowly through the large familiar rooms and it was as if she had never been away. She had not realized how much she had missed this place. It seemed to Elizabeth that the few happy memories of her childhood had been here. It felt strange to be alone in this labyrinth where there had always been half a dozen servants bustling around, cooking, cleaning, polishing. Now there was only herself. And the echoes of the past.

She left Sam's attaché case in the downstairs hallway and carried her suitcase upstairs. With the habit of long years, she started to head for her bedroom in the centre of the hallway, then stopped. Her father's room was at the far end. Elizabeth turned and walked towards it. She opened the door slowly, because while her mind understood the reality, some deep, atavistic instinct made her half expect to see Sam there, to hear the sound of his voice.

The room was empty, of course, and nothing had changed since Elizabeth had last seen it. It contained a large double bed, a beautiful tallboy, a dressing-table, two comfortable upholstered chairs, and a couch in front of the fireplace. Elizabeth put down her suitcase and walked over to the window. The iron shutters had been closed against the late September sun, and the curtains were drawn. She opened them wide and let the fresh mountain air flow in, soft and cool with the promise of fall. She would sleep in this room.

Elizabeth returned downstairs and went into the library. She sat down in one of the comfortable leather chairs, rubbing her hands along the sides. This was where Rhys always sat when he had a conference with her father.

She thought about Rhys and wished that he were here with her. She remembered the night he had brought her back to school after the dinner in Paris, and how she had gone back to her room and had written "Mrs Rhys Williams" over and over. On an impulse Elizabeth walked over to the desk, picked up a pen and slowly wrote "Mrs Rhys Williams". She looked at it and smiled. "I wonder," she mocked herself aloud, "how many other idiots are doing the same thing right now?"

She turned her thoughts away from Rhys, but still he was at the back of her mind, pleasantly comforting. She got up and wandered around the house. She explored the large, old-fashioned kitchen, with its wood-burning stove, and two ovens.

She walked over to the refrigerator and opened it. It was empty. She should have anticipated that, with the house shut down. Because the refrigerator was empty, she became suddenly hungry. She searched the cupboards. There were two small cans of tuna fish, a half-filled jar of Nescafé, and an unopened packet of biscuits. If she was going to be here for a long weekend, Elizabeth decided, she had better do some planning. Rather than drive into town for every meal, she would shop at one of the little markets in Cali di Volpe and stock enough food for several days. A utility jeep was always kept in the carport and she wondered if it was still there. She went to the back of the kitchen and through the door that led to the carport, and there was the jeep. Elizabeth walked back into the kitchen, where, on a board behind the cupboard, were hooks with labelled keys on them. She found the key to the jeep and returned to the carport. Would there be petrol in it? She turned the key and pressed the starter. Almost immediately the motor sparked into life. So *that* problem was eliminated. In the morning she would drive into town and pick up whatever groceries she needed.

She went back into the house. As she walked across the tiled floor of the reception hall, she could hear the echo of her footsteps, and it was a hollow, lonely sound. She wished that Alec would call, and even as she was thinking it the telephone rang, startling her. She walked to it and picked it up. "Hello."

"Elizabeth. It's Alec here."

Elizabeth laughed aloud.

"What's so funny?"

"You wouldn't believe me if I told you. Where are you?"

"Down in Gloucester." And Elizabeth felt a sudden, urgent impulse to see him, to tell him her decision about the company. But not over the telephone. "Would you do me a favour, Alec?"

"You know I will."

"Could you fly down here for the weekend? I'd like to discuss something with you."

There was only the slightest hesitation, and then Alec said, "Of course."

Not a word about what engagements he would have to break, how inconvenient it might be. Just "Of course." That was Alec.

Elizabeth forced herself to say, "And bring Vivian."

"I'm afraid she won't be able to come. She's – ah – rather involved in London. I can arrive tomorrow morning. Will that do?"

"Perfect. Let me know what time, and I'll pick you up at the airport."

"It will be simpler if I just take a taxi."

"All right. Thank you, Alec. Very much."

When Elizabeth replaced the receiver, she was feeling infinitely better.

She knew she had made the right decision. She was in this position only because Sam had died before he had had the time to name his successor.

Elizabeth wondered who the next president of Roffe and Sons would be. The board could decide that for themselves. She thought about it from Sam's point of view, and the name that sprang instantly to mind was Rhys Williams. The others were competent in their own areas, but Rhys was the only one who had a working knowledge of the company's complete global operation. He was brilliant and effective. The problem, of course, was that Rhys was not eligible to be president. Because he was not a Roffe, or married to a Roffe, he could not even sit on the board.

Elizabeth walked into the hallway and saw her father's attaché case. She hesitated. There was hardly any point in her going through it now. She could give it to Alec when he arrived in the morning. Still, if there *was* something personal in it . . . She carried it into the library, set it on the desk, untaped the key and opened the little locks on each side. In the centre of the case lay a large manila envelope. Elizabeth opened it and removed a sheaf of typewritten papers lying loosely in a cardboard cover labelled:

MR SAM ROFFE
CONFIDENTIAL
NO COPIES

It was obviously a report of some kind, but without anyone's name on it so that Elizabeth could not know who had drawn it. She started to skim through the report, then slowed down, then stopped. She could not believe what she was reading. She carried the papers over to an armchair, kicked off her shoes, curled her legs up underneath her and turned to page one again.

This time she read every word, and she was filled with horror. It was an astonishing document, a confidential report of an investigation into a series of events that had occurred over the past year.

In Chile a chemical plant owned by Roffe and Sons had exploded, sending tons of poisonous materials spouting over a ten-square-mile area. A dozen people had been killed, hundreds more had been taken to hospitals. All the livestock had died, the vegetation was poisoned. The entire region had had to be evacuated. The lawsuits filed against Roffe and Sons had run into hundreds of millions of dollars. But the shocking thing was that the explosion had been deliberate. The report read "The Chilean government's investigation into the accident was cursory. The official attitude seems to be: the Company is rich, the people are poor, let the Company pay. There is no question in the minds of our investigating staff but that it was an act of sabotage, by a person or persons unknown, using plastic explosives. Because of the antagonistic official attitude here, it will be impossible to prove."

Elizabeth remembered the incident only too well. Newspapers and magazines had been full of horror stories complete with photographs of the victims, and the world's press had attacked Roffe and Sons, accusing it of being careless and indifferent to human suffering. It had damaged the image of the company badly.

The next section of the report dealt with major research projects that Roffe and Sons' scientists had been working on for a number of years. There were four projects listed, each of them of inestimable potential value. Combined, they had cost more than fifty million dollars to develop. In each case a rival pharmaceutical firm had applied for a patent for one of the products, just ahead of Roffe and Sons, using the identical formula. The report continued: "One isolated incident might have been put down as coincidence. In a field where dozens of companies are working in related areas, it is inevitable that several companies might be working on the same type of product. But four such incidents in a period of a few months force us to the conclusion that someone in the employ of Roffe and

Sons gave or sold the research material to the competitive firms. Because of the secret nature of the experiments, and the fact that they were conducted in widely separated laboratories under conditions of maximum security, our investigation indicates that the person, or persons, behind this would need to have access to top security clearances. We therefore conclude that whoever is responsible is someone in the highest executive echelon of Roffe and Sons."

There was more.

A large batch of toxic drugs had been mislabelled and shipped. Before they could be recalled there were several deaths, and more bad publicity for the company. No-one could learn where the wrong labels had come from.

A deadly toxin had disappeared from a heavily guarded laboratory. Within an hour an unidentified person had leaked the story to the newspapers and started a scare.

The afternoon shadows had long since lengthened into evening, and the night air had turned chilly. Elizabeth remained totally absorbed in the document she held in her hands. When the study became dark, she switched on a lamp and continued to read, the horror piled on horror.

Not even the dry, terse tone of the report could conceal the drama in it. One thing was clear. Someone was methodically attempting to damage or destroy Roffe and Sons.

Someone in the highest echelon of the company. On the last page was a marginal note in her father's neat, precise handwriting. "Additional pressure on me to let the company go public? Trap the bastard."

She remembered now how worried Sam had been, and his sudden secrecy. He had not known whom to trust.

Elizabeth looked at the front page of the report again. "NO COPIES".

Elizabeth was sure the report had been done by an outside investigative agency. So in all probability no one had been aware of this report but Sam. And now herself. The guilty person had no idea he was under suspicion. Had Sam known who he was? Had Sam confronted him before his accident? Elizabeth had no way of knowing. All she knew was that there was a traitor.

Someone in the highest echelon of the company.

No one else would have the opportunity or the ability to carry out so much destruction on so many different levels. Was that why Sam had refused to let the company go public? Was he trying to find the guilty person first? Once the company was sold, it would be impossible to conduct a secret investigation, with every move being reported to a group of strangers.

Elizabeth thought about the board meeting, and how they had urged her to sell. All of them.

Elizabeth suddenly felt very alone in the house. The loud ringing of the telephone made her jump. She walked over to it and picked it up. "Hello?"

"Liz? It's Rhys. I just received your message."

She was glad to hear his voice, but she suddenly remembered why she had called him. To tell him that she was going to sign the papers, let the company be sold. In a few short hours everything had completely changed. Elizabeth glanced out into the hallway, at the portrait of old Samuel. He had founded this company and had fought for it. Elizabeth's father had built it up, helped turn it into a giant, and lived for it, dedicated himself to it.

"Rhys," Elizabeth said, "I'd like to have a board meeting Tuesday. Two o'clock. Would you please arrange for everyone to be there?"

"Tuesday at two o'clock," Rhys agreed. "Anything else?"

She hesitated. "No. That's all. Thank you."

Elizabeth slowly replaced the receiver. She was going to fight them.

She was high on a mountain with her father, climbing at his side. *Don't look down*, Sam kept saying, and Elizabeth disobeyed, and there was nothing below but thousands of feet of empty space. There was a loud rumble of thunder, and a bolt of lightning came hurtling towards them. It hit Sam's rope and set it on fire, and Sam started falling through space. Elizabeth watched her father's body tumble end over end, and she began to scream, but her screams were drowned by the roar of the thunder.

Elizabeth awakened suddenly, her nightgown drenched with perspiration, her heart pounding wildly. There was a loud clap of thunder, and she looked towards the window and saw that it was pouring outside. The wind was driving the rain into the bedroom through the open French doors. Quickly, Elizabeth got out of bed, crossed to the doors and pushed them tightly shut. She looked out at the storm clouds that filled the sky, and at the lightning flashes across the horizon, but she was not seeing them.

She was thinking about her dream.

In the morning the storm had passed over the island, leaving only a light drizzle. Elizabeth hoped that the weather would not delay Alec's arrival. After reading the report she desperately needed someone to talk to. In the meantime she decided it would be a good idea to put it away in a secure place. There was a safe up in the tower room. She would keep it there. Elizabeth bathed, put on a pair of old slacks and a sweater, and went down into the library to get the report.

It was gone.

19

The room looked as though a hurricane had swept through it. The storm had blown open the French doors during the night, and the wind and the rain had wreaked havoc, scattering everything before it. A few loose pages of the report lay on the wet rug, but the rest of the pages had obviously been carried away by the wind.

Elizabeth stepped to the French windows and looked out. She could see no papers on the lawn, but the wind could easily have blown them over the cliff. That must have been what happened.

NO COPIES. She must find out the name of the investigator Sam had hired. Perhaps Kate Erling would know. But Elizabeth could not be sure now that Sam had trusted Kate. This had become like a terrible game, where no one could trust anybody. She would have to move very carefully.

Elizabeth suddenly remembered that there was no food in the house. She could shop at Cala di Volpe and be back before Alec arrived. She went to the hall closet and got her raincoat and a scarf for her hair. Later, when the rain let up, she would search the grounds for the missing papers. She went into the kitchen and took the key to the jeep from the key rack. She walked out the back door that led to the carport.

Elizabeth started the engine and carefully backed the jeep out of the carport. She turned it round and headed out of the private driveway, braking to slow down because of the wet surface. At the bottom of the driveway she turned right, on to the narrow mountain road that led to the little village of Cala di Volpe below. There was no traffic on the road at this hour, but there seldom was, for few houses had been built up this high. Elizabeth glanced down to her left and saw that the sea below had become dark and angry, swollen with the night storm.

She drove slowly, for this part of the road became treacherous. It was narrow, with two lanes that had been cut into the side of the mountain, along a sheer precipice. On the inside lane was the solid rock of the mountain, and on the outside, a drop of hundreds of feet to the sea below. Elizabeth kept as close as she could to the inside lane, braking to fight the momentum of the steep mountain gradient.

The car was approaching a sharp curve. Automatically, Elizabeth put her foot on the brakes to slow the jeep down.

The brakes were dead.

It took a long moment to register. Elizabeth pressed again, harder, pushing down on the pedal with all her strength, and her heart began to pound as the jeep kept gathering speed. It took the curve and was moving faster now, racing down the steep mountain road, gaining momentum with each second. She pressed down on the brakes again. They were useless.

Another curve lay ahead. Elizabeth was afraid to take her eyes off the road to look at the speedometer, but out of the corner of her eye she could see the needle racing upward and she was filled with an icy terror. She reached the curve and skidded round it, much too fast. The back wheels slid towards the edge of the precipice, then the tyres found their traction and the jeep plunged forward again, hurtling down the steep road ahead. There was nothing to stop it now, no barriers, no controls, only the swift roller-coaster ride down, and the deadly, beckoning curves ahead.

Elizabeth's mind raced frantically, seeking some escape. She thought of jumping. She risked a quick look at the speedometer. She was doing seventy miles an hour now, and building up speed every moment, trapped between the solid mountain wall on one side and the deadly drop into space on the other. She was going to die. And in an instant revelation Elizabeth knew that she was being murdered, and that her father had been murdered. Sam had read the report, and he had been killed. As she was going to be killed. And she had no idea who her murderer was, who hated them enough to do this terrible thing. Somehow she could have borne it better if it had been a stranger. But it was someone she knew, someone who knew her. Faces flashed through her mind. Alec . . . Ivo . . . Walther . . . Charles . . . It had to be one of them. *Someone in the highest echelon of the company.*

Her death would be listed as an accident, as Sam's had been. Elizabeth was crying now, silently, her tears mixing with the fine mist of rain that was falling, but she was not even aware of it. The jeep was beginning to skid out of control on the wet surface, and Elizabeth fought to keep the wheels on the road. She knew it was only a matter of seconds before she hurtled over the cliff, into oblivion. Her body became rigid, and her hands were numb from gripping the steering-wheel. There was nothing in the universe now but herself, careering down the mountain road, with the roaring wind tugging at her, saying *Come join me*, tearing at the car, trying to push it over the brink of the cliff. The jeep started into another skid, and Elizabeth fought desperately to straighten it out, remembering what she had been taught. *Steer into the skid, always into the skid*, and the rear wheels straightened out and the car continued racing downhill. Elizabeth stole another quick glance at the speedometer . . . eighty miles an hour. She was catapulting towards a steep hairpin curve ahead, and she knew she was not going to make this one.

Something in her mind seemed to freeze, and it was as if there was a thin veil between her and reality. She heard her father's voice saying, *What are you doing down here alone in the dark?* and he was picking her up and carrying her to bed and she was on stage dancing and turning and turning and she could not stop, and Mme Netturova was screaming at her (or was it the wind?) and Rhys was there, saying, *How many times does a girl have her twenty-first birthday?* And Elizabeth thought, I'll never see Rhys again, and she screamed his name and the veil disappeared, but the nightmare was still there. The sharp curve was looming closer now, the car speeding towards it like a bullet. She would go over the cliff. *Let it happen quickly*, she prayed silently.

At that moment, to the right, just before the hairpin curve, Elizabeth caught a glimpse of a small firebreak trail that had been cut through the rock, going up the mountainside. She had to make a decision in a split second. She had no idea where the trail led. All she knew was that it went *upward*, that it might slow her momentum, give her a chance. And she took it. At the last instant, as the jeep reached the trail, Elizabeth swung the wheel hard to the right. The rear wheels started to skid, but the front wheels were on the gravel road and the momentum gave them enough traction to hold. The jeep was now hurtling upward, and Elizabeth was fighting the wheel, trying to keep the car on the narrow trail. There was a thin line of trees and their branches were slashing at her as she raced by them, tearing at her face and her hands. She looked ahead, and to her horror, she could see the Tyrrhenian Sea below. The path had merely led to the other side of the cliff. There was no safety here at all.

She was getting closer and closer to the brink now, moving too fast to jump from the jeep. The edge of the cliff was just ahead of her, the sea hundreds of feet below. As the jeep hurtled towards the edge, it went into a wild skid, and the last thing Elizabeth remembered was a tree looming up in front of her and then an explosion that seemed to fill the universe.

After that the world became still and white and peaceful and silent.

20

She opened her eyes and she was in a hospital bed and the first thing she saw was Alec Nichols.

"There's nothing in the house for you to eat," she whispered, and started to cry.

Alec's eyes filled with pain, and he put his arms around her and held her close. "Elizabeth!"

And she mumbled, "It's all right, Alec. Everything is fine."

And it was. Every inch of her body felt bruised and beaten, but she was alive, and she could not believe it. She remembered the terror of that drive down the mountain, and her body went cold.

"How long have I been here?" Her voice was weak and hoarse.

"They brought you in two days ago. You've been unconscious since then. The doctor says it was a miracle. According to everybody who saw the scene of the accident, you should be dead. A service crew came across you and rushed you in here. You have a concussion and a hell of a lot of bruises, but, thank the Lord, there's nothing broken." He looked at her, puzzled, and said, "What were you doing up there on that firebreak road?"

Elizabeth told him. She could see the horror on his face as he lived through the terrible ride with her. He kept repeating, "Oh, my God," over and over. When Elizabeth had finished, Alec was pale. "What a stupid, terrible accident!"

"It wasn't an accident, Alec."

He looked at her, puzzled. "I don't understand."

How could he? He had not read the report. Elizabeth said, "Someone tampered with the brakes."

He shook his head incredulously. "Why would anyone do that?"

"Because – " She could not tell him. Not yet. She trusted Alec more than she trusted anyone else, but she was not ready to talk. Not until she felt stronger, not until she had had time to think.

"I don't know," she said evasively. "I'm just sure someone did."

She watched him and she could read the changing expressions on his face. They went from disbelief to puzzlement to anger.

"Well, we're certainly going to find out." His voice was grim.

He picked up the telephone, and a few minutes later he was talking to the Chief of Police in Olbia. "This is Alec Nichols," he said. "I – Yes, she's fine, thank you . . . Thank you. I'll tell her. I'm calling about the jeep she was driving. Could you tell me where it is? . . . Would you keep it there, please? And I'd like you to get hold of a good mechanic. I'll be there in half an hour." He replaced the receiver. "It's in the police garage. I'm going over."

"I'm coming with you."

He looked at her in surprise. "The doctor said you must stay in bed for at least another day or two. You can't – "

"I'm coming with you," she insisted stubbornly.

Forty-five minutes later Elizabeth checked her bruised and swollen body out of the hospital over a doctor's protests, and was on her way to the police garage with Alec Nichols.

Luigi Ferraro, the Chief of Police of Olbia, was a swarthy, middle-aged Sardo, with a large stomach and bandy legs. Next to him was Detective Bruno Campagna, who towered over his chief. Campagna was a muscularly built man in his fifties, with an air of solid competence. He stood next to Elizabeth and Alec, watching a mechanic examine the underside of a jeep that was raised on a hydraulic hoist. The left front fender and radiator had been smashed, and they were streaked with the sap of the trees they had crashed into. Elizabeth had felt faint at her first sight of the car, and she had had to lean on Alec for support. He looked at her with concern. "Are you sure you're up to this?"

"I feel fine," Elizabeth lied. She felt weak and terribly tired. But she had to see for herself.

The mechanic wiped his hands on a greasy cloth and walked over to the group. "They don't build them like that no more," he said.

Thank God, Elizabeth thought.

"Any other car woulda been in bits and pieces."

"What about the brakes?" Alec asked.

"The brakes? They're in perfect condition."

Elizabeth felt a sudden sense of unreality engulfing her. "What – what do you mean?"

"They're workin' fine. The accident didn't hurt them at all. That's what I meant when I said that they don't build – "

"That's impossible," Elizabeth interrupted. "The brakes were not working on that jeep."

"Miss Roffe believes that someone tampered with them," Chief Ferraro explained.

The mechanic shook his head. "No, sir." He walked back to the jeep and pointed to the underside. "There's only two ways you can *fregare* – " He turned to Elizabeth. "Excuse me, signorina – screw up the brakes on a jeep. You can either cut the brake links or you can loosen this nut" – he indicated a piece of metal on the underside – "and let the brake fluid run out. You can see for yourself that this link is solid, and I checked the brake drum. It's full."

Chief Ferraro said to Elizabeth soothingly, "I can understand how in your condition it could – "

"Just a moment," Alec interrupted. He turned to the mechanic. "Isn't it possible that those links were cut and then replaced or that someone drained the brake fluid and then filled it again?"

The mechanic shook his head stubbornly. "Mister, those links ain't been touched." He took his rag again and carefully wiped off the oil around the nut that held the brake fluid. "See this nut? If anyone had loosened it, there'd be fresh wrench marks on it. I'll guarantee that no one's touched it in the last six months. There's not a thing wrong with these brakes. I'll show you."

He walked over to the wall and pulled a switch. There was a whirring sound and the hydraulic lift began to lower the jeep to the floor. They watched as the mechanic got in it, started the engine and backed the jeep up. When it was touching the back wall, he put the jeep in first gear and pressed down on the accelerator. The car raced towards Detective Campagna. Elizabeth opened her mouth to scream, and at that instant the jeep jerked to a stop an inch away from him. The mechanic ignored the look the detective gave him and said, "See? These brakes are perfect."

They were all looking at Elizabeth now, and she knew what they were thinking. But that did not change the terror of that ride down the mountain. She could feel her foot pressing on the brakes, and nothing happening. Yet the police mechanic had proved that they worked. Unless he was in on it. And that meant the Chief of Police probably knew too. I'm becoming paranoiac, Elizabeth thought.

Alec said helplessly, "Elizabeth – "

"When I drove that jeep, those brakes were not working."

Alec studied her for a moment, then said to the mechanic, "Let's suppose that someone did arrange it so that the brakes on this jeep wouldn't work. How else could it have been done?"

Detective Campagna spoke up. "They could have wet the brake lining."

Elizabeth could feel an excitement stirring in her. "What would happen if they did that?"

Detective Campagna said, "When the brake lining pressed against the drum, it would have no traction."

The mechanic nodded. "He's right. The only thing is – " He turned to Elizabeth. "Were your brakes working when you started driving?"

Elizabeth remembered using the brakes to back out of the carport, and braking again later when she came to the first curves. "Yes," she said, "they were working."

"There's your answer," the mechanic said triumphantly. "Your brakes got wet in the rain."

"Hold on," Alec objected. "Why couldn't someone have wet them before she started?"

"Because," the mechanic said patiently, "if anyone had wet them before she started, she wouldn'ta had no brakes at all."

The Chief of Police turned to Elizabeth. "Rain can be very dangerous, Miss Roffe. Particularly on these narrow mountain roads. This sort of thing happens all too often."

Alec was watching Elizabeth, not knowing what to do next. She felt like a fool. It *had* been an accident after all. She wanted to get out of here. She looked at the Chief of Police. "I – I'm sorry to have put you to all this trouble."

"*Please*. It is a pleasure. I mean – I am distressed about the circumstances, but it is always a pleasure to be of service. Detective Campagna will drive you back to your villa."

Alec said to her, "If you don't mind my saying so, old girl, you look ghastly. Now, I want you to hop into your bed and stay there for a few days. I'll order some groceries by telephone."

"If I stay in bed, who's going to cook?"

"I am," Alec declared.

That evening he prepared dinner and served it to Elizabeth in bed.

"I'm afraid I'm not a very good cook," he said cheerfully, as he set a tray down in front of Elizabeth.

It was the understatement of the year, Elizabeth thought. Alec was a terrible cook. Every dish was either burned, underdone or oversalted. But she managed to eat, partly because she was starving, and partly because she did not want to hurt Alec's feelings. He sat with her, making careful small talk. Not a word about what a fool she had made of herself at the police garage. She loved him for it.

The two of them spent the next few days at the villa, with Elizabeth remaining in bed, and Alec fussing over her, cooking all the meals, reading to her. During that time it seemed to Elizabeth that the telephone never stopped ringing. Ivo and Simonetta called every day to see how she was, and Hélène and Charles, and

Walter. Even Vivian called. They all offered to come and stay with her.

"I'm really all right," she told them. "There's no reason for you to come. I'll be returning to Zurich in a few days."

Rhys Williams called. Elizabeth had not realized how much she had missed him until she heard the sound of his voice.

"I hear you decided to give Hélène some competition," he said. But she could hear the concern in his voice.

"Wrong. I only race on mountains, downhill." It was incredible to her that she could joke about it now.

Rhys said, "I'm glad you're all right, Liz."

His tone, as much as his words, warmed her. She wondered if he was with another woman now, and who she was. It would be someone beautiful, of course.

Damn her.

"Did you know you made the headlines?" Rhys asked.

"No."

" 'Heiress narrowly escapes death in car accident. Only a few weeks after her father, the well-known – ' You can write the rest of the story yourself."

They spoke on the phone for half an hour, and when Elizabeth hung up she was feeling much better. Rhys seemed so genuinely interested in her, and concerned. She wondered whether he made every woman he knew feel that way about him. It was part of his charm. She remembered how they had celebrated her birthday together. *Mrs Rhys Williams.*

Alec walked into the bedroom. He said, "You look like the Cheshire cat."

"Do I?"

Rhys had always been able to make her feel that way. Perhaps, she thought, I should tell Rhys about the confidential report.

Alec had arranged for one of the company planes to fly them back to Zurich.

"I hate to take you back so soon," he said apologetically, "but there are some rather urgent decisions that have to be made."

The flight to Zurich was uneventful. There were reporters at the airport. Elizabeth made a brief statement about her accident, and then Alec had her safely inside the limousine and they were on their way to the company headquarters.

She was in the conference room with all the members of the board, and Rhys, present. The meeting had been going on for the past three hours, and the air was stale with cigar and cigarette smoke. Elizabeth was still shaken from her experience, and she had a pounding headache – *Nothing to be concerned about, Miss Roffe. When the concussion wears off, the headaches will go away.*

She looked round the room, at the tense, angry faces. "I've decided not to sell," Elizabeth had told them. They thought she was being arbitrary and stubborn. If they only knew how close she had come to giving in. But now it was impossible. Someone in this room was an enemy. If she quit now, it would be his victory.

They had all tried to convince her, each in his own fashion.

Alec said reasonably, "Roffe and Sons needs an experienced president, Elizabeth. Particularly now. For your own sake, as well as everyone else's, I would like to see you walk away from this."

Ivo used his charm. "You're a beautiful young girl, *carissima*. The whole world is yours. Why do you want to become a slave to something as dull as business when you could be out, having a wonderful time, travelling – "

"I've travelled," Elizabeth said.

Charles used Gallic logic. "You happen to hold the controlling stock through a tragic accident, but it makes no sense for you to try to run the company. We have serious problems. You will only make them worse."

Walther spoke bluntly. "The company is in enough trouble. You have no idea how much trouble. If you do not sell now, it will be too late."

Elizabeth felt as though she were under siege. She listened to them all, studying them, evaluating what they were telling her. Each of them based his argument on the good of the company – yet one of them was working to destroy it.

One thing was clear. They all wanted her to get out, to let them sell their stock, and bring in outsiders to take over Roffe and Sons. Elizabeth knew that the moment she did that, her chances of finding out who was behind this were finished. As long as she stayed here, on the inside, there was the possibility that she could learn who was sabotaging the company. She would stay only as long as she had to. She had not spent the last three years with Sam without learning something about the business. With the help of the experienced staff he had built up, she would continue to carry out her father's policies. The insistence from all the board members that she get out now only made her more stubbornly determined to remain.

She decided it was time to end the meeting.

"I've made my decision," Elizabeth said. "I don't plan to run this company alone. I'm aware of how much I have to learn. I know I can count on all of you to help me. We'll deal with the problems one by one."

She sat at the head of the table, still pale from her accident, looking small and defenceless.

Ivo threw up his hands helplessly. "Can't anyone talk some logic into her?"

Rhys turned to Elizabeth and smiled. "I think everyone's going to have to go along with whatever the lady wants to do."

"Thank you, Rhys." Elizabeth looked at the others. "There's one thing more. Since I'm taking my father's place, I think it would be best to make it official."

Charles stared at her. "You mean – you want to become president?"

"In effect," Alec reminded him dryly, "Elizabeth is already president. She's merely showing us the courtesy of letting us handle the situation gracefully."

Charles hesitated, then said, "All right. I move that Elizabeth Roffe be nominated president of Roffe and Sons."

"I second the motion." Walther.

The motion was carried.

It was such a bad time for presidents, he thought sadly. *So many were being assassinated.*

21

No-one was more aware than Elizabeth of the enormous responsibility she had assumed. As long as she was running the company, the jobs of thousands of people depended upon her. She needed help, but she had no idea whom she could trust. Alec and Rhys and Ivo were the ones she most wanted to confide in, but she was not ready yet. It was too soon. She sent for Kate Erling.

"Yes, Miss Roffe?"

Elizabeth hesitated, wondering how to begin. Kate Erling had worked for Elizabeth's father for many years. She would have a sense of the undercurrents that flowed beneath the deceptively calm surface. She would know about the inner workings of the company, about Sam Roffe's feelings, his plans. Kate Erling would make a strong ally.

Elizabeth said, "My father was having some kind of confidential report drawn up for him, Kate. Do you know anything about it?"

Kate Erling frowned in concentration, then shook her head. "He never discussed it with me, Miss Roffe."

Elizabeth tried another approach. "If my father had wanted a confidential investigation, to whom would he have gone?"

This time the answer was unhesitating. "Our security division."

The last place Sam would have gone to. "Thank you," Elizabeth said.

There was no-one she could talk to.

There was a current financial report on her desk. Elizabeth read it with growing dismay, and then sent for the company comptroller. His name was Wilton Kraus. He was younger than Elizabeth had expected. Bright, eager, an air of faint superiority. The Wharton School, she decided, or perhaps Harvard.

Elizabeth began without preamble. "How can a company like Roffe and Sons be in financial difficulty?"

Kraus looked at her and shrugged. He was obviously not used to reporting to a woman. He said condescendingly, "Well, putting it in words of one syllable – "

"Let's begin with the fact," Elizabeth said curtly, "that up until two years ago Roffe and Sons had always done its own capital financing."

She watched his expression change, trying to adjust. "Well – yes, ma'am."

"Then why are we so heavily indebted to banks now?"

He swallowed and said, "A few years ago, we went through a period of unusually heavy expansion. Your father and the other members of the board felt that it would be wise to raise that money by borrowing from banks on short-term loans. We have current net commitments to various banks for six hundred and fifty million dollars. Some of those loans are now due."

"Overdue," Elizabeth corrected him.

"Yes, ma'am. Overdue."

"We're paying the prime rate, plus one per cent, plus penalty interest. Why haven't we paid off the overdue loans and reduced the principal on the others?"

He was beyond surprise now. "Because of – er – certain unfortunate recent occurrences, the company's cash-flow position is considerably less than we had anticipated. Under ordinary circumstances we would go to the banks and ask for extensions. However, with our current problems, the various litigation settlements, the write-offs in our experimental laboratory, and . . ." His voice trailed off.

Elizabeth sat there, studying him, wondering whose side he was on. She looked down at the balance sheets again, trying to pinpoint where things had gone wrong. The statement showed a sharp decline over the past three quarters, largely because of the heavy lawsuit payoffs listed under the column "Extraordinary Expenses (Non-recurring)". In her mind's eye she saw the explosion in Chile, the cloud of poisonous chemicals spouting into the air. She could hear the screams of the victims. A dozen people dead. Hundreds more taken to hospitals. And in the end all the human pain and misery had been reduced to money, to Extraordinary Expenses (Non-recurring).

She looked up at Wilton Kraus. "According to your report, Mr Kraus, our problems are of a temporary nature. We are Roffe and Sons. We're still a first-class risk for any bank in the world."

It was his turn to study her. His supercilious air was gone, but he was wary now.

"You must realize, Miss Roffe," he began cautiously, "that a drug firm's reputation is as important as its products."

Who had said that to her before? Her father? Alec? She remembered. Rhys.

"Go on."

"Our problems are becoming too well-known. The business world is a jungle. If your competitors suspect that you've been wounded, they move in for the kill." He hesitated, then added, "They're moving in for the kill."

"In other words," Elizabeth replied, "our competitors bank with our bankers, too."

He gave her a brief congratulatory smile. "Exactly. The banks have a limited amount of funds to loan out. If they're convinced that A is a better risk than B – "

"And *do* they think that?"

He ran his fingers through his hair, nervously. "Since your father's death I've had several calls from Herr Julius Badrutt. He heads the banking consortium we're dealing with."

"What did Herr Badrutt want?" She knew what was coming.

"He wanted to know who was going to be the new president of Roffe and Sons."

"Do you know who the new president is?" Elizabeth asked.

"No, ma'am."

"I am." She watched him try to conceal his surprise. "What do you think will happen when Herr Badrutt learns the news?"

"He'll pull the plug on us," Wilton Kraus blurted out.

"I'll talk to him," Elizabeth said. She leaned back in her chair and smiled. "Would you care for some coffee?"

"Why, that's – that's very kind of you. Yes, thank you."

Elizabeth watched him relax. He had sensed that she had been testing him, and he felt that he had passed the test.

"I'd like your advice," Elizabeth said. "If you were in my position, Dr Kraus, what would you do?"

That faintly patronizing air was back. "Well," he said confidently, "that's very simple. Roffe and Sons has enormous assets. If we sold off a substantial block of stock to the public, we could easily raise more than enough money to satisfy all our bank loans."

She knew now whose side he was on.

22

Hamburg
Friday, October 1
2 a.m.

The wind was blowing from the sea, and the early-morning air was chill and damp. In the Reeperbahn section of Hamburg the streets were crowded with visitors eager to experience the forbidden pleasures of the city of sin. The Reeperbahn catered for all tastes impartially. Drinks, drugs, girls or boys – they were all available at a price.

The garishly lighted hostess bars were on the main street, while the Grosse Freiheit featured the lewd strip shows. The Herbertstrasse, one block away, was for pedestrians only, and both sides of the street were lined with prostitutes sitting in the windows of their flats, displaying their wares through flimsy, soiled nightgowns that concealed nothing. The Reeperbahn was a vast market, a human butcher shop, where you could select any piece of meat you could afford to pay for. For the strait-laced there was simple sex, missionary style; for those who enjoyed a bit of variety there was cunnilingus and analingus and sodomy. On the Reeperbahn you could buy a twelve-year-old boy or girl, or get into bed with a mother and daughter. If your tastes ran that way, you could watch a woman being serviced by a Great Dane, or get yourself whipped until you achieved orgasm. You could hire a toothless crone to perform fellatio on you in a busy alley or buy yourself an orgy in an elaborately mirrored bedroom with as many girls or boys as your libido required. The Reeperbahn prided itself on having something for everyone. Younger whores in short skirts and tight-fitting blouses cruised the pavements, propositioning men, women and couples impartially.

The cameraman walked down the street slowly, the target for a dozen girls and brightly rouged boys. He ignored them all until he came to a girl who looked to be no more than eighteen. She had blonde hair. She was leaning against a wall, talking to a girl friend. She turned as the man approached, and smiled. "Would you like a party, *liebchen?* My friend and I will give you a good time."

The man studied the girl and said, "Just you."

The other girl shrugged and moved off.

"What's your name?"

"Hildy."

"Would you like to be in the movies, Hildy?" the cameraman asked.

The young girl studied him with cold eyes. "*Herrgott!* You're not going to give me that old Hollywood *Scheiss?*"

He smiled reassuringly. "No, no. This is a genuine offer. It's a porno film. I make them for a friend of mine."

"It will cost you five hundred marks. In advance."

"*Gut.*"

She regretted instantly that she had not asked for more. Well, she would find some way to get a bonus out of him. "What do I have to do?" Hildy asked.

Hildy was nervous.

She lay sprawled out naked on the bed in the small, shabbily furnished apartment, watching the three people in the room, and thinking, There's something wrong here. Her instincts had been sharpened on the streets of Berlin and Munich and Hamburg. She had learned to rely on them. There was something about these people she did not trust. She would have liked to have walked out before it started, but they had already paid her five hundred marks, and promised her another five hundred if she did a good job. She would do a good job. She was a professional and she took a pride in her work. She turned to the naked man in bed beside her. He was strong and well-built; his body was hairless. What bothered Hildy was his face. He was too old for this sort of film. But it was the spectator who sat quietly at the back of the room who disturbed Hildy the most. The spectator wore a long coat, a large hat and dark glasses. Hildy could not even tell if it was a man or a woman. The vibrations were bad. Hildy fingered the red ribbon tied around her neck, wondering why they had asked her to wear it. The cameraman said, "All right. We're ready now. Action."

The camera began whirring. Hildy had been told what to do. The man was lying on his back. Hildy went to work.

She started with a trip around the world, skilfully using her tongue and lips on the man's ears and neck, moving down across his chest and stomach and belly, lightly flicking her tongue in quick butterfly strokes against his groin and penis, then each leg, down to his toes, slowly licking each toe, watching his erection begin. She rolled him over on his stomach, and her tongue began to work its way back up his body, moving slowly, expertly, finding all the erotic crevices and sensitive areas and exploring them. The man was fully aroused now, rock-hard.

"Get inside her," the cameraman said. The man rolled her over and was on top of her, forcing her thighs apart, his penis swollen to an enormous tumescence, and as he entered her, Hildy forgot her earlier fear. It felt wonderful.

"Shove it in me, *liebchen!*" she cried.

The man was deep, deep inside her, rocking back and forth, and Hildy started to move with him, her hips writhing in quickening spasms. In the back of the room the spectator was leaning forward, watching every movement. The girl on the bed closed her eyes.

She was spoiling it!

"Her eyes!" the spectator shouted.

The director called out, "*Offne die Augen!*"

Startled, Hildy opened her eyes. She watched the man on top of her. He was good. It was the kind of sex she liked. Hard and thrusting. He was moving faster now, and she began to respond to him. Usually she did not have orgasms, except with her girl friend. With customers she always faked it, and they never knew the difference. But the cameraman had warned her that if she did not have an orgasm, she would not be paid the bonus. And so now she relaxed and let herself think about all the beautiful things she was going to buy with the money, and she felt herself beginning to climax.

"*Schneller!*" she cried. "*Schneller!*"

Her body began to shudder. "*Ah, jetzt!*" she screamed. "*Es kommt! Es kommt!*"

The spectator nodded, and the cameraman cried, "Now!"

The man's hands moved up towards the girl's neck. His enormous fingers closed over her windpipe and squeezed. She looked up into his eyes and saw what was there, and she was filled with terror. She tried to scream, but she was unable to breathe. She fought desperately to fight free, her body jerking in great, orgiastic spasms, but he had her pinned down. There was no escape.

The spectator sat there drinking it in, feasting on it, looking into the dying girl's eyes, watching her being punished.

The girl's body shuddered once, and then was still.

23

Zurich
Monday, October 4
10 a.m.

When Elizabeth arrived at her office, a sealed envelope marked "CONFIDENTIAL", with her name on it, was lying on her desk. She opened it. In it was a report from the chemical laboratory. It was signed "Emil Joeppli". It was full of technical terms, and Elizabeth read it through without understanding it. Then she read it again. And again. Each time more slowly. When finally she had grasped its significance, she said to Kate, "I'll be back in an hour.'And she went to find Emil Joeppli.

He was a tall man, about thirty-five, with a thin, freckled face, and a scalp that was bald except for a tonsure of bright red hair. He fidgeted uncomfortably, as though unused to having visitors in his little laboratory.

"I read your report," Elizabeth told him. "There's a great deal in it that I don't understand. I wonder if you would mind explaining it to me."

Instantly, Joeppli's nervousness vanished. He leaned forward in his chair, sure and confident, and began to speak rapidly. "I've been experimenting with a method of inhibiting rapid differentiation of the collagens, by using mucopolysaccharides and enzyme blocking techniques. Collagen, of course, is the fundamental protein basis of all connective tissue."

"Of course," Elizabeth said.

She did not even try to understand the technical part of what Joeplli was saying. What Elizabeth did understand was that the project he was working on could retard the ageing process. It was a breathtaking concept.

She sat there, silent, listening, thinking about what this could mean in terms of revolutionizing the lives of men and women all over the world. According to Joeplli, there was no reason why everyone could not live to be a hundred, or a hundred and fifty, or even two hundred years old.

"It would not even be necessary to have injections," Joeppli told Elizabeth. "With this formula the ingredients could be taken orally in a pill or a capsule."

The possibilities were staggering. It would mean nothing less than a social revolution. And billions of dollars for Roffe and Sons. They would manufacture it themselves, and license it out to other companies as well. There was no one over fifty years of age who would not take a pill that would keep him or her young. It was difficult for Elizabeth to conceal her excitement.

"How far along are you on this project?"

"As I wrote in my report, I've been doing tests with animals for the last four years. All the recent results have been positive. It's just about ready for testing on human beings." She liked his enthusiasm.

"Who else knows about this?" Elizabeth asked.

"Your father knew. It's a Red Folder project. Top security. That means that I report only to the president of the company and to one member of the board."

Elizabeth suddenly felt chilled. "Which member?"

"Mr Walther Gassner."

Elizabeth was silent for a moment. "From this time on," she said, "I want you to report directly to me. And only to me."

Joeppli looked at her in surprise. "Yes, Miss Roffe."

"How soon could we have this on the market?"

"If everything goes well, eighteen to twenty-four months from now."

"Fine. If you need anything – money, extra help, equipment – let me know. I want you to move as quickly as possible."

"Yes, ma'am."

Elizabeth rose, and instantly Emil Joeppli jumped to his feet.

"It's a pleasure meeting you." He smiled, and added shyly, "I liked your father."

"Thank you," Elizabeth said. Sam had known about this project. Was that another reason he refused to sell the company?

At the door Emil Joeppli turned to Elizabeth.

"It's going to work on people!"

"Yes," Elizabeth said. "Of course it will."

It had to.

"How is a Red Folder project handled?"

Kate Erling asked, "From the beginning?"

"From the beginning."

"Well. As you know, we have several hundred new products in various experimental stages. They – "

"Who authorizes them?"

"Up to a certain amount of money, the heads of the different departments involved," Kate Erling said.

"What amount of money?"

"Fifty thousand dollars."

"And after that?"

"There must be board approval. Of course, a project does not come into the Red Folder category until it has passed its initial tests."

"You mean until it looks like it has a chance of being successful?" Elizabeth asked.

"That's right."

"How is it protected?"

"If it's an important project, all the work is transferred to one of our high-security laboratories. All the papers are removed from the general files and put into a Red Folder file. Only three people have access to that. The scientist in charge of the project, the president of the company, and one member of the board."

"Who decides who that member will be?" Elizabeth asked.

"Your father selected Walther Gassner."

The moment the words were out of her mouth, Kate realized her mistake.

The two women looked at each other, and Elizabeth said, "Thank you, Kate. That will be all."

Elizabeth had made no mention of Joeppli's project. Yet Kate had known what Elizabeth was talking about. There were two possibilities. Either Sam had trusted her and told her about Joeppli's project, or she had learned about it on her own. For someone else.

This was too important to allow anything to go wrong. She would check on the security herself. And she had to speak to Walther Gassner. She reached for the telephone, then stopped. There was a better way.

Late that afternoon Elizabeth was on a commercial airliner to Berlin.

Walther Gassner was nervous.

They were seated at a corner booth in the upstairs dining-room of the Papillon on the Kurfürstendamm. Whenever Elizabeth had visited Berlin in the past, Walther had always insisted that Elizabeth have dinner at his home, with Anna and him. This time there had been no mention of that. He had suggested instead that they meet at this restaurant. And he had come without Anna.

Walther Gassner still had the clear-cut, boyish, movie-star handsomeness, but the surface gloss had begun to crack. There were lines of tension in his face, and his hands never stopped moving. He seemed to be under some extraordinary tension. When Elizabeth asked about Anna, Walther was vague. "Anna's not feeling well. She couldn't come."

"Is it anything serious?"

"No, no. She'll be fine. She's at home, resting."

"I'll call her and – "

"Better not to disturb her."

It was a puzzling conversation, totally unlike Walther, whom Elizabeth had always found so open and outgoing.

She brought up the subject of Emil Joeppli. "We need what he's working on very badly," Elizabeth said.

Walther nodded. "It's going to be big."

"I've asked him not to report to you any more," Elizabeth told him.

Walther's hands suddenly went very still. It was like a shout. He looked at Elizabeth and asked, "Why did you do that?"

"It has nothing to do with you, Walther. I would have done exactly the same thing with any other board member working with him. I simply want to handle this in my own way."

He nodded. "I see." But his hands remained motionless on the table. "You have a right, of course." He forced a smile and she could see what it was costing him. "Elizabeth," he said, "Anna has a lot of stock in the company. She can't sell it unless you vote yes. It's very important. I – "

"I'm sorry, Walther, I can't let the stock be sold now."

His hands suddenly began to move again.

24

Herr Julius Badrutt was a thin, brittle man who resembled a praying mantis in a black suit. He was like a stick figure drawn by a child, with angular arms and legs, and a dry, unfinished face sketched on top of his body. He was seated stiffly at the conference table of the Roffe and Sons boardroom, facing Elizabeth. There were five other bankers with him. They all wore black suits with waistcoats, white shirts and dark ties. They appeared, Elizabeth thought, not so much *dressed* as in uniform. Looking round at the cold, impassive eyes at the table, Elizabeth was filled with a sense of misgiving. Before the meeting had begun, Kate had brought in a tray of coffee and delicious, freshly baked pastries. The men had all declined. Just as they had declined Elizabeth's invitation to come to lunch. She decided it was a bad sign. They were there to get the money that was owed them.

Elizabeth said, "First of all, I wish to thank all of you for coming here today."

There were polite, meaningless murmurs in response.

She took a deep breath. "I asked you here to discuss an extension on the loans owed to you by Roffe and Sons."

Julius Bradrutt shook his head in tiny, jerky movements. "I am sorry, Miss Roffe. We have already informed – "

"I haven't finished," Elizabeth said. She glanced round the room. "If I were you, gentlemen, I would refuse."

They stared at her, then looked at one another in confusion.

Elizabeth continued, "If you were concerned about the loans when my father was running this company – and he was a brilliant businessman – why would you extend them for a woman who is inexperienced in business?"

Julius Badrutt said dryly, "I think you have answered your own question, Miss Roffe. We have no intention of – "

Elizabeth said, "I haven't finished."

They were eyeing her more warily now. She looked at each of them in turn, making sure she had their full attention. They were Swiss bankers, admired, respected and envied by their lesser colleagues in other parts of the financial world. They were leaning forward now, listening carefully, their attitude of impatience and boredom replaced by curiosity.

"You have all known Roffe and Sons for a long time," Elizabeth went on. "I am sure most of you knew my father and, if you did, you must have respected him."

There were nods of agreement from some of the men.

"I imagine," Elizabeth continued, "that you gentlemen must have choked over your morning coffee when you learned that I was taking his place here."

One of the bankers smiled, then laughed aloud, and said, "You are quite right, Miss Roffe. I do not mean to be ungallant, but I think I am speaking for the rest of my colleagues when I say that – what were your words? – we choked over our morning coffee."

Elizabeth smiled ingenuously. "I don't blame you. I'm sure I would have reacted in exactly the same way."

Another banker spoke up. "I am curious, Miss Roffe. Since we are all in agreement about the outcome of this meeting" – he spread his hands expressively – "why are we here?"

"You're here," Elizabeth said, "because in this room are some of the greatest bankers in the world. I can't believe that you became so successful by looking at everything only in dollars and cents. If that were true, then any of your bookkeepers could run your business for you. I am sure that there is much more to banking than that."

"Of course there is," another banker murmured, "but we're businessmen, Miss Roffe, and – "

"And Roffe and Sons is a business. It's a great business. I didn't know how great until I sat behind my father's desk. I had no idea how many lives this company has saved in countries all over the world. Or of the enormous contributions we've made to medicine. Or how many thousands of people depend on this company for their livelihood. If – "

Julius Badrutt interrupted. "That is all very commendable, but we seem to be getting off the point. I understand that it has been suggested to you that if you release the company stock, there will be more than sufficient monies to satisfy our loans."

His first mistake, Elizabeth thought. *I understand that it has been suggested to you.*

The suggestion had been made in the privacy of a board of directors' meeting, where everything was confidential. Someone at that meeting had talked. Someone who was trying to put pressure on her. She intended to find out who, but that would have to come later.

"I want to ask you a question," Elizabeth said. "If your loans are repaid, would it matter to you where the money came from?"

Julius Badrutt studied her, his mind circling the question, looking for a trap. Finally he said, "No. Not as long as we receive the money due to us."

Elizabeth leaned forward and said earnestly, "So it doesn't matter whether you're paid from the sale of company stock to outsiders, or from our own financial resources. All of you know that Roffe and Sons isn't going out of business. Not today. Not tomorrow. Not ever. All I'm asking is the courtesy of a little extra time."

Julius Badrutt smacked his dry lips and said, "Believe me, Miss Roffe, we are most sympathetic. We understand the terrible emotional stress you have gone through, but we cannot – "

"Three months," Elizabeth said. "Ninety days. With your getting additional penalty interest, of course."

There was a silence around the table. But it was a negative silence. Elizabeth could see their cold, hostile faces. She decided on one last desperate gamble.

"I – I don't know whether it's proper for me to reveal this," she said with deliberate hesitation, "and I must ask you to keep it confidential." She looked around and saw that she had their interest again. "Roffe and Sons is on the verge of a breakthrough that's going to revolutionize the entire pharmaceutical industry." She paused to heighten the suspense. "The company is about to reveal a new product that our projections show will *far outsell every drug available on the market today.*"

She could feel the change in the atmosphere.

It was Julius Badrutt who rose to the bait first. "What – er – type of – ?"

Elizabeth shook her head. "I'm sorry, Herr Badrutt. Perhaps I've already said too much. I can only tell you that it will be the biggest innovation in the history of this business. It will require a tremendous expansion of our facilities. We'll have to double them, perhaps triple them. Of course, we'll be looking for new financing on a large scale."

The bankers were glancing at one another, exchanging silent signals. The silence was broken by Herr Badrutt. "If we *were* to give you a ninety-day extension, we would naturally expect to act as the prime bankers for Roffe and Sons in all future transactions."

"Naturally."

Another exchange of meaningful looks. It's like a form of jungle drums, Elizabeth thought.

"In the meantime," Herr Badrutt said, "we would have your assurance that at the end of ninety days all your outstanding notes will be met in full?"

"Yes."

Herr Badrutt sat there, staring into space. He looked at Elizabeth, then looked around at the others, and received their silent signals. "For my part, I am willing to agree. I do not think a delay – with penalty interest – will do any harm."

One of the other bankers nodded. "If you think we should go along, Julius . . ."

And it was done. Elizabeth leaned back in her chair, trying to conceal the feeling of relief flooding through her. She had gained ninety days.

She would need every minute of that time.

25

It was like being in the eye of a hurricane.

Everything flowed across Elizabeth's desk from the hundreds of departments at headquarters, from the factories in Zaire, the laboratories in Greenland, the offices in Australia and Thailand, from the four corners of the earth. There were reports on new products, sales, statistical projections, advertising campaigns, experimental programmes.

There were decisions to be made on building new factories, selling old ones, acquiring companies, hiring and firing executives. Elizabeth had expert advice on every phase of the business, but all final decisions had to be made by her. As they had once been made by Sam. She was grateful now for the three years she had worked with her father. She knew much more about the company than she had realized, and much less. Its very scope was awesome. Elizabeth had once thought of it as a kingdom, but it was a *series* of kingdoms, run by viceroys, with the president's office as the throne room. Each of her cousins had charge of his own domain, but in addition they supervised other overseas territories, so that they were all travelling constantly.

Elizabeth soon learned that she had a special problem. She was a woman in a man's world, and she discovered that it made a difference. She had never really believed that men subscribed to the myth of the inferiority of women, but she quickly learned better. No one ever put it into words or acted overtly, but Elizabeth was faced with it every day. It was an attitude born of ancient prejudices and it was inescapable. The men did not like taking orders from a woman. They resented the idea of a woman questioning their judgements, trying to improve on their ideas. The fact that Elizabeth was young and attractive made it worse. They tried to make her feel that she should be at home, in a bed or kitchen, and that she should leave serious business matters to the men.

Elizabeth scheduled meetings with different department heads every day. Not all were hostile. Some were predatory. A beautiful girl sitting behind the president's desk was a challenge to the male ego. Their minds were easy to read: If I can fuck her, I can control her.

Like the grown-up version of the boys in Sardinia.

The men went after the wrong part of Elizabeth. They should have gone after her mind, because in the end that was where she controlled them. They underestimated her intelligence, and that was their mistake.

They miscalculated her capacity to assume authority, and that was another error.

And they misjudged her strength, and that was their greatest mistake. She was a Roffe, with the bloodline of old Samuel and her father in her, and she had their determination and spirit.

While the men round her were trying to use Elizabeth, she used them.

She tapped the knowledge and the experience and the insights that they had accumulated, and she made them her own. She let the men talk, and she listened. She asked questions, and she remembered the answers.

She learned.

Every night Elizabeth took home two heavy briefcases filled with reports to be studied. Sometimes she worked until four in the morning. One evening a newspaper photographer snapped a picture of Elizabeth walking out of the building with a secretary carrying her two briefcases. The photograph appeared in the newspapers the next day. The caption read: "Working Heiress".

Elizabeth had become an international celebrity overnight. The story of a beautiful young girl inheriting a multi-billion-dollar corporation and then taking command was irresistible. The press jumped at it. Elizabeth was lovely, intelligent, and down-to-earth, a combination they rarely came across in celebrities. She made herself available to them whenever possible, trying to build up the damaged image of the company, and they appreciated it. When she didn't know the answer to a reporter's question, she was not afraid to pick up a telephone and ask someone. Her cousins flew into Zurich once a week for meetings and Elizabeth spent as much time with them as possible. She saw them together, and one at a time. She talked to them and studied them, searching for a clue as to which one of them had allowed innocent people to die in an explosion, had sold secrets to competitors, and which one of them was trying to destroy Roffe and Sons. One of her cousins.

Ivo Palazzi, with his irresistible warmth and charmth.

Alec Nichols, a correct and proper gentleman, and gentle man, always helpful when Elizabeth had needed him.

Charles Martel, a dominated, frightened man. And frightened men could be dangerous when cornered.

Walther Gassner. The All-German boy. Beautiful-looking and friendly on the outside. What was he like on the inside? He had married Anna, an heiress, thirteen years his senior. Had he married for love or money?

When Elizabeth was with them, she watched, and listened, and probed. She mentioned the explosion in Chile and studied their reactions, and she talked about the patents that Roffe had lost to other companies, and she discussed the impending government lawsuits.

She learned nothing. Whoever it was, he was too clever to give himself away. He would have to be trapped. Elizabeth recalled Sam's marginal note on the report. *Trap the bastard*. She would have to find a way.

Elizabeth found herself becoming more and more fascinated by the inside operation of the pharmaceutical business.

Bad news was deliberately spread. If there was a report that a patient had died from a competitor's medication, within half an hour a dozen men were placing telephone calls all around the world. "By the way, did you happen to hear about . . . ?"

Yet on the surface all the companies appeared to be on the best of terms. The heads of some of the large firms held regular informal get-togethers, and Elizabeth was invited to one. She was the only woman present. They talked about their mutual problems.

The president of one of the large companies, a pompous, middle-aged roué, who had been following Elizabeth around all evening, said, "Government restrictions get more unreasonable every goddamned day. If some genius invented aspirin tomorrow, the government would never okay it." He gave Elizabeth a superior smile. "And do you have any idea, little lady, how long we've had aspirin?"

Little lady replied, "Since four hundred BC, when Hippocrates discovered salicin in the bark of the willow tree."

He stared at her a moment, and the smile died. "Right." He walked away.

The company heads all agreed that one of their biggest problems was the me-too firms, the copycat houses that stole the formulas of successful products, changed the names and rushed them on to the market. It was costing the reputable drug firms hundreds of millions of dollars a year.

In Italy it was not even necessary to steal.

"Italy is one of the countries that has no patent regulations protecting new drugs," one of the executives told Elizabeth. "For a bribe of a few hundred thousand lire, anyone can buy the formulas and pirate them under another name. We spend millions of dollars on research – they walk off with the profits."

"Is it just Italy?" Elizabeth asked.

"Italy and Spain are the worst. France and West Germany aren't bad. England and the United States are clean."

Elizabeth looked around at all these indignant, moral men and wondered if any of them was involved in the thefts of the patents of Roffe and Sons.

It seemed to Elizabeth that she spent most of her time in aeroplanes. She kept her passport in the top drawer of her desk. At least once a week there was a frantic call from Cairo or Guatemala or Tokyo, and within a few hours Elizabeth would find herself in a plane with half a dozen members of her staff, to cope with some emergency.

She met factory managers and their families in large cities like Bombay, and at remote outposts like Puerto Vallarta, and gradually Roffe and Sons began to take on a new perspective. It was no longer an impersonal mass of reports and statistics. A report headed "Guatemala" now meant Emil Nunoz and his fat, happy wife and their twelve children; "Copenhagen" was Nils Bjorn and the crippled mother with whom he lived; "Rio de Janeiro" was an evening spent with Alessandro Duval and his exquisite mistress.

Elizabeth kept in regular touch with Emil Joeppli. She always telephoned him on her private line, calling him at his little flat on Aussersihl in the evenings.

She was cautious even over the telephone.

"How are things going?"

"A little slower than I hoped, Miss Roffe."

"Do you need anything?"

"No. Just time. I ran into a little problem but I think it's solved now."

"Good. Call me if you need anything – anything at all."

"I will. Thank you, Miss Roffe."

Elizabeth hung up. She had an urge to push him, to tell him to hurry, for she knew that her time with the banks was running out. She desperately needed what Emil Joeppli was working on, but pressing him was not the answer, and so she kept her impatience to herself. Elizabeth knew that the experiments could not possibly be completed by the time the bank notes were due. But she had a plan. She intended to let Julius Badrutt into the secret, take him into the laboratory and let him see for himself what was happening. The banks would give them all the time they needed.

Elizabeth found herself working with Rhys Williams more and more closely, sometimes late into the night. They often worked alone, just the two of them, having dinner in her private dining-room at the office, or at the elegant apartment she had taken. It was a modern condominium in Zurichberg, overlooking the Lake of Zurich, and it was large and airy and bright. Elizabeth was more aware than ever of the strong animal magnetism of Rhys, but if he felt an attraction for her, he was careful not to show it. He was always polite and friendly. *Avuncular* was the word that came into Elizabeth's mind, and somehow it had a pejorative sound. She wanted to lean on him, confide in him, and yet she knew she had to be careful. More than once she had found herself on the verge of telling Rhys about the efforts to sabotage the company, but something held her back. She was not ready to discuss it with anyone yet. Not until she knew more.

Elizabeth was gaining more confidence in herself. At a sales meeting they were discussing a new hair conditioner that was selling badly. Elizabeth had tried it,' and she knew that it was superior to similar products on the markets.

"We're getting heavy returns from drugstores," one of the sales executives complained. "It's just not catching on. We need more advertising."

"We're already over our advertising budget," Rhys objected. "We'll have to find a different approach."

Elizabeth said, "Take it out of the drugstores."

They all looked at her. "What?"

"It's too available." She turned to Rhys. "I think we should continue the advertising campaign, but sell it only at beauty salons. Make it exclusive, hard to get. That's the image it should have."

Rhys thought for a moment, then nodded and said, "I like it. Let's try it."

It became a big seller overnight.

Afterwards Rhys had complimented her. "You're not just another pretty face," he had said, grinning.

So he *was* beginning to notice!

26

London
Friday, November 2
5 p.m.

Alec Nichols was alone in the club sauna when the door opened and a man walked into the steam-filled room, wearing a towel around his waist. He sat down on the wooden bench, next to Alec. "Hot as a witch's tit in here, ain't it, Sir Alec?"

Alec turned. It was Jon Swinton. "How did you get in here?"

Swinton winked. "I said you were expectin' me." He looked into Alec's eyes and asked, "You was expectin' me, wasn't you, Sir Alec?"

"No," Alec replied. "I told you I need more time."

"You also told us your little cousin was going to sell the stock, and you'd give us our money."

"She – she changed her mind."

"Ah, then you'd better change it back for her, hadn't you?"

"I'm trying. It's a question of – "

"It's a question of how much more horseshit we're going to take from you." Jon Swinton was moving closer, forcing Alec to slide along the bench. "We don't want to get rough with you 'cause it's nice to have a good friend like you in Parliament. You know what I mean? But there's a limit." He was leaning against Alec now, and Alec slid further away from him. "We did you a favour. Now it's time to pay us back. You're gonna get hold of a shipment of drugs for us."

"No! That's impossible," Alec said. "I can't. There's no way – "

Alec suddenly found that he had been crowded to the end of the bench, next to the large metal container filled with hot rocks. "Be careful," Alec said. "I – "

Swinton grabbed hold of Alec's arm and twisted it, forcing it towards the bed of rocks. Alec could feel the hair on his arm begin to singe.

"No!"

The next instant his arm was pressed down on to the rocks, and he screamed with pain and fell to the floor in agony. Swinton was standing over him.

"You find a way. We'll be in touch."

27

Berlin
Saturday, November 3
6 p.m.

Anna Roffe Gassner did not know how much longer she would be able to stand it.

She had become a prisoner in her own home. Except for the cleaning woman who came in for a few hours once a week, Anna and the children were alone, completely at Walther's mercy. He no longer bothered to conceal his hatred. Anna had been in the children's room as they listened together to one of their favourite records.

"Welch ein Singen, Musizieren,
Pfeifen, Zwitschken, Tiriliern . . ."

Walther had stormed in. "I'm sick of that!" he had yelled.

And he had smashed the record, while the children cowered in terror.

Anna had tried to placate him. "I – I'm sorry, Walther. I – I didn't know you were home. Can I do something for you?"

He had walked up to her, his eyes blazing, and he said, "We're going to get rid of the children, Anna."

In front of them!

He put his hands on her shoulders. "What happens in this house must be our secret." *Our secret. Our secret. Our secret.*

She could feel the words reverberating in her head, and his arms started to crush her until she could not breathe. She fainted.

When Anna woke up, she was lying in her bed. The shades were drawn. She looked at the bedside clock. Six p.m. The house was quiet. Too quiet. Her first thought was of the children, and terror swept through her. She rose from the bed on shaky legs, and stumbled over to the door. It was locked from the outside. She pressed her ear hard against the panel, listening. There should have been the sounds of the children. They should have come up to see her.

If they had been able to. If they were still alive.

Her legs were trembling so hard that she could barely walk to the telephone. She breathed a silent prayer, then picked it up. She heard the familiar dialling tone. She hesitated, dreading the thought of what Walther would do to her if he caught her again. Without giving herself a chance to think, Anna began to dial 110. Her hands shook so badly that she dialled a wrong number. And another. She began to sob. There was so little time left. Fighting her growing hysteria, she tried again, willing her fingers to move slowly. She heard a ringing, then miraculously a man's voice said, "*Hier ist der Notruf der Polizei.*"

Anna could not find her voice.

"*Hier ist der Notruf der Polizei. Kann ich Ihnen helfen?*"

"*Ja!*" It was a high-pitched sob. "*Ja, bitte! Ich bin in grosser Gefahr. Bitte schicken sie jemanden –* "

Walther loomed in front of her, ripping the telephone out of her hand and hurling her against the bed. He slammed down the receiver, breathing hard, tore the cord out of the wall, and turned to Anna.

"The children," she whispered. "What have you done with the children?"

Walther did not answer.

The Central Division of the Berlin Kriminalpolizei was located at 2832 Keithstrasse in a district of ordinary-looking apartment houses and office buildings. The emergency number of the *Deltk ans Mensch* department was equipped with an automatic hold system, so that a caller was unable to disconnect until the line had been electronically released by the switchboard. In this way every number calling in could be traced, no matter how brief the conversation. It was a sophisticated piece of equipment of which the department was proud.

Within five minutes of Anna Gassner's telephone call, Detective Paul Lange walked into the office of his chief, Major Wageman, carrying a cassette player.

"I would like you to listen to this." Detective Lange pressed a button. A metallic male voice said, "*Heir ist der Notruf der Polizei. Kann ich Ihnen helfen?*"

Then a woman's voice, filled with terror. "*Ja! Ja, bitte! Ich bin in grosser Gefahr. Bitte schicken sie jemanden –* "

There was the sound of a thud, a click, and the line went dead. Major Wageman looked up at Detective Lange. "You've traced the call?"

"We know whose residence it came from," Detective Lange replied carefully.

"Then what's the problem?" Major Wageman demanded impatiently. "Have Central send a car to investigate."

"I wanted your authority first." Detective Lange placed a slip of paper on the desk in front of the major.

"*Scheiss!*" Major Wageman stared at him. "Are you sure?"

"Yes, Major."

Major Wageman looked down at the slip of paper again. The telephone was listed in the name of Gassner, Walther. Head of the German division of Roffe and Sons, one of the industrial giants of Germany.

There was no need to discuss the implications. Only an idiot could miss them. One wrong move and they would both be walking the streets, looking for a job. Major Wageman thought for a moment and then said, "All right. Check it out. I want you to go there yourself. And walk on fucking eggs. Do you understand?"

"I understand, Major."

The Gassner estate was in Wannsee, an exclusive suburb in south-west Berlin.

Detective Lange took the longer Hohenzollerndamm instead of the speedier autobahn, because the traffic was lighter. He went through the Clayalle, past the CIA building, hidden behind half a mile of barbed wire fences. He passed the American Army Headquarters and turned right on what was once known as Road One, the longest road in Germany, running from East Prussia to the Belgian border. On his right was the Brücke der Einheit, the Bridge of Unity, where the spy Abel had been exchanged for the American U-2 pilot Gary Powers. Detective Lange turned the car off the highway into the wooded hills of Wannsee.

The houses were beautiful, impressive. On Sundays, Detective Lange sometimes took his wife out here, just to look at the outsides of the houses and the grounds.

He found the address he was looking for and turned into the long driveway leading to the Gassner estate. The estate represented something more than money: it represented power. The Roffe dynasty was big enough to make governments fall. Major Wageman had been right: he would be very careful.

Detective Lange drove to the front door of the three-storey stone house, got out of the car, took off his hat and pressed the doorbell. He waited. There was the heavy hanging silence of a house that has been deserted. He knew that was impossible. He rang again. Nothing but that still, oppressive silence. He was debating whether to go round to the back when the door unexpectedly opened. A woman stood in the doorway. She was middle-aged, plain-looking, wearing a wrinkled dressing-gown. Detective Lange took her for the housekeeper. He pulled out his identification. "I'd like to see Mrs Walther Gassner. Please tell her Detective Lange."

"I am Mrs Gassner," the woman said.

Detective Lange tried to conceal his surprise. She was totally unlike his image of the lady of this house.

"I – we received a telephone call at police headquarters a short time ago," he began.

She watched him, her face blank, disinterested. Detective Lange felt that he was handling this badly, but he did not know why. He had a feeling that he was missing something important.

"Did you make that call, Mrs Gassner?" he asked.

"Yes," she answered. "It was a mistake."

There was a dead, remote quality to her voice that was disturbing. He remembered the shrill, hysterical voice on the tape recorder half an hour earlier.

"Just for our records, may I ask what kind of mistake?"

Her hesitation was barely perceptible. "There was – I thought that a piece of my jewellery was missing. I found it."

The emergency number was for murder, rape, mayhem. *Walk on fucking eggs.*

"I see." Detective Lange hesitated, wanting to get inside the house, wanting to find out what she was covering up. But there was nothing more he could say or do. "Thank you, Mrs Gassner. I'm sorry to have troubled you."

He stood there, frustrated, and watched the door close in his face. He slowly got into his car and drove off.

Behind the door Anna turned.

Walther nodded and said softly, "You did very well, Anna. Now we're going back upstairs."

He turned towards the stairway, and Anna pulled out a pair of shears that had been concealed in the folds of her dressing-gown and plunged them into his back.

28

Rome
Sunday, November 4
Noon

It was a perfect day, Ivo Palazzi thought, for visiting the Villa d'Este with Simonetta and their three beautiful daughters. As Ivo strolled through the fabled Tivoli Gardens arm in arm with his wife, watching the girls race ahead from fountain to splashing fountain, he idly wondered whether Pirro Ligorio, who had built the park for his patrons, the d'Este family, had ever dreamed how much joy he would one day give to millions of sightseers. The Villa d'Este was a short distance north-east of Rome, nestled high in the Sabine Hills. Ivo had been there often, but it always gave him a feeling of special pleasure to stand at the very top level and look down on the dozens of sparkling fountains below, each one cunningly designed, each one different from the others.

In the past Ivo had taken Donatella and his three sons here. How they had adored it! The thought of them made Ivo sad. He had not seen or talked to Donatella since the horrifying afternoon at the apartment. He still remembered vividly the terrible scratches she had inflicted on him. He knew what remorse she must be going through, and how she must be longing for him. Well, it would do her good to suffer for a while, as he had suffered. In his mind he could hear Donatella's voice, and she was saying, "Come along. This way, boys."

It was so clear it seemed almost real. He could hear her say, "Faster, Francesco!" and Ivo turned and Donatella was behind him, with their three boys, moving determinedly towards him and Simonetta and the three girls. Ivo's first thought was that Donatella had happened to be here at the Tivoli Gardens by coincidence, but the instant he saw the expression on her face, he knew better. The *putana* was trying to bring his two families together, trying to destroy him! Ivo rose to the occasion like a madman.

He shouted to Simonetta. "There's something I must show you. Quickly, everybody."

And he swept his family down the long, winding stone steps towards a lower level, pushing tourists aside, casting frantic glances over his shoulder. Above, Donatella and the boys were moving towards the steps. Ivo knew that if the boys saw him, everything was lost. All it needed was for one of them to shout "Papa!" and he might as well drown himself in the fountains. He hurried Simonetta and the girls along, not giving them a chance to pause, not daring to let them stop for an instant.

"Where are we rushing to?" Simonetta gasped. "What's the hurry?"

"It's a surprise," Ivo said gaily. "You'll see."

He risked another quick glance back. Donatella and the three boys were out of sight for the moment. Ahead was a labyrinth, with one set of stairs leading up and another leading down. Ivo chose the stairs going up.

"Come along," he called to the girls. "Whoever gets to the top first gets a prize!"

"Ivo! I'm exhausted!" Simonetta complained. "Can't we rest aminute?"

He looked at her in shock. "*Rest?* That would spoil the surprise. Hurry!"

He took Simonetta's arm and dragged her up the steep steps, his three daughters racing ahead of them. Ivo found himself gasping for breath. It would serve them all right, he thought bitterly, if I had a heart attack and died right here. Goddamn women! You can't trust any of them. How could she do this to me? She adores me. I'll kill the bitch for this.

He could visualize himself strangling Donatella in her bed. She was wearing nothing but a flimsy negligée. He ripped it off and began to mount her, while she screamed for mercy. Ivo could feel himself getting an erection.

"Can we stop now?" Simonetta begged.

"No! We're almost there!"

They had reached the upper level again. Ivo took a hasty look around. Donatella and the boys were nowhere in sight.

"Where are you taking us?" Simonetta demanded.

"You'll see," Ivo said hysterically. "Follow me!" He shoved them towards the exit.

Isabella, the oldest girl, said, "Are we leaving, Papa? We just got here!"

"We're going to a better place," Ivo panted. He glanced back. Coming into sight, climbing the stairs, were Donatella and the boys.

"Faster, girls!"

A moment later Ivo and one of his families were outside the gate of the Villa d'Este, racing towards their car on the large square.

"I've never seen you like this," Simonetta gasped.

"I've never been like this," Ivo said truthfully. He had the motor going before the car doors were closed, and he raced out of the parking lot as though the devil was pursuing him.

"Ivo!"

He patted Simonetta's hand. "I want everybody to relax now. As a special treat I'm – I'm taking you to lunch at the Hassler."

They sat at a picture window overlooking the Spanish Steps, with Saint Peter's looming gloriously in the distance.

Simonetta and the children had a marvellous time. The food was delicious. Ivo could have been eating cardboard. His hands were trembling so badly that he could hardly hold his knife and fork. I can't stand much more of this, he thought. I'm not going to let her ruin my life.

For he had no doubt now that that was exactly what Donatella intended to do. *Il giuoco è stata fatto.* The game was up. Unless he could find a way to give Donatella the money she was demanding.

He had to get it. It did not matter how.

29

Paris
Monday, November 5
6 p.m.

The instant Charles Martel arrived home he knew he was in trouble. Hélène was waiting for him, and with her was Pierre Richaud, the jeweller who had made the replicas of her stolen jewellery. Charles stood in the doorway, in a state of shock.

"Come in, Charles," Hélène said. There was an undercurrent in her voice that terrified him. "I believe that you and M. Richaud know each other."

Charles stared, knowing that whatever he said would hang him. The jeweller was studying the floor in embarrassment, obviously ill at ease.

"Sit down, Charles." It was a command. Charles sat down.

Hélène said, "What you're facing, *mon cher mari*, is a criminal charge of grand theft. You have been stealing my jewellery and replacing the pieces with clumsy imitation paste, made by M. Richaud."

To his horror Charles found himself wetting his pants, a thing he had not done since he was a small boy. He blushed. He wished desperately that he could leave the room for a moment to clean himself. No, he wanted to flee and never return.

Hélène knew everything. It did not matter how she had found him out. There would be no escape and no mercy. It was terrifying enough that Hélène had discovered he had been stealing from her. Wait until she learned his motive! Wait until she found out that he had been planning to use the money to run away from her! Hell was going to have a new meaning. No-one knew Hélène as Charles did. She was *une sauvage*, capable of anything. She would destroy him, without a moment's thought, turn him into a *clochard*, one of those sad bums who sleep on the streets of Paris in rags. His life had suddenly turned into an *emmerdement*, a shower of shit.

"Did you really think you could get away with anything so stupid?" Hélène was asking.

Charles remained miserably silent. He could feel his pants getting wetter, but he did not dare look down.

"I have persuaded M. Richaud to give me all the facts."

Persuaded. Charles dreaded to think how.

"I have photostat copies of the receipts for the money you stole from me. I can put you in prison for the next twenty years." She paused, and added, "If I choose to."

Her words only served to increase Charles's panic. Experience had taught him that a generous Hélène was a dangerous Hélène. Charles was afraid to meet her glance. He wondered what it was she would demand from him. Something monstrous.

Hélène turned to Pierre Richaud. "You will say nothing of this to anyone until I have made up my mind what I wish to do."

"Of course, Mme Roffe-Martel, of course, of course." The man was babbling. He looked hopefully towards the door. "May I – ?"

Hélène nodded, and Pierre Richaud scurried out.

Hélène watched him go, then swung round to study her husband. She could smell his fear. And something else. Urine. She smiled. Charles had pissed himself out of fear. She had taught him well. Hélène was pleased with Charles. It was a very satisfying marriage. She had broken Charles, then made him her creature. The innovations he had brought to Roffe and Sons were brilliant, for they had all come from Hélène. She ruled a small part of Roffe and Sons through her husband, but now it was not enough. She was a Roffe. She was wealthy in her own right; her earlier marriages had made her even wealthier. But it was not money she was interested in. It was the control of the company. She had planned to use her stock to acquire more stock, to buy up the interest of the others. She had already discussed it with them. They were willing to go along with her, to form a minority group. First, Sam had stood in the way of her plan, and now Elizabeth. But Hélène had no intention of allowing Elizabeth or anyone else to keep her from getting what she wanted. Charles was going to get it for her. If anything went wrong, he would be her scapegoat.

Now, of course, he must be punished for his *petite révolte*. She watched his face and said, "No-one steals from me, Charles. No-one. You're finished. Unless I decide to save you."

He sat there, silent, wishing her dead, terrified of her. She walked over to where he sat, her thighs brushing against his face.

She said, "Would you like me to save you, Charles?"

"Yes," he said hoarsely. She was stepping out of her skirt, her eyes vicious, and he thought, *Oh, my God! Not now!*

"Then listen to me. Roffe and Sons is my company. I want the controlling interest."

He looked up at her miserably and said, "You know Elizabeth won't sell."

Hélène slipped out of her blouse and pants. She stood there, animal naked, her body lean and magnificent, her nipples hard. "Then you must do something about her. Or spend the next twenty years of your life in prison. Don't worry. I'll tell you what you will do. But first, come here, Charles."

30

The following morning, at ten o'clock, Elizabeth's private phone rang. It was Emil Joeppli. She had given him the number so that no one would be aware of their conversations. "I wonder if I could see you," he said. He sounded excited.

"I'll be there in fifteen minutes."

Kate Erling looked up in surprise as Elizabeth came out of her office wearing a coat. "You have an appointment at – "

"Cancel everything for the next hour," Elizabeth said, and walked out.

In the Development Building an armed guard examined Elizabeth's pass. "Last door to the left, Miss Roffe."

Elizabeth found Joeppli alone in his laboratory. He greeted her with enthusiasm.

"I finished the final tests last night. It works. The enzymes completely inhibit the ageing process. Look."

He led her to a cage holding four young rabbits, alert and filled with restless vitality. Next to it was another cage containing four more rabbits, quieter, more mature.

"This is the five hundredth generation to receive the enzyme," Joeppli said.

Elizabeth stood in front of the cage. "They look healthy."

Joeppli smiled. "*That's* part of the control group. He pointed to the cage on the left. "*Those* are the senior citizens."

Elizabeth stared at the energetic rabbits, frisking around in the cage like newborn bunnies, and she could not believe it.

"They'll outlive the others by at least three to one," Joeppli told her.

When you applied that ratio to human beings, the implications were staggering. She could barely contain her excitement.

"When – when will you be ready to start testing it on people?"

"I'm getting my final notes together. After that, another three or four weeks at the most."

"Emil, don't discuss this with anyone," Elizabeth warned.

Emil Joeppli nodded. "I won't, Miss Roffe. I'm working alone. I'm being very careful."

The entire afternoon had been taken up with a board meeting, and it had gone well. Walther had not appeared. Charles had again brought up the subject of selling the stock, but Elizabeth had firmly vetoed it. After that, Ivo had been his charming self, as had Alec. Charles seemed unusually tense. Elizabeth wished she knew why.

She invited them all to stay in Zurich and have dinner with her. As casually as possible, Elizabeth brought up the problems that had been mentioned in the report, watching for a reaction of some kind, but she could detect no sign of nervousness or guilt. And everyone who could have been involved, except for Walther, was seated at that table.

Rhys had not attended the meeting or the dinner. "I have some urgent business to take care of," he had said, and Elizabeth had wondered if it was a girl. Elizabeth was aware that whenever Rhys stayed late at night to work with her, he had had to cancel a date. Once, when he had been unable to reach the girl in time, she had appeared at the office. She was a stunning redhead, with a figure that made Elizabeth feel like a boy. The girl had been furious at being stood up, and she had not bothered to hide her displeasure. Rhys had escorted her to the lift and returned.

"Sorry about that," he had said.

Elizabeth could not help herself. "She's charming," she said sweetly. "What does she do?"

"She's a brain surgeon," Rhys had replied earnestly, and Elizabeth had laughed. The following day Elizabeth had learned that the girl *was* a brain surgeon.

There were others, and Elizabeth found herself resenting all of them. She wished that she understood Rhys better. She knew the gregarious and public Rhys Williams; she wanted to meet the private Rhys Williams, the self he kept hidden. More than once, Elizabeth had thought, Rhys should be running this company instead of taking orders from me. I wonder how he really feels about it?

That evening after dinner, when the members of the board had dispersed to catch trains and planes back to their homes, Rhys walked into Elizabeth's office where she was working with Kate. "Thought I ought to give you a hand," Rhys said lightly.

No explanation of where he had been. Why should there be? Elizabeth thought. He doesn't have to account to me.

They all set to work and the time flew. Elizabeth watched Rhys now, bent over some papers, rapidly scanning them, his eyes quick and alert. He had found several flaws in some important contracts that the attorneys had missed. Now Rhys straightened up, stretched and glanced at his watch.

"Oops! It's after midnight. I'm afraid I have an appointment. I'll come in early tomorrow and finish checking these agreements."

Elizabeth wondered if his appointment was with the brain surgeon or with one of his other – She stopped herself. What Rhys Williams did with his private life was his own business.

"I'm sorry," Elizabeth said. "I didn't realize it was so late. You run along. Kate and I will finish reading these papers."

Rhys nodded. "See you in the morning. Good night, Kate."

"Good night, Mr Williams."

Elizabeth watched Rhys leave, then forced her mind back to the contracts. But a moment later her thoughts were on Rhys again. She had been eager to tell him about the progress that Emil Joeppli was making on the new drug, to share it with him, yet she had held back. Soon, she told herself.

By one o'clock in the morning, they were finished.

Kate Erling said, "Will there be anything else, Miss Roffe?"

"No, I think that's all. Thank you, Kate. Come in late tomorrow."

Elizabeth stood up, and realized how stiff her body felt from sitting so long.

"Thank you. I'll have everything typed for you by tomorrow afternoon."

"That will be fine."

Elizabeth got her coat and purse, waited for Kate, and they walked to the door. They went out into the corridor together and headed towards the private express lift that stood there, door open, waiting. The two of them stepped inside the lift. As Elizabeth reached for the lobby button, they heard the sudden ringing of the telephone from the office.

"I'll answer it, Miss Roffe," Kate Erling said. "You go on ahead." She stepped out of the car.

Downstairs the night guard on duty in the lobby looked up at the elevator control board as a red light at the top of the board flashed on and began descending. It was the signal light for the private lift. That meant Miss Roffe was on her way down. Her chauffeur was sitting in a chair in a corner, drowsing over a newspaper.

"The boss is coming," the guard said.

The chauffeur stretched, and started lazily to his feet.

An alarm bell suddenly shattered the peace of the lobby.

The guard's eyes flashed to the control board. The red light was moving in a quick plunging pattern, gathering speed, marking the descent of the lift.

It was out of control.

"Oh, Jesus!" the guard mumbled.

He hurried to the board, jerked open a panel and pulled the emergency switch to activate the safety brake. The red light continued its downward plunge. The chauffeur had hurried over to the control panel. He saw the look on the guard's face.

"What's going – ?"

"Get away!" the guard yelled. "It's going to crash!"

They ran from the row of lifts towards the farthest wall. The lobby was beginning to vibrate with the speed of the runaway car inside the shaft, and the guard thought, *Don't let her be in it*, and as the plunging lift shot past the lobby, he heard the terrified screams from inside.

An instant later, there was a loud roar, and the building shuddered as though it had been hit by an earthquake.

31

Chief Inspector Otto Schmied of the Zurich Kriminalpolizei was seated at his desk, eyes closed, taking deep yoga breaths, trying to calm himself, trying to control the fury that filled him.

In police procedure there were rules that were so basic, so obvious, that no-one had thought it even necessary to put them in the police manual. They were simply taken for granted, like eating, or sleeping, or breathing. For example, when an accident-related fatality occurred, the first thing the investigating detective did – the *very* first thing a detective did, the simple, obvious, you-don't-have-to-draw-it-on-a-fucking-blackboard thing he did – was to visit the scene of the accident. Nothing could be more elementary than that. Yet staring up at Chief Inspector Otto Schmied from his desk was a report from Detective Max Hornung that violated every element of police procedure. I should have expected it, the Inspector told himself bitterly. Why am I even surprised?

Detective Hornung was Inspector Schmied's albatross, his *bête noire*, his – Inspector Schmied was an ardent admirer of Melville – his Moby Dick. The inspector took another deep breath and slowly exhaled. Then, only slightly less agitated, he picked up Detective Hornung's report and read it again from the beginning.

BRANDTOUR OFFIZIER REPORT

Wednesday, November 7

TIME	1.15 AM
SUBJECT	Report from central switchboard of accident at Roffe and Sons administration building at Eichenbahn factory
TYPE OF ACCIDENT	Unknown
CAUSE OF ACCIDENT	Unknown
NUMBER OF INJURED OR DECEASED	Unknown

TIME	1.27 AM
SUBJECT	Second message from central switchboard re accident at Roffe and Sons
TYPE OF ACCIDENT	Lift crash
CAUSE OF ACCIDENT	Unknown
NUMBER OF INJURED OR DECEASED	One female, deceased

I began an immediate investigation. By 1.35 AM I obtained the name of the superintendent of the Roffe and Sons administration building and from him got the name of the chief architect of the building.

2.30 AM I located the chief architect. He was celebrating his birthday at La Puce. He gave me the name of the company that had installed the lifts in the building. Rudolf Schatz, A.G.

At 3.15 AM I telephoned Mr Rudolf Schatz at his home and requested him to immediately locate the plans for the lifts. I also requested the master budget sheets along with preliminary estimates, final estimates and final costs; also requested a complete inventory of all mechanical and electrical materials used.

At this point Inspector Schmied could feel a familiar twitch starting in his right cheek. He took several deep breaths and read on.

6.15 AM the requested documents were delivered to me at police headquarters by Mr Schatz's wife. After an examination of the preliminary budget and final costs I was satisfied that:
a) no inferior materials were substituted in building the lifts;
b) because of the reputation of the builders, inferior workmanship could be ruled out as a cause of the crash;
c) the safety measures built into the lifts were adequate;
d) my conclusion therefore was that the cause of the crash was not an accident.
[Signed] Max Hornung, CID

NB Since my phone calls took place during the course of the night and early morning, it is possible that you may receive one or two complaints from some of the people I might have awakened.

Inspector Schmied savagely slammed the report down on his desk. "It is possible"! "Might have awakened"! The chief inspector had been under attack the entire morning by half of the officials of the Swiss government. What did he think he was running – a gestapo? How dare he awaken the president of a respectable building corporation and order him to deliver documents in the middle of the night? How dare he impugn the integrity of a reputable firm like Rudolf Schatz? And on and on and on.

But the thing that was so stunning – that was so incredible – was that Detective Max Hornung had not even *appeared* at the scene of the accident until *fourteen hours* after it was reported! By the time he arrived the victim had been removed, identified and autopsied. Half a dozen other detectives had examined the scene of the accident, had questioned witnesses and had filed their reports.

When Chief Inspector Schmied finished rereading Detective Max Hornung's report, he summoned him to his office.

The very sight of Detective Max Hornung was anathema to the chief inspector. Max Hornung was a dumpy, wistful-looking man, egg-bald, with a face that had been put together by an absent-minded prankster. His head was too large, his ears were too small, and his mouth was a raisin stuck in the middle of a pudding face. Detective Max Hornung was six inches too short to meet the rigid standards of the Zurich Kriminalpolizei, fifteen pounds too light, and hopelessly nearsighted. To top it all off, he was arrogant. All the men in the force felt unanimously about Detective Hornung: they hated him.

"Why don't you fire him?" the chief inspector's wife had asked, and he had almost struck her.

The reason that Max Hornung was in the Zurich detective force was that he had single-handedly contributed more to the Swiss national income than all the chocolate and watch factories combined. Max Hornung was an accountant, a mathematical genius with an encyclopaedic knowledge of fiscal matters, an instinct for the chicanery of man, and a patience that would have made Job weep with envy. Max had been a clerk in the Betrug Abteilung, the department set up to investigate financial frauds, irregularities in stock sales and banking transactions, and the ebb and flow of currency in and out of Switzerland. It was Max Hornung who had brought the smuggling of illegal money into Switzerland to a standstill, who had ferreted out billions of dollars' worth of ingenious but illicit financial schemes, and who had put half a dozen of the world's respected business leaders in prison. No matter how cunningly assets were concealed, mingled, remingled, sent to the Seychelles to be laundered, transferred and retransferred through a complex series of dummy corporations, in the end Max Hornung would ferret out the truth. In short, he had made himself the terror of the Swiss financial community.

Above all things that they held sacred and dear, the Swiss valued their privacy. With Max Hornung on the loose, there was no privacy.

Max's salary as a financial watchdog was meagre. He had been offered bribes of a million francs in numbered bank accounts, a chalet at Cortina d'Ampezzo, a yacht, and in half a dozen instances beautiful, nubile women. In each case the bribe had been rejected and the authorities promptly notified. Max Hornung cared nothing for money. He could have become a millionaire simply by applying his financial skills to the stock market, but the idea never even occurred to him. Max Hornung was interested in but one thing: catching those who strayed from the path of financial probity. Ah, yes, there was one other wish that consumed Max Hornung, and in the end it proved to be a blessing to the business community. For reasons which no one could fathom, Max Hornung wanted to be a police detective. He envisaged himself as a kind of Sherlock Holmes or Maigret, patiently following a labyrinth of clues, relentlessly stalking the criminal to his lair. When one of Switzerland's leading financiers accidentally learned of Max Hornung's ambitions to be a sleuth, he immediately got together with a few powerful friends and within forty-eight hours Max Hornung was offered a job in the Zurich police force as a detective. Max could not believe his good fortune. He accepted with alacrity, and the entire business community breathed a collective sigh of relief and resumed its arcane activities.

Chief Inspector Schmied had not even been consulted about the matter. He had received a telephone call from the most powerful political leader in Switzerland, had been given his instructions, and there the matter had ended. Or, to be more accurate, there it had begun. For the chief inspector, it was the beginning of a Gethsemane that showed no sign of ending. He had honestly tried to get over his resentment at having a detective – an inexperienced and unqualified one at that – forced upon him. He assumed that there had to be some strong political motivation for such an unheard of move. Very well, he was determined to cooperate, confident that he could handle the situation easily. His confidence was shaken the moment Max Hornung reported to him. The detective's appearance was ridiculous enough. But what stunned Inspector Schmied as he looked at this lump of humanity was the man's attitude of superiority. He exuded an air that said: Max Hornung is here – now you can all relax and stop worrying.

Inspector Schmied's thoughts of any easy cooperation vanished. Instead he devised another approach. He tried to sweep Max Hornung under the rug, as it were, by transferring him from department to department, assigning him unimportant jobs. Max worked in the Kriminal-Tech Abteilung, the fingerprint and identification division, and the Fahndungsabteilung, the division for stolen property and missing persons. But always Max Hornung kept returning, like a bad centime.

There was a rule that every detective had to work as Brandtour Offizier, on the night emergency desk, one week out of every twelve. Without fail, each time Max was on duty, something important would occur, and while Inspector Schmied's other detectives ran around trying to track down clues, Max would solve the case. It was infuriating.

He knew absolutely nothing about police procedure, criminology, forensics, ballistics, or criminal psychology – all the things that the other detectives were experienced in – and yet he kept solving cases that baffled everyone else. Chief Inspector Schmied came to the conclusion that Max Hornung was the luckiest man who ever lived.

In reality, luck had nothing to do with it. Detective Max Hornung solved criminal cases in exactly the same way that accountant Max Hornung had exposed a hundred ingenious schemes to defraud banks and the government. Max Hornung had a single-track mind, and it was a very narrow-gauge track at that. All he needed was one loose thread, one tiny piece that did not fit into the rest of the fabric, and once he had that he would begin to unravel it, until somebody's brilliant, foolproof scheme fell apart at the seams.

The fact that Max had a photographic memory drove his colleagues crazy. Max could instantly recall anything he had ever heard, read or seen.

Another mark against him, if indeed one was needed, was that his expense accounts were an embarrassment to the entire detective squadron. The first time he had turned in an expense sheet, the Oberleutnant had summoned him to his office and said genially, "You've obviously made a mistake in your figures here, Max."

The equivalent of informing Capablanca that he had sacrificed his queen through stupidity.

Max blinked. "A mistake in my figures?"

"Yes. Several, in fact." The Oberleutnant pointed to the paper in front of him. "Transportation across town, eighty centimes. Return, eighty centimes." He looked up and said, "The minimum taxi fare would be thirty-four francs each way."

"Yes, sir. That's why I used the bus."

The Oberleutnant stared at him. "A *bus?*"

None of the detectives was required to ride buses while on a case. It was unheard of. The only reply he could think of was, "Well, it's – it's not necessary. I mean – we naturally don't encourage spendthrifts in this department, Hornung, but we do have a decent expense budget. Another thing. You were out in the field on this case for three days. You forgot to include meals."

"No, Herr Oberleutnant. I only take coffee in the morning and I prepare my own lunches and carry a lunch bag. My dinners are listed there."

And so they were. Three dinners, total: sixteen francs. He must have eaten at the Salvation Army kitchen.

The Oberleutnant said coldly, "Detective Hornung, this department existed for a hundred years before you joined it, and it will exist for a hundred years after you leave it. There are certain traditions that we observe here." He shoved the expense account back to Max. "You must think about your colleagues, you know. Now take this, revise it, and return it."

"Yes, Herr Oberleutnant. I – I'm sorry if I did it incorrectly."

A generous wave of the hand. "Quite all right. After all, you're new here."

Thirty minutes later Detective Max Hornung turned in his revised account. He had decreased his expenses by another three per cent.

Now, on this day in November, Chief Inspector Schmied was holding Detective Max Hornung's report in his hand while the author of the report stood before him. Detective Hornung was wearing a bright blue suit, brown shoes and white socks. In spite of his resolves, and the calming yoga breathing exercises, Inspector Schmied found himself yelling. "You were in charge here when that report came in. It was *your* job to investigate the accident and you arrived on the scene *fourteen hours later!* The whole fucking New Zealand police force could have been flown here and been back home in that time."

"Oh, no, sir. The flying time from New Zealand to Zurich by jet is – "

"Oh, shut up!"

Chief Inspector Schmied ran his hands through his thick, rapidly greying hair, trying to think what to say to this man. You could not insult him, you could not reason with him. He was an idiot, shot with luck.

Chief Inspector Schmied barked, "I will not tolerate incompetence in my department, Hornung. When the other detectives came on duty and saw the report, they immediately went to the scene to inspect the accident. They called an ambulance, had the body taken to the morgue, identified it – " He knew he was talking too fast again, and he forced himself to calm down. "In short, Hornung, they did everything a good detective is supposed to do. While you were sitting in your office waking up half of the most important men in Switzerland, in the middle of the night."

"I thought – "

"Don't! I've been on the phone apologizing the whole damned morning because of you."

"I had to find out – "

"Oh, get out of here, Hornung!"

"Yes, sir. Is it all right if I attend the funeral? It's this morning."

"Yes! Go!"

"Thank you, sir. I – "

"Just go!"

It was thirty minutes before Chief Inspector Schmied was breathing normally again.

32

The funeral parlour at Sihlfeld was crowded. It was an ornate, old-fashioned building of stone and marble, with preparation rooms and a crematorium. Inside the large chapel two dozen executives and employees of Roffe and Sons occupied the front row of seats. Towards the rear were the friends, the community representatives and the press. Detective Hornung was seated in the last row, thinking that death was illogical. Man reached his prime and then, when he had the most to give, the most to live for, he died. It was inefficient.

The coffin was mahogany and covered with flowers. More waste, Detective Hornung thought. The coffin had been ordered sealed. Max could understand why. The minister was speaking in a doomsday voice, " . . . death in the midst of life, born in sin, ashes to ashes." Max Hornung paid little attention. He was studying those in the chapel.

"The Lord giveth, and the Lord taketh away," and people were beginning to stand and head for the exit. The service was over.

Max stood near the door, and as a man and a woman approached him he stepped in front of the woman and said, "Miss Elizabeth Roffe? I wonder if I might have a word with you?"

Detective Max Hornung was seated with Elizabeth Roffe and Rhys Williams in a booth at a Konditorei across from the funeral parlour. Through the window they could see the coffin being loaded into a grey hearse. Elizabeth looked away. Her eyes were haunted.

"What's this all about?" Rhys demanded. "Miss Roffe has already given her statement to the police."

Detective Max Hornung said, "Mr Williams, isn't it? There are just a few little details I want to check out."

"Can't they wait? Miss Roffe has been through a very trying – "

Elizabeth put her hand on Rhys's. "It's all right. If I can be of any help – " She turned to Max. "What would you like to know, Detective Hornung?"

Max stared at Elizabeth, and for the first time in his life he was at a loss for words. Women were as foreign to Max as creatures from an alien planet. They were illogical and unpredictable, subject to emotional reactions rather than rational ones. They did not compute. Max had few sexual stirrings, for he was mind-oriented, but he could appreciate the precise logic of sex. It was the mechanical construction of moving parts fitting together into a coordinated, functioning whole that excited him. That, for Max, was the poetry of loving. The sheer dynamics of it. Max felt that the poets had all missed the point. Emotions were imprecise and untidy, a waste of energy that could not move the smallest grain of sand one inch, while logic could move the world. What was puzzling Max now was that he felt comfortable with Elizabeth. It made him uneasy. No woman had ever affected him that way before. She did not seem to think he was an ugly, ridiculous little man, the way other women did. He forced himself to look away from her eyes so that he could concentrate.

"Were you in the habit of working late at night, Miss Roffe?"

"Very often. Elizabeth said. "Yes."

"How late?"

"It varied. Sometimes until ten. Sometimes until midnight, or after."

"So it was a kind of pattern? That is, people around you would have known about it?"

She was studying him, puzzled. "I suppose so."

"On the night the lift crashed, you and Mr Williams and Kate Erling were all working late?"

"Yes."

"But you didn't leave together?"

Rhys said, "I left early. I had an engagement."

Max regarded him a moment, then turned back to Elizabeth. "How long after Mr Williams left did you leave?"

"I think it was about an hour."

"Did you and Kate Erling leave together?"

"Yes. We got our coats and went out into the hall." Elizabeth's voice faltered. "The – the lift was there, waiting for us."

The special express lift.

"What happened then?"

"We both got in. The telephone in the office rang. Kate – Miss Erling – said,

'I'll answer it,' and she started to get out. But I was expecting an overseas call I had placed earlier, so I told her I would answer it." Elizabeth stopped, her eyes brimming with tears. "I got out of the lift. She asked if she should wait, and I said, 'No, go ahead.' She pressed the lobby button. I started back to the office, and as I was opening the door, I heard – I heard the screaming, then – " She was unable to go on.

Rhys turned to Max Hornung, his face clouded with anger. "That's enough. Will you tell us what this is all about?"

It was about murder, Max thought. Someone had tried to kill Elizabeth Roffe. Max sat there concentrating, recalling everything he had learned in the past forty-eight hours about Roffe and Sons. It was a deeply plagued company, forced to pay astronomical damages in lawsuits, swamped by bad publicity, losing customers, owing enormous sums of money to banks that had grown impatient. A company ripe for a change. Its president, Sam Roffe, who had held the controlling vote, had died. An expert mountain climber who had been killed in a climbing accident. The controlling stock had gone to his daughter, Elizabeth, who had almost died in a jeep accident in Sardinia, and had narrowly missed being killed in a lift that had passed a recent inspection. Someone was playing deadly games.

Detective Max Hornung should have been a happy man. He had found a loose thread. But now he had met Elizabeth Roffe, and she was no longer simply a name, an equation in a mathematical puzzle. There was something very special about her. Max felt an urge to shield her, to protect her.

Rhys said, "I asked what this – "

Max looked at him and said vaguely, "Er – police procedure, Mr Williams. Just routine." He rose. "Excuse me."

He had some urgent work to do.

33

Chief Inspector Schmied had had a full morning. There had been a political demonstration in front of Iberia Air Lines, three men detained for questioning. A fire of suspicious origin at a paper factory in Brunau. It was being investigated. A girl had been raped in Platzspitz Park. A smash-and-grab job at Guebelin and another at Grima, next to the Baur-au-Lac. And if that weren't enough, Detective Max Hornung was back, filled with some kind of nonsensical theory. Chief Inspector Schmied found himself starting to hyperventilate again.

"The lift cable drum was cracked," Max was saying. "When it collapsed, all the safety controls went out. Someone – "

"I saw the reports, Hornung. Normal wear and tear."

"No, Chief Inspector. I examined the specifications for the cable drum. It should have lasted another five or six years."

Chief Inspector Schmied felt the tic in his cheek. "What are you trying to say?"

"Someone tampered with the lift."

Not, I think someone tampered with the lift, or, In my opinion someone tampered with the lift. Oh, no! Someone tampered with the lift.

"Why would they do that?"

"That's what I would like to find out."

"You want to go back to Roffe and Sons?"

Detective Max Hornung looked at Inspector Schmied in genuine surprise. "No, sir. I want to go to Chamonix."

The town of Chamonix lies forty miles south-east of Geneva, 3400 feet above sea level in the French department of Haute-Savoie, between the Mont Blanc massif and the Aiguille Rouge range, with one of the most breathtaking vistas in the world.

Detective Max Hornung was completely unaware of the scenery as he debouched from the train at the Chamonix station, carrying a battered cardboard suitcase. He waved a taxi away and headed on foot for the local police station, a small building situated on the main square in the centre of town. Max entered, feeling instantly at home, revelling in the warm camaraderie that he shared with the fraternity of policemen all over the world. He was one of *them.*

The French sergeant behind the desk looked up and asked, "*Est-ce qu'on peut vous aider?*"

"*Oui.*" Max beamed. And he started to talk. Max approached all foreign languages in the same fashion: he slashed his way through the impenetrable thicket of irregular verbs and tenses and participles, using his tongue like a machete. As he spoke, the expression on the desk sergeant's face changed from puzzlement to disbelief. It had taken the French people hundreds of years to develop their tongues and soft palates and larynxes to form the glorious music that was the French language. And now this man standing before him was somehow managing to turn it into a series of horrible incomprehensible noises.

The desk sergeant could bear no more. He interrupted. "What – what are you trying to *say?*"

Max replied, "What do you mean? I'm speaking French."

The desk sergeant leaned forward and asked with unabashed curiosity, "Are you speaking it *now?*"

The fool doesn't even speak his own language, Max thought. He pulled out his warrant card and handed it to the sergeant. The sergeant read it through twice, looked up to study Max, and then read it again. It was impossible to believe that the man standing before him was a detective.

Reluctantly he handed the identification back to Max. "What can I do for you?"

"I'm investigating a climbing accident that happened here two months ago. The victim's name was Sam Roffe."

The sergeant nodded. "Yes, I remember."

"I would like to talk to someone who can give me some information about what happened."

"That would be the mountain-rescue organization. It is called the Société Chamoniarde de Secours en Montagne. You will find it in Place du Mont Blanc. The telephone number is five-three-one-six-eight-nine. Or they might have some information at the clinic. That's in Rue du Valais. The telephone number there is five-three-zero-one-eight-two. Here. I'll write all this down for you." He reached for a pen.

"That won't be necessary," Max said, "Société Chamoniarde de Secours en Montagne, Place du Mont Blanc, five-three-one-six-eight-nine. Or the clinic in Rue du Valais, five-three-zero-one-eight-two."

The sergeant was still staring long after Max had disappeared through the door.

The Société Chamoniarde de Secours was in the charge of a dark, athletic-looking young man seated behind a battered pine desk. He looked up as Max walked in, and his instant thought was that he hoped this odd-looking visitor did not plan to climb a mountain.

"Can I help you?"

"Detective Max Hornung." He showed his warrant card.

"What can I do for you, Detective Hornung?"

"I am investigating the death of a man named Sam Roffe," Max said.

The man behind the desk sighed. "Ah, yes. I liked Mr Roffe very much. It was an unfortunate accident."

"Did you see it happen?"

A shake of the head. "No. I took my rescue team up as soon as we received their distress signal, but there was nothing we could do. Mr Roffe's body had fallen into a crevasse. It will never be found."

"How did it happen?"

"There were four climbers in the party. The guide and Mr Roffe were last. As I understand it, they were traversing an icy moraine. Mr Roffe slipped and fell."

"Wasn't he wearing a harness?"

"Of course. His rope broke."

"Does a thing like that happen often?"

"Only once." He smiled at his little joke, then saw the detective's look and added quickly. "Experienced climbers always check their equipment thoroughly, but accidents still happen."

Max stood there a moment, thinking. "I'd like to speak to the guide."

"Mr Roffe's regular guide didn't make the climb that day."

Max blinked, "Oh? Why not?"

"As I recall, he was ill. Another guide took his place."

"Do you have his name?"

"If you'll wait a minute, I can look it up for you." The man disappeared into an inner office. In a few minutes he returned with a slip of paper in his hand. "The guide's name was Hans Bergmann."

"Where can I find him?"

"He's not a local." He consulted the piece of paper. "He comes from a village called Lesgets. It's about sixty kilometres from here."

Before Max left Chamonix, he stopped at the desk of the Kleine Scheidegg hotel and talked to the room clerk. "Were you on duty when Mr Roffe was staying here?"

"Yes," the clerk said. "The accident was a terrible thing, terrible."

"Mr Roffe was alone here?"

The clerk shook his head. "No. He had a friend with him."

Max stared. "A friend?"

"Yes. Mr Roffe made the reservation for both of them."

"Could you give me the name of his friend?"

"Certainly," the clerk said. He pulled out a large ledger from beneath the desk and began to turn back the pages. He stopped, ran his finger down a page and said, "Ah, here we are . . ."

It took almost three hours for Max to drive to Lesgets in a Volkswagen, the cheapest rental car he could find, and he almost passed through it. It was not even a village. The place consisted of a few shops, a small alpine lodge, and a general store with a single petrol pump in front of it.

Max parked in front of the lodge and walked in. There were half a dozen men seated in front of an open fireplace, talking. The conversation trailed off as Max entered.

"Excuse me," he said, "I'm looking for Herr Hans Bergmann."

"Who?"

"Hans Bergmann. The guide. He comes from this village."

An elderly man with a face that was a weather map of his years spat into the fireplace and said, "Somebody's been kidding you, mister. I was born in Lesgets. I never heard of any Hans Bergmann."

34

It was the first day that Elizabeth had gone to the office since the death of Kate Erling a week earlier. Elizabeth entered the downstairs lobby with trepidation, responding mechanically to the greetings of the doorman and guards. At the far end of the lobby she saw workmen replacing the smashed lift car. She thought about Kate Erling, and Elizabeth could visualize the terror she must have felt as she plunged twelve interminable storeys to her death. She knew that she could never ride in that lift again.

When she walked into her office, her mail had already been opened by Henriette, the second secretary, and neatly placed on her desk. Elizabeth went through it quickly, initialling some memos, writing questions on others, or marking them for various department heads. At the bottom of the pile was a large sealed envelope marked "Elizabeth Roffe – Personal". Elizabeth took a letter-opener and slit the envelope across the top. She reached in and took out an 8–by-10 photograph. It was a close-up of a mongoloid child, its bulging eyes staring out of its encephalic head. Attached to the picture was a note printed in crayon: THIS IS MY BEAUTIFUL SON JOHN. YOUR DRUGS DID THIS TO HIM. I AM GOING TO KILL YOU.

Elizabeth dropped the note and the picture, and found that her hands were trembling. Henriette walked in with a handful of papers.

"These are ready to be signed, Miss – " She saw the look on Elizabeth's face. "Is something wrong?"

Elizabeth said, "Please – ask Mr Williams to come in here." Her eyes went back to the picture on her desk.

Roffe and Sons could not be responsible for anything so dreadful.

"It was our fault," Rhys said. "A shipment of drugs was mislabelled. We managed to recall most of it, but – " He raised his hands expressively.

"How long ago did this happen?"

"Almost four years ago."

"How many people were affected?"

"About a hundred." He saw the expression on her face and added quickly, "They received compensation. They weren't all like this, Liz. Look, we're damned careful here. We take every safety precaution we can devise, but people are human. Mistakes are sometimes made."

Elizabeth sat staring at the picture of the child. "It's horrible."

"They shouldn't have shown you the letter." Rhys ran his fingers through his thick black hair and said, "This is a hell of a time to bring it up, but we have a few other problems more important than this."

She wondered what could be more important. "Yes?"

"The FDA just gave a decision against us on our aerosol sprays. There's going to be a complete ban on aerosols within two years."

"How will that affect us?"

"It's going to hurt us badly. It means we'll have to close down half a dozen factories around the world and lose one of our most profitable divisions."

Elizabeth thought about Emil Joeppli and the culture he was working on, but she said nothing. "What else?"

"Have you seen the morning papers?"

"No."

"A government minister's wife in Belgium, Mme van den Logh, took some Benexan."

"That's one of our drugs?"

"Yes. It's an antihistamine. It's contra-indicated for anyone with essential hypertension. Our label carries a clear warning. She ignored it."

Elizabeth felt her body beginning to tense. "What happened to her?"

Rhys said, "She's in a coma. She may not live. The newspaper stories mention that it's our product. Cancellations on orders are pouring in from all over the world. The FDA notified us that it's starting an investigation, but that will take at least a year. Until they finish, we can keep selling the drug."

Elizabeth said, "I want it taken off the market."

"There's no reason to do that. It's a damned effective drug for – "

"Have any other people been hurt by it?"

"Hundreds of thousands of people have been helped by it." Rhys's tone was cool. "It's one of our most effective – "

"You haven't answered my question."

"A few isolated cases, I suppose, yes. But – "

"I want it taken off the market. Now."

He sat there, fighting his anger, then he said, "Right. Would you like to know what that will cost the company?"

"No," Elizabeth said.

Rhys nodded. "So far you've only heard the good news. The bad news is that the bankers want a meeting with you. Now. They're calling in their loans."

Elizabeth sat in her office alone, thinking about the mongoloid child, and about the woman who lay in a coma because of a drug that Roffe and Sons had sold her. Elizabeth was well aware that these kinds of tragedies involved other pharmaceutical firms as well as Roffe and Sons. There were almost daily stories in the newspapers about similar cases, but they had not touched her as this had. She felt responsible. She was determined to have a talk with the department heads who were in charge of safety measures to see if they could not be improved.

This is my beautiful son John.

Mme van den Logh is in a coma. She may not live.

The bankers want a meeting with you. Now. They've decided to call in their loans.

She felt choked, as though everything was beginning to close in on her at once. For the first time Elizabeth wondered if she was going to be able to cope. The burdens were too heavy, and they were piling up too fast. She swung round in her chair to look up at the portrait of old Samuel hanging on the wall. He looked so competent, so sure. But she knew about his doubts and uncertainties, and his black despairs. Yet he had come through. She would survive somehow, too. She was a Roffe.

She noticed that the portrait was askew. Probably as a result of the lift crash. Elizabeth got up to straighten it. As she tilted the picture, the hook holding it gave way, and the painting crashed to the floor. Elizabeth did not even look at it. She was staring at the place where the painting had hung. Taped to the wall was a tiny microphone.

It was 4 a.m., and Emil Joeppli was working late again. It had become a habit of his recently. Even though Elizabeth Roffe had not given him a specific deadline, Joeppli knew how important this project was to the company and he was pushing to get it finished as quickly as possible. He had heard disturbing rumours about Roffe and Sons lately. He wanted to do everything he could to help the company. It had been good to him. It gave him a handsome salary and complete freedom. He had liked Sam Roffe, and he liked his daughter too. Elizabeth Roffe would never know, but these late hours were Joeppli's gift to her. He was hunched over his small desk, checking out the results of his last experiment. They were even better than he had anticipated. He sat there, deep in concentration, unaware of the foetid smell of the caged animals in the laboratory or the cloying humidity of the room or the lateness of the hour. The door opened, and the guard on the graveyard shift, Sepp Nolan, walked in. Nolan hated this shift. There was something eerie about the deserted experimental laboratories at night. The smell of the caged animals made him ill. Nolan wondered whether all the animals they had killed here had souls and came back to haunt these corridors. I ought to put in for spook pay, he thought. Everyone in the building had long since gone home. Except for this fucking mad scientist with his cages full of rabbits and cats and hamsters.

"How long you gonna be, Doc?" Nolan asked.

Joeppli looked up, aware of Nolan for the first time. "What?"

"If you're gonna be here awhile, I can bring you back a sandwich or something. I'm gonna run over to the commissary for a quick bite."

Joeppli said, "Just coffee, please." He turned back to his charts.

Nolan said, "I'll lock the outside door behind me when I leave the building. Be right back."

Joeppli did not even hear him.

Ten minutes later the door to the laboratory opened, and a voice said, "You're working late, Emil."

Joeppli looked up, startled. When he saw who it was, he got to his feet, flustered, and said, "Yes, sir." He felt flattered that this man had dropped in to see him.

The Fountain of Youth project, top secret, eh?"

Emil hesitated. Miss Roffe had said no one was supposed to know about it. But, of course, that did not include his visitor. It was this man who had brought him into the company. So Emil Joeppli smiled and said, "Yes, sir. Top secret."

"Good. Let's keep it that way. How is it going?"

"Wonderfully, sir."

The visitor wandered over to one of the rabbit cages. Emil Joeppli followed him. "Is there anything I can explain to you?"

The man smiled. "No, I'm pretty familiar with it, Emil." As the visitor started to turn away, he brushed against an empty feeding dish on the ledge and it fell to the floor. "Sorry."

"Don't worry about it, sir. I'll get it." Emil Joeppli reached down to pick it up and the back of his head seemed to explode in a shower of red, and the last thing he saw was the floor racing up to meet him.

The insistent ringing of the telephone awakened Elizabeth. She sat up in bed, heavy with sleep, and looked at the digital clock on the little table. Five a.m. She fumbled the telephone off the hook. A frantic voice said, "Miss Roffe? This is the security guard at the plant. There's been an explosion at one of the laboratories. It was completely destroyed."

Instantly she was wide awake. "Was anybody hurt?" "Yes, ma'am. One of the scientists was burned to death."

He did not have to tell Elizabeth the name.

35

Detective Max Hornung was thinking. The detective bureau was filled with the noise of typewriters clattering, voices raised in argument, telephones ringing, but Hornung saw and heard nothing of these things. He had the single-minded concentration of a computer. He was thinking about the charter of Roffe and Sons, as old Samuel had set it up, keeping control within the family. Ingenious, Max thought. And dangerous. It reminded him of the tontine, the Italian insurance plan devised by the banker Lorenzo Tonti in 1695. Every member of the tontine put in an equal amount of money, and as each member died, the survivors inherited his share. It provided a powerful motive to eliminate the other members. Like Roffe and Sons. It was too much of a temptation to let people inherit stock worth millions, and then tell them they could not sell it unless everyone agreed.

Max had learned that Sam Roffe had not agreed. He was dead. Elizabeth Roffe had not agreed. She had narrowly escaped death twice. Too many accidents. Detective Max Hornung did not believe in accidents. He went to see Chief Inspector Schmied.

The chief inspector listened to Max Hornung's report on Sam Roffe's climbing accident and growled, "So there's been a mix-up about the name of a guide. That hardly constitutes a case for murder, Hornung. Not in *my* department, it doesn't."

The little detective said patiently, "I think there's more to it. Roffe and Sons is having big internal problems. Perhaps someone thought that getting rid of Sam Roffe would solve them."

Chief Inspector Schmied sat back and eyed Detective Hornung. He was certain that there was nothing to his theories. But the idea of having Detective Max Hornung out of sight for a while filled Chief Inspector Schmied with a deep pleasure. His absence would be a boost to the morale of the entire department. And there was something else to consider: The people Max Hornung wanted to investigate. No less than the powerful Roffe family. Ordinarily, Schmied would have ordered Max Hornung to keep a million miles away from them. If Detective Hornung irritated them – and how could he not! – they had enough power to have him thrown out of the force. And no one could blame Chief Inspector Schmied. Hadn't the little detective been forced on him? And so he said to Max Hornung, "The case is yours. Take your time."

"Thank you," Max said happily.

As Max was walking through the corridor towards his office, he ran into the coroner. "Hornung! Can I borrow your memory for a minute?"

Max blinked. "I beg your pardon?"

"The river patrol has just fished a girl out of the river. Will you take a look at her?"

Max swallowed and said, "If you wish."

This was not a part of the job that Max enjoyed, but he felt that it was his duty.

She lay in the impersonal metal drawer in the chill of the morgue. She had blonde hair and was in her late teens or early twenties. Her body was bloated from the water, and naked, except for a red ribbon knotted around her neck.

"There are signs of sexual intercourse just before death. She was strangled and then dumped into the river," the coroner said. "There's no water in her lungs. We can't get any fingerprints on her. Ever seen her before?"

Detective Max Hornung looked down at the girl's face and said, "No."

He left to catch his bus to the airport.

36

When Detective Max Hornung landed at the Costa Smeralda airport in Sardinia, he rented the cheapest car available, a Fiat 500, and drove into Olbia. Unlike the rest of Sardinia, Olbia was an industrial city, and the outskirts were an ugly sprawl of mills and factories, a city dump and a giant graveyard of once-beautiful automobiles, now useless old hulks, good only for scrap. Every city in the world had its automobile junkyards, Max thought. Monuments to civilization.

Max reached the centre of town and drove up in front of a building with a sign that read: "QUESTURA DI SASSARI COMMISSARIATO DI POLIZIA OLBIA." The moment Max entered, he felt that familiar sense of identity, of belonging. He showed his warrant card to the desk sergeant, and a few minutes later he was ushered into the office of the Chief of Police, Luigi Ferraro. Ferraro rose to his feet, a welcoming smile on his face. It died as he saw his visitor. There was something about Max that did not spell "detective".

"Could I see your identification?" Chief Ferraro asked politely.

"Certainly," Max said. He pulled out his warrant card and Chief Ferraro examined both sides of it carefully, then returned it. His immediate conclusion was that Switzerland must be very hard up for detectives. He took a seat behind his desk and said, "What can I do for you?"

Max started to explain, in fluent Italian. The problem was that it took Chief Ferraro some moments to figure out what language Max was speaking. When he realized what it was supposed to be, he held up a horrified hand and said, "*Basta!* Do you speak English?"

"Of course," Max replied.

"Then I beg of you! Let us speak in English."

When Max was through talking, Chief Ferraro said, "You are mistaken, signore. I can tell you that you are wasting your time. My mechanics have already examined the jeep. Everyone is agreed that it was an accident."

Max nodded, unperturbed. "*I* haven't looked at it."

Chief Ferraro said, "Very well. It is in a public garage now, up for sale. I will have one of my men take you there. Would you like to see the scene of the accident?"

Max blinked and said, "What for?"

Detective Bruno Campagna was elected as Max's escort. "We've already checked it out. It was an accident," Campagna said.

"No," Max replied.

The jeep was in a corner of the garage, its front still dented and splashed with dried green sap.

"I haven't had time to work on it yet," the mechanic explained.

Max walked around the jeep, examining it. "How were the brakes tampered with?" he asked.

The mechanic said, "*Gesù!* You, too?" A note of irritation crept into his voice. "I have been a mechanic for twenty-five years, signore. I examined this jeep myself. The last time anyone touched these brakes was when this car left the factory."

"Someone tampered with them," Max said.

"How?" The mechanic was spluttering.

"I don't know yet, but I will," Max assured him confidently. He took a last look at the jeep, then turned and walked out of the garage.

Chief of Police Luigi Ferraro looked at Detective Bruno Campagna and demanded, "What did you *do* with him?"

"I didn't do anything. I took him to the garage, he made an ass of himself with the mechanic, then he said he wanted to go for a stroll by himself."

"*Incredibile!*"

Max was standing on the shore, staring out at the emerald Tyrrhenian waters, seeing nothing. He was concentrating, his mind busily putting the pieces together. It was like working on a giant jigsaw puzzle. Everything always went neatly into place when you knew where it fitted. The jeep was a small but important part of the puzzle. Its brakes had been examined by expert mechanics. Max had no reason to doubt either their honesty or competence. He therefore accepted the fact that the brakes of the jeep had not been tampered with. Because Elizabeth had been driving the jeep and someone wanted her dead, he also accepted the fact that they *had* been tampered with. There was no way it could have been done. Yet someone had done it. Max was up against someone clever. It made things more interesting.

Max stepped out on to the sandy beach, sat down on a large rock, closed his eyes and began to concentrate again, focusing on the pieces, shifting, dissecting, rearranging the bits of the puzzle.

Twenty minutes later the last piece clicked into place. Max's eyes flew open and he thought admiringly, Bravo! I must meet the man who thought of this.

After that, Detective Max Hornung had two stops to make, the first just outside Olbia and the second in the mountains. He caught the late afternoon plane back to Zurich.

Economy class.

37

The head of the security forces of Roffe and Sons said to Elizabeth, "It all happened too fast, Miss Roffe. There was nothing we could do. By the time the fire-fighting equipment got into action, the whole laboratory was gone."

They had found the remains of Emil Joeppli's charred body. There was no way of knowing whether his formula had been removed from the laboratory before the explosion.

Elizabeth asked, "The Development Building was under twenty-four-hour guard, was it not?"

"Yes, ma' am. We – "

"How long have you been in charge of our security department?"

"Five years. I – "

"You're fired."

He started to say something in protest, then changed his mind. "Yes, ma'am."

"How many men are there on your staff?"

"Sixty-five."

Sixty-five! And they could not save Emil Joeppli. "I'm giving them twenty-four hours' notice," Elizabeth said. "I want them all out of here."

He looked at her a moment. "Miss Roffe, do you think you're being fair?"

She thought of Emil Joeppli, and the priceless formula that had been stolen, and of the bug that had been planted in her office that she had ground under the heel of her shoe.

"Get out," Elizabeth said.

She filled every minute that morning, trying to wipe out the vision of the charred body of Emil Joeppli and his laboratory full of burned animals. She tried not to think about what the loss of that formula was going to cost the company. There was a chance a rival company might patent it and there was nothing Elizabeth could do about it. It *was* a jungle. When your competitors thought you were weak, they moved in for the kill. But this wasn't a competitor doing this. This was a friend. A deadly friend.

Elizabeth arranged for a professional security force to take over immediately. She would feel safer with strangers around her.

She phoned the Hôpital Internationale in Brussels to check on the condition of Mme van den Logh, the wife of the Belgian minister. They reported that she was still in a coma. They did not know whether she would live.

Elizabeth was thinking about Emil Joeppli and the mongoloid child and the minister's wife when Rhys walked in. He looked at her face and said gently, "As bad as that?"

She nodded, miserably.

Rhys walked over to her and studied her. She looked tired, drained. He wondered how much more she could stand. He took her hands in his and asked gently, "Is there anything I can do to help?"

Everything, Elizabeth thought. She needed Rhys desperately. She needed his strength and his help and his love. Their eyes met and she was ready to go into his arms, to tell him everything that had happened, that was happening.

Rhys said, "There's nothing new on Mme van den Logh?"

And the moment had passed.

"No," Elizabeth said.

He asked, "Have you had any calls yet on the *Wall Street Journal* story?"

"What story?"

"You haven't seen it?"

"No."

Rhys sent to his office for a copy. The article enumerated all the recent troubles of Roffe and Sons, but the major theme of the story was that the company needed someone experienced to run it. Elizabeth put the newspaper down. "How much damage will this do?"

Rhys shrugged. "The damage has already been done. They're just reporting it. We're beginning to lose a lot of our markets. We – "

The intercom buzzed. Elizabeth pressed the switch. "Yes?"

"Herr Julius Badrutt is on line two, Miss Roffe. He says it's urgent."

Elizabeth looked up at Rhys. She had been postponing the meeting with the bankers. "Put him on." She picked up the phone. "Good morning, Herr Badrutt."

"Good morning." Over the phone his voice sounded dry and brittle. "Are you free this afternoon?"

"Well, I'm – "

"Fine. Will four o'clock be satisfactory?"

Elizabeth hesitated. "Yes. Four o'clock."

There was a dry, rustling sound over the phone and Elizabeth realized that Herr Badrutt was clearing his throat. "I was sorry to hear about Mr Joeppli," he said.

Joeppli's name had not been mentioned in the newspaper accounts of the explosion.

She hung up slowly, and found that Rhys was watching her.

"The sharks smell blood," Rhys said.

The afternoon was filled with phone calls. Alec telephoned. "Elizabeth, did you see the story in the newspaper this morning?"

"Yes," Elizabeth said. "*The Wall Street Journal* was exaggerating."

There was a pause, and then Alec said, "I'm not talking about *The Wall Street Journal*. The *Financial Times* has a headline story on Roffe and Sons. It's not good. My phones haven't stopped ringing. We're getting heavy cancellations. What are we going to do?"

"I'll get back to you, Alec," Elizabeth promised.

Ivo called. "*Carissima*, I think you'd better prepare yourself for a shock."

I'm prepared, Elizabeth thought wryly. "What is it?"

Ivo said, "An Italian minister was arrested a few hours ago for accepting bribes."

Elizabeth had a sudden feeling of what was coming. "Go on."

There was a note of apology in Ivo's voice. "It wasn't our fault," Ivo said. "He got greedy and he was careless. They caught him at the airport, trying to smuggle money out of Italy. They've traced the money to us."

Even though Elizabeth was prepared for it, she still felt a shock of disbelief. "Why were we bribing him?"

Ivo said matter-of-factly, "So that we could do business in Italy. It's a way of life here. Our crime was not in bribing the minister, *cara* – it was in getting caught."

She sat back in her chair, her head beginning to pound.

"What happens now?"

"I would suggest that we meet with the company attorney as quickly as possible," Ivo said. "Don't worry. Only the poor go to jail in Italy."

Charles called from Paris, his voice frantic with worry. The French press was full of Roffe and Sons. Charles urged Elizabeth to sell the company while it still had a reputation.

"Our customers are losing faith," Charles said. "Without that, there is no company."

Elizabeth thought about the phone calls, the bankers, her cousins, the press. Too much was happening too quickly. Someone was making it happen. She *had* to find out who.

The name was still in Elizabeth's private telephone book. Maria Martinelli. It brought back long-ago memories of the tall, leggy Italian girl who had been a classmate of Elizabeth's in Switzerland. They had corresponded from time to time. Maria had become a model and she had written to Elizabeth that she was engaged to marry an Italian newspaper publisher in Milan. It took Elizabeth fifteen minutes to reach Maria. When the social amenities had been disposed of, Elizabeth said into the phone, "Are you still engaged to that newspaper publisher?"

"Of course. The minute Tony gets his divorce, we're going to be married."

"I want you to do me a favour, Maria."

"Name it."

Less than one hour later Maria Martinelli called back. "I got that information you wanted. The banker who was caught trying to smuggle money out of Italy was set up. Tony says a man tipped off the border police."

"Was he able to find out the name of the man?"

"Ivo Palazzi."

Detective Max Hornung had made an interesting discovery. He had learned that not only was the explosion at the Roffe and Sons laboratory arranged deliberately, but that it had been caused by an explosive called Rylar X, made exclusively for the military, and not available to anyone else. What intrigued Max was that Rylar X was manufactured at one of the factories of Roffe and Sons. It took Max only one telephone call to learn which one.

The factory outside Paris.

At exactly 4 p.m. Herr Julius Badrutt lowered his angular figure into a chair and said without preamble, "As much as we would like to accommodate you, Miss Roffe, I am afraid our responsibility towards our stockholders must take precedence."

It was the kind of statement, Elizabeth thought, that bankers made to widows and orphans before they foreclosed their mortgages. But this time she was ready for Herr Badrutt.

"My board of directors has therefore instructed me to inform you that our bank is calling in the notes on Roffe and Sons immediately."

"I was told I had ninety days," Elizabeth said.

"Unfortunately, we feel that the circumstances have changed for the worse. I should also inform you that the other banks you are dealing with have reached the same decision."

With the banks refusing to help her, there would be no way to keep the company private.

"I'm sorry to bring you such bad news, Miss Roffe, but I felt that I should tell you personally."

"You know, of course, that Roffe and Sons is still a very strong and healthy company."

Herr Julius Badrutt nodded his head, once. "Of course. It's a great company."

"Yet you won't give us more time."

Herr Badrutt looked at her for a moment, then said, "The bank thinks your problems are manageable, Miss Roffe. But . . ." He hesitated.

"But you don't think there's anyone to manage them?"

"I'm afraid that is correct." He started to rise.

"What if someone else were president of Roffe and Sons?" Elizabeth asked.

He shook his head. "We have discussed that possibility. We don't feel that any of the present members of the board have the overall ability to cope with – "

She said, "I was thinking of Rhys Williams."

38

Constable Thomas Hiller of the Thames Marine Police Division was in terrible shape. He was sleepy, hungry, horny and wet; and he could not decide which was the greatest of his miseries.

He was sleepy because his fiancée, Flo, had kept him awake all night, fighting; he was hungry because by the time she was through screaming at him, he was late for duty, and he had had no time to pick up a bite; he was horny because she had refused to let him touch her, and he was wet because the thirty-foot police boat on which he was travelling had been built for service, not comfort, and a rising wind was driving the rain into the small wheelhouse where he stood. On days like this there was bloody little to see and even bloody less to do. The Thames Division covered fifty-four miles of river from Dartford Creek to Staines Bridge, and ordinarily Constable Hiller enjoyed patrol duty. But not when he was in this shape. Damn all women! He thought about Flo in bed, naked as a pouter pigeon, her large tits waving up and down as she yelled at him. He glanced at his watch. Another half-hour and this miserable tour would be finished. The boat had turned and was headed back towards Waterloo Pier. His only problem now was deciding what to do first: sleep, eat, or jump in the kip with Flo. Maybe all three at once, he thought. He rubbed his eyes to force the sleep out of them, and turned to look at the muddy, swollen river pimpled by the rain.

It seemed to loom out of nowhere. It looked like a large white fish floating belly up, and Constable Hiller's first thought was: If we haul it aboard, we're going to stink of it. It was about ten yards to starboard and the boat was moving away from it. If he opened his mouth, the bloody fish was going to delay his getting off duty. They would have to stop and grapple it, and either pull it over the side or tow it in. Whichever they did would delay his getting to Flo. Well, he didn't *have* to report it. What if he had not seen it? What if – ? They were moving farther away.

Constable Hiller called out, "Sergeant, there's a floating fish twenty degrees off starboard. Looks like a big shark."

The hundred-horsepower diesel engine suddenly changed rhythm, and the boat began to slow. Sergeant Gaskins stepped to one side. "Where is it?" he asked.

The dim shape was gone now, buried in the rain. "It was over there."

Sergeant Gaskins hesitated. He too was anxious to get home. His impulse was to ignore the damned fish.

"Was it big enough to menace navigation?" he asked.

Constable Hiller fought with himself and lost. "Yes," he said.

And so the patrol boat turned and slowly headed towards where the object had last been seen. It materialized again unexpectedly, almost under the bow, and they both stood there, staring down at it. It was the body of a young blonde girl.

She was naked, except for a red ribbon tied around her swollen neck.

39

At the moment when Constable Hiller and Sergeant Gaskins were fishing the body of the murdered girl out of the Thames, ten miles on the other side of London, Detective Max Hornung was entering a grey and white marble lobby of New Scotland Yard. Just walking through the storied portals gave him a sense of pride. They were all part of the same great fraternity. He enjoyed the fact that the Yard's cable address was HANDCUFFS. Max was very fond of the English. His only problem concerned their ability to communicate with him. The English spoke their native language so strangely.

The policeman behind the reception desk asked, "Can I help you, sir?"

Max turned. "I have an appointment with Inspector Davidson."

"Name, sir?"

Max said, slowly and distinctly, "Inspector Davidson."

The guard looked at him with interest. "Your name is Inspector Davidson?"

"My name is *not* Inspector Davidson. My name is Max Hornung."

The policeman behind the desk said apologetically, "Excuse me, sir, but do you speak any English?"

Five minutes later Max was seated in the office of Inspector Davidson, a large, middle-aged man with a florid face and uneven yellow teeth. Typically British-looking, Max thought happily.

"Over the phone you said you were interested in information on Sir Alec Nichols as a possible suspect in a murder case."

"He's one of half a dozen."

Inspector Davidson stared at him. "His wanted toes are frozen?"

Max sighed. He repeated what he had just said, slowly and carefully.

"Ah." The inspector thought for a moment. "Tell you what I'll do. I'll turn you over to C-Four Criminal Records Department. If they have nothing on him, we'll try C-Eleven and C-Thirteen – Criminal Intelligence."

Sir Alec Nichols' name was not listed in any of the files. But Max Knew where he could get the information he wanted.

Earlier that morning Max had phoned a number of executives who worked in the City, the financial centre of London.

Their reactions were identical. When Max announced his name, they were filled with trepidation, for everyone doing business in the City had *something* to hide, and Max Hornung's reputation as a financial avenging angel was international. The moment that Max informed them that he was seeking information about someone else, they fell over themselves to co-operate with him.

Max spent two days visiting banks and financial companies, credit rating organizations and vital statistics offices. He was not interested in talking to the people at those places: he was interested in talking to their computers.

Max was a genius with computers. He would sit before the console board and play the machines like a virtuoso. It did not matter what language the computer had been taught, for Max spoke all of them. He talked to digital computers and low-level and high-level language computers. He was at ease with FORTRAN and FORTRAN IV, the giant IBM 370s and the PDP 10s and 11s and ALGOL 68.

He was at home with COBOL, programmed for business, and BASIC, used by the police, and the high speed APL, which conversed solely in charts and graphs. Max talked to LISP and APT, and the PL-1. He held conversations in the binary code, and questioned the arithmetic units and the CPV units, and the high-speed printer answered his questions at the rate of eleven hundred lines a minute. The giant computers had spent their lives sucking up information like insatiable pumps, storing it, analysing it, remembering it, and now they were spewing it out in Max's ear, whispering their secrets to him in their secluded air-conditioned crypts.

Nothing was sacred, nothing was safe. Privacy in today's civilization was a delusion, a myth. Every citizen was exposed, his deepest secrets laid bare, waiting to be read. People were on record if they had a social security number, an insurance policy, a driving licence or a bank account. They were listed if they had paid taxes, drawn unemployment benefit or welfare funds. Their names were stored in computers if they were covered by private medical insurance, had made mortgage payments on a house, owned a car or motor bicycle, or had a deposit or current account. The computer knew their names if they had been in hospital, or had done military service; had a gun or a fishing licence; had applied for a passport, a telephone or electricity; or if they had been born, married or divorced.

If one knew where to look, and if one was patient, all the facts were available.

Max Hornung and the computers had a wonderful rapport. They did not laugh at Max's accent, or the way he looked, or dressed. To the computers Max was a giant. They respected his intelligence, admired him, loved him. They happily gave up their secrets to him, sharing their delicious gossip about the fools that mortals made of themselves. It was like old friends chatting.

"Let's talk about Sir Alec Nichols," Max said.

The computers began. They gave Max a mathematical sketch of Sir Alec, drawn in digits and binary codes and charts. In two hours Max had a composite picture of the man, a financial identi-kit.

Copies of bank receipts and cancelled cheques and bills were all laid before him. The first puzzling item that caught Max's eye was a series of cheques for large amounts, all made out to "Bearer", cashed by Sir Alec Nichols. Where had the money gone? Max looked to see if it had been reported as a business or personal expense, or as a tax deduction. Negative. He went back over the lists of expenditures again: a cheque to White's club, a meat-market bill, unpaid . . . an evening gown from John Bates . . . the Guinea . . . a dentist's bill, unpaid . . . Annabelle's . . . one challis robe from Saint Laurent in Paris . . . a bill from the White Elephant, unpaid . . . a rates bill . . . John Wyndham, the hairdresser, unpaid . . . four dresses from Yves Saint Laurent, Rive Gauche . . . household salaries.

Max asked a question of the computer at the Motor Vehicle Licensing Centre.

Affirmative. *Sir Alec owns a Bentley and a Morris.*

Something was missing. There was no mechanic's bill.

Max had the computers search their memories. In seven years no such bill existed.

Did we forget something? the computers asked.

No, Max replied, *you didn't forget.*

Sir Alec did not use a mechanic. He repaired his own cars. A man with that mechanical ability would have no trouble causing a lift, or a jeep, to crash. Max Hornung pored over the arcane figures that his friends set before him, with the eagerness of an Egyptologist translating a set of newly discovered hieroglyphics. He found further mysteries. Sir Alec was spending a great deal more than his income.

Another loose thread.

Max's friends in the City had connections in many quarters. Within two days Max learned that Sir Alec had been borrowing money from Tod Michaels, the owner of a club in Soho.

Max turned to the police computers and asked questions. They listened, and they replied. *Yes, we have Tod Michaels for you. Has been charged with several crimes, but never convicted. Suspected of being involved in blackmail, dope, prostitution and loan-sharking.*

Max went down to Soho and asked more questions. He found out that Sir Alec Nichols did not gamble. But his wife did.

When Max was finished, there was no doubt in his mind that Sir Alec Nichols was being blackmailed. He had unpaid bills, he needed money fast. He had stock that would be worth millions, if he could sell it. Sam Roffe had stood in his way, and now Elizabeth Roffe.

Sir Alec Nichols had a motive for murder.

Max checked out Rhys Williams. The machines tried, but the information proved too sketchy.

The computers informed Max that Rhys Williams was male, born in Wales, thirty-four years of age, unmarried. An executive of Roffe and Sons. Salary eighty thousand dollars a year, plus bonuses. A London savings account with a balance of twenty-five thousand pounds, a current account with an average balance of eight hundred pounds. A safe-deposit box in Zurich, contents unknown.

All major charge accounts and credit cards. Many of the items purchased with them were for women. Rhys Williams had no criminal record. He had been employed at Roffe and Sons for nine years.

Not enough, Max thought. Not nearly enough. It was as though Rhys Williams was hiding behind the computers. Max remembered how protective the man had been when Max had questioned Elizabeth, after Kate Erling's funeral. Whom had he been protecting? Elizabeth Roffe? Or himself?

At six o'clock that evening Max booked himself on an Alitalia economy flight to Rome.

40

Ivo Palazzi had spent almost ten years carefully and skilfully building an intricate double life that not even his closest associates had penetrated.

It took Max Hornung and his computer friends in Rome less than twenty-four hours. Max held discussions with the computer at the Anagrafe Building, where vital statistics and city-administration data were kept, and he visited the computers at SID, and went to call on the bank computers.

They all welcomed Max.

Tell me about Ivo Palazzi, Max said.

Happily, they replied.

The conversations began.

A grocery bill from Amici . . . a beauty salon bill from Sergio in the Via Condotti . . . one blue suit from Angelo . . . flowers from Carducci . . . two evening dresses from Irene Galitzine . . . shoes from Gucci . . . a Pucci purse . . . utility bills.

Max kept reading the print-outs, examining, analysing, smelling. Something smells wrong. There were tuition fees for six children.

Have you made an error? Max asked.

Sorry. What type of error?

The computers at Anagrafe told me that Ivo Palazzi is registered as the father of three children. Do you verify six tuition fees?

We do.

You show Ivo Palazzi's address as being in Olgiata?

That is correct.

But he is paying for an apartment in Via Montemignaio?

Yes.

Are there two Ivo Palazzis?

No. One man. Two families. Three daughters by his wife. Three sons by Donatella Spolini.

Before Max was through, he knew the tastes of Ivo's mistress, her age, the name of her hairdresser, and the names of Ivo's illegitimate children. He knew that Simonetta was a blonde, and Donatella a brunette. He knew what size dresses and bras and shoes each wore and how much they cost.

Among the expenses several interesting items caught Max's eye. The amounts were small, but they stood out like beacons. There was a receipted cheque for a lathe, a plane and a saw. Ivo Palazzi liked to work with his hands. Max thought about the fact that an architect would probably know something about lifts.

Ivo Palazzi applied for a large bank loan recently, the computers informed Max.

Did he receive it?

No. The bank asked him to have his wife co-sign. He withdrew the request.

Thank you.

Max took a bus to the Polizia Scientifica centre in EUR, where the giant computer was kept in a. large round room.

Does Ivo Palazzi have a criminal record? Max asked.

Affirmative. Ivo Palazzi was convicted on an assault and battery charge at age twenty-three. His victim went to hospital. Palazzi went to jail for two months. Anything else?

Ivo Palazzi keeps a mistress at Via Montemignaio.

Thank you. I know.

There are several police reports of complaints from neighbours.

What sort of complaints?

Disturbing the peace. Fighting, yelling. One night she smashed all the dishes. Is that important?

Very, Max said. *Thank you.*

So Ivo Palazzi had a temper. And Donatella Spolini had a temper. Had something happened between her and Ivo? Was she threatening to expose him? Was that why he had suddenly gone to the bank for a large loan? How far would a man like Ivo Palazzi go to protect his marriage, his family, his way of life?

There was one final item that caught the little detective's attention. A large payment had been made to Ivo Palazzi by the financial section of the Italian security police. It was a reward, a percentage of the money found on the banker whom Ivo had turned in. If Ivo Palazzi was that desperate for money, what else would he do for it?

Max bade farewell to his computers and caught a noon flight to Paris on Air France.

41

The taxi fare from Charles de Gaulle Airport to the Notre Dame area is seventy francs, not including a tip. The fare by city bus Number 351, to the same area, is seven and a half francs, no tip required. Detective Max Hornung took the bus. He checked into the inexpensive Hôtel Meublé and began making phone calls.

He talked to the people who held in their hands the secrets of the citizens of France. The French were normally more suspicious than even the Swiss, but they were eager to cooperate with Max Hornung. There were two reasons. The first was that Max Hornung was a virtuoso in his field, greatly admired, and it was an honour to co-operate with such a man. The second was that they were terrified of him. There were no secrets from Max. The odd-looking little man with the funny accent stripped everyone naked. "Certainly," they told Max. "You're welcome to use our computers. Everything to be kept confidential, of course."

"Of course."

Max dropped in at the Inspecteurs des Finances, the Crédit Lyonnais, and the Assurance Nationale and chatted with the tax computers. He visited the computers at the *gendarmerie* at Rosny-sous-Bois and the ones at the Prefecture of Police at Ile de la Cité.

They started off with the light, easy gossip of old friends. *Who are Charles and Hélène Roffe-Martel?* Max asked.

Charles and Hélène Roffe-Martel, residence Rue François Premier 5, Vésinet, married May 24, 1970, at the Mairie in Neuilly, children none, Hélène three times divorced, maiden name Roffe, bank account at the Crédit Lyonnais in Avenue Montaigne in name of Hélène Roffe-Martel, average balance in excess of twenty thousand francs.

Expenditures?

With pleasure. A bill from Librairie Marceau for books . . . a dental bill for root-canal work for Charles Martel . . . hospital bills for Charles Martel . . . doctor's bill for examination of Charles Martel.

Do you have result of diagnosis?

Can you wait? I will have to speak to another computer.

Yes, please. Max waited.

The machine containing the doctor's report began to speak. *I have the diagnosis.*

Go ahead.

A nervous condition.

Anything else?

Severe bruises and contusions on thighs and buttocks.

Any explanation?

None given.

Go on, please.

A bill for a pair of men's shoes from Pinet . . . one hat from Rose Valois . . . foie gras from Fauchon . . . Carita beauty salon . . . Maxim's, dinner party for eight . . . flat silver from Christofle . . . a man's robe from Sulka . . . Max stopped the computer. Something was bothering him. Something about the bills. He realized what it was. Every purchase had been signed by Mme Roffe-Martel. The bill for men's clothes, the restaurant bills – all the accounts were in her name. Interesting.

And then the first loose thread.

A company named Belle Paix had purchased a land tax stamp. One of the owners of Belle Paix was named Charles Dessain. Charles Dessain's Social Security number was the same as Charles Martel's. Concealment.

Tell me about Belle Paix , Max said.

Belle Paix is owned by René Duchamps and Charles Dessain, also known as Charles Martel.

What does Belle Paix do?

It owns a vineyard.

How much is the company capitalized at?

Four million francs.

Where did Charles Martel get his share of the money?

From Chez ma tante.

The house of your aunt?

Sorry. A French slang expression. The proper name is Crédit Municipal.

Is the vineyard profitable?

No. It failed.

Max needed more. He kept talking to his friends, probing, cajoling, demanding. It was the insurance computer that confided to Max that there was a warning on file of a possible insurance fraud. Max felt something delicious stir within him.

Tell me about it, he said.

And they talked, like two women gossiping back and forth over the Monday wash.

When Max was through he went to see a jeweller named Pierre Richaud.

In thirty minutes Max knew to a franc how much of Hélène Roffe-Martel's jewellery had been duplicated. It came to just over two million francs, the amount Charles Martel had invested in the vineyard. So Charles Dessain-Martel had been desperate enough to steal his wife's jewellery.

What other acts of desperation had he committed?

There was one other entry that interested Max. It might be of little significance, but Max methodically filed it away in his mind. It was a bill for the purchase of one pair of mountain-climbing boots. It made Max pause, because mountain climbing did not fit in with his image of Charles Martel-Dessain, a man who was so dominated by his wife that he was allowed no charge accounts of his own, had no bank account in his name, and was forced to steal in order to make an investment.

No, Max could not visualize Charles Martel challenging a mountain. Max went back to his computers.

The bill you showed me yesterday from Timwear Sports Shop. I would like to see an itemized statement, please.

Certainly.

It flashed on the screen before him. There was the bill for the boots. Size *36A*. A woman's size. It was Hélène Roffe-Martel who was the mountain climber.

Sam Roffe had been killed on a mountain.

42

Rue Armengaud was a quiet Paris street lined with one- and two-storey private residences, each with its sloping guttered roof. Towering above its neighbours was Number 26, an eight-storey, modern structure of glass, steel and stone, the headquarters of Interpol, the clearing house for information on international criminal activities.

Detective Max Hornung was talking to a computer in the huge, air-conditioned basement room when one of the staff members walked in and said, "They're running a snuff film upstairs. Want to see it?"

Max looked up and said, "I don't know. What is a snuff film?"

"Come and take a look."

Two dozen men and women were seated in the large screening room on the third floor of the building. There were members of the Interpol staff, police inspectors from the Sûreté, plainclothes detectives and a scattering of uniformed policemen.

Standing at the front of the room next to a blank screen, René Almedin, an assistant to the secretary of Interpol, was speaking. Max entered and found a seat in the back row.

René Almedin was saying, " . . . for the last several years we have been hearing increasing rumours of snuff films, pornographic films in which at the end of the sexual act the victim is murdered on camera. There has never been proof that such films actually existed. The reason, of course, is obvious. These films would not have been made for the public. They would have been made to be shown privately to wealthy individuals who got their pleasure in twisted, sadistic ways." René Almedin carefully removed his glasses. "As I have said, everything has been rumour and speculation. That has now changed, however. In a moment you are going to see footage from an actual snuff film." There was an expectant stir from the audience. "Two days ago, a male pedestrian carrying an attaché case was struck down in a hit-and-run accident in Passy. The man died on the way to the hospital. He is still unidentified. The Sûreté found this reel of film in his attaché case and turned it over to the laboratory, where it was developed." He gave a signal and the lights began to dim. The film began.

The blonde girl could not have been more than eighteen. There was something unreal about watching that young face and budding woman's body performing fellatio, analingus and a variety of other sexual acts with the large hairless man in bed with her. The camera moved in to a close-up to show his enormous penis driving into her body, then pulled back to show her face. Max Hornung had never seen her face before. But he had seen something else that was familiar. His eyes were fixed on the ribbon that the girl was wearing around her neck. It triggered a memory. A red ribbon. Where? Slowly, the girl on the screen began to build to a peak, and as she started to climax, the man's fingers went around her throat and began to squeeze. The look on the girl's face changed from ecstasy to horror. She fought wildly to escape, but his hands pressed tighter, until at the final moment of orgasm the girl died. The camera moved in for a close-up of her face. The film ended. The lights suddenly came on in the room. Max remembered.

The girl who had been fished out of the river in Zurich.

At Interpol headquarters in Paris, replies from urgent inquiry cables were beginning to arrive from all over Europe. Six similar murders had taken place – in Zurich, London, Rome, Portugal, Hamburg and Paris.

René Almedin said to Max, "The descriptions match exactly. The victims were all blonde, female, young; they were strangled during sexual intercourse and their bodies were nude except for a red ribbon around their necks. We're dealing with a mass murderer. Someone who has a passport, and is either affluent enough to travel extensively on his own or is on an expense account."

A man in plain clothes walked into the office and said, "We ran into some good luck. The raw stock of the film is manufactured by a small outfit in Brussels. This particular batch had a colour-balance problem, which makes it easy for them to identify. We're getting a list of the customers they sold it to."

Max said, "I would like to see that list when you have it."

"Of course," René Almedin said. He studied the little detective. Max Hornung looked like no detective he had ever seen. And yet it was Max Hornung who had tied the snuff murders together.

"We owe you a debt of gratitude," Almedin said.

Max Hornung looked at him and blinked. "What for?" he asked.

43

Alec Nichols had not wanted to attend the banquet, but he had not wished Elizabeth to go alone. They were both scheduled to speak. The banquet was in Glasgow, a city Alec hated. A car was outside the hotel, waiting to take them to the airport as soon as they could decently make their excuses. He had already given his speech but his mind had been elsewhere. He was tense and nervous, and his stomach was upset. Some fool had had the bad judgement to serve haggis. Alec had barely tasted it. Elizabeth was seated next to him. "Are you all right, Alec?"

"Fine." He patted her hand reassuringly.

The speeches were almost finished when a waiter came up to Alec and whispered, "Excuse me, sir. There's a trunk call for you. You can take it in the office."

Alec followed the waiter out of the large dining-room into the small office behind the reception desk. He picked up the telephone. "Hello?"

Swinton's voice said, "This is your last warning!" The line went dead.

44

The last city on Detective Max Hornung's agenda was Berlin.

His friends the computers were waiting for him. Max spoke to the exclusive Nixdorf computer, to which one had access only with a specially punched card. He talked to the great computers at Allianz and Schuffa and to the ones at the Bundeskriminalamt at Wiesbaden, the collection point for all criminal activity in Germany.

What can we do for you? they asked.

Tell me about Walther Gassner.

And they told him. When they were through telling Max Hornung their secrets, Walther Gassner's life was spread out before Max in beautiful mathematical symbols. Max could see the man as clearly as if he were looking at a photograph of him. He knew his taste in clothes, wines, food, hotels. A handsome young ski instructor who had lived off women and had married an heiress much older than himself.

There was one item that Max found curious: a cancelled cheque made out to a Dr Heissen, for two hundred marks. On the cheque was written "For consultation". What kind of consultation? The cheque had been cashed at the

Dresdener Bank in Düsseldorf. Fifteen minutes later Max was speaking to the branch manager of the bank. Yes, of course the branch manager knew Dr Heissen. He was a valued client of the bank.

What kind of doctor was he?

A psychiatrist.

When Max had hung up, he sat back, his eyes closed, thinking. A loose thread. He picked up the telephone and put through a call to Dr Heissen in Düsseldorf.

An officious receptionist told Max that the doctor could not be disturbed. When Max insisted, Dr Heissen got on the telephone and rudely informed Max that he never revealed any information about his patients, and that he would certainly not dream of discussing such matters over the telephone. He hung up on the detective.

Max went back to the computers. *Tell me about Dr Heissen*, he said.

Three hours later Max was speaking to Dr Heissen on the telephone again.

"I told you before," the doctor snapped, "that if you want any information about any of my patients, you will have to come to my office with a court order."

"It is inconvenient for me to come to Düsseldorf just now," the detective explained.

"That's your problem. Anything else? I'm a busy man."

"I know you are. I have in front of me your income tax reports for the past five years."

"So?"

Max said, "Doctor, I don't want to make trouble for you. But you are illegally concealing twenty-five per cent of your income. If you prefer, I can just forward your files to the German income tax authorities and tell them where to look. They could start with your safe-deposit box in Munich, or your numbered bank account in Basle."

There was a long silence, and then the doctor's voice asked, "Who did you say you were?"

"Detective Max Hornung of the Swiss Kriminalpolizei."

There was another pause. The doctor said politely, "And what is it exactly you wish to know?"

Max told him.

Once Dr Heissen began talking, there was no stopping him. Yes, of course he remembered Walther Gassner. The man had barged in without an appointment and had insisted on seeing him. He had refused to give his name. He had used the pretext that he wanted to discuss the problems of a friend.

"Of course, that alerted me instantly," Dr Heissen confided to Max. "It is a classic syndrome of people unwilling or afraid to face their problems."

"What *was* the problem?" Max asked.

"He said his friend was schizophrenic and homicidal, and would probably kill someone unless he could be stopped. He asked if there was some kind of treatment that could help. He said he could not bear to have his friend locked away in an insane asylum."

"What did you tell him?"

"I told him that first, of course, I would have to examine his friend, that some types of mental illness could be helped with modern drugs and other psychiatric and therapeutic treatments, and that other types were incurable. I also mentioned that in a case such as he described, treatment might be necessary for an extended period of time."

"What happened then?" Max asked.

"Nothing. That was really all. I never saw the man again. I would like to have helped him. He was very distraught. His coming to me was obviously a cry for help. It is similar to a killer who writes on the wall of his victim's apartment, 'Stop me before I kill again!' "

There was one thing still puzzling Max. "Doctor, you said he wouldn't give you his name, and yet he gave you a cheque and signed it."

Dr Heissen explained, "He had forgotten to bring any money with him. He was very upset about that. In the end he had to write a cheque. That's how I happened to learn his name. Is there anything else you need to know, sir?"

"No."

Something was disturbing Max, a loose thread dangling tantalizingly out of reach. It would come to him – meanwhile, he had finished with the computers. The rest was up to him now.

When Max returned to Zurich the following morning, he found a teletype on his desk from Interpol. It contained a list of customers who had purchased the batch of raw stock used to make the snuff murder film.

There were eight names on the list.

Among them was Roffe and Sons.

Chief Inspector Schmied was listening to Detective Max Hornung make his report. There was no doubt about it. The lucky little detective had stumbled on to another big case.

"It's one of five people," Max was saying. "They all have a motive and they had the opportunity. They were all in Zurich for a board meeting the day the lift crashed. Any one of them could have been in Sardinia at the time of the jeep accident."

Chief Inspector Schmied frowned, "You said there were five suspects. Aside from Elizabeth Roffe, there are only four members of the board. Who's your other suspect?"

Max blinked and said patiently, "The man who was in Chamonix with Sam Roffe when he was murdered. Rhys Williams."

45

Mrs Rhys Williams.

Elizabeth could not believe it. The whole thing had an air of unreality. It was something out of a blissful girlhood dream. Elizabeth remembered how she had written in her exercise book, over and over, *Mrs Rhys Williams, Mrs Rhys Williams.* She glanced down now at the wedding ring on her finger.

Rhys said, "What are you grinning about?" He was seated in an easy chair across from her in the luxurious Boeing 707–320. They were thirty-five thousand feet somewhere above the Atlantic ocean, dining on Iranian caviar and drinking chilled Dom Perignon, and it was such a cliché of *La Dolce Vita* that Elizabeth had to laugh aloud.

Rhys smiled. "Something I said?"

Elizabeth shook her head. She looked at him and marvelled at how attractive he was. Her husband. "I'm just happy."

He would never know how happy. How could she tell him how much this marriage meant to her? He would not understand, because to Rhys it was not a marriage, it was a business proposition. But she loved Rhys. It seemed to Elizabeth that she had always loved him. She wanted to spend the rest of her life with him, have his children, belong to him, have him belong to her. Elizabeth looked over at Rhys again and thought wryly, But first I have to solve one small problem. I have to find a way to make him fall in love with me.

Elizabeth had proposed to Rhys the day of her meeting with Julius Badrutt. After the banker had left, Elizabeth had carefully brushed her hair, walked into Rhys's office, taken a deep breath and said, "Rhys – would you marry me?"

She had seen the look of surprise on his face, and before he could speak, she had gone hurriedly on, trying to sound efficient and cool. "It would be a purely business arrangement. The banks are willing to extend our loans if you take over as president of Roffe and Sons. The only way you can do that" – to Elizabeth's horror her voice had cracked – "is to marry a member of the family, and I – I seem to be the only one available."

She felt her face flush. She could not look at him.

"It wouldn't be a real marriage, of course," Elizabeth had said, "in the sense that – I mean – you'd be free to – to come and go as you pleased."

He had watched her, not helping her. Elizabeth wished he would say something. Anything.

"Rhys – "

"Sorry. You took me by surprise." He had smiled. "It isn't every day a man gets proposed to by a beautiful girl."

He was stalling, trying to get out of this without hurting her feelings. *I'm sorry, Elizabeth, but –*

"You have a deal," Rhys said.

And Elizabeth had suddenly felt as though a heavy burden had been lifted from her. She had not realized until that moment how important this had been. She had bought time now to learn who the enemy was. Together she and Rhys could stop all the terrible things that had been happening. There was one thing she had to make clear to him.

"You will be president of the company," she had said, "but the voting control of the stock will remain in my hands."

Rhys had frowned. "If I'm running the company – "

"You will be," Elizabeth had assured him.

"But the controlling stock – "

"Stays in my name. I want to make sure that it can't be sold."

"I see."

She could sense his disapproval. She had wanted to tell him that she had reached a decision. She had decided that the company should go public, that the members of the board should be able to sell their shares. With Rhys as president, Elizabeth would no longer have any fears about strangers coming in and taking over. Rhys would be strong enough to handle them. But Elizabeth could not let that happen until she found out who was trying to destroy the company. She had wanted desperately to tell Rhys all these things, but she knew that now was not the time, and so all she said was "Other than that, you'll have complete control."

Rhys had stood there, silently studying her for what seemed a long time. When he spoke, he said, "When would you like to get married?"

"As soon as possible."

Except for Anna, and Walther, who was at home, ill, they all came to Zurich for the wedding. Alec and Vivian, Hélène and Charles, Simonetta and Ivo. They seemed delighted for Elizabeth, and their pleasure made her feel like a fraud. She had not made a marriage, she had made a business deal.

Alec hugged her and said, "You know I wish you everything wonderful."

"I know, Alec. Thank you."

Ivo waxed ecstatic. "*Carissima, tanti auguri e fig maschi*. 'To find riches is a beggar's dream, but to find love is the dream of kings.' "

Elizabeth smiled. "Who said that?"

"I did," Ivo declared. "I hope Rhys appreciates what a lucky man he is."

"I keep telling him," she said lightly.

Hélène took Elizabeth aside. "You are full of surprises, *ma chère*. I had no idea that you and Rhys were interested in each other."

"It happened suddenly."

Hélène studied her with cool, calculating eyes. "Yes. I'm sure it did." And she walked away.

After the ceremony there was a wedding reception at the Baur-au-Lac. On the surface it was gay and festive, but Elizabeth felt the undercurrents. There was something evil in the room, a malediction, but she could not tell from whom it was coming. All she knew was that someone in the room hated her. She could feel it, deep down inside her, yet when she looked around, all she saw were smiles and friendly faces. Charles raising his glass in a toast to her . . . Elizabeth had received a report on the laboratory explosion. *The explosive was manufactured by your factory outside Paris.*

Ivo, a happy grin on his face . . . *The banker who was caught trying to smuggle money out of Italy was set up. A man tipped off the border police. Ivo Palazzi.*

Alec? Walther? Which? Elizabeth wondered.

The following morning a board meeting was held, and Rhys Williams was unanimously elected president and chief operating officer of Roffe and Sons. Charles raised the question that was on everyone's mind. "Now that you are running the company, are we going to be allowed to sell our stock?"

Elizabeth could feel the sudden tension in the room. "The controlling stock is still in Elizabeth's hands," Rhys informed them. "It's her decision."

Every head turned towards Elizabeth.

"We're not selling," she announced.

When Elizabeth and Rhys were alone, he said, "How would you like to honeymoon in Rio?"

Elizabeth looked at him, and her heart soared. He added matter-of-factly, "Our manager there is threatening to quit. We cannot afford to lose him. I was planning to fly there tomorrow to straighten things out. It would look a bit strange if I went without my bride."

Elizabeth nodded and said, "Yes, of course." You're a fool, she told herself. This was your idea. It's an arrangement, not a marriage. You have no right to expect anything from Rhys. And still, a small voice, deep inside her, said, Who knows what can happen? . . .

When they got off the plane at the Galeão airport, the air was surprisingly warm, and Elizabeth realized that in Rio it was summer. A Mercedes 600 was waiting for them. The chauffeur was a thin, dark-skinned man in his late twenties. When they got into the car, Rhys asked the driver, "Where's Luis?"

"Luis is sick, Mr Williams. I'll be driving you and Mrs Williams."

"Tell Luis I hope he'll be better soon."

The driver studied them in the rearview mirror and said, "I will."

Half an hour later they were driving along the esplanade, over the colourful tiles of the broad avenue along the Copacabana Beach. They pulled up in front of the modern Princessa Sugarloaf Hotel and a moment later, their luggage was being attended to. They were ushered into an enormous suite with four bed-rooms, a beautiful living-room, a kitchen, and a huge terrace overlooking the bay. The suite had been stocked with flowers in silver vases, champagne, whisky, and boxes of chocolates. The manager himself had escorted them to their suite.

"If there is anything at all we can do for you – anything – I am personally at your service twenty-four hours a day." And he bowed himself out.

"They're certainly friendly," Elizabeth said.

Rhys laughed and replied, "They should be. You own this hotel."

Elizabeth felt herself colour. "Oh. I – I didn't know."

"Hungry?"

"I – No, thank you," Elizabeth replied.

"Some wine?"

"Yes, thank you."

In her own ears her voice sounded stilted and unnatural. She was not certain how she was supposed to behave, or what to expect from Rhys. He had suddenly become a stranger, and she felt terribly conscious of the fact that they were alone in the honeymoon suite of a hotel, that it was getting late, and that it would soon be time for bed.

She watched Rhys as he deftly opened a bottle of champagne. He did everything so smoothly, with the easy assurance of a man who knows exactly what he wants and how to get it. What did he want?

Rhys carried a glass of champagne to Elizabeth and raised his own glass in a toast. "To beginnings," he said.

"To beginnings," Elizabeth echoed. *And happy endings*, she added silently.

They drank.

We should smash our glasses into a fireplace, Elizabeth thought, to celebrate. She gulped down the rest of her champagne.

They were in Rio on their honeymoon, and she wanted Rhys. Not just for now, but forever.

The phone rang. Rhys picked it up and spoke into it briefly. When he finished he hung up and said to Elizabeth, "It's late. Why don't you get ready for bed?"

It seemed to Elizabeth that the word "bed" hung heavily in the air.

"Right," she said weakly. She turned and went into the bedroom where the bellboys had put their luggage. There was a large double bed in the centre of the room. A maid had unpacked their suitcases and prepared the bed. On one side was a sheer silk nightgown of Elizabeth's and on the other side a pair of men's blue pyjamas. She hesitated a moment, then began to undress. When she was naked, she walked into the large mirrored dressing-room and carefully removed her make-up. She wrapped a Turkish towel around her head, went into the bathroom and showered, slowly lathering her body and feeling the warm soapy water running between her breasts and down her belly and thighs, like warm wet fingers.

All the time she was trying not to think about Rhys, and she could think of nothing else. She thought of his arms around her and his body on hers. Had she married Rhys to help save the company, or was she using the company as an excuse because she wanted him? She no longer knew. Her desire had turned into one burning, all-consuming need. It was as though the fifteen-year-old child had been waiting for him all these years without being aware of it, and the need had turned into a hunger. She stepped out of the shower, dried herself with a soft warmed towel, put on the sheer silk nightgown, let her hair fall loose and free and climbed into bed. She lay there waiting, thinking about what was going to happen, wondering what he would be like, and she found that her heart was beginning to pound faster. She heard a sound and looked up. Rhys was standing in the doorway. He was fully dressed.

"I'll be going out now," he said.

Elizabeth sat up. "Where – where are you going?"

"It's a business problem I have to take care of." And he was gone.

Elizabeth lay awake all that night, tossing and turning, filled with conflicting emotions, telling herself how grateful she was that Rhys had kept to their agreement, feeling like a fool for what she had been anticipating, furious with him for rejecting her.

It was dawn when Elizabeth heard Rhys return. His footsteps moved towards the bedroom, and Elizabeth closed her eyes, pretending to be asleep. She could hear Rhys's breathing as he came over to the bed. He stood there, watching her for a long time. Then he turned and walked into the other room.

A few minutes later Elizabeth was asleep.

In the late morning they had breakfast on the terrace. Rhys was pleasant and chatty, telling her what the city was like at carnival time. But he volunteered no information about where he had spent the night, and Elizabeth did not ask. One waiter took their order for breakfast. Elizabeth noticed that it was a different waiter who served it. She thought no more about it, nor about the maids who were constantly in and out of the suite.

Elizabeth and Rhys were at the Roffe and Sons factory on the outskirts of Rio, seated in the office of the plant manager, Senhor Tumas, a middle-aged, frog-faced man, who perspired copiously.

He was addressing Rhys. "You must understand how it is. Roffe and Sons is dearer to me than my own life. It is my family. When I leave here, it will be like leaving home. A part of my heart will be torn out. More than anything in the world, I want to stay here." He stopped to wipe his brow. "But 1 have a better offer from another company, and I have my wife and children and mother-in-law to think of. You understand?"

Rhys was leaning back in his chair, his legs casually stretched out before him. "Of course, Roberto. I know how much this company means to you. You have spent many years here. Still, a man has to think of his family."

"Thank you," Roberto said gratefully. "I knew I could count on you, Rhys."

"What about your contract with us?"

Tumas shrugged. "A piece of paper. We will tear it up, no? What good is a contract if a man is unhappy in his heart?"

Rhys nodded. "That's why we flew down here, Roberto – to make you happy in your heart."

Tumas sighed. "Ah, if only it were not too late. But I have already agreed to go to work for this other company."

"Do they know you're going to prison?" Rhys asked conversationally.

Tumas gaped at him. "Prison?"

Rhys said, "The United States government has ordered every company doing business overseas to turn in a list of all foreign bribes they've paid over the past ten years. Unfortunately, you're heavily involved in that, Roberto. You've broken a few laws here. We had planned to protect you – as a faithful member of the family – but if you're not with us, there's no longer any reason to, is there?"

All the colour had drained from Roberto's face.

"But – but it was for the company that I did it," he protested. "I was only following orders."

Rhys nodded sympathetically. "Of course. You can explain that to the government at your trial." He rose to his feet and said to Elizabeth, "We'd better be starting back."

"Wait a minute," Roberto yelled. "You can't walk out and leave me like this."

Rhys said, "I think you're confused. *You're* the one who's leaving."

Tumas was mopping his brow again, his lips twitching uncontrollably. He walked over to the window and looked out. A heavy silence hung over the room. Finally, without turning, he said, "If I stay with the company – will I be protected?"

"All the way," Rhys assured him.

They were in the Mercedes, the thin, dark chauffeur at the wheel, driving back to the city. "You blackmailed him," Elizabeth declared.

Rhys nodded. "We couldn't afford to lose him. He was going over to a competitor. He knows too much about our business. He would have sold us out."

Elizabeth looked at Rhys and thought, I have so much to learn about him.

That evening they went to Mirander for dinner, and Rhys was charming and amusing and impersonal. Elizabeth felt as though he were hiding behind a façade of words, putting up a verbal smoke-screen to conceal his feelings. When they finished dinner, it was after midnight. Elizabeth wanted to be alone with Rhys. She had hoped they would return to the hotel. Instead he said, "I'm going to show you some of the night life in Rio."

They made the rounds of nightclubs, and everyone seemed to know Rhys. Wherever they went, he was the centre of attention, charming everyone. They were invited to join couples at other tables, and groups of people joined them at their table. Elizabeth and Rhys were never alone for a moment. It seemed to Elizabeth that it was intentional, that Rhys was deliberately putting a wall of people between them. They had been friends before, and now they were – what? Elizabeth only knew that there was some unseen barrier between them. What was he afraid of and why?

At the fourth nightclub, where they had joined a table with half a dozen of Rhys's friends, Elizabeth decided she had had enough. She broke into the conversation between Rhys and a lovely-looking Spanish girl. "I haven't had a chance to dance with my husband. I'm sure you'll excuse us."

Rhys looked at her in quick surprise, then rose to his feet. "I'm afraid I've been neglecting my bride," he said lightly to the others. He took Elizabeth's arm and led her out to the dance floor. She was holding herself stiffly, and he looked at her face and said, "You're angry."

He was right, but it was an anger directed at herself. She had made the rules, and was upset now because Rhys would not break them. But it was more than that, of course. It was not knowing how Rhys felt. Was he sticking to their agreement because of a sense of honour, or because he was simply not interested in her? She had to know.

Rhys said, "Sorry about all these people, Liz, but they're in the business, and in one way or another they can be helpful to us."

So he was aware of her feelings. She could feel his arms around her, his body against hers. She thought, It feels right. Everything about Rhys was right for her. They belonged together. She knew it. But did he know how much she wanted him? Elizabeth's pride would not let her tell him. And yet he must feel something. She closed her eyes and pressed closer to him. Time had stopped and there was nothing but the two of them and the soft music and the magic of this moment. She could have gone on dancing forever in Rhys's arms. She relaxed and gave herself up to him completely and she began to feel his male hardness pressing against her thighs. She opened her eyes and looked up at him and there was something in his eyes she had never seen there before, an urgency, a wanting, that was a reflection of her own.

When he spoke, his voice was hoarse. He said, "Let's go back to the hotel."

And she could not speak.

When he helped her on with her wrap, his fingers burned her skin. They sat apart in the back of the limousine, afraid to touch. Elizabeth felt as if she were on fire. It seemed to her that it took an eternity for them to reach their suite. She did not think she could wait another moment. As the door closed, they came together in a wonderful wild hunger that swept through both of them. She was in his arms and there was a ferocity in him that she had never known. He picked her up and carried her into the bedroom. They could not get their clothes off quickly enough. We're like eager children, Elizabeth thought, and she wondered why it had taken Rhys all this time. But it did not matter now. Nothing mattered except their nakedness and the wonderful feel of his body against hers. They were in bed, exploring each other, and Elizabeth gently pulled away from his embrace and started kissing him, her tongue moving down his lean, taut body, embracing him with her lips, feeling his velvet hardness inside her mouth. His hands were on her hips, turning her on her side, and his mouth was running down between her thighs, parting them to his tongue and thrusting into the sweetness there, and when neither of them could bear it an instant longer, he moved on top of her and slowly slid inside her, thrusting deep and making gently circling motions and she began to move to his rhythm, their rhythm, the rhythm of the universe, and everything began to move faster and faster, spinning out of control, until there was a vast ecstatic explosion and the earth became still and peaceful again.

They lay there, holding each other close, and Elizabeth thought joyfully, *Mrs Rhys Williams.*

46

"Excuse me, Mrs Williams," Henriette's voice said on the intercom, "there's a Detective Hornung here to see you. He says it's urgent."

Elizabeth turned to look up at Rhys, puzzled. They had just returned from Rio to Zurich the evening before, and they had only been in the office a few minutes. Rhys shrugged. "Tell her to send the man in. Let's find out what's so important."

A few moments later the three of them were seated in Elizabeth's office. "What did you want to see me about?" Elizabeth asked.

Max Hornung had no small talk. He said, "Someone is trying to murder you." As he watched the colour drain from Elizabeth's face, Max was genuinely distressed, wondering if there might have been a more tactful way he could have phrased it.

Rhys Williams said, "What the hell are you talking about?"

Max continued to address himself to Elizabeth. "There have already been two attempts on your life. There will probably be more."

Elizabeth stammered, "I – you must be mistaken."

"No, ma'am. That lift crash was meant to kill you."

She stared at him in silence, her dark eyes filled with bewilderment, and some other emotion buried deeper, that Max could not define. "So was the jeep."

Elizabeth found her voice again. "You're wrong. That was an accident. There was nothing the matter with the jeep. The police in Sardinia examined it."

"No."

"I saw them," Elizabeth insisted.

"No, ma'am. You saw them examine *a* jeep. It wasn't yours."

They were both staring at him now.

Max went on, "Your jeep was never in that garage. I found it in an auto junkyard at Olbia. The bolt that sealed the master cylinder had been loosened, and the brake fluid had run out. That's why you had no brakes. The left front fender was still bashed in and there were green markings on it from the sap of the trees you ran into. The lab checked it out. It matches."

The nightmare was back. Elizabeth felt it sweep through her, as though the floodgates of her hidden fears had suddenly opened, and she was filled again with the terror of that ride down the mountains.

Rhys was saying, "I don't understand. How could anyone – ?"

Max turned to look at Rhys. "All jeeps look alike. That's what they were counting on. When she crashed instead of going off the mountain, they had to improvise. They couldn't let anyone examine that jeep because it had to look like an accident. They had expected it to be at the bottom of the sea. They probably would have finished her off there, but a maintenance crew came along, found her and took her to the hospital. They got hold of another jeep, smashed it up a little and made the switch before the police came."

Rhys said, "You keep saying 'they'."

"Whoever was behind it had help."

"Who – who would want to kill me?" Elizabeth asked.

"The same person who killed your father."

She had a sudden feeling of unreality, as if none of this was happening. It was all a nightmare that would go away.

"Your father was murdered," Max went on. "He was set up with a phony guide who killed him. Your father didn't go to Chamonix alone. There was someone with him."

When Elizabeth spoke, her voice was a hollow whisper. "Who?"

Max looked at Rhys and said, "Your husband."

The words echoed in her ears. They seemed to come from far away, fading in and out, and she wondered if she was losing her mind.

"Liz," Rhys said, "I wasn't there with Sam when he was killed."

"You were in Chamonix with him, Mr Williams," Max insisted.

"That's true." Rhys was talking to Elizabeth now. "I left before Sam went on his climb."

She turned to look at him. "Why didn't you tell me?"

He hesitated a moment, then seemed to make a decision. "It's something I couldn't discuss with anyone. For the past year someone has been sabotaging Roffe and Sons. It was done very cleverly, so that it seemed to be a series of accidents. But I began to see a pattern. I went to Sam with it, and we decided to hire an outside agency to investigate."

Elizabeth knew then what was coming, and she was simultaneously filled with a deep sense of relief and a feeling of guilt. Rhys had known about the report all along. She should have trusted him enough to tell him about it, instead of keeping her fears to herself.

Rhys turned to Max Hornung, "Sam Roffe got a report that confirmed my suspicions. He asked me to go up to Chamonix to discuss it with him. I went. We decided to keep it just between the two of us until we could find out who was responsible for what was happening." When he continued, there was a note of bitterness in his voice. "Obviously, it wasn't kept quiet enough. Sam was killed because someone knew we were getting on to him. The report is missing."

"I had it," Elizabeth said. Rhys looked at her in surprise. "It was with Sam's personal effects." She said to Max, "The report indicates that it was someone on the board of Roffe and Sons, but they all have stock in the company. Why would they want to destroy it?"

Max explained, "They're not trying to destroy it, Mrs Williams. They're trying to cause enough trouble to make the banks nervous enough to start calling in their loans. They wanted to force your father to sell the stock and go public. Whoever is behind this hasn't got what he wanted yet. Your life is still in danger."

"Then you've got to give her police protection," Rhys demanded.

Max blinked and said tonelessly, "I wouldn't worry about that, Mr Williams. She hasn't been out of our sight since she married you."

47

Berlin
Monday, December 1
10 a.m.

The pain was unbearable and he had lived with it for four weeks.

The doctor had left some pills for him, but Walther Gassner was afraid to take them. He had to stay constantly alert to see that Anna did not try to kill him again, or to escape.

"You should go straight to a hospital," the doctor had told him. "You've lost a good deal of blood – "

"No!" That was the last thing Walther wanted. Stab wounds were reported to the police. Walther had sent for the company doctor because he knew he would not report it. Walther could not afford to have the police snooping around. Not now. The doctor had silently stitched up the gaping wound, his eyes filled with curiosity. When he had finished, he had asked, "Would you like me to send a nurse to the house, Mr Gassner?"

"No. My – my wife will take care of me."

That had been a month ago. Walther had telephoned his secretary and told her that he had had an accident and would be staying at home.

He thought about that terrible moment when Anna had tried to kill him with the shears. He had turned just in time to catch the blade in his shoulder instead of through the heart. He had almost fainted from the pain and shock, but he had retained consciousness long enough to drag Anna to her bedroom and lock her in. And all the while she was screaming, "What have you done with the children? What have you done with the children? . . ."

Since then Walther had kept her in the bedroom. He prepared all her meals. He would take a tray up to Anna's room, unlock the door and enter. She would be huddled in a corner, cringing from him, and she would whisper, "What have you done with the children?"

Sometimes he would open the bedroom door and find her with her ear pressed against the wall, listening for the sounds of their son and daughter. The house was silent now, except for the two of them. Walther knew there was very little time left. His thoughts were interrupted by a faint noise. He listened. And then he heard it again. *Someone was moving around in the hallway upstairs. There was not supposed to be anyone in the house. He had locked all the doors himself.*

Upstairs, Frau Mendler was dusting. She was a day-worker, and this was only her second time in this house. She did not like it. When she had worked here on Wednesday the week before, Herr Gassner had followed her around as though expecting her to steal something. When she had tried to go upstairs to clean, he had angrily stopped her, given her her wages and sent her away. There was something about his manner that frightened her.

Today he was nowhere in sight, *Gott sei Dank*. Frau Mendler had let herself in with the key she had taken the week before, and she had gone upstairs. The house was unnaturally silent, and she decided that no-one was at home. She had cleaned one bedroom and had found some loose change lying around, and a gold pillbox. She started down the hallway towards the next bedroom and tried to open the door. It was locked. Strange. She wondered if they kept something valuable inside. She turned the handle again, and a woman's voice from behind the door whispered, "Who is it?"

Frau Mendler jerked her hand away from the knob, startled.

"Who is it? Who's out there?"

"Frau Mendler, the cleaning lady. Do you want me to do your bedroom?"

"You can't. I'm locked in." The voice was louder now, filled with hysteria. "Help me! Please! Call the police. Tell them my husband has killed our children. He's going to kill me. Hurry! Get away from here before he – "

A hand spun Frau Mendler around and she found herself staring up into the face of Herr Gassner. He looked as pale as death.

"What are you sneaking around here for?" he demanded. He was holding her arm, hurting it.

"I – I'm not sneaking," she said. "Today is my day to clean. The agency – "

"I told the agency I didn't want anyone here. I – " He stopped. Had he telephoned the agency? He had meant to, but he was in such pain that he could no longer remember. Frau Mendler looked into his eyes and she was terrified by what she saw there.

"They never told me," she said.

He stood still, listening for sounds from behind the locked door. Silence.

He turned to Frau Mendler. "Get out of here. Don't come back."
She could not leave the house fast enough. He had not paid her, but she had the gold pillbox and the coins she had found on the dresser. She felt sorry for the poor woman behind the door. She wished she could help her, but she could not afford to get involved. She had a police record.

In Zurich, Detective Max Hornung was reading a teletype from Interpol headquarters in Paris.

INVOICE NUMBER OF SNUFF FILM RAW STOCK USED FOR ROFFE AND SONS GENERAL EXECUTIVE ACCOUNT. PURCHASING AGENT NO LONGER WITH COMPANY. TRYING TO TRACE. WILL KEEP YOU INFORMED. END MESSAGE.

In Paris the police were fishing a nude body out of the Seine. She was a blonde in her late teens. She wore a red ribbon around her neck.

In Zurich, Elizabeth Williams had been placed under twenty-four-hour police protection.

48

The white light flashed, signalling a call on Rhys's private line. Fewer than half a dozen people had the number. He picked up the telephone. "Hello."
"Good morning, darling." There was no mistaking the husky, distinctive voice.
"You shouldn't be calling me."
She laughed. "You never used to worry about things like that. Don't tell me that Elizabeth has tamed you already."
"What do you want?" Rhys asked.
"I want to see you this afternoon."
"That's impossible."
"Don't make me cross, Rhys. Shall I come to Zurich or – ?"
"No, I can't see you here." He hesitated. "I'll come there."
"That's better. Our usual place, *chéri*."
And Hélène Roffe-Martel hung up.
Rhys replaced the receiver slowly and sat thinking. As far as he was concerned, he had had a brief physical affair, with an exciting woman, and it had been finished for some time. But Hélène was not a woman who let go easily. She was

bored with Charles, and she wanted Rhys. "You and I would make a perfect team," she had said, and Hélène Roffe-Martel could be very determined. And very dangerous. Rhys decided the trip to Paris was necessary. He had to make her understand once and for all that there could be nothing further between them.

A few moments later he walked into Elizabeth's office, and her eyes brightened. She put her arms around him and whispered, "I've been thinking about you. Let's go home and play hooky this afternoon."

He grinned. "You're becoming a sex maniac."

She held him closer. "I know. Isn't it lovely?"

"I'm afraid I have to fly to Paris this afternoon, Liz."

She tried to conceal her disappointment. "Shall I come with you?"

"No point. It's just a minor business problem. I'll be back tonight. We'll have a late supper."

When Rhys walked into the familiar small hotel on the Left Bank, Hélène was already there, seated in the dining-room, waiting for him. Rhys had never known her to be late. She was organized and efficient, extraordinarily beautiful, intelligent, a wonderful lover; and yet something was missing. Hélène was a woman without compassion. There was a ruthlessness about her, a killer's instinct. Rhys had seen others hurt by it. He had no intention of becoming one of her victims. He sat down at the table.

She said, "You're looking well, darling. Marriage agrees with you. Is Elizabeth taking good care of you in bed?"

He smiled to take the sting out of his words. "That's none of your business."

Hélène leaned forward and took one of his hands, "Ah, but it is, *chéri*. It is *our* business."

She began stroking his hand, and he thought of her in bed. A tigress, wild, skilled and insatiable. He withdrew his hand.

Hélène's eyes chilled. She said, "Tell me, Rhys. How does it feel to be president of Roffe and Sons?"

He had almost forgotten how ambitious she was, how greedy. He remembered the long conversations they had once had. She was obsessed by the idea of taking control of the company. *You and I, Rhys. If Sam were out of the way, we could run it.*

Even in the midst of their lovemaking: *It's my company, darling. Samuel Roffe's blood is in me. It's mine. I want it. Fuck me, Rhys.*

Power was Hélène's aphrodisiac. And danger. "What did you want to see me about?" Rhys asked.

"I think it's time you and I made some plans."

"I don't know what you're talking about."

She said maliciously, "I know you too well, darling. You're as ambitious as I am. Why did you serve as Sam's shadow all those years when you had dozens of offers to run other companies? Because you knew that one day you would be running Roffe and Sons."

"I stayed because I liked Sam."

She grinned. "Of course, *chéri*. And now you've married his charming little girl." She took a thin black cigar from her purse and lit it with a platinum lighter. "Charles tells me that Elizabeth has arranged to keep control of the stock and that she refuses to sell."

"That's right, Hélène."

"It's occurred to you, of course, that if she had an accident, you would inherit her estate."

Rhys stared at her for a long time.

49

In his home in Olgiata, Ivo Palazzi was casually looking out the window of his living-room when he saw a terrifying sight. Coming up the driveway were Donatella and their three sons. Simonetta was upstairs, taking a nap. Ivo hurried out of the front door and went to meet his second family. He was filled with such rage that he could have killed. He had been so wonderful to this woman, so kind, so loving, and now she was deliberately trying to destroy his career, his marriage, his life. He watched Donatella get out of the Lancia Flavia he had so generously given her. Ivo thought she had never looked more beautiful. The boys climbed out of the car, and were hugging and kissing him. Oh, how Ivo loved them. Oh, how he hoped that Simonetta would not wake up from her nap!

"I came to see your wife," Donatella said stiffly. She turned to the boys. "Come on, boys."

"No!" Ivo commanded.

"How are you going to stop me? If I don't see her today, I'll see her tomorrow."

Ivo was cornered. There was no way out. Yet he knew that he could not let her or anyone else ruin everything he had worked so hard for. Ivo thought of himself as a decent man, and he hated what he knew he must do. Not just for himself, but for Simonetta and Donatella and all his children.

"You will have your money," Ivo promised. "Give me five days."

Donatella looked into his eyes. "Five days," she said.

In London, Sir Alec Nichols was taking part in a serious debate in the House of Commons. He had been chosen to make a major policy speech dealing with the crucial subject of the labour strikes that were crippling the British economy. But it was difficult for him to concentrate. He was thinking about the series of telephone calls he had received over the past few weeks. They had managed to find him wherever he was, at his club, at his barber, restaurants, business meetings. And each time Alec had hung up on them. He knew that what they were asking was only the beginning. Once they controlled him, they would find a way to take over his stock, they would own a piece of a gigantic pharmaceutical company that manufactured drugs of every description. He could not let that happen. They had begun telephoning him four and five times a day until his nerves were stretched to the breaking-point. What worried Alec now was that on this day he had *not* heard from them. He had expected a call at breakfast, and then again when he had lunched at White's. But there were no calls and somehow he could not shake off the feeling that the silence was more ominous than the threats. He tried to push these thoughts away now as he addressed the House.

"No man has been a stauncher friend of labour than I. Our labour force is what makes our country great. Workers feed our mills, turn the wheels in our factories. They are the true élite of this country, the backbone that makes England stand tall and strong among nations." He paused. "However, there comes a time in the fortunes of every nation when certain sacrifices must be made . . ."

He spoke by rote. He was wondering whether he had frightened them off by calling their bluff. After all, they were just small-time hoodlums. He was Sir Alec Nichols, MP. What could they do to him? In all probability he would not hear from them again. From now on they would leave him in peace. Sir Alec finished his speech amid vociferous applause from the back benches.

He was on his way out when an attendant came up to him and said, "I have a message for you, Sir Alec."

Alec turned. "Yes?"

"You're to go home as quickly as possible. There has been an accident."

They were carrying Vivian into the ambulance when Alec arrived at the house. The doctor was at her side. Alec slammed the car against the kerb and was out running before it had stopped. He took one look at Vivian's white, unconscious face and turned to the doctor. "What happened?"

The doctor said helplessly, "I don't know, Sir Alec. I received an anonymous call that there had been an accident. When I got here, I found Lady Nichols on the floor of her bedroom. Her – her kneecaps had been hammered to the floor with spikes."

Alec closed his eyes, fighting off the spasm of nausea that gripped him. He could feel the bile rising in his throat.

"We'll do everything we can, of course, but I think you had better be prepared. It's unlikely that she'll ever walk again."

Alec felt as though he could not breathe. He started towards the ambulance.

"She's under heavy sedation," the doctor said. "I don't think she'll recognize you."

Alec did not even hear him. He climbed into the ambulance and sat in a jump seat, staring down at his wife, oblivious of the back doors being closed, the sound of the siren, and the ambulance beginning to move. He took Vivian's cold hands in his. Her eyes opened. "Alec." Her voice was a slurred whisper.

Alec's eyes filled with tears. "Oh, my darling, my darling . . ."

"Two men . . . wore masks . . . they held me down . . . broke my legs . . . I'll never be able to dance again . . . I'm going to be a cripple, Alec . . . Will you still want me?"

He buried his head in her shoulder and wept. They were tears of despair and agony, and yet there was something else, something he hardly dared admit to himself. He felt a sense of relief. If Vivian were crippled, he would be able to take care of her, she could never leave him for anyone else.

But Alec knew that this was not over. They were not finished with him. This was only their warning. The only way he would ever get rid of them was to give them what they wanted.

Quickly.

50

Zurich
Thursday, December 4

It was exactly noon when the call came through the switchboard at the Kriminalpolizei headquarters in Zurich. It was routed through to Chief Inspector Schmied's office, and when the chief inspector had finished talking he went to find Detective Max Hornung.

"It's all over," he told Max. "The Roffe case has been solved. They've found the killer. Get out to the airport. You've just got time to catch your plane."

Max blinked at him. "Where am I going?"

"To Berlin."

Chief Inspector Schmied telephoned Elizabeth Williams. "I am calling to bring you some good news," he said. "You will no longer need a bodyguard. The murderer has been caught."

Elizabeth found herself gripping the telephone. At long last she was going to learn the name of her faceless enemy. "Who is it?" she asked.

"Walther Gassner."

They were speeding along the autobahn, heading for Wannsee. Max was in the back seat, next to Major Wageman, and two detectives sat in front. They had met Max at Tempelhof Airport, and Major Wageman had briefed Max on the situation as they drove. "The house is surrounded, but we have to be careful how we move in. He's holding his wife hostage."

Max asked, "How did you get on to Walther Gassner?"

"Through you. That's why I thought you would like to be here."

Max was puzzled. "Through me?"

"You told me about the psychiatrist he visited. On a hunch, I sent out Gassner's description to other psychiatrists and found out that he had gone to half a dozen of them, looking for help. Each time he used a different name, then ran away. He knew how ill he was. His wife had phoned us for help a couple of months ago, but when one of our men went out to investigate, she sent him away."

They were turning off the autobahn now, only a few minutes from the house. "This morning we received a call from a cleaning woman, a Frau Mendler. She told us she was working at the Gassner house on Monday and that she talked to Mrs Gassner through the locked door of her bedroom. Mrs Gassner told her that her husband had killed their two children and was going to kill her."

Max blinked. "This happened on *Monday?* And the woman didn't call you until this morning?"

"Frau Mendler has a long police record. She was afraid to come to us. Last night she told her boy friend what had happened, and this morning they decided to call us."

They had reached the Wannsee. The car pulled up a block away from the entrance to the Gassner estate, behind an unmarked car. A man got out of the vehicle and hurried towards Major Wageman and Max. "He's still inside the house, Major. I have men all round the grounds."

"Do you know if the woman is still alive?"

The man hesitated, "No, sir. All the blinds are drawn."

"All right. Let's make it fast and quiet. Get everyone in place. Five minutes."

The man hurried off. Major Wageman reached into the car and pulled out a small walkie-talkie. He began rapidly to issue orders. Max was not listening. He was thinking of something that Major Wageman had said to him a few minutes ago. Something that made no sense. But there was no time to ask him about it now. Men were starting to move towards the house, using trees and shrubs as cover. Major Wageman turned to Max. "Coming, Hornung?"

It seemed to Max that there was an army of men infiltrating the garden. Some of them were supplied with telescopic rifles and armoured vests; others carried snub-nosed tear gas rifles. The operation was carried out with mathematical precision. At a signal from Major Wageman, tear gas grenades were simultaneously hurled through the downstairs and upstairs windows of the house and at the same instant the front and rear doors were smashed in by men wearing gas masks. Behind them came more detectives with drawn guns.

When Max and Major Wageman ran through the open front door, the hallway was filled with acrid smoke, but it was rapidly being dispersed by the open windows and doors. Two detectives were bringing Walther Gassner into the hallway in handcuffs. He was wearing a robe and pyjamas and he was unshaven and his face looked gaunt and his eyes swollen.

Max stared at him, seeing him for the first time in person. Somehow he seemed unreal to Max. It was the *other* Walther Gassner who was real, the man in the computer, whose life had been spelled out in digits. Which was the shadow and which was the substance?

Major Wageman said, "You're under arrest, Herr Gassner. Where is your wife?"

Walther Gassner said hoarsely, "She's not here. She's gone! I – "

Upstairs there was the sound of a door being forced open, and a moment later a detective called down, "I've found her. She was locked in her room."

The detective appeared on the staircase, supporting a trembling Anna Gassner. Her hair was stringy and her face was streaked and blotchy, and she was sobbing.

"Oh, thank God," she said. "Thank God you've come!"

Gently the detective led her downstairs towards the group standing in the enormous reception hall. When Anna Gassner looked up and saw her husband, she began to scream.

"It's all right, Frau Gassner," Major Wageman said soothingly. "He can't harm you any more."

"My children," she cried. "He killed my children!"

Max was watching Walther Gassner's face. He was staring at his wife with an expression of utter hopelessness. He looked broken and lifeless.

"Anna," he whispered. "Oh, Anna."

Major Wageman said, "You have the right to remain silent or to ask for a lawyer. For your own sake I hope you will co-operate with us."

Walther was not listening. "Why did you have to call them, Anna?" he pleaded. "Why? Weren't we happy together?"

"The children are dead," Anna Gassner shrieked. "They're dead."

Major Wageman looked at Walther Gassner and asked, "Is that true?"

Walther nodded, and his eyes looked old and defeated. "Yes . . . They're dead."

"Murderer! Murderer!" his wife was shrieking.

Major Wageman said, "We would like you to show us the bodies. Will you do that?"

Walther Gassner was crying now, the tears rolling down his cheeks. He could not speak.

Major Wageman said, "Where are they?"

It was Max who answered. "The children are buried in Saint Paul's graveyard."

Everyone in the room turned to stare at him. "They died at birth five years ago," Max explained.

"Murderer!" Anna Gassner screamed at her husband.

And they turned and saw the madness blazing out of her eyes.

51

Zurich
Thursday, December 4
8 p.m.

The cold winter night had fallen, snuffing out the brief twilight. It had begun to snow, a soft, windblown powder that dusted the city. In the administration building at Roffe and Sons the lights of the deserted offices flowed against the darkness like pale yellow moons.

In her office Elizabeth was alone, working late, waiting for Rhys to return from Geneva, where he had gone for a meeting. She wished that he would hurry. Everyone had long since left the building. Elizabeth felt restless, unable to concentrate. She could not get Walther and Anna out of her mind. She remembered Walther as she had first met him, boyish and handsome and madly in love with Anna. Or pretending to be. It was so hard to believe that Walther was responsible for all those terrible acts. Elizabeth's heart went out to Anna. Elizabeth had tried several times to telephone her, but there had been no answer. She would fly to Berlin, to give her whatever comfort she could. The telephone rang, startling her. She picked it up. It was Alec on the other end of the line, and Elizabeth was pleased to hear his voice.

"You've heard about Walther?" Alec asked.

"Yes. It's horrible. I can't believe it."

"Don't, Elizabeth."

She thought she had misunderstood him. "What?"

"Don't believe it. Walther's not guilty."

"The police said – "

"They've made a mistake. Walther was the first person Sam and I checked out. We cleared him. He's not the one we are looking for."

Elizabeth stared at the phone, filled with a sense of confusion. *He's not the one we were looking for.* She said, "I – I don't understand what you're saying."

Alec replied hesitantly, "It's awkward doing this over a telephone, Elizabeth, but I haven't had an opportunity to speak to you alone."

"Speak to me about what?" Elizabeth asked.

"For the past year," Alec said, "someone has been sabotaging the company. There was an explosion in one of our South American factories, patents have been stolen, dangerous drugs have been mislabelled. There isn't time to go into it all now. I went to Sam and suggested that we engage an outside investigating agency to try to find out who was behind it. We agreed not to discuss it with anyone else."

It was as though the earth had suddenly stopped and time was frozen. A dizzying feeling of *déjà vu* swept through Elizabeth. Alec's words were coming through the telephone, but it was Rhys's voice she was hearing. Rhys saying, *Someone has been sabotaging Roffe and Sons. It was done very cleverly, so that it seemed to be a series of accidents. But I began to see a pattern. I went to Sam with it and we decided to hire an outside agency to investigate.*

Alec's voice was going on. "They finished their report and Sam took it with him to Chamonix. We discussed it over the telephone."

Elizabeth could hear Rhys's voice saying, *Sam asked me to come up to Chamonix to discuss it with him . . . We decided to keep it just between the two of us until we could find out who was responsible for what was happening.*

Elizabeth was suddenly finding it hard to breathe. When she spoke, she tried to make her voice sound normal. "Alec, who – who else knew about the report beside you and Sam?"

"No one. That was the whole point. According to Sam, the report showed that whoever was guilty had to be someone high up in the company."

The highest echelon. And Rhys had not mentioned being in Chamonix until the detective had brought it up.

She asked slowly, the words dragged out of her, "Could Sam have told Rhys about it?"

"No. Why?"

There was only one way Rhys could have known what was in the report. He had stolen it. There was only one reason he could have gone to Chamonix. To kill Sam. Elizabeth did not hear the rest of what Alec was saying. The loud roaring in her ears drowned his words. She dropped the receiver, her head spinning, fighting off the horror that was starting to engulf her. Her mind was a series of chaotic jumbled images. At the time she had had the jeep accident she had left a message for Rhys that she would be in Sardinia. The night of the lift crash, Rhys had not been at the board meeting, but he had appeared later when she and Kate were alone. *Thought I ought to give you a hand.* And soon afterwards he had left the building. *Or had he?* Her body was trembling now. It had to be some terrible mistake. Not Rhys. *No!* It was a scream in her mind.

Elizabeth rose from the desk and on unsteady legs walked through the connecting door to Rhys's office. The room was dark. She turned on the lights and stood looking around uncertainly, not sure what she expected to find. She was not searching for evidence of Rhys's guilt, she was looking for evidence of his innocence. It was unbearable to think that the man she loved, the man who had held her in his arms and made love to her, could be a cold-blooded murderer.

There was an engagement book on Rhys's desk. Elizabeth opened it, turning the pages back to September, to the holiday weekend of the jeep accident. Nairobi was marked on his calendar. She would need to check his passport to see if he had gone there. She started to look through Rhys's desk for the passport, feeling guilty, knowing that somehow there had to be an innocent explanation.

The bottom drawer of Rhys's desk was locked. Elizabeth hesitated. She knew she had no right to break into it. Somehow it was a violation of faith, the crossing of a forbidden boundary, from which there could be no return. Rhys would know that she had done this and she would have to tell him why. And yet Elizabeth had to know. She picked up a letter opener from the desk and broke the lock, splintering the wood.

In the drawer were stacks of notes and memoranda. She lifted them out. There was an envelope addressed to Rhys Williams in a woman's handwriting. It was postmarked a few days earlier, from Paris. Elizabeth hesitated a moment, then opened it. The letter was from Hélène. It began, "*Chéri*, I tried to reach you by phone. It is urgent that we meet again soon to make our plans . . ." Elizabeth did not finish the letter.

She was staring at the stolen report in the drawer.

MR SAM ROFFE
CONFIDENTIAL
NO COPIES

She felt the room begin to spin and she clutched the edge of the desk for support. She stood there for ever, eyes closed, waiting for the dizziness to pass. Her killer had a face now. It was the face of her husband. The silence was broken by the insistent ringing of a distant telephone. It took Elizabeth a long time to realize where the sound was coming from. Slowly she walked back to her office. She picked up the telephone.

It was the attendant in the lobby, his voice cheerful. "Just checkin' that you're still there, Mrs Williams. Mr Williams is on his way up to you."

To stage another accident.

Her life was all that stood between Rhys and the control of Roffe and Sons. She could not face him, could not pretend that nothing was wrong. The moment he saw her, he would know. She had to escape. In a blind panic, Elizabeth grabbed her purse and coat and started out of the office. She stopped. She had forgotten something. Her passport. She had to get far away from Rhys, some place where he could not find her. She hurried back to her desk, found the passport and ran out into the corridor, her heart pounding as though it would burst. The indicator on the private lift was swinging upward.

Eight . . . nine . . . ten . . .

Elizabeth began racing down the stairs, running for her life.

52

There was a ferryboat that ran between Civitavecchia and Sardinia, carrying passengers and automobiles. Elizabeth drove aboard in a rental car, lost among a dozen other cars. Airports kept records, but the huge boat was anonymous. Elizabeth was one of a hundred passengers crossing over to the island of Sardinia for a holiday. She was sure she could not have been followed, and yet she was filled with an unreasoning fear. Rhys had gone too far to let anything stop him now. She was the only one who could expose him. He would have to get rid of her.

When Elizabeth had fled from the building, she had had no idea where she was going. She knew only that she must get out of Zurich and hide somewhere, that she would not be safe until Rhys was caught. *Sardinia*. It was the first place she thought of. She had rented a small car and had stopped at a phone booth along the auto route to Italy and had tried to call Alec. He was out. She left a message for him to call her in Sardinia. Unable to reach Detective Max Hornung, she left the same message for him.

She would be at the villa in Sardinia. But this time she would not be alone. The police would be there to protect her.

When the ferryboat landed in Olbia, Elizabeth found that it would not be necessary to go to the police. They were waiting for her in the person of Bruno Campagna, the detective she had met with Chief of Police Ferraro. It had been Campagna who had taken her to look at the jeep following the accident. The detective hurried over to Elizabeth's car and said, "We were beginning to get very worried about you, Mrs Williams."

Elizabeth looked at him, surprised.

"We received a call from the Swiss police," Campagna explained, "asking us to keep an eye out for you. We've been covering all the boats and airports."

Elizabeth was filled with a feeling of gratitude. Max Hornung! He had got her message. Detective Campagna looked at her tired, drawn face. "Would you like me to drive?"

"Please," Elizabeth said gratefully.

She slid over to the passenger seat, and the tall detective got behind the wheel. "Where would you rather wait – the police station or your villa?"

"The villa, if someone could stay with me. I'd – I'd rather not be there alone."

Campagna nodded reassuringly. "Don't worry. We have orders to keep you well guarded. I'll stay there with you tonight, and we'll have a radio car stationed at the driveway leading to your place. No one will be able to get near you."

His confidence was enough to let Elizabeth relax. Detective Campagna drove swiftly and expertly, winding through the little streets of Olbia, heading up the mountain road that led to the Costa Smeralda. Every place they passed reminded her of Rhys.

Elizabeth asked, "Has there been any – any news of my husband?"

Detective Campagna gave her a quick, compassionate glance, then turned his eyes back to the road. "He's on the run, but he won't get far. They expect to have him in custody by morning."

Elizabeth knew that she should feel a sense of relief, and instead the words brought a terrible, aching pain. It was Rhys they were talking about, Rhys who was being hunted like some animal. He had placed her in this terrible nightmare, and now he was caught up in his own nightmare, fighting for his life, as he had made her fight for hers. And how she had trusted him! How she had believed in his kindness and his gentleness and his love! She shuddered. Detective Campagna asked her, "Are you cold?"

"No. I'm fine." She felt feverish. A warm wind seemed to be whistling through the car, setting her nerves on edge. At first she thought it was her imagination until Detective Campagna said, "I'm afraid we're in for a sirocco. It's going to be a busy night."

Elizabeth understood what he meant. The sirocco could drive people and animals crazy. The wind blew in from the Sahara, hot and dry and grainy with sand, with a macabre keening sound that had an eerie, unbalancing effect on the nerves. The crime rate always went up during a sirocco, and the judges treated criminals leniently.

An hour later, out of the dark, the villa loomed ahead of them. Detective Campagna turned into the driveway, drove into the empty carport and turned off the engine. He walked round to the side of the car and opened Elizabeth's door. "I'd like you to stay right behind me, Mrs Williams," he said. "Just in case."

"All right," Elizabeth replied.

They moved towards the front door of the darkened villa. Detective Campagna said, "I'm sure he's not here but we won't take any chances. May I have your key?"

Elizabeth handed him the key. He gently edged her to one side of the door, inserted the key and opened the door, his other hand hovering near his gun. He reached inside and flicked on the light switch, and the hallway was suddenly flooded with brilliant light.

"I'd like you to show me the house," Detective Campagna said. "Make sure we cover every room. Okay?"

"Yes."

They started walking through the house, and everywhere they went the huge detective turned the lights on. He looked in all the closets and corners and checked to make sure the windows and doors were locked. There was no one else in the house. When they returned to the living-room downstairs, Detective Campagna said, "If you don't mind, I'd like to call headquarters."

"Of course," Elizabeth said. She led him into the study.

He picked up the telephone and dialled. A moment later he said, "Detective Campagna. We're at the villa. I'll camp here for the night. You can send a cruiser up to park at the foot of the driveway." He listened a moment, then said into the phone, "She's fine. Just a little tired. I'll check in later." He replaced the receiver.

Elizabeth sank into a chair. She was feeling tense and nervous, but she knew that it was going to be worse tomorrow. Much worse. She would be safe but Rhys would be either dead or in prison. Somehow, in spite of everything he had done, she could not bear the thought of that.

Detective Campagna was studying her, a look of concern on his face. "I could use a cup of coffee," he said. "How about you?"

She nodded. "I'll make some." She started to rise.

"You stay where you are, Mrs Williams. My wife says I make the best coffee in the world."

Elizabeth managed a smile. "Thank you." She sank back gratefully. She had not realized how emotionally drained she felt. For the first time now, Elizabeth admitted to herself that even during the telephone conversation with Alec she had felt that there might be some mistake, some explanation, that Rhys must be innocent. Even while she was fleeing, she had held on to the thought that he could not have done all those terrible things, that he could not have killed her father and then made love to her and tried to kill her. It would take a monster to do those things. And so she had kept that tiny ember of hope flickering in her. It had died when Detective Campagna had said, *He's on the run, but he won't get far. They expect to have him in custody by morning.*

She could not bear to think about it any more, but she could think of nothing else. How long had Rhys been planning to take over the company? Probably from the moment he had met that impressionable fifteen-year-old girl, alone and lonely in a Swiss boarding school. That was when he must have decided how he was going to outwit Sam – through his daughter. How easy it had been for him. The dinner at Maxim's and the long friendly talks during the years, and the charm – oh, the incredible charm! He had been patient. He had waited until she had become a woman, and the greatest irony of all was that Rhys did not even have to woo her. She had wooed *him*. How he must have laughed at her. He and Hélène. Elizabeth wondered whether they were in it together, and she wondered where Rhys was now, and whether the police would kill him when they caught him. She began to weep uncontrollably.

"Mrs Williams . . ." Detective Campagna was standing over her, holding out a cup of coffee.

"Drink this," he said. "You'll feel better."

"I – I'm sorry," Elizabeth apologized. "I don't usually carry on this way."

He said to her gently, "I think you're doing *molto bene*."

Elizabeth took a sip of the hot coffee. He had put something in it. She looked up at him, and he grinned. "I decided a shot of Scotch wouldn't do you any harm."

He sat down across from her in a companionable silence. She was grateful for his company. She could never have stayed here alone. Not until she knew what had happened to Rhys, not until she knew whether he was dead or alive. She finished her coffee.

Detective Campagna looked at his watch. "The patrol car should be here any minute. There'll be two men in it on guard duty all night. I'll stay downstairs. I suggest you go up to bed now and try to get some sleep."

Elizabeth shivered. "I couldn't sleep." But even as she said it, her body was filled with an enormous lassitude. The long drive and the tremendous strain she had been under for so long were finally taking their toll.

"Maybe I'll just lie down for a bit," she said. She found it difficult to get the words out.

Elizabeth lay in her bed, fighting against sleep. Somehow it did not seem fair that she should be asleep while Rhys was being hunted. She visualized him being shot down on some cold, dark street and she shuddered. She tried to keep her eyes open, but they were heavy weights, and the instant they closed she began to feel herself sinking down, down, into a soft cushion of nothingness.

Some time later she was awakened by the screams.

53

Elizabeth sat up in bed, her heart beating wildly, not knowing what it was that had awakened her. Then she heard it again. An eerie, high-pitched scream that seemed to come from right outside her window, the sound of someone in the agony of death. Elizabeth arose and stumbled over to the window and looked out into the night. It was a landscape by Daumier, lit by a chill winter moon. The trees were black and stark, their branches whipped by a wild wind. In the distance, far below, the sea was a boiling cauldron.

The scream came again. And again. And Elizabeth realized what it was. The singing rocks. The sirocco had risen in intensity and was blowing through them, making that terrible keening sound, over and over. And it became Rhys's voice she was hearing, crying out for her, begging her to help him. She could not stand it. She covered her ears with her hands, but the sound would not go away.

Elizabeth started towards the bedroom door, and she was surprised at how weak she was. Her mind was hazy with exhaustion. She walked out into the hallway and started down the stairs. She felt dazed, as though she had been drugged. She tried to call out to Detective Campagna, but her voice was a hoarse croak. She kept descending the long flight of stairs, fighting to keep her balance. She called aloud, "Detective Campagna."

There was no answer. Elizabeth stumbled into the living-room. He was not there. She moved from room to room, holding on to furniture to keep from falling down.

Detective Campagna was not in the house.

She was alone.

Elizabeth stood in the hallway, her mind confused, trying to force herself to think. The detective had stepped outside to talk to the policemen in the patrol car. Of course that was it. She walked to the front door and opened it and looked outside.

No-one was there. Only the black night and the screaming wind. With a growing feeling of fear, Elizabeth turned and made her way back to the study. She would call the police station and find out what had happened. She picked up the telephone, and the line was dead.

It was at that instant that all the lights went out.

54

In London, at Westminster Hospital, Vivian Nichols regained consciousness as she was being wheeled out of the operating room, down the long, bleak corridor. The operation had taken eight hours. In spite of everything the skilled surgeons had been able to do, she would never walk again. She woke in agonizing pain, whispering Alec's name over and over. She needed him, she needed to have him at her side, to have him promise that he would still love her.

The hospital staff was unable to locate Alec.

In Zurich, in the communications room of the Kriminalpolizei, an Interpol message was received from Australia. The former film purchasing agent for Roffe and Sons had been located in Sydney. He had died of a heart attack three days earlier. His ashes were being shipped home. Interpol had been unable to obtain any information regarding the purchase of the film. They were awaiting further instructions.

In Berlin, Walther Gassner was seated in the discreet waiting-room of an exclusive, private sanatorium in a pleasant suburb outside the city. He had been there, motionless, for almost ten hours. From time to time a nurse or an attendant would stop to speak to him and offer him something to eat or drink. Walther paid no attention to them. He was waiting for his Anna.

It would be a long wait.

In Olgiata, Simonetta Palazzi was listening to a woman's voice on the telephone. "My name is Donatella Spolini," the voice said. "We've never met, Mrs Palazzi, but we have a great deal in common. I suggest we meet for luncheon at the Bolognese in the Piazza del Popolo. Shall we say one o'clock tomorrow?"

Simonetta had a conflicting appointment at the beauty parlour the next day, but she adored mysteries. "I'll be there," she said. "How will I know you?"

"I'll have my three sons with me."

In her villa in Le Vésinet, Hélène Roffe-Martel was reading a note she had found waiting for her on the mantelpiece in the drawing-room. It was from Charles. He had left her, run away. "You will never see me again," the note said. "Don't try to find me." Hélène tore the note into small pieces. She would see him again. She would find him.

In Rome, Max Hornung was at Leonardo da Vinci Airport. For the past two hours he had been trying to get a message through to Sardinia, but because of the storm all communications were down. Max went back to the flight operations office to talk to the airport manager again. "You've *got* to get me on a plane to Sardinia," Max said. "Believe me, it's a matter of life and death."

The airport manager said, "I believe you, signore, but there is nothing I can do about it. Sardinia is shut up tight. The airports are closed. Even the boats have stopped running. Nothing is going in or out of that island until the sirocco is over."

"When will that be?" Max asked.

The airport manager turned to study the large weather map on the wall. "It looks like it's good for at least another twelve hours."

Elizabeth Williams would not be alive in twelve hours.

55

The dark was hostile, filled with invisible enemies waiting to strike at her. And Elizabeth realized now that she was completely at their mercy. Detective Campagna had brought her here to be murdered. He was Rhys's man. Elizabeth remembered Max Hornung explaining about switching the jeeps. *Whoever did it had help. Someone who knew the island.* How convincing Detective Campagna had been. *We've been covering all the boats and airports.* Because Rhys had known she would come here to hide. *Where would you like to wait – at the police station or your villa?* Detective Campagna had had no intention of letting her go to the police. It had not been headquarters he had phoned. It had been Rhys. *We're at the villa.*

Elizabeth knew she had to flee, but she no longer had the strength. She was fighting to keep her eyes open, and her arms and legs felt heavy. She suddenly realized why. He had drugged her coffee. Elizabeth turned and made her way into the dark kitchen. She opened a cabinet and fumbled around until she found what she wanted. She took down a bottle of vinegar and splashed some into a glass with water and forced herself to drink it. Immediately she began to retch into the sink. In a few minutes she felt a little better, but she was still weak. Her brain refused to function. It was as if all the circuits inside her had already closed down, were preparing for the darkness of death.

"No," she told herself fiercely. "You're not going to die like that. You're going to fight. They're going to have to kill you." She raised her voice and said, "Rhys, come and kill me," but her voice was barely a whisper. She turned and headed for the hallway, feeling her way by instinct. She stopped under the portrait of old Samuel, while outside the moaning, alien wind tore against the house, screaming at her, taunting her, warning her. She stood there in the blackness, alone, facing a choice of terrors. She could go outside, into the unknown, and try to escape from Rhys, or she could stay here and try to fight him. But how?

Her mind was trying to tell her something but she was still dazed by the drug. She could not concentrate. Something about an accident.

She remembered then and said aloud, "He has to make it look like an accident."

You must stop him, Elizabeth. Had Samuel spoken? Or was it in her mind?

"I can't. It's too late." Her eyes were closing, and her face was pressed against the coolness of the portrait. It would be so wonderful to go to sleep. But there was something she had to do. She tried to remember what it was, but it kept slipping away.

Don't let it look like an accident. Make it look like murder. Then the company will never belong to him.

Elizabeth knew what she had to do. She walked into the study. She stood there a moment, then reached for a table lamp and hurled it against a mirror. She could hear them both smash. She lifted a small chair and pounded it against the wall until the chair began to splinter. She moved over to the bookcase and began ripping pages out of the books, scattering them around the room. She tore the useless telephone cord out of the wall. Let Rhys explain this to the police, she thought. Do not go gentle into that good night. Well, she would not go gentle. They would have to take her by force.

A sudden gale swept through the room, swirling the papers through the air, then died away. It took Elizabeth a moment to realize what had happened.

She was no longer alone in the house.

At Leonardo da Vinci Airport, near the *merci* area where freight was handled, Detective Max Hornung was watching a helicopter land. By the time the pilot had his door open Max was at his side. "Can you fly me to Sardinia?" he asked.

The pilot stared at him. "What's going on? I just flew somebody there. There's a bad storm blowing."

"Will you take me?"

"It'll cost you triple."

Max did not even hesitate. He climbed into the helicopter. As they took off, Max turned to the pilot and asked, "Who was the passenger you took to Sardinia?"

"His name was Williams."

The dark was Elizabeth's ally now, concealing her from her killer. It was too late to get away. She had to try to find a place to hide somewhere in the house. She went upstairs, putting distance between herself and Rhys. At the top of the stairs she hesitated, then turned towards Sam's bedroom. Something leaped at her out of the dark, and she started to scream, but it was only the shadow of a wind-whipped tree through the window. Her heart was pounding so hard that she was sure that Rhys would be able to hear it downstairs.

Delay him, her mind said. *But how?* Her head felt heavy. Everything was fuzzy. Think! she told herself. What would old Samuel have done? She walked to the bedroom at the end of the hall, took the key from the inside and locked the door from the outside. Then she locked the other doors and they were the doors of the gates of the ghetto in Krakow, and Elizabeth was not sure why she was doing it, and then she remembered that she had killed Aram and that they must not catch her. She saw the beam of a flashlight below, starting to move up the stairs, and her heart leaped. Rhys was coming for her. Elizabeth began to climb the tower stairs, and halfway up, her knees began to buckle. She slid to the floor and crawled the rest of the way on her hands and knees. She reached the top of the stairs and dragged herself upright. She opened the door to the tower room and went in. *The door*, Samuel said. *Lock the door.*

Elizabeth locked the door, but she knew that that would not keep Rhys out. At least, she thought, he will have to break it down. More violence to explain. Her death was going to look like murder. She pushed furniture against the door, moving slowly, as though the darkness were a heavy sea dragging her down. She pushed a table against the door, then an armchair and another table, working like an automaton, fighting for time, building her pitiable fortress against death. From the floor below she heard a crash and a moment later another and then a third. Rhys was breaking down the bedroom doors, looking for her. Signs of an attack, a trail for the police to follow. She had tricked him, as he had tricked her. Yet something was vaguely bothering her. If Rhys had to make her death look like an accident, why was he breaking down doors? She moved to the French doors and looked outside, listening to the mad wind singing a dirge to her. Beyond the balcony there was a sheer drop to the sea below. There was no escape from this room. This was where Rhys would have to come to get her. Elizabeth felt around for a weapon, but there was nothing that could help her.

She waited in the dark for her killer.

What was Rhys waiting for? Why didn't he break the door down and get it over with? *Break the door down*. Something was wrong. Even if he took her body away from here and disposed of it somewhere else, Rhys would still not be able to explain the violence of the house, the smashed mirror, the broken doors. Elizabeth tried to put herself in Rhys's mind, to figure out what plan he could have that would explain all those things without the police suspecting him of her death. There was only one way.

And even as Elizabeth thought of it, she could smell the smoke.

56

From the helicopter Max could see the coast of Sardinia, thickly blanketed by a cloud of swirling red dust. The pilot shouted above the din of the rotor blades, "It's got worse. I don't know if I can land."

"You've got to!" Max yelled. "Head for Porto Cervo."

The pilot turned to look at Max. "That's at the top of a fucking mountain."

"I know," Max said. "Can you do it?"

"Our chances are about seventy-thirty."

"Which way?"

"Against."

The smoke was seeping in under the door, coming up from below through the floorboards, and a new sound had been added to the shrieking of the wind. The roar of flames. Elizabeth knew now, she had the answer, but it was too late to save her life. She was trapped here. Of course it did not matter whether doors and mirrors and furniture had been smashed, because in a few minutes nothing would be left of this house or of her. Everything would be ruined by the fire, as the laboratory and Emil Joeppli had been destroyed, and Rhys would have an alibi in some other place, so that he could not be blamed. He had beaten her. He had beaten them all.

The smoke was beginning to billow into the room now – yellow, acrid fumes that made Elizabeth choke. She could see the edges of flame start to lick at the cracks of the door, and she began to feel the heat.

It was her anger that gave Elizabeth the strength to move.

Through the blinding haze of smoke she felt her way towards the French doors. She pushed them open and stepped on to the balcony. The instant the doors opened, the flames from the hallway leaped into the room, licking at the walls. Elizabeth stood on the balcony, gratefully gulping in deep breaths of fresh air as the wind tore at her clothes. She looked down. The balcony protruded from the side of the building, a tiny island hanging over an abyss. There was no hope, no escape.

Unless . . . Elizabeth looked up at the sloping slate roof above her head. If there was some way for her to reach the roof and get to the other side of the house that was not burning yet, she might get away. She stretched her arms as high as she could, but the eave of the roof was beyond her reach. The flames were beginning to move closer now, enveloping the room. There was one slender chance. Elizabeth took it. She forced herself to go back into the blazing, smoke-filled room, choking from the acrid fumes. She grabbed the chair behind her father's desk and dragged it on to the balcony. Fighting to keep her balance, she positioned the chair and stood on top of it. Her fingers could reach the roof now, but they could not find a grip. She fumbled blindly, vainly, searching to get a purchase.

Inside, the flames had reached the curtains and were dancing all around the room, attacking the books and the carpet and the furniture, moving towards the balcony. Elizabeth's fingers suddenly found a grip on a protruding slate. Her arms were leaden; she was not sure she could hold on. She started to pull herself up, and the chair began to slip away from her. With her last remaining strength she pulled herself up and held on. She was climbing the walls of the ghetto now, fighting for her life. She kept pulling and straining and suddenly she found herself lying on the sloping roof, gasping for breath. She forced herself to move, inching her way upward, pressing her body hard against the steep pitch of the roof, aware that one slip would hurtle her into the black abyss below. She reached the peak of the roof and paused to catch her breath and take her bearings. The balcony she had just escaped from was blazing. There could be no turning back.

Looking down on the far side of the house, Elizabeth could see the balcony of one of the guest bedrooms. There were no flames there yet. But Elizabeth did not know whether she would be able to reach it. The roof slanted sharply downward, the slates were loose, the wind was pulling madly at her. If she slipped, there would be nothing to stop her fall. She stayed where she was, frozen, afraid to try it. And then, like a sudden miracle, a figure appeared on the guest balcony, and it was Alec, and he was looking up and calling out calmly, "You can make it, old girl. Nice and easy."

And Elizabeth's heart soared within her.

"Take it slow," Alec counselled. "One step at a time. It's a piece of cake."

And Elizabeth began to let herself move towards him, carefully, sliding down inch by inch, not letting go of one slate until she had found a firm grip on another. It seemed to take for ever. And all the while she heard Alec's encouraging voice, urging her on. She was almost there now, sliding towards the balcony. A slate loosened, and she started to fall.

"Hold on!" Alec called.

Elizabeth found another hold, grabbing it fiercely. She had reached the edge of the roof now, with nothing below her but endless space. She would have to drop down on to the balcony where Alec stood waiting. If she missed. . .

Alec was looking up at her, his face filled with quiet confidence. "Don't look down," he said. "Close your eyes, and let yourself go. I'll catch you."

She tried. She took a deep breath, and then another. She knew she had to let go and yet she could not bring herself to do it. Her fingers were frozen to the tiles.

"Now!" Alec called, and Elizabeth let herself drop and she was falling into space, and suddenly she was caught in Alec's arms as he pulled her to safety. She closed her eyes in relief.

"Well done," Alec said.

And she felt the muzzle of the gun against her head.

57

The helicopter pilot was flying as low as he dared over the island, skimming the treetops, trying to avoid the punishing winds. Even at that altitude the air was filled with turbulence. In the distance ahead the pilot saw the mountain peak of Porto Cervo. Max saw it at the same moment. "There it is!" Max shouted. "I can see the villa." And then he saw something else that made his heart jump. "It's on fire!"

On the balcony Elizabeth heard the sound of the approaching helicopter over the wind, and she looked up. Alec paid no attention. He was watching Elizabeth, his eyes filled with pain. "It was for Vivian. I had to do it for Vivian. You see that, don't you? They have to find you in the fire."

Elizabeth was not listening. She could only think, *It wasn't Rhys. It wasn't Rhys.* All the time it had been Alec. Alec had killed her father and had tried to kill her. He had stolen the report and then tried to frame Rhys with it. He had terrified her into running away from Rhys because Alec had known that she would come here.

The helicopter had disappeared from sight now, beyond some nearby trees.

Alec said, "Close your eyes, Elizabeth."

She said fiercely, "No!"

And Rhys's voice suddenly called, "Drop the gun, Alec!"

They both looked down, and on the lawn below, in the light of the flickering flames, they saw Rhys and Chief of Police Luigi Ferraro and half a dozen detectives, armed with rifles.

"It's finished, Alec," Rhys shouted. "Let her go."

One of the detectives with a telescopic rifle said, "I can't shoot at him unless she moves out of the way."

Move, Rhys prayed. *Move!*

From behind the trees across the lawn Max Hornung came hurrying up to Rhys. He stopped as he saw the tableau above. Rhys said, "I got your message. I was too late."

They were both staring up at the two figures on the balcony, puppets, backlit by the rising flames coming from the far side of the villa. The wind was whipping the house into a gigantic torch, lighting the surrounding mountains, turning the night into an inferno, a blazing Valhalla.

Elizabeth turned and looked into Alec's face, and it was a mask of death, his eyes unseeing. He moved away from her towards the balcony door.

On the ground the detective said, "I've got him," and raised his rifle. He fired once. Alec staggered, then disappeared through the door into the house.

One moment there were two figures on the balcony, and then only one.

Elizabeth screamed, "Rhys!"

But he was already racing towards her.

Everything after that happened in a quick, confused kaleidoscope of motion. Rhys was picking her up and carrying her down to safety, and she clung tightly to him and could not hold him close enough.

She was lying on the grass, with her eyes closed, and Rhys was holding her in his arms, saying, "I love you, Liz. I love you, my darling."

She listened to his voice washing over her, caressing her. She could not speak. She looked into his eyes and saw all the love and anguish, and there was so much she wanted to tell him. She was filled with guilt for all of her terrible suspicions. She would spend the rest of her life making it up to him.

She was too weary to think about it now, too weary to think about any of it. It was as though it had all happened to someone else in some other place, at some other time.

The only important thing was that she and Rhys were together. She felt his strong arms holding her close, for ever, and it was enough.

58

It was like stepping into a blazing corner of hell. The smoke was getting thicker, filling the room with dancing chimeras that kept vanishing. The fire leaped down at Alec, fondling his hair, and the crackle of the flames became Vivian's voice calling to him in an irresistible siren song.

In a sudden flare of brightness, he saw her. She was stretched out on the bed, her beautiful body naked except for the scarlet ribbon tied around her neck, the same red ribbon she had worn the first time he had made love to her. She called his name again, her voice filled with longing. And this time she wanted *him*, not the others. He moved closer, and she whispered, "You're the only one I ever loved."

And Alec believed it. He had had to punish her because of the things she had done. But he had been clever – he had made those others pay for her sins. The terrible things he had done had been for her. As he moved towards her, Vivian whispered again, "You're the only one I ever loved, Alec," and he knew that it was true.

She was holding out her beckoning arms to him, and he sank down beside her. He embraced her, and they became one. He was inside her, and he *was* her. And this time he was able to satisfy her. And he felt such pleasure that it became an exquisite pain beyond bearing. He could feel the heat from her body consuming him, and even as he watched in wonder, the ribbon around Vivian's neck turned into a vivid tongue of flame caressing him, licking at him. In the next instant, a blazing beam from the ceiling crashed on top of him in a fiery pyre.

Alec died as the others had. In ecstasy.

Master of the Game

For my brother,
Richard
the Lion-Hearted

My appreciation goes to Miss Geraldine Hunter for her endless patience and assistance in preparing this manuscript.

"And hence one master-passion in the breast,
Like Aaron's serpent, swallows up the rest."

— Alexander Pope,
Essay on Man, Epistle II

"Diamonds resist blows to such an extent that an iron hammer may be split in two and even the anvil itself may be displaced. This invincible force, which defies Nature's two most violent forces, iron and fire, can be broken by ram's blood. But it must be steeped in blood that is fresh and warm and, even so, many blows are needed."

— Pliny the Elder

Prologue

Kate
1982

The large ballroom was crowded with familiar ghosts come to help celebrate her birthday. Kate Blackwell watched them mingle with the flesh-and-blood people, and in her mind, the scene was a dreamlike fantasy as the visitors from another time and place glided around the dance floor with the unsuspecting guests in black tie and long, shimmering evening gowns. There were one hundred people at the party at Cedar Hill House, in Dark Harbor, Maine. *Not counting the ghosts*, Kate Blackwell thought wryly.

She was a slim, petite woman, with a regal bearing that made her appear taller than she was. She had a face that one remembered. A proud bone structure, dawn-gray eyes and a stubborn chin, a blending of her Scottish and Dutch ancestors. She had fine, white hair that once had been a luxuriant black cascade, and against the graceful folds of her ivory velvet dress, her skin had the soft translucence old age sometimes brings.

I don't feel ninety, Kate Blackwell thought. *Where have all the years gone?* She watched the dancing ghosts. *They know. They were there. They were a part of those years, a part of my life.* She saw Banda, his proud black face beaming. And there was her David, dear David, looking tall and young and handsome, the way he looked when she first fell in love with him, and he was smiling at her, and she thought, *Soon, my darling, soon.* And she wished David could have lived to know his great grand-son.

Kate's eyes searched the large room until she saw him. He was standing near the orchestra, watching the musicians. He was a strikingly handsome boy, almost eight years old, fair-haired, dressed in a black velvet jacket and tartan trousers. Robert was a replica of his great-great-grandfather, Jamie McGregor, the man in the painting above the marble fireplace. As though sensing her eyes on him, Robert turned, and Kate beckoned him to her with a wave of her fingers, the perfect twenty-carat diamond her father had scooped up on a sandy beach almost a hundred years ago scintillating in the radiance of the crystal chandelier. Kate watched with pleasure as Robert threaded his way through the dancers.

I am the past, Kate thought. *He is the future. My great-grandson will take over Kruger-Brent Limited one day.* He reached her side, and she made room for him on the seat beside her.

"Are you having a nice birthday, Gran?"

"Yes. Thank you, Robert."

"That's a super orchestra. The conductor's really *bad*."

Kate looked at him in momentary confusion, then her brow cleared. "Ah. I presume that means he's good."

Robert grinned at her. "Right. You sure don't seem ninety."

Kate Blackwell laughed. "Just between the two of us, I don't feel it."

He slipped his hand in hers, and they sat there in a contented silence, the eighty-two-year difference between them giving them a comfortable affinity. Kate turned to watch her grand-daughter dancing. She and her husband were without doubt the handsomest couple on the floor.

Robert's mother saw her son and grandmother seated together and she thought, *What an incredible woman. She's ageless. No one would ever guess all she has lived through.*

The music stopped, and the conductor said, "Ladies and gentlemen, it's my pleasure to present young Master Robert."

Robert squeezed his great-grandmother's hand, stood up and walked over to the piano. He sat down, his face serious and intent, and then his fingers began to race across the keyboard. He played Scriabin, and it was like the ripping of moonlight on water.

His mother listened and thought, *He's a genius. He'll grow up to be a geat musician.* He was no longer her baby. He was going to belong to the world. When Robert finished, the applause was enthusiastic and genuine.

Earlier, dinner had been served outdoors. the large and formal garden had been festively decorated with lanterns and ribbons and balloons. Musicians played from the terrace while butlers and maids hovered over tables, silent and efficient, making sure the Baccarat glasses and Limoges dishes were kept filled. A telegram was read from the President of the United States. A Supreme Court justice toasted Kate.

The government eulogized her. ". . . One of the most remarkable women in the history of this nation. Kate Blackwell's endowments to hundreds of charitable causes around the world are legendary. The Blackwell Foundation has contributed to the health and well-being of people in more than fifty countries. to paraphrase the late Sir Winston Churchill, 'Never have so many owed so much to one person.' I have had the privilege of knowing Kate Blackwell . . ."

Bloody hell! Kate thought. *No one knows me. He sounds like he's talking about some saint. What would all these people say if they knew the real Kate Blackwell? Sired by a thief and kidnapped before I was a year old. What would they think if I showed them the bullet scars on my body?*

She turned her head and looked at the man who had once tried to kill her. Kate's eyes moved past him to linger on a figure in the shadows, wearing a veil to conceal her face. Over a distant clap of thunder, Kate heard the governor finish his speech and introduce her. She rose to her feet and looked out at the assembled guests. When she spoke, her voice was firm and strong. "I've lived longer than any of you. As youngsters today would say, 'That's no big deal.' But I'm glad I made it to this age, because otherwise I wouldn't be here with all you dear friends. I know some of you have traveled from distant countries to be with me tonight, and you must be tired from your journey. It wouldn't be fair for me to expect everyone to have my energy." There was a roar of laughter, and they applauded her.

"Thank you for making this such a memorable evening. I shall never forget it.

For those of you who wish to retire, your rooms are ready. For the others, there will be dancing in the ballroom." There was another clap of thunder. "I suggest we all move indoors before we get caught in one of our famous Maine storms."

Now the dinner and dancing were over, the guests had retired and Kate was alone with her ghosts. She sat in the library, drifting back into the past, and she suddenly felt depressed. *There's no one left to call me Kate*, she thought. *They've all gone.* Her world had shrunk. Wasn't it Longfellow who said, "The leaves of memory make a mournful rustle in the dark"? She would be entering the dark soon, but not yet. *I still have to do the most important thing of my life*, Kate thought. *Be patient, David I'll be with you soon.*

"Gran . . ."

Kate opened her eyes. The family had come into the room. She looked at them, one by one, her eyes a pitiless camera, missing nothing. *My family*, Kate thought. *My immortality. A murderer, a grotesque and a psychotic. The Blackwell skeletons. Was this what all the years of hope and pain and suffering had finally come to?*

Her granddaughter stood beside her. "Are you all right, Gran?"

"I'm a little tired, children. I think I'll go to bed." She rose to her feet and started toward the stairs, and at that moment there was a violent roar of thunder and the storm broke, the rain rattling against the windows like machine-gun fire. Her family watched as the old woman reached the top of the stairway, a proud, erect figure. There was a blaze of lightning and seconds later a loud clap of thunder. Kate Blackwell turned to look down at them, and when she spoke, it was with the accent of her ancestors. "In South Africa, we used to call this a *donderstorm*."

The past and present began to merge once again, and she walked down the hallway to her bedroom, surrounded by the familiar, comfortable ghosts.

Book One

Jamie
1883–1906

1

"By God, this is a real *donderstorm!*" Jamie McGregor said. He had grown up amid the wild storms of the Scottish Highlands, but he had never witnessed anything as violent as this. The afternoon sky had been suddenly obliterated by enormous clouds of sand, instantly turning day into night. The dusty sky was fit by flashes of lightning – *weerlig* the Afrikaners called it – that scorched the air, followed by *donderslag* – thunder. Then the deluge. Sheets of rain that smashed against the army of tents and tin huts and turned the dirt streets of Klipdrift into frenzied streams of mud. The sky was aroar with rolling peals of thunder, one following the other like artillery in some celestial war.

Jamie McGregor quickly stepped aside as a house built of raw brick dissolved into mud, and he wondered whether the town of Klipdrift was going to survive.

Klipdrift was not really a town. It was a sprawling canvas village, a seething mass of tents and huts and wagons crowding the banks of the Vaal River, populated by wild-eyed dreamers drawn to South Africa from all parts of the world by the same obsession: diamonds.

Jamie McGregor was one of the dreamers. He was barely eighteen, a handsome lad, tall and fair-haired, with startlingly light gray eyes. There was an attractive ingenuousness about him, an eagerness to please that was endearing. He had a lighthearted disposition and a soul filled with optimism.

He had traveled almost eight thousand miles from his father's farm in the Highlands of Scotland to Edinburgh, London, Cape Town and now Klipdrift. He had given up his rights to the share of the farm that he and his brothers tilled with their father, but Jamie McGregor had no regrets. He knew he was going to be rewarded ten thousand times over. He had left the security of the only life he had ever known and had come to this distant, desolate place because he dreamed of being rich. Jamie was not afraid of hard work, but the rewards of tilling the rocky little farm north of Aberdeen were meager. He worked from sunup to sundown, along with his brothers, his sister, Mary, and his mother and his father, and they had little to show for it. He had once attended a fair in Edinburgh and had seen the wondrous things of beauty that money could buy. Money was to make your life easy when you were well, and to take care of your needs when you were ailing. Jamie had seen too many friends and neighbors live and die in poverty.

He remembered his excitement when he first heard about the latest diamond strike in South Africa. The biggest diamond in the world had been found there, lying loose in the sand, and the whole area was rumored to be a great treasure chest waiting to be opened.

He had broken the news to his family after dinner on a Saturday night. They were seated around an uncleared table in the rude, timbered kitchen when Jamie spoke, his voice shy and at the same time proud. "I'm going to South Africa to find diamonds. I'll be on my way next week."

Five pairs of eyes stared at him as though he were crazy.

"You're goin' chasing after diamonds?" his father asked. "You must be daft, lad. That's all a fairy tale – a temptation of the devil to keep men from doin' an honest day's work."

"Why do you nae tell us where you're gettin' the money to go?" his brother Ian asked. "It's halfway 'round the world. You hae no money."

"If I had money," Jamie retorted, "I wouldn't have to go looking for diamonds, would I? Nobody there has money. I'll be an equal with all of them. I've got brains and a strong back. I'll not fail."

His sister, Mary, said, "Annie Cord will be disappointed. She expects to be your bride one day, Jamie."

Jamie adored his sister. She was older than he. Twenty-four, and she looked forty. She had never owned a beautiful thing in her life. *I'll change that*, Jamie promised himself.

His mother silently picked up the platter that held the remains of the steaming haggis and walked over to the iron sink.

Late that night she came to Jamie's bedside. She gently placed one hand on Jamie's shoulder, and her strength flooded into him. "You do what you must, Son. I dinna ken if there be diamonds there, but if there be, you'll find them." She brought out from behind her a worn leather pouch. "I've put by a few pounds. You needn't say nothin' to the others. God bless you, Jamie."

When he left for Edinburgh, he had fifty pounds in the pouch.

It was an arduous journey to South Africa, and it took Jamie McGregor almost a year to make it. He got a job as a waiter in a workingman's restaurant in Edinburgh until he added another fifty pounds to the pouch. Then it was on to London. Jamie was awed by the size of the city, the huge crowds, the noise and the large horse-drawn omnibuses that raced along at five miles an hour. There were hansom cabs everywhere, carrying beautiful women in large hats and swirling skirts and dainty little high-button shoes. He watched in wonder as the ladies alighted from the cabs and carriages to shop at Burlington Arcade, a dazzling cornucopia of silver and dishes and dresses and furs and pottery and apothecary shops crammed with mysterious bottles and jars.

Jamie found lodging at a house at 32 Fitzroy Street. It cost ten shillings a week, but it was the cheapest he could find. He spent his days at the docks, seeking a ship that would take him to South Africa, and his evenings seeing the wondrous sights of London town. One evening he caught a glimpse of Edward, the Prince of Wales, entering a restaurant near Covent Garden by the side door, a beautiful young lady on his arm. She wore a large flowered hat, and Jamie thought how nice it would look on his sister.

Jamie attended a concert at the Crystal Palace, built for The Great Exposition in 1851. He visited Drury Lane and at intermission sneaked into the Savoy

Theatre, where they had installed the first electric lighting in a British public building. Some streets were lighted by electricity, and Jamie heard that it was possible to talk to someone on the other side of town by means of a wonderful new machine, the telephone. Jamie felt that he was looking at the future.

In spite of all the innovations and activity, England was in the midst of a growing economic crisis that winter. The streets were filled with the unemployed and the hungry, and there were mass demonstrations and street fighting. *I've got to get away from here*, Jamie thought. I *came to escape poverty.* The following day, Jamie signed on as a steward on the *Walmer Castle*, bound for Cape Town, South Africa.

The sea journey lasted three weeks, with stops at Madeira and St. Helena to take on more coal for fuel. It was a rough, turbulent voyage in the dead of winter, and Jamie was seasick from the moment the ship sailed. But he never lost his cheerfulness, for every day brought him nearer to his treasure chest. As the ship moved toward the equator, the climate changed. Miraculously, winter began to thaw into summer, and as they approached the African coast, the days and nights became hot and steamy.

The *Walmer Castle* arrived in Cape Town at early dawn, moving carefully through the narrow channel that divided the great leper settlement of Robben Island from the mainland, and dropped anchor in Table Bay.

Jamie was on deck before sunrise. He watched, mesmerized, as the early-morning fog lifted and revealed the grand spectacle of Table Mountain looming high over the city. He had arrived.

The moment the ship made fast to the wharf, the decks were overrun by a horde of the strangest-looking people Jamie had ever seen. There were touts for all the different hotels – black men, yellow men, brown men and red men frantically offering to bear away luggage – and small boys running back and forth with newspapers and sweets and fruits for sale. Hansom drivers who were half-castes, Parsis or blacks were yelling their eagerness to be hired. Vendors and men pushing drinking carts called attention to their wares. The air was thick with huge black flies. Sailors and porters hustled and halloaed their way through the crowd while passengers vainly tried to keep their luggage together and in sight. It was a babel of voices and noise. People spoke to one another in a language Jamie had never heard.

"*Yulle kom van de Kaap, neh?*"

"*Het julle mine papa zyn wagen gezien?*"

"*Wat bedui'di?*"

"*Huistoe!*"

He did not understand a word.

*

Cape Town was utterly unlike anything Jamie had ever seen. No two houses were alike. Next to a large warehouse two or three stories high, built of bricks or stone, was a small canteen of galvanized iron, then a jeweler's shop with hand-blown plate-glass windows and abutting it a small greengrocer's and next to that a tumble-down tobacconist's.

Jamie was mesmerized by the men, women and children who thronged the streets. He saw a kaffir clad in an old pair of 78th Highland trews and wearing as a coat a sack with slits cut for the arms and head. The kaffir walked behind two Chinese men, hand in hand, who were wearing blue smock frocks, their pigtails carefully coiled up under their conical straw hats. There were stout, red-faced Boer farmers with sun-bleached hair, their wagons loaded with potatoes, corn and leafy vegetables. Men dressed in brown velveteen trousers and coats, with broad-brimmed, soft-felt hats on their heads and long clay pipes in their mouths, strode ahead of their *vraws*, attired in black, with thick black veils and large black-silk poke bonnets. Parsi washerwomen with large bundles of soiled clothes on their heads pushed past soldiers in red coats and helmets. It was a fascinating spectacle.

The first thing Jamie did was to seek out an inexpensive boardinghouse recommended to him by a sailor aboard ship. The landlady was a dumpy, ample-bosomed, middle-aged widow.

She looked Jamie over and smiled. "*Zoek yulle goud?*"

He blushed. "I'm sorry – I don't understand."

"English, yes? You are here to hunt gold? Diamonds?"

"Diamonds. Yes, ma'am."

She pulled him inside. "You will like it here. I have all the convenience for young men like you."

Jamie wondered whether she was one of them. He hoped not.

"I'm Mrs. Venster," she said coyly, "but my friends call me 'Dee-Dee' " She smiled, revealing a gold tooth in front. "I have a feeling we are going to be very good friends. Ask of me anything."

"That's very kind of you," Jamie said. "Can you tell me where I can get a map of the city?"

With map in hand, Jamie went exploring. On one side of the city were the landward suburbs of Rondebosch, Claremont and Wynberg, stretching along nine miles of thinning plantations and vineyards. On the other side were the marine suburbs of Sea Point and Green Point. Jamie walked through the rich residential area, down Strand Street and Bree Street, admiring the large, two-story buildings with their flat roofs and peaked stuccoed fronts – steep terraces rising from the street. He walked until he was finally driven indoors by the flies that seemed to have a personal vendetta against him. They were large and black and attacked in swarms. When Jamie returned to his boardinghouse, he found his room filled with them. They covered the walls and table and bed.

He went to see the landlady. "Mrs. Venster, isn't there anything you can do about the flies in my room? They're – "

She gave a fat, jiggling laugh and pinched Jamie's cheek. "*Myn magtig.* You'll get used to them. You'll see."

The sanitary arrangements in Cape Town were both primitive and inadequate, and when the sun set, an odoriferous vapor covered the city like a noxious blanket. It was unbearable. But Jamie knew that he would bear it. He needed more money before he could leave. "You can't survive in the diamond fields without money," he had been warned. "They'll charge you just for breathin'."

On his second day in Cape Town, Jamie found a job driving a team of horses for a delivery firm. On the third day he started working in a restaurant after dinner, washing dishes. He lived on the leftover food that he squirreled away and took back to the boardinghouse, but it tasted strange to him and he longed for his mother's cock-a-leekie and oatcakes and hot, fresh-made baps. He did not complain, even to himself, as he sacrificed both food and comfort to increase his grubstake. He had made his choice and nothing was going to stop him, not the exhausting labor, or the foul air he breathed or the flies that kept him awake most of the night. He felt desperately lonely. He knew no one in this strange place, and he missed his friends and family. Jamie enjoyed solitude, but loneliness was a constant ache.

At last, the magic day arrived. His pouch held the magnificent sum of two hundred pounds. He was ready. He would leave Cape Town the following morning for the diamond fields.

Reservations for passenger wagons to the diamond fields at Klipdrift were booked by the Inland Transport Company at a small wooden depot near the docks. When Jamie arrived at 7:00 A.M., the depot was already so crowded that he could not get near it. There were hundreds of fortune seekers fighting for seats on the wagons. They had come from as far away as Russia and America, Australia, Germany and England. They shouted in a dozen different tongues, pleading with the besieged ticket sellers to find spaces for them. Jamie watched as a burly Irishman angrily pushed his way out of the office onto the sidewalk, fighting to get through the mob.

"Excuse me," Jamie said. "What's going on in there?"

"Nothin'," the Irishman grunted in disgust. "The bloody wagons are all booked up for the next six weeks." He saw the look of dismay on Jamie's face. "That's not the worst of it, lad. The heathen bastards are chargin' fifty pounds a head."

It was incredible! "There must be another way to get to the diamond fields."

"Two ways. You can go Dutch Express, or you can go by foot."

"What's Dutch Express?"

"Bullock wagon. They travel two miles an hour. By the time you get there, the damned diamonds will all be gone."

Jamie McGregor had no intention of being delayed until the diamonds were gone. He spent the rest of the morning looking for another means of transportation. Just before noon, he found it. He was passing a livery stable with a sign in front that said MAIL DEPOT. On an impulse, he went inside, where the thinnest man he had ever seen was loading large mail sacks into a dogcart. Jamie watched him a moment.

"Excuse me," Jamie said. "Do you carry mail to Klipdrift?"

"That's right. Loadin' up now."

Jamie felt a sudden surge of hope. "Do you take passengers?"

"Sometimes." He looked up and studied Jamie. "How old are you?"

An odd question. "Eighteen. Why?"

"We don't take anyone over twenty-one or twenty-two. You in good health?"

An even odder question. "Yes, sir."

The thin man straightened up. "I guess you're fit. I'm leavin' in an hour. The fare's twenty pounds."

Jamie could not believe his good fortune. "That's wonderful! I'll get my suitcase and – "

"No suitcase. All you got room for is one shirt and a toothbrush."

Jamie took a closer look at the dogcart. It was small and roughly built. The body formed a well in which the mail was stored, and over the well was a narrow, cramped space where a person could sit back to back behind the driver. It was going to be an uncomfortable journey.

"It's a deal," Jamie said. "I'll fetch my shirt and toothbrush."

When Jamie returned, the driver was hitching up a horse to the open cart. There were two large young men standing near the cart: One was short and dark, the other was a tall, blond Swede. The men were handing the driver some money.

"Wait a minute," Jamie called to the driver. "You said *I* was going."

"You're all goin'," the driver said. "Hop in."

"The *three* of us?"

"That's right."

Jamie had no idea how the driver expected them all to fit in the small cart, but he knew he was going to be on it when it pulled out.

Jamie introduced himself to his two fellow passengers. "I'm Jamie McGregor."

"Wallach," the short, dark man said.

"Pederson," the tall blond replied.

Jamie said, "We're lucky we discovered this, aren't we? It's a good thing everybody doesn't know about it."

Pederson said, "Oh, they know about the post carts, McGregor. There just aren't that many fit enough or desperate enough to travel in them."

Before Jamie could ask what he meant, the driver said, "Let's go."

The three men – Jamie in the middle – squeezed into the seat, crowded against each other, their knees cramped, their backs pressing hard against the wooden back of the driver's seat. There was no room to move or breathe. *It's not bad*, Jamie reassured himself.

"Hold on!" the driver sang out, and a moment later they were racing through the streets of Cape Town on their way to the diamond fields at Klipdrift.

By bullock wagon, the journey was relatively comfortable. The wagons transporting passengers from Cape Town to the diamond fields were large and roomy, with tent covers to ward off the blazing winter sun. Each wagon accommodated a dozen passengers and was drawn by teams of horses or mules. Refreshments were provided at regular stations, and the journey took ten days.

The mail cart was different. It never stopped, except to change horses and drivers. The pace was a full gallop, over rough roads and fields and rutted trails. There were no springs on the cart, and each bounce was like the blow of a horse's hoof. Jamie gritted his teeth and thought, *I can stand it until we stop for the night. I'll eat and get some sleep, and in the morning I'll be fine*. But when nighttime came, there was a ten-minute halt for a change of horse and driver, and they were off again at a full gallop.

"When do we stop to eat?" Jamie asked.

"We don't," the new driver grunted. "We go straight through. We're carryin' the mails, mister."

They raced through the long night, traveling over dusty, bumpy roads by moonlight, the little cart bouncing up the rises, plunging down the valleys, springing over the flats. Every inch of Jamie's body was battered and bruised from the constant jolting. He was exhausted, but it was impossible to sleep. Every time he started to dose off, he was jarred awake. His body was cramped and miserable and there was no room to stretch. He was starving and motion-sick. He had no idea how many days it would be before his next meal. It was a six-hundred-mile journey, and Jamie McGregor was not sure he was going to live through it. Neither was he sure that he wanted to.

By the end of the second day and night, the misery had turned to agony. Jamie's traveling companions were in the same sorry state, no longer even able to complain. Jamie understood now why the company insisted that its passengers be young and strong.

When the next dawn came, they entered the Great Karroo, where the real wilderness began. Stretching to infinity, the monstrous veld lay flat and forbidding under a pitiless sun. The passengers were smothered in heat, dust and flies.

Occasionally, through a miasmic haze, Jamie saw groups of men slogging along on foot. There were solitary riders on horseback, and dozens of bullock wagons drawn by eighteen or twenty oxen, handled by drivers and *voorlopers*, with their sjamboks, the whips with long leather thongs, crying, "Trek! Trek!" The huge wagons were laden with a thousand pounds of produce and goods, tents and digging equipment and wood-burning stoves, flour and coal and oil lamps. They carried coffee and rice, Russian hemp, sugar and wines, whiskey and boots and Belfast candles, and blankets. They were the lifeline to the fortune seekers at Klipdrift.

It was not until the mail cart crossed the Orange River that there was a change from the deadly monotony of the veld. The scrub gradually became taller and tinged with green. The earth was redder, patches of grass rippled in the breeze, and low thorn trees began to appear.

I'm going to make it, Jamie thought dully. *I'm going to make it.*

And he could feel hope begin to creep into his tired body.

They had been on the road for four continuous days and nights when they finally arrived at the outskirts of Klipdrift.

Young Jamie McGregor had not known what to expect, but the scene that met his weary, bloodshot eyes was like nothing he ever could have imagined. Klipdrift was a vast panorama of tents and wagons lined up on the main streets and on the shores of the Vaal River. The dirt roadway swarmed with kaffirs, naked except for brightly colored jackets, and bearded prospectors, butchers, bakers, thieves, teachers. In the center of Klipdrift, rows of wooden and iron shacks served as shops, canteens, billiard rooms, eating houses, diamond-buying offices and lawyers' rooms. On a corner stood the ramshackle Royal Arch Hotel, a long chain of rooms without windows.

Jamie stepped out of the cart, and promptly fell to the ground, his cramped legs refusing to hold him up. He lay there, his head spinning, until he had strength enough to rise. He stumbled toward the hotel, pushing through the boisterous crowds that thronged the sidewalks and streets. The room they gave him was small, stifling hot and swarming with flies. But it had a cot. Jamie fell onto it, fully dressed, and was asleep instantly. He slept for eighteen hours.

Jamie awoke, his body unbelievably stiff and sore, but his soul filled with exultation. *I am here! I have made it!* Ravenously hungry, he went in search of food. The hotel served none, but there was a small, crowded restaurant across the street, where he devoured fried snook, a large fish resembling pike; carbon-aatje, thinly sliced mutton grilled on a spit over a wood fire; a haunch of bok and, for dessert, *koeksister*, a dough deep-fried and soaked in syrup.

Jamie's stomach, so long without food, began to give off alarming symptoms. He decided to let it rest before he continued eating, and turned his attention to his surroundings. At tables all around him, prospectors were feverishly discussing the subject uppermost in everyone's mind: diamonds.

" . . . There's still a few diamonds left around Hopetown, but the mother lode's at New Rush. . . ."

" . . . Kimberley's got a bigger population than Joburg. . . ."

" . . . About the find up at Dutoitspan last week? They say there's more diamonds there than a man can carry. . . ."

" . . . There's a new strike at Christiana. I'm goin' up there tomorrow."

So it was true. There were diamonds everywhere! Young Jamie was so excited he could hardly finish his huge mug of coffee. He was staggered by the amount of the bill. Two pounds, three shillings for one meal! *I'll have to be very careful*, he thought, as he walked out onto the crowded, noisy street.

A voice behind him said, "Still planning to get rich, McGregor?"

Jamie turned. It was Pederson, the Swedish boy who had traveled on the dogcart with him.

"I certainly am," Jamie said.

"Then let's go where the diamonds are." He pointed. "The Vaal River's that way."

They began to walk.

Klipdrift was in a basin, surrounded by hills, and as far as Jamie could see, everything was barren, without a blade of grass or shrub in sight. Red dust rose thick in the air, making it difficult to breathe. The Vaal River was a quarter of a mile away, and as they got closer to it, the air became cooler. Hundreds of prospectors lined both sides of the riverbank, some of them digging for diamonds, others meshing stones in rocking cradles, still others sorting stones at rickety, makeshift tables. The equipment ranged from scientific earth-washing apparatus to old tub boxes and pails. The men were sunburned, unshaven and roughly dressed in a weird assortment of collarless, colored and striped flannel shirts, corduroy trousers and rubber boots, riding breeches and laced leggings and wide-brimmed felt hats or pith helmets. They all wore broad leather belts with pockets for diamonds or money.

Jamie and Pederson walked to the edge of the riverbank and watched a young boy and an older man struggling to remove a huge ironstone boulder so they could get at the gravel around it. Their shirts were soaked with sweat. Nearby, another team loaded gravel onto a cart to be sieved in a cradle. One of the diggers rocked the cradle while another poured buckets of water into it to wash away the silt. The large pebbles were then emptied onto an improvised sorting table, where they were excitedly inspected.

"It looks easy," Jamie grinned.

"Don't count on it, McGregor. I've been talking to some of the diggers who have been here a while. I think we've bought a sack of pups."

"What do you mean?"

"Do you know how many diggers there are in these parts, all hoping to get rich? Twenty bloody thousand! And there aren't enough diamonds to go around, chum. Even if there were, I'm beginning to wonder if it's worth it. You broil in winter, freeze in summer, get drenched in their damned *donderstormen*, and try to cope with the dust and the flies and the stink. You can't get a bath or a decent bed, and there are no sanitary arrangements in this damned town. There are drownings in the Vaal River every week. Some are accidental, but I was told that for most of them it's a way out, the only escape from this hellhole. I don't know why these people keep hanging on."

"I do." Jamie looked at the hopeful young boy with the stained shirt. "The next shovelful of dirt."

But as they headed back to town, Jamie had to admit that Pederson had a point. They passed carcasses of slaughtered oxen, sheep and goats left to rot outside the tents, next to wide-open trenches that served as lavatories. The place stank to the heavens. Pederson was watching him. "What are you going to do now?"

"Get some prospecting equipment."

In the center of town was a store with a rusted hanging sign that read: SALOMON VAN DER MERWE, GENERAL STORE. A tall black man about Jamie's age was unloading a wagon in front of the store. He was broad-shouldered and heavily muscled, one of the most handsome men Jamie had ever seen. He had soot-black eyes, an aquiline nose and a proud chin. There was a dignity about him, a quiet aloofness. He lifted a heavy wooden box of rifles to his shoulder and, as he turned, he slipped on a leaf fallen from a crate of cabbage. Jamie instinctively reached out an arm to steady him. The black man did not acknowledge Jamie's presence. He turned and walked into the store. A Boer prospector hitching up a mule spat and said distastefully, "That's Banda, from the Barolong tribe. Works for Mr. van der Merwe. I don't know why he keeps that uppity black. Those fuckin' Bantus think they own the earth."

The store was cool and dark inside, a welcome relief from the hot, bright street, and it was filled with exotic odors. It seemed to Jamie that every inch of space was crammed with merchandise. He walked through the store, marveling. There were agricultural implements, beer, cans of milk and crocks of butter, cement, fuses and dynamite and gunpowder, crockery, furniture, guns and haberdashery, oil and paint and varnish, bacon and dried fruit, saddlery and harness, sheep-dip and soap, spirits and stationery and paper, sugar and tea and tobacco and snuff and cigars . . . A dozen shelves were filled from top to bottom with flannel shirts and blankets, shoes, poke bonnets and saddles. *Whoever owns all this*, Jamie thought, *is a rich man.*

A soft voice behind him said, "Can I help you?"

Jamie turned and found himself facing a young girl. He judged she was about fifteen. She had an interesting face, fine-boned and heart-shaped, like a valentine, a pert nose and intense green eyes. Her hair was dark and curling. Jamie, looking at her figure, decided she might be closer to sixteen.

"I'm a prospector," Jamie announced. "I'm here to buy some equipment."

"What is it you need?"

For some reason, Jamie felt he had to impress this girl. "I – er – you know – the usual."

She smiled, and there was mischief in her eyes. "What is the usual, sir?"

"Well . . ." He hesitated. "A shovel."

"Will that be all?"

Jamie saw that she was teasing him. He grinned and confessed, "To tell you the truth, I'm new at this. I don't know what I need."

She smiled at him, and it was the smile of a woman. "It depends on where you're planning to prospect, Mr. – ?"

"McGregor. Jamie McGregor."

"I'm Margaret van der Merwe." She glanced nervously toward the rear of the store.

"I'm pleased to meet you, Miss van der Merwe."

"Did you just arrive?"

"Aye. Yesterday. On the post cart."

"Someone should have warned you about that. Passengers have died on that trip." There was anger in her eyes.

Jamie grinned. "I can't blame them. But I'm very much alive, thank you."

"And going out to hunt for *mooi klippe*."

"Mooi klippe?"

"That's our Dutch word for diamonds. Pretty pebbles."

"You're Dutch?"

"My family's from Holland."

"I'm from Scotland."

"I could tell that." Her eyes flicked warily toward the back of the store again. "There are diamonds around, Mr. McGregor, but you must be choosy where you look for them. Most of the diggers are running around chasing their own tails. When someone makes a strike, the rest scavenge off the leavings. If you want to get rich, you have to find a strike of your own."

"How do I do that?"

"My father might be the one to help you with that. He knows everything. He'll be free in an hour."

"I'll be back," Jamie assured her. "Thank you, Miss van der Merwe."

He went out into the sunshine, filled with a sense of euphoria, his aches and pains forgotten. If Salomon van der Merwe would advise him where to find diamonds, there was no way Jamie could fail. He would have the jump on all of them. He laughed aloud, with the sheer joy of being young and alive and on his way to riches.

Jamie walked down the main street, passing a blacksmith's, a billiard hall and half a dozen saloons. He came to a sign in front of a decrepit-looking hotel and stopped. The sign read:

R-D MILLER, WARM AND COLD BATHS.
OPEN DAILY FROM 6 A.M. TO 8 P.M.,
WITH THE COMFORTS OF A NEAT
DRESSING ROOM

Jamie thought, *When did I have my last bath? Well, I took a bucket bath on the boat. That was* – He was suddenly aware of how he must smell. He thought of the weekly tub baths in the kitchen at home, and he could hear his mother's voice calling, "Be sure to wash down below, Jamie."

He turned and entered the baths. There were two doors inside, one for women and one for men. Jamie entered the men's section and walked up to the aged attendant. "How much is a bath?"

"Ten shillings for a cold bath, fifteen for a hot."

Jamie hesitated. The idea of a hot bath after his long journey was almost irresistible. "Cold," he said. He could not afford to throw away his money on luxuries. He had mining equipment to buy.

The attendant handed him a small bar of yellow lye soap and a threadbare hand towel and pointed. "In there, mate."

Jamie stepped into a small room that contained nothing except a large galvanized-iron bathtub in the center and a few pegs on the wall. The attendant began filling the tub from a large wooden bucket.

"All ready for you, mister. Just hang your clothes on those pegs."

Jamie waited until the attendant left and then undressed. He looked down at his grime-covered body and put one foot in the tub. The water was cold, as advertised. He gritted his teeth and plunged in, soaping himself furiously from head to foot. When he finally stepped out of the tub, the water was black. He dried himself as best he could with the worn linen towel and started to get dressed. His pants and shirt were stiff with dirt, and he hated to put them back on. He would have to buy a change of clothes, and this reminded him once more of how little money he had. And he was hungry again.

Jamie left the bathhouse and pushed his way down the crowded street to a saloon called the Sundowner. He ordered a beer and lunch. Lamb cutlets with tomatoes, and sausage and potato salad and pickles. While he ate, he listened to the hopeful conversations around him.

". . . I hear they found a stone near Colesberg weighin' twenty-one carats. Mark you, if there's *one* diamond up there, there's plenty more. . . ."

". . . There's a new diamond find up in Hebron. I'm thinkin' of goin' there. . . ."

"You're a fool. The big diamonds are in the Orange River. . . ."

At the bar, a bearded customer in a collarless, striped-flannel shirt and corduroy trousers was nursing a shandygaff in a large glass. "I got cleaned out in Hebron," he confided to the bartender. "I need me a grubstake."

The bartender was a large, fleshy, bald-headed man with a broken, twisted nose and ferret eyes. He laughed. "Hell, man, who doesn't? Why do you think I'm tendin' bar? As soon as I have enough money, I'm gonna hightail it up the Orange myself." He wiped the bar with a dirty rag. "But I'll tell you what you might do, mister. See Salomon ven der Merwe. He owns the general store and half the town."

"What good'll that do me?"

"If he likes you, he might stake you."

The customer looked at him. "Yeah? You really think he might?"

"He's done it for a few fellows I know of. You put up your labor, he puts up the money. You split fifty-fifty."

Jamie McGregor's thoughts leaped ahead. He had been confident that the hundred and twenty pounds he had left would be enough to buy the equipment and food he would need to survive, but the prices in Klipdrift were astonishing. He had noticed in Van der Merwe's store that a hundred-pound sack of Australian flour cost five pounds. One pound of sugar cost a shilling. A bottle of beer cost five shillings. Biscuits were three shillings a pound, and fresh eggs sold for seven shillings a dozen. At that rate, his money would not last long. *My God*, Jamie thought, *at home we could live for a year on what three meals cost here.* But if he could get the backing of someone wealthy, like Mr. van der . . . Jamie hastily paid for his food and hurried back to the general store.

Salomon van der Merwe was behind the counter, removing the rifles from a wooden crate. He was a small man, with a thin, pinched face framed by Dundreary whiskers. He had sandy hair, tiny black eyes, a bulbous nose and pursed lips. *His daughter must take after her mother*, Jamie thought. "Excuse me, sir . . ."

Van der Merwe looked up. "*Ja?*"

"Mr. van der Merwe? My name is Jamie McGregor, sir. I'm from Scotland. I came here to find diamonds."

"*Ja?* So?"

"I hear you sometimes back prospectors."

Van der Merwe grumbled, "*Myn magtig!* Who spreads these stories? I help out a few diggers, and everyone thinks I'm Santa Claus."

"I've saved a hundred and twenty pounds," Jamie said earnestly. "But I see that it's not going to buy me much here. I'll go out to the bush with just a shovel if I have to, but I figure my chances would be a lot better if I had a mule and some proper equipment."

Van der Merwe was studying him with those small, black eyes. "*Wat denk ye?* What makes you think *you* can find diamonds?"

"I've come halfway around the world, Mr. van der Merwe, and I'm not going to leave here until I'm rich. If the diamonds are out there, I'll find them. If you help me, I'll make us both rich."

Van der Merwe grunted, turned his back on Jamie and continued unloading the rifles. Jamie stood there awkwardly, not knowing what more to say. When Van der Merwe spoke again, his question caught Jamie off guard. "You travel here by bullock wagon, *ja?*"

"No. Post cart."

The old man turned to study the boy again. He said, finally, "We talk about it."

They talked about it at dinner that evening in the room in back of the store that was the Van der Merwe living quarters. It was a small room that served as a kitchen, dining room and sleeping quarters, with a curtain separating two cots. The lower half of the walls was built of mud and stone, and the upper half was faced with cardboard boxes that had once contained provisions. A square hole, where a piece of wall had been cut out, served as a window. In wet weather it could be closed by placing a board in front of it. The dining table consisted of a long plank stretched across two wooden crates. A large box, turned on its side, served as a cupboard. Jamie guessed that Van der Merwe was not a man who parted easily with his money.

Van der Meerwe's daughter moved silently about, preparing dinner. From time to time she cast quick glances at her father, but she never once looked at Jamie. *Why is she so frightened?* Jamie wondered.

When they were seated at the table, Van der Merwe began, "Let us have a blessing. We thank Thee, O Lord, for the bounty we receive at Thy hands. We thank Thee for forgiving us our sins and showing us the path of righteousness and delivering us from life's temptations. We thank Thee for a long and fruitful life, and for smiting dead all those who offend Thee. Amen." And without a breath between, "Pass me the meat," he said to his daughter.

The dinner was frugal: a small roast pork, three boiled potatoes and a dish of turnip greens. The portions he served to Jamie were small. The two men talked little during the meal, and Margaret did not speak at all.

When they had finished eating, Van der Merwe said, "That was fine, Daughter," and there was pride in his voice. He turned to Jamie. "We get down to business, *ja?*"

"Yes, sir."

Van der Merwe picked up a long clay pipe from the top of the wooden cabinet. He filled it with a sweet-smelling tobacco from a small pouch and lighted the pipe. His sharp eyes peered intently at Jamie through the wreaths of smoke.

"The diggers here at Klipdrift are fools. Too few diamonds, too many diggers. A man could break his back here for a year and have nothing to show for it but *schlenters.*"

"I – I'm afraid I'm not familiar with that word, sir."

"Fools' diamonds. Worthless. Do you follow me?"

"I – Yes, sir. I think so. But what's the answer, sir?"

"The Griquas."

Jamie looked at him blankly.

"They're an African tribe up north. *They* find diamonds – big ones – and sometimes they bring them to me and I trade them for goods." The Dutchman lowered his voice to a conspiratorial whisper. "I know where they find them."

"But could you nae go after them yourself, Mr. van der Merwe?"

Van der Merwe sighed. "No. I can't leave the store. People would steal me blind. I need someone I can trust to go up there and bring the stones back. When I find the right man, I'll supply him with all the equipment he needs." He paused to take a long drag on the pipe. "And I'll tell him where the diamonds are."

Jamie leaped to his feet, his heart pounding. "Mr. van der Merwe, *I'm* the person you're looking for. Believe me, sir, I'll work night and day." His voice was charged with excitement. "I'll bring you back more diamonds than you can count."

Van der Merwe silently studied him for what seemed to Jamie to be an eternity.

When Van der Merwe finally spoke, he said only one word. "*Ja.*"

Jamie signed the contract the following morning. It was written in Afrikaans.

"I'll have to explain it to you," Van der Merwe said. "It says we're full partners. I put up the capital – you put up the labor. We share everything equally."

Jamie looked at the contract in Van der Merwe's hand. In the middle of all the incomprehensible foreign words he recognized only a sum: *two pounds.*

Jamie pointed to it. "What is that for, Mr. van der Merwe?"

"It means that in addition to your owning half the diamonds you find, you'll get an extra two pounds for every week you work. Even though I know the diamonds are out there, it's possible you might not find anything, lad. This way you'll at least get something for your labor."

The man was being more than fair. "Thank you. Thank you very much, sir." Jamie could have hugged him.

Van der Merwe said, "Now let's get you outfitted."

It took two hours to select the equipment that Jamie would take into the bush with him: a small tent, bedding, cooking utensils, two sieves and a washing cradle, a pick, two shovels, three buckets and one change of socks and underwear. There was an ax and a lantern and paraffin oil, matches and arsenical soap. There were tins of food, biltong, fruit, sugar, coffee and salt. At last everything was in readiness. The black servant, Banda, silently helped Jamie stow everything into backpacks. The huge man never glanced at Jamie and never spoke one word. *He doesn't speak English*, Jamie decided. Margaret was in the store waiting on customers, but if she knew Jamie was there, she gave no indication.

Van der Merwe came over to Jamie. "Your mule's in front," he said. "Banda will help you load up."

"Thank you, Mr. van der Merwe," Jamie said. "I – "

Van der Merwe consulted a piece of paper covered with figures. "That will be one hundred and twenty pounds."

Jamie looked at him blankly. "W – what? This is part of our deal. We – "

"*Wat bedui'di?*" Van der Merwe's thin face darkened with anger. "You expect me to *give* you all this, and a fine mule, and make you a partner, and give you two pounds a week on top of *that?* If you're looking for something for nothing, you've come to the wrong place." He began to unload one of the backpacks.

Jamie said quickly, "No! Please, Mr. van der Merwe. I – I just didn't understand. It's perfectly all right. I have the money right here." He reached in his pouch and put the last of his savings on the counter.

Van der Merwe hesitated. "All right," he said grudgingly. "Perhaps it was a misunderstanding, neh? This town is full of cheaters. I have to be careful who I do business with."

"Yes, sir. Of course you do," Jamie agreed. In his excitement, he had misunderstood the deal. *I'm lucky he's giving me another chance*, Jamie thought.

Van der Merwe reached into his pocket and pulled out a small, wrinkled, hand-drawn map. "Here is where you'll find the *mooi klippe*. North of here at Magerdam on the northern bank of the Vaal."

Jamie studied the map, and his heart began to beat faster. "How many miles is it?"

"Here we measure distance by time. With the mule, you should make the journey in four or five days. Coming back will be slower because of the weight of the diamonds."

Jamie grinned. "*Ja.*"

When Jamie McGregor stepped back out onto the streets of Klipdrift, he was no longer a tourist. He was a prospector, a digger, on his way to his fortune. Banda had finished loading the supplies onto the back of a frail-looking mule tethered to the hitching post in front of the store.

"Thanks." Jamie smiled.

Banda turned and looked him in the eye, then silently walked away. Jamie unhitched the reins and said to the mule, "Let's go, partner. It's *mooi klippe* time."

They headed north.

Jamie pitched camp near a stream at nightfall, unloaded and watered and fed the mule, and fixed himself some beef jerky, dried apricots and coffee. The night was filled with strange noises. He heard the grunts and howls and padding of wild animals moving down to the water. He was unprotected, surrounded by the most dangerous beasts in the world, in a strange, primitive country. He jumped at every sound. At any moment he expected to be attacked by fangs and claws leaping at him from out of the darkness. His mind began to drift. He thought of his snug bed at home and the comfort and safety he had always taken for granted. He slept fitfully, his dreams filled with charging lions and elephants, and large, bearded men trying to take an enormous diamond away from him.

At dawn when Jamie awakened, the mule was dead.

2

He could not believe it. He looked for a wound of some kind, thinking it must have been attacked by a wild animal during the night, but there was nothing. The beast had died in its sleep. *Mr. van der Merwe will hold me responsible for this*, Jamie thought. *But when I bring him diamonds, it won't matter.*

There was no turning back. He would go on to Magerdam without the mule.

He heard a sound in the air and looked up. Giant black vultures were beginning to circle high above. Jamie shuddered. Working as quickly as possible, he rearranged his gear, deciding what he had to leave behind, then stowed everything he could carry into a backpack and started off. When he looked back five minutes later, the enormous vultures had covered the body of the dead animal. All that was visible was one long ear. Jamie quickened his step.

It was December, summer in South Africa, and the trek across the veld under the huge orange sun was a horror. Jamie had started out from Klipdrift with a brisk step and a light heart, but as the minutes turned into hours and the hours into days, his steps got slower and his heart became heavier. As far as the eye could see, the monotonous veld shimmered flat and forbidding under the blazing sun and there seemed no end to the gray, stony, desolate plains.

Jamie made camp whenever he came to a watering hole, and he slept with the eerie, nocturnal sounds of the animals all around him. The sounds no longer bothered him. They were proof that there was life in this barren hell, and they made him feel less lonely. One dawn Jamie came across a pride of lions. He watched from a distance as the lioness moved toward her mate and their cubs, carrying a baby impala in her powerful jaws. She dropped the animal in front of the male and moved away while he fed. A reckless cub leaped forward and dug his teeth into the impala. With one motion, the male raised a paw and swiped the cub across the face, killing it instantly, then went back to his feeding. When he finished, the rest of the family was permitted to move in for the remains of the feast. Jamie slowly backed away from the scene and continued walking.

It took him almost two weeks to cross the Karroo. More than once he was ready to give up. He was not sure he could finish the journey. *I'm a fool. I should have returned to Klipdrift to ask Mr. van der Merwe for another mule. But what if Van der Merwe had called off the deal? No, I did the right thing.*

And so, Jamie kept moving, one step at a time. One day, he saw four figures in the distance, coming toward him. *I'm delirious*, Jamie thought. *Its a mirage.* But the figures came closer, and Jamie's heart began to thud alarmingly. *Men! There is human life here!* He wondered if he had forgotten how to speak. He tried out his voice on the afternoon air, and it sounded as if it belonged to someone long dead. The four men reached him, prospectors returning to Klipdrift, tired and defeated.

"Hello," Jamie said.

They nodded. One of them said, "There ain't nothin' ahead, boy. We looked. You're wastin' your time. Go back."

And they were gone.

Jamie shut his mind to everything but the trackless waste ahead of him. The sun and the black flies were unbearable and there was no place to hide. There were thorn trees, but their branches had been laid waste by the elephants. Jamie was almost totally blinded by the sun. His fair skin was burned raw, and he was constantly dizzy. Each time he took a breath of air, his lungs seemed to explode. He was no longer walking, he was stumbling, putting one foot in front of the other, mindlessly lurching ahead. One afternoon, with the midday sun beating down on him, he slipped off his backpack and slumped to the ground, too tired to take another step. He closed his eyes and dreamed he was in a giant crucible and the sun was a huge, bright diamond blazing down on him, melting him. He awoke in the middle of the night trembling from the cold. He forced himself to take a few bites of biltong and a drink of tepid water. He knew he must get up and start moving before the sun rose, while the earth and sky were cool. He tried, but the effort was too great. It would be so easy just to lie there forever and never have to take another step. *I'll just sleep for a little while longer*, Jamie thought. But some voice deep within him told him he would never wake up again. They would find his body there as they had found hundreds of others. He remembered the vultures and thought, *No, not my body – my bones.* Slowly and painfully, he forced himself to his feet. His backpack was so heavy he could not lift it. Jamie started walking again, dragging the pack behind him. He had no recollection of how many times he fell onto the sand and staggered to his feet again. Once he screamed into the predawn sky, "I'm Jamie McGregor, and I'm going to make it. I'm going to live. Do you hear me, God? I'm going to live. . . ." Voices were exploding in his head.

You're goin' chasin' diamonds? You must be daft, son. That's a fairy tale – a temptation of the devil to keep men from doin' an honest day's work.

Why do you nae tell us where you're gettin' the money to go? Its halfway 'round the world. You hae no money.

Mr. van der Merwe, I'm the person you're looking for. Believe me, sir, I'll work night and day. I'll bring you back more diamonds than you can count.

And he was finished before he had even started. *You have two choices*, Jamie told himself. *You can go on or you can stay here and die . . . and die . . . and die . . .*

The words echoed endlessly in his head. *You can take one more step*, Jamie thought. *Come on, Jamie boy. One more step. One more step . . .*

Two days later Jamie McGregor stumbled into the village of Magerdam. The sunburn had long since become infected and his body oozed blood and sera. Both eyes were swollen almost completely shut. He collapsed in the middle of the street, a pile of crumpled clothes holding him together. When sympathetic diggers tried to relieve him of his backpack, Jamie fought them with what little strength he had left, raving deliriously. "No! Get away from my diamonds. Get away from my diamonds. . . ."

He awakened in a small, bare room three days later, naked except for the bandages that covered his body. The first thing he saw when he opened his eyes was a buxom, middle-aged woman seated at the side of his cot.

"Wh – ?" His voice was a croak. He could not get the words out.

"Easy, dear. You've been sick." She gently lifted his swathed head and gave him a sip of water from a tin cup.

Jamie managed to prop himself up on one elbow. "Where – ?" He swallowed and tried again. "Where am I?"

"You're in Magerdam. I'm Alice Jardine. This is my boarding house. You're going to be fine. You just need a good rest. Now lie back."

Jamie remembered the strangers who tried to take his backpack away, and he was filled with panic. "My things, where – ?" He tried to rise from the cot, but the woman's gentle voice stopped him.

"Everything's safe. Not to worry, son." She pointed to his backpack in a corner of the room.

Jamie lay back on the clean white sheets. *I got here. I made it. Everything is going to be all right now.*

Alice Jardine was a blessing, not only to Jamie McGregor, but to half of Magerdam. In that mining town filled with adventurers, all sharing the same dream, she fed them, nursed them, encouraged them. She was an Englishwoman who had come to South Africa with her husband, when he decided to give up his teaching job in Leeds and join the diamond rush. He had died of fever three weeks after they arrived, but she had decided to stay on. The miners had become the children she never had.

She kept Jamie in bed for four more days, feeding him, changing his bandages and helping him regain his strength. By the fifth day, Jamie was ready to get up.

"I want you to know how grateful I am to you, Mrs. Jardine. I can't pay you anything. Not yet. But you'll have a big diamond from me one day soon. That's a promise from Jamie McGregor."

She smiled at the intensity of the handsome young boy. He was still twenty pounds too thin, and his gray eyes were filled with the horror he had been through, but there was a strength about him, a determination that was awesome. *He's different from the others*, Mrs. Jardine thought.

Jamie, dressed in his freshly washed clothes, went out to explore the town. It was Klipdrift on a smaller scale. There were the same tents and wagons and dusty streets, the flimsily built shops and the crowds of prospectors. As Jamie passed a saloon, he heard a roar from inside and entered. A noisy crowd had gathered around a red-shirted Irishman.

"What's going on?" Jamie asked.

"He's going to wet his find."

"He's what?"

"He struck it rich today, so he stands treat for the whole saloon. He pays for as much liquor as a saloon-full of thirsty men can swallow."

Jamie joined in a conversation with several disgruntled diggers sitting at a round table.

"Where you from, McGregor?"

"Scotland."

"Well, I don't know what horseshit they fed you in Scotland, but there ain't enough diamonds in this fuckin' country to pay expenses."

They talked of other camps: Gong Gong, Forlorn Hope, Delports, Poormans Kopje, Sixpenny Rush . . .

The diggers all told the same story – of months doing the backbreaking work of moving boulders, digging into the hard soil and squatting over the riverbank sifting the dirt for diamonds. Each day a few diamonds were found; not enough to make a man rich, but enough to keep his dreams alive. The mood of the town was a strange mixture of optimism and pessimism. The optimists were arriving; the pessimists were leaving.

Jamie knew which side he was on.

He approached the red-shirted Irishman, now bleary-eyed with drink, and showed him Van der Merwe's map.

The man glanced at it and tossed it back to Jamie. "Worthless. That whole area's been picked over. If I was you, I'd try Bad Hope."

Jamie could not believe it. Van der Merwe's map was what had brought him there, the lodestar that was going to make him rich.

Another digger said, "Head for Colesberg. That's where they're findin' diamonds, son."

"Gilfillans Kop – *that's* the place to dig."

"You'll try Moonlight Rush, if you want my opinion."

At supper that night, Alice Jardine said, "Jamie, one place is as big a gamble as another. Pick your own spot, dig in your pickax and pray. That's all these other *experts* are doing."

After a night of sleepless self-debate, Jamie decided he would forget Van der Merwe's map. Against everyone's advice, he decided to head east, along the Modder River. The following morning Jamie said good-bye to Mrs. Jardine and set off.

He walked for three days and two nights, and when he came to a likely-looking spot, he set up his small tent. Huge boulders lay along both sides of the riverbank, and Jamie, using thick branches as levers, laboriously moved them out of the way to get at the gravel that lay beneath.

He dug from dawn until dusk, looking for the yellow clay or the blue diamondiferous soil that would tell him he had found a diamond pipe. But the earth was barren. He dug for a week without finding a single stone. At the end of the week, he moved on.

One day as he walked along, he saw in the distance what looked like & silver house, glowing dazzlingly in the sun. *I'm going blind*, Jamie thought. But as he got closer, he saw that he was approaching a village, and all the houses seemed to be made of silver. Crowds of Indian men, women and children dressed in rags swarmed through the streets. Jamie stared in amazement. The silver houses glistening in the sun were made of tin jam pots, flattened out, fastened together and nailed over the crude shacks. He walked on, and an hour later, when he looked back, he could still see the glow of the village. It was a sight he never forgot.

Jamie kept moving north. He followed the riverbank where the diamonds might be, digging until his arms refused to lift the heavy pick, then sifting the wet gravel through the hand sieve. When it got dark, he slept as though drugged.

At the end of the second week, he moved upstream again, just north of a small settlement called Paardspan. He stopped near a bend in the river and fixed himself a meal of carbonaatje, grilled on a spit over a wood fire, and hot tea, then sat in front of his tent, looking up at the wheeling stars in the vast sky. He had not seen a human being in two weeks, and an eddy of loneliness washed over him. *What the hell am I doing here?* he wondered. *Sitting in the middle of a blasted wilderness like a bloody fool, killing myself breaking rocks and digging up dirt? I was better off at the farm. Come Saturday, if I don't find a diamond, I'm going home.* He looked up at the uncaring stars and yelled, "Do you hear me, damn you?" *Oh, Jesus,* he thought, *I'm losing my mind.*

Jamie sat there, idly sifting the sand through his' fingers. They closed on a large stone, and he looked at it a moment, then threw it away. He had seen a thousand worthless stones like it in the past weeks. What was it Van der Merwe had called them? *Schlenters.* Yet, there was something about this one that belatedly caught Jamie's attention. He rose, went over to it and picked it up. It was much larger than the other stones and of an odd shape. He rubbed some of the dirt off it against the leg of his trousers and examined it more closely. It *looked* like a diamond. The only thing that made Jamie doubt his senses was the size of it. It was almost as large as a hen's egg. *Oh, God. If it is a diamond . . .* He suddenly had difficulty breathing. He grabbed his lantern and began searching the ground around him. In fifteen minutes he had found four more like it. None of them was as large as the first one, but they were large enough to fill him with a wild excitement.

He was up before dawn, digging like a madman, and by noon he had found half a dozen more diamonds. He spent the next week feverishly digging up diamonds and burying them at night in a safe place where no passers-by could find them. There were fresh diamonds every day, and as Jamie watched his fortune pile up, he was filled with an ineffable joy. Only half of this treasure was his, but it was enough to make him rich beyond anything he had ever dared to dream.

At the end of the week, Jamie made a note on his map and staked out his claim by carefully marking the boundaries with his pick. He dug up his hidden treasure, carefully stored it deep down in his backpack and headed back to Magerdam.

The sign outside the small building read: DIAMANT KOOPER.

Jamie walked into the office, a small, airless room, and he was filled with a sudden sense of trepidation. He had heard dozens of stories of prospectors who had found diamonds that had turned out to be worthless stones. *What if I'm wrong? What if – ?*

The assayer was seated at a cluttered desk in the tiny office. "Somethin' I can do for you?"

Jamie took a deep breath. "Yes, sir. I would like to have these valued, please."

Under the watchful eye of the assayer, Jamie started laying the stones on his desk. When he was finished, there was a total of twenty-seven, and the assayer was gazing at them in astonishment.

"Where – where did you find these?"

"I'll tell you after you tell me whether they're diamonds."

The assayer picked up the largest stone and examined it with a jeweler's loupe. "My God!" he said. "This is the biggest diamond I've ever seen!" And Jamie realized he had been holding his breath. He could have yelled aloud with joy.

"Where – " the man begged, "where did these come from?"

"Meet me in the canteen in fifteen minutes," Jamie grinned, "and I'll tell you."

Jamie gathered up the diamonds, put them in his pockets and strode out. He headed for the registration office two doors down the street. "I want to register a claim," he said. "In the names of Salomon van der Merwe and Jamie McGregor."

He had walked through that door a penniless farm boy and walked out a multimillionaire.

The assayer was in the canteen waiting when Jamie McGregor entered. He had obviously spread the news, because when Jamie walked in there was a sudden, respectful hush. There was a single unspoken question on everyone's mind. Jamie walked up to the bar and said to the bartender, "I'm here to wet my find." He turned and faced the crowd. "Paardspan."

Alice Jardine was having a cup of tea when Jamie walked into the kitchen. Her face lighted up when she saw him. "Jamie! Oh, thank God you're back safely!" She took in his disheveled appearance and flushed face. "It didn't go well, did it? Never you mind. Have a nice cup of tea with me, dear, and you'll feel better."

Without a word, Jamie reached into his pocket and pulled out a large diamond. He placed it in Mrs. Jardine's hand.

"I've kept my promise," Jamie said.

She stared at the stone for a long time, and her blue eyes became moist. "No, Jamie. No." Her voice was very soft. "I don't want it. Don't you see, child? It would spoil everything . . ."

When Jamie McGregor returned to Klipdrift, he did it in style. He traded one of his smaller diamonds for a horse and carriage, and made a careful note of what he had spent, so that his partner would not be cheated. The trip back to Klipdrift was easy and comfortable, and when Jamie thought of the hell he had gone through on this same journey, he was filled with a sense of wonder. *That's the difference between the rich and the poor*, he thought. *The poor walk; the rich ride in carriages.*

He gave the horse a small flick of the whip and rode on contentedly through the darkening veld.

3

Klipdrift had not changed, but Jamie McGregor had. People stared as he rode into town and stopped in front of Van der Merwe's general store. It was not just the expensive horse and carriage that drew the attention of the passers-by; it was the air of jubilation about the young man. They had seen it before in other prospectors who had struck it rich, and it always filled them with a renewed sense of hope for themselves. They stood back and watched as Jamie jumped out of the carriage.

The same large black man was there. Jamie grinned at him. "Hello! I'm back."

Banda tied the reins to a hitching post without comment and went inside the store. Jamie followed him.

Salomon van der Merwe was waiting on a customer. The little Dutchman looked up and smiled, and Jamie knew that somehow Van der Merwe had already heard the news. No one could explain it, but news of a diamond strike flashed across the continent with the speed of light.

When Van der Merwe had finished with the customer, he nodded his head toward the back of the store. "Come, Mr. McGregor."

Jamie followed him. Van der Merwe's daughter was at the stove, preparing lunch. "Hello, Margaret."

She flushed and looked away.

"Well! I hear there is good news." Van der Merwe beamed. He seated himself at the table and pushed the plate and silverware away, clearing a place in front of him.

"That's right, sir." Proudly, Jamie took a large leather pouch from his jacket pocket and poured the diamonds on the kitchen table. Van der Merwe stared at them, hypnotized, then picked them up slowly, one by one, savoring each one, saving the largest until last. Then he scooped up the diamonds, put them in a chamois bag and put the bag in a large iron safe in the corner and locked it.

When he spoke, there was a note of deep satisfaction in his voice. "You've done well, Mr. McGregor. Very well, indeed."

"Thank you, sir. This is only the beginning. There are hundreds more there. I don't even dare think about how much they're worth."

"And you've staked out the claim properly?"

"Yes, sir." Jamie reached in his pocket and pulled out the registration slip. "It's registered in both our names."

Van der Merwe studied the slip, then put it in his pocket. "You deserve a bonus. Wait here." He started toward the doorway that led into the shop. "Come along, Margaret."

She followed him meekly, and Jamie thought, *She's like a frightened kitten.*

A few minutes later, Van der Merwe returned, alone. "Here we are." He opened a purse and carefully counted out fifty pounds.

Jamie looked at him, puzzled. "What's this for, sir?"

"For you, son. All of it."

"I – I don't understand."

"You've been gone twenty-four weeks. At two pounds a week, that's forty-eight pounds, and I'm giving you an extra two pounds as a bonus."

Jamie laughed. "I don't need a bonus. I have my share of the diamonds."

"Your share of the diamonds?"

"Why, yes, sir. My fifty percent. We're partners."

Van der Merwe was staring at him. "Partners? Where did you get that idea?"

"Where did I – ?" Jamie looked at the Dutchman in bewilderment. "We have a contract."

"That is correct. Have you read it?"

"Well, no, sir. It's in Afrikaans, but you said we were fifty-fifty partners."

The older man shook his head. "You misunderstood me, Mr. McGregor. I don't need any partners. You were working for me. I outfitted you and sent you to find diamonds for me."

Jamie could feel a slow rage boiling up within him. "You gave me nothing. I paid you a hundred and twenty pounds for that equipment."

The old man shrugged. "I won't waste my valuable time quibbling. Tell you what I'll do. I'll give you an extra five pounds, and we'll call the whole thing quits. I think that's very generous."

Jamie exploded in a fury. "We'll nae call the whole thing quits!" In his anger his Scottish burr came back. "I'm entitled to half that claim. And Ill get it. I registered it in *both* our names."

Van der Merwe smiled thinly. "Then you tried to cheat me. I could have you arrested for that." He shoved the money into Jamie's hand. "Now take your wages and get out."

"I'll fight you!"

"Do you have money for a lawyer? I own them all in these parts, boy."

This isn't happening to me, Jamie thought. *It's a nightmare.* The agony he had gone through, the weeks and months of the burning desert, the punishing physical labor from sunrise to sunset – it all came flooding back. He had nearly died, and now this man was trying to cheat him out of what was his.

He looked Van der Merwe in the eye. "I'll not let you get away with this. I'm not going to leave Klipdrift. I'll tell everybody here what you've done. I'm going to get my share of those diamonds."

Van der Merwe started to turn away from the fury in the pale-gray eyes. "You'd better find a doctor, boy," he muttered. "I think the sun has addled your wits."

In a second, Jamie was towering over Van der Merwe. He pulled the thin figure into the air and held him up to eye level. "I'm going to make you sorry you ever laid eyes on me." He dropped Van der Merwe to his feet, flung the money on the table and stormed out.

When Jamie McGregor walked into the Sundowner Saloon, it was almost deserted, for most of the prospectors were on their way to Paardspan. Jamie was filled with anger and despair. *It's incredible*, he thought. *One minute I'm as rich as Croesus, and the next minute I'm dead broke. Van der Merwe is a thief and I'm going to find a way to punish him. But how?* Van der Merwe was right. Jamie could not even afford a lawyer to fight his case. He was a stranger there, and Van der Merwe was a respected member of the community. The only weapon Jamie had was the truth. He would let everyone in South Africa know what Van der Merwe had done.

Smit, the bartender, greeted him. "Welcome back. Everything's on the house, Mr. McGregor. What would you like?"

"A whiskey."

Smit poured a double and set it in front of Jamie. Jamie downed it in one gulp. He was not used to drinking, and the hard liquor scorched his throat and stomach.

"Another, please."

"Comin' up. I've always said the Scots could drink anybody under the table."

The second drink went down easier. Jamie remembered that it was the bartender who had told a digger to go to Van der Merwe for help. "Did you know Old Man Van der Merwe is a crook? He's trying to cheat me out of my diamonds."

Smit was sympathetic. "What? That's terrible. I'm sorry to hear that."

"He'll nae get away with it." Jamie's voice was slurred. "Half those diamonds are mine. He's a thief and I'm gonna see that everybody knows it."

"Careful. Van der Merwe's an important man in this town," the bartender warned. "If you're goin' up against him, you'll need help. In fact, I know just the person. He hates Van der Merwe as much as you do." He looked around to make sure no one could overhear him. "There's an old barn at the end of the street. I'll arrange everything. Be there at ten o'clock tonight."

"Thanks," Jamie said gratefully. "I won't forget you."

"Ten o'clock. The old barn."

The barn was a hastily thrown-together structure built of corrugated tin, off the main street at the edge of town. At ten o'clock Jamie arrived there. It was dark, and he felt his way carefully. He could see no one around. He stepped inside. "Hello . . ."

There was no reply. Jamie went slowly forward. He could make out the dim shapes of horses moving restlessly in their stalls. Then he heard a sound behind him, and as he started to turn, an iron bar crashed across his shoulder blades, knocking him to the ground. A club thudded against his head, and a giant hand picked him up and held him while fists and boots smashed into his body. The beating seemed to last forever. When the pain became too much to bear and he lost consciousness, cold water was thrown in his face. His eyes fluttered open. He thought he caught a glimpse of Van der Merwe's servant, Banda, and the beating began anew. Jamie could feel his ribs breaking. Something smashed into his leg, and he heard the crunch of bone.

That was when he lost consciousness again.

His body was on fire. Someone was scraping his face with sandpaper, and he vainly tried to lift a hand to protest. He made an effort to open his eyes, but they were swollen shut. Jamie lay there, every fiber of his being screaming with pain, as he tried to remember where he was. He shifted, and the scraping began again. He put out his hand blindly and felt sand. His raw face was lying in hot sand. Slowly, every move an agony, he managed to draw himself up on his knees. He tried to see through his swollen eyes, but he could make out only hazy images. He was somewhere in the middle of the trackless Karroo, naked. It was early morning, but he could feel the sun starting to burn through his body. He felt around blindly for food or a billy can of water. There was nothing. They had left him there for dead. *Salomon van der Merwe. And, of course, Smit, the bartender.* Jamie had threatened Van der Merwe, and Van der Merwe had punished him as easily as one punished a small child. *But he'll find out I'm no child,* Jamie promised himself. *Not anymore. I'm an avenger. They'll pay. They will pay.* The hatred that coursed through Jamie gave him the strength to sit up. It was a torture for him to breathe. How many ribs had they broken? *I must be careful so they don't puncture my lungs.* Jamie tried to stand up, but fell down with a scream. His right leg was broken and lay at an unnatural angle. He was unable to walk.

But he could crawl.

Jamie McGregor had no idea where he was. They would have taken him to some place off the beaten track, where his body would not be found except by the desert scavengers, the hyenas and secretary birds and vultures. The desert was a vast charnel house. He had seen the bones of men's bodies that had been scavenged, and there had not been a scrap of meat left on the skeleton. Even as Jamie was thinking about it, he heard the rustle of wings above him and the shrill hiss of the vultures. He felt a flood of terror. He was blind. He could not see them. But he could smell them.

He began to crawl.

He made himself concentrate on the pain. His body was aflame with it, and each small movement brought exquisite rivers of agony. If he moved in a certain way, his broken leg would send out stabbing pains. If he shifted his position slightly to favor his leg, he could feel his ribs grinding against each other. He could not stand the torture of lying still; he could not stand the agony of moving.

He kept crawling.

He could hear them circling above, waiting for him with an ancient, timeless patience. His mind started to wander. He was in the cool kirk at Aberdeen, neatly dressed in his Sunday suit, seated between his two brothers. His sister, Mary, and Annie Cord were wearing beautiful white summer dresses, and Annie Cord was looking at him and smiling. Jamie started to get up and go to her, and his brothers held him back and began to pinch him. The pinches became excruciating shafts of pain, and he was crawling through the desert again, naked, his body broken. The cries of the vultures were louder now, impatient.

Jamie tried to force his eyes open, to see how close they were. He could see nothing except vague, shimmering objects that his terrified imagination turned into feral hyenas and jackals. The wind became their hot, fetid breath caressing his face.

He kept crawling, for he knew that the moment he stopped they would be upon him. He was burning with fever and pain and his body was flayed by the hot sand. And still, he could not give up, not as long as Van der Merwe was unpunished – not as long as Van der Merwe was alive.

He lost all awareness of time. He guessed that he had traveled a mile. In truth, he had moved less than ten yards, crawling in a circle. He could not see where he had been or where he was going. He focused his mind on only one thing: Salomon van der Merwe.

He slipped into unconsciousness and was awakened by a shrieking agony beyond bearing. Someone was stabbing at his leg, and it took Jamie a second to remember where he was and what was happening. He pulled one swollen eye open. An enormous hooded black vulture was attacking his leg, savagely tearing at his flesh, eating him alive with its sharp beak. Jamie saw its beady eyes and the dirty ruff around its neck. He smelled the foul odor of the bird as it sat on his body. Jamie tried to scream, but no sound came out. Frantically he jerked himself forward, and felt the warm flow of blood pouring from his leg. He could see the shadows of the giant birds all around him, moving in for the kill. He knew that the next time he lost consciousness would be the last time. The instant he stopped, the carrion birds would be at his flesh again. He kept crawling. His mind began to wander into delirium. He heard the loud flapping wings of the birds as they moved closer, forming a circle around him. He was too weak now to fight them off; he had no strength left to resist. He stopped moving and lay still on the burning sand.

The giant birds closed in for their feast.

4

Saturday was market day in Cape Town and the streets were crowded with shoppers looking for bargains, meeting friends and lovers. Boers and Frenchmen, soldiers in colorful uniforms and English ladies in flounced skirts and ruffled blouses mingled in front of the bazaars set up in the town squares at Braameonstein and Park Town and Burgersdorp. Everything was for sale: furniture, horses and carriages and fresh fruit. One could purchase dresses and chessboards, or meat or books in a dozen different languages. On Saturdays, Cape Town was a noisy, bustling fair.

Banda walked along slowly through the crowd, careful not to make eye contact with the whites. It was too dangerous. The streets were filled with blacks, Indians and coloreds, but the white minority ruled. Banda hated them. This was his land, and the whites were the *uitlanders*. There were many tribes in southern Africa: the Basutos, Zulus, Bechuanas, the Matabele – all of them Bantu. The very word *bantu* came from *abantu – the people*. But the Barolongs – Banda's tribe – were the aristocracy. Banda remembered the tales his grandmother told him of the great black kingdom that had once ruled South Africa. *Their* kingdom, *their* country. And now they were enslaved by a handful of white jackals. The whites had pushed them into smaller and smaller territories, until their freedom had been eroded. Now, the only way a black could exist was by *slim*, subservient on the surface, but cunning and clever beneath.

Banda did not know how old he was, for natives had no birth certificates. Their ages were measured by tribal lore: wars and battles, and births and deaths of great chiefs, comets and blizzards and earthquakes, Adam Kok's trek, the death of Chaka and the cattle-killing revolution. But the number of his years made no difference. Banda knew he was the son of a chief, and that he was destined to do something for his people. Once again, the Bantus would rise and rule because of him. The thought of his mission made him walk taller and straighter for a moment, until he felt the eyes of a white man upon him.

Banda hurried east toward the outskirts of town, the district allotted to the blacks. The large homes and attractive shops gradually gave way to tin shacks and lean-tos and huts. He moved down a dirt street, looking over his shoulder to make certain he was not followed. He reached a wooden shack, took one last look around, rapped twice on the door and entered. A thin black woman was seated in a chair in a corner of the room sewing on a dress. Banda nodded to her and then continued on into the bedroom in back.

He looked down at the figure lying on the cot.

Six weeks earlier Jamie McGregor had regained consciousness and found himself on a cot in a strange house. Memory came flooding back. He was in the Karroo again, his body broken, helpless. The vultures . . .

Then Banda had walked into the tiny bedroom, and Jamie knew he had come to kill him. Van der Merwe had somehow learned Jamie was still alive and had sent his servant to finish him off.

"Why didn't your master come himself?" Jamie croaked.

"I have no master."

"Van der Merwe. He didn't send you?"

"No. He would kill us both if he knew."

None of this made any sense. "Where am I? I want to know where I am."

"Cape Town."

"That's impossible. How did I get here?"

"I brought you."

Jamie stared into the black eyes for a long moment before he spoke. "Why?"

"I need you. I want vengeance."

"What do you – ?"

Banda moved closer. "Not for me. I do not care about me. Van der Merwe raped my sister. She died giving birth to his baby. My sister was eleven years old."

Jamie lay back, stunned. "My God!"

"Since the day she died I have been looking for a white man to help me. I found him that night in the barn where I helped beat you up, Mr. McGregor. We dumped you in the Karroo. I was ordered to kill you. I told the others you were dead, and I returned to get you as soon as I could. I was almost too late."

Jamie could not repress a shudder. He could feel again the foul-smelling carrion bird digging into his flesh.

"The birds were already starting to feast. I carried you to the wagon and hid you at the house of my people. One of our doctors taped your ribs and set your leg and tended to your wounds."

"And after that?"

"A wagonful of my relatives was leaving for Cape Town. We took you with us. You were out of your head most of the time. Each time you fell asleep, I was afraid you were not going to wake up again."

Jamie looked into the eyes of the man who had almost murdered him. He had to think. He did not trust this man – and yet he had saved his life. Banda wanted to get at Van der Merwe through him. *That can work both ways*, Jamie decided. More than anything in the world, Jamie wanted to make Van der Merwe pay for what he had done to him.

"All right," Jamie told Banda. "I'll find a way to pay Van der Merwe back for both of us."

For the first time, a thin smile appeared on Banda's face. "Is he going to die?"

"No," Jamie told him. "He's going to live."

Jamie got out of bed that afternoon for the first time, dizzy and weak. His leg still had not completely healed, and he walked with a slight limp. Banda tried to assist him.

"Let go of me. I can make it on my own."

Banda watched as Jamie carefully moved across the room.

"I'd like a mirror," Jamie said. *I must look terrible*, he thought. *How long has it been since I've had a shave?*

Banda returned with a hand mirror, and Jamie held it up to his face. He was looking at a total stranger. His hair had turned snow-white. He had a full, unkempt white beard. His nose had been broken and a ridge of bone pushed it to one side. His face had aged twenty years. There were deep ridges along his sunken cheeks and a livid scar across his chin. But the biggest change was in his eyes. They were eyes that had seen too much pain, felt too much, hated too much. He slowly put down the mirror.

"I'm going out for a walk," Jamie said.

"Sorry, Mr. McGregor. That's not possible."

"Why not?"

"White men do not come to this part of town, just as blacks never go into the white places. My neighbors do not know you are here. We brought you in at night."

"How do I leave?"

"I will move you out tonight."

For the first time, Jamie began to realize how much Banda had risked for him. Embarrassed, Jamie said, "I have no money. I need a job."

"I took a job at the shipyard. They are always looking for men." He took some money from his pocket. "Here."

Jamie took the money. "I'll pay it back."

"You will pay my sister back," Banda told him.

It was midnight when Banda led Jamie out of the shack. Jamie looked around. He was in the middle of a shantytown, a jungle of rusty, corrugated iron shacks and lean-tos, made from rotting planks and torn sacking. The ground, muddy from a recent rain, gave off a rank odor. Jamie wondered how people as proud as Banda could bear spending their lives in a place such as this. "Isn't there some – ?"

"Don't talk, please," Banda whispered. "My neighbors are inquisitive." He led Jamie outside the compound and pointed. "The center of town is in that direction. I will see you at the shipyard."

Jamie checked into the same boardinghouse where he had stayed on his arrival from England. Mrs. Venster was behind the desk.

"I'd like a room," Jamie said.

"Certainly, sir." She smiled, revealing her gold tooth. "I'm Mrs. Venster."

"I know."

"Now how would you know a thing like that?" she asked coyly. "Have your men friends been tellin' tales out of school?"

"Mrs. Venster, don't you remember me? I stayed here last year."

She took a close look at his scarred face, his broken nose and his white beard, and there was not the slightest sign of recognition. "I never forget a face, dearie. And I've never seen yours before. But that don't mean we're not going to be good friends, does it? My friends call me 'Dee-Dee.' What's your name, love?"

And Jamie heard himself saying, "Travis. Ian Travis."

The following morning Jamie went to see about work at the shipyard.

The busy foreman said, "We need strong backs. The problem is you might be a bit old for this kind of work."

"I'm only nineteen – " Jamie started to say and stopped himself. He remembered that face in the mirror. "Try me," he said.

He went to work as a stevedore at nine shillings a day, loading and unloading the ships that came into the harbor. He learned that Banda and the other black stevedores received six shillings a day.

At the first opportunity, Jamie pulled Banda aside and said, "We have to talk."

"Not here, Mr. McGregor. There's an abandoned warehouse at the end of the docks. I'll meet you there when the shift is over."

Banda was waiting when Jamie arrived at the deserted warehouse.

"Tell me about Salomon van der Merwe," Jamie said.

"What do you want to know?"

"Everything."

Banda spat. "He came to South Africa from Holland. From stories I heard, his wife was ugly, but wealthy. She died of some sickness and Van der Merwe took her money and went up to Klipdrift and opened his general store. He got rich cheating diggers."

"The way he cheated me?"

"That's only one of his ways. Diggers who strike it lucky go to him for money to help them work their claim, and before they know it Van der Merwe owns them."

"Hasn't anyone ever tried to fight back?"

"How can they? The town clerk's on his payroll. The law says that if forty-five days go by without working a claim, it's open. The town clerk tips off Van der Merwe and he grabs it. There's another trick he uses. Claims have to be staked out at each boundary line with pegs pointing straight up in the air. If the pegs fall down, a jumper can claim the property. Well, when Van der Merwe sees a claim he likes, he sends someone around at night, and in the morning the stakes are on the ground."

"Jesus!"

"He's made a deal with the bartender, Smit. Smit sends likely-looking prospectors to Van der Merwe, and they sign partnership contracts and if they find diamonds, Van der Merwe takes everything for himself. If they become troublesome, he's got a lot of men on his payroll who follow his orders."

"I know about that," Jamie said grimly. "What else?"

"He's a religious fanatic. He's always praying for the souls of sinners."

"What about his daughter?" She had to be involved in this.

"Miss Margaret? She's frightened to death of her father. If she even looked at a man, Van der Merwe would kill them both."

Jamie turned his back and walked over to the door, where he stood looking out at the harbor. He had a lot to think about. "We'll talk again tomorrow."

It was in Cape Town that Jamie became aware of the enormous schism between the blacks and whites. The blacks had no rights except the few they were given by those in power. They were herded into conclaves that were ghettos and were allowed to leave only to work for the white man.

"How do you stand it?" Jamie asked Banda one day.

"The hungry lion hides its claws. We will change all this someday. The white man accepts the black man because his muscles are needed, but he must also learn to accept his brain. The more he drives us into a corner, the more he fears us because he knows that one day there may be discrimination and humiliation in reverse. He cannot hear the thought of that. But we will survive because of *isiko.*"

"Who is *isiko?*"

Banda shook his head. "Not a *who.* A *what.* It is difficult to explain, Mr. McGregor. *Isiko* is our roots. It is the feeling of belonging to a nation that has given its name to the great Zambezi River. Generations ago my ancestors entered the waters of the Zambezi naked, driving their herds before them. Their weakest members were lost, the prey of the swirling waters or hungry crocodiles, but the survivors emerged from the waters stronger and more virile. When a Bantu dies, *isiko* demands that the members of his family retire to the forest so that the rest of the community will not have to share their distress. *Isiko* is the scorn felt for a slave who cringes, the belief that a man can look anyone in the face, that he is worth no more and no less than any other man. Have you heard of John Tengo Jabavu?" He pronounced the name with reverence.

"No."

"You will, Mr. McGregor," Banda promised. "You will." And Banda changed the subject.

Jamie began to feel a growing admiration for Banda. In the beginning there was a wariness between the two men. Jamie had to learn to trust a man who had almost killed him. And Banda had to learn to trust an age-old enemy – a white man. Unlike most of the blacks Jamie had met, Banda was educated.

"Where did you go to school?" Jamie asked.

"Nowhere. I've worked since I was a small boy. My grandmother educated me. She worked for a Boer schoolteacher. She learned to read and write so she could teach me to read and write. I owe her everything."

It was on a late Saturday afternoon after work that Jamie first heard of the Namib Desert in Great Namaqualand. He and Banda were in the deserted warehouse on the docks, sharing an impala stew Banda's mother had cooked. It was good – a little gamey for Jamie's taste, but his bowl was soon empty, and he lay back on some old sacks to question Banda.

"When did you first meet Van der Merwe?"

"When I was working at the diamond beach on the Namib Desert. He owns the beach with two partners. He had just stolen his share from some poor prospector, and he was down there visiting it."

"If Van der Merwe is so rich, why does he still work at his store?"

"The store is his bait. That's how he gets new prospectors to come to him. And he grows richer."

Jamie thought of how easily he himself had been cheated. How trusting that naive young boy had been! He could see Margaret's oval-shaped face as she said, *My father might be the one to help you.* He had thought she was a child until he had noticed her breasts and Jamie suddenly jumped to his feet, a smile on his face, and the up-turning of his lips made the livid scar across his chin ripple.

"Tell me how you happened to go to work for Van der Merwe."

"On the day he came to the beach with his daughter – she was about eleven then – I suppose she got bored sitting around and she went into the water and the tide grabbed her. I jumped in and pulled her out. I was a young boy, but I thought Van der Merwe was going to kill me."

Jamie stared at him. "Why?"

"Because I had my arms around her. Not because I was black, but because I was a *male.* He can't stand the thought of any man touching his daughter. Someone finally calmed him down and reminded him that I had saved her life. He brought me back to Klipdrift as his servant." Banda hesitated a moment, then continued. "Two months later, my sister came to visit me." His voice was very quiet. "She was the same age as Van der Merwe's daughter."

There was nothing Jamie could say.

Finally Banda broke the silence. "I should have stayed in the Namib Desert. That was an easy job. We'd crawl along the beach picking up diamonds and putting them in little jam tins."

"Wait a minute. Are you saying that the diamonds are just lying there, on top of the sand?"

"That's what I'm saying, Mr. McGregor. But forget what you're thinking. Nobody can get near that field. It's on the ocean, and the waves are up to thirty feet high. They don't even bother guarding the shore. A lot of people have tried to sneak in by sea. They've all been killed by the waves or the reefs."

"There must be some other way to get in."

"No. The Namib Desert runs right down to the ocean's shore."

"What about the entrance to the diamond field?"

"There's a guard tower and a barbed-wire fence. Inside the fence are guards with guns and dogs that'll tear a man to pieces. And they have a new kind of explosive called a land mine. They're buried all over the field. If you don't have a map of the land mines, you'll get blown to bits."

"How large is the diamond field?"

"It runs for about thirty-five miles."

Thirty-five miles of diamonds just lying on the sand . . . "My God!"

"You aren't the first one to get excited about the diamond fields at the Namib, and you won't be the last. I've picked up what was left of people who tried to come in by boat and got torn apart by the reefs. I've seen what those land mines do if a man takes one wrong step, and I've watched those dogs rip out a man's throat. Forget it, Mr. McGregor. I've been there. There's no way in and there's no way out – not alive, that is."

Jamie was unable to sleep that night. He kept visualizing thirty-five miles of sand sprinkled with enormous diamonds belonging to Van der Merwe. He thought of the sea and the jagged reefs, the dogs hungry to kill, the guards and the land mines. He was not afraid of the danger; he was not afraid of dying. He was only afraid of dying before he repaid Salomon van der Merwe.

On the following Monday Jamie went into a cartographer's shop and bought a map of Great Namaqualand. There was the beach, off the South Atlantic Ocean between Luderitz to the north and the Orange River Estuary to the south. The area was marked in red: SPERRGEBIET – Forbidden.

Jamie examined every detail of the area on the map, going over it again and again. There were three thousand miles of ocean flowing from South America to South Africa, with nothing to impede the waves, so that their full fury was spent on the deadly reefs of the South Atlantic shore. Forty miles south, down the coastline, was an open beach. *That must be where the poor bastards launched their boats to sail into the forbidden area*, Jamie decided. Looking at the map, he could understand why the shore was not guarded. The reefs would make a landing impossible.

Jamie turned his attention to the land entrance to the diamond field. According to Banda, the area was fenced in with barbed wire and patrolled twenty-four hours a day by armed guards. At the entrance itself was a manned watchtower. And even if one did somehow manage to slip past the watchtower into the diamond area, there would be the land mines and guard dogs.

The following day when Jamie met Banda, he asked, "You said there was a land-mine map of the field?"

"In the Namib Desert? The supervisors have the maps, and they lead the diggers to work. Everybody walks in a single file so no one gets blown up." His eyes filled with a memory. "One day my uncle was walking in front of me and he stumbled on a rock and fell on top of a land mine. There wasn't enough left of him to take home to his family."

Jamie shuddered.

"And then there's the sea *mis*, Mr. McGregor. You've never seen a *mis* until you've been in one in the Namib. It rolls in from the ocean and blows all the way across the desert to the mountains and it blots out everything. If you're caught in one of them, you don't dare move. The land-mine maps are no good then because you can't see where you're going. Everybody just sits quietly until the *mis* lifts."

"How long do they last?"

Banda shrugged. "Sometimes a few hours, sometimes a few days."

"Banda, have you ever *seen* a map of those land mines?"

"They're closely guarded." A worried look crossed his face. "I'm telling you again, no one can get away with what you're thinking. Once in a while workers will try to smuggle out a diamond. There is a special tree for hanging them. It's a lesson to everybody not to try to steal from the company."

The whole thing looked impossible. Even if he could manage to get into Van der Merwe's diamond field, there was no way out. Banda was right. He would have to forget about it.

The next day he asked Banda, "How does Van der Merwe keep the workers from stealing diamonds when they come off their shifts?"

"They're searched. They strip them down mother-naked and then they look up and down every hole they've got. I've seen workers cut gashes in their legs and try to smuggle diamonds out in them. Some drill out their back teeth and stick diamonds up there. They've tried every trick you can think of." He looked at Jamie and said, "If you want to live, you'll get that diamond field off your mind."

Jamie tried. But the idea kept coming back to him, taunting him. Van der Merwe's diamonds just lying on the sand waiting. *Waiting for him.*

The solution came to Jamie that night. He could hardly contain his impatience until he saw Banda. Without preamble, Jamie said, "Tell me about the boats that have tried to land on the beach."

"What about them?"

"What kind of boats were they?"

"Every kind you can think of. A schooner. A tugboat. A big motorboat. Sailboat. Four men even tried it in a rowboat. While I worked the field, there were half a dozen tries. The reefs just chewed the boats to pieces. Everybody drowned."

Jamie took a deep breath. "Did anyone ever try to get in by raft?"

Banda was staring at him. "*Raft?*"

"Yes." Jamie's excitement was growing. "Think about it. No one ever made it to the shore because the bottoms of their boats were torn out by the reefs. But a *raft* will glide right over those reefs and onto the shore. And it can get out the same way."

Banda looked at him for a long time. When he spoke, there was a different note in his voice. "You know, Mr. McGregor, you might just have an idea there . . ."

It started as a game, a possible solution to an unsolvable puzzle. But the more Jamie and Banda discussed it, the more excited they became. What had started as idle conversation began to take concrete shape as a plan of action. Because the diamonds were lying on top of the sand, no equipment would be required. They could build their raft, with a sail, on the free beach forty miles south of the *Sperrgebiet* and sail it in at night, unobserved. There were no land mines along the unguarded shore, and the guards and patrols only operated inland. The two men could roam the beach freely, gathering up all the diamonds they could carry.

"We can be on our way out before dawn," Jamie said, "with our pockets full of Van der Merwe's diamonds."

"How do we get out?"

"The same way we got in. We'll paddle the raft over the reefs to the open sea, put up the sail and we're home free."

Under Jamie's persuasive arguments, Banda's doubts began to melt. He tried to poke holes in the plan and every time he came up with an objection, Jamie answered it. The plan *could* work. The beautiful part of it was its simplicity, and the fact that it would require no money. Only a great deal of nerve.

"All we need is a big bag to put the diamonds in," Jamie said. His enthusiasm was infectious.

Banda grinned. "Let's make that *two* big bags."

The following week they quit their jobs and boarded a bullock wagon to Port Nolloth, the coastal village forty miles south of the forbidden area where they were headed.

At Port Nolloth, they disembarked and looked around. The village was small and primitive, with shanties and tin huts and a few stores, and a pristine white beach that seemed to stretch on forever. There were no reefs here, and the waves lapped gently at the shore. It was a perfect place to launch their raft.

There was no hotel, but the little market rented a room in back to Jamie. Banda found himself a bed in the black quarter of the village.

"We have to find a place to build our raft in secret," Jamie told Banda. "We don't want anyone reporting us to the authorities."

That afternoon they came across an old, abandoned warehouse.

"This will be perfect," Jamie decided. "Let's get to work on the raft."

"Not yet," Banda told him. "We'll wait. Buy a bottle of whiskey."

"What for?"

"You'll see."

The following morning, Jamie was visited by the district constable, a florid, heavy-set man with a large nose covered with the telltale broken veins of a tippler.

"Mornin'," he greeted Jamie. "I heard we had a visitor. Thought I'd stop by and say hello. I'm Constable Mundy."

"Ian Travis," Jamie replied.

"Headin' north, Mr. Travis?"

"South. My servant and I are on our way to Cape Town."

"An. I was in Cape Town once. Too bloody big, too bloody noisy."

"I agree. Can I offer you a drink, Constable?"

"I never drink on duty." Constable Mundy paused, making a decision. "However, just this once, I might make an exception I suppose."

"Fine." Jamie brought out the bottle of whiskey, wondering how Banda could have known. He poured out two fingers into a dirty tooth glass and handed it to the constable.

"Thank you, Mr. Travis. Where's yours?"

"I can't drink," Jamie said ruefully. "Malaria. That's why I'm going to Cape Town. To get medical attention. I'm stopping off here a few days to rest. Traveling's very hard on me."

Constable Mundy was studying him. "You look pretty healthy."

"You should see me when the chills start."

The constable's glass was empty. Jamie filled it.

"Thank you. Don't mind if I do." He finished the second drink in one swallow and stood up. "I'd best be gettin' along. You said you and your man will be movin' on in a day or two?"

"As soon as I'm feeling stronger."

"I'll come back and check on you Friday," Constable Mundy said.

That night, Jamie and Banda went to work on the raft in the deserted warehouse.

"Banda, have you ever built a raft?"

"Well, to tell you the truth, Mr. McGregor, no."

"Neither have I." The two men stared at each other. "How difficult can it be?"

They stole four empty, fifty-gallon wooden oil barrels from behind the market and carried them to the warehouse. When they had them assembled, they spaced them out in a square. Next they gathered four empty crates and placed one over each oil barrel.

Banda looked dubious. "It doesn't look like a raft to me."

"We're not finished yet," Jamie assured him.

There was no planking available so they covered the top layer with whatever was at hand: branches from the stinkwood tree, limbs from the Cape beech, large leaves from the marula. They lashed everything down with thick hemp rope, tying each knot with careful precision.

When they were finished, Banda looked it over. "It still doesn't look like a raft."

"It will look better when we get the sail up," Jamie promised.

They made a mast from a fallen yellowwood tree, and picked up two flat branches for paddles.

"Now all we need is a sail. We need it fast. I'd like to get out of here tonight. Constable Mundy's coming back tomorrow."

It was Banda who found the sail. He came back late that evening with an enormous piece of blue cloth. "How's this, Mr. McGregor?"

"Perfect. Where did you get it?"

Banda grinned. "Don't ask. We're in enough trouble."

They rigged up a square sail with a boom below and a yard on top, and at last it was ready.

"We'll take off at two in the morning when the village is asleep," Jamie told Banda. "Better get some rest until then."

But neither man was able to sleep. Each was filled with the excitement of the adventure that lay ahead.

At two A.M. they met at the warehouse. There was an eagerness in both of them, and an unspoken fear. They were embarking on a journey that would either make them rich or bring them death. There was no middle way.

"It's time," Jamie announced.

They stepped outside. Nothing was stirring. The night was still and peaceful, with a vast canopy of blue overhead. A sliver of moon appeared high in the sky. *Good*, Jamie thought. *There won't be much light to see us by.* Their timetable was complicated by the fact that they had to leave the village at night so no one would be aware of their departure, and arrive at the diamond beach the next night so they could slip into the field and be safely back at sea before dawn.

"The Benguela current should carry us to the diamond fields sometime in the late afternoon," Jamie said. "But we can't go in by daylight. We'll have to stay out of sight at sea until dark."

Banda nodded. "We can hide out at one of the little islands off the coast."

"What islands?"

"There are dozens of them – Mercury, Ichabod, Plum Pudding . . ."

Jamie gave him a strange look. "*Plum Pudding?*"

"There's also a Roast Beef Island."

Jamie took out his creased map and consulted it. "This doesn't show any of those."

"They're guano islands. The British harvest the bird droppings for fertilizer."

"Anyone live on those islands?"

"Can't. The smell's too bad. In places the guano is a hundred feet thick. The government uses gangs of deserters and prisoners to pick it up. Some of them die on the island and they just leave the bodies there."

"That's where we'll hide out," Jamie decided.

Working quietly, the two men slid open the door to the warehouse and started to lift the raft. It was too heavy to move. They sweated and tugged, but in vain.

"Wait here," Banda said.

He hurried out. Half an hour later, he returned with a large, round log. "We'll use this. I'll pick up one end and you slide the log underneath."

Jamie marveled at Banda's strength as the black man picked up one end of the raft. Quickly, Jamie shoved the log under it. Together they lifted the back end of the raft and it moved easily down the log. When the log had rolled out from under the back end, they repeated the procedure. It was strenuous work, and by the time they got to the beach they were both soaked in perspiration. The operation had taken much longer than Jamie had anticipated. It was almost dawn now. They had to be away before the villagers discovered them and reported what they were doing. Quickly, Jamie attached the sail and checked to make sure everything was working properly. He had a nagging feeling he was forgetting something. He suddenly realized what was bothering him and laughed aloud.

Banda watched him, puzzled. "Something funny?"

"Before, when I went looking for diamonds I had a ton of equipment. Now all I'm carrying is a compass. It seems too easy."

Banda said quietly, "I don't think that's going to be our problem, Mr. McGregor."

"It's time you called me Jamie."

Banda shook his head in wonder. "You *really* come from a faraway country." He grinned, showing even white teeth. "What the hell – they can hang me only once." He tasted the name on his lips, then said it aloud. "Jamie."

"Let's go get those diamonds."

They pushed the raft off the sand into the shallow water and both men leaped aboard and started paddling. It took them a few minutes to get adjusted to the pitching and yawing of their strange craft. It was like riding a bobbing cork, but it was going to work. The raft was responding perfectly, moving north with the swift current. Jamie raised the sail and headed out to sea. By the time the villagers awoke, the raft was well over the horizon.

"We've done it!" Jamie said.

Banda shook his head. "It's not over yet." He trailed a hand in the cold Benguela current. "It's just beginning."

They sailed on, due north past Alexander Bay and the mouth of the Orange River, seeing no signs of life except for flocks of Cape cormorants heading home, and a flight of colorful greater flamingos. Although there were tins of beef and cold rice, and fruit and two canteens of water aboard, they were too nervous to eat. Jamie refused to let his imagination linger on the dangers that lay ahead, but Banda could not help it. He had been there. He was remembering the brutal guards with guns and the dogs and the terrible flesh-tearing land mines, and he wondered how he had ever allowed himself to be talked into this insane venture. He looked over at the Scotsman and thought, *He is the bigger fool. If I die, I die for my baby sister. What does he die for?*

At noon the sharks came. There were half a dozen of them, their fins cutting through the water as they sped toward the raft.

"Black-fin sharks," Banda announced. "They're man-eaters."

Jamie watched the fins skimming closer to the raft. "What do we do?"

Banda swallowed nervously. "Truthfully, Jamie, this is my very first experience of this nature."

The back of a shark nudged the raft, and it almost capsized. The two men grabbed the mast for support. Jamie picked up a paddle and shoved it at a shark, and an instant later the paddle was bitten in two. The sharks surrounded the raft now, swimming in lazy circles, their enormous bodies rubbing up close against the small craft. Each nudge tilted the raft at a precarious angle. It was going to capsize at any moment.

"We've got to get rid of them before they sink us."

"Get rid of them with what?" Banda asked.

"Hand me a tin of beef."

"You must be joking. A tin of beef won't satisfy them. They want *us!*"

There was another jolt, and the raft heeled over.

"The beef!" Jamie yelled. "Get it!"

A second later Banda placed a tin in Jamie's hand. The raft lurched sickeningly.

"Open it halfway. Hurry!"

Banda pulled out his pocketknife and pried the top of the can half open. Jamie took it from him. He felt the sharp, broken edges of the metal with his finger.

"Hold tight!" Jamie warned.

He knelt down at the edge of the raft and waited. Almost immediately, a shark approached the raft, its huge mouth wide open, revealing long rows of evil, grinning teeth. Jamie went for the eyes. With all his strength, he reached out with both hands and scraped the edge of the broken metal against the eye of the shark, ripping it open. The shark lifted its great body, and for an instant the raft stood on end. The water around them was suddenly stained red. There was a giant thrashing as the sharks moved in on the wounded member of the school. The raft was forgotten. Jamie and Banda watched the great sharks tearing at their helpless victim as the raft sailed farther and farther away until finally the sharks were out of sight.

Banda took a deep breath and said softly, "One day I'm going to tell my grandchildren about this. Do you think they'll believe me?"

And they laughed until the tears streamed down their faces.

Late that afternoon, Jamie checked his pocket watch. "We should be off the diamond beach around midnight. Sunrise is at six-fifteen. That means we'll have four hours to pick up the diamonds and two hours to get back to sea and out of sight. Will four hours be enough, Banda?"

"A hundred men couldn't live long enough to spend what you can pick up on that beach in four hours." *I just hope we live long enough to pick them up. . . .*

They sailed steadily north for the rest of that day, carried by the wind and the tide. Toward evening a small island loomed ahead of them. It looked to be no more than two hundred yards in circumference. As they approached the island, the acrid smell of ammonia grew strong, bringing tears to their eyes. Jamie could understand why no one lived here. The stench was overpowering. But it would make a perfect place for them to hide until nightfall. Jamie adjusted the sail, and the small raft bumped against the rocky shore of the low-lying island. Banda made the raft fast, and the two men stepped ashore. The entire island was covered with what appeared to be millions of birds: cormorants, pelicans, gannets, penguins and flamingos. The thick air was so noisome that it was impossible to breathe. They took half a dozen steps and were thigh deep in guano.

"Let's get back to the raft," Jamie gasped.

Without a word, Banda followed him.

As they turned to retreat, a flock of pelicans took to the air, revealing an open space on the ground. Lying there were three men. There was no telling how long they had been dead. Their corpses had been perfectly preserved by the ammonia in the air, and their hair had turned a bright red.

A minute later Jamie and Banda were back on the raft, headed out to sea.

They lay off the coast, sail lowered, waiting.

"We'll stay out here until midnight. Then we go in."

They sat together in silence, each in his own way preparing for whatever lay ahead. The sun was low on the western horizon, painting the dying sky with the wild colors of a mad artist. Then suddenly they were blanketed in darkness.

They waited for two more hours, and Jamie hoisted the sail. The raft began to move east toward the unseen shore. Overhead, clouds parted and a thin wash of moonlight paled down. The raft picked up speed. In the distance the two men could begin to see the faint smudge of the coast. The wind blew stronger, snapping at the sail, pushing the raft toward the shore at an ever-increasing speed. Soon, they could clearly make out the outline of the land, a gigantic parapet of rock. Even from that distance it was possible to see and hear the enormous whitecaps that exploded like thunder over the reefs. It was a terrifying sight from afar, and Jamie wondered what it would be like up close.

He found himself whispering. "You're sure the beach side isn't guarded?"

Banda did not answer. He pointed to the reefs ahead. Jamie knew what he meant. The reefs were more deadly than any trap man could devise. They were the guardians of the sea, and they never relaxed, never slept. They lay there, patiently waiting for their prey to come to them. *Well*, Jamie thought, *were going to outsmart you. We're going to float over you.*

The raft had carried them that far. It would carry them the rest of the way. The shore was racing toward them now, and they began to feel the heavy swell of the giant combers. Banda was holding tightly to the mast.

"We're moving pretty fast."

"Don't worry," Jamie reassured him. "When we get closer, I'll lower the sail. That will cut our speed. We'll slide over the reefs nice and easy."

The momentum of the wind and the waves was picking up, hurtling the raft toward the deadly reefs. Jamie quickly estimated the remaining distance and decided the waves would carry them in to shore without the help of the sail. Hurriedly, he lowered it. Their momentum did not even slow. The raft was completely in the grip of the huge waves now, out of control, hurled forward from one giant crest to the next. The raft was rocking so violently that the men had to cling to it with both hands. Jamie had expected the entrance to be difficult, but he was totally unprepared for the fury of the seething maelstrom they faced. The reefs loomed in front of them with startling clarity. They could see the waves rushing in against the jagged rocks and exploding into huge, angry geysers. The entire success of the plan depended on bringing the raft over the reefs intact so that they could use it for their escape. Without it, they were dead men.

They were bearing down on the reefs now, propelled by the terrifying power of the waves. The roar of the wind was deafening. The raft was suddenly lifted high in the air by an enormous wave and flung toward the rocks.

"Hold on, Banda!" Jamie shouted. "We're going in!"

The giant breaker picked up the raft like a matchstick and started to carry it toward shore, over the reef. Both men were hanging on for their lives, fighting the violent bucking motion that threatened to sweep them into the water. Jamie glanced down and caught a glimpse of the razor-sharp reefs below them. In another moment they would be sailing over them, safe in the haven of the shore.

At that instant there was a sudden, tearing wrench as a reef caught one of the barrels underneath the raft and ripped it away. The raft gave a sharp lurch, and another barrel was torn away, and then another. The wind and the pounding waves and the hungry reef were playing with the raft like a toy, tossing it backward and forward, spinning it wildly in the air. Jamie and Banda felt the thin wood begin to split beneath their feet.

"Jump!" Jamie yelled.

He dived over the side of the raft, and a giant wave picked him up and shot him toward the beach at the speed of a catapult. He was caught in the grip of an element that was powerful beyond belief. He had no control over what was happening. He was a part of the wave. It was over him and under him and inside him. His body was twisting and turning and his lungs were bursting. Lights began to explode in his head. Jamie thought, *I'm drowning.* And his body was thrown up onto the sandy shore. Jamie lay there gasping, fighting for breath, filling his lungs with the cool, fresh sea air. His chest and legs were scraped raw from the sand, and his clothes were in shreds. Slowly, he sat up and looked around for Banda. He was crouching ten yards away, vomiting seawater. Jamie got to his feet and staggered over to him.

"You all right?"

Banda nodded. He took a deep, shuddering breath and looked up at Jamie. "I can't swim."

Jamie helped him to his feet. The two men turned to look at the reef. There was not a sign of their raft. It had been torn to pieces in the wild ocean. They had gotten into the diamond field.

There was no way to get out.

5

Behind them was the raging ocean. Ahead was unbroken desert from the sea to the foothills of the distant, rugged, purple mountains of the Richterveld escarpment, a world of kloofs and canyons and twisted peaks, lit by the pale moon. At the foot of the mountains was the Hexenkessel Valley – "the witch's cauldron" – a bleak wind trap. It was a primeval, desolate landscape that went back to the beginning of time itself. The only clue that man had ever set foot in this place was a crudely printed sign pounded into the sand. By the light of the moon, they read:

VERBODE GEBIED
SPERRGEBIET

Forbidden.

There was no escape toward the sea. The only direction left open to them was the Namib Desert.

"We'll have to try to cross it and take our chances," Jamie said.

Banda shook his head. "The guards will shoot us on sight or hang us. Even if we were lucky enough to slip by the guards and dogs, there's no way to get by the land mines. We're dead men." There was no fear in him, only a resigned acceptance of his fate.

Jamie looked at Banda and felt a sense of deep regret. He had brought the black man into this, and not once had Banda complained. Even now, knowing there was no escape for them, he did not utter one word of reproach.

Jamie turned to look at the wall of angry waves smashing at the shore, and he thought it was a miracle that they had gotten as far as they had. It was two A.M., four hours before dawn and discovery, and they were both still in one piece. *I'll be damned if I'm ready to give up*, Jamie thought.

"Let's go to work, Banda."

Banda blinked. "Doing what?"

"We came here to get diamonds, didn't we? Let's get them."

Banda stared at the wild-eyed man with his white hair plastered to his skull and his sopping trousers hanging in shreds around his legs. "What are you talking about?"

"You said they're going to kill us on sight, right? Well, they might as well kill us rich as poor. A miracle got us in here. Maybe a miracle will get us out. And if we do get out, I damned well don't plan to leave empty-handed."

"You're crazy," Banda said softly.

"Or we wouldn't be here," Jamie reminded him.

Banda shrugged. "What the hell. I have nothing else to do until they find us."

Jamie stripped off his tattered shirt, and Banda understood and did the same.

"Now. Where are all these big diamonds that you've been talking about?"

"They're everywhere," Banda promised. And he added, "Like the guards and the dogs."

"We'll worry about them later. When do they come down to the beach?"

"When it gets light."

Jamie thought for a moment. "Is there a part of the beach where they *don't* come? Someplace we could hide?"

"There's no part of this beach they don't come to, and there's no place you could hide a fly."

Jamie slapped Banda on the shoulder. "Right, then. Let's go."

Jamie watched as Banda got down on his hands and knees and began slowly crawling along the beach, his fingers sifting sand as he moved. In less than two minutes, he stopped and held up a stone. "I found one!"

Jamie lowered himself to the sand and began moving. The first two stones he found were small. The third must have weighed over fifteen carats. He sat there looking at it for a long moment. It was incredible to him that such a fortune could be picked up so easily. And it all belonged to Salomon van der Merwe and his partners. Jamie kept moving.

In the next three hours, the two men collected more than forty diamonds ranging from two carats to thirty carats. The sky in the east was beginning to lighten. It was the time Jamie had planned to leave, to jump back on the raft, sail over the reefs and make their escape. It was useless to think about that now.

"It will be dawn soon," Jamie said. "Let's see how many more diamonds we can find."

"We're not going to live to spend any of *this*. You want to die *very rich*, don't you?"

"I don't want to die at all."

They resumed their search, mindlessly scooping up diamond after diamond, and it was as though a madness had taken possession of them. Their piles of diamonds increased, until sixty diamonds worth a king's ransom lay in their torn shirts.

"Do you want me to carry these?" Banda asked.

"No. We can both – " And then Jamie realized what was on Banda's mind.

The one caught in actual possession of the diamonds would die more slowly and painfully.

"I'll take them," Jamie said. He dumped the diamonds into the rag that was left of his shirt, and carefully tied it in a knot. The horizon was light gray now, and the east was becoming stained with the colors of the rising sun.

What next? That was the question! What was the answer? They could stand there and die, or they could move inland toward the desert and die.

"Let's move."

Jamie and Banda slowly began walking away from the sea, side by side.

"Where do the land mines start?"

"About a hundred yards up ahead." In the far distance, they heard a dog bark. "I don't think we're going to have to worry about the land mines. The dogs are heading this way. The morning shift is coming to work."

"How soon before they reach us?"

"Fifteen minutes. Maybe ten."

It was almost full dawn now. What had been vague, shimmering patterns turned into small sand dunes and distant mountains. There was no place to hide.

"How many guards are on a shift?"

Banda thought for a moment. "About ten."

"Ten guards aren't many for a beach this big."

"*One* guard is plenty. They've got guns and dogs. The guards aren't blind, and we're not invisible."

The sound of the barking was closer now. Jamie said, "Banda, I'm sorry. I should never have gotten you into this."

"You didn't."

And Jamie understood what he meant.

They could hear voices calling in the distance.

Jamie and Banda reached a small dune. "What if we buried ourselves in the sand?"

"That has been tried. The dogs would find us and rip our throats out. I want my death to be quick. I'm going to let them see me, then start running. That way they'll shoot me. I – I don't want the dogs to get me."

Jamie gripped Banda's arm. "We may die, but I'll be damned if we're going to *run* to our deaths. Let's make them work for it."

They could begin to distinguish words in the distance. "Keep moving, you lazy bastards," a voice was yelling. "Follow me . . . stay in line. . . . You've all had a good night's sleep. . . . Now let's get some work done. . . ."

In spite of his brave words, Jamie found he was retreating from the voice. He turned to look at the sea again. *Was drowning an easier way to die?* He watched the reefs tearing viciously at the demon waves breaking over them and he suddenly saw something else, something beyond the waves. He could not understand what it was. "Banda, look . . ."

Far out at sea an impenetrable gray wall was moving toward them, blown by the powerful westerly winds.

"It's the sea *mis!*" Banda exclaimed. "It comes in two or three times a week."

While they were talking, the *mis* moved closer, like a gigantic gray curtain sweeping across the horizon, blotting out the sky.

The voices had moved closer, too. "*Den dousant!* Damn this *mis!* Another slowdown. The bosses ain't gonna like this . . ."

"We've got a chance!" Jamie said. He was whispering now.

"What chance?"

"The *mis!* They won't be able to see us."

"That's no help. It's going to lift sometime, and when it does we're still going to be right here. If the guards can't move through the land mines, neither can we. You try to cross this desert in the *mis* and you won't go ten yards before you're blown to pieces. You're looking for one of your miracles."

"You're damned right I am," Jamie said.

The sky was darkening overhead. The *mis* was closer, covering the sea, ready to swallow up the shore. It had an eerie, menacing look about it as it rolled toward them, but Jamie thought exultantly, *Its going to save us!*

A voice suddenly called out, "Hey! You two! What the hell are you doin' there?"

Jamie and Banda turned. At the top of a dune about a hundred yards away was a uniformed guard carrying a rifle. Jamie looked back at the shore. The *mis* was closing in fast.

"You! You two! Come here," the guard yelled. He lifted his rifle.

Jamie raised his hands. "I twisted my foot," he called out. "I can't walk."

"Stay where you are," the guard ordered. "I'm comin" to get you." He lowered his rifle and started moving toward them. A quick look back showed that the *mis* had reached the edge of the shore, and was coming in swiftly.

"Run!" Jamie whispered. He turned and raced toward the beach, Banda running close behind him.

"Stop!"

A second later they heard the sharp crack of a rifle, and the sand ahead of them exploded. They kept running, racing to meet the great dark wall of the fog. There was another rifle shot, closer this time, and another, and the next moment the two men were in total darkness. The sea *mis* licked at them, chilling them, smothering them. It was like being buried in cotton. It was impossible to see anything.

The voices were muffled now and distant, bouncing off the *mis* and coming from all directions. They could hear other voices calling to one another.

"Kruger! . . . It's Brent. . . . Can you hear me?"

"I hear you, Kruger . . ."

"There're two of them," the first voice yelled. "A white man and a black. They're on the beach. Spread your men out. *Skiet hom!* Shoot to kill."

"Hang on to me," Jamie whispered.

Banda gripped his arm. "Where are you going?"

"We're getting out of here."

Jamie brought his compass up to his face. He could barely see it. He turned until the compass was pointing east. "This way . . ."

"Wait! We can't walk. Even if we don't bump into a guard or a dog, we're going to set off a land mine."

"You said there are a hundred yards before the mines start. Let's get away from the beach."

They started moving toward the desert, slowly and unsteadily, blind men in an unknown land. Jamie paced off the yards. Whenever they stumbled in the soft sand, they picked themselves up and kept moving. Jamie stopped to check the compass every few feet. When he estimated they had traveled almost a hundred yards, he stopped.

"This should be about where the land mines start. Is there any pattern to the way they're placed? Anything you can think of that could help us?"

"Prayer," Banda answered. "Nobody's ever gotten past those land mines, Jamie. They're scattered all over the field, buried about six inches down. We're going to have to stay here until the *mis* lifts and give ourselves up."

Jamie listened to the cotton-wrapped voices ricocheting around them.

"Kruger! Keep in voice contact. . . ."

"Right, Brent. . . ."

"Kruger . . ."

"Brent . . ."

Disembodied voices calling to each other in the blinding fog. Jamie's mind was racing, desperately exploring every possible avenue of escape. If they stayed where they were, they would be killed the instant the *mis* lifted. If they tried moving through the field of mines, they would be blown to bits.

"Have you ever seen the land mines?" Jamie whispered.

"I helped bury some of them."

"What sets them off?"

"A man's weight. Anything over eighty pounds will explode them. That way they don't kill the dogs."

Jamie took a deep breath. "Banda, I may have a way for us to get out of here. It might not work. Do you want to gamble with me?"

"What have you got in mind?"

"We're going to cross the mine fields on our bellies. That way we'll distribute our weight across the sand."

"Oh, Jesus!"

"What do you think?"

"I think I was crazy for ever leaving Cape Town."

"Are you with me?" He could barely make out Banda's face next to him.

"You don't leave a man a lot of choice, do you?"

"Come on then."

Jamie carefully stretched himself out flat on the sand. Banda looked at him a moment, took a deep breath and joined him. Slowly the two men began crawling across the sand, toward the mine field.

"When you move," Jamie whispered, "don't press down with your hands or your legs. Use your whole body."

There was no reply. Banda was busy concentrating on staying alive.

They were in a smothering, gray vacuum that made it impossible to see anything. At any instant they could bump into a guard, a dog or one of the land mines. Jamie forced all this out of his mind. Their progress was painfully slow. Both men were shirtless, and the sand scraped against their stomachs as they inched forward. Jamie was aware of how overwhelming the odds were against them. Even if by some chance they did succeed in crossing the desert without getting shot or blown up, they would be confronted by the barbed-wire fence and the armed guards at the watchtower at the entrance. And there was no telling how long the *mis* would last. It could lift at any second, exposing them.

They kept crawling, mindlessly sliding forward until they lost all track of time. The inches became feet, and the feet became yards, and the yards became miles. They had no idea how long they had been traveling. They were forced to keep their heads close to the ground, and their eyes and ears and noses became filled with sand. Breathing was an effort.

In the distance was the constant echo of the guards' voices. "*Kruger . . . Brent . . . Kruger . . . Brent . . .*"

The two men stopped to rest and check the compass every few minutes, then moved on, beginning their endless crawl again. There was an almost overwhelming temptation to move faster, but that would mean pressing down harder, and Jamie could visualize the metal fragments exploding under him and ripping into his belly. He kept the pace slow. From time to time they could hear other voices around them, but the words' were muffled by the fog and it was impossible to tell where they were coming from. *It's a big desert*, Jamie thought hopefully. *Were not going to stumble into anyone*.

Out of nowhere, a large, furry shape leaped at him. It happened so swiftly that Jamie was caught off guard. He felt the huge Alsatian's teeth sinking into his arm. He dropped the bundle of diamonds and tried to pry open the dog's jaw, but he had only one free hand and it was impossible. He felt the warm blood running down his arm. The dog was sinking its teeth in harder now, silent and deadly. Jamie felt himself begin to faint. He heard a dull thud, and then another, and the dog's jaw loosened and its eyes glazed over. Through the mist of pain, Jamie saw Banda smashing the sack of diamonds against the dog's skull. The dog whimpered once and lay still.

"You all right?" Banda breathed anxiously.

Jamie could not speak. He lay there, waiting for the waves of pain to recede. Banda ripped off a piece of his trousers and tied a strip tightly around Jamie's arm to stop the bleeding.

"We've got to keep moving," Banda warned. "If there's one of them around, there are more."

Jamie nodded. Slowly he slid his body forward, fighting against the terrible throbbing in his arm.

He remembered nothing of the rest of the trek. He was semiconscious, an automaton. Something outside him directed his movements. *Arms forward, pull . . . Arms forward, pull . . . Arms forward pull . . .* It was endless, an odyssey of agony. It was Banda who followed the compass now, and when Jamie started to crawl in the wrong direction Banda gently turned him around. They were surrounded by guards and dogs and land mines and only the *mis* kept them safe. They kept moving, crawling for their lives, until the time came when neither man had the strength to move another inch.

They slept.

When Jamie opened his eyes, something had changed. He lay there on the sand, his body stiff and aching, trying to remember where he was. He could see Banda asleep six feet away, and it all came flooding in. The raft crashing on the reefs . . . the sea *mis* . . . But something was wrong. Jamie sat up, trying to figure out what it was. And his stomach lurched. *He could see Banda! That was what was wrong. The* mis *was lifting.* Jamie heard voices nearby. He peered through the thin mists of the dissipating fog. They had crawled near the entrance to the diamond field. There was the high guard tower and the barbed-wire fence Banda had described. A crowd of about sixty black workers was moving away from the diamond field toward the gate. They had finished their shift and the next shift was coming in. Jamie got on his knees and crawled over to Banda and shook him. Banda sat up, instantly awake. His eyes turned to the watchtower and the gate.

"Damn!" he said incredulously. "We almost made it."

"We *did* make it! Give me those diamonds!"

Banda handed him the folded shirt. "What do you – ?"

"Follow me."

"Those guards with the guns at the gate," Banda said in a low voice, "they'll know we don't belong here."

"That's what I'm counting on," Jamie told him.

The two men moved toward the guards, drifting between the line of departing workers and the line of arriving workers who were yelling at one another, exchanging good-natured catcalls.

"You fellas gonna work your asses off, man. We got a nice sleep in the *mis*. . . ."

"How did you arrange for the *mis*, you lucky bastards . . . ?"

"God listens to me. He ain't gonna listen to you. You're bad . . . ."

Jamie and Banda reached the gate. Two huge armed guards stood inside, herding the departing workers over to a small tin hut where they would be thoroughly searched. *They strip them down mother-naked and then they look up and down every hole they've got.* Jamie clutched the tattered shirt in his hand more tightly. He pushed through the line of workers and walked up to a guard. "Excuse me, sir," Jamie said. "Who do we see about a job here?"

Banda was staring at him, petrified.

The guard turned to face Jamie. "What the hell are you doin' inside the fence?"

"We came in to look for work. I heard there was an opening for a guard, and my servant can dig. I thought – "

The guard eyed the two ragged, disreputable-looking figures. "Get the hell back outside!"

"We don't want to go outside," Jamie protested. "We need jobs, and I was told – "

"This is a restricted area, mister. Didn't you see the signs? Now get the hell out. Both of you!" He pointed to a large bullock wagon outside the fence, filling with the workers who had finished their shift. "That wagon'll take you to Port Nolloth. If you want a job, you have to apply at the company office there."

"Oh. Thank you, sir," Jamie said. He beckoned to Banda, and the two men moved out through the gate to freedom.

The guard glared after them. "Stupid idiots."

Ten minutes later, Jamie and Banda were on their way to Port Nolloth. They were carrying with them diamonds worth half a million pounds.

6

The expensive carriage rolled down the dusty main street of Klipdrift, drawn by two beautiful matched bays. At the reins was a slender, athletic-looking man with snow-white hair, a white beard and mustache. He was dressed in a fashionably tailored gray suit and ruffled shirt, and in his black cravat was a diamond stickpin. He wore a gray top hat, and on his little finger was a large, sparkling diamond ring. He appeared to be a stranger to the town, but he was not.

Klipdrift had changed considerably since Jamie McGregor had left it a year earlier. It was 1884, and it had grown from a camp to a township. The railway had been completed from Cape Town to Hopetown, with a branch running to Klipdrift, and this had created a whole new wave of immigrants. The town was even more crowded than Jamie remembered, but the people seemed different. There were still many prospectors, but there were also men in business suits and well-dressed matrons walking in and out of stores. Klipdrift had acquired a patina of respectability.

Jamie passed three new dance halls and half a dozen new saloons. He drove by a recently built church and barbershop, and a large hotel called the Grand. He stopped in front of a bank and alighted from the carriage, carelessly tossing the reins to a native boy.

"Water them."

Jamie entered the bank and said to the manager in a loud voice, "I wish to deposit one hundred thousand pounds in your bank."

The word spread quickly, as Jamie had known it would, and by the time he left the bank and entered the Sundowner Saloon, he was the center of interest. The interior of the saloon had not changed. It was crowded, and curious eyes followed Jamie as he walked up to the bar. Smit nodded deferentially. "What would you like, sir?" There was no recognition on the bartender's face.

"Whiskey. The best you have."

"Yes, sir." He poured the drink. "You're new in town?"

"Yes."

"Just passin' through, are you?"

"No. I've heard this is a good town for a man looking for investments."

The bartender's eyes lighted up. "You couldn't find better! A man with a hundred – A man with money can do real well for hisself. Matter of fact, I might be of some service to you, sir."

"Really? How is that?"

Smit leaned forward, his tone conspiratorial. "I know the man who runs this town. He's chairman of the Borough Council and head of the Citizen's Committee. He's the most important man in this part of the country. Name of Salomon van der Merwe."

Jamie took a sip of his drink. "Never heard of him."

"He owns that big general store across the street. He can put you on to some good deals. It'd be worth your while to meet him."

Jamie McGregor took another sip of his drink. "Have him come over here."

The bartender glanced at the large diamond ring on Jamie's finger, and at his diamond stickpin. "Yes, sir. Can I tell him your name?"

"Travis. Ian Travis."

"Right, Mr. Travis. I'm sure Mr. van der Merwe will want to meet you." He poured out another drink. "Have this while you're waitin'. It's on the house."

Jamie sat at the bar sipping the whiskey, aware that everyone in the saloon was watching him. Men had departed from Klipdrift wealthy, but no one of such obvious wealth had ever arrived there before. It was something new in their experience.

Fifteen minutes later, the bartender was back, accompanied by Salomon van der Merwe.

Van der Merwe walked up to the bearded, white-haired stranger, held out his hand and smiled. "Mr. Travis, I'm Salomon van der Merwe."

"Ian Travis."

Jamie waited for a flicker of recognition, a sign that Van der Merwe found something familiar about him. There was nothing. *But then, why should there be?* Jamie thought. There was nothing left of that naïve, idealistic, eighteen-year-old boy he had been. Smit obsequiously led the two men to a corner table.

As soon as they were seated, Van der Merwe said, "I understand you're looking for some investments in Klipdrift, Mr. Travis."

"Possibly."

"I might be able to be of some service. One has to be careful. There are many immoral people around."

Jamie looked at him and said, "I'm sure there are."

It was unreal, sitting there carrying on a polite conversation with the man who had cheated him out of a fortune and then tried to murder him. His hatred for Van der Merwe had consumed him for the last year, his thirst for vengeance was all that had sustained him, kept him alive. And now Van der Merwe was about to feel that vengeance.

"If you don't mind my asking, Mr. Travis, how much money were you planning on investing?"

"Oh, around a hundred thousand pounds to begin with," Jamie said carelessly. He watched Van der Merwe wet his lips. "Then perhaps three or four hundred thousand more."

"Er – you should be able to do very well with that, very well, indeed. With the right guidance, of course," he added quickly. "Do you have any idea what you might want to invest in?"

"I thought I'd look around and see what opportunities there were."

"That's very wise of you." Van der Merwe nodded sagely. "Perhaps you would like to come to dinner tonight and we can discuss it? My daughter's an excellent cook. It would be an honor to have you."

Jamie smiled. "I'd enjoy that, Mr. van der Merwe." *You have no idea how much I'd enjoy that*, he thought.

It had started.

The journey from the diamond fields of Namib to Cape Town had been uneventful. Jamie and Banda had hiked inland to a small village where a doctor treated Jamie's arm, and they had gotten a lift on a wagon bound for Cape Town. It was a long, difficult ride, but they were oblivious to the discomfort. At Cape Town, Jamie checked into the ornate Royal Hotel on Plein Street – "Patronized by HRH, the Duke of Edinburgh" – and was escorted to the Royal Suite.

"I want you to send up the best barber in town," Jamie told the manager. "Then I want a tailor and a bootmaker up here."

"At once, sir," the manager said.

It's wonderful what money can do, Jamie thought.

The bath in the Royal Suite was heaven. Jamie lay back in the hot water, soaking the tiredness out of his body, thinking back over the past incredible weeks. Had it been only weeks since he and Banda had built that raft? It seemed like years. Jamie thought about the raft sailing them to the *Sperrgebiet*, and the sharks, and the demon waves and the reefs tearing the raft to pieces. The sea *mis* and the crawling over the land mines, and the huge dog on top of him . . . The eerie, muffled cries that would ring in his ears forever: *Kruger . . . Brent . . . Kruger . . . Brent . . .*

But most of all, he thought of Banda. His friend.

When they had reached Cape Town, Jamie had urged, "Stay with me."

Banda smiled, showing his beautiful white teeth. "Life's too dull with you, Jamie. I have to go somewhere and find a little excitement."

"What will you do now?"

"Well, thanks to you and your wonderful plan about how easy it is to float a raft over the reef, I'm going to buy a farm, find a wife and have a lot of children."

"All right. Let's go to the *diamant kooper* so I can give you your share of the diamonds."

"No," Banda said. "I don't want it."

Jamie frowned. "What are you talking about? Half the diamonds are yours. You're a millionaire."

"No. Look at my skin, Jamie. If I became a millionaire, my life would not be worth a tickey."

"You can hide some of the diamonds away. You can – "

"All I need is enough to buy a morgen of farmland and two oxen to trade for a wife. Two or three little diamonds will get me everything I'll ever want. The rest are yours."

"That's impossible. You can't give me your share."

"Yes, I can, Jamie. Because you're going to give me Salomon van der Merwe."

Jamie looked at Banda for a long moment. "I promise."

"Then I'll say good-bye, my friend."

The two men clasped hands.

"We'll meet again," Banda said. "Next time think of something *really* exciting for us to do."

Banda walked away with three small diamonds carefully tucked in his pocket.

Jamie sent off a bank draft amounting to twenty thousand pounds to his parents, bought the finest carriage and team he could find and headed back to Klipdrift.

The time had come for revenge.

That evening when Jamie McGregor entered Van der Merwe's store, he was gripped by a sensation so unpleasant and so violent that he had to pause to regain control of himself.

Van der Merwe hurried out of the back of the shop, and when he saw who it was, his face lighted up in a big smile. "Mr. Travis!" he said. "Welcome."

"Thank you, mister – er – sorry, I don't remember your name . . ."

"Van der Merwe. Salomon van der Merwe. Don't apologize. Dutch names are difficult to remember. Dinner is ready. Margaret!" he called as he led Jamie into the back room. Nothing had changed. Margaret was standing at the stove over a frying pan, her back to them.

"Margaret, this is our guest I spoke of – Mr. Travis."

Margaret turned. "How do you do?"

There was not a flicker of recognition.

"I'm pleased to meet you." Jamie nodded.

The customer bell rang and Van der Merwe said, "Excuse me, I'll be right back. Please make yourself at home, Mr. Travis." He hurried out.

Margaret carried a steaming bowl of vegetables and meat over to the table, and as she hurried to take the bread from the oven Jamie stood there, silently looking at her. She had blossomed in the year since he had seen her. She had become a woman, with a smoldering sexuality that had been lacking before.

"Your father tells me you're an excellent cook."

Margaret blushed. "I – I hope so, sir."

"It's been a long time since I've tasted home cooking. I'm looking forward to this." Jamie took a large butter dish from Margaret and placed it on the table for her. Margaret was so surprised she almost dropped the plate in her hands. She had never heard of a man who helped in woman's work. She lifted her startled eyes to his face. A broken nose and a scar spoiled what would otherwise have been a too-handsome face. His eyes were light gray and shone with intelligence and a burning intensity. His white hair told her that he was not a young man, and yet there was something very youthful about him. He was tall and strong and – Margaret turned away, embarrassed by his gaze.

Van der Merwe hurried back into the room, rubbing his hands. "I've closed the shop," he said. "Let's sit down and have a fine dinner."

Jamie was given the place of honor at the table. "We'll say grace," Van der Merwe said.

They closed their eyes. Margaret slyly opened hers again, so that she could continue her scrutiny of the elegant stranger while her father's voice droned on. "We are all sinners in your eyes, O Lord, and must be punished. Give us the strength to bear our hardships on this earth, so that we may enjoy the fruits of heaven when we are called. Thank you, Lord, for helping those of us who deserve to prosper. Amen."

Salomon van der Merwe began serving. This time the portions he served Jamie were more than generous. They talked as they ate. "Is this your first time out this way, Mr. Travis?"

"Yes," Jamie said. "First time."

"You didn't bring Mrs. Travis along, I understand."

"There is no Mrs. Travis. I haven't found anyone who'd have me." Jamie smiled.

What fool of a woman would refuse him? Margaret wondered. She lowered her eyes, afraid the stranger might read her wicked thoughts.

"Klipdrift is a town of great opportunity, Mr. Travis. *Great* opportunity."

"I'm willing to be shown." He looked at Margaret, and she blushed.

"If it isn't too personal, Mr. Travis, may I ask how you acquired your fortune?"

Margaret was embarrassed by her father's blunt questions, but the stranger did not seem to mind.

"I inherited it from my father," Jamie said easily.

"Ah, but I'm sure you've had a lot of business experience."

"Very little, I'm afraid. I need a lot of guidance."

Van der Merwe brightened. "It's fate that we met, Mr. Travis. I have some very profitable connections. Very profitable, indeed. I can almost guarantee that I can double your money for you in just a few months." He leaned over and patted Jamie's arm. "I have a feeling this is a big day for both of us."

Jamie just smiled.

"I suppose you're staying at the Grand Hotel?"

"That's right."

"It's criminally expensive. But I suppose to a man of your means . . ." He beamed at Jamie.

Jamie said, "I'm told the countryside around here is interesting. Would it be an imposition to ask you to let your daughter show me around a bit tomorrow?"

Margaret felt her heart stop for a second.

Van der Merwe frowned. "I don't know. She – "

It was an iron-clad rule of Salomon van der Merwe's never to permit any man to be alone with his daughter. In the case of Mr. Travis, however, he decided there would be no harm in making an exception. With so much at stake, he did not want to appear inhospitable. "I can spare Margaret from the store for a short time. You will show our guest around, Margaret?"

"If you wish, Father," she said quietly.

"That's settled then." Jamie smiled. "Shall we say ten o'clock in the morning?"

After the tall, elegantly dressed guest left, Margaret cleared away the table and washed the dishes, in a complete daze. *He must think I'm an idiot.* She went over and over in her mind everything she had contributed to the conversation. Nothing. She had been completely tongue-tied. Why was that? Hadn't she waited on hundreds of men in the store without becoming a stupid fool? Of course they had not looked at her the way Ian Travis had. *Men all have the devil in them, Margaret. I'll not let them corrupt your innocence.* Her father's voice echoed in her mind. Could that be it? The weakness and trembling she had felt when the stranger had looked at her? Was he corrupting her innocence? The thought of it sent a delicious thrill through her body. She looked down at the plate she had dried three times and sat down at the table. She wished her mother were still alive.

Her mother would have understood. Margaret loved her father, but sometimes she had the oppressive feeling that she was his prisoner. It worried her that he never allowed a man to come near her. *I'll never get married*, Margaret thought.

Not until he dies. Her rebellious thoughts filled her with guilt, and she hurriedly left the room and went into the store, where her father sat behind a desk, working on his accounts.

"Good night, Father."

Van der Merwe took off his gold-framed spectacles and rubbed his eyes before he raised his arms to embrace his daughter good-night. Margaret did not know why she pulled away.

Alone in the curtained-off alcove that served as her bedroom, Margaret studied her face in the small, round mirror that hung on the wall. She had no illusions about her looks. She was not pretty. She was interesting-looking. Nice eyes. High cheekbones. A good figure. She drew nearer to the mirror. What had Ian Travis seen when he looked at her? She began getting undressed. And Ian Travis was in the room with her, watching her, his eyes burning into her. She stepped out of her muslin drawers and camisole and stood naked before him. Her hands slowly caressed the swell of her breasts and felt her hardening nipples. Her fingers slid down across her flat belly and his hands became entwined with hers, moving slowly downward. They were between her legs now, gently touching, stroking, rubbing, harder now, faster and faster until she was caught up in a frantic whirlpool of sensation that finally exploded inside her and she gasped his name and fell to the bed.

They rode out in Jamie's carriage, and he was amazed once more at the changes that had taken place. Where before there had been only a sea of tents, now there were substantial-looking houses, constructed of timber with roofs of corrugated iron or thatch.

"Klipdrift seems very prosperous," Jamie said as they rode along the main street.

"I suppose it would be interesting for a newcomer," Margaret said. And she thought, *I've hated it until now.*

They left the town and drove out toward the mining camps along the Vaal River. The seasonal rains had turned the countryside into an enormous, colorful garden, filled with the luxuriant bush Karroo, and the spreading Rhenoster bush and heaths and diosmas plants that could be found nowhere else in the world. As they drove past a group of prospectors, Jamie asked, "Have there been any big diamond finds lately?"

"Oh, yes, a few. Every time the news gets out, hundreds of new diggers come pouring in. Most of them leave poor and heartbroken." Margaret felt she had to warn him of the danger here. "Father would not like to hear me say this, but I think it's a terrible business, Mr. Travis."

"For some, probably," Jamie agreed. "For some."

"Do you plan to stay on a while?"

"Yes."

Margaret felt her heart singing. "Good." Then added quickly, "Father will be pleased."

They drove around all morning, and from time to time they stopped and Jamie chatted with prospectors. Many of them recognized Margaret and spoke respectfully. There was a warmth to her and an easy friendliness that she did not reveal when she was around her father.

As they drove on, Jamie said, "Everyone seems to know you."

She blushed. "That's because they do business with Father. He supplies most of the diggers."

Jamie made no comment. He was keenly interested in what he was seeing. The railroad had made an enormous difference. A new combine called De Beers, named after the farmer in whose field the first diamond discovery was made, had bought out its chief rival, a colorful entrepreneur named Barney Barnato, and De Beers was busily consolidating the hundreds of small claims into one organization. Gold had been discovered recently, not far from Kimberley, along with manganese and zinc. Jamie was convinced this was only the beginning, that South Africa was a treasure-house of minerals. There were incredible opportunities here for a man with foresight.

When Jamie and Margaret returned, it was late afternoon. Jamie stopped the carriage in front of Van der Merwe's store and said, "I would be honored if you and your father would be my guests at dinner tonight."

Margaret glowed. "I'll ask Father. I do so hope he'll say yes. Thank you for a lovely day, Mr. Travis."

And she fled.

The three of them had dinner in the large, square dining room of the new Grand Hotel.

The room was crowded, and Van der Merwe grumbled, "I don't see how these people can afford to eat here."

Jamie picked up a menu and glanced at it. A steak cost one pound four shillings, a potato was four shillings and a piece of apple pie ten shillings.

"They're robbers!" Van der Merwe complained. "A few meals here and a man could eat himself into the poorhouse."

Jamie wondered what it would take to put Salomon van der Merwe in the poorhouse. He intended to find out. They ordered, and Jamie noticed that Van der Merwe ordered the most expensive items on the menu. Margaret ordered a clear soup. She was too excited to eat. She looked at her hands, remembered what they had done the night before and felt guilty.

"I can afford dinner," Jamie teased her. "Order anything you like."

She blushed. "Thank you, but I'm – I'm not really very hungry."

Van der Merwe noticed the blush and looked sharply from Margaret to Jamie. "My daughter is a rare girl, a rare girl, Mr. Travis."

Jamie nodded. "I couldn't agree with you more, Mr. van der Merwe."

His words made Margaret so happy that when their dinner was served, she could not even eat the soup. The effect Ian Travis had on her was incredible. She read hidden meanings into his every word and gesture. If he smiled at her, it meant he liked her a lot; if he frowned, it meant he hated her. Margaret's feelings were an emotional thermometer that kept going up and down.

"Did you see anything of interest today?" Van der Merwe asked Jamie.

"No, nothing special," Jamie said casually.

Van der Merwe leaned forward. "Mark my words, sir, this is going to be the fastest-growing area in the world. A man would be smart to invest here now. The new railway's going to turn this place into a second Cape Town."

"I don't know," Jamie said dubiously. "I've heard of too many boomtowns like this going bust. I'm not interested in putting my money into a ghost town."

"Not Klipdrift," Van der Merwe assured him. "They're finding more diamonds all the time. And gold."

Jamie shrugged. "How long will that last?"

"Well, nobody can be sure of that, of course, but – "

"Exactly."

"Don't make any hasty decisions," Van der Merwe urged. "I wouldn't like to see you lose out on a great opportunity."

Jamie thought that over. "Perhaps I am being hasty. Margaret, could you show me around again tomorrow?"

Van der Merwe opened his mouth to object, then closed it. He remembered the words of Mr. Thorenson, the banker: *He walked in here and deposited a hundred thousand pounds, cool as you please, Salomon, and he said there'd be a lot more coming?*

Greed got the better of Van der Merwe. "Of course she could."

The following morning, Margaret put on her Sunday dress, ready to meet Jamie. When her father walked in and saw her, his face turned red. "Do you want the man to think you're some kind of fallen woman – dressin' up to attract him? This is business, girl. Take that off and put on your workin' clothes."

"But, Papa – "

"Do as I say!"

She did not argue with him. "Yes, Papa."

Van der Merwe watched Margaret and Jamie drive away twenty minutes later. He wondered if he could be making a mistake.

This time Jamie headed the carriage in the opposite direction. There were exciting signs of new developments and building everywhere. *If the mineral discoveries keep up*, Jamie thought – and there was every reason to believe they would – *there is more money to be made here in real estate than in diamonds or gold. Klipdrift will need more banks, hotels, saloons, shops, brothels* . . . The list was endless. So were the opportunities.

Jamie was conscious of Margaret staring at him. "Is something wrong?" he asked.

"Oh, no," she said, and quickly looked away.

Jamie studied her now, and noticed the radiance about her. Margaret was aware of his closeness, his maleness. He sensed her feelings. She was a woman without a man.

At noon Jamie drove off the main road down to a wooded area near a stream and stopped under a large baobab tree. He had had the hotel pack a picnic lunch. Margaret put down a tablecloth, unpacked the basket and spread out the food. There was cold roast lamb, fried chicken, yellow saffron rice, quince jam and tangerines and peaches and *soetekoekjes*, almond-topped spice cookies.

"This is a banquet!" Margaret exclaimed. "I'm afraid I don't deserve all this, Mr. Travis."

"You deserve much more," Jamie assured her.

Margaret turned away, busying herself with the food.

Jamie took her face between his hands. "Margaret . . . look at me."

"Oh! Please. I – " She was trembling.

"Look at me."

Slowly she lifted her head and looked into his eyes. He pulled her into his arms, and his lips found hers and he held her close, pressing his body against hers.

After a few moments she struggled free, shook her head and said, "Oh, my God. We mustn't. Oh, we mustn't. We'll go to hell."

"Heaven."

"I'm afraid."

"There's nothing to be afraid of. Do you see my eyes? They can look right inside you. And you know what I see, don't you? You want me to make love to you. And I'm going to. And there's nothing to fear, because you belong to me. You know that, don't you? You belong to me, Margaret. You say it. I belong to Ian. Go on. I – belong – to Ian."

"I belong – to Ian."

His lips were on hers again, and he began to undo the hooks on the back of her bodice. In a moment she stood naked in the soft breeze, and he lowered her gently down to the ground. And the tremulous passage from girlhood to womanhood became an exciting, soaring experience that made Margaret feel more alive than she had ever felt in her life. *I'll remember this moment forever*, she thought. The bed of leaves and the warm caressing breeze on her naked skin, the shadow of the baobab tree that dappled their bodies. They made love again, and it was even more wonderful. She thought, *No woman could ever love anyone as much as I love this man*.

When they were spent, Jamie held her in his strong arms, and she wished she could be there forever. She looked up at him and whispered, "What are you thinking?"

He grinned and whispered back, "That I'm bloody starving."

She laughed, and they rose and had their lunch under the shelter of the trees.

Afterward they swam and lay down to let the hot sun dry them. Jamie took Margaret again, and she thought, *I want this day to go on forever.*

That evening, Jamie and Van der Merwe were seated at a corner table at the Sundowner. "You were right," Jamie announced. "The possibilities here may be greater than I thought."

Van der Merwe beamed. "I knew you were too clever a man not to see that, Mr. Travis."

"What exactly would you advise me to do?" Jamie asked.

Van der Merwe glanced around and lowered his voice. "Just today I got some information on a big new diamond strike north of Pniel. There are ten claims still available. We can divide them up between us. I'll put up fifty thousand pounds for five claims, and you put up fifty thousand pounds for the other five. There are diamonds there by the bushel. We can make millions overnight. What do you think?"

Jamie knew exactly what he thought. Van der Merwe would keep the claims that were profitable and Jamie would end up with the others. In addition, Jamie would have been willing to bet his life that Van der Merwe was not putting up one shilling.

"It sounds interesting," Jamie said. "How many prospectors are involved?"

"Only two."

"Why does it take so much money?" he asked innocently.

"Ah, that's an intelligent question." He leaned forward in his chair. "You see, they know the value of their claim, but they don't have the money to operate it. That's where you and I come in. We give them one hundred thousand pounds and let them keep twenty percent of their fields."

He slipped the twenty percent in so smoothly that it almost went by unnoticed. Jamie was certain the prospectors would be cheated of their diamonds and their money. It would all flow to Van der Merwe.

"We'll have to move fast," Van der Merwe warned. "As soon as word of this leaks out – "

"Let's not lose it," Jamie urged.

Van der Merwe smiled. "Don't worry, I'll have the contracts drawn up right away."

In *Afrikaans*, Jamie thought.

"Now, there are a few other deals I find very interesting, Ian."

Because it was important to keep his new partner happy, Van der Merwe no longer objected when Jamie asked that Margaret show him around the countryside. Margaret was more in love with Jamie every day. He was the last thing she thought of when she went to bed at night, and the first thing she thought of when she opened her eyes in the morning. Jamie had loosed a sensuality in her that she had not even known existed. It was as though she had suddenly discovered what her body was for, and all the things she had been taught to be ashamed of became glorious gifts to bring pleasure to Jamie. And to herself. Love was a wonderful new country to be explored. A sensual land of hidden valleys and exciting dales and glens and rivers of honey. She could not get enough of it.

In the vast sweep of the countryside, it was easy to find isolated places where they could make love, and each time for Margaret was as exciting as the first time.

The old guilt about her father haunted her. Salomon van der Merwe was an elder of the Dutch Reformed Church, and Margaret knew if he ever found out what she was doing, there would be no forgiveness. Even in the rough frontier community where they lived, where men took their pleasures where they found them, there would be no understanding. There were only two kinds of women in the world – nice girls and whores – and a nice girl did not let a man touch her unless she was married to him. So she would be labeled a whore. *It's so unfair*, she thought. *The giving and taking of love is too beautiful to be evil.* But her growing concern finally made Margaret bring up the subject of marriage.

They were driving along the Vaal River when Margaret spoke. "Ian, you know how much I – " She did not know how to go on. "That is, you and I – " In desperation she blurted out, How do you feel about marriage?"

Jamie laughed. "I'm all for it, Margaret. I'm all for it."

She joined him in his laughter. It was the happiest moment of her life.

On Sunday morning, Salomon van der Merwe invited Jamie to accompany him and Margaret to church. The Nederduits Hervormde Kerk was a large, impressive building done in bastard Gothic, with the pulpit at one end and a huge organ at the other. When they walked in the door, Van der Merwe was greeted with great respect.

"I helped build this church," he told Jamie proudly. "I'm a deacon here."

The service was brimstone and hellfire, and Van der Merwe sat there, rapt, nodding eagerly, accepting the minister's every word.

He's God's man on Sunday, Jamie thought, *and the rest of the week he belongs to the devil.*

Van der Merwe had placed himself between the two young people, but Margaret was conscious of Jamie's nearness all through the service. *Its a good thing* – she smiled nervously to herself – *that the minister doesn't know what I'm thinking about.*

That evening, Jamie went to visit the Sundowner Saloon. Smit was behind the bar serving drinks. His face brightened when he saw Jamie.

"Good evenin', Mr. Travis. What will you have, sir? The usual?"

"Not tonight, Smit. I want to talk to you. In the back room."

"Certainly, sir." Smit scented money to be made. He turned to his assistant. "Mind the bar."

The back room of the Sundowner was no more than a closet, but it afforded privacy. It contained a round table with four chairs, and in the center of the table was a lantern. Smit lit it.

"Sit down," Jamie said.

Smit took a chair. "Yes, sir. How can I help you?"

"It's you I've come to help, Smit."

Smit beamed. "Really, sir?"

"Yes." Jamie took out a long, thin cigar and lighted it. "I've decided to let you live."

An uncertain look flickered over Smit's face. "I – I don't understand, Mr. Travis."

"Not Travis. The name is McGregor. Jamie McGregor. Remember? A year ago you set me up to be killed. At the barn. For Van der Merwe."

Smit was frowning now, suddenly wary. "I don't know what – "

"Shut up and listen to me." Jamie's voice was like a whiplash.

Jamie could see the wheels turning in Smit's mind. He was trying to reconcile the face of the white-haired man in front of him with the eager youth of a year before.

"I'm still alive, and I'm rich – rich enough to hire men to burn this place down and you with it. Are you with me so far, Smit?"

Smit started to protest his ignorance, but he looked into Jamie McGregor's eyes and saw the danger there. Smit said cautiously, "Yes, sir. . . ."

"Van der Merwe pays you to send prospectors to him so he can cheat them out of what they find. That's an interesting little partnership. How much does he pay you?"

There was a silence. Smit was caught between two powerful forces. He did not know which way to jump.

"How much?"

"Two percent," he said reluctantly.

"I'll give you five. From now on when a likely prospect comes in, you'll send him to me. I'll finance him. The difference is that he'll get his fair share and you'll get yours. Did you really think Van der Merwe was paying you two percent of what he made? You're a fool."

Smit nodded. "Right, Mr. Trav – Mr. McGregor. I understand."

Jamie rose to his feet. "Not completely." He leaned over the table. "You're thinking of going to Van der Merwe and telling him about our little conversation. That way, you can collect from both of us. There's only one problem with that, Smit." His voice dropped to a whisper. "If you do, you're a dead man."

7

Jamie was getting dressed when he heard a tentative knock at the door. He listened, and it was repeated. He walked over to the door and opened it. Margaret stood there.

"Come in, Maggie," Jamie said. "Is something wrong?" It was the first time she had come to his hotel room. She stepped inside, but now that she was face to face with him, she found it difficult to speak. She had lain awake all night, wondering how to tell him the news. She was afraid he might never want to see her again.

She looked into his eyes. "Ian, I'm going to have your baby."

His face was so still that Margaret was terrified that she had lost him. And suddenly his expression changed to such joy that all her doubts were instantly wiped out. He grabbed her arms and said, "That's wonderful, Maggie! Wonderful! Have you told your father?"

Margaret pulled back in alarm. "Oh, no! He – " She walked over to the Victorian green-plush sofa and sat down. "You don't know Father. He – he would never understand."

Jamie was hurriedly putting on his shirt. "Come on, we're going to tell him together."

"Are you sure everything will be all right, Ian?"

"I've never been surer of anything in my life."

Salomon van der Merwe was measuring out strips of biltong for a prospector when Jamie and Margaret strode into the shop. "An, Ian! I'll be with you in a moment." He hurriedly finished with the customer and walked over to Jamie. "And how is everything this fine day?" Van der Merwe asked.

"It couldn't be better," Jamie said happily. "Your Maggie's going to have a baby."

There was a sudden stillness in the air. "I – I don't understand," Van der Merwe stuttered.

"It's very simple. I've gotten her pregnant."

The color drained from Van der Merwe's face. He turned wildly from one to the other. "This – this isn't true?" A maelstrom of conflicting emotions whirled through Salomon van der Merwe's head. The terrible shock of his precious daughter losing her virginity . . . getting pregnant . . . He would be the laughing stock of the town. But Ian Travis was a very wealthy man. And if they got married quickly . . .

Van der Merwe turned to Jamie. "You'll get married immediately, of course."

Jamie looked at him in surprise. "*Married?* You'd allow Maggie to marry a stupid bairn who let you cheat him out of what belonged to him?"

Van der Merwe's head was spinning. "What are you talking about, Ian? I never – "

"My name's not Ian," Jamie said harshly. "I'm Jamie McGregor. Dinna you recognize me?" He saw the bewildered expression on Van der Merwe's face. "Nae, a course you don't. That boy is dead. You killed him. But I'm not a man to hold a grudge, Van der Merwe. So I'm giving you a gift. My seed in your daughter's belly."

And Jamie turned and walked out, leaving the two of them staring after him, stunned.

Margaret had listened in shocked disbelief. He could not mean what he had just said. *He loved her! He –*

Salomon van der Merwe turned on his daughter, in the throes of a terrible rage. "You whore!" he screamed. "*Whore! Get out! Get out of here!*"

Margaret stood stock-still, unable to grasp the meaning of the awful thing that was happening. Ian blamed her for something her father had done. Ian thought she was part of something bad. *Who was Jamie McGregor? Who – ?*

"Go!" Van der Merwe hit her hard across the face. "I never want to see you again as long as I live."

Margaret stood there, rooted, her heart pounding, gasping for breath. Her father's face was that of a madman. She turned and fled from the store, not looking back.

Salomon van der Merwe stood there watching her go, gripped by despair. He had seen what happened to other men's daughters who had disgraced themselves. They had been forced to stand up in church and be publicly pilloried and then exiled from the community. It was proper and fitting punishment, exactly what they deserved. But his Margaret had been given a decent, God-fearing upbringing. *How could she have betrayed him like this?* Van der Merwe visualized his daughter's naked body, coupling with that man, writhing in heat like animals, and he began to have an erection.

He put a Closed sign on the front door of the store and lay on his bed without the strength or the will to move. When word got around town, he would become an object of derision. He would be either pitied or blamed for his daughter's depravity. Either way, it would be unbearable. He had to make certain no one learned about it. He would send the whore out of his sight forever. He knelt and prayed: *O, God! How could you do this to me, your loyal servant? Why have you forsaken me? Let her die, O Lord. Let them both die . . . .*

The Sundowner Saloon was crowded with noon trade when Jamie entered. He walked over to the bar and turned to face the room. "Your attention, please!" The conversation tapered off into silence. "Drinks on the house for everybody."

"What is it?" Smit asked. "A new strike?"

Jamie laughed. "In a way, my friend. Salomon van der Merwe's unmarried daughter is pregnant. Mr. van der Merwe wants everybody to help him celebrate."

Smit whispered, "Oh, Jesus!"

"Jesus had nothing to do with it. Just Jamie McGregor."

Within an hour, everyone in Klipdrift had heard the news. How Ian Travis was really Jamie McGregor, and how he had gotten Van der Merwe's daughter pregnant. Margaret van der Merwe had fooled the whole town.

"She doesn't look like the kind, does she?"

"Still waters run deep, they say."

"I wonder how many other men in this town have dipped their wick in that well?"

"She's a shapely girl. I could use a piece of that myself."

"Why don't you ask her? She's givin' it away."

And the men laughed.

When Salomon van der Merwe left his store that afternoon, he had come to terms with the dreadful catastrophe that had befallen him. He would send Margaret to Cape Town on the next coach. She could have her bastard there, and there was no need for anyone in Klipdrift to know his shame. Van der Merwe stepped out into the street, hugging his secret, a smile pasted on his lips.

"Afternoon, Mr. van der Merwe. I hear you might be stockin' some extra baby clothes."

"Good day, Salomon. Hear you're gonna get a little helper for your store soon."

"Hello there, Salomon. I hear a bird watcher just spotted a new species out near the Vaal River. Yes, sir, a stork!"

Salomon van der Merwe turned and blindly stumbled back into his shop, bolting the door behind him.

At the Sundowner Saloon, Jamie was having a whiskey, listening to the flood of gossip around him. It was the biggest scandal Klipdrift had ever had, and the pleasure the townspeople took in it was intense. *I wish*, Jamie thought, *that Banda were here with me to enjoy this.* This was payment for what Salomon van der Merwe had done to Banda's sister, what he had done to Jamie and to – how many others? But this was only part payment for all the things Salomon van der Merwe had done, just the beginning. Jamie's vengeance would not be complete until Van der Merwe had been totally destroyed. As for Margaret, he had no sympathy for her. She was in on it. What had she said the first day they met? *My father might be the one to help you. He knows everything.* She was a Van der Merwe too, and Jamie would destroy both of them.

Smit walked over to where Jamie was sitting. "Kin I talk to you a minute, Mr. McGregor?"

"What is it?"

Smit cleared his throat self-consciously. "I know a couple of prospectors who have ten claims up near Pniel. They're producin' diamonds, but these fellas don't have the money to get the proper equipment to work their claim. They're lookin' for a partner. I thought you might be interested."

Jamie studied him. "These are the men you talked to Van der Merwe about, right?"

Smit nodded, surprised. "Yes, sir. But I been thinkin' over your proposition. I'd rather do business with you."

Jamie pulled out a long, thin cigar, and Smit hastened to light it. "Keep talking."

Smit did.

In the beginning, prostitution in Klipdrift was on a haphazard basis. The prostitutes were mostly black women, working in sleazy, back-street brothels. The first white prostitutes to arrive in town were part-time barmaids. But as diamond strikes increased and the town prospered, more white prostitutes appeared.

There were now half a dozen sporting houses on the outskirts of Klipdrift, wooden railway huts with tin roofs. The one exception was Madam Agnes's, a respectable-looking two-story frame structure on Bree Street, off Loop Street, the main thoroughfare, where the wives of the townspeople would not be offended by having to pass in front of it. It was patronized by the husbands of those wives, and by any strangers in town who could afford it. It was expensive, but the women were young and uninhibited, and gave good value for the money. Drinks were served in a reasonably well-decorated drawing room, and it was a rule of Madam Agnes's that no customer was ever rushed or shortchanged. Madam Agnes herself was a cheerful, robust redhead in her mid-thirties. She had worked at a brothel in London and been attracted to South Africa by the tales of easy money to be picked up in a mining town like Klipdrift. She had saved enough to open her own establishment, and business had flourished from the beginning.

Madam Agnes prided herself on her understanding of men, but Jamie McGregor was a puzzle to her. He visited often, spent money freely and was always pleasant to the women, but he seemed withdrawn, remote and untouchable. His eyes were what fascinated Agnes. They were pale, bottomless pools, cold. Unlike the other patrons of her house, he never spoke about himself or his past. Madam Agnes had heard hours earlier that Jamie McGregor had deliberately gotten Salomon van der Merwe's daughter pregnant and then refused to marry her. *The bastard!* Madam Agnes thought. But she had to admit that he was an attractive bastard. She watched Jamie now as he walked down the red-carpeted stairs, politely said good night and left.

When Jamie arrived back at his hotel, Margaret was in his room, staring out the window. She turned as Jamie walked in.

"Hello, Jamie." Her voice was atremble.

"What are you doing here?"

"I had to talk to you."

"We have nothing to talk about."

"I know why you're doing this. You hate my father." Margaret moved closer to him. "But you have to know that whatever it was he did to you, I knew nothing about. Please – I beg of you – believe that. Don't hate me. I love you too much."

Jamie looked at her coldly. "That's *your* problem, isn't it?"

"Please don't look at me like that. You love me, too. . . ."

He was not listening. He was again taking the terrible journey to Paardspan where he had almost died . . . and moving the boulders on the riverbanks until he was ready to drop . . . and finally, miraculously, finding the diamonds. . . . Handing them to Van der Merwe and hearing Van der Merwe's voice saying, *You misunderstood me, boy. I don't need any partners. You're working for me . . . I'm giving you twenty-four hours to get out of town.* And then the savage beating . . . He was smelling the vultures again, feeling their sharp beaks tear into his flesh. . . .

As though from a distance, he heard Margaret's voice. "Don't you remember? I belong – to – you. . . . I love you."

He shook himself out of his reverie and looked at her. *Love.* He no longer had any idea what the word meant. Van der Merwe had burned every emotion out of him except hate. He lived on that. It was his elixir, his lifeblood. It was what had kept him alive when he fought the sharks and crossed the reef, and crawled over the mines at the diamond fields of the Namib Desert. Poets wrote about love, and singers sang about it, and perhaps it was real, perhaps it existed. But love was for other men. Not for Jamie McGregor.

"You're Salomon van der Merwe's daughter. You're carrying his grandchild in your belly. Get out."

There was nowhere for Margaret to go. She loved her father, and she needed his forgiveness, but she knew he would never – could never – forgive her. He would make her life a living hell. But she had no choice. She had to go to someone.

Margaret left the hotel and walked toward her father's store. She felt that everyone she passed was staring at her. Some of the men smiled insinuatingly, and she held her head high and walked on. When she reached the store, she hesitated, then stepped inside. The store was deserted. Her father came out from the back.

"Father . . ."

"*You!*" The contempt in his voice was a physical slap. He moved closer, and she could smell the whiskey on his breath. "I want you to get out of this town. Now. Tonight. You're never to come near here again. Do you hear me? Never!"

He pulled some bills from his pocket and threw them on the floor. "Take them and get out."

"I'm carrying your grandchild."

"You're carrying the devil's child!" He moved closer to her, and his hands were knotted into fists. "Every time people see you strutting around like a whore, they'll think of my shame. When you're gone, they'll forget it."

She looked at him for a long, lost moment, then turned and blindly stumbled out the door.

"The money, whore!" he yelled. "You forgot the money!"

There was a cheap boardinghouse at the outskirts of town, and Margaret made her way to it, her mind in a turmoil. When she reached it, she went looking for Mrs. Owens, the landlady. Mrs. Owens was a plump, pleasant-faced woman in her fifties, whose husband had brought her to Klipdrift and abandoned her. A lesser woman would have crumbled, but Mrs. Owens was a survivor. She had seen a good many people in trouble in this town, but never anyone in more trouble than the seventeen-year-old girl who stood before her now.

"You wanted to see me?"

"Yes. I was wondering if – if perhaps you had a job for me here."

"A job? Doing what?"

"Anything. I'm a good cook. I can wait on tables. I'll make the beds. I – I'll – " There was desperation in her voice. "Oh, please," she begged. "Anything!"

Mrs. Owens looked at the trembling girl standing there in front of her, and it broke her heart. "I suppose I could use an extra hand. How soon can you start?" She could see the relief that lighted Margaret's face.

"Now."

"I can pay you only – " She thought of a figure and added to it. "One pound two shillings eleven pence a month, with board and lodging."

"That will be fine," Margaret said gratefully.

Salomon van der Merwe seldom appeared now on the streets of Klipdrift. More and more often, his customers found a Closed sign on the front door of his store at all hours of the day. After a while, they took their business elsewhere.

But Salomon van der Merwe still went to church every Sunday. He went not to pray, but to demand of God that He right this terrible iniquity that had been heaped upon the shoulders of his obedient servant. The other parishioners had always looked up to Salomon van der Merwe with the respect due a wealthy and powerful man, but now he could feel the stares and whispers behind his back. The family that occupied the pew next to him moved to another pew. He was a pariah. What broke his spirit completely was the minister's thundering sermon artfully combining Exodus and Ezekiel and Leviticus. "I, the Lord thy God, am a jealous God, visiting the iniquity of the fathers upon the children. Wherefor, O harlot, hear the word of the Lord. Because thy filthiness was poured out, and thy nakedness discovered through thy whoredoms with thy lovers. . . . And the Lord spake unto Moses, saying, 'Do not prostitute thy daughter, to cause her to be a whore; lest the land fall to whoredom and the land become full of wickedness. . . .' "

Van der Merwe never set foot in church again after that Sunday.

As Salomon van der Merwe's business deteriorated, Jamie McGregor's prospered. The expense of mining for diamonds increased as the digging got deeper, and miners with working claims found they were unable to afford the elaborate equipment needed. The word quickly spread that Jamie McGregor would provide financing in exchange for a share in the mines, and in time Jamie bought out his partners. He invested in real estate and businesses and gold. He was meticulously honest in his dealings, and as his reputation spread, more people came to him to do business.

There were two banks in town, and when one of them failed because of inept management, Jamie bought it, putting in his own people and keeping his name out of the transaction.

Everything Jamie touched seemed to prosper. He was successful and wealthy beyond his boyhood dreams, but it meant little to him. He measured his successes only by Salomon van der Merwe's failures. His revenge had still only begun.

From time to time, Jamie passed Margaret on the street. He took no notice of her.

Jamie had no idea what those chance encounters did to Margaret. The sight of him took her breath away, and she had to stop until she regained control of herself. She still loved him, completely and utterly. Nothing could ever change that. He had used her body to punish her father, but Margaret knew that that could be a double-edged sword. Soon she would have Jamie's baby, and when he saw that baby, his own flesh and blood, he would marry her and give his child a name. Margaret would become Mrs. Jamie McGregor, and she asked nothing more from life. At night before Margaret went to sleep, she would touch her swollen belly and whisper, "Our son." It was probably foolish to think she could influence its sex, but she did not want to overlook any possibility. Every man wanted a son.

As her womb swelled, Margaret became more frightened. She wished she had someone to talk to. But the women of the town did not speak to her. Their religion taught them punishment, not forgiveness. She was alone, surrounded by strangers, and she wept in the night for herself and for her unborn baby.

Jamie McGregor had bought a two-story building in the heart of Klipdrift, and he used it as headquarters for his growing enterprises. One day, Harry McMillan, Jamie's chief accountant, had a talk with him.

"We're combining your companies," he told Jamie, "and we need a corporate name. Do you have any suggestions?"

"I'll think about it."

Jamie thought about it. In his mind he kept hearing the sound of long-ago echoes piercing the sea *mis* on the diamond field in the Namib Desert, and he knew there was only one name he wanted. He summoned the accountant. "We're going to call the new company Kruger-Brent. Kruger-Brent Limited."

Alvin Cory, Jamie's bank manager, stopped in to visit him. "It's about Mr. van der Merwe's loans," he said. "He's fallen very far behind. In the past he's been a good risk, but his situation has drastically changed, Mr. McGregor. I think we should call in his loans."

"No."

Cory looked at Jamie in surprise. "He came in this morning trying to borrow more money to – "

"Give it to him. Give him everything he wants."

The manager got to his feet. "Whatever you say, Mr. McGregor. I'll tell him that you – "

"Tell him nothing. Just give him the money."

Every morning Margaret arose at five o'clock to bake large loaves of wonderful-smelling bread and sourdough biscuits, and when the boarders trooped into the dining room for breakfast, she served them porridge and ham and eggs, buckwheat cakes, sweet rolls and pots of steaming coffee and *naartje*. The majority of the guests at the boardinghouse were prospectors on their way to and from their claims. They would stop off in Klipdrift long enough to have their diamonds appraised, have a bath, get drunk and visit one of the town's brothels – usually in that order. They were for the most part rough, illiterate adventurers.

There was an unwritten law in Klipdrift that nice women were not to be molested. If a man wanted sex, he went to a whore. Margaret van der Merwe, however, was a challenge, for she fit into neither category. Nice girls who were single did not get pregnant, and the theory went that since Margaret had fallen once, she was probably eager to bed everyone else. All they had to do was ask. They did.

Some of the prospectors were open and blatant; others were leering and furtive. Margaret handled them all with quiet dignity. But one night as Mrs. Owens was preparing for bed, she heard screams coming from Margaret's room at the back of the house. The landlady flung the door open and rushed in. One of the guests, a drunken prospector, had ripped off Margaret's nightgown and had her pinned down on the bed.

Mrs. Owens was on him like a tiger. She picked up a flatiron and began hitting him with it. She was half the size of the prospector, but it made no difference. Filled with an overpowering rage, she knocked the prospector unconscious and dragged him into the hallway and out to the street. Then she turned and hurried back to Margaret's room. Margaret was wiping the blood off her lips from where the man had bitten her. Her hands were trembling.

"Are you all right, Maggie?"

"Yes. I – thank you, Mrs. Owens."

Unbidden tears sprang into Margaret's eyes. In a town where few people even spoke to her, here was someone who had shown kindness.

Mrs. Owens studied Margaret's swollen belly and thought, *The poor dreamer. Jamie McGregor will never marry her.*

The time of confinement was drawing close. Margaret tired easily now, and bending down and getting up again was an effort. Her only joy was when she felt her baby stir inside her. She and her son were completely alone in the world, and she talked to him hour after hour, telling him all the wonderful things that life had in store for him.

Late one evening, shortly after supper, a young black boy appeared at the boardinghouse and handed Margaret a sealed letter.

"I'm to wait for an answer," the boy told her.

Margaret read the letter, then read it again, very slowly. "Yes," she said. "The answer is yes."

The following Friday, promptly at noon, Margaret arrived in front of Madam Agnes's bordello. A sign on the front door read Closed. Margaret rapped tentatively on the door, ignoring the startled glances of the passers-by. She wondered if she had made a mistake by coming here. It had been a difficult decision, and she had accepted only out of a terrible loneliness. The letter had read:

Dear Miss van der Merwe:

It's none of my business, but my girls and me have been discussing your unfortunate and unfair situation, and we think it's a damned shame. We would like to help you and your baby. If it would not embarrass you, we would be honored to have you come to lunch. Would Friday at noon be convenient?

Respectfully yours,

Madam Agnes

P.S. We would be very discreet.

Margaret was debating whether to leave, when the door was opened by Madam Agnes.

She took Margaret's arm and said, "Come in, dearie. Let's get you out of this damned heat."

She led her into the parlor, furnished with Victorian red-plush couches and chairs and tables. The room had been decorated with ribbons and streamers and – from God knows where – brightly colored balloons. Crudely lettered cardboard signs hanging from the ceiling read: WELCOME BABY . . . IT'S GOING TO BE A BOY . . . HAPPY BIRTHDAY.

In the parlor were eight of Madam Agnes's girls, in a variety of sizes, ages and colors. They had all dressed for the occasion under Madam Agnes's tutelage. They wore conservative afternoon gowns and no makeup. They *look*, Margaret thought in wonder, *more respectable than most of the wives in this town.*

Margaret stared at the roomful of prostitutes, not quite knowing what to do. Some of the faces were familiar. Margaret had waited on them when she worked in her father's store. Some of the girls were young and quite beautiful. A few were older and fleshy, with obviously dyed hair. But they all had one thing in common – they *cared*. They were friendly and warm and kind, and they wanted to make her happy.

They hovered around Margaret self-consciously, afraid of saying or doing the wrong thing. No matter what the townspeople said, they knew this was a lady, and they were aware of the difference between Margaret and themselves. They were honored that she had come to them, and they were determined not to let anything spoil this party for her.

"We fixed you a nice lunch, honey," Madam Agnes said. "I hope you're hungry."

They led her into the dining room, where a table had been festively set, with a bottle of champagne at Margaret's place. As they walked through the hallway, Margaret glanced toward the stairs that led to the bedrooms on the second floor. She knew Jamie visited here, and she wondered which of the girls he chose. All of them, perhaps. And she studied them again and wondered what it was they had for Jamie that she did hot.

The luncheon turned out to be a banquet. It began with a delicious cold soup and salad, followed by fresh carp. After that came mutton and duck with potatoes and vegetables. There was a tipsy cake and cheese and fruit and coffee. Margaret found herself eating heartily and enjoying herself immensely. She was seated at the head of the table, Madam Agnes on her right, and Maggie, a lovely blond girl who could have been no more than sixteen, on her left. In the beginning the conversation was stilted. The girls had dozens of amusing, bawdy stories to tell, but they were not the kind they felt Margaret should hear. And so they talked about the weather and about how Klipdrift was growing, and about the future of South Africa. They were knowledgeable about politics and the economy and diamonds because they got their information firsthand from experts.

Once, the pretty blonde, Maggie, said, "Jamie's just found a new diamond field at – " And as the room went suddenly silent and she realized her gaffe, she added nervously, "That's my *Uncle* Jamie. He's – he's married to my aunt."

Margaret was surprised by the sudden wave of jealousy that swept through her. Madam Agnes hastily changed the subject.

When the luncheon was finished, Madam Agnes rose and said, "This way, honey."

Margaret and the girls followed her into a second parlor which Margaret had not seen before. It was filled with dozens of gifts, all of them beautifully wrapped. Margaret could not believe her eyes.

"I – I don't know what to say."

"Open them," Madam Agnes told Margaret.

There was a rocking cradle, handmade bootees, sacques, embroidered bonnets, a long, embroidered cashmere cloak. There were French-kid button shoes, a child's silver cup, gold-lined, and a comb and brush with solid sterling-silver handles. There were solid-gold baby bib pins with beaded edges, a celluloid baby rattle and rubber teething ring and a rocking horse painted dapple gray. There were toy soldiers, brightly colored wooden blocks and the most beautiful thing of all: a long, white christening dress.

It was like Christmas. It was beyond anything Margaret had ever expected. All the bottled-up loneliness and unhappiness of the past months exploded in her, and she burst into sobs.

Madam Agnes put her arms around her and said to the other girls. "Get out."

They quietly left the room. Madam Agnes led Margaret to a couch and sat there holding her until the sobs subsided.

"I – I'm so sorry," Margaret stammered. "I – I don't know what came over me."

"It's all right, honey. This room has seen a lot of problems come and go. And you know what I've learned? Somehow, in the end everything always gets sorted out. You and your baby are gonna be just fine."

"Thank you," Margaret whispered. She gestured toward the piles of presents. "I can never thank you and your friends enough for – "

Madam Agnes squeezed Margaret's hand. "Don't. You don't have no idea how much fun the girls and me had gettin' all this together. We don't get a chance to do this kind of thing very often. When one of *us* gets pregnant, it's a fuckin' tragedy." Her hands flew to her mouth and she said, "Oh! Excuse me!"

Margaret smiled. "I just want you to know that this has been one of the nicest days of my life."

"We're real honored that you came to visit us, honey. As far as I'm concerned, you're worth all the women in this town put together. Those damned bitches! I could kill them for the way they're behavin' to you. And if you don't mind my sayin' so, Jamie McGregor is a damned fool." She rose to her feet. "Men! It would be a wonderful world if we could live without the bastards. Or maybe it wouldn't. Who knows?"

Margaret had recovered her composure. She rose to her feet and took Madam Agnes's hand in hers. "I'll never forget this. Not as long as I live. Someday, when my son is old enough, I'll tell him about this day."

Madam Agnes frowned. "You really think you should?"

Margaret smiled. "I really think I should."

Madam Agnes saw Margaret to the door. "I'll have a wagon deliver all the gifts to your boardinghouse, and – good luck to you."

"Thank you. Oh, thank you."

And she was gone.

Madam Agnes stood there a moment watching Margaret walk clumsily down the street. Then she turned inside and called loudly, "All right, ladies. Let's go to work."

One hour later, Madam Agnes's was open for business as usual.

8

It was time to spring the trap. Over the previous six months, Jamie McGregor had quietly bought out Van der Merwe's partners in his various enterprises so that Jamie now had control of them. But his obsession was to own Van der Merwe's diamond fields in the Namib. He had paid for those fields a hundred times over with his blood and guts, and very nearly with his life. He had used the diamonds he and Banda had stolen there to build an empire from which to crush Salomon van der Merwe. The task had not yet been completed. Now, Jamie was ready to finish it.

Van der Merwe had gone deeper and deeper into debt. Everyone in town refused to lend him money, except the bank Jamie secretly owned. His standing instruction to his bank manager was, "Give Salomon van der Merwe everything he wants."

The general store was almost never open now. Van der Merwe began drinking early in the morning, and in the afternoon he would go to Madam Agnes's and sometimes spend the night there.

One morning Margaret stood at the butcher's counter waiting for the spring chickens Mrs. Owens had ordered, when she glanced out the window and saw her father leaving the brothel. She could hardly recognize the unkempt old man shuffling along the street. *I did this to him. Oh, God, forgive me, I did this!*

Salomon van der Merwe had no idea what was happening to him. He knew that somehow, through no fault of his own, his life was being destroyed. God had chosen him – as He had once chosen Job – to test the mettle of his faith. Van der Merwe was certain he would triumph over his unseen enemies in the end. All he needed was a little time – time and more money. He had put up his general store as security, the shares he had in six small diamond fields, even his horse and wagon. Finally, there was nothing left but the diamond field in the Namib, and the day he put that up as collateral, Jamie pounced.

"Pull in all his notes," Jamie ordered his bank manager. "Give him twenty-four hours to pay up in full, or foreclose."

"Mr. McGregor, he can't possibly come up with that kind of money. He – "

"Twenty-four hours."

At exactly four o'clock the following afternoon, the assistant manager of the bank appeared at the general store with the marshal and a writ to confiscate all of Salomon van der Merwe's worldly possessions. From his office building across the street, Jamie watched Van der Merwe being evicted from his store. The old man stood outside, blinking helplessly in the sun, not knowing what to do or where to turn. He had been stripped of everything. Jamie's vengeance was complete. *Why is it*, Jamie wondered, *that I feel no sense of triumph?* He was empty inside. The man he destroyed had destroyed him first.

When Jamie walked into Madam Agnes's that night, she said, "Have you heard the news, Jamie? Salomon van der Merwe blew his brains out an hour ago."

The funeral was held at the dreary, windswept cemetery outside town. Besides the burying crew, there were only two people in attendance: Margaret and Jamie McGregor. Margaret wore a shapeless black dress to cover her protruding figure. She looked pale and unwell. Jamie stood tall and elegant, withdrawn and remote. The two stood at opposite sides of the grave watching the crude pine-box coffin lowered into the ground. The clods of earth clattered against the coffin, and to Margaret they seemed to say, *Whore! . . . Whore! . . .*

She looked across her father's grave at Jamie, and their eyes met. Jamie's glance was cool and impersonal, as though she were a stranger. Margaret hated him then. *You stand there feeling nothing, and you're as guilty as I am. We killed him, you and I. In God's eyes, I'm your wife. But we're partners in evil.* She looked down at the open grave and watched the last shovelful of dirt cover the pine box. "Rest," she whispered. "Rest."

When she looked up, Jamie was gone.

There were two wooden buildings in Klipdrift that served as hospitals, but they were so filthy and unsanitary that more patients died there than lived. Babies were born at home. As Margaret's time for delivery drew closer, Mrs. Owens arranged for a black midwife, Hannah. Labor began at three A.M.

"Now you just bear down," Hannah instructed. "Nature'll do the rest."

The first pain brought a smile to Margaret's lips. She was bringing her son into the world, and he would have a name. She would see to it that Jamie McGregor recognized his child. Her son was not going to be punished.

The labor went on, hour after hour, and when some of the boarders stepped into Margaret's bedroom to watch the proceedings, they were sent packing.

"This is personal," Hannah told Margaret. "Between you and God and the devil who got you into this trouble."

"Is it going to be a boy?" Margaret gasped.

Hannah mopped Margaret's brow with a damp cloth. "I'll let you know as soon as I check out the plumbin'. Now press down. Real hard! Hard! Harder!"

The contractions began to come closer together and the pain tore through Margaret's body. *Oh, my God, something's wrong*, Margaret thought.

"Bear down!" Hannah said. And suddenly there was a note of alarm in her voice. "It's twisted around," she cried. "I – I can't get it out!"

Through a red mist, Margaret saw Hannah bend down and twist her body, and the room began to fade out, and suddenly there was no more pain. She was floating in space and there was a bright light at the end of a tunnel and someone was beckoning to her, and it was Jamie. *I'm here, Maggie, darling. You're going to give me a fine son.* He had come back to her. She no longer hated him. She knew then she had never hated him. She heard a voice saying, "It's almost over," and there was a tearing inside her, and the pain made her scream aloud.

"Now!" Hannah said. "It's coming."

And a second later, Margaret felt a wet rush between her legs and there was a triumphant cry from Hannah. She held up a red bundle and said, "Welcome to Klipdrift. Honey, you got yourself a son."

She named him Jamie.

Margaret knew the news about the baby would reach Jamie quickly, and she waited for him to call on her or send for her. When several weeks had passed and Margaret had not heard anything, she sent a message to him. The messenger returned thirty minutes later.

Margaret was in a fever of impatience. "Did you see Mr. McGregor?"

"Yes, ma'am."

"And you gave him the message?"

"Yes, ma'am."

"What did he *say?*" she demanded.

The boy was embarrassed. "He – he said he has no son, Miss van der Merwe."

She locked herself and her baby in her room all that day and all that night and refused to come out. "Your father's upset just now, Jamie. He thinks your mother did something bad to him. But you're his son, and when he sees you, he's going to take us to live in his house and he's going to love both of us very much. You'll see, darling. Everything is going to be fine."

In the morning when Mrs. Owens knocked on the door, Margaret opened it. She seemed strangely calm.

"Are you all right, Maggie?"

"I'm fine, thank you." She was dressing Jamie in one of his new outfits. "I'm going to take Jamie out in his carriage this morning."

The carriage, from Madam Agnes and her girls, was a thing of beauty. It was made of the finest grade of reed, with a strong cane bottom and solid, bentwood handles. It was upholstered in imported brocade, with piped rolls of silk plush, and it had a parasol hooked on at the back, with a deep ruffle.

Margaret pushed the baby carriage down the narrow sidewalks of Loop Street. An occasional stranger stopped to smile at the baby, but the women of the town averted their eyes or crossed to the other side of the street to avoid Margaret.

Margaret did not even notice. She was looking for one person. Every day that the weather was fine, Margaret dressed the baby in one of his beautiful outfits and took him out in the baby carriage. At the end of a week, when Margaret had not once encountered Jamie on the streets, she realized he was deliberately avoiding her. *Well, if he won't come to see his son, his son will go to see him*, Margaret decided.

The following morning, Margaret found Mrs. Owens in the parlor. "I'm taking a little trip, Mrs. Owens. I'll be back in a week."

"The baby's too young to travel, Maggie. He – "

"The baby will be staying in town."

Mrs. Owens frowned. "You mean *here?*"

"No, Mrs. Owens. Not here."

Jamie McGregor had built his house on a kopje, one of the hills overlooking Klipdrift. It was a low, steep-roofed bungalow with two large wings attached to the main building by wide verandas. The house was surrounded by green lawns studded with trees and a lush rose garden. In back was the carriage house and separate quarters for the servants. The domestic arrangements were in the charge of Eugenia Talley, a formidable middle-aged widow with six grown children in England.

Margaret arrived at the house with her infant son in her arms at ten in the morning, when she knew Jamie would be at his office. Mrs. Talley opened the door and stared in surprise at Margaret and the baby. As did everyone else within a radius of a hundred miles, Mrs. Talley knew who they were.

"I'm sorry, but Mr. McGregor is not at home," the housekeeper said, and started to close the door.

Margaret stopped her. "I didn't come to see Mr. McGregor. I brought him his son."

"I'm afraid I don't know anything about that. You – "

"I'll be gone for one week. I'll return for him then." She held the baby out. "His name is Jamie."

A horrified look came over Mrs. Talley's face. "You can't leave him here! Why, Mr. McGregor would – "

"You have a choice," Margaret informed her. "You can either take him in the house or have me leave him here on your doorstep. Mr. McGregor wouldn't like *that* either."

Without another word, she thrust the baby into the arms of the housekeeper and walked away.

"Wait! You can't – ! Come back here! Miss – !"

Margaret never turned around. Mrs. Talley stood there, holding the tiny bundle and thinking, *Oh, my God! Mr. McGregor is going to be furious!*

She had never seen him in such a state. "How could you have been so *stupid?*" he yelled. "All you had to do was slam the door in her face!"

"She didn't give me a chance, Mr. McGregor. She – "

"I will not have her child in my house!"

In his agitation he paced up and down, pausing to stop in front of the hapless housekeeper from time to time. "I should fire you for this."

"She's coming back to pick him up in a week. I – "

"I don't care when she's coming back," Jamie shouted. "Get that child out of here. Now! Get rid of it!"

"How do you suggest I do that, Mr. McGregor?" she asked stiffly.

"Drop it off in town. There must be someplace you can leave it."

"Where?"

"How the devil do I know!"

Mrs. Talley looked at the tiny bundle she was holding in her arms. The shouting had started the baby crying. "There are no orphanages in Klipdrift." She began to rock the baby in her arms, but the screams grew louder. "Someone has to take care of him."

Jamie ran his hands through his hair in frustration. "Damn! All right," he decided. "You're the one who so generously took the baby. *You* take care of him."

"Yes, sir."

"And stop that unbearable wailing. Understand something, Mrs. Talley. I want it kept out of my sight. I don't want to know it's in this house. And when its mother picks it up next week, I don't want to see her. Is that clear?"

The baby started up with renewed vigor.

"Perfectly, Mr. McGregor." And Mrs. Talley hurried from the room.

Jamie McGregor sat alone in his den sipping a brandy and smoking a cigar. *The stupid woman. The sight of her baby is supposed to melt my heart, make me go rushing to her and say, "I love you. I love the baby. I want to marry you."* Well, he had not even bothered looking at the infant. It had nothing to do with him. He had not sired it out of love, or even lust. It had been sired out of vengeance. He would forever remember the look on Salomon van der Merwe's face when he had told him Margaret was pregnant. That was the beginning. The end was the dirt being thrown onto the wooden coffin. He must find Banda and let him know their mission was finished.

Jamie felt an emptiness. *I need to set new goals*, he thought. He was already wealthy beyond belief. He had acquired hundreds of acres of mineral land. He had bought it for the diamonds that might be found there, and had ended up owning gold, platinum and half a dozen other rare minerals. His bank held mortgages on half the properties in Klipdrift, and his land-holdings extended from the Namib to Cape Town. He felt a satisfaction in this, but it was not enough. He had asked his parents to come and join him, but they did not want to leave Scotland. His brothers and sister had married. Jamie sent large sums of money back to his parents, and that gave him pleasure, but his life was at a plateau. A few years earlier it had consisted of exciting highs and lows. He had felt alive. He was alive when he and Banda sailed their raft through the reefs of the *Sperrgebiet*. He was alive crawling over the land mines through the desert sand. It seemed to Jamie that he had not been alive in a long time. He did not admit to himself that he was lonely.

He reached again for the decanter of brandy and saw that it was empty. He had either drunk more than he realized or Mrs. Talley was getting careless. Jamie rose from his chair, picked up the brandy snifter and wandered out to the butler's pantry where the liquor was kept. He was opening the bottle when he heard the cooing of an infant. *It! Mrs. Talley must have the baby in her quarters, off the kitchen.* She had obeyed his orders to the letter. He had neither seen nor heard the infant in the two days it had been trespassing in his home. Jamie could hear Mrs. Talley talking to it in the singsong tone that women used to talk to infants.

"You're a handsome little fellow, aren't you?" she was saying. "You're just an angel. Yes, you are. An angel."

The baby cooed again. Jamie walked over to Mrs. Talley's open bedroom door and looked inside. From somewhere the housekeeper had obtained a crib and the baby was lying in it. Mrs. Talley was leaning over him, and the infant's fist was tightly wrapped around her finger.

"You're a strong little devil, Jamie. You're going to grow up to be a big – " She broke off in surprise as she became aware of her employer standing in the doorway.

"Oh," she said. "I – is there something I can get for you, Mr. McGregor?"

"No." He walked over to the crib. "I was disturbed by the noise in here." And Jamie took his first look at his son. The baby was bigger than he had expected, and well formed. He seemed to be smiling up at Jamie.

"Oh, I'm sorry, Mr. McGregor. He's really such a good baby. And healthy. Just give him your finger and feel how strong he is."

Without a word, Jamie turned and walked out of the room.

Jamie McGregor had a staff of over fifty employees working on his various enterprises. There was not an employee from the mail boy to the highest executive who did not know how Kruger-Brent, Ltd., got its name, and they all took fierce pride in working for Jamie McGregor. He had recently hired David Blackwell, the sixteen-year-old son of one of his foremen, an American from Oregon who had come to South Africa looking for diamonds. When Blackwell's money ran out, Jamie had hired him to supervise one of the mines. The son went to work for the company one summer, and Jamie found him such a good worker that he offered him a permanent job. Young David Blackwell was intelligent and attractive and had initiative. Jamie knew he could also keep his mouth shut, which is why he chose him to run this particular errand.

"David, I want you to go to Mrs. Owens's boardinghouse. There's a woman living there named Margaret van der Merwe."

If David Blackwell was familiar with the name or her circumstances, he gave no indication of it. "Yes, sir."

"You're to speak only to her. She left her baby with my housekeeper. Tell her I want her to pick it up today and get it out of my house."

"Yes, Mr. McGregor."

Half an hour later, David Blackwell returned. Jamie looked up from his desk.

"Sir, I'm afraid I couldn't do what you asked."

Jamie rose to his feet. "Why not?" he demanded. "It was a simple enough job."

"Miss van der Merwe wasn't there, sir."

"Then find her."

"She left Klipdrift two days ago. She's expected back in five days. If you'd like me to make further inquiries – "

"No." That was the last thing Jamie wanted. "Never mind. That's all, David."

"Yes, sir." The boy left the office.

Damn that woman! When she returned, she was going to have a surprise coming. She was going to get her baby back!

That evening, Jamie dined at home alone. He was having his brandy in the study when Mrs. Talley came in to discuss a household problem. In the middle of a sentence, she suddenly stopped to listen and said, "Excuse me, Mr. McGregor. I hear Jamie crying." And she hurried out of the room.

Jamie slammed down his brandy snifter, spilling the brandy. *That goddamned baby! And she had the nerve to name him* Jamie. *He didn't look like a Jamie. He didn't look like anything.*

Ten minutes later, Mrs. Talley returned to the study. She saw the spilled drink. "Shall I get you another brandy?"

"That won't be necessary," Jamie said coldly. "What *is* necessary is that you remember who you're working for. I will not be interrupted because of that bastard. Is that quite clear, Mrs. Talley?"

"Yes, sir."

"The sooner that infant you brought into this house is gone, the better it will be for all of us. Do you understand?"

Her lips tightened. "Yes, sir. Is there anything else?"

"No."

She turned to leave.

"Mrs. Talley . . ."

"Yes, Mr. McGregor?"

"You said it was crying. It's not ill, is it?"

"No, sir. Just wet. He needed a change."

Jamie found the idea revolting. "That will be all."

Jamie would have been furious had he been aware that the servants in the house spent hour upon hour discussing him and his son. They all agreed that the master was behaving unreasonably, but they also knew that even to mention the subject would mean instant dismissal. Jamie McGregor was not a man who took kindly to advice from anyone.

The following evening Jamie had a late business meeting. He had made an investment in a new railroad. It was a small one, to be sure, running from his mines in the Namib Desert to De Aar, linking up with the Cape Town–Kimberley line, but it would now be much cheaper to transport his diamonds and gold to the port. The first South Africa Railway had been opened in 1860, running from Dunbar to the Point, and since then new lines had been run from Cape Town to Wellington. Railroads were going to be the steel veins that allowed goods and people to flow freely through the heart of South Africa, and Jamie intended to be a part of them. That was only the beginning of his plan. *After that*, Jamie thought, *ships. My own ships to carry the minerals across the ocean.*

He arrived home after midnight, undressed and got into bed. He had had a decorator from London design a large, masculine bedroom with a huge bed that had been carved in Cape Town. There was an old Spanish chest in one corner of the room and two enormous wardrobes which held more than fifty suits and thirty pairs of shoes. Jamie cared nothing about clothes, but it was important to him that they be there. He had spent too many days and nights wearing rags.

He was just dozing off when he thought he heard a cry. He sat up and listened. Nothing. Was it the baby? It might have fallen out of its crib. Jamie knew that Mrs. Talley was a sound sleeper. It would be dreadful if something happened to the infant while it was in Jamie's house. Then it could become his responsibility. *Damn that woman!* Jamie thought.

He put on a robe and slippers and went through the house to Mrs. Talley's room. He listened at her closed door and could hear nothing. Quietly, Jamie pushed open the door. Mrs. Talley was sound asleep, huddled under the covers, snoring. Jamie walked over to the crib. The baby lay on its back, its eyes wide open. Jamie moved closer and looked down. There *was* a resemblance, by God! It definitely had Jamie's mouth and chin. Its eyes were blue now, but all babies were born with blue eyes. Jamie could tell by looking at it that it was going to have gray eyes. It moved its little hands in the air and made a cooing sound and smiled up at Jamie. *Now, that's a brave lad*, Jamie thought, *lying there, not making any noise, not screaming like other babies would do.* He peered closer. *Yes, he's a McGregor, all right.*

Tentatively, Jamie reached down and held out a finger. The infant grabbed it with both hands and squeezed tightly. *He's as strong as a bull*, Jamie thought. At that moment, a strained look came over the infant's face, and Jamie could smell a sour odor.

"Mrs. Talley!"

She leaped up in bed, filled with alarm. "What – what is it?"

"The baby needs attention. Do I have to do everything around here?"

And Jamie McGregor stalked out of the room.

"David, do you know anything about babies?"

"In what respect, sir?" David Blackwell asked.

"Well, you know. What they like to play with, things like that."

The young American said, "I think when they're very young they enjoy rattles, Mr. McGregor."

"Pick up a dozen," Jamie ordered.

"Yes, sir."

No unnecessary questions. Jamie liked that. David Blackwell was going to go far.

That evening when Jamie arrived home with a small brown package, Mrs. Talley said, "I want to apologize for last night, Mr. McGregor. I don't know how I could have slept through it. The baby must have been screaming something terrible for you to have heard it all the way in your room."

"Don't worry about it," Jamie said generously. "As long as one of us heard it." He handed her the package. "Give this to it. Some rattles for him to play with. Can't be much fun for him to be a prisoner in that crib all day."

"Oh, he's not a prisoner, sir. I take him out."

"Where do you take him?"

"Just in the garden, where I can keep an eye on him."

Jamie frowned. "He didn't look well to me last night."

"He didn't?"

"No. His color's not good. It wouldn't do for him to get sick before his mother picks him up."

"Oh, no, sir."

"Perhaps I'd better have another look at him."

"Yes, sir. Shall I bring him in here?"

"Do that, Mrs. Talley."

"Right away, Mr. McGregor."

She was back in a few minutes with little Jamie in her arms. The baby was clutching a blue rattle. "His color looks fine to me."

"Well, I could have been wrong. Give him to me."

Carefully, she held the baby out and Jamie took his son in his arms for the first time. The feeling that swept over him took him completely by surprise. It was as though he had been longing for this moment, living for this moment, without ever knowing it. This was his flesh and blood he was holding in his arms – his son, Jamie McGregor, Jr. What was the point of building an empire, a dynasty, of having diamonds and gold and railroads if you had no one to pass them on to? *What a bloody fool I've been!* Jamie thought. It had never occurred to him until now what was missing. He had been too blinded by his hatred. Looking down into the tiny face, a hardness somewhere deep in the core of him vanished.

"Move Jamie's crib into my bedroom, Mrs. Talley."

Three days later when Margaret appeared at the front door of Jamie's house, Mrs. Talley said, "Mr. McGregor is away at his office, Miss van der Merwe, but he asked me to send for him when you came for the baby. He wishes to speak with you."

Margaret waited in the living room, holding little Jamie in her arms. She had missed him terribly. Several times during the week she had almost lost her resolve and rushed back to Klipdrift, afraid that something might have happened to the baby, that he might have become ill or had an accident. But she had forced herself to stay away, and her plan had worked. Jamie wanted to talk to her! Everything was going to be wonderful. The three of them would be together now.

The moment Jamie walked into the living room, Margaret felt again the familiar rush of emotion. Oh, God, she thought, *I love him so much.*

"Hello, Maggie."

She smiled, a warm, happy smile. "Hello, Jamie."

"I want my son."

Margaret's heart sang. "Of course you want your son, Jamie. I never doubted it."

"I'll see to it that he's brought up properly. He'll have every advantage I can give him and, naturally, I'll see that you're taken care of."

Margaret looked at him in confusion. "I – I don't understand."

"I said I want my son."

"I thought – I mean – you and I – "

"No. It's only the boy I want."

Margaret was filled with a sudden outrage. "I see. Well, I'll not let you take him away from me."

Jamie studied her a moment. "Very well. We'll work out a compromise. You can stay on here with Jamie. You can be his – his governess." He saw the look on her face. "What *do* you want?"

"I want my son to have a name," she said fiercely. "His father's name."

"All right. I'll adopt him."

Margaret looked at him scornfully. "Adopt my baby? Oh, no. You will not have my son. I feel sorry for you. The great Jamie McGregor. With all your money and power, you have' nothing. You're a thing of pity."

And Jamie stood there watching as Margaret turned and walked out of the house, carrying his son in her arms.

The following morning, Margaret made preparations to leave for America.

"Running away won't solve anything," Mrs. Owens argued.

"I'm not running away. I'm going someplace where my baby and I can have a new life."

She could no longer subject herself and her baby to the humiliation Jamie McGregor offered them.

"When will you leave?"

"As soon as possible. We'll take a coach to Worcester and the train from there to Cape Town. I've saved enough to get us to New York."

"That's a long way to go."

"It will be worth it. They call America the land of opportunity, don't they? That's all we need."

Jamie had always prided himself on being a man who remained calm under pressure. Now he went around yelling at everyone in sight. His office was in a constant uproar. Nothing anyone did pleased him. He roared and complained about everything, unable to control himself. He had not slept in three nights. He kept thinking about the conversation with Margaret. *Damn her!* He should have known she would try to push him into marriage. Tricky, just like her father. He had mishandled the negotiations. He had told her he would take care of her, but he had not been specific. Of course. *Money!* He should have offered her money. A thousand pounds – ten thousand pounds more.

"I have a delicate task for you," he told David Blackwell.

"Yes, sir."

"I want you to talk to Miss van der Merwe. Tell her I'm offering her twenty thousand pounds. She'll know what I want in exchange." Jamie wrote out a check. He had long ago learned the lure of money in hand. "Give this to her."

"Right, sir." And David Blackwell was gone.

He returned fifteen minutes later and handed the check back to his employer. It had been torn in half. Jamie could feel his face getting red. "Thank you, David. That will be all."

So Margaret was holding out for more money. Very well. He would give it to her. But this time he would handle it himself.

Late that afternoon, Jamie McGregor went to Mrs. Owens's boardinghouse. "I want to see Miss van der Merwe," Jamie said.

"I'm afraid that's not possible," Mrs. Owens informed him. "She's on her way to America."

Jamie felt as though he had been hit in the stomach. "She can't be! When did she leave?"

"She and her son took the noon coach to Worcester."

The train sitting at the station in Worcester was filled to capacity, the seats and aisles crowded with noisy travelers on their way to Cape Town. There were merchants and their wives, salesmen, prospectors, kaffirs and soldiers and sailors reporting back for duty. Most of them were riding a train for the first time and there was a festive atmosphere among the passengers. Margaret had been able to get a seat near a window, where Jamie would not be crushed by the crowd. She sat there holding her baby close to her, oblivious to those around her, thinking about the new life that lay ahead of them. It would not be easy. Wherever she went, she would be an unmarried woman with a child, an offense to society. But she would find a way to make sure her son had his chance at a decent life. She heard the conductor call, "All aboard!"

She looked up, and Jamie was standing there. "Collect your things," he ordered. "You're getting off the train."

He still thinks he can buy me, Margaret thought. "How much are you offering this time?"

Jamie looked down at his son, peacefully asleep in Margaret's arms. "I'm offering you marriage."

9

They were married three days later in a brief, private ceremony. The only witness was David Blackwell.

During the wedding ceremony, Jamie McGregor was filled with mixed emotions. He was a man who had grown used to controlling and manipulating others, and this time it was he who had been manipulated. He glanced at Margaret. Standing next to him, she looked almost beautiful. He remembered her passion and abandon, but it was only a memory, nothing more, without heat or emotion. He had used Margaret as an instrument of vengeance, and she had produced his heir.

The minister was saying, "I now pronounce you man and wife. You may kiss the bride."

Jamie leaned forward and briefly touched his lips to Margaret's cheek.

"Let's go home," Jamie said. His son was waiting for him.

When they returned to the house, Jamie showed Margaret to a bedroom in one of the wings.

"This is your bedroom," Jamie informed her.

"I see."

"I'll hire another housekeeper and put Mrs. Talley in charge of Jamie. If there's anything you require, tell David Blackwell."

Margaret felt as though he had struck her. He was treating her like a servant. But that was not important. *My son has a name. That is enough for me.*

Jamie did not return home for dinner. Margaret waited for him, then finally dined alone. That night she lay awake in her bed, aware of every sound in the house. At four o'clock in the morning, she finally fell asleep. Her last thought was to wonder which of the women at Madam Agnes's he had chosen.

If Margaret's relationship with Jamie was unchanged since their marriage, her relationship with the townspeople of Klipdrift underwent a miraculous transformation. Overnight, Margaret went from being an outcast to becoming

Klipdrift's social arbiter. Most of the people in town depended for their living in one way or another on Jamie McGregor and Kruger-Brent, Ltd. They decided that if Margaret van der Merwe was good enough for Jamie McGregor, she was good enough for them. Now when Margaret took little Jamie for an outing, she was met with smiles and cheery greetings. Invitations poured in. She was invited to teas, charity luncheons and dinners and urged to head civic committees. When she dressed her hair in a different way, dozens of women in town instantly followed suit. She bought a new yellow dress, and yellow dresses were suddenly popular. Margaret handled their fawning in the same manner she had handled their hostility – with quiet dignity.

Jamie came home only to spend time with his son. His attitude toward Margaret remained distant and polite. Each morning at breakfast she played the role of happy wife for the servants' benefit, despite the cool indifference of the man sitting across the table from her. But when Jamie had gone and she could escape to her room, she would be drenched in perspiration. She hated herself. Where was her pride? Because Margaret knew she still loved Jamie. *I'll always love him*, she thought. *God help me.*

Jamie was in Cape Town on a three-day business trip. As he came out of the Royal Hotel, a liveried black driver said, "Carriage, sir?"

"No," Jamie said. "I'll walk."

"Banda thought you might like to ride."

Jamie stopped and looked sharply at the man. "Banda?"

"Yes, Mr. McGregor."

Jamie got into the carriage. The driver flicked his whip and they started off. Jamie sat back in his seat, thinking of Banda, his courage, his friendship. He had tried many times to find him in the last two years, with no success. Now he was on his way to meet his friend.

The driver turned the carriage toward the waterfront, and Jamie knew instantly where they were going. Fifteen minutes later the carriage stopped in front of the deserted warehouse where Jamie and Banda had once planned their adventure into the Namib. *What reckless young fools we were*, Jamie thought. He stepped out of the carriage and approached the warehouse. Banda was waiting for him. He looked exactly the same, except that now he was neatly dressed in a suit and shirt and tie.

They stood there, silently grinning at each other, then they embraced.

"You look prosperous," Jamie smiled.

Banda nodded. "I've not done badly. I bought that farm we talked about. I have a wife and two sons, and I raise wheat and ostriches."

"*Ostriches?*"

"Their feathers bring in lots of money."

"Ah. I want to meet your family, Banda."

Jamie thought of his own family in Scotland, and of how much he missed them. He had been away from home for four years.

"I've been trying to find you."

"I've been busy, Jamie." Banda moved closer. "I had to see you to give you a warning. There's going to be trouble for you."

Jamie studied him. "What kind of trouble?"

"The man in charge of the Namib field – Hans Zimmerman – he's bad. The workers hate him. They're talking about walking out. If they do, your guards will try to stop them and there will be a riot."

Jamie never took his eyes from Banda's face.

"Do you remember I once mentioned a man to you – John Tengo Javabu?"

"Yes. He's a political leader. I've been reading about him. He's been stirring up a *donderstorm*."

"I'm one of his followers."

Jamie nodded. "I see. I'll do what has to be done," Jamie promised.

"Good. You've become a powerful man, Jamie. I'm glad."

"Thank you, Banda."

"And you have a fine-looking son."

Jamie could not conceal his surprise. "How do you know that?"

"I like to keep track of my friends." Banda rose to his feet. "I have a meeting to go to, Jamie. I'll tell them things will be straightened out at the Namib."

"Yes. I'll attend to it." He followed the large black man to the door. "When will I see you again?"

Banda smiled. "I'll be around. You can't get rid of me that easily."

And Banda was gone.

When Jamie returned to Klipdrift, he sent for young David Blackwell. "Has there been any trouble at the Namib field, David?"

"No, Mr. McGregor." He hesitated. "But I have heard rumors that there might be."

"The supervisor there is Hans Zimmerman. Find out if he's mistreating the workers. If he is, put a stop to it. I want you to go up there yourself."

"I'll leave in the morning."

When David arrived at the diamond field at the Namib, he spent two hours quietly talking to the guards and the workers. What he heard filled him with a cold fury. When he had learned what he wanted to know, he went to see Hans Zimmerman.

Hans Zimmerman was a goliath of a man. He weighed three hundred pounds and was six feet, six inches tall. He had a sweaty, porcine face and red-veined eyes, and was one of the most unattractive men David Blackwell had ever seen. He was also one of the most efficient supervisors employed by Kruger-Brent,

Ltd. He was seated at a desk in his small office, dwarfing the room, when David walked in.

Zimmerman rose and shook David's hand. "Pleasure to see you, Mr. Blackwell. You should have told me you was comin'."

David was sure that word of his arrival had already reached Zimmerman.

"Whiskey?"

"No, thank you."

Zimmerman leaned back in his chair and grinned. "What can I do for you? Ain't we diggin' up enough diamonds to suit the boss?"

Both men knew that the diamond production at the Namib was excellent. "I get more work out of my kaffirs than anyone else in the company," was Zimmerman's boast.

"We've been getting some complaints about conditions here," David said.

The smile faded from Zimmerman's face. "What kind of complaints?"

"That the men here are being treated badly and – "

Zimmerman leaped to his feet, moving with surprising agility. His face was flushed with anger. "These ain't men. These are kaffirs. You people sit on your asses at headquarters and – "

"Listen to me," David said. "There's no – "

"You listen to *me!* I produce more fuckin' diamonds than anybody else in the company, and you know why? Because I put the fear of God into these bastards."

"At our other mines," David said, "we're paying fifty-nine shillings a month and keep. You're paying your workers only fifty shillings a month."

"You complainin' 'cause I made a better deal for you? The only thing that counts is profit."

"Jamie McGregor doesn't agree," David replied. "Raise their wages."

Zimmerman said sullenly, "Right. It's the boss's money."

"I hear there's a lot of whipping going on."

Zimmerman snorted. "Christ, you can't hurt a native, mister. Their hides are so thick they don't even feel the goddamned whip. It just scares them."

"Then you've scared three workers to death, Mr. Zimmerman."

Zimmerman shrugged. "There's plenty more where they came from."

He's a bloody animal, David thought. *And a dangerous one*. He looked up at the huge supervisor. "If there's any more trouble here, you're going to be replaced." He rose to his feet. "You'll start treating your men like human beings. The punishments are to stop immediately. I've inspected their living quarters. They're pigsties. Clean them up."

Hans Zimmerman was glaring at him, fighting to control his temper. "Anything else?" he finally managed to say.

"Yes. I'll be back here in three months. If I don't like what I see, you can find yourself a job with another company. Good day." David turned and walked out.

Hans Zimmerman stood there for a long time, filled with a simmering rage. The *fools*, he thought. *Uitlanders*. Zimmerman was a Boer, and his father had been a Boer. The land belonged to them and God had put the blacks there to serve them. If God had meant them to be treated like human beings, he would not have made their skins black. Jamie McGregor did not understand that. But what could you expect from an *uitlander*, a native-lover? Hans Zimmerman knew he would have to be a little more careful in the future. But he would show them who was in charge at the Namib.

Kruger-Brent, Ltd., was expanding, and Jamie McGregor was away a good deal of the time. He bought a paper mill in Canada and a shipyard in Australia. When he was home, Jamie spent all his time with his son, who looked more like his father each day. Jamie felt an inordinate pride in the boy. He wanted to take the child with him on his long trips, but Margaret refused to let him.

"He's much too young to travel. When he's older, he can go with you. If you want to be with him, you'll see him here."

Before Jamie had realized it, his son had had his first birthday, and then his second, and Jamie marveled at how the time raced by. It was 1887.

To Margaret, the last two years had dragged by. Once a week Jamie would invite guests to dinner and Margaret was his gracious hostess. The other men found her witty and intelligent and enjoyed talking to her. She knew that several of the men found her very attractive indeed, but of course they never made an overt move, for she was the wife of Jamie McGregor.

When the last of the guests had gone, Margaret would ask, "Did the evening go well for you?"

Jamie would invariably answer, "Fine. Good night," and be off to look in on little Jamie. A few minutes later, Margaret would hear the front door close as Jamie left the house.

Night after night, Margaret McGregor lay in her bed thinking about her life. She knew how much she was envied by the women in town, and it made her ache, knowing how little there was to envy. She was living out a charade with a husband who treated her worse than a stranger. If only he would notice her! She wondered what he would do if one morning at breakfast she took up the bowl that contained his oatmeal especially imported from Scotland and poured it over his stupid head. She could visualize the expression on his face, and the fantasy tickled her so much that she began to giggle, and the laughter turned into deep, wrenching sobs. *I don't want to love him any more. I won't. I'll stop, somehow, before I'm destroyed . . . .*

By 1890, Klipdrift had more than lived up to Jamie's expectations. In the seven years he had been there, it had become a full-fledged boomtown, with prospectors pouring in from every part of the world. It was the same old story. They came by coach and in wagons and on foot. They came with nothing but the rags they wore. They needed food and equipment and shelter and grubstake money, and Jamie McGregor was there to supply it all. He had shares in dozens of producing diamond and gold mines, and his name and reputation grew.

One morning Jamie received a visit from an attorney for De Beers, the giant conglomerate that controlled the huge diamond mines at Kimberley.

"What can I do for you?" Jamie asked.

"I've been sent to make you an offer, Mr. McGregor. De Beers would like to buy you out. Name your price."

It was a heady moment. Jamie grinned and said, "Name *yours*."

David Blackwell was becoming more and more important to Jamie. In the young American Jamie McGregor saw himself as he once had been. The boy was honest, intelligent and loyal. Jamie made David his secretary, then his personal assistant and, finally, when the boy was twenty-one, his general manager.

To David Blackwell, Jamie McGregor was a surrogate father. When David's own father suffered a heart attack, it was Jamie who arranged for a hospital and paid for the doctors, and when David's father died, Jamie McGregor took care of the funeral arrangements. In the five years David had worked for Kruger-Brent, Ltd., he had come to admire Jamie more than any man he had ever known. He was aware of the problem between Jamie and Margaret, and deeply regretted it, because he liked them both. *But its none of my business*, David told himself. *My job is to help Jamie in any way I can.*

Jamie spent more and more time with his son. The boy was five now, and the first time Jamie took him down in the mines, young Jamie talked of nothing else for a week. They went on camping trips, and they slept in a tent under the stars. Jamie was used to the skies of Scotland, where the stars knew their rightful places in the firmament. Here in South Africa, the constellations were confusing. In January Canopus shone brilliantly overhead, while in May it was the Southern Cross that was near the zenith. In June, which was South Africa's winter, Scorpio was the glory of the heavens. It was puzzling. Still, it was a very special feeling for Jamie to lie on the warm earth and look up at the timeless sky with his son at his side and know they were part of the same eternity.

They rose at dawn and shot game for the pot: partridge, guinea fowl, reedbuck and oribi. Little Jamie had his own pony, and father and son rode along the veld carefully avoiding the six-foot holes dug by the ant bear, deep enough to engulf a horse and rider, and the smaller holes dug by the mere-cat.

There was danger on the veld. On one trip Jamie and his son were camped at a riverbed where they were almost killed by a band of migrating springbok. The first sign of trouble was a faint cloud of dust on the horizon. Hares and jackals and merecats raced past and large snakes came out of the brush looking for rocks under which to hide. Jamie looked at the horizon again. The dust cloud was coming closer.

"Let's get out of here," he said.

"Our tent – "

"Leave it!"

The two of them quickly mounted and headed for the top of a high hill. They heard the drumming of hooves and then they could see the front rank of the springbok, racing in a line at least three miles long. There were more than half a million of them, sweeping away everything in their path. Trees were torn down and shrubs were pulverized, and in the wake of the relentless tide were the bodies of hundreds of small animals. Hares, snakes, jackals and guinea fowl were crushed beneath the deadly hooves. The air was filled with dust and thunder, and when it was finally over, Jamie estimated that it had lasted more than three hours.

On Jamie's sixth birthday, his father said, "I'm going to take you to Cape Town next week and show you what a real city looks like."

"Can Mother go with us?" Jamie asked. "She doesn't like shooting, but she likes cities."

His father ruffled the boy's hair and said, "She's busy here, Son. Just the two of us men, eh?"

The child was disturbed by the fact that his mother and father seemed so distant with each other, but then he did not understand it.

They made the journey in Jamie's private railway car. By the year 1891, railways were becoming the pre-eminent means of travel in South Africa, for trains were inexpensive, convenient and fast. The private railway car Jamie ordered built for himself was seventy-one feet long and had four paneled staterooms that could accommodate twelve persons, a salon that could be used as an office, a dining compartment, a bar-room and a fully equipped kitchen. The staterooms had brass beds, Pintsch gas lamps and wide picture windows.

"Where are all the passengers?" the young boy asked.

Jamie laughed. "We're all the passengers. It's your train, Son."

Young Jamie spent most of the trip staring out the window, marveling at the endless expanse of land speeding past.

"This is God's land," his father told him. "He filled it with precious minerals for us. They're all in the ground, waiting to be discovered. What's been found so far is only the beginning, Jamie."

When they arrived at Cape Town, young Jamie was awed by the crowds and the huge buildings. Jamie took his son down to the McGregor Shipping Line, and pointed out half a dozen ships loading and unloading in the harbor. "You see those? They belong to us."

When they returned to Klipdrift, young Jamie was bursting with the news of all he had seen. "Papa owns the whole city!" the boy exclaimed. "You'd love it, Mama. You'll see it next time."

Margaret hugged her son to her. "Yes, darling."

Jamie spent many nights away from home, and Margaret knew he was at Madam Agnes's. She had heard he had bought a house for one of the women so that he could visit her privately. She had no way of knowing whether it was true. Margaret only knew that whoever she was, she wanted to kill her.

To retain her sanity, Margaret forced herself to take an interest in the town. She raised funds to build a new church and started a mission to help the families of prospectors who were in dire need. She demanded that Jamie use one of his railroad cars to transport prospectors free of charge back to Cape Town when they had run out of money and hope.

"You're asking me to throw away good money, woman," he growled. "Let 'em walk back the same way they came."

"They're in no condition to walk," Margaret argued. "And if they stay, the town will have to bear the cost of clothing and feeding them."

"All right," Jamie finally grumbled. "But it's a damn fool idea."

"Thank you, Jamie."

He watched Margaret march out of his office, and, in spite of himself, he could not help feeling a certain pride in her. *She'd make a fine wife for someone*, Jamie thought.

The name of the woman Jamie set up in a private house was Maggie, the pretty prostitute who had sat next to Margaret at the baby shower. It was ironic, Jamie thought, that she should bear his wife's name. They were nothing alike. This Maggie was a twenty-one-year-old blonde with a pert face and a lush body – a tigress in bed. Jamie had paid Madam Agnes well for letting him take the girl, and he gave Maggie a generous allowance. Jamie was very discreet when he visited the small house. It was almost always at night, and he was certain he was unobserved. In fact, he was observed by many people, but not one of them cared to comment about it. It was Jamie McGregor's town, and he had the right to do anything he pleased.

On this particular evening, Jamie was finding no joy. He had gone to the house anticipating pleasure, but Maggie was in a foul mood. She lay sprawled across the large bed, her rose-colored dressing gown not quite concealing her ripe breasts or the silky, golden triangle between her thighs. "I'm sick of stayin' locked up in this damned house," she said. "It's like I'm a slave or somethin'! At least at Madam Agnes's there was somethin' goin' on all the time. Why don't you ever take me with you when you travel?"

"I've explained that, Maggie. I can't – "

She leaped out of bed and stood defiantly before him, her dressing gown wide open. "Horseshit! You take your *son* everywhere. Ain't I as good as your son?"

"No," Jamie said. His voice was dangerously quiet. "You're not." He walked over to the bar and poured himself a brandy. It was his fourth – much more than he usually drank.

"I don't mean a damned thing to you," Maggie screamed. "I'm just a piece of arse." She threw her head back and laughed derisively. "Big, moral Scotchman!"

"Scot – not Scotchman."

"For Christ's sake, will you stop criticizin' me? Everythin' I do ain't good enough. Who the hell do you think you are, my bloody father?"

Jamie had had enough. "You can go back to Madam Agnes's tomorrow. I'll tell her you're coming." He picked up his hat and headed for the door.

"You can't get rid of me like this, you bastard!" She followed him, wild with anger.

Jamie stopped at the door. "I just did." And he disappeared into the night.

To his surprise, he found he was walking unsteadily. His mind seemed fuzzy. Perhaps he had had more than four brandies. He was not sure. He thought about Maggie's naked body in bed that evening, and how she had flaunted it, teasing him, then withdrawing. She had played with him stroking him and running her soft tongue over his body until he was hard and eager for her. And then she had begun the fight, leaving him inflamed and unsatisfied.

When Jamie reached home, he entered the front hall, and as he started toward his room, he passed the closed door of Margaret's bedroom. There was a light from under the door. She was still awake. Jamie suddenly began to picture Margaret in bed, wearing a thin nightgown. Or perhaps nothing. He remembered how her rich, full body had writhed beneath him under the trees by the Orange River. With the liquor guiding him, he opened Margaret's bedroom door and entered.

She was in bed reading by the light of a kerosene lamp. She looked up in surprise. "Jamie . . . is something wrong?"

"'Cause I decide to pay my wife a l'il visit?" His words were slurred.

She was wearing a sheer nightgown, and Jamie could see her ripe breasts straining against the fabric. God, *she has a lovely body!* He began to take off his clothes.

Margaret leaped out of bed, her eyes very wide. "What are you doing?"

Jamie kicked the door shut behind him and walked over to her. In a moment, he had thrown her onto the bed and he was next to her, naked. "God, I want you, Maggie."

In his drunken confusion, he was not sure which Maggie he wanted. How she fought him! Yes, this was his little wildcat. He laughed as he finally managed to subdue her flailing arms and legs, and she was suddenly open to him and pulling him close and saying, "Oh, my darling, my darling Jamie. I need you so much," and he thought, *I shouldn't have been so mean to you. In the morning I'm gonna tell you you don't have to go back to Madam Agnes . . .*

When Margaret awoke the next morning, she was alone in bed. She could still feel Jamie's strong male body inside hers and she heard him saying, God, *I want you, Maggie*, and she was filled with a wild, complete joy. She had been right all along. He did love her. It had been worth the wait, worth the years of pain and loneliness and humiliation.

Margaret spent the rest of the day in a state of rapture. She bathed and washed her hair and changed her mind a dozen times about which dress would please Jamie most. She sent the cook away so that she herself could prepare Jamie's favorite dishes. She set the dining-room table again and again before she was satisfied with the candles and flowers. She wanted this to be a perfect evening.

Jamie did not come home for dinner. Nor did he come home all night. Margaret sat in the library waiting for him until three o'clock in the morning, and then she went to her bed, alone.

When Jamie returned home the following evening, he nodded politely to Margaret and walked on to his son's room. Margaret stood staring after him in stunned bewilderment, and then slowly turned to look at herself in the mirror. The mirror told her that she had never looked as beautiful, but when she looked closer she could not recognize the eyes. They were the eyes of a stranger.

10

"Well, I have some wonderful news for you, Mrs. McGregor," Dr. Teeger beamed. "You're going to have a baby."

Margaret felt the shock of his words and did not know whether to laugh or cry. *Wonderful news?* To bring another child into a loveless marriage was impossible. Margaret could no longer bear the humiliation. She would have to find a way out, and even as she was thinking it, she felt a sudden wave of nausea that left her drenched in perspiration.

Dr. Teeger was saying, "Morning sickness?"

"A bit."

He handed her some pills. "Take these. They'll help. You're in excellent condition, Mrs. McGregor. Not a thing to worry about. You run along home and tell the good news to your husband."

"Yes," she said dully. "I'll do that."

They were at the dinner table when she said, "I saw the doctor today. I'm going to have a baby."

Without a word, Jamie threw down his napkin, arose from his chair and stormed out of the room. That was the moment when Margaret learned she could hate Jamie McGregor as deeply as she could love him.

It was a difficult pregnancy, and Margaret spent much of the time in bed, weak and tired. She lay there hour after hour, fantasizing, visualizing Jamie at her feet, begging for forgiveness, making wild love to her again. But they were only fantasies. The reality was that she was trapped. She had nowhere to go, and even if she could leave, he would never allow her to take her son with her.

Jamie was seven now, a healthy, handsome boy with a quick mind and a sense of humor. He had drawn closer to his mother, as though somehow sensing the unhappiness in her. He made little gifts for her in school and brought them home, and Margaret would smile and thank him and try to lift herself out of her depression. When young Jamie asked why his father stayed away nights and never took her out, Margaret would reply, "Your father is a very important man, Jamie, doing important things, and he's very busy."

What's between his father and me is my problem, Margaret thought, *and I'll not have Jamie hating his father because of it.*

Margaret's pregnancy became more and more apparent. When she went out on the street, acquaintances would stop her and say, "It won't be long now, will it, Mrs. McGregor? I'll bet it's going to be a fine boy like little Jamie. Your husband must be a happy man."

Behind her back, they said, "Poor thing. She's lookin" peaked – she must have found out about the whore he's taken as his mistress . . ."

Margaret tried to prepare young Jamie for the new arrival. "You're going to have a new brother or sister, darling. Then you'll have someone to play with all the time. Won't that be nice?"

Jamie hugged her and said, "It will be more company for you, Mother."

And Margaret fought to keep back the tears.

The labor pains began at four o'clock in the morning. Mrs. Talley sent for Hannah, and the baby was delivered at noon. It was a healthy baby girl, with her mother's mouth and her father's chin, and black hair curling around her little red face. Margaret named her Kate. *It's a good, strong name*, Margaret thought. *And she's going to need her strength. We all are. I've got to take the children away from here. I don't know how yet, but I must find a way.*

David Blackwell burst into Jamie McGregor's office without knocking, and Jamie looked up in surprise. "What the hell – ?"

"They're rioting at the Namib!"

Jamie stood up. "*What?* What happened?"

"One of the black boys was caught trying to steal a diamond. He cut a hole under his armpit and hid the stone inside it. As a lesson, Hans Zimmerman flogged him in front of the other workers. The boy died. He was twelve years old."

Jamie's face filled with rage. "Sweet Jesus! I ordered a stop to flogging at all the mines."

"I warned Zimmerman."

"Get rid of the bastard."

"We can't find him."
"Why not?"
"The blacks have him. The situation's out of control."
Jamie grabbed his hat. "Stay here and take care of things until I get back."
"I don't think it's safe for you to go up there, Mr. McGregor. The native that Zimmerman killed was from the Barolong tribe. They don't forgive, and they don't forget. I could – "
But Jamie was gone.

When Jamie McGregor was ten miles away from the diamond field, he could see the smoke. All the huts at the Namib had been set to the torch. *The damned fools!* Jamie thought. *They're burning their own houses.* As his carriage drew closer, he heard the sounds of gunshots and screams. Amid the mass confusion, uniformed constables were shooting at blacks and coloreds who were desperately trying to flee. The whites were outnumbered ten to one, but they had the weapons.
When the chief constable, Bernard Sothey, saw Jamie McGregor, he hurried up to him and said, "Don't worry, Mr. McGregor. We'll get every last one of the bastards."
"The hell you will," Jamie cried. "Order your men to stop shooting."
"*What?* If we – "
"Do as I say!" Jamie watched, sick with rage, as a black woman fell under a hail of bullets. "Call your men off."
"As you say, sir." The chief constable gave orders to an aide, and three minutes later all shooting had stopped.
There were bodies on the ground everywhere. "If you want my advice," Sothey said, "I'd – "
"I don't want your advice. Bring me their leader."
Two policemen brought a young black up to where Jamie was standing. He was handcuffed and covered with blood, but there was no fear in him. He stood tall and straight, his eyes blazing, and Jamie remembered Banda's word for Bantu pride: *isiko.*
"I'm Jamie McGregor."
The man spat.
"What happened here was not my doing. I want to make it up to your men."
"Tell that to their widows."
Jamie turned to Sothey. "Where's Hans Zimmerman?"
"We're still looking for him, sir."
Jamie saw the gleam in the black man's eyes, and he knew that Hans Zimmerman was not going to be found.
He said to the man, "I'm closing the diamond field down for three days. I want you to talk to your people. Make a list of your complaints, and I'll look

at it. I promise you I'll be fair. I'll change everything here that's not right."

The man studied him, a look of skepticism on his face.

"There will be a new foreman in charge here, and decent working conditions. But I'll expect your men back at work in three days."

The chief constable said, incredulously, "You mean you're gonna let him go? He killed some of my men."

"There will be a full investigation, and – "

There was the sound of a horse galloping toward them, ad Jamie turned. It was David Blackwell, and the unexpected sight of him sounded an alarm in Jamie's mind.

David leaped off his horse. "Mr. McGregor, your son has disappeared."

The world suddenly grew cold.

Half the population of Klipdrift turned out to join in the search. They covered the countryside, looking through gulleys, ravines and klops. There was no trace of the boy.

Jamie was like a man possessed. *He's wandered away somewhere, that's all. He'll be back.*

He went into Margaret's bedroom. She was lying in bed, nursing the baby.

"Is there any news?" she demanded.

"Not yet, but I'll find him." He looked at his baby daughter for an instant, then turned and walked out without another word.

Mrs. Talley came into the room, twisting her hands in her apron. "Don't you worry, Mrs. McGregor. Jamie is a big boy. He knows how to take care of himself."

Margaret's eyes were blinded by tears. *No one would harm little Jamie, would they? Of course not.*

Mrs. Talley reached down and took Kate from Margaret's arms.

"Try to sleep."

She took the baby into the nursery and laid her down in her crib. Kate was looking up at her, smiling.

"You'd better get some sleep too, little one. You've got a busy life ahead of you."

Mrs. Talley walked out of the room, closing the door behind her.

At midnight, the bedroom window silently slid open and a man climbed into the room. He walked over to the crib, threw a blanket over the infant's head and scooped her up in his arms.

Banda was gone as quickly as he had come.

It was Mrs. Talley who discovered that Kate was missing. Her first thought was that Mrs. McGregor had come in the night and taken her. She walked into Margaret's bedroom and asked, "Where's the baby?"

And from the look on Margaret's face, she knew instantly what had happened.

*

As another day went by with no trace of his son, Jamie was on the verge of collapsing. He approached David Blackwell. "You don't think anything had has happened to him?" His voice was barely under control.

David tried to sound convincing. "I'm sure not, Mr. McGregor."

But he *was* sure. He had warned Jamie McGregor that the Bantus neither forgave nor forgot, and it was a Bantu who had been cruelly murdered. David was certain of one thing: If the Bantus had taken little Jamie, he had died a horrible death, for they would exact their vengeance in kind.

Jamie returned home at dawn, drained. He had led a search party of towns-people, diggers and constables, and they had spent the night looking without success in every conceivable place for the young boy.

David was waiting when Jamie walked into the study. David rose to his feet. "Mr. McGregor, your daughter has been kidnapped."

Jamie stared at him in silence, his face pale. Then he turned and walked into his bedroom.

Jamie had not been to bed for forty-eight hours, and he fell into bed, utterly exhausted, and slept. He was under the shade of a large baobab tree and in the distance across the trackless veld a lion was moving toward him. Young Jamie was shaking him. *Wake up, Papa, a lion is coming.* The animal was moving toward them faster now. His son was shaking him harder. *Wake up!*

Jamie opened his eyes. Banda was standing over him. Jamie started to speak, but Banda put a hand over Jamie's mouth.

"Quiet!" He allowed Jamie to sit up.

"Where's my son?" Jamie demanded.

"He's dead."

The room began to spin.

"I'm sorry. I was too late to stop them. Your people spilled Bantu blood. My people demanded vengeance."

Jamie buried his face in his hands. "Oh, my God! What did they do to him?"

There was a bottomless sorrow in Banda's voice. "They left him out in the desert. I – I found his body and buried him."

"Oh, no! Oh, please, no!"

"I tried to save him, Jamie."

Jamie slowly nodded, accepting it. Then dully, "What about my daughter?"

"I took her away before they could get her. She's back in her bedroom, asleep. She'll be all right if you do what you promised."

Jamie looked up, and his face was a mask of hatred. "I'll keep my promise. But I want the men who killed my son. They're going to pay."

Banda said quietly, "Then you will have to kill my whole tribe, Jamie."

Banda was gone.

It was only a nightmare, but she kept her eyes tightly closed, because she knew if she opened them the nightmare would become real and her children would be dead. So she played a game. She would keep her eyes squeezed shut until she felt little Jamie's hand on hers saying, "It's all right, Mother. We're here. We're safe."

She had been in bed for three days, refusing to talk to anyone or see anyone. Dr. Teeger came and went, and Margaret was not even aware of it. In the middle of the night Margaret was lying in bed with her eyes shut when she heard a loud crash from her son's room. She opened her eyes and listened. There was another sound. Little Jamie was back!

Margaret hurriedly got out of bed and ran down the corridor toward the closed door of her son's room. Through the door, she could hear strange animal sounds. Her heart pounding wildly, she pushed the door open.

Her husband lay on the floor, his face and body contorted. One eye was closed and the other stared up at her grotesquely. He was trying to speak, and the words came out as slobbering animal sounds.

Margaret whispered, "Oh, Jamie – Jamie!"

Dr. Teeger said, "I'm afraid the news is bad, Mrs. McGregor. Your husband has had a severe stroke. There's a fifty-fifty chance he'll live – but if he does, he'll be a vegetable. I'll make arrangements to get him into a private sanitarium where he can get the proper care."

"No."

He looked at Margaret in surprise. "No . . . what?"

"No hospital. I want him here with me."

The doctor considered for a moment. "All right. You'll need a nurse. I'll arrange – "

"I don't want a nurse. I'll take care of Jamie myself."

Dr. Teeger shook his head. "That won't be possible, Mrs. McGregor. You don't know what's involved. Your husband is no longer a functioning human being. He's completely paralyzed and will be for as long as he lives."

Margaret said, "I'll take care of him."

Now Jamie finally, truly, belonged to her.

11

Jamie McGregor lived for exactly one year from the day he was taken ill, and it was the happiest time of Margaret's life. Jamie was totally helpless. He could neither talk nor move. Margaret cared for her husband, tended to all his needs, and kept him at her side day and night. During the day, she propped him up in a wheelchair in the sewing room, and while she knitted sweaters and throw-robes for him, she talked to him. She discussed all the little household problems he had never had time to listen to before, and she told him how well little Kate was getting along. At night she carried Jamie's skeletal body to her bedroom and gently lay him in bed next to her. Margaret tucked him in and they had their one-sided chat until Margaret was ready to go to sleep.

David Blackwell was running Kruger-Brent, Ltd. From time to time, David came to the house with papers for Margaret to sign, and it was painful for David to see the helpless condition Jamie was in. *I owe this man everything*, David thought.

"You chose well, Jamie," Margaret told her husband. "David is a fine man." She put down her knitting and smiled. "He reminds me of you a bit. Of course, there was never anyone as clever as you, my darling, and there never will be again. You were so fair to look at, Jamie, and so kind and strong. And you weren't afraid to dream. Now all your dreams have come true. The company is getting bigger every day." She picked up her knitting again. "Little Kate is beginning to talk. I'll swear she said 'mama' this morning . . ."

Jamie sat there, propped up in his chair, one eye staring ahead.

"She has your eyes and your mouth. She's going to grow up to be a beauty . . ."

The following morning when Margaret awakened, Jamie McGregor was dead. She took him in her arms and held him close to her.

"Rest, my darling, rest. I've always loved you so much, Jamie. I hope you know that. Good-bye, my own dear love."

She was alone now. Her husband and her son had left her. There was only herself and her daughter. Margaret walked into the baby's room and looked down at Kate, sleeping in her crib. *Katherine. Kate*. The name came from the Greek, and it meant clear or pure. It was a name given to saints and nuns and queens.

Margaret said aloud, "Which are you going to be, Kate?"

It was a time of great expansion in South Africa, but it was also a time of great strife. There was a long-standing Transvaal dispute between the Boers and the British, and it finally came to a head. On Thursday, October 12, 1899, on Kate's seventh birthday, the British declared war on the Boers, and three days later the Orange Free State was under attack. David tried to persuade Margaret to take Kate and leave South Africa, but Margaret refused to go.

"My husband is here," she said.

There was nothing David could do to dissuade her. "I'm going to join with the Boers," David told her. "Will you be all right?"

"Yes, of course," Margaret said. "I'll try to keep the company going."

The next morning David was gone.

The British had expected a quick and easy war, no more than a mopping-up operation, and they began with a confident, lighthearted holiday spirit. At the

Hyde Park Barracks in London, a send-off supper was given, with a special menu showing a British soldier holding up the head of a boar on a tray. The menu read:

SEND-OFF SUPPER

To the CAPE SQUADRON,
November 27, 1899

MENU

Oysters – Blue Points
Compo Soup
Toady in the Hole
Sandy Sole
Mafeking Mutton
Transvaal Turnips. Cape Sauce
Pretoria Pheasants
White Sauce
Tinker Taters
Peace Pudding. Massa Ices
Dutch Cheese
Dessert

(You are requested not to throw shells under the tables)

Boer Whines – Long Tom
Hollands-in-Skin
Orange Wine

The British were in for a surprise. The Boers were on their own home territory, and they were tough and determined. The first battle of the war took place in Mafeking, hardly more than a village, and for the first time, the British began to realize what they were up against. More troops were quickly sent over from England. They laid siege to Kimberley, and it was only after a fierce and bloody fight that they went on to take Ladysmith. The cannons of the Boers had a longer range than those of the British, so long-range guns were removed from British warships, moved inland and manned by sailors hundreds of miles from their ships.

In Klipdrift, Margaret listened eagerly for news of each battle, and she and those around her lived on rumors, their moods varying from elation to despair, depending on the news. And then one morning one of Margaret's employees came running into her office and said, "I just heard a report that the British are advancing on Klipdrift. They're going to kill us all!"

"Nonsense. They wouldn't dare touch us."

Five hours later, Margaret McGregor was a prisoner of war.

Margaret and Kate were taken to Paardeberg, one of the hundreds of prison camps that had sprung up all over South Africa. The prisoners were kept inside an enormous open field, ringed by barbed wire and guarded by armed British soldiers. The conditions were deplorable.

Margaret took Kate in her arms and said, "Don't worry, darling, nothing's going to happen to you."

But neither of them believed it. Each day became a calendar of horrors. They watched those around them die by the tens and the hundreds and then by the thousands as fever swept through the camp. There were no doctors or medication for the wounded, and food was scarce. It was a constant nightmare that went on for almost three harrowing years. The worst of it was the feeling of utter helplessness. Margaret and Kate were at the complete mercy of their captors. They were dependent upon them for meals and shelter, for their very lives. Kate lived in terror. She watched the children around her die, and she was afraid that she would be next. She was powerless to protect her mother or herself, and it was a lesson she was never to forget. *Power.* If you had power, you had food. You had medicine. You had freedom. She saw those around her fall ill and die, and she equated power with life. *One day*, Kate thought, *I'll have power. No one will be able to do this to me again.*

The violent battles went on – Belmont and Graspan and Stormberg and Spioenkop – but in the end, the brave Boers were no match for the might of the British Empire. In 1902, after nearly three years of bloody war, the Boers surrendered. Fifty-five thousand Boers fought, and thirty-four thousand of their soldiers, women and children died. But what filled the survivors with a deep savage bitterness was the knowledge that twenty-eight thousand of those died in British concentration camps.

On the day the gates of the camp were flung open, Margaret and Kate returned to Klipdrift. A few weeks later, on a quiet Sunday, David Blackwell arrived. The war had matured him, but he was still the same grave, thoughtful David Margaret had learned to rely upon. David had spent these hellish years fighting and worrying about whether Margaret and Kate were dead or alive. When he found them safe at home, he was filled with joy.

"I wish I could have protected you both," David told Margaret:

"That's all past, David. We must think only of the future."

And the future was Kruger-Brent, Ltd.

For the world, the year 1900 was a clean slate on which history was going to be written, a new era that promised peace and limitless hope for everyone. A new century had begun, and it brought with it a series of astonishing inventions that reshaped life around the globe. Steam and electric automobiles were replaced by the combustion engine. There were submarines and airplanes. The world population exploded to a billion and a half people. It was a time to grow and expand, and during the next six years, Margaret and David took full advantage of every opportunity.

During those years, Kate grew up with almost no supervision. Her mother was too busy running the company with David to pay much attention to her. She was a wild child, stubborn and opinionated and intractable. One afternoon when Margaret came home from a business meeting, she saw her fourteen-year-old daughter in the muddy yard in a fistfight with two boys. Margaret stared in horrified disbelief.

"Bloody hell!" she said under her breath. "That's the girl who one day is going to run Kruger-Brent, Limited! God help us all!"

Book Two

Kate and David
1906–1914

12

On a hot summer night in 1914, Kate McGregor was working alone in her office at the new Kruger-Brent, Ltd., headquarters building in Johannesburg when she heard the sound of approaching automobiles. She put down the papers she had been studying, walked over to the window and looked out. Two cars of police and a paddy wagon had come to a stop in front of the building. Kate watched, frowning, as half a dozen uniformed policemen leaped from the cars and hurried to cover the two entrances and exits to the building. It was late, and the streets were deserted. Kate caught a wavy reflection of herself in the window. She was a beautiful woman, with her father's light-gray eyes and her mother's full figure.

There was a knock at the office door and Kate called, "Come in."

The door opened and two uniformed men entered. One wore the bars of a superintendent of police.

"What on earth is going on?" Kate demanded.

"I apologize for disturbing you at this late hour, Miss McGregor. I'm Superintendent Cominsky."

"What's the problem, Superintendent?"

"We've had a report that an escaped killer was seen entering this building a short time ago."

There was a shocked look on Kate's face. "Entering *this* building?"

"Yes, ma'am. He's armed and dangerous."

Kate said nervously, "Then I would very much appreciate it, Superintendent, if you would find him and get him out of here."

"That's exactly what we intend to do, Miss McGregor. You haven't seen or heard anything suspicious, have you?"

"No. But I'm alone here, and there are a lot of places a person could hide. I'd like you to have your men search this place thoroughly."

"We'll get started immediately, ma'am."

The superintendent turned and called to the men in the hallway, "Spread out. Start at the basement and work your way up to the roof." He turned to Kate. "Are any of the offices locked?"

"I don't believe so," Kate said, "but if they are, I'll open them for you."

Superintendent Cominsky could see how nervous she was, and he did not blame her. She would be even more nervous if she knew how desperate the man was for whom they were looking. "We'll find him," the superintendent assured Kate.

Kate picked up the report she had been working on, but she was unable to concentrate. She could hear the police moving through the building, going from office to office. *Would they find him?* She shivered.

The policemen moved slowly, methodically searching every possible hiding place from the basement to the roof. Forty-five minutes later, Superintendent Cominsky returned to Kate's office.

She looked at his face. "You didn't find him."

"Not yet, ma'am, but don't worry – "

"I *am* worried, Superintendent. If there is an escaped killer in this building, I want you to find him."

"We will, Miss McGregor. We have tracking dogs."

From the corridor came the sound of barking and a moment later a handler came into the office with two large German shepherds on leashes.

"The dogs have been all over the building, sir. They've searched every place but this office."

The superintendent turned to Kate. "Have you been out of this office anytime in the past hour or so?"

"Yes. I went to look up some records in the file room. Do you think he could have – ?" She shuddered. "I'd like you to check this office, please."

The superintendent gave a signal and the handler slipped the leashes off the dogs and gave the command, "Track."

The dogs went crazy. They raced to a closed door and began barking wildly.

"Oh, my God!" Kate cried. "He's in there!"

The superintendent pulled out his gun. "Open it," he ordered.

The two policemen moved to the closet door with drawn guns and pulled the door open. The closet was empty. One of the dogs raced to another door and pawed excitedly at it.

"Where does that door lead?" Superintendent Cominsky asked.

"To a washroom."

The two policemen took up places on either side of the door and yanked it open. There was no one inside.

The handler was baffled. "They've never behaved this way before." The dogs were racing around the room frantically. "They've got the scent," the handler said. "But where is he?"

Both dogs ran to the drawer of Kate's desk and continued their barking.

"There's your answer," Kate tried to laugh. "He's in the drawer."

Superintendent Cominsky was embarrassed. "I'm sorry to have troubled you, Miss McGregor." He turned to the handler and snapped, "Take these dogs out of here."

"You're not leaving?" There was concern in Kate's voice.

"Miss McGregor, I can assure you you're perfectly safe. My men have covered every inch of this building. You have my personal guarantee that he's not here. I'm afraid it was a false alarm. My apologies."

Kate swallowed. "You certainly know how to bring excitement to a woman's evening."

Kate stood looking out the window, watching the last of the police vehicles drive away. When they were out of sight, she opened her desk drawer and pulled out a blood-stained pair of canvas shoes. She carried them down the corridor to a door marked *Private, Authorized Personnel Only*, and entered. The room was bare except for a large, locked, walk-in safe built into the wall, the vault where Kruger-Brent, Ltd., stored its diamonds before shipping. Quickly, Kate dialed the combination on the safe and pulled open the giant door. Dozens of metal safe-deposit boxes were built into the sides of the vault, all crammed with diamonds. In the center of the room, lying on the floor half-conscious, was Banda.

Kate knelt beside him. "They've gone."

Banda slowly opened his eyes and managed a weak grin. "If I had a way out of this vault, do you know how rich I'd be, Kate?"

Kate carefully helped him to his feet. He winced with pain as she touched his arm. She had wrapped a bandage around it, but blood was seeping through.

"Can you put your shoes on?" She had taken them from him earlier, and, to confuse the tracking dogs she knew would be brought in, she had walked around her office in them and then hidden them in her drawer.

Now Kate said, "Come on. We have to get you out of here."

Banda shook his head. "I'll make it on my own. If they catch you helping me, you'll be in more trouble than you can handle."

"Let me worry about that."

Banda took a last look around the vault.

"Do you want any samples?" Kate asked. "You can help yourself."

Banda looked at her and saw that she was serious. "Your daddy made me that offer once, a long time ago."

Kate smiled wryly. "I know."

"I don't need money. I just have to leave town for a while."

"How do you think you're going to get out of Johannesburg?"

"I'll find a way."

"Listen to me. The police have roadblocks out by now. Every exit from the city will be watched. You won't have a chance by yourself."

He said stubbornly, "You've done enough." He had managed to put his shoes on. He was a forlorn-looking figure, standing there in a torn, bloodied shirt and jacket. His face was seamed and his hair was gray, but when Kate looked at him she saw the tall, handsome figure she had first met as a child.

"Banda, if they catch you, they'll kill you," Kate said quietly. "You're coming with me."

She knew she was right about the roadblocks. Every exit from Johannesburg would be guarded by police patrols. Banda's capture was a top priority and the authorities had orders to bring him in dead or alive. The railroad stations and roads would be watched.

"I hope you have a better plan than your daddy had," Banda said. His voice was weak. Kate wondered how much blood he had lost.

"Don't talk. Save your strength. Just leave everything to me." Kate sounded more confident than she felt. Banda's life was in her hands, and she could not bear it if anything happened to him. She wished again, for the hundredth time, that David was not away. Well, she would simply have to manage without him.

"I'm going to bring my automobile around to the alley," Kate said. "Give me ten minutes, then come outside. I'll have the back door of the car open. Get in and lie on the floor. There will be a blanket to cover yourself with."

"Kate, they're going to search every automobile leaving the city. If – "

"We're not going by automobile. There's a train leaving for Cape Town at eight A.M. I ordered my private car connected to it."

"You're getting me out of here in your private railroad car?"

"That's right."

Banda managed a grin. "You McGregors really like excitement."

Thirty minutes later, Kate drove into the railroad yards. Banda was on the floor of the backseat, concealed by a blanket. They had had no trouble passing the roadblocks in the city, but now as Kate's car turned into the train yards, a light suddenly flashed on, and Kate saw that her way was blocked by several policemen. A familiar figure walked toward Kate's car.

"Superintendent Cominsky!"

He registered surprise. "Miss McGregor, what are you doing here?"

Kate gave him a quick, apprehensive smile. "You'll think I'm just a silly, weak female, Superintendent, but to tell you the truth, what happened back at the office scared the wits out of me. I decided to leave town until you catch this killer you're looking for. Or have you found him?"

"Not yet, ma'am, but we will. I have a feeling he'll make for these railroad yards. Wherever he runs, we'll catch him."

"I certainly hope so!"

"Where are you headed?"

"My railway car is on a siding up ahead. I'm taking it to Cape Town."

"Would you like one of my men to escort you?"

"Oh, thank you, Superintendent, but that won't be necessary. Now that I know where you and your men are, I'll breathe a lot easier, believe me."

Five minutes later, Kate and Banda were safely inside the private railway car. It was pitch black.

"Sorry about the dark," Kate said. "I don't want to light any lamps."

She helped Banda onto a bed. "You'll be fine here until morning. When we start to pull out, you'll hide out in the washroom."

Banda nodded. "Thank you."

Kate drew the shades. "Have you a doctor who will take care of you when we get to Cape Town?"

He looked up into her eyes. "*We?*"

"You didn't think I was going to let you travel alone while I missed all the fun?"

Banda threw back his head and laughed. *She's her father's daughter, all right.*

*

As dawn was breaking, an engine pulled up to the private railroad car and shunted it onto the main track in back of the train that was leaving for Cape Town. The car rocked back and forth as the connection was made.

At exactly eight o'clock, the train pulled out of the station. Kate had left word that she did not wish to be disturbed. Banda's wound was bleeding again, and Kate attended to it. She had not had a chance to talk to Banda since earlier that evening, when he had stumbled half-dead into her office. Now she said, "Tell me what happened, Banda."

Banda looked at her and thought, *Where can I begin?* How could he explain to her the *trekboers* who pushed the Bantus from their ancestral land? Had it started with them? Or had it started with the giant Oom Paul Kruger, President of the Transvaal, who said in a speech to the South African Parliament, "We must be the lords over the blacks and let them be a subject race . . ." Or had it begun with the great empire-builder Cecil Rhodes, whose motto was, "Africa for the whites?" How could he sum up the history of his people in a sentence? He thought of a way. "The police murdered my son," Banda said.

The story came pouring out. Banda's older son, Ntombenthle, was attending a political rally when the police charged in to break it up. Some shots were fired, and a riot began. Ntombenthle was arrested, and the next morning he was found hanged in his cell. "They said it was suicide," Banda told Kate. "But I know my son. It was murder."

"My God, he was so young," Kate breathed. She thought of all the times they had played together, laughed together. Ntombenthle had been such a handsome boy. "I'm sorry, Banda. I'm so sorry. But why are they after you?"

"After they killed him I began to rally the blacks. I had to fight back, Kate. I couldn't just sit and do nothing. The police called me an enemy of the state. They arrested me for a robbery I did not commit and sentenced me to prison for twenty years. Four of us made a break. A guard was shot and killed, and they're blaming me. I've never carried a gun in my life."

"I believe you," Kate said. "The first thing we have to do is get you somewhere where you'll be safe."

"I'm sorry to involve you in all this."

"You didn't involve me in anything. You're my friend."

He smiled. "You know the first white man I ever heard call me friend? Your daddy." He sighed. "How do you think you're going to sneak me off the train at Cape Town?"

"We're not going to Cape Town."

"But you said – "

"I'm a woman. I have a right to change my mind."

In the middle of the night when the train stopped at the station at Worcester, Kate arranged to have her private railroad car disconnected and shunted to a siding. When Kate woke up in the morning, she went over to Banda's cot. It was empty. Banda was gone. He had refused to compromise her any further. Kate was sorry, but she was sure he would be safe. He had many friends to take care of him. *David will be proud of me*, Kate thought.

"I can't believe you could be so stupid!" David roared, when Kate returned to Johannesburg and told him the news. "You not only jeopardized your own safety, but you put the company in danger. If the police had found Banda here, do you know what they would have done?"

Kate said defiantly, "Yes. They would have killed him."

David rubbed his forehead in frustration. "Don't you understand anything?"

"You're bloody right, I do! I understand that you're cold and unfeeling." Her eyes were ablaze with fury.

"You're still a child."

She raised her hand to strike him, and David grabbed her arms. "Kate, you've got to learn to control your temper."

The words reverberated in Kate's head. *Kate, you've got to learn to control your temper . . .*

It was so long ago. She was four years old, in the middle of a fistfight with a boy who had dared tease her. When David appeared, the boy ran away. Kate started to chase him, and David grabbed her. "Hold it, Kate. You've got to learn to control your temper. Young ladies don't get into fistfights."

"I'm not a young lady," Kate snapped. "Let go of me." David released her.

The pink frock she was wearing was muddied and torn, and her cheek was bruised.

"We'd better get you cleaned up before your mother sees you," David told her.

Kate looked after the retreating boy with regret. "I could have licked him if you had left me alone."

David looked down into the passionate little face and laughed. "You probably could have."

Mollified, Kate allowed him to pick her up and carry her into her house. She liked being in David's arms. She liked everything about David. He was the only grown-up who understood her. Whenever he was in town, he spent time with her. In relaxed moments, Jamie had told young David about his adventures with Banda, and now David told the stories to Kate. She could not get enough of them.

"Tell me again about the raft they built."

And David would tell her.

"Tell me about the sharks . . . Tell me about the sea *mis* . . . Tell me about the day . . ."

Kate did not see very much of her mother. Margaret was too involved in running the affairs of Kruger-Brent, Ltd. She did it for Jamie.

Margaret talked to Jamie every night, just as she had during the year before he died. "David is such a great help, Jamie, and he'll be around when Kate's running the company. I don't want to worry you, but I don't know what to do with that child . . ."

Kate was stubborn and willful and impossible. She refused to obey her mother or Mrs. Talley. If they chose a dress for her to wear, Kate would discard it for another. She would not eat properly. She ate what she wanted to, when she wanted to, and no threat or bribe could sway her. When Kate was forced to go to a birthday party, she found ways to disrupt it. She had no girl friends. She refused to go to dancing class and instead spent her time playing rugby with teen-age boys. When Kate finally started school, she set a record for mischief. Margaret found herself going to see the headmistress at least once a month to persuade her to forgive Kate and let her remain in school.

"I don't understand her, Mrs. McGregor," the headmistress sighed. "She's extremely bright, but she rebels against simply everything. I don't know what to do with her."

Neither did Margaret.

The only one who could handle Kate was David. "I understand you're invited to a birthday party this afternoon," David said.

"I hate birthday parties."

David stooped down until he was at her eye level. "I know you do, Kate. But the father of the little girl who's having the birthday party is a friend of mine. It will make me look bad if you don't attend and behave like a lady."

Kate stared at him. "Is he a *good* friend of yours?"

"Yes."

"I'll go."

Her manners that afternoon were impeccable.

"I don't know how you do it," Margaret told David. "It's magic."

"She's just high-spirited," David laughed. "She'll grow out of it. The important thing is to be careful not to break that spirit."

"I'll tell you a secret," Margaret said grimly, "half the time I'd like to break her neck."

When Kate was ten, she said to David, "I want to meet Banda."

David looked at her in surprise. "I'm afraid that's not possible, Kate. Banda's farm is a long way from here."

"Are you going to take me there, David, or do you want me to go by myself?"

The following week David took Kate to Banda's farm. It was a good-sized piece of land, two morgens, and on it Banda raised wheat, sheep and ostriches. The living accommodations were circular huts with walls made of dried mud. Poles supported a cone-shaped roof covered with thatches. Banda stood in front, watching as Kate and David drove up and got out of the carriage. Banda looked at the gangling, serious-faced girl at David's side and said, "I'd have known you were Jamie McGregor's daughter."

"And I'd have known you were Banda," Kate said gravely. "I came to thank you for saving my father's life."

Banda laughed. "Someone's been telling you stories. Come in and meet my family."

Banda's wife was a beautiful Bantu woman named Ntame. Banda had two sons, Ntombenthle, seven years older than Kate, and Magena, six years older. Ntombenthle was a miniature of his father. He had the same handsome features and proud bearing and an inner dignity.

Kate spent the entire afternoon playing with the two boys. They had dinner in the kitchen of the small, neat farmhouse. David felt uncomfortable eating with a black family. He respected Banda, but it was traditional that there was no socializing between the two races. In addition to that, David was concerned about Banda's political activities. There were reports that he was a disciple of John Tengo Javabu, who was fighting for drastic social changes. Because mine owners could not get enough natives to work for them, the government had imposed a tax of ten shillings on all natives who did not work as mine laborers, and there were riots all over South Africa.

In the late afternoon, David said, "We'd better get started home, Kate. We have a long ride."

"Not yet." Kate turned to Banda. "Tell me about the sharks . . ."

From that time on, whenever David was in town, Kate made him take her to visit Banda and his family.

David's assurance that Kate would grow out of her high-spiritedness showed no signs of coming to pass. If anything, she grew more willful every day. She flatly refused to take part in any of the activities that other girls her age participated in. She insisted on going into the mines with David, and he took her hunting and fishing and camping. Kate adored it. One day when Kate and David were fishing the Vaal, and Kate gleefully pulled in a trout larger than anything David had caught, he said, "You should have been born a boy."

She turned to him in annoyance. "Don't be silly, David. Then I couldn't marry you."

David laughed.

"We *are* going to be married, you know."

"I'm afraid not, Kate. I'm twenty-two years older than you. Old enough to be your father. You'll meet a boy one day, a nice young man – "

— I don't want a nice young man," she said wickedly. "I want you."

"If you're really serious," David said, "then I'll tell you the secret to a man's heart."

"Tell me!" Kate said eagerly.

"Through his stomach. Clean that trout and let's have lunch."

There was not the slightest doubt in Kate's mind that she was going to marry David Blackwell. He was the only man in the world for her.

Once a week Margaret invited David to dinner at the big house. As a rule, Kate preferred to eat dinner in the kitchen with the servants, where she did not have to mind her manners. But on Friday nights when David came, Kate sat in the big dining-room. David usually came alone, but occasionally he would bring a female guest and Kate would hate her instantly.

Kate would get David alone for a moment and say, with sweet innocence, "I've never seen hair that shade of blond," or, "She certainly has peculiar taste in dresses, hasn't she?" or, "Did she use to be one of Madam Agnes's girls?"

When Kate was fourteen, her headmistress sent for Margaret. "I run a respectable school, Mrs. McGregor. I'm afraid your Kate is a bad influence."

Margaret sighed. "What's she done now?"

"She's teaching the other children words they've never heard before." Her face was grim. "I might add, Mrs. McGregor, that I've never heard some of the words before. I can't imagine where the child picked them up."

Margaret could. Kate picked them up from her street friends. *Well*, Margaret decided, *it is time to end all that.*

The headmistress was saying, "I do wish you would speak to her. We'll give her another chance, but – "

"No. I have a better idea. I'm going to send Kate away to school."

When Margaret told David her idea, he grinned. "She's not going to like that."

"I can't help it. Now the headmistress is complaining about the language Kate uses. She gets it from those prospectors she's always following around. My daughter's starting to sound like them, look like them and smell like them. Frankly, David, I don't understand her at all. I don't know why she behaves as she does. She's pretty, she's bright, she's – "

"Maybe she's too bright."

"Well, too bright or not, she's going away to school."

When Kate arrived home that afternoon, Margaret broke the news to her.

Kate was furious. "You're trying to get rid of me!"

"Of course I'm not, darling. I just think you'd be better off – "

"I'm better off *here*. All my friends are here. You're trying to separate me from my friends."

"If you're talking about that riffraff you – "

"They're *not* riffraff. They're as good as anybody."

"Kate, I'm not going to argue with you. You're going away to a boarding school for young ladies, and that's that."

"I'll kill myself," Kate promised.

"All right, darling. There's a razor upstairs, and if you look around, I'm sure you'll find various poisons in the house."

Kate burst into tears. "Please don't do this to me, Mother."

Margaret took her in her arms. "It's for your own good, Kate. You'll be a young woman soon. You'll be ready for marriage. No man is going to marry a girl who talks and dresses and behaves the way you do."

"That's not true," Kate sniffled. "David doesn't mind."

"What does David have to do with this?"

"We're going to be married."

Margaret sighed. "I'll have Mrs. Talley pack your things."

There were half a dozen good English boarding schools for young girls. Margaret decided that Cheltenham, in Gloucestershire, was best suited for Kate. It was a school noted for its rigid discipline. It was set on acres of land surrounded by high battlements and, according to its charter, was founded for the daughters of noblemen and gentlemen. David did business with the husband of the headmistress, Mrs. Keaton, and he had no trouble arranging for Kate to be enrolled there.

When Kate heard where she was going, she exploded anew. "I've heard about that school! It's awful. I'll come back like one of those stuffed English dolls. Is that what you'd like?"

"What I would like is for you to learn some manners," Margaret told her.

"I don't need manners. I've got brains."

"That's not the first thing a man looks for in a woman," Margaret said dryly, "and you're becoming a woman."

"I don't want to become a woman," Kate screamed. "Why the bloody hell can't you just leave me alone?"

"I will not have you using that language."

And so it went until the morning arrived when Kate was to leave. Since David was going to London on a business trip, Margaret asked, "Would you mind seeing that Kate gets to school safely? The Lord only knows where she'll end up if she goes on her own."

"I'll be happy to," David said.

"You! You're as bad as my mother! You can't wait to get rid of me."

David grinned. "You're wrong. I can wait."

They traveled by private railway car from Klipdrift to Cape Town and from there by ship to Southampton. The journey took four weeks. Kate's pride would not let her admit it, but she was thrilled to be traveling with David. *Its like a honeymoon*, she thought, *except that we're not married. Not yet.*

Aboard ship, David spent a great deal of time working in his stateroom. Kate curled up on the couch, silently watching him, content to be near him.

Once she asked, "Don't you get bored working on all those figures, David?"

He put down his pen and looked at her. "They're not just figures, Kate. They're stories."

"What kind of stories?"

"If you know how to read them, they're stories about companies we're buying or selling, people who work for us. Thousands of people all over the world earn a living because of the company your father founded."

"Am I anything like my father?"

"In many ways, yes. He was a stubborn, independent man."

"Am I a stubborn, independent woman?"

"You're a spoiled brat. The man who marries you is going to have one hell of a life."

Kate smiled dreamily. *Poor David.*

In the dining room, on their last night at sea, David asked, "Why are you so difficult, Kate?"

"Am I?"

"You know you are. You drive your poor mother crazy." Kate put her hand over his.

"Do I drive you crazy?"

David's face reddened. "Stop that. I don't understand you."

"Yes, you do."

"Why can't you be like other girls your age?"

"I'd rather die first. I don't want to be like anybody else."

"God knows you're not!"

"You won't marry anyone else until I'm grown up enough for you, will you, David? I'll get older as fast as I can. I promise. Just don't meet anybody you love, please."

He was touched by her earnestness. He took her hand in his and said, "Kate, when I get married, I'd like my daughter to be exactly like you."

Kate rose to her feet and said in a voice that rang through the dining salon, "You can bloody well go to hell, David Blackwell!" And she stormed out of the room, as everyone stared.

They had three days together in London, and Kate loved every minute of it.

"I have a treat for you," David told her. "I got two tickets for *Mrs. Wiggs of the Cabbage Patch.*"

"Thank you, David. I want to go to the Gaiety."

"You can't. That's a – a music-hall revue. That's not for you."

"I won't know until I see it, will I?" she said stubbornly.

They went to the Gaiety.

Kate loved the look of London. The mixture of motorcars and carriages, the ladies beautifully dressed in lace and tulle and light satins and glittering jewelry, and the men in dinner clothes with piqué waistcoats and white shirtfronts. They had dinner at the Ritz, and a late supper at the Savoy. And when it was time to leave, Kate thought, *We'll come back here. David and I will come back here.*

When they arrived at Cheltenham, they were ushered into the office of Mrs. Keaton.

"I want to thank you for enrolling Kate," David said.

"I'm sure we'll enjoy having her. And it's a pleasure to accommodate a friend of my husband."

At that moment, Kate knew she had been deceived. It was *David* who had wanted her sent away and had arranged for her to come here.

She was so furious and hurt she refused to say good-bye to him.

13

Cheltenham School was unbearable. There were rules and regulations for everything. The girls had to wear identical uniforms, down to their knickers. The school day was ten hours long, and every minute was rigidly structured. Mrs. Keaton ruled the pupils and her staff with a rod of iron. The girls were there to learn manners and discipline, etiquette and decorum, so that they could one day attract desirable husbands.

Kate wrote her mother, "It's a bloody prison. The girls here are awful. All they ever talk about are bloody clothes and bloody boys. The bloody teachers are monsters. They'll never keep me here. I'm going to escape."

Kate managed to run away from the school three times, and each time she was caught and brought back, unrepentant.

At a weekly staff meeting, when Kate's name was brought up, one of the teachers said, "The child is uncontrollable. I think we should send her back to South Africa."

Mrs. Keaton replied, "I'm inclined to agree with you, but let's look upon it as a challenge. If we can succeed in disciplining Kate McGregor, we can succeed in disciplining anyone."

Kate remained in school.

To the amazement of her teachers, Kate became interested in the farm that the school maintained. The farm had vegetable gardens, chickens, cows, pigs and horses. Kate spent as much time as possible there, and when Mrs. Keaton learned of this, she was immensely pleased.

"You see," the headmistress told her staff, "it was simply a question of patience. Kate has finally found her interest in life. One day she will marry a landowner and be of enormous assistance to him."

The following morning, Oscar Denker, the man in charge of running the farm, came to see the headmistress. "One of your students," he said, "that Kate McGregor – I wish you'd keep her away from my farm."

"Whatever are you talking about?" Mrs. Keaton asked. "I happen to know she's very interested."

"Sure she is, but do you know what she's interested in? The animals fornicating, if you'll excuse my language."

"*What?*"

"That's right. She stands around all day, just watching the animals do it to each other."

"Bloody hell!" Mrs. Keaton said.

Kate still had not forgiven David for sending her into exile, but she missed him terribly. *It's my fate*, she thought gloomily, *to be in love with a man I hate*. She counted the days she was away from him, like a prisoner marking time until the day of release. Kate was afraid he would do something dreadful, like marry another woman while she was trapped in the bloody school. *If he does*, Kate thought, *I'll kill them both. No. I'll just kill her. They'll arrest me and hang me, and when I'm on the gallows, he'll realize that he loves me. But it will be too late. He'll beg me to forgive him. "Yes, David, my darling. I forgive you. You were too foolish to know when you held a great love in the palm of your hand. You let it fly away like a little bird. Now that little bird is about to be hanged. Good-bye, David." But at the last minute she would be reprieved and David would take her in his arms and carry her off to some exotic country where the food was better than the bloody slop they served at bloody Cheltenham.*

Kate received a note from David saying he was going to be in London and would come to visit her. Kate's imagination was inflamed. She found a dozen hidden meanings in his note. *Why was he going to be in England? To be near her, of course. Why was he coming to visit her? Because he finally knew he loved her and could not bear to be away from her any longer. He was going to sweep her off her feet and take her out of this terrible place*. She could scarcely contain her happiness. Kate's fantasy was so real that the day David arrived, Kate went around saying good-bye to her classmates. "My lover is coming to take me out of here," she told them.

The girls looked at her in silent disbelief. All except Georgina Christy, who scoffed, "You're lying again: Kate McGregor."

"Just wait and see. He's tall and handsome, and he's mad about me."

When David arrived, he was puzzled by the fact that all the girls in the school seemed to be staring at him. They looked at him and whispered and giggled, and the minute they caught his eye, they blushed and turned away.

"They act as though they've never seen a man before," David told Kate. He looked at her suspiciously. "Have you been saying anything about me?"

"Of course not," Kate said haughtily. "Why would I do that?"

They ate in the school's large dining room, and David brought Kate up to date on everything that was happening at home. "Your mother sends her love. She's expecting you home for the summer holiday."

"How is mother?"

"She's fine. She's working hard."

"Is the company doing well, David?"

He was surprised by her sudden interest. "It's doing very well. Why?"

Because, Kate thought, *someday it will belong to me, and you and I will share it.* "I was just curious."

He looked at her untouched plate. "You're not eating."

Kate was not interested in food. She was waiting for the magic moment, the moment when David would say, "*Come away with me, Kate. You're a woman now, and I want you. We're going to be married.*"

The dessert came and went. Coffee came and went, and still no magic words from David.

It was not until he looked at his watch and said, "Well, I'd better he going or I'll miss my train," that Kate realized with a feeling of horror that he had not come to take her away at all. The bastard was going to leave her there to rot!

David had enjoyed his visit with Kate. She was a bright and amusing child, and the waywardness she had once shown was now under control. David patted Kate's hand fondly and asked, "Is there anything I can do for you before I leave, Kate?"

She looked him in the eye and said sweetly, "Yes, David, there is. You can do me an enormous favor. *Get out of my bloody life!*" And she walked out of the room with great dignity, her head held high, leaving him sitting there, mouth agape.

Margaret found that she missed Kate. The girl was unruly and contrary, but Margaret realized that she was the only living person she loved. *She's going to be a great woman*, Margaret thought with pride. *But I want her to have the manners of a lady.*

Kate came home for summer vacation. "How are you getting along in school?" Margaret asked.

"I hate it! It's like being surrounded by a hundred nannies."

Margaret studied her daughter. "Do the other girls feel the same way, Kate?"

"What do *they* know?" she said contemptuously. "You should *see* the girls at that school! They've been sheltered all their lives. They don't know a damn thing about life."

"Oh, dear," Margaret said. "That must be awful for you."

"Don't laugh at me, please. The've never even been to South Africa. The only animals they've seen have been in zoos. None of them has ever seen a diamond mine or a gold mine."

"Underprivileged."

Kate said, "All right. But when I turn out like them, you're going to be bloody sorry."

"Do you think you'll turn out like them?"

Kate grinned wickedly. "Of course not! Are you mad?"

An hour after Kate arrived home, she was outside playing rugby with the children of the servants. Margaret watched her through the window and thought, *I'm wasting my money. She's never going to change.*

That evening, at dinner, Kate asked casually, "Is David in town?"

"He's been in Australia. He'll be back tomorrow, I think."

"Is he coming to dinner Friday night?"

"Probably." She studied Kate and said, "You like David, don't you?"

She shrugged. "He's all right, I suppose."

"I see," Margaret said. She smiled to herself as she remembered Kate's vow to marry David.

"I don't *dislike* him, Mother. I mean, I like him as a human being. I just can't stand him as a *man*."

When David arrived for dinner Friday night, Kate flew to the door to greet him. She hugged him and whispered in his ear, "I forgive you. Oh, I've missed you so much, David! Have you missed me?"

Automatically he said, "Yes." And then he thought with astonishment, *By God, I have missed her.* He had never known anyone like this child. He had watched her grow up, and each time he encountered her she was a revelation to him. She was almost sixteen years old and she had started to fill out. She had let her black hair grow long, and it fell softly over her shoulders. Her features had matured, and there was a sensuality about her that he had not noticed before. She was a beauty, with a quick intelligence and a strong will. *She's going to be a handful for some man*, David thought.

At dinner David asked, "How are you getting along in school, Kate?"

"Oh, I just love it," she gushed. "I'm really learning a lot. The teachers are wonderful, and I've made a lot of great friends."

Margaret sat in stunned silence.

"David, will you take me to the mines with you?"

"Is that how you want to waste your vacation?"

"Yes, please."

A trip down into the mines took a full day, and that meant she would be with David all that time.

"If your mother says it's all right – "

"Please, mother!"

"All right, darling. As long as you're with David, I know you'll be safe." Margaret hoped David would be safe.

The Kruger-Brent Diamond Mine near Bloemfontein was a gigantic operation, with hundreds of workers engaged in digging, engineering, washing or sorting.

"This is one of the company's most profitable mines," David told Kate. They were above ground in the manager's office, waiting for an escort to take them down into the mine. Against one wall was a showcase filled with diamonds of all colors and sizes.

"Each diamond has a distinct characteristic," David explained. "The original diamonds from the banks of the Vaal are alluvial, and their sides are worn down from the abrasion of centuries."

He's more handsome than ever, Kate thought. *I love his eyebrows.*

"These stones all come from different mines, but they can be easily identified by their appearance. See this one? You can tell by the size and yellow cast that it comes from Paardspan. De Beers's diamonds have an oily-looking surface and are dodecahedral in shape."

He's brilliant. He knows everything.

"You can tell this one is from the mine at Kimberley because it's an octahedron. Their diamonds range from smoky-glassy to pure white."

I wonder if the manager thinks David is my lover. I hope so.

"The color of a diamond helps determine its value. The colors are named on a scale of one to ten. At the top is the tone blue-white, and at the bottom is the draw, which is a brown color."

He smells so wonderful. Its such a – such a male smell. I love his arms and shoulders. I wish –

"Kate!"

She said guiltily, "Yes, David?"

"Are you listening to me?"

"Of course I am." There was indignation in her voice. "I've heard every word."

They spent the next two hours in the bowels of the mine, and then had lunch. It was Kate's idea of a heavenly day.

When Kate returned home late in the afternoon, Margaret said, "Did you enjoy yourself?"

"It was wonderful. Mining is really fascinating."

Half an hour later, Margaret happened to glance out the window. Kate was on the ground wrestling with the son of one of the gardeners.

The following year, Kate's letters from school were cautiously optimistic. She had been made captain of the hockey and lacrosse teams, and was at the head of her class scholastically. The school was not really all *that* bad, she wrote, and there were even a few girls in her classes who were reasonably nice. She asked permission to bring two of her friends home for the summer vacation, and Margaret was delighted. The house would be alive again with the sound of youthful laughter. She could not wait for her daughter to come home. Her dreams were all for Kate now. *Jamie and I are the past*, Maggie thought. *Kate is the future. And what a wonderful, bright future it will be!*

When Kate was home during her vacation, all the eligible young men of Klipdrift flocked around besieging her for dates, but Kate was not interested in any of them. David was in America, and she impatiently awaited his return. When he came to the house, Kate greeted him at the door. She wore a white dress circled in by a black velvet belt that accentuated her lovely bosom. When David embraced her, he was astonished by the warmth of her response. He drew back and looked at her. There was something different about her, something knowing. There was an expression in her eyes he could not define, and it made him vaguely uneasy.

The few times David saw Kate during that vacation she was surrounded by boys, and he found himself wondering which would be the lucky one. David was called back to Australia on business, and when he returned to Klipdrift, Kate was on her way to England.

In Kate's last year of school, David appeared unexpectedly one evening. Usually his visits were preceded by a letter or a telephone call. This time there had been no warming.

"David! What a wonderful surprise!" Kate hugged him. "You should have told me you were coming. I would have –"

"Kate, I've come to take you home."

She pulled back and looked up at him. "Is something wrong?"

"I'm afraid your mother is very ill."

Kate stood stark still for a moment. "I'll get ready."

Kate was shocked by her mother's appearance. She had seen her only a few months earlier, and Margaret had seemed to be in robust health. Now she was pale and emaciated, and the bright spirit had gone out of her eyes. It was as though the cancer that was eating at her flesh had also eaten at her soul.

Kate sat at the side of the bed and held her mother's hand in hers. "Oh, Mother," she said. "I'm so bloody sorry."

Margaret squeezed her daughter's hand. "I'm ready, darling. I suppose I've been ready ever since your father died." She looked up at Kate. "Do you want to hear something silly? I've never told this to a living soul before." She hesitated, then went on. "I've always been worried that there was no one to take proper care of your father. Now I can do it."

Margaret was buried three days later. Her mother's death shook Kate deeply. She had lost her father and a brother, but she had never known them; they were only storied figments of the past. Her mother's death was real and painful. Kate was eighteen years old and suddenly alone in the world, and the thought of that was frightening.

David watched her standing at her mother's graveside, bravely fighting not to cry. But when they returned to the house, Kate broke down, unable to stop sobbing. "She was always so w-wonderful to me, David, and I was such a r-rotten daughter."

David tried to console her. "You've been a wonderful daughter, Kate."

"I was n-nothing b-but trouble. I'd give anything if I could m-make it up to her. I didn't want her to die, David! Why did God do this to her?"

He waited, letting Kate cry herself out. When she was calmer, David said, "I know it's hard to believe now, but one day this pain will go away. And you know what you'll be left with, Kate? Happy memories. You'll remember all the good things you and your mother had."

"I suppose so. Only right now it hurts so b-bloody much."

The following morning they discussed Kate's future.

"You have family in Scotland," David reminded her.

"No!" Kate replied sharply. "They're not family. They're relatives." Her voice was bitter. "When Father wanted to come to this country, they laughed at him. No one would help him except his mother, and she's dead. No. I won't have anything to do with them."

David sat there thinking. "Do you plan to finish out the school term?" Before Kate could answer, David went on. "I think your mother would have wanted you to."

"Then I'll do it." She looked down at the floor, her eyes unseeing. "Bloody hell," Kate said.

"I know," David said gently. "I know."

Kate finished the school term as class valedictorian, and David was there for the graduation.

Riding from Johannesburg to Klipdrift in the private railway car, David said, "You know, all this will belong to you in a few years. This car, the mines, the company – it's yours. You're a very rich young woman. You can sell the company for many millions of pounds." He looked at her and added, "Or you can keep it. You'll have to think about it."

"I have thought about it," Kate told him. She looked at him and smiled. "My father was a pirate, David. A wonderful old pirate. I wish I could have known him. I'm not going to sell this company. Do you know why? Because the pirate named it after two guards who were trying to kill him. Wasn't that a lovely thing to do? Sometimes at night when I can't sleep, I think about my father and Banda crawling through the sea *mis*, and I can hear the voices of the guards: *Kruger . . . Brent . . .* " She looked up at David. "No, I'll never sell my father's company. Not as long as you'll stay on and run it."

David said quietly, "I'll stay as long as you need me."

"I've decided to enroll in a business school."

"A business school?" There was surprise in his voice.

"This is 1910," Kate reminded him. "They have business schools in Johannesburg where women are allowed to attend."

"But – "

"You asked me what I wanted to do with my money." She looked him in the eye and said, "I want to earn it."

14

Business school was an exciting new adventure. When Kate had gone to Cheltenham, it had been a chore, a necessary evil. This was different. Every class taught her something useful, something that would help her when she ran the company. The courses included accounting, management, international trade and business administration. Once a week David telephoned to see how she was getting along.

"I love it," Kate told him. "It's really exciting, David."

One day she and David would be working together, side by side, late at night, all by themselves. *And one of those nights, David would turn to her and say, "Kate, darling, I've been such a blind fool. Will you* marry me?" *And an instant later, she would be in his arms . . .*

But that would have to wait. In the meantime, she had a lot to learn. Resolutely, Kate turned to her homework.

The business course lasted two years, and Kate returned to Klipdrift in time to celebrate her twentieth birthday. David met her at the station. Impulsively, Kate flung her arms around him ad hugged him. "Oh, David, I'm so happy to see you."

He pulled away and said awkwardly, "It's nice to see you, Kate." There was an uncomfortable stiffness in his manner.

"Is something wrong?"

"No. It's – it's just that young ladies don't go around hugging men in public."

She looked at him a moment. "I see. I promise not to embarrass you again."

As they drove to the house, David covertly studied Kate. She was a hauntingly beautiful girl, innocent and vulnerable, and David was determined that he would never take advantage of that.

On Monday morning Kate moved into her new office at Kruger-Brent, Ltd. It was like suddenly being plunged into some exotic and bizarre universe that had its own customs and its own language. There was a bewildering array of divisions, subsidiaries, regional departments, franchises and foreign branches. The products that the company manufactured or owned seemed endless. There were steel mills, cattle ranches, a railroad, a shipping line and, of course, the foundation of the family fortune: diamonds and gold, zinc and platinum and magnesium, mined each hour around the clock, pouring into the coffers of the company.

Power.

It was almost too much to take in. Kate sat in David's office listening to him make decisions that affected thousands of people around the world. The general managers of the various divisions made recommendations, but as often as not, David overruled them.

"Why do you do that? Don't they know their jobs?" Kate asked.

"Of course they do, but that's not the point," David explained. "Each manager sees his own division as the center of the world, and that's as it should be. But someone has to have an overall view and decide what's best for the company. Come on. We're having lunch with someone I want you to meet."

David took Kate into the large, private dining room adjoining Kate's office. A young, raw-boned man with a lean face and inquisitive brown eyes was waiting for them.

"This is Brad Rogers," David said. "Brad, meet your new boss, Kate McGregor."

Brad Rogers held out his hand. "I'm pleased to meet you, Miss McGregor."

"Brad is our secret weapon," David said. "He knows as much about Kruger-Brent, Limited, as I do. If I ever leave, you don't have to worry. Brad will be here."

If I ever leave. The thought of it sent a wave of panic through Kate. *Of course, David would never leave the company.* Kate could think of nothing else through lunch, and when it was over she had no idea what she had eaten.

After lunch, they discussed South Africa.

"We're going to run into trouble soon," David warned. "The government has just imposed poll taxes."

"Exactly what does that mean?" Kate asked.

"It means that blacks, coloreds and Indians have to pay two pounds each for every member of their family. That's more than a month's wages for them."

Kate thought about Banda and was filled with a sense of apprehension. The discussion moved on to other topics.

Kate enjoyed her new life tremendously. Every decision involved a gamble of millions of pounds. Big business was a matching of wits, the courage to gamble and the instinct to know when to quit and when to press ahead.

"Business is a game," David told Kate, "played for fantastic stakes, and you're in competition with experts. If you want to win, you have to learn to be a master of the game."

And that was what Kate was determined to do. Learn.

Kate lived alone in the big house, except for the servants. She and David continued their ritual Friday-night dinners, but when Kate invited him over on any other night, he invariably found an excuse not to come. During business hours they were together constantly, but even then David seemed to have erected a barrier between them, a wall that Kate was unable to penetrate.

On her twenty-first birthday, all the shares in Kruger-Brent, Ltd., were turned over to Kate. She now officially had control of the company. "Let's have dinner tonight to celebrate," she suggested to David.

"I'm sorry, Kate, I have a lot of work to catch up on."

Kate dined alone that night, wondering why. *Was it she, or was it David?* He would have to be deaf, dumb and blind not to know how she felt about him, how she had always felt about him. She would have to do something about it.

The company was negotiating for a shipping line in the United States.

"Why don't you and Brad go to New York and close the deal?" David suggested to Kate. "It will be good experience for you."

Kate would have liked for David to have gone with her, but she was too proud to say so. She would handle this without him. Besides, she had never been to America. She looked forward to the experience.

The closing of the shipping-line deal went smoothly. "While you're over there," David had told her, "you should see something of the country."

Kate and Brad visited company subsidiaries in Detroit, Chicago, Pittsburgh and New York, and Kate was amazed by the size and energy of the United States. The highlight of Kate's trip was a visit to Dark Harbor, Maine, on an enchanting little island called Islesboro, in Penobscot Bay. She had been invited to dinner at the home of Charles Dana Gibson, the artist. There were twelve people at dinner and, except for Kate, they all had homes on the island.

"This place has an interesting history," Gibson told Kate. "Years ago, residents used to get here by small coasting vessels from Boston. When the boat landed, they'd be met by a buggy and taken to their houses."

"How many people live on this island?" Kate asked.

"About fifty families. Did you see the lighthouse when the ferry docked?"

"Yes."

"It's run by a lighthouse keeper and his dog. When a boat goes by the dog goes out and rings the bell."

Kate laughed. "You're joking."

"No, ma'am. The funny thing is the dog is deaf as a stone. He puts his ear against the bell to feel if there's any vibration."

Kate smiled. "It sounds as if you have a fascinating island here."

"It might be worth your while staying over and taking a look around in the morning."

On a impulse, Kate said, "Why not?"

She spent the night at the island's only hotel, the Islesboro Inn. In the morning she hired a horse and carriage, driven by one of the islanders. They left the center of Dark Harbor, which consisted of a general store, a hardware store and a small restaurant, and a few minutes later they were driving through a beautiful wooded area. Kate noticed that none of the little winding roads had names, nor were there any names on the mailboxes. She turned to her guide. "Don't people get lost here without any signs?"

"Nope. The islanders know where everythin' is."

Kate gave him a sidelong look. "I see."

At the lower end of the island, they passed a burial ground.

"Would you stop, please?" Kate asked.

She stepped out of the carriage and walked over to the old cemetery and wandered around looking at the tombstones.

JOB PENDLETON, DIED JANUARY 25, 1794, AGE 47. The epitaph read: *Beneath this stone, I rest my head in slumber sweet; Christ blessed the bed.* JANE, WIFE OF THOMAS PENDLETON, DIED FEBRUARY 25, 1802, AGE 47.

There were spirits here from another century, from an era long gone. CAPTAIN WILLIAM HATCH DROWNED IN LONG ISLAND SOUND, OCTOBER 1866, AGE 30 YEARS. The epitaph on his stone read: *Storms all weathered and life's seas crossed.*

Kate stayed there a long time, enjoying the quiet and peace. Finally, she returned to the carriage and they drove on.

"What is it like here in the winter?" Kate asked.

"Cold. The bay used to freeze solid, and they'd come from the mainland by sleigh. Now a' course, we got the ferry."

They rounded a curve, and there, next to the water below, was a beautiful white-shingled, two-story house surrounded by delphinium, wild roses and poppies. The shutters on the eight front windows were painted green, and next to the double doors were white benches and six pots of red geraniums. It looked like something out of a fairy tale.

"Who owns that house?"

"That's the old Dreben house. Mrs. Dreben died a few months back."

"Who lives there now?"

"Nobody, I reckon."

"Do you know if it's for sale?"

The guide looked at Kate and said, "If it is, it'll probably be bought by the son of one of the families already livin' here. The islanders don't take kindly to strangers."

It was the wrong thing to say to Kate.

One hour later, she was speaking to a lawyer for the estate. "It's about the Dreben house," Kate said. "Is it for sale?"

The lawyer pursed his lips. "Well, yes, and no."

"What does that mean?"

"It's for sale, but a few people are already interested in buying it."

The old families on the island, Kate thought. "Have they made an offer?"

"Not yet, but – "

"I'm making one," Kate said.

He said condescendingly, "That's an expensive house."

"Name your price."

"Fifty thousand dollars."

"Let's go look at it."

The inside of the house was even more enchanting than Kate had anticipated. The large, lovely hall faced the sea through a wall of glass. On one side of the hall was a large ballroom, and on the other side, a living room with fruitwood paneling stained by time and an enormous fireplace. There was a library, and a huge kitchen with an iron stove and a large pine worktable, and off of that was a butler's pantry and laundry room. Downstairs, the house had six bedrooms for the servants and one bathroom. Upstairs was a master bedroom suite and four smaller bedrooms. It was a much larger house than Kate had expected. *But when David and I have our children*, she thought, *we'll need all these rooms.* The grounds ran all the way down to the bay, where there was a private dock.

Kate turned to the lawyer. "I'll take it."

She decided to name it Cedar Hill House.

She could not wait to get back to Klipdrift to break the news to David.

On the way back to South Africa, Kate was filled with a wild excitement. The house in Dark Harbor was a sign, a symbol that she and David would be married. She knew he would love the house as much as she did.

On the afternoon Kate and Brad arrived back in Klipdrift, Kate hurried to David's office. He was seated at his desk, working, and the sight of him set Kate's heart pounding. She had not realized how much she had missed him.

David rose to his feet. "Kate! Welcome home!" And before she could speak, he said, "I wanted you to be the first to know. I'm getting married."

15

It had begun casually six weeks earlier. In the middle of a hectic day, David received a message that Tim O'Neil, the friend of an important American diamond buyer, was in Klipdrift and asking if David would be good enough to welcome him and perhaps take him to dinner. David had no time to waste on tourists, but he did not want to offend his customer. He would have asked Kate to entertain the visitor, but she was on a tour of the company's plants in North America with Brad Rogers. *I'm stuck*, David decided. He called the hotel where O'Neil was staying and invited him to dinner that evening.

"My daughter is with me," O'Neil told him. "I hope you don't mind if I bring her along?"

David was in no mood to spend the evening with a child. "Not at all," he said politely. He would make sure the evening was a short one.

They met at the Grand Hotel, in the dining room. When David arrived, O'Neil and his daughter were already seated at the table. O'Neil was a handsome, gray-haired Irish-American in his early fifties. His daughter, Josephine, was the most beautiful woman David had ever seen. She was in her early thirties, with a stunning figure, soft blond hair and clear blue eyes. The breath went out of David at the sight of her.

"I – I'm sorry I'm late," he said. "Some last-minute business."

Josephine watched his reaction to her with amusement. "Sometimes that's the most exciting kind," she said innocently. "My father tells me you're a very important man, Mr. Blackwell."

"Not really – and it's David."

She nodded. "That's a good name. It suggests great strength."

Before the dinner was over, David decided that Josephine O'Neil was much more than just a beautiful woman. She was intelligent, had a sense of humor and was skillful at making him feel at ease. David felt she was genuinely interested in him. She asked him questions about himself that no one had ever asked before. By the time the evening ended, he was already half in love with her.

"Where's your home?" David asked Tim O'Neil.

"San Francisco."

"Will you be going back soon?" He made it sound as casual as he could.

"Next week."

Josephine smiled at David. "If Klipdrift is as interesting as it promises to be, I might persuade Father to stay a little longer."

"I intend to make it as interesting as possible," David assured her. "How would you like to go down into a diamond mine?"

"We'd love it," Josephine answered. "Thank you."

At one time David had personally escorted important visitors down into the mines, but he had long since delegated that task to subordinates. Now he heard himself saying, "Would tomorrow morning be convenient?" He had half a dozen meetings scheduled for the morning, but they suddenly seemed unimportant.

He took the O'Neils down a rockshaft, twelve hundred feet below ground. The shaft was six feet wide and twenty feet long, divided into four compartments, one for pumping, two for hoisting the blue diamondiferous earth and one with a double-decked cage to carry the miners to and from work.

"I've always been curious about something," Josephine said. "Why are diamonds measured in carats?"

"The carat was named for the carob seed," David explained, "because of its consistency in weight. One carat equals two hundred milligrams, or one one-hundred-forty-second of an ounce."

Josephine said, "I'm absolutely fascinated, David."

And he wondered if she was referring only to the diamonds. Her nearness was intoxicating. Every time he looked at Josephine, David felt a fresh sense of excitement.

"You really should see something of the countryside," David told the O'Neils. "If you're free tomorrow, I'd be happy to take you around."

Before her father could say anything, Josephine replied, "That would be lovely."

David was with Josephine and her father every day after that, and each day David fell more deeply in love. He had never known anyone as bewitching.

When David arrived to pick up the O'Neils for dinner one evening and Tim O'Neil said, "I'm a bit tired tonight, David. Would you mind if I didn't go along?" David tried to hide his pleasure.

"No, sir. I understand."

Josephine gave David a mischievous smile. "I'll try to keep you entertained," she promised.

David took her to a restaurant in a hotel that had just opened. The room was crowded, but David was recognized and given a table immediately. A three-piece ensemble was playing American music.

David asked, "Would you like to dance?"

"I'd love to."

A moment later, Josephine was in his arms on the dance floor, and it was magic. David held her lovely body close to his, and he could feel her respond.

"Josephine, I'm in love with you."

She put a finger to his lips. "Please, David . . . don't . . ."

"Why?"

"Because I couldn't marry you."

"Do you love me?"

She smiled up at him, her blue eyes sparkling. "I'm crazy about you, my darling. Can't you tell?"

"Then why?"

"Because I could never live in Klipdrift. I'd go mad."

"You could give it a try."

"David, I'm tempted, but I know what would happen. If I married you and had to live here, I'd turn into a screaming shrew and we'd end up hating each other. I'd rather we said good-bye this way."

"I don't want to say good-bye."

She looked up into his face, and David felt her body melt into his. "David, is there any chance that you could live in San Francisco?"

It was an impossible idea. "What would I do there?"

"Let's have breakfast in the morning. I want you to talk to Father."

Tim O'Neil said, "Josephine has told me about your conversation last night. Looks like you two have a problem. But I might have a solution, if you're interested."

"I'm very interested, sir."

O'Neil picked up a brown-leather briefcase and removed some blueprints. "Do you know anything about frozen foods?"

"I'm afraid I don't."

"They first started freezing food in the United States in 1865. The problem was transporting it long distances without the food thawing out. We've got refrigerated railway cars, but no one's been able to come up with a way to refrigerate trucks." O'Neil tapped the blueprints. "Until now. I just received a patent on it. This is going to revolutionize the entire food industry, David."

David glanced at the blueprints. "I'm afraid these don't mean much to me, Mr. O'Neil."

"That doesn't matter. I'm not looking for a technical expert. I have plenty of those. What I'm looking for is financing and someone to run the business. This isn't some wild pipe dream. I've talked to the top food processors in the business. This is going to be big – bigger than you can imagine. I need someone like you."

"The company headquarters will be in San Francisco," Josephine added.

David sat there silent, digesting what he had just heard. "You say you've been given a patent on this?"

"That's right. I'm all set to move."

"Would you mind if I borrowed these blueprints and showed them to someone?"

"I have no objection at all."

The first thing David did was to check on Tim O'Neil. He learned that O'Neil had a solid reputation in San Francisco. He had been head of the science department at a Berkeley College there and was highly regarded. David knew nothing. about the freezing of food, but he intended to find out.

"I'll be back in five days, darling. I want you and your father to wait for me."

"As long as you like. I'll miss you," Josephine said.

"I'll miss you, too." And he meant it more than she knew.

David took the train to Johannesburg and made an appointment to see Edward Broderick, the owner of the largest meat-packing plant in South Africa.

"I want your opinion on something." David handed him the blueprints. "I need to know if this can work."

"I don't know a damned thing about frozen foods or trucks, but I know people who do. If you come back this afternoon, I'll have a couple of experts here for you, David."

At four o'clock that afternoon David returned to the packing plant. He found that he was nervous, in a state of uncertainty, because he was not sure bow he wanted the meeting to go. Two weeks earlier, he would have laughed if anyone had even suggested he would ever leave Kruger-Brent, Ltd. It was a part of him. He would have laughed even harder if they had told him he would have considered heading a little food company in San Francisco. It was insane, except for one thing: Josephine O'Neil.

There were two men in the room with Edward Broderick. "This is Dr. Crawford and Mr. Kaufman. David Blackwell."

They exchanged greetings. David asked, "Have you gentlemen had a chance to look at the blueprints?"

Dr. Crawford replied, "We certainly have, Mr. Blackwell. We've been over them thoroughly."

David took a deep breath. "And?"

"I understand that the United States Patent Office has granted a patent on this?"

"That's right."

"Well, Mr. Blackwell, whoever got that patent is going to be one very rich man."

David nodded slowly, filled with conflicting emotions.

"It's like all great inventions – it's so simple you wonder why someone didn't think of it sooner. This one can't miss."

David did not know how to react. He had half-hoped that the decision would be taken out of his hands. If Tim O'Neil's invention was useless, there was a chance of persuading Josephine to stay in South Africa. But what O'Neil had told him was true. It *did* work. Now David had to make his decision.

He thought of nothing else on the journey back to Klipdrift. If he accepted, it would mean leaving the company, starting up a new, untried business. He was an American, but America was a foreign country to him. He held an important position in one of the most powerful companies in the world. He loved his job. Jamie and Margaret McGregor had been very good to him. And then there was Kate. He had cared for her since she was a baby. He had watched her grow up from a stubborn, dirty-faced tomboy to a lovely young woman. Her life was a photo album in his mind. He turned the pages and there was Kate at four, eight, ten, fourteen, twenty-one – vulnerable, unpredictable . . .

By the time the train arrived at Klipdrift, David had made up his mind. He was not going to leave Kruger-Brent, Ltd.

He drove directly to the Grand Hotel and went up to the O'Neils" suite. Josephine opened the door for him.

"David!"

He took her in his arms and kissed her hungrily, feeling her warm body pressing against his.

"Oh, David, I've missed you so much. I don't ever want to be away from you again."

"You won't have to," David said slowly. "I'm going to San Francisco . . ."

David had waited with growing anxiety for Kate to return from the United States. Now that he had made his decision, he was eager to get started on his new life, impatient to marry Josephine.

And now Kate was back, and he was standing in front of her saying, "I'm getting married."

Kate heard the words through a roaring in her ears. She felt suddenly faint, and she gripped the edge of the desk for support. *I want to die*, she thought. *Please let me die.*

Somehow, from some deep wellspring of will, she managed a smile. "Tell me about her, David." She was proud of how calm her voice sounded. "Who is she?"

"Her name is Josephine O'Neil. She's been visiting here with her father. I know you two will be good friends, Kate. She's a fine woman."

"She must be, if you love her, David."

He hesitated. "There's one more thing, Kate. I'm going to be leaving the company."

The world was falling in on her. "Just because you're getting married, doesn't mean you have to – "

"It isn't that. Josephine's father is starting a new business in San Francisco. They need me."

"So – so you'll be living in San Francisco."

"Yes. Brad Rogers can handle my job easily, and we'll pick a top management team to back him up. Kate, I – I can't tell you what a difficult decision this was for me."

"Of course, David. You – you must love her very much. When do I get to meet the bride?"

David smiled, pleased at how well Kate was taking the news. "Tonight, if you're free for dinner."

"Yes, I'm free."

She would not let the tears come until she was alone.

The four of them had dinner at the McGregor mansion. The moment Kate saw Josephine, she blanched, *Oh God! No wonder he's in love with her!* She was dazzling. Just being in her presence made Kate feel awkward and ugly. And to make matters worse, Josephine was gracious and charming. And obviously very much in love with David. *Bloody hell!*

During dinner Tim O'Neil told Kate about the new company.

"It sounds very interesting," Kate said.

"I'm afraid it's no Kruger-Brent, Limited, Miss McGregor. We'll have to start small, but with David running it, we'll do all right."

"With David running it, you can't miss," Kate assured him.

The evening was an agony. In the same cataclysmic moment, she had lost the man she loved and the one person who was indispensable to Kruger-Brent, Ltd. She carried on a conversation and managed to get through the evening, but afterward she had no recollection of what she said or did. She only knew that every time David and Josephine looked at each other or touched, she wanted to kill herself.

On the way back to the hotel, Josephine said, "She's in love with you, David."

He smiled. "Kate? No. We're friends. We have been since she was a baby. She liked you a lot."

Josephine smiled. *Men are so naïve.*

In David's office the following morning, Tim O'Neil and David sat facing each other. "I'll need about two months to get my affairs in order here," David said. "I've been thinking about the financing we'll need to begin with. If we go to one of the big companies, they'll swallow us up and give us a small share. It won't belong to us anymore. I think we should finance it ourselves. I figure It will cost eighty thousand dollars to get started. I've saved the equivalent of about forty thousand dollars. We'll need forty thousand more."

"I have ten thousand dollars," Tim O'Neil said. "And I have a brother who will loan me another five thousand."

"So, we're twenty-five thousand dollars short," David said. "We'll try to borrow that from a bank."

"We'll leave for San Francisco right away," O'Neil told David, "and get everything set up for you."

Josephine and her father left for the United States two days later. "Send them to Cape Town in the private railway car, David," Kate offered.

"That's very generous of you, Kate."

The morning Josephine left, David felt as though a piece of his life had been taken away. He could not wait to join her in San Francisco.

The next few weeks were taken up with a search for a management team to back up Brad Rogers. A list of possible candidates was carefully drawn up, and Kate and David and Brad spent hours discussing each one.

" . . . Taylor is a good technician, but he's weak on management."

"What about Simmons?"

"He's good, but he's not ready yet," Brad decided. "Give him another five years."

"Babcock?"

"Not a bad choice. Let's discuss him."

"What about Peterson?"

"Not enough of a company man," David said. "He's too concerned with himself." And even as he said it, he felt a pang of guilt because he was deserting Kate.

They continued on with the list of names. By the end of the month, they had narrowed the choice to four men to work with Brad Rogers. All of them were working abroad, and they were sent for so that they could be interviewed. The first two interviews went well. "I'd be satisfied with either one of them," Kate assured David and Brad.

On the morning the third interview was to take place, David walked into Kate's office, his face pale. "Is my job still open?"

Kate looked at his expression and stood up in alarm. "What is it, David?"

"I–I – " He sank into a chair. "Something has happened."

Kate was out from behind the desk and by his side in an instant. "Tell me!"

"I just got a letter from Tim O'Neil. He's sold the business."

"What do you mean?"

"Exactly what I said. He accepted an offer of two hundred thousand dollars and a royalty for his patent from the Three Star Meat Packing Company in Chicago." David's voice was filled with bitterness. "The company would like to hire me to manage it for them. He regrets any inconvenience to me, but he couldn't turn down that kind of money."

Kate looked at him intently. "And Josephine? What does she say? She must be furious with her father."

"There was a letter from her, too. We'll marry as soon as I come to San Francisco."

"And you're not going?"

"Of course I'm not going!" David exploded. "Before, I had something to offer. I could have built it into a great company. But they were in too much of a damned hurry for the money."

"David, you're not being fair when you say 'they.' Just be – "

"O'Neil would never have made that deal without Josephine's approval."

"I – I don't know what to say, David."

"There is nothing to say. Except that I almost made the biggest mistake of my life."

Kate walked over to the desk and picked up the list of candidates. Slowly, she began to tear it up.

In the weeks that followed, David plunged himself deeply into his work, trying to forget his bitterness and hurt. He received several letters from Josephine O'Neil, and he threw them all away, unread. But he could not get her out of his mind. Kate, deeply aware of David's pain, let him know she was there if he needed her.

Six months had passed since David received the letter from Tim O'Neil. During that time, Kate and David continued to work closely together, travel together and be alone together much of the time. Kate tried to please him in every way she could. She dressed for him, planned things he would enjoy and went out of her way to make his life as happy as possible. As far as she could tell, it was having no effect at all. And finally she lost her patience.

She and David were in Rio de Janeiro, checking on a new mineral find. They had had dinner at their hotel and were in Kate's room going over some figures late at night. Kate had changed to a comfortable kimono and slippers. When they finished, David stretched and said, "Well, that's it for tonight. I guess I'll go on to bed."

Kate said quietly, "Isn't it time you came out of mourning, David?"

He looked at her in surprise. "Mourning?"

"For Josephine O'Neil."

"She's out of my life."

"Then act like it."

"Just what would you like me to do, Kate?" he asked curtly.

Kate was angry now. Angry at David's blindness, angry about all the wasted time. "I'll tell you what I'd like you to do – kiss me."

"What?"

"Bloody hell, David! I'm your boss, damn it!" She moved close to him. "Kiss me." And she pressed her lips against his and put her arms around him. She felt him resist and start to draw back. And then slowly his arms circled her body, and he kissed her.

"Kate . . ."

She whispered against his lips. "I thought you'd never ask . . ."

They were married six weeks later. It was the biggest wedding Klipdrift had ever seen or would see again. It was held in the town's largest church and afterward there was a reception in the town hall and everyone was invited. There were mountains of food and uncounted cases of beer and whiskey and champagne, and musicians played and the festivities lasted until dawn. When the sun came up, Kate and David slipped away.

"I'll go home and finish packing," Kate said. "Pick me up in an hour."

In the pale dawn light, Kate entered the huge house alone and went upstairs to her bedroom. She walked over to a painting on the wall and pressed against the frame. The painting flew back, revealing a wall safe. She opened it and brought out a contract. It was for the purchase of the Three Star Meat Packing Company of Chicago by Kate McGregor. Next to it was a contract from the Three Star Meat Packing Company purchasing the rights to Tim O'Neil's freezing process for two hundred thousand dollars. Kate hesitated a moment, then returned the papers to the safe and locked it. David belonged to her now. He had always belonged to her. And to Kruger-Brent, Ltd. Together, they would build it into the biggest, most powerful company in the world.

Just as Jamie and Margaret McGregor would have wanted it.

Book Three

Kruger–Brent, Ltd.
1914–1945

16

They were in the library, where Jamie had once liked to sit with his brandy glass in front of him. David was arguing that there was no time for a real honeymoon. "Someone has to mind the store, Kate."

"Yes, Mr. Blackwell. But who's going to mind me?" She curled up in David's lap, and he felt the warmth of her through her thin dress. The documents he had been reading fell to the floor. Her arms were around him, and he felt her hands sliding down his body. She pressed her hips against him, making slow, small circles, and the papers on the floor were forgotten. She felt him respond, and she rose and slipped out of her dress. David watched her, marveling at her loveliness. How could he have been so blind for so long? She was undressing him now, and there was a sudden urgency in him. They were both naked, and their bodies were pressed together. He stroked her, his fingers lightly touching her face and her neck, down to the swell of her breasts. She was moaning, and his hands moved down until he felt the velvety softness between her legs. His fingers stroked her and she whispered, "Take me, David," and they were on the deep, soft rug and she felt the strength of his body on top of her. There was a long, sweet thrust and he was inside her, filling her, and she moved to his rhythm. It became a great tidal wave, sweeping her up higher and higher until she thought she could not bear the ecstasy of it. There was a sudden, glorious explosion deep inside her and another and another, and she thought, *I've died and gone to heaven.*

They traveled all over the world, to Paris and Zurich and Sydney and New York, taking care of company business, but wherever they went they carved out moments of time for themselves. They talked late into the night and made love and explored each other's minds and bodies. Kate was an inexhaustible delight to David. She would awaken him in the morning to make wild and pagan love to him, and a few hours later she would be at his side at a business conference, making more sense than anyone else there. She had a natural flair for business that was as rare as it was unexpected. Women were few in the top echelons of the business world. In the beginning Kate was treated with a tolerant condescension, but the attitude quickly changed to a wary respect. Kate took a delight in the maneuvering and machinations of the game. David watched her outwit men with much greater experience. She had the instincts of a winner. She knew what she wanted and how to get it. *Power.*

They ended their honeymoon with a glorious week in Cedar Hill House at Dark Harbor.

*

It was on June 28, 1914, that the first talk of war was heard. Kate and David were guests at a country estate in Sussex. It was the age of country-house living and weekend guests were expected to conform to a ritual. Men dressed for breakfast, changed for midmorning lounging, changed for lunch, changed for tea – to a velvet jacket with satin piping – and changed to a formal jacket for dinner.

"For God's sake," David protested to Kate. "I feel like a damned peacock."

"You're a very handsome peacock, my darling," Kate assured him. "When you get home, you can walk around naked."

He took her in his arms. "I can't wait."

At dinner, the news came that Francis Ferdinand, heir to the Austrian-Hungarian throne, and his wife, Sophie, had been slain by an assassin.

Their host, Lord Maney, said, "Nasty business, shooting a woman, what? But no one is going to war over some little Balkan country."

And the conversation moved on to cricket.

Later in bed, Kate said, "Do you think there's going to be a war, David?"

"Over some minor archduke being assassinated? No."

It proved to be a bad guess. Austria-Hungary, suspecting that its neighbor, Serbia, had instigated the plot to assassinate Ferdinand, declared war on Serbia, and by October, most of the world's major powers were at war. It was a new kind of warfare. For the first time, mechanized vehicles were used – airplanes, airships and submarines.

The day Germany declared war, Kate said, "This can be a wonderful opportunity for us, David."

David frowned. "What are you talking about?"

"Nations are going to need guns and ammunition and – "

"They're not getting them from us," David interrupted firmly. "We have enough business, Kate. We don't have to make profits from anyone's blood."

"Aren't you being a bit dramatic? Someone has to make guns."

"As long as I'm with this company, it won't be us. We won't discuss it again, Kate. The subject is closed."

And Kate thought, *The bloody hell it is.* For the first time in their marriage, they slept apart. Kate thought, *How can David be such an idealistic ninny?*

And David thought, *How can she be so cold-blooded? The business has changed her.* The days that followed were miserable for both of them. David regretted the emotional chasm between them, but he did not know how to bridge it. Kate was too proud and headstrong to give in to him because she knew she was right.

President Woodrow Wilson had promised to keep the United States out of the war, but as German submarines began torpedoing unarmed passenger ships, and stories of German atrocities spread, pressure began to build up for America to help the Allies. "Make the world safe for democracy," was the slogan.

David had learned to fly in the bush country of South Africa, and when the

Lafayette Escadrille was formed in France with American pilots, David went to Kate. "I've got to enlist."

She was appalled. "No! It's not your war!"

"It's going to be," David said quietly. "The United States can't stay out. I'm an American. I want to help now."

"You're forty-six years old!"

"I can still fly a plane, Kate. And they need all the help they can get."

There was no way Kate could dissuade him. They spent the last few days together quietly, their differences forgotten. They loved each other, and that was all that mattered.

The night before David was to leave for France, he said, "You and Brad Rogers can run the business as well as I can, maybe better."

"What if something happens to you? I couldn't bear it."

He held her close. "Nothing will happen to me, Kate. I'll come back to you with all kind, of medals."

He left the following morning.

David's absence was death for Kate. It had taken her so long to win him, and now every second of her day there was the ugly, creeping fear of losing him. He was always with her. She found him in the cadence of a stranger's voice, the sudden laughter on a quiet street, a phrase, a scent, a song. He was everywhere. She wrote him long letters every day. Whenever she received a letter from him, she reread it until it was in tatters. He was well, he wrote. The Germans had air superiority, but that would change. There were rumors that America would be helping soon. He would write again when he could. He loved her.

Don't let anything happen to you, my darling. I'll hate you forever if you do.

She tried to forget her loneliness and misery by plunging into work. At the beginning of the war, France and Germany had the best-equipped fighting forces in Europe, but the Allies had far greater manpower, resources and materials. Russia, with the largest army, was badly equipped and poorly commanded.

"They all need help," Kate told Brad Rogers. "They need tanks and guns and ammunition."

Brad Rogers was uncomfortable. "Kate, David doesn't think – "

"David isn't here, Brad. It's up to you and me."

But Brad Rogers knew that what Kate meant was, *Its up to me.*

Kate could not understand David's attitude about manufacturing armaments. The Allies needed weapons, and Kate felt it was her patriotic duty to supply them. She conferred with the heads of half a dozen friendly nations, and within a year Kruger-Brent, Ltd., was manufacturing guns and tanks, bombs and ammunition. The company supplied trains and tanks and uniforms and guns. Kruger-Brent was rapidly becoming one of the fastest-growing conglomerates in the world. When Kate saw the most recent revenue figures, she said to Brad Rogers, "Have you seen these? David will have to admit he was mistaken."

South Africa, meanwhile, was in turmoil. The party leaders had pledged their support to the Allies and accepted responsibility for defending South Africa against Germany, but the majority of Afrikaners opposed the country's support of Great Britain. They could not forget the past so quickly.

In Europe the war was going badly for the Allies. Fighting on the western front reached a standstill. Both sides dug in, protected by trenches that stretched across France and Belgium, and the soldiers were miserable. Rain filled the dugouts with water and mud, and rats swarmed through the vermin-infested trenches. Kate gas grateful that David was fighting his war in the air.

On April 6, 1917, President Wilson declared war, and David's prediction came true. America began to mobilize.

The first American Expeditionary Force under General John J. Pershing began landing in France on June 26, 1917. New place names became a part of everyone's vocabulary: Saint-Mihiel . . . Château-Thierry . . . the Meuse-Argonne . . . Belleau Hood . . . Verdun . . . The Allies had become an irresistible force, and on November 11, 1918, the war was finally over. The world was safe for democracy.

David was on his way home.

When David disembarked from the troop ship in New York, Kate was there to meet him. They stood staring at each other for one eternal moment, ignoring the noise and the crowds around them, then Kate was in David's arms. He was thinner and tired-looking, and Kate thought, *Oh, God. I've missed him so.* She had a thousand questions to ask him, but they could wait. "I'm taking you to Cedar Hill House," Kate told him. "It's a perfect place for you to rest."

Kate had done a great deal with the house in anticipation of David's arrival home. The large, airy living room had been furnished with twin sofas covered in old rose-and-green floral chintz. Matching down-filled armchairs were grouped around the fireplace. Over the fireplace was a Vlaminck floral canvas, and, on each side of it, doré sconces. Two sets of French doors opened out onto the veranda, which ran the entire length of the house on three sides, covered with a striped awning. The rooms were bright and airy, and the view of the harbor spectacular.

Kate led David through the house, chattering away happily. He seemed strangely quiet. When they had completed the tour, Kate asked, "Do you like what I've done with it, darling?"

"It's beautiful, Kate. Now, sit down. I want to talk to you."

She had a sudden sinking feeling. "Is anything wrong?"

"We seem to have become a munitions supplier for half the world."

"Wait until you look at the books," Kate began. "Our profit has – "

"I'm talking about something else. As I recall, our profit was pretty good before I left. I thought we agreed we wouldn't get involved in manufacturing war supplies."

Kate felt an anger rising in her. "You agreed. I didn't." She fought to control it. "Times change, David. We have to change with them."

He looked at her and asked quietly, "Have you changed?"

Lying in bed that night, Kate asked herself whether it was she who had changed, or David. Had she become stronger, or had David become weaker? She thought about his argument against manufacturing armaments. It was a weak argument. After all, *someone* was going to supply the merchandise to the Allies, and there was an enormous profit in it. What had happened to David's business sense? She had always looked up to him as one of the cleverest men she knew. But now, she felt that she was more capable of running the business than David. She spent a sleepless night.

In the morning Kate and David had breakfast and walked around the grounds.

"It's really lovely," David told her. "I'm glad to be here."

Kate said, "About our conversation last night – "

"It's done. I was away, and you did what you thought was right."

Would I have done the same thing if you had been here? Kate wondered. But she did not say the words aloud. She had done what she had for the sake of the company. *Does the company mean more to me than my marriage?* She was afraid to answer the question.

17

The next five years witnessed a period of incredible worldwide growth. Kruger-Brent Ltd., had been founded on diamonds and gold, but it had diversified and expanded all over the world, so that its center was no longer South Africa. The company recently had acquired a publishing empire, an insurance company and half a million acres of timberland.

One night Kate nudged David awake. "Darling, let's move the company headquarters."

David sat up groggily. "W – what?"

"The business center of the world today is New York. That's where our headquarters should be. South Africa's too far away from everything. Besides, now that we have the telephone and cable, we can communicate with any of our offices in minutes."

"Now why didn't I think of that?" David mumbled. And he went back to sleep.

New York was an exciting new world. On her previous visits there, Kate had felt the quick pulse of the city, but living there was like being caught up at the center of a matrix. The earth seemed to spin faster, everything moved at a more rapid pace.

Kate and David selected a site for the new company headquarters on Wall Street, and the architects went to work. Kate chose another architect to design a sixteenth-century French Renaissance mansion on Fifth Avenue.

"This city is so damned *noisy,*" David complained.

And it was true. The chatter of riveters filled the air in every part of the city as skyscrapers began to soar into the heavens. New York had become the mecca for trade from all over the world, the headquarters for shipping, insurance, communications and transportation. It was a city bursting with a unique vitality. Kate loved it, but she sensed David's unhappiness.

"David, this is the future. This place is growing, and we'll grow with it."

"My God, Kate, how much more do you want?"

And without thinking, she replied, "All there is."

She could not understand why David had even asked the question. The name of the game was to win, and you won by beating everyone else. It seemed so obvious to her. Why couldn't David see it? David was a good businessman, but there was something missing in him, a hunger, a compulsion to conquer, to be the biggest and the best. Her father had had that spirit, and she had it. Kate was not sure exactly when it had happened, but at some point in her life, the company had become the master, and she the slave. It owned her more than she owned it.

When she tried to explain her feelings to David, he laughed and said, "You're working too hard." *She's so much like her father*, David thought. And he was not sure why he found that vaguely disturbing.

How could one work too hard? Kate wondered. There was no greater joy in life. It was when she felt most alive. Each day brought a new set of problems, and each problem was a challenge, a puzzle to be solved, a new game to be won. And she was wonderful at it. She was caught up in something beyond imagination. It had nothing to do with money or achievement; it had to do with *power.* A power that controlled the lives of thousands of people in every corner of the earth. Just as her life had once been controlled. As long as she had power, she would never truly need anyone. It was a weapon that was awesome beyond belief.

Kate was invited to dine with kings and queens and presidents, all seeking her favor, her goodwill. A new Kruger-Brent factory could mean the difference between poverty and riches. *Power.* The company was alive, a growing giant that had to be fed, and sometimes sacrifices were necessary, for the giant could not be shackled. Kate understood that now. It had a rhythm, a pulse, and it had become her own.

In March, a year after they had moved to New York, Kate felt unwell. David persuaded her to see a doctor.

"His name is John Harley. He's a young doctor with a good reputation."

Reluctantly, Kate went to see him. John Harley was a thin, serious-looking young Bostonian about twenty-six, five years younger than Kate.

"I warn you," Kate informed him, "I don't have time to be sick."

"I'll bear that in mind, Mrs. Blackwell. Meanwhile, let's have a look at you."

Dr. Harley examined her, made some tests and said, "I'm sure it's nothing serious. I'll have the results in a day or two. Give me a call on Wednesday."

Early Wednesday morning Kate telephoned Dr. Harley. "I have good news for you, Mrs. Blackwell," he said cheerfully. "You're going to have a baby."

It was one of the most exciting moments of Kate's life. She could not wait to tell David.

She had never seen David so thrilled. He scooped her up in his strong arms and said, "It's going to be a girl, and she'll look exactly like you." He was thinking, *This is exactly what Kate needs. Now she'll stay home more. She'll be more of a wife.*

And Kate was thinking, *It will be a boy. One day he'll take over Kruger-Brent.*

As the time for the birth of the baby drew nearer, Kate worked shorter hours, but she still went to the office every day.

"Forget about the business and relax," David advised her.

What he did not understand was that the business *was* Kate's relaxation.

The baby was due in December. "I'll try for the twenty-fifth," Kate promised David. "He'll be our Christmas present."

Its *going to be a perfect Christmas*, Kate thought. She was head of a great conglomerate, she was married to the man she loved and she was going to have his baby. If there was irony in the order of her priorities, Kate was not aware of it.

Her body had grown large and clumsy, and it was getting more and more difficult for Kate to go to the office, but whenever David or Brad Rogers suggested she stay home, her answer was, "My brain is still working." Two months before the baby was due, David was in South Africa on an inspection tour of the mine at Pniel. He was scheduled to return to New York the following week.

Kate was at her desk when Brad Rogers walked in unannounced. She looked at the grim expression on his face and said, "We lost the Shannon deal!"

"No. I – Kate, I just got word. There's been an accident. A mine explosion."

She felt a sharp pang. "Where? Was it bad? Was anyone killed?"

Brad took a deep breath. "Half a dozen. Kate – David was with them."

The words seemed to fill the room and reverberate against the paneled walls, growing louder and louder, until it was a screaming in her ears, a Niagara of sound that was drowning her, and she felt herself being sucked into its center, deeper and deeper, until she could no longer breathe.

And everything became dark and silent.

*

The baby was born one hour later, two months premature. Kate named him Anthony James Blackwell, after David's father. *I'll love you, my son, for me, and I'll love you for your father.*

One month later the new Fifth Avenue mansion was ready, and Kate and the baby and a staff of servants moved into it. Two castles in Italy had been stripped to furnish the house. It was a showplace, with elaborately carved sixteenth-century Italian walnut furniture and rose-marble floors bordered with sienna-red marble. The paneled library boasted a magnificent eighteenth-century fireplace over which hung a rare Holbein. There was a trophy room with David's gun collection, and an art gallery that Kate filled with Rembrandts and Vermeers and Velazquezes and Bellinis. There was a ballroom and a sun room and a formal dining room and a nursery next to Kate's room, and uncounted bedrooms. In the large formal gardens were statues by Rodin, Augustus Saint-Gaudens and Maillol. It was a palace fit for a king. *And the king is growing up in it*, Kate thought happily.

In 1928, when Tony was four, Kate sent him to nursery school. He was a handsome, solemn little boy, with his mother's gray eyes and stubborn chin. He was given music lessons, and when he was five he attended dancing school. Some of the best times the two of them spent together were at Cedar Hill House in Dark Harbor. Kate bought a yacht, an eighty-foot motor sailer she named the *Corsair*, and she and Tony cruised the waters along the coast of Maine. Tony adored it. But it was the work that gave Kate her greatest pleasure.

There was something mystic about the company Jamie McGregor had founded. It was alive, consuming. It was her lover, and it would never die on a winter day and leave her alone. It would live forever. She would see to it. And one day she would give it to her son.

The only disturbing factor in Kate's life was her homeland. She cared deeply about South Africa. The racial problems there were growing, and Kate was troubled. There were two political camps: the *verkramptes* – the narrow ones, the pro-segregationists – and the *verligtes* – the enlightened ones, who wanted to improve the position of the blacks. Prime Minister James Hertzog and Jan Smuts had formed a coalition and combined their power to have the New Land Act passed. Blacks were removed from the rolls and were no longer able to vote or own land. Millions of people belonging to different minority groups were disrupted by the new law. The areas that had no minerals, Industrial centers or ports were assigned to coloreds, blacks and Indians.

Kate arranged a meeting in South Africa with several high government officials. "This is a time bomb," Kate told them. "What you're doing is trying to keep eight million people in slavery."

"It's not slavery, Mrs. Blackwell. We're doing this for their own good."

"Really? How would you explain that?"

"Each race has something to contribute. If the blacks mingle with the whites, they'll lose their individuality. We're trying to protect them."

"That's bloody nonsense," Kate retorted. "South Africa has become a racist hell."

"That's not true. Blacks from other countries come thousands of miles in order to enter this country. They pay as much as fifty-six pounds for a forged pass. The black is better off here than anywhere else on earth."

"Then I pity them," Kate retorted.

"They're primitive children, Mrs. Blackwell. It's for their own good."

Kate left the meeting frustrated and deeply fearful for her country.

Kate was also concerned about Banda. He was in the news a good deal. The South African newspapers were calling him the *Scarlet Pimpernel*, and there was a grudging admiration in their stories. He escaped the police by disguising himself as a laborer, a chauffeur, a janitor. He had organized a guerrilla army and he headed the police's most-wanted list. One article in the *Cape Times* told of his being carried triumphantly through the streets of a black village on the shoulders of demonstrators. He went from village to village addressing crowds of students, but every time the police got wind of his presence, Banda disappeared. He was said to have a personal bodyguard of hundreds of friends and followers, and he slept at a different house every night. Kate knew that nothing would stop him but death.

She had to get in touch with him. She summoned one of her veteran black foremen, a man she trusted. "William, do you think you can find Banda?"

"Only if he wishes to be found."

"Try. I want to meet with him."

"I'll see what I can do."

The following morning the foreman said, "If you are free this evening, a car will be waiting to take you out to the country."

Kate was driven to a small village seventy miles north of Johannesburg. The driver stopped in front of a small frame house, and Kate went inside. Banda was waiting for her. He looked exactly the same as when Kate had last seen him. *And he must be sixty years old*, Kate thought. He had been on the run from the police for years, and yet he appeared serene and calm.

He hugged Kate and said, "You look more beautiful every time I see you."

She laughed. "I'm getting old. I'm going to be forty in a few years."

"The years sit lightly on you, Kate."

They went into the kitchen, and while Banda fixed coffee, Kate said, "I don't like what's happening, Banda. Where is it going to lead?"

"It will get worse," Banda said simply. "The government will not allow us to speak with them. The whites have destroyed the bridges between us and them, and one day they will find they need those bridges to reach us. We have our heroes now, Kate. Nehemiah Tile, Mokone, Richard Msimang. The whites goad us and move us around like cattle to pasture."

"Not all whites think like that," Kate assured him. "You have friends who are fighting to change things. It will happen one day, Banda, but it will take time."

"Time is like sand in an hourglass. It runs out."

"Banda, what's happened to Ntame and to Magena?"

"My wife and son are in hiding," Banda said sadly. "The police are still very busy looking for me."

"What can I do to help? I can't just sit by and do nothing. Will money help?"

"Money always helps."

"I will arrange it. What else?"

"Pray. Pray for all of us."

The following morning, Kate returned to New York.

When Tony was old enough to travel, Kate took him on business trips during his school holidays. He was fond of museums, and he could stand for hours looking at the paintings and statues of the great masters. At home, Tony sketched copies of the paintings on the wall, but he was too self-conscious to let his mother see his work.

He was sweet and bright and fun to be with, and there was a shyness about him that people found appealing. Kate was proud of her son. He was always first in his class. "You beat all of them, didn't you, darling?" And she would laugh and hold him fiercely in her arms.

And young Tony would try even harder to live up to his mother's expectations.

In 1936, on Tony's twelfth birthday, Kate returned from a trip to the Middle East. She had missed Tony and was eager to see him. He was at home waiting for her. She took him in her arms and hugged him. "Happy birthday, darling! Has it been a good day?"

"Y-yes, m-ma'am. It's b-b-been wonderful."

Kate pulled back and looked at him. She had never noticed him stutter before. "Are you all right, Tony?"

"F-fine, thank you, M-mother."

"You mustn't stammer," she told him. "Speak more slowly."

"Yes, M-mother."

Over the next few weeks, it got worse. Kate decided to talk to Dr. Harley. When he finished the examination, John Harley said, "Physically, there's nothing wrong with the boy, Kate. Is he under any kind of pressure?"

"My son? Of course not. How can you ask that?"

"Tony's a sensitive boy. Stuttering is very often a physical manifestation of frustration, an inability to cope."

"You're wrong, John. Tony is at the very top of all the achievement tests in school. Last term he won three awards. Best all-around athlete, best all-around scholar and best student in the arts. I'd hardly call that unable to cope."

"I see." He studied her. "What do you do when Tony stammers, Kate?"

"I correct him, of course."

"I would suggest that you don't. That will only make him more tense."

Kate was stung to anger. "If Tony has any psychological problems, as you seem to think, I can assure you it's not because of his mother. I adore him. And he's aware that I think he's the most fantastic child on earth."

And that was the core of the problem. No child could live up to that. Dr. Harley glanced down at his chart. "Let's see now. Tony is twelve?"

"Yes."

"Perhaps it might be good for him if he went away for a while. Maybe a private school somewhere."

Kate just stared at him.

"Let him be on his own a bit. Just until he finishes high school. They have some excellent schools in Switzerland."

Switzerland! The idea of Tony being so far away from her was appalling. He was too young, he was not ready yet, he – Dr. Harley was watching her. "I'll think about it," Kate told him.

That afternoon she canceled a board meeting and went home early. Tony was in his room, doing homework.

Tony said, "I g-g-got all A's t-today, M-mother."

"What would you think of going to school in Switzerland, darling?"

And his eyes lit up and he said, "M-m-may I?"

Six weeks later, Kate put Tony aboard a ship. He was on his way to the Institute Le Rosey in Rolle, a small town on the shore of Lake Geneva. Kate stood at the New York pier and watched until the huge liner cut loose from the tugboats. *Bloody hell! I'm going to miss him.* Then she turned and walked back to the limousine waiting to take her to the office.

Kate enjoyed working with Brad Rogers. He was forty-six, two years older than Kate. They had become good friends through the years, and she loved him for his devotion to Kruger-Brent. Brad was unmarried and had a variety of attractive girl friends, but gradually Kate became aware that he was half in love with her. More than once he made studiously ambiguous remarks, but she chose to keep their relationship on an impersonal, business level. She broke that pattern only once.

Brad had started seeing someone regularly. He stayed out late every night and came into morning meetings tired and distracted, his mind elsewhere. It was bad for the company. When a month went by and his behavior was becoming more flagrant, Kate decided that something had to be done. She remembered how close David had come to quitting the company because of a woman. She would not let that happen with Brad.

Kate had planned to travel to Paris alone to acquire an import-export company, but at the last minute she asked Brad to accompany her. They spent the day of their arrival in meetings and that evening had dinner at the Grand Véfour. Afterward, Kate suggested that Brad join her in her suite at the George V to go over the reports on the new company. When he arrived, Kate was waiting for him in a filmy negligee.

"I brought the revised offer with me," Brad began, "so we – "

"That can wait," Kate said softly. There was an invitation in her voice that made him look at her again. "I wanted us to be alone, Brad."

"Kate – "

She moved into his arms and held him close.

"My God!" he said. "I've wanted you for so long."

"And I you, Brad."

And they moved into the bedroom.

Kate was a sensual woman, but all of her sexual energy had long since been harnessed into other channels. She was completely fulfilled by her work. She needed Brad for other reasons.

He was on top of her, and she moved her legs apart and felt his hardness in her, and it was neither pleasant nor unpleasant.

"Kate, I've loved you for so long . . ."

He was pressing into her, moving in and out in an ancient, timeless rhythm, and she thought, *They're asking too bloody much for the company. They're going to hold out because they know I really want it.*

Brad was whispering words of endearment in her ear.

I could call off the negotiations and wait for them to come back to me. But what if they don't? Do I dare risk *losing the deal?*

His rhythm was faster now, and Kate moved her hips, thrusting against his body.

No. They could easily find another buyer. Better to pay them what they want. I'll make up for it by selling off one of their subsidiaries.

Brad was moaning, in a frenzy of delight, and Kate moved faster, bringing him to a climax.

I'll tell them I've decided to meet their terms.

There was a long, shuddering gasp, and Brad said, "Oh, God, Kate, it was wonderful. Was it good for you, darling?"

"It was heaven."

She lay in Brad's arms all night, thinking and planning, while he slept. In the morning when he woke up, she said, "Brad, that woman you've been seeing – "

"My God! You're jealous!" He laughed happily. "Forget about her. I'll never see her again, I promise."

Kate never went to bed with Brad again. When he could not understand why she refused him, all she said was, "You don't know how much I want to, Brad, but I'm afraid we wouldn't be able to work together any longer. We must both make a sacrifice."

And he was forced to live with that.

As the company kept expanding, Kate set up charitable foundations that contributed to colleges, churches and schools. She kept adding to her art collection.

She acquired the great Renaissance and post-Renaissance artists Raphael and Titian, Tintoretto and El Greco; and the baroque painters Rubens, Caravaggio and Vandyck.

The Blackwell collection was reputed to be the most valuable private collection in the world. *Reputed*, because no one outside of invited guests was permitted to see it. Kate would not allow it to be photographed, nor would she discuss it with the press. She had strict, inflexible rules about the press. The personal life of the Blackwell family was off limits. Neither servants nor employees of the company were permitted to discuss the Blackwell family. It was impossible, of course, to stop rumors and speculation, for Kate Blackwell was an intriguing enigma – one of the richest, most powerful women in the world. There were a thousand questions about her, but few answers.

Kate telephoned the headmistress at Le Rosey. "I'm calling to find out how Tony is."

"Ah, he is doing very well, Mrs. Blackwell. Your son is a superb student. He – "

"I wasn't referring to that. I meant – " She hesitated, as though reluctant to admit there could be a weakness in the Blackwell family. "I meant his stammering."

"Madame, there is no sign of any stammering. He is perfectly fine."

Kate heaved an inward sigh of relief. She had known all along that it was only temporary, a passing phase of some kind. So much for doctors!

Tony arrived home four weeks later, and Kate was at the airport to meet him. He looked fit and handsome, and Kate felt a surge of pride. "Hello, my love. How are you?"

"I'm f-f-fine, M-m-mother. How are y-y-you?"

On his vacations at home, Tony eagerly looked forward to examining the new paintings his mother had acquired while he was away. He was awed by the masters, and enchanted by the French Impressionists: Monet, Renoir, Manet and Morisot. They evoked a magic world for Tony. He bought a set of paints and an easel and went to work. He thought his paintings were terrible, and he still refused to show them to anyone. How could they compare with the exquisite masterpieces?

Kate told him, "One day all these paintings will belong to you, darling."

The thought of it filled the thirteen-year-old boy with a sense of unease. His mother did not understand. They could never be truly his, because he had done nothing to earn them. He had a fierce determination somehow to earn his own way. He had ambivalent feelings about being away from his mother, for everything around her was always exciting. She was at the center of a whirlwind, giving orders, making incredible deals, taking him to exotic places, introducing him to interesting people. She was an awesome figure, and Tony was inordinately proud of her. He thought she was the most fascinating woman in the world. He felt guilty because it was only in her presence that he stuttered.

Kate had no idea how deeply her son was in awe of her until one day when he was home on vacation he asked, "M-mmother, do you r-r-run the world?"

And she had laughed and said, "Of course not. What made you ask such a silly question?"

"All my f-friends at school talk about you. Boy, you're really s-something."

"I am something," Kate said. "I'm your mother."

Tony wanted more than anything in the world to please Kate. He knew how much the company meant to her, how much she planned on his running it one day, and he was filled with regret, because he knew he could not. That was not what he intended to do with his life.

When he tried to explain this to his mother, she would laugh, "Nonsense, Tony. You're much too young to know what you want to do with your future."

And he would begin to stammer.

The idea of being a painter excited Tony. To be able to capture beauty and freeze it for all eternity; that was something worthwhile. He wanted to go abroad and study in Paris, but he knew he would have to broach the subject to his mother very carefully.

They had wonderful times together. Kate was the châtelaine of vast estates. She had acquired homes in Palm Beach and South Carolina, and a stud farm in Kentucky, and she and Tony visited all of them during his vacations. They watched the America's Cup races in Newport, and when they were in New York, they had lunch at Delmonico's and tea at the Plaza and Sunday dinner at Lüchow's. Kate was interested in horse racing, and her stable became one of the finest in the world. When one of Kate's horses was running and Tony was home from school, Kate would take him to the track with her. They would sit in her box and Tony would watch in wonder as his mother cheered until she was hoarse. He knew her excitement had nothing to do with money.

"It's winning, Tony. Remember that. Winning is what's important."

They had quiet, lazy times at Dark Harbor. They shopped at Pendleton and Coffin, and had ice-cream sodas at the Dark Harbor Shop. In summer they went sailing and hiking and visited art galleries. In the winter there was skiing and skating and sleigh riding. They would sit in front of a fire in the large fireplace in the library, and Kate would tell her son all the old family stories about his grandfather and Banda, and about the baby shower Madam Agnes and her girls gave for Tony's grandmother. It was a colorful family, a family to be proud of, to cherish.

"Kruger-Brent, Limited, will be yours one day, Tony. You'll run it and – "

"I d-don't want to r-run it, Mother. I'm not interested in big business or p-power."

And Kate exploded. "You bloody fool! What do you know about big business or power? Do you think I go around the world spreading evil? Hurting people? Do you think Kruger-Brent is some kind of ruthless money machine crushing anything that gets in its way? Well, let me tell you something, Son. It's the next best thing to Jesus Christ. We're the resurrection, Tony. We save lives by the hundreds of thousands. When we open a factory in a depressed community or country, those people can afford to build schools and libraries and churches, and give their children decent food and clothing and recreation facilities." She was breathing hard, carried away by her anger. "We build factories where people are hungry and out of work, and because of us they're able to live decent lives and hold up their heads. We become their saviors. Don't ever again let me hear you sneer at big business and power."

All Tony could say was, "I'm s-s-sorry, M-m-mother."

And he thought stubbornly: *I'm going to be an artist.*

When Tony was fifteen, Kate suggested he spend his summer vacation in South Africa. He had never been there. "I can't get away just now, Tony, but you'll find it a fascinating place. I'll make all the arrangements for you."

"I was s-sort of h-hoping to spend my vacation at Dark Harbor, M-mother."

"Next summer," Kate said firmly. "This summer I would like you to go to Johannesburg."

Kate carefully briefed the company superintendent in Johannesburg, and together they laid out an itinerary for Tony. Each day was planned with one objective in view: to make this trip as exciting as possible for Tony, to make him realize his future lay with the company.

Kate received a daily report about her son. He had been taken into one of the gold mines. He had spent two days in the diamond fields. He had been on a guided tour of the Kruger-Brent plants, and had gone on a safari in Kenya.

A few days before Tony's vacation ended, Kate telephoned the company manager in Johannesburg. "How is Tony getting along?"

"Oh, he's having a great time, Mrs. Blackwell. In fact, this morning he asked if he couldn't stay on a little longer."

Kate felt a surge of pleasure. "That's wonderful! Thank you."

When Tony's vacation was over, he went to Southampton, England, where he boarded a Pan American Airways System plane for the United States. Kate flew Pan American whenever possible. It spoiled her for other airlines.

Kate left an important meeting to greet her son when he arrived at the Pan American terminal at the newly built La Guardia Airport in New York. His handsome face was filled with enthusiasm.

"Did you have a good time, darling?"

"South Africa's a f-fantastic country, M-mother. Did you know they f-flew me to the Namib Desert where grandfather s-stole those diamonds from Great-grandfather v-van der Merwe?"

"He didn't steal them, Tony," Kate corrected him. "He merely took what was his."

"Sure," Tony scoffed. "Anyway, I was th-there. There was no sea *mis*, but they s-still have the guards and dogs and everything." He grinned. "They wouldn't give me any s-samples."

Kate laughed happily. "They don't have to give you any samples, darling. One day they will all be yours."

"*You* t-tell them. They wouldn't l-listen to me."

She hugged him. "You *did* enjoy it, didn't you?" She was enormously pleased that at last Tony was excited about his heritage.

"You know what I loved m-most?"

Kate smiled lovingly. "What?"

"The colors. I p-painted a lot of landscapes th-there. I hated to leave. I want to go back there and p-paint."

"Paint?" Kate tried to sound enthusiastic. "That sounds like a wonderful hobby, Tony."

"No. I don't m – mean as a hobby, Mother. I want to be a p-painter. I've been thinking a lot about it. I'm going to P-paris to study. I really think I might have some talent."

Kate felt herself tensing. "You don't want to spend the rest of your life painting."

"Yes, I do, M-mother. It's the only thing I really c-care about."

And Kate knew she had lost.

He has a right to live his own life Kate thought. *But how can I let him make such a terrible mistake?*

In September, the decision was taken out of both their hands. Europe went to war.

"I want you to enroll in the Wharton School of Finance and Commerce," Kate informed Tony. "In two years if you still want to be an artist, you'll have my blessing." Kate was certain that by then Tony would change his mind. It was inconceivable that her son would choose to spend his life slapping daubs of color on bits of canvas when he could head the most exciting conglomerate in the world. He was, after all, her son.

To Kate Blackwell, World War II was another great opportunity. There were worldwide shortages of military supplies and materials, and Kruger-Brent was able to furnish them. One division of the company provided equipment for the armed forces, while another division took care of civilian needs. The company factories were working twenty-four hours a day.

Kate was certain the United States was not going to be able to remain neutral. President Franklin D. Roosevelt called upon the country to be the great arsenal of democracy, and on March 11, 1941, the Lend-Lease Bill was pushed through Congress. Allied shipping across the Atlantic was menaced by the German blockade. U-boats, the German submarines, attacked and sank scores of Allied ships, fighting in wolf packs of eight.

Germany was a juggernaut that seemingly could not be stopped. In defiance of the Versailles Treaty, Adolf Hitler had built up one of the greatest war machines in history. In a new *blitzkrieg* technique, Germany attacked Poland,

Belgium and the Netherlands, and in rapid succession, the German machine crushed Denmark, Norway, Luxembourg and France.

Kate went into action when she received word that Jews working in the Nazi-confiscated Kruger-Brent, Ltd., factories were being arrested and deported to concentration camps. She made two telephone calls, and the following week she was on her way to Switzerland. When she arrived at the Baur au Lac Hotel in Zurich, there was a message that Colonel Brinkmann wished to see her. Brinkmann had been a manager of the Berlin branch of Kruger-Brent, Ltd. When the factory had been taken over by the Nazi government, Brinkmann was given the rank of colonel and kept in charge.

He came to see Kate at the hotel. He was a thin, precise man with blond hair combed carefully over his balding skull. "I am delighted to see you, Frau Blackwell. I have a message for you from my government. I am authorized to assure you that as soon as we have won the war, your factories will be returned to you. Germany is going to be the greatest industrial power the world has ever known, and we welcome the collaboration of people such as yourself."

"What if Germany loses?"

Colonel Brinkmann allowed a small smile to play on his lips. "We both know that cannot happen, Frau Blackwell. The United States is wise to stay out of Europe's business. I hope it continues to do so."

"I'm sure you do, Colonel." She leaned forward. "I've heard rumors about Jews being sent to concentration camps and being exterminated. Is that true?"

"British propaganda, I assure you. It is true that *die Juden* are sent to work camps, but I give you my word as an officer that they are being treated as they should be."

Kate wondered exactly what those words meant. She intended to find out.

The following day Kate made an appointment with a prominent German merchant named Otto Bueller. Bueller was in his fifties, a distinguished-looking man with a compassionate face and eyes that had known deep suffering. They met at a small café near the *bahnhof.* Herr Bueller selected a table in a deserted corner.

"I've been told," Kate said softly, "that you've started an underground to help smuggle Jews into neutral countries. Is that true?"

"It's not true, Mrs. Blackwell. Such an act would be treason against the Third Reich."

"I have also heard that you're in need of funds to run it."

Herr Bueller shrugged. "Since there is no underground, I have no need of funds to run it, is that not so?"

His eyes kept nervously darting around the café. This was a man who breathed and slept with danger each day of his life.

"I was hoping I might be of some help," Kate said carefully. "Kruger-Brent, Limited, has factories in many neutral and Allied countries. If someone could get the refugees there, I would arrange for them to have employment."

Herr Bueller sat there sipping a bitter coffee. Finally, he said, "I know nothing about these things. Politics are dangerous these days. But if you are interested in helping someone in distress, I have an uncle in England who suffers from a terrible, debilitating disease. His doctor bills are very high."

"How high?"

"Fifty thousand dollars a month. Arrangements would have to be made to deposit the money for his medical expenses in London and transfer the deposits to a Swiss bank."

"That can be arranged."

"My uncle would be very pleased."

Some eight weeks later, a small but steady stream of Jewish refugees began to arrive in Allied countries to go to work in Kruger-Brent factories.

Tony quit school at the end of two years. He went up to Kate's office to tell her the news. "I t-tried, M-mother. I really d-did. But I've m-made up m-my mind. I want to s-study p-painting. When the w-war is over, I'm g-going to P-paris."

Each word was like a hammerblow.

"I kn-know you're d-disappointed, but I have to l-live my own life. I think I can be good – *really* good." He saw the look on Kate's face. "I've done what you've asked me to do. Now you've got to g-give me my chance. They've accepted me at the Art I-institute in Chicago."

Kate's mind was in a turmoil. What Tony wanted to do was such a bloody *waste*. All she could say was, "When do you plan to leave?"

"Enrollment starts on the fifteenth."

"What's the date today?"

"D-december sixth."

On Sunday, December 7, 1941, squadrons of Nakajima bombers and Zero fighter planes from the Imperial Japanese Navy attacked Pearl Harbor, and the following day, the United States was at war. That afternoon Tony enlisted in the United States Marine Corps. He was sent to Quantico, Virginia, where he was graduated from Officers' Training School and from there to the South Pacific.

Kate felt as though she were living on the edge of an abyss. Her working day was filled with the pressures of running the company, but every moment at the back of her mind was the fear that she would receive some dreaded news about Tony – that he had been wounded or killed.

The war with Japan was going badly. Japanese bombers struck at American bases on Guam, Midway and Wake islands. They took Singapore in February 1942, and quickly overran New Britain, New Ireland and the Admiralty and Solomon islands. General Douglas MacArthur was forced to withdraw from the Philippines. The powerful forces of the Axis were slowly conquering the world, and the shadows were darkening everywhere. Kate was afraid that Tony might be taken prisoner of war and tortured. With all her power and influence, there was nothing she could do except pray. Every letter from Tony was a beacon of hope, a sign that, a few short weeks before, he had been alive. "They keep us in the dark here," Tony wrote. "Are the Russians still holding on? The Japanese soldier is brutal, but you have to respect him. He's not afraid to die . . ."

"What's happening in the States? Are factory workers really striking for more money? . . ."

"The PT boats are doing a wonderful job here. Those boys are all heroes . . ."

"You have great connections, Mother. Send us a few hundred F4U's, the new Navy fighters. Miss you. . . ."

On August 7, 1942, the Allies began their first offensive action in the Pacific. United States Marines landed on Guadalcanal in the Solomon Islands, and from then on they kept moving to take back the islands the Japanese had conquered.

In Europe, the Allies were enjoying an almost unbroken string of victories. On June 6, 1944, the Allied invasion of Western Europe was launched with landings by American, British and Canadian troops on the Normandy beaches, and a year later, on May 7, 1945, Germany surrendered unconditionally.

In Japan, on August 6, 1945, an atomic bomb with a destructive force of more than twenty thousand tons of TNT was dropped on Hiroshima. Three days later, another atomic bomb destroyed the city of Nagasaki. On August 14, the Japanese surrendered. The long and bloody war was finally over.

Three months later, Tony returned home. He and Kate were at Dark Harbor, sitting on the terrace looking over the bay dotted with graceful white sails.

The war has changed him, Kate thought. There was a new maturity about Tony. He had grown a small mustache, and looked tanned and fit and handsome. There were lines about his eyes that had not been there before. Kate was sure the years overseas had given him time to reconsider his decision about not going into the company.

"What are your plans now, Son?" Kate asked.

Tony smiled. "As I was saying before we were so rudely interrupted, Mother – I'm going to P-paris."

Book Four

Tony
1946–1950

18

Tony had been to Paris before, but this time the circumstances were different. The City of Light had been dimmed by the German occupation, but had been saved from destruction when it was declared an open city. The people had suffered a great deal, and though the Nazis had looted the Louvre, Tony found Paris relatively untouched. Besides, this time he was going to live there, to be a part of the city, rather than be a tourist. He could have stayed at Kate's penthouse on Avenue du Maréchal Foch, which had not been damaged during the occupation. Instead, he rented an unfurnished flat in an old converted house behind Grand Montparnasse. The apartment consisted of a living room with a fireplace, a small bedroom and a tiny kitchen that had no refrigerator. Between the bedroom and the kitchen crouched a bathroom with a claw-footed tub and small stained bidet and a temperamental toilet with a broken seat.

When the landlady started to make apologies, Tony stopped her. "It's perfect."

He spent all day Saturday at the flea market. Monday and Tuesday he toured the secondhand shops along the Left Bank, and by Wednesday he had the basic furniture he needed. A sofa bed, a scarred table, two overstuffed chairs, an old, ornately carved wardrobe, lamps and a rickety kitchen table and two straight chairs. *Mother would be horrified*, Tony thought. He could have had his apartment crammed with priceless antiques, but that would have been *playing* the part of a young American artist in Paris. He intended to *live* it.

The next step was getting into a good art school. The most prestigious art school in all of France was the École des Beaux-Arts of Paris. Its standards were high, and few Americans were admitted. Tony applied for a place there. *They'll never accept me*, he thought. *But if they do!* Somehow, he had to show his mother he had made the right decision. He submitted three of his paintings and waited four weeks to hear whether he had been accepted. At the end of the fourth week, his concierge handed him a letter from the school. He was to report the following Monday.

The École des Beaux-Arts was a large stone building, two stories high, with a dozen classrooms filled with students. Tony reported to the head of the school, Maître Gessand, a towering, bitter-looking man with no neck and the thinnest lips Tony had ever seen.

"Your paintings are amateurish," he told Tony. "But they show promise. Our committee selected you more for what was *not* in the paintings than for what *was* in them. Do you understand?"

"Not exactly, maître."

"You will, in time. I am assigning you to Maître Cantal. He will be your teacher for the next five years – if you last that long."

I'll last that long, Tony promised himself.

Maître Cantal was a very short man, with a totally bald head which he covered with a purple beret. He had dark-brown eyes, a large, bulbous nose and lips like sausages. He greeted Tony with, "Americans are dilettantes, barbarians. Why are you here?"

"To learn, maître."

Maître Cantal grunted.

There were twenty-five pupils in the class, most of them French. Easels had been set up around the room, and Tony selected one near the window that overlooked a workingman's bistro. Scattered around the room were plaster casts of various parts of the human anatomy taken from Greek statues. Tony looked around for the model. He could see no one.

"You will begin," Maître Cantal told the class.

"Excuse me," Tony said. "I – I didn't bring my paints with me."

"You will not need paints. You will spend the first year learning to draw properly."

The maître pointed to the Greek statuary. "You will draw those. If it seems too simple for you, let me warn you: Before the year is over, more than half of you will be eliminated." He warmed to his speech. "You will spend the first year learning anatomy. The second year – for those of you who pass the course – you will draw from live models, working with oils. The third year – and I assure you there will be fewer of you – you will paint with me, in my style, greatly improving on it, naturally. In the fourth and fifth years, you will find your own style, your own voice. Now let us get to work."

The class went to work.

The maître went around the room, stopping at each easel to make criticisms or comments. When he came to the drawing Tony was working on, he said curtly, "No! That will not do. What I see is the *outside* of an arm. I want to see the *inside*. Muscles, bones, ligaments. I want to know there is *blood* flowing underneath. Do you know how to do that?"

"Yes, maître. You think it, see it, feel it, and then you draw it."

When Tony was not in class, he was usually in his apartment sketching. He could have painted from dawn to dawn. Painting gave him a sense of freedom he had never known before. The simple act of sitting in front of an easel with a paintbrush in his hand made him feel godlike. He could create whole worlds with one hand. He could make a tree, a flower, a human, a universe. It was a heady experience. He had been born for this. When he was not painting, he was out on the streets of Paris exploring the fabulous city. Now it was *his* city, the place where his art was being born. There were two Parises, divided by the Seine into the Left Bank and the Right Bank, and they were worlds apart. The Right Bank was for the wealthy, the established. The Left Bank belonged to the students, the artists, the struggling. It was Montparnasse and the Boulevard Raspail and Saint-Germain-des-Prés. It was the Café Flore and Henry Miller and Elliot Paul. For Tony, it was home. He would sit for hours at the Boule Blanche or La Coupole with fellow students, discussing their arcane world.

"I understand the art director of the Guggenheim Museum is in Paris, buying up everything in sight."

"Tell him to wait for me!"

They all read the same magazines and shared them because they were expensive: *Studio* and *Cahiers d'Art*, *Formes et Couleurs* and *Gazette des Beaux-Arts.*

Tony had learned French at Le Rosey, and he found it easy to make friends with the other students in his class, for they all shared a common passion. They had no idea who Tony's family was, and they accepted him as one of them. Poor and struggling artists gathered at Café Flore and Les Deux Magots on Boulevard Saint-Germain, and ate at Le Pot d'Etian on the Rue des Canettes or at the Rue de l'Université. None of the others had ever seen the inside of Lasserre or Maxim's.

In 1946, giants were practicing their art in Paris. From time to time, Tony caught glimpses of Pablo Picasso, and one day Tony and a friend saw Marc Chagall, a large, flamboyant man in his fifties, with a wild mop of hair just beginning to turn gray. Chagall was seated at a table across the café, in earnest conversation with a group of people.

"We're lucky to see him," Tony's friend whispered. "He comes to Paris very seldom. His home is at Vence, near the Mediterranean coast."

There was Max Ernst sipping an aperitif at a sidewalk café, and the great Alberto Giacometti walking down the Rue de Rivoli, looking like one of his own sculptures, tall and thin and gnarled. Tony was surprised to note he was clubfooted. Tony met Hans Belmer, who was making a name for himself with erotic paintings of young girls turning into dismembered dolls. But perhaps Tony's most exciting moment came when he was introduced to Braque. The artist was cordial, but Tony was tongue-tied.

The future geniuses haunted the new art galleries, studying their competition. The Drouant-David Gallery was exhibiting an unknown young artist named Bernard Buffet, who had studied at the École des Beaux-Arts, and Soutine, Utrillo and Dufy. The students congregated at the Salon d'Automne and the Charpentier Gallery and Mlle. Roussa's Gallery on the Rue de Seine, and spent their spare time gossiping about their successful rivals.

The first time Kate saw Tony's apartment, she was stunned. She wisely made no comment, but she thought, *Bloody hell! How can a son of mine live in this dreary closet?* Aloud she said, "It has great charm, Tony. I don't see a refrigerator. Where do you keep your food?"

"Out on the w-windowsill."

Kate walked over to the window, opened it and selected an apple from the sill outside. "I'm not eating one of your subjects, am I?"

Tony laughed. "N-no, Mother."

Kate took a bite. "Now," she demanded, "tell me about your painting."

"There's n-not much to t-tell yet," Tony confessed. "We're just doing d-drawings this year."

"Do you like this Maître Cantal?"

"He's m-marvelous. The important question is whether he l-likes *me*. Only about one-third of the class is going to m-make it to next year."

Not once did Kate mention Tony's joining the company.

Maître Cantal was not a man to lavish praise. The biggest compliment Tony would get would be a grudging, "I suppose I've seen worse," or, "I'm almost beginning to see *underneath*."

At the end of the school term, Tony was among the eight advanced to the second-year class. To celebrate, Tony and the other relieved students went to a nightclub in Montmartre, got drunk and spent the night with some young English women who were on a tour of France.

When school started again, Tony began to work with oils and live models. It was like being released from kindergarten. After one year of sketching parts of anatomy, Tony felt he knew every muscle, nerve and gland in the human body. That wasn't drawing – it was *copying*. Now, with a paintbrush in his hand and a live model in front of him, Tony began to create. Even Maître Cantal was impressed.

"You have the *feel*," he said grudgingly. "Now we must work on the technique."

There were about a dozen models who sat for classes at the school. The ones Maître Cantal used most frequently were Carlos, a young man working his way through medical school; Annette, a short, buxom brunette with a clump of red pubic hair and an acne-scarred back; and Dominique Masson, a beautiful, young, willowy blonde with delicate cheekbones and deep-green eyes. Dominique also posed for several well-known painters. She was everyone's favorite. Every day after class the male students would gather around her, trying to make a date.

"I never mix pleasure with business," she told them. "Anyway," she teased, "it would not be fair. You have all seen what I have to offer. How do I know what you have to offer?"

And the ribald conversation would go on. But Dominique never went out with anyone at the school.

Late one afternoon when all the other students had left and Tony was finishing a painting of Dominique, she came up behind him unexpectedly. "My nose is too long."

Tony was flustered. "Oh. I'm sorry, I'll change it."

"No, no. The nose in the painting is fine. It is *my* nose that is too long."

Tony smiled. "I'm afraid I can't do much about that."

"A Frenchman would have said, 'Your nose is perfect, *chérie.*' "

"I like your nose, and I'm not French."

"Obviously. You have never asked me out. I wonder why."

Tony was taken aback. "I – I don't know. I guess it's because everyone else has, and you never go out with anybody."

Dominique smiled. "*Everybody* goes out with somebody. Good night."

And she was gone.

Tony noticed that whenever he stayed late, Dominique dressed and then returned to stand behind him and watched him paint.

"You are very good," she announced one afternoon. "You are going to be an important painter."

"Thank you, Dominique. I hope you're right."

"Painting is very serious to you, *oui?*"

"Oui."

"Would a man who is going to be an important painter like to buy me dinner?" She saw the look of surprise on his face. "I do not eat much. I must keep my figure."

Tony laughed. "Certainly. It would be a pleasure."

They ate at a bistro near Sacré-Coeur, and they discussed painters and painting. Tony was fascinated with her stories of the well-known artists for whom she posed. As they were having *café au lait*, Dominique said, "I must tell you, you are as good as any of them."

Tony was inordinately pleased, but all he said was, "I have a long way to go."

Outside the café, Dominique asked, "Are you going to invite me to see your apartment?"

"If you'd like to. I'm afraid it isn't much."

When they arrived, Dominique looked around the tiny, messy apartment and shook her head. "You were right. It is not much. Who takes care of you?"

"A cleaning lady comes in once a week."

"Fire her. This place is filthy. Don't you have a girl friend?"

"No."

She studied him a moment. "You're not queer?"

"No."

"Good. It would be a terrible waste. Find me a pail of water and some soap."

Dominique went to work on the apartment, cleaning and scrubbing and finally tidying up. When she had finished, she said, "That will have to do for now. My God, I need a bath."

She went into the tiny bathroom and ran water in the tub. "How do you fit yourself in this?" she called out.

"I pull up my legs."

She laughed. "I would like to see that."

Fifteen minutes later, she came out of the bathroom with only a towel around her waist, her blond hair damp and curling. She had a beautiful figure, full breasts, a narrow waist and long, tapering legs. Tony had been unaware of her as a woman before. She had been merely a nude figure to be portrayed on canvas. Oddly enough, the towel changed everything. He felt a sudden rush of blood to his loins.

Dominique was watching him. "Would you like to make love to me?"

"Very much."

She slowly removed the towel. "Show me."

Tony had never known a woman like Dominique. She gave him everything and asked for nothing. She came over almost every evening to cook for Tony. When they went out to dinner, Dominique insisted on going to inexpensive bistros or sandwich bars. "You must save your money," she scolded him. "It is very difficult even for a good artist to get started. And you are good, *chéri.*"

They went to Les Halles in the small hours of the morning and had onion soup at Pied de Cochon. They went to the Musée Carnavalet and out-of-the-way places where tourists did not go, like Cimetiére Pére-Lachaise – the final resting place of Oscar Wilde, Frédéric Chopin, Honoré de Balzac and Marcel Proust. They visited the catacombs and spent a lazy holiday week going down the Seine on a barge owned by a friend of Dominique's.

Dominique was a delight to be with. She had a quixotic sense of humor, and whenever Tony was depressed, she would laugh him out of it. She seemed to know everyone in Paris, and she took Tony to interesting parties where he met some of the most prominent figures of the day, like the poet Paul Éluard, and André Breton, in charge of the prestigious Galerie Maeght.

Dominique was a source of constant encouragement. "You are going to be better than all of them, *chéri*. Believe me. I know."

If Tony was in the mood to paint at night, Dominique would cheerfully pose for him, even though she had been working all day. *God, I'm lucky,* Tony thought. This was the first time he had been sure someone loved him for what he was, not who he was, and it was a feeling he cherished. Tony was afraid to tell Dominique he was the heir to one of the world's largest fortunes, afraid she would change, afraid they would lose what they had. But for her birthday Tony could not resist buying her a Russian lynx coat.

"It's the most beautiful thing I've ever seen in my life!" Dominique swirled the coat around her and danced around the room. She stopped in the middle of a spin. "Where did it come from? Tony, where did you get the money to buy this coat?"

He was ready for her. "It's hot – stolen. I bought it from a little man outside the Rodin Museum. He was anxious to get rid of it. It didn't cost me much more than a good cloth coat would cost at Au Printemps."

Dominique stared at him a moment, then burst out laughing. "I'll wear it even if we both go to prison!"

Then she threw her arms around Tony and started to cry. "Oh, Tony, you idiot. You darling, fantastic idiot."

It was well worth the lie, Tony decided.

One night Dominique suggested to Tony that he move in with her. Between working at the École des Beaux-Arts and modeling for some of the better-known artists in Paris, Dominique was able to rent a large, modern apartment on Rue Prêtres-Saint Severin. "You should not be living in a place like this, Tony. It is dreadful. Live with me, and you will not have to pay any rent. I can do your laundry, cook for you and – "

"No, Dominique. Thank you."

"But why?"

How could he explain? In the beginning he might have told her he was rich, but now it was too late. She would feel he had been making a fool of her. So he said, "It would be like living off you. You've already given me too much."

"Then I'm giving up my apartment and moving in here. I want to be with you."

She moved in the following day.

There was a wonderful, easy intimacy between them. They spent weekends in the country and stopped at little hostels where Tony would set up his easel and paint landscapes, and when they got hungry Dominique would spread out a picnic lunch she had prepared and they would eat in a meadow. Afterward, they made long, sweet love. Tony had never been so completely happy.

His work was progressing beautifully. One morning Maître Cantal held up one of Tony's paintings and said to the class, "Look at that body. You can see it *breathing.*"

Tony could hardly wait to tell Dominique that night. "You know how I got the breathing just right? I hold the model in my arms every night."

Dominique laughed in excitement and then grew serious. "Tony, I do not think you need three more years of school. You are ready now. Everyone at the school sees that, even Cantal."

Tony's fear was that he was not good enough, that he was just another painter, that his work would be lost in the flood of pictures turned out by thousands of artists all over the world every day. He could not bear the thought of it. *Winning is what's important, Tony. Remember that.*

Sometimes when Tony finished a painting he would be filled with a sense of elation and think, *I have talent. I really have talent.* At other times he would look at his work and think, *I'm a bloody amateur.*

With Dominique's encouragement, Tony was gaining more and more confidence in his work. He had finished almost two dozen paintings on his own. Landscapes, still lifes. There was a painting of Dominique lying nude under a tree, the sun dappling her body. A man's jacket and shirt were in the foreground, and the viewer knew the woman awaited her lover.

When Dominique saw the painting, she cried, "You must have an exhibition!"

"You're mad, Dominique! I'm not ready."

"You're wrong, *mon cher.*"

Tony arrived home late the next afternoon to find that Dominique was not alone. Anton Goerg, a thin man with an enormous potbelly and protuberant hazel eyes, was with her. He was the owner and proprietor of the Goerg Gallery, a modest gallery on the Rue Dauphine. Tony's paintings were spread around the room.

"What's going on?" Tony asked.

"What's going on, monsieur," Anton Goerg exclaimed, "is that I think your work is brilliant." He clapped Tony on the back. "I would be honored to give you a showing in my gallery."

Tony looked over at Dominique, and she was beaming at him.

"I – I don't know what to say."

"You have already said it," Goerg replied. "On these canvases."

Tony and Dominique stayed up half the night discussing it.

"I don't feel I'm ready. The critics will crucify me."

"You're wrong, *chéri*. This is perfect for you. It is a small gallery. Only the local people will come and judge you. There is no way you can get hurt. Monsieur Goerg would never offer to give you an exhibition if he did not believe in you. He agrees with me that you are going to be a very important artist."

"All right," Tony finally said. "Who knows? I might even sell a painting."

The cable read: ARRIVING PARIS SATURDAY. PLEASE JOIN ME FOR DINNER. LOVE, MOTHER.

Tony's first thought as he watched his mother walk into the studio was, *What a handsome woman she is.* She was in her mid-fifties, hair untinted, with white strands laced through the black. There was a charged vitality about her. Tony had once asked her why she had not remarried. She had answered quietly, "Only two men were ever important in my life. Your father and you."

Now, standing in the little apartment in Paris, facing his mother, Tony said, "It's g-good to see you, M-mother."

"Tony, you look absolutely wonderful! The beard is new." She laughed and ran her fingers through it. "You look like a young Abe Lincoln." Her eyes swept the small apartment. "Thank God, you've gotten a good cleaning woman. It looks like a different place."

Kate walked over to the easel, where Tony had been working on a painting, and she stopped and stared at it for a long time. He stood there, nervously awaiting his mother's reaction.

When Kate spoke, her voice was very soft. "It's brilliant, Tony. Really brilliant." There was no effort to conceal the pride she felt. She could not be deceived about art, and there was a fierce exultation in her that her son was so talented.

She turned to face him. "Let me see more!"

They spent the next two hours going through his stack of paintings. Kate discussed each one in great detail. There was no condescension in her voice. She had failed in her attempt to control his life, and Tony admired her for taking her defeat so gracefully.

Kate said, "I'll arrange for a showing. I know a few dealers who – "

"Thanks, M-mother, but you d-don't have to. I'm having a showing next F-friday. A g-gallery is giving me an exhibition."

Kate threw her arms around Tony. "That's wonderful! Which gallery?"

"The G-goerg Gallery."

"I don't believe I know it."

"It's s-small, but I'm not ready for Hammer or W-wildenstein yet."

She pointed to the painting of Dominique under the tree. "You're wrong, Tony. I think this – "

There was the sound of the front door opening. "I'm horny, *chéri*. Take off your – " Dominique saw Kate. "Oh, *merde!* I'm sorry. I – I didn't know you had company, Tony."

There was a moment of frozen silence.

"Dominique, this is my m-mother. M-mother, may I present D-dominique Masson."

The two women stood there, studying each other.

"How do you do, Mrs. Blackwell."

Kate said, "I've been admiring my son's portrait of you." The rest was left unspoken.

There was another awkward silence.

"Did Tony tell you he's going to have an exhibition, Mrs. Blackwell?"

"Yes, he did. It's wonderful news."

"Can you s-stay for it, Mother?"

"I'd give anything to be able to be there, but I have a board meeting the day after tomorrow in Johannesburg and there's no way I can miss it. I wish I'd known about it sooner, I'd have rearranged my schedule."

"It's all r-right," Tony said. "I understand." Tony was nervous that his mother might say more about the company in front of Dominique, but Kate's mind was on the paintings.

"It's important for the right people to see your exhibition."

"Who are the right people, Mrs. Blackwell?"

Kate turned to Dominique. "Opinion-makers, critics. Someone like André d'Usseau – he should be there."

André d'Usseau was the most respected art critic in France. He was a ferocious lion guarding the temple of art, and a single review from him could make or break an artist overnight. D'Usseau was invited to the opening of every exhibition, but he attended only the major ones. Gallery owners and artists trembled, waiting for his reviews to appear. He was a master of the *bon mot*, and his quips flew around Paris on poisoned wings. André d'Usseau was the most hated man in Parisian art circles, and the most respected. His mordant wit and savage criticism were tolerated because of his expertise.

Tony turned to Dominique. "That's a m-mother for you." Then to Kate, "André d'Usseau doesn't g-go to little galleries."

"Oh, Tony, he *must* come. He can make you famous overnight."

"Or b-break me."

"Don't you believe in yourself?" Kate was watching her son.

"Of course he does," Dominique said. "But we couldn't dare hope that Monsieur d'Usseau would come."

"I could probably find some friends who know him."

Dominique's face lighted up. "That would be fantastic!" She turned to Tony. "*Chéri*, do you know what it would mean if he came to your opening?"

"Oblivion?"

"Be serious. I know his taste, Tony. I know what he likes. He will adore your paintings."

Kate said, "I won't try to arrange for him to come unless you want me to, Tony."

"Of course he wants it, Mrs. Blackwell."

Tony took a deep breath. "I'm s-scared, but what the hell! L-let's try."

"I'll see what I can do." Kate looked at the painting on the easel for a long, long time, then turned back to Tony. There was a sadness in her eyes. "Son, I must leave Paris tomorrow. Can we have dinner tonight?"

Tony replied, "Yes, of course, Mother. *We're* f-free."

Kate turned to Dominique and said graciously, "Would you like to have dinner at Maxim's or – "

Tony said quickly, "Dominique and I know a w-wonderful little café not f-far from here."

They went to a bistro at the Place Victoire. The food was good and the wine was excellent. The two women seemed to get along well, and Tony was terribly proud of both of them. *Its one of the best nights of my life*, he thought. *I'm with my mother and the woman I'm going to marry.*

The next morning Kate telephoned from the airport. "I've made a half a dozen phone calls," she told Tony. "No one could give me a definite answer about André d' Usseau. But whichever way it goes, darling, I'm proud of you. The paintings are wonderful. Tony, I love you."

"I l-love you, too, M-mother."

The Goerg Gallery was just large enough to escape being called *intime*. Two dozen of Tony's paintings were being hung on the walls in frantic, last-minute preparation for the opening. On a marble sideboard were slabs of cheese and biscuits and bottles of Chablis. The gallery was empty except for Anton Goerg, Tony, Dominique and a young female assistant who was hanging the last of the paintings.

Anton Goerg looked at his watch. "The invitations said 'seven o'clock.' People should start to arrive at any moment now."

Tony had not expected to be nervous. And *I'm not nervous*, he told himself. *I'm panicky!*

"What if no one shows up?" he asked. "I mean, what if not one single, bloody person shows up?"

Dominique smiled and stroked his cheek. "Then we'll have all this cheese and wine for ourselves."

People began to arrive. Slowly at first, and then in larger numbers. Monsieur Goerg was at the door, effusively greeting them. *They don't look like art buyers to me*, Tony thought grimly. His discerning eye divided them into three categories: There were the artists and art students who attended each exhibition to evaluate the competition; the art dealers who came to every exhibition so they could spread derogatory news about aspiring painters; and the *arty* crowd, consisting to a large extent of homosexuals and lesbians who seemed to spend their lives around the fringes of the art world. *I'm not going to sell a single, goddamned picture*, Tony decided.

Monsieur Goerg was beckoning to Tony from across the room.

"I don't think I want to meet any of these people," Tony whispered to Dominique. "They're here to rip me apart."

"Nonsense. They came here to meet you. Now be charming, Tony."

And so, he was charming. He met everybody, smiled a lot and uttered all the appropriate phrases in response to the compliments that were paid him. *But were they really compliments?* Tony wondered. Over the years a vocabulary had developed in art circles to cover exhibitions of unknown painters. Phrases that said everything and nothing.

"You really feel you're there . . ."

"I've never seen a style quite like yours . . ."

"Now, that's a painting! . . ."

"It speaks to me . . ."

"You couldn't have done it any better . . ."

People kept arriving, and Tony wondered whether the attraction was curiosity about his paintings or the free wine and cheese. So far, not one of his paintings had sold, but the wine and cheese were being consumed rapaciously.

"Be patient," Monsieur Goerg whispered to Tony. "They are interested. First they must get a smell of the paintings. They see one they like, they keep wandering back to it. Pretty soon they ask the price, and when they nibble, *voilà!* The hook is set!"

"Jesus! I feel like I'm on a fishing cruise," Tony told Dominique.

Monsieur Goerg bustled up to Tony. "We've sold one!" he exclaimed. "The Normandy landscape. Five hundred francs."

It was a moment that Tony would remember as long as he lived. Someone had bought a painting of his! Someone had thought enough of his work to pay money for it, to hang it in his home or office, to look at it, live with it, show it to friends. It was a small piece of immortality. It was a way of living more than one life, of being in more than one place at the same time. A successful artist was in hundreds of homes and offices and museums all over the world, bringing pleasure to thousands – sometimes millions of people. Tony felt as though he had stepped into the pantheon of Da Vinci and Michelangelo and Rembrandt. He was no longer an amateur painter, he was a professional. Someone had paid money for his work.

Dominique hurried up to him, her eyes bright with excitement. "You've just sold another one, Tony."

"Which one?" he asked eagerly.

"The floral."

The small gallery was filled now with people and loud chatter and the clink of glasses; and suddenly a stillness came over the room. There was an undercurrent of whispers and all eyes turned to the door.

André d'Usseau was entering the gallery. He was in his middle fifties, taller than the average Frenchman, with a strong, leonine face and a mane of white hair. He wore a flowing inverness cape and Borsalino hat, and behind him came an entourage of hangers-on. Automatically, everyone in the room began to make way for d'Usseau. There was not one person present who did not know who he was.

Dominique squeezed Tony's hand. "He's come!" she said. "He's here!"

Such an honor had never befallen Monsieur Goerg before, and he was beside himself, bowing and scraping before the great man, doing everything but tugging at his forelock.

"Monsieur d'Usseau," he babbled. "What a great pleasure this is! What an honor! May I offer you some wine, some cheese?" He cursed himself for not having bought a decent wine.

"Thank you," the great man replied. "I have come to feast only my eyes. I would like to meet the artist."

Tony was too stunned to move. Dominique pushed him forward.

"Here he is," Monsieur Goerg said. "Mr. André d'Usseau, this is Tony Blackwell."

Tony found his voice. "How do you do, sir? I – thank you for coming."

André d'Usseau bowed slightly and moved toward the paintings on the walls. Everyone pushed back to give him room. He made his way slowly, looking at each painting long and carefully, then moving on to the next one. Tony tried to read his face, but he could tell nothing. D'Usseau neither frowned nor smiled. He stopped for a long time at one particular painting, a nude of Dominique, then moved on. He made a complete circle of the room, missing nothing. Tony was perspiring profusely.

When André d'Usseau had finished, he walked over to Tony. "I am glad I came," was all he said.

Within minutes after the famous critic had left, every painting in the gallery was sold. A great new artist was being born, and everyone wanted to be in at the birth.

"I have never seen anything like it," Monsieur Goerg exclaimed. "André d'Usseau came to my gallery. *My* gallery! All Paris will read about it tomorrow. 'I am glad I came.' André d'Usseau is not a man to waste words. This calls for champagne. Let us celebrate."

Later that night, Tony and Dominique had their own private celebration. Dominique snuggled in his arms. "I've slept with painters before," she said, "but never anyone as famous as you're going to be. Tomorrow everyone in Paris will know who you are."

And Dominique was right.

*

At five o'clock the following morning, Tony and Dominique hurriedly got dressed and went out to get the first edition of the morning paper. It had just arrived at the kiosk. Tony snatched up the paper and turned to the art section. His review was the headline article under the by-line of André d'Usseau. Tony read it aloud:

"An exhibition by a young American painter, Anthony Blackwell, opened last night at the Goerg Gallery. It was a great learning experience for this critic. I have attended so many exhibitions of talented painters that I had forgotten what truly bad paintings looked like. I was forcibly reminded last night . . ."

Tony's face turned ashen.

"Please don't read any more," Dominique begged. She tried to take the paper from Tony.

"Let go!" he commanded.

He read on.

"At first I thought a joke was being perpetrated. I could not seriously believe that anyone would have the nerve to hang such amateurish paintings and dare to call them art. I searched for the tiniest glimmering of talent. Alas, there was none. They should have hung the painter instead of his paintings. I would earnestly advise that the confused Mr. Blackwell return to his real profession, which I can only assume is that of house painter."

"I can't believe it," Dominique whispered. "I can't believe he couldn't see it. Oh, that bastard!" Dominique began to cry helplessly.

Tony felt as though his chest were filled with lead. He had difficulty breathing. "He saw it," he said. "And he does know, Dominique. He does know." His voice was filled with pain. "That's what hurts so much. Christ! What a fool I was!" He started to move away.

"Where are you going, Tony?"

"I don't know."

He wandered around the cold, dawn streets, unaware of the tears running down his face. Within a few hours, everyone in Paris would have read that review. He would be an object of ridicule. But what hurt more was that he had deluded himself. He had really believed he had a career ahead of him as a painter. At least André d'Usseau had saved him from that mistake. *Pieces of posterity*, Tony thought grimly. *Pieces of shit!* He walked into the first open bar and proceeded to get mindlessly drunk.

When Tony finally returned to his apartment, it was five o'clock the following morning.

Dominique was waiting for him, frantic. "Where have you been, Tony? Your mother has been trying to get in touch with you. She's sick with worry."

"Did you read it to her?"

"Yes, she insisted. I – "

The telephone rang. Dominique looked at Tony, and picked up the receiver.

"Hello? Yes, Mrs. Blackwell. He just walked in." She held the receiver out to Tony. He hesitated, then took it.

"Hello, M-mother."

Kate's voice was filled with distress. "Tony, darling, listen to me. I can make him print a retraction. I – "

"Mother," Tony said wearily, "this isn't a b-business transaction. This is a c-critic expressing an opinion. His opinion is that I should be h-hanged."

"Darling, I hate to have you hurt like this. I don't think I can stand – " She broke off, unable to continue.

"It's all right, M-mother. I've had my little f-fling. I tried it and it didn't w-work. I don't have what it t-takes. It's as simple as that. I h-hate d'Usseau's guts, but he's the best g-goddamned art critic in the world, I have to g-give him that. He saved me from making a t-terrible mistake."

"Tony, I wish there was something I could say . . ."

"D'Usseau s-said it all. It's b-better that I f-found it out now instead of t-ten years from now, isn't it? I've got to g-get out of this town."

"Wait there for me, darling. I'll leave Johannesburg tomorrow and we'll go back to New York together."

"All right," Tony said. He replaced the receiver and turned toward Dominique. "I'm sorry, Dominique. You picked the wrong fellow."

Dominique said nothing. She just looked at him with eyes filled with an unspeakable sorrow.

The following afternoon at Kruger-Brent's office on Rue Matignon, Kate Blackwell was writing out a check. The man seated across the desk from her sighed. "It is a pity. Your son has talent, Mrs. Blackwell. He could have become an important painter."

Kate stared at him coldly. "Mr. d'Usseau, there are tens of thousands of painters in the world. My son was not meant to be one of the crowd." She passed the check across the desk. "You fulfilled your part of the bargain, I'm prepared to fulfill mine. Kruger-Brent, Limited, will sponsor art museums in Johannesburg, London and New York. You will be in charge of selecting the paintings – with a handsome commission, of course."

But long after d'Usseau had gone, Kate sat at her desk, filled with a deep sadness. She loved her son so much. If he ever found out . . . She knew the risk she had taken. But she could not stand by and let Tony throw away his inheritance. No matter what it might cost her, he had to be protected. The company had to be protected. Kate rose, feeling suddenly very tired. It was time to pick up Tony and take him home. She would help him get over this, so he could get on with what he had been born to do.

Run the company.

19

For the next two years, Tony Blackwell felt he was on a giant treadmill that was taking him nowhere. He was the heir apparent to an awesome conglomerate. Kruger-Brent's empire had expanded to include paper mills, an airline, banks and a chain of hospitals. Tony learned that a name is a key that opens all doors. There are clubs and organizations and social cliques where the coin of the realm is not money or influence, but the proper name. Tony was accepted for membership in the Union Club, The Brook and The Links Club. He was catered to everywhere he went, but he felt like an imposter. He had done nothing to deserve any of it. He was in the giant shadow of his grandfather, and he felt he was constantly being measured against him. It was unfair, for there were no more mine fields to crawl over, no guards shooting at him, no sharks threatening him. The ancient tales of derring-do had nothing to do with Tony. They belonged to a past century, another time, another place, heroic acts committed by a stranger.

Tony worked twice as hard as anyone else at Kruger-Brent, Ltd. He drove himself mercilessly, trying to rid himself of memories too searing to bear. He wrote to Dominique, but his letters were returned unopened. He telephoned Maître Cantal, but Dominique no longer modeled at the school. She had disappeared.

Tony handled his job expertly and methodically, with neither passion nor love, and if he felt a deep emptiness inside himself, no one suspected it. Not even Kate. She received weekly reports on Tony, and she was pleased with them.

"He has a natural aptitude for business," she told Brad Rogers.

To Kate, the long hours her son worked were proof of how much he loved what he was doing. When Kate thought of how Tony had almost thrown his future away, she shuddered and was grateful she had saved him.

In 1948 the Nationalist Party was in full power in South Africa, with segregation in all public places. Migration was strictly controlled, and families were split up to suit the convenience of the government. Every black man had to carry a *bewyshoek*, and it was more than a pass, it was a lifeline, his birth certificate, his work permit, his tax receipt. It regulated his movements and his life. There were increasing riots in South Africa, and they were ruthlessly put down by the police. From time to time, Kate read newspaper stories about sabotage and unrest, and Banda's name was always prominently mentioned. He was still a leader in the underground, despite his age. *Of course he would fight for his people*, Kate thought. *He's Banda.*

Kate celebrated her fifty-sixth birthday alone with Tony at the house on Fifth Avenue. She thought, *This handsome twenty-four-year-old man across the table can't be my son. I'm too young.* And he was toasting her, "To m-my f-fantastic m-mother. Happy b-birthday!"

"You should make that to my fantastic *old* mother." *Soon I'll be retiring*, Kate thought, *but my son will take my place. My son!*

At Kate's insistence, Tony had moved into the mansion on Fifth Avenue.

"The place is too bloody large for me to rattle around in alone," Kate told him. "You'll have the whole east wing to yourself and all the privacy you need." It was easier for Tony to give in than to argue.

Tony and Kate had breakfast together every morning, and the topic of conversation was always Kruger-Brent, Ltd. Tony marveled that his mother could care so passionately for a faceless, soulless entity, an amorphous collection of buildings and machines and bookkeeping figures. *Where did the magic lie?* With all the myriad mysteries of the world to explore, why would anyone want to waste a lifetime accumulating wealth to pile on more wealth, gathering power that was beyond power? Tony did not understand his mother But he loved her. And he tried to live up to what she expected of him.

The Pan American flight from Rome to New York had been uneventful. Tony liked the airline. It was pleasant and efficient. He worked on his overseas acquisitions reports from the time the plane took off, skipping dinner and ignoring the stewardesses who kept offering him drinks, pillows or whatever else might appeal to their attractive passenger.

"Thank you, miss. I'm fine."

"If there's *anything at* all, Mr. Blackwell . . ."

"Thank you."

A middle-aged woman in the seat next to Tony was reading a fashion magazine. As she turned a page, Tony happened to glance over, and he froze. There was a picture of a model wearing a ball gown. It was Dominique. There was no question about it. There were the high, delicate cheekbones and the deep-green eyes, the luxuriant blond hair. Tony's pulse began to race.

"Excuse me," Tony said to his seat companion. "May I borrow that page?"

Early the following morning, Tony called the dress shop and got the name of their advertising agency. He telephoned them. I'm trying to locate one of your models," he told the switchboard operator. "Could you – "

"One moment, please."

A man's voice came on. "May I help you?"

"I saw a photograph in this month's issue of *Vogue*. A model advertising a ball gown for the Rothman stores. Is that your account?"

"Yes."

"Can you give me the name of your model agency?"

"That would be the Carleton Blessing Agency." He gave Tony the telephone number.

A minute later, Tony was talking to a woman at the Blessing Agency. "I'm trying to locate one of your models," he said. "Dominique Masson."

"I'm sorry. It is our policy not to give out personal information." And the line went dead.

Tony sat there, staring at the receiver. There *had* to be a way to get in touch with Dominique. He went into Brad Rogers's office.

"Morning, Tony. Coffee?"

"No, thanks. Brad, have you heard of the Carleton Blessing Model Agency?"

"I should think so. We own it."

"*What?*"

"It's under the umbrella of one of our subsidiaries."

"When did we acquire it?"

"A couple of years ago. Just about the time you joined the company. What's your interest in it?"

"I'm trying to locate one of their models. She's an old friend."

"No problem. I'll call and – "

"Never mind. I'll do it. Thanks, Brad."

A feeling of warm anticipation was building up inside Tony.

Late that afternoon, Tony went uptown to the offices of the Carleton Blessing Agency and gave his name. Sixty seconds later, he was seated in the office of the president, a Mr. Tilton.

"This is certainly an honor, Mr. Blackwell. I hope there's no problem. Our profits for the last quarter – "

"No problem. I'm interested in one of your models. Dominique Masson."

Tilton's face lighted up. "She's turned out to be one of our very best. Your mother has a good eye."

Tony thought he had misunderstood him. "I beg your pardon?"

"Your mother personally requested that we engage Dominique. It was part of our deal when Kruger-Brent, Limited, took us over. It's all in our file, if you'd care to – "

"No." Tony could make no sense of what he was hearing. *Why would his mother – ?* "May I have Dominique's address, please?"

"Certainly, Mr. Blackwell. She's doing a layout in Vermont today, but she should be back" – he glanced at a schedule on his desk – "tomorrow afternoon."

Tony was waiting outside Dominique's apartment building when a black sedan pulled up and Dominique stepped out. With her was a large, athletic-looking man carrying Dominique's suitcase. Dominique stopped dead when she saw Tony.

"Tony! My God! What – what are you doing here?"

"I need to talk to you."

"Some other time, buddy," the athlete said. "We have a busy afternoon."

Tony did not even look at him. "Tell your friend to go away."

"Hey! Who the hell do you think – ?"

Dominique turned to the man. "Please go, Ben. I'll call you this evening."

He hesitated a moment, then shrugged. "Okay." He glared at Tony, got back in the car and roared off.

Dominique turned to Tony. "You'd better come inside."

The apartment was a large duplex with white rugs and drapes and modern furniture. It must have cost a fortune.

"You're doing well," Tony said.

"Yes. I've been lucky." Dominique's fingers were picking nervously at her blouse. "Would you like a drink?"

"No, thanks. I tried to get in touch with you after I left Paris."

"I moved."

"To America?"

"Yes."

"How did you get a job with the Carleton Blessing Agency?"

"I – I answered a newspaper advertisement," she said lamely.

"When did you first meet my mother, Dominique?"

"I – at your apartment in Paris. Remember? We – "

"No more games," Tony said. He felt a wild rage building in him. "It's over. I've never hit a woman in my life, but if you tell me one more lie, I promise you your face won't be fit to photograph."

Dominique started to speak, but the fury in Tony's eyes stopped her.

"I'll ask you once more. When did you first meet my mother?"

This time there was no hesitation. "When you were accepted at École des Beaux-Arts. Your mother arranged for me to model there."

He felt sick to his stomach. He forced himself to go on. "So I could meet you?"

"Yes, I – "

"And she paid you to become my mistress, to pretend to love me?"

"Yes. It was just after the war – it was terrible. I had no money. Don't you see? But Tony, believe me, I cared. I really cared – "

"Just answer my questions." The savagery in his voice frightened her. This was a stranger before her, a man capable of untold violence.

"What was the point of it?"

"Your mother wanted me to keep an eye on you."

He thought of Dominique's tenderness and her lovemaking – bought and paid for, courtesy of his mother – and he was sick with shame. All along, he had been his mother's puppet, controlled, manipulated. His mother had never given a damn about him. He was not her son. He was her crown prince, her heir apparent. All that mattered to her was the company. He took one last look at Dominique, then turned and stumbled out. She looked after him, her eyes blinded by tears, and she thought, *I didn't lie about loving you, Tony. I didn't lie about that.*

Kate was in the library when Tony walked in, very drunk.

"I t-talked to D-dominique," he said. "You t-two m-must have had a w-wonderful time l-laughing at me behind my back."

Kate felt a quick sense of alarm. "Tony – "

"From now on I want you to s-stay out of my p-personal l-life. Do you hear me?" And he turned and staggered out of the room.

Kate watched him go, and she was suddenly filled with a terrible sense of foreboding.

20

The following day, Tony took an apartment in Greenwich Village. There were no more sociable dinners with his mother. He kept his relationship with Kate on an impersonal, businesslike basis. From time to time Kate made conciliatory overtures, which Tony ignored.

Kate's heart ached. But she had done what was right for Tony. Just as she had once done what was right for David. She could not have let either of them leave the company. Tony was the one human being in the world Kate loved, and she watched as he became more and more insular, drawing deep within himself, rejecting everyone. He had no friends. Where once he had been warm and outgoing, he was now cool and reserved. He had built a wall around himself that no one was able to breach. *He needs a wife to care for him*, Kate thought. *And a son to carry on. I must help him. I must.*

Brad Rogers came into Kate's office and said, "I'm afraid we're in for some more trouble, Kate."

"What's happened?"

He put a cable on her desk. "The South African Parliament has outlawed the Natives' Representative Council and passed the Communist Act."

Kate said, "My God!" The act had nothing to do with communism. It stated that anyone who disagreed with any government policy and tried to change it in any way was guilty under the Communist Act and could be imprisoned.

"It's their way of breaking the black resistance movement," she said. "If – " She was interrupted by her secretary.

"There's an overseas call for you. It's Mr. Pierce in Johannesburg."

Jonathan Pierce was the manager of the Johannesburg branch office. Kate picked up the phone. "Hello, Johnny. How are you?"

"Fine, Kate. I have some news I thought you'd better be aware of."

"What's that?"

"I've just received a report that the police have captured Banda."

7

Kate was on the next flight to Johannesburg. She had alerted the company lawyers to see what could be done for Banda. Even the power and prestige of Kruger-Brent, Ltd., might not be able to help him. He had been designated an enemy of the state, and she dreaded to think what his punishment would be. At least she must see him and talk to him and offer what support she could.

When the plane landed in Johannesburg, Kate went to her office and telephoned the director of prisons.

"He's in an isolation block, Mrs. Blackwell, and he's allowed no visitors. However, in your case, I will see what can be done . . ."

The following morning, Kate was at the Johannesburg prison, face to face with Banda. He was manacled and shackled, and there was a glass partition between them. His hair was completely white. Kate had not known what to expect – despair, defiance – but Banda grinned when he saw her and said, "I knew you'd come. You're just like your daddy. You can't stay away from trouble, can you?"

"Look who's talking," Kate retorted. "Bloody hell! How do we get you out of here?"

"In a box. That's the only way they're going to let me go."

"I have a lot of fancy lawyers who – "

"Forget it, Kate. They caught me fair and square. Now I've got to get away fair and square."

"What are you talking about?"

"I don't like cages, I never did. And they haven't built one yet that can keep me."

Kate said, "Banda, don't try it. Please. They'll kill you."

"Nothing can kill me," Banda said. "You're talking to a man who lived through sharks and land mines and guard dogs." A soft gleam came into his eyes. "You know something, Kate? I think maybe that was the best time of my life."

When Kate went to visit Banda the next day, the superintendent said, "I'm sorry, Mrs. Blackwell. We've had to move him for security reasons."

"Where is he?"

"I'm not at liberty to say."

When Kate woke up the following morning, she saw the headline in the newspaper carried in with her breakfast tray. It read: REBEL LEADER KILLED WHILE TRYING TO ESCAPE PRISON. She was at the prison an hour later, in the superintendent's office.

"He was shot during an attempted prison break, Mrs. Blackwell. That's all there is to it."

You're wrong thought Kate, *there's more. Much more.* Banda was dead, but was his dream of freedom for his people dead?

Two days later, after making the funeral arrangements, Kate was on the plane to New York. She looked out the window to take one last look at her beloved land. The soil was red and rich and fertile, and in the bowels of its earth were treasures beyond man's dreams. This was God's chosen land, and He had been lavish in his generosity. But there was a curse upon the country. *I'll never come back here again*, Kate thought sadly. *Never.*

One of Brad Rogers's responsibilities was to oversee the Long-Range Planning Department of Kruger-Brent, Ltd. He was brilliant at finding businesses that would make profitable acquisitions.

One day in early May, he walked into Kate Blackwell's office. "I've come across something interesting, Kate." He placed two folders on her desk. "Two companies. If we could pick up either one of them, it would be a coup."

"Thanks, Brad. I'll look them over tonight."

That evening, Kate dined alone and studied Brad Rogers's confidential reports on the two companies – Wyatt Oil & Tool and International Technology. The reports were long and detailed, and both ended with the letters NIS, the company code for *Not Interested in Selling*, which meant that if the companies were to be acquired, it would take more than a straightforward business transaction to accomplish it. *And*, Kate thought, *they're well worth taking over.* Each company was privately controlled by a wealthy and strong-minded individual, which eliminated any possibility of a takeover attempt. It was a challenge, and it had been a long time since Kate had faced a challenge. The more she thought about it, the more the possibilities began to excite her. She studied again the confidential balance sheets. Wyatt Oil & Tool was owned by a Texan, Charlie Wyatt, and the company's assets included producing oil wells, a utility company and dozens of potentially profitable oil leases. There was no question about it, Wyatt Oil & Tool would make a handsome acquisition for Kruger-Brent, Ltd.

Kate turned her attention to the second company. International Technology was owned by a German, Count Frederick Hoffman. The company had started with a small steel mill in Essen, and over the years had expanded into a huge conglomerate, with shipyards, petrochemical plants, a fleet of oil tankers and a computer division.

As large as Kruger-Brent, Ltd., was, it could digest only one of these giants. She knew which company she was going after. NIS, the sheet read.

We'll see about that, Kate thought.

Early the following morning, she sent for Brad Rogers. "I'd love to know how you got hold of those confidential balance sheets," Kate grinned. "Tell me about Charlie Wyatt and Frederick Hoffman."

Brad had done his homework. "Charlie Wyatt was born in Dallas. Flamboyant, loud, runs his own empire, smart as hell. He started with nothing, got lucky in oil wildcatting, kept expanding and now he owns about half of Texas."

"How old is he?"
"Forty-seven."
"Children?"
"One daughter, twenty-five. From what I hear, she's a raving beauty."
"Is she married?"
"Divorced."
"Frederick Hoffman."
"Hoffman's a couple of years younger than Charlie Wyatt. He's a count, comes from a distinguished German family going back to the Middle Ages. He's a widower. His grandfather started with a small steel mill. Frederick Hoffman inherited it from his father and built it into a conglomerate. He was one of the first to get into the computer field. He holds a lot of patents on microprocessors. Every time we use a computer, Count Hoffman gets a royalty."
"Children?"
"A daughter, twenty-three."
"What is she like?"
"I couldn't find out," Brad Rogers apologized. "It's a very buttoned-up family. They travel in their own little circles." He hesitated. "We're probably wasting our time on this, Kate. I had a few drinks with a couple of top executives in both companies. Neither Wyatt nor Hoffman has the slightest interest in a sale, merger or joint venture. As you can see from their financials, they'd be crazy even to think about it."
That feeling of challenge was there in Kate again, tugging at her.

Ten days later Kate was invited by the President of the United States to a Washington conference of leading international industrialists to discuss assistance to underdeveloped countries. Kate made a telephone call, and shortly afterward Charlie Wyatt and Count Frederick Hoffman received invitations to attend the conference.

Kate had formed a mental impression of both the Texan and the German, and they fitted her preconceived notions almost precisely. She had never met a shy Texan, and Charlie Wyatt was no exception. He was a huge man – almost six feet four inches – with enormous shoulders and a football player's body that had gone to fat. His face was large and ruddy, and his voice loud and booming. He came off as a good ol' boy – or would have if Kate had not known better. Charlie Wyatt had not built his empire by luck. He was a business genius. Kate had talked to him for less than ten minutes when she knew that there was no way this man could be persuaded to do anything he did not want to do. He was opinionated, and he had a deep stubborn streak. No one was going to cajole him, threaten him or con him out of his company. But Kate had found his Achilles' heel, and that was enough.

Frederick Hoffman was Charlie Wyatt's opposite. He was a handsome man, with an aristocratic face and soft brown hair tinged with gray at the temples. He was punctiliously correct and filled with a sense of old-fashioned courtesy. On the surface, Frederick Hoffman was pleasant and debonair; on the inside Kate sensed a core of steel.

The conference in Washington lasted three days, and it went well. The meetings were chaired by the Vice-President, and the President made a brief appearance. Everyone there was impressed with Kate Blackwell. She was an attractive, charismatic woman, head of a corporate empire she had helped build, and they were fascinated, as Kate meant them to be.

When Kate got Charlie Wyatt alone for a moment, she asked innocently, "Is your family with you, Mr. Wyatt?"

"I brought my daughter along. She has a little shoppin' to do."

"Oh, really? How nice." No one would have suspected that Kate not only knew his daughter was with him, but what kind of dress she had bought at Garfinckel's that morning. "I'm giving a little dinner party at Dark Harbor Friday. I'd be pleased if you and your daughter would join us for the weekend."

Wyatt did not hesitate. "I've heard a lot about your spread, Mrs. Blackwell. I'd sure like to see it."

Kate smiled. "Good. I'll make arrangements for you to be flown up there tomorrow night."

Ten minutes later, Kate was speaking to Frederick Hoffman. "Are you alone in Washington, Mr. Hoffman?" she asked. "Or is your wife with you?"

"My wife died a few years ago," Frederick Hoffman told her. "I'm here with my daughter."

Kate knew they were staying at the Hay-Adams Hotel in Suite 418. "I'm giving a little dinner party at Dark Harbor. I would be delighted if you and your daughter could join us tomorrow for the weekend."

"I should be getting back to Germany," Hoffman replied. He studied her a moment, and smiled. "I suppose another day or two won't make much difference."

"Wonderful. I'll arrange transportation for you."

It was Kate's custom to give a party at the Dark Harbor estate once every two months. Some of the most interesting and powerful people in the world came to these gatherings, and the get-togethers were always fruitful. Kate intended to see to it that this one was a very special party. Her problem was to make sure Tony attended. During the past year, he had seldom bothered to show up, and when he did he had made a perfunctory appearance and left. This time it was imperative that he come and that he stay.

When Kate mentioned the weekend to Tony, he said curtly, "I c-can't make it. I'm leaving for C-canada Monday and I have a lot of w-work to clean up before I go."

"This is important," Kate told him. "Charlie Wyatt and Count Hoffman are going to be there and they're – "

"I know who they are," he interrupted. "I t-talked to Brad Rogers. We haven't got a p-prayer of acquiring either one of those companies."

"I want to give it a try."

He looked at her and asked, "W-which one are you after?"

"Wyatt Oil and Tool. It could increase our profits as much as fifteen percent, perhaps more. When the Arab countries realize they have the world by the throat, they're going to form a cartel, and oil prices will skyrocket. Oil is going to turn into liquid gold."

"What about International T-t-technology?"

Kate shrugged. "It's a good company, but the plum is Wyatt Oil and Tool. It's a perfect acquisition for us. I need you there, Tony. Canada can wait a few days."

Tony loathed parties. He hated the endless, boring conversations, the boastful men and the predatory women. But this was business. "All right."

All the pieces were in place.

The Wyatts were flown to Maine in a company Cessna, and from the ferry were driven to Cedar Hill House in a limousine. Kate was at the door to greet them. Brad Rogers had been right about Charlie Wyatt's daughter, Lucy. She was strikingly beautiful. She was tall, with black hair and gold-flecked brown eyes, set in almost perfect features. Her sleek Galanos dress outlined a firm, stunning figure. She had, Brad informed Kate, been divorced from a wealthy Italian playboy two years earlier. Kate introduced Lucy to Tony and watched for her son's reaction. There was none. He greeted both the Wyatts with equal courtesy and led them into the bar, where a bartender was waiting to mix drinks.

"What a lovely room," Lucy exclaimed. Her voice was unexpectedly soft and mellow, with no trace of a Texas accent. "Do you spend much time here?" she asked Tony.

"No."

She waited for him to go on. Then, "Did you grow up here?"

"Partly."

Kate picked up the conversation, adroitly smoothing over Tony's silence. "Some of Tony's happiest memories are of this house. The poor man is so busy he doesn't get much chance to come back here and enjoy it, do you, Tony?"

He gave his mother a cool look and said, "No. As a matter of fact, I should be in C-canada – "

"But he postponed it so he could meet both of you," Kate finished for him.

"Well, I'm mighty pleased," Charlie Wyatt said. "I've heard a lot about you, son." He grinned. "You wouldn't want to come to work for me, would you?"

"I don't think that's q-quite what my mother had in mind, Mr. Wyatt."

Charlie Wyatt grinned again. "I know." He turned to look at Kate. "Your mother's quite a lady. You should have seen her rope and hog-tie everybody at that White House meetin'. She – " He stopped as Frederick Hoffman and his daughter, Marianne, entered the room. Marianne Hoffman was a pale version of her father. She had the same aristocratic features and she had long, blond hair. She wore an off-white chiffon dress. Next to Lucy Wyatt she looked washed out.

"May I present my daughter, Marianne?" Count Hoffman said. "I'm sorry we're late," He apologized. "The plane was delayed at La Guardia."

"Oh, what a shame," Kate said. Tony was aware that Kate had arranged the delay. She had had the Wyatts and the Hoffmans flown up to Maine in separate planes, so that the Wyatts would arrive early and the Hoffmans late. "We were just having a drink. What would you like?"

"A Scotch, please," Count Hoffman said.

Kate turned to Marianne. "And you, my dear?"

"Nothing, thank you."

A few minutes later, the other guests began to arrive, and Tony circulated among them, playing the part of the gracious host. No one except Kate could have guessed how little the festivities meant to him. It was not, Kate knew, that Tony was bored. It was simply that he was completely removed from what was happening around him. He had lost his pleasure in people. It worried Kate.

Two tables had been set in the large dining room. Kate seated Marianne Hoffman between a Supreme Court justice and a senator at one table, and she seated Lucy Wyatt on Tony's right at the other table. All the men in the room – married and unmarried – were eyeing Lucy. Kate listened to Lucy trying to draw Tony into conversation. It was obvious that she liked him. Kate smiled to herself. It was a good beginning.

The following morning, Saturday, at breakfast, Charlie Wyatt said to Kate, "That's a mighty pretty yacht you've got sittin' out there, Mrs. Blackwell. How big is it?"

"I'm really not quite sure." Kate turned to her son. "Tony, how large is the *Corsair?*"

His mother knew exactly how large it was, but Tony said politely, "Eighty f-feet."

"We don't go in much for boats in Texas. We're in too much of a hurry. We do most of our travelin' in planes." Wyatt gave a booming laugh. "Guess maybe I'll try it and get my feet wet."

Kate smiled. "I was hoping you would let me show you around the island. We could go out on the boat tomorrow."

Charlie Wyatt looked at her thoughtfully and said, "That's mighty kind of you, Mrs. Blackwell."

Tony quietly watched the two of them and said nothing. The first move had just been made, and he wondered whether Charlie Wyatt was aware of it. Probably not. He was a clever businessman, but he had never come up against anyone like Kate Blackwell.

Kate turned to Tony and Lucy. "It's such a beautiful day. Why don't you two go for a sail in the catboat?"

Before Tony could refuse, Lucy said, "Oh, I'd love that."

"I'm s-sorry," Tony said curtly. "I'm expecting s-some overseas calls." Tony could feel his mother's disapproving eyes on him.

Kate turned to Marianne Hoffman. "I haven't seen your father this morning."

"He's out exploring the island. He's an early riser."

"I understand you like to ride. We have a fine stable here."

"Thank you, Mrs. Blackwell. I'll just wander around, if you don't mind."

"Of course not." Kate turned back to Tony. "Are you sure you won't change your mind about taking Miss Wyatt for a sail?" There was steel in her voice.

"I'm s-sure."

It was a small victory, but it was a victory nevertheless. The battle was joined, and Tony had no intention of losing it. Not this time. His mother no longer had the power to deceive him. She had used him as a pawn once, and he was fully aware she was planning to try it again; but this time she would fail. She wanted the Wyatt Oil & Tool Company. Charlie Wyatt had no intention of merging or selling his company. But every man has a weakness, and Kate had found his: his daughter. If Lucy were to marry into the Blackwell family, a merger of some kind would become inevitable. Tony looked across the breakfast table at his mother, despising her. She had baited the trap well. Lucy was not only beautiful, she was intelligent and charming. But she was as much of a pawn in this sick game as Tony was, and nothing in the world could induce him to touch her. This was a battle between his mother and himself.

When breakfast was over, Kate rose. "Tony, before your phone call comes in, why don't you show Miss Wyatt the gardens?"

There was no way Tony could refuse graciously. "All right." He would make it short.

Kate turned to Charlie Wyatt. "Are you interested in rare books? We have quite a collection in the library."

"I'm interested in anything you want to show me," the Texan said.

Almost as an afterthought, Kate turned back to Marianne Hoffman. "Will you be all right, dear?"

"I'll be fine, thank you, Mrs. Blackwell. Please don't worry about me."

"I won't," Kate said.

And Tony knew she meant it. Miss Hoffman was of no use to Kate, and so she dismissed her. It was done with a light charm and a smile, but beneath it was a single-minded ruthlessness that Tony detested.

Lucy was watching him. "Are you ready, Tony?"

"Yes."

Tony and Lucy moved toward the door. They were not quite out of earshot when Tony heard his mother say, "Don't they make a lovely couple?"

The two of them walked through the large, formal gardens toward the dock where the *Corsair* was tied up. There were acres and acres of wildly colored flowers staining the summer air with their scent.

"This is a heavenly place," Lucy said.

"Yes."

"We don't have flowers like these in Texas."

"No?"

"It's so quiet and peaceful here."

"Yes."

Lucy stopped abruptly and turned to face Tony.

He saw the anger in her face. "Have I said something to offend you?" he asked.

"You haven't said anything. That's what I find offensive. All I can get out of you is a yes or a no. You make me feel as though I'm – I'm chasing you."

"Are you?"

She laughed. "Yes. If I could only teach you to talk, I think we might have something."

Tony grinned.

"What are you thinking?" Lucy asked.

"Nothing."

He was thinking of his mother, and how much she hated losing.

Kate was showing Charlie Wyatt the large, oak-paneled library. On the shelves were first editions of Oliver Goldsmith, Laurence Sterne, Tobias Smollett and John Donne, along with a Ben Jonson first folio. There was Samuel Butler and John Bunyan, and the rare 1813 privately printed edition of *Queen Mab.* Wyatt walked along the shelves of treasures, his eyes gleaming. He paused in front of a beautifully bound edition of John Keats's *Endymion*.

"This is a Roseberg copy," Charlie Wyatt said.

Kate looked at him in surprise. "Yes. There are only two known copies."

"I have the other one," Wyatt told her.

"I should have known," Kate laughed. "That 'good ol' Texas boy' act you put on had me fooled."

Wyatt grinned. "Did it? It's good camouflage."

"Where did you go to school?"

"Colorado School of Mining, then Oxford on a Rhodes Scholarship." He studied Kate a moment. "I'm told it was you who got me invited to that White House conference."

She shrugged. "I merely mentioned your name. They were delighted to have you."

"That was mighty kind of you, Kate. Now, as long as you and I are alone, why don't you tell me exactly what's on your mind?"

Tony was at work in his private study, a small room off the main downstairs hallway. He was seated in a deep armchair when he heard the door open and someone come in. He turned to look. It was Marianne Hoffman. Before Tony could open his mouth to make his presence known, he heard her gasp.

She was looking at the paintings on the wall. They were Tony's paintings – the few he had brought back from his apartment in Paris, and this was the only room in the house where he would allow them to be hung. He watched her walk around the room, going from painting to painting, and it was too late to say anything.

"I don't believe it," she murmured.

And Tony felt a sudden anger within him. He knew they were not *that* bad. As he moved, the leather of his chair creaked, and Marianne turned and saw him.

"Oh! I'm sorry," she apologized. "I didn't know anyone was in here."

Tony rose. "That's quite all right." His tone was rude. He disliked having his sanctuary invaded. "Were you looking for something?"

"No. I – I was just wandering around. Your collection of paintings belongs in a museum."

"Except for these," Tony heard himself saying.

She was puzzled by the hostility in his voice. She turned to look at the paintings again. She saw the signature. "*You* painted these?"

"I'm sorry if they don't appeal to you."

"They're fantastic!" She moved toward him. "I don't understand. If you can do this, why would you ever want to do anything else? You're wonderful. I don't mean you're good. I mean you're *wonderful*."

Tony stood there, not listening, just wanting her to get out.

"I wanted to be a painter," Marianne said. "I studied with Oskar Kokoschka for a year. I finally quit because I knew I never could be as good as I wanted to be. But you!" She turned to the paintings again. "Did you study in Paris?"

He wished she would leave him alone. "Yes."

"And you quit – just like that?"

"Yes."

"What a pity. You – "

"*There* you are!"

They both turned. Kate was standing in the doorway. She eyed the two of them a moment, then walked over to Marianne. "I've been looking everywhere for you, Marianne. Your father mentioned that you like orchids. You must see our greenhouse."

"Thank you," Marianne murmured. "I'm really – "

Kate turned to Tony. "Tony, perhaps you should see to your other guests." There was a note of sharp displeasure in her voice.

She took Marianne's arm, and they were gone.

There was a fascination to watching his mother maneuver people. It was done so smoothly. Not a move was wasted. It had started with the Wyatts arriving early and the Hoffmans arriving late. Lucy being placed next to him at every meal. The private conferences with Charlie Wyatt. It was so damned obvious, and yet Tony had to admit to himself that it was obvious only because he had the key. He knew his mother and the way her mind worked. Lucy Wyatt was a lovely girl. She would make a wonderful wife for someone, but not for him. Not with Kate Blackwell as her sponsor. His mother was a ruthless, calculating bitch, and as long as Tony remembered that, he was safe from her machinations. He wondered what her next move would be.

He did not have to wait long to find out.

They were on the terrace having cocktails. "Mr. Wyatt has been kind enough to invite us to his ranch next weekend," Kate told Tony. "Isn't that lovely?" Her face radiated her pleasure. "I've never seen a Texas ranch."

Kruger-Brent *owned* a ranch in Texas, and it was probably twice as big as the Wyatt spread.

"You will come, won't you, Tony?" Charlie Wyatt asked.

Lucy said, "Please do."

They were ganging up on him. It was a challenge. He decided to accept it. "I'd be d-delighted."

"Good." There was real pleasure on Lucy's face. And on Kate's.

If Lucy is planning to seduce me, Tony thought, *she is wasting her time*. The hurt done to Tony by his mother and Dominique had implanted in him such a deep distrust of females that his only association with them now was with high-priced call girls. Of all the female species, they were the most honest. All they wanted was money and told you how much up front. You paid for what you got, and you got what you paid for. No complications, no tears, no deceit.

Lucy Wyatt was in for a surprise.

Early Sunday morning, Tony went down to the pool for a swim. Marianne Hoffman was already in the water, wearing a white maillot. She had a lovely figure, tall and slender and graceful. Tony stood there watching her cutting cleanly through the water, her arms flashing up and down in a regular, graceful rhythm. She saw Tony and swam over to him.

"Good morning."

"Morning. You're good," Tony said.

Marianne smiled. "I love sports. I get that from my father." She pulled herself up to the edge of the pool, and Tony handed her a towel. He watched as she unselfconsciously dried her hair.

"Have you had breakfast?" Tony asked.

"No. I wasn't sure the cook would be up this early."

"This is a hotel. There's twenty-four-hour service."

She smiled up at him. "Nice."

"Where is your home?"

"Mostly in Munich. We live in an old *schloss* – a castle – outside the city."

"Where were you brought up?"

Marianne sighed. "That's a long story. During the war, I was sent away to school in Switzerland. After that, I went to Oxford, studied at the Sorbonne and lived in London for a few years." She looked directly into his eyes. "That's where I've been. Where have you been?"

"Oh, New York, Maine, Switzerland, South Africa, a few years in the South

Pacific during the war, Paris . . ." He broke off abruptly, as though he were saying too much.

"Forgive me if I seem to pry, but I can't imagine why you stopped painting."

"It's not important," Tony said curtly. "Let's have breakfast."

They ate alone on the terrace overlooking the sparkling sweep of the bay. She was easy to talk to. There was a dignity about her, a gentleness that Tony found appealing. She did not flirt, she did not chatter. She seemed genuinely interested in him. Tony found himself attracted to this quiet, sensitive woman. He could not help wondering how much of that attraction was due to the thought that it would spite his mother.

"When do you go back to Germany?"

"Next week," Marianne replied. "I'm getting married."

Her words caught him off guard. "Oh," Tony said lamely. "That's great. Who is he?"

"He's a doctor. I've known him all my life." *Why had she added that? Did it have some significance?*

On an impulse, Tony asked, "Will you have dinner with me in New York?"

She studied him, weighing her answer. "I would enjoy that."

Tony smiled, pleased. "It's a date."

They had dinner at a little seashore restaurant on Long Island. Tony wanted Marianne to himself, away from the eyes of his mother. It was an innocent evening, but Tony knew that if his mother learned about it, she would find some way to poison it. This was a private thing between him and Marianne, and for the brief time it existed, Tony wanted nothing to spoil it. Tony enjoyed Marianne's company even more than he had anticipated. She had a quick, sly sense of humor, and Tony found himself laughing more than he had laughed since he left Paris. She made him feel lighthearted and carefree.

When do you go back to Germany?

Next week . . . I'm getting married.

During the next five days, Tony saw a great deal of Marianne. He canceled his trip to Canada, and he was not certain why. He had thought it might be a form of rebellion against his mother's plan, a petty vengeance, but if that had been true in the beginning, it was no longer true. He found himself drawn to Marianne more and more strongly. He loved her honesty. It was a quality he had despaired of ever finding.

Since Marianne was a tourist in New York, Tony took her everywhere. They climbed the Statue of Liberty and rode the ferry to Staten Island, went to the top of the Empire State Building, and ate in Chinatown. They spent an entire day at the Metropolitan Museum of Art, and an afternoon at the Frick Collection. They shared the same tastes. They carefully avoided speaking of any personal things, and yet both were conscious of the powerful sexual undercurrent between them. The days spilled into one another, and it was Friday, the day Tony was to leave for the Wyatt Ranch.

"When do you fly back to Germany?"

"Monday morning." There was no joy in her voice.

Tony left for Houston that afternoon. He could have gone with his mother in one of the company planes, but he preferred to avoid any situation where he and Kate would be alone together. As far as he was concerned, his mother was solely a business partner: brilliant and powerful, devious and dangerous.

There was a Rolls-Royce to pick up Tony at the William P. Hobby Airport in Houston, and he was driven to the ranch by a chauffeur dressed in Levi's and a colorful sport shirt.

"Most folks like to fly direct to the ranch," the driver told Tony. "Mr. Wyatt's got a big landin' strip there. From here, it's 'bout an hour's drive to the gate, then another half hour before we git to the main house."

Tony thought he was exaggerating, but he was wrong. The Wyatt Ranch turned out to be more of a town than a ranch. They drove through the main gate onto a private road, and after thirty minutes they began to pass generator buildings and barns and corrals and guest houses and servants' bungalows. The main house was an enormous one-story ranch house that seemed to go on forever. Tony thought it was depressingly ugly.

Kate had already arrived. She and Charlie Wyatt were seated on the terrace overlooking a swimming pool the size of a small lake. They were in the midst of an intense conversation when Tony appeared. When Wyatt saw him, he broke off abruptly in the middle of a sentence. Tony sensed that he had been the subject of their discussion.

"Here's our boy! Have a good trip, Tony?"

"Yes, th-thank you."

"Lucy was hopin' you'd be able to catch an earlier plane," Kate said.

Tony turned to look at his mother. "Was sh-she?"

Charlie Wyatt clapped Tony on the shoulder. "We're puttin' on a whoppin' barbecue in honor of you and Kate. *Everybody's* flyin' in for it."

"That's very k-kind of you," Tony said. *If they're planning to serve fatted calf* he thought, *they're going to go hungry.*

Lucy appeared, wearing a white shirt and tight-fitting, well-worn jeans, and Tony had to admit she was breathtakingly lovely.

She went up to him and took his arm. "Tony! I was wondering if you were coming."

"S-sorry I'm late," Tony said. "I had some b-business to finish up."

Lucy gave him a warm smile. "It doesn't matter, as long as you're here. What would you like to do this afternoon?"

"What do you have to offer?"

Lucy looked him in the eye. "Anything you want," she said softly.

Kate Blackwell and Charlie Wyatt beamed.

The barbecue was spectacular, even by Texas standards. Approximately two hundred guests had arrived by private plane, Mercedes or Rolls-Royce. Two bands were playing simultaneously in different areas of the grounds. Half a dozen bartenders dispensed champagne, whiskey, soft drinks and beer, while four chefs busily prepared food over outdoor fires. There was barbecued beef, lamb, steaks, chicken and duck. There were bubbling earthen pots of chili, and whole lobsters; crabs and corn on the cob were cooking in the ground. There were baked potatoes and yams and fresh peas in the pod, six kinds of salads, homemade hot biscuits, and corn bread with honey and jam. Four dessert tables were laden with freshly baked pies, cakes and puddings, and a dozen flavors of homemade ice cream. It was the most conspicuous waste Tony had ever seen. It was, he supposed, the difference between new money and old money. Old money's motto was, *If you have it, hide it*. New money's motto was, *If you have it, flaunt it*.

This was flaunting on a scale that was unbelievable. The women were dressed in daring gowns, and the display of jewelry was blinding. Tony stood to one side watching the guests gorging themselves, calling out noisily to old friends. He felt as though he were attending some mindless, decadent rite. Every time he turned around, Tony found himself confronted with a waiter carrying a tray containing large crocks of beluga caviar or paté or champagne. It seemed to Tony that there were almost as many servants as guests. He listened to conversations around him.

"He came out here from New York to sell me a bill of goods, and I said, 'You're wastin' your time, mister. No good oil deal gets east of Houston . . .' "

"You gotta watch out for the smooth talkers. They're all hat and no cattle . . ."

Lucy appeared at Tony's side. "You're not eating." She was watching him intently. "Is anything wrong, Tony?"

"No, everything's fine. It's quite a party."

She grinned. "You ain't seen nothin' yet, pardner. Wait until you see the fireworks display."

"The fireworks display?"

"Uh-huh." She touched Tony's arm. "Sorry about the mob scene. It's not always like this. Daddy wanted to impress your mother." She smiled. "Tomorrow they'll all be gone."

So will I, Tony thought grimly. It had been a mistake for him to come here. If his mother wanted the Wyatt Oil & Tool Company so badly, she would have to figure out some other way to get it. His eyes searched the crowd for his mother, and he saw her in the middle of an admiring group. She was beautiful. She was almost sixty years old, but she looked ten years younger. Her face was unlined, and her body was firm and trim, thanks to exercise and daily massage. She was as disciplined with herself as with everyone around her, and in a perverse way,

Tony admired her. To a casual onlooker, Kate Blackwell seemed to be having a marvelous time. She was chatting with the guests, beaming, laughing. *She's loathing every moment of this*, Tony thought. *There isn't anything she won't suffer to get what she wants.* He thought of Marianne and of how much she would have hated this kind of senseless orgy. The thought of her was a sudden ache in him.

I'm marrying a doctor. I've known him all my life.

Half an hour later when Lucy came looking for Tony, he was on his way back to New York.

He called Marianne from a telephone booth at the airport. "I want to see you."

There was no hesitation. "Yes."

Tony had not been able to get Marianne Hoffman out of his thoughts. He had been alone for a long time, but he had not felt lonely. Being away from Marianne was a loneliness, a feeling that a part of him was missing. Being with her was a warmth, a celebration of life, a chasing away of the ugly dark shadows that had been haunting him. He had the terrifying feeling that if he let Marianne go, he would be lost. He needed her as he had never needed anyone in his life.

Marianne met him at his apartment, and as she walked in the door, there was a hunger in Tony that he had thought forever dead. And looking at her, he knew the hunger was hers, too, and there were no words for the miracle of it.

She went into his arms, and their emotion was an irresistible riptide that caught them both up and swept them away in a glorious explosion, an eruption, and a contentment beyond words. They were floating together in a velvety softness that knew no time or place, lost in the wondrous glory and magic of each other. Later they lay spent, holding each other, her hair soft against his face.

"I'm going to marry you, Marianne."

She took his face in her hands and looked searchingly into his eyes. "Are you sure, Tony?" Her voice was gentle. "There's a problem, darling."

"Your engagement?"

"No. I'll break it off. I'm concerned about your mother."

"She has nothing to do with – "

"No. Let me finish, Tony. She's planning for you to marry Lucy Wyatt."

"That's *her* plan." He took her in his arms again. "*My* plans are right here."

"She'll hate me, Tony. I don't want that."

"Do you know what I want?" Tony whispered.

And the miracle started all over again.

It was another forty-eight hours before Kate Blackwell heard from Tony. He had disappeared from the Wyatt Ranch without an explanation or good-bye and had flown back to New York. Charlie Wyatt was baffled, and Lucy Wyatt was furious. Kate had made awkward apologies and had taken the company plane back to New York that night. When she reached home, she telephoned Tony at his apartment. There was no answer. Nor was there any answer the following day.

Kate was in her office when the private phone on her desk rang. She knew who it was before she picked it up.

"Tony, are you all right?"

"I'm f-fine, Mother."

"Where are you?"

"On my h-honeymoon. Marianne Hoffman and I were m-married yesterday." There was a long, long silence. "Are you there, M-mother?"

"Yes. I'm here."

"You might s-say congratulations, or m-much happiness or one of those c-customary phrases." There was a mocking bitterness in his voice.

Kate said, "Yes. Yes, of course, I wish you much happiness, Son."

"Thank you, M-mother." And the line went dead.

Kate replaced the receiver and pressed down an intercom button. "Would you please come in, Brad?"

When Brad Rogers walked into the office, Kate said, "Tony just called."

Brad took one look at Kate's face and said, "Jesus! Don't tell me you did it!"

"*Tony* did it," Kate smiled. "We've got the Hoffman empire in our lap."

Brad Rogers sank into a chair. "I can't believe it! I know how stubborn Tony can be. How did you ever get him to marry Marianne Hoffman?"

"It was really very simple," Kate sighed. "I pushed him in the wrong direction."

But she knew it was really the right direction. Marianne would be a wonderful wife for Tony. She would dispel the darkness in him.

Lucy had had a hysterectomy.

Marianne would give him a son.

21

Six months from the day Tony and Marianne were married, the Hoffman company was absorbed into Kruger-Brent, Ltd. The formal signing of the contracts took place in Munich as a gesture to Frederick Hoffman, who would run the subsidiary from Germany. Tony had been surprised by the meekness with which his mother accepted his marriage. It was not like her to lose gracefully, yet she had been cordial to Marianne when Tony and his bride returned from their honeymoon in the Bahamas, and had told Tony how pleased she was with the marriage. What puzzled Tony was that her sentiments seemed genuine. It was too quick a turnaround, out of character for her. Perhaps, Tony decided, he did not understand his mother as well as he thought he did.

The marriage was a brilliant success from the beginning. Marianne filled a long-felt need in Tony, and everyone around him noticed the change in him – specially Kate.

When Tony took business trips, Marianne accompanied him. They played together, they laughed together, they truly enjoyed each other. Watching them, Kate thought happily, *I have done well for my son.*

It was Marianne who succeeded in healing the breach between Tony and his mother. When they returned from their honeymoon, Marianne said, "I want to invite your mother to dinner."

"No. You don't know her, Marianne. She – "

"I want to get to know her. Please, Tony."

He hated the idea, but in the end he gave in. Tony had been prepared for a grim evening, but he had been surprised. Kate had been touchingly happy to be with them. The following week Kate invited them to the house for dinner, and after that it became a weekly ritual.

Kate and Marianne became friends. They spoke to each other over the telephone several times a week, and lunched together at least once a week.

They were meeting for lunch at Lutéce, and the moment Marianne walked in, Kate knew something was wrong.

"I'd like a double whiskey, please," Marianne told the captain. "Over ice."

As a rule, Marianne drank only wine.

"What's happened, Marianne?"

"I've been to see Dr. Harley."

Kate felt a sudden stab of alarm. "You're not ill, are you?"

"No. I'm just fine. Only . . ." The whole story came tumbling out.

It had begun a few days earlier. Marianne had not been feeling well, and she had made an appointment with John Harley. . . .

"You look healthy enough," Dr. Harley smiled. "How old are you, Mrs. Blackwell?"

"Twenty-three."

"Any history of heart disease in your family?"

"No."

He was making notes. "Cancer?"

"No."

"Are your parents alive?"

"My father is. My mother died in an accident."

"Have you ever had mumps?"

"No."

"Measles?"

"Yes. When I was ten."

"Whooping cough?"

"No."

"Any surgery?"

"Tonsils. I was nine."

"Other than that, you've never been hospitalized for anything?"

"No. Well, yes – that is, once. Briefly."

"What was that for?"

"I was on the girls' hockey team at school and during a game I blacked out. I woke up in a hospital. I was only there two days. It was really nothing."

"Did you suffer an injury during the game?"

"No. I – I just blacked out."

"How old were you then?"

"Sixteen. The doctor said it was probably some kind of adolescent glandular upset."

John Harley sat forward in his chair. "When you woke up, do you remember if you felt any weakness on either side of your body?"

Marianne thought a moment. "As a matter of fact, yes. My right side. But it went away in a few days. I haven't had anything like it since."

"Did you have headaches? Blurred vision?"

"Yes. But they went away, too." She was beginning to be alarmed. "Do you think there's something wrong with me, Dr. Harley?"

"I'm not sure. I'd like to make a few tests – just to be on the safe side."

"What kind of tests?"

"I'd like to do a cerebral angiogram. Nothing to be concerned about. We can have it done right away."

Three days later, Marianne received a call from Dr. Harley's nurse asking her to come in. John Harley was waiting for her in his office. "Well, we've solved the mystery."

"Is it something bad?"

"Not really. The angiogram showed that what you had, Mrs. Blackwell, was a small stroke. Medically, it's called a berry aneurysm, and it's very common in women – particularly in teenage girls. A small blood vessel in the brain broke and leaked small amounts of blood. The pressure is what caused the headaches and blurred vision. Fortunately, those things are self-healing."

Marianne sat there listening, her mind fighting panic. "What – what does all this mean, exactly? Could it happen again?"

"It's very unlikely." He smiled. "Unless you're planning to go out for the hockey team again, you can live an absolutely normal life."

"Tony and I like to ride and play tennis. Is that – ?"

"As long as you don't overdo, everything goes. From tennis to sex. No problem."

She smiled in relief. "Thank God."

As Marianne rose, John Harley said, "There is one thing, Mrs. Blackwell. If you and Tony are planning to have children, I would advise adopting them."

Marianne froze. "You said I was perfectly normal."

"You are. Unfortunately, pregnancy increases the vascular volume enormously. And during the last six to eight weeks of pregnancy, there's an additional increase in blood pressure. With the history of that aneurysm, the risk factor would be unacceptably high. It would not only be dangerous – it could be fatal. Adoptions are really quite easy these days. I can arrange – "

But Marianne was no longer listening. She was hearing Tony's voice: *I want us to have a baby. A little girl who looks exactly like you.*

" . . . I couldn't bear to hear any more," Marianne told Kate. "I ran out of his office and came straight here."

Kate made a tremendous effort not to let her feelings show. It was a stunning blow. But there had to be a way. There was always a way.

She managed a smile and said, "Well! I was afraid it was going to be something much worse."

"But, Kate, Tony and I want so much to have a baby."

"Marianne, Dr. Harley is an alarmist. You had a minor problem years ago, and Harley's trying to turn it into something important. You know how doctors are." She took Marianne's hand. "You feel well, don't you, darling?"

"I felt wonderful until – "

"Well, there you are. You aren't going around having any fainting spells?"

"No."

"Because it's all over. He said himself that those things are self-healing."

"He said the risks – "

Kate sighed. "Marianne, every time a woman gets pregnant, there's always a risk. Life is full of risks. The important thing in life is to decide which risks are the ones worth taking, don't you agree?"

"Yes." Marianne sat there thinking. She made her decision. "You're right. Let's not say anything to Tony. It would only worry him. We'll keep it our secret."

Kate thought, *I could bloody well kill John Harley for scaring her to death.* "It will be our secret," Kate agreed.

Three months later, Marianne became pregnant. Tony was thrilled. Kate was quietly triumphant. Dr. John Harley was horrified.

"I'll arrange for an immediate abortion," he told Marianne.

"No, Dr. Harley. I feel fine. I'm going to have the baby."

When Marianne told Kate about her visit, Kate stormed into John Harley's office. "How dare you suggest my daughter-in-law have an abortion?"

"Kate, I told her that if she carries that baby to term, there's a chance it might kill her."

"You don't *know* that. She's going to be fine. Stop alarming her."

Eight months later, at four A.M. In early February, Marianne's labor pains began prematurely. Her moans awakened Tony.

He began hurriedly dressing. "Don't worry, darling. I'll have you at the hospital in no time."

The pains were agonizing. "Please hurry."

She wondered whether she should have told Tony about her conversations with Dr. Harley. No, Kate had been right. It was her decision to make. Life was so wonderful that God would not let anything bad happen to her.

When Marianne and Tony arrived at the hospital, everything was in readiness. Tony was escorted to a waiting room. Marianne was taken into an examining room. The obstetrician, Dr. Mattson, took Marianne's blood pressure. He frowned and took it again. He looked up and said to his nurse, "Get her into the operating room – fast!"

Tony was at the cigarette machine in the hospital corridor when a voice behind him said, "Well, well, if it isn't Rembrandt." Tony turned. He recognized the man who had been with Dominique in front of her apartment building. What had she called him? Ben. The man was staring at Tony, an antagonistic expression on his face. Jealousy? What had Dominique told him? At that moment, Dominique appeared. She said to Ben, "The nurse said Michelline is in intensive care. We'll come – " She saw Tony, and stopped.

"Tony! What are you doing here?"

"My wife is having a baby."

"Did your mother arrange it?" Ben asked.

"What's that supposed to mean?"

"Dominique told me your mother arranges everything for you, sonny."

"Ben! Stop it!"

"Why? It's the truth, isn't it, baby? Isn't that what you said?"

Tony turned to Dominique. "What is he talking about?"

"Nothing," she said quickly. "Ben, let's get out of here."

But Ben was enjoying himself. "I wish I had a mother like yours, buddy boy. You want a beautiful model to sleep with, she buys you one. You want to have an art exhibition in Paris, she arranges it for you. You – "

"You're crazy."

"Am I?" Ben turned to Dominique. "Doesn't he know?"

"Don't I know what?" Tony demanded.

"Nothing, Tony."

"He said my mother arranged the exhibition in Paris. That's a lie, isn't it?" He saw the expression on Dominique's face.

"*Isn't* it?"

"No," Dominique said reluctantly.

"You mean she had to pay Goerg to – to show my paintings?"

"Tony, he really liked your paintings."

"Tell him about the art critic," Ben urged.

"That's enough, Ben!" Dominique turned to go. Tony grabbed her arm. "Wait! What about him? Did my mother arrange for him to be at the exhibit?"

"Yes." Dominique's voice had dropped to a whisper.

"But he *hated* my paintings."

She could hear the pain in his voice. "No, Tony. He didn't. André d'Usseau told your mother you could have become a great artist."

And he was face to face with the unbelievable. "My mother paid d'Usseau to destroy me?"

"Not to destroy you. She believed she was doing it for your own good."

The enormity of what his mother had done was staggering. *Everything she had told him was a lie. She had never intended to let him live his own life.* And André d'Usseau! How could a man like that be bought? But of course Kate would know the price of any man. Wilde could have been referring to Kate when he talked of someone who knew the price of everything, the value of nothing. Everything had always been for the company. And the company was Kate Blackwell. Tony turned and walked blindly down the corridor.

In the operating room, the doctors were fighting desperately to save Marianne's life. Her blood pressure was alarmingly low, and her heartbeat was erratic. She was given oxygen and a blood transfusion, but it was useless. Marianne was unconscious from a cerebral hemorrhage when the first baby was delivered, and dead three minutes later when the second twin was taken.

Tony heard a voice calling, "Mr. Blackwell." He turned. Dr. Mattson was at his side.

"You have two beautiful, healthy twin daughters, Mr. Blackwell."

Tony saw the look in his eyes. "Marianne – she's all right, isn't she?"

Dr. Mattson took a deep breath. "I'm so sorry. We did everything we could. She died on the – "

"She *what?*" It was a scream. Tony grabbed Dr. Mattson's lapels and shook him. "You're lying! She's *not* dead."

"Mr. Blackwell – "

"Where is she? I want to see her."

"You can't go in just now. They're preparing her – "

Tony cried out, "You killed her, you bastard! You killed her." He began attacking the doctor. Two interns hurried in and grabbed Tony's arms.

"Now take it easy, Mr. Blackwell."

Tony fought like a madman. "I want to see my wife!"

Dr. John Harley hurried up to the group. "Let him go," he commanded. "Leave us alone."

Dr. Mattson and the interns left. Tony was weeping brokenly. "John, they k-killed Marianne. They m-murdered her."

"She's dead, Tony, and I'm sorry. But no one murdered her. I told her months ago if she went ahead with this pregnancy it could kill her."

It took a long moment for the words to sink in. "What are you talking about?"

"Marianne didn't tell you? Your mother didn't say anything?"

Tony was staring at him, his eyes uncomprehending. "My mother?"

"She thought I was being an alarmist. She advised Marianne to go ahead with it. I'm so sorry, Tony. I've seen the twins. They're beautiful. Wouldn't you like to – ?"

Tony was gone.

Kate's butler opened the door for Tony.

"Good morning, Mr. Blackwell."

"Good morning, Lester."

The butler took in Tony's disheveled appearance. "Is everything all right, sir?"

"Everything is fine. Would you make me a cup of coffee, Lester?"

"Certainly, sir."

Tony watched the butler move toward the kitchen. Now, *Tony*, the voice in his head commanded.

Yes. Now. Tony turned and walked into the trophy room. He went to the cabinet that held the gun collection, and he stared at the gleaming array of instruments of death.

Open the cabinet, Tony.

He opened it. He selected a revolver from the gun rack and checked the barrel to make sure it was loaded.

She'll be upstairs, Tony.

Tony turned and started up the stairs. He knew now that it was not his mother's fault that she was evil. She was possessed, and he was going to cure her. The company had taken her soul, and Kate was not responsible for what she did. His mother and the company had become one, and when he killed her, the company would die.

He was outside Kate's bedroom door.

Open the door, the voice commanded.

Tony opened the door. Kate was dressing in front of a mirror when she heard the door open.

"Tony! What on earth – "

He carefully aimed the gun at her and began squeezing the trigger.

22

The right of primogeniture – the claim of the first-born to a family title or estate – is deeply rooted in history. Among royal families in Europe a high official is present at every birth of a possible heir to a queen or princess so that should twins be born, the right of succession will not be in dispute. Dr. Mattson was careful to note which twin had been delivered first.

Everyone agreed that the Blackwell twins were the most beautiful babies they had ever seen. They were healthy and unusually lively, and the nurses at the hospital kept finding excuses to go in and look at them. Part of the fascination, although none of the nurses would have admitted it, was the mysterious stories that were circulating about the twins' family. Their mother had died during childbirth. The twins' father had disappeared, and there were rumors he had murdered his mother, but no one was able to substantiate the reports. There was nothing about it in the newspapers, save for a brief item that Tony Blackwell had suffered a nervous breakdown over the death of his wife and was in seclusion. When the press tried to question Dr. Harley, he gave them a brusque, "No comment."

The past few days had been hell for John Harley. As long as he lived, he would remember the scene when he reached Kate Blackwell's bedroom after a frantic phone call from the butler. Kate was lying on the floor in a coma, bullet wounds in her neck and chest, her blood spilling onto the white rug. Tony was going through her closets, slashing his mother's clothes to shreds with a pair of scissors.

Dr. Harley took one quick look at Kate and hurriedly telephoned for an ambulance. He knelt at Kate's side and felt her pulse. It was weak and thready, and her face was turning blue. She was going into shock. He swiftly gave her an injection of adrenaline and sodium bicarbonate.

"What happened?" Dr. Harley asked.

The butler was soaked in perspiration. "I – I don't know. Mr. Blackwell asked me to make him some coffee. I was in the kitchen when I heard the sound of gunfire. I ran upstairs and found Mrs. Blackwell on the floor, like this. Mr. Blackwell was standing over her, saying "It can't hurt you anymore, Mother. I killed it." And he went into the closet and started cutting her dresses."

Dr. Harley turned to Tony. "What are you doing, Tony?"

A savage slash. "I'm helping Mother. I'm destroying the company. It killed Marianne, you know." He continued slashing at the dresses in Kate's closet.

Kate was rushed to the emergency ward of a midtown private hospital owned by Kruger-Brent, Ltd. She was given four blood transfusions during the operation to remove the bullets.

It took three male nurses to force Tony into an ambulance, and it was only after Dr. Harley gave him an injection that Tony was quiet. A police unit had responded to the ambulance call, and Dr. Harley summoned Brad Rogers to deal with them. Through means that Dr. Harley did not understand, there was no mention in the media of the shooting.

Dr. Harley went to the hospital to visit Kate in intensive care. Her first words were a whispered, "Where's my son?"

"He's being taken care of, Kate. He's all right."

Tony had been taken to a private sanitarium in Connecticut.

"John, why did he try to kill me? Why?" The anguish in her voice was unbearable.

"He blames you for Marianne's death."

"That's insane!"

John Harley made no comment.

He blames you for Marianne's death.

Long after Dr. Harley had left, Kate lay there, refusing to accept those words. She had loved Marianne because she made Tony happy. *Everything I have done has been for you, my son. All my dreams were for you. How could you not know that?* And he hated her so much he had tried to kill her. She was filled with such a deep agony that she wanted to die. But she would not let herself die. She had done what was right. They were wrong. Tony was a weakling. They had all been weaklings. Her father had been too weak to face his son's death. Her mother had been too weak to face life alone. *But I am not weak*, Kate thought. *I can face this. I can face anything. I'm going to live. I'll survive. The company will survive.*

Book Five

Eve and Alexandra
1950–1975

23

Kate recuperated at Dark Harbor, letting the sun and the sea heal her.

Tony was in a private asylum, where he could get the best care possible. Kate had psychiatrists flown in from Paris, Vienna and Berlin, but when all the examinations and tests had been completed, the diagnosis was the same: Her son was a homicidal schizophrenic and paranoiac.

"He doesn't respond to drugs or psychiatric treatment, and he's violent. We have to keep him under restraint."

"What kind of restraint?" Kate asked.

"He's in a padded cell. Most of the time we have to keep him in a strait-jacket."

"Is that necessary?"

"Without it, Mrs. Blackwell, he would kill anyone who got near him."

She closed her eyes in pain. This was not her sweet, gentle Tony they were talking about. It was a stranger, someone possessed. She opened her eyes. "Is there nothing that can be done?"

"Not if we can't reach his mind. We're keeping him on drugs, but the moment they wear off, he gets manic again. We can't continue this treatment indefinitely."

Kate stood very straight. "What do you suggest, Doctor?"

"In similar cases, we've found that removing a small portion of the brain has produced remarkable results."

Kate swallowed. "A lobotomy?"

"That is correct. Your son will still be able to function in every way, except that he will no longer have any strong dysfunctional emotions."

Kate sat there, her mind and body chilled. Dr. Morris, a young doctor from the Menninger Clinic, broke the silence. "I know how difficult this must be for you, Mrs. Blackwell. If you'd like to think about – "

"If that's the only thing that will stop his torment," Kate said, "do it."

Frederick Hoffman wanted his granddaughters. "I will take them back to Germany with me."

It seemed to Kate that he had aged twenty years since Marianne's death. Kate felt sorry for him, but she had no intention of giving up Tony's children. "They need a woman's care, Frederick. Marianne would have wanted them brought up here. You'll come and visit them often."

And he was finally persuaded.

The twins were moved into Kate's home, and a nursery suite was set up for them. Kate interviewed governesses, and finally hired a young French woman named Solange Dunas.

Kate named the first-born Eve, and her twin, Alexandra. They were identical – impossible to tell apart. Seeing them together was like looking at an image in a mirror, and Kate marveled at the double miracle that her son and Marianne had created. They were both bright babies, quick and responsive, but even after a few weeks, Eve seemed more mature than Alexandra. Eve was the first to crawl and talk and walk. Alexandra followed quickly, but from the beginning it was Eve who was the leader. Alexandra adored her sister and tried to imitate everything she did. Kate spent as much time with her granddaughters as possible. They made her feel young. And Kate began to dream again. One *day, when I'm old and ready to retire . . .*

On the twins' first birthday, Kate gave them a party. They each had an identical birthday cake, and there were dozens of presents from friends, company employees and the household staff. Their second birthday party seemed to follow almost immediately. Kate could not believe how rapidly the time went by and how quickly the twins were growing. She was able to discern even more clearly the differences in their personalities: Eve, the stronger, was more daring, Alexandra was softer, content to follow her sister's lead. *With no mother or father, Kate* thought repeatedly, *its a blessing that they have each other and love each other so much.*

The night before their fifth birthday, Eve tried to murder Alexandra.

It is written in Genesis 25:22–23:

> And the children struggled together within her . . .
> And the Lord said unto her, Two [nations] are in thy womb, and two manner of people shall be separated from thy bowels; and the one [people] shall be stronger than the other [people]; and the elder shall serve the younger.

In the case of Eve and Alexandra, Eve had no intention of serving her younger sister.

Eve had hated her sister for as long as she could remember. She went into a silent rage when someone picked up Alexandra, or petted her or gave her a present. Eve felt she was being cheated. She wanted it all for herself – all the love and the beautiful things that surrounded the two of them. She could not have even a birthday of her own. She hated Alexandra for looking like her, dressing like her, stealing the part of her grandmother's love that belonged to her. Alexandra adored Eve, and Eve despised her for that. Alexandra was generous, eager to give up her toys and dolls, and that filled Eve with still more contempt. Eve shared nothing. What was hers belonged to her; but it was not enough. She wanted everything Alexandra had. At night, under the watchful eye of Solange Dunas, both girls would say their prayers aloud, but Eve always added a silent prayer begging God to strike Alexandra dead. When the prayer went unanswered, Eve decided she would have to take care of it herself. Their fifth birthday was only a few days away, and Eve could not bear the thought of sharing another party with Alexandra. They were *her* friends, and *her* gifts that her sister was stealing from her. She had to kill Alexandra soon.

On the night before their birthday, Eve lay in her bed, wide awake. When she was sure the household was asleep, she went over to Alexandra's bed and awakened her. "Alex," she whispered, "let's go down to the kitchen and see our birthday cakes."

Alexandra said sleepily, "Everybody's sleeping."

"We won't wake anyone up."

"Mademoiselle Dunas won't like it. Why don't we look at the cakes in the morning?"

"Because I want to look at them now. Are you coming or not?"

Alexandra rubbed the sleep out of her eyes. She had no interest in seeing the birthday cakes, but she did not want to hurt her sister's feelings. "I'm coming," she said.

Alexandra got out of bed and put on a pair of slippers. Both girls wore pink nylon nightgowns.

"Come on," Eve said. "And don't make any noise."

"I won't," Alexandra promised.

They tiptoed out of their bedroom, into the long corridor, past the closed door of Mademoiselle Dunas's bedroom, down the steep back stairs that led to the kitchen. It was an enormous kitchen, with two large gas stoves, six ovens, three refrigerators and a walk-in freezer.

In the refrigerator Eve found the birthday cakes that the cook, Mrs. Tyler, had made. One of them said Happy Birthday, Alexandra. The other said Happy Birthday, Eve.

Next year, Eve thought happily, *there will only be one.*

Eve took Alexandra's cake out of the refrigerator and placed it on the wooden chopping block in the middle of the kitchen. She opened a drawer and took out a package of brightly colored candles.

"What are you doing?" Alexandra asked.

"I want to see how it looks with the candles all lighted." Eve began pressing the candles into the icing of the cake.

"I don't think you should do that, Eve. You'll ruin the cake. Mrs. Tyler is going to be angry."

"She won't mind." Eve opened another drawer and took out two large boxes of kitchen matches. "Come on, help me."

"I want to go back to bed."

Eve turned on her angrily. "All right. Go back to bed, scaredy cat. I'll do it alone."

Alexandra hesitated. "What do you want me to do?"

Eve handed her one of the boxes of matches. "Start lighting the candles."

Alexandra was afraid of fire. Both girls had been warned again and again about the danger of playing with matches. They knew the horror stories about children who had disobeyed that rule. But Alexandra did not want to disappoint Eve, and so she obediently began lighting the candles.

Eve watched her a moment. "You're leaving out the ones on the other side, silly," she said.

Alexandra leaned over to reach the candles at the far side of the cake, her back to Eve. Quickly, Eve struck a match and touched it to the matches in the box she was holding. As they burst into flames, Eve dropped the box at Alexandra's feet, so that the bottom of Alexandra's nightgown caught fire. It was an instant before Alexandra was aware of what was happening. When she felt the first agonizing pain against her legs, she looked down and screamed, "Help! Help me!"

Eve stared at the flaming nightgown a moment, awed by the extent of her success. Alexandra was standing there, petrified, frozen with fear.

"Don't move!" Eve said. "I'll get a bucket of water." She hurried off to the butler's pantry, her heart pounding with a fearful joy.

It was a horror movie that saved Alexandra's life. Mrs. Tyler, the Blackwells' cook, had been escorted to the cinema by a police sergeant whose bed she shared from time to time. On this particular evening, the motion-picture screen was so filled with dead and mutilated bodies that finally Mrs. Tyler could bear it no longer. In the middle of a beheading, she said, "This may all be in a day's work for you, Richard, but I've had enough."

Sergeant Richard Dougherty reluctantly followed her out of the theater.

They arrived back at the Blackwell mansion an hour earlier than they had expected to, and as Mrs. Tyler opened the back door, she heard Alexandra's screams coming from the kitchen. Mrs. Tyler and Sergeant Dougherty rushed in, took one horrified look at the scene before them and went into action. The sergeant leaped at Alexandra and ripped off her flaming nightgown. Her legs and hips were blistered, but the flames had not reached her hair or the front of her body. Alexandra fell to the floor, unconscious. Mrs. Tyler filled a large pot with water and poured it over the flames licking at the floor.

"Call an ambulance," Sergeant Dougherty ordered. "Is Mrs. Blackwell home?"

"She should be upstairs asleep."

"Wake her up."

As Mrs. Tyler finished phoning for an ambulance, there was a cry from the butler's pantry, and Eve ran in carrying a pan of water, sobbing hysterically.

"Is Alexandra dead?" Eve screamed. "Is she dead?"

Mrs. Tyler took Eve in her arms to soothe her. "No, darling, she's all right. She's going to be just fine."

"It was my fault," Eve sobbed. "She wanted to light the candles on her birthday cake. I shouldn't have let her do it."

Mrs. Tyler stroked Eve's back. "It's all right. You mustn't blame yourself."

"The m-matches fell out of my hand, and Alex caught on fire. It was t-terrible."

Sergeant Dougherty looked at Eve and said sympathetically, "Poor child."

"Alexandra has second-degree burns on her legs and back," Dr. Harley told Kate, "but she's going to be fine. We can do amazing things with burns these days. Believe me, this could have been a terrible tragedy."

"I know," Kate said. She had seen Alexandra's burns, and they had filled her with horror. She hesitated a moment. "John, I think I'm even more concerned about Eve."

"Was Eve hurt?"

"Not physically, but the poor child blames herself for the accident. She's having terrible nightmares. The last three nights I've had to go in and hold her in my arms before she could go back to sleep. I don't want this to become more traumatic. Eve is very sensitive."

"Kids get over things pretty quickly, Kate. If there's any problem, let me know, and I'll recommend a child therapist."

"Thank you," Kate said gratefully.

Eve was terribly upset. The birthday party had been canceled. *Alexandra cheated me out of that*, Eve thought bitterly.

Alexandra healed perfectly, with no signs of scars. Eve got over her feelings of guilt with remarkable ease. As Kate assured her, "Accidents can happen to anybody, darling. You mustn't blame yourself."

Eve didn't. She blamed Mrs. Tyler. Why did she have to come home and spoil everything? It had been a perfect plan.

The sanitarium where Tony was confined was in a peaceful, wooded area in Connecticut. Kate was driven out to see him once a month. The lobotomy had been successful. There was no longer the slightest sign of aggression in Tony. He recognized Kate and he always politely asked about Eve and Alexandra, but he showed no interest in seeing them. He showed very little interest in anything. He seemed happy. *No, not happy*, Kate corrected herself. *Content. But content – to do what?*

Kate asked Mr. Burger, the superintendent of the asylum, "Doesn't my son *do* anything all day?"

"Oh, yes, Mrs. Blackwell. He sits by the hour and paints."

Her son, who could have owned the world, sat and painted all day. Kate tried not to think of the waste, that brilliant mind gone forever. "What does he paint?"

The man was embarrassed. "No one can quite figure it out."

24

During the next two years, Kate became seriously concerned about Alexandra. The child was definitely accident-prone. During Eve and Alexandra's summer vacation at the Blackwell estate in the Bahamas, Alexandra almost drowned while playing with Eve in the pool, and it was only the prompt intervention of a gardener that saved her. The following year when the two girls were on a picnic in the Palisades, Alexandra somehow slipped off the edge of a cliff and saved herself by clinging to a shrub growing out of the steep mountainside.

"I wish you would keep a closer eye on your sister," Kate told Eve. "She can't seem to take care of herself the way you can."

"I know," Eve said solemnly. "I'll watch her, Gran."

Kate loved both her granddaughters, but in different ways. They were seven years old now, and identically beautiful, with long, soft blond hair, exquisite features and the McGregor eyes. They looked alike, but their personalities were quite different. Alexandra's gentleness reminded Kate of Tony, while Eve was more like her, headstrong and self-sufficient.

A chauffeur drove them to school in the family Rolls-Royce. Alexandra was embarrassed to have her classmates see her with the car and chauffeur; Eve reveled in it. Kate gave each girl a weekly allowance, and ordered them to keep a record of how they spent it. Eve invariably ran short of money before the week was out and borrowed from Alexandra. Eve learned to adjust the books so that Gran would not know. But Kate knew, and she could hardly hold back her smile. Seven years old and already a creative accountant!

In the beginning, Kate had nurtured a secret dream that one day Tony would be well again, that he would leave the asylum and return to Kruger-Brent. But as time passed, the dream slowly faded. It was tacitly understood that while Tony might leave the asylum for short visits, accompanied by a male nurse, he would never again be able to participate in the outside world.

It was 1962, and as Kruger-Brent, Ltd., prospered and expanded, the demands for new leadership grew more urgent. Kate celebrated her seventieth birthday. Her hair was white now, and she was a remarkable figure of a woman, strong and erect and vital. She was aware that the attrition of time would overtake her. She had to be prepared. The company had to be safeguarded for the family. Brad Rogers was a good manager, but he was not a Blackwell. *I have to last until the twins can take over.* She thought of Cecil Rhodes's last words: "So little done – so much to do."

The twins were twelve years old, on the verge of becoming young ladies. Kate had spent as much time with them as she possibly could, but now she turned even more of her attention to them. It was time to make an important decision.

During Easter week, Kate and the twins flew to Dark Harbor in a company plane. The girls had visited all the family estates except the one in Johannesburg, and of them all, Dark Harbor was their favorite. They enjoyed the wild freedom and the seclusion of the island. They loved to sail and swim and water-ski, and Dark Harbor held all these things for them. Eve asked if she could bring some schoolmates along, as she had in the past, but this time her grandmother refused. Grandmother; that powerful, imposing figure who swept in and out, dropping off a present here, a kiss on the cheek there, with occasional admonitions about how young ladies behaved, wanted to be alone with them. This time the girls sensed that something different was happening. Their grandmother was with them at every meal. She took them boating and swimming and even riding. Kate handled her horse with the sureness of an expert.

The girls still looked amazingly alike, two golden beauties, but Kate was interested less in their similarities than in their differences. Sitting on the veranda watching them as they finished a tennis game, Kate summed them up in her mind. Eve was the leader, Alexandra the follower. Eve had a stubborn streak. Alexandra was flexible. Eve was a natural athlete. Alexandra was still having accidents. Only a few days before, when the two girls were out alone in a small sailboat with Eve at the rudder, the wind had come behind the sail and the sail had luffed, swinging it crashing toward Alexandra's head. She had not gotten out of the way in time and had been swept overboard and nearly drowned. Another boat nearby had assisted Eve in rescuing her sister. Kate wondered whether all these things could have anything to do with Alexandra having been born three minutes later than Eve, but the reasons did not matter. Kate had made her decision. There was no longer any question in her mind. She was putting her money on Eve, and it was a ten-billion-dollar bet. She would find a perfect consort for Eve, and when Kate retired, Eve would run Kruger-Brent. As for Alexandra, she would have a life of wealth and comfort. She might be very good working on the charitable grants Kate had set up. Yes, that would be perfect for Alexandra. She was such a sweet and compassionate child.

The first step toward implementing Kate's plan was to see that Eve got into the proper school. Kate chose Briarcrest, an excellent school in South Carolina. "Both my granddaughters are delightful," Kate informed Mrs. Chandler, the headmistress. "But you'll find that Eve is the clever one. She's an extraordinary girl, and I'm sure you'll see to it that she has every advantage here."

"All our students have every advantage here, Mrs. Blackwell. You spoke of Eve. What about her sister?"

"Alexandra? A lovely girl." It was a pejorative. Kate stood up. "I shall be checking their progress regularly."

In some odd way, the headmistress felt the words were a warning.

Eve and Alexandra adored the new school, particularly Eve. She enjoyed the freedom of being away from home, of not having to account to her grandmother and Solange Dunas. The rules at Briarcrest were strict, but that did not bother

Eve, for she was adept at getting around rules. The only thing that disturbed her was that Alexandra was there with her. When Eve first heard the news about Briarcrest, she begged, "May I go alone? Please, Gran?"

And Kate said, "No, darling. I think it's better if Alexandra goes with you."

Eve concealed her resentment. "Whatever you say, Gran."

She was always very polite and affectionate around her grandmother. Eve knew where the power lay. Their father was a crazy man, locked up in an insane asylum. Their mother was dead. It was their grandmother who controlled the money. Eve knew they were rich. She had no idea how much money there was, but it was a lot – enough to buy all the beautiful things she wanted. Eve loved beautiful things. There was only one problem: Alexandra.

One of the twins' favorite activities at Briarcrest School was the morning riding class. Most of the girls owned their own jumpers, and Kate had given each twin one for her twelfth birthday. Jerome Davis, the riding instructor, watched as his pupils went through their paces in the ring, jumping over a one-foot stile, then a two-foot stile and finally a four-foot stile. Davis was one of the best riding teachers in the country. Several of his former pupils had gone on to win gold medals, and he was adept at spotting a natural-born rider. The new girl, Eve Blackwell, was a natural. She did not have to think about what she was doing, how to hold the reins or post in the saddle. She and her horse were one, and as they sailed over the hurdles, Eve's golden hair flying in the wind, it was a beautiful sight to behold. *Nothings going to stop that one*, Mr. Davis thought.

Tommy, the young groom, favored Alexandra. Mr. Davis watched Alexandra saddle up her horse, preparing for her turn. Alexandra and Eve wore different-colored ribbons on their sleeves so he could tell them apart. Eve was helping Alexandra saddle her horse while Tommy was busy with another student. Davis was summoned to the main building for a telephone call, and what happened after that was a matter of great confusion.

From what Jerome Davis was able to piece together later, Alexandra mounted her horse, circled the ring and started toward the first low jump. Her horse inexplicably began rearing and bucking, and threw Alexandra into a wall. She was knocked unconscious, and it was only by inches that the wild horse's hooves missed her face. Tommy carried Alexandra to the infirmary, where the school doctor diagnosed a mild concussion.

"Nothing broken, nothing serious," he said. "By tomorrow morning, she'll be right as rain, ready to get up on her horse again."

"But she could have been killed!" Eve screamed.

Eve refused to leave Alexandra's side. Mrs. Chandler thought she had never seen such devotion in a sister. It was truly touching.

When Mr. Davis was finally able to corral Alexandra's horse to unsaddle it, he found the saddle blanket stained with blood. He lifted it off and discovered a large piece of jagged metal from a beer can still protruding from the horse's back, where it had been pressed down by the saddle. When he reported this to

Mrs. Chandler, she started an immediate investigation. All the girls who had been in the vicinity of the stable were questioned.

"I'm sure," Mrs. Chandler said, "that whoever put that piece of metal there thought she was playing a harmless prank, but it could have led to very serious consequences. I want the name of the girl who did it."

When no one volunteered, Mrs. Chandler talked to them in her office, one by one. Each girl denied any knowledge of what had happened. When it was Eve's turn to be questioned, she seemed oddly ill at ease.

"Do you have any idea who could have done this to your sister?" Mrs. Chandler asked.

Eve looked down at the rug. "I'd rather not say," she mumbled.

"Then you *did* see something?"

"Please, Mrs. Chandler . . ."

"Eve, Alexandra could have been seriously hurt. The girl who did this must be punished so that it does not happen again."

"It wasn't one of the girls."

"what do you mean?"

"It was Tommy."

"The *groom?*"

"Yes, ma'am. I saw him. I thought he was just tightening the cinch. I'm sure he didn't mean any harm. Alexandra orders him around a lot, and I guess he wanted to teach her a lesson. Oh, Mrs. Chandler, I wish you hadn't made me tell you. I don't want to get anyone in trouble." The poor child was on the verge of hysteria.

Mrs. Chandler walked around the desk and put her arm around her. "It's all right, Eve. You did right to tell me. Now you just forget about everything. I'll take care of it."

The following morning when the girls went out to the stables, there was a new groom.

A few months later, there was another unpleasant incident at the school. Several of the girls had been caught smoking marijuana and one of them accused Eve of supplying it and selling it. Eve angrily denied it. A search by Mrs. Chandler revealed marijuana hidden in Alexandra's locker.

"I don't believe she did it," Eve said stoutly. "Someone put it there. I know it."

An account of the incident was sent to Kate by the headmistress, and Kate admired Eve's loyalty in shielding her sister. She was a McGregor, all right.

On the twins' fifteenth birthday, Kate took them to the estate in South Carolina, where she gave a large party for them. It was not too early to see to it that Eve was exposed to the proper young men, and every eligible young man around was invited to the girls' party.

The boys were at the awkward age where they were not yet seriously interested in girls, but Kate made it her business to see that acquaintances were made and friendships formed. Somewhere among these young boys could be the man in Eve's future, the future of Kruger-Brent, Ltd.

Alexandra did not enjoy parties, but she always pretended she was having a good time in order not to disappoint her grandmother. Eve adored parties. She loved dressing up, being admired. Alexandra preferred reading and painting. She spent hours looking at her father's paintings at Dark Harbor, and she wished she could have known him before he became ill. He appeared at the house on holidays with his male companion, but Alexandra found it impossible to reach her father. He was a pleasant, amiable stranger who wanted to please, but had nothing to say. Their grandfather, Frederick Hoffman, lived in Germany, but was ill. The twins seldom saw him.

In her second year at school, Eve became pregnant. For several weeks she had been pale and listless and had missed some morning classes. When she began to have frequent periods of nausea, she was sent to the infirmary and examined. Mrs. Chandler had been hastily summoned.

"Eve is pregnant," the doctor told her.

"But – that's impossible! How could it have happened?"

The doctor replied mildly, "In the usual fashion, I would presume."

"But she's just a child."

"Well, this child is going to be a mother."

Eve bravely refused to talk. "I don't want to get anyone in trouble," she kept saying.

It was the kind of answer Mrs. Chandler expected from Eve.

"Eve, dear, you must tell me what happened."

And so at last Eve broke down. "I was raped," she said, and burst into tears.

Mrs. Chandler was shocked. She held Eve's trembling body close to her and demanded, "Who was it?"

"Mr. Parkinson."

Her English teacher.

If it had been anyone else but Eve, Mrs. Chandler would not have believed it. Joseph Parkinson was a quiet man with a wife and three children. He had taught at Briarcrest School for eight years, and he was the last one Mrs. Chandler would have ever suspected. She called him into her office, and she knew instantly that Eve had told the truth. He sat facing her, his face twitching with nervousness.

"You know why I've sent for you, Mr. Parkinson?"

"I – I think so."

"It concerns Eve."

"Yes. I – I guessed that."

"She says you raped her."

Parkinson looked at her in disbelief. "*Raped* her? My God! If anyone was raped, it was me." In his excitement he lapsed into the ungrammatical.

Mrs. Chandler said contemptuously, "Do you know what you're saying? That child is – "

"She's *not* a child." His voice was venomous. "She's a devil." He wiped the perspiration from his brow. "All semester she sat in the front row of my class, with her dress hiked up. After class she would come up and ask a lot of meaningless questions while she rubbed herself against me. I didn't take her seriously. Then one afternoon about six weeks ago she came over to my house when my wife and children were away and – " His voice broke. "oh, Jesus! I couldn't help it." He burst into tears.

They brought Eve into the office. Her manner was composed. She looked into Mr. Parkinson's eyes, and it was he who turned away first. In the office were Mrs. Chandler, the assistant principal and the chief of police of the small town where the school was located.

The chief of police said gently, "Do you want to tell us what happened, Eve?"

"Yes, sir." Eve's voice was calm. "Mr. Parkinson said he wanted to discuss my English work with me. He asked me to come to his house on a Sunday afternoon. He was alone in the house. He said he wanted to show me something in the bedroom, so I followed him upstairs. He forced me onto the bed, and he – "

"It's a lie!" Parkinson yelled. "That's not the way it happened. That's not the way it happened . . ."

Kate was sent for, and the situation was explained to her. It was decided that it was in everyone's interest to keep the incident quiet. Mr. Parkinson was dismissed from the school and given forty-eight hours to leave the state. An abortion was discreetly arranged for Eve.

Kate quietly bought up the school mortgage, carried by a local bank, and foreclosed.

When Eve heard the news, she sighed, "I'm so sorry, Gran. I really liked that school."

A few weeks later when Eve had recovered from her operation, she and Alexandra were registered at L'Institut Fernwood, a Swiss finishing school near Lausanne.

25

There was a fire burning in Eve that was so fierce she could not put it out. It was not sex alone: That was only a small part of it. It was a rage to live, a need to do everything, be everything. Life was a lover, and Eve was desperate to possess it with all she had in her. She was jealous of everyone. She went to the ballet and hated the ballerina because she herself was not up there dancing and winning the cheers of the audience. She wanted to be a scientist, a singer, a surgeon, a pilot, an actress. She wanted to do everything, and do it better than anyone else had ever done it. She wanted it all, and she could not wait.

Across the valley from L'Institut Fernwood was a boys' military school. By the time Eve was seventeen, nearly every student and almost half the instructors were involved with her. She flirted outrageously and had affairs indiscriminately, but this time she took proper precautions, for she had no intention of ever getting pregnant again. She enjoyed sex, but it was not the act itself Eve loved, it was the power it gave her. She was the one in control. She gloated over the pleading looks of the boys and men who wanted to take her to bed and make love to her. She enjoyed teasing them and watching their hunger grow. She enjoyed the lying promises they made in order to possess her. But most of all, Eve enjoyed the power she had over their bodies. She could bring them to an erection with a kiss, and wither them with a word. She did not need them, they needed her. She controlled them totally, and it was a tremendous feeling. Within minutes she could measure a man's strengths and weaknesses. She decided men were fools, all of them.

Eve was beautiful and intelligent and an heiress to one of the world's great fortunes, and she had had more than a dozen serious proposals of marriage. She was not interested. The only boys who attracted her were the ones Alexandra liked.

At a Saturday-night school dance, Alexandra met an attentive young French student named Rene Mallot. He was not handsome, but he was intelligent and sensitive, and Alexandra thought he was wonderful. They arranged to meet in town the following Saturday.

"Seven o'clock," Rene said.

"I'll be waiting."

In their room that night, Alexandra told Eve about her new friend. "He's not like the other boys. He's rather shy and sweet. We're going to the theater Saturday."

"You like him a lot, don't you, little sister?" Eve teased.

Alexandra blushed. "I just met him, but he seems – Well, you know."

Eve lay back on her bed, hands clasped behind her head. "No, I don't know. Tell me. Did he try to take you to bed?"

"Eve! He's not that kind of boy at all. I told you . . . he's – he's shy."

"Well, well. My little sister's in love."

"Of course I'm not! Now I wish I hadn't told you."

"I'm glad you did," Eve said sincerely.

When Alexandra arrived in front of the theater the following Saturday, Rene was nowhere in sight. Alexandra waited on the street corner for more than an hour, ignoring the stares of passers-by, feeling like a fool. Finally she had a bad dinner alone in a small café and returned to school, miserable. Eve was not in their room. Alexandra read until curfew and then turned out the lights. It was almost two A.M. when Alexandra heard Eve sneak into the room.

"I was getting worried about you," Alexandra whispered.

"I ran into some old friends. How was your evening – divine?"
"It was dreadful. He never even bothered to show up."
"That's a shame," Eve said sympathetically. "But you must learn never to trust a man."
"You don't think anything could have happened to him?"
"No, Alex. I think he probably found somebody he liked better."
Of course he did, Alexandra thought. She was not really surprised. She had no idea how beautiful she was, or how admirable. She had lived all her life in the shadow of her twin sister. She adored her, and it seemed only right to Alexandra that everyone should be attracted to Eve. She felt inferior to Eve, but it never occurred to her that her sister had been carefully nourishing that feeling since they were children.

There were other broken dates. Boys Alexandra liked would seem to respond to her, and then she would never see them again. One weekend she ran into Rene unexpectedly on the streets of Lausanne. He hurried up to her and said, "What happened? You promised you would call me."
"Call you? What are you talking about?"
He stepped back, suddenly wary. "Eve . . . ?"
"No, Alexandra."
His face flushed. "I – I'm sorry. I have to go." And he hurried away, leaving her staring after him in confusion.
That evening when Alexandra told Eve about the incident, Eve shrugged and said, "He's obviously *fou*. You're much better off without him, Alex."

In spite of her feeling of expertise about men, there was one male weakness of which Eve was unaware, and it almost proved to be her undoing. From the beginning of time, men have boasted of their conquests, and the students at the military school were no different. They discussed Eve Blackwell with admiration and awe.
"When she was through with me, I couldn't move . . ."
"I never thought I'd have a piece of ass like that . . ."
"She's got a pussy that *talks* to you . . ."
"God, she's like a tigress in bed!"
Since at least two dozen boys and half a dozen teachers were praising Eve's libidinous talents, it soon became the school's worst-kept secret. One of the instructors at the military school mentioned the gossip to a teacher at L'Institut Fernwood, and she in turn reported it to Mrs. Collins, the headmistress. A discreet investigation was begun, and the result was a meeting between the headmistress and Eve.
"I think it would be better for the reputation of this school if you left immediately."

Eve stared at Mrs. Collins as though the lady were demented. "What on earth are you talking about?"

"I'm talking about the fact that you have been servicing half the military academy. The other half seems to be lined up, eagerly waiting."

"I've never heard such terrible lies in my whole life." Eve's voice was quivering with indignation. "Don't think I'm not going to report this to my grandmother. When she hears – "

"I will spare you the trouble," the headmistress interrupted. "I would prefer to avoid embarrassment to L'Institut Fernwood, but if you do not leave quietly, I have a list of names I intend to send to your grandmother."

"I'd like to see that list!"

Mrs. Collins handed it to Eve without a word. It was a long list. Eve studied it and noted that at least seven names were missing. She sat there, quietly thinking.

Finally she looked up and said imperiously, "This is obviously some kind of plot against my family. Someone is trying to embarrass my grandmother through me. Rather than let that happen, I will leave."

"A very wise decision," Mrs. Collins said dryly. "A car will drive you to the airport in the morning. I'll cable your grandmother that you're coming home. You're dismissed."

Eve turned and started for the door, then suddenly thought of something. "What about my sister?"

"Alexandra may remain here."

When Alexandra returned to the dormitory after her last class, she found Eve packing. "What are you doing?"

"I'm going home."

"Home? In the middle of the term?"

Eve turned to face her sister. "Alex, don't you really have any idea what a waste this school is? We're not learning anything here. We're just killing time."

Alexandra was listening in surprise. "I had no idea you felt that way, Eve."

"I've felt like this every damn day for the whole bloody year. The only reason I stuck it out was because of you. You seemed to be enjoying it so much."

"I am, but – "

"I'm sorry, Alex. I just can't take it any longer. I want to get back to New York. I want to go home where *we* belong."

"Have you told Mrs. Collins?"

"A few minutes ago."

"How did she take it?"

"How did you expect her to take it? She was miserable – afraid it would make her school look bad. She begged me to stay."

Alexandra sat down on the edge of the bed. "I don't know what to say."

"You don't have to say anything. This has nothing to do with you."

"Of course it has. If you're that unhappy here – " She stopped. "You're probably right. It is a bloody waste of time. Who needs to conjugate Latin verbs?"

"Right. Or who gives a fig about Hannibal or his bloody brother, Hasdrubal?"

Alexandra walked over to the closet, took out her suitcase and put it on the bed.

Eve smiled. "I wasn't going to ask you to leave here, Alex, but I'm really glad we're going home together."

Alexandra pressed her sister's hand. "So am I."

Eve said casually, "Tell you what. While I finish packing, call Gran and tell her we'll be on the plane home tomorrow. Tell her we can't stand this place. Will you do that?"

"Yes." Alexandra hesitated. "I don't think she's going to like it."

"Don't worry about the old lady," Eve said confidently. "I can handle her."

And Alexandra had no reason to doubt it. Eve was able to make Gran do pretty much what she wanted. *But then*, Alexandra thought, *how could anyone refuse Eve anything?*

She went to make the phone call.

Kate Blackwell had friends and enemies and business associates in high places, and for the last few months disturbing rumors had been coming to her ears. In the beginning she had ignored them as petty jealousies. But they persisted. Eve was seeing too much of the boys at a military school in Switzerland. Eve had an abortion. Eve was being treated for a social disease.

Thus, it was with a degree of relief that Kate learned that her granddaughters were coming home. She intended to get to the bottom of the vile rumors.

The day the girls arrived, Kate was at home waiting for them. She took Eve into the sitting room off her bedroom. "I've been hearing some distressing stories," she said. "I want to know why you were thrown out of school." Her eyes bored into those of her granddaughter.

"We weren't thrown out," Eve replied. "Alex and I decided to leave."

"Because of some incidents with boys?"

Eve said, "Please, Grandmother. I'd rather not talk about it."

"I'm afraid you're going to have to. What have you been doing?"

"I haven't been doing anything. It is Alex who – " She broke off.

"Alex who what?" Kate was relentless.

"Please don't blame her," Eve said quickly. "I'm sure she couldn't help it. She likes to play this childish game of pretending to be me. I had no idea what she was up to until the girls started gossiping about it. It seems she was seeing a lot of boys – " Eve broke off in embarrassment.

"Pretending to be you?" Kate was stunned. "Why didn't you put a stop to it?"

"I tried," Eve said miserably. "She threatened to kill herself. Oh, Gran, I think Alexandra is a bit" – she forced herself to say the word – "unstable. If you even discuss any of this with her, I'm afraid of what she might do." There was naked agony in the child's tear-filled eyes.

Kate's heart felt heavy at Eve's deep unhappiness. "Eve, don't. Don't cry, darling. I won't say anything to Alexandra. This will be just between the two of us."

"I – I didn't want you to know. Oh, Gran," she sobbed, "I knew how much it would hurt you."

Later, over tea, Kate studied Alexandra. *She's beautiful outside and rotten inside*, Kate thought. It was bad enough that Alexandra was involved in a series of sordid affairs, but to try to put the blame on her sister! Kate was appalled.

During the next two years, while Eve and Alexandra finished school at Miss Porter's, Eve was very discreet. She had been frightened by the close call. Nothing must jeopardize the relationship with her grandmother. The old lady could not last much longer – she was seventy-nine! – and Eve intended to make sure that she was Gran's heiress.

For the girls' twenty-first birthday, Kate took her granddaughters to Paris and bought them new wardrobes at Coco Chanel.

At a small dinner party at Le Petit Bedouin, Eve and Alexandra met Count Alfred Maurier and his wife, the Countess Vivien. The count was a distinguished-looking man in his fifties, with iron-gray hair and the disciplined body of an athlete. His wife was a pleasant-looking woman with a reputation as an international hostess.

Eve would have paid no particular attention to either of them, except for a remark she overheard someone make to the countess. "I envy you and Alfred. You're the happiest married couple I know. How many years have you been married? Twenty-five?"

"It will be twenty-six next month," Alfred replied for her. "And I may be the only Frenchman in history who has never been unfaithful to his wife."

Everyone laughed except Eve. During the rest of the dinner, she studied Count Maurier and his wife. Eve could not imagine what the count saw in that flabby, middle-aged woman with her crepey neck. Count Maurier had probably never known what real lovemaking was. That boast of his was stupid. Count Alfred Maurier was a challenge.

The following day, Eve telephoned Maurier at his office. "This is Eve Blackwell. You probably don't remember me, but – "

"How could I forget you, child? You are one of the beautiful granddaughters of my friend Kate."

"I'm flattered that you remember, Count. Forgive me for disturbing you, but I was told you're an expert on wines. I'm planning a surprise dinner party for Grandmother." She gave a rueful little laugh. "I know what I want to serve, but I don't know a thing about wines. I wondered whether you'd be kind enough to advise me."

"I would be delighted," he said, flattered. "It depends on what you are serving. If you are starting with a fish, a nice, light Chablis would be – "

"Oh, I'm afraid I could never remember all this. Would it be possible for me to see you so that we could discuss it? If you're free for lunch today . . . ?"

"For an old friend, I can arrange that."

"Oh, good." Eve replaced the receiver slowly. It would be a lunch the count would remember the rest of his life.

They met at Lasserre. The discussion on wines was brief. Eve listened to Maurier's boring discourse impatiently, and then interrupted. "I'm in love with you, Alfred."

The count stopped dead in the middle of a sentence. "I beg your pardon?"

"I said I'm in love with you."

He took a sip of wine. "A vintage year." He patted Eve's hand and smiled. "All good friends should love one another."

"I'm not talking about that kind of love, Alfred."

And the count looked into Eve's eyes and knew exactly what kind of love she was talking about. It made him decidedly nervous. This girl was twenty-one years old, and he was past middle age, a happily married man. He simply could not understand what got into young girls these days. He felt uneasy sitting across from her, listening to what she was saying, and he felt even uneasier because she was probably the most beautiful, desirable young woman he had ever seen. She was wearing a beige pleated skirt and a soft green sweater that revealed the outline of a full, rich bosom. She was not wearing a brassiere, and he could see the thrust of her nipples. He looked at her innocent young face, and he was at a loss for words. "You – you don't even know me."

"I've dreamed about you from the time I was a little girl. I imagined a man in shining armor who was tall and handsome and – "

"I'm afraid my armor's a little rusty. I – "

"Please don't make fun of me," Eve begged. "When I saw you at dinner last night, I couldn't take my eyes off you. I haven't been able to think of anything else. I haven't slept. I haven't been able to get you out of my mind for a moment." Which was almost true.

"I – I don't know what to say to you, Eve. I am a happily married man. I – "

"Oh, I can't tell you how I envy your wife! She's the luckiest woman in the world. I wonder if she realizes that, Alfred."

"Of course she does. I tell her all the time." He smiled nervously, and wondered how to change the subject.

"Does she *really* appreciate you? Does she know how sensitive you are? Does she worry about your happiness? I would."

The count was becoming increasingly uncomfortable. "You're a beautiful young woman," he said. "And one day you re going to find your knight in shining, *unrusted* armor, and then – "

"I've found him and I want to go to bed with him."

He looked around, afraid that someone might have overheard. "Eve! Please!"

She leaned forward. "That's all I ask. The memory will last me for the rest of my life."

The count said firmly, "This is impossible. You are placing me in a most embarrassing position. Young women should not go around propositioning strangers."

Slowly, Eve's eyes filled with tears. "Is that what you think of me? That I go around – I've known only one man in my life. We were engaged to be married." She did not bother to brush the tears away. "He was kind and loving and gentle. He was killed in a mountain-climbing accident. I saw it happen. It was awful."

Count Maurier put his hand over hers. "I am so sorry."

"You remind me so much of him. When I saw you, it was as though Bill had returned to me. If you would give me just one hour, I would never bother you again. You'd never even have to see me again. Please, Alfred!"

The count looked at Eve for a long time, weighing his decision.

After all, he was French.

They spent the afternoon in a small hotel on Rue Sainte-Anne. In all his experience before his marriage, Count Maurier had never bedded anyone like Eve. She was a hurricane, a nymphet, a devil. She knew too much. By the end of the afternoon, Count Maurier was completely exhausted.

As they were getting dressed, Eve said, "When will I see you again, darling?"

"I'll telephone you," Maurier said.

He did not plan ever to see this woman again. There was something about her that was frightening – almost evil. She was what the Americans so appropriately called *bad news*, and he had no intention of becoming involved further with her.

The matter would have ended there, had they not been seen coming out of the hotel together by Alicia Vanderlake, who had served on a charity committee with Kate Blackwell the previous year. Mrs. Vanderlake was a social climber, and this was a heaven-sent ladder. She had seen newspaper photographs of Count Maurier and his wife, and she had seen photographs of the Blackwell twins. She was not sure which twin this was, but that was not important. Mrs. Vanderlake knew where her duty lay. She looked in her private telephone book and found Kate Blackwell's number.

The butler answered the telephone. "*Bonjour.*"

"I would like to speak with Mrs. Blackwell, please."

"May I tell her who is calling?"

"Mrs. Vanderlake. It's a personal matter."

A minute later, Kate Blackwell was on the phone. "Who is this?"

"This is Alicia Vanderlake, Mrs. Blackwell. I'm sure you'll remember me. We served on a committee together last year and – "

"If it's for a donation, call my – "

"No, no," Mrs. Vanderlake said hastily. "It's personal. It's about your granddaughter."

Kate Blackwell would invite her over to tea, and they would discuss it, woman to woman. It would be the beginning of a warm friendship.

Kate Blackwell said, "What about her?"

Mrs. Vanderlake had had no intention of discussing the matter over the telephone, but Kate Blackwell's unfriendly tone left her no choice. "Well, I thought it my duty to tell you that a few minutes ago I saw her sneaking out of a hotel with Count Alfred Maurier. It was an obvious assignation."

Kate's voice was icy. "I find this difficult to believe. Which one of my granddaughters?"

Mrs. Vanderlake gave an uncertain laugh. "I – I don't know. I can't tell them apart. But then, no one can, can they? It – "

"Thank you for the information." And Kate hung up.

She stood there digesting the information she had just heard. Only the evening before they had dined together. Kate had known Alfred Maurier for fifteen years, and what she had just been told was entirely out of character for him, unthinkable. And yet, men were susceptible. If Alexandra had set out to lure Alfred into bed . . .

Kate picked up the telephone and said to the operator, "I wish to place a call to Switzerland. L'Institut Fernwood at Lausanne."

When Eve returned home late that afternoon, she was flushed with satisfaction, not because she had enjoyed sex with Count Maurier, but because of her victory over him. *If I can have him so easily, Eve* thought, *I can have anyone. I can own the world.* She walked into the library and found Kate there.

"Hello, Gran. Did you have a lovely day?"

Kate stood there studying her lovely young granddaughter. "Not a very good one, I'm afraid. What about you?"

"Oh, I did a little shopping. I didn't see anything more I really wanted. You bought me everything. You always – "

"Close the door, Eve."

Something in Kate's voice sent out a warning signal. Eve closed the large oak door.

"Sit down."

"Is something wrong, Gran?"

"That's what you're going to tell me. I was going to invite Alfred Maurier here, but I decided to spare us all that humiliation."

Eve's brain began to spin. *This was impossible! There was no way anyone could have found out about her and Alfred Maurier.* She had left him only an hour earlier. "I – I don't understand what you're talking about."

"Then let me put it bluntly. You were in bed this afternoon with Count Maurier."

Tears sprang to Eve's eyes. "I – I was hoping you'd never find out what he did to me, because he's your friend." She fought to keep her voice steady. "It was terrible. He telephoned and invited me to lunch and got me drunk and – "

"Shut up!" Kate's voice was like a whiplash. Her eyes were filled with loathing. "You're despicable."

Kate had spent the most painful hour of her life, coming to a realization of the truth about her granddaughter. She could hear again the voice of the headmistress saying, *Mrs. Blackwell, young women will be young women, and if one of them has a discreet affair, it is none of my business. But Eve was so blatantly promiscuous that for the good of the school . . .*

And Eve had blamed Alexandra.

Kate started to remember the accidents. The fire, when Alexandra almost burned to death. Alexandra's fall from the cliff. Alexandra being knocked out of the boat Eve was sailing, and almost drowning. Kate could hear Eve's voice recounting the details of her "rape" by her English teacher: *Mr. Parkinson said he wanted to discuss my English work with me. He asked me to come to his house on a Sunday afternoon. When I got there, he was alone in the house. He said he wanted to show me something in the bedroom. I followed him upstairs. He forced me onto the bed, and he . . .*

Kate remembered the incident at Briarcrest when Eve was accused of selling marijuana and the blame had been put on Alexandra. Eve had not *blamed* Alexandra, she had *defended* her. That was Eve's technique – to be the villain and play the heroine. Oh, she was clever.

Now Kate studied the beautiful, angel-faced monster in front of her. *I built all my future plans around you. It was you who was going to take control of Kruger-Brent one day. It was you I loved and cherished.* Kate said, "I want you to leave this house. I never want to see you again."

Eve had gone very pale.

"You're a whore. I think I could live with that. But you're also deceitful and cunning and a psychopathic liar. I cannot live with that."

It was all happening too fast. Eve said desperately, "Gran, if Alexandra has been telling you lies about me – "

"Alexandra doesn't know anything about this. I just had a long talk with Mrs. Collins."

"Is *that* all?" Eve forced a note of relief in her voice. "Mrs. Collins hates me because – "

Kate was filled with a sudden weariness. "It won't work, Eve. Not anymore. It's over. I've sent for my lawyer. I'm disinheriting you."

Eve felt her world crumbling around her. "You can't. How – how will I live?"

"You will be given a small allowance. From now on, you will live your own life. Do anything you please." Kate's voice hardened. "But if I ever hear or read one word of scandal about you, if you ever disgrace the Blackwell name in any way, your allowance will stop forever. Is that clear?"

Eve looked into her grandmother's eyes and knew this time there would be no reprieve. A dozen excuses sprang to her lips, but they died there.

Kate rose to her feet and said in an unsteady voice, "I don't suppose this will mean anything to you, but this is – this is the most difficult thing I've ever had to do in my life."

And Kate turned and walked out of the room, her back stiff and straight.

Kate sat in her darkened bedroom alone, wondering why everything had gone wrong.

If David had not been killed, and Tony could have known his father . . .

If Tony had not wanted to be an artist . . .

If Marianne had lived . . .

If. A two-letter word for futility.

The future was clay, to be molded day by day, but the past was bedrock, immutable. *Everyone I've loved has betrayed me*, Kate thought. *Tony. Marianne. Eve. Sartre said it well: "Hell is other people."* She wondered when the pain would go away.

If Kate was filled with pain, Eve was filled with fury. All she had done was to enjoy herself in bed for an hour or two, and her grandmother acted as though Eve had committed some unspeakable crime. *The old-fashioned bitch!* No, not old-fashioned: *senile*. That was it. She was senile. Eve would find a good attorney and have the new will laughed out of court. Her father and grandmother were both insane. No one was going to disinherit her. Kruger-Brent was *her* company. How many times had her grandmother told her that one day it would belong to her. And Alexandra! All this time Alexandra had been undermining her, whispering God-knows-what poison into their grandmother's ears. Alexandra wanted the company for herself. The terrible part was that now she would probably get it. What had happened this afternoon was bad enough, but the thought of Alexandra gaining control was unbearable. *I can't let that happen*, Eve thought. *I'll find a way to stop her.* She closed the snaps on her suitcase and went to find her sister.

Alexandra was in the garden reading. She looked up as Eve approached.

"Alex, I've decided to go back to New York."

Alexandra looked at her sister in surprise. "*Now?* Gran's planning a cruise to the Dalmatian coast next week. You – "

"Who cares about the Dalmatian coast? I've been thinking a lot about this. It's time I had my own apartment." She smiled. "I'm a big girl now. So I'm going to find the most divine little apartment, and if you're good, I'll let you spend the night once in a while." *That's just the right note,* Eve thought. *Friendly, but not gushy. Don't let her know you're on to her.*

Alexandra was studying her sister with concern. "Does Gran know?"

"I told her this afternoon. She hates the idea, of course, but she understands. I wanted to get a job, but she insisted on giving me an allowance."

Alexandra asked, "Would you like me to come with you?"

The goddamned, two faced bitch! First she forced her out of the house, and now she was pretending she wanted to go with her. *Well, they're not going to dispose of little Eve so easily. I'll show them all.* She would have her own apartment – she would find some fabulous decorator to do it – and she would have complete freedom to come and go as she pleased. She could invite men up to her place and have them spend the night. She would be truly free for the first time in her life. It was an exhilarating thought.

Now she said, "You're sweet, Alex, but I'd like to be on my own for a while."

Alexandra looked at her sister and felt a deep sense of loss. It would be the first time they had ever been parted. "We'll see each other often, won't we?"

"Of course we will," Eve promised. "More than you imagine."

26

When Eve returned to New York, she checked into a midtown hotel, as she had been instructed. An hour later, Brad Rogers telephoned.

"Your grandmother called from Paris, Eve. Apparently there's some problem between you two."

"Not really," Eve laughed. "It's just a little family – " She was about to launch into an elaborate defense when she suddenly realized the danger that lay in that direction. From now on, she would have to be very careful. She had never had to think about money. It had always been there. Now it loomed large in her thoughts. She had no idea how large her allowance was going to be and for the first time in her life Eve felt fear.

"She told you she's having a new will drawn up?" Brad asked.

"Yes, she mentioned something about it." She was determined to play it cool.

"I think we had better discuss this in person. How's Monday at three?"

"That will be fine, Brad."

"My office. All right?"

"I'll be there."

At five minutes before three, Eve entered the Kruger-Brent, Ltd., Building. She was greeted deferentially by the security guard, the elevator starter and even the elevator operator. *Everyone knows me*, Eve thought. *I'm a Blackwell.* The elevator took her to the executive floor, and a few moments later Eve was seated in Brad Rogers's office.

Brad had been surprised when Kate telephoned him to say she was going to disinherit Eve, for he knew how much Kate cared about this particular granddaughter and what plans she had for her. Brad could not imagine what had happened. Well, it was none of his business. If Kate wanted to discuss it with him, she would. His job was to carry out her orders. He felt a momentary flash of pity for the lovely young woman before him. Kate had not been much older when he had first met her. Neither had he. And now he was a gray-haired old fool, still hoping that one day Kate Blackwell would realize there was someone who loved her very deeply.

He said to Eve, "I have some papers for you to sign. If you'll just read them over and – "

"That won't be necessary."

"Eve, it's important that you understand." He began to explain. "Under your grandmother's will, you're the beneficiary of an irrevocable trust fund currently in excess of five million dollars. Your grandmother is the executor. At her discretion, the money can be paid to you at any time from the age of twenty-one to thirty-five." He cleared his throat. "She has elected to give it to you when you reach age thirty-five."

It was a slap in the face.

"Beginning today, you will receive a weekly allowance of two hundred fifty dollars."

It was impossible! One decent dress cost more than that. There was no way she could live on $250 a week. This was being done to humiliate her. This bastard was probably in on it with her grandmother. He was sitting behind his big desk, enjoying himself, laughing. She wanted to pick up the large bronze paperweight in front of him and smash his head in. She could almost feel the crunch of bone under her hand.

Brad droned on. "You are not to have any charge accounts, private or otherwise, and you are not to use the Blackwell name at any stores. Anything you purchase must be paid for in cash."

The nightmare was getting worse and worse.

"Next. If there is any gossip connected with your name in any newspaper or magazine – local or foreign – your weekly income will be stopped. Is that clear?"

"Yes." Her voice was a whisper.

"You and your sister Alexandra were issued insurance policies on your grandmother's life for five million dollars apiece. The policy you hold was canceled as of this morning. At the end of one year," Brad went on, "if your grandmother is satisfied with your behavior, your weekly allowance will be doubled." He hesitated. "There is one final stipulation."

She wants to hang me in public by my thumbs. "Yes?"

Brad Rogers looked uncomfortable. "Your grandmother does not wish ever to see you again, Eve."

Well, I want to see you one more time, old woman. I want to see you dying in agony.

Brad's voice trickled through to the cauldron of Eve's mind. "If you have any problems, you are to telephone me. She does not want you to come to this building again, or to visit any of the family estates."

He had tried to argue with Kate about that. "My God, Kate, she's your granddaughter, your flesh and blood. You're treating her like a leper."

"She *is* a leper."

And the discussion had ended.

Now Brad said awkwardly, "Well, I think that covers everything. Are there any questions, Eve?"

"No." She was in shock.

"Then if you'll just sign these papers . . ."

Ten minutes later, Eve was on the street again. There was a check for $250 in her purse.

The following morning Eve called on a real-estate agent and began looking for an apartment. In her fantasies, she had envisioned a beautiful penthouse overlooking Central Park, the rooms done in white with modern furniture, and a terrace where she could entertain guests. Reality came as a stunning blow. It seemed there were no Park Avenue penthouses available for someone with an income of $250 a week. What *was* available was a one-room studio apartment in Little Italy with a couch that became a bed, a nook that the real-estate agent euphemistically referred to as the "library," a small kitchenette and a tiny bathroom with stained tile.

"Is – is this the best you have?" Eve asked.

"No," the agent informed her. "I've got a twenty-room townhouse on Sutton Place for a half a million dollars, plus maintenance."

You bastard! Eve thought.

Real despair did not hit Eve until the following afternoon when she moved in. It was a prison. Her dressing room at home had been as large as this entire apartment. She thought of Alexandra enjoying herself in the huge house on Fifth Avenue. *My God, why couldn't Alexandra have burned to death? It had been so close!* If she had died and Eve had been the only heiress, things would have been different. Her grandmother would not have dared disinherit her.

But if Kate Blackwell thought that Eve intended to give up her heritage that easily, she did not know her granddaughter. Eve had no intention of trying to live on $250 a week. There was five million dollars that belonged to her, sitting in a bank, and that vicious old woman was keeping it from her. *There has to be a way to get my hands on that money. I will find it.*

The solution came the following day.

"And what can I do for you, Miss Blackwell?" Alvin Seagram asked deferentially. He was vice-president of the National Union Bank, and he was, in fact, prepared to do almost anything. What kind Fates had brought this young woman to him? If he could secure the Kruger-Brent account, or any part of it, his career would rise like a rocket.

"There's some money in trust for me," Eve explained. "Five million dollars. Because of the rules of the trust, it won't come to me until I'm thirty-five years old." She smiled ingenuously. "That seems so long from now."

"At your age, I'm sure it does," the banker smiled. "You're – nineteen?"

"Twenty-one."

"And beautiful, if you'll permit me to say so, Miss Blackwell."

Eve smiled demurely. "Thank you, Mr. Seagram." It was going to be simpler than she thought. *The man's an idiot.*

He could feel the rapport between them. *She likes me.* "How exactly may we help you?"

"Well, I was wondering if it would be possible to borrow an advance on my trust fund. You see, I need the money now more than I'll need it later. I'm engaged to be married. My fiancé is a construction engineer working in Israel, and he won't be back in this country for another three years."

Alvin Seagram was all sympathy. "I understand perfectly." His heart was pounding wildly. *Of course, he could grant her request.* Money was advanced against trust funds all the time. And when he had satisfied her, she would sent him other members of the Blackwell family, and he would satisfy them. Oh, how he would satisfy them! After that, there would be no stopping him. He would be made a member of the executive board of National Union. Perhaps one day its chairman. And he owed all this to the delicious little blonde seated across the desk.

"No problem at all," Alvin Seagram assured Eve. "It's a very simple transaction. You understand that we could not loan you the entire amount, but we could certainly let you have, say, a million immediately. Would that be satisfactory?"

"Perfectly," Eve said, trying not to show her exhilaration.

"Fine. If you'll just give me the details of the trust . . ." He picked up a pen.

"You can get in touch with Brad Rogers at Kruger-Brent. He'll give you all the information you need."

"I'll give him a call right away."

Eve rose. "How long will it take?"

"No more than a day or two. I'll rush it through personally."

She held out a lovely, delicate hand. "You're very kind."

The moment Eve was out of the office, Alvin Seagram picked up the telephone. "Get me Mr. Brad Rogers at Kruger-Brent, Limited." The very name sent a delicious shiver up his spine.

Two days later Eve returned to the bank and was ushered into Alvin Seagram's office. His first words were, "I'm afraid I can't help you, Miss Blackwell."

Eve could not believe what she was hearing. "I don't understand. You said it was simple. You said – "

"I'm sorry. I was not in possession of all the facts."

How vividly he recalled the conversation with Brad Rogers. "Yes, there is a five-million-dollar trust fund in Eve Blackwell's name. Your bank is perfectly free to advance any amount of money you wish against it. However, I think it only fair to caution you that Kate Blackwell would consider it an unfriendly act."

There was no need for Brad Rogers to spell out what the consequences could be. Kruger-Brent had powerful friends everywhere. And if those friends started pulling money out of National Union, Alvin Seagram did not have to guess what it would do to his career.

"I'm sorry," he repeated to Eve. "There's nothing I can do."

Eve looked at him, frustrated. But she would not let this man know what a blow he had dealt her. "Thank you for your trouble. There are other banks in New York. Good day."

"Miss Blackwell," Alvin Seagram told her, "there isn't a bank in the world that will loan you one penny against that trust."

Alexandra was puzzled. In the past, her grandmother had made it obvious in a hundred ways that she favored Eve. Now, overnight everything had changed. She knew something terrible had happened between Kate and Eve, but she had no idea what it could have been.

Whenever Alexandra tried to bring up the subject, her grandmother would say, "There is nothing to discuss. Eve chose her own life."

Nor could Alexandra get anything out of Eve.

Kate Blackwell began spending a great deal of time with Alexandra. Alexandra was intrigued. She was not merely in her grandmother's presence, she was becoming an actual part of her life. It was as though her grandmother were seeing her for the first time. Alexandra had an odd feeing she was being evaluated.

Kate *was* seeing her granddaughter for the first time, and because she had been bitterly deceived once, she was doubly careful in forming an opinion about Eve's twin. She spent every possible moment with Alexandra, and she probed and questioned and listened. And in the end she was satisfied.

It was not easy to know Alexandra. She was a private person, more reserved than Eve. Alexandra had a quick, lively intelligence, and her innocence, combined with her beauty, made her all the more endearing. She had always received countless invitations to parties and dinners and the theater, but now it was Kate who decided which invitations Alexandra should accept and which ones she should refuse. The fact that a suitor was eligible was not enough – not nearly enough. What Kate was looking for was a man capable of helping Alexandra run Kate's dynasty. She said nothing of this to Alexandra. There would be time enough for that when Kate found the right man for her granddaughter. Sometimes, in the lonely early-morning hours when Kate had trouble sleeping, she thought about Eve.

Eve was doing beautifully. The episode with her grandmother had bruised her ego so badly that for a short time she had forgotten something very important: She had forgotten how attractive she was to men. At the first party she was invited to after she moved into her own apartment, she gave her telephone number to six men – four of them married – and within twenty-four hours she had heard from all six of them. From that day on, Eve knew she would no longer have to worry about money. She was showered with gifts: expensive jewelry, paintings and, more often, cash.

"I've just ordered a new credenza, and my allowance check hasn't come. Would you mind, darling?"

And they never minded.

When Eve went out in public, she made sure she was escorted by men who were single. Married men she saw afternoons at her apartment. Eve was very discreet. She was careful to see that her name was kept out of gossip columns, not because she was any longer concerned about her allowance being stopped, but because she was determined that one day her grandmother was going to come crawling to her. Kate Blackwell needed an heir to take over Kruger-Brent. *Alexandra is not equipped to be anything but a stupid housewife*, Eve gloated.

One afternoon, leafing through a new issue of *Town and Country*, Eve came across a photograph of Alexandra dancing with an attractive man. Eve was not looking at Alexandra, she was looking at the man. And realizing that if Alexandra married and had a son, it would be a disaster for Eve and her plans.

She stared at the picture a long time.

Over a period of a year, Alexandra had called Eve regularly, for lunch or dinner, and Eve had always put her off with excuses. Now Eve decided it was time to have a talk with her sister. She invited Alexandra to her apartment.

Alexandra had not seen the apartment before, and Eve braced herself for pity. But all Alexandra said was, "It's charming, Eve. It's very cozy, isn't it?"

Eve smiled. "It suits me. I wanted something *intime.*" She had pawned enough jewelry and paintings so that she could have moved into a beautiful apartment, but Kate would have learned of it and would have demanded to know where the money had come from. For the moment, the watchword was *discretion*.

"How is Gran?" Eve asked.

"She's fine." Alexandra hesitated. "Eve, I don't know what happened between you two, but you know if there's anything I can do to help, I'll – "

Eve sighed. "She didn't tell you?"

"No. She won't discuss it."

"I don't blame her. The poor dear probably feels as guilty as hell. I met a wonderful young doctor. We were going to be married. We went to bed together. Gran found out about it. She told me to get out of the house, that she never wanted to see me again. I'm afraid our grandmother is very old-fashioned, Alex."

She watched the look of dismay on Alexandra's face. "That's terrible! The two of you must go to Gran. I'm sure she would – "

"He was killed in an airplane accident."

"Oh, Eve! Why didn't you tell me this before?"

"I was too ashamed to tell anyone, even you." She squeezed her sister's hand. "And you know I tell you everything."

"Let me talk to Gran. I'll explain – "

"No! I have too much pride. Promise me you'll never discuss this with her. Ever!"

"But I'm sure she would – "

"Promise!"

Alexandra sighed. "All right."

"Believe me, I'm very happy here. I come and go as I please. It's great!"

Alexandra looked at her sister and thought how much she had missed Eve.

Eve put her arm around Alexandra and began to tease. "Now, enough about me. Tell me what's going on in your life. Have you met Prince Charming yet? I'll bet you have!"

"No."

Eve studied her sister. It was a mirror image of herself, and she was determined to destroy it. "You will, darling."

"I'm in no hurry. I decided it's time I started earning a living. I talked to Gran about it. Next week I'm going to meet with the head of an advertising agency about a job."

They had lunch at a little bistro near Eve's apartment, and Eve insisted on paying. She wanted nothing from her sister.

When they were bidding each other good-bye, Alexandra said, "Eve, if you need any money – "

"Don't be silly, darling. I have more than enough."

Alexandra persisted. "Still, if you run short, you can have anything I've got."

Eve looked into Alexandra's eyes and said, "I'm counting on that." She smiled. "But I really don't need a thing, Alex." She did not need crumbs. She intended to have the whole cake. The question was: How was she going to get it?

There was a weekend party in Nassau.

"It wouldn't be the same without you, Eve. All your friends will be here."

The caller was Nita Ludwig, a girl whom Eve had known at school in Switzerland.

She would meet some new men. The present crop was tiresome.

"It sounds like fun," Eve said. "I'll be there."

That afternoon she pawned an emerald bracelet she had been given a week earlier by an infatuated insurance executive with a wife and three children, and bought some new summer outfits at Lord & Taylor and a round-trip ticket to Nassau. She was on the plane the following morning.

The Ludwig estate was a large, sprawling mansion on the beach. The main house had thirty rooms, and the smallest was larger than Eve's entire apartment. Eve was escorted to her room by a uniformed maid, who unpacked for her while Eve freshened up. Then she went down to meet her fellow guests.

There were sixteen people in the drawing room, and they had one thing in common: They were wealthy. Nita Ludwig was a firm believer in the "birds of a feather" philosophy. These people felt the same way about the same things; they were comfortable with one another because they spoke the same language. They shared the commonality of the best boarding schools and colleges, luxurious estates, yachts, private jets and tax problems. A columnist had dubbed them the "jet set," an appellation they derided publicly and enjoyed privately. They were the privileged, the chosen few, set apart from all others by a discriminating god. Let the rest of the world believe that money could not buy everything. These people knew better. Money bought them beauty and love and luxury and a place in heaven. And it was from all this that Eve had been excluded by the whim of a narrow-minded old lady. *But not for long*, Eve thought.

She entered the drawing room and the conversation dropped as Eve walked in. In a room full of beautiful women, she was the most beautiful of all. Nita took Eve around to greet her friends, and to introduce her to the people she did not know. Eve was charming and pleasant, and she studied each man with a knowing eye, expertly selecting her targets. Most of the older men were married, but that only made it easier.

A bald-headed man dressed in plaid slacks and Hawaiian sport shirt came up to her. "I'll bet you get tired of people telling you you're beautiful, honey."

Eve rewarded him with a warm smile. "I never get tired of that, Mr. – ?"

"Peterson. Call me Dan. You should be a Hollywood star."

"I'm afraid I have no talent for acting."

"I'll bet you've got a lot of other talents, though."

Eve smiled enigmatically. "You never know until you try, do you, Dan?"

He wet his lips. "You down here alone?"

"Yes."

"I've got my yacht anchored in the bay. Maybe you and I could take a little cruise tomorrow?"

"That sounds lovely," Eve said.

He grinned. "I don't know why we've never met before. I've known your grandmother, Kate, for years."

The smile stayed on Eve's face, but it took a great effort. "Gran's a darling," Eve said. "I think we'd better join the others."

"Sure, honey." He winked. "Remember tomorrow."

*

From that moment on, he was unable to get Eve alone again. She avoided him at lunch, and after lunch she borrowed one of the automobiles kept in the garage for guests and drove into town. She drove past Blackbeard's Tower and the lovely Ardastra Gardens where the colorful flamingos were on parade. She stopped at the waterfront to watch the fishing boats unload their catch of giant turtles, enormous lobsters, tropical fish and a brilliantly colored variety of conch shells, which would be polished and sold to the tourists.

The bay was smooth, and the sea sparkled like diamonds. Across the water Eve could see the crescent curve of Paradise Island Beach. A motorboat was leaving the dock at the beach, and as it picked up speed, the figure of a man suddenly rose into the sky, trailing behind the boat. It was a startling sight. He appeared to be hanging on to a metal bar fastened to a blue sail, his long, lean body stretched against the wind. *Para-sailing.* Eve watched, fascinated, as the motorboat roared toward the harbor, and the airborne figure swept closer. The boat approached the dock and made a sharp turn, and for an instant Eve caught a glimpse of the dark, handsome face of the man in the air, and then he was gone.

He walked into Nita Ludwig's drawing room five hours later, and Eve felt as though she had willed him there. She had known he would appear. Up close he was even more handsome. He was six foot three, with perfectly sculptured, tanned features, black eyes and a trim, athletic body. When he smiled, he revealed white, even teeth. He smiled down at Eve as Nita introduced him.

"This is George Mellis. Eve Blackwell."

"My God, you belong in the Louvre," George Mellis said. His voice was deep and husky, with the trace of an indefinable accent.

"Come along, darling," Nita commanded. "I'll introduce you to the other guests."

He waved her away. "Don't bother. I just met everybody."

Nita looked at the two of them thoughtfully. "I see. Well, if I can do anything, call me." She walked away.

"Weren't you a little rude to her?" Eve asked.

He grinned. "I'm not responsible for what I say or do. I'm in love."

Eve laughed.

"I mean it. You're the most beautiful thing I've ever seen in my life."

"I was thinking the same about you."

Eve did not care whether this man had money or not. She was fascinated by him. It was more than his looks. There was a magnetism, a sense of power that excited her. No man had ever affected her this way before. "Who are you?" Eve asked.

"Nita told you. George Mellis."

"Who are you?" she repeated.

"Ah, you mean in the philosophical sense. The *real* me. Nothing colorful to tell, I'm afraid. I'm Greek. My family grows olives and other things."

That Mellis! The Mellis food brands could be found in every corner grocery store and supermarket in America.

"Are you married?" Eve asked.

He grinned. "Are you always this direct?"

"No."

"I'm not married."

The answer gave her an unexpected feeling of pleasure. Just looking at him made Eve want to possess him, to be possessed. "Why did you miss dinner?"

"The truth?"

"Yes."

"It's very personal."

She waited.

"I was busy persuading a young lady not to commit suicide." He said it matter-of-factly, as though it were a common occurrence.

"I hope you succeeded."

"For now. I hope you're not the suicidal type.?"

"No. I hope *you're* not."

George Mellis laughed aloud. "I love you," he said. "I really love you." He took Eve's arm, and his touch made her shiver.

He stayed at Eve's side all evening, and he was totally attentive to her, oblivious to everyone else. He had long, delicate hands, and they were constantly doing things for Eve: bringing her a drink, lighting her cigarette, touching her discreetly. His nearness set her body afire, and she could not wait to be alone with him.

Just after midnight when the guests began to retire to their rooms, George Mellis asked, "Which is your bedroom?"

"At the end of the north hall."

He nodded, his long-lashed eyes boring into hers.

Eve undressed and bathed and put on a new sheer, black negligee that clung to her figure. At one A.M. there was a discreet tap on the door. She hurried to open it, and George Mellis stepped in.

He stood there, his eyes filled with admiration. "*Matia mou*, you make the *Venus de Milo* look like a hag."

"I have an advantage over her," Eve whispered. "I have two arms."

And she put both arms around George Mellis and drew him to her. His kiss made something explode inside her. His lips pressed hard against hers, and she felt his tongue exploring her mouth.

"Oh, my God!" Eve moaned.

He started to strip off his jacket, and she helped him. In a moment he was free of his trousers and French shorts, and he was naked before her. He had the most glorious physique Eve had ever seen. He was hard and erect.

"Quick," Eve said. "Make love to me." She moved onto the bed, her body on fire.

He commanded, "Turn over. Give me your ass."

She looked up at him. "I – I don't – "

And he hit her on the mouth. She stared up at him in shock.

"Turn over."

"No."

He hit her again, harder, and the room began to swim in front of her.

"Please, no."

He hit her again, savagely. She felt his powerful hands turning her over, pulling her up on her knees.

"For God's sake," she gasped, "stop it! I'll scream."

He smashed his arm across the back of her neck, and Eve started to lose consciousness. Dimly, she felt him raise her hips higher into the air. He pulled her cheeks apart, and his body pressed against hers. There was a sudden, excruciating pain as he plunged deep inside her. She opened her mouth to scream, but she stopped in terror of what he might do to her.

She begged, "Oh, please, you're hurting me . . ."

She tried to pull away from him, but he was holding her hips tightly, plunging into her again and again, tearing her apart with his enormous penis. The pain was unbearable.

"Oh, God, no!" she whispered. "Stop it! Please stop it!"

He kept moving in, deeper and faster, and the last thing Eve remembered was a wild groan that came from deep inside him and seemed to explode in her ears.

When she regained consciousness and opened her eyes, George Mellis was sitting in a chair, fully dressed, smoking a cigarette. He moved over to the bed and stroked her forehead. She cringed from his touch.

"How do you feel, darling?"

Eve tried to sit up, but the pain was too great. She felt as though she had been ripped apart. "You goddamned animal . . ." Her voice was a ragged whisper.

He laughed. "I was gentle with you."

She looked at him in disbelief.

He smiled. "I can sometimes be very rough." He stroked her hair again. "But I love you, so I was kind. You'll get used to it, *Hree-se'e-moo.* I promise you."

If she had had a weapon at that moment, Eve would have killed him. "You're insane!"

She saw the gleam that came into his eyes, and she saw his hand clench into a fist, and in that instant she knew stark terror. He *was* insane.

She said quickly, "I didn't mean it. It's just that I – I've never experienced anything like that before. Please, I'd like to go to sleep now. Please."

George Mellis stared at her for a long moment, and then relaxed. He rose and walked over to the dressing table where Eve had put her jewelry. There was a platinum bracelet and an expensive diamond necklace lying there. He scooped up the necklace, examined it and slipped it into his pocket. "I'll keep this as a little souvenir."

She was afraid to open her mouth to protest.

"Good night, darling." And he walked back to the bed, leaned over and gently kissed Eve's lips.

She waited until he had gone, and then crawled out of bed, her body burning with pain. Every step was an agony. It was not until she had locked the bedroom door that she felt safe again. She was not sure she would be able to make it to the bathroom, and she fell back onto the bed, waiting for the pain to recede. She couldn't believe the enormity of the rage she felt. He had sodomized her – horribly and brutally. She wondered what he had done to that other girl who had wanted to commit suicide.

When Eve finally dragged herself into the bathroom and looked in the mirror, she was aghast. Her face was bruised and discolored where he had hit her, and one eye was almost swollen shut. She ran a hot bath and crawled into it like a wounded animal, letting the soothing water wash away the pain. Eve lay there for a long time, and, finally, when the water was starting to cool, she got out of the tub and took a few tentative steps. The pain had lessened, but it was still agonizing. She lay awake for the rest of the night, terrified that he might return.

When Eve arose at dawn, she saw that the sheets were stained with her blood. She was going to make him pay for that. She walked into the bathroom, moving carefully, and ran another hot bath. Her face was even more swollen and the bruises were livid. She dipped a washcloth into cold water and applied it to her cheek and eye. Then she lay in the tub, thinking about George Mellis. There was something puzzling about his behavior that had nothing to do with his sadism. And she suddenly realized what it was. The necklace. Why had he taken it?

Two hours later, Eve went downstairs to join the other guests for breakfast, even though she had no appetite. She badly needed to talk to Nita Ludwig.

"My God! What happened to your face?" Nita asked.

Eve smiled ruefully. "The silliest thing. I got up in the middle of the night to go to the loo, and I didn't bother turning on the light. I walked right into one of your fancy doors."

"Would you like to have a doctor look at that?"

"It's nothing," Eve assured her. "It's just a little bruise." Eve looked around. "Where's George Mellis?"

"He's out playing tennis. He's one of the top-seeded players. He said to tell you he'd see you at lunch. I think he really likes you, darling."

"Tell me about him," Eve said casually. "What's his background?"

"George? He comes from a long line of wealthy Greeks. He's the oldest son, and he's filthy rich. He works at a New York brokerage firm, Hanson and Hanson."

"He's not in the family business?"

"No. He probably hates olives. Anyway, with the Mellis fortune, he doesn't have to work. I suppose he does it just to occupy his days." She grinned and said, "His nights are full enough."

"Are they?"

"Darling, George Mellis is the most eligible bachelor around. The girls can't wait to pull their little panties down for him. They all see themselves as the future Mrs. Mellis. Frankly, if my husband weren't so damned jealous, I'd go for George myself. Isn't he a gorgeous hunk of animal?"

"Gorgeous," Eve said.

George Mellis walked onto the terrace where Eve was seated alone, and in spite of herself, she felt a stab of fear.

He walked up to her and said, "Good morning, Eve. Are you all right?" His face was filled with genuine concern. He touched her bruised cheek gently. "My darling, you are so beautiful." He pulled up a chair and straddled it, sitting across from her, and gestured toward the sparkling sea. "Have you ever seen anything so lovely?"

It was as though the previous night had never happened. She listened to George Mellis as he went on talking, and she felt once again the powerful magnetism of the man. Even after the nightmare she had experienced, she could still feel *that*. It was incredible. *He looks like a Greek god. He belongs in a museum. He belongs in an insane asylum.*

"I have to return to New York tonight," George Mellis was saying. "Where can I call you?"

"I just moved," Eve said quickly. "I don't have a telephone yet. Let me call you."

"All right, my darling." He grinned. "You really enjoyed last night, didn't you?"

Eve could not believe her ears.

"I have many things to teach you, Eve," he whispered.

And I have something to teach you, Mr. Mellis, Eve promised herself.

The moment she returned home, Eve telephoned Dorothy Hollister. In New York, where an insatiable segment of the media covered the comings and goings of the so-called beautiful people, Dorothy was the fountainhead of information. She had been married to a socialite, and when he divorced her for his twenty-one-year-old secretary, Dorothy Hollister was forced to go to work. She took a job that suited her talents well: She became a gossip columnist. Because she knew everyone in the milieu she was writing about, and because they believed she could be trusted, few people kept any secrets from her.

If anyone could tell Eve about George Mellis, it would be Dorothy Hollister. Eve invited her to lunch at La Pyramide. Hollister was a heavy-set woman with a fleshy face, dyed red hair, a loud, raucous voice and a braying laugh. She was loaded down with jewelry – all fake.

When they had ordered, Eve said casually, "I was in the Bahamas last week. It was lovely there."

"I know you were," Dorothy Hollister said. "I have Nita Ludwig's guest list. Was it a fun party?"

Eve shrugged. "I saw a lot of old friends. I met an interesting man named" she paused, her brow wrinkled in thought – "George somebody. Miller, I think. A Greek."

Dorothy Hollister laughed, a loud, booming laugh that could be heard across the room. "Mellis, dear. George Mellis."

"That's right. Mellis. Do you know him?"

"I've seen him. I thought I was going to turn into a pillar of salt. My God, he's fantastic looking."

"What's his background, Dorothy?"

Dorothy Hollister looked around, then leaned forward confidentially. "No one knows this, but you'll keep it to yourself, won't you? George is the black sheep of the family. His family is in the wholesale food business, and they're too rich for words, my dear. George was supposed to take over the business, but he got in so many scrapes over there with girls and boys and goats, for all I know, that his father and his brothers finally got fed up and shipped him out of the country."

Eve was absorbing every word.

"They cut the poor boy off without a drachma, so he had to go to work to support himself."

So that explained the necklace!

"Of course, he doesn't have to worry. One of these days George will marry rich." She looked over at Eve and asked, "Are you interested, sweetie?"

"Not really."

Eve was more than interested. George Mellis might be the key she had been looking for. The key to her fortune.

Early the next morning, she telephoned him at the brokerage firm where he worked. He recognized her voice immediately.

"I've been going mad waiting for your call, Eve. We'll have dinner tonight and – "

"No. Lunch, tomorrow."

He hesitated, surprised. "All right. I was supposed to have lunch with a customer, but I'll put him off."

Eve did not believe it was a *him*. "Come to my apartment," Eve said. She gave him the address. "I'll see you at twelve-thirty."

"I'll be there." She could hear the smug satisfaction in his voice.

George Mellis was due for a surprise.

He arrived thirty minutes late, and Eve realized it was a pattern with him. It was not a deliberate rudeness, it was an indifference, the knowledge that people would always wait for him. His pleasures would be there for him whenever he bothered to reach out and take them. With his incredible looks and charm, the world belonged to him. Except for one thing: He was poor. That was his vulnerable point.

George looked around the little apartment, expertly appraising the value of its contents. "Very pleasant."

He moved toward Eve, his arms outstretched. "I've thought about you every minute."

She evaded his embrace. "Wait. I have something to tell you, George."

His black eyes bored into hers. "We'll talk later."

"We'll talk now." She spoke slowly and distinctly. "If you ever touch me like that again, I'm going to kill you."

He looked at her, his lips curved in a half smile. "What kind of joke is that?"

"It's not a joke. I mean it. I have a business proposition for you."

There was a puzzled expression on his face. "You called me here to discuss business?"

"Yes. I don't know how much you make conning silly old ladies into buying stocks and bonds, but I'm sure it's not enough."

His face went dark with anger. "Are you crazy? My family – "

"Your family is rich – you're not. My family is rich – I'm not. We're both in the same leaky rowboat, darling. I know a way we can turn it into a yacht." She stood there, watching his curiosity get the better of his anger.

"You'd better tell me what you're talking about."

"It's quite simple. I've been disinherited from a very large fortune. My sister Alexandra hasn't."

"What does that have to do with me?"

"If you married Alexandra, that fortune would be yours – ours."

"Sorry. I could never stand the idea of being tied down to anyone."

"As it happens," Eve assured him, "that's no problem. My sister has always been accident-prone."

27

Berkley and Mathews Advertising Agency was the diadem in Madison Avenue's roster of agencies. Its annual billings exceeded the combined billings of its two nearest competitors, chiefly because its major account was Kruger-Brent, Ltd., and its dozens of worldwide subsidiaries. More than seventy-five account executives, copywriters, creative directors, photographers, engravers, artists and media experts were employed on the Kruger-Brent account alone. It came as no surprise, therefore, that when Kate Blackwell telephoned Aaron Berkley to ask him if he could find a position in his agency for Alexandra, a place was found for her instantly. If Kate Blackwell had desired it, they would probably have made Alexandra president of the agency.

"I believe my granddaughter is interested in being a copywriter," Kate informed Aaron Berkley.

Berkley assured Kate that there just happened to be a copywriter vacancy, and that Alexandra could start any time she wished.

She went to work the following Monday.

Few Madison Avenue advertising agencies are actually located on Madison Avenue, but Berkley and Mathews was an exception. The agency owned a large, modern building at the corner of Madison and Fifty-seventh Street. The agency occupied eight floors of the building and leased the other floors. In order to save a salary, Aaron Berkley and his partner, Norman Mathews, decided Alexandra Blackwell would replace a young copywriter hired six months earlier. The word spread rapidly. When the staff learned the young woman who was fired was being replaced by the granddaughter of the agency's biggest client, there was general indignation. Without even having met Alexandra, the consensus was that she was a spoiled bitch who had probably been sent there to spy on them.

When Alexandra reported for work, she was escorted to the huge, modern office of Aaron Berkley, where both Berkley and Mathews waited to greet her. The two partners looked nothing alike. Berkley was tall and thin, with a full head of white hair, and Mathews was short, tubby and completely bald. They had two things in common: They were brilliant advertising men who had created some of the most famous slogans of the past decade; and they were absolute tyrants. They treated their employees like chattels, and the only reason the employees stood for such treatment was that anyone who had worked for Berkley and Mathews could work at any advertising agency in the world. It was *the* training ground.

Also present in the office when Alexandra arrived was Lucas Pinkerton, a vice-president of the firm, a smiling man with an obsequious manner and cold eyes. Pinkerton was younger than the senior partners, but what he lacked in age, he made up for in vindictiveness toward the men and women who worked under him.

Aaron Berkley ushered Alexandra to a comfortable armchair. "What can I get you, Miss Blackwell? Would you like some coffee, tea?"

"Nothing, thank you."

"So. You're going to work with us here as a copywriter."

"I really appreciate your giving me this opportunity, Mr. Berkley. I know I have a great deal to learn, but I'll work very hard."

"No need for that," Norman Mathews said quickly. He caught himself. "I mean – you can't rush a learning experience like this. You take all the time you want."

"I'm sure you'll be very happy here," Aaron Berkley added. "You'll be working with the best people in the business."

One hour later, Alexandra was thinking, *They may be the best, but they're certainly not the friendliest.* Lucas Pinkerton had taken Alexandra around to introduce her to the staff, and the reception everywhere had been icy. They acknowledged her presence and then quickly found other things to do. Alexandra sensed their resentment, but she had no idea what had caused it. Pinkerton led her into a smoke-filled conference room. Against one wall was a cabinet filled with Clios and Art Directors' awards. Seated around a table were a woman and two men, all of them chain-smoking. The woman was short and dumpy, with rust-colored hair. The men were in their middle thirties, pale and harassed-looking.

Pinkerton said, "This is the creative team you'll be working with. Alice Koppel, Vince Barnes and Marty Bergheimer. This is Miss Blackwell."

The three of them stared at Alexandra.

"Well, I'll leave you to get acquainted with one another," Pinkerton said. He turned to Vince Barnes. "I'll expect the new perfume copy on my desk by tomorrow morning. See that Miss Blackwell has everything she needs." And he left.

"What do you need?" Vince Barnes asked.

The question caught Alexandra off guard. "I – I guess I just need to learn the advertising business."

Alice Koppel said sweetly, "You've come to the right place, Miss Blackwell. We're dying to play teacher."

"Lay off," Marty Bergheimer told her.

Alexandra was puzzled. "Have I done something to offend any of you?"

Marty Bergheimer replied, "No, Miss Blackwell. We're just under a lot of pressure here. We're working on a perfume campaign, and so far Mr. Berkley and Mr. Mathews are underwhelmed by what we've delivered.",

"I'll try not to be a bother," Alexandra promised.

"That would be peachy," Alice Koppel said.

The rest of the day went no better. There was not a smile in the place. One of their co-workers had been summarily fired because of this rich bitch, and they were going to make her pay.

At the end of Alexandra's first day, Aaron Berkley and Norman Mathews came into the little office Alexandra had been assigned, to make sure she was comfortable. The gesture was not lost on Alexandra's fellow workers.

*

Everyone in the agency was on a first-name basis – except for Alexandra. She was Miss Blackwell to everyone.

"Alexandra," she said.

"Right."

And the next time they addressed her, it was "Miss Blackwell."

Alexandra was eager to learn and to make a contribution. She attended think-tank meetings where the copywriters brain-stormed ideas. She watched art editors draw up their designs. She listened to Lucas Pinkerton tear apart the copy that was brought to him for approval. He was a nasty, mean-spirited man, and Alexandra felt sorry for the copywriters who suffered under him. Alexandra found herself shuttling from floor to floor for meetings with department heads, meetings with clients, photographic sessions, strategy discussion meetings. She kept her mouth shut, listened and learned. At the end of her first week, she felt as though she had been there a month. She came home exhausted, not from the work but from the tension that her presence seemed to create.

When Kate asked how the job was going, Alexandra replied, "Fine, Gran. It's very interesting."

"I'm sure you'll do well, Alex. If you have any problems, just see Mr. Berkley or Mr. Mathews."

That was the last thing Alexandra intended to do.

On the following Monday Alexandra went to work determined to find a way to solve her problem. There were daily morning and afternoon coffee breaks, and the conversation was easy and casual.

"Did you hear what happened over at National Media? Some genius there wanted to call attention to the great year they had, so he printed their financial report in *The New York Times* in red ink!"

"Remember that airline promotion: *Fly Your Wife Free?* It was a smash until the airline sent letters of appreciation to the wives and got back a flood of mail demanding to know who their husbands had flown with. They – "

Alexandra walked in, and the conversation stopped dead.

"Can I get you some coffee, Miss Blackwell?"

"Thank you. I can get it."

There was silence while Alexandra fed a quarter into the coffee machine. When she left, the conversation started again.

"Did you hear about the Pure Soap foul-up? The angelic-looking model they used turned out to be a porno star . . ."

At noon Alexandra said to Alice Koppel, "If you're free for lunch, I thought we might – "

"Sorry. I have a date."

Alexandra looked at Vince Barnes. "Me, too," he said.

She looked at Marty Bergheimer. "I'm all booked up."

Alexandra was too upset to eat lunch. They were making her feel as though she were a pariah, and she found herself getting angry. She did not intend to give up. She was going to find a way to reach them, to let them know that deep down under the Blackwell name she was one of *them*. She sat at meetings and listened to Aaron Berkley and Norman Mathews and Lucas Pinkerton tongue-lash the creators who were merely trying to do their jobs as well as they could. Alexandra sympathized, but they did not want her sympathy. Or her.

Alexandra waited three days before trying again. She said to Alice Koppel, "I heard of a wonderful little Italian restaurant near here – "

"I don't eat Italian food."

She turned to Vince Barnes. "I'm on a diet."

Alexandra looked at Marty Bergheimer. "I'm going to eat Chinese."

Alexandra's face was flushed. They did not want to be seen with her. *Well, to hell with them. To hell with all of them.* She had had enough. She had gone out of her way to try to make friends, and each time she had been slapped down. Working there was a mistake. She would find another job somewhere with a company that her grandmother had nothing to do with. She would quit at the end of the week. *But I'm going to make you all remember I was here*, Alexandra thought grimly.

At 1:00 P.M. on Thursday, everyone except the receptionist at the switchboard was out to lunch. Alexandra stayed behind. She had observed that in the executive offices there were intercoms connecting the various departments, so that if an executive wanted to talk to an underling, all he had to do was press a button on the talk box where the employee's name was written on a card. Alexandra slipped into the deserted offices of Aaron Berkley and Norman Mathews and Lucas Pinkerton and spent the next hour changing all the cards around. Thus it was that early that afternoon Lucas Pinkerton pressed down the key that connected him to his chief copywriter and said, "Get your ass in here. Now!"

There was a moment of stunned silence, then Norman Mathews's voice bellowed, "What did you say?"

Pinkerton stared at the machine, transfixed. "Mr. Mathews, is that you?"

"You're damned right it is. Get *your* fucking ass in *here. Now!*"

A minute later, a copywriter pressed down a button on the machine on his desk and said, "I've got some copy for you to run downstairs."

Aaron Berkley's voice roared back at him. "You *what?*"

It was the beginning of pandemonium. It took four hours to straighten out the mess that Alexandra had created, and it was the best four hours that the employees of Berkley and Mathews had ever known. Each time a fresh incident occurred, they whooped with joy. The executives were being buzzed to run errands, fetch cigarettes and repair a broken toilet. Aaron Berkley and Norman

Mathews and Lucas Pinkerton turned the place upside down trying to find out who the culprit was, but no one knew anything.

The only one who had seen Alexandra go into the various offices was Fran, the woman on the switchboard, but she hated her bosses more than she hated Alexandra, so all she would say was, "I didn't see a soul."

That night when Fran was in bed with Vince Barnes, she related what had happened.

He sat up in bed. "The *Blackwell* girl did it? I'll be a sonofabitch!"

The following morning when Alexandra walked into her office, Vince Barnes, Alice Koppel and Marty Bergheimer were there, waiting. They stared at her in silence. "Is something wrong?" Alexandra asked.

"Not a thing, Alex," Alice Koppel said. "The boys and I were just wondering if you'd like to join us for lunch. We know this great little Italian joint near here . . ."

28

From the time she was a little girl, Eve Blackwell had been aware of her ability to manipulate people. Before, it had always been a game with her, but now it was deadly serious. She had been treated shabbily, deprived of a vast fortune that was rightfully hers, by her scheming sister and her vindictive old grandmother. They were going to pay in full for what they had done to her, and the thought of it gave Eve such intense pleasure that it almost brought her to orgasm. Their lives were now in her hands.

Eve worked out her plan carefully and meticulously, orchestrating every move. In the beginning, George Mellis had been a reluctant conspirator.

"Christ, it's too dangerous. I don't need to get involved in anything like this," he argued. "I can get all the money I need."

"How?" Eve asked contemptuously. "By laying a lot of fat women with blue hair? Is that how you want to spend the rest of your life? What happens when you put on a little weight and start to get a few wrinkles around your eyes? No, George, you'll never have another opportunity like this. If you listen to me, you and I can own one of the largest conglomerates in the world. You hear me? *Own* it."

"How do you know this plan will work?"

"Because I'm the greatest living expert on my grandmother and my sister. Believe me, it will work."

Eve sounded confident, but she had reservations and they concerned George Mellis. Eve knew she could do her part, but she was not sure George would be able to do his. He was unstable, and there was no room for error. One mistake, and the whole plan would fall apart.

She said to him now, "Make up your mind. Are you in or out?"

He studied her for a long time. "I'm in." He moved close to her and stroked her shoulders. His voice was husky. "I want to be all the way in."

Eve felt a sexual thrill go through her. "All right," she whispered, "but we do it my way."

They were in bed. Naked, he was the most magnificent animal Eve had ever seen. And the most dangerous, but that only added to her excitement. She had the weapon now to control him. She nibbled at his body, slowly moving down toward his groin, tiny, teasing bites that made his penis grow stiff and hard.

"Fuck me, George," Eve said.

"Turn over."

"No. My way."

"I don't enjoy that."

"I know. You'd like me to be a tight-assed little boy, wouldn't you, darling? I'm not. I'm a woman. Get on top of me."

He mounted her and put his tumescent penis inside her. "I can't be satisfied this way, Eve."

She laughed. "I don't care, sweetheart. *I* can."

She began to move her hips, thrusting against him, feeling him going deeper and deeper inside her. She had orgasm after orgasm, and watched his frustration grow. He wanted to hurt her, to make her scream with pain, but he dared not . . .

"Again!" Eve commanded. And he pounded his body into her until she moaned aloud with pleasure. "Ahh-h-h . . . that's enough for now."

He withdrew and lay at her side. He reached for her breasts. "Now it's my – "

And she said curtly, "Get dressed."

He rose from the bed, trembling with frustration and rage. Eve lay in bed watching him put on his clothes, a tight smile on her face. "You've been a good boy, George. It's time you got your reward. I'm going to turn Alexandra over to you."

Overnight; everything had changed for Alexandra. What was to have been her last day at Berkley and Mathews had turned into a triumph for her. She had gone from outcast to heroine. News of her caper spread all over Madison Avenue.

"You're a legend in your own time," Vince Barnes grinned.

Now she was one of them.

Alexandra enjoyed her work, particularly the creative sessions that went on every morning. She knew this was not what she wanted to do for the rest of her life, but she was not sure what she wanted. She had had at least a dozen proposals of marriage, and she had been tempted by one or two of them, but something had been lacking. She simply had not found the right man.

On Friday morning, Eve telephoned to invite Alexandra to lunch. "There's a new French restaurant that just opened. I hear the food is marvelous."

Alexandra was delighted to hear from her sister. She was concerned about Eve. Alexandra telephoned her two or three times a week, but Eve was either out or too busy to see her. So now, even though Alexandra had an engagement, she said, "I'd love to have lunch with you."

The restaurant was chic and expensive, and the bar was filled with patrons waiting for tables. Eve had had to use her grandmother's name in order to get a reservation. It galled her, and she thought, *Just wait. One day you'll be begging me to eat at your crummy restaurant*. Eve was already seated when Alexandra arrived. She watched Alexandra as the maître d' escorted her to the table, and she had the odd sensation she was watching herself approach the table.

Eve greeted her sister with a kiss on the cheek. "You look absolutely marvelous, Alex. Work must agree with you."

They ordered, and then caught up with each other's lives.

"How's the job going?" Eve asked.

Alexandra told Eve everything that was happening to her, and Eve gave Alexandra a carefully edited version of her own life. In the midst of their conversation, Eve glanced up. George Mellis was standing there. He was looking at the two of them, momentarily confused. *My God*, Eve realized, *he doesn't know which one I am!*

"George!" she said.

He turned to her in relief. "Eve!"

Eve said, "What a pleasant surprise." She nodded toward Alexandra. "I don't believe you've met my sister. Alex, may I present George Mellis."

George took Alexandra's hand and said, "Enchanted." Eve had mentioned that her sister was a twin, but it had not occurred to him that they would be identical twins.

Alexandra was staring at George, fascinated.

Eve said, "Won't you join us?"

"I wish I could. I'm afraid I'm late for an appointment. Another time, perhaps." He looked at Alexandra. "And soon, I hope."

They watched him leave. "Good heavens!" Alexandra said. "Who was *that?*"

"Oh, he's a friend of Nita Ludwig. I met him at her house party."

"Am I crazy, or is he as stunning as I think he is?"

Eve laughed. "He's not my type, but women seem to find him attractive."

"I would think so! Is he married?"

"No. But it's not because they aren't out there trying, darling. George is very rich. You might say he has everything: looks, money, social background." And Eve skillfully changed the subject.

When Eve asked for the check, the captain told her it had been taken care of by Mr. Mellis.

Alexandra was unable to stop thinking about George Mellis.

On Monday afternoon, Eve called Alexandra and said, "Well, it looks like you made a hit, darling. George Mellis called me and asked for your telephone number. Is it all right to give it to him?"

Alexandra was surprised to find that she was smiling. "If you're sure *you're* not interested in – "

"I told you, Alex, he's not my type."

"Then I don't mind if you give him my number."

They chatted a few minutes more, and Eve hung up. She replaced the receiver and looked up at George, who was lying next to her on the bed, naked. "The lady said yes."

"How soon?"

"When I tell you."

Alexandra tried to forget that George Mellis was going to telephone her, but the more she tried to put him out of her mind, the more she thought about him. She had never been particularly attracted to handsome men, for she had found that most of them were self-centered. But George Mellis, Alexandra thought, seemed different. There was an overpowering quality about him. The mere touch of his hand had stirred her. *You're crazy*, she told herself. *You've only seen the man for two minutes.*

He did not call all that week, and Alexandra's emotions went from impatience to frustration to anger. *To hell with him*, she thought. *He's found someone else. Good!*

When the phone rang at the end of the following week and Alexandra heard his deep, husky voice, her anger dissipated as if by magic.

"This is George Mellis," he said. "We met briefly when you and your sister were having lunch. Eve said you wouldn't mind if I telephoned you."

"She did mention that you might call," Alexandra said casually. "By the way, thank you for the lunch."

"You deserve a feast. You deserve a monument."

Alexandra laughed, enjoying his extravagance.

"I wonder if you would care to have dinner with me one evening?"

"Why – I – yes. That would be nice."

"Wonderful. If you had said no, I should have killed myself."

"Please don't," Alexandra said. "I hate eating alone."

"So do I. I know a little restaurant on Mulberry Street: Matoon's. It's very obscure, but the food is – "

"*Matoons!* I love it!" Alexandra exclaimed. "It's my favorite."

"You know it?" There was surprise in his voice.

"oh, yes."

George looked over at Eve and grinned. He had to admire her ingenuity. She had briefed him on all of Alexandra's likes and dislikes. George Mellis knew everything there was to know about Eve's sister.

When George finally replaced the receiver, Eve thought, *It's started.*

It was the most enchanting evening of Alexandra's life. One hour before George Mellis was due, a dozen pink balloons arrived, with an orchid attached. Alexandra had been filled with a fear that her imagination might have led her to expect too much, but the moment she saw George Mellis again, all her doubts were swept away. She felt once again his overpowering magnetism.

They had a drink at the house and then went on to the restaurant.

"Would you like to look at the menu?" George asked. "Or shall I order for you?"

Alexandra had her favorite dishes here, but she wanted to please George. "Why don't you order?"

He chose every one of Alexandra's favorites, and she had the heady feeling he was reading her mind. They dined on stuffed artichokes, veal Matoon, a specialty of the house, and angel hair, a delicate pasta. They had a salad that George mixed at the table with a deft skill.

"Do you cook?" Alexandra asked.

"Ah, it's one of the passions of my life. My mother taught me. She was a brilliant cook."

"Are you close to your family, George?"

He smiled, and Alexandra thought it was the most attractive smile she had ever seen.

"I'm Greek," he said simply. "I'm the oldest of three brothers and two sisters, and we are like one." A look of sadness came into his eyes. "Leaving them was the most difficult thing I ever had to do. My father and my brothers begged me to stay. We have a large business, and they felt I was needed there."

"Why didn't you stay?"

"I will probably seem a fool to you, but I prefer to make my own way. It has always been difficult for me to accept gifts from anyone, and the business was a gift handed down from my grandfather to my father. No, I will take nothing from my father. Let my brothers have my share."

How Alexandra admired him.

"Besides," George added softly, "if I had stayed in Greece, I never would have met you."

Alexandra felt herself blushing. "You've never been married?"

"No. I used to get engaged once a day," he teased, "but at the last moment I always felt there was something wrong." He leaned forward, and his voice was earnest. "Beautiful Alexandra, you are going to think me very old-fashioned, but when I get married, it will be forever. One woman is enough for me, but it must be the right woman."

"I think that's lovely," she murmured.

"And you?" George Mellis asked. "Have you ever been in love?"

"No."

"How unlucky for someone," he said. "But how lucky for – "

At that moment, the waiter appeared with dessert. Alexandra was dying to ask George to finish the sentence, but she was afraid to.

Alexandra had never felt so completely at ease with anyone. George Mellis seemed so genuinely interested in her that she found herself telling him about her childhood, her life, the experiences she had stored up and treasured.

George Mellis prided himself on being an expert on women. He knew that beautiful women were usually the most insecure, for men concentrated on that beauty, leaving the women feeling like objects rather than human beings. When George was with a beautiful woman, he never mentioned her looks. He made the woman feel that he was interested in her mind, her feelings, that he was a soul mate sharing her dreams. It was an extraordinary experience for Alexandra. She told George about Kate, and about Eve.

"Your sister does not live with you and your grandmother?"

"No. She – Eve wanted an apartment of her own."

Alexandra could not imagine why George Mellis had not been attracted to her sister. Whatever the reason, Alexandra was grateful. During the course of the dinner, Alexandra noted that every woman in the place was aware of George, but not once did he look around or take his eyes from her.

Over coffee, George said, "I don't know if you like jazz, but there's a club on St. Marks Place called the Five Spot . . ."

"Where Cecil Taylor plays!"

He looked at Alexandra in astonishment. "You've been there?"

"Often!" Alexandra laughed. "I love him! It's incredible how we share the same tastes."

George replied quietly, "It's like some kind of miracle."

They listened to Cecil Taylor's spellbinding piano playing, long solos that rocked the room with arpeggios and rippling glissandi. From there they went to a bar on Bleecker Street, where the customers drank, ate popcorn, threw darts and listened to good piano music. Alexandra watched as George got into a dart contest with one of the regular patrons. The man was good, but he never had a chance. George played with a grim intensity that was almost frightening. It was only a game, but he played it as though it meant life or death. *He's a man who has to win*, Alexandra thought.

It was 2:00 A.M. when they left the bar, and Alexandra hated for the evening to end.

George sat beside Alexandra in the chauffeur-driven Rolls-Royce he had rented. He did not speak. He just looked at her. The resemblance between the two sisters was startling. *I wonder if their bodies are alike*. He visualized Alexandra in bed with him, writhing and screaming with pain.

"What are you thinking?" Alexandra asked.

He looked away from her so she could not read his eyes. "You'll laugh at me."

"I won't. I promise."

"I wouldn't blame you if you did. I suppose I'm considered something of a playboy. You know the life – yachting trips and parties, and all the rest of it."

"Yes . . ."

He fixed his dark eyes on Alexandra. "I think you are the one woman who could change all that. Forever."

Alexandra felt her pulse quicken. "I – I don't know what to say."

"Please. Don't say anything." His lips were very close to hers, and Alexandra was ready. But he made no move. *Don't make any advances*, Eve had warned. *Not on the first night. If you do, you become one of a long line of Romeos dying to get their hands on her and her fortune. She has to make the first move.*

And so, George Mellis merely held Alexandra's hand in his until the car glided to a smooth stop in front of the Blackwell mansion. George escorted Alexandra to her front door. She turned to him and said, "I can't tell you how much I've enjoyed this evening."

"It was magic for me."

Alexandra's smile was bright enough to light up the street. "Good night, George," she whispered. And she disappeared inside.

Fifteen minutes later, Alexandra's phone rang. "Do you know what I just did? I telephoned my family. I told them about the wonderful woman I was with tonight. Sleep well, lovely Alexandra."

When he hung up, George Mellis thought, *After we're married, I will call my family. And I'll tell them all to go fuck themselves.*

29

Alexandra did not hear from George Mellis again. Not that day, or the next, or the rest of that week. Every time the phone rang, she rushed to pick it up, but she was always disappointed. She could not imagine what had gone wrong. She kept replaying the evening in her mind: *I think you are the one woman who could change all that forever*, and *I telephoned my mother and father and brothers and told them about the wonderful woman I was with tonight*. Alexandra went through a litany of reasons why he had not telephoned her.

She had offended him in some way without realizing it.

He liked her too much, was afraid of falling in love with her and had made up his mind never to see her again.

He had decided she was not his type.

He had been in a terrible accident and was lying helpless in a hospital somewhere.

He was dead.

When Alexandra could stand it no longer, she telephoned Eve. Alexandra forced herself to make small talk for a full minute before she blurted out, "Eve, you haven't heard from George Mellis lately, by any chance, have you?"

"Why, no. I thought he was going to call you about dinner."

"We did have dinner – last week."

"And you haven't heard from him since?"

"No."

"He's probably busy."

No one is that busy, Alexandra thought. Aloud she said, "Probably."

"Forget about George Mellis, darling. There's a very attractive Canadian I'd like you to meet. He owns an airline and . . ."

When Eve had hung up, she sat back, smiling. She wished her grandmother could have known how beautifully she had planned everything.

"Hey, what's eating you?" Alice Koppel asked.

"I'm sorry," Alexandra replied.

She had been snapping at everyone all morning. It had been two full weeks since she had heard from George Mellis, and Alexandra was angry – not with him, but with herself for not being able to forget him. He owed her nothing. They were strangers who had shared an evening together, and she was acting as though she expected him to marry her, for God's sake. George Mellis could have any woman in the world. Why on earth would he want her?

Even her grandmother had noticed how irritable she had become. "What's the matter with you, child? Are they working you too hard at that agency?"

"No, Gran. It's just that I – I haven't been sleeping well lately."

When she did sleep, she had erotic dreams about George Mellis. *Damn him!* She wished Eve had never introduced him to her.

The call came at the office the following afternoon. "Alex? George Mellis." As though she didn't hear that deep voice in her dreams.

"Alex? Are you there?"

"Yes, I'm here." She was filled with mixed emotions. She did not know whether to laugh or cry. He was a thoughtless, selfish egotist, and she did not care whether she ever saw him again.

"I wanted to call you sooner," George apologized, "but I just returned from Athens a few minutes ago."

Alexandra's heart melted. "You've been in Athens?"

"Yes. Remember the evening we had dinner together?"

Alexandra remembered.

"The next morning Steve, my brother, telephoned me – My father had a heart attack."

"Oh, George!" She felt so guilty for having thought such terrible things about him. "How is he?"

"He's going to be all right, thank God. But I felt as though I was being torn in pieces. He begged me to come back to Greece and take over the family business."

"Are you going to?" She was holding her breath.

"No."

She exhaled.

"I know now that my place is here. There isn't one day or one hour that's gone by that I haven't thought about you. When can I see you?"

Now! "I'm free for dinner this evening."

He was almost tempted to name another of Alexandra's favorite restaurants. Instead he said, "Wonderful. Where would you like to dine?"

"Anywhere. I don't care. Would you like to have dinner at the house?"

"No." He was not ready to meet Kate yet. *Whatever you do, stay away from Kate Blackwell for now. She's your biggest obstacle.* "I'll pick you up at eight o'clock," George told her.

Alexandra hung up, kissed Alice Koppel, Vince Barnes and Marty Bergheimer and said, "I'm off to the hairdresser. I'll see you all tomorrow."

They watched her race out of the office.

"It's a man," Alice Koppel said.

They had dinner at Maxwell's Plum. A captain led them past the crowded horseshoe bar near the front door and up the stairs to the dining room. They ordered.

"Did you think about me while I was away?" George asked.

"Yes." She felt she had to be completely honest with this man – this man who was so open, so vulnerable. "When I didn't hear from you, I thought something terrible might have happened. I – I got panicky. I don't think I could have stood it another day."

Full marks for Eve, George thought. *Sit tight*, Eve had said. *I'll tell you when to call her. For* the first time George had the feeling the plan really was going to work. Until now he had let it nibble at the edges of his mind, toying with the idea of controlling the incredible Blackwell fortune, but he had not really dared believe it. It had been merely a game that he and Eve had been playing. Looking at Alexandra now, seated across from him, her eyes filled with naked adoration, George Mellis knew it was no longer just a game. Alexandra was his. That was the first step in the plan. The other steps might be dangerous, but with Eve's help, he would handle them.

We're in this together all the way, George, and we'll share everything right down the middle.

George Mellis did not believe in partners. When he had what he wanted, when he had disposed of Alexandra, then he would take care of Eve. That thought gave him enormous pleasure.

"You're smiling," Alexandra said.

He put his hand over hers, and his touch warmed her. "I was thinking how nice it was our being here together. About our being *anywhere* together." He reached into his pocket and pulled out a jewel box. "I brought something for you from Greece."

"Oh, George – "

"Open it, Alex."

Inside the box was an exquisite diamond necklace.

"It's beautiful."

It was the one he had taken from Eve. *Its safe to give it to her, Eve* had told him. *She's never seen it.*

"It's too much. Really."

"It's not nearly enough. I'll enjoy watching you wear it."

"I – " Alexandra was trembling. "Thank you."

He looked at her plate. "You haven't eaten anything."

"I'm not hungry."

He saw the look in her eyes again and felt the familiar soaring sense of power. He had seen that look in the eyes of so many women: beautiful women, ugly women, rich women, poor women. He had used them. In one way or another, they had all given him something. But this one was going to give him more than all of them put together.

"What would you like to do?" His husky voice was an invitation.

She accepted it, simply and openly. "I want to be with you."

George Mellis had every right to be proud of his apartment. It was a tasteful jewel of a place, furnished by grateful lovers – men and women – who had tried to buy his affection with expensive gifts, and had succeeded, always temporarily.

"It's a lovely apartment," Alexandra exclaimed.

He went over to her and slowly turned her around so that the diamond necklace twinkled in the subdued lighting of the room. "It becomes you, darling."

And he kissed her gently, and then more urgently, and Alexandra was hardly aware when he led her into the bedroom. The room was done in tones of blue, with tasteful, masculine furniture. In the center of the room stood a large, king-size bed. George took Alexandra in his arms again and found that she was shaking. "Are you all right, *kale' mou?*"

"I – I'm a little nervous." She was terrified that she would disappoint this man. She took a deep breath and started to unbutton her dress.

George whispered, "Let me." He began to undress the exquisite blonde standing before him, and he remembered Eve's words: *Control yourself. If you hurt Alexandra, if she finds out what a pig you really are, you'll never see her again.*

Do you understand that? Save your fists for your whores and your pretty little boys.

And so George tenderly undressed Alexandra and studied her nakedness. Her body was exactly the same as Eve's: beautiful and ripe and full. He had an overwhelming desire to bruise the white, delicate skin; to hit her, choke her, make her scream. *If you hurt her, you'll never see her again.*

He undressed and drew Alexandra close to his body. They stood there together, looking into each other's eyes, and then George gently led Alexandra to the bed and began to kiss her, slowly and lovingly, his tongue and fingers expertly exploring every crevice of her body until she was unable to wait another moment.

"Oh, please," she said. "Now. Now!"

He mounted her then, and she was plunged into an ecstasy that was almost unbearable. When finally Alexandra lay still in his arms and sighed, "Oh, my darling. I hope it was as wonderful for you," he lied and said, "It was."

She held him close and wept, and she did not know why she was weeping, only that she was grateful for the glory and the joy of it.

"There, there," George said soothingly. "Everything is marvelous."

And it was.

Eve would have been so proud of him.

In every love affair, there are misunderstandings, jealousies, small hurts, but not in the romance between George and Alexandra. With Eve's careful coaching, George was able to play skillfully on Alexandra's every emotion. George knew Alexandra's fears, her fantasies, her passions and aversions, and he was always there, ready to give her exactly what she needed. He knew what made her laugh, and what made her cry. Alexandra was thrilled by his lovemaking, but George found it frustrating. When he was in bed with Alexandra, listening to her animal cries, her excitement aroused him to a fever pitch. He wanted to savage her, make her scream for mercy so he could have his own relief. But he knew if he did that he would destroy everything. His frustration kept growing. The more they made love, the more he grew to despise Alexandra.

There were certain places where George Mellis could find satisfaction, but he knew he had to be cautious. Late at night he haunted anonymous singles' bars and gay discos, and he picked up lonely widows looking for an evening's comfort, gay boys hungry for love, prostitutes hungry for money. George took them to a series of seedy hotels on the West Side, in the Bowery and in Greenwich Village. He never returned to the same hotel twice, nor would he have been welcomed back. His sexual partners usually were found either unconscious or semi-conscious, their bodies battered and sometimes covered with cigarette burns.

George avoided masochists. They enjoyed the pain he inflicted, and that took away his pleasure. No, he had to hear them scream and beg for mercy, as his father had made him scream and beg for mercy when George was a small boy. His punishments for the smallest infractions were beatings that often left him unconscious. When George was eight years old and his father caught him and a neighbor's son naked together, George's father beat him until the blood ran from his ears and nose, and to make sure the boy never sinned again, his father pressed a lighted cigar to George's penis. The scar healed, but the deeper scar inside festered.

George Mellis had the wild, passionate nature of his Hellenic ancestors. He could not bear the thought of being controlled by anyone. He put up with the taunting humiliation Eve Blackwell inflicted upon him only because he needed her. When he had the Blackwell fortune in his hands, he intended to punish her until she begged him to kill her. Meeting Eve was the luckiest thing that had ever happened to him. *Lucky for me*, George mused. *Unlucky for her.*

Alexandra continually marveled at how George always knew just what flowers to send her, what records to buy, what books would please her. When he took her to a museum, he was excited about the same paintings she loved. It was incredible to Alexandra how identical their tastes were. She looked for a single flaw in George Mellis, and she could find none. He was perfect. She grew more and more eager for Kate to meet him.

But George always found an excuse to avoid meeting Kate Blackwell.

"Why, darling? You'll love her. Besides, I want to show you off."

"I'm sure she's wonderful," George said boyishly. "I'm terrified she'll think I'm not good enough for you."

"That's ridiculous!" His modesty touched her. "Gran will adore you."

"Soon," he told Alexandra. "As soon as I get up my courage."

He discussed it with Eve one night.

She thought about it. "All right. You'll have to get it over with sooner or later. But you'll have to watch yourself every second. She's a bitch, but she's a smart bitch. Don't underestimate her for a second. If she suspects you're after anything, she'll cut your heart out and feed it to her dogs."

"Why do we need her?" George asked.

"Because if you do anything to make Alexandra antagonize her, we'll all be out in the cold."

Alexandra had never been so nervous. They were going to dine together for the first time, George and Kate and Alexandra, and Alexandra prayed that nothing would go wrong. She wanted more than anything in the world for her grandmother and George to like each other, for her grandmother to see what a wonderful person George was and for George to appreciate Kate Blackwell.

Kate had never seen her granddaughter so happy. Alexandra had met some of the most eligible young men in the world, and none of them had interested her. Kate intended to take a very close look at the man who had captivated her granddaughter. Kate had had long years of experience with fortune hunters, and she had no intention of allowing Alexandra to be taken in by one.

She was eagerly looking forward to meeting Mr. George Mellis. She had a feeling he had been reluctant to meet her, and she wondered why.

Kate heard the front doorbell ring, and a minute later Alexandra came into the drawing room leading a tall, classically handsome stranger by the hand.

"Gran, this is George Mellis."

"At last," Kate said. "I was beginning to think you were avoiding me, Mr. Mellis."

"On the contrary, Mrs. Blackwell, you have no idea how much I've been looking forward to this moment." He was about to say, "You're even more beautiful than Alex told me," but he stopped himself.

Be careful. No flattery, George. It's like a red flag to the old lady.

A butler came in, fixed drinks and discreetly withdrew.

"Please sit down, Mr. Mellis."

"Thank you."

Alexandra sat beside him on the couch, facing her grandmother.

"I understand you've been seeing quite a bit of my granddaughter."

"That's been my pleasure, yes."

Kate was studying him with her pale-gray eyes. "Alexandra tells me you're employed by a brokerage firm."

"Yes."

"Frankly, I find it strange, Mr. Mellis, that you should choose to work as a salaried employee when you could be heading a very profitable family business."

"Gran, I explained that – "

"I would like to hear it from Mr. Mellis, Alexandra."

Be polite, but for Christ's sake, don't kowtow to her. If you show the slightest sign of weakness, she'll tear you apart.

"Mrs. Blackwell, I'm not in the habit of discussing my personal life." He hesitated, as though making a decision. "However, under the circumstances, I suppose . . ." He looked Kate Blackwell in the eye and said, "I'm a very independent man. I don't accept charity. If I had founded Mellis and Company, I would be running it today. But it was founded by my grandfather and built into a very profitable business by my father. It does not need me. I have three brothers who are perfectly capable of running it. I prefer being a salaried employee, as you call it, until I find something that I can build up myself and take pride in."

Kate nodded slowly. This man was not what she had expected at all. She had been prepared for a playboy, a fortune hunter, the kind who had been pursuing her granddaughters ever since Kate could remember. This one appeared to be different. And yet, there was something disturbing about him that Kate could not define. He seemed almost *too* perfect.

"I understand your family is wealthy."

All she has to believe is that you're filthy rich, and madly in love with Alex. Be charming. Keep your temper under control, and you've got it made.

"Money is a necessity, of course, Mrs. Blackwell. But there are a hundred things that interest me more."

Kate had checked on the net worth of Mellis and Company. According to the Dun & Bradstreet report, it was in excess of thirty million dollars.

"Are you close to your family, Mr. Mellis?"

George's face lighted up. "Perhaps too close." He allowed a smile to play on his lips. "We have a saying in our family, Mrs. Blackwell. When one of us cuts his finger, the rest of us bleed. We are in touch with each other constantly." He had not spoken to any member of his family for more than three years.

Kate nodded approvingly. "I believe in closely knit families."

Kate glanced at her granddaughter. There was a look of adoration on Alexandra's face. For one fleeting instant, it reminded Kate of herself and David in those long-ago days when they were so much in love. The years had not dimmed the memory of how she had felt.

Lester came into the room. "Dinner is served, madame."

The conversation at dinner seemed more casual, but Kate's questions were pointed. George was prepared for the most important question when it came.

"Do you like children, Mr. Mellis?"

She's desperate for a great-grandson. . . . She wants that more than anything in the world.

George turned toward Kate in surprise. "Like children? What is a man without sons and daughters? I am afraid that when I marry, my poor wife will be kept very busy. In Greece, a man's worth is measured by the number of children he has sired."

He seems genuine, Kate thought. *But, one can't be too careful. Tomorrow I'll have Brad Rogers run a check on his personal finances.*

Before Alexandra went to bed, she telephoned Eve. She had told Eve that George Mellis was coming to dinner.

"I can't wait to hear all about it, darling," Eve had said. "You must call me the moment he leaves. I want a full report."

And now Alexandra was reporting. "I think Gran liked him a lot."

Eve felt a small frisson of satisfaction. "What did she say?"

"She asked George a hundred personal questions. He handled himself beautifully."

So he had behaved.

"Ah! Are you two lovebirds going to get married?"

"I – He hasn't asked me yet, Eve, but I think he's going to."

She could hear the happiness in Alexandra's voice. "And Gran will approve?"

"Oh, I'm sure she will. She's going to check on George's personal finances, but of course that will be no problem."

Eve felt her heart lurch.

Alexandra was saying, "You know how cautious Gran is."

"Yes," Eve said slowly. "I know."

They were finished. Unless she could think of something quickly.

"Keep me posted," Eve said.

"I will. Good night."

The moment Eve replaced the receiver, she dialed George Mellis's number. He had not reached home yet. She called him every ten minutes, and when he finally answered Eve said, "Can you get your hands on a million dollars in a hurry?"

"What the hell are you talking about?"

"Kate is checking out your finances."

"She knows what my family is worth. She – "

"I'm not talking about your family. I'm talking about you. I told you she's no fool."

There was a silence. "Where would I get hold of a million dollars?"

"I have an idea," Eve told him.

When Kate arrived at her office the following morning, she said to her assistant, "Ask Brad Rogers to run a personal financial check on George Mellis. He's employed by Hanson and Hanson."

"Mr. Rogers is out of town until tomorrow, Mrs. Blackwell. Can it wait until then or – ?"

"Tomorrow will be fine."

At the lower end of Manhattan on Wall Street, George Mellis was seated at his desk at the brokerage firm of Hanson and Hanson. The stock exchanges were open, and the huge office was a bedlam of noise and activity. There were 225 employees working at the firm's headquarters: brokers, analysts, accountants, operators and customer representatives, and everyone was working at a feverish speed. Except for George Mellis. He was frozen at his desk, in a panic. What he was about to do would put him in prison if he failed. If he succeeded, he would own the world.

"Aren't you going to answer your phone?"

One of the partners was standing over him, and George realized that his phone had been ringing for – how long? He must act normally and not do anything that might arouse suspicion. He scooped up the phone. "George Mellis," and smiled reassuringly at the partner.

George spent the morning taking buy and sell orders, but his mind was on Eve's plan to steal a million dollars. *It's simple, George. All you have to do is borrow some stock certificates for one night. You can return them in the morning, and no one will be the wiser.*

Every stock brokerage firm has millions of dollars in stocks and bonds stored in its vaults as a convenience to customers. Some of the stock certificates bear the name of the owner, but the vast majority are street-name stocks with a coded CUSIP number – the Committee on Uniform Security Identification Procedures – that identifies the owner. The stock certificates are not negotiable, but George Mellis did not plan to cash them in. He had something else in mind. At Hanson and Hanson, the stocks were kept in a huge vault on the seventh floor in a security area guarded by an armed policeman in front of a gate that could only be opened by a coded plastic access card. George Mellis had no such card. But he knew someone who did.

Helen Thatcher was a lonely widow in her forties. She had a pleasant face and a reasonably good figure, and she was a remarkable cook. She had been married for twenty-three years, and the death of her husband had left a void in her life. She needed a man to take care of her. Her problem was that most of the women who worked at Hanson and Hanson were younger than she, and more attractive to the brokers at the office. No one asked Helen out.

She worked in the accounting department on the floor above George Mellis. From the first time Helen had seen George, she had decided he would make a perfect husband for her. Half a dozen times she had invited him to a home-cooked evening, as she phrased it, and had hinted that he would be served more than dinner, but George had always found an excuse. On this particular morning, when her telephone rang and she said, "Accounting, Mrs. Thatcher," George Mellis's voice came over the line. "Helen? This is George." His voice was warm, and she thrilled to it. "What can I do for you, George?"

"I have a little surprise for you. Can you come down to my office?"

"Now?"

"Yes."

"I'm afraid I'm in the middle of – "

"Oh, if you're too busy, never mind. It will keep."

"No, no. I – I'll be right down."

George's phone was ringing again. He ignored it. He picked up a handful of papers and walked toward the bank of elevators. Looking around to make sure no one was observing him, he walked past the elevators and took the backstairs. When he reached the floor above, he checked to make sure Helen had left her office, then casually walked in as though he had business there. If he was caught – but he could not think of that. He opened the middle drawer where he knew Helen kept her access card to the vault. There it was. He picked it up, slipped it in his pocket, left the office and hurried downstairs. When he reached his desk, Helen was there, looking around for him.

"Sorry," George said. "I was called away for a minute."

"Oh, that's all right. Tell me what the surprise is."

"Well, a little bird told me it's your birthday," George said, "and I want to take you to lunch today." He watched the expression on her face. She was torn between telling him the truth and missing the chance of a lunch date with him.

"That's – very nice of you," she said. "I'd love to have lunch with you."

"All right," he told her. "I'll meet you at Tony's at one o'clock." It was a date he could have made with her over the telephone, but Helen Thatcher was too thrilled to even question it. He watched as she left.

The minute she was gone, George went into action. He had a lot to accomplish before he returned the plastic card. He took the elevator to the seventh floor and walked over to the security area where the guard stood in front of the closed grilled gate. George inserted the plastic card and the gate opened. As he started inside, the guard said, "I don't think I've seen you here before."

George's heart began to beat faster. He smiled. "No. This isn't my usual territory. One of my customers suddenly decided he wanted to see his stock certificates, so I've got to dig them out. I hope it doesn't take me the whole blasted afternoon."

The guard smiled sympathetically. "Good luck." He watched as George walked into the vault.

The room was concrete, thirty feet by fifteen feet. George walked back to the fireproof file cabinets that contained the stocks and opened the steel drawers. Inside were hundreds of stock certificates that represented shares of every company on the New York and American stock exchanges. The number of shares represented by each certificate was printed on the face of the certificate and ranged from one share to one hundred thousand shares. George went through them swiftly and expertly. He selected certificates of various blue-chip companies, representing a value of one million dollars. He slipped the pieces of paper into his inside jacket pocket, closed the drawer and walked back to the guard.

"That was fast," the guard said.

George shook his head. "The computers came up with the wrong numbers. I'll have to straighten it out in the morning."

"Those damned computers," the guard commiserated. "They'll be the ruination of us all yet."

When George returned to his desk, he found he was soaked with perspiration. *But so far so good.* He picked up the telephone and called Alexandra.

"Darling," he said, "I want to see you and your grandmother tonight."

"I thought you had a business engagement tonight, George."

"I did, but I canceled it. I have something very important to tell you."

At exactly 1:00 P.M. George was in Helen Thatcher's office returning the access card to her desk drawer, while she waited for him at the restaurant. He desperately wanted to hang on to the card, for he would need it again, but he knew that every card that was not turned in each night was invalidated by the computer the next morning. At ten minutes past one, George was lunching with Helen Thatcher.

He took her hand in his. "I want us to do this more often," George said, looking at her searchingly. "Are you free for lunch tomorrow?"

She beamed. "Oh, yes, George."

*

When George Mellis walked out of his office that afternoon, he was carrying with him one-million-dollars' worth of stock certificates.

He arrived at the Blackwell house promptly at seven o'clock and was ushered into the library, where Kate and Alexandra were waiting for him.

"Good evening," George said. "I hope this is not an intrusion, but I had to speak to you both." He turned to Kate. "I know this is very old-fashioned of me, Mrs. Blackwell, but I would like your permission for your granddaughter's hand in marriage. I love Alexandra, and I believe she loves me. But it would make both of us happy if you would give us your blessing." He reached into his jacket pocket, brought out the stock certificates and tossed them on the table in front of Kate. "I'm giving her a million dollars as a wedding present. She won't need any of your money. But we both need your blessing."

Kate glanced down at the stock certificates George had carelessly scattered on the table. She recognized the names of every one of the companies. Alexandra had moved to George, her eyes shining. "Oh, darling!" She turned to her grandmother, her eyes imploring, "Gran?"

Kate looked at the two of them standing together, and there was no way she could deny them. For a brief instant, she envied them. "You have my blessing," she said.

George grinned and walked over to Kate. "May I?" He kissed her on the cheek.

For the next two hours they talked excitedly about wedding plans. "I don't want a large wedding, Gran," Alexandra said. We don't have to do that, do we?"

"I agree," George replied. "Love is a private matter."

In the end, they decided on a small ceremony, with a judge marrying them.

"Will your father be coming over for the wedding?" Kate inquired.

George laughed. "You couldn't keep him away. My father, my three brothers and my two sisters will all be here."

"I'll be looking forward to meeting them."

"You'll like them, I know." Then his eyes turned back to Alexandra.

Kate was very touched by the whole evening. She was thrilled for her granddaughter – pleased that she was getting a man who loved her so much. *I must remember*, Kate thought, *to tell Brad not to bother about that financial rundown on George.*

Before George left, and he was alone with Alexandra, he said casually, "I don't think it's a good idea to have a million dollars in securities lying around the house. I'll put them in my safe-deposit box for now."

"Would you?" Alexandra asked.

George picked up the certificates and put them back into his jacket pocket.

*

The following morning George repeated the procedure with Helen Thatcher. While she was on her way downstairs to see him ("I have a little something for you"), he was in her office getting the access card. He gave her a Gucci scarf – "a belated birthday present" – and confirmed his luncheon date with her. This time getting into the vault seemed easier. He replaced the stock certificates, returned the access card and met Helen Thatcher at a nearby restaurant.

She held his hand and said, "George, why don't I fix a nice dinner for the two of us tonight?"

And George replied, "I'm afraid that's impossible, Helen. I'm getting married."

Three days before the wedding ceremony was to take place, George arrived at the Blackwell house, his face filled with distress. "I've just had terrible news," he said. "My father suffered another heart attack."

"Oh, I'm so sorry," Kate said. "Is he going to be all right?"

"I've been on the phone with the family all night. They think he'll pull through, but of course they won't be able to attend the wedding."

"We could go to Athens on our honeymoon and see them," Alexandra suggested.

George stroked her cheek. "I have other plans for our honeymoon, *matia mou*. No family, just us."

The marriage ceremony was held in the drawing room of the Blackwell mansion. There were fewer than a dozen guests in attendance, among them Vince Barnes, Alice Koppel and Marty Bergheimer. Alexandra had pleaded with her grandmother to let Eve attend the wedding, but Kate was adamant. "Your sister will never be welcome in this house again."

Alexandra's eyes filled with tears. "Gran, you're being cruel. I love you both. Can't you forgive her?"

For an instant, Kate was tempted to blurt out the whole story of Eve's disloyalty, but she stopped herself. "I'm doing what I think is best for everyone."

A photographer took pictures of the ceremony, and Kate heard George ask him to make up some extra prints to send to his family. *What a considerate man he is*, Kate thought.

After the cake-cutting ceremony, George whispered to Alexandra, "Darling, I'm going to have to disappear for an hour or so."

"Is anything wrong?"

"Of course not. But the only way I could persuade the office to let me take time off for our honeymoon was to promise to finish up some business for an important client. I won't be long. Our plane doesn't leave until five o'clock."

She smiled. "Hurry back. I don't want to go on our honeymoon without you."

When George arrived at Eve's apartment, she was waiting for him, wearing a filmy negligee. "Did you enjoy your wedding, darling?"

"Yes, thank you. It was small but elegant. It went off without a hitch."
"Do you know why, George? Because of me. Never forget that."
He looked at her and said slowly, "I won't."
"We're partners all the way."
"Of course."
Eve smiled. "Well, well. So you're married to my little sister."
George looked at his watch. "Yes. And I must get back."
"Not yet," Eve told him.
"Why not?"
"Because you're going to make love to me first, darling. I want to fuck my sister's husband."

30

Eve had planned the honeymoon. It was expensive, but she told George, "You mustn't stint on anything."

She sold three pieces of jewelry she had acquired from an ardent admirer and gave the money to George.

"I appreciate this, Eve," he said. "I . . ."

"I'll get it back."

The honeymoon was perfection. George and Alexandra stayed at Round Hill on Montego Bay, in the northern part of Jamaica. The lobby of the hotel was a small, white building set in the center of approximately two dozen beautiful, privately owned bungalows that sprawled down a hill toward the clear, blue sea. The Mellises had the Noel Coward bungalow, with its own swimming pool and a maid to prepare their breakfast, which they ate in the open-air dining room. George rented a small boat and they went sailing and fishing. They swam and read and played backgammon and made love. Alexandra did everything she could think of to please George in bed, and when she heard him moaning at the climax of their lovemaking, she was thrilled that she was able to bring him such pleasure.

On the fifth day, George said, "Alex, I have to drive into Kingston on business. The firm has a branch office there and they asked me to look in on it."

"Fine," Alexandra said. "I'll go with you."

He frowned. "I'd love you to, darling, but I'm expecting an overseas call. You'll have to stay and take the message."

Alexandra was disappointed. "Can't the desk take it?"

"It's too important. I can't trust them."

"All right, then. Of course I'll stay."

George rented a car and drove to Kingston. It was late afternoon when he arrived. The streets of the capital city were swarming with colorfully dressed tourists from the cruise ships, shopping at the straw market and in small bazaars. Kingston is a city of commerce, with refineries, warehouses and fisheries, but with its landlocked harbor it is also a city of beautiful old buildings and museums and libraries.

George was interested in none of these things. He was filled with a desperate need that had been building up in him for weeks and had to be satisfied. He walked into the first bar he saw and spoke to the bartender. Five minutes later George was accompanying a fifteen-year-old black prostitute up the stairs of a cheap hotel. He was with her for two hours. When George left the room, he left alone, got into the car and drove back to Montego Bay, where Alexandra told him the urgent telephone call he was expecting had not come through.

The following morning the Kingston newspapers reported that a tourist had beaten up and mutilated a prostitute, and that she was near death.

At Hanson and Hanson, the senior partners were discussing George Mellis. There had been complaints from a number of clients about the way he handled their securities accounts. A decision had been reached to fire him. Now, however, there were second thoughts.

"He's married to one of Kate Blackwell's granddaughters," a senior partner said. "That puts things in a new light."

A second partner added, "It certainly does. If we could acquire the Blackwell account . . ."

The greed in the air was almost palpable. They decided George Mellis deserved another chance.

When Alexandra and George returned from their honeymoon, Kate told them, "I'd like you to move in here with me. This is an enormous house, and we wouldn't be in one another's way. You – "

George interrupted. "That's very kind of you," he said. "But I think it would be best if Alex and I had our own place."

He had no intention of living under the same roof with the old woman hovering over him, spying on his every move.

"I understand," Kate replied. "In that case, please let me buy a house for you. That will be my wedding present."

George put his arms around Kate and hugged her. "That's very generous of you." His voice was hoarse with emotion. "Alex and I accept with gratitude."

"Thank you, Gran," Alexandra said. "We'll look for a place not too far away."

"Right," George agreed. "We want to be close enough to keep an eye on you. You're a damned attractive woman, you know!"

Within a week they found a beautiful old brownstone near the park, a dozen blocks away from the Blackwell mansion. It was a charming three-story house, with a master bedroom, two guest bedrooms, servants' quarters, a huge old kitchen, a paneled dining room, an elegant living room and a library.

"You're going to have to do the decorating by yourself, darling," George told Alexandra. "I'm all tied up with clients."

The truth was that he spent almost no time at the office, and very little time with clients. His days were occupied with more interesting matters. The police were receiving a string of assault reports from male and female prostitutes and lonely women who visited singles' bars. The victims described their attacker as handsome and cultured, and coming from a foreign background, possibly Latin. Those who were willing to look at police mug shots were unable to come up with an identification.

Eve and George were having lunch in a small downtown restaurant where there was no chance of their being recognized.

"You've got to get Alex to make a new will without Kate knowing about it."

"How the hell do I do that?"

"I'm going to tell you, darling . . ."

The following evening George met Alexandra for dinner at Le Plaisir, one of New York's finest French restaurants. He was almost thirty minutes late.

Pierre Jourdan, the owner, escorted him to the table where Alexandra was waiting. "Forgive me, angel," George said breathlessly. "I was at my attorneys', and you know how they are. They make everything so complicated."

Alexandra asked, "Is anything wrong, George?"

"No. I just changed my will." He took her hands in his. "If anything should happen to me now, everything I have will belong to you."

"Darling, I don't want – "

"Oh, it's not much compared to the Blackwell fortune, but it would keep you very comfortably."

"Nothing's going to happen to you. Not ever."

"Of course not, Alex. But sometimes life plays funny tricks. These things aren't pleasant to face, but it's better to plan ahead and be prepared, don't you think?"

She sat there thoughtfully for a moment. "I should change my will, too, shouldn't I?"

"What for?" He sounded surprised.

"You're my husband. Everything I have is yours."

He withdrew his hand. "Alex, I don't give a damn about your money."

"I know that, George, but you're right. It *is* better to look ahead and be prepared." Her eyes filled with tears. "I know I'm an idiot, but I'm so happy that

I can't bear to think of anything happening to either of us. I want us to go on forever."

"We will," George murmured.

"I'll talk to Brad Rogers tomorrow about changing my will."

He shrugged. "If that's what you wish, darling." Then, as an afterthought, "Come to think of it, it might be better if my lawyer made the change. He's familiar with my estate. He can coordinate everything."

"Whatever you like. Gran thinks – "

He caressed her cheek. "Let's keep your grandmother out of this. I adore her, but don't you think we should keep our personal affairs personal?"

"You're right, darling. I won't say anything to Gran. Could you make an appointment for me to see your attorney tomorrow?"

"Remind me to call him. Now, I'm starved. Why don't we start with the crab . . . ?"

One week later George met Eve at her apartment.

"Did Alex sign the new will?" Eve asked.

"This morning. She inherits her share of the company next week on her birthday."

The following week, 49 percent of the shares of Kruger-Brent, Ltd., were transferred to Alexandra. George called to tell Eve the news. She said, "Wonderful! Come over tonight. We'll celebrate."

"I can't. Kate's giving a birthday party for Alex."

There was a silence. "What are they serving?"

"How the hell do I know?"

"Find out." The line went dead.

Forty-five minutes later George called Eve back. "I don't know why you're so interested in the menu," he said nastily, "since you aren't invited to the party, but it's *Coquille Saint-Jacques, Chateaubriand*, a bibb lettuce salad, *Brie, cappuccino* and a birthday cake with Alex's favorite ice cream, Neapolitan. Satisfied?"

"Yes, George. I'll see you tonight."

"No, Eve. There's no way I can walk out in the middle of Alex's – "

"You'll think of something."

God damn the bitch! George hung up the phone and looked at his watch. *God damn everything!* He had an appointment with an important client he had stood up twice already. Now he was late. He knew the partners were keeping him on only because he had married into the Blackwell family. He could not afford to do anything to jeopardize his position. He had created an image for Alexandra and Kate, and it was imperative that nothing destroy that. Soon he would not need any of them.

He had sent his father a wedding invitation, and the old man had not even bothered to reply. Not one word of congratulations. *I never want to see you again*, his father had told him. *You're dead, you understand? Dead.* Well, his father was in for a surprise. The prodigal son was going to come to life again.

Alexandra's twenty-third birthday party was a great success. There were forty guests. She had asked George to invite some of his friends, but he had demurred. "Its your party, Alex," he said. "Let's just have your friends."

The truth was that George had no friends. He was a loner, he told himself proudly. People who were dependent on other people were weaklings. He watched as Alexandra blew out the candles on her cake and made a silent wish. He knew the wish involved him, and he thought, *You should have wished for a longer life, darling.* He had to admit that Alexandra was exquisite looking. She was wearing a long white chiffon dress with delicate silver slippers and a diamond necklace, a present from Kate. The large, pear-shaped stones were strung together on a platinum chain, and they sparkled in the candlelight.

Kate looked at them and thought, *I remember our first anniversary, when David put that necklace on me and told me how much he loved me.*

And George thought, *That necklace must be worth a hundred and fifty thousand dollars.*

George had been aware all evening that several of Alexandra's female guests were eyeing him, smiling at him invitingly, touching him as they talked to him. *Horny bitches*, he thought contemptuously. Under other circumstances, he might have been tempted to risk it, but not with Alexandra's friends. They might not dare complain to Alexandra, but there was a chance they could go to the police. No, things were moving along too smoothly to take any unnecessary chances.

At one minute before ten o'clock, George positioned himself near the telephone. When it rang a minute later, he picked it up. "Hello."

"Mr. Mellis?"

"Yes."

"This is your answering service. You asked me to call you at ten o'clock."

Alexandra was standing near him. He looked over at her and frowned. "What time did he call?"

"Is this Mr. Mellis?"

"Yes."

"You left a ten o'clock call, sir."

Alexandra was at his side.

"Very well," he said into the phone. "Tell him I'm on my way. I'll meet him at the Pan Am Clipper Club."

George slammed the phone down.

"What's the matter, darling?"

He turned to Alexandra. "One of the idiot partners is on his way to Singapore and he left some contracts at the office that he needs to take with him. I've got to pick them up and get them to him before his plane leaves."

"*Now?*" Alexandra's voice was filled with dismay. "Can't someone else do it?"

"I'm the only one they trust," George sighed. "You'd think I was the only capable one in the whole office." He put his arms around her. "I'm sorry, darling. Don't let me spoil your party. You go on and I'll get back as soon as I can."

She managed a smile. "I'll miss you."

Alexandra watched him go, then looked around the room to make sure all her guests were enjoying themselves.

She wondered what Eve was doing on their birthday.

Eve opened the door to let George in. "You managed," she said. "You're such a clever man."

"I can't stay, Eve. Alex is – "

She took his hand. "Come, darling. I have a surprise for you." She led him into the small dining room. The table was set for two, with beautiful silver and white napery and lighted candles in the center of the table.

"What's this for?"

"It's my birthday, George."

"Of course," he said lamely. "I – I'm afraid I didn't bring you a present."

She stroked his cheek. "Yes you did, love. You'll give it to me later. Sit down."

"Thanks," George said. "I couldn't eat anything. I just had a big dinner."

"Sit down." There was no inflection to her voice.

George looked into her eyes, and sat down.

Dinner consisted of *Coquille Saint-Jacques, Chateaubriand*, a bibb lettuce salad, *Brie, cappuccino* and a birthday cake with Neapolitan ice cream.

Eve sat across from him, watching George force the food down. "Alex and I have always shared everything," Eve told him. "Tonight I'm sharing her birthday dinner. But next year there will be just one of us having a birthday party. The time has come, darling, for my sister to have an accident. And after that, poor old Gran is going to die of grief. It's going to be all ours, George. Now, come into the bedroom and give me my birthday present."

He had been dreading this moment. He was a man, strong and vigorous, and Eve dominated him and made him feel impotent. She had him undress her slowly, and then she undressed him and skillfully excited him to an erection.

"There you are, darling." She got astride him and began slowly moving her hips. "Ah, that feels so good. . . . You can't have an orgasm, can you, poor baby? Do you know why? Because you're a freak. You don't like women, do you, George? You only enjoy hurting them. You'd like to hurt me, wouldn't you? Tell me you'd like to hurt me."

"I'd like to kill you."

Eve laughed. "But you won't, because you want to own the company as much as I do. . . . You'll never hurt me, George, because if anything ever happens to me, a friend of mine is holding a letter that will be delivered to the police."

He did not believe her. "You're bluffing."

Eve raked a long, sharp nail down his naked chest. "There's only one way you can find out, isn't there?" she taunted.

And he suddenly knew she was telling the truth. He was never going to be able to get rid of her! She was always going to be there to taunt him, to enslave him. He could not bear the idea of being at this bitch's mercy for the rest of his life. And something inside him exploded. A red film descended over his eyes, and from that moment on he had no idea what he was doing. It was as though someone outside himself was controlling him. Everything happened in slow motion. He remembered shoving Eve off him, pulling her legs apart and her cries of pain. He was battering at something over and over, and it was indescribably wonderful. The whole center of his being was racked with a long spasm of unbearable bliss, and then another, and another, and he thought, *Oh, God! I've waited so long for this.* From somewhere in the far distance, someone was screaming. The red film slowly started to clear, and he looked down. Eve was lying on the bed, covered with blood. Her nose was smashed in, her body was covered with bruises and cigarette burns and her eyes were swollen shut. Her jaw was broken, and she was whimpering out of the side of her mouth. "Stop it, stop it, stop it . . . ,"

George shook his head to clear it. As the reality of the situation hit him, he was filled with sudden panic. There was no way he could ever explain what he had done. He had thrown everything away. Everything!

He leaned over her. "Eve?"

She opened one swollen eye. "Doctor . . . Get . . . a . . . doctor . . ." Each word was a drop of pain. "Harley . . . John Harley."

All George Mellis said on the phone was, "Can you come right away? Eve Blackwell has had an accident."

When Dr. John Harley walked into the room, he took one look at Eve and the blood-spattered bed and walls and said, "Oh, my God!" He felt Eve's fluttering pulse, and turned to George. "Call the police. Tell them we need an ambulance."

Through the mist of pain, Eve whispered, "John . . ."

John Harley leaned over the bed. "You're going to be all right. We'll get you to the hospital."

She reached out and found his hand. "No police . . ."

"I have to report this. I – "

Her grip tightened. "No . . . police . . ."

He looked at her shattered cheekbone, her broken jaw and the cigarette burns on her body. "Don't try to talk."

The pain was excruciating, but Eve was fighting for her life. "Please . . ." It took a long time to get the words out. "Private . . . Gran would never . . . forgive me. . . . No . . . police. . . . Hit . . . run . . . accident . . ."

There was no time to argue. Dr. Harley walked over to the telephone and dialed. "This is Dr. Harley." He gave Eve's address. "I want an ambulance sent here immediately. Find Dr. Keith Webster and ask him to meet me at the hospital. Tell him it's an emergency. Have a room prepared for surgery." He listened a moment, then said, "A hit-and-run accident." He slammed down the receiver.

"Thank you, Doctor," George breathed.

Dr. Harley turned to look at Alexandra's husband, his eyes filled with loathing: George's clothes had been hastily donned, but his knuckles were raw, and his hands and face were still spattered with blood. "Don't thank me. I'm doing this for the Blackwells. But on one condition. That you agree to see a psychiatrist."

"I don't need a – "

"Then I'm calling the police, you sonofabitch. You're not fit to be running around loose." Dr. Harley reached for the telephone again.

"Wait a minute!" George stood there, thinking. He had almost thrown everything away, but now, miraculously, he was being given a second chance. "All right. I'll see a psychiatrist."

In the far distance they heard the wail of a siren.

She was being rushed down a long tunnel, and colored lights were flashing on and off. Her body felt light and airy, and she thought, *I can fly if I want to*, and she tried to move her arms, but something was holding them down. She opened her eyes, and she was speeding down a white corridor on a gurney being wheeled by two men in green gowns and caps. *I'm starring in a play*, Eve thought. *I can't remember my lines. What are my lines?* When she opened her eyes again, she was in a large white room on an operating table.

A small, thin man in a green surgical gown was leaning over her. "My name is Keith Webster. I'm going to operate on you."

"I don't want to be ugly," Eve whispered. It was difficult to talk. "Don't let me be . . . ugly."

"Not a chance," Dr. Webster promised. "I'm going to put you to sleep now. Just relax."

He gave a signal to the anesthesiologist.

George managed to wash the blood off himself and clean up in Eve's bathroom, but he cursed as he glanced at his wristwatch. It was three o'clock in the morning. He hoped Alexandra was asleep, but when he walked into their living room, she was waiting for him.

"Darling! I've been frantic! Are you all right?"

"I'm fine, Alex."

She went up to him and hugged him. "I was getting ready to call the police. I thought something terrible had happened."

How right you are, George thought.

"Did you bring him the contracts?"

"Contracts?" He suddenly remembered. "Oh, those. Yes. I did." That seemed like years ago, a lie from the distant past.

"What on earth kept you so late?"

"His plane was delayed," George said glibly. "He wanted me to stay with him. I kept thinking he'd take off at any minute, and then finally it got too late for me to telephone you. I'm sorry."

"It's all right, now that you're here."

George thought of Eve as she was being carried out on the stretcher. Out of her broken, twisted mouth, she had gasped, "Go . . . home . . . nothing . . . happened. . . ." But what if Eve died? He would be arrested for murder. If Eve lived, everything would be all right; it would be just as it was before. Eve would forgive him because she needed him.

George lay awake the rest of the night. He was thinking about Eve and the way she had screamed and begged for mercy. He felt her bones crunch again beneath his fists, and he smelled her burning flesh, and at that moment he was very close to loving her.

It was a stroke of great luck that John Harley was able to obtain the services of Keith Webster for Eve. Dr. Webster was one of the foremost plastic surgeons in the world. He had a private practice on Park Avenue and his own clinic in lower Manhattan, where he specialized in taking care of those who had been born with disfigurements. The people who came to the clinic paid only what they could afford. Dr. Webster was used to treating accident cases, but his first sight of Eve Blackwell's battered face had shocked him. He had seen photographs of her in magazines, and to see that much beauty deliberately disfigured filled him with a deep anger.

"Who's responsible for this, John?"

"It was a hit-and-run accident, Keith."

Keith Webster snorted. "And then the driver stopped to strip her and snuff out his cigarette on her behind? What's the real story?"

"I'm afraid I can't discuss it. Can you put her back together again?"

"That's what I do, John, put them back together again."

It was almost noon when Dr. Webster finally said to his assistants, "We're finished. Get her into intensive care. Call me at the slightest sign of anything going wrong."

The operation had taken nine hours.

Eve was moved out of intensive care forty-eight hours later. George went to the hospital. He had to see Eve, to talk to her, to make sure she was not plotting some terrible vengeance against him.

"I'm Miss Blackwell's attorney," George told the duty nurse. "She asked to see me. I'll only stay a moment."

The nurse took one look at this handsome man and said, "She's not supposed to have visitors, but I'm sure it's all right if you go in."

Eve was in a private room, lying in bed, flat on her back, swathed in bandages, tubes connected to her body like obscene appendages. The only parts of her face visible were her eyes and her lips.

"Hello, Eve . . ."

"George . . ." Her voice was a scratchy whisper. He had to lean close to hear what she said.

"You didn't . . . tell Alex?"

"No, of course not." He sat down on the edge of the bed. "I came because – "

"I know why you came. . . . We're . . . going ahead with it . . ."

He had a feeling of indescribable relief. "I'm sorry about this, Eve. I really am. I – "

"Have someone call Alex . . . and tell her I've gone away . . . on a trip . . . back in a few . . . weeks . . ."

"All right."

Two bloodshot eyes looked up at him. "George . . . do me a favor."

"Yes?"

"Die painfully. . . ."

She slept. When she awakened, Dr. Keith Webster was at her bedside.

"How are you feeling?" His voice was gentle and soothing.

"Very tired . . . What was the . . . matter with me?"

Dr. Webster hesitated. The X rays had shown a fractured zygoma and a blowout fracture. There was a depressed zygomatic arch impinging on the temporal muscle, so that she was unable to open or close her mouth without pain. Her nose was broken. There were two broken ribs and deep cigarette burns on her posterior and on the soles of her feet.

"What?" Eve repeated.

Dr. Webster said, as gently as possible, "You had a fractured cheekbone. Your nose was broken. The bony floor where your eye sits had been shifted. There was pressure on the muscle that opens and closes your mouth. There were cigarette burns. Everything has been taken care of."

"I want to see a mirror," Eve whispered.

That was the last thing he would allow. "I'm sorry," he smiled. "We're fresh out."

She was afraid to ask the next question. "How am I – how am I going to look when these bandages come off?"

"You're going to look terrific. Exactly the way you did before your accident."

"I don't believe you."

"You'll see. Now, do you want to tell me what happened? I have to write up a police report."

There was a long silence. "I was hit by a truck."

Dr. Keith Webster wondered again how anyone could have tried to destroy this fragile beauty, but he had long since given up pondering the vagaries of the human race and its capacity for cruelty. "I'll need a name," he said gently. "Who did it?"

"Mack."

"And the last name?"

"Truck."

Dr. Webster was puzzled by the conspiracy of silence. First John Harley, now Eve Blackwell.

"In cases of criminal assault," Keith Webster told Eve, "I'm required by law to file a police report."

Eve reached out for his hand and grasped it and held it tightly. "Please, if my grandmother or sister knew, it would kill them. If you tell the police . . . the newspapers will know. You mustn't . . . please. . . ."

"I can't report it as a hit-and-run accident. Ladies don't usually run out in the street without any clothes on."

"Please!"

He looked down at her, and was filled with pity. "I suppose you could have tripped and fallen down the stairs of your home."

She squeezed his hand tighter. "That's exactly what happened . . ."

Dr. Webster sighed. "That's what I thought."

Dr. Keith Webster visited Eve every day after that, sometimes stopping by two or three times a day. He brought her flowers and small presents from the hospital gift shop. Each day Eve would ask him anxiously, "I just lie here all day. Why isn't anyone doing anything?"

"My partner's working on you," Dr. Webster told her.

"'Your partner'?"

"Mother Nature. Under all those frightening-looking bandages, you're healing beautifully."

Every few days he would remove the bandages and examine her.

"Let me have a mirror," Eve pleaded.

But his answer was always the same: "Not yet."

He was the only company Eve had, and she began to look forward to his visits. He was an unprepossessing man, small and thin, with sandy, sparse hair and myopic brown eyes that constantly blinked. He was shy in Eve's presence, and it amused her.

"Have you ever been married?" she asked.

"No."

"Why not?"

"I – I don't know. I guess I wouldn't make a very good husband. I'm on emergency call a lot."

"But you must have a girl friend."

He was actually blushing. "Well, you know . . ."
"Tell me," Eve teased him.
"I don't have a regular girl friend."
"I'll bet all the nurses are crazy about you."
"No. I'm afraid I'm not a very romantic kind of person."
To say the least, Eve thought. And yet, when she discussed Keith Webster with the nurses and interns who came in to perform various indignities on her body, they spoke of him as though he were some kind of god.
"The man is a miracle worker," one intern said. "There's nothing he can't do with a human face."
They told her about his work with deformed children and criminals, but when Eve asked Keith Webster about it, he dismissed the subject with, "Unfortunately, the world judges people by their looks. I try to help those who were born with physical deficiencies. It can make a big difference in their lives."
Eve was puzzled by him. He was not doing it for the money or the glory. He was totally selfless. She had never met anyone like him, and she wondered what motivated him. But it was an idle curiosity. She had no interest in Keith Webster, except for what he could do for her.

Fifteen days after Eve checked into the hospital, she was moved to a private clinic in upstate New York.
"You'll be more comfortable here," Dr. Webster assured her.
Eve knew it was much farther for him to travel to see her, and yet he still appeared every day.
"Don't you have any other patients?" Eve asked.
"Not like you."

Five weeks after Eve entered the clinic, Keith Webster removed the bandages. He turned her head from side to side. "Do you feel any pain?" he asked.
"No."
"Any tightness?"
"No."
Dr. Webster looked up at the nurse. "Bring Miss Blackwell a mirror."
Eve was filled with a sudden fear. For weeks she had been longing to look at herself in a mirror. Now that the moment was here, she was terrified. She wanted her own face, not the face of some stranger.
When Dr. Webster handed her the mirror, she said faintly, "I'm afraid – "
"Look at yourself," he said gently.
She raised the mirror slowly. It was a miracle! There was no change at all; it was her face. She searched for the signs of scars. There were none. Her eyes filled with tears.
She looked up and said, "Thank you," and reached out to give Keith Webster

a kiss. It was meant to be a brief thank-you kiss, but she could feel his lips hungry on hers.

He pulled away, suddenly embarrassed. "I'm – I'm glad you're pleased," he said.

Pleased! "Everyone was right. You *are* a miracle worker."

He said shyly, "Look what I had to work with."

31

George Mellis had been badly shaken by what had happened. He had come perilously close to destroying everything he wanted. George had not been fully aware before of how much the control of Kruger-Brent, Ltd., meant to him. He had been satisfied to live on gifts from lonely ladies, but he was married to a Blackwell now, and within his reach was a company larger than anything his father had ever conceived of. *Look at me, Papa. I'm alive again. I own a company bigger than yours.* It was no longer a game. He knew he would kill to get what he wanted.

George devoted himself to creating the image of the perfect husband. He spent every possible moment with Alexandra. They breakfasted together, he took her out to lunch and he made it a point to be home early every evening. On weekends they went to the beach house Kate Blackwell owned in East Hampton, on Long Island, or flew to Dark Harbor in the company Cessna 620. Dark Harbor was George's favorite. He loved the rambling old house, with its beautiful antiques and priceless paintings. He wandered through the vast rooms. *Soon all this will be mine*, he thought. It was a heady feeling.

George was also the perfect grandson-in-law. He paid a great deal of attention to Kate. She was eighty-one, chairman of the board of Kruger-Brent, Ltd., and a remarkably strong, vital woman. George saw to it that he and Alexandra dined with her once a week, and he telephoned the old woman every few days to chat with her. He was carefully building up the picture of a loving husband and caring grandson-in-law.

No one would ever suspect him of murdering two people he loved so much.

George Mellis's sense of satisfaction was abruptly shattered by a telephone call from Dr. John Harley.

"I've made arrangements for you to see a psychiatrist. Dr. Peter Templeton."

George made his voice warm and ingratiating. "That's really not necessary any more, Dr. Harley. I think – "

"I don't give a damn what you think. We have an agreement – I don't report you to the police, and you consult a psychiatrist. If you wish to break that agree – ”

"No, no," George said hastily. "If that's what you want, fine."

"Dr. Templeton's telephone number is five-five-five-three-one-six-one. He's expecting your call. Today." And Dr. Harley slammed down the receiver.

The damned busybody, George thought angrily. The last thing in the world he needed was to waste time with a shrink, but he could not risk Dr. Harley's talking. He would call this Dr. Templeton, see him once or twice and that would be the end of it.

Eve telephoned George at the office. "I'm home."

"Are you – ?" He was afraid to ask. "All right?"

"Come and see for yourself. Tonight."

"It's difficult for me to get away just now. Alex and I – "

"Eight o'clock."

He could hardly believe it. Eve stood in front of him, looking just as beautiful as ever. He studied her face closely and could find no sign of the terrible damage he had inflicted upon her.

"It's incredible! You – you look exactly the same."

"Yes. I'm still beautiful, aren't I, George?" She smiled, a cat smile, thinking of what she planned to do to him. He was a sick animal, not fit to live. He would pay in full for what he had done to her, but not yet. She still needed him. They stood there, smiling at each other.

"Eve, I can't tell you how sorry I – "

She held up a hand. "Let's not discuss it. It's over. Nothing has changed."

But George remembered that something had changed. "I got a call from Harley," he said. "He's arranged for me to see some damned psychiatrist."

Eve shook her head. "No. Tell him you haven't time."

"I tried. If I don't go, he'll turn in a report of the – the accident to the police."

"Damn!"

She stood there, deep in thought. "Who is he?"

"The psychiatrist? Someone named Templeton. Peter Templeton."

"I've heard of him. He has a good reputation."

"Don't worry. I can just lie on his couch for fifty minutes and say nothing. If – "

Eve was not listening. An idea had come to her, and she was exploring it.

She turned to George. "This may be the best thing that could have happened."

Peter Templeton was in his middle thirties, just over six feet, with broad shoulders, clean-cut features and inquisitive blue eyes, and he looked more like a quarterback than a doctor. At the moment, he was frowning at a notation on his schedule: *George Mellis – grandson-in-law of Kate Blackwell.*

The problems of the rich held no interest for Peter Templeton. Most of his colleagues were delighted to get socially prominent patients. When Peter Templeton had first begun his practice, he had had his share, but he had quickly found he was unable to sympathize with their problems. He had dowagers in his office literally screaming because they had not been invited to some social event, financiers threatening to commit suicide because they had lost money in the stock market, overweight matrons who alternated between feasting and fat farms. The world was full of problems, and Peter Templeton had long since decided that these were not the problems he was interested in helping to solve.

George Mellis. Peter had reluctantly agreed to see him only because of his respect for Dr. John Harley. "I wish you'd send him somewhere else, John," Peter Templeton had said. "I really have a full schedule."

"Consider this a favor, Peter."

"What's his problem?"

"That's your department. I'm just an old country doctor."

"All right," Peter had agreed. "Have him call me."

Now he was here. Dr. Templeton pressed down the button on the intercom on his desk. "Send Mr. Mellis in."

Peter Templeton had seen photographs of George Mellis in newspapers and magazines, but he was still unprepared for the overpowering vitality of the man. He gave new meaning to the word *charisma*.

They shook hands. Peter said, "Sit down, Mr. Mellis."

George looked at the couch. "Over there?"

"Wherever you're comfortable."

George took the chair opposite the desk. George looked at Peter Templeton and smiled. He had thought he would dread this moment, but after his talk with Eve, he had changed his mind. Dr. Templeton was going to be his ally, his witness.

Peter studied the man opposite him. When patients came to see him for the first time, they were invariably nervous. Some covered it up with bravado, others were silent or talkative or defensive. Peter could detect no signs of nervousness in this man. On the contrary, he seemed to be enjoying himself. *Curious*, Peter thought.

"Dr. Harley tells me you have a problem."

George sighed. "I'm afraid I have two."

"Why don't you tell me about them?"

"I feel so ashamed. That's why I – I insisted on coming to see you." He leaned forward in his chair and said earnestly, "I did something I've never done before in my life, Doctor. I struck a woman."

Peter waited.

"We were having an argument and I blacked out, and when I came to, I had . . . hit her." He let his voice break' slightly. "It was terrible."

Peter Templeton's inner voice told him he already knew what George Mellis's problem was. He enjoyed beating up women.

"Was it your wife you struck?"

"My sister-in-law."

Peter had occasionally come across items about the Blackwell twins in newspapers or magazines when they appeared at charity events or society affairs. They were identical, Peter recalled, and strikingly beautiful. So this man had hit his sister-in-law. Peter found that mildly interesting. He also found it interesting that George Mellis made it sound as though he had merely slapped her once or twice. If that had been true, John Harley would not have insisted that Peter see Mellis.

"You say you hit her. Did you hurt her?"

"As a matter of fact, I hurt her pretty badly. As I told you, Doctor, I blacked out. When I came to, I – I couldn't believe it."

When I came to. The classic defense. I didn't do it, my subconscious did it.

"Do you have any idea what caused that reaction?"

"I've been under a terrible strain lately. My father has been seriously ill. He's had several heart attacks. I've been deeply concerned about him. We're a close family."

"Is your father here?"

"He's in Greece."

That Mellis. "You said you had two problems."

"Yes. My wife, Alexandra . . ." He stopped.

"You're having marital problems?"

"Not in the sense you mean. We love each other very much. It's just that – " He hesitated. "Alexandra hasn't been well lately."

"Physically?"

"Emotionally. She's constantly depressed. She keeps talking about suicide."

"Has she sought professional help?"

George smiled sadly. "She refuses."

Too bad, Peter thought. *Some Park Avenue doctor is being cheated out of a fortune*. "Have you discussed this with Dr. Harley?"

"No."

"Since he's the family doctor, I would suggest you speak with him. If he feels it's necessary, he'll recommend a psychiatrist."

George Mellis said nervously, "No. I don't want Alexandra to feel I'm discussing her behind her back. I'm afraid Dr. Harley would – "

"That's all right, Mr. Mellis. I'll give him a call."

"Eve, we're in trouble," George snapped. "Big trouble."

"What happened?"

"I did exactly as you told me. I said I was concerned about Alexandra, that she was suicidal."

"And?"

"The sonofabitch is going to call John Harley and discuss it with him!"

"Oh, Christ! We can't let him."

Eve began to pace. She stopped suddenly. "All right. I'll handle Harley. Do you have another appointment with Templeton?"

"Yes."

"Keep it."

The following morning Eve went to see Dr. Harley at his office. John Harley liked the Blackwell family. He had watched the children grow up. He had gone through the tragedy of Marianne's death and the attack on Kate, and putting Tony away in a sanitarium. Kate had suffered so much. And then the rift between Kate and Eve. He could not imagine what had caused it, but it was none of his business. His business was to keep the family physically healthy.

When Eve walked into his office, Dr. Harley looked at her and said, "Keith Webster did a fantastic job!" The only telltale mark was a very thin, barely visible red scar across her forehead. Eve said, "Dr. Webster is going to remove the scar in a month or so."

Dr. Harley patted Eve's arm. "It only makes you more beautiful, Eve. I'm very pleased." He motioned her to a chair. "What can I do for you?"

"This isn't about me, John. It's about Alex."

Dr. Harley frowned. "Is she having a problem? Something to do with George?"

"Oh, no," Eve said quickly. "George is behaving perfectly. In fact, it's George who's concerned about her. Alex has been acting strangely lately. She's been very depressed. Suicidal, even."

Dr. Harley looked at Eve and said flatly, "I don't believe it. That doesn't sound like Alexandra."

"I know. I didn't believe it either, so I went to see her. I was shocked by the change in her. She's in a state of deep depression. I'm really worried, John. I can't go to Gran about it – That's why I came to you. You've got to do something." Her eyes misted. "I've lost my grandmother. I couldn't bear to lose my sister."

"How long has this been going on?"

"I'm not sure. I pleaded with her to talk to you about it. At first she refused, but I finally persuaded her. You've got to help her."

"Of course I will. Have her come in tomorrow morning. And try not to worry, Eve. There are new medications that work miracles."

Dr. Harley walked her to the door of his office. He wished Kate were not so unforgiving. Eve was such a caring person.

When Eve returned to her apartment, she carefully cold-creamed away the red scar on her forehead.

*

The following morning at ten o'clock, Dr. Harley's receptionist announced, "Mrs. George Mellis is here to see you, Doctor."

"Send her in."

She walked in slowly, unsure of herself. She was pale, and there were dark circles under her eyes.

John Harley took her hand and said, "It's good to see you, Alexandra. Now what's this I hear about your having problems?"

Her voice was low. "I feel foolish bothering you, John. I'm sure there's nothing wrong with me. If Eve hadn't insisted, I never would have come. I feel fine, physically."

"What about emotionally?"

She hesitated. "I don't sleep very well."

"What else?"

"You'll think I'm a hypochondriac. . . ."

"I know you better than that, Alexandra."

She lowered her eyes. "I feel depressed all the time. Sort of anxious and . . . tired. George goes out of his way to make me happy and to think up things for us to do together and places for us to go. The problem is that I don't feel like doing anything or going anywhere. Everything seems so-hopeless."

He was listening to every word, studying her. "Anything else?"

"I – I think about killing myself." Her voice was so soft he could barely hear her. She looked up at him and said, "Am I going crazy?"

He shook his head. "No. I don't think you're going crazy. Have you ever heard of anhedonia?"

She shook her head.

"It's a biological disturbance that causes the symptoms you've described. It's a fairly common condition, and there are some new drugs that make it easy to treat. These drugs have no side effects, and they're effective. I'm going to examine you, but I'm sure we won't find anything really wrong."

When the examination was completed and she had gotten dressed again, Dr. Harley said, "I'm going to give you a prescription for Wellbutrin. It's part of a new generation of anti-depressants – one of the new wonder drugs."

She watched listlessly as he wrote out a prescription.

"I want you to come back and see me a week from today. In the meantime, if you have any problems, call me, day or night." He handed her the prescription.

"Thank you, John," she said. "I just hope these will stop the dream."

"What dream?"

"Oh, I thought I told you. It's the same one every night. I'm on a boat and it's windy, and I hear the sea calling. I walk to the rail and I look down and I see myself in the water, drowning. . . ."

She walked out of Dr. Harley's office and onto the street. She leaned against the building, taking deep breaths. *I did it*, Eve thought exultantly. *I got away with it*. She threw the prescription away.

32

Kate Blackwell was tired. The meeting had gone on too long. She looked around the conference table at the three men and three women on the executive board. They all seemed fresh and vital. *So its not the meeting that has been going on too long*, Kate thought. *I've gone on too long. I'll be eighty-two. I'm getting old.* The thought depressed her, not because she had any fear of dying, but because she was not ready yet. She refused to die until Kruger-Brent, Ltd., had a member of the Blackwell family running it. After the bitter disappointment with Eve, Kate had tried to build her future plans around Alexandra.

"You know I would do anything for you, Gran, but I'm simply not interested in becoming involved with the company. George would be an excellent executive . . ."

"Do you agree, Kate?" Brad Rogers was addressing her.

The question shook Kate out of her reverie. She looked toward Brad guiltily. "I'm sorry. What was the question?"

"We were discussing the Deleco merger." His voice was patient. Brad Rogers was concerned about Kate Blackwell. In recent months she had started day-dreaming during board meetings, and then just when Brad Rogers decided Kate was becoming senile and should retire from the board, she would come up with some stunning insight that would make everyone wonder why *he* had not thought of it. She was an amazing woman. He thought of their brief, long-ago affair and wondered again why it had ended so abruptly.

It was George Mellis's second visit to Peter Templeton. "Has there been much violence in your past, Mr. Mellis?"

George shook his head. "No. I abhor violence." *Make a note of that, you smug sonofabitch. The coroner is going to ask you about that.*

"You told me your mother and father never physically punished you."

"That is correct."

"Would you say you were an obedient child?"

Careful. There are traps here. "About average, I suppose."

"The average child usually gets punished at some time or another for breaking the rules of the grown-up world."

George gave him a deprecating smile. "I guess I didn't break any rules."

He's lying, Peter Templeton thought. *The question is why? What is he concealing?* He recalled the conversation he had had with Dr. Harley after the first session with George Mellis.

"He said he hit his sister-in-law, John, and – "

"*Hit* her!" John Harley's voice was filled with indignation. "It was butchery, Peter. He smashed her cheekbone, broke her nose and three ribs, and burned her buttocks and the soles of her feet with cigarettes."

Peter Templeton felt a wave of disgust wash over him. "He didn't mention that to me."

"I'll bet he didn't," Dr. Harley snapped. "I told him if he didn't go to you, I was going to report him to the police."

Peter remembered George's words: *I feel ashamed. That's why I insisted on coming to see you.* So he had lied about that, too.

"Mellis told me his wife is suffering from depression, that she's talking about suicide."

"Yes, I can vouch for that. Alexandra came to see me a few days ago. I prescribed Wellbutrin. I'm quite concerned about her. What's your impression of George Mellis?"

Peter said slowly, "I don't know yet. I have a feeling he's dangerous."

Dr. Keith Webster was unable to get Eve Blackwell out of his mind. She was like a beautiful goddess, unreal and untouchable. She was outgoing and vivacious and stimulating, while he was shy and dull and drab. Keith Webster had never married, because he had never found a woman he felt was unworthy enough to be his wife. Apart from his work, his self-esteem was negligible. He had grown up with a fiercely domineering mother and a weak, bullied father. Keith Webster's sexual drive was low, and what little there was of it was sublimated in his work. But now he began to dream about Eve Blackwell, and when he recalled the dreams in the morning, he was embarrassed. She was completely healed and there was no reason for him to see her anymore, yet he knew he had to see her.

He telephoned her at her apartment. "Eve? This is Keith Webster. I hope I'm not disturbing you. I – er – I was thinking about you the other day, and I – I was just wondering how you were getting along?"

"Fine, thank you, Keith. How are *you* getting along?" There was that teasing note in her voice again.

"Jus – just fine," he said. There was a silence. He summoned up his nerve. "I guess you're probably too busy to have lunch with me."

Eve smiled to herself. He was such a deliciously timid little man. It would be amusing. "I'd love to, Keith."

"Would you really?" She could hear the note of surprise in his voice. "When?"

"What about tomorrow?"

"It's a date." He spoke quickly, before she could change her mind.

Eve enjoyed the luncheon. Dr. Keith Webster acted like a young schoolboy in love. He dropped his napkin, spilled his wine and knocked over a vase of flowers. Watching him, Eve thought with amusement, *No one would ever guess what a brilliant surgeon he is.*

When the luncheon was over, Keith Webster asked shyly, "Could we – could we do this again sometime?"

She replied with a straight face, "We'd better not, Keith. I'm afraid I might fall in love with you."

He blushed wildly, not knowing what to say.

Eve patted his hand. "I'll never forget you."

He knocked over the vase of flowers again.

John Harley was having lunch at the hospital cafeteria when Keith Webster joined him.

Keith said, "John, I promise to keep it confidential; but I'd feel a lot better if you told me the truth about what happened to Eve Blackwell."

Harley hesitated, then shrugged. "All right. It was her brother-in-law, George Mellis."

And Keith Webster felt that now he was sharing a part of Eve's secret world.

George Mellis was impatient. "The money is there, the will has been changed – What the hell are we waiting for?"

Eve sat on the couch, her long legs curled up under her, watching him as he paced.

"I want to get this thing over with, Eve."

He's losing his nerve, Eve thought. He was like a deadly coiled snake. Dangerous. She had made a mistake with him once by goading him too far, and it had almost cost her her life. She would not make that mistake again.

"I agree with you," she said slowly. "I think it's time."

He stopped pacing. "When?"

"Next week."

The session was almost over and George Mellis had not once mentioned his wife. Now, suddenly he said, "I'm worried about Alexandra, Dr. Templeton. Her depression seems to be worse. Last night she kept talking about drowning. I don't know what to do."

"I spoke to John Harley. He's given her some medication he thinks will help her."

"I hope so, Doctor," George said earnestly. "I couldn't stand it if anything happened to her."

And Peter Templeton, his ear attuned to the unspoken words, had the uneasy feeling he was witnessing a charade. There was a deadly violence in this man. "Mr. Mellis, how would you describe your past relationships with women?"

"Normal."

"Did you ever get angry with any of them, lose your temper?"

George Mellis saw where the questions were leading. "Never." *I'm too damned smart for you, Doc.* "I told you, I don't believe in violence."

It was butchery, Peter. He smashed her cheekbone, broke her nose and three ribs, and burned her buttocks and the soles of her feet with cigarettes.

"Sometimes," Peter said, "to some people violence provides a necessary outlet, an emotional release."

"I know what you mean. I have a friend who beats up whores."

I have a friend. An alarm signal. "Tell me about your friend."

"He hates prostitutes. They're always trying to rip him off. So when he finishes with them, he roughs them up a little – just to teach them a lesson." He looked at Peter's face, but saw no disapproval there. Emboldened, George went on. "I remember once he and I were in Jamaica together. This little black hooker took him up to a hotel room, and after she got his pants off, she told him she wanted more money." George smiled. "He beat the shit out of her. I'll bet she won't try that on anyone again."

He's psychotic, Peter Templeton decided. There was no friend, of course. He was boasting about himself, hiding behind an alter ego. The man was a megalomaniac, and a dangerous one.

Peter decided he had better have another talk with John Harley as quickly as possible.

The two men met for lunch at the Harvard Club. Peter Templeton was in a difficult position. He needed to get all the information he could about George Mellis without breaching the confidentiality of the doctor-patient relationship.

"What can you tell me about George Mellis's wife?" he asked Harley.

"Alexandra? She's lovely. I've taken care of her and her sister, Eve, since they were babies." He chuckled. "You hear about identical twins, but you never really appreciate what that means until you see those two together."

Peter asked slowly, "They're identical twins?"

"Nobody could ever tell them apart. They used to play all kinds of pranks when they were little tykes. I remember once when Eve was sick and supposed to get a shot, I somehow wound up giving it to Alexandra." He took a sip of his drink. "It's amazing. Now they're grown up, and I still can't tell one from the other."

Peter thought about that. "You said Alexandra came to see you because she was feeling suicidal."

"That's right."

"John, how do you know it was Alexandra?"

"That's easy," Dr. Harley said. "Eve still has a little scar on her forehead from the surgery after the beating George Mellis gave her."

So that was a blind alley. "I see."

"How are you getting along with Mellis?"

Peter hesitated, wondering how much he could say. "I haven't reached him. He's hiding behind a facade. I'm trying to break it down."

"Be careful, Peter. If you want my opinion, the man's insane." He was remembering Eve lying in bed, in a pool of blood.

"Both sisters are heir to a large fortune, aren't they?" Peter asked.

Now it was John Harley's turn to hesitate. "Well, it's private family business," he said, "but the answer is no. Their grandmother cut off Eve without a dime. Alexandra inherits everything."

I'm worried about Alexandra, Dr. Templeton. Her depression seems to be worse. She keeps talking about drowning. I couldn't stand it if anything happened to her.

It had sounded to Peter Templeton like a classic setup for murder – except that George Mellis was the heir to a large fortune of his own. There would be no reason for him to kill anyone for money. *You're imagining things*, Peter chided himself.

A woman was drowning in the cold sea, and he was trying to swim to her side, but the waves were too high, and she kept sinking under them and rising again. *Hold on*, he shouted. *I'm coming.* He tried to swim faster, but his arms and legs seemed leaden, and he watched as she went down again. When he reached the place where she had disappeared, he looked around and saw an enormous white shark bearing down on him. Peter Templeton woke up. He turned on the lights and sat up in bed, thinking about his dream.

Early the following morning, he telephoned Detective Lieutenant Nick Pappas.

Nick Pappas was a huge man, six feet four inches and weighing almost three hundred pounds. As any number of criminals could testify, not an ounce of it was fat. Lieutenant Pappas was with the homicide task force in the "silk stocking" district in Manhattan. Peter had met him several years earlier while testifying as a psychiatric expert in a murder trial, and he and Pappas had become friends. Pappas's passion was chess, and the two met once a month to play.

Nick answered the phone. "Homicide. Pappas."

"It's Peter, Nick."

"My friend! How go the mysteries of the mind?"

"Still trying to unravel them, Nick. How's Tina?"

"Fantastic. What can I do for you?"

"I need some information. Do you still have connections in Greece?"

"Do I!" Pappas moaned. "I got a hundred relatives over there, and they all need money. The stupid part is I send it to them. Maybe you oughta analyze me."

"Too late," Peter told him. "You're a hopeless case."
"That's what Tina keeps telling me. What information do you need?"
"Have you ever heard of George Mellis?"
"The food family?"
"Yes."
"He's not exactly on my beat, but I know who he is. What about him?"
"I'd like to know if he has any money."
"You must be kiddin". His family – "
"I mean money of his own."
"I'll check it out, Peter, but it'll be a waste of time. The Mellises are rich – rich."
"By the way, if you have anyone question George Mellis's father, tell him to handle it gently. The old man's had several heart attacks."
"Okay. I'll put it out on the wire."
Peter remembered the dream. "Nick, would you mind making a telephone call instead? Today?"
There was a different note in Pappas's voice. "Is there anything you'd like to tell me, Peter?"
"There's nothing to tell. I just want to satisfy my curiosity. Charge the phone call to me."
"Damn right I will – and the dinner you're gonna buy me when you tell me what the fuck this is all about."
"Deal." Peter Templeton hung up. He felt a little better.

Kate Blackwell was not feeling well. She was at her desk talking on the telephone when she felt the sudden attack. The room started to spin, and she gripped her desk tightly until everything righted itself again.
Brad came into the office. He took one look at her pale face and asked, "Are you all right, Kate?"
She let go of the desk. "Just a little dizzy spell. Nothing important."
"How long since you've had a medical checkup?"
"I don't have time for that nonsense, Brad."
"Find time. I'm going to have Annette call and make an appointment for you with John Harley."
"Bloody hell, Brad. Stop fussing, will you please?"
"Will you go see him?"
"If it will get you off my back."

The following morning Peter Templeton's secretary said, "Detective Pappas is calling on line one."
Peter picked up the phone. "Hello, Nick."
"I think you and I better have a little talk, my friend."

Peter felt a sudden anxiety stirring in him. "Did you talk to someone about Mellis?"

"I talked to Old Man Mellis himself. First of all, he's never had a heart attack in his life, and second, he said as far as he's concerned, his son George is dead. He cut him off without a dime a few years ago. When I asked why, the old man hung up on me. Then I called one of my old buddies at headquarters in Athens. Your George Mellis is a real beauty. The police know him well. He gets his kicks beating up girls and boys. His last victim before he left Greece was a fifteen-year-old male prostitute. They found his body in a hotel, and tied him in with Mellis. The old man bought somebody off, and Georgie boy got his ass kicked out of Greece. For good. Does that satisfy you?"

It did more than satisfy Peter; it terrified him. "Thanks, Nick. I owe you one."

"Oh, no, pal. I think I'd like to collect on *this* one. If your boy's on the loose again, you'd better tell me."

"I will as soon as I can, Nick. Give my love to Tina." And Peter hung up. He had a lot to think about. George Mellis was coming in at noon.

Dr. John Harley was in the middle of an examination when his receptionist said, "Mrs. George Mellis is here to see you, Doctor. She has no appointment, and I told her your schedule is – "

John Harley said, "Bring her in the side door and put her in my office."

Her face was paler than the last time, and the shadows under her eyes were darker. "I'm sorry to barge in on you like this, John, but – "

"That's all right, Alexandra. What's the problem?"

"Everything. I – I feel awful."

"Have you been taking the Wellbutrin regularly?"

"Yes."

"And you still feel depressed?"

Her hands were clenched. "It's worse than depression. It's – I feel desperate. I feel as though I have no control over anything anymore. I can't stand myself. I'm afraid I'm – I'm going to do something terrible."

Dr. Harley said reassuringly, "There's nothing physically wrong with you. I'll stake my reputation on that. It's all emotional. I'm going to switch you to another drug, Nomifensine. It's very effective. You should notice a change within a few days." He wrote out a prescription and handed it to her. "If you don't feel better by Friday, I want you to call me. I may want to send you to a psychiatrist."

Thirty minutes later, back in her apartment, Eve removed the pale foundation cream from her face and wiped away the smudges under her eyes.

The pace was quickening.

*

George Mellis sat opposite Peter Templeton, smiling and confident.

"How are you feeling today?"

"Much better, Doctor. These few sessions we've had have helped more than you know."

"Have they? In what way?"

"Oh, just having someone to talk to. That's the principle the Catholic Church is built on, isn't it? Confession?"

"I'm glad you feel the sessions have been helpful. Is your wife feeling better?"

George frowned. "I'm afraid not. She saw Dr. Harley again, but she's talking about suicide more and more. I may take her away somewhere. I think she needs a change."

It seemed to Peter that there was an ominous foreboding in those words. Could it be his imagination?

"Greece is a very relaxing place," Peter said casually. "Have you taken her there to meet your family?"

"Not yet. They're dying to meet Alex." He grinned. "The only problem is that every time Pop and I get together, he keeps trying to talk me into coming back and taking over the family business."

And at that moment, Peter knew that Alexandra Mellis was in real danger.

Long after George Mellis had left, Peter Templeton sat in his office going over his notes. Finally, he reached for the telephone and dialed a number.

"I want you to do me a favor, John. Can you find out where George Mellis took his wife on their honeymoon?"

"I can tell you right now. I gave them some shots before they left. They went to Jamaica."

I have a friend who beats up whores. . . . I remember once we were in Jamaica together. This little black whore took him up to a hotel room, and after she got his pants off she told him she wanted more . . . . He beat the shit out of her. I'll bet she won't try that on anyone again.

Still, there was no proof that George Mellis was planning to kill his wife. John Harley had verified that Alexandra Mellis was suicidal. *Its not my problem*, Peter tried to tell himself. But he knew it was his problem.

Peter Templeton had had to work his way through school. His father had been the caretaker of a college in a small town in Nebraska, and even with a scholarship, Peter had not been able to afford to go to one of the Ivy League medical schools. He had been graduated from the University of Nebraska with honors and had gone on to study psychiatry. He had been successful from the start. His secret was that he genuinely liked people; he cared what happened to them. Alexandra Mellis was not a patient, yet he was involved with her. She was a missing part of the puzzle, and meeting her face-to-face might help him solve it. He took out George Mellis's file, found his home number and telephoned Alexandra Mellis. A maid summoned her to the phone.

"Mrs. Mellis, my name is Peter Templeton. I'm – "

"Oh, I know who you are, Doctor. George has told me about you."

Peter was surprised. He would have bet that George Mellis would not have mentioned him to his wife. "I wondered if we could meet. Perhaps lunch?"

"Is it about George? Is something wrong?"

"No, nothing. I just thought we might have a talk."

"Yes, certainly, Dr. Templeton."

They made an appointment for the following day.

They were seated at a corner table at La Grenouille. From the moment Alexandra had walked into the restaurant, Peter had been unable to take his eyes off her. She was dressed simply in a white skirt and blouse that showed off her figure, and she wore a single strand of pearls around her neck. Peter looked for signs of the tiredness and depression Dr. Harley had mentioned. There were none. If Alexandra was aware of Peter's stare, she gave no sign of it.

"My husband is all right, isn't he, Dr. Templeton?"

"Yes." This was going to be much more difficult than Peter had anticipated. He was walking a very fine line. He had no right to violate the sanctity of the doctor-patient relationship, yet at the same time he felt that Alexandra Mellis must be warned.

After they had ordered, Peter said, "Did your husband tell you why he's seeing me, Mrs. Mellis?"

"Yes. He's been under a great strain lately. His partners at the brokerage firm where he works put most of the responsibility on his shoulders. George is very conscientious, as you probably know, Doctor."

It was incredible. She was completely unaware of the attack on her sister. *Why had no one told her?*

"George told me how much better he felt having someone he could discuss his problems with." She gave Peter a grateful smile. "I'm very pleased that you're helping him."

She was so innocent! She obviously idolized her husband. What Peter had to say could destroy her. How could he inform her that her husband was a psychopath who had murdered a young male prostitute, who had been banished by his family and who had brutally assaulted her sister? Yet, how could he not?

"It must be very satisfying being a psychiatrist," Alexandra went on. "You're able to help so many people."

"Sometimes we can," Peter said carefully. "Sometimes we can't."

The food arrived. They talked as they ate, and there was an easy rapport between them. Peter found himself enchanted by her. He suddenly became uncomfortably aware that he was envious of George Mellis.

"I'm enjoying this luncheon very much," Alexandra finally said, "but you wanted to see me for a reason, didn't you, Dr. Templeton?"

The moment of truth had arrived.

"As a matter of fact, yes. I – "

Peter stopped. His next words could shatter her life. He had come to this luncheon determined to tell her of his suspicions and suggest that her husband be put in an institution. Now that he had met Alexandra, he found it was not so simple. He thought again of George Mellis's words: *She's not any better. It's the suicidal thing that worries me*. Peter thought he had never seen a happier, more normal person. Was that a result of the medication she was taking? At least he could ask her about that. He said, "John Harley told me that you're taking – "

And George Mellis's voice boomed out. "There you are, darling! I called the house and they told me you'd be here." He turned to Peter. "Nice to see you, Dr. Templeton. May I join you?"

And the opportunity vanished.

"*Why* did he want to meet Alex?" Eve demanded.

"I haven't the slightest idea," George said. "Thank God she left a message where she would be in case I wanted her. With Peter Templeton, for Christ's sake! I got over there fast!"

"I don't like it."

"Believe me, there was no harm done. I questioned her afterward, and she told me they didn't discuss anything in particular."

"I think we'd better move up our plan."

George Mellis felt an almost sexual thrill at her words. He had been waiting so long for this moment. "When?"

"Now."

33

The dizzy spells were getting worse, and things were beginning to blur in Kate's mind. She would sit at her desk considering a proposed merger and suddenly realize the merger had taken place ten years earlier. It frightened her. She finally decided to take Brad Rogers's advice to see John Harley.

It had been a long time since Dr. Harley had been able to persuade Kate Blackwell to have a checkup, and he took full advantage of her visit. He examined her thoroughly, and when he finished he asked her to wait for him in his office. John Harley was disturbed. Kate Blackwell was remarkably alert for her age, but there were disquieting signs. There was a definite hardening of the arteries, which would account for her occasional dizziness and weakened memory. She should have retired years ago, and yet she hung on tenaciously, unwilling to give the reins to anyone else. *Who am I to talk?* he thought. *I should have retired ages ago.*

Now, with the results of the examination in front of him, John Harley said, "I wish I were in your condition, Kate."

"Cut the soft-soap, John. What's my problem?"

"Age, mostly. There's a little hardening of the arteries, and – "

"Arteriosclerosis?"

"Oh. Is that the medical term for it?" Dr. Harley asked. "Whatever it is, you've got it."

"How bad is it?"

"For your age, I'd say it was pretty normal. These things are all relative."

"Can you give me something to stop these bloody dizzy spells? I hate fainting in front of a roomful of men. It looks bad for my sex."

He nodded. "I don't think that will be any problem. When are you going to retire, Kate?"

"When I have a great-grandson to take over the business."

The two old friends who had known each other for so many years sized each other up across the desk. John Harley had not always agreed with Kate, but he had always admired her courage.

As though reading his mind, Kate sighed, "Do you know one of the great disappointments of my life, John? Eve. I really cared for that child. I wanted to give her the world, but she never gave a damn about anyone but herself."

"You're wrong, Kate. Eve cares a great deal about you."

"Like bloody hell she does."

"I'm in a position to know. Recently she" – he had to choose his words carefully – "suffered a terrible accident. She almost died."

Kate felt her heart lurch. "Why – why didn't you tell me?"

"She wouldn't let me. She was so concerned you would be worried that she made me swear not to say a word."

"Oh, my God." It was an agonized whisper. "Is – is she all right?" Kate's voice was hoarse.

"She's fine now."

Kate sat, staring into space. "Thank you for telling me, John. Thank you."

"I'll write out a prescription for those pills." When he finished writing the prescription, he looked up. Kate Blackwell had left.

Eve opened the door and stared unbelievingly. Her grandmother was standing there, stiff and straight as always, allowing no sign of frailty to show.

"May I come in?" Kate asked.

Eve stepped aside, unable to take in what was happening. "Of course."

Kate walked in and looked around the small apartment, but she made no comment. "May I sit down?"

"I'm sorry. Please do. Forgive me – this is so – Can I get you something? Tea, coffee, anything?"

"No, thank you. Are you well, Eve?"

"Yes, thank you. I'm fine."

"I just came from Dr. John. He told me you had been in a terrible accident."

Eve watched her grandmother cautiously, not sure what was coming. "Yes . . ."

"He said you were . . . near death. And that you would not allow him to tell me because you didn't want to worry me."

So that was it. Eve was on surer ground now. "Yes, Gran."

"That would indicate to me," Kate's voice was suddenly choked, "that – that you cared."

Eve started to cry from relief. "Of course I care. I've always cared."

And an instant later, Eve was in her grandmother's arms. Kate held Eve very close and pressed her lips to the blond head in her lap. Then she whispered, "I've been such a damned old fool. Can you ever forgive me?" Kate pulled out a linen handkerchief and blew her nose. "I was too hard on you," she declared. "I couldn't bear it if anything had happened to you."

Eve stroked her grandmother's blue-veined hand soothingly and said, "I'm all right, Gran. Everything's fine."

Kate was on her feet, blinking back tears. "We'll have a fresh start, all right?" She pulled Eve up to face her. "I've been stubborn and unbending, like my father. I'm going to make amends for that. The first thing I'm going to do is put you back in my will, where you belong."

What was happening was too good to be true! "I – I don't care about the money. I only care about you."

"You're my heiress – you and Alexandra. You two are all the family I have."

"I'm getting along fine," Eve said, "but if it will make you happy – "

"It will make me very happy, darling. Very happy, indeed. When can you move back into the house?"

Eve hesitated for only a moment. "I think it would be better if I stayed here, but I'll see you as often as you want to see me. Oh, Gran, you don't know how lonely I've been."

Kate took her granddaughter's hand and said, "Can you forgive me?"

Eve looked her in the eye and said solemnly, "Of course, I can forgive you."

The moment Kate left, Eve mixed herself a stiff Scotch and water and sank down onto the couch to relive the incredible scene that had just occurred. She could have shouted aloud with joy. She and Alexandra were now the sole heirs to the Blackwell fortune. It would be easy enough to get rid of Alexandra. It was George Mellis Eve was concerned about. He had suddenly become a hindrance.

"There's been a change of plans," Eve told George. "Kate has put me back in her will."

George paused in the middle of lighting a cigarette. "Really? Congratulations."

"If anything happened to Alexandra now, it would look suspicious. So we'll take care of her later when – "

"I'm afraid later doesn't suit me."

"What do you mean?"

"I'm not stupid, darling. If anything happens to Alexandra, *I'll* inherit her stock. You want me out of the picture, don't you?"

Eve shrugged. "Let's say you're an unnecessary complication. I'm willing to make a deal with you. Get a divorce, and as soon as I come into the money, I'll give you – "

He laughed. "You're funny. It's no good, baby. Nothing has changed. Alex and I have a date in Dark Harbor Friday night. I intend to keep it."

Alexandra was overjoyed when she heard the news about Eve and her grandmother. "Now we're a family again," she said.

The telephone.

"Hello. I hope I'm not disturbing you, Eve. It's Keith Webster."

He had started telephoning her two or three times a week. At first his clumsy ardor had amused Eve, but lately he had become a nuisance.

"I can't talk to you now," Eve said. "I was just going out the door."

"Oh." His voice was apologetic. "Then I won't keep you. I have two tickets for the horse show next week. I know you love horses, and I thought – "

"Sorry. I will probably be out of town next week."

"I see." She could hear the disappointment in his voice. "Perhaps the following week, then. I'll get tickets to a play. What would you like to see?"

"I've seen them all," Eve said curtly. "I have to run." She replaced the receiver. It was time to get dressed. She was meeting Rory McKenna, a young actor she had seen in an off-Broadway play. He was five years younger than she, and he was like an insatiable wild stallion! Eve visualized his making love to her, and she felt a moisture between her legs. She looked forward to an exciting evening.

On his way home, George Mellis stopped to buy flowers for Alexandra. He was in an exuberant mood. It was a delicious irony that the old lady had put Eve back in her will, but it changed nothing. After Alexandra's accident, he would take care of Eve. The arrangements were all made. On Friday Alexandra would be waiting for him at Dark Harbor. "Just the two of us," he had pleaded as he kissed her. "Get rid of all the servants, darling."

Peter Templeton was unable to get Alexandra Mellis out of his mind. He heard the echo of George Mellis's words: *I may take her away somewhere. I think she needs a change.* Every instinct told Peter that Alexandra was in danger, yet he was powerless to act. He could not go to Nick Pappas with his suspicions. He had no proof.

Across town, in the executive offices of Kruger-Brent, Ltd., Kate Blackwell was signing a new will, leaving the bulk of her estate to her two granddaughters.

In upstate New York, Tony Blackwell was standing before his easel in the garden of the sanitarium. The painting on the easel was a jumble of colors, the kind of painting an untalented child might do. Tony stepped back to look at it and smiled with pleasure.

Friday. 10:57 A.M.

At La Guardia Airport, a taxi pulled up in front of the Eastern Airlines shuttle terminal and Eve Blackwell got out. She handed the driver a hundred-dollar bill.

"Hey, I can't change this, lady," he said. "Have you got anything smaller?"

"No."

"Then you'll have to get change inside."

"I haven't time. I have to catch the next shuttle to Washington." She looked at the Baume & Mercier watch on her wrist and made a decision. "Keep the hundred dollars," she told the startled driver.

Eve hurried into the terminal. She half-walked and half-ran to the departure gate marked Washington Shuttle. "One round trip to Washington," Eve said breathlessly.

The man looked at the clock above his head. "You missed this one by two minutes. It's just taking off."

"I've got to be on that plane. I'm meeting – Isn't there anything you can do?" She was near panic.

"Take it easy, miss. There's another shuttle leaving in an hour."

"That's to – Damn it!"

He watched her regain control of herself.

"Very well. I'll wait. Is there a coffee shop around here?"

"No, ma'am. But there's a coffee machine down the corridor."

"Thank you."

He looked after her and thought, *What a beauty. I sure envy the guy she's in such a hurry to meet.*

*

Friday. 2:00 P.M.

It will be a second honeymoon, Alexandra thought. The idea excited her. *Get rid of all the servants. I want it to be just the two of us, angel. We'll have a lovely weekend.* And now Alexandra was leaving the brownstone, on her way to Dark Harbor to meet George. She was running behind schedule. She had had a luncheon engagement, and it had taken longer than Alexandra had planned. She said to the maid, "I'm going now. I'll be back Monday morning."

As Alexandra reached the front door, the telephone rang. *I'm late. Let it ring*, she thought, and hurried out the door.

Friday. 7:00 P.M.

George Mellis had examined Eve's plan over and over. There was not a single flaw in it. *There will be a motor launch waiting for you at Philbrook Cove. Take it to Dark Harbor and make sure you're not seen. Tie it to the stern of the Corsair. You'll take Alexandra for a moonlight sail. When you're out at sea, do whatever turns you on, George – just don't leave any traces of blood. Dump the body overboard, get into the launch and leave the* Corsair *adrift. You'll take the launch back to Philbrook Cove, then catch the Lincolnville ferry to Dark Harbor. Take a taxi to the house. Use some excuse to get the driver to go in so that you'll both notice the* Corsair *is missing from the dock. When you see that Alexandra is gone, you'll call the police. They'll never find Alexandra's body. The tide will wash it out to sea. Two eminent doctors will testify it was a probable suicide.*

He found the motorboat moored at Philbrook Cove, waiting for him, according to plan.

George crossed the bay without running lights, using the light of the moon to steer by. He passed a number of moored boats without being detected, and arrived at the dock at the Blackwell estate. He cut the motor and made the line fast to the *Corsair*, the large motor sailer.

She was talking on the telephone, waiting for him in the living room when George walked in. She waved to him, covered the receiver with her hand and mouthed, "It's Eve." She listened a moment, then, "I have to go now, Eve. My darling just arrived. I'll see you at lunch next week." She replaced the receiver and hurried over to hug George. "You're early. I'm so pleased."

"I got lonely for you, so I just dropped everything and came."

She kissed him. "I love you."

"I love you, *matia mou*. Did you get rid of the servants?"

She smiled. "It's just the two of us. Guess what? I made moussaka for you."

He traced a finger lightly across the nipples straining against her silk blouse. "Do you know what I've been thinking about all afternoon at that dreary office? Going for a sail with you. There's a brisk wind. Why don't we go out for an hour or two?"

"If you like. But my moussaka is – "

He cupped his hand over her breast. "Dinner can wait. I can't."

She laughed. "All right. I'll go change. It won't take me a minute."

"I'll race you."

He went upstairs to his clothes closet, changed into a pair of slacks, a sweater and boat shoes. Now that the moment was here, he was filled with a sense of wild anticipation, a feeling of excitement that was almost an explosion.

He heard her voice. "I'm ready, darling."

He turned. She stood in the doorway, dressed in a sweater, a pair of black slacks and canvas shoes. Her long, blond hair was tied back with a little blue ribbon. *My God, she's beautiful!* he thought. It seemed almost a shame to waste that beauty.

"So am I," George told her.

She noticed the motor launch secured to the stern of the yacht. "What's that for, darling?"

"There's a little island at the end of the bay that I've always wanted to explore," George explained. "We'll take the launch over to it so we won't have to worry about rocks."

He cast off the lines and powered slowly out of the slip. He nosed into the wind to raise the mainsail and jib, and the boat fell off on a starboard tack. The wind caught the large sails and the *Corsair* surged forward. George headed out to sea. As they cleared the breakwater, they were met with a stiff force-five wind, and the boat started heeling, its lee rail running under.

"It's wild and lovely," she called out. "I'm so happy, darling."

He smiled. "So am I."

In an odd way, it gave George Mellis pleasure that Alexandra was happy, that she was going to die happy. He scanned the horizon to make certain no other boats were close by. There were only faint lights from afar. It was time.

He put the boat on automatic pilot, took one last look around the empty horizon and walked over to the lee railing, his heart beginning to pound with excitement.

"Alex," he called. "Come look at this."

She made her way over to him and looked down at the cold, dark water racing below them.

"Come to me." His voice was a harsh command.

She moved into his arms, and he kissed her hard on the lips. His arms closed around her, hugging her, and he felt her body relax. He flexed his muscles and began to lift her in the air toward the railing.

She was fighting him suddenly. "George!"

He lifted her higher, and he felt her try to pull away, but he was too strong for her. She was almost on top of the railing now, her feet kicking wildly, and he braced himself to shove her over the side. At that instant, he felt a sudden white-hot pain in his chest. His first thought was, *I'm having a heart attack*. He opened his mouth to speak and blood came spurting out. He dropped his arms and looked down at his chest in disbelief. Blood was pouring from a gaping wound in it. He looked up, and she was standing there with a bloody knife in her hand, smiling at him.

George Mellis's last thought was, *Eve* . . .

34

It was ten o'clock in the evening when Alexandra arrived at the house at Dark Harbor. She had tried telephoning George there several times, but there had been no answer. She hoped he would not be angry because she had been detained. It had been a stupid mix-up. Early that afternoon, as Alexandra was leaving for Dark Harbor, the phone had rung. She had thought, *I'm late. Let it ring*, and had gone out to the car. The maid had come hurrying after her.

"Mrs. Mellis! It's your sister. She says it is urgent."

When Alexandra picked up the telephone, Eve said, "Darling, I'm in Washington, D.C. I'm having a terrible problem. I have to see you."

"Of course," Alexandra said instantly. "I'm leaving for Dark Harbor now to meet George, but I'll be back Monday morning and – "

"This can't wait." Eve sounded desperate. "Will you meet me at La Guardia Airport? I'll be on the five o'clock plane."

"I'd like to, Eve, but I told George – "

"This is an emergency, Alex. But, of course, if you're too busy . . ."

"Wait! All right. I'll be there."

"Thanks, darling. I knew I could count on you."

It was so seldom that Eve asked her for a favor, she could not refuse her. She would catch a later plane to the island. She telephoned George at the office to tell him she would be detained, but he was not in. She left a message with his secretary. An hour later she took a taxi to La Guardia in time to meet the five o'clock plane from Washington. Eve was not on it. Alexandra waited for two hours, and there was still no sign of Eve. Alexandra had no idea where to reach Eve in Washington. Finally, because there was nothing else she could do, Alexandra took a plane to the island. Now as she approached Cedar Hill House, she found it dark. Surely George should have arrived by now. Alexandra went from room to room, turning on the lights.

"George?"

There was no sign of him. She telephoned her home in Manhattan. The maid answered.

"Is Mr. Mellis there?" Alexandra asked.

"Why, no, Mrs. Mellis. He said you would both be away for the weekend."

"Thank you, Marie. He must have been detained somewhere."

There had to be a logical reason for his absence. Obviously some business had come up at the last minute and, as usual, the partners had asked George to handle it. He would be along at any moment. She dialed Eve's number.

"Eve!" Alexandra exclaimed. "What on earth happened to you?"

"What happened, to *you*? I waited at Kennedy, and when you didn't show up – "

"*Kennedy!* You said *La Guardia*."

"No, darling, Kennedy."

"But – " It did not matter any longer. "I'm sorry," Alexandra said. "I must have misunderstood. Are you all right?"

Eve said, "I am now. I've had a hellish time. I got involved with a man who's a big political figure in Washington. He's insanely jealous and – " She laughed. "I can't go into the details over the telephone. The phone company will take out both our phones. I'll tell you all about it Monday."

"All right," Alexandra said. She was enormously relieved.

"Have a nice weekend," Eve told her. "How's George?"

"He's not here." Alexandra tried to keep the note of concern out of her voice. "I suppose he got tied up on business and hasn't had a chance to call me."

"I'm sure you'll hear from him soon. Good night, darling."

"Good night, Eve."

Alexandra replaced the receiver and thought, *It would be nice if Eve found someone really wonderful. Someone as good and kind as George.* She looked at her watch. It was almost eleven o'clock. Surely he would have had a chance to call by now. She picked up the telephone and dialed the number of the brokerage firm. There was no answer. She telephoned his club. No, they had not seen Mr. Mellis. By midnight, Alexandra was alarmed, and by one A.M. she was in a state of panic. She was not sure what to do. It was possible that George was out with a client and could not get to a telephone, or perhaps he had had to fly somewhere and had not been able to reach her before he left. There was some simple explanation. If she called the police and George walked in, she would feel like a fool.

At 2:00 A.M. she telephoned the police. There was no police force on the island of Islesboro itself, and the closest station was in Waldo County.

A sleepy voice said, "Waldo County Sheriff's Department. Sergeant Lambert."

"This is Mrs. George Mellis at Cedar Hill House."

"Yes, Mrs. Mellis." The voice was instantly alert. "What can I do for you?"

"To tell you the truth, I'm not sure," Alexandra said hesitantly. "My husband was supposed to have met me at the house earlier this evening, and he – he hasn't shown up."

"I see"." There were all kinds of implications in that phrase. The sergeant knew at least three reasons why a husband could be away from home at two A.M. in the morning: blondes, brunets and redheads.

He said tactfully, "Is it possible he was detained on business somewhere?"

"He – he usually calls."

"Well, you know how it is, Mrs. Mellis. Sometimes you get in a situation where you can't call. I'm sure you'll be hearing from him."

Now she *did* feel like a fool. Of course there was nothing the police could do. She had read somewhere that a person had to be missing for twenty-four hours before the police would even start looking for him, and George was not *missing*, for heaven's sake. He was just late.

"I'm sure you're right," Alexandra said into the telephone. "I'm sorry to have troubled you."

"Not at all, Mrs. Mellis. I'll bet he'll be on the seven o'clock ferry first thing in the morning."

He was not on the seven o'clock ferry, or the one after that. Alexandra telephoned the Manhattan house again. George was not there.

A feeling of disaster began to grip Alexandra. George had been in an accident; he was in a hospital somewhere, ill or dead. If only there had not been the mix-up with Eve at the airport. Perhaps George had arrived at the house, and when he found she was not there, he had gone. But that left too many things unexplained. He would have left a note. He could have surprised burglars and been attacked or kidnapped. Alexandra went through the house, room by room, looking for any possible clue. Everything was intact. She went down to the dock. The *Corsair* was there, safely moored.

She telephoned the Waldo County Sheriff's Department again. Lieutenant Philip Ingram, a twenty-year veteran of the force, was on morning duty. He was already aware that George Mellis had not been home all night. It had been the chief topic of conversation around the station all morning, most of it ribald.

Now he said to Alexandra, "There's no trace of him at all, Mrs. Mellis? All rift. I'll come out there myself." He knew it would he a waste of time. Her old man was probably tomcatting around in some alley. *But when the Blackwells call, the peasants come* running, he thought wryly. Anyway, this was a nice lady. He had met her a few times over the years.

"Back in an hour or so," he told the desk sergeant.

Lieutenant Ingram listened to Alexandra's story, checked the house and the dock and reached the conclusion that Alexandra Mellis had a problem on her hands. George Mellis was to have met his wife the evening before at Dark Harbor, but he had not shown up. While it was not Lieutenant Ingram's problem, he knew it would do him no harm to be helpful to a member of the Blackwell family. Ingram telephoned the island airport and the ferry terminal at Lincolnville. George Mellis had used neither facility within the past twenty-four hours. "He didn't come to Dark Harbor," the lieutenant told Alexandra. *And where the hell did that leave things? Why would the man have dropped out of sight? In* the lieutenant's considered opinion, no man in his right mind would voluntarily leave a woman like Alexandra.

"We'll check the hospitals and mor – " He caught himself. "And other places, and I'll put out an APB on him."

Alexandra was trying to control her emotions, but he could see what an effort it was. "Thank you, Lieutenant. I don't have to tell you how much I'll appreciate anything you can do."

"That's my job," Lieutenant Ingram replied.

When Lieutenant Ingram returned to the station, he began calling hospitals and morgues. The responses were negative. There was no accident report on George Mellis. Lieutenant Ingram's next move was to call a reporter friend on the *Maine Courier*. After that, the lieutenant sent out a missing person all-points-bulletin.

The afternoon newspapers carried the story in headlines: HUSBAND OF BLACKWELL HEIRESS MISSING.

Peter Templeton first heard the news from Detective Nick Pappas.

"Peter, remember askin' me a while ago to do some checkin' on George Mellis?"

"Yes . . ."

"He's done a vanishing act."

"He's *what*?"

"Disappeared, vamoosed, gone." He waited while Peter digested the news.

"Did he take anything with him? Money, clothes, passport?"

"Nope. According to the report we got from Maine, Mr. Mellis just melted into thin air. You're his shrink. I thought you might have some idea why our boy would do a thing like that."

Peter said truthfully, "I haven't any idea, Nick."

"If you think of anything, let me know. There's gonna be a lot of heat on this."

"Yes," Peter promised. "I will."

Thirty minutes later, Alexandra Mellis telephoned Peter Templeton, and he could hear the shrill edge of panic in her voice. "I – George is missing. No one seems to know what happened to him. I was hoping he might have told you something that might have given you a clue or – " She broke off.

"I'm sorry, Mrs. Mellis. He didn't. I have no idea what could have happened."

"Oh."

Peter wished there was some way he could comfort her. "If I think of anything, I'll call you back. Where can I reach you?"

"I'm at Dark Harbor now, but I'm going to return to New York this evening. I'll be at my grandmother's."

Alexandra could not bear the thought of being alone. She had talked to Kate several times that morning. "Oh, darling, I'm sure there's nothing to worry about," Kate said. "He probably went off on some business deal and forgot to tell you."

Neither of them believed it.

Eve saw the story of George's disappearance on television. There were photographs of the exterior of Cedar Hill House, and pictures of Alexandra and George after their wedding ceremony. There was a close-up of George, looking upward, with his eyes wide. Somehow it reminded Eve of the look of surprise on his face just before he died.

The television commentator was saying, "There has been no evidence of foul play and no ransom demands have been made. The police speculate that George Mellis was possibly the victim of an accident and may be suffering from amnesia." Eve smiled in satisfaction.

They would never find the body. It had been swept out to sea with the tide. Poor George. He had followed her plan perfectly. But she had changed it. She had flown up to Maine and rented a motorboat at Philbrook Cove, to be held for "a friend." She had then rented a second boat from a nearby dock and taken it to Dark Harbor, where she had waited for George. He had been totally unsuspecting. She had been careful to wipe the deck clean before she returned the yacht to the dock. After that, it had been a simple matter to tow George's rented motorboat back to its pier, return her boat and fly back to New York to await the telephone call she knew Alexandra would make.

It was a perfect crime. The police would list it as a mysterious disappearance.

The announcer was saying, "In other news . . ." Eve switched the television set off.

She did not want to be late for her date with Rory McKenna.

At six o'clock the following morning, a fishing boat found George Mellis's body pinned against the breakwater at the mouth of Penebscot Bay. The early news reports called it a drowning and accidental death, but as more information came in, the tenor of the stories began to change. From the coroner's office came reports that what at first had been thought to have been shark bites were actually stab wounds. The evening newspaper editions screamed: MURDER SUSPECTED IN GEORGE MELLIS MYSTERY DEATH . . . MILLIONAIRE FOUND STABBED TO DEATH.

Lieutenant Ingram was studying the tide charts for the previous evening. When he was finished, he leaned back in his chair, a perplexed expression on his face. George Mellis's body would have been swept out to sea had it not been caught against the breakwater. What puzzled the lieutenant was that the body had to have been carried by the tide from the direction of Dark Harbor. Where George Mellis was not supposed to have been.

Detective Nick Pappas flew up to Maine to have a talk with Lieutenant Ingram.

"I think my department might be of some help to you in this case," Nick said. "We have some interesting background information on George Mellis. I know this is out of our jurisdiction, but if you were to ask for our cooperation, we'd be happy to give it to you, Lieutenant."

In the twenty years Lieutenant Ingram had been with the Waldo County Sheriff's Department, the only real excitement he had seen was when a drunken tourist shot a moose head off the wall of a local curio shop. The George Mellis murder was front-page news, and Lieutenant Ingram sensed a chance to make a name for himself. With a little luck, it could lead to a job as a detective in the New York City Police Department, where the action was. And so now he looked at Nick Pappas and murmured, "I don't know . . ."

As though reading his mind, Nick Pappas said, "We're not looking for credit. There's gonna be a hell of a lot of pressure on this one, and it would make life easier for us if we could wrap it up fast. I could start by filling you in on George Mellis's background."

Lieutenant Ingram decided he had nothing to lose. "OK, you've got a deal."

Alexandra was in bed, heavily sedated. Her mind stubbornly refused to accept the fact that George had been murdered. How could he have been? There was no reason in the world for anyone to kill him. The police had talked of a knife wound, but they were wrong about that. It had to be some kind of accident. *No one would want to kill him. . . . No one would want to kill him. . . .* The opiate Dr. Harley gave her finally took hold. She slept.

Eve had been stunned at the news that George's body had been found. *But perhaps it's a good thing*, Eve thought. *Alexandra will be the one under suspicion. She was there, on the island.*

Kate was seated next to Eve on the couch in the drawing room. The news had been a tremendous shock to Kate.

"Why would anyone want to murder George?" she asked.

Eve sighed. "I don't know, Gran. I just don't know. My heart breaks for poor Alex."

Lieutenant Philip Ingram was questioning the attendant on the Lincolnville-Islesboro ferry. "Are you positive neither Mr. or Mrs. Mellis came over on the ferry Friday afternoon?"

"They didn't come over on my shift, Phil, and I checked with the morning man, and he didn't see 'em neither. They had to have come in by plane."

"One more question, Lew. Did *any* strangers take the ferry across on Friday?"

"Hell," the attendant said, "you know we don't get no strangers goin' to the island this time of year. There might be a few tourists in the summer – but in *November?* She-e-e-it!"

Lieutenant Ingram went to talk to the manager of the Islesboro airport. "George Mellis sure didn't fly in that evening, Phil. He musta come over to the island by ferry."

"Lew said he didn't see him."

"Well, hell, he couldn't a *swum* over, now could he?"

"What about Mrs. Mellis?"

"Yep. She come in here in her Beechcraft about ten o'clock. I had my son, Charley, run her over to Cedar Hill from the airport."

"What kind of mood did Mrs. Mellis seem to be in?"

"Funny you should ask. She was as nervous as spit on a hot kettle. Even my boy noticed it. Usually she's calm, always has a pleasant word for everybody. But that night she was in a tearin' hurry."

"One more question. Did any strangers fly in that afternoon or evening? Any unfamiliar faces?"

He shook his head. "Nope. Just the regulars."

An hour later, Lieutenant Ingram was on the phone talking to Nick Pappas. "What I've got so far," he told the New York detective, "is damned confusing. Friday night Mrs. Mellis arrived by private plane at the Islesboro airport around ten o'clock, but her husband wasn't with her, and he didn't come in by plane or ferry. In fact, there's nothin' to show he was on the island at all that night."

"Except the tide."

"Yeah."

"Whoever killed him probably threw him overboard from a boat, figuring the tide would carry him out to sea. Did you check the *Corsair?*"

"I looked it over. No sign of violence, no bloodstains."

"I'd like to bring a forensics expert up there. Would you mind?"

"Not as long as you remember our little deal."

"I'll remember. See you tomorrow."

Nick Pappas and a team of experts arrived the following morning. Lieutenant Ingram escorted them to the Blackwell dock, where the *Corsair* was tied up. Two hours later, the forensics expert said, "Looks like we hit the jackpot, Nick. There are some bloodstains on the underside of the lee rail."

That afternoon, the police laboratory verified that the stains matched George Mellis's blood type.

Manhattan's "silk stocking" police precinct was busier than usual. A series of all-night drug busts had filled the prisoners' cage to capacity, and the holding cells were crowded with prostitutes, drunks and sex offenders. The noise and the stench competed for Peter Templeton's attention, as he was escorted through the din to Lieutenant Detective Pappas's office.

"Hey, Peter. Nice of you to drop by."

On the phone Pappas had said, "You're holdin' out on me, chum. Be at my office before six o'clock, or I'll send a fuckin' SWAT team to bring you in."

When his escort left the office, Peter asked, "What's this all about, Nick? What's bothering you?"

"I'll tell you what's botherin' me. Someone's being clever. Do you know what we've got? A dead man who vanished from an island he never went to."

"That doesn't make sense."

"Tell me about it, pal. The ferryboat operator and the guy who runs the airport swear they never saw George Mellis on the night he disappeared. The only other way he could have gotten to Dark Harbor was by motorboat. We checked all the boat operators in the area. Zilch."

"Perhaps he wasn't at Dark Harbor that night."

"The forensic lab says different. They found evidence that Mellis was at the house and changed from a business suit into the sailing clothes he was wearin' when his body was found."

"Was he killed at the house?"

"On the Blackwell yacht. His body was dumped overboard. Whoever did it figured the current would carry the body to China."

"How did – ?"

Nick Pappas raised a beefy hand. "My turn. Mellis was your patient. He must have talked to you about his wife."

"What does she have to do with this?"

"Everything. She's my first, second and third choice."

"You're crazy."

"Hey, I thought shrinks never used words like *crazy*."

"Nick, what makes you think Alexandra Mellis killed her husband?"

"She was there, and she had a motive. She arrived at the island late that night with some cockamamy excuse about being delayed because she was waitin' at the wrong airport to meet her sister."

"What does her sister say?"

"Give me a break. What the hell would you expect her to say? They're *twins*. We know George Mellis was at the house that night, but his wife swears she never saw him. It's a big house, Peter, but it's not *that* big. Next, Mrs. M gave all the servants the weekend off. When I asked her why, she said it was George's idea. George's lips, of course, are sealed."

Peter sat there, deep in thought. "You said she had a motive. What?"

"You have a short memory span. You're the one who put me on the track. The lady was married to a psycho who got his kicks sexually abusing everything he could lay his fists on. He was probably slapping her around pretty good. Let's say she decided she didn't want to play anymore. She asked for a divorce. He wouldn't give it to her. Why should he? He had it made. She wouldn't dare take him to court – it would touch off too juicy a scandal. She had no choice. She had to kill him." He leaned back in his chair.

"What do you want from me?" Peter asked.

"Information. You had lunch with Mellis's wife ten days ago." He pressed the button on a tape recorder on the desk. "We're going on the record now, Peter.

Tell me about that lunch. How did Alexandra Mellis behave? Was she tense? Angry? Hysterical?"

"Nick, I've never seen a more relaxed, happily married lady."

Nick Pappas glared at him and snapped off the tape recorder. "Don't shaft me, my friend. I went to see Dr. John Harley this morning. He's been giving Alexandra Mellis medication to stop her from committing suicide, for Christ's sake!"

Dr. John Harley had been greatly disturbed by his meeting with Lieutenant Pappas. The detective had gotten right to the point. "Has Mrs. Mellis consulted you professionally recently?"

"I'm sorry," Dr. Harley said. "I'm not at liberty to discuss my patients. I'm afraid I can't help you."

"All right, Doc. I understand. You're old friends. You'd like to keep the whole thing quiet. That's okay with me." He rose to his feet. "This is a homicide case. I'll be back in an hour with a warrant for your appointment records. When I find out what I want to know, I'm going to feed it to the newspapers."

Dr. Harley was studying him.

"We can handle it that way, or you can tell me now what I want to know, and I'll do what I can to keep it quiet. Well?"

"Sit down," Dr. Harley said. Nick Pappas sat. "Alexandra has been having some emotional problems lately."

"What kind of emotional problems?"

"She's been in a severe depression. She was talking about committing suicide."

"Did she mention using a knife?"

"No. She said she had a recurrent dream about drowning. I gave her Wellbutrin. She came back and told me it didn't seem to be helping, and I prescribed Nomifensine. I – I don't know whether it helped or not."

Nick Pappas sat there, putting things together in his mind. Finally he looked up. "Anything else?"

"That's everything, Lieutenant."

But there was more, and John Harley's conscience was bothering him. He had deliberately refrained from mentioning the brutal attack George Mellis had made on Eve Blackwell. Part of his concern was that he should have reported it to the police at the time it happened, but mainly Dr. Harley wanted to protect the Blackwell family. He had no way of knowing whether there was a connection between the attack on Eve and George Mellis's murder, but his instincts told him that it was better not to bring up the subject. He intended to do everything possible to protect Kate Blackwell.

*

Fifteen minutes after he made that decision, his nurse said, "Dr. Keith Webster is on line two, Doctor."

It was as if his conscience was prodding him.

Keith Webster said, "John, I'd like to stop by this afternoon and see you. Are you free?"

"I'll make myself free. What time?"

"How's five o'clock?"

"Fine, Keith. I'll see you then."

So, the matter was not going to be laid to rest so easily.

At five o'clock, Dr. Harley ushered Keith Webster into his office. "Would you like a drink?"

"No, thank you, John. I don't drink. Forgive me for barging in on you like this."

It seemed to John Harley that every time he saw him, Keith Webster was apologizing about something. He was such a mild, little man, so inoffensive and eager to please – a puppy waiting to be patted on the head. It was incredible to John Harley that within that pale, colorless persona there lurked such a brilliant surgeon.

"What can I do for you, Keith?"

Keith Webster drew a deep breath. "It's about that – you know – that beating George Mellis gave Eve Blackwell."

"What about it?"

"You're aware she almost died?"

"Yes."

"Well, it was never reported to the police. In view of what's happened – Mellis's murder and everything – I was wondering if maybe I shouldn't tell the police about it."

So there it was. There seemed no way to escape the problem.

"You have to do whatever you think best, Keith."

Keith Webster said gloomily, "I know. It's just that I'd hate to do anything that might hurt Eve Blackwell. She's a very special person."

Dr. Harley was watching him cautiously. "Yes, she is."

Keith Webster sighed. "The only thing is, John, if I do keep quiet about it now and the police find out later, it's going to look bad for me."

For both of us, John Harley thought. He saw a possible out. He said casually, "It's not very likely the police would find out, is it? Eve certainly would never mention it, and you fixed her up perfectly. Except for that little scar, you'd never know she'd been disfigured."

Keith Webster blinked. "What little scar?"

"The red scar on her forehead. She told me you said you were going to remove it in a month or two."

Dr. Webster was blinking faster now. It was some kind of nervous tic, Dr. Harley decided.

"I don't re – When did you last see Eve?"

"She came in about ten days ago to talk about a problem involving her sister.

As a matter of fact, the scar was the only way I could tell it was Eve instead of Alexandra. They're identical twins, you know."

Keith Webster nodded slowly. "Yes. I've seen photographs of Eve's sister in the newspapers. There's an amazing likeness. And you say the only way you could tell them apart was by the scar on Eve's forehead from the operation I performed?"

"That's right."

Dr. Webster sat there, silent, chewing on his lower lip. Finally he said, "Perhaps I shouldn't go to the police just yet. I'd like to think about this a little more."

"Frankly, I think that's wise, Keith. They're both lovely young women. The newspapers are hinting that the police think Alexandra killed George. That's impossible. I remember when they were little girls . . ."

Dr. Webster was no longer listening.

When he left Dr. Harley, Keith Webster was lost in thought. He had certainly not left even the trace of a scar on that beautiful face. Yet, John Harley had seen it. It was possible that Eve could have gotten a scar afterward in another accident, but then why had she lied? It made no sense.

He examined it from every angle, going over all the different possibilities, and when he had come to a conclusion, he thought, *If I'm right, this is going to change my whole. . . .*

Early the following morning, Keith Webster called Dr. Harley. "John," he began, "excuse me for disturbing you. You said that Eve Blackwell came in to talk to you about her sister, Alexandra?"

"That's right."

"After Eve's visit, did Alexandra happen to come in to see you?"

"Yes. As a matter of fact, she came to my office the following day. Why?"

"Just curious. Can you tell me what Eve's sister came to see you about?"

"Alexandra was in a deep depression. Eve was trying to help her."

Eve had been beaten and almost killed by Alexandra's husband. And now the man had been murdered and it was Alexandra who was being blamed.

Keith Webster had always known he was not brilliant. In school he had had to work very hard in order to achieve barely passing grades. He was the perennial butt of his classmates' jokes. He was neither an athlete nor a scholar, and he was socially inept. He was as close as one could come to being a nonentity. No one was more surprised than his own family when Keith Webster was admitted to medical school. When he elected to become a surgeon, neither his peers nor his teachers expected him to become a competent one, let alone a great one. But he had surprised them all. There was a talent deep inside him that was nothing short of genius. He was like some exquisite sculptor working his magic with living flesh instead of clay, and in a short time Keith Webster's reputation spread. In spite of his success, however, he was never able to overcome the trauma of his childhood. Inside he was still the little boy who bored everyone, the one at whom the girls laughed.

When he finally reached Eve, Keith's hands were slippery with sweat. She answered the phone on the first ring. "Rory?" Her voice was low and sultry.

"No. This is Keith Webster."

"Oh. Hello."

He heard the change in her voice. "How've you been?" he asked.

"Fine."

He could sense her impatience. "I – I'd like to see you."

"I'm not seeing anyone. If you read the papers, you'll know my brother-in-law was murdered. I'm in mourning."

He wiped his hands on his trousers. "That's what I want to see you about, Eve. I have some information you should know about."

"What kind of information?"

"I would prefer not to discuss it on the telephone." He could almost hear Eve's mind working.

"Very well. When?".

"Now, if it's convenient."

When he arrived at Eve's apartment thirty minutes later, Eve opened the door for him. "I'm very busy. What did you want to see me about?"

"About this," Keith Webster said apologetically. He opened a manila envelope he was clutching, took out a photograph and diffidently handed it to Eve. It was a photograph of herself.

She looked at it, puzzled. "Well?"

"It's a picture of you."

"I can see that," she said curtly. "What about it?"

"It was taken after your operation."

"So?"

"There's no scar on your forehead, Eve."

He watched the change that came over her face.

"Sit down, Keith."

He sat opposite her, on the edge of the couch, and he could not keep from staring at her. He had seen many beautiful women in his practice, but Eve Blackwell totally bewitched him. He had never known anyone like her.

"I think you'd better tell me what this is all about."

He started at the beginning. He told her about his visit to Dr. Harley and about the mysterious scar, and as Keith Webster talked, he watched Eve's eyes. They were expressionless.

When Keith Webster finished, Eve said, "I don't know what you're thinking, but whatever it is, you're wasting my time. As for the scar, I was playing a little joke on my sister. It's as simple as that. Now, if you've quite finished, I have a great deal to do."

He remained seated. "I'm sorry to have bothered you. I just thought I should talk to you before I went to the police." He could see that he really had her attention now.

"Why on earth would you go to the police?"

"I'm obliged to report the attack George Mellis made on you. Then there's that business about you and the scar. I don't understand it, but I'm sure you can explain it to them."

Eve felt the first stab of fear. This stupid, dreary little man in front of her had no idea what had really happened, but he knew enough to start the police asking questions.

George Mellis had been a frequent visitor to the apartment. The police could probably find witnesses who had seen him. She had lied about being in Washington the night of George's murder. She had no real alibi. She had never thought she would need one. If the police learned that George had almost killed her, it would give them a motive. The whole scheme would begin to unravel. She had to silence this man.

"What is it you want? Money?"

"No!"

She saw the indignation on his face. "What, then?"

Dr. Webster looked down at the rug, his face red with embarrassment. "I – I like you so much, Eve. I would hate it if anything bad happened to you."

She forced a smile. "Nothing bad is going to happen to me, Keith. I haven't done anything wrong. Believe me, none of this has anything to do with George Mellis's murder." She reached out and took his hand. "I would really appreciate it very much if you would forget about this. All right?"

He covered her hand and squeezed it. "I'd like to, Eve. I really would. But they're holding the coroner's inquest Saturday. I'm a doctor. I'm afraid it's my duty to testify at that inquest and tell them everything I know."

He saw the alarm that appeared in her eyes.

"You don't have to do that!"

He stroked her hand. "Yes, I do, Eve. It's my sworn obligation. There's only one thing that could prevent me from doing it." He watched her leap to the bait of his words.

"What is that?"

His voice was very gentle. "A husband can't be forced to testify against his wife."

35

The wedding took place two days before the coroner's inquest. They were married by a judge in his private chambers. The mere idea of being married to Keith Webster made Eve's skin crawl, but she had no choice. *The fool thinks I'm going to stay married to him.* As soon as the inquest was over, she would get an annulment and that would be the end of it.

Detective Lieutenant Nick Pappas had a problem. He was sure he knew who the murderer of George Mellis was, but he could not prove it. He was confronted by a conspiracy of silence around the Blackwell family that he could not break through. He discussed the problem with his superior, Captain Harold Cohn, a street-wise cop who had worked his way up from the ranks.

Cohn quietly listened to Pappas and said, "It's all smoke, Nick. You haven't got a fucking bit of evidence. They'd laugh us out of court."

"I know," Lieutenant Pappas sighed. "But I'm right." He sat there a moment, thinking. "Would you mind if I talked to Kate Blackwell?"

"Jesus! What for?"

"It'll be a little fishing expedition. She runs that family. She might have some information she doesn't even know she has."

"You'll have to watch your step."

"I will."

"And go easy with her, Nick. Remember, she's an old lady."

"That's what I'm counting on," Detective Pappas said.

The meeting took place that afternoon in Kate Blackwell's office. Nick Pappas guessed that Kate was somewhere in her eighties, but she carried her age remarkably well. She showed little of the strain the detective knew she must be feeling. She was a very private person, and she had been forced to watch the Blackwell name become a source of public speculation and scandal.

"My secretary said you wished to see me about a matter of some urgency, Lieutenant."

"Yes, ma'am. There's a coroner's inquest tomorrow on the death of George Mellis. I have reason to think your granddaughter is involved in his murder."

Kate went absolutely rigid. "I don't believe it."

"Please hear me out, Mrs. Blackwell. Every police investigation begins with the question of motive. George Mellis was a fortune hunter and a vicious sadist." He saw the reaction on her face, but he pressed on. "He married your granddaughter and suddenly found himself with his hands on a large fortune. I figured he beat up Alexandra once too often and when she asked for a divorce, he refused. Her only way to get rid of him was to kill him."

Kate was staring at him, her face pale.

"I began looking around for evidence to back up my theory. We knew George Mellis was at Cedar Hill House before he disappeared. There are only two ways to get to Dark Harbor from the mainland – plane or ferryboat. According to the local sheriffs office, George Mellis didn't use either. I don't believe in miracles, and I figured Mellis wasn't the kind of man who could walk on water. The only possibility left was that he took a boat from somewhere else along the coast. I started checking out boat-rental places, and I struck pay dirt at Gilkey Harbor. At four P.M. on the afternoon of the day George Mellis was murdered, a woman rented a motor launch there and said a friend would be picking it up later. She paid cash, but she had to sign the rental slip. She used the name Solange Dunas. Does that ring a bell?"

"Yes. She – she was the governess who took care of the twins when they were children. She returned to France years ago."

Pappas nodded, a look of satisfaction on his face. "A little farther up the coast, the same woman rented a second boat. She took it out and returned it three hours later. She signed her name Solange Dunas again. I showed both attendants a photograph of Alexandra. They were pretty sure it was her, but they couldn't be positive, because the woman who rented the boats was a brunet."

"Then what makes you think – ?"

"She wore a wig."

Kate said stiffly, "I don't believe Alexandra killed her husband."

"I don't either, Mrs. Blackwell," Lieutenant Pappas told her. "It was her sister, Eve."

Kate Blackwell was as still as stone.

"Alexandra couldn't have done it. I checked on her movements the day of the murder. She spent the early part of the day in New York with a friend, then she flew directly from New York up to the island. There's no way she could have rented those two motorboats." He leaned forward. "So I was left with Alexandra's look-alike, who signed the name Solange Dunas. It had to be Eve. I started looking around for her motive. I showed a photograph of George Mellis to the tenants of the apartment house Eve lives in, and it turned out that Mellis was a frequent visitor there. The superintendent of the building told me that one night when Mellis was there, Eve was almost beaten to death. Did you know that?"

"No." Kate's voice was a whisper.

"Mellis did it. It fits his pattern. And that was Eve's motive – vengeance. She lured him out to Dark Harbor and murdered him." He looked at Kate, and felt a pang of guilt at taking advantage of this old woman. "Eve's alibi is that she was in Washington, D.C., that day. She gave the cab driver who took her to the airport a hundred-dollar bill so he would be sure to remember her, and she made a big fuss about missing the Washington shuttle. But I don't think she went to Washington. I believe she put on a dark wig and took a commercial plane to Maine, where she rented those boats. She killed Mellis, dumped his body overboard, then docked the yacht and towed the extra motorboat back to the rental dock, which was closed by then."

Kate looked at him, a long moment. Then she said, slowly, "All the evidence you have is circumstantial, isn't it?"

"Yes." He was ready to move in for the kill. "I need concrete evidence for the coroner's inquest. You know your granddaughter better than anyone in the world, Mrs. Blackwell. I want you to tell me anything you can that might be helpful."

She sat there quietly, making up her mind. Finally she said, "I think I can give you some information for the inquest."

And Nick Pappas's heart began to beat faster. He had taken a long shot, and it had paid off. The old lady had come through. He unconsciously leaned forward. "Yes, Mrs. Blackwell?"

Kate spoke slowly and distinctly. "On the day George Mellis was murdered, Lieutenant, my granddaughter Eve and I were in Washington, D.C., together."

She saw the surprised expression on his face. *You fool*, Kate Blackwell thought. *Did you really think I would offer up a Blackwell as a sacrifice to you? That I would let the press have a Roman holiday with the Blackwell name? No. I will punish Eve in my own way.*

The verdict from the coroner's jury was death at the hands of an unknown assailant or assailants.

To Alexandra's surprise and gratitude, Peter Templeton was at the inquest at the county courthouse.

"Just here to lend moral support," he told her. Peter thought Alexandra was holding up remarkably well, but the strain showed in her face and in her eyes. During a recess, he took her to lunch at the Lobster Pound, a little restaurant facing the bay in Lincolnville.

"When this is over," Peter said, "I think it would be good for you to take a trip, get away for a while."

"Yes. Eve has asked me to go away with her." Alexandra's eyes were red with pain. "I still can't believe George is dead. I know it has happened, but it – it still seems unreal."

"It's nature's way of cushioning the shock until the pain becomes bearable."

"It's so senseless. He was such a fine man." She looked up at Peter. "You spent time with him. He talked to you. Wasn't he a wonderful person?"

"Yes," Peter said slowly. "Yes, he was."

Eve said, "I want an annulment, Keith."

Keith Webster blinked at his wife in surprise. "Why on earth would you want an annulment?"

"Oh, come on, Keith. You didn't really think I was going to stay married to you, did you?"

"Of course. You're my wife, Eve."

"What are you after? The Blackwell money?"

"I don't need money, darling. I make an excellent living. I can give you anything you want."

"I told you what I want. An annulment."

He shook his head regretfully. "I'm afraid I can't give you it."

"Then I'm going to file for divorce."

"I don't think that would be advisable. You see, nothing has really changed, Eve. The police haven't found out who killed your brother-in-law, so the case is still open. There's no statute of limitations on murder. If you divorced me, I'd be forced to . . ." He raised his hands helplessly.

"You're talking as though *I* killed him."

"You did, Eve."

Her voice was scornful. "How the hell do *you* know?"

"It's the only reason you would have married me."

She looked at him, filled with loathing. "You bastard! How can you do this to me?"

"It's very simple. I love you."

"I hate you. Do you understand that? I despise you!"

He smiled sadly. "I love you so much"

The trip with Alexandra was called off. "I'm going to Barbados on my honeymoon," Eve told her.

Barbados was Keith's idea.

"I won't go," Eve told him flatly. The idea of a honeymoon with him was disgusting.

"It will look strange. if we don't have a honeymoon," he said shyly. "And we don't want people asking a lot of awkward questions, do we, dear?"

Alexandra began to see Peter Templeton for lunch once a week. In the beginning, it was because she wanted to talk about George, and there was no one else she could discuss him with. But after several months, Alexandra admitted to herself that she enjoyed Peter Templeton's company immensely. There was a dependability about him that she desperately needed. He was sensitive to her moods, and he was intelligent and entertaining.

"When I was an intern," he told Alexandra, "I went out on my first house call in the dead of winter. The patient was a frail old man in bed with a terrible cough. I was going to examine his chest with my stethoscope, but I didn't want to shock him, so I decided to warm it first. I put it on the radiator while I examined his throat and his eyes. Then I got my stethoscope and put it to his chest. The old man leaped out of bed like a scalded cat. His cough went away, but it took two weeks for the burn to heal."

Alexandra laughed. It was the first time she had laughed in a long time.

"Can we do this again next week?" Peter asked.

"Yes, please."

*

Eve's honeymoon turned out much better than she had anticipated. Because of Keith's pale, sensitive skin, he was afraid to go out in the sun, so Eve went down to the beach alone every day. She was never alone for long. She was surrounded by amorous lifeguards, beach bums, tycoons and playboys. It was like feasting at a wonderful smorgasbord, and Eve chose a different dish each day. She enjoyed her sexual escapades twice as much because she knew her husband was upstairs in their suite waiting for her. He could not do enough for her. He fetched and carried for her like a little lapdog, and waited on her hand and foot. If Eve expressed a wish, it was instantly gratified. She did everything she could think of to insult him, anger him, to turn him against her so that he would let her go, but his love was unshakable. The idea of letting Keith make love to her sickened Eve, and she was grateful that he had a weak libido.

The years are beginning to catch up with me, Kate Blackwell thought. There were so many of them, and they had been so full and rich.

Kruger-Brent, Ltd., needed a strong hand at the helm. It needed someone with Blackwell blood. *There's no one to carry on after I'm gone*, Kate thought. *All the working and planning and fighting for the company. And for what? For strangers to take over one day. Bloody hell! I can't let that happen.*

A week after they returned from their honeymoon, Keith said apologetically, "I'm afraid I'm going to have to go back to work, dear. I have a lot of operations scheduled. Will you be all right during the day without me?"

Eve barely managed to keep a straight face. "I'll try."

Keith was up and out early every morning long before Eve awakened, and when she went into the kitchen she found he had made coffee and laid out all the breakfast things for her. He opened a generous bank account in Eve's name and kept it replenished. She spent his money recklessly. As long as she was enjoying herself, Keith was happy. Eve bought expensive jewelry for Rory, with whom she spent almost every afternoon. He worked very little.

"I can't take just any part," he complained to Eve. "It would hurt my image."

"I understand, darling."

"Do you? What the fuck do you know about show business? You were born with a silver spoon up your ass."

And Eve would buy him an extra-nice present to placate him. She paid Rory's rent and bought him clothes for interviews, and paid for his dinners at expensive restaurants so that he could be seen by important producers. She wanted to be with him twenty-four hours a day, but there was her husband. Eve would arrive home at seven or eight o'clock at night, and Keith would be in the kitchen preparing dinner for her in his "Kiss the Cook" apron. He never questioned her about where she had been.

*

During the following year, Alexandra and Peter Templeton saw each other more and more often. Each had become an important part of the other's life. Peter accompanied Alexandra when she went to visit her father at the asylum, and somehow the sharing made the pain easier to bear.

Peter met Kate one evening when he arrived to pick up Alexandra. "So you're a doctor, eh? I've buried a dozen doctors, and I'm still around. Do you know anything about business?"

"Not a great deal, Mrs. Blackwell."

"Are you a corporation?" Kate asked.

"No."

She snorted. "Bloody hell. You don't know anything. You need a good tax man. I'll set up an appointment for you with mine. The first thing he'll do is incorporate you and – "

"Thank you, Mrs. Blackwell. I'm getting along just fine."

"My husband was a stubborn man, too," Kate said. She turned to Alexandra. "Invite him to dinner. Maybe I can talk some sense into him."

Outside, Peter said, "Your grandmother hates me."

Alexandra laughed. "She likes you. You should *hear* how Gran behaves with people she hates."

"I wonder how she would feel if I told her that I want to marry you, Alex . . . ?"

And she looked up at him and beamed. "We'd both feel wonderful, Peter!"

Kate had watched the progress of Alexandra's romance with Peter Templeton with a great deal of interest. She liked the young doctor, and she decided he would be a good husband for Alexandra. But she was a trader at heart. Now she sat in front of the fireplace facing the two of them.

"I must tell you," Kate lied, "that this comes as a complete surprise. I always expected Alexandra to marry an executive who would take over Kruger-Brent."

"This isn't a business proposition, Mrs. Blackwell. Alexandra and I want to get married."

"On the other hand," Kate continued, as if there had been no interruption, "you're a psychiatrist. You understand the way people's minds and emotions work. You would probably be a great negotiator. I would like you to become involved with the company. You can – "

"No," Peter said firmly. "I'm a doctor. I'm not interested in going into a business."

"This isn't 'going into a business'," "Kate snapped. "We're not talking about some corner grocery store. You'll be part of the family, and I need someone to run – "

"I'm sorry." There was a finality in Peter's tone. "I'll have nothing to do with Kruger-Brent. You'll have to find someone else for that. . . ."

Kate turned to Alexandra. "What do you have to say to that?"

"I want whatever makes Peter happy, Gran."

"Damned ingratitude," Kate glowered. "Selfish, the both of you." She sighed. "Ah, well. Who knows? You might change your mind one day." And she added innocently, "Are you planning to have children?"

Peter laughed. "That's a private matter. I have a feeling you're a great manipulator, Mrs. Blackwell, but Alex and I are going to live our own lives, and our children – if we have children – will live *their* lives."

Kate smiled sweetly. "I wouldn't have it any other way, Peter. I've made it a lifelong rule never to interfere in other people's lives."

Two months later when Alexandra and Peter returned from their honeymoon, Alexandra was pregnant. When Kate heard the news, she thought, *Good. It will be a boy.*

Eve lay in bed watching Rory walk out of the bathroom naked. He had a beautiful body, lean and trim. Eve adored the way he made love to her. She could not get enough of him. She suspected he might have other bedmates, but she was afraid to ask, afraid to say anything that might upset him. Now, as he reached the bed, he ran his finger along her skin, just below the eyes, and said, "Hey, baby, you're gettin' a few wrinkles. They're cute."

Each word was a stab, a reminder of the age difference between them and the fact that she was twenty-five years old. They made love again, but for the first time Eve's mind was elsewhere.

It was almost nine o'clock when Eve arrived home. Keith was basting a roast in the oven.

He kissed her on the cheek. "Hello, dear. I've made some of your favorite dishes. We're having – "

"Keith, I want you to remove these wrinkles."

He blinked. "What wrinkles?"

She pointed to the area around her eyes. "These."

"Those are laugh lines, darling. I love them."

"*I* don't! I hate them!" she yelled.

"Believe me, Eve, they're not – "

"For Christ's sake, just get rid of them. That *is* what you do for a living, isn't it?"

"Yes, but – All right," he said placatingly, "if it will make you happy, dear."

"When?"

"In about six weeks. My schedule is full right – "

"I'm not one of your goddamned patients," Eve snapped. "I'm your wife. I want you to do it now – tomorrow."

"The clinic is closed on Saturdays."

"Then open it!" *He was so stupid.* God, she could not wait to get rid of him. And she would. One way or another. And soon.

"Come into the other room for a moment." He took her into the dressing room.

She sat in a chair under a strong light while he carefully examined her face. In an instant he was transformed from a bumbling little milquetoast to a brilliant surgeon, and Eve could sense the transformation. She remembered the miraculous job he had done on her face. This operation might seem unnecessary to Keith, but he was wrong. It was vital. Eve could not bear the thought of losing Rory.

Keith turned off the light. "No problem," he assured her. "I'll do it in the morning."

The following morning, the two of them went to the clinic. "I usually have a nurse assist me," Keith told her, "but with something as minor as this, it won't be necessary."

"You might as well do something with this while you're at it." Eve tugged at a bit of skin at her throat.

"If you wish, dear. I'll give you something to put you to sleep so you won't feel any discomfort. I don't want my darling to have any pain."

Eve watched as he filled a hypodermic and skillfully gave her an injection. She would not have minded if there had been pain. She was doing this for Rory. Darling Rory. She thought of his rock-hard body and the look in his eyes when he was hungry for her. . . . She drifted off to sleep.

She woke up in a bed in the back room of the clinic. Keith was seated in a chair next to the bed.

"How did it go?" Her voice was thick with sleep.

"Beautifully," Keith smiled.

Eve nodded, and was asleep again.

Keith was there when she woke up later. "We'll leave the bandages on for a few days. I'll keep you here where you can be properly cared for."

"All right."

He checked her each day, examined her face, nodded. "Perfect."

"When can I look?"

"It should be all healed by Friday," he assured her.

She ordered the head nurse to have a private telephone installed by the bedside. The first call she made was to Rory.

"Hey, baby, where the hell are you?" he asked. "I'm horny."

"So am I, darling. I'm still tied up with his damned medical convention in Florida, but I'll be back next week."

"You'd better be."

"Have you missed me?"

"Like crazy."

Eve heard whispering in the background. "Is there someone there with you?"

"Yeah. We're havin' a little orgy." Rory loved to make jokes. "Gotta go." The line went dead.

Eve telephoned Alexandra and listened, bored, to Alexandra's excited talk about her pregnancy. "I can't wait," Eve told her. "I've always wanted to be an aunt."

Eve seldom saw her grandmother. A coolness had developed that Eve did not understand. *She'll come around*, Eve thought.

Kate never asked about Keith, and Eve did not blame her, for he was a nothing. Perhaps one day Eve would talk to Rory about helping her get rid of Keith. That would tie Rory to her forever. It was incredible to Eve that she could cuckold her husband every day and that he neither suspected nor cared. Well, thank God he had a talent for *something*. The bandages were coming off on Friday.

Eve awakened early on Friday and waited impatiently for Keith.

"It's almost noon," she complained. "Where the hell have you been?"

"I'm sorry, darling," he apologized. "I've been in surgery all morning and – "

"I don't give a damn about that. Take these bandages off. I want to see."

"Very well."

Eve sat up and was still, as he deftly cut the bandages away from her face. He stood back to study her, and she saw the satisfaction in his eyes. "Perfect."

"Give me a mirror."

He hurried out of the room and returned a moment later with a hand mirror. With a proud smile, he presented it to her.

Eve raised the mirror slowly and looked at her reflection.

And screamed.

Epilogue

Kate
1982

36

It seemed to Kate that the wheel of time was spinning faster, hurrying the days along, blending winter into spring and summer into autumn, until all the seasons and years blurred into one. She was in her late eighties now. Eighty what? Sometimes she forgot her exact age. She could face growing old, but she could not face the idea of growing old and slovenly, and she took great pains with her appearance. When she looked in the mirror, she saw a neat, erect figure of a woman, proud and indomitable.

She still went to her office every day, but it was a gesture, a ruse to ward off death. She attended every board meeting, but things were no longer as clear as they once had been. Everyone around her seemed to be speaking too rapidly. The most disturbing thing to Kate was that her mind played tricks on her. The past and present were constantly intermingling. Her world was closing in, becoming smaller and smaller.

If there was a lifeline that Kate clutched, a driving force that kept her alive, it was her passionate conviction that someone in the family must one day take charge of Kruger-Brent. Kate had no intention of letting outsiders take over what Jamie McGregor and Margaret and she and David had suffered and toiled so long and so hard for. Eve, on whom Kate had twice pinned such high hopes, was a murderer. And a *grotesque*. Kate had not had to punish her. She had seen Eve once. What had been done to her was punishment enough.

On the day Eve had seen her face in the mirror, she had tried to commit suicide. She had swallowed a bottle of sleeping pills, but Keith had pumped out her stomach and brought her home, where he hovered over her constantly. When he had to be at the hospital, day and night nurses guarded her.

"Please let me die," Eve begged her husband. "Please, Keith! I don't want to live like this."

"You belong to me now," Keith told her, "and I'll always love you."

The image of what her face looked like was etched in Eve's brain. She persuaded Keith to dismiss the nurses. She did not want anyone around her looking at her, staring at her.

Alexandra called again and again, but Eve refused to see her. All deliveries were left outside the front door so no one could see her face. The only person who saw her was Keith. He was, finally, the only one she had left. He was her only link with the world, and she became terrified that he would leave her, that she would be left alone with nothing but her ugliness – her unbearable ugliness.

Every morning at five o'clock, Keith arose to go to the hospital or clinic, and Eve was always up before him to fix his breakfast. She cooked dinner for him every night, and when he was late, she was filled with apprehension. *What if he had found some other woman? What if he did not return to her?*

When she heard his key in the door, she would rush to open it and go into his arms, holding him tightly. She never suggested they make love because she was afraid he might refuse, but when he did make love to her, Eve felt as though he was bestowing upon her a wonderful kindness.

Once she asked, timidly, "Darling, haven't you punished me enough? Won't you repair my face?"

He looked at her and said proudly, "It can never be repaired."

As time went on, Keith became more demanding, more peremptory, until Eve was finally and completely a slave to him, catering to his every whim. Her ugliness bound her to him more strongly than iron chains.

Alexandra and Peter had had a son, Robert, a bright, handsome boy. He reminded Kate of Tony when he was a child. Robert was almost eight now, and precocious for his age. *Very precocious indeed*, Kate thought. *A really remarkable boy.*

All the members of the family received their invitations on the same day. The invitation read: MRS. KATE BLACKWELL REQUESTS THE HONOR OF YOUR PRESENCE TO CELEBRATE HER NINETIETH BIRTHDAY AT CEDAR HILL HOUSE, DARK HARBOR, MAINE, ON SEPTEMBER 24, 1982, AT EIGHT O'CLOCK. BLACK TIE.

When Keith read the invitation, he looked at Eve and said, "We're going."

"Oh, no! I can't! You go. I'll – "

He said, "We're both going."

Tony Blackwell was in the garden of the sanitarium, painting, when his companion approached. "A letter for you, Tony."

Tony opened the envelope, and a vague smile lighted his face. "That's nice," he said. "I like birthday parties."

Peter Templeton studied the invitation. "I can't believe the old girl's ninety years old. She's really amazing."

"Yes, isn't she?" Alexandra agreed. And she added thoughtfully, "Do you know something sweet? Robert received his own invitation, addressed to him."

37

The overnight guests had long since departed by ferry and plane, and the family was gathered in the library at Cedar Hill. Kate looked at those in the room, one by one, and she saw each with remarkable clarity. Tony, the smiling, vaguely amiable vegetable who had tried to kill her, the son who had been so full of promise and hope. Eve, the murderer, who could have owned the world if she had not had the seed of evil in her. How ironic it was, Kate thought, that her terrible punishment had come from the meek little nonentity she married. And then there was Alexandra. Beautiful, affectionate and kind – the bitterest disappointment of all. She had put her own happiness before the welfare of the company. She was not interested in Kruger-Brent and had chosen a husband who refused to have anything to do with the company. Traitors, both of them. Had all the pain of the past gone for nothing? *No*, Kate thought. *I won't let it end like this. It's not all been wasted. I've built a proud dynasty. A hospital in Cape Town is named after me. I've built schools and libraries and helped Banda's people.* Her head was beginning to hurt. The room was slowly filling with ghosts. Jamie McGregor and Margaret – looking so beautiful – and Banda smiling at her. And dear, wonderful David, holding out his arms. Kate shook her head to clear it. She was not ready for any of them yet. *Soon*, she thought. *Soon*.

There was one more member of the family in the room. She turned to her handsome young great-grandson and said, "Come here, darling."

Robert walked up to her and took her hand.

"It sure was a great birthday party, Gran."

"Thank you, Robert. I'm glad you enjoyed it. How are you getting along in school?"

"All A's, like you told me to get. I'm at the head of my class."

Kate looked at Peter. "You should send Robert to the Wharton School when he's old enough. It's the best – "

Peter laughed. "For God's sake, Kate, my darling, don't you ever give up? Robert's going to do exactly what he likes. He has a remarkable musical talent, and he wants to be a classical musician. He's going to choose his own life."

"You're right," Kate sighed. "I'm an old woman, and I have no right to interfere. If he wants to be a musician, that's what he should be." She turned to the boy, and her eyes shone with love. "Mind you, Robert, I can't promise anything, but I'm going to try to help you. I know someone who's a dear friend of Zubin Mehta."